THE COUNT OF MONTE CRISTO

The name of ALEXANDRE DUMAS is synonymous with romance and adventure. His father, son of a French marquis and a Saint Domingo negress, was one of Napoleon's  Alexandre was brought up by his miles from Paris, where he was bc employment as a clerk, he settled name as an author. By 1829 he leaders of the new Romantic mc had turned his attention away from a series of historical romances which he hoped would make him the French Walter Scott. *The Three Musketeers* (1844) and its sequels, together with *The Count of Monte Cristo* (1844–6), his most enduring novels, have not only delighted generations of readers but made history exciting. His output was prodigious and fills more than 300 volumes in the standard French edition. First serialized in the new, cheap newspapers before appearing in volume form, his books brought him enormous popularity and extraordinary wealth which he readily gave away to anyone who asked, or squandered on a succession of mistresses and on follies like the 'Château de Monte Cristo', his monument to his own grandeur at Marly. He was an inveterate traveller and a cook of genius. He courted princes and loved wearing medals (some of which he bought himself), but was at heart a republican with a strong sense of social justice. He took part in the July Revolution of 1830 and gave spirited support to Garibaldi's efforts to create Italian independence in 1860. Many envied Dumas, some accused him of employing others to write the books he signed, but few ever spoke ill of this generous, open-handed, and disarming man. He lived just long enough to survive his talent and died of a stroke at Puy, near Dieppe, in 1870.

DAVID COWARD is Senior Fellow and Emeritus Professor of French Literature at the University of Leeds. He is the author of studies of Marivaux, Marguerite Duras, Marcel Pagnol, and Restif de la Bretonne. For Oxford World's Classics, he has edited eight novels by Alexandre Dumas, including the whole of the Musketeer saga, and translated Dumas *fils' La Dame aux Camélias*, two selections of Maupassant short stories, Sade's *Misfortunes of Virtue and Other Early Tales*, and Diderot's *Jacques the Fatalist*. Winner of the 1996 Scott-Moncrieff prize for translation, he reviews regularly for the *Times Literary Supplement*.

OXFORD WORLD'S CLASSICS

*For over 100 years Oxford World's Classics have brought
readers closer to the world's great literature. Now with over 700
titles—from the 4,000-year-old myths of Mesopotamia to the
twentieth century's greatest novels—the series makes available
lesser-known as well as celebrated writing.*

*The pocket-sized hardbacks of the early years contained
introductions by Virginia Woolf, T. S. Eliot, Graham Greene,
and other literary figures which enriched the experience of reading.
Today the series is recognized for its fine scholarship and
reliability in texts that span world literature, drama and poetry,
religion, philosophy and politics. Each edition includes perceptive
commentary and essential background information to meet the
changing needs of readers.*

OXFORD WORLD'S CLASSICS

ALEXANDRE DUMAS

The Count of Monte Cristo

Edited with an Introduction and Notes by
DAVID COWARD

OXFORD
UNIVERSITY PRESS

OXFORD

UNIVERSITY PRESS

Great Clarendon Street, Oxford OX2 6DP

Oxford University Press is a department of the University of Oxford.
It furthers the University's objective of excellence in research, scholarship,
and education by publishing worldwide in

Oxford New York

Auckland Bangkok Buenos Aires Cape Town Chennai
Dar es Salaam Delhi Hong Kong Istanbul Karachi Kolkata
Kuala Lumpur Madrid Melbourne Mexico City Mumbai Nairobi
São Paulo Shanghai Singapore Taipei Tokyo Toronto

Oxford is a registered trade mark of Oxford University Press
in the UK and in certain other countries

Published in the United States
by Oxford University Press Inc., New York

Introduction, Select Bibliography, Chronology, and Explanatory Notes
© David Coward 1990

First published as a World's Classics paperback 1990
Reissued as an Oxford World's Classics paperback 1998

British Library Cataloguing in Publication Data

Data available

Library of Congress Cataloging in Publication Data

Data available

ISBN–13: 978–0–19–283395–2
ISBN–10: 0–19–283395–2

12

Printed in Great Britain by
Clays Ltd, St Ives plc

CONTENTS

THE COUNT OF MONTE CRISTO

INTRODUCTION

Alexandre Dumas was a force of nature. A robust, roaring man of vast appetites and even vaster energies, he cries out to be measured in cubits rather than the feet and inches that are used for mere mortals. For forty years, sparks from his mighty anvil lit fires which inflamed the world and burn still. D'Artagnan and Edmond Dantès are the stuff of dreams.

He was born in 1802 at Villers-Cotterêts, about fifty miles north-east of Paris, the second child of an innkeeper's daughter and of one of Napoleon's most remarkable generals. Thomas-Alexandre Davy de la Pailleterie was born at Saint Domingo in 1762, the son of a French marquis and Marie-Cessette Dumas, a negress. Disowned by his father, he took his mother's name, enlisted as a private soldier in 1786 and rose rapidly through the ranks during the early Revolutionary campaigns. A courageous and dashing field officer, he usually had more to say for himself than was politic. In 1799, he quarrelled with Napoleon and never regained his favour, nor did he receive the army pay that was due to him. He died poor in 1806, leaving his wife and children to manage as they could.

At the schools which he attended with no great enthusiasm, young Alexandre, who inherited all his father's drive and (as caricaturists were later to emphasize) some of his negroid features, learned at least to write a good hand. It was for his handwriting rather than through his father's old friends that he found work as a none-too-diligent minor clerk in 1823. He had left Villers-Cotterêts for good and was determined to make his way in Paris as an author. While waiting for his hour to come, he set about laying the foundations of his future life. He spent more money than he earned, developed a habit of collaborating with other writers and kept up a steady stream of affairs: by Catherine Lebay, a seamstress, he had a son in 1824, also called Alexandre, who later became famous as the author of *La Dame aux Camélias* before turning into the self-appointed guardian of the nation's morality and censor of his father's excesses. Many plays and numerous mistresses later, Dumas scored an enormous success with *Henry III and His Court* (1829), a play which helped to inaugurate the new 'Romantic' drama which was a potent expression of the reaction against the ultra-conservative political, moral, and cultural climate of the Restoration. He threw himself unbidden into the July Revolution of 1830 and single-handedly captured a powder magazine at Soissons. He persuaded Lafayette, the liberal hero of old Revolutionary struggles who had helped set the constitutionally-minded Louis-Philippe on the throne of France, to appoint him organizer of the National Guard in the Vendée, but Dumas, a natural republican, soon gave up when he encountered strong local Royalist opposition. He returned to Paris where he resumed his position as one of the age's leading theatrical lights.

Dumas tackled contemporary subjects in plays like *Antony* (1831), a lurid story of marital infidelity, but as a dramatist was always temperamentally attracted by historical anecdotes, which he unfailingly exploited for their melodramatic potential. He also re-wrote, with or without permission, plays by other hands and soon acquired a suspect reputation for his nonchalant attitude to literary property. By the mid-1830s, however, conscious of the inadequacy of his education, he began reading history seriously with a view to creating the French 'historical novel' which would be as respected and successful as the English historical novels of Walter Scott. In the meantime he accepted whatever commissions came his way. It was thus that he undertook a walking tour of the South of France in 1834 to collect material for a series of articles which he later published as the first of his books of travel impressions. As a travel writer, Dumas gave short historical and geographical measure, but always succeeded in interesting his reader with local lore coaxed out of chance acquaintances, and with amazing anecdotes of his personal perils and astounding adventures. (The Romantic poet Lamartine once remarked that while some men spent their lives looking for the secret of perpetual motion, Dumas had invented 'perpetual astonishment'.) His journeys were not always motivated by commissions—in 1832, when his republican sympathies had become dangerous, he prudently left Paris for Switzerland. Surrounded by mistresses, fending off creditors, and habitually working fourteen hours a day at his desk to meet his many commitments, he remained as yet a man of the theatre and consolidated his position with the triumph of *Kean* in 1836.

But by the late 1830s he was turning to the novel, partly because he was interested in the possibilities of fiction and partly because the market was favourable. The appearance in 1836 of *La Presse* and *Le Siècle*, the first of a new breed of cheap newspapers financed almost entirely by advertising revenues, had revolutionized the newspaper industry. Editors found that they could increase circulation by running novels in serial form, though not all writers were able to provide the thrilling climax to each episode which ensured that readers would buy the next issue. Where Balzac failed, Eugène Sue succeeded: when *Le Constitutionnel* outbid its rivals for Sue's *Le Juif errant* (*The Wandering Jew*) in 1843, the number of copies sold daily soared within three weeks from 4,000 to 24,000. Dumas's gift for melodrama and the speed at which he worked ensured that he made the most of his opportunities and on occasions was writing three or even four serial novels simultaneously. When the episodes were collected (as they at first were by opportunist Belgian publishers who paid no royalties) and sold in multi-volume sets, he became not merely France's best-known writer but also the most famous Frenchman of his day, a star who was recognized wherever he travelled.

He throve on fame and success and lived up to the image

of extravagance, indestructibility, and recklessness which he himself encouraged. He married an actress in 1840 from whom he separated in 1844. By this time he was growing close to his son, Alexandre, whom he undertook to initiate into the literary and social life of the capital. With Alexandre, he set off for Spain in 1846—simply abandoning a number of novels he was writing on the grounds that he needed to rest—and thence travelled to Algeria, with an official commission to write one of his inimitable travel books which the government hoped would make North Africa attractive to potential colonizers. In 1847 he moved to Marly, to the 'Chateau de Monte Cristo' which was to have been a modest residence but had grown into a costly palace which symbolized his success. The same year, he inaugurated the 'Théâtre historique' where he hoped to reap enormous financial rewards by staging mainly his own plays. Meanwhile the stream of historical romances continued to feed the presses of the Paris newspapers and he commanded huge fees, which he squandered. Dumas had no financial acumen and the horde of social and literary spongers took full advantage of his generosity.

Though he courted kings and princes, his democratic (or rather meritocratic) leanings prompted him to stand, unsuccessfully, as a republican candidate in the 1848 elections. But while he welcomed the change of regime, the Revolution which ended Louis-Philippe's bourgeois monarchy also ruined the market for his novels and plays and he was never thereafter to earn the vast sums he needed to finance his lavish adventures. In 1850 the 'Chateau de Monte Cristo', which had cost him 400,000 francs was sold to an American dentist for 30,000. The 'Théâtre historique' failed and Dumas fled to Brussels to avoid his creditors. His reputation still made him attractive to women who more often than not counted on him to advance their careers. His son grew increasingly embarrassed by his self-indulgence. He continued to write indefatigably and to travel, notably to Russia

in 1859. In 1860, he met Garibaldi and was swept up enthusiastically into the cause of Italian independence. In 1867
he began his final liaison, with the American acrobat Ada
Mencken, and published his last significant novel, *La Terreur
prussienne* (*The Prussian Terror*), which carried a clear-sighted
warning of the threat looming from across the Rhine. He
lived long enough to be saddened by the decline of his powers
and to witness the Franco–Prussian War he had predicted.
In September 1870 he suffered a stroke and lingered until 5
December when he died at the home of his son at Puy, near
Dieppe.

Dumas, who had earned millions, was not a rich man
when he died. He had no financial sense, nor indeed much of
a sense of property. He kept money in drawers and tobacco
jars and was as ready to give large sums away as he was
unembarrassed when borrowing his cab-fare or annexing
sections of a neighbour's land to complete his estate at
Marly. This open-handedness helps to explain his cavalier
attitude to literary property. Early in his career, comments
were made about his use of collaborators, and even friends
and fellow authors found it hard to believe that any one man
could, unaided, write or even dictate all the vast novels he
signed. In 1845 a journalist named Jacquot attempted to
expose Dumas, accusing him of directing a 'fiction-factory'
which employed writers to turn out the serials and volumes
to which he put his signature. Dumas took him to court and
won his case.

But though his good faith cannot be doubted, the question
of Dumas's authorship of his works cannot be left there. He
never tried to hide his debts to others and was always eager
to acknowledge the contribution of collaborators. As a playwright in the 1830s, he had been in the habit of working with
one or more experienced hands. Sometimes plays which had
not found a home would be brought to him for rewriting: *La
Tour de Nesle* (*The Tower of Nesle*) (1832) was the result of one
such proposal. He might call too upon others to supply the

historical and documentary background for his romances: for *Georges* (1843) he talked to a Mauritian who gave him enough information for Dumas to describe the island as vividly as though he had been there. His most regular collaborator, however, was Auguste Maquet (1813–88), a failed author of a scholarly disposition, with whom he discussed the direction his plots should take and who furnished him with historical and other materials which Dumas duly incorporated into the books that continued to appear under his name. Dumas's contemporaries raised an eyebrow at this practice, but his collaborative working habits certainly help to explain just why he was able to publish over 300 plays, novels, travel books, and memoirs: 1,348 volumes, in all, it has been calculated. Of this total, it is likely that one or two titles were never even read by Dumas who on occasions agreed to lend his name to help a struggling writer: the name of Dumas could sell anything. But there can be no doubt that he wrote all his books himself, though with the kind of help enjoyed by modern script-writers. Some of his collaborators would nowadays be called 'researchers'. Others, providing no more than secretarial assistance, recopied his manuscripts, adding punctuation and correcting inconsistencies. Others still— Maquet in particular—were involved in what would nowadays be called 'script-conferences', discussing story-lines, the development of characters, and ways of grafting fictional events onto solid historical stock. But only Dumas had the 'Dumas touch', and he alone was ultimately responsible for the final tone, tension, and form of his romances. The writing of *Monte Cristo* is a case in point.

In an article published in his own newspaper, *Le Monte Cristo*, in April 1857, Dumas explained that in 1842 he had accompanied Prince Napoleon on a sailing expedition to Elba. It was then that he first saw the Island of Monte Cristo which so took his imagination that he promised the Prince that he would one day write a novel in which it would feature. In 1843 he signed a contract with the publishers Béthune and

Plon for eight volumes of 'Impressions of Paris'. But the success of Eugène Sue's *Mystères de Paris* gave the publishers second thoughts and they subsequently informed Dumas that they now wanted a novel rather than the historical and archaeological guide they had originally commissioned. Having received an advance but not yet having written a word, Dumas was only too happy to oblige. He dusted down an 'anecdote' which he had found in the *Mémoires historiques tirés des archives de la police de Paris* (1838, 6 vols.) by Jacques Peuchet (1758–1830), a former police archivist, who had written accounts of a number of intriguing cases in the manner designed to thrill, titillate, and horrify.

The affair that had attracted Dumas was entitled 'Le Diamant et la vengeance' ('Revenge and the Diamond') and began in Paris in 1807 where four friends from the Midi, François Picaud, Gervais Chaubard, Guilhem Solari, and Antoine Allut were in the habit of meeting regularly at the café run by one Mathieu Loupian, a widower with two children. When Picaud, a cobbler, announced that he was to marry Marguerite Vigoroux, a pretty girl with a handsome dowry, the envious Loupian persuaded the others that Picaud needed to be taught a lesson. With only Allut dissenting from what he considered to be a dangerous jest, they denounced Picaud as an English spy. He was arrested and disappeared from sight. Seven years later, in April 1814, Picaud was released from the prison of Fenestrelles in Piedmont. While serving his sentence, he had grown close to another prisoner, a Milanese cleric abandoned by his family, who had come to regard him as a son. Before his death in January 1814, the cleric made over to him a vast fortune which included a secret hoard of three million gold coins. Picaud returned to Paris an extremely rich man on 15 February 1815.

There he learned that Marguerite had waited for him for two years before marrying Loupian who had used her dowry to open what had become one of the most fashionable cafés in

Paris. Following the trail, he travelled to see Allut who had retired to Nîmes. Calling himself the abbé Baldini, he explained that he had shared a cell in a Naples jail with Picaud who was now dead. For services rendered to a wealthy English prisoner, Picaud had acquired a diamond worth 50,000 francs and had charged the abbé to give it to Allut, the only member of the conspiracy to demur, on condition that he reveal the identity of those who had denounced him. Their names were to be engraved on his tombstone. Allut hesitated but was brow-beaten into accepting by his greedy, shrewish wife. Subsequently the merchant who bought the diamond resold it for 100,000 francs, thus incurring the anger of the Alluts. When he was found dead, Allut was charged with murder and jailed.

At about the same time in Paris, an old lady approached Loupian and offered him a small regular payment to employ an old family servant named Prosper. Shortly afterwards, Chaubard, one of the original four friends, was found stabbed on the Pont des Arts. Attached to the handle of the murder-weapon was a note which read: 'Number One'. It was the first of a series of sinister incidents. Loupian's dog and his wife's parrot were poisoned. Mademoiselle Loupian was seduced and promised marriage by a rich nobleman who proved to be a former galley-slave who promptly absconded. The café burned down and Loupian was ruined. One night Solari was taken violently ill and died in agony. A note pinned to the body proclaimed: 'Number Two'. Loupian's son was lured into bad company, took to crime, and was jailed for twenty years. Marguerite died and Loupian's daughter, now destitute, was forced into prostitution by Prosper.

One night in the Jardin des Tuileries, Loupian was surprised by old Prosper who revealed that he was Picaud, the architect of the catastrophes which had befallen him, his purpose being to ruin the man who had ruined his life. Picaud stabbed his victim to death but was himself overpowered by a stranger who locked him up in a lonely cellar. The stranger was Allut who had followed the trail of the 'abbé Baldini' but had arrived too late to warn Loupian. He too now wanted revenge for the time he had spent in prison and demanded 25,000 francs every time Picaud asked for food. Though he was worth 16 millions, Picaud had grown avaricious and refused to pay. Finally Allut lost patience and murdered him before fleeing to England where he revealed the full story on his death-bed in 1828.

Dumas retained the tripartite structure of Picaud's revenge which he decided initially was the essence of the anecdote. From Monte Cristo's disguises to Vampa's treatment of his prisoner Danglars—but not the character of Marguerite/ Mercédès, who is given a central role—he relied heavily on Peuchet's sombre version of events. He began by setting his story in Rome at what is now Chapter 31. Working quickly, he took events up to the return of Albert de Morcerf and Franz d'Epinay to Paris—though his chronicle was at this stage written in the first person from Franz's point of view. He then showed what he had written to Maquet who asked why the most dramatic part of the story—the betrayal, imprisonment, and escape of the hero—had been omitted. The tale would have to be related at some point to justify the theme of vengeance: it was too long to be introduced retrospectively and too interesting to be summarized. Dumas agreed and the next day decided that the novel should fall into three parts: Marseilles, Rome, and Paris (that is, Chapters 1–30, 31–9, and 40–117 in this translation). Subsequent 'script conferences' prompted Maquet to write out a kind of story-board which Dumas was only too happy to follow.

The 'first part' appeared in *Le Journal des débats* between 28 August and 18 October. The 'Roman' section followed immediately but 'Part III' was delayed by Dumas's other commitments: in addition to deadlines for *L'Histoire d'une casse-noisette* (*The History of a Nutcracker*) (1845) and a number of similar smaller commissions, he had contracted to write *La Dame de Monsoreau* for *Le Constitutionnel*, and *Les Quarante-Cinq* (*The Forty-Five Guardsmen*) and *Le Chevalier de Maison-Rouge* for *La Démocratie pacifique*. As a result, Part III did not appear until June 1845 and the final instalment, beginning at Chapter 63 of the present edition, ran more or less smoothly until 15 January 1846. It is hardly surprising that Dumas, who regularly over-committed himself in this way, glady accepted whatever help he could get.

But if Maquet had given him a line to follow, it was Dumas who breathed his own life into the saga of Edmond Dantès, which retains many features of Peuchet's anecdote and yet is quite different from its mood. From his stay in Marseilles in 1834, he recalled the Morrel family, the Catalan community, and his visit to the Chateau d'If where he had inspected the cell once occupied by Mirabeau. He remembered too the stories he had heard of the strange and learned abbé Faria who had died in 1819 (see note to p. 104). To give a ring of authenticity to the murders perpetrated by Mme de Villefort, the wife of the magistrate who sent Dantès to the Chateau d'If, he borrowed scientific details from the trial of the poisoner Castaing and the experiments he and a friend named Thibaut had carried out with toxic substances (see notes to p. 348 and 712). He drew on his own experience for his descriptions of If, Monte Cristo, and Rome, while his picture of Paris—and Dumas thought of the book as essentially a novel of contemporary manners—was rooted in his own observation. But more important than the way the story was put together or the memories of places and people which made it authentic and immediate, Dumas's imagination took his melodramatic plot into the realm of legend. The first part especially has an extra, special, magnetic charge. In Italy and Paris, Monte Cristo the avenger burns like ice, but Edmond Dantès, the super-hero of the Chateau d'If, generates a sense of wonder and simply makes off with the reader. Balzac or Stendhal, who were greater novelists, never achieved as much, and only Hugo's archetypes, Jean Valjean and Quasimodo, have a comparable epic presence.

Yet for all the oriental and magical aura of his tale, events are rooted in real life, as the explanatory notes at the end of the present edition serve to show. Dumas parades his knowledge of horticulture, art, architecture, literature, and history and in so doing attaches his tale to the common-place, common-sense world. His characters live at real addresses, patronize well-known stables and watchmakers, see the operas and plays which everyone who was someone had seen, live in authentic social milieus in the Chaussée d'Antin or the Faubourg Saint-Germain and adopt attitudes appropriate to their age and rank. Politically they live in the shadow first of Napoleon, then of the conservative Restoration before emerging into the kind of society where opportunists like Danglars made fortunes by speculating in the new railways and the nascent industrial revolution, and where canny politicians like Villefort or Debray always stayed on the winning side.

Against the forces of conservatism stands the idealism which had made Greece independent, sought a just settlement in Carlist Spain, and turned Mehemet Ali and Ali Pacha into heroes in the struggle against tyranny in general and the British in particular. Dumas, who took pride in being the friend of Kings and Princes, was a paradoxical democrat and his mixed liberal sympathies give the novel an ambiguous political colour. His contempt for the ambition of the representatives of the people who despise the voters who elected them is as clear as his sympathy for Faria's belief in the inevitability of national and personal freedom. Edmond Dantès is not merely the victim of the envy of Danglars but a pawn in a game of political intrigue: the clothes and titles may be different, but France is as firmly under the control of sultans and viziers as the Orient where the outward forms of tyranny were at least openly acknowledged. Yet Monte Cristo speaks out against 'the socialists' and rejects all loyalty to a society hostile to the idea of justice: is not Villefort 'the living statue of the law?' Dantès the victim turns himself through his own efforts into a hardened individualist who, though he never forgets the rights of man, has relied on his own energies, brains, and will to overcome impossible odds.

At this level *Monte Cristo* shares the nascent habit of realism best exemplified by Balzac: indeed, the novel is sometimes thought of as a kind of 'Comédie humaine' in its own right. Then again, Dumas's protagonist, a superman who tastes disillusionment, belongs with those disintegrating, self-doubting heroes who so fired the Romantic imagination. He suffers the fate of those who live to see their wishes come true: the heady wine of vengeance turns to dust in his mouth. But Dantès's trials and his heaven-sent opportunity to revenge the wrongs done him also cripple him emotionally. His first thought on returning to France may well be to reward the good, and Morrel's business is duly saved. But he is doomed to engineer human happiness in which he cannot share: he is a man apart, an outsider. And the terrible toll he takes of those who wronged him leaves him empty rather than fulfilled. Vengeance may be a meal best eaten cold, but cold meats do not satisfy him. He is as lonely as Vigny's Moses who is abandoned by God. Monte Cristo does not simply live above the society which he judges, he is cut off from it, without human contact, a solitary figure chained to the destiny of his mission. He believes that he is God's agent through whom just punishment is meted out to those who have sinned against man and heaven. But as time passes, even he begins to doubt that anyone can really be 'the angel of Providence'. As Mercédès points out, self-appointed Hammers of the Lord are not always able to distinguish between Justice and Anger: why does Monte Cristo remember crimes that Providence has forgotten? It is only when Villefort has gone mad, and Morcerf is destroyed that Monte Cristo understands that he is not the privileged instrument of God's providence but a victim of Fate like all the others. Only then does he abandon his obsession: the crimes of Mme de Villefort and the death of Edward, which he had not foreseen, do not simply teach him that Fate is beyond his control but finally sicken him. Monte Cristo's ultimate victory is not the defeat of his enemies but the spiritual re-birth which enables him to rejoin the human race and sail away in hope with Haydée.

Thus to historical realism and strong social types is added a level of psychological depth which is also present in the bold sketch of the lesbian Eugénie, say, or in the mixture of puritanism and sadism which explains so much of Villefort's later conduct. ('I am on the earth to punish', he says). But *Monte Cristo* is also a highly moral book. François Picaud revenged himself by acts which were criminal; Monte Cristo, as the agent of Providence, remains neutral, refuses to intervene, and settles for laying traps in which his prey entangle themselves through greed or ambition. His victims are made responsible for bringing about their own downfall and their fate is a punishment not for what they once did to Edmond Dantès but for the crimes they have since committed against moral and social law: Danglers for his financial opportunism, Fernand for betraying Ali Pacha, and Villefort for applying the law without mercy. Behind events is a vigorous defence of Justice.

But of course it is not Dumas's moral lessons or social and psychological realism nor the solitary Romantic anguish of the hero which explain the novel's lasting popularity. For most readers, *Monte Cristo* is not about Justice at all, but about Injustice. It is a tale of Revenge and Retribution which does not lead back to the Paris of the 1840s but opens into a world of magic, of fabulous treasure buried on desert islands, of bandits and dark intrigue, of wizardry and splendours borrowed from the *Arabian Nights*. The fearless Monte Cristo is a super-hero who overcomes all the odds. A master of disguise, he has the secret of all knowledge, immense physical strength, endless resourcefulness, and complete power to

punish the wicked. Heroes do not come any taller. He is the
stuff of adolescent dreams and will retain his fascination, as
Swinburne said, 'while the boy's heart beats in man'. It was
for 'the Great Dumas'' capacity to stir the emotions and
carry his reader into a world of excitement and adventure
that Thackeray was kept 'on the stretch for nearly nine hours
one day' in July 1849. In September 1853 he wrote to a
friend: 'began to read Monte Christo [*sic*] at six one morning
and never stopped until eleven at night'. Shaw placed
Dumas with Dickens and Scott 'in the second order because,
though they are immensely entertaining, their morality is
ready made', and commented reproachfully that Dumas
'made French history like an opera by Meyerbeer for me'.
But the niggards and carpers (and they have never been in
short supply) will always lose hands down. With *Monte Cristo*,
Dumas, King of Romance and Prince of Story-tellers,
achieved what he also managed in *The Three Musketeers*: he
manufactured a folk legend.

Where in that extrovert, amiable, and engaging personality Dumas found the resources to deal with such sombre
subjects as treachery and revenge remains a mystery. Part of
the answer surely lies in the exuberance of his imagination
which was equalled in his own age only by that of Victor
Hugo. Hugo's literary gifts were undoubtedly the greater but
even he deferred to Dumas. After Dumas's death, he wrote:
'The name of Alexandre Dumas is more than French, it is
European; and it is more than European, it is universal'.

For even during his lifetime, *The Count of Monte Cristo* had
travelled far beyond the frontiers of France. It was quickly
translated into German, Spanish, and Italian and subsequently into countless languages from Arabic to Swedish.
The first English version was made in 1846 by Emma Hardy
for the inexpensive Parlour Novelist series published in Bel-
fast, but it was the anonymous translation published by
Chapman and Hall the same year which was to flood the
English-speaking world. It differs in some respects from the

standard French text (there are a few omissions and the chapter arrangement varies) but it is as readable as it is faithful. With one or two exceptions, the small number of 'new' translations since made have drawn heavily upon it and it is this classic version which we publish here. Routledge secured the rights in 1852 and reprinted it at least twenty times before 1900. Thereafter it was adopted by Nelson, Dent's Everyman Library, and Collins, and has been more or less permanently available every since. It first appeared in the United States in 1846 and was subsequently reissued many times by T. B. Peterson of Philadelphia, Routledge's New York office, and Little, Brown and Company of Boston. When, by 1890, the popularity of *Monte Cristo* began to decline in France, the Anglo-Saxon world was afflicted by Dumas-mania. Thirty English editions appeared between 1890 and 1910, while in the United States the figure approaches 50. Thereafter, save for a revival in the 1920s, sales declined though this is not to say that Dumas's popularity has waned. The silent cinema projected Monte Cristo's revenge onto the world's screens where it seemed even more tremendous than on the printed page. The first filmed *Monte Cristo* was made by William Selig in 1907 and there have since been about thirty different versions. But the tale has also worked its magic on radio—the latest six-hour version was broadcast by the BBC in 1988—and on television. Monte Cristo, master of disguise, has left the printed page only to reappear with the face of Robert Donat, Louis Hayward, Jean Marais, and Louis Jourdan, or the voice of Andrew Sachs.

Dumas, collaborating still with Maquet, adapted his novel for the stage in four parts (1848–52) and for a moment contemplated writing a sequel. Others have since written continuations of the saga—with J. Le Prince and Jules Lermina as principal perpetrators—but none have captured the secret of Monte Cristo, man of mystery. '"I say he is a myth"', says Albert de Morcerf on p. 320, '"and never had an existence."'

"And what may a myth be?" enquired Pastrini. "The explanation would be too long, my dear landlord," replied Franz'. And too dreary. The simplest course is to admit to the plain fact that Monte Cristo is quite simply irresistible.

SELECT BIBLIOGRAPHY

Le Comte de Monte Cristo was serialized in *Le Journal des Débats* between 28 August 1844 and 15 January 1846 and was first published in Paris by Pétion (18 vols., 1844–5). The standard French editions are those prepared by J.-H. Bornèque for the Classiques Garnier series (2 vols., Paris, 1956) and by Gilbert Sigaux for La Pléiade (Paris, 1981). The most valiant attempt at resolving the complex printing history of Dumas's writings is still Frank W. Reed *A Bibliography of Dumas père* (London, 1933). Reed's other unpublished researches are listed in Léon-François Hoffman's edition of *Georges* (Paris, 1974), a novel (1843) which has structural and thematic similarities to *Monte Cristo*. Anglo-Saxon readers will also be interested in Douglas Munro's *Alexandre Dumas père: A Bibliography of Works Translated into English to 1910* (New York and London, 1978).

Dumas's autobiography (*Mes Mémoires* (1852–5), 5 vols., ed. Pierre Josserand, (Paris, 1954–68); English translation (London, 1907–9) is entertaining but highly romanced and does not proceed beyond 1832. The best French biographies are by Henri Clouard, *Alexandre Dumas* (Paris, 1955), Claude Schopp, *Alexandre Dumas* (Paris, 1985), and André Maurois, *Les Trois Dumas* (Paris, 1957; English translation, London, 1958). Gilles Henry, *Monte Cristo, ou l'extraordinaire aventure des ancêtres d'Alexandre Dumas* (Paris, 1976) is especially interesting for the light thrown on the Davy–Dumas family. Isabelle Jan, *Dumas romancier* (Paris, 1973) offers the fullest study of the novels.

Of the many books in English devoted to Dumas, still helpful are Francis Gribble, *Dumas, Father and Son* (London, 1930) and A. Craig Bell, *Alexandre Dumas* (London, 1950). Richard Stowe's *Dumas* (Boston, 1976) provides a general introduction and Michael Ross (*Alexandre Dumas* (Newton Abbot, 1981)) gives a sympathetic account of Dumas's life. The most balanced and comprehensive guide, however, is F. W. J. Hemmings's excellent *The King of Romance* (London, 1979).

Useful too are special numbers of literary magazines devoted to Dumas: *Europe*, 490–1 (February–March 1970); *Le Magazine littéraire*, 72 (January 1973); and *L'Arc*, 71 (1978).

A CHRONOLOGY OF ALEXANDRE DUMAS

1762   25 March: Birth at Saint Domingo of Thomas-Alexandre, son of the Marquis Davy de la Pailleterie and a mulatto, Marie-Cessette Dumas. He returns to France with his father in 1780.

1792   28 November: Colonel Dumas marries Marie-Louise-Elizabeth Labouret, daughter of an inn-keeper, at Villers-Cotterêts.

1801   1 May: General Dumas returns to France from prison in Italy.

1802   24 July: Birth of Alexandre Dumas at Villers-Cotterêts.

1806   26 February: Death of General Dumas who had been refused an army pension by Napoleon who disliked his independent spirit.

1812   Dumas goes to school at Villers-Cotterêts.

1814   Madame Dumas given a licence to run a tobacco-shop.

1817   Dumas becomes a lawyer's office-boy.

1819   Dumas falls in love with Adèle Dalvin who subsequently marries a wealthy man older than herself. Meets Adolphe de Leuven, with whom he collaborates in writing unsuccessful plays.

1822   Visits Leuven in Paris, meets Talma and resolves to become a playwright.

1823   Moves to Paris. Enters the service of the Duke d'Orléans. Falls in love with a seamstress, Catherine Labay.

1824   27 July: Birth of Alexandre Dumas *fils*.

1825   22 September: Dumas's first play, *La Chasse et l'amour* (*The Chase and Love*), written in collaboration with Leuven and Rousseau, makes no impact.

1826   Publication of *Les Nouvelles contemporaines* (*Tales of Today*), Dumas's first solo composition. It sells four copies.

1827 A company of English actors, which includes Kean, Kemble, and Mrs Smithson, performs Shakespeare in English to enthusiastic Paris audiences: Dumas is deeply impressed. Liaison with Mélanie Waldor.

1828–9 Liaison with the actress Virginie Bourbier. Dumas enters Parisian literary circles through Charles Nodier.

1829 11 February: First of about fifty performances of *Henri III et sa cour* (*Henry III and His Court*) which makes Dumas famous and thrusts him into the front line of the Romantic revolution in literature. Dumas meets Victor Hugo.

1830 30 March: First performance of *Christine* (written in 1828). In May start of an affair with the actress Belle Krelsamer. Active in the July Revolution: Dumas single-handedly captures a gunpowder magazine at Soissons and is sent by Lafayette to promote the National Guard in the Vendée: he makes little headway against strong local royalist loyalties.

1831 5 March: Birth of Marie, his daughter by Belle Krelsamer. 17 March: Dumas acknowledges Alexandre, his son by Catherine Lebay. First performance of *Napoléon Bonaparte* (10 January), *Antony*, starring Marie Dorval (3 May), *Charles VII et ses grands vassaux* (*Charles VII and the Barons*, 20 October), and *Richard Darlington* (10 December).

1832 6 February: Start of his affair with the acresss Ida Ferrier. 15 April: Dumas succumbs to the cholera which kills 20,000 Parisians. First performance of *La Tour de Nesle* (*The Tower of Nesle*, 29 May): Gaillardet accuses Dumas of plagiarism. In July, suspected of republicanism, Dumas leaves for a three-month stay in Switzerland where he meets Chateaubriand. After the spectacular failure of his next play, *Le Fils de l'émigré* (*The Son of the Emigré*, 28 August), he begins to take an interest in the literary possibilities of French history.

1833 Start of serial publication of the first of Dumas's many travel books: *Impressions de voyage: En Suisse* (*Travel Impressions: Switzerland*).

1834–5 October: Dumas travels in the Midi with the landscape painter Godefroy Jadin. There he meets the Catalans, visits the Chateau d'If and inspects the cell once occupied by Mirabeau. From the Riviera, he embarks on the first of many journeys to Italy.

1836   31 August: Dumas returns triumphantly to the theatre with *Kean*, with Frederick Lemaître in the title role.

1837   Becomes a *chevalier* of the Legion of Honour.

1838   Death of Dumas's mother. Travels along the Rhine with Gérard de Nerval who introduces him to Auguste Maquet in December.

1840   1 February: Dumas marries Ida Ferrier, travels to Italy and publishes *Le Capitaine Pamphile*, the best of his children's books.

1840–2   Dividing his time between Paris and Italy, Dumas increasingly abandons the theatre for the novel.

1842   June: During a cruise in the Mediterranean with Prince Napoleon (son of Jérôme Bonaparte, ex-King of Westphalia), Dumas visits Elba and sails round the Ile of Monte Cristo. He publishes a travelogue, *Le Speronare* and the first of the romances written in collaboration with Maquet: *Le Chevalier d'Harmental*. Subsequently he enlisted Maquet's support for his most famous novels: *The Three Musketeers*, *Vingt Ans Après* (*Twenty Years After*), *The Count of Monte Cristo*, *La Reine Margot* (*Queen Margot*), *Joseph Balsamo* (*Memoirs of a Physician*), *Le Vicomte de Bragelonne*, etc. 2 August: Dumas hurries back to Paris for the funeral of the Duke d'Orléans.

1843   A particularly prolific year for plays and novels which include *Georges*, a tale of vengeance which anticipates *The Count of Monte Cristo*. Dumas quarrels with the theatre critic Jules Janin and a duel is narrowly averted.

1844   Publication of *The Three Musketeers* and the start of the serialization of *The Count of Monte Cristo* in *Le Journal des débats*. 15 October: amicable separation from Ida Ferrier.

1845   Dumas signs contracts with *La Presse* and *Le Constitutionnel* to write nine volumes of fiction a year. He wins his suit against the journalist Jacquot, author of *Fabrique de romans: Maison Alexandre Dumas et Cie* (*A Fiction Factory: The Firm of Alexandre Dumas and Co.*), in which he accused him of publishing other men's work under his own name.

1846 Separates from Ida Ferrier. Brief liaison with Lola Montès. November–January: travels with his son to Spain and North Africa.

1847 Completion of the 'Château de Monte Cristo' at Marly-le-Roi. 20 February: opening of the 'Théâtre historique'. Questions asked in the House about Dumas's use of the Navy vessel, *Le Véloce*, during his visit to North Africa. Loses a lawsuit brought by newspaper proprietors for not producing copy for which he had received considerable advances.

1848 1 March: Founds a newspaper, *Le Mois*, which he personally edits until Dumas puts up, unsuccessfully, as a parliamentary candidate. Votes for Louis-Napoleon in the December elections.

1850 Beginning of a nine-year liaison with Isabella Constant. 20 March: the 'Théâtre historique' is declared bankrupt. The Château de Monte Cristo is sold for 30,000 Francs.

1851 Michel Lévy begins to bring out the first volumes of Dumas's complete works which will eventually fill 301 volumes. 7 December: using Louis-Napoleon's *coup d'état* as an excuse, Dumas flees to Belgium to avoid his creditors.

1852 Publication of the first volumes of *Mes Mémoires*. Dumas declared bankrupt with debts of 100,000 Francs.

1853 November: After making a settlement with his creditors, Dumas returns to Paris and founds a periodical, *Le Mousquetaire* (last issue 7 February 1857) for which he writes most of the copy himself.

1857 23 April: Founds a literary weekly, *Le Monte Cristo* which, with one break, survives until 1862.

1858 15 June: Dumas leaves for Russia where he travels until March 1859.

1859 11 March: Death of Ida Ferrier. Beginning of a liaison with

Emilie Cordier which lasts until 1864. Spends two days with Victor Hugo in exile on Guernsey.

1860   Meets Garibaldi at Turin and just misses the taking of Sicily (June). He returns to Marseilles where he buys guns for the Italian cause and is in Naples just after the city falls in September. Garibaldi stands, by proxy, as godfather to Dumas's daughter by Emile Cordier. 11 October: founds *L'Indipendente*, a literary and political periodical published half in French and half in Italian.

1863   The works of Dumas are placed on the Index by the Catholic Church.

1864   April: Dumas returns to Paris.

1865   Further travels in Italy, Germany, and Austria.

1867   Publishes *Le Terreur prussienne* (*The Prussian Terror*), a novel, to warn France against Prussian might. Begins a last liaison, with Ada Menken, an American actress (d. 1868).

1869   10 March: First performance of Dumas's last play, *Les Blancs et les Bleus* (*The Whites and the Blues*)

1870   5 December: Dumas dies at Puy, near Dieppe, after a stroke in September.

1872   Dumas's remains transferred to Villers-Cotterêts.

1883   Unveiling of a statue to Dumas in Paris.

THE COUNT OF
MONTE CRISTO

The arrival at Marseilles

ON the 24th of February, 1815, the lookout of Notre-Dame de la Garde signalled the three-master, the *Pharaon*, from Smyrna, Trieste, and Naples.

As usual, a pilot put off immediately, and rounding the Château d'If, got on board the vessel between Cape Morgion and the Isle of Rion.

Immediately, and according to custom, the platform of Fort Saint-Jean was covered with spectators; it is always an event at Marseilles for a ship to come into port, especially when this ship, like the *Pharaon*, had been built, rigged, and laden on the stocks of the old Phocée, and belonged to an owner of the city.

The ship drew on: it had safely passed the strait, which some volcanic shock has made between the Isle of Calasareigne and the Isle of Jaros; had doubled Pomègue, and approached the harbour under topsails, jib, and foresail, but so slowly and sedately that the idlers, with that instinct which misfortune sends before it, asked one another what misfortune could have happened on board. However, those experienced in navigation saw plainly that if any accident had occurred, it was not to the vessel herself, for she bore down with all the evidence of being skilfully handled, the anchor ready to be dropped, the bowsprit-shrouds loose, and beside the pilot, who was steering the *Pharaon* by the narrow entrance of the port of Marseilles, was a young man, who with activity and vigilant eye, watched every motion of the ship, and repeated each direction of the pilot.

The vague disquietude which prevailed amongst the spectators had so much affected one of the crowd that he did not await the arrival of the vessel in harbour, but jumping into a small skiff, desired to be pulled alongside the *Pharaon*, which he reached as she rounded the creek of La Rèserve.

When the young man on board saw this individual approach, he left his station by the pilot, and came, hat in hand, to the side of the ship's bulwarks.

He was a fine, tall, slim young fellow, with black eyes, and hair as dark as the raven's wing; and his whole appearance bespoke that calmness and resolution peculiar to men accustomed from their cradle to contend with danger.

"Ah! is it you, Dantès?" cried the man in the skiff. "What's the matter? and why have you such an air of sadness aboard?"

"A great misfortune, M. Morrel," replied the young man,— "a great misfortune, for me especially! Off Civita Vecchia we lost our brave Captain Leclere."

"And the cargo?" inquired the owner eagerly.

"Is all safe, M. Morrel; and I think you will be satisfied on that head. But poor Captain Leclere——"

"What happened to him?" asked the owner, with an air of considerable resignation. "What happened to the worthy captain?"

"He died."

"Fell into the sea?"

"No, sir, he died of brain-fever in dreadful agony." Then turning to the crew, he said:

"Look out there! all ready to drop anchor!"

All hands obeyed. At the same moment the eight or ten seamen, who composed the crew, sprung some to the main-sheets, others to the braces, others to the halyards, others to the jib-ropes, and others to the topsail brails.

The young sailor gave a look to see that his orders were promptly and accurately obeyed, and then turned again to the owner.

"And how did this misfortune occur?" he inquired, resuming the inquiry suspended for a moment.

"Alas, sir, in the most unexpected manner. After a long conversation with the harbour-master, Captain Leclere left Naples greatly disturbed in his mind. At the end of twenty-four hours he was attacked by a fever, and died three days afterwards. We performed the usual burial service, and he is at his rest, sewn up in his hammock, with two bullets of thirty-six pounds each at his head and heels, off the Island of El Giglio. We bring to his widow his sword and cross of honour. It was worth while, truly." added the young man, with a melancholy smile, "to make war against the English for ten years, and to die in his bed at last, like everybody else."

"Why, you see, Edmond," replied the owner, who appeared more comforted at every moment, "we are all mortal, and the old must make way for the young. If not, why, there would be no promotion; and as you have assured me that the cargo——"

"Is all safe and sound, M. Morrel, take my word for it; and I advise you not to take £1000 for the profits of the voyage."

Then, as they were just passing the Round Tower, the young man shouted out, "Ready, there, to lower topsails, foresail, and jib!"

The order was executed as promptly as if on board a man-of-war.

" Let go—and brail all! "

At this last word all the sails were lowered, and the bark moved almost imperceptibly onwards.

" Now, if you will come on board, M. Morrel," said Dantès, observing the owner's impatience, " here is your supercargo, M. Danglars, coming out of his cabin, who will furnish you with every particular. As for me, I must look after the anchoring, and dress the ship in mourning."

The owner did not wait to be twice invited. He seized a rope which Dantès flung to him, and with an activity that would have done credit to a sailor, climbed up the side of the ship, whilst the young man, going to his task, left the conversation to the individual whom he had announced under the name of Danglars, who now came towards the owner. He was a man of twenty-five or twenty-six years of age, of unprepossessing countenance, obsequious to his superiors, insolent to his inferiors; and then, besides his position as responsible agent on board, which is always obnoxious to the sailors, he was as much disliked by the crew, as Edmond Dantès was beloved by them.

" Well, M. Morrel," said Danglars, " you have heard of the misfortune that has befallen us? "

" Yes—yes: poor Captain Leclere! He was a brave and an honest man! "

" And a first-rate seaman, grown old between sky and ocean, as should a man charged with the interests of a house so important as that of Morrel and Son," replied Danglars.

" But," replied the owner, following with his look Dantès, who was watching the anchoring of his vessel, " it seems to me that a sailor needs not to be so old as you say, Danglars, to understand his business; for our friend Edmond seems to understand it thoroughly, and not to require instruction from any one."

" Yes," said Danglars, casting towards Edmond a look in which a feeling of envy was strongly visible. " Yes, he is young, and youth is invariably self-confident. Scarcely was the captain's breath out of his body than he assumed the command without consulting any one, and he caused us to lose a day and a half at the Isle of Elba, instead of making for Marseilles direct."

" As to taking the command of the vessel," replied Morrel, " that was his duty as captain's mate; as to losing a day and a half off the Isle of Elba, he was wrong, unless the ship wanted some repair."

" The ship was as well as I am, and as, I hope, you are, M.

Morrel, and this day and a half was lost from pure whim, for the pleasure of going ashore, and nothing else."

" Dantès," said the shipowner, turning towards the young man, " come this way! "

" In a moment, sir," answered Dantès, " and I'm with you! ". Then calling to the crew, he said:

" Let go! "

The anchor was instantly dropped, and the chain ran rattling through the port-hole. Dantès continued at his post, in spite of the presence of the pilot, until this manœuvre was completed, and then he added, " Lower the pennant half-mast high—put the ensign in a weft, and slope the yards! "

" You see," said Danglars, " he fancies himself captain already, upon my word."

" And so, in fact, he is," said the owner.

" Except your signature and your partner's, M. Morrel."

" And why should he not have this? " asked the owner; " he is young, it is true, but he seems to me a thorough seaman, and of full experience."

A cloud passed over Danglars' brow.

" Your pardon, M. Morrel," said Dantès, approaching, " the ship now rides at anchor, and I am at your service. You hailed me, I think? "

Danglars retreated a step or two.

" I wish to inquire why you stopped at the Isle of Elba? "

" I do not know, sir; it was to fulfil a last instruction of Captain Leclere, who, when dying, gave me a packet for the Maréchal Bertrand."*

" Then did you see him, Edmond? "

" Who? "

" The maréchal? "

" Yes."

Morrel looked around him, and then, drawing Dantès on one side, he said suddenly:

" And how is the emperor? "

" Very well, as far as I could judge from my eyes."

" You saw the emperor, then? "

" He entered the maréchal's apartment whilst I was there."

" And you spoke to him? "

" Why, it was he who spoke to me, sir," said Dantès, with a smile.

" And what did he say to you? "

" Asked me questions about the ship, the time it left Marseilles, the course she had taken, and what was her cargo. I believe, if she had not been laden, and I had been master, he would have bought her. But I told him I was only mate, and that she belonged to the firm of Morrel and Son. ' Ah! ah! ' he said. ' I know them! The Morrels have been shipowners from father to son; and there was a Morrel who served in the same regiment with me when I was in garrison at Valence.' "

" *Pardieu!* and that is true! " cried the owner, greatly delighted. " And that was Policar Morrel, my uncle, who was afterwards a captain. Dantès, you must tell my uncle that the emperor remembered him, and you will see it will bring tears into the old soldier's eyes. Come, come! " continued he, patting Edmond's shoulder kindly. " You did very right, Dantès, to follow Captain Leclere's instruction, and touch at the Isle of Elba, although, if it were known, that you had conveyed a packet to the maréchal and had conversed with the emperor, it might bring you into trouble."

" How could that bring me into trouble, sir? " asked Dantès; " for I did not even know of what I was the bearer; and the emperor merely made such inquiries as he would of the first comer. But your pardon; here are the officers of health and the customs coming alongside! " and the young man went to the gangway. As he departed, Danglars approached, and said:

" Well, it appears that he has given you satisfactory reasons for his landing at Porto-Ferrajo? "

" Yes, most satisfactory, my dear Danglars."

" Well, so much the better," said the supercargo; " for it is always painful to see a comrade who does not do his duty."

" Dantès has done his," replied the owner, " and that is not saying much. It was Captain Leclere who gave orders for this delay."

" Talking of Captain Leclere, has not Dantès given you a letter from him? "

" To me?—no—was there one?"

" I believe that, besides the packet, Captain Leclere had confided a letter to his care."

" Of what packet are you speaking, Danglars? "

" Why, that which Dantès left at Porto-Ferrajo."

" How do you know he had a packet to leave at Porto-Ferrajo? " Danglars turned very red.

" I was passing close to the door of the captain's cabin, which was half open, and I saw him give the packet and letter to Dantès."

" He did not speak to me of it," replied the shipowner; " but if there be any letter he will give it to me."

Danglars reflected for a moment.

" Then, M. Morrel, I beg of you," said he, " not to say a word to Dantès on the subject, I may have been mistaken."

At this moment the young man returned, and Danglars retreated as before.

" Well, my dear Dantès, are you now free? " inquired the owner.

" Yes, sir."

" You have not been long detained? "

" No. I gave the custom-house officers a copy of our bill of lading; and as to the other papers, they sent a man off with the pilot, to whom I gave them."

" Then you have nothing more to do here? "

" No, all is arranged now."

" Then you can come and dine with me? "

" Excuse me, M. Morrel, excuse me, if you please; but my first visit is due to my father, though I am not the less grateful for the honour you have done me."

" Right, Dantès, quite right. I always knew you were a good son."

" And," inquired Dantès, with some hesitation, " do you know how my father is? "

" Well, I believe, my dear Edmond, although I have not seen him lately."

" Yes, he likes to keep himself shut up in his little room."

" That proves, at least, that he has wanted for nothing during your absence."

Dantès smiled.

" My father is proud, sir; and if he had not a meal left, I doubt if he would have asked anything from any one, except God."

" Well, then, after this first visit has been made we rely on you."

" I must again excuse myself, M. Morrel; for after this first visit has been paid I have another, which I am most anxious to pay."

" True, Dantès, I forgot that there was at the Catalans some one who expects you no less impatiently than your father—the lovely Mercédès."

Dantès blushed.

" Ah! ah! " said the shipowner, " that does not astonish me, for she has been to me three times, inquiring if there were any news of the *Pharaon*. *Peste!* Edmond, you have a very handsome mistress! "

" She is not my mistress," replied the young sailor gravely, " she is my betrothed."

" Sometimes one and the same thing," said Morrel, with a smile.

" Not with us, sir," replied Dantès.

" Well, well, my dear Edmond," continued the owner, " do not let me detain you. You have managed my affairs so well, that I ought to allow you all the time you require for your own. Do you want any money ? "

" No, sir; I have all my pay to take,—nearly three months' wages."

" You are a careful fellow, Edmond."

" Say I have a poor father, sir."

" Yes, yes, I know how good a son you are, so now haste away to see your father. I have a son too, and I should be very wroth with those who detained him from me after a three months' voyage."

" Then I have your leave, sir? "

" Yes, if you have nothing more to say to me."

" Nothing."

" Captain Leclere did not, before he died, give you a letter for me? "

" He was unable to write, sir. But that reminds me that I must ask your leave of absence for some days."

" To get married? "

" Yes, first, and then to go to Paris."

" Very good; have what time you require, Dantès. It will take quite six weeks to unload the cargo, and we cannot get you ready for sea until three months after that; only be back again in three months, for the *Pharaon*," added the owner, patting the young sailor on the back, " cannot sail without her captain."

" Without her captain! " cried Dantès, his eyes sparkling with animation; " pray mind what you say, for you are touching on the most secret wishes of my heart. Is it really your intention to nominate me captain of the *Pharaon*? "

" If I were sole owner I would nominate you this moment, my dear Dantès, and say it is settled; but I have a partner, and you know the Italian proverb—*Che a compagno a padrone*—' He who has a partner has a master.' But the thing is at least half done, as you have one out of two voices. Rely on me to procure you the other; I will do my best."

" Ah, M. Morrel," exclaimed the young seaman, with tears in his eyes, and grasping the owner's hand, " M. Morrel, I thank you in the name of my father and of Mercédès."

" Good, good! Edmond. There's a sweet little cherub that sits up aloft that keeps a good watch for good fellows! Go to your father: go and see Mercédès, and come to me afterwards."

" Shall I row you on shore? "

" No, I thank you; I shall remain and look over the accounts with Danglars. Have you been satisfied with him this voyage? "

" That is according to the sense you attach to the question, sir. Do you mean is he a good comrade? No, for I think he never liked me since the day when I was silly enough, after a little quarrel we had, to propose to him to stop for ten minutes at the Isle of Monte Cristo to settle the dispute, a proposition which I was wrong to suggest, and he quite right to refuse. If you mean as responsible agent that you ask me the question, I believe there is nothing to say against him, and that you will be content with the way in which he has performed his duty."

" But tell me, Dantès, if you had the command of the *Pharaon*, should you have pleasure in retaining Danglars? "

" Captain or mate, M. Morrel," replied Dantès, " I shall always have the greatest respect for those who possess our owners' confidences."

" Good! good! Dantès. I see you are a thorough good fellow, and will detain you no longer. Go, for I see how impatient you are."

" Then I have leave? "

" Go, I tell you."

" May I have the use of your skiff? "

" Certainly."

" Then for the present, M. Morrel, farewell, and a thousand thanks! "

" I hope soon to see you again, my dear Edmond. Good luck to you! "

The young sailor jumped into the skiff, and sat down in the stern, desiring to be put ashore at the Canebière. The two rowers bent to their work, and the little boat glided away as rapidly as possible in the midst of the thousand vessels which choke up the narrow way which leads between the two rows of ships from the mouth of the harbour to the Quai d'Orléans.

The shipowner, smiling, followed him with his eyes, until he saw him spring out on the quay, and disappear in the midst of the throng which, from five o'clock in the morning until nine o'clock at night, choke up this famous street of La Canebière, of which the modern Phocéens are so proud, and say with all the gravity in the world, and with that accent which gives so much character to what is said, " If Paris had La Canebière, Paris would be a second Marseilles."' On turning round, the owner saw Danglars behind him, who apparently attended his orders; but in reality followed, as he did, the young sailor with his eyes, only there was a great difference in the expression of the looks of the two men who thus watched the movements of Edmond Dantès.

2

Father and Son

WE will leave Danglars struggling with the feelings of hatred, and endeavouring to insinuate in the ear of the shipowner, Morrel, some evil suspicions against his comrade, and follow Dantès; who, after having traversed the Canebière, took the Rue de Noailles, and entering into a small house, situated on the left side of the Allées de Meillan, rapidly ascended four stories of a dark staircase, holding the baluster in his hand, whilst with the other he repressed the beatings of his heart, and paused before a half-opened door, which revealed all the interior of a small apartment.

This apartment was occupied by Dantès' father.

The news of the arrival of the *Pharaon* had not yet reached the old man, who, mounted on a chair, was amusing himself with staking some nasturtiums with tremulous hand, which, mingled with clematis, formed a kind of trellis at his window.

Suddenly he felt an arm thrown round his body, and a well-known voice behind him exclaimed, " Father! dear father! "

The old man uttered a cry, and turned round; then, seeing his son, he fell into his arms, pale and trembling.

" What ails you, my dearest father? Are you ill? " inquired the young man, much alarmed.

" No, no, my dear Edmond—my boy—my son!—no; but I did not expect you; and joy, the surprise of seeing you so suddenly—— Ah! I really seem as if I were going to die! "

" Come, come, cheer up, my dear father! 'Tis I—really I! They say joy never hurts, and so I come to you without any warning. Come now, look cheerfully at me, instead of gazing as you do with your eyes so wide. Here I am back again, and we will now be happy."

" Yes, yes, my boy, so we will—so we will," replied the old man, " but how shall we be happy?—Will you never leave me again? —Come, tell me all the good fortune that has befallen you."

" God forgive me," said the young man, " for rejoicing at happiness derived from the misery of others; but Heaven knows I did not seek this good fortune: it has happened, and I really cannot affect to lament it. The good Captain Leclere is dead, father, and it is probable that, with the aid of M. Morrel, I shall have his place. Do you understand, father? Only imagine me a captain at twenty, with a hundred louis pay, and a share in the profits! Is this not more than a poor sailor, like me, could have hoped for?"

"Yes, my dear boy," replied the old man, "and much more than you could have expected."

"Well, then, with the first money I touch, I mean you to have a small house, with a garden to plant your clematis, your nasturtiums, and your honeysuckles. But what ails you, father? Are not you well?"

"'Tis nothing, nothing; it will soon pass away;" and as he said so the old man's strength failed him, and he fell backwards.

"Come, come," said the young man, "a glass of wine, father, will revive you. Where do you keep your wine?"

"No, no; thank ye. You need not look for it; I do not want it," said the old man.

"Yes, yes, father, tell me where it is;" and he opened two or three cupboards.

"It is no use," said the old man; "there is no wine."

"What! no wine?" said Dantès, turning pale, and looking alternately at the hollow cheeks of the old man and the empty cupboards. "What! no wine? Have you wanted money, father?"

"I want nothing now you are here," said the old man.

"Yet," stammered Dantès, wiping the perspiration from his brow—"yet I gave you two hundred francs when I left three months ago."

"Yes, yes, Edmond, that is true, but you forgot at that time a little debt to our neighbour Caderousse. He reminded me of it, telling me if I did not pay for you, he would be paid by M. Morrel; and so, you see, lest he might do you an injury——"

"Well?"

"Why, I paid him."

"But," cried Dantès, "it was a hundred and forty francs I owed Caderousse."

"Yes," stammered the old man.

"And you paid him out of the two hundred francs I left you?"

The old man made a sign in the affirmative.

"So that you have lived for three months on sixty francs?" muttered the young man.

"You know how little I require," said the old man.

"Heaven pardon me," cried Edmond, falling on his knees before the old man.

" What are you doing? "

" You have wounded my very heart."

" Never mind it, for I see you once more," said the old man; " and now all is forgotten—all is well again."

" Yes, here I am," said the young man, " with a happy prospect and a little money. Here, father ! here! " he said, " take this— take it, and send for something immediately."

And he emptied his pockets on the table, whose contents consisted of a dozen pieces of gold, five or six crowns, and some smaller coin.

The countenance of old Dantès brightened.

" Whom does this belong to? " he inquired.

" To me! to you! to us! Take it; buy some provisions; be happy, and to-morrow we shall have more."

" Gently, gently," said the old man, with a smile; " and by your leave I will use your purse moderately, for they would say, if they saw me buy too many things at a time, that I had been obliged to await your return, in order to be able to purchase them."

" Do as you please; but, first of all, pray have a servant, father. I will not have you left alone so long. I have some smuggled coffee, and most capital tobacco, in a small chest in the hold, which you shall have to-morrow. But, hush! here comes somebody."

" 'Tis Caderousse, who has heard of your arrival, and, no doubt, comes to congratulate you on your fortunate return."

" Ah! lips that say one thing, whilst the heart thinks another," murmured Edmond. " But never mind, he is a neighbour who has done us a service on a time, so he's welcome."

As Edmond finished his sentence in a low voice, there appeared at the door the black and shock head of Caderousse. He was a man of twenty-five or twenty-six years of age, and held in his hand a morsel of cloth, which, in his capacity as a tailor, he was about to turn into the lining of a coat.

" What! is it you, Edmond, returned?" said he, with a broad Marseillaise accent, and a grin that displayed his teeth as white as ivory.

" Yes, as you see, neighbour Caderousse; and ready to be agreeable to you in any and every way," replied Dantès, but ill concealing his feeling under this appearance of civility.

" Thanks—thanks; but, fortunately, I do not want for anything; and it chances that at times there are others who have need of me." Dantès made a gesture. " I do not allude to you, my boy. No!—no! I lent you money, and you returned it; that's like good neighbours, and we are quits."

" We are never quits with those who oblige us," was Dantès' reply; " for when we do not owe them money, we owe them gratitude."

" What's the use of mentioning that? What is done is done. Let us talk of your happy return, my boy. I had gone on the quay to match a piece of mulberry cloth, when I met friend Danglars.

" ' What! you at Marseilles? '

" ' Yes,' says he.

" ' I thought you were at Smyrna.'

" ' I was; but am now back again.'

" ' And where is the dear boy, our little Edmond? '

" ' Why, with his father, no doubt,' replied Danglars. And so I came," added Caderousse, " as fast as I could to have the pleasure of shaking hands with a friend."

" Worthy Caderousse! " said the old man, " he is so much attached to us! "

" Yes, to be sure I am. I love and esteem you, because honest folks are so rare. But it seems you have come back rich, my boy," continued the tailor, looking askance at the handful of gold and silver which Dantès had thrown on the table.

The young man remarked the greedy glance which shone in the dark eyes of his neighbour.

" Eh!" he said negligently, " this money is not mine: I was expressing to my father my fears that he had wanted many things in my absence, and to convince me he emptied his purse on the table. Come, father," added Dantès, " put this money back in your box—unless neighbour Caderousse wants anything, and in that case it is at his service."

" No, my boy, no," said Caderousse. " I am not in any want, thank God! the state nourishes me. Keep your money—keep it, I say;—one never has too much;—but at the same time, my boy, I am as much obliged by your offer as if I took advantage of it."

" It was offered with goodwill," said Dantès.

" No doubt, my boy; no doubt. Well, you stand well with M. Morrel, I hear,—you insinuating dog, you! "

" M. Morrel has always been exceedingly kind to me," replied Dantès.

" Then you were wrong to refuse to dine with him."

" What! did you refuse to dine with him? " said old Dantès; " and did he invite you to dine? "

" Yes, my dear father," replied Edmond, smiling at his father's astonishment at the excessive honour paid to his son.

" And why did you refuse, my son? " inquired the old man.

"That I might the sooner see you again, my dear father," replied the young man. "I was most anxious to see you."

"But it must have vexed M. Morrel, good, worthy man," said Caderousse. "And when you are looking forward to be captain, it was wrong to annoy the owner."

"But I explained to him the cause of my refusal," replied Dantès; "and I hope he fully understood it."

"Yes, but to be captain one must give way a little to one's patrons."

"I hope to be captain without that," said Dantès.

"So much the better—so much the better! Nothing will give greater pleasure to all your old friends; and I know one down there behind the citadel of Saint Nicolas, who will not be sorry to hear it."

"Mercédès?" said the old man.

"Yes, my dear father, and with your permission, now I have seen you, and know you are well, and have all you require, I will ask your consent to go and pay a visit to the Catalans."

"Go, my dear boy," said old Dantès; "and Heaven bless you in your wife, as it has blessed me in my son!"

"His wife!" said Caderousse; "why, how fast you go on, father Dantès; she is not his wife yet, it appears."

"No, but according to all probability she soon will be," replied Edmond.

"Yes—yes," said Caderousse; "but you were right to return as soon as possible, my boy."

"And why?"

"Because Mercédès is a very fine girl, and fine girls never lack lovers; she, particularly, has them by dozens."

"Really?" answered Edmond, with a smile which had in it traces of slight uneasiness.

"Ah, yes," continued Caderousse, "and capital offers too; but you know you will be captain, and who could refuse you then?"

"Meaning to say," replied Dantès, with a smile which but ill concealed his trouble, "that if I were not a captain——"

"Eh—eh!" said Caderousse, shaking his head.

"Come, come," said the sailor, "I have a better opinion than you of women in general, and of Mercédès in particular; and I am certain that, captain or not, she will remain ever faithful to me."

"So much the better—so much the better," said Caderousse. "When one is going to be married, there is nothing like implicit confidence; but never mind that, my boy,—but go and announce your arrival, and let her know all your hopes and prospects."

" I will go directly," was Edmond's reply; and, embracing his father, and saluting Caderousse, he left the apartment.

Caderousse lingered for a moment, then taking leave of old Dantès, he went downstairs to rejoin Danglars, who awaited him at the corner of the Rue Senac.

" Well," said Danglars, " did you see him? "

" I have just left him," answered Caderousse.

" Did he allude to his hope of being captain? "

" He spoke of it as a thing already decided."

" Patience! " said Danglars, " he is in too much hurry, it appears to me."

" Why, it seems M. Morrel has promised him the thing."

" So that he is quite elate about it."

" That is to say, he is actually insolent on the matter—has already offered me his patronage, as if he were a grand personage, and proffered me a loan of money, as though he were a banker."

" Which you refused."

" Most assuredly; although I might easily have accepted, for it was I who put into his hands the first silver he ever earned; but now M. Dantès has no longer any occasion for assistance— he is about to become a captain."

" Pooh! " said Danglars, " he is not one yet."

" Ma foi!—and it will be as well he never should be," answered Caderousse; " for if he should be, there will be really no speaking to him."

" If we choose," replied Danglars, " he will remain what he is, and, perhaps, become even less than he is."

" What do you mean? "

" Nothing—I was speaking to myself. And is he still in love with the Catalane? "

" Over head and ears: but, unless I am much mistaken, there will be a storm in that quarter."

" Explain yourself."

" Why should I? "

" It is more important than you think, perhaps. You do not love Dantès? "

" I never like upstarts."

" Then tell me all you know relative to the Catalane."

" I know nothing for certain; only I have seen things which induce me to believe, as I told you, that the future captain will find some annoyance in the environs of the Vieilles Infirmeries."

" What do you know?—come, tell me! "

" Well, every time I have seen Mercédès come into the city, she has been accompanied by a tall, strapping, black-eyed Catalan, with a red complexion, brown skin, and fierce air, whom she calls cousin."

" Really; and you think this cousin pays her attentions? "

" I only suppose so. What else can a strapping chap of twenty-one mean with a fine wench of seventeen? "

" And you say Dantès has gone to the Catalans? "

" He went before I came down."

" Let us go the same way; we will stop at La Réserve, and we can drink a glass of La Malgue whilst we wait for news."

" Come along," said Caderousse; " but mind you pay the shot."

" Certainly," replied Danglars; and going quickly to the spot alluded to, they called for a bottle of wine and two glasses.

Père Pamphile had seen Dantès pass not ten minutes before; and assured that he was at the Catalans, they sat down under the budding foliage of the planes and sycamores, in the branches of which the birds were joyously singing on a lovely day in early spring.

3

The Catalans

ABOUT a hundred paces from the spot where the two friends were, with their looks fixed on the distance, and their ears attentive, whilst they imbibed the sparkling wine of La Malgue, behind a bare, and torn, and weather-worn wall, was the small village of the Catalans.

One day a mysterious colony quitted Spain, and settled on the tongue of land on which it is to this day. It arrived from no one knew where, and spoke an unknown tongue. One of its chiefs, who understood Provençal, begged the commune of Marseilles to give them this bare and barren promontory, on which, like the sailors of the ancient times, they had run their boats ashore. The request was granted, and three months afterwards, around the twelve or fifteen small vessels which had brought these gipsies of the sea, a small village sprung up.

This village, constructed in a singular and picturesque manner, half Moorish, half Spanish, is that which we behold at the present day inhabited by the descendants of those men who speak the language of their fathers. For three or four centuries they remained faithful to this small promontory, on which they had settled like a flight of sea-birds, without mixing with the Marseillaise population, intermarrying, and preserving their original customs and the costume of their mother country, as they have preserved its language.

Our readers will follow us along the only street of this little village, and enter with us into one of the houses, on the outside of which the sun had stamped that beautiful colour of the dead leaf peculiar to the buildings of the country, and within a coat of limewash, of that white tint which forms the only ornament of Spanish posadas.

A young and beautiful girl, with hair as black as jet, her eyes as velvety as the gazelle's, was leaning with her back against the wainscot, rubbing in her slender fingers, moulded after the antique, a bunch of heath-blossoms, the flowers of which she was picking off, and strewing on the floor; her arms bare to the elbow, embrowned, and resembling those of the Venus at Arles, moved with a kind of restless impatience, and she tapped the earth with her pliant and well-formed foot so as to display the pure and full shape of her well-turned leg, in its red cotton stocking with gray and blue clocks.

At three paces from her, seated in a chair which he balanced on two legs, leaning his elbow on an old worm-eaten table, was a tall young man of twenty or two-and-twenty, who was looking at her with an air in which vexation and uneasiness were mingled. He questioned her with his eyes, but the firm and steady gaze of the young girl controlled his look.

" You see, Mercédès," said the young man, " here is Easter come round again; tell me, is this the moment for a wedding? "

" I have answered you a hundred times, Fernand, and really you must be your own enemy to ask me again."

" Well, repeat it,—repeat it, I beg of you, that I may at last believe it! Tell me for the hundredth time that you refuse my love, which had your mother's sanction. Make me fully comprehend that you are trifling with my happiness, that my life or death are immaterial to you. Ah! to have dreamed for ten years of being your husband, Mercédès, and to lose that hope, which was the only stay of my existence! "

" At least it was not I who ever encouraged you in that hope, Fernand," replied Mercédès; " you cannot reproach me with the slightest coquetry. I have always said to you, I love you as a brother, but do not ask from me more than sisterly affection, for my heart is another's. Is not this true, Fernand? "

" Yes, I know it well, Mercédès," replied the young man. " Yes, you have been cruelly frank with me; but do you forget that it is among the Catalans a sacred law to intermarry? "

" You mistake. Fernand, it is not a law, but merely a custom;

and, I pray of you, do not cite this custom in your favour. You are included in the conscription, Fernand, and are only at liberty on sufferance, liable at any moment to be called upon to take up arms. Once a soldier, what would you do with me, a poor orphan, forlorn, without fortune, with nothing but a hut, half in ruins, containing some ragged nets, a miserable inheritance left by my father to my mother, and by my mother to me? She has been dead a year, and you know, Fernand, I have subsisted almost entirely on public charity. Sometimes you pretend I am useful to you, and that is an excuse to share with me the produce of your fishing; and I accept it, Fernand, because you are the son of my father's brother, because we were brought up together, and still more because it would give you so much pain if I refuse. But I feel very deeply that this fish which I go and sell, and with the produce of which I buy the flax, I spin,—I feel very keenly, Fernand, that this is charity!"

"And if it were, Mercédès, poor and lone as you are, you suit me as well as the daughter of the first shipowner, or the richest banker of Marseilles! What do such as we desire but a good wife and careful housekeeper, and where can I look for these better than in you?"

"Fernand," answered Mercédès, shaking her head, "a woman becomes a bad manager, and who shall say she will remain an honest woman, when she loves another man better than her husband? Rest content with my friendship, for I repeat to you that is all I can promise, and I will promise no more than I can bestow."

"I understand," replied Fernand, "you can endure your own wretchedness patiently, but you are afraid of mine. Well, Mercédès, beloved by you, I would tempt fortune; you would bring me good luck, and I should become rich. I could extend my occupation as a fisherman, might get a place as clerk in a warehouse, and become myself a dealer in time."

"You could do no such thing, Fernand; you are a soldier, and if you remain at the Catalans it is because there is not a war; so remain a fisherman, and contented with my friendship, as I cannot give you more."

"Well, you are right, Mercédès. I will be a sailor; instead of the costume of our fathers, which you despise, I will wear a varnished hat, a striped shirt, and a blue jacket with an anchor on the buttons. Would not that dress please you?"

"What do you mean?" asked Mercédès, darting at him an angry glance,—"what do you mean? I do not understand you."

"I mean, Mercédès, that you are thus harsh and cruel with me, because you are expecting some one who is thus attired;

but, perhaps, he you await is inconstant, or, if he is not, the sea is so to him."

"Fernand!" cried Mercédès, "I believed you were good hearted, and I was mistaken! Fernand, you are wicked to call to your aid jealousy and the anger of God! Yes, I will not deny it, I do await, and I do love him to whom you allude; and, if he does not return, instead of accusing him of the inconstancy which you insinuate, I will tell you that he died loving me and me only."

The young Catalan made a gesture of rage.

"I understand you, Fernand; you would be revenged on him because I do not love you; you would cross your Catalan knife with his dirk. What end would that answer? To lose you my friendship if he were conquered, and see that friendship changed into hate if you were conqueror. Believe me, to seek a quarrel with a man is a bad method of pleasing the woman who loves that man. No, Fernand, you will not thus give way to evil thoughts. Unable to have me for your wife, you will content yourself with having me for your friend and sister; and besides," she added, her eyes troubled and moistened with tears, "wait, wait, Fernand, you said just now that the sea was treacherous, and he has been gone four months, and during these four months we have had some terrible storms."

Fernand made no reply, nor did he attempt to check the tears which flowed down the cheeks of Mercédès, although for each of these tears he would have shed his heart's blood; but these tears flowed for another. He arose, paced awhile up and down the hut, and then, suddenly stopping before Mercédès, with his eyes glowing and his hands clenched:

"Say, Mercédès," he said, "once for all, is this your final determination?"

"I love Edmond Dantès," the young girl calmly replied, "and none but Edmond shall ever be my husband."

"And you will always love him?"

"As long as I live."

Fernand let fall his head like a defeated man, heaved a sigh which resembled a groan, and then, suddenly looking her full in the face, with clenched teeth and expanded nostrils, said:

"But if he is dead——"

"If he is dead, I shall die too."

"If he has forgotten you——"

"Mercédès!" cried a voice joyously, outside the house,— "Mercédès!"

"Ah!" exclaimed the young girl, blushing with delight, and springing up with love, "you see he has not forgotten me, for 'here he is!'" And rushing towards the door, she opened it, saying, " Here, Edmond, here I am!"

Fernand, pale and trembling, receded like a traveller at the sight of a serpent, and fell into a chair beside him.

Edmond and Mercédès were clasped in each other's arms. The burning sun of Marseilles, which penetrated the room by the open door, covered them with a flood of light. At first they saw nothing around them. Their intense happiness isolated them from all the rest of the world, and they only spoke in broken words, which are the tokens of a joy so extreme that they seem rather the expression of sorrow.

Suddenly Edmond saw the gloomy countenance of Fernand, as it was defined in the shadow, pale and threatening. By a movement, for which he could scarcely account to himself, the young Catalan placed his hands on the knife at his belt.

" Ah! your pardon," said Dantès, frowning in his turn. " I did not perceive that there were three of us." Then, turning to Mercédès, he inquired, " Who is this gentleman? "

" One who will be your best friend, Dantès, for he is my friend, my cousin, my brother,—it is Fernand—the man whom, after you, Edmond, I love the most in the world. Do you not remember him? "

" Yes," said Edmond, and without relinquishing Mercédès' hand clasped in one of his own, he extended the other to the Catalan with a cordial air.

But Fernand, instead of responding to this amicable gesture, remained mute and trembling.

Edmond then cast his eyes scrutinisingly at Mercédès, agitated and embarrassed, and then again on Fernand, gloomy and menacing.

" I did not know, when I came with such haste to you, that I was to meet an enemy here."

" An enemy! " cried Mercédès, with an angry look at her cousin. " An enemy in my house, do you say, Edmond! If I believed that, I would place my arm under yours and go with you to Marseilles, leaving the house to return to it no more."

Fernand's eye darted lightning.

" And, should any misfortune occur to you, dear Edmond," she continued, with the same calmness, which proved to Fernand that the young girl had read the very innermost depths of his sinister thought, " if misfortune should occur to you, I would ascend the highest point of the Cape de Morgion, and cast myself headlong from it."

Fernand became deadly pale.

" But you are deceived, Edmond," she continued. " You have

no enemy here—there is no one but Fernand, my brother, who will grasp your hand as a devoted friend."

And at these words the young girl fixed her imperious look on the Catalan, who, as if fascinated by it, came slowly towards Edmond, and offered him his hand.

His hatred, like a powerless though furious wave, was broken against the strong ascendancy which Mercédès exercised over him.

Scarcely, however, had he touched Edmond's hand than he felt he had done all he could do, and rushed hastily out of the house.

" Oh! " he exclaimed, running furiously and tearing his hair— " oh ! who will deliver me from this man? Wretched—wretched that I am! "

" Hallo, Catalan! Hallo, Fernand! where are you running to? " exclaimed a voice.

The young man stopped suddenly, looked around him, and perceived Caderousse sitting at table with Danglars under an arbour.

" Well," said Caderousse, " why don't you come? Are you really in such a hurry that you have not time to say, ' how do ' to your friends? "

" Particularly when they have still a full bottle before them," added Danglars. Fernand looked at them both with a stupefied air, but did not say a word.

" He seems besotted," said Danglars, pushing Caderousse with his knee. " Are we mistaken, and is Dantès triumphant in spite of all we have believed? "

" Why, we must inquire into that," was Caderousse's reply; and turning towards the young man, said, " Well, Catalan, can't you make up your mind? "

Fernand wiped away the perspiration steaming from his brow, and slowly entered the arbour, whose shade seemed to restore somewhat of calmness to his senses, and whose coolness, somewhat of refreshment to his exhausted body.

" Good day," said he. " You called me, didn't you? " And he fell rather than sat down on one of the seats which surrounded the table.

" I called you because you were running like a madman; and I was afraid you would throw yourself into the sea," said Caderousse, laughing. " Why! when a man has friends, they are not only to offer him a glass of wine, but, moreover, to prevent his swallowing three or four pints of water unnecessarily! "

Fernand gave a groan, which resembled a sob, and dropped his head into his hands, his elbows leaning on the table.

" Well, Fernand, I must say," said Caderousse, beginning the conversation, with that brutality of the common people, in which curiosity destroys all diplomacy, " you look uncommonly like a rejected lover; " and he burst into a hoarse laugh.

" Bah! " said Danglars, " a lad of his make was not born to be unhappy in love. You are laughing at him, Caderousse! "

" No," he replied, " only hark how he sighs! Come, come, Fernand! " said Caderousse, " hold up your head and answer us. It's not polite not to reply to friends who ask news of your health."

" My health is well enough," said Fernand, clenching his hands without raising his head.

" Ah! you see, Danglars," said Caderousse, winking at his friend, " this it is, Fernand whom you see here is a good and brave Catalan, one of the best fishermen in Marseilles, and he is in love with a very fine girl, named Mercédès; but it appears, unfortunately, that the fine girl is in love with the second in command on board the *Pharaon*; and, as the *Pharaon* arrived to-day—why, you understand! "

" No, I do not understand," said Danglars.

" Poor Fernand has been dismissed," continued Caderousse.

" Well, and what then? " said Fernand, lifting up his head, and looking at Caderousse like a man who looks for some one on whom to vent his anger; " Mercédès is not accountable to any person, is she? Is she not free to love whomsoever she will? "

" Oh! if you take it in that sense," said Caderousse, " it is another thing! But I thought you were a Catalan, and they told me the Catalans were not men to allow themselves to be supplanted by a rival. It was even told me that Fernand, especially, was terrible in his vengeance."

Fernand smiled piteously. " A lover is never terrible," he said.

" Poor fellow! " remarked Danglars, affecting to pity the young man from the bottom of his heart. " Why, you see, he did not expect to see Dantès return so suddenly! he thought he was dead, perhaps; or, perchance, faithless! These things always come on us more severely when they come suddenly."

" Ah, *ma foi*, under any circumstances! " said Caderousse, who drank as he spoke, and on whom the fumes of the wine of La Malgue began to take effect,—" under any circumstances Fernand is not the only person put out by the fortunate arrival of Dantès; is he, Danglars? "

" No, you are right—and I should say that would bring him ill luck."

" Well, never mind," answered Caderousse, pouring out a glass of wine for Fernand, and filling his own for the eighth or

ninth time, whilst Danglars had merely sipped his. " Never mind
—in the meantime he marries Mercédès—the lovely Mercédès—
at least, he returns to do that."

During this time Danglars fixed his piercing glance on the young
man, on whose heart Caderousse's words fell like molten lead.

" And when is the wedding to be? " he asked.

" Oh, it is not yet fixed! " murmured Fernand.

" No, but it will be," said Caderousse, " as surely as Dantès
will be captain of the *Pharaon*—eh, Danglars? "

Danglars shuddered at this unexpected attack, and turned to
Caderousse, whose countenance he scrutinised to try and detect
whether the blow was premeditated; but he read nothing but
envy in a countenance already rendered brutal and stupid by
drunkenness.

" Well," said he, filling the glasses, " let us drink to Captain
Edmond Dantès, husband of the beautiful Catalane! "

Caderousse raised his glass to his mouth with unsteady hand,
and swallowed the contents at a gulp. Fernand dashed his on the
ground.

" Eh! eh! eh! " stammered Caderousse. " What do I see down
there by the wall in the direction of the Catalans? Look, Fernand!
your eyes are better than mine. I believe I see double. You know
wine is a deceiver; but I should say it was two lovers walking
side by side, and hand in hand. Heaven forgive me! they do not
know that we can see them, and they are actually embracing! "

Danglars did not lose one pang that Fernand endured.

" Do you know them, M. Fernand? " he said.

" Yes," was the reply, in a low voice. " It is M. Edmond and
Mademoiselle Mercédès! "

" Ah! see there, now! " said Caderousse; " and I did not
recognise them! Holla, Dantès! holla, lovely damsel! Come this
way, and let us know when the wedding is to be, for M. Fernand
here is so obstinate he will not tell us! "

" Hold your tongue! will you? " said Danglars, pretending
to restrain Caderousse, who, with the tenacity of drunkards,
leaned out of the arbour. " Try to stand upright, and let the
lovers make love without interruption. See, look at M. Fernand,
and follow his example—he is well behaved! "

Fernand, probably excited beyond bearing, pricked by
Danglars, as the bull is by the banderilleros, was about to rush
out; for he had risen from his seat, and seemed to be collecting
himself to dash headlong upon his rival, when Mercédès, smiling
and graceful, lifted up her lovely head, and showed her clear and
bright eye. At this Fernand recollected her threat of dying if
Edmond died, and dropped again heavily on his seat.

Danglars looked at the two men, one after the other, the one brutalised by liquor, the other overwhelmed with love.

" I shall extract nothing from these fools," he muttered; " and I am very much afraid of being here between a drunkard and a coward. Yet this Catalan has eyes that glisten like the Spaniards, Sicilians, and Calabrians, who practise revenge so well. Unquestionably, Edmond's star is in the ascendant, and he will marry the splendid girl—he will be captain, too, and laugh at us all, unless"—a sinister smile passed over Danglar's lips—" unless I take a hand in the affair," he added.

" Hallo! " continued Caderousse, half rising, and with his fist on the table, " hallo, Edmond! do you not see your friends, or are you too proud to speak to them? "

" No, my dear fellow! " replied Dantès, " I am not proud, but I am happy; and happiness blinds, I think, more than pride."

" Ah! very well, that's an explanation! " said Caderousse. " Well, good day, Madame Dantès! "

Mercédès curtseyed gravely, and said:

" That is not my name, and in my country it bodes ill fortune, they say, to call young girls by the name of their betrothed before he becomes their husband. Call me, then, Mercédès, if you please."

" We must excuse our worthy neighbour, Caderousse," said Dantès, " he is so easily mistaken."

" So, then, the wedding is to take place immediately, M. Dantès," said Danglars, bowing to the young couple.

" As soon as possible, M. Danglars; to-day all preliminaries will be arranged at my father's, and to-morrow, or next day at latest, the wedding festival here at La Réserve. My friends will be there, I hope; that is to say, you are invited, M. Danglars, and you, Caderousse."

" And Fernand," said Caderousse, with a chuckle; " Fernand, too, is invited! "

" My wife's brother, is my brother" said Edmond; " and we, Mercédès and I, should be very sorry if he were absent at such a time."

Fernand opened his mouth to reply, but his voice died on his lips, and he could not utter a word.

" To-day the preliminaries, to-morrow or next day the ceremony! you are in a hurry, captain! "

" Danglars," said Edmond, smiling, " I will say to you as Mercédès said just now to Caderousse, ' Do not give me a title which does not belong to me; ' that may bring me bad luck."

" Your pardon," replied Danglars; " I merely said you seemed in a hurry, and we have lots of time, the *Pharaon* cannot be under weigh again in less than three months."

"We are always in a hurry to be happy, M. Danglars; for when we have suffered a long time, we have great difficulty in believing in good fortune. But it is not selfishness alone that makes me thus in haste; I must go to Paris."

"To Paris! really! and will it be the first time you have ever been there, Dantès?"

"Yes."

"Have you business there?"

"Not of my own; the last commission of poor Captain Leclere; you know to what I allude, Danglars; it is sacred. Besides, I shall only take the time to go and return."

"Yes, yes, I understand," said Danglars; and then in a low tone, he added, "To Paris, no doubt to deliver the letter which the Grand Marshal gave him. Ah! this letter gives me an idea, —a capital idea! Ah! Dantès, my friend, you are not yet registered number One on board the good ship *Pharaon*;" then turning towards Edmond, who was walking away, "Good journey," he cried.

"Thank ye," said Edmond, with a friendly nod, and the two lovers continued their route, calm and joyous.

4

The Plotters

DANGLARS followed Edmond and Mercédès with his eyes until the two lovers disappeared behind one of the angles of Fort Saint Nicolas, then turning round, he perceived Fernand, who had fallen pale and trembling into his chair, whilst Caderousse stammered out the words of a drinking song.

"Well, my dear sir," said Danglars to Fernand, "here is a marriage which does not appear to make everybody happy."

"It drives me to despair," said Fernand.

"Do you, then, love Mercédès?"

"I adore her!"

"Have you loved her long?"

"Ever since I have known her."

"And you sit there, tearing your hair, instead of seeking to remedy your condition! I did not think it was thus your nation acted."

" What would you have me do? " said Fernand.

" How do I know? Is it my affair? I am not in love with Mademoiselle Mercédès, but for you—seek, and you shall find."

" I have found already."

" What? "

" I would stab the man, but the woman told me that if any misfortune happened to her betrothed she would kill herself."

" Pooh! women say those things, but never do them."

" You do not know Mercédès; what she threatens she will do."

" Idiot! " muttered Danglars, " whether she kills herself or not, what matter provided Dantès is not captain? "

" Before Mercédès should die," replied Fernand, with the accents of unshaken resolution, " I would die myself! "

" That's what I call love! " said Caderousse, with a voice more tipsy than ever. " That's love, or I don't know what love is."

" Come," said Danglars, " you appear to me a good sort of fellow, and hang me! but I should like to help you, but——"

" Yes," said Caderousse, " but how? "

" My dear fellow," replied Danglars, " you are three parts drunk; finish the bottle, and you will be completely so. Drink, then, and do not meddle with what we are discussing, for that requires all one's wit and cool judgment."

" I—drunk? " said Caderousse; " well, that's a good one! I could drink four more such bottles; they are no bigger than eau-de-Cologne flasks. Père Pamphile, more wine! " and Caderousse rattled his glass upon the table.

" You were saying, sir——" said Fernand, awaiting with great anxiety the end of this interrupted remark.

" What was I saying? I forget. This drunken Caderousse has made me lose the thread of my thoughts."

" Drunk, if you like; so much the worse for those who fear wine, for it is because they have some bad thoughts which they are afraid the liquor will extract from their hearts; " and Caderousse began to sing the two last lines of a song very popular at the time:

> Tous les méchants sont beuveurs d'eau;
> C'est bien prouvé par le déluge.*

" You said, sir, you would like to help me, but——"

" Yes; but I added, to help you it would be sufficient that Dantès did not marry her you love; and the marriage may easily be thwarted, methinks, and yet Dantès need not die."

" Death alone can separate them," remarked Fernand.

" You talk like a noodle, my friend," said Caderousse, " and here is Danglars, who is a wide-awake, clever, deep fellow, who will prove to you that you are wrong. Prove it, Danglars. I have answered for you. Say there is no need why Dantès should die: it would, indeed, be a pity he should. Dantès is a good fellow; I like Dantes! Dantès, your health! "

Fernand rose impatiently.

" Let him run on," said Danglars, restraining the young man; " drunk as he is, he is not much out in what he says. Absence severs as well as death, and if the walls of a prison were between Edmond and Mercédès they would be as effectually separated as if they lay under a tombstone."

" Yes; only people get out of prison," said Caderousse, who, with what sense was left him, listened eagerly to the conversation, " and when they get out, and their names are Edmond Dantès, they revenge——"

" What matters that? " muttered Fernand.

" And why, I should like to know," persisted Caderousse, " should they put Dantès in prison; he has neither robbed, nor killed, nor murdered."

" Hold your tongue! " said Danglars.

" I won't hold my tongue! " replied Caderousse; " I say I want to know why they should put Dantès in prison; I like Dantès; Dantès your, health! " and he swallowed another glass of wine.

Danglars saw in the muddled look of the tailor the progress of his intoxication, and turning towards Fernand, said:

" Well, you understand there is no need to kill him."

" Certainly not, if, as you said just now, you have the means of having Dantès arrested. Have you that means? "

" It is to be found for the searching. But, why should I meddle in the matter? it is no affair of mine."

" I know not why you meddle," said Fernand, seizing his arm, " but this I know, you have some motive of personal hatred against Dantès, for he who himself hates, is never mistaken in the sentiments of others."

" I! motives of hatred against Dantès? None, on my word! I saw you were unhappy, and your unhappiness interested me; that's all; but the moment you believe I act for my own account, adieu, my dear friend, get out of the affair as best you may; " and Danglars rose as if he meant to depart.

" No, no," said Fernand, restraining him, " stay! It is of very little consequence to me in the long-run whether you have any angry feelings or not against Dantès. I hate him! I confess it openly. Do you find the means, I will execute it, provided it is not to kill the man, for Mercédès has declared she will kill herself if Dantès is killed."

Caderousse, who had let his head drop on the table, now raised it, and looking at Fernand with his dull and fishy eyes, he said:

" Kill Dantès! who talks of killing Dantès? I won't have him killed—I won't! He's my friend, and this morning offered to share his money with me, as I shared mine with him. I won't have Dantès killed—I won't! "

" And who has said a word about killing him, muddlehead! " replied Danglars. " We were merely joking: drink to his health," he added, filling Caderousse's glass, " and do not interfere with us."

" Yes, yes, Dantès' good health! " said Caderousse, emptying his glass, " here's to his health! his health!—hurrah! ".

" But the means—the means? " said Fernand.

" Have you not hit upon any? "

" No!—you undertook to do so."

" True," replied Danglars; " the French have the superiority over the Spaniards, that the Spaniards ruminate whilst the French invent."

" Do you invent, then? " said Fernand impatiently.

" Waiter," said Danglars, " pen, ink, and paper."

" Pen, ink, and paper," muttered Fernand.

" Yes; I am a supercargo; pen, ink, and paper are my tools, and without my tools I am fit for nothing."

" Pen, ink, and paper! " then called Fernand loudly.

" All you require is a table," said the waiter, pointing to the writing materials.

" Bring them here."

The waiter did as he was desired.

" When one thinks," said Caderousse, letting his hand drop on the paper, " there is here wherewithal to kill a man more sure than if we waited at the corner of a wood to assassinate him. I have always had more dread of a pen, a bottle of ink, and a sheet of paper, than of a sword or pistol."

" The fellow is not so drunk as he appears to be," said Danglars. " Give him some more wine, Fernand." Fernand filled Caderousse's glass, who, toper as he was, lifted his hand from the paper and seized the glass.

The Catalan watched him until Caderousse, almost overcome by this fresh assault on his senses, rested, or rather allowed his glass to fall upon the table.

" Well! " resumed the Catalan, as he saw the final glimmer of Caderousse's reason vanishing before the last glass of wine.

" Well, then, I should say, for instance," resumed Danglars,

" that if after a voyage such as Dantès has just made, and in which he touched the Isle of Elba, some one were to denounce him to the king's procureur as a Bonapartist agent——"

" I will denounce him! " exclaimed the young man hastily.

" Yes, but they will make you then sign your declaration, and confront you with him you have denounced; I will supply you with the means of supporting your accusation, for I know the fact well. But Dantès cannot remain for ever in prison, and one day or other he will leave it, and the day when he comes out, woe betide him who was the cause of his incarceration! "

" Oh, I should wish nothing better than that he would come and seek a quarrel with me."

" Yes, and Mercédès! Mercédès, who will detest you if you have only the misfortune to scratch the skin of her dearly beloved Edmond! "

" True! " said Fernand.

" No! no! " continued Danglars; " if we resolve on such a step, it would be much better to take, as I now do, this pen, dip it into this ink, and write with the left hand (that the writing may not be recognised) the denunciation we propose." And Danglars, uniting practice with theory, wrote with his left hand, and in a writing reversed from his usual style, and totally unlike it, the following lines which he handed to Fernand, and which Fernand read in an undertone:—

" Monsieur,—The procureur du roi is informed by a friend of the throne and religion, that one Edmond Dantès, mate of the ship *Pharaon*, arrived this morning from Smyrna, after having touched at Naples and Porto-Ferrajo, has been intrusted by Murat* with a letter for the usurper, and by the usurper with a letter for the Bonapartist committee in Paris.

" Proof of this crime will be found on arresting him, for the letter will be found upon him, or at his father's, or in his cabin on board the *Pharaon*."

" Very good," resumed Danglars; " now your revenge looks like common sense, for in no way can it revert to yourself, and the matter will thus work its own way; there is nothing to do now but fold the letter as I am doing, and write upon it, ' To M. le Procureur Royal,' and that's all settled."

And Danglars wrote the address as he spoke.

" Yes, and that's all settled! " exclaimed Caderousse, who, by a last effort of intellect, had followed the reading of the letter, and instinctively comprehended all the misery which such a denunciation must entail. " Yes, and that's all settled: only it will be an infamous shame; " and he stretched out his hand to reach the letter.

"Yes," said Danglars, taking it from beyond his reach; "and as what I say and do is merely in jest, and I amongst the first and foremost should be sorry if anything happened to Dantès—the worthy Dantès—look here!"

And taking the letter he squeezed it up in his hands, and threw it into a corner of the arbour.

"All right!" said Caderousse. "Dantès is my friend, and I won't have him ill-used."

"And who thinks of using him ill? Certainly neither I nor Fernand!" said Danglars, rising, and looking at the young man, who still remained seated, but whose eye was fixed on the denunciatory sheet of paper flung into the corner.

"In this case," replied Caderousse, "let's have some more wine. I wish to drink to the health of Edmond and the lovely Mercédès."

"You have had too much already, drunkard," said Danglars; "and if you continue you will be compelled to sleep here, because you will be unable to stand on your legs."

"I?" said Caderousse, rising with all the offended dignity of a drunken man, "I can't keep on my legs! Why, I'll bet a wager I go up into the belfry of the Acoules, and without staggering, too!"

"Well done!" said Danglars, "I'll take your bet; but to-morrow—to-day it is time to return. Give me your arm, and let us go."

"Very well, let us go," said Caderousse; "but I don't want your arm at all. Come, Fernand, won't you return to Marseilles with us?"

"No," said Fernand; "I shall return to the Catalans."

"You're wrong. Come with us to Marseilles—come along."

"I will not."

"What do you mean? you will not? Well, just as you like, my prince; there's liberty for all the world. Come along, Danglars, and let the young gentleman return to the Catalans if he chooses."

Danglars took advantage of Caderousse's temper at the moment, to take him off towards Marseilles by the Porte-Saint-Victor, staggering as he went.

When they had advanced about twenty yards, Danglars looked back and saw Fernand stoop, pick up the crumpled paper, and, putting it into his pocket, then rush out of the arbour towards Pillon.

"Well," said Caderousse, "why, what a lie he told! He said he was going to the Catalans, and he is going to the city. Holloa, Fernand!"

"Oh, you see wrong," said Danglars; "he's gone right enough."

"Well," said Caderousse, "I should have said not—how treacherous wine is!"

"Come, come," said Danglars to himself, "now the thing is at work, and it will effect its purpose unassisted."

5

The Betrothal Feast

THE morning's sun rose clear and resplendent, gilding the heavens, and even the foamy waves with its bright refulgent beams.

The plenteous feast had been prepared at La Réserve, with whose arbour the reader is already familiar. The apartment destined for the purpose was spacious, and lighted by a number of windows, over each of which was written in golden letters the name of one of the principal cities of France; beneath these windows a wooden balcony extended the entire length of the house. And although the entertainment was fixed for twelve o'clock at noon, an hour previous to that time the balcony was filled with impatient and expectant guests consisting of the favoured part of the crew of the *Pharaon*, and other personal friends of the bridegroom, the whole of whom had arrayed themselves in their choicest costumes, in order to do greater honour to the day.

Various rumours were afloat to the effect that the owners of the *Pharaon* had promised to attend the nuptial feast; but all seemed unanimous in doubting that an act of such rare and exceeding condescension could possibly be intended.

Danglars, however, who now made his appearance, accompanied by Caderousse, effectually confirmed the report, stating, that he had recently conversed with M. Morrel, who had himself assured him he intended joining the festive party upon the occasion of their second officer's marriage.

Even while relating this aloud, an enthusiastic burst of applause from the crew of the *Pharaon* announced the presence of M. Morrel, who hailed the visit of the shipowner as a sure indication that the man whose wedding-feast he thus delighted to honour, would ere long be first in command of the *Pharaon*; and as Dantès was universally beloved on board his vessel,

the sailors put no restraint on the tumultuous joy at fin
opinion and choice of their superiors so exactly coincide
their own.

This noisy though hearty welcome over, Danglars and Caderousse were despatched to the residence of the bridegroom to
convey to him the intelligence of the arrival of the important
personage who had recently joined them, and to desire he would
hasten to receive his honourable guest.

The above-mentioned individuals started off upon their errand
at full speed; but ere they had gone many steps they perceived
a group advancing towards them, composed of the betrothed
pair, a party of young girls in attendance on the bride, by whose
side walked Dantès' father; the whole brought up by Fernand,
whose lips wore their usual sinister smile.

Neither Mercédès nor Edmond observed the strange expression
of his countenance; basking in the sunshine of each other's love,
they heeded not the dark louring look that scowled on their
innocent felicity.

Having acquitted themselves of their errand, and exchanged a
hearty shake of the hand with Edmond, Danglars and Caderousse
took their places beside Fernand and old Dantès,—the latter of
whom attracted universal notice. The old man was attired in a
suit of black, trimmed with steel buttons, beautifully cut and
polished. His thin but still powerful legs were arrayed in a pair
of richly embroidered· clocked stockings, evidently of English
manufacture; while from his three-cornered hat depended a
long streaming knot of white and blue ribands. Thus he came
along, supporting himself on a curiously-carved stick, his aged
countenance lit up with happiness, while beside him crept
Caderousse, whose desire to partake of the good things provided
for the wedding party had induced him to become reconciled to
the Dantès' father and son, although there still lingered in his
mind a faint and imperfect recollection of the events of the
preceding night; just as the brain retains on waking the dim and
misty outline of the dream.

As Danglars approached the disappointed lover, he cast on him
a look of deep meaning, while Fernand, as he slowly paced behind
the happy pair, who seemed, in their own unmixed content, to
have entirely forgotten that such a being as himself existed, was
pale and abstracted: occasionally, however, a deep flush would
overspread his countenance, and a nervous contraction distort
his features, while, with an agitated and restless gaze, he would
glance in the direction of Marseilles, like one who either anticipated or foresaw some great and important event.

Dantès himself was simply, though becomingly, clad in the

merchant-service,—a costume somewhat
a civil garb; and with his fine countenance,
happiness, a more perfect specimen of manly
be imagined.

eeks of Cyprus or Chios, Mercédès boasted
shing eyes of jet, and ripe, round, coral lips.
d in the arts of great cities would have hid
her blushes h a veil, or, at least, have cast down her thickly
fringed lashes, so as to have concealed the liquid lustre of her
animated eyes; but, on the contrary, the delighted girl looked
around her with a smile that seemed to invite all who saw her to
behold, and beholding, to rejoice with her in her exceeding
happiness.

Immediately the bridal cortège came in sight of La Réserve,
M. Morrel came forth to meet it, followed by the soldiers and
sailors there assembled, to whom he had repeated the promise
already given, that Dantès should be the successor to the late
Captain Leclere. Edmond, at the approach of his patron, respectfully placed the arm of his affianced bride within that of M.
Morrel, who forthwith conducting her up the flight of wooden
steps leading to the chamber in which the feast was prepared,
was gaily followed by the guests, beneath whose thronging
numbers the slight structure creaked and groaned as though
alarmed at the unusual pressure.

" Father," said Mercédès, stopping when she had reached the
centre of the table, " sit, I pray you, on my right hand; on my
left I will place him who has ever been as a brother to me,"
pointing with a soft and gentle smile to Fernand; but her words
and look seemed to inflict the direst torture on him, for his lips
became ghastly pale, and even beneath the dark hue of his complexion the blood might be seen retreating as though some sudden
pang drove it back to the heart.

During this time, Dantès, at the opposite side of the table, had
been occupied in similarly placing his most honoured guests.
M. Morrel was seated at his right hand, Danglars, at his left
while at a sign from Edmond, the rest of the company arranged
themselves as they found it most agreeable.

And now commenced the work of devastation upon the many
good things with which the table was loaded. Sausages of Arles,
with their delicate seasoning and piquant flavour, lobsters in
their dazzling red cuirasses, prawns of large size and brilliant
colour, the echinus, with its prickly outside and dainty morsel
within; the clovis, esteemed by the epicures of the south as more
than rivalling the exquisite flavour of the oyster. All these,
in conjunction with the numerous delicacies cast up by the

wash of waters on the sandy beach, and styled by the grateful fishermen " sea fruits," served to furnish forth this marriage-table.

" A pretty silence, truly! " said the old father of the bride-groom, as he carried to his lips a glass of wine of the hue and brightness of the topaz, and which had just been placed before Mercédès herself. " Now, would anybody think that this room contained a happy, merry party, who desire nothing better than to laugh and dance the hours away? "

" Ah! " sighed Caderousse, " a man cannot always feel happy because he is about to be married! "

" The truth is," replied Dantès, " that I am too happy for noisy mirth; if that is what you meant by your observation, my worthy friend, you were right; joy takes a strange effect at times, it seems to oppress us almost the same as sorrow."

Danglars looked towards Fernand, whose excitable nature received and betrayed each fresh impression.

" Why, what ails you? " asked he of Edmond. " Do you fear any approaching evil? I should say that you were the happiest man alive at this instant."

" And that is the very thing that alarms me," returned Dantès. " Man does not appear to me to be intended to enjoy felicity so unmixed; happiness is like the enchanted palaces we read of in our childhood,¹ where fierce, fiery dragons defend the entrance and approach; and monsters of all shapes and kinds, requiring to be overcome ere victory is ours. I own that I am lost in wonder to find myself promoted to an honour of which I feel myself unworthy,—that of being the husband of Mercédès."

" Nay, nay! " cried Caderousse, smiling, " you have not attained that honour yet. Mercédès is not yet your wife. Just assume the tone and manner of a husband, and see how she will remind you that your hour has not yet come! "

The bride blushed, and seemed half inclined to be angry, while Fernand, restless and uneasy, seemed to start at every fresh sound, occasionally applying his handkerchief to his brow to wipe away the large drops of perspiration that gathered again, almost as soon as they were removed.

" Well, never mind that, neighbour Caderousse, it is not worth while to contradict me for such a trifle as that. 'Tis true that Mercédès is not actually my wife; but," added he, drawing out his watch, "in an hour and a half from this she will be as fast and firm as holy church can make her."

A general exclamation of surprise ran round the table, with the exception of the elder Dantès, whose laugh displayed the still perfect beauty of his large white teeth. Mercédès looked pleased and gratified, while Fernand grasped the handle of his knife with a convulsive clutch.

" In an hour? " inquired Danglars, turning pale. " How is that, my friend? "

" Why, thus it is," replied Dantès. " Thanks to the influence of M. Morrel, to whom, next to my father, I owe every blessing I enjoy, every difficulty has been removed. We have purchased permission to waive the usual delay; and at half-past two o'clock the mayor of Marseilles will be waiting for us at the Hotel-de-Ville. Now, as a quarter-past one has already struck, I do not consider I have asserted too much in saying, that in another hour and thirty minutes Mercédès will have become Madame Dantès." .

Fernand closed his eyes, a burning sensation passed across his brow, and he was compelled to support himself by the table to prevent his falling from his chair; but in spite of all his efforts, he could not refrain from uttering a deep groan, which, however, was lost amid the noisy felicitations of the company.

" Upon my word," cried the old man, " you make short work of these kind of affairs. Arrived here only yesterday morning, and married to-day at three o'clock! Commend me to a sailor for going the quick way to work! "

" But," asked Danglars, in a timid tone, " how did you manage about the other formalities—the contract—the settlement! "

" Oh, bless you! " answered Dantès laughingly, " our papers were soon drawn up. Mercédès has no fortune; I have none to settle on her. So, you see, our papers were quickly written out, and certainly do not come very expensive."

This joke elicited a fresh burst of applause.

" So that what we presumed to be merely the betrothal feast turns out to be the actual wedding-dinner! " said Danglars.

" No, no! " answered Dantès; " don't imagine I am going to put you off in that shabby manner. To-morrow morning I start for Paris: five days to go, and the same to return, with one day to discharge the commission entrusted to me, is all the time I shall be absent. I shall be back here by the 12th of March, and the next day I give my real marriage-feast."

This prospect of fresh festivity redoubled the hilarity of the guests to such a degree, that the elder Dantès who at the commencement of the repast had commented upon the silence that prevailed, now found it difficult, amid the general din of voices, to obtain a moment's tranquillity in which to drink to the health and prosperity of the bride and bridegroom.

Dantès, perceiving the affectionate eagerness of his father, responded by a look of grateful pleasure, while Mercédès, whose eyes had been constantly consulting the pendule which decked the chamber, made an expressive gesture to Edmond.

Around the festive board reigned that mirthful freedom from all restraint which is usually found at the termination of social meetings, among those at least whose inferior station in the world gives them a happy dispensation from the frigid rules of etiquette; and so it was with the party now assembled. Such as at the commencement of the repast had not been able to seat themselves according to their inclination, rose unceremoniously, and exchanged their place for the more immediate proximity of some preferred individual, male or female, as the case might be. All spoke at the same time, and yet none heeded a reply, but appeared as though merely addressing their own thoughts.

The paleness of Fernand appeared to have communicated itself to Danglars. As for Fernand himself, he seemed as though undergoing the tortures of the damned; unable to rest, he was among the first to quit the table, and as though seeking to avoid the hilarious mirth that rose in such deafening sounds, he continued, in utter silence, to pace the farther end of the salon.

Caderousse approached him just as Danglars, whom Fernand seemed most anxious to avoid, had joined him in a corner of the room.

"Upon my word," said Caderousse, from whose mind the friendly treatment of Dantès, united with the effect of the excellent wine he had partaken of, had effaced every feeling of envy or jealousy at Dantès' good fortune,—"upon my word Dantès is a downright good fellow, and when I see him sitting there beside his pretty wife that is so soon to be, I cannot help thinking it would have been a great pity to have served him that trick you were planning yesterday."

"Oh, there was no harm meant!" answered Danglars; "at first I certainly did feel somewhat uneasy as regarded what Fernand might be tempted to do, but when I saw how completely he had mastered his feelings, even so far as to become one of his rival's bride's-men, I knew there was no further cause for apprehension."

Caderousse looked full at Fernand—he was ghastly pale.

"Certainly," continued Danglars, "the sacrifice was no trifling one when the beauty of the bride is considered. Upon my soul, that future captain of mine is a lucky dog! Gad! I only wish he would let me take his place!"

"Shall we not set forth?" asked the sweet, silvery voice of Mercédès; "two o'clock has just struck, and you know we are expected at the Hotel-de-Ville in a quarter of an hour."

" To be sure!—to be sure! " cried Dantès, eagerly quitting the table; " let us go directly! "

His words were re-echoed by the whole party, who rose with a simultaneous cheer, and commenced forming themselves into procession.

At this moment Danglars, who had been incessantly observing every change in Fernand's look and manner, perceived him stagger and fall back, with an almost convulsive spasm, against a seat placed near one of the open windows. At the same instant the ear caught a sort of indistinct sound on the stairs, followed by the measured tread of soldiery, with the clanking of swords and military accoutrements! then came a hum and buzz of many voices, so as to deaden even the noisy mirth of the bridal party, among whom a vague feeling of curiosity and apprehension quelled every disposition to talk, and almost instantaneously the most deathlike stillness prevailed.

Nearer and nearer came those sounds of terror. Three distinct knocks, as though from the hilt of a sword, against the door, increased the fears of the before gay party. Each looked inquiringly in the countenance of his neighbour, while all wished themselves quietly and safely at home.

" I demand admittance," said a loud voice outside the room, " in the name of the law! "

As no attempt was made to prevent it, the door was opened, and a magistrate, wearing his official scarf, presented himself, followed by four soldiers and a corporal. Uneasiness now yielded to the most extreme dread on the part of those present.

" May I venture to inquire the reason of this unexpected visit? " said M. Morrel, addressing the magistrate, whom he evidently knew; " there is doubtless some mistake easily explained."

" If it be so," replied the magistrate, " rely upon every reparation being made; meanwhile, I am the bearer of an order of arrest, and although I most reluctantly perform the task assigned to me, it must, nevertheless, be fulfilled. Who among the persons here assembled answers to the name of Edmond Dantès? "

Every eye was turned towards the individual so described, who, spite of the agitation he could not but feel, advanced with dignity, and said, in a firm voice, " I am he! what is your pleasure with me? "

" Edmond Dantès," replied the magistrate, " I arrest you in the name of the law! "

" Me! " repeated Edmond, slightly changing colour, " and wherefore, I pray? "

" I cannot inform you, but you will be duly acquainted with

the reasons that have rendered such a step necessary at your first examination."

M. Morrel felt that further resistance or remonstrance was useless. He saw before him an officer delegated to enforce the law, and perfectly well knew that it would be as unavailing to seek pity from a magistrate decked with his official scarf as to address a petition to some cold, marble effigy. Old Dantès, however, saw not all this. His paternal heart could not contemplate the idea of such an outrage as consigned his beloved child to prison amid the joys of his wedding feast. Rushing forwards, therefore, he threw himself at the magistrate's feet, and prayed and supplicated in terms so moving, that even the officer was touched; and, although firm to his duty, he kindly said, " My worthy friend, let me beg of you to calm your apprehensions. Your son has probably neglected some prescribed form or attention in registering his cargo, and it is more than probable he will be set at liberty directly he has given the information required, whether touching the health of his crew, or the value of his freight."

" What is the meaning of all this? " inquired Caderousse frowningly, of Danglars, who had assumed an air of utter surprise.

" How can I tell you? " replied he; " I am, like yourself, utterly bewildered at all that is going on, not a word of which do I understand."

Caderousse then looked around for Fernand, but he had disappeared.

The scene of the previous night now came back to his mind with startling accuracy. The painful catastrophe he had just witnessed appeared effectually to have rent away the veil which the intoxication of the evening before had raised between himself and his memory.

" So! so " said he, in a hoarse and choking voice, to Danglars, " this, then, I suppose, is a part of the trick you were concerting yesterday? All I can say is, that if it be so, 'tis an ill turn, and well deserves to bring double evil on those who have projected it."

" Nonsense! " returned Danglars, " I tell you again I have nothing whatever to do with it; besides, you know very well that I tore the paper to pieces."

" No, you did not! " answered Caderousse, " you merely threw it by—I saw it lying in a corner."

" Hold your tongue, you fool!—what should you know about it?—why, you were drunk! "

" Where is Fernand? " inquired Caderousse.

" How do I know? " replied Danglars; " gone, as every prudent man ought to do, to look after his own affairs, most likely. Never mind where he is, let you and I go and see what is to be done for our poor friends in this their affliction."

During this conversation, Dantès, after having exchanged a cheerful shake of the hand with all his sympathising friends, had surrendered himself to the officer sent to arrest him, merely saying, " Make yourselves quite easy, my good fellows, there is some little mistake to clear up, that's all, depend upon it! and very likely I may not have to go so far as the prison to effect that."

" Oh, to be sure! " responded Danglars, who had now approached the group, " nothing more than a mistake, I feel quite certain."

Dantès descended the staircase, preceded by the magistrate, and followed by the soldiers. A carriage awaited him at the door; he got in, followed by two soldiers and the magistrate, and the vehicle drove off towards Marseilles.

" Adieu! adieu! dearest Edmond! " cried Mercédès, stretching out her arms to him from the balcony.

The prisoner, whose ready ear caught the despairing accents of his betrothed, felt as though the chill hand of death pressed on his heart, as, leaning from the coach, he tried to reply in cheerful tones.

" Good-bye, my sweet Mercédès!—we shall soon meet again! "

The rapid progress of the vehicle, which disappeared round one of the turnings of Fort Saint-Nicolas, prevented his adding more.

" Wait for me, here, all of you! " cried M. Morrel; " I will take the first conveyance I find, and hurry to Marseilles, whence I will bring you word how all is going on."

" That's right! " exclaimed a multitude of voices, " go, and return as quickly as you can! "

This second departure was followed by a long and fearful state of terrified silence on the part of those who were left behind. The old father and Mercédès remained for some time apart, each absorbed in their separate griefs; but at length the two poor victims of the same blow raised their eyes, and with a simultaneous burst of feeling rushed into each other's arms.

Meanwhile Fernand made his reappearance, poured out for himself a glass of water with a trembling hand, then hastily swallowing it, went to sit down on the first vacant chair he perceived; and this was, by mere chance, placed next to the seat on which poor Mercédès had fallen, half fainting, when released from the warm and affectionate embrace of old Dantès. Instinctively Fernand drew back his chair.

" He is the cause of all this misery—I am quite sure of it," whispered Caderousse, who had never taken his eyes off Fernand, to Danglars.

" I really do not think so," answered the other; " he is too stupid to imagine such a scheme. I only hope the mischief will fall upon the head of whoever wrought it."

" You don't mention those who aided and abetted the cruel deed, any more than of those who advised it," said Caderousse.

" Surely," answered Danglars, " one cannot be expected to become responsible for all the idle words one may have been obliged to listen to in the course of our lives."

Meantime the subject of the arrest was being canvassed in every different form.

" What think you, Danglars," said one of the party, turning towards him, " of the late unfortunate event? "

" Why upon, my word, I know not what to say," replied he. " I think, however, that it is just possible Dantès may have been detected with some trifling article on board ship considered here as contraband."

" But how could he have done so without your knowledge, Danglars, who was the ship's supercargo? "

" Why, as for that, I could only know what I was told respecting the merchandise with which the vessel was laden. I know she was loaded with cotton, and that she took in her freight at Alexandria from the magazine of M. Pastret, and at Smyrna from M. Pascal's; that is all I was obliged to know, and I beg I may not be asked for any further particulars."

" Now, I recollect! " cried the afflicted old father; " my poor boy told me yesterday he had got a small case of coffee, and another of tobacco, for me! "

" There you see! " exclaimed Danglars. " Now the mischief is out; depend upon it the custom-house people went rummaging about the ship in our absence, and discovered poor Dantès' hidden treasures."

Mercédès, however, paid no heed to this explanation of her lover's arrest. Her grief, which she had hitherto tried to restrain, now burst out in a violent fit of hysterical sobbing.

" Come, come," said the old man, " be comforted, my poor child; there is still hope! "

" Hope! " repeated Danglars.

" Hope! " faintly murmured Fernand; but the word seemed to die away on his pale, agitated lips, and a convulsive spasm passed over his countenance.

" Good news! good news! " shouted forth one of the party stationed in the balcony on the look-out. " Here comes M. Morrel back. No doubt, now, we shall hear that our friend is released! "

Mercédès and the old man rushed to meet the person from

whom they hoped so much; but the first glance of the pale, desponding countenance of M. Morrel prepared them for evil tidings.

" What news? " exclaimed a general burst of voices.

" Alas! my friends," replied M. Morrel, with a mournful shake of his head, " the thing has assumed a more serious aspect than I expected."

" Oh! indeed—indeed, sir, he is innocent! " sobbed forth Mercédès.

" That I believe! " answered M. Morrel; " but still he is charged——"

" With what? " inquired the elder Dantès.

" With being an agent of the Bonapartist faction! "

Many of my readers may be able to recollect how formidable such an accusation became in the period at which our story is dated.

A despairing cry escaped the pale lips of Mercédès, while the heart-broken father fell listlessly into a chair, kindly placed for him by one of the pitying guests.

" Ah, Danglars! " whispered Caderousse, " you have deceived me—the trick you spoke of last night has been played off, I see; but I cannot suffer a poor old man or an innocent girl to die of grief through your fault. I am determined to tell them all about it."

" Be silent, you simpleton! " cried Danglars, grasping him by the arm, " or I will not answer even for your own safety. Who can tell whether Dantès be innocent or guilty? The vessel did touch at Elba, where he quitted it, and passed a whole day in the island. Now, should any letters or other documents of a compromising character be found upon him, will it not be taken for granted that all who uphold him are his accomplices? "

With the rapid instinct of selfishness, Caderousse readily perceived the solidity of this mode of reasoning; he gazed doubtfully, wistfully on Danglars, and then insensibly continued to retreat from the dangerous proximity in which he found himself.

" Suppose we wait a while, and see what comes of it! " said he, casting a bewildered look on his companion.

" To be sure! " answered Danglars. " Let us wait, by all means. If he be innocent, of course he will be set at liberty; if guilty, why, it is no use involving ourselves in his conspiracy."

" Then let us go hence. I cannot stay to endure the sight of that old man's distress."

" With all my heart! " replied Danglars, but too pleased to find a partner in his retreat. " Let us take ourselves out of the way, and leave every one else to do the same thing, if they please."

After their departure, Fernand, who had now again become the only friend and protector poor Mercédès could find in this trying hour, led the weeping girl back to her home, which she had quitted with such different hopes and feelings in the morning, while some friends of Dantès conducted the poor heart-broken parent to his childless and dreary abode.

The rumour of Edmond's arrest as a Bonapartist agent was not slow in circulating throughout the city.

" Could you ever have credited such a thing, my dear Danglars? " asked M. Morrel, as on his return to the port for the purpose of gleaning fresh tidings of Dantès, he overtook his supercargo and Caderousse. " Could you have believed such a thing possible? "

" Why, you know I told you," replied Danglars, " that I considered the circumstance of his having anchored in the Isle of Elba as a very suspicious circumstance."

" And did you mention these suspicions to any person besides myself? "

" Certainly not! " returned Danglars. Then added in a low whisper, " You understand that, on account of your uncle, M. Policar Morrel, who served under the other government, and who does not altogether conceal what he thinks on the subject, you are strongly suspected of regretting the abdication of Napoleon. I should have feared to injure both Edmond and yourself, had I divulged my own apprehensions to a soul. I am too well aware that though a subordinate, like myself, is bound to acquaint the shipowner with everything that occurs, there are many things he ought most carefully to conceal from all else."

" 'Tis well, Danglars—'tis well! " replied M. Morrel. " You are a worthy fellow; and I had already thought of your interests in the event of poor Edmond having become captain of the *Pharaon*."

" Is it possible you were so kind? "

" Yes, indeed; I had previously inquired of Dantès what was his opinion of you, and if he should have any reluctance to continue you in your post, for somehow I have perceived a sort of coolness between you two that led me to believe that he would rather have another in your place as supercargo."

" And what was his reply? "

" That he certainly did think he had given you offence in an affair which he merely referred to without entering into particulars, but that whoever possessed the good opinion and confidence of the ship's owners would have his preference also."

" The hypocrite! " murmured Danglars, between his teeth.

" Poor Dantès! " said Caderousse. " No one can deny his being a noble-hearted young fellow! "

" But in the midst of all our trouble," continued M. Morrel, " we must not forget that the *Pharaon* has at present no captain."

" Oh! " replied Danglars, " since we cannot leave this port for the next three months, let us hope that ere the expiration of that period Dantès will be set at liberty."

" Of that I entertain no doubt; but in the meantime what are we to do? "

" I am entirely at your service, M. Morrel," answered Danglars. " You know that I am as capable of managing a ship as the most experienced captain in the service; and it will be so far advantageous to you to accept my services, that upon Edmond's release from prison no further change will be requisite on board the *Pharaon* than for Dantès and myself each to resume our respective posts."

" Thanks! thanks! my good friend, for your excellent idea and acceptable proposition—that will smooth all difficulties. I fully authorise you at once to assume the command of the *Pharaon*, and look carefully to the unloading of her freight. Private misfortunes must never induce us to neglect public affairs."

" Depend upon my zeal and attention, M. Morrel; but when do you think it likely we may be permitted to visit our poor friend in his prison? "

" I will let you know that directly I have seen M. de Villefort, whom I shall endeavour to interest in Edmond's favour. I am aware he is a furious royalist; but, spite of that, and of his being the king's procureur, he is a man like ourselves, and I fancy not a bad sort of one! "

" Perhaps not," replied Danglars; " but he is universally spoken of as extremely ambitious, and ambition is a sore hardener of the heart! "

" Well, well! " returned M. Morrel, " we shall see! But now hasten on board. I will join you there ere long." So saying, the worthy shipowner quitted the two allies, and proceeded in the direction of the Palais de Justice.

" You see," said Danglars, addressing Caderousse, " the turn things have taken. Do you still feel any desire to stand up in his defence? "

" Not the slightest, but yet it seems to me a shocking thing a mere joke should lead to such frightful consequences."

" But who perpetrated that joke, let me ask? neither you nor myself, but Fernand: you know very well that I threw the paper into a corner of the room,—indeed, I fancied I had destroyed it."

" Oh, no! " replied Caderousse, " that I can answer for, you did not. I only wish I could see it now as plainly as I saw it lying all crushed and crumpled in a corner of the arbour."

"Well, then, if you did, depend upon it, Fernand picked it up, and either copied it or caused it to be copied; perhaps, even, he did not take the trouble of recopying it. And now I think of it, by heavens! he has sent the letter itself! Fortunately, for me, the handwriting was disguised."

"Then you were aware of Dantès being engaged in a conspiracy?"

"Not I. As I before said, I thought the whole thing was a joke, nothing more. It seems, however, that I have unconsciously stumbled upon the truth."

"Still," argued Caderousse, "I would give a great deal if nothing of the kind had happened, or, at least, that I had had no hand in it. You will see, Danglars, that it will turn out an unlucky job for both of us."

"Nonsense! If any harm comes of it, it should fall on the guilty person; and that, you know, is Fernand. How can we be implicated in any way? All we have got to do is, to keep our own counsel, and remain perfectly quiet, not breathing a word to any living soul; and you will see that the storm will pass away without in the least affecting us."

"Amen!" responded Caderousse, waving his hand in token of adieu to Danglars, and bending his steps towards the Alleés de Meillan, moving his head to and fro, and muttering as he went, after the manner of one whose mind was overcharged with one absorbing idea.

"So far, then," said Danglars mentally, "all has gone as I would have it! I am temporarily commander of the *Pharaon*, with the certainty of being permanently so, if that fool of a Caderousse can be persuaded to hold his tongue. My only fear is the chance of Dantès being released. But bah! he is in the hands of justice; and," added he, with a smile, "she will take her own."

So saying, he leaped into a boat, desiring to be rowed on board the *Pharaon*, where M. Morrel had appointed to meet him.

6

The Deputy Procureur

In one of the large aristocratical mansions, situated in the Rue du Grand Cours, opposite the fountain of Medusa, a second marriage-feast was being celebrated, almost at the same hour with the ill-fated nuptial repast given by Dantès.

In this case, however, although the occasion of the entertainment was similar, the company assembled formed a striking difference. Instead of a rude mixture of sailors, soldiers, and those belonging to the humblest grade of life, the present assembly was composed of the very flower of Marseilles society. Magistrates who had resigned their office during the usurper's reign; officers who, scorning to fight under his banners, had offered their services to foreign powers, with younger members of the family, brought up to hate and execrate the man whom five years of exile would have converted into a martyr, and fifteen of restoration elevated to the rank of a demigod.

The guests were still at table, and the heated and energetic conversation that prevailed betrayed the violent and vindictive passions that then agitated each dweller of the south, where, unhappily, religious strife* had long given increased bitterness to the violence of party feeling.

The emperor, now king of the petty Isle of Elba, after having held sovereign sway over one half of the world, counting us, his subjects, a small population of twenty millions, after having been accustomed to hear the " *Vive Napoleons* " of, at least, six times that number of human beings, uttered in nearly every language of the globe,—was looked upon among the *haute société* of Marseilles as a ruined man, separated for ever from any fresh connection with France or claim to her throne.

The magistrates freely discussed their political views; the military part of the company talked unreservedly of Moscow and Leipsic, while the females indulged in open comment upon the divorce of the Empress Josephine.*

All seemed to evince that in this focus of royalism it was not over the downfall of one man they rejoiced, but in the bright and cheering prospect of a revivified political existence for themselves.

An old man, decorated with the cross of Saint Louis, now rose and proposed the health of King Louis XVIII. This aged individual was the Marquis de Saint-Méran.

This toast, recalling at once the patient exile of Hartwell, and the peace-loving king of France, excited universal enthusiasm; glasses were elevated in the air à l'Anglais; and the ladies, snatching their bouquets from their fair bosoms, strewed the table with their floral treasures. In a word, an almost poetical fervour prevailed.

"Ah!" said the Marquise de Saint-Méran, a woman with a stern, forbidding eye, though still noble and elegant-looking, despite her having reached her fiftieth year—"Ah! these revolutionists, who have driven us from those very possessions they afterwards purchased for a mere trifle during the Reign of Terror, would be compelled to own, were they here, that all true devotion was on our side, since we were content to follow the fortunes of a falling monarch, while they, on the contrary, made their fortune by worshipping the rising sun;—yes, yes, they could not help admitting that the king, for whom we sacrificed rank, wealth, and station, was truly our ' Louis the Well-beloved! ' while their wretched usurper has been, and ever will be, to them their evil genius, their ' Napoleon the Accursed! ' Am I not right, Villefort? "

"I beg your pardon, madame! I really must pray you to excuse me—but—in truth—I was not attending to the conversation."

"Marquise!—marquise! " interposed the same elderly personage who had proposed the toast, " let the young people alone; let me tell you, on one's wedding day there are more agreeable subjects of conversation than dry politics! "

"Never mind, dearest mother," said a young and lovely girl, with a profusion of light brown hair, and eyes that seemed to float in liquid crystal; " 'tis all my fault for seizing upon M. de Villefort, so as to prevent his listening to what you said. But there—now take him—he is all your own, for as long as you like. M. Villefort, I beg to remind you my mother speaks to you."

"If Madame la Marquise will deign to repeat the words I but imperfectly caught, I shall be delighted to answer," said M. de Villefort.

"Never mind, Renée," replied the marquise, with such a look of tenderness, as all were astonished to see her harsh dry features capable of expressing; for, however all other feelings may be withered in a woman's nature, there is always one bright smiling spot in the maternal breast, and that is where a dearly-beloved child is concerned, " I forgive you. What I was saying, Villefort, was, that the Bonapartists had neither our sincerity, enthusiasm, nor devotion."

"They had, however, what supplied the place of those fine

qualities," replied the young man, "and that was fanaticism. Napoleon is the Mahomet of the West, and is worshipped by his commonplace but ambitious followers, not only as a leader and law-giver, but also as the personification of equality."

"He!" cried the marquise,—"Napoleon the type of equality! —for mercy's sake, then, what would you call Robespierre?— Come, come, do not strip the latter of his just rights to bestow them on one who has usurped enough, methinks."

"Nay, madame! I would place each of these heroes on his right pedestal—that of Robespierre to be built where his scaffold was erected; that of Napoleon on the column of the Place Vendôme. The only difference consists in the opposite character of the equality supported by these two men; the one advocates the equality that elevates, the other professes the equality that depresses;—the one brings a king within reach of the guillotine, the other elevates the people to a level with the throne. Observe," said Villefort, smiling, "I do not mean to deny, that both the individuals we have been referring to were revolutionary scoundrels, and that the 9th Thermidor and 4th of April*were lucky days for France, worthy of being gratefully remembered by every friend to monarchy and civil order; and that explains how it comes to pass, that, fallen as I trust he is for ever, Napoleon has still preserved a train of parasitical satellites. Still, marquise, it has been so with other usurpers; Cromwell, for instance, who was not half so bad as Napoleon, had his partisans and advocates."

"Do you know, Villefort, that you are talking in a most dreadfully revolutionary strain?—but I excuse it—it is impossible to expect the son of a Girondin to be free from a small spice of the old leaven."

A deep crimson suffused the countenance of Villefort. "'Tis true, madame," answered he, "that my father was a Girondin, but he was not among the number of those who voted for the king's death; he was an equal sufferer with yourself during the Reign of Terror, and had well-nigh lost his head on the same scaffold as your own father."

"True!" replied the marquise, without wincing in the slightest degree at the tragical remembrance thus called up; "but bear in mind, if you please, that our respective parents underwent persecution and proscription from diametrically opposite principles; in proof of which I may remark, that while my family remained among the stanchest adherents of the exiled princes, your father lost no time in joining the new government; and that after the Citizen Noirtier had become a Girondin, the Count Noirtier appeared as a senator and statesman."

"Dear mother!" interposed Renée, "you know very well it

was agreed that all these disagreeable reminiscences should for ever be laid aside."

"Suffer me, also, madame, to add my earnest request that you will kindly allow the veil of oblivion to cover and conceal the past. What avails retrospection and recrimination touching circumstances wholly past recall? for my own part, I have laid aside even the name of my father, and altogether disown his political principles. He was—nay, probably may still be—a Bonapartist, and is called Noirtier; I, on the contrary, am a stanch royalist, and style myself de Villefort. Let what may remain of revolutionary sap exhaust itself and die away with the old trunk, and condescend only to regard the young shoot which has started up at a distance from the parent tree, without having the power, any more than the wish, to separate entirely from the stock from which it sprung."

"Bravo, Villefort!" cried the marquis; "excellently well said! Come, now, I have hopes of obtaining what I have been for years endeavouring to persuade the marquise to promise—namely, a perfect amnesty and forgetfulness of the past."

"With all my heart," replied the marquise; "let the past be for ever forgotten! I promise you it affords *me* as little pleasure to revive it as it does you. All I ask, is, that Villefort will be firm and inflexible for the future in marking his political principles. Remember also, Villefort, that we have pledged ourselves to his majesty for your fealty and strict loyalty, and that at our recommendation, the king consented to forget the past, as I do" (and here she extended to him her hand), "as I now do at your entreaty. But bear in mind, that should there fall in your way any one guilty of conspiring against the government, you will be so much the more bound to visit the offence with rigorous punishment, as it is known you belong to a suspected family."

"Alas! madame," returned Villefort, "my profession, as well as the times in which we live, compel me to be severe. I have already successfully conducted several public prosecutions, and brought the offenders to merited punishment. But we have not done with the thing yet."

"Do you, indeed, think so?" inquired the marquise.

"I am, at least, fearful of it. Napoleon, in the island of Elba, is too near France, and his proximity keeps up the hopes of his partisans. Marseilles is filled with half-pay officers, who are daily, under one frivolous pretext or other, getting up quarrels with the royalists; from hence arise continual and fatal duels among the higher classes of persons, and assassinations in the lower."

"You have heard, perhaps," said the Comte de Salvieux, one of M. de Saint-Méran's oldest friends, and chamberlain to the Count d'Artois, " that the Holy Alliance purpose removing him from thence? "

" Ah! they were talking about it when we left Paris," said M. de Saint Méran; " and where is it decided to transfer him? "

" To Saint.Helena! "

" For Heaven's sake, where is that? " asked the marquise.

" An island situated on the other side of the equator, at least two thousand leagues from hence," replied the count.

" So much the better! As Villefort observes, it is a great act of folly to have left such a man between Corsica, where he was born, Naples, of which his brother-in-law is king, and Italy, the sovereignty of which he coveted for his son."

" Well," said the marquise, " it seems probable, that by the aid of the Holy Alliance, we shall be rid of Napoleon; and we must trust to the vigilance of M. de Villefort to purify Marseilles of his partisans. The king is either a king or no king; if he be acknowledged as sovereign of France, he should be upheld in peace and tranquillity, and this can best be effected by employing the most inflexible agents to put down every attempt at conspiracy—'tis the best and surest means of preventing mischief."

" Unfortunately, madame," answered Villefort, " the strong arm of the law is not called upon to interfere until the evil has taken place."

" Then all he has got to do is to endeavour to repair it."

" Nay, madame, the law is frequently powerless to effect this; all it can do is to avenge the wrong done."

" Oh! M. de Villefort," cried a beautiful young creature, daughter to Comte de Salvieux, and the cherished friend of Mademoiselle de Saint-Méran,—" do try and get up some famous trial while we are at Marseilles. I never was in a law court; I am told it is so very amusing! "

" Amusing, certainly! " replied the young man, " inasmuch as, instead of shedding tears as at the fictitious tale of woe produced at a theatre, you behold in a law court a case of real and genuine distress—a drama of life. The prisoner whom you there see pale, agitated, and alarmed, instead of—as is the case when the curtain falls on a tragedy—going home to sup peacefully with his family, and then retiring to rest, that he may recommence his mimic woes on the morrow, is removed from your sight merely to be reconducted to his prison and delivered up to the executioner. I leave you to judge how far your nerves are calculated to bear you through such a scene. Of this, however, be assured, that should any favourable opportunity present itself, I will not fail to offer you the choice of being present at it."

" For shame, M. de Villefort! " said Renée, becoming quite

pale; "don't you see how you are frightening us?—and yet you laugh."

"Why, I stand almost in the light of one engaged in a duel. I have already recorded sentence of death, five or six times, against the movers of political conspiracies, and who can say how many daggers may be ready sharpened, and only waiting a favourable opportunity to be buried in my heart?"

"Gracious heavens! M. de Villefort," said Renée, becoming more and more terrified; "you surely are not in earnest."

"Indeed, I am," replied the young magistrate, with a smile; "and in the interesting trial that young lady is anxious to witness, the case would only be still more aggravated. Suppose, for instance, the prisoner, as is more than probable, to have served under Napoleon—well, can you expect for an instant, that one accustomed, at the word of his commander, to rush fearlessly on the very bayonets of his foe, will scruple more to drive a stiletto into the heart of one he knows to be his personal enemy, than to slaughter his fellow-creatures, merely because bidden to do so by one he is bound to obey? Besides, one requires the excitement of being hateful in the eyes of the accused, in order to lash oneself into a state of sufficient vehemence and power. I would not choose to see the man against whom I pleaded smile, as though in mockery of my words. No! my pride is to see the accused pale, agitated, and as though beaten out of all composure by the fire of my eloquence."

"Bravo!" cried one of the guests, "that is what I call talking to some purpose."

"Just the person we require at a time like the present," said a second.

"What a splendid business that last cause of yours was, my dear Villefort!" remarked a third. "I mean the trial of the man for murdering his father. Upon my word you killed him ere the executioner had laid his hand upon him."

"Oh! as for parricides, and such dreadful people as that," interposed Renée, "it matters very little what is done to them; but as regards poor unfortunate creatures whose only crime consists in having mixed themselves up in political intrigues——"

"Why, that is the very worst offence they could possibly commit; for, don't you see, Renée, the king is the father of his people, and he who shall plot or contrive aught against the life and safety of the parent of thirty-two millions of souls, is a parricide upon a fearfully great scale?"

"I don't know anything about that," replied Renée; "but M. de Villefort, you have promised me—have you not?—always to show mercy to those I plead for."

"Make yourself quite easy on that point," answered Villefort, with one of his sweetest smiles, "you and I will always consult upon our verdicts."

"My love," said the marquise, "attend to your doves, your lapdogs, and embroidery, but do not meddle with what you understand not. Nowadays the military profession has rest, and its brave sons repose under their well-earned laurels. Now is the time for those of the long robe, like M. de Villefort, to achieve a splendid notoriety; seek not, therefore, to cross the brilliant career your betrothed husband may otherwise pursue."

"Well," said Renée, "I cannot help regretting you had not chosen some other profession than your own—a physician, for instance. Do you know I always felt a shudder at the idea of even a *destroying* angel?"

"Dear good Renée!" whispered Villefort, as he gazed with unutterable tenderness on the lovely speaker.

"Let us hope, my child," cried the marquis, "that M. de Villefort may prove the moral and political physician of this province; if so, he will have achieved a noble work."

"And one which will go far to efface the recollection of his father's conduct," added the incorrigible marquise.

"Madame," replied Villefort, with a mournful smile, "I have already had the honour to observe, that my father has (at least I hope so) abjured his past errors, and that he is, at the present moment, a firm and zealous friend to religion and order, a better royalist possibly than his son, for he has to atone for past dereliction, while I have no other impulse than warm, decided preference and conviction."

Having made this well-turned speech, Villefort looked carefully round to mark the effect of his oratory, much as he would have done had he been addressing the bench in open court.

"Do you know, my dear Villefort," cried the Comte de Salvieux, "that is as nearly as possible what I myself said the other day at the Tuileries, when questioned by his majesty's principal chamberlain, touching the singularity of an alliance between the son of a Girondin, and the daughter of an officer of the Duc de Condé; and I assure you he seemed fully to comprehend that this mode of reconciling political differences was based upon sound and excellent principles. Then the king, who, without our suspecting it, had overheard our conversation, interrupted us by saying, 'Villefort,'—observe that the king did not pronounce the word Noirtier, but on the contrary placed considerable emphasis on that of Villefort,—'Villefort,' said his majesty, is a 'young man of great judgment and discretion, who will be sure to make a figure in his profession. I like him much, and it gave me great pleasure to hear that he was about to become the son-in-law of M. le Marquis and Madame la Marquise de Saint-Méran. I should myself have recommended the match, had not the noble marquis anticipated my wishes by requesting my consent to it.' "

" Is it possible the king could have condescended so far as to express himself so favourably of me? " asked the enraptured Villefort.

" I give you his very words; and if the marquis chooses to be candid, he will confess that they perfectly agree with what his majesty said to him, when he went six months ago to consult him upon the subject of your espousing his daughter."

" Certainly," answered the marquis; " you state but the truth."

" How much do I owe this gracious prince! What is there I would not do to evince my earnest gratitude? "

" That is right," cried the marquise. " I love to see you thus. Now, then, were a conspirator to fall into your hands he would be most welcome."

" For my part, dear mother," interposed Renée, " I trust your wishes will not prosper, and that Providence will only permit petty offenders, poor debtors, and miserable cheats, to fall into M. de Villefort's hands, then I shall be contented."

" Just the same as though you prayed that a physician might only be called upon to prescribe for headaches, measles, and the stings of wasps, or any other slight affection of the epidermis. If you wish to see me the king's procureur, you must desire for me some of those violent and dangerous diseases from the cure of which so much honour redounds to the physician."

At this moment, and as though the utterance of Villefort's wish had sufficed to effect its accomplishment, a servant entered the room and whispered a few words in his ear. Villefort immediately rose from table and quitted the room upon the plea of urgent business: he soon, however, returned, his whole face beaming with delight.

Renée regarded him with fond affection; and certainly his handsome features, lit up as they then were with more than usual fire and animation, seemed formed to excite the innocent admiration with which she gazed on her graceful and intelligent lover.

" You were wishing just now," said Villefort, addressing her, " that I were a doctor instead of a lawyer. Well, I at least resemble the disciples of Esculapius in one thing, that of not being able to call a day my own, not even that of my betrothal."

" And wherefore were you called away just now? " asked Mademoiselle de Saint-Méran, with an air of deep interest.

"For a very serious affair, which bids well to afford our executioner here some work."

"How dreadful!" exclaimed Renée, her cheeks, that were before glowing with emotion, becoming pale as marble.

"Is it possible?" burst simultaneously from all who were near enough to the magistrate to hear his words.

"Why, if my information prove correct, a sort of Bonaparte conspiracy has just been discovered."

"Can I believe my ears?" cried the marquise.

"I will read you the letter containing the accusation at least," said Villefort:—

"'The procureur du roi is informed by a friend to the throne and the religious institutions of his country, that an individual, named Edmond Dantès, second in command on board the *Pharaon*, this day arrived from Smyrna, after having touched at Naples and Porto-Ferrajo, has been the bearer of a letter from Murat to the usurper, and again taken charge of another letter from the usurper to the Bonapartist club in Paris. Ample corroboration of this statement may be obtained by arresting the above-mentioned Edmond Dantès, who either carries the letter for Paris about with him, or has it at his father's abode. Should it not be found in the possession of father or son, then it will assuredly be discovered in the cabin belonging to the said Dantès, on board the *Pharaon*.'"

"But," said Renée, "this letter, which, after all, is but an anonymous scrawl, is not even addressed to you, but to the procureur du roi."

"True; but that gentleman being absent, his secretary, by his orders, opened his letters; thinking this one of importance, he sent for me, but not finding me, took upon himself to give the necessary orders for arresting the accused party."

"Then the guilty person is absolutely in custody?" said the marquise.

"Nay, dear mother, say the accused person. You know we cannot yet pronounce him guilty."

"He is in safe custody," answered Villefort; "and rely upon it, if the letter alluded to is found, he will not be likely to be trusted abroad again, unless he goes forth under the especial protection of the headsman."

"And where is the unfortunate being?" asked Renée.

"He is at my house!"

"Come, come, my friend," interrupted the marquis, "do not neglect your duty to linger with us. You are the king's servant, and must go whithersoever that service calls you."

"Oh, Villefort!" cried Renée, clasping her hands, and looking towards her lover with piteous earnestness, " be merciful on this day of our betrothal."

The young man passed round to the side of the table where the fair pleader sat, and leaning over her chair said tenderly:

" To give you pleasure, my sweet Renée, I promise to show all the lenity in my power; but if the charges brought against this Bonapartean hero prove correct, why, then, you really must give me leave to order his head to be cut off."

Renée, with an almost convulsive shudder, turned away her head, as though the very mention of killing a fellow-creature in cold blood was more than her tender nature could endure.

" Never mind that foolish girl, Villefort," said the marquise, " she will soon get over these things."

So saying, Madame de Saint Méran extended her dry bony hand to Villefort, who, while imprinting a son-in-law's respectful salute on it, looked at Renée, as much as to say, " I must try and fancy 'tis your dear hand I kiss, as it should have been."

" These are mournful auspices to accompany a betrothal! " sighed poor Renée.

" Upon my word, child! " exclaimed the angry marquise, " your folly exceeds all bounds. I should be glad to know what connection there can possibly be between your sickly sentiment-ality and the affairs of state! "

" Oh, mother! " murmured Renée.

" Nay, madame, I pray you pardon this little traitor; I promise you, that to make up for her want of loyalty I will be most inflexibly severe; " then casting an expressive glance at his betrothed, which seemed to say, " Fear not, for your dear sake my justice shall be tempered with mercy," and receiving a sweet and approving smile in return Villefort quitted the room.

7

The Examination

NO sooner had Villefort left the saloon, than he assumed the grave air of a man who holds the balance of life and death in his hands. Except the recollection of the line of politics his father had adopted, and which might interfere, unless he acted with the greatest prudence, with his own career, Villefort was as happy as a man could be. Already rich, he held a high official situation, though only twenty-seven. He was about to marry a young and charming woman, and besides her personal attractions, which were very great, Mademoiselle de Saint-Méran's family possessed considerable political influence, which they would of course exert in his favour. The dowry of his wife amounted to six thousand pounds, besides the prospect of inheriting twenty thousand more at her father's death.

At the door he met the commissary of police, who was waiting for him. The sight of this officer recalled Villefort from the third heaven to earth; he composed his face as we have before described, and said, " I have read the letter, monsieur, and you have acted rightly in arresting this man; now inform me what you have discovered concerning him and the conspiracy."

" We know nothing as yet of the conspiracy, monsieur; all the papers found have been sealed up and placed on your bureau. The prisoner himself is named Edmond Dantès, mate on board the threemaster, the *Pharaon*, trading in cotton with Alexandria and Smyrna, and belonging to Morrel and Son, of Marseilles."

" Before he entered the navy had he ever served in the marines? "

" Oh, no, monsieur, he is very young."

" How old? "

" Nineteen or twenty at the most."

At this moment, and as Villefort had arrived at the corner of the Rue des Conseils, a man, who seemed to have been waiting for him, approached: it was M. Morrel.

" Ah, M. de Villefort," cried he, " I am delighted to see you. Some of your people have committed the strangest mistake— they have just arrested Edmond Dantès, the mate of my ship."

" I know it, monsieur," replied Villefort, " and I am now going to examine him."

" Oh," said Morrel, carried away by his friendship, " you do not know him, and I do. He is the most estimable, the most trustworthy creature in the world, and I will venture to say, there is not a better seaman in all the merchant-service. Oh, M. de Villefort, I beseech your indulgence for him."

Villefort, as we have seen, belonged to the aristocratic party at Marseilles, Morrel to the plebeian; the first was a royalist, the other suspected of Bonapartism. Villefort looked disdainfully at Morrel, and replied:

" You are aware, monsieur, that a man may be estimable and trustworthy in private life, and the best seaman in the merchant-service, and yet be, politically speaking, a great criminal. Is it not true? "

The magistrate laid emphasis on these words, as if he wished to apply them to the owner himself, whilst his eyes seemed to plunge into the heart of him who, whilst he interceded for another, had himself need of indulgence. Morrel reddened, for his own conscience was not quite clear on politics; besides, what Dantès had told him of his interview with the grand-marshal, and what the emperor had said to him, embarrassed him. He replied, however:

" I entreat you, M. de Villefort, be, as you always are, kind and equitable, and give him back to us soon."

This *give us* sounded revolutionary in the subprefect's ears.

" Ah! ah! " murmured he, " is Dantès then a member of some Carbonari society, that his protector thus employs the collective form? He was, if I recollect, arrested in a cabaret, in company with a great many others." Then he added, " Monsieur, you may rest assured I shall perform my duty impartially, and that if he be innocent you shall not have appealed to me in vain; should he, however, be guilty, in this present epoch, impunity would furnish a dangerous example and I must do my duty."

As he had now arrived at the door of his own house, which adjoined the Palais de Justice, he entered, after having saluted the shipowner, who stood, as if petrified, on the spot where Villefort had left him.

The antechamber was full of agents of police and gendarmes, in the midst of whom, carefully watched, but calm and smiling, stood the prisoner. Villefort traversed the antechamber, cast a side glance at Dantès, and taking a packet which a gendarme offered him, disappeared, saying, " Bring in the prisoner."

Rapid as had been Villefort's glance, it had served to give him an idea of the man he was about to interrogate. He had recognised intelligence in the high forehead, courage in the dark eye and bent brow, and frankness in the thick lips that showed a set of pearly teeth.

Villefort's first impression was favourable, but he had been so often warned to mistrust first impulses that he applied the maxim to the impression, forgetting the difference between the two words. He stifled, therefore, the feelings of compassion that were rising, composed his features, and sat down at his bureau. An instant after Dantès entered.

He was pale, but calm and collected, and saluting his judge with easy politeness, looked round for a seat, as if he had been in the saloon of M. Morrel.

It was then that he encountered, for the first time, Villefort's look, that look peculiar to justice; which, whilst it seems to read the culprit's thoughts, betrays nought of its own.

"Who and what are you?" demanded Villefort, turning over a pile of papers, containing information relative to the prisoner that an agent of police had given to him on his entry.

"My name is Edmond Dantès," replied the young man calmly. "I am mate of the *Pharaon*, belonging to Messrs. Morrel and Son."

"Your age?" continued Villefort.

"Nineteen," returned Dantès.

"What were you doing at the moment you were arrested?"

"I was at the festival of my marriage, monsieur," said the young man, his voice slightly tremulous, so great was the contrast between that happy moment and the painful ceremony he was now undergoing; so great was the contrast between the sombre aspect of M. de Villefort and the radiant face of Mercédès.

"You were at the festival of your marriage?" said the deputy, shuddering in spite of himself.

"Yes, monsieur, I am on the point of marrying a young girl I have been attached to for three years."

Villefort, impassive as he was, was struck with this coincidence; and the tremulous voice of Dantès, surprised in the midst of his happiness, struck a sympathetic chord in his own bosom; he also was on the point of being married, and he was summoned from his own happiness to destroy that of another.

This philosophic reflection, thought he, will make a great sensation at M. de Saint-Méran's, and he arranged mentally, whilst Dantès awaited further questions, the antitheses by which orators often create a reputation for eloquence.

When this speech was arranged, Villefort turned to Dantès.

"Continue, sir," said he.

"What would you have me continue?"

"To give all the information in your power."

"Tell me on which point you desire information, and I will tell all I know; only," added he, with a smile, "I warn you I know very little."

"Have you served under the usurper?"

"I was about to be incorporated in the royal marines when he fell."

"It is reported your political opinions are extreme," said Villefort, who had never heard anything of the kind, but was not sorry to make this inquiry, as if it were an accusation.

"My political opinions!" replied Dantès. "Alas! sir, I never had any opinions. I am hardly nineteen; I know nothing; I have no part to play. If I obtain the situation I desire, I shall owe it to M. Morrel. Thus all my opinions—I will not say public, but private, are confined to these three sentiments—I love my father, I respect M. Morrel, and I adore Mercédès. This, sir, is all I can tell you, and you see how uninteresting it is."

As Dantès spoke, Villefort gazed at his ingenuous and open countenance, and recollected the words of Renée, who, without knowing who the culprit was, had besought his indulgence for him. With the deputy's knowledge of crime and criminals, every word the young man uttered convinced him more and more of his innocence.

This lad, for he was scarcely a man, simple, natural, eloquent with that eloquence of the heart, never found when sought for, full of affection for everybody, because he was happy, and because happiness renders even the wicked good, extended his affection even to his judge, spite of Villefort's severe look and stern accent. Dantès seemed full of kindness.

"*Pardieu!*" said Villefort, "he is a noble fellow! I hope I shall gain Renée's favour easily by obeying the first command she ever imposed on me. I shall have at least a pressure of the hand in public, and a sweet kiss in private."

Full of this idea, Villefort's face became so joyous that, when he turned to Dantès, the latter, who had watched the change on his physiognomy, was smiling also.

"Sir," said Villefort, "have you any enemies, at least that you know?"

"Enemies?" replied Dantès; "my position is not sufficiently elevated for that. As for my character, that is, perhaps, somewhat too hasty, but I have striven to repress it. I have had ten or twelve sailors under me; and if you question them, they will tell you that they love and respect me, not as a father, for I am too young, but as an elder brother."

"But instead of enemies you may have excited jealousy. You are about to become captain at nineteen, an elevated post; you are about to marry a pretty girl, who loves you, and these two pieces of good fortune may have excited the envy of some one."

"You are right; you know men better than I do, and what you say may possibly be the case, I confess; I prefer not knowing them, because then I should be forced to hate them."

"You are wrong; you should always strive to see clearly around you. You seem a worthy young man; I will depart from the strict line of my duty to aid you in discovering the author of this accusation. Here is the paper; do you know the writing?"

As he spoke, Villefort drew the letter from his pocket, and presented it to Dantès. Dantès read it. A cloud passed over his brow as he said:

"No, monsieur, I do not know the writing, and yet it is tolerably plain. Whoever did it writes well. I am very fortunate," added he, looking gratefully at Villefort, "to be examined by such a man as you, for this envious person is a real enemy."

And by the rapid glance that the young man's eyes shot forth, Villefort saw how much energy lay hid beneath this mildness.

"Now," said the deputy, "answer me frankly, not as a prisoner to a judge, but as one man to another who takes an interest in him, what truth is there in the accusation contained in this anonymous letter?"

And Villefort threw disdainfully on his bureau the letter Dantès had just given back to him.

"None at all. I will tell you the real facts. I swear by my honour as a sailor, by my love for Mercédès, by the life of my father——"

"Speak, monsieur," said Villefort. Then, internally. "If Renée could see me, I hope she would be satisfied, and would no longer call me a decapitator."

"Well, when we quitted Naples, Captain Leclere was attacked with a brain fever. As we had no doctor on board, and he was so anxious to arrive at Elba, that he would not touch at any other port, his disorder rose to such a height, that at the end of the third day, feeling he was dying, he called me to him. 'My dear Dantès,' said he, 'swear to perform what I am going to tell you, for it is a matter of the deepest importance.'

"'I swear, captain,' replied I.

"'Well, as after my death the command devolves on you as mate, assume the command, and bear up for the Isle of Elba, disembark at Porto-Ferrajo, ask for the grand-marshal, give him this letter, perhaps they will give you another letter, and charge you with a commission. You will accomplish what I was to have done, and derive all the honour and profit from it.'

" ' I will do it, captain; but, perhaps, I shall not be admitted to the grand-marshal's presence as easily as you expect? '

" ' Here is a ring that will obtain audience of him, and remove every difficulty,' said the captain.

" At these words he gave me a ring. It was time: two hours after he was delirious; the next day he died."

" And what did you do then? "

" What I ought to have done, and what every one would have done in my place. Everywhere the last requests of a dying man are sacred; but amongst sailors the last requests of his superior are commands. I sailed for the Isle of Elba, where I arrived the next day; I ordered everybody to remain on board, and went on shore alone. As I had expected, I found some difficulty in obtaining access to the grand-marshal; but I sent the ring I had received from the captain to him, and was instantly admitted. He questioned me concerning Captain Leclere's death; and, as the latter had told me, gave me a letter to carry on to a person in Paris. I undertook it because it was what my captain had bade me do. I landed here, regulated the affairs of the vessel, and hastened to visit my affianced bride, whom I found more lovely than ever. Thanks to M. Morrel, all the forms were got over; in a word, I was, as I told you, at my marriage-feast, and I should have been married in an hour, and to-morrow I intended to start for Paris."

" Ah! " said Villefort, " this seems to me the truth. If you have been culpable, it was imprudence, and this imprudence was legitimised by the orders of your captain. Give up this letter you have brought from Elba, and pass your word you will appear should you be required, and go and rejoin your friends."

" I am free, then sir? " cried Dantès joyfully.

" Yes; but first give me this letter."

" You have it already; for it was taken from me with some others which I see in that packet."

" Stop a moment," said the deputy, as Dantès took his hat and gloves. " To whom is it addressed? "

" To Monsieur Noirtier, Rue Coq-Héron, Paris."

Had a thunderbolt fallen into the room, Villefort could not have been more stupefied. He sank into his seat, and hastily turning over the packet, drew forth the fatal letter, at which he glanced with an expression of terror.

" M. Noirtier, Rue Coq-Héron, No, 13," murmured he, growing still paler.

" Yes," said Dantès; " do you then know him? "

" No," replied Villefort; " a faithful servant of the king does not know conspirators."

" It is a conspiracy, then? " asked Dantès, who, after believing himself free, now began to feel a tenfold alarm. " I have already told you, however, sir, I was ignorant of the contents of the letter."

" Yes, but you knew the name of the person to whom it was addressed? " said Villefort.

" I was forced to read the address to know whom to give it."

" Have you shown this letter to any one? " asked Villefort, becoming still more pale.

" To no one, on my honour."

" Everybody is ignorant that you are the bearer of a letter from the Isle of Elba, and addressed to M. Noirtier? "

" Everybody, except the person who gave it to me."

" This is too much," murmured Villefort.

Villefort's brow darkened more and more, his white lips and clenched teeth filled Dantès with apprehension.

After reading the letter, Villefort covered his face with his hands.

" Oh! " said Dantès timidly, " what is the matter? "

Villefort made no answer, but raised his head at the expiration of a few seconds, and again perused the letter.

" You give me your honour that you are ignorant of the contents of this letter? "

" I give you my honour, sir," said Dantès, " but what is the matter? You are ill;—shall I ring for assistance?—shall I call? "

" No," said Villefort, rising hastily; " stay where you are. It is for me to give orders here, and not you."

" Monsieur," replied Dantès proudly, " it was only to summon assistance for you,"

" I want none; it was a temporary indisposition. Attend to yourself; answer me."

Dantès waited, expecting a question, but in vain. Villefort fell back on his chair, passed his hand over his brow, moist with perspiration, and, for the third time, read the letter.

" Oh! if he knows the contents of this! " murmured he, " and that Noirtier is the father of Villefort, I am lost! " And he fixed his eyes upon Edmond as if he would have penetrated his thoughts.

" Oh! it is impossible to doubt it," cried he suddenly.

" In Heaven's name! " cried the unhappy young man, " if you doubt me, question me; I will answer you,"

Villefort made a violent effort, and in a tone he strove to render firm:

" Sir," said he, " I am no longer able, as I had hoped, to restore you immediately to liberty; before doing so, I must consult the judge of instruction; but you see how I behave towards you."

" Oh! monsieur," cried Dantès, " you have been rather a friend than a judge."

" Well, I must detain you some time longer, but I will strive to make it as short as possible. The principal charge against you is this letter, and you see——"

Villefort approached the fire, cast it in, and waited until it was entirely consumed.

" You see, I destroy it? "

" Oh! " exclaimed Dantès, " you are goodness itself."

" Listen," continued Villefort, " you can now have confidence in me after what I have done."

" Oh! order me, and I will obey."

" Listen! this is not an order, but a counsel I give you."

" Speak, and I will follow your advice."

" I shall detain you until this evening in the Palais de Justice. Should any one else interrogate you, do not breathe a word of this letter."

" I promise."

It was Villefort who seemed to entreat, and the prisoner who reassured him.

" You see," continued he, " the letter is destroyed; you and I alone knew of its existence: should you, therefore, be questioned, deny all knowledge of it."

" Fear nothing, I will deny it."

" It was the only letter you had? "

" It was."

" Swear it."

" I swear it."

Villefort rang. An agent of police entered. Villefort whispered some words in his ear, to which the officer replied by a motion of his head.

" Follow him," said Villefort to Dantès.

Dantès saluted Villefort and retired.

Hardly had the door closed, than Villefort threw himself into a chair.

" Alas! alas! " murmured he, " if the procureur de roi had been at Marseilles, I should have been ruined. This accursed letter would have destroyed all my hopes. Oh! my father, must your past career always interfere with my successes? "

Suddenly a light passed over his face, a smile played round his mouth, and his lips became unclenched.

" This will do," said he, " and from this letter, which might have ruined me, I will make my fortune."

And after having assured himself the prisoner was gone, the deputy procureur hastened to the house of his bride.

8

The Château d'If

THE commissary of police, as he traversed the antechamber, made a sign to two gendarmes, who placed themselves one on Dantès right and the other on his left. A door that communicated with the Palais de Justice was opened, and they traversed a long range of gloomy corridors, whose appearance might have made even the boldest shudder.

The Palais de Justice communicated with the prison,—a sombre edifice, that from its grated windows looks on the clock-tower of the Accoules.

After numberless windings, Dantès saw an iron door. The commissary knocked thrice, every blow seeming to Dantès as if struck on his heart. The door opened, the two gendarmes gently pushed him forward, and the door closed with a loud sound behind him. The air he inhaled was no longer pure, but thick and mephitic,—he was in prison.

He was conducted to a tolerably neat chamber, but grated and barred, and its appearance, therefore, did not greatly alarm him; besides the words of Villefort, who seemed to interest himself so much, resounded still in his ears like a promise of freedom.

It was four o'clock when Dantès was placed in this chamber. It was, as we have said, the 1st of March, and the prisoner was soon buried in darkness.

The obscurity augmented the acuteness of his hearing: at the slightest sound he rose and hastened to the door, convinced they were about to liberate him, but the sound died away, and Dantès sank again into his seat.

At last, about ten o'clock, and just as Dantès began to despair, steps were heard in the corridor, a key turned in the lock, the bolts creaked, the massive oaken door flew open, and a flood of light from two torches pervaded the apartment.

By the torchlight Dantès saw the glittering sabres and carbines of four gendarmes. He had advanced at first, but stopped at the sight of this fresh accession of force.

" Are you come to fetch me? " asked he.

" Yes," replied a gendarme.

" By the orders of the deputy of the king's procureur? "

" I believe so."

The conviction that they came from M. de Villefort relieved all Dantès' apprehensions, he advanced calmly and placed himself in the centre of the escort.

A carriage waited at the door, the coachman was on the box, and an exempt seated behind him.

" Is this carriage for me? " said Dantès.

" It is for you," replied a gendarme.

Dantès was about to speak, but feeling himself urged forward, and having neither the power nor the intention to resist, he mounted the steps, and was in an instant seated inside between two gendarmes, the two others took their places opposite, and the carriage rolled heavily over the stones.

The prisoner glanced at the windows, they were grated; he had changed his prison for another that was conveying him he knew not whither. Through the grating, however, Dantès saw they were passing through the Rue Caisserie, and by the Quay Saint-Laurent and the Rue Taramis, to the port.

The carriage stopped, the exempt descended, approached the guard-house, a dozen soldiers came out and formed themselves in order; Dantès saw the reflection of their muskets by the light of the lamps on the quay.

" Can all this force be summoned on my account? " thought he.

The exempt opened the door, which was locked, and, without speaking a word, answered Dantès' question, for he saw between the ranks of the soldiers a passage formed from the carriage to the port.

The two gendarmes who were opposite to him descended first. then he was ordered to alight, and the gendarmes on each side of him followed his example. They advanced towards a boat, which a custom-house officer held by a chain, near the quay.

The soldiers looked at Dantès with an air of stupid curiosity. In an instant he was placed in the sternsheets of the boat between the gendarmes, whilst the exempt stationed himself at the bow; a shove sent the boat adrift, and four sturdy oarsmen impelled it rapidly towards the Pilon. At a shout from the boat the chain that closes the mouth of the port was lowered, and in a second they were outside the harbour.

The prisoner's first feeling was joy at again breathing the pure air, for air is freedom; but he soon sighed, for he passed before La Réserve, where he had that morning been so happy, and now through the open windows came the laughter and revelry of a ball.

Dantès folded his hands, raised his eyes to heaven, and prayed fervently.

The boat continued her voyage. They had passed the Tête de More, were now in front of the lighthouse, and about to double the battery; this manœuvre was incomprehensible to Dantès.

" Whither are you taking me? " asked he.

" You will soon know."

" But still——"

" We are forbidden to give you any explanation."

Dantès knew that nothing would be more absurd than to question subordinates, who were forbidden to reply, and remained silent.

The most vague and wild thoughts passed through his mind. The boat they were in could not make a long voyage, there was no vessel at anchor outside the harbour; he thought, perhaps, they were going to leave him on some distant point. He was not bound, nor had they made any attempt to handcuff him; this seemed a good augury. Besides, had not the deputy who had been so kind to him told him that provided he did not pronounce the dreaded name of Noirtier, he had nothing to apprehend. Had not Villefort in his presence destroyed the fatal letter, the only proof against him? He waited silently, striving to pierce through the darkness.

They had left the Ile Ratonneau, where the lighthouse stood, on the right, and were now opposite the Point des Catalans. It seemed to the prisoner that he could distinguish a female form on the beach, for it was there Mercédès dwelt.

How was it that a presentiment did not warn Mercédès her lover was near her?

One light alone was visible, and Dantès recognised it as coming from the chamber of Mercédès. A loud cry could be heard by her. He did not utter it. What would his guards think if they heard him shout like a madman?

He remained silent, his eyes fixed upon the light; the boat went on, but the prisoner only thought of Mercédès. A rising ground hid the light. Dantès turned and perceived they had got out to sea. Whilst he had been absorbed in thought they hoisted the sail.

In spite of his repugnance to address the guards, Dantès turned to the nearest gendarme, and taking his hand:

" Comrade," said he, " I adjure you as a Christian and a soldier, to tell me where we are going. I am Captain Dantès, a loyal Frenchman though, accused of treason; tell me where you are conducting me, and I promise you on my honour I will submit to my fate."

The gendarme looked irresolutely at his companion, who returned for answer a sigh that said, " I see no great harm in telling him now," and the gendarme replied:

" You are a native of Marseilles and a sailor, and yet you do not know where you are going? "

" On my honour, I have no idea."

" That is impossible."

" I swear to you it is true. Tell me, I entreat."

" But my orders."

" Your orders do not forbid your telling me what I must know in ten minutes, in half an hour, or an hour. You see I cannot escape, even if I intended."

" Unless you are blind, or have never been outside the harbour you must know."

" I do not."

" Look round you then."

Dantès rose and looked forward, when he saw rise within a hundred yards of him the black and frowning rock on which stands the Château d'If.* This gloomy fortress, which has for more than three hundred years furnished food for so many wild legends, seemed to Dantès like a scaffold to a malefactor.

" The Château d'If! " cried he; " what are we going there for? "

The gendarme smiled.

" I am not going there to be imprisoned," said Dantès; " it is only used for political prisoners. I have committed no crime. Are there any magistrates or judges at the Château d'If? "

" There are only," said the gendarme, " a govenor, a garrison, turnkeys, and good thick walls. Come, come, do not look so astonished, or you will make me think you are laughing at me in return for my good nature."

Dantès pressed the gendarme's hand as though he would crush it.

" You think, then," said he, " that I am conducted to the Château to be imprisoned there? "

" It is probable; but there is no occasion to squeeze so hard."

" Without any formality."

" All the formalities have been gone through."

" In spite of M. de Villefort's promises? "

" I do not know what M. de Villefort promised you," said the gendarme, " but I know we are taking you to the Château d'If. But what are you doing? Help! comrades, help! "

By a rapid movement, which the gendarme's practised eye had perceived, Dantès sprang forward to precipitate himself into the sea, but four vigorous arms seized him as his feet quitted the flooring of the boat. He fell back foaming with rage.

" Good! " said the gendarme, placing his knee on his chest; " believe soft-spoken gentlemen again! Harkye, my friend, I have disobeyed my first order, but I will not disobey the second, and if you move I lodge a bullet in your brain."

And he levelled his carbine at Dantès, who felt the muzzle touch his head.

For a moment the idea of struggling crossed his mind, and so end the unexpected evil that had overtaken him. But he bethought him of M. de Villefort's promise; and, besides, death in a boat from the hand of a gendarme seemed too terrible. He remained motionless, but gnashing his teeth with fury.

At this moment a violent shock made the bark tremble. One of the sailors leaped on shore, a cord creaked as it ran through a pulley, and Dantès guessed they were at the end of the voyage.

His guardians, taking hold of his arms, forced him to rise, and dragged him towards the steps that lead to the gate of the fortress, while the exempt followed, armed with a carbine and bayonet.

Dantès made no resistance, he was like a man in a dream, he saw soldiers who stationed themselves on the sides, he felt himself forced up fresh stairs, he perceived he passed through a door, and the door closed behind him; but all this as mechanically as through a mist, nothing distinctly.

They halted for a minute, during which he strove to collect his thoughts; he looked around; he was in a court surrounded by high walls; he heard the measured tread of sentinels, and as they passed before the light he saw the barrels of their muskets shine.

They waited upwards of ten minutes. Captain Dantès could not escape, the gendarmes released him; they seemed awaiting orders. The orders arrived.

" Where is the prisoner? " said a voice.

" Here," replied the gendarmes.

" Let him follow me; I am going to conduct him to his room."

" Go! " said the gendarmes, pushing Dantès.

The prisoner followed his conductor, who led him into a room almost under ground, whose bare and reeking walls seemed as though impregnated with tears; a lamp placed on a stool illumined the apartment faintly, and showed Dantès the features of his conductor; an under-gaoler, ill-clothed, and of sullen appearance.

" Here is your chamber for to-night," said he. " It is late, and Monsieur le Gouverneur is asleep; to-morrow, perhaps, he may change you. In the meantime there is bread, water, and fresh straw, and that is all a prisoner can wish for. Good night!"

And before Dantès could open his mouth,—before he had noticed where the gaoler placed his bread or the water,—before he had glanced towards the corner where the straw was, the gaoler disappeared, taking with him the lamp.

Dantès was alone in darkness and in silence: cold as the shadows that he felt breathe on his burning forehead.

With the first dawn of day the gaoler returned, with orders to leave Dantès where he was. He found the prisoner in the same position, as if fixed there,—his eyes swollen with weeping.

He had passed the night standing and without sleep.

The gaoler advanced; Dantès appeared not to perceive him. He touched him on the shoulder: Edmond started.

"Have you not slept?" said the gaoler.

"I do not know," replied Dantès.

The gaoler stared.

"Are you hungry?" continued he.

"I do not know."

"Do you wish for anything?"

"I wish to see the governor."

The gaoler shrugged his shoulders and left the chamber.

Dantès followed him with his eyes, and stretched forth his hands towards the open door; but the door closed.

All his emotion then burst forth; he cast himself on the ground, weeping bitterly, and asking himself what crime he had committed that he was thus punished.

The day passed thus; he scarcely tasted food, but walked round and round the cell like a wild beast in its cage.

One thought in particular tormented him, namely, that during his journey hither he had sat so still, whereas he might, a dozen times, have plunged into the sea, and, thanks to his powers of swimming, for which he was famous, have gained the shore, concealed himself until the arrival of a Genoese or Spanish vessel; escaped to Spain or Italy, where Mercédès and his father could have joined him. He had no fears as to how he should live; good seamen are welcome everywhere; he spoke Italian like a Tuscan, and Spanish like a Castilian; he would have then been happy, whereas he was now confined in the Château d'If, ignorant of the future destiny of his father and Mercédès; and all this because he had trusted to Villefort's promise. The thought was maddening, and Dantès threw himself furiously down on his straw.

The next morning the gaoler made his appearance.

"Well," said the gaoler, "are you more reasonable to-day?"

Dantès made no reply.

" Come, take courage, do you want anything in my power to do for you? "

" I wish to see the governor."

" I have already told you it was impossible."

" Why so? "

" Because it is not allowed by the rules."

" What is allowed, then? "

" Better fare, if you pay for it, books, and leave to walk about."

" I do not want books, I am satisfied with my food, and I do not care to walk about; but I wish to see the governor."

" If you worry me by repeating the same thing I will not bring you any more to eat."

" Well, then," said Edmond, " if you do not, I shall die of famine, that is all."

The gaoler saw by his tone he would be happy to die; and, as every prisoner is worth sixpence a day to his gaoler, he replied in a more subdued tone:

" What you ask is impossible; but if you are very well behaved you will be allowed to walk about, and some day you will meet the governor; and if he chooses to reply, that is his affair."

" But," asked Dantès, " how long shall I have to wait? "

" Ah! a month—six months—a year."

" It is too long a time. I wish to see him at once."

" Ah! " said the gaoler, " do not always brood over what is impossible, or you will be mad in a fortnight."

" You think so? "

" Yes, we have an instance here; it was by always offering a million of francs to the governor for his liberty that an abbé became mad, who was in this chamber before you."

" How long has he left it? "

" Two years."

" Was he liberated then? "

" No; he was put in a dungeon."

" Listen! " said Dantès. " I am not an abbé, I am not mad; perhaps I shall be; but at present, unfortunately, I am not. I will make you another offer."

" What is that? "

" I do not offer you a million, because I have it not; but I will give you a hundred crowns if the first time you go to Marseilles you will seek out a young girl, named Mercédès, at the Catalans, and give her two lines from me."

" If I took them, and were detected, I should lose my place, which is worth two thousand francs a year; so that I should be a great fool to run such a risk for three hundred."

" Well," said Dantès, " mark this, if you refuse, at least, to tell Mercédès I am here, I will some day hide myself behind the door, and when you enter, I will dash out your brains with this stool."

" Threats! " cried the gaoler, retreating, and putting himself on the defensive; " you are certainly going mad. The abbé began like you; and in three days you will want a strait-waistcoat; but, fortunately, there are dungeons here."

Dantès whirled the stool round his head.

" Oh! " said the gaoler, " you shall see the governor at once."

" That is right," returned Dantès, dropping the stool, and sitting on it as if he were in reality mad.

The gaoler went out, and returned in an instant with a corporal and four soldiers.

" By the governor's orders," said he, " conduct the prisoner to the story beneath."

" To the dungeon, then," said the corporal.

" Yes, we must put the madman with the madmen."

The soldiers seized Dantès, who followed passively.

He descended fifteen steps, and the door of a dungeon was opened, and he was thrust in.

The door closed, and Dantès advanced with outstretched hands until he touched the wall; he then sat down in the corner until his eyes became accustomed to the darkness.

The gaoler was right; Dantès wanted but little of being utterly mad.

9

The Evening of the Betrothal

VILLEFORT had, as we have said, hastened back to the Place du Grand Cours, and on entering the house found all the guests in the salon at coffee. Renée was, with all the rest of the company, anxiously awaiting him, and his entrance was followed by a general exclamation.

" Well, Decapitator, Guardian of the State, Brutus, what is the matter? " said one.

" Are we threatened with a fresh Reign of Terror? " asked another.

" Has the Corsican ogre broke loose? " cried a third.

" Madame la Marquise," said Villefort, approaching his future mother-in-law, " I request your pardon for thus leaving you. M. le Marquis, honour me by a few moments' private conversation!"

"Ah! this affair is really serious, then?" asked the marquis, remarking the cloud on Villefort's brow.

"So serious, that I must take leave of you for a few days; so," added he, turning to Renée, "judge for yourself if it be not important?"

"You are going to leave us?" cried Renée, unable to hide her emotion.

"Alas!" returned Villefort, "I must!"

"Where, then, are you going?" asked the marquise.

"That, madame, is the secret of justice, but if you have any commissions for Paris, a friend of mine is going there to-night."

The guests looked at each other.

"You wish to speak to me alone?" said the marquis.

"Yes, let us go into your cabinet."

The marquis took his arm, and left the salon.

"Well!" asked he, as soon as they were in his closet, "tell me, what is it?"

"An affair of the greatest importance, that demands my immediate presence in Paris. Now, excuse the indiscretion, marquis, but have you any funded property?"

"All my fortune is in the funds; seven or eight hundred thousand francs."

"Then sell out,—sell out, marquis, as soon as you can."

"Eh! how can I sell out here?"

"You have a broker, have you not?"

"Yes."

"Then give me a letter to him, and tell him to sell out without an instant's delay, perhaps even now I shall arrive too late."

"What say you?" said the marquis, "let us lose no time, then!"

And, sitting down, he wrote a letter to his broker, ordering him to sell out at any loss.

"Now, then," said Villefort, placing the letter in his pocket-book, "write another!"

"To whom?"

"To the king."

"I dare not write to his majesty."

"I do not ask you to write to his majesty, but ask M. de Salvieux to do so. I want a letter that will enable me to reach the king's presence without all the formalities of demanding an audience, that would occasion a loss of time."

"But address yourself to the keeper of the seals, he has the right of entry, and can procure you audience."

" Doubtless; but there is no occasion to divide the merit of my discovery with him. The keeper would leave me in the background, and take all the honour to himself. I tell you, marquis, my fortune is made if I only reach the Tuileries the first, for the king will not forget the service I do him."

" In that case make your preparations, and I will write the letter."

" Be as quick as possible, I must be *en route* in a quarter of an hour."

" Make your carriage stop at the door."

" You will present my excuses to the marquise and Mademoiselle Renée, whom I leave on such a day with great regret."

" They are both in my room, you can say all this for yourself."

" A thousand thanks, busy yourself with the letter."

The marquis rang, a servant entered.

" Inform the Comte de Salvieux I am waiting for him."

" Now, then, go! " said the marquis.

" I only go for a few moments."

Villefort hastily quitted the apartment, but reflecting that the sight of the deputy procureur running through the streets would be enough to throw the whole city into confusion, he resumed his ordinary pace. At his door he perceived a figure in the shadow that seemed to wait for him. It was Mercédès, who, hearing no news of her lover, had come herself to inquire after him.

As Villefort drew near, she advanced and stood before him. Dantès had spoken of his bride, and Villefort instantly recognised her. Her beauty and high bearing surprised him, and when she inquired what had become of her lover, it seemed to him that she was the judge, and he the accused.

" The young man you speak of," said Villefort abruptly, " is a great criminal, and I can do nothing for him, mademoiselle."

Mercédès burst into tears, and, as Villefort strove to pass her, again addressed him.

" But, at least, tell me where he is, that I may learn if he is alive or dead," said she.

" I do not know, he is no longer in my hands," replied Villefort.

And desirous of putting an end to the interview, he pushed by her, and closed the door, as if to exclude the pain he felt. But remorse is not thus banished; like the wounded hero of Virgil, arrow remained in the wound, and, arrived at the salon, Villefort, in his turn, burst into tears, and sank into a chair.

The man he sacrificed to his ambition, that innocent victim he made pay the penalty of his father's faults, appeared to him pale and threatening, leading his affianced bride by the hand, and bringing with him remorse, not such as the ancients figured, furious and terrible, but that slow and consuming agony, whose pangs cease only with life. Then he had a moment's hesitation. He had frequently called for capital punishment on criminals, and owing to his irresistible eloquence they had been condemned, and yet the slightest shadow of remorse had never clouded Villefort's brow, because they were guilty; at least, he believed so; but here was an innocent man whose happiness he had destroyed: in this case he was not the judge, but the executioner.

As he thus reflected, he felt the sensation we have described, and which had hitherto been unknown to him, arise in his bosom, and fill him with vague apprehensions. It is thus that a wounded man trembles instinctively at the approach of the finger to his wound until it be healed, but Villefort's was one of those that never close, or if they do, only close to reopen more agonising than ever. If at this moment the sweet voice of Renée had sounded in his ears pleading for mercy, or the fair Mercédès had entered and said, " In the name of God, I conjure you to restore me my affianced husband," his cold and trembling hands would have signed his release; but no voice broke the stillness of the chamber, and the door was opened only by Villefort's valet, who came to tell him the travelling-carriage was in readiness.

Villefort rose, or rather sprang, from his chair, hastily opened one of the drawers of his *sécrétaire*, emptied all the gold it contained into his pocket, stood motionless an instant, his hand pressed to his head, muttered a few inarticulate sounds, and then perceiving his servant had placed his cloak on his shoulders, he sprang into the carriage, ordering the postilions to go, Rue du Grand Cours, to the house of M. de Saint-Méran.

As the marquis had promised, Villefort found the letter. He started when he saw Renée, for he fancied she was again about to plead for Dantès. Alas! she was thinking only of Villefort's departure.

She loved Villefort, and he left her at the moment he was about to become her husband. Villefort knew not when he should return, and Renée, far from pleading for Dantès, hated the man whose crime separated her from her lover. What had Mercédès to say ?

Mercédès had met Fernand at the corner of the Rue de la Loge; she had returned to the Catalans, and had despairingly cast herself on her couch. Fernand, kneeling by her side, took her hand, and covered it with kisses that Mercédès did not even feel.

She passed the night thus, and the day returned without her noticing it. Grief had made her blind to all but one object, that was Edmond.

" Ah! you are there," said she, at length.

" I have not quitted you since yesterday," returned Fernand sorrowfully.

M. Morrel had learned that Dantès had been conducted to prison, and he had gone to all his friends, and the influential persons of the city, but the report was already in circulation that Dantès was arrested as a Bonapartist agent; and as the most sanguine looked upon any attempt of Napoleon to remount the throne as impossible, he met with nothing but refusal, and had returned home in despair.

Caderousse was equally restless and uneasy, but instead of seeking to aid Dantès, he had shut himself up with two bottles of wine, in the hope of drowning reflection. But he did not succeed, and became too intoxicated to fetch any more wine, and yet not so intoxicated as to forget what had happened.

Danglars alone was content and joyous, he had got rid of an enemy and preserved his situation on board the *Pharaon*; Danglars was one of those men born with a pen behind the ear, and an inkstand in place of a heart. Everything with him was multiplication or subtraction, and he estimated the life of a man as less precious than a figure, when that figure could increase, and that life would diminish, the total of the amount.

Villefort, after having received M. de Salvieux' letter, embraced Renée, kissed the marquise's hand, and shaken hands with the marquis, started for Paris.

Old Dantès was dying with anxiety to know what had become of Edmond.

10

The Little Room in the Tuileries

WE will leave Villefort on the road to Paris, travelling with all speed, and penetrating the two or three apartments which precede it, enter the small cabinet of the Tuileries with the arched window, so well known as having been the favourite cabinet of Napoleon and Louis XVIII, as also that of Louis Philippe.

There, in this closet, seated before a walnut-tree table he had brought with him from Hartwell, and to which, from one of those fancies not uncommon to great people, he was particularly attached, the king, Louis XVIII, was carelessly listening to a

man of fifty or fifty-two years of age, with gray hairs, aristocratic
bearing, and exceedingly gentlemanly attire, whilst he was making
a note in a volume of Horace, Gryphius's* edition, which was
much indebted to the sagacious observations of the philosophical
monarch.

"You say, sir——" said the king.

"That I am exceedingly disquieted, sire."

"Really, have you had a visit of the seven fat kine and seven
lean kine?"

"No, sire, for that would only betoken for us seven years of
plenty and seven years of scarcity, and with a king as full of
foresight as your majesty, scarcity is not a thing to be feared."

"Then of what other scourge are you afraid, my dear Blacas?"*

"Sire, I have every reason to believe that a storm is brewing in
the south."

"Well, my dear duke," replied Louis XVIII, "I think you
are wrongly informed, and know positively that, on the contrary,
it is very fine weather in that direction."

Man of ability as he was, Louis XVIII liked a pleasant jest.

"Sire," continued M. de Blacas, "if it only be to reassure a
faithful servant, will your majesty send into Languedoc, Provence,
and Dauphiné, trusty men who will bring you back a faithful
report as to the feeling in these three provinces?"

"*Canimus surdis!*"*replied the king, continuing the annotations
in his Horace.

"Sire," replied the courtier, laughing, in order that he might
seem to comprehend the quotation, "your majesty may be perfectly right in relying on the good feeling of France, but I fear I
am not altogether wrong in dreading some desperate attempt."

"By whom?"

"By Bonaparte, or, at least, his party."

"My dear Blacas," said the king, "you with your alarms
prevent me from working."

"And you, sire, prevent me from sleeping with your security."

"Wait, my dear sir, wait a moment, for I have such a delightful
note on the *Pastor quùm traheret,*—wait, and I will listen to you
afterwards."

There was a brief pause, during which Louis XVIII wrote,
in a hand as small as possible, another note on the margin of his
Horace, and then looking at the duke with the air of a man
who thinks he has an idea of his own, whilst he is but commenting
upon the idea of another, he said:

"Go on, my dear duke, go on—I listen."

"Sire," said Blacas, who had for a moment the hope of
sacrificing Villefort to his own profit, "I am compelled to tell you

that these are not mere rumours destitute of foundation which
thus disquiet me; but a reflective man, deserving all my confidence, and charged by me to watch over the south " (the duke
hesitated as he pronounced these words), " has arrived post to
tell me a great peril threatens the king, and then I hastened to
you, sire."

" *Mala ducis avi domum*,"*continued Louis XVIII, still annotating.

" Does your majesty wish me to cease as to this subject? "

" By no means, dear duke; but just stretch out your hand,"

" Which? "

" Whichever you please—there to the left."

" Hère, sire? "

" I tell you to the left, and you seek the right,—I mean on my
right!—yes, there! You will find the report of the minister of
police of yesterday. But here is M. Dandré himself; " and M.
Dandré,* announced by the chamberlain in waiting, entered.

" Come in," said Louis XVIII, with an imperceptible smile,
" come in, baron, and tell the duke all you know—the latest
news of M. de Bonaparte; do not conceal anything, however
serious—let us see the island of Elba is a volcano, and we may
expect to have issuing thence flaming and bristling war,—*bella,
horrida bella!* "*

M. Dandré leaned very respectfully on the back of a chair
with his two hands, and said:

" Has your majesty perused yesterday's report? "

" Yes, yes! but tell the duke himself, who cannot find anything, what the report contains; give him the particulars of what
the usurper is doing in his islet."

" Monsieur," said the baron to the duke, " all the servants of
his majesty must approve of the latest intelligence which we have
from the island of Elba. Bonaparte "—M. Dandré looked at
Louis XVIII, who, employed in writing a note, did not even
raise his head—" Bonaparte," continued the baron ," is mortally
wearied, and passes whole days in watching his miners at work
at Porto-Longone."

" And scratches himself for amusement," added the king.

" Scratches himself? " inquired the duke, " what does your
majesty mean? "

" Yes, indeed, my dear duke; did you forget that this great
man, this hero, this demigod, is attacked with a malady of the
skin which worries him to death, *prurigo*? "*

" And moreover, M. le Duc," continued the minister of
police, " we are almost assured that, in a very short time, the
usurper will be insane."

" Insane? "

" Insane to a degree; his head becomes weaker. Sometimes he weeps bitterly, sometimes laughs boisterously; at other times he passes hours on the seashore, flinging stones in the water, and when the flint makes ' duck-and-drake ' five or six times he appears as delighted as if he had gained another Marengo or Austerlitz. Now you must agree these are indubitable symptoms of weakness? "

" Or of wisdom, M. le Baron—or of wisdom," said Louis XVIII, laughing; " the greatest captains of antiquity recreated themselves with casting pebbles into the ocean: see Plutarch's life of Scipio Africanus."

M. de Blacas pondered deeply in this blind repose of monarch and minister. Villefort, who did not choose to reveal the whole secret, lest another should reap all the benefit of the disclosure, had yet communicated enough to cause him the greatest uneasiness.

" Well, well, Dandré," said Louis XVIII, " Blacas is not yet convinced, let us proceed, therefore, to the usurper's conversion."

The minister of police bowed.

" The usurper's conversion! " murmured the duke, looking at the king and Dandré, who spoke alternately, like Virgil's shepherds—" the usurper converted! "

" Decidedly, my dear duke."

" In what way converted? "

" To good principles; explain all about it, baron."

" Why this it is, M. le Duc," said the minister, with the gravest air in the world: " Napoleon lately had a review, and as two or three of his old veterans testified a desire to return to France he gave them their dismissal, and exhorted them to ' serve the good king '; these were his own words, M. le Duc, I am certain of that. "

" Well, Blacas, what think you of this? " inquired the king triumphantly, and pausing for a moment from the voluminous scholiast before him.

" I say, sire, that the minister of police is greatly deceived, or I am; and as it is impossible it can be the minister of police, as he has the guardianship of the safety and honour of your majesty, it is probable I am in error. However, sire, if I might advise, your majesty will interrogate the person of whom I spoke to you, and I will urge your majesty to do him this honour."

" Most willingly, duke; under your auspices I will receive any person you please, but with arms in hand. M. le Ministre, have you any report more recent than this, dated the 20th February, and this is the 4th of March? "

"No, sire, but I am hourly expecting one; it may have arrived since I left my office."

"Go thither, and if there be none—well, well," continued Louis XVIII, "make one; that is the usual way, is it not?" and the king laughed facetiously.

"Oh, sire," replied the minister, "we have no occasion to invent any: every day our desks are loaded with most circumstantial denunciations, coming from crowds of individuals who hope for some return for services which they seek to render, but cannot: they trust to fortune, and rely that some unexpected event will give a kind of reality to their predictions."

"Well, sir, go," said Louis XVIII, "and remember that I am waiting for you."

"I will but go and return, sire; I shall be back in ten minutes."

"And I, sire," said M. de Blacas, "will go and find my messenger."

"Wait, sir, wait," said Louis XVIII; "really, M. de Blacas, I must change your armorial bearings; I will give you an eagle with outstretched wings, holding in its claws a prey which tries in vain to escape, and bearing this device, *Tenax.*"

"Sire, I listen," said de Blacas, biting his nails with impatience.

"I wish to consult you on this passage, '*Molli fugies anhelitu*';* you know it refers to a stag flying from a wolf. Are you not a sportsman and a great wolf-hunter? Well, then, what do you think of the *molli anhelitu?*"

"Admirable, sire; but my messenger is like the stag you refer to, for he has posted two hundred and twenty leagues in little more than three days."

"Which is undergoing great fatigue and anxiety, my dear duke, when we have a telegraph*which corresponds in three or four hours, and that without putting it the least in the world out of breath."

"Ah, sire, you recompense but badly this poor young man, who has come so far, and with so much ardour to give your majesty useful information. If only for the sake of M. de Salvieux, who recommends him to me, I entreat your majesty to receive him graciously."

"M. de Salvieux, my brother's chamberlain?"

"Yes, sire."

"He is at Marseilles."

"And writes me thence."

"Does he speak to you of this conspiracy?"

"No, but strongly recommends M. de Villefort, and begs me to present him to your majesty."

" M. de Villefort! " cried the king, " is the messenger's name M. de Villefort? "

" Yes, sire."

" And he comes from Marseilles? "

" In person."

" Why did you not mention his name at once? " replied the king, betraying some uneasiness.

" Sire, I thought his name was unknown to your majesty."

" No, no, Blacas; he is a man of strong and elevated understanding, ambitious too, and, *pardieu!* you know his father's name! "

" His father? "

" Yes, Noirtier."

" Noirtier the Girondin?—Noirtier the senator? "*

" He himself."

" And your majesty has employed the son of such a man? "

" Blacas, my friend, you have but limited comprehension. I told you Villefort was ambitious, and to attain his ambition Villefort would sacrifice everything, even his father."

" Then, sire, may I present him? "

" This instant, duke! Where is he? "

" Waiting below, in my carriage."

" Seek him at once."

" I hasten to do so."

The duke left the royal presence with the speed of a young man; his really sincere royalism made him youthful again. Louis XVIII remained alone, and turning his eyes on his half-opened Horace, muttered, " *Justum et tenacem propositi virum.*"*

M. de Blacas returned with the same rapidity he had descended, but in the antechamber he was forced to appeal to the king's authority. Villefort's dusty garb, his costume, which was not of courtly cut, excited the susceptibility of M. de Brezé, who was all astonishment at finding that this young man had the pretension to enter before the king in such attire. The duke, however, superseded all difficulties with a word—his majesty's order, and, in spite of the observations which the master of the ceremonies made for the honour of his office and principles, Villefort was introduced.

The king was seated in the same place where the duke had left him. On opening the door, Villefort found himself facing him, and the young magistrate's first impulse was to pause.

" Come in, M. de Villefort," said the king, " come in."

Villefort bowed, and, advancing a few steps, waited until the king should interrogate him.

" M. de Villefort," said Louis XVIII, " the Duc de Blacas

assures me you have some interesting information to communicate."

"Sire, the duke is right, and I believe your majesty will think it equally important."

"In the first place, and before everything else, sir, is the bad news as great in your opinion as it is wished to make me believe?"

"Sire, I believe it to be most urgent, but I hope, by the speed I have used, that it is not irreparable."

"Speak as fully as you please, sir," said the king, who began to give way to the emotion which had showed itself in Blacas' face and affected Villefort's voice,—"speak, sir, and pray begin at the beginning; I like order in everything."

"Sire," said Villefort, "I will render a faithful report to your majesty, but I must entreat your forgiveness if my anxiety creates some obscurity in my language."

A glance at the king after this discreet and subtle exordium assured Villefort of the benignity of his august auditor, and he continued:

"Sire, I have come as rapidly to Paris as possible, to inform your majesty that I have discovered, in the exercise of my duties, not a commonplace and insignificant plot, such as is every day got up in the lower ranks of the people and in the army, but an actual conspiracy, a storm which menaces no less than the throne of your majesty. Sire, the usurper is arming three ships, he meditates some project, which, however mad, is yet, perhaps, terrible. At this moment he will have left Elba, to go whither I know not, but assuredly to attempt a landing either at Naples, or on the coast of Tuscany, or, perhaps, on the shore of France. Your majesty is well aware that the sovereign of the Isle of Elba has maintained his relations with Italy and France?"

"I am, sir," said the king, much agitated; "and recently we have had information that the Bonapartist clubs have had meetings in the Rue Saint-Jacques. But proceed, I beg of you; how did you obtain these details?"

"Sire, they are the results of an examination which I have made of a man of Marseilles, whom I have watched for some time, and arrested on the day of my departure. This person, a sailor, of turbulent character, and whom I suspected of Bonapartism, has been secretly to the Isle of Elba. There he saw the grand-marshal, who charged him with a verbal mission to a Bonapartist in Paris, whose name I could not extract from him; but this mission was to prepare men's minds for a return (it is the man who says this, sire),—a return which will soon occur."

"And where is this man?"

"In prison, sire."

" And the matter seems serious to you? "

" So serious, sire, that when the circumstance surprised me in the midst of a family festival, on the very day of my betrothal, I left my bride and friends, postponing everything, that I might hasten to lay at your majesty's feet the fears which impressed me, and the assurance of my devotion."

" True," said Louis XVIII, "was there not a marriage engagement between you and Mademoiselle de Saint-Méran? "

" Daughter of one of your majesty's most faithful servants."

" Yes, yes; but let us talk of this plot, M. de Villefort."

" Sire, I fear it is more than a plot; I fear it is a conspiracy."

" A conspiracy in these times," said Louis XVIII, smiling, " is a thing very easy to meditate, but more difficult to conduct to an end; inasmuch as re-established so recently on the throne of our ancestors, we have our eyes open at once upon the past, the present, and the future. For the last ten months my ministers have redoubled their vigilance, in order to watch the shore of the Mediterranean. If Bonaparte landed at Naples, the whole coalition would be on foot before he could even reach Piombino; if he land in Tuscany, he will be in an unfriendly territory; if he land in France, it must be with a handful of men, and the result of that is easily foretold, execrated as he is by the population. Take courage, sir; but at the same time rely on our royal gratitude."

" And, here is M. Dandré! " cried de Blacas.

At this instant the minister of police appeared at the door, pale, trembling, and as if ready to faint.

Villefort was about to retire, but M. de Blacas, taking his hand, restrained him.

11

The Corsican Ogre

A T the sight of this agitation Louis XVIII pushed from him
violently the table at which he was writing.

" What ails you, M. le Baron? " he exclaimed. " You appear
quite aghast. This trouble—this hesitation—have they anything
to do with what M. de Blacas has told me, and M. de Villefort
has just confirmed? "

M. de Blacas moved suddenly towards the baron, but the fright
of the courtier precluded the triumph of the statesman; and
besides, as matters were, it was much more to his advantage that
the prefect of police should triumph over him than that he should
humiliate the prefect.

" Sire—— " stammered the baron.

" Well, what is it? " asked Louis XVIII.

The minister of police, giving way to an impulse of despair, was
about to throw himself at the feet of Louis XVIII, who retreated
a step and frowned.

" Will you speak? " he said.

" Oh! sire, what a dreadful misfortune! I am indeed, to be
pitied. I can never forgive myself! "

" Monsieur," said Louis XVIII, " I command you to speak."

" Well, sire, the usurper left Elba on the 26th February, and
landed on the 1st of March."*

" And where? In Italy? " asked the king eagerly.

" In France, sire, at a small port near Antibes, in the Gulf
of Juan."

" The usurper landed in France near Antibes, in the Gulf of
Juan, 250 leagues from Paris, on the 1st of March, and you only
acquired this information to-day, the 4th of March! Well, sir,
what you tell me is impossible. You must have received a false
report, or you have gone mad."

" Alas! sire, it is but too true! "

Louis made a gesture of indescribable anger and alarm, and
then drew himself up as if this sudden blow had struck him at
the same moment in heart and countenance.

" In France! " he cried, " the usurper in France! Then they
did not watch over this man. Who knows? they were, perhaps,
in league with him."

" Oh, sire! " exclaimed the Duc de Blacas, " M. Dandré is not a man to be accused of treason! Sire, we have all been blind, and the minister of police has shared the general blindness, that is all."

" But——" said Villefort, and then suddenly checking himself, he was silent; then he continued, " Your pardon, sire," he said, bowing, " my zeal carried me away. Will your majesty deign to excuse me? "

" Speak, sir, speak boldly," replied Louis. " You alone forewarned us of the evil; now try and aid us with the remedy! "

" Sire," said Villefort, " the usurper is detested in the south; and it seems to me that if he ventured into the south, it would be easy to raise Languedoc and Provence against him."

" Yes, assuredly," replied the minister; " but he is advancing by Gap and Sisteron."

" Advancing! he is advancing! " said Louis XVIII. " Is he then advancing on Paris? "

The minister of police kept a silence which was equivalent to a complete avowal.

" And Dauphiné, sir? " inquired the king, of Villefort. " Do you think it possible to rouse that as well as Provence? "

" Sire, I am sorry to tell your majesty a cruel fact; but the feeling in Dauphiné is far from resembling that of Provence or Languedoc. The mountaineers are Bonapartists, sire."

" Then," murmured Louis, " he was well informed. And how many men had he with him? "

" I do not know, sire," answered the minister of police.

" What! you do not know? Have you neglected to obtain information of this circumstance? It is true this is of small importance," he added, with a withering smile.

" Sire, it was impossible to learn; the despatch simply stated the fact of the landing and the route taken by the usurper."

" And how did this despatch reach you? " inquired the king.

The minister bowed his head, and whilst a deep colour overspread his cheeks he stammered out:

" By the telegraph, sire."

Louis XVIII advanced a step, and folded his arms over his chest as Napoleon would have done.

" So then! " he exclaimed, turning pale with anger, " seven conjoined and allied armies overthrew that man. A miracle of Heaven replaced me on the throne of my fathers after five-and-twenty years of exile. I have, during those five-and-twenty years, studied, sounded, analysed the men and things of that France which was promised to me; and when I have attained the end of all my wishes, the power I hold in my hands bursts and shatters me to atoms! "

" Sire, it is fatality! " murmured the minister, feeling that such a pressure, however light for destiny, was sufficient to overwhelm a man.

" What our enemies say of us is then true. We have learnt nothing, forgotten nothing!* If I were betrayed as he was, I would console myself; but to be in the midst of persons elevated by myself to dignities, who ought to watch over me more preciously than over themselves; for my fortune is theirs!—before me they were nothing—after me they will be nothing, and perish miserably from incapacity—ineptitude! Oh, yes, sir! you are right—it is fatality! "

The minister was bowed beneath this crushing sarcasm. M. de Blacas wiped the moisture from his brow. Villefort smiled within himself, for he felt his increased importance.

" To fall! " continued King Louis, who at the first glance had sounded the abyss on which the monarchy hung suspended,— " to fall, and learn that fall by the telegraph! Oh! I would rather mount the scaffold of my brother, Louis XVI, than thus descend the staircase of the Tuileries driven away by ridicule. Ridicule, sir—why, you know not its power in France, and yet you ought to know it! "

" Sire, sire, " murmured the minister, " for pity's——"

" Approach, M. de Villefort, " resumed the king, addressing the young man, who, motionless and breathless, was listening to a conversation on which depended the destiny of a kingdom. " Approach, and tell monsieur that it is possible to know beforehand all that he has not known. "

" Sire, it was really impossible to learn secrets which that man concealed from all the world. "

" Really impossible! Yes—that is a great word, sir. Unfortunately, there are great words, as there are great men; I have measured them. Really impossible for a minister who has an office, agents, spies, and fifteen hundred thousand francs for secret service money, to know what is going on at sixty leagues from the coast of France! Well, then, see, here is a gentleman who had none of these resources at his disposal—a gentleman, only a simple magistrate, who learned more than you with all your police, and who would have saved my crown, if, like you, he had the power of directing a telegraph. "

The look of the minister of police was turned with concentrated spite on Villefort, who bent his head with the modesty of triumph.

" I do not mean that for you, Blacas, " continued Louis XVIII; " for if you have discovered nothing, at least you have had the good sense to persevere in your suspicions. Any other than your-self would have considered the disclosure of M. de Villefort as insignificant, or else dictated by a venal ambition."

These words were meant to allude to those which the minister of police had uttered with so much confidence an hour before.

Villefort understood the drift of the king. Any other person would, perhaps, have been too much overcome by the intoxication of praise; but he feared to make for himself a mortal enemy of the police minister, although he perceived Dandré was irrevocably lost. In fact, the minister who, in the plenitude of his power, had been unable to penetrate Napoleon's secret, might in the convulsions of his dying throes penetrate his (Villefort's) secret, for which end he had but to interrogate Dantès. He therefore, came to the rescue of the crestfallen minister, instead of aiding to crush him.

" Sire," said Villefort, " the rapidity of the event must prove to your majesty that God alone can prevent it, by raising a tempest; what your majesty is pleased to attribute to me as profound perspicacity is simply owing to chance; and I have profited by that chance, like a good and devoted servant, that's all. Do not attribute to me more than I deserve, sire, that your majesty may never have occasion to recall the first opinion you have been pleased to form of me."

The minister of police thanked the young man by an eloquent look, and Villefort understood that he had succeeded in his design; that is to say, that without forfeiting the gratitude of the king, he had made a friend of one on whom, in case of necessity, he might rely.

" 'Tis well! " resumed the king. " And now, gentlemen," he continued, turning towards M. de Blacas and the minister of police, " I have no further occasion for you, and you may retire; what now remains to do is in the department of the minister of war."

" Fortunately, sire," said M. de Blacas, " we can rely on the army; your majesty knows how every report confirms their loyalty and attachment."

" Do not mention reports, sir, to me! for I know now what confidence to place in them. Yet, apropos of reports, M. le Baron, what intelligence have you as to our affair in the Rue Saint-Jacques? "

" The affair in the Rue Saint-Jacques! " exclaimed Villefort, unable to repress an exclamation. Then, suddenly pausing, he added, " Your pardon, sire, but my devotion to your majesty has made me forget, not the respect I have, for that is too deeply engraven in my heart, but the rules of etiquette."

" Say and act, sir! " replied the king; " you have acquired the right to inquire."

" Sire," replied the minister of police, " I came this moment to give your majesty fresh information which I had obtained on this head, when your majesty's attention was attracted by this terrible affair of the gulf, and now these facts will cease to interest your majesty."

" On the contrary, sir,—on the contrary," said Louis XVIII, " this affair seems to me to have a decided connection with that which occupies our attention; and the death of General Quesnel* will, perhaps, put us on the direct track of a great internal conspiracy."

At the name of General Quesnel, Villefort trembled.

" All combines, sir," said the minister of police, " to ensure the probability that this death is not the result of a suicide, as we at first believed, but of an assassination. General Quesnel had quitted, as it appears, a Bonapartist club when he disappeared. An unknown person had been with him that morning, and made an appointment with him in the Rue Saint-Jacques; unfortunately, the general's valet-de-chambre, who was dressing his hair at the moment when the stranger entered, heard the street mentioned, but did not catch the number."

As the police minister related this to the king, Villefort, who seemed as if his very existence hung on his lips, turned alternately red and pale. The king looked towards him.

" Do you not think with me, M. de Villefort, that General Quesnel, whom they believed attached to the usurper, but who was really entirely devoted to me, has perished the victim of a Bonapartist ambush? "

" It is probable, sire," replied Villefort. " But is this all that is known? "

" They are on the traces of the man who appointed the meeting with him."

" On his traces? " said Villefort.

" Yes, the servant has given his description. He is a man of from fifty to fifty-two years of age, brown, with black eyes, covered with shaggy eyebrows, and a thick moustache. He was dressed in a blue frockcoat, buttoned up to the chin, and wore at his buttonhole the rosette of an officer of the Legion of Honour.* Yesterday an individual was followed exactly corresponding with this description, but he was lost sight of at the corner of the Rue de la Jussienne and the Rue Coq-Héron."

Villefort leaned on the back of an arm-chair, for in proportion as the minister of police spoke, he felt his legs bend under him;

but when he learnt that the unknown had escaped the vigilance of the agent who followed him, he breathed again.

"Continue to seek for this man, sir," said the king to the minister of police; "for if, as all conspires to convince me, General Quesnel, who would have been so useful to us at this moment, has been murdered, his assassins, Bonapartists or not, shall be cruelly punished."

It required all Villefort's *sang-froid* not to betray the terror with which this declaration of the king inspired him.

"How strange!" continued the king, with some asperity, "the police thinks all is said when it says, 'A murder has been committed,' and particularly when it adds, 'And we are on the trace of the guilty persons.'"

"Sire, your majesty will, I trust, be amply satisfied on this point, at least."

"We shall see; I will no longer detain you, baron. M. de Villefort, you must be fatigued after so long a journey, go and repose yourself. Of course you stopped at your father's?"

A faintness came over Villefort.

"No, sire," he replied, "I alighted at the Hôtel de Madrid, in the Rue de Tournon."

"But you have seen him?"

"Sire, I went straight to the Duc de Blacas."

"But you will see him, then?"

"I think not, sire."

"Ah, I forgot," said Louis, smiling in a manner which proved that all these questions were not made without a motive,—"I forgot you and M. Noirtier are not on the best terms possible, and that this is another sacrifice made to the royal cause, and for which you should be recompensed."

"Sire, the kindness your majesty deigns to evince towards me is a recompense which so far surpasses my utmost ambition that I have nothing more to request."

"Never mind, sir, we will not forget you, make your mind easy. In the meanwhile" (the king here detached the cross of the Legion of Honour he usually wore over his blue coat, near the cross of Saint Louis, above the order of Notre-Dame-du-Mont-Carmel and Saint Lazare, and gave it to Villefort)—"in the meanwhile take this cross."

"Sire," said Villefort, "your majesty mistakes, this cross is that of an officer."

"*Ma foi!*" said Louis XVIII, "take it, such as it is, for I have not the time to procure you another. Blacas, let it be your care to see that the brevet is made out and sent to M. de Villefort."

Villefort's eyes were filled with tears of joy and pride; he took the cross and kissed it.

" And now," he said, " may I inquire what are the orders with which your majesty deigns to honour me? "

" Take what rest you require, and remember that, unable to serve me here in Paris, you may be of the greatest service to me at Marseilles."

" Sire," replied Villefort, bowing, " in an hour I shall have quitted Paris."

" Go, sir," said the king; " and should I forget you (kings' memories are short), do not be afraid to bring yourself to my recollection. M. le Baron, send for the minister of war. Blacas, remain."

" Ah, sir," said the minister of police to Villefort, as they left the Tuileries, " you enter by the right door, and your fortune is made."

" Will it be long first? " muttered Villefort, saluting the minister, whose career was ended, and looking about him for a hackney-coach. One passed at the moment, which he hailed: he gave his address to the driver, and springing in, threw himself on the seat, and gave loose to dreams of ambition.

Ten minutes afterwards Villefort reached his hotel, ordered his horses in two hours, and desired to have his breakfast brought to him. He was about to commence his repast when the sound of the bell, rung by a free and firm hand, was heard. The valet opened the door, and Villefort heard his name pronounced.

" Who could know that I was here already? " said the young man.

The valet entered.

" Well," said Villefort, " what is it?—Who rang?—Who asked for me? "

" A stranger, who will not send in his name."

" A stranger who will not send in his name! What can he want with me? "

" He wishes to speak to you."

" To me? "

" Yes."

" Did he mention my name? "

" Yes."

" What sort of person is he? "

" Why, sir, a man of about fifty."

" Short or tall? "

" About your own height, sir."

" Dark or fair? "

"Dark—very dark: with black eyes, black hair, black eyebrows."

"And how dressed?" asked Villefort quickly.

"In a blue frock-coat, buttoned up close, decorated with the Legion of Honour."

"It is he!" said Villefort, turning pale.

"Eh, *pardieu!*" said the individual whose description we have twice given, entering the door, "what a great deal of ceremony! Is it the custom in Marseilles for sons to keep their fathers waiting in their anterooms?"

"Father!" cried Villefort, "then I was not deceived; I felt sure it must be you."

"Well, then, if you felt so sure," replied the newcomer, putting his cane in a corner and his hat on a chair, "allow me to say, my dear Gérard, that it was not very filial of you to keep me waiting at the door."

"Leave us, Germain," said Villefort.

The servant quitted the apartment with evident signs of astonishment.

12

Father and Son

M NOIRTIER—for it was, indeed, he who entered—followed with his eyes the servant until he had closed the door, and then, fearing, no doubt, that he might be overheard in the antechamber, he opened the door again; nor was the precaution useless, as appeared from the rapid retreat of Germain, who proved that he was not exempt from the sin which ruined our first parents.

M. Noirtier then took the trouble to close carefully the door of the antechamber, then that of the bedchamber, and then extended his hand to Villefort, who had followed all his motions with surprise which he could not conceal.

"Well, now, my dear Gérard," said he to the young man, with a very significant look, "do you know you seem as if you were not very glad to see me?"

"My dear father," said Villefort, "I am, on the contrary, delighted, but I so little expected your visit, that it has somewhat overcome me."

"But, my dear fellow," replied M. Noirtier, seating himself, "I might say the same thing to you when you announce to me your wedding for the 28th of February, and on the 4th of March here you are in Paris."

" And if I have come, my dear father," said Gérard, drawing closer, to M. Noirtier, " do not complain, for it is for you that I came, and my journey will save you."

" Ah, indeed! " said M. Noirtier, stretching himself out at his ease in the chair. " Really, pray, tell me all about it, M. le Magistrat, for it must be interesting."

" Father, you have heard tell of a certain club of Bonapartists held in the Rue Saint-Jacques? "

" No. 53: yes, I am vice-president."

" Father, your coolness makes me shudder."

" Why, my dear boy, when a man has been proscribed by the mountaineers, has escaped from Paris in a hay-cart, been hunted in the *landes* of Bordeaux by M. Robespierre's bloodhounds, he becomes accustomed to most things. But go on, what about the club in the Rue Saint-Jacques? "

" Why, they induced General Quesnel to go there, and General Quesnel, who quitted his own house at nine o'clock in the evening, was found the next day in the Seine."

" And who told you this fine story? "

" The king himself."

" Well, then, in return for your story," continued Noirtier, " I will tell you one."

" My dear father, I think I already know what you are about to tell me."

" Ah, you have heard of the landing of the emperor? "

" Not so loud, father, I entreat of you—for your own sake as well as mine. Yes, I heard this news, and knew it even before you could; for three days ago I posted from Marseilles to Paris with all possible speed, and half desperate because I could not send with a wish two hundred leagues ahead of me the thought which was agitating my brain."

" Three days ago? you are crazy. Why, three days ago the emperor had not landed."

" No matter, I was aware of his project."

" How did you learn it? "

" By a letter addressed to you from the Isle of Elba."

" To me? "

" To you, and which I discovered in the pocket-book of the messenger; had that letter fallen into the hands of another, you, my dear father, would, probably, ere this have been shot."

Villefort's father laughed.

" Come, come," said he, " it appears that the Restoration has learned from the Empire the mode of settling affairs speedily. Shot, my dear boy! you go ahead with a vengeance. Where is this letter you talk about? I know you too well to suppose you would allow such a thing to pass you."

" I burnt it, for fear that even a fragment should remain; for that letter must have effected your condemnation."

" And the destruction of your future prospects," replied Noirtier; " yes, I can easily comprehend that. But I have nothing to fear whilst I have you to protect me."

" I do better than that, sir—I save you."

" You do? why, really, the thing becomes more and more dramatic—explain yourself."

" I must refer again to the club in the Rue Saint-Jacques."

" It appears that this club is rather a bore to the police. Why didn't they search more vigilantly? they would have found——"

" They have not found, but they are on the track."

" Yes, that's the usual phrase, I know it well. When the police is at fault, it declares that it is on the track, and the government patiently awaits the day when it comes to say, with a sneaking air, that the track is lost."

" Yes, but they have found a corpse; the general has been killed, and in all countries they call that a murder."

" A murder do you call it? why, there is nothing to prove that the general was murdered. People are found every day in the Seine, having thrown themselves in, or having been drowned from not knowing how to swim."

" Father, you know very well that the general was not a man to drown himself in despair, and people do not bathe in the Seine in the month of January. No, no, do not mistake, this death was a murder in every sense of the word."

" And who thus designated it? "

" The king himself."

" The king! I thought he was philosopher enough to allow that there was no murder in politics. In politics, my dear fellow, you know, as well as I do, there are no men, but ideas—no feelings, but interests; in politics we do not kill a man, we only remove an obstacle, that is all. Would you like to know how matters have progressed? well, I will tell you. It was thought reliance might be placed in General Quesnel, he was recommended to us from the Isle of Elba; one of us went to him and invited him to the Rue Saint-Jacques, where he would find some friends. He came there, and the plan was unfolded to him of the leaving Elba, the projected landing, etc, When he had heard and comprehended all to the fullest extent, he replied that he was a royalist. Then all looked at each other,—he was made to take an oath, and did so, but with such an ill grace that it was really tempting Providence to swear thus, and yet, in spite of that, the general was allowed to depart free—perfectly free. Yet he did not return home. What could that mean? why, my dear fellow, that on leaving us he lost his way, that's all. A murder! really, Villefort, you surprise me. You, a deputy procureur, to found an accusation on such bad premises! Did I ever say to you, when you were fulfilling your character as a royalist, and cut off the head of one of my party, ' My son, you have committed a murder'? No, I said, ' Very well, sir, you have gained the victory, to-morrow, perchance, it will be our turn.' "

" But, father, take care when our turn comes, our revenge will be sweeping."

" I do not understand you."

" You rely on the usurper's return? "

" We do."

" You are mistaken, he will not advance two leagues into the interior of France without being followed, tracked, and caught like a wild beast."

" My dear fellow, the emperor is at this moment on the way to Grenoble, on the 10th or 12th he will be at Lyons, and on the 20th or 25th at Paris."*

" The population will rise."

" Yes, to go and meet him."

" He has but a handful of men with him, and armies will be despatched against him."

" Yes, to escort him into the capital. Really, my dear Gérard, you are but a child; you think yourself well informed because a telegraph has told you three days after the landing, ' The usurper has landed at Cannes with several men. He is pursued.' But where is he? what is he doing? You do not know well, and in this way they will pursue him to Paris without drawing a trigger."

" Grenoble and Lyons are faithful cities, and will oppose to him an impassable barrier."

" Grenoble will open her gates to him with enthusiasm—all Lyons will hasten to welcome him. Believe me, we are as well informed as you, and our police is as good as your own. Would you like a proof of it? well, you wished to conceal your journey from me, and yet I knew of your arrival half an hour after you had passed the barrier. You gave your direction to no one but your postilion, yet I have your address, and in proof I am here the very instant you are going to sit at table. Ring, then, if you please, for a second knife, fork and plate, and we will dine together."

"Indeed!" replied Villefort, looking at his father with astonishment, "you really do seem very well informed."

"Eh? the thing is simple enough. You who are in power have only the means that money produces—we who are in expectation have those which devotion prompts."

"Devotion!" said Villefort, with a sneer.

"Yes, devotion, for that is, I believe, the phrase for hopeful ambition."

And Villefort's father extended his hand to the bell-rope, to summon the servant whom his son had not called. Villefort arrested his arm.

"Wait, my dear father," said the young man, "one other word."

"Say it."

"However ill-conducted the royalist police is, they yet know one terrible thing."

"What is that?"

"The description of the man who, on the morning of the day when General Quesnel disappeared, presented himself at his house."

"Oh, the admirable police have found out that, have they? And what may be that description?"

"Brown complexion; hair, eyebrows, and whiskers, black; blue frock-coat, buttoned up to the chin; rosette of an officer of the Legion of Honour in his button-hole, a hat with wide brim, and a cane."

"Ah! ah! that is it, is it?" said Noirtier, "and why, then, have they not laid hands on the individual?"

"Because yesterday, or the day before, they lost sight of him at the corner of the Rue-Coq-Héron."

"Didn't I say your police was good for nothing?"

"Yes, but still it may lay hands on him."

"True," said Noirtier, looking carelessly around him, "true, if this individual were not warned as he is;" and he added with a smile, "he will consequently change looks and costume."

At these words he rose, and put off his frock-coat and cravat, went towards a table on which lay all the requisites of the toilette for his son, lathered his face, took a razor, and, with a firm hand, cut off the whiskers that might have compromised him and gave the police so decided a trace. Villefort watched him with alarm, not divested of admiration.

His whiskers cut off, Noirtier gave another turn to his hair, took, instead of his black cravat, a coloured neckerchief, which lay at the top of an open portmanteau, put on in lieu of his blue and high-buttoned frock-coat a coat of Villefort's, of dark brown.

and sloped away in front, tried on before the glass a narrow-brimmed hat of his son's, which appeared to fit him perfectly, and leaving his cane in the corner where he had deposited it, he made to whistle in his powerful hand a small bamboo switch, which the dandy deputy used when he walked, and which aided in giving him that easy swagger, which was one of his principal characteristics.

" Well," he said, turning towards his wondering son, when this disguise was completed,—" well, do you think your police will recognise me now? "

" No, father," stammered Villefort, " at least, I hope not."

" And now, my dear boy," continued Noirtier, " I rely on your prudence to remove all the things which I leave in your care."

" Oh, rely on me," said Villefort.

" Yes, yes! and now I believe you are right, and that you have really saved my life, but be assured I will return the obligation to you hereafter."

Villefort shook his head.

" You are not convinced yet? "

" I hope, at least, that you may be mistaken."

" Shall you see the king again? "

" Perhaps."

" Would you pass in his eyes for a prophet? "

" Prophets of evil are not in favour at the court, father."

" True, but some day they do them justice; and supposing a second restoration, you would then pass for a great man."

" Well, what should I say to the king? "

" Say this to him:—' Sire you, are deceived as to the feeling in France, as to the opinions of the towns, and the prejudices of the army; he whom in Paris you call the Corsican ogre, who at Nevers is styled the usurper, is already saluted as Bonaparte at Lyons, and emperor at Grenoble. You think he is tracked, pursued, captured: he is advancing as rapidly as his own eagles. The soldiers you believe dying with hunger, worn out with fatigue, ready to desert, increase like atoms of snow about the rolling ball which hastens onward. Sire, go, leave France to its real master, to him who did not buy, but acquired it—go, sire, not that you incur any risk, for your adversary is powerful enough to show you mercy, but because it would be humilating for a grandson of Saint Louis to owe his life to the man of Arcola, Marengo, Austerlitz.' Tell him this, Gérard, or, rather, tell him nothing. Keep your journey a secret, do not boast of what you have come to Paris to do, or have done; return with all speed, enter Marseilles at night, and your house by the back-door, and there remain, quiet, submissive, secret, and, above all, inoffensive, for this time I swear to you we shall act like powerful men who know their enemies. Go, my son—go, my dear Gérard, and by your obedience to my paternal orders, or, if you prefer it, friendly counsels, we will keep you in your place. This will be," added Noirtier, with a smile, " one means by which you may a second time save me, if the political balance should one day place you high and me low. Adieu, my dear Gérard, and at your next journey alight at my door."

Noirtier left the room when he had finished, with the same calmness that had characterised him during the whole of this remarkable and trying conversation.

Villefort, pale and agitated, ran to the window, put aside the curtain, and saw him pass, cool and collected, by two or three ill-looking men at the corner of the street, who were there, perhaps, to arrest a man with black whiskers, and a blue frock-coat, and hat with broad brim.

Villefort stood watching, breathless, until his father had disappeared at the Rue Bussy. Then he turned to the various articles he had left behind him, put at the bottom of his portmanteau his black cravat and blue frock-coat, threw the hat into a dark closet, broke the cane into small bits, and flung it in the fire, put on his travelling-cap, and calling his valet, checked with a look the thousand questions he was ready to ask, paid his bill, sprung into his carriage, which was ready, learned at Lyons that Bonaparte had entered Grenoble, and in the midst of the tumult which prevailed along the road, at length reached Marseilles, a prey to all the hopes and fears which enter into the heart of man with ambition and its first successes.

13

The Hundred Days*

M NOIRTIER was a true prophet, and things progressed rapidly . as he had predicted. Every one knows the history of the famous return from Elba, a return which, without example in the past, will probably remain without imitation in the future.

Louis XVIII made but a faint attempt to parry this unexpected blow; the monarchy he had scarcely reconstructed tottered on its precarious foundation, and it needed but a sign of the emperor to hurl to the ground all this edifice composed of ancient prejudices and new ideas. Villefort therefore gained nothing save the king's gratitude (which was rather likely to injure him at the present time), and the cross of the Legion of Honour, which he had the prudence not to wear, although M. de Blacas had duly forwarded the brevet.

Napoleon would, doubtless, have deprived Villefort of his office had it not been for Noirtier, who was all-powerful at the court; and thus the Girondin of '93 and the Senator of 1806 protected him who so lately had been his protector.

All Villefort's influence barely enabled him to stifle the secret Dantès had so nearly divulged.

The king's procureur alone was deprived of his office, being suspected of royalism.

However, scarcely was the imperial power established, that is, scarcely had the emperor re-entered the Tuileries and issued his numerous orders from that little cabinet into which we have introduced our readers, and on the table of which he found Louis XVIII's snuff-box, half full, than Marseilles began to rekindle the flames of civil war, and it required but little to excite the populace to acts of far greater violence than the shouts and insults with which they assailed the royalists whenever they ventured abroad.

Owing to this change, the worthy shipowner became at that moment, we will not say all-powerful—because Morrel was a prudent and rather a timid man, so much so, that many of the most zealous partisans of Bonaparte accused him of "moderation," —but sufficiently influential to make a demand in favour of Dantès.

Villefort retained his place, but his marriage was put off until a more favourable opportunity. If the emperor remained on the throne, Gérard required a different alliance to aid his career; if Louis XVIII returned, the influence of M. Saint-Méran and himself became double, and the marriage must be still more suitable.

The deputy-procureur was, therefore, the first magistrate of Marseilles, when one morning his door opened, and M. Morrel was announced.

Any one else would have hastened to receive him, but Villefort was a man of ability, and he knew this would be a sign of weakness. He made Morrel wait in the antechamber, although he had no one with him, for the simple reason that the king's procureur always makes every one wait; and after a quarter of an hour passed in reading the papers, he ordered M. Morrel to be admitted. ·

Morrel expected Villefort would be dejected; he found him, as he had found him six weeks before, calm, firm, and full of that glacial politeness, that most insurmountable barrier which separates the well-bred and the vulgar man.

He had penetrated into Villefort's cabinet, convinced the magistrate would tremble at the sight of him; on the contrary, he felt a cold shudder all over him when he beheld Villefort seated, his elbow on his desk, and his head leaning on his hand. He stopped at the door; Villefort gazed at him, as if he had some difficulty in recognising him; then, after a brief interval, during which the honest shipowner turned his hat in his hands,—

" M. Morrel, I believe? " said Villefort.

" Yes, sir."

" Come nearer," said the magistrate, with a patronising wave of the hand; " and tell me to what circumstance I owe the honour of this visit."

" Do you not guess, monsieur? " asked Morrel.

" Not in the least; but if I can serve you in any way I shall be delighted."

" Everything depends on you."

" Explain yourself, pray."

" Monsieur," said Morrel, recovering his assurance as he proceeded, " do you recollect that a few days before the landing of his majesty the emperor, I came to intercede for a young man, the mate of my ship, who was accused of being concerned in a correspondence with the Isle of Elba, and what was the other day a crime is to-day a title to favour; you then served Louis XVIII, and you did not show any favour—it was your duty; to-day you serve Napoleon, and you ought to protect him—it is equally your duty; I come, therefore, to ask what has become of him? "

Villefort made a violent effort. "What is his name?" said he; "tell me his name."

"Edmond Dantès."

Villefort would evidently rather have stood opposite the muzzle of a pistol, at five-and-twenty paces, than have heard this name pronounced; but he betrayed no emotion.

"Dantès!" repeated he; "Edmond Dantès?"

"Yes, monsieur."

Villefort opened a large register, then went to a table, from the table turned to his registers, and then turning to Morrel,—

"Are you quite sure you are not mistaken, monsieur?" said he, in the most natural tone in the world.

Had Morrel been a more quick-sighted man, or better versed in these matters, he would have been surprised at the king's procureur answering him on such a subject, instead of referring him to the governors of the prison or the prefect of the department. But Morrel, disappointed in his expectations of exciting fear, saw only in its place condescension. Villefort had calculated rightly.

"No," said Morrel, "I am not mistaken. I have known him ten years, and the last four he has been in my service. Do not you recollect, I came about six weeks ago to beseech your clemency, as I come to-day to beseech your justice; you received me very coldly? Oh! the royalists were very severe with the Bonapartists in those days."

"Monsieur," returned Villefort, "I was then a royalist, because I believed the Bourbons not only the heirs to the throne but the chosen of the nation. The miraculous return of Napoleon has conquered me; the legitimate monarch is he who is loved by his people."

"That's right!" cried Morrel. "I like to hear you speak thus; and I augur well for Edmond from it."

"Wait a moment," said Villefort, turning over the leaves of a register.

"I have it!—a sailor, who was about to marry a young Catalan girl. I recollect now, it was a very serious charge."

"How so?"

"You know that when he left here he was taken to the Palais de Justice."

"Well?"

"I made my report to the authorities at Paris, and a week after he was carried off."

"Carried off!" said Morrel. "What can they have done with him?"

"Oh! he has been taken to Fenestrelles, to Pignerol, or to the Iles Sainte-Marguerite.* Some fine morning he will return to assume the command of your vessel."

"Come when he will, it shall be kept for him. But how is it he is not already returned? It seems to me the first care of government should be to set at liberty those who have suffered for their adherence to it."

"Do not be too hasty, M. Morrel," replied Villefort. "The order of imprisonment came from high authority, and the order for his liberation must proceed from the same source: and, as Napoleon has scarcely been reinstated a fortnight, the letters have not yet been forwarded."

"But," said Morrel, "is there no way of expediting all these formalities of releasing him from his arrest?"

"There has been no arrest."

"How?"

"It is sometimes essential to government to cause a man's disappearance without leaving any traces, so that no written forms or documents may defeat their wishes."

"It might be so under the Bourbons; but at present——"

"It has always been the same, my dear Morrel, since the reign of Louis XIV. The emperor is more strict in prison discipline than even Louis himself, and the number of prisoners whose names are not on the register is incalculable."

Had Morrel even any suspicions, so much kindness would have dispelled them.

"Well, M. de Villefort, how would you advise me to act?" asked he.

"Petition the minister."

"Oh, I know what that is; the minister receives two hundred every day, and does not read three."

"That is true; but he will read a petition countersigned and presented by me."

"And will you undertake to deliver it?"

"With the greatest pleasure. Dantès was then guilty, and now he is innocent; and it is as much my duty to free him as it was to condemn him."

"But how shall I address the minister?"

"Sit down there," said Villefort, giving up his place to Morrel, "and write what I dictate."

"Will you be so good?"

"Certainly. But lose no time; we have lost too much already."

"That is true. Only think that perhaps this poor young man is pining in captivity."

Villefort shuddered at this picture: but he was too far gone to recede: Dantès must be crushed beneath the weight of Villefort's ambition.

Villefort dictated a petition, in which, from an excellent intention no doubt, Dantès' services were exaggerated, and he was made out one of the most active agents of Napoleon's return. It was evident that at the sight of this document the minister would instantly release him.

The petition finished, Villefort read it aloud.

" That will do," said he; " leave the rest to me."

" Will the petition go soon? "

" To-day."

" Countersigned by you? "

" The best thing I can do will be to certify the truth of the contents of your petition."

And sitting, down, Villefort wrote the certificate at the bottom.

" What more is to be done? "

" I will answer for everything."

This assurance charmed Morrel, who took leave of Villefort, and hastened to announce to old Dantès that he would soon see his son.

As for Villefort, instead of sending to Paris, he carefully preserved the petition that so fearfully compromised Dantès, in the hopes of an event that seemed not unlikely, that is, a second restoration.

Dantès remained a prisoner, and heard not the noise of the fall of Louis XVIII's throne.

Twice during the Hundred Days had Morrel renewed his demand, and twice had Villefort soothed him with promises. At last there was Waterloo, and Morrel came no more: he had done all that was in his power, and any fresh attempt would only compromise himself uselessly.

Louis XVIII remounted the throne, Villefort demanded and obtained the situation of king's procureur at Toulouse, and a fortnight afterwards married Renée.

Danglars comprehended the full extent of the wretched fate that overwhelmed Dantès, and, like all men of small abilities, he termed this *a decree of Providence*. But when Napoleon returned to Paris, Danglars' heart failed him, and he feared at every instant to behold Dantès eager for vengeance; he therefore informed M. Morrel of his wish to quit the sea, and obtained a recommendation from him to a Spanish merchant, into whose service he entered at the end of March, that is, ten or twelve days after Napoleon's return. He then left for Madrid, and was no more heard of.

Fernand understood nothing except that Dantès was absent. What had become of him? He cared not to inquire. Only during the respite the absence of his rival afforded him, he reflected partly on the means of deceiving Mercédès as to the cause of his absence, partly on plans of emigration and abduction, as from time to time he sat sad and motionless on the summit of Cape Pharo, at the spot from whence Marseilles and the village des Catalans are visible, watching for the apparition of a young and handsome man, who was for him also the messenger of vengeance. Fernand's mind was made up: he would shoot Dantès, and then kill himself. But Fernand was mistaken; a man of his disposition never kills himself, for he constantly hopes.

During this time the empire made a last appeal, and every man in France capable of bearing arms rushed to obey the summons of their emperor.

Fernand departed with the rest, bearing with him the terrible thought, that perhaps his rival was behind him, and would marry Mercédès.

Had Fernand really meant to kill himself, he would have done so when he parted from Mercédès. His devotion, and the compassion he showed for her misfortunes, produced the effect they always produce on noble minds; Mercédès had always had a sincere regard for Fernand, and this was now strengthened by gratitude.

" My brother," said she, as she placed his knapsack on his shoulders, " be careful of yourself, for if you are killed I shall be alone in the world."

These words infused a ray of hope into Fernand's heart. Should Dantès not return, Mercédès might one day be his.

Mercédès remained alone upon this bare plain, which to her eyes never appeared so barren as now, with the mighty sea stretching to the horizon. Quite dissolved in tears, like Niobe, she wandered without ceasing, about the little Catalan village, halting at one time under the fierce heat of the southern sun, standing upright, motionless and dumb as a statue, her gaze fixed on Marseilles; at another, sitting on the shore, listening to the moaning of the sea, eternal as grief itself, and asking herself continually whether she would not be better to cast herself in, to let the deep open and engulf her, rather than to suffer thus all the cruelties of waiting without hope.

It was not want of courage that prevented her putting this resolution into execution; but her religious feelings came to her aid and saved her.

Caderousse was, like Fernand, enrolled in the army; but being married, and eight years older, he was merely sent to the frontier.

Old Dantès, who was only sustained by hope, lost all hope at Napoleon's downfall. Five months after he had been separated from his son, and almost at the very hour at which he was arrested, he breathed his last in Mercédès' arms.

M. Morrel paid the expenses of his funeral, and a few small debts the poor old man had contracted.

There was more than benevolence in this action; there was courage; for to assist, even on his death-bed, the father of so dangerous a Bonapartist as Dantès was stigmatised as a crime.

14

In the Dungeons

A YEAR after the restoration of Louis XVIII, a visit was made by the inspector-general of prisons.

Dantès heard from the recesses of his cell the noises made by the preparations for receiving him,—sounds that at the depth where he lay would have been inaudible to any but the ear of a prisoner, who could distinguish the plash of the drop of water that every hour fell from the roof of his dungeon. He guessed something uncommon was passing among the living; but he had so long ceased to have any intercourse with the world, that he looked upon himself as dead.

The inspector visited the cells and dungeons, one after another, of several of the prisoners, whose good behaviour or stupidity recommended them to the clemency of the government; the inspector inquired how they were fed, and if they had anything to demand. The universal response was, that the fare was detestable, and that they required their freedom.

The inspector asked if they had anything else to demand. They shook their heads! What could they desire beyond their liberty?

The inspector turned smilingly to the governor.

" I do not know what reason government can assign for these useless visits; when you see one prisoner you see all—always the same thing—ill-fed and innocent. Are there any others? "

" Yes; the dangerous and mad prisoners are in the dungeons."

" Let us visit them," said the inspector, with an air of fatigue. " I must fulfil my mission. Let us descend."

" Let us first send for two soldiers," said the governor. " The prisoners sometimes, through mere uneasiness of life, and in order to be sentenced to death, commit acts of useless violence, and you might fall a victim."

" Take all needful precautions," replied the inspector.

Two soldiers were accordingly sent for, and the inspector descended a stair so foul, so humid, so dark, that the very sight affected the eye, the smell, and the respiration.

" Oh," cried the inspector, " who can live here? "

" A most dangerous conspirator, a man we are ordered to keep the most strict watch over, as he is daring and resolute."

" He is alone? "

" Certainly."

" How long has he been there? "

" Nearly a year."

" Was he placed here when he first arrived? "

" No, not until he attempted to kill the turnkey."

" To kill the turnkey! "

" Yes, the very one who is lighting us. Is it not true, Antoine? " asked the governor.

" True enough; he wanted to kill me! " replied the turnkey.

" He must be mad," said the inspector.

" He is worse than that; he is a devil! " returned the turnkey.

" Shall I complain of him? " demanded the inspector.

" Oh, no; it is useless. Besides, he is almost mad now, and in another year he will be quite so."

" So much the better for him; he will suffer less," said the inspector.

He was, as this remark shows, a man full of philanthropy, and in every way fit for his office.

" You are right, sir," replied the governor; " and this remark proves that you have deeply considered the subject. Now we have in a dungeon about twenty feet distant, and to which you descend by another stair, an abbé, ancient leader of a party in Italy, who has been here since 1811, and in 1813 he went mad, and the change is astonishing. He used to weep, he now laughs; he grew thin, he now grows fat. You had better see him, for his madness is amusing."

" I will see them both," returned the inspector; " I must conscientiously perform my duty."

This was the inspector's first visit: he wished to display his authority.

" Let us visit this one first," added he.

" Willingly," replied the governor, and he signed to the turnkey to open the door. At the sound of the key turning in the lock, and the creaking of the hinges, Dantès, who was crouched in a corner of the dungeon, raised his head.

At the sight of a stranger, lighted by two turnkeys, accompanied by two soldiers, and to whom the governor spoke bareheaded,

Dantès, who guessed the truth, and that the moment to address himself to the superior authorities was come, sprang forward with clasped hands.

The soldiers presented their bayonets, for they thought he was about to attack the inspector, and the latter recoiled two or three steps. Dantès saw he was represented as a dangerous prisoner. Then infusing all the humility he possessed into his eyes and voice, he addressed the inspector, and sought to inspire him with pity.

The inspector listened attentively; then turning to the governor, observed, " He will become religious—he is already more gentle; he is afraid, and retreated before the bayonets— madmen are not afraid of anything; I made some curious observations on this at Charenton." Then turning to the prisoner, " What do you demand? " said he.

" What crime I have committed—to be tried; and if I am guilty, may be shot; if innocent, I may be set at liberty."

" Are you well fed? " said the inspector.

" I believe so—I know not, but that matters little; what matters really, not only to me, but to every one, is that an innocent man should languish in prison, the victim of an infamous denunciation."

" You are very humble to-day," remarked the governor; " you are not so always; the other day, for instance, when you tried to kill the turnkey."

" It is true, sir, and I beg his pardon, for he has always been very good to me: but I was mad."

" And you are not so any longer? "

" No! captivity has subdued me—I have been here so long."

" So long?—when were you arrested, then? " asked the inspector.

" The 28th of February, 1815, at half-past two in the afternoon."

" To-day is the 30th of June, 1816; why, it is but seventeen months."

" Only seventeen months! " replied Dantès; " oh, you do not know what is seventeen months in prison!—seventeen ages rather, especially to a man who, like me, had arrived at the summit of his ambition—to a man who, like me, was on the point of marrying a woman he adored, who saw an honourable career open before him, and who loses all in an instant, who sees his prospects destroyed, and is ignorant of the fate of his affianced wife, and whether his aged father be still living! Seventeen months' captivity to a sailor accustomed to the boundless ocean is a worse punishment than human crime ever merited. Have pity on me, then, and ask for me, not indulgence, but a trial—let me know my crime and my sentence, for incertitude is worse than all."

" We shall see," said the inspector; then turning to the governor, " On my word, the poor devil touches me; you must show me the proofs against him."

" Certainly, but you will find terrible notes against him."

" Monsieur," continued Dantès, " I know it is not in your power to release me, but you can plead for me, you can have me tried, and that is all I ask."

" Light me," said the inspector.

" Monsieur," cried Dantès, " I can tell by your voice you are touched with pity; tell me at least to hope."

" I cannot tell you that," replied the inspector; " I can only promise to examine into your case."

" Oh, I am free!—then I am saved! "

" Who arrested you? "

" M. Villefort; see him, and hear what he says."

" M. Villefort is no longer at Marseilles, he is now at Toulouse."

" I am no longer surprised at my detention," murmured Dantès, " since my only protector is removed."

" Had M. de Villefort any cause of personal dislike to you? "

" None; on the contrary, he was very kind to me."

" I can then rely on the notes he has left concerning you? "

" Entirely."

" That is well; wait patiently, then."

Dantès fell on his knees, and prayed earnestly. The door closed, but this time a fresh inmate was left with Dantès. Hope.

" Will you see the register at once," asked the governor, " or proceed to the other cell? "

" Let us visit them all," said the inspector; " if I once mounted the stairs, I should never have the courage to descend."

" Ah, this one is not like the other, and his madness is less affecting than the reason of his neighbour."

" What is his folly? "

" He fancies he possesses an immense treasure: the first year he offered government a million of francs (£40,000) for his release, the second two, the third three, and so on progressively, he is now in his fifth year of captivity, he will ask to speak to you in private, and offer you five millions."

" How curious! what is his name? "

" L'Abbé Faria."*

" No. 27," said the inspector.

" It is here; unlock the door, Antoine."

The turnkey obeyed, and the inspector gazed curiously into the chamber of the *mad abbé*.

In the centre of the cell, in a circle traced with a fragment of plaster detached from the wall, sat a man whose tattered garments scarcely covered him. He was drawing in this circle geometrical lines, and seemed as much absorbed in his problem as Archimedes when the soldier of Marcellus slew him.*

He did not move at the sound of the door, and continued his problem until the flash of the torches lighted up with an unwonted glare the sombre walls of his cell, then raising his head he perceived with astonishment the number of persons in his cell.

He hastily seized the coverlid of his bed, and wrapt it round him.

" What do you demand? " said the inspector.

" I monsieur,! " replied the abbé, with an air of surprise, " I demand nothing."

" You do not understand," continued the inspector; " I am sent here by government to visit the prisoners, and hear the requests of the prisoners."

" Oh, that is different," cried the abbé; " and we shall understand each other, I hope."

" There now," whispered the governor, " it is just as I told you."

" Monsieur," continued the prisoner, " I am the Abbé Faria, born at Rome. I was for twenty years Cardinal Spada's secretary ;* I was arrested, why I know not, in 1811, since then I have demanded my liberty from the Italian and French government."

" Why from the French government? "

" Because I was arrested at Piombino, and I presume that, like Milan and Florence, Piombino has become the capital of some French department."

" Ah! " said the inspector, " you have not the latest intelligence from Italy."

" They date from the day on which I was arrested," returned the Abbé Faria; " and as the emperor had created the kingdom of Rome for his infant son, I presume that he has realised the dream of Machiavel and Cæsar Borgia, which was to make Italy one vast kingdom."

" Monsieur," returned the inspector, " Providence has changed this gigantic plan you advocate so warmly."

" It is the only means of rendering Italy happy and independent."

" Very possibly; only I am not come to discuss politics, but to inquire if you have anything to ask or to complain of."

" The food is the same as in other prisons,—that is, very bad, the lodging is very unwholesome, but on the whole passable for a dungeon, but it is not that which I speak of, but a secret I have to reveal of the greatest importance."

" We are coming to the point," whispered the governor.

" It is for that reason I am delighted to see you," continued the abbé, " although you have disturbed me in a most important calculation, which if it succeeded would possibly change Newton's system. Could you allow me a few words in private? "

" What did I tell you? " said the governor.

" You knew him," returned the inspector.

" What you ask is impossible, monsieur," continued he, addressing Faria.

" But," said the abbé, " I would speak to you of a large sum, amounting to five millions."

" The very sum you named," whispered in his turn the inspector.

" However," continued Faria, perceiving the inspector was about to depart, " it is not absolutely necessary we should be alone; monsieur the governor can be present."

" Unfortunately," said the governor, " I know beforehand what you are about to say; it concerns your treasures, does it not? "

Faria fixed his eyes on him with an expression that would have convinced any one else of his sanity.

" Doubtless," said he; " of what else should I speak? "

" Monsieur l'Inspecteur," continued the governor, " I can tell you the story as well, for it has been dinned in my ears for the last four or five years."

" That proves," returned the abbé, " that you are like the idols of Holy Writ, who have ears and hear not."

" The government does not want your treasures," replied the inspector; " keep them until you are liberated."

The abbé's eyes glistened; he seized the inspector's hand.

" But what if I am not liberated," cried he, " and am detained here until my death? Had not government better profit by it? I will offer six millions, and I will content myself with the rest."

" On my word," said the inspector, in a low tone, " had I not been told beforehand this man was mad I should believe what he says,"

" I am not mad! " replied Faria, with that acuteness of hearing peculiar to prisoners. " The treasure I speak of really exists, and I offer to sign a treaty with you, in which I promise to lead you to the spot you shall dig, and if I deceive you, bring me here again,—I ask no more."

The governor laughed. " Is the spot far from here? "

" A hundred leagues."

" It is not a bad idea," said the governor.

" If every prisoner took it into his head to travel a hundred leagues, and their guardians consented to accompany them, they would have a capital chance of escaping."

" The scheme is well known," said the governor; " and M. l'Abbé has not even the merit of its invention."

Then turning to Faria,—

" I inquired if you are well fed? " said he.

" Swear to me," replied Faria, " to free me if what I tell you prove true, and I will stay here whilst you go to the spot."

" Are you well fed? " repeated the inspector.

" Monsieur, you run no risk, for, as I told you, I will stay here, so there is no chance of my escaping."

" You do not reply to my question," replied the inspector impatiently.

" Nor you to mine," cried the abbé. " You will not accept my gold; I will keep it for myself. You refuse me my liberty; God will give it me."

And the abbé, casting away his coverlid, resumed his place, and continued his calculations.

" What is he doing there? " said the inspector.

" Counting his treasures," replied the governor.

Faria replied to this sarcasm by a glance of profound contempt.

" He has been wealthy once, perhaps? " said the inspector.

" Or dreamed he was, and awoke mad."

" After all," said the inspector, " if he had been rich he would not have been here."

Thus finished the adventure of the Abbé Faria. He remained in his cell, and this visit only increased the belief of his insanity.

Caligula or Nero, those treasure-seekers, those desirers of the impossible, would have accorded to the poor wretch, in exchange for his wealth, the liberty and the air he so earnestly prayed for.

But the kings of modern ages, retained within the limits of probability, have neither the courage nor the desire. They fear the ear that hears their orders, and the eye that scrutinises their actions. Formerly they believed themselves sprung from Jupiter, and shielded by their birth; but, nowadays, they are not inviolable.

It has always been against the policy of despotic governments to suffer the victims of their policy to reappear. As the Inquisition rarely suffered their victims to be seen with their limbs distorted, and their flesh lacerated by torture, so madness is always concealed in its cell, from whence, should it depart, it is conveyed to some gloomy hospital, where the doctor recognises neither man nor mind in the mutilated being the gaoler delivers to him.

The very madness of the Abbé Faria, gone mad in prison, condemned him to perpetual captivity.

The inspector kept his word with Dantès: he examined the register, and found the following note concerning him:—

EDMOND DANTÈS. { Violent Bonapartist; took an active part in the return from Elba.

The greatest watchfulness and care to be excercised.

This note was in a different hand from the rest, which proved it had been added since his confinement.

The inspector could not contend against this accusation; he simply wrote: " Nothing to be done."

This visit had infused new vigour into Dantès; he had, till then, forgotten the date; but now, with a fragment of plaster, he wrote the date, 30th July, 1816; and made a mark every day, in order not to lose his reckoning again. Days and weeks passed away, then months; Dantès still waited; he at first expected to be freed in a fortnight. This fortnight expired; he reflected the inspector would do nothing until his return to Paris, and that he would not reach there until his circuit was finished; he, therefore, fixed three months: three months passed away, then six more. During these ten months no favourable change had taken place; and Dantès began to fancy the inspector's visit was but a dream, an illusion of the brain.

At the expiration of a year the governor was changed; he had obtained the government of Ham.* He took with him several of his subordinates, and amongst them Dantès gaoler. A fresh governor arrived; it would have been too tedious to acquire the names of the prisoners; he learned their numbers instead.

This horrible place consisted of fifty chambers; their inhabitants were designated by the number of their chamber; and the unhappy young man was no longer called Edmond Dantès—he was now number 34.

15

Number 34 and Number 27

DANTÈS passed through all the degrees of misfortune that prisoners, forgotten in their dungeon, suffer. He commenced with pride, a natural consequence of hope, and a consciousness of innocence; then he began to doubt his own innocence, which justified in some measure the governor's belief in his mental alienation; and then falling into the opposite extreme, he supplicated, not Heaven, but his gaoler.

Dantès entreated to be removed from his present dungeon into another; for a change, however disadvantageous, was still a change, and could afford him some amusement. He entreated to be allowed to walk about, to have books and instruments. Nothing was granted; no matter, he asked all the same. He accustomed himself to speak to his fresh gaoler, although he was, if possible, more taciturn than the former; but still, to speak to a man, even though mute, was something. Dantès spoke for the sake of hearing his own voice; he had tried to speak when alone, but the sound of his voice terrified him. Often before his captivity Dantès' mind had revolted at the idea of those assemblages of prisoners, composed of thieves, vagabonds, and murderers. He now wished to be amongst them, in order to see some other face besides that of his gaoler; he sighed for the galleys, with their infamous costume, their chain, and the brand on the shoulder. The galley-slaves breathed the fresh air of heaven, and saw each other. They were very happy.

He besought the gaoler one day to let him have a companion, were it even the mad abbé.

The gaoler, though rude and hardened by the constant sight of so much suffering, was yet a man. At the bottom of his heart he had often compassionated the unhappy young man who suffered thus; and he laid the request of number 34 before the governor; but the latter sapiently imagined that Dantès wished to conspire, or attempt an escape, and refused his request.

Dantès had exhausted all human resources; and he then turned to God.

All the pious ideas that had been so long forgotten returned; he recollected the prayers his mother had taught him, and discovered a new meaning in every word. For in prosperity prayers seem but a mere assemblage of words until the day when misfortune comes to explain to the unhappy sufferer the sublime language by which he invokes the pity of Heaven! He prayed, and prayed aloud, no longer terrified at the sound of his voice; for he fell into a species of ecstasy. He laid every action of his life before the Almighty, proposed tasks to accomplish, and at the end of every prayer introduced the entreaty oftener addressed to man than to God, "Forgive us our trespasses as we forgive them that trespass against us." Yet in spite of his earnest prayers, Dantès remained a prisoner.

Then a gloomy feeling took possession of him. He was simple and without education; he could not, therefore, in the solitude of his dungeon, and of his own thoughts, reconstruct the ages that had passed, reanimate the nations that had perished, and rebuild the ancient cities that imagination renders so vast and stupendous, and that pass before our eyes, illuminated by the fires of heaven, as in Martin's pictures.* He could not do this, he whose past life was so short, whose present so melancholy, and his future so doubtful. Nineteen years of light to reflect upon in eternal darkness. No distraction could come to his aid; his energetic spirit that would have exulted in thus revisiting the past was imprisoned like an eagle in a cage. He clung to one idea, that of his happiness, destroyed without apparent cause by an unheard-of-fatality; he considered and reconsidered this idea, devoured it (so to speak) as Ugolino devours the skull of the Archbishop Roger in the Inferno of Dante.*

Rage succeeded this. Dantès uttered blasphemies that made his gaoler recoil with horror, dashed himself furiously against the walls of his prison, attacked everything, and chiefly himself, and the least thing,—a grain of sand, a straw, or a breath of air that had annoyed him. Then the letter he had seen that Villefort had showed to him recurred to his mind, and every line seemed visible in fiery letters on the wall, like the *Mene Tekel Upharsin* of Belshazzar. He said that it was the vengeance of man, and not of Heaven, that had thus plunged him into the deepest misery. He devoted these unknown persecutors to the most horrible tortures he could imagine, and found them all insufficient, because after torture came death, and after death, if not repose, at least that insensibility that resembles it.

By dint of constantly dwelling on the idea that repose was death, and in order to punish, other tortures than death must be invented, he began to reflect of suicide. Unhappy he, who, on the brink of misfortune, broods over these ideas!

It is one of those dead seas that seem clear and smooth to the eye; but he who unwarily ventures within its embrace finds himself entangled in a quagmire that attracts and swallows him. Once thus ensnared, unless the protecting hand of God snatch him thence, all is over, and his struggles but tend to hasten his destruction. This state of mental anguish is, however, less terrible than the sufferings that precede, and the punishment that awaits it. A sort of consolation that points to the yawning abyss, at the bottom of which is darkness and obscurity.

Edmond found some solace in these ideas. All his sorrows, all his sufferings, with their train of gloomy spectres, fled from his cell, where the angel of death seemed about to enter. Dantès reviewed with composure his past life, and looking forward with terror to his future existence, chose that middle line that seemed to afford him a refuge.

" Sometimes," said he, " in my voyages, when I was a man and commanded other men, I have seen the heavens become overcast, the sea rage and foam, the storm arise, and, like a monstrous bird, cover the sky with its wings. Then I felt that my vessel was a vain refuge that trembled and shook before the tempest. Soon the fury of the waves, and the sight of the sharp rocks, announced the approach of death, and death then terrified me, and I used all my skill and intelligence as a man and a sailor to escape. But I did so because I was happy, because I had not courted death, because this repose on a bed of rocks and sea-weed seemed terrible, because I was unwilling that I, a creature made for the service of God, should serve for food to the gulls and ravens. But now it is different. I have lost all that bound me to life; death smiles and invites me to repose; I die after my own manner, I die exhausted and broken-spirited, as I fall asleep when I have paced three thousand times round my cell."

No sooner had this idea taken possession of him than he became more composed, arranged his couch to the best of his power, ate little, and slept less, and found this existence almost supportable, because he felt he could throw it off at pleasure, like a worn-out garment. He had two means of dying; the one was to hang himself with his handkerchief to the stanchions of the window; the other, to refuse food and starve himself. But the former means was repugnant to him. Dantès had always entertained the greatest horror of pirates, who are hung up to the yard-arm; he would not die by what seemed an infamous death. He resolved to adopt the second, and began that day to execute his resolve. Nearly four years had passed away; at the end of the second he had ceased to mark the lapse of time.

Dantès said, " I wish to die," and had chosen the manner of his death; and fearful of changing his mind, he had taken an oath to die. " When my morning and evening meals are brought," thought he, " I will cast them out of the window, and I shall be believed to have eaten them."

He kept his word; twice a day he cast out, by the barred aperture, the provisions his gaoler brought him, at first gaily, then with deliberation, and at last with regret; nothing but the recollection of his oath gave him strength to proceed. Hunger rendered these viands, once so repugnant, acceptable to him; he held the plate in his hand for an hour at a time, and gazed on the morsel of bad meat, of tainted fish, of black and mouldy bread. It was the last struggle of life, which occasionally vanquished his resolve; then his dungeon seemed less sombre, his prospects less desperate. He was still young, he was only four or five and twenty, he had nearly fifty years to live. What unforeseen events might not open his prison door and restore him to liberty? Then he raised to his lips the repast that, like a voluntary Tantalus, he refused himself; but he thought of his oath, and he would not break it. He persisted until, at last, he had not sufficient force to cast his supper out of the loophole.

The next morning he could not see or hear; the gaoler feared he was dangerously ill. Edmond hoped he was dying.

The day passed away thus: Edmond felt a species of stupor creeping over him; the gnawing pain at his stomach had ceased; his thirst had abated; when he closed his eyes he saw myriads of lights dancing before them, like the meteors that play about the marshes. It was the twilight of that mysterious country called Death!

Suddenly, about nine o'clock in the evening, Edmond heard a hollow sound in the wall against which he was lying.

So many loathsome animals inhabited the prison, that their noise did not, in general, awake him; but whether abstinence had quickened his faculties, or whether the noise was really louder than usual, Edmond raised his head and listened.

It was a continual scratching, as if made by a huge claw, a powerful tooth, or some iron instrument, attacking the stones.

Although weakened, the young man's brain instantly recurred to the idea that haunts all prisoners—liberty! It seemed to him that Heaven had at length taken pity on him, and had sent this noise to warn him on the very brink of the abyss. Perhaps one of those beloved ones he had so often thought of was thinking of him, and striving to diminish the distance that separated them.

No! no! doubtless he was deceived, and it was but one of those dreams that forerun death!

Edmond still heard the sound. It lasted nearly three hours; he then heard a noise of something falling, and all was silent.

Some hours afterwards, it began nearer and more distinct;

Edmond became already interested in that labour, when the gaoler entered.

For a week that he had resolved to die, and for four days that he put this resolution into execution, Edmond had not spoken to this man, had not answered him when he inquired what was the matter with him, and turned his face to the wall when he looked too curiously at him; but now the gaoler might hear this noise and put an end to it, thus destroying a ray of something like hope that soothed his last moments.

The gaoler brought him his breakfast. Dantès raised himself up, and began to speak on everything; on the bad quality of his food, on the coldness of his dungeon, grumbling and complaining, in order to have an excuse for speaking louder, and wearying the patience of his gaoler, who had solicited some broth and white bread for his prisoner, and who had brought it.

Fortunately he fancied Dantès was delirious; and placing his food on the rickety table, he withdrew.

Edmond listened, and the sound became more and more distinct.

There can be no doubt, thought he, it is some prisoner who is striving to obtain his freedom.

Suddenly another idea took possession of his mind, so used to misfortune, that it could scarcely understand hope; yet this idea possessed him, that the noise arose from the workmen the governor had ordered to repair the neighbouring dungeon.

It was easy to ascertain this; but how could he risk the question? It was easy to call his gaoler's attention to the noise, and watch his countenance as he listened, but might he not by this means betray interests far more precious than this short-lived satisfaction? Unfortunately Edmond's brain was still so feeble that he could not bend his thoughts to anything in particular.

He saw but one means of restoring lucidity and clearness to his judgment. He turned his eyes towards the soup his gaoler had brought him, rose, staggered towards it, raised the vessel to his lips and drank off the contents with a feeling of indescribable pleasure. He had often heard that shipwrecked persons had died through having eagerly devoured too much food; Edmond replaced on the table the bread he was about to devour, and returned to his couch; he did not wish to die. He soon felt that his ideas became again collected, he could think and strengthen his thoughts by reasoning. Then he said to himself, " I must put this to the test, but without compromising anybody. If it is a workman, I need but knock against the wall, and he will cease to work in order to find out who is knocking, and why he does so; but as his occupation is sanctioned by the governor, he will soon resume it. If, on the contrary, it is a prisoner, the noise I make will alarm him, he will cease, and not recommence until he thinks every one is asleep."

Edmond rose again, but this time his legs did not tremble, and his eyes were free from mists: he advanced to a corner of his dungeon, detached a stone, and with it knocked against the wall where the sound came. He struck thrice.

At the first blow the sound ceased, as if by magic.

Edmond listened intently; an hour passed, two hours passed, and no sound was heard from the wall; all was silent there.

Full of hope, Edmond swallowed a few mouthfuls of bread and water, and, thanks to the excellence of his constitution, found himself well-nigh recovered.

The day passed away in utter silence—night came without the noise having recommenced.

" It is a prisoner," said Edmond joyfully.

The night passed in perfect silence. Edmond did not close his eyes.

In the morning the gaoler brought him fresh provisions—he had already devoured those of the previous day; he ate these, listening anxiously for the sound, walking round and round his cell, shaking the iron bars of the loophole, restoring by exercise vigour and agility to his limbs, and preparing himself thus for his future destiny. At intervals he listened if the noise had not begun again, and grew impatient at the prudence of the prisoner, who did not guess he had been disturbed by a captive as anxious for liberty as himself.

Three days passed—seventy-two long tedious hours!

At length one evening, as the gaoler was visiting him for the last time that night, Dantès fancied he heard an almost imperceptible movement among the stones.

Edmond recoiled from the wall, walked up and down his cell to collect his thoughts, and replaced his ear against the wall.

There could be no doubt something was passing on the other side; the prisoner had discovered the danger, and had substituted the lever for the chisel.

Encouraged by this discovery, Edmond determined to assist the indefatigable labourer; he began by moving his bed, and sought with his eyes for anything with which he could pierce the wall, penetrate the cement and, displace a stone.

He saw nothing, he had no knife or sharp instrument, the grating of his window alone was of iron, and he had too often assured himself of its solidity. All his furniture consisted of a bed, a chair, a table, a pail, and a jug. The bed had iron clamps, but they were screwed to the wood, and it would have required a screw-driver to take them off. The table and chair had nothing, the pail had had a handle, but that had been removed.

Dantès had but one resource, which was to break the jug, and with one of the sharp fragments attack the wall. He let the jug fall on the floor, and it broke in pieces.

Dantès concealed two or three of the sharpest fragments in his bed, leaving the rest on the floor. The breaking of his jug was too natural an accident to excite suspicion; Edmond had all the night to work in, but in the darkness he could not do much, and he soon felt his instrument was blunted against something hard; he pushed back his bed and awaited the day.

All night he heard the subterranean workman, who continued to mine his way. The day came, the gaoler entered. Dantès told him the jug had fallen from his hands in drinking, and the gaoler went grumblingly to fetch another, without giving himself the trouble to remove the fragments of the broken one.

He returned speedily, recommended the prisoner to be more careful, and departed.

Dantès heard joyfully the key grate in the lock, he listened until the sound of steps died away, and then, hastily displacing his bed, saw by the faint light that penetrated into his cell, that he had laboured uselessly the previous evening, in attacking the stone instead of removing the plaster that surrounded it.

The damp had rendered it friable, and Dantès saw joyfully the plaster detach itself; in small morsels, it is true, but at the end of half an hour he had scraped off a handful: a mathematician might have calculated that in two years, supposing that the rock was not encountered, a passage, twenty feet long, and two feet broad, might be formed.

The prisoner reproached himself with not having thus employed the hours he had passed in prayers and despair.

In six years (the space he had been confined) what might he not have accomplished?

In three days he had succeeded, with the utmost precaution, in removing the cement, and exposing the stone; the wall was formed of rough stones, to give solidity to which were embedded, at intervals, blocks of hewn stone. It was one of these he had uncovered, and which he must remove from its socket.

Dantès strove to do so with his nails, but they were too weak. The fragments of the jug broke, and after an hour of useless toil, Dantès paused.

Was he to be thus stopped at the beginning, and was he to wait inactive until his fellow-workman had completed his toils?

Suddenly an idea occurred to him; he smiled, and the perspiration dried on his forehead.

The gaoler always brought Dantès' soup in an iron saucepan; this saucepan contained the soup of a second prisoner, for Dantès had remarked that it was either quite full, or half empty, according as the turnkey gave it to himself or his companion first.

The handle of this saucepan was of iron; Dantès would have given ten years of his life in exchange for it.

The gaoler poured the contents of this saucepan into Dantès' plate, who, after eating his soup with a wooden spoon, washed the plate, which thus served for every day. In the evening Dantès placed his plate on the ground near the door; the gaoler as he entered stepped on it and broke it.

This time he could not blame Dantès. He was wrong to leave it there, but the gaoler was wrong not to have looked before him.

The gaoler, therefore, contented himself with grumbling. Then he looked about him for something to pour the soup into; Dantès' whole furniture consisted of one plate; there was no alternative.

" Leave the saucepan," said Dantès, " you can take it away when you bring me my breakfast."

This advice was to the gaoler's taste, as it spared him the necessity of ascending, descending, and ascending again.

He left the saucepan.

Dantès was beside himself with joy. He rapidly devoured his food, and after waiting an hour lest the gaoler should change his mind and return, he removed his bed, took the handle of the saucepan, inserted the point between the hewn stone and rough stones of the wall, and employed it as a lever. A slight oscillation showed Dantès all went well.

At the end of an hour the stone was extricated from the wall, leaving a cavity of a foot and a half in diameter.

Dantès carefully collected the plaster, carried it into the corners of his cell, and covered it with earth. Then wishing to make the best use of this night, in which chance, or rather, his own stratagem, had placed so precious an instrument in his hands, he continued to work without ceasing.

At the dawn of day he replaced the stone, pushed his bed against the wall, and lay down.

The breakfast consisted of a piece of bread; the gaoler entered and placed the bread on the table.

" Well, you do not bring me another plate? " said Dantès.

" No," replied the turnkey, " you destroy everything. First, you break your jug, then you make me break your plate. If all the prisoners followed your example, the government would be ruined. I shall leave you the saucepan, and pour your soup into

that, so for the future I hope you will not be so destructive to
your furniture."

Dantès raised his eyes to heaven, clasped his hands beneath
the coverlid, and prayed.

He felt more gratitude for the possession of this piece of iron
than he had ever felt for anything; he had, however, remarked
that the prisoner on the other side had ceased to labour.

No matter, this was a greater reason for proceeding; if his
neighbour would not come to him, he would go to him.

All day he toiled on untiringly, and by the evening he had
succeeded in extracting ten handfuls of plaster and fragments
of stone.

When the hour for his gaoler's visit arrived, Dantès straightened
the handle of the saucepan as well as he could, and placed it in its
accustomed place. The turnkey poured his ration of soup into
it, together with the fish, for thrice a week the prisoners were
made to abstain from meat: this would have been a method of
reckoning time, had not Dantès long ceased to do so.

Having poured out the soup, the turnkey retired.

Dantès wished to ascertain whether his neighbour had really
ceased to work.

He listened.

All was silent as it had been for the last three days.

Dantès sighed: it was evident that his neighbour distrusted
him.

However, he toiled on all the night, without being discouraged;
but after two or three hours he encountered an obstacle.

The iron made no impression, but met with a smooth surface;
Dantès touched it, and found it was a beam.

This beam crossed, or rather blocked up, the hole Dantès
had made.

It was necessary, therefore, to dig above or under it.

The unhappy young man had not thought of this.

" Oh, my God! my God! " murmured he, " I have so earnestly
prayed to you, that I hoped you would have heard me. After
having deprived me of my liberty, after having deprived me of
death, after having recalled me to existence, my God! have pity
on me, and do not let me die in despair."

" Who talks of God and despair at the same time? " said a
voice that seemed to come from beneath the earth, and, deadened
by the distance, sounded hollow and sepulchral in the young
man's ears.

Edmond's hair stood on end, and he rose on his knees.

" Ah! " said he " I hear a human voice." Edmond had not
heard any one speak save his gaoler for four or five years, and a

gaoler is not a man to a prisoner, he is a living door added to his door of oak, a barrier of flesh and blood added to his barriers of iron.

" In the name of Heaven," cried Dantès, " speak again, though the sound of your voice terrifies me."

" Who are you? " said the voice.

" An unhappy prisoner," replied Dantès, who made no hesitation in answering.

" Of what country? "

" A Frenchman."

" Your name? "

" Edmond Dantès."

" Your profession? "

" A sailor."

" How long have you been here? "

" Since the 28th of February, 1815."

" Your crime? "

" I am innocent."

" But of what are you accused? "

" Of having conspired to aid the emperor's return."

" How for the emperor's return? the emperor is no longer on the throne then? "

" He abdicated at Fontainebleau in 1814, and was sent to the island of Elba; but how long have you been here that you are ignorant of all this? "

" Since 1811."

Dantès shuddered; this man had been four years longer than himself in prison.

" Do not dig any more," said the voice; " only tell me how high up is your excavation? "

" On a level with the floor."

" How is it concealed? "

" Behind my bed."

" Has your bed been moved since you have been a prisoner? "

" No."

" What does your chamber open on? "

" A corridor."

" And the corridor? "

" On a court."

" Alas! " murmured the voice.

" Oh, what is the matter? " said Dantès.

" I am deceived, and the imperfection of my plans has ruined all. An error of a line in the plan has been equivalent to fifteen feet in reality, and I took the wall you are mining for the wall of the fortress."

" But then you were close to the sea? "

" That is what I hoped."

" And supposing you succeeded? "

" I should have thrown myself into the sea, gained one of the islands near here,—the Isle de Daume or the Isle de Tiboulen, and then I was safe."

" Could you have swam so far? "

" Heaven would have given me strength; but now all is lost."

" All? "

" Yes; stop up your excavation carefully : do not work any more, and wait until you hear from me."

" Tell me, at least, who you are? "

" I am—I am Number 27."

" You mistrust me, then? " said Dantès.

Edmond fancied he heard a bitter laugh proceed from the unknown.

" Oh! I am a Christian," cried Dantès, guessing instinctively that this man meant to abandon him. " I swear to you by Him who died for us that nought shall induce me to breathe one syllable to my gaolers, but I conjure you do not abandon me. If you do, I swear to you that I will dash my brains out against the wall, and you will have my death to reproach yourself with."

" How old are you? Your voice is that of a young man."

" I do not know my age, for I have not counted the years I have been here. All I do know is, that I was just nineteen when I was arrested the 28th of February, 1815."

" Not quite twenty-six! " murmured the voice; " at that age he cannot be a traitor."

" Oh! no, no! " cried Dantès. " I swear to you again, rather than betray you they shall hew me to pieces! "

" You have done well to speak to me, and entreat me, for I was about to form another plan, and leave you; but your age reassures me. I will not forget you; expect me."

" When? "

" I must calculate our chances; I will give you the signal."

" But you will not leave me; you will come to me, or you will let me come to you. We will escape, and if we cannot escape we will talk, you of those whom you love, and I of those whom I love. You must love somebody? "

" No, I am alone in the world."

" Then you will love me. If you are young, I will be your comrade; if you are old, I will be your son. I have a father who is seventy if he yet lives; I only love him and a young girl called Mercédès. My father has not yet forgotten me, I am sure; but

God alone knows if she loves me still: I shall love you as I love my father."

" It is well," returned the voice; " to-morrow."

These few words were uttered with an accent that left no doubt of his sincerity; Dantès rose, dispersed the fragments with the same precaution as before, and pushed back his bed against the wall. He then gave himself up to his happiness: he would no longer be alone. He was, perhaps, about to regain his liberty; at the worst, he would have a companion, and captivity that is shared is but half captivity.

All day Dantès walked up and down his cell. He sat down occasionally on his bed, pressing his hand on his heart. At the slightest noise he bounded towards the door. Once or twice the thought crossed his mind that he might be separated from this unknown, whom he loved already, and then his mind was made up,—when the gaoler moved his bed and stooped to examine the opening, he would kill him with his water-jug.

He would be condemned to die; but he was about to die of grief and despair when this miraculous noise recalled him to life.

The gaoler came in the evening: Dantès was on his bed. It seemed to him that thus he better guarded the unfinished opening. Doubtless there was a strange expression in his eyes, for the gaoler said, " Come, are you going mad again? "

Dantès did not answer: he feared that the emotion of his voice would betray him.

The gaoler retired, shaking his head.

The night came. Dantès hoped that his neighbour would profit by the silence to address him, but he was mistaken. The next morning, however, just as he removed his bed from the wall, he heard three knocks; he threw himself on his knees.

" Is it you? " said he: I am here."

" Is your gaoler gone? "

" Yes," said Dantès, " he will not return until the evening, so that we have twelve hours before us."

" I can work then" said the voice.

" Oh! yes, yes, this instant, I entreat you."

In an instant the portion of the floor on which Dantès (half buried in the opening) was leaning his two hands, gave way; he cast himself back, whilst a mass of stones and earth disappeared in a hole that opened beneath the aperture he himself had formed. Then from the bottom of this passage, the depth of which it was impossible to measure, he saw appear, first, the head, then the shoulders, and lastly the body of a man, who sprang lightly into his cell.

16

A Learned Italian

RUSHING towards the friend so long and ardently desired, Dantès almost carried him towards the window, in order to obtain a better view of his features by the aid of the imperfect light that struggled through the grating of the prison.

He was a man of small stature, with hair blanched rather by suffering and sorrow than years. A deepset, penetrating eye, almost buried beneath the thick gray eyebrow, and a long (and still black) beard reaching down to his breast.

The meagreness of his features, deeply furrowed by care, joined to the bold outline of his strongly marked features, announced a man more accustomed to exercise his moral faculties than his physical strength. Large drops of perspiration were now standing on his brow, while his garments hung about him in such rags as to render it useless to form a guess as to their primitive description.

The stranger might have numbered sixty or sixty-five years, but a certain briskness and appearance of vigour in his movements made it probable that he was aged more from captivity than the course of time. He received the enthusiastic greeting of his young acquaintance with evident pleasure, as though his chilled affections seemed rekindled and invigorated by his contact with one so warm and ardent. He thanked him with grateful cordiality for his kindly welcome, although he must at that moment have been suffering bitterly to find another dungeon where he had fondly reckoned on discovering a means of regaining his liberty.

" Let us first see," said he, " whether it is possible to remove the traces of my entrance here—our future comforts depend upon our gaolers being entirely ignorant of it." Advancing to the opening, he stooped and raised the stone as easily as though it had not weighed an ounce; then fitting it into its place, he said:

" You removed this stone very carelessly; but I suppose you had no tools to aid you."

" Why ! " exclaimed Dantès, with astonishment, " do you possess any ? "

" I made myself some; and with the exception of a file, I have all that are necessary—a chisel, pincers, and lever."

" Oh! how I should like to see these products of your industry and patience! "

" Well! in the first place, here is my chisel! "

So saying, he displayed a sharp strong blade, with a handle made of beechwood.

" And with what did you contrive to make that? " inquired Dantès.

" With one of the clamps of my bedstead; and this very tool has sufficed me to hollow out the road by which I came hither, a distance of at least fifty feet."

" Fifty feet! ! " re-echoed Dantès, with a species of terror.

" Do not speak so loud, young man!—don't speak so loud! It frequently occurs in a state prison like this, that persons are stationed outside the doors of the cells purposely to overhear the conversation of the prisoners."

" But they believe I am shut up alone here! "

" That makes no difference."

" And you say that you penetrated a length of fifty feet to arrive here? "

" I do; that is about the distance that separates your chamber from mine—only unfortunately I did not curve aright: for want of the necessary geometrical instruments to calculate my scale of proportion, instead of taking an ellipsis of forty feet, I have made fifty. I expected, as I told you, to reach the outer wall, pierce through it, and throw myself into the sea; I have, however, kept along the corridor on which your chamber opens, instead of going beneath it. My labour is all in vain, for I find that the corridor looks into a courtyard filled with soldiers."

" That's true," said Dantès; " but the corridor you speak of only bounds one side of my cell: there are three others,—do you know anything of their situation? "

" This one is built against the solid rock, and it would take ten experienced miners, duly furnished with the requisite tools, as many years to perforate it;—this adjoins the lower part of the governor's apartments, and were we to work our way through, we should only get into some lock-up cellars, where we must necessarily be recaptured;—the fourth and last side of your cell looks out—looks out—stop a minute, now where does it open to? "

The side which thus excited curiosity was the one in which was fixed the loophole by which the light was admitted into the chamber. This loophole, which gradually diminished as it approached the outside, until only an opening through which a child could not have passed, was, for better security, furnished with three iron bars, so as to quiet all apprehensions even in the mind of the most suspicious gaoler as to the possibility of a prisoners' escape.

As the stranger finished his self-put question, he dragged the table beneath the window.

" Climb up," said he to Dantès.—The young man obeyed, mounted on the table, and, divining the intentions of his companion, placed his back securely against the wall, and held out both hands. The stranger, whom as yet Dantès knew only by his assumed title of the number of his cell, sprang up with an agility by no means to be expected in a person of his years, and, light and steady as the bound of a cat or a lizard, climbed from the table to the outstretched hands of Dantès, and from them to his shoulders; then, almost doubling himself in two, for the ceiling of the dungeon prevented his holding himself erect, he managed to slip his head through the top bar of the window, so as to be able to command a perfect view from top to bottom.

An instant afterwards he hastily drew back his head, saying, " I thought so! " and sliding from the shoulders of Dantès, as dexterously as he had ascended, he nimbly leapt from the table to the ground.

" What made you say those words? " asked the young man, in an anxious tone, in his turn descending from the table.

The elder prisoner appeared to meditate. " Yes," said he at length, " it is so. This side of your chamber looks out upon a kind of open gallery, where patrols are continually passing, and sentries keep watch day and night."

" Are you quite sure of that? "

" Certain. I saw the soldier's shako and the top of his musket: that made me draw in my head so quickly, for I was fearful he might also see me."

" Well? " inquired Dantès.

" You perceive, then, the utter impossibility of escaping through your dungeon? "

" Then," pursued the young man eagerly——

" Then," answered the elder prisoner, " the will of God be done! " and as the old man slowly pronounced those words, an air of profound resignation spread itself over his care-worn countenance.

Dantès gazed on the individual who could thus philosophically resign hopes so long and ardently nourished with an astonishment mingled with admiration.

" Tell me, I entreat of you, who and what you are? " said he at length; " never have I met with so remarkable a person as yourself."

" Willingly," answered the stranger; " if, indeed, you feel any curiosity respecting one, now, alas! powerless to aid you in any way! "

" Say not so; you can console and support me by the strength of your own powerful mind. Pray let me know who you really are? "

The stranger smiled a melancholy smile. " Then listen," said he; " I am the Abbé Faria, and have been imprisoned in this Château d'If since the year 1811; previously to which I had been confined for three years in the fortress of Fenestrelle. In the year 1811 I was transferred to Piedmont in France; it was at this period I learned that the destiny which seemed subservient to every wish formed by Napoleon had bestowed on him a son, named King of Rome even in his cradle. I was very far then from expecting the change you have just informed me of, namely, that four years afterwards this colossus of power would be overthrown. Then who reigns in France at this moment? Napoleon II ? "

" No, Louis XVIII ! "

" The brother of Louis XVI !—How inscrutable are the ways of Providence!—for what great and mysterious purpose has it pleased Heaven to abase the man once so elevated, and raise up the individual so beaten down and depressed? "

Dantès' whole attention was riveted on a man who could thus forget his own misfortunes while occupying himself with the destinies of others.

" But so it was," continued he, " in England. After Charles I came Cromwell; to Cromwell succeeded Charles II, and then James II, who was succeeded by some son-in-law or relation. Ah! my friend! " said the abbé, turning towards Dantès, and surveying him with the kindling gaze of a prophet; " these are the changes and vicissitudes that give liberty to a nation. Mark what I say!—you are young, and may see my words come to pass that such will be the case with France—you will see it, I say! "

" Probably, if ever I get out of prison! "

" True," replied Faria, " we are prisoners; but I forget this sometimes, and there are even moments when my mental vision transports me beyond these walls, and I fancy myself at liberty."

" But wherefore are you here? "

" Because in 1807 I meditated the very scheme Napoleon wished to realise in 1811;* because, like Machiavel, I desired to alter the political face of Italy, and instead of allowing it to be split up into a quantity of petty principalities, each held by some weak or tyrannical ruler, I sought to form one large, compact, and powerful empire; and, lastly, because I fancied I had found my Cæsar Borgia in a crowned simpleton, who feigned to enter into my views only to betray me. It was projected equally by Alexander VI and Clement VII, but it will never succeed now, for they attempted it fruitlessly, and Napoleon was unable to complete his work. Italy seems fated to be unlucky." The old man uttered these last words in a tone of deep dejection, and his head fell listlessly on his breast.

To Dantès all this was perfectly incomprehensible. In the first place, he could not understand a man risking his life and liberty for such unimportant matters as the division of a kingdom; then, again, the persons referred to were wholly unknown to him. Napoleon certainly he knew something of, inasmuch as he had seen and spoken with him; but the other individuals alluded to were strangers to him even by name.

" Pray excuse my question," said Dantès, beginning to partake of the gaoler's opinion touching the state of the abbé's brain; " but are you not the priest who is considered throughout the Château d'If—to—be—ill? "

" Mad, you mean, don't you? "

" I did not like to say so," answered Dantès, smiling.

" Well, then," resumed Faria, with a bitter smile. " let me answer your question in full, by acknowledging that I am the poor mad prisoner of the Château d'If; for many years permitted to amuse the different visitants to the prison with what is said to be my insanity; and, in all probability, I should be promoted to the honour of making sport for the children, if such innocent beings could be found in an abode devoted like this to suffering and despair."

Dantès remained for a short time mute and motionless; at length he said, " Then you abandon all hope of flight? "

" I perceive its utter impossibility; and I consider it impious to attempt that which the Almighty evidently does not approve."

" Nay, be not discouraged. Would it not be expecting too much to hope to succeed at your first attempt? Why not try to find an opening in another direction to that which had so unfortunately failed? "

" Alas! it shows how little notion you can have of all it has cost me to effect a purpose so unexpectedly frustrated that you talk of beginning over again. In the first place, I was four years making the tools I possess; and have been two years scraping and digging out earth, hard as granite itself; then what toil and fatigue has it not been to remove huge stones I should once have deemed impossible to loosen! Whole days have I passed in these Titanic efforts, considering my labour well repaid if by night-time I have contrived to carry away a square inch of this hardbound cement, changed by ages into a substance unyielding as the stones themselves; then to conceal the mass of earth and rubbish I dug up, I was compelled to break through a staircase, and throw the fruits of my labour into the hollow part of it; but the well is now so completely choked up, that I scarcely think it would be possible to add another handful of dust without leading to a discovery. Consider also that I fully believed I had accomplished the end and aim of my undertaking, for which I had so exactly husbanded my strength as to make it just hold out to the termination of my enterprise; and just at the moment when I reckoned upon success, my hopes are for ever dashed from me. No, I repeat, again, that nothing shall induce me to renew attempts evidently at variance with the Almighty's pleasure."

Dantès held down his head, that his companion might not perceive how little of real regret at the failure of the scheme was expressed on his countenance; but, in truth, the young man could entertain no other feeling than delight at finding his prison would be no longer solitary or uncheered by human participation.

The abbé sunk upon Edmond's bed, while Edmond himself remained standing, lost in a train of deep meditation. Flight had never once occurred to him.—There are, indeed, some things which appear so morally impossible that the mind does not dwell on them for an instant. To undermine the ground for fifty feet—to devote three years to a labour which, if successful, would conduct you to a precipice overhanging the sea—to plunge into the waves at a height of fifty or sixty feet, at the risk of being dashed to pieces against the rocks, should you have been fortunate enough to have escaped the balls from the sentinel's musket; and even, supposing all these perils past, then to have to swim for your life a distance of at least three miles ere you could reach the shore— were difficulties so startling and formidable that Dantès had never even dreamed of such a scheme, but resigned himself to his fate. But the sight of an old man clinging to life with so desperate a courage, gave a fresh turn to his ideas, and inspired him with new courage and energy. An instance was before him of one less adroit, as well as weaker and older, having devised a plan which nothing but an unfortunate mistake in geometrical calculation could have rendered abortive. This same individual, with almost incredible patience and perseverance, had contrived to provide himself with tools requisite for so unparalleled an attempt. If, then, one man had already conquered the seeming impossibility, why should not he, Dantès, also try to regain his liberty? Faria had made his way through fifty feet of the prison, Dantès resolved to penetrate through double that distance. Faria, at the age of fifty, had devoted three years to the task; he, who was but half as old, would sacrifice six. Faria, a churchman and philosopher, had not shrunk from risking his life by trying to swim a distance of three miles to reach the isles of Daume, Rattonneau, or Lemaire; should a hardy sailor, and experienced diver, like himself, shrink from a similar task; should he, who had so often for mere amusement's sake plunged to the bottom of the sea to fetch up the bright coral-branch, hesitate to swim a distance of three miles? He could do it in an hour, and how many times had he for pure pastime continued in the water for more than twice as long! At once Dantès resolved to follow the brave example of his energetic companion, and to remember that what has once been done may be done again.

After continuing some time in profound meditation, the young man suddenly exclaimed, " I have found what you were in search of! "

Faria started: " Have you indeed? " cried he, raising his head with quick anxiety; " pray let me know what it is you have discovered? "

" The corridor through which you have bored your way from the cell you occupy here extends in the same direction as the outer gallery, does it not? "

" It does! "

" And is not above fifteen steps from it? "

" About that! "

" Well, then, I will tell you what we must do. We must pierce through the corridor by forming a side opening about the middle, as it were the top part of a cross. This time you will lay your plans more accurately; we shall get out into the gallery you have described; kill the sentinel who guards it, and make our escape. All we require to ensure success is courage, and that you possess, and strength, which I am not deficient in; as for patience, you have abundantly proved yours—you shall now see me prove mine."

" One instant, my dear friend," replied the abbé; " it is clear you do not understand the nature of the courage with which I am endowed, and what use I intend making of my strength. As for patience, I consider I have abundantly exercised that on recommencing every morning the task of the overnight, and every night beginning again the task of the day. But then, young man (and I pray of you to give me your full attention), then I thought I could not be doing anything displeasing to the Almighty in trying to set an innocent being at liberty,—one who had committed no offence, and merited not condemnation."

" And have your notions changed? " asked Dantès. with much surprise; " do you think yourself more guilty in making the attempt since you have encountered me? "

" No; neither do I wish to incur guilt. Hitherto I have fancied myself merely waging war against circumstances, not men. I have thought it no sin to bore through a wall, or destroy a staircase, but I cannot so easily peruade myself to pierce a heart or take away a life."

A slight movement of surprise escaped Dantès.

" Is it possible," said he, " that where your liberty is at stake you can allow any such scruple to deter you from obtaining it?."

" Tell me," replied Faria, " what has hindered you from knocking down your gaoler with a piece of wood torn from your bedstead, dressing yourself in his clothes, and endeavouring to escape? "

" Simply that I never thought of such a scheme," answered Dantès.

" Because," said the old man, " the natural repugnance to the commission of such a crime prevented its bare idea from occurring to you; and so it ever is with all simple and allowable things. Our natural instincts keep us from deviating from the strict line of duty. The tiger, whose nature teaches him to delight in shedding blood, needs but the organ of smelling to know when his prey is within his reach; and by following this instinct he is enabled to measure the leap necessary to enable him to spring on his victim; but man, on the contrary, loathes the idea of blood;—it is not alone that the laws of social life inspire him with a shrinking dread of taking life; his natural construction and physiological formation——"

Dantès remained confused and silenced by this explanation of the thoughts which had unconsciously been working in his mind, or rather soul; for there are two distinct sorts of ideas, those that proceed from the head and those that emanate from the heart.

" Since my imprisonment," said Faria, " I have thought over all the most celebrated cases of escape recorded. Among the many that have failed in obtaining the ultimate release of the prisoner, I consider there has been a precipitation—a haste wholly incompatible with such undertakings. Those escapes that have been crowned with full success have been long meditated upon and carefully arranged—such, for instance, as the escape of the Duc de Beaufort from the Château de Vincennes, that of the Abbé Dubuquoi from For l'Evêque; Latude's from the Bastille, with similar cases of successful evasion;* and I have come to the conclusion, that chance frequently affords opportunities we should never ourselves have thought of. Let us, therefore, wait patiently for some favourable moment; rely upon it, you will not find me more backward than yourself in seizing it."

" Ah! " said Dantès, " you might well endure the tedious delay; you were constantly occupied in the task you set yourself, and when weary with toil, you had your hopes to refresh and encourage you."

" I assure you," replied the old man, " I did not turn to that source for recreation or support."

" What did you do then? "

" I wrote or studied."

" Were you then permitted the use of pens, ink, and paper? "

" Oh, no! " answered the abbé; " I had none but what I made for myself."

" Do you mean to tell me," exclaimed Dantès, " that you could invent all those things—for real ones you could not procure unaided? "

" I do, indeed, truly say so."

Dantès gazed with kindling eyes and rapidly increasing admiration on the wonderful being whose hand seemed gifted with the power of a magician's wand; some doubt, however, still lingered in his mind, which was quickly perceived by the penetrating eye of the abbé.

" When you pay me a visit in my cell, my young friend," said he, " I will show you an entire work, the fruits of the thoughts and reflections of my whole life; many of them meditated over in the ruins of the Coliseum of Rome, at the foot of St. Mark's Column at Venice, and on the borders of the Arno at Florence, little imagining at the time that they would be arranged in order within the walls of the Château d'If. The work I speak of is called *A Treatise on the Practicability of forming Italy into one General Monarchy*, and will make one large quarto volume."

" And on what have you written all this? "

" On two of my shirts. I invented a preparation that makes linen as smooth and as easy to write on as parchment."

" You are, then, a chemist? "

" Somewhat:—I know Lavoisier, and was the intimate friend of Cabanis."*

" But for such a work you must have needed books;—had you any? "

" I possessed nearly 5000 volumes in my library at Rome, but after reading them over many times, I found out that with 150 well-chosen books a man possesses a complete analysis of all human knowledge, or at least all that is either useful or desirable to be acquainted with. I devoted three years of my life to reading and studying these 150 volumes, till I knew them nearly by heart;

so that since I have been in prison, a very slight effort of memory has enabled me to recall their contents as readily as though the pages were open before me. I could recite you the whole of Thucydides, Xenophon, Plutarch, Titus Livius, Tacitus, Strada, Jornandès, Dante, Montaigne, Shakespeare, Spinoza, Machiavel, and Bossuet. Observe, I merely quote the most important names and writers."

" You are, doubtless, acquainted with a variety of languages, so as to have been able to read all these? "

" Yes; I speak five of the modern tongues; that is to say, German, French, Italian, English, and Spanish; by the aid of ancient Greek I learned modern Greek—I don't speak it so well as I could wish, but I am still trying to improve myself."

" Improve yourself! " repeated Dantès; " why, how can you manage to do so? "

" Why, I made a vocabulary of the words I knew; turned, returned, and arranged them, so as to enable me to express my thoughts through their medium. I know nearly one thousand words, which is all that is absolutely necessary, although I believe there are nearly one hundred thousand in the dictionaries. I cannot hope to be very fluent, but I certainly should have no difficulty in explaining my wants and wishes; and that would be quite as much as I should ever require."

Stronger grew the wonder of Dantès, who almost fancied he had to do with one gifted with supernatural powers; still hoping to find some imperfection which might bring him down to a level with human beings, he added, " Then if you were not furnished with pens, how did you manage to write the work you speak of? "

" I made myself some excellent ones, which would be universally preferred to all others, if once known. You are aware what huge whitings are served to us on maigre days. Well, I selected the cartilages of the heads of these fishes, and you can scarcely imagine the delight with which I welcomed the arrival of each Wednesday, Friday, and Saturday, as affording me the means of increasing my stock of pens; for I will freely confess that my historical labours have been my greatest solace and relief. While retracing the past, I forget the present; and while following the free and independent course of historical record, I cease to remember that I am myself immured within the gloomy walls of a dungeon."

" But the ink requisite for copying down your ideas," said Dantès; " how have you procured that? "

" I will tell you," replied Faria. " There was formerly a fire-place in my dungeon, but it was closed up long before I became an occupant of this prison. Still it must have been many years in use, for it was thickly covered with a coating of soot. This soot I dissolved in a portion of the wine brought to me every Sunday; and I assure you a better ink cannot be desired. For very important notes, for which closer attention is required, I have pricked one of my fingers, and written the facts claiming notice in blood."

" And when," asked Dantès, " will you show me all this? "

" Whenever you please," replied the abbé.

" Oh, then! let it be directly," exclaimed the young man.

" Follow me, then," said the abbé, as he re-entered the subterranean passage, in which he soon disappeared, followed by Dantès.

17

In the Abbé's cell

AFTER having passed with tolerable ease through the subterranean passage, which, however, did not permit of their holding themselves erect, the two friends reached the farther end of the corridor, into which the cell of the abbé opened. From that point, the opening became much narrower, barely permitting an individual to creep through on his hands and knees. The floor of the abbé's cell was paved, and it had been by raising one of the stones in the most obscure corner that Faria had been able to commence the laborious task of which Dantès had witnessed the completion.

As he entered the chamber of his friend, Dantès cast around one eager and searching glance in quest of the expected marvels; but nothing more than common met his view.

" It is well," said the abbé, " we have some hours before us; it is now just a quarter past twelve o'clock."

Instinctively Dantès turned round to observe by what watch or clock the abbé had been able so accurately to specify the hour.

" Look at this ray of light, which enters by my window," said the abbé, " and then observe the lines traced on the wall. Well, by means of these lines, which are in accordance with the double motion of the earth, as well as the ellipses it describes round the sun, I am enabled to ascertain the precise hour with more minuteness than if I possessed a watch, for that might be broken or deranged in its movements, while the sun and earth never vary in their appointed paths."

This last explanation was wholly lost upon Dantès, who had

always imagined, from seeing the sun rise from behind the mountains and set in the Mediterranean, that it moved, and not the earth. A double movement in the globe he inhabited, and of which he could feel nothing, appeared to him perfectly impossible; still, though unable to comprehend the full meaning of his companion's allusions, each word that fell from his lips seemed fraught with the wonders of science, as admirable deserving of being brought fully to light as were the glittering treasures he could just recollect having visited during his earliest youth in a voyage he made to Guzerat and Golconda.

" Come! " said he to the abbé, " show me the wonderful inventions you told me of—I am all impatience to behold them."

The abbé smiled, and proceeding to the disused fireplace, raised, by the help of his chisel, a long stone which had doubtless been the hearth, beneath which was a cavity of considerable depth, serving as a safe depository of the articles mentioned to Dantès.

" What do you wish to see first? " asked the abbé.

" Oh! your great work on the monarchy of Italy! "

Faria then drew forth from its hiding-place three or four rolls of linen, laid one over the other, like the folds of papyrus found in mummy-cases; these rolls consisted of slips of cloth about four inches wide, and eighteen long; they were all carefully numbered and closely covered with writing, so legible that Dantès could easily read it, as well as make out the sense—it being in Italian, a language he, as a Provençal, perfectly understood.

" There! " said he, " there is the work complete—I wrote the word *finis* at the end of the last page about a week ago. I have torn up two of my shirts, and as many handkerchiefs as I was master of, to complete the precious pages. Should I ever get out of prison, and find a printer courageous enough to publish what I have composed, my literary reputation is for ever secured."

" I see," answered Dantès. " Now let me behold the curious pens with which you have written your work."

" Look! " said Faria, showing to the young man a slender stick about six inches long, and much resembling the size of the handle of a fine painting-brush, to the end of which was tied by a piece of thread one of those cartilages of which the abbé had before spoken to Dantès—it was pointed, and divided at the nib like an ordinary pen.

Dantès examined it with intense admiration; then looked around to see the instrument with which it had been shaped so correctly into form.

" Ah, I see! " said Faria; " you are wondering where I found my penknife, are not you? Well, I must confess that I look upon that article of my ingenuity as the very perfection of all my handiworks. I made it, as well as this knife, out of an old iron candlestick." The penknife was sharp and keen as a razor;—as for the other knife, it possessed the double advantage of being capable of serving either as a dagger or a knife.

Dantès examined the various articles shown to him with the same attention he had bestowed on the curiosities and strange tools exhibited in the shops at Marseilles as the works of the savages in the South Seas, from whence they had been brought by the different trading vessels.

"As for the ink," said Faria, "I told you how I managed to obtain that—and I only just make it from time to time, as I require it."

"There is one thing puzzles me still," observed Dantès, "and that is how you managed to do all this by daylight?"

"I worked at night also," replied Faria.

"Night!—why, for Heaven's sake, are your eyes like cats', that you can see to work in the dark?"

"Indeed they are not; but a beneficent Creator has supplied man with intelligence and ability to supply the want of the power you allude to. I furnished myself with a light quite as good as that possessed by the cat."

"You did?—Pray tell me how."

"I separated the fat from the meat served to me, melted it, and made a most capital oil; here is my lamp." So saying, the abbé exhibited a sort of vessel very similar to those employed upon the occasion of public illuminations.

"But how do you procure a light?"

"Oh, here are two flints, and a morsel of burnt linen."

"And your matches?"

"Were easily prepared,—I feigned a disorder of the skin, and asked for a little sulphur, which was readily supplied."

Dantès laid the different things he had been looking at gently on the table, and stood with his head drooping on his breast, as though overwhelmed by the persevering spirit and strength of character developed in each fresh trait of his new-found friend's conduct.

"You have not seen all yet," continued Faria, "for I did not think it wise to trust all my treasures in the same hiding-place; let us shut this one up, and then you shall see what else I have to display."

Dantès helped him to replace the stone as they first found it; the abbé sprinkled a little dust over it to conceal the traces of its having been removed, rubbed his foot well on it to make it assume the same appearance as the other, and then, going towards his bed, he removed it from the spot it stood in. Behind the head of the bed, and concealed by a stone fitting in so closely as to defy all suspicion, was a hollow space, and in this space a ladder of cords between twenty-five and thirty feet in length.

Dantès closely and eagerly examined it,—he found it firm, solid, and compact enough to bear any weight.

" Who supplied you with the materials for making this wonderful work? " asked Dantès.

" No one but myself. I tore up several of my shirts, and unravelled the sheets of my bed, during my three years' imprisonment at Fenestrelle; and when I was removed to the Château d'If, I managed to bring the ravellings with me, so that I have been able to finish my work here."

" And was it not discovered that your sheets were unhemmed? "

" Oh, no! for when I had taken out the thread I required, I hemmed the edges over again."

" With what? "

" With this needle! " said the abbé, as, opening his ragged vestments, he showed Dantès a long, sharp fish-bone, with a small perforated eye for the thread, a small portion of which still remained in it. " I once thought," continued Faria, " of removing these iron bars, and letting myself down from the window, which, as you see, is somewhat wider than yours—although I should have enlarged it still more preparatory to my flight;—however, I discovered that I should merely have dropped into a sort of inner court, and I therefore renounced the project altogether as too full of risk and danger. Nevertheless, I carefully preserved my ladder against one of those unforeseen opportunities of which I spoke just now, and which sudden chance frequently brings about."

While affecting to be deeply engaged in examining the ladder, the mind of Dantès was, in fact, busily occupied by the idea that a person so intelligent, ingenious, and clear-sighted as the abbé, might probably be enabled to dive into the dark recesses of his own misfortunes, and cause that light to shine upon the mystery connected with them he had in vain sought to elicit.

" What are you thinking of? " asked the abbé smilingly, imputing the deep abstraction in which his visitor was plunged to the excess of his awe and wonder.

" I was reflecting, in the first place," replied Dantès, " upon the enormous degree of intelligence and ability you must have employed to reach the high perfection to which you have attained; —if you thus surpass all mankind while but a prisoner, what would you not have accomplished free? "

" Possibly nothing at all;—the overflow of my brain would

probably, in a state of freedom, have evaporated in a thousand follies; it needs trouble and difficulty and danger to hollow out various mysterious and hidden mines of human intelligence. Pressure is required, you know, to ignite powder: captivity has collected into one single focus all the floating faculties of my mind; they have come into close contact in the narrow space in which they have been wedged, and you are well aware that from the collision of clouds electricity is produced—from electricity comes the lightning, from whose flash we have light amid our greatest darkness."

" Alas, no! " replied Dantès; " I know not that these things follow in such natural order. Oh, I am very ignorant; and you must be blessed, indeed, to possess the knowledge you have."

The abbé smiled. " Well," said he, " but you had another subject for your thoughts besides admiration for me; did you not say so just now? "

" I did! "

" You have told me as yet but one of them,—let me hear the other."

" It was this:—that while you had related to me all the particulars of your past life, you were perfectly unacquainted with mine."

" Your life, my young friend. has not been of sufficient length to admit of your having passed through any very important events."

" It has been long enough to inflict on me a misfortune so great, so crushingly overwhelming, that unconscious as I am of having in any way deserved it, I would fain know who, of all mankind, has been the accursed author of it, that I may no longer accuse Heaven, as I have done in my fury and despair, of wilful injustice towards an innocent and injured man."

" Then you profess ignorance of the crime with which you are charged? "

" I do, indeed; and this I swear by the two beings most dear to me upon earth—my father and Mercédès."

" Come," said the abbé, closing his hiding-place, and pushing the bed back to its original situation, " let me hear your story."

Dantès obeyed, and commenced what he called his history, but which consisted only of the account of a voyage to India and two or three in the Levant, until he arrived at the recital of his last cruise, with the death of Captain Leclere, and the receipt of a packet to be delivered by himself to the grand-maréchal; his interview with that personage, and his receiving in place of the packet brought a letter addressed to M. Noirtier—his arrival at Marseilles and interview with his father—his affection for Mercédès and their nuptial fête—his arrest and subsequent examination in the temporary prison of the Palais de Justice, ending in his final imprisonment in the Château d'If. From the period of his arrival all was a blank to Dantès—he knew nothing, not even the length of time he had been imprisoned. His recital finished, the abbé reflected long and earnestly.

"There is," said he, at the end of his meditations, "a clever maxim which bears upon what I was saying to you some little while ago, and that is, that unless wicked ideas take root in a naturally depraved mind, human nature, in a right and wholesome state, revolts at crime. Still, from an artificial civilisation have originated wants, vices, and false tastes, which occasionally become so powerful as to stifle within us all good feelings, and ultimately to lead us into guilt and wickedness—from this view of things then comes the axiom I allude to—that if you wish to discover the author of any bad action, seek first to discover the person to whom the perpetration of that bad action could be in any way advantageous. Now, to apply it in your case:—to whom could your disappearance have been serviceable?"

"To no breathing soul. Why, who could have cared about the removal of so insignificant a person as myself?"

"Do not speak thus, for your reply evinces neither logic nor philosophy. Everything is relative, my dear young friend, from the king who obstructs his successor's immediate possession of the throne, to the occupant of a place for which the supernumerary to whom it has been promised ardently longs. Now, in the event of the king's death, his successor inherits a crown;—when the placeman dies, the supernumerary steps into his shoes, and receives his salary of twelve thousand livres. Well, these twelve thousand livres are his civil list, and are as essential to him as the twelve millions of a king. Every individual, from the highest to the lowest degree, has his place in the ladder of social life, and around him are grouped a little world of interests, composed of stormy passions and conflicting atoms; but let us return to your world. You say you were on the point of being appointed captain of the *Pharaon*?"

"I was."

"And about to become the husband of a young and lovely girl?"

"True."

"Now could any one have had an interest in preventing the accomplishment of these two circumstances? But let us first settle the question as to its being the interest of any one to hinder you from being captain of the *Pharaon*. What say you?"

" I cannot believe such was the case. I was generally liked on board; and had the sailors possessed the right of selecting a captain themselves, I feel convinced their choice would have fallen on me. There was only one person among the crew who had any feeling of ill-will towards me. I had quarrelled with him some time previously, and had even challenged him to fight me; but he refused."

" Now we are getting on. And what was this man's name? "

" Danglars."

" What rank did he hold on board? "

" He was supercargo."

" And, had you been captain, should you have retained him in his employment? "

" Not if the choice had remained with me; for I had frequently observed inaccuracies in his accounts."

" Good again! Now then, tell me, was any person present during your last conversation with Captain Leclere? "

" No; we were quite alone."

" Could your conversation be overheard by any one? "

" It might, for the cabin-door was open;—and—stay; now I recollect,—Danglars himself passed by just as Captain Leclere was giving me the packet for the grand-maréchal."

" That will do," cried the abbé; " now we are on the right scent. Did you take anybody with you when you put into the port of Elba? "

" Nobody."

" Somebody there received your packet, and gave you a letter in place of it, I think? "

" Yes, the grand-maréchal did."

" And what did you do with that letter? "

" Put it into my pocket-book."

" Ah! indeed! You had your pocket-book with you, then? Now, how could a pocket-book, large enough to contain an official letter, find sufficient room in the pockets of a sailor? "

" You are right: I had it not with me,—it was left on board."

" Then it was not till your return to the ship that you placed the letter in the pocket-book? "

" No."

" And what did you do with this same letter while returning from Porto-Ferrajo to your vessel? "

" I carried it in my hand."

" So that when you went on board the *Pharaon*, everybody could perceive you held a letter in your hand? "

" To be sure they could."

" Danglars, as well as the rest? "

"Yes; he as well as others."

"Now, listen to me, and try to recall every circumstance attending your arrest. Do you recollect the words in which the information against you was couched?"

"Oh, yes! I read it over three times, and the words sunk deeply into my memory."

"Repeat it to me."

Dantès paused a few instants as though collecting his ideas, then said, "This is it, word for word:—' M. le Procureur du Roi is informed by a friend to the throne and religion, that an individual, named Edmond Dantès, second in command on board the *Pharaon*, this day arrived from Smyrna, after having touched at Naples and Porto-Ferrajo, has been charged by Murat with a packet for the usurper; again, by the usurper, with a letter for the Bonapartist Club in Paris. This proof of his guilt may be procured by his immediate arrest, as the letter will be found either about his person, at his father's residence, or in his cabin on board the *Pharaon*.'"

The abbé shrugged up his shoulders. "The thing is clear as day," said he; "and you must have had a very unsuspecting nature, as well as a good heart, not to have suspected the origin of the whole affair."

"Do you really think so? Ah, that would, indeed, be the treachery of a villian!"

"How did Danglars usually write?"

"Oh! extremely well."

"And how was the anonymous letter written?"

"All the wrong way—backwards, you know."

Again the abbé smiled. "In fact it was a disguised hand?"

"I don't know; it was very boldly written, if disguised."

"Stop a bit," said the abbé, taking up what he called his pen and, after dipping it into the ink, he wrote on a morsel of prepared linen, with his left hand, the first two or three words of the accusation. Dantès drew back, and gazed on the abbé with a sensation almost amounting to terror.

"How very astonishing!" cried he, at length. "Why, your writing exactly resembles that of the accusation!"

"Simply because that accusation had been written with the left hand; and I have always remarked one thing——"

"What is that?"

"That whereas all writing done with the right hand varies, that performed with the left hand is invariably similar."

"You have evidently seen and observed everything."

"Let us proceed."

"Oh! yes, yes! Let us go on."

"Now as regards the second question. Was there any person whose interest it was to prevent your marriage with Mercédès?"

"Yes, a young man who loved her."

"And his name was——?"

"Fernand."

"That is a Spanish name, I think?"

"He was a Catalan."

"You imagine him capable of writing the letter?"

"Oh, no! he would more likely have got rid of me by sticking a knife into me."

"That is in strict accordance with the Spanish character; an assassination they will unhesitatingly commit, but an act of cowardice never."

"Besides," said Dantès, "the various circumstances mentioned in the letter were wholly unknown to him."

"You had never spoken of them yourself to any one?"

"To no person whatever."

"Not even to your mistress?"

"No, not even to my betrothed bride."

"Then it is Danglars beyond a doubt."

"I feel quite sure of it, now."

"Wait a little. Pray was Danglars acquainted with Fernand?"

"No—yes, he was. Now I recollect——"

"What?"

"To have seen them both sitting at table together beneath an arbour at Père Pamphile the evening before the day fixed for my wedding. They were in earnest conversation. Danglars was joking in a friendly way, but Fernand looked pale and agitated."

"Were they alone?"

"There was a third person with them whom I knew perfectly well, and who had, in all probability, made their acquaintance; he was a tailor named Caderousse, but he was quite intoxicated. Stay!—stay!—How strange that it should not have occurred to me before! Now I remember quite well that on the table round which they were sitting were pens, ink, and paper. Oh! the heartless, treacherous scoundrels!" exclaimed Dantès, pressing his hand to his throbbing brows.

"Is there anything else I can assist you in discovering, besides the villainy of your friends?" inquired the abbé.

"Yes, yes," replied Dantès eagerly; "I would beg of you, who see so completely to the depths of things, and to whom the greatest mystery seems but an easy riddle, to explain to me how it was that I underwent no second examination, was never brought to trial, and, above all, my being condemned without ever having had sentence passed on me?"

" That is altogether a different and more serious matter," responded the abbé. " The ways of justice are frequently too dark and mysterious to be easily penetrated. All we have hitherto done in the matter has been child's play. If you wish me to enter upon the more difficult part of the business, you must assist me by the most minute information on every point."

" That I will, gladly. So pray begin, my dear abbé, and ask me whatever questions you please; for, in good truth, you seem to turn over the pages of my past life far better than I could do myself."

" In the first place, then, who examined you,—the procureur du roi, his deputy, or a magistrate? "

" The deputy."

" Was he young or old? "

" About six or seven-and-twenty years of age, I should say."

" To be sure," answered the abbé. " Old enough to be ambitious, but not sufficiently so to have hardened his heart. And how did he treat you? "

" With more of mildness than severity."

" Did you tell him your whole story? "

" I did."

" And did his conduct change at all in the course of your examination? "

" Yes; certainly he did appear much disturbed when he read the letter that had brought me into this scrape. He seemed quite overcome at the thoughts of the danger I was in."

" *You* were in? "

" Yes; for whom else could he have felt any apprehensions? "

" Then you feel quite convinced he sincerely pitied your misfortune? "

" Why, he gave me one great proof of his sympathy, at least."

" And what was that? "

" He burnt the sole proof that could at all have criminated me."

" Do you mean the letter of accusation? "

" Oh, no! the letter I was entrusted to convey to Paris."

" Are you sure he burnt it? "

" He did so, before my eyes."

" Ay, indeed! that alters the case, and leads to the conclusion, that this man might, after all, be a greater scoundrel than I at first believed."

" Upon my word," said Dantès, " you make me shudder. If I listen much longer to you, I shall believe the world is filled with tigers and crocodiles."

" Only remember that two-legged tigers and crocodiles are more dangerous than those that walk on four."

" Never mind, let us go on."

" With all my heart! You tell me he burnt the letter in your presence? "

" He did; saying at the same time, ' You see I thus destroy the only proof existing against you.' "

" This action is somewhat too sublime to be natural."

" You think so? "

" I am sure of it. To whom was this letter addressed? "

" To M. Noirtier, No. 13, Rue Coq-Héron, Paris."

" Now can you conceive any interest your heroic deputy-procureur could by possibility have had in the destruction of that letter? "

" Why, it is not altogether impossible he might have had, for he made me promise several times never to speak of that letter to any one, assuring me he so advised me for my own interest; and more than this, he insisted on my taking a solemn oath never to utter the name mentioned in the address."

" Noirtier! " repeated the abbé; " Noirtier!—I knew a person of that name at the court of the Queen of Etruria,—a Noirtier, who had been a Girondin during the revolution! What was your deputy called? "

" De Villefort! "

The abbé burst into a fit of laughter; while Dantés gazed on him in utter astonishment.

" What ails you? " said he, at length.

" Do you see this ray of light? "

" I do."

" Well! I see my way into the full meaning of all the proceedings against you more clearly than you even discern that sunbeam. Poor fellow! poor young man! And you tell me this magistrate expressed great sympathy and commiseration for you? "

" He did! "

" And the worthy man destroyed your compromising letter? "

" He burnt it before me! "

" And then made you swear never to utter the name of Noirtier? "

" Certainly! "

" Why, you poor short-sighted simpleton, can you not guess who this Noirtier was, whose very name he was so careful to keep concealed? "

" Indeed, I cannot! "

"No other than the father of your sympathetic deputy-procureur."

Had a thunderbolt fallen at the feet of Dantès, or hell opened its yawning gulf before him, he could not have been more completely transfixed with horror than at the sound of words so wholly unexpected, revealing as they did the fiendish perfidy which had consigned him to wear out his days in the dark cell of a prison, that was to him as a living grave. Starting up, he clasped his hands around his head as though to prevent his very brain from bursting, as in a choked and almost inarticulate voice, he exclaimed, "His father! oh, no! not his father, surely!"

"His own father, I assure you," replied the abbé; "his right name was Noirtier de Villefort!"

At this instant a bright light shot through the mind of Dantès, and cleared up all that had been dark and obscure before. The change that had come over Villefort during the examination; the destruction of the letter, the exacted promise, the almost supplicating tones of the magistrate, who seemed rather to implore mercy than denounce punishment,—all returned with a stunning force to his memory. A cry of mental agony escaped his lips, and he staggered against the wall almost like a drunken man; then, as the paroxysm passed away, he hurried to the opening conducting from the abbé's cell to his own, and said:

"I must be alone to think over all this."

When he regained his dungeon he threw himself on his bed, where the turnkey found him at his evening visit, sitting, with fixed gaze and contracted features, still and motionless as a statue; but, during hours of deep meditation, which to him had seemed but as minutes, he had formed a fearful resolution, and bound himself to its fulfilment by a solemn oath.

Dantès was at length roused from his reverie by the voice of Faria, who, having also been visited by his gaoler, had come to invite his fellow-sufferer to share his supper.

The reputation of being out of his mind, though harmlessly, and even amusingly so, had procured for the abbé greater privileges than were allowed to prisoners in general. He was supplied with bread of a finer, whiter description than the usual prison fare, and even regaled each Sunday with a small quantity of wine: the present day chanced to be Sunday, and the abbé came delighted at having such luxuries to offer his new friend.

Dantès followed him with a firm and assured step; his features had lost their almost spasmodic contraction, and now wore their usual expression; but there was that in his whole appearance that bespoke one who had come to a fixed and desperate resolve. Faria bent on him his penetrating eye: "I regret now," said he, "having helped you in your late inquiries, or having given you the information I did."

"Why so?" inquired Dantès.

"Because it has instilled a new passion in your heart—that of vengeance."

A bitter smile played over the features of the young man: "Let us talk of something else," said he.

Again the abbé looked at him, then mournfully shook his head; but, in accordance with Dantès' request, he began to speak of other matters.

The elder prisoner was one of those persons whose conversation, like that of all who have experienced many trials, contained many useful and important hints as well as sound information; but it was never egotistical, for the unfortunate man never alluded to his own sorrows.

Dantès listened with admiring attention to all he said; some of his remarks corresponded with what he already knew, or applied to the sort of knowledge his nautical life had enabled him to acquire. A part of the good abbé's words, however, were wholly incomprehensible to him; but, like those auroræ which serve to light the navigators in southern latitudes, they sufficed to open fresh views to the inquiring mind of the listener, and to give a glimpse of new horizons, illumined by the wild meteoric flash, enabling him justly to estimate the delight an intellectual mind would have in following the high and towering spirit of one so richly gifted as Faria in all the giddiest heights or lowest depths of science.

"You must teach me a small part of what you know," said Dantès, "if only to prevent your growing weary of me. I can well believe that so learned a person as yourself would prefer absolute solitude to being tormented with the company of one as ignorant and uninformed as myself. If you will only agree to my request, I promise you never to mention another word about escaping."

The abbé smiled. "Alas! my child," said he, "human knowledge is confined within very narrow limits; and when I have taught you mathematics, physics, history, and the three or four modern languages with which I am acquainted, you will know as much as I do myself. Now, it will scarcely require two years for me to communicate to you the stock of learning I possess."

"Two years!" exclaimed Dantès; "do you really believe I can acquire all these things in so short a time?"

"Not their application, certainly, but their principles you may; to learn is not to know; there are the learners and the learned. Memory makes the one, philosophy the other."

"But can I not learn philosophy as well as other things?"

"My son, philosophy, as I understand it, is reducible to no rules by which it can be learned; it is the amalgamation of all the sciences, the golden cloud which bears the soul to heaven."

"Well, then," said Dantès, "leaving philosophy out of the question, tell me what you shall teach me first? I feel my great need of scientific knowledge, and long to begin the work of improvement; say, when shall we commence?"

"Directly, if you will," said the abbé.

And that very evening the prisoners sketched a plan of education to be entered upon the following day.

Dantès possessed a prodigious memory, combined with an astonishing quickness and readiness of conception. The mathematical turn of his mind rendered him apt at all kinds of calculation, while his naturally poetical feelings threw a light and pleasing veil over the dry reality of arithmetical computation or the rigid severity of lines. He already knew Italian, and had also picked up a little of the Romaic dialect, during his different voyages to the East; and by the aid of these two languages he easily comprehended the construction of all the others, so that at the end of six months he began to speak Spanish, English, and German.

In strict accordance with the promise made to the abbé, Dantès never even alluded to flight; it might have been that the delight his studies afforded him supplied the place of liberty; or, probably, the recollection of his pledged word (a point, as we have already seen, to which he paid a rigid attention) kept him from reverting to any plan for escape: but absorbed in the acquisition of knowledge, days, even months, passed by unheeded in one rapid and instructive course. Time flew on, and at the end of a year Dantès was a new man. With Faria, on the contrary, Dantès remarked, that, spite of the relief his society afforded, he daily grew sadder: one thought seemed incessantly to harass and distract his mind. Sometimes he would fall into long reveries, sigh heavily and involuntarily, then suddenly rise, and, with folded arms, begin pacing the confined space of his dungeon.

One day he stopped all at once in the midst of these so often repeated promenades, and exclaimed, "Ah! if there were no sentinel!"

"There shall not be one a minute longer than you please," said Dantès, who had followed the working of his thoughts as accurately as though his brain were enclosed in crystal, so clear as to display its minutest operations.

"I have already told you," answered the abbé, "that I loathe the idea of shedding blood."

"Still, in our case the death we should bestow would not be

dictated by any wild or savage propensity, but as a necessary step to secure our own personal safety and preservation."

"No matter! I could never agree to it!"

"Still, you have thought of it?"

"Incessantly, alas!" cried the abbé.

"And you have discovered a means of regaining our freedom; have you not?" asked Dantès eagerly.

"I have; if it were only possible to place a deaf and blind sentinel in the gallery beyond us."

"I will undertake to make him both," replied the young man, with an air of determined resolution that made his companion shudder.

"No, no!" cried the abbé; "I tell you the thing is impossible: name it no more!"

In vain did Dantès endeavour to renew the subject; the abbé shook his head in token of disapproval, but refused any further conversation respecting it.

Three months passed away.

"Do you feel yourself strong?" inquired the abbé of Dantès.

The young man, in reply, took up the chisel, bent it into the form of a horseshoe, and then as readily straightened it.

"And will you engage not to do any harm to the sentry, except as a last extremity?"

"I promise on my honour not to hurt a hair of his head, unless positively obliged for our mutual preservation."

"Then," said the abbé, "we may hope to put our design into execution."

"And how long shall we be in accomplishing the necessary work?"

"At least a year."

"And shall we begin at once?"

"Directly!"

"We have lost a year to no purpose," cried Dantès.

"Do you consider the last twelve months as wasted?" asked the abbé, in a tone of mild reproach.

"Forgive me!" cried Edmond, blushing deeply; "I am indeed ungrateful to have hinted such a thing."

"Tut! tut!" answered the abbé: "man is but man at last, and you are about the best specimen of the genus I have ever known. Come, let me show you my plan."

The abbé then showed Dantès the sketch he had made for their escape: it consisted of a plan of his own cell and that of Dantès, with the corridor which united them. In this passage he proposed to form a tunnel, such as is employed in mines; this tunnel would conduct the two prisoners immediately beneath the gallery where the sentry kept watch; once there, a large excavation would be made, and one of the flag-stones with which the gallery was paved be so completely loosened, that at the desired moment it would give way beneath the soldier's feet, who falling into the excavation below, would be immediately bound and gagged, ere, stunned by the effects of his fall, he had power to offer resistance. The prisoners were then to make their way through one of the gallery windows, and to let themselves down from the outer walls by means of the abbé's ladder of cords. The eyes of Dantès sparkled with joy, and he rubbed his hands with delight at the idea of a plan so simple yet apparently so certain to succeed.

That very day the miners commenced their labours; and that with so much more vigour and alacrity as it succeeded to a long rest from fatigue, and was destined, in all probability, to carry out the dearest wish of the heart of each.

Nothing interrupted the progress of their work except the necessity of returning to their respective cells against the hour in which their jailor was in the habit of visiting them; they had learned to distinguish the most imperceptible sound of his footsteps, as he descended towards their dungeons, and happily never failed being prepared for his coming.

The fresh earth excavated during their present work, and which would have entirely blocked up the old passage, was thrown, by degrees and with the utmost precaution, out of the window in either Faria's or Dantès' cell; the rubbish being first pulverised so finely that the night wind carried it far away without permitting the smallest trace to remain.

More than a year had been consumed in this undertaking; the only tools for which had been a chisel, a knife, and a wooden lever. Faria, still continuing to instruct Dantès by conversing with him, sometimes in one language, sometimes in another; at others relating to him the history of nations and great men who from time to time have left behind them one of those bright tracks called glory.

The abbé was a man of the world, and had, moreover, mixed in the first society of the day; his appearance was impressed with that air of melancholy dignity, which Dantès, thanks to the imitative powers bestowed on him by nature, easily acquired, as well as that outward polish and politeness he had before been wanting in, and which is seldom possessed except by those who have been placed in constant intercourse with persons of high birth and breeding.

At the end of fifteen months the tunnel was made, and the excavation completed beneath the gallery, and the two workmen could distinctly hear the measured tread of the sentinel as he paced to and fro over their heads.

Compelled, as they were, to await a night sufficiently dark to favour their flight, they were obliged to defer their final attempt till that auspicious moment should arrive; their greatest dread now was lest the stone through which the sentry was doomed to fall should give way before its right time, and this they had in some measure provided against, by placing under it, as a kind of prop, a sort of bearer they had discovered among the foundations through which they had worked their way. Dantès was occupied in arranging this piece of wood when he heard Faria, who had remained in Edmond's cell for the purpose of cutting a peg to secure their rope-ladder, call to him in accents of pain and suffering. Dantès hastened to his dungeon, where he found him standing in the middle of the room, pale as death, his forehead streaming with perspiration and, his hands clenched tightly together.

" Gracious heavens! " exclaimed Dantès; " what is the matter? what has happened? "

" Quick! quick! " returned the abbé; " listen to what I have to say."

Dantès looked in fear and wonder at the livid countenance of Faria, whose eyes, already dull and sunken, were circled by a halo of a bluish cast, his lips were white as those of a corpse, and his very hair seemed to stand on end.

" For God's sake! " cried Dantès. " what is the meaning of this? Tell me, I beseech you, what ails you? "

" Alas! " faltered out the abbé, " all is over with me. I am seized with a terrible, perhaps mortal illness; I can feel that the paroxysm is fast approaching: I had a similar attack the year previous to my imprisonment. This malady admits but of one remedy; I will tell you what that is; go into my cell as quickly as you can—draw out one of the feet that support the bed, you will find it has been hollowed out for the purpose of containing a small phial you will see there half filled with a red-looking fluid, bring it to me—or rather no, no!—I may be found here, therefore help me back to my room while I have any strength to drag myself along; who knows what may happen? or how long the fit may last? "

In spite of the magnitude of the misfortune which thus suddenly frustrated his hopes, Dantès lost not his presence of mind, but descended into the corridor dragging his unfortunate companion with him; then half carrying, half supporting him, he managed to reach the abbé's chamber, when he immediately laid the sufferer on his bed.

"Thanks!" said the poor abbé, shivering as though his veins were filled with ice. "Now that I am safely here, let me explain to you the nature of my attack, and the appearance it will present. I am seized with a fit of catalepsy; when it comes to its height, I may probably lie still and motionless as though dead, uttering neither sigh nor groan. On the other hand, the symptoms may be much more violent and cause me to fall into fearful convulsions, cover my lips with foaming, and force from me the most piercing shrieks;—this last evil you must carefully guard against, for, were my cries to be heard, it is more than probable I should be removed to another part of the prison, and we be separated for ever. When I become quite motionless, cold, and rigid as a corpse, then, and not before—you understand—force open my teeth with a chisel, pour from eight to ten drops of the liquor contained in the phial down my throat, and I may perhaps revive."

"Perhaps!" exclaimed Dantès, in grief-stricken tones.

"Help! help!" cried the abbé; "I—I—die—I——"

So sudden and violent was the fit, that the unfortunate prisoner was unable to complete the sentence began: a violent convulsion shook his whole frame, his eyes started from their sockets, his mouth was drawn on one side, his cheeks became purple, he struggled, foamed, dashed himself about, and uttered the most dreadful cries, which, however, Dantès prevented from being heard by covering his head with the blanket; the fit lasted two hours, then, more helpless than an infant, and colder and paler than marble, more crushed and broken than a reed trampled under foot, he stretched himself out as though in the agonies of death, and became of the ghastly hue of the tomb.

Edmond waited till life seemed extinct in the body of his friend; then taking up the chisel, he with difficulty forced open the closely fixed jaws carefully poured the appointed number of drops down the rigid throat, and anxiously awaited the result.

An hour passed away without the old man's giving the least sign of returning animation; Dantès began to fear he had delayed too long ere he administered the remedy, and, thrusting his hands into his hair, continued gazing on the lifeless features of his friend in an agony of despair. At length a slight colour tinged the livid cheeks, consciousness returned to the dull, open eyeballs; a faint sigh issued from the lips, and the sufferer made a feeble effort to move.

"He is saved!—he is saved!" cried Dantès, in a paroxysm of delight.

The sick man was not yet able to speak, but he pointed with evident anxiety towards the door. Dantès listened, and plainly distinguished the approaching steps of the gaoler; it was therefore near seven o'clock; but Edmond's anxiety had put all thoughts of time out of his head.

The young man sprang to the entrance, darted through it, carefully drawing the stone over the opening, and hurried to his cell. He had scarcely done so before the door opened and disclosed to the gaoler's inquisitorial gaze the prisoner seated as usual on the side of his bed.

Almost before the key had turned in the lock, and before the departing steps of the gaoler had died away in the long corridor he had to traverse, Dantès, whose restless anxiety concerning his friend left him no desire to touch the food brought him, hurried back to the abbé's chamber, and raising the stone by pressing his head against it, was soon beside the sick man's couch.

Faria had now fully regained his consciousness, but he still lay helpless and exhausted on his miserable bed.

" I did not expect to see you again," said he feebly to Dantès.

" And why not? " asked the young man; " did you fancy yourself dying? "

" No, I had no such idea; but, knowing that all was ready for your flight, I considered you had availed yourself of it and were gone."

The deep glow of indignation suffused the cheeks of Dantès.

" And did you really think so meanly of me," cried he, " as to believe I would depart without you? "

" At least," said the abbé, " I now see how wrong such an opinion would have been. Alas! alas! I am fearfully exhausted and debilitated by this attack."

" Be of good cheer! " replied Dantès. " Your strength will return; " and as he spoke he seated himself on the bed beside Faria and tenderly chafed his chilled hands. The abbé shook his head.

" The former of these fits," said he, " lasted but half an hour. At the termination of which I experienced no other feeling than a great sensation of hunger; and I rose from my bed without requiring the least help. Now I can neither move my right arm nor leg, and my head seems uncomfortable, proving a rush of blood to the brain. The next of these fits will either carry me off or leave me paralysed for life."

" No, no," cried Dantès. " You are mistaken—you will not die! And your third attack (if, indeed, you should have another) will find you at liberty. We shall save you another time, as we have done this, only with a better chance, because we shall be able to command every requisite assistance."

" My good Edmond," answered the abbé, " be not deceived. The attack which has just passed away condemns me for ever to the walls of a prison. None can fly from their dungeon but those who can walk."

" Well, well, perhaps just now you are not in a condition to effect your escape; but there is no hurry; we have waited so long we can very easily defer our purpose a little longer; say a week, a month,—two, if necessary; by that time you will be quite well and strong; and as it only remains with us to fix the hour and minute, we will choose the first instant that you feel able to swim, to execute our project."

" I shall never swim again," replied Faria. " This arm is paralysed; not for a time, but for ever. Lift it, and judge by its weight if I am mistaken."

The young man raised the arm, which fell back by its own weight perfectly inanimate and helpless. A sigh escaped him.

" You are convinced now, Edmond, are you not? " asked the abbé. " Depend upon it, I know what I say. Since the first attack I experienced of this malady I have continually reflected on it. Indeed, I expected it, for it is a family inheritance; both my father and grandfather having been taken off by it. The physician who prepared for me the remedy I have twice successfully taken was no other than the celebrated Cabanis; and he predicted a similar end for me."

" The physician may be mistaken! " exclaimed Dantès. " And as for your poor arm, what difference will that make in our escape? Never mind, if you cannot swim I can take you on my shoulders and swim for both of us."

" My son," said the abbé, " you who are a sailor and a swimmer must know as well as I do, that a man so loaded would sink ere he had advanced fifty yards in the sea. Cease, then, to allow yourself to be duped by vain hopes, that even your own excellent heart refuses to believe in. Here I shall remain till the hour of my deliverance arrives: and that in all human probability, will be the hour of my death. As for you, who are young and active, delay not on my account, but fly—go—I give you back your promise."

" It is well," said Dantès. " And, now hear my determination also." Then rising and extending his hand with an air of solemnity over the old man's head, he slowly added, " Here I swear to remain with you so long as life is spared to you, and that death only shall divide us."

Faria gazed fondly on his noble-minded but single-hearted young friend, and read in his honest, open countenance, ample confirmation of truthfulness, as well as sincere, affectionate, and faithful devotion.

" Thanks, my child," murmured the invalid, extending the

one hand of which he still retained the use. " Thanks for your generous offer, which I accept as frankly as it was made." Then, after a short pause, he added, " You may one of these days reap the reward of your disinterested devotion; but as I cannot, and you will not, quit this place, it becomes necessary to fill up the excavation beneath the soldier's gallery; he might, by chance, find out the hollow sound produced by his footsteps over the excavated ground, and call the attention of his officer to the circumstance; that would bring about a discovery which would inevitably lead to our being separated. Go, then, and set about this work, in which, unhappily, I can offer you no assistance; keep at it all night, if necessary, and do not return here to-morrow till after the gaoler has visited me. I shall have something of the greatest importance to communicate to you."

Dantès took the hand of the abbé in his, and affectionately pressed it. Faria smiled encouragingly on him, and the young man retired to his task filled with a religious determination faithfully and unflinchingly to discharge the vow which bound him to his afflicted friend.

18

The Treasure

WHEN Dantès returned next morning to the chamber of his companion in captivity, he found Faria seated and looking composed. In the ray of light which entered by the narrow window of his cell, he held open in his left hand, of which alone, it will be recollected, he retained the use, a morsel of paper, which, from being constantly rolled into a small compass, had the form of a cylinder, and was not easily kept open. He did not speak, but showed the paper to Dantès.

" What is that? " he inquired.

" Look at it," said the abbé, with a smile.

" I have looked at it with all possible attention, said Dantès, " and I only see a half-burnt paper on which are traces of Gothic characters traced with peculiar kind of ink."

" This paper, my friend," said Faria, " I may now avow to you, since I have proved you,—this paper is my treasure, of which, from this day forth, one half belongs to you."

A cold damp started to Dantès brow. Until this day,—and what a space of time!—he had avoided talking to the abbé of this treasure, the source whence accusation of madness against the poor abbé was derived. With his instinctive delicacy Edmond had preferred avoiding any touch on this painful chord, and Faria had been equally silent. He had taken the silence of the old man for a return to reason, and now these few words uttered by Faria, after so painful a crisis, seemed to announce a serious relapse of mental alienation.

"Your treasure?" stammered Dantès. Faria smiled.

"Yes," said he. "You are, indeed, a noble heart, Edmond; and I see by your paleness and your shudder what is passing in your heart at this moment. No, be assured, I am not mad. This treasure exists, Dantès; and if I have not been allowed to possess it you will. Yes—you. No one would listen to me or believe me because they thought me mad; but you, who must know that I am not, listen to me, and believe me afterwards if you will."

"Alas!" murmured Edmond to himself, "this is a terrible relapse! There was only this blow wanting." Then he said aloud, "My dear friend, your attack has, perhaps fatigued you, had you not better repose a while! To-morrow, if you will, I will hear your narrative; but to-day I wish to nurse you carefully. Besides," he said, "a treasure is not a thing we need hurry."

"On the contrary, it must be hurried, Edmond!" replied the old man. "Who knows if to-morrow, or the next day after, the third attack may not come on? and then must not all be finished? Yes, indeed, I have often thought with a bitter joy that these riches, which would make the wealth of a dozen families, will be for ever lost to those men who persecute me. This idea was one of vengeance to me, and I tasted it slowly in the night of my dungeon and the despair of my captivity. But now I have forgiven the world for the love of you; now I see you young and full of hope and prospect,—now that I think of all that may result to you in the good fortune of such a disclosure, I shudder at any delay, and tremble lest I should not assure to one so worthy as yourself the possession of so vast an amount of hidden treasure."

Edmond turned away his head with a sigh.

"You persist in your incredulity, Edmond," continued Faria. "My words have not convinced you. I see you require proofs. Well, then, read this paper which I have never shown to any one."

"To-morrow, my dear friend," said Edmond, desirous of not yielding to the old man's madness. "I thought it was understood that we should not talk of that until to-morrow."

"Then we will not talk of it until to-morrow; but read this paper to-day."

"I will not irritate him," thought Edmond, and taking the

paper, of which half was wanting, having been burnt, no doubt, by some accident, he read:

" This treasure, which may amount to two
of Roman crowns in the most distant a
of the second opening wh
declare to belong to him alo
heir.
" 25th April, 149 "

" Well! " said Faria, when the young man had finished reading it.

" Why," replied Dantès, " I see nothing but broken lines and unconnected words, which are rendered illegible by fire."

" Yes, to you, my friend, who read them for the first time, but not for me, who have grown pale over them by many nights' study, and have reconstructed every phrase, completed every thought."

" And do you believe you have discovered the concealed sense? "

" I am sure I have, and you shall judge for yourself; but first listen to the history of this paper."

" Silence! " exclaimed Dantès. " Steps approach, I go, adieu."

And Dantès, happy to escape the history and explanation which could not fail to confirm to him his friend's malady, glided like a snake along the narrow passage, whilst Faria, restored by his alarm to a kind of activity, pushed with his foot the stone into its place, and covered it with a mat in order the more effectually to avoid discovery.

It was the governor, who, hearing of Faria's accident from the gaoler, had come in person to see him.

Faria sat up to receive him, and continued to conceal from the governor the paralysis that had already half stricken him with death. His fear was, lest the governor touched, with pity, might order him to be removed to a prison more wholesome, and thus separate him from his young companion; but fortunately this was not the case, and the governor left him convinced that the poor madman, for whom in his heart he felt a kind of affection, was only affected with a slight indisposition.

During this time, Edmond, seated on his bed with his head in his hands, tried to collect his scattered thoughts. All was so rational, so grand, so logical, with Faria, since he had known him, that he could not understand how so much wisdom on all points could be allied to madness in any one;—was Faria deceived as to his treasure, or was all the world deceived as to Faria?

Dantès remained in his cell all day, not daring to return to his friend, thinking thus to defer the moment when he should acquire the certainty that the abbé was mad—such a conviction would be so terrible!

But, towards the evening, after the usual visitation, Faria, not seeing the young man appear, tried to move, and get over the distance which separated them. Edmond shuddered when he heard the painful efforts which the old man made to drag himself along; his leg was inert, and he could no longer make use of one arm. Edmond was compelled to draw him towards himself, for otherwise he could not enter by the small aperture which led to Dantès' chamber.

" Here I am, pursuing you remorselessly," he said, with a benignant smile. " You thought to escape my munificence, but it is in vain. Listen to me."

Edmond saw there was no escape, and placing the old man on his bed, he seated himself on the stool beside him.

" You know," said the abbé, " that I was the secretary and intimate friend of the Cardinal Spada, the last of the princes of that name. I owe to this worthy lord all the happiness I ever knew. He was not rich, although the wealth of his family had passed into a proverb, and I heard the phrase very often, ' As rich as a Spada.' But he, like public rumour, lived on this reputation for wealth; his palace was my paradise. I instructed his nephews, who are dead, and when he was alone in the world I returned to him, by an absolute devotion to his will, all he had done for me during ten years.

" The house of the cardinal had no secrets for me. I had often seen my noble patron annotating ancient volumes, and eagerly searching amongst dusty family manuscripts. One day when I was reproaching him for his unavailing searches, and the kind of prostration of mind that followed them, he looked at me, and, smiling bitterly, opened a volume relating to the History of the City of Rome.* There, in the twenty-ninth chapter of the Life of Pope Alexander VI, were the following lines, which I can never forget:—

" ' The great wars of Romagne had ended; Cæsar Borgia, who had completed his conquest, had need of money to purchase all Italy. The pope had also need of money to conclude with Louis, the twelfth king of France, formidable still in spite of his recent reverses; and it was necessary, therefore, to have recourse to some profitable speculation, which was a matter of great difficulty in the impoverished condition of exhausted Italy. His holiness had an idea. He determined to make two cardinals.'

" By choosing two of the greatest personages of Rome, especially rich men,—*this* was the return the holy father looked for from his speculation. In the first place, he had to sell the great appointments and splendid offices which the cardinals already held, and then he had the two hats to sell besides.

" There was a third view in the speculation, which will appear hereafter.

" The pope and Cæsar Borgia first found the two future cardinals; they were Jean Rospigliosi, who held four of the highest dignities of the holy seat; and Cæsar Spada, one of the noblest and richest of the Roman nobility; both felt the high honour of such a favour from the pope. They were ambitious: and these found, Cæsar Borgia soon found purchasers for their appointments.

" The result was that Rospigliosi and Spada paid for being cardinals, and eight other persons paid for the offices the cardinals held before their elevation, and thus eight hundred thousand crowns entered into the coffers of the speculators.

" It is time now to proceed to the last part of the speculation. The pope having almost smothered Rospigliosi and Spada with caresses, having bestowed upon them the insignia of cardinal, and induced them to realise their fortunes, and fix themselves at Rome, the pope and Cæsar Borgia invited the two cardinals to dinner.

" This was a matter of dispute between the holy father and his son. Cæsar thought they could make use of one of the means which he always had ready for his friends; that is to say, in the first place the famous key with which they requested certain persons to go and open a particular cupboard. This key was furnished with a small iron point,—a negligence on the part of the locksmith. When this was pressed to effect the opening of the cupboard, of which the lock was difficult, the person was pricked by this small point, and died next day. Then there was the ring with the lion's head, which Cæsar wore when he meant to give certain squeezes of the hand. The lion bit the hand thus favoured, and at the end of twenty-four hours, the bite was mortal.

" Cæsar then proposed to his father, either to ask the cardinals to open the cupboard, or give each a cordial squeeze of the hand, but Alexander VI replied to him:

" ' Whilst we are thinking of those worthy cardinals, Spada and Rospigliosi, let us ask both of them to a dinner. Something tells me that we shall regain this money. Besides, you forget, Cæsar, an indigestion declares itself immediately, whilst a prick or a bite occasions a day or two's delay.'

" Cæsar gave way before such cogent reasoning, and the cardinals were consequently invited to dinner.

" The table was laid in a vineyard belonging to the pope, near Saint-Pierre-ès-Liens, a charming retreat which the cardinals knew very well by report.

" Rospigliosi, quite giddy with his dignity, prepared his stomach, and assumed his best looks. Spada, a prudent man, and greatly attached to his only nephew, a young captain of highest promise, took paper and pen and made his will.

" He then sent to his nephew to await him in the vicinity of the vineyard, but it appeared the servant did not find him.

" Spada knew the nature of these invitations; since Christianity, so eminently civilising, had made progress in Rome, it was no longer a centurion who came from the tyrant with a message, ' Cæsar wills that you die,' but it was a legate *à latere*, who came with a smile on his lips to say from the pope, ' His holiness requests you will dine with him.'

" Spada set out about two o'clock to Saint-Pierre-ès-Liens. The pope awaited him. The first figure that struck the eyes of Spada was that of his nephew, in full costume, and Cæsar Borgia paying him most marked attentions. Spada turned pale, as Cæsar looked at him with an ironical air, which proved that he had anticipated all, and that the snare was well spread.

" They began dinner, and Spada was only able to inquire of his nephew if he had received his message. The nephew replied no, perfectly comprehending the meaning of the question. It was too late, for he had already drank a glass of excellent wine, placed for him expressly by the pope's butler. Spada at the same moment saw another bottle approach him, which he was pressed to taste. An hour afterwards a physician declared they were both poisoned through eating mushrooms. Spada died on the threshold of the vineyard; the nephew expired at his own door, making signs which his wife could not comprehend.

" Then Cæsar and the pope hastened to lay hands on the heritage, under pretence of seeking for the papers of the dead man. But the inheritance consisted in this only, a scrap of paper on which Spada had written:

" ' I bequeath to my beloved nephew my coffers, my books, and, amongst other my breviary and the gold corners, which I beg he will preserve in remembrance of his affectionate uncle.'

" The heirs sought everywhere, admired the breviary, laid hands on the furniture, and were greatly astonished that Spada, the rich man, was really the most miserable of uncles—no treasures —unless they were those of science composed in the library and laboratories. This was all. Cæsar and his father searched, examined, scrutinised, but found nothing, or at least very little; not exceeding a few thousand crowns in plate, and about the same in ready money; but the nephew had time to say to his wife before he expired:

"'Look well among my uncle's papers; there is a will.'

"They sought even more thoroughly than the august heirs had done, but it was fruitless. There were two palaces and a vineyard behind the Palatine Hill, but in these days landed property had not much value, and the two palaces and the vineyard remained to the family as beneath the rapacity of the pope and his son.

"Months and years rolled on. Alexander VI died poisoned,—you know by what mistake. Cæsar, poisoned at the same time, escaped with colouring his skin like a snake, and assumed a new cuticle, on which the poison left spots like those we see on the skin of a tiger; then, compelled to quit Rome, he went and killed himself in obscurity in a night skirmish, scarcely noticed in history.

"After the pope's death and his son's exile, it was supposed the Spada family would again make the splendid figure they had before the cardinal's time; but this was not the case. The Spadas remained in doubtful ease, a mystery hung over this dark affair, and the public rumour was, that Cæsar, a better politician than his father, had carried off from the pope the fortune of the two cardinals. I say the two, because Cardinal Rospigliosi, who had not taken any precaution, was completely despoiled.

"Up to this time," said Faria, interrupting the thread of his narrative, "this seems to you very ridiculous, no doubt, eh?"

"Oh! my friend," said Dantès, "on the contrary, it seems as if I were reading a most interesting narrative; go on, I pray of you."

"I will.

"The family began to feel accustomed to this obscurity. Years rolled on, and amongst the descendants some were soldiers, others diplomatists, some churchmen, some bankers, some grew rich, and some were ruined. I come now to the last of the family, whose secretary I was,—the Comte de Spada.

"I had often heard him complain of the disproportion of his rank with his fortune; and I advised him to sink all he had in an annuity. He did so, and thus doubled his income.

"The celebrated breviary remained in the family, and was in the comte's possession. It had been handed down from father to son, for the singular clause of the only will that had been found, had rendered it a real relic, preserved in the family with superstitious veneration. It was an illuminated book with beautiful Gothic characters, and so weighty with gold, that a servant always carried it before the cardinal on days of great solemnity.

"At the sight of papers of all sorts, titles, contracts, parchments, which were kept in the archives of the family, all descending from the poisoned cardinal, I, like twenty servitors, stewards, secretaries before me, in my turn examined the immense bundles of documents; but in spite of the most accurate researches, I found—nothing. Yet I had read, I had even written a precise history of the Borgia family, for the sole purpose of assuring myself whether any increase of fortune had occurred to them on the death of the Cardinal Cæsar Spada; but could only trace the acquisition of the property of the Cardinal Rospigliosi, his companion in misfortune.

" I was then almost assured that the inheritance had neither profited the Borgias nor the family, but had remained unpossessed like the treasures of the Arabian Nights, which slept in the bosom of the earth under the eyes of a genie. I searched, ransacked, counted, calculated a thousand and a thousand times the income and expenditure of the family for three hundred years. It was useless. I remained in my ignorance, and the Comte de Spada in his poverty.

" My patron died. He had reserved from his annuity his family papers, his library composed of 5000 volumes, and his famous breviary. All these he bequeathed to me, with a thousand Roman crowns, which he had in ready money, on condition, that I would have said anniversary masses for the repose of his soul, and that I would draw up a genealogical tree and history of his house; all this I did scrupulously.

" Be easy, my dear Edmond, we are near the conclusion.

" In 1807, a month before I was arrested, and fifteen days after the death of Comte de Spada, on the 25th of December (you will see presently how the date became fixed in my memory), I was reading, for the thousandth time, the papers I was arranging, for the palace was sold to a stranger; and I was going to leave Rome and settle at Florence, intending to take with me twelve thousand francs I possessed, my library, and famous breviary; when, tired with my constant labour at the same thing, and overcome by a heavy dinner I had eaten, my head dropped on my hands, and I fell asleep about three o'clock in the afternoon.

" I awoke as the clock was striking six.

" I raised my head, all was in darkness. I rang for a light, but as no one came, I determined to find one for myself. It was indeed the habit of a philosopher which I should soon be under the necessity of adopting. I took a wax candle in one hand, and with the other groped about for a piece of paper (my match-box being empty), with which I hoped to produce a light from the small flame still playing on the embers. Fearing, however, to make use of any valuable piece of paper, I hesitated for a moment, then recollected that I had seen in the famous breviary which was on the table beside me, an old paper quite yellow with age, and which had served as a marker for centuries, kept there by the request of the heirs. I felt for it, found it, twisted it up together, and putting it into the expiring flame, set light to it.

" But beneath my fingers as if by magic, in proportion as the fire ascended, I saw yellowish characters appear on the paper; I grasped it in my hand, put out the flame as quickly as I could, lighted my taper in the fire itself, and opened the crumpled paper with inexpressible emotion, recognising, when I had done so that these characters had been traced in mysterious and sympathetic ink, only appearing when exposed to the fire: nearly one-third of the paper had been consumed by the flame. It was that paper you read this morning; read it again, Dantès, and then I will complete for you the incomplete words and unconnected sense."

Faria, with an air of triumph, offered the paper to Dantès, who this time read the following words traced with an ink of a colour which most nearly resembled rust:—

" This 25th day of April, 1498, be . . .
Alexander VI, and fearing that not . . .
he may desire to become my heir, and re . . .
and Bentivoglio, who were poisoned, . . .
my sole heir, that I have bu . . .
and has visited with me, that is, in . . .
island of Monte Cristo, all I poss . . .
jewels, diamonds, gems; that I alone . . .
may amount to nearly two mil . . .
will find on raising the twentieth ro . . .
creek to the east in a right line. Two open . . .
in these caves; the treasure is in the furthest a . . .
which treasure I bequeath and leave en . . .
as my sole heir.

                                            " Cæs . . .

    " 25th April, 1498."

" And now," said the abbé, " read this other paper; " and he presented to Dantès a second leaf with fragments of lines written on it which Edmond read as follows:—

                    . . . ing invited to dine with his Holiness
                . . . content with making me pay for my hat,
            . . . serves for me the fate of Cardinals Caprara
                . . . I declare to my nephew, Guido Spada,

. . . ried in a place he knows
. . . the caves of the small
. . . essed of ingots, gold money,
. . . know of the existence of this treasure, which
. . . lions of Roman crowns, and which he
. . . ck from the small
. . . ings have been made
. . . ngle in the second;
. . . tire to him
AR † SPADA."

Faria followed him with excited look.

"And now," he said, when he saw Dantès had read the last line, "put the two fragments together, and judge for yourself."

Dantès obeyed, and the conjoined pieces gave the following:—

"This 25th day of April, 1498, be . . ing invited to dine with his Holiness Alexander VI, and fearing that not . . content with making me pay for my hat, he may desire to become my heir, and re . . serves for me the fate of Cardinals Caprara and Bentivoglio, who were poisoned, . . I declare to my nephew, Guido Spada, my sole heir, that I have bu . . ried in a place he knows and has visited with me, . . that is, in . . the caves of the small island of Monte Cristo, all I poss . . essed of ingots, gold, money, jewels, diamonds, gems; that I alone . . know of the existence of this treasure, which may amount to nearly two mil . . lions of Roman crowns, and which he will find on raising the twentieth ro . . ck from the small creek to the east in a right line. Two open . . ings have been made in these caves; the treasure is in the furthest a . . ngle in the second; which treasure I bequeath and leave en . . tire to him as my sole heir.

"CÆS . . AR † SPADA"

"25th April, 1498."

"Well, do you comprehend now?" inquired Faria.

"It is the declaration of Cardinal Spada, and the will so long sought for," replied Edmond, still incredulous.

"Of course; what else could it be?"

"And who completed it as it now is?"

"I did. Aided by the remaining fragment, I guessed the rest; measuring the length of the lines by those of the paper, and divining the hidden meaning, by means of what was in part revealed, as we are guided in a cavern by the small ray of light above us."

" And what did you do when you arrived at this conclusion? "

" I resolved to set out, and did set out that very instant, carrying with me the beginning of my great work on forming Italy into one kingdom; but for some time the infernal police (who at this period quite contrary to what Napoleon desired so soon as he had a son born to him, wished for a partition of provinces) had their eyes on me and my hasty departure, the cause of which they were unable to guess. Having aroused their suspicions, I was arrested at the very moment I was leaving Piombino.

" Now," continued Faria, addressing Dantès with an almost paternal expression,—" now, my dear fellow, you know as much as I do myself. If we ever escape together, half this treasure is yours; if I die here, and you escape alone, the whole belongs to you."

" But," inquired Dantès, hesitating, " has this treasure no more legitimate possessor in this world than ourselves? "

" No, no, be easy on that score; the family is extinct. The last Comte de Spada, moreover, made me his heir; bequeathing to me this symbolic breviary, he bequeathed to me all it contained: no, no, make your mind satisfied on that point. If we lay hands on this fortune, we may enjoy it without remorse."

" And you say this treasure amounts to——"

" Two millions of Roman crowns; nearly thirteen millions of our money."

" Impossible! " said Dantès, staggered at the enormous amount.

" Impossible! and why? " asked the old man. " The Spada family was one of the oldest and most powerful families of the fifteenth century; and in these times, when all speculation and occupation were wanting, those accumulations of gold and jewels were by no means rare; there are at this day Roman families perishing of hunger, though possessed of nearly a million in diamonds and jewels, handed down as heirlooms, and which they cannot touch."

Edmond thought he was in a dream—he wavered between incredulity and joy.

" I have only kept this secret so long from you," continued Faria, " that I might prove you, and then surprise you. Had we escaped before my attack of catalepsy, I should have conducted you to Monte Cristo; now," he added, with a sigh, " it is you who will conduct me thither. Well! Dantès, you do not thank me? "

" This treasure belongs to you, my dear friend," replied Dantès, " and to you only. I have no right to it. I am no relation of yours."

" You are my son, Dantès," exclaimed the old man. " You

are the child of my captivity. My profession condemns me to celibacy. God has sent you to me to console, at one and the same time, the man who could not be a father and the prisoner who could not get free."

And Faria extended the arm of which alone the use remained to him to the young man, who threw himself upon his neck and wept bitterly.

19

The Death of the Abbé

Now that this treasure which had so long been the object of the abbé's meditations could ensure the future happiness of him whom Faria really loved as a son, it had doubled its value in his eyes, and every day he expatiated on the amount, explaining to Dantès all the good which with thirteen or fourteen millions of francs a man could do in these days to his friends; and then Dantès' countenance became gloomy, for the oath of vengeance he had taken recurred to his memory, and he reflected how much ill in these times a man with thirteen or fourteen millions could do to his enemies.

The abbé did not know the Isle of Monte Cristo,* but Dantès knew it, and had often passed it, situated twenty-five miles from Pianosa, between Corsica and the Isle of Elba, and had once touched at it. This island was, always had been, and still is, completely deserted. It is a rock of almost conical form, which seems as though produced by some volcanic effort from the depth to the surface of the ocean.

Dantès traced a plan of the island to Faria, and Faria gave Dantès advice as to the means he should employ to recover the treasure.

But Dantès was far from being as enthusiastic and confident as the old man. It was past a question now that Faria was not a lunatic, and the way in which he had achieved the discovery, which had given rise to the suspicion of his madness, increased his admiration of him; but at the same time he could not believe that that deposit, supposing it had ever existed, still existed, and though he considered the treasure as by no means chimerical, he yet believed it was no longer there.

However, as if fate resolved on depriving the prisoners of their last chance, and making them understand that they were condemned to perpetual imprisonment, a new misfortune befell them; the gallery on the seaside, which had long been in ruins, was rebuilt. They had repaired it completely, and stopped up, with vast masses of stone, the hole Dantès had partly filled in. But for this precaution, which it will be remembered the abbé had made to Edmond, the misfortune would have been still greater, for their attempt to escape would have been detected, and they would undoubtedly have been separated. Thus, a fresh and even stronger door was closed upon them.

"You see," said the young man, with an air of sorrowful resignation, to Faria, "that God deems it right to take from me even what you call my devotion to you. I have promised you to remain for ever with you, and now I could not break my promise if I would. I shall no more have the treasure than you, and neither of us will quit this prison. But my real treasure is not that, my dear friend, which awaits me beneath the sombre rocks of Monte Cristo, but it is your presence, our living together five or six hours a day, in spite of our gaolers; it is those rays of intelligence you have elicited from my brain, the languages you have implanted in my memory, and which spring there with all their philological ramifications. These different sciences that you have made so easy to me by the depth of the knowledge you possess of them, and the clearness of the principles to which you have reduced them,—this is my treasure, my beloved friend, and with this you have made me rich and happy. Believe me, and take comfort, this is better for me than tons of gold and cases of diamonds, even were they not as problematical as the clouds we see in the morning floating over the sea which we take for *terra firma*, and which evaporate and vanish as we draw near to them. To have you as long as possible near me, to hear your eloquent voice which I trust embellishes my mind, strengthens my soul, and makes my whole frame capable of great and terrible things, if I should ever be free, so fills my whole existence, that the despair to which I was just on the point of yielding when I knew you, has no longer any hold over me: and this—this is my fortune—not chimerical but actual. I owe you my real good, my present happiness; and all the sovereigns of the earth, were they Cæsar Borgias, could not deprive me of this."

Thus, if not actually happy, yet the days these two unfortunates passed together went quickly. Faria, who for so long a time had kept silence as to the treasure, now perpetually talked of it. As he had said, he remained paralysed in the right arm and the left leg, and had given up all hope of ever enjoying it himself. But he was continually thinking over some means of escape for his young companion, and he enjoyed it for him. For fear the letter might be some day lost or abstracted, he compelled Dantès to learn it by heart, and he thus knew it from one end to the other.

Then he destroyed the second portion, assured that if the first were seized, no one would be able to penetrate its real meaning. Whole hours sometimes passed whilst Faria was giving instructions to Dantès—instructions which were to serve him when he was at liberty. Then, once free, from the day and hour and moment when he was so, he could have but one only thought, which was, to gain Monte Cristo by some means, and remain there alone under some pretext which would give no suspicions, and once there to endeavour to find the wonderful caverns, and search in the appointed spot. The appointed spot, be it remembered, being the farthest angle in the second opening.

In the meanwhile the hours passed, if not rapidly, at least tolerably. Faria, as we have said, without having recovered the use of his hand and foot, had resumed all the clearness of his understanding; and had gradually, besides the moral instructions we have detailed taught his youthful companion the patient and sublime duty of a prisoner, who learns to make something from nothing. They were thus perpetually employed. Faria, that he might not see himself grow old; Dantès, for fear of recalling the almost extinct past which now only floated in his memory like a distant light wandering in the night. All went on as if in existences in which misfortune has deranged nothing, and which glide on mechanically and tranquilly beneath the eye of Providence.

But beneath this superficial calm there were in the heart of the young man, and, perhaps, in that of the old man, many repressed desires, many stifled sighs, which found vent when Faria was left alone, and when Edmond returned to his cell.

One night Edmond awoke suddenly, believing he heard some one calling him.

He opened his eyes and tried to pierce through the gloom.

His name, or rather a plaintive voice, which essayed to pronounce his name, reached him.

" Alas! " murmured Edmond, " can it be? "

He moved his bed, drew up the stone, rushed into the passage, and reached the opposite extremity; the secret entrance was open.

By the light of the wretched and wavering lamp, of which we have spoken, Dantès saw the old man, pale, but yet erect, clinging to the bedstead. His features were writhing with those horrible symptoms which he already knew, and which had so seriously alarmed him when he saw them for the first time.

"Alas! my dear friend," said Faria in a resigned tone, "you understand, do you not, and I need not attempt to explain to you?"

Edmond uttered a cry of agony, and, quite out of his senses, rushed towards the door, exclaiming

"Help! help!"

Faria had just sufficient strength to retain him.

"Silence!" he said, "or you are lost. Think now of yourself; only, my dear friend, act so as to render your captivity supportable or your flight possible. It would require years to renew only what I have done here, and which would be instantly destroyed if our gaolers knew we had communicated with each other. Besides, be assured, my dear Edmond, the dungeon I am about to leave will not long remain empty; some other unfortunate being will soon take my place, and to him you will appear like an angel of salvation. Perhaps he will be young, strong, and enduring, like yourself, and will aid you in your escape, whilst I have been but a hindrance. You will no longer have half a dead body tied to you to paralyse all your movements. At length Providence has done something for you; he restores to you more than he takes away, and it was time I should die."

Edmond could only clasp his hands and exclaim:

"Oh, my friend! my friend! speak not thus!" and then resuming all his presence of mind, which had for a moment staggered under this blow, and his strength, which had failed at the words of the old man, he said:

"Oh! I have saved you once, and I will save you a second time!"

And raising the foot of the bed he drew out the phial, still a third filled with the red liquor.

"See!" he exclaimed, "there remains still some of this saving draught. Quick! quick! tell me what I must do this time,—are there any fresh instructions? Speak, my friend, I listen."

"There is not a hope," replied Faria, shaking his head; "but no matter, God wills it that man whom he has created, and in whose heart he has so profoundly rooted the love of life, should do all in his power to preserve that existence which, however painful it may be, is yet always so dear."

"Oh! yes, yes!" exclaimed Dantès, "and I tell you you shall be saved!"

"Well, then, try! the cold gains upon me. I feel the blood flowing towards my brain. This horrible trembling, which makes my teeth chatter, and seems to dislocate my bones, begins to pervade my whole frame; in five minutes the malady will reach its height, and in a quarter of an hour there will be nothing left of me but a dead corpse."

"Oh!" exclaimed Dantès, his heart wrung with anguish.

"Do as you did before, only do not wait so long. All the springs of life are now exhausted in me, and death," he continued, looking at his paralysed arm and leg, "has but half its work to do. If, after having made me swallow twelve drops instead of ten, you see that I do not recover, then pour the rest down my throat. Now lift me on my bed, for I can no longer support myself."

Edmond took the old man in his arms, and laid him on the bed.

"And now, my dear friend," said Faria, "sole consolation of my wretched existence,—you whom Heaven gave me somewhat late, but still gave me, a priceless gift, and for which I am most grateful, at the moment of separating from you for ever, I wish you all the happiness and all the prosperity you so well deserve. My son, I bless thee!"

The young man cast himself on his knees, leaning his head against the old man's bed.

"Listen, now, to what I say in this my dying moment. The treasure of the Spadas exists. God grants me that there no longer exists for me distance or obstacle. I see it in the depths of the inner cavern. My eyes pierce the inmost recesses of the earth, and are dazzled at the sight of so much riches. If you do escape, remember that the poor abbé, whom all the world called mad, was not so. Hasten to Monte Cristo—avail yourself of the fortune—for you have indeed suffered long enough."

A violent shock interrupted the old man. Dantès raised his head and saw Faria's eyes injected with blood. It seemed as if a flow of blood had ascended from the chest to the head.

"Adieu! adieu!" murmured the old man, clasping Edmond's hand convulsively—"adieu!"

"Oh, no—no, not yet," he cried, "do not forsake me! Oh! succour him! Help!—help!—help!"

"Hush! hush!" murmured the dying man, "that they may not separate us if you save me!"

"You are right. Oh, yes, yes! be assured I shall save you! Besides, although you suffer much, you do not seem in such agony as before."

"Do not mistake! I suffer less because there is in me less strength to endure it. At your age we have faith in life; it is the privilege of youth to believe and hope, but old men see death more clearly. Oh! 'tis here—'tis here—'tis over—my sight is gone—my reason escapes! Your hand, Dantès! Adieu!—adieu!"

And raising himself by a final effort, in which he summoned all his faculties, he said:

" Monte Cristo! forget not Monte Cristo! "

And he fell back in his bed.

The crisis was terrible; his twisted limbs, his swollen eyelids, a foam of blood and froth in his lips; a frame quite rigid was soon extended on this bed of agony in place of the intellectual being who was there but so lately.

Dantès took the lamp, placed it on a projecting stone above the bed, whence its tremulous light fell with strange and fantastic ray on this discomposed countenance and this motionless and stiffened body.

With fixed eyes he awaited boldly the moment for administering the hoped-for restorative.

When he believed the instant had arrived, he took the knife, unclosed the teeth, which offered less resistance than before, counted one after the other twelve drops, and watched; the phial contained, perhaps, twice as much more.

He waited ten minutes, a quarter of an hour, half an hour, nothing moved. Trembling, his hair erect, his brow bathed with perspiration, he counted the seconds by the beatings of his heart.

Then he thought it was time to make the last trial, and he put the phial to the violet lips of Faria, and without having occasion to force open his jaws, which had remained extended, he poured the whole of the liquid down his throat.

The draught produced a galvanic effect, a violent trembling pervaded the old man's limbs, his eyes opened until it was fearful to gaze upon them, he heaved a sigh which resembled a shriek, and then all this vibrating frame returned gradually to its state of immobility, only the eyes remaining open.

Half an hour, an hour, an hour and a half elapsed, and during this time of anguish Edmond leaned over his friend, his hand applied to his heart, and felt the body gradually grow cold, and the heart's pulsation become more and more deep and dull, until at length all stopped; the last movement of the heart ceased, the face became livid, the eyes remained open, but the look was glazed.

It was six o'clock in the morning, the dawn was just breaking, and its weak ray came into the dungeon, and paled the ineffectual light of the lamp. Singular shadows passed over the countenance of the dead man, which at times gave it the appearance of life. Whilst this struggle between day and night lasted, Dantès still doubted; but as soon as the daylight gained the pre-eminence, he saw that he was alone with a corpse.

Then an invincible and extreme terror seized upon him, and

he dared not again press the hand that hung out of bed, he dared no longer to gaze on those fixed and vacant eyes which he tried many times to close, but in vain—they opened again as soon as shut. He extinguished the lamp, carefully concealed it, and then went away, closing as well as he could the entrance to the secret passage by the large stone as he descended.

It was time, for the gaoler was coming. On this occasion he began his rounds at Dantès cell, and on leaving him he went on to Faria's dungeon, where he was taking breakfast and some linen.

Nothing betokened that the man knew anything of what had occurred. He went on his way.

Dantès was then seized with an indescribable desire to know what was going on in the dungeon of his unfortunate friend. He therefore returned by the subterraneous gallery, and arrived in time to hear the exclamations of the turnkey who called out for help.

Other turnkeys came, and then was heard the regular tramp of soldiers even when not on duty—behind them came the governor.

Edmond heard the creaking of the bed in which they were moving the corpse, heard the voice of the governor, who desired them to throw water on the face, and seeing that in spite of this application the prisoner did not recover, sent for the doctor.

The governor then went out, and some words of pity fell on Dantès listening ears, mingled with brutal laughter.

" Well! well! " said one, " the madman has gone to look after his treasure. Good journey to him! "

" With all his millions, he will not have enough to pay for his shroud! " said another.

" Oh! " added a third voice " the shrouds of the Château d'If are not dear! "

" Perhaps," said one of the previous speakers, " as he was a churchman, they may go to some expense in his behalf."

" They may give him the honours of the sack."

Edmond did not lose a word, but comprehended very little of what was said. The voices soon ceased, and it seemed to him as if the persons had all left the cell. Still he dared not to enter, as they might have left some turnkey to watch the dead.

He remained, therefore, mute and motionless, restraining even his respiration.

At the end of an hour, he heard a faint noise, which increased. It was the governor, who returned, followed by the doctor and other attendants.

There was a moment's silence—it was evident that the doctor was examining the dead body.

The inquiries soon commenced.

The doctor analysed the symptoms of the malady under which the prisoner had sunk, and declared he was dead.

Questions and answers followed in a manner that made Dantès indignant, for he felt that all the world should experience for the poor abbé the love he bore him.

" I am very sorry for what you tell me," said the governor, replying to the assurance of the doctor, " that the old man is really dead, for he was a quiet, inoffensive prisoner, happy in his folly, and required no watching."

" Ah! " added the turnkey, " there was no occasion for watching him; he would have stayed here fifty years, I'll answer for it, without any attempt to escape."

" Still," said the governor, " I believe it will be requisite, notwithstanding your certainty, and not that I doubt your science, but for my own responsibility's sake, that we should be perfectly assured that the prisoner is dead "

There was a moment of complete silence, during which Dantès, still listening, felt assured that the doctor was examining and touching the corpse a second time.

" You may make your mind easy," said the doctor; " he is dead. I will answer for that." .

" You know, sir," said the governor, persisting, " that we are not content in such cases as this with such a simple examination. In spite of all appearances, be so kind, therefore, as finish your duty by fulfilling the formalities prescribed by law."

" Let the irons be heated," said the doctor; " but really it is a useless precaution."

This order to heat the irons made Dantès shudder. He heard hasty steps, the creaking of a door, people going and coming, and some minutes afterwards a turnkey entered, saying:

" Here is the brazier lighted."

There was a moment's silence, and then was heard the noise made by burning flesh, of which the peculiar and nauseous smell penetrated even behind the wall where Dantès was listening horrified.

At this smell of human flesh carbonised, the damp came over the young man's brow, and he felt as if he should faint.

" You see, sir, he is really dead," said the doctor; " this burn in the heel is decisive; the poor fool is cured of his folly, and delivered from his captivity."

" Wasn't his name Faria? " inquired one of the officers who accompanied the governor.

" Yes, sir; and as he said, it was an ancient name; he was, too, very learned, and rational enough on all points which did not relate to his treasure; but on that, indeed, he was obstinate."

"It is the sort of malady which we call monomania," said the doctor.

"You had never anything to complain of?" said the governor to the gaoler who had charge of the abbé.

"Never, sir," replied the gaoler, "never—on the contrary, he sometimes amused me very much by telling me stories. One day, too, when my wife was ill, he gave me a prescription which cured her."

"Ah, ah!" said the doctor, "I was ignorant that I had a competitor; but I hope, M. le Governeur, that you will show him all proper respect in consequence."

"Yes, yes; make your mind easy; he shall be decently interred in the newest sack we can find. Will that satisfy you?"

"Must we do this last formality in your presence, sir?" inquired a turnkey.

"Certainly. But make haste. I cannot stay here all day."

Fresh footsteps, going and coming, were now heard, and a moment afterwards the noise of cloth being rubbed reached Dantès' ears, the bed creaked on its hinges, and the heavy foot of a man, who lifts a weight, resounded on the floor; then the bed again creaked under the weight deposited upon it.

"In the evening!" said the governor.

"Will there be any mass?" asked one of the attendants.

"That is impossible," replied the governor. "The chaplain of the Château came to me yesterday to beg for leave of absence in order to take a trip to Hyères for a week. I told him I would attend to the prisoners in his absence. If the poor abbé had not been in such a hurry he might have had his requiem."

"Pooh! pooh!" said the doctor, with the accustomed impiety of persons of his profession, "he is a churchman. God will respect his profession, and not give the devil the wicked delight of sending him a priest."

A shout of laughter followed this brutal jest.

During this time the operation of putting the body in the sack was going on.

"This evening," said the governor, when the task was ended.

"At what o'clock?" inquired a turnkey.

"Why, about ten or eleven o'clock."

"Shall we watch by the corpse?"

"Of what use would it be? Shut the dungeon as if he were alive—that is all."

Then the steps retreated, and the voices died away in the distance; the noise of the door with its creaking hinges and bolts ceased, and a silence duller than any solitude ensued, the silence of death, which pervaded all, and struck its icy chill through the young man's whole frame. Then he raised the flagstone cautiously with his head, and looked carefully round the chamber.

It was empty, and Dantès, quitting the passage, entered it.

20

The Cemetery of the Château d'If

ON the bed, at full length, and faintly lighted by the pale ray that penetrated the window, was visible a sack of coarse cloth, under the large folds of which were stretched a long and stiffened form; it was Faria's last winding-sheet—a winding-sheet which, as the turnkey said, cost so little. All then was completed. A material separation had taken place between Dantès and his old friend,—he could no longer see those eyes which had remained open as if to look even beyond death,—he could no longer clasp that hand of industry which had lifted for him the veil that had concealed hidden and obscure things. Faria, the usual and the good companion, with whom he was accustomed to live so intimately, no longer breathed. He seated himself on the edge of that terrible bed, and fell into a melancholy and gloomy reverie.

Alone! he was alone again! again relapsed into silence! he found himself once again in the presence of nothingness!

Alone! no longer to see,—no longer to hear the voice of the only human being who attached him to life! Was it not better, like Faria, to seek the presence of his Maker and learn the enigma of life at the risk of passing through the mournful gate of intense suffering?

The idea of suicide, driven away by his friend, and forgotten in his presence whilst living, arose like a phantom before him in presence of his dead body.

" If I could die," he said, " I should go where he goes, and should assuredly find him again. But how to die? It is very easy," he continued, with a smile of bitterness; " I will remain here, rush on the first person that opens the door, will strangle him, and then they will guillotine me."

But as it happens that in excessive griefs, as in great tempests, the abyss is found between the tops of the loftiest waves, Dantès recoiled from the idea of this infamous death, and passed suddenly from despair to an ardent desire for life and liberty.

" Die! oh, no," he exclaimed, " not die now, after having lived and suffered so long and so much! Die! yes, had I died years since; but now it would be indeed to give way to my bitter destiny. No, I desire to live, I desire to struggle to the very last, I wish to reconquer the happiness of which I have been deprived. Before I die, I must not forget that I have my executioners to punish, and, perhaps, too, who knows, some friends to reward. Yet they will forget me here, and I shall die in my dungeon like Faria."

As he said this, he remained motionless, his eyes fixed like a man struck with a sudden idea, but whom this idea fills with amazement. Suddenly he rose, lifted his hand to his brow as if his brain were giddy, paced twice or thrice round his chamber, and then paused abruptly at the bed.

" Ah! ah!" he muttered, " who inspires me with this thought? Is that thou, gracious God? Since none but the dead pass freely from this dungeon, let me assume the place of the dead!"

Without giving himself time to reconsider his decision, and, indeed, that he might not allow his thoughts to be distracted from his desperate resolution, he bent over the appalling sack, opened it with the knife which Faria had made, drew the corpse from the sack, and transported it along the gallery to his own chamber, laid it on his couch, passed round its head the rag he wore at night round his own, covered it with his counterpane, once again kissed the ice-cold brow, and tried vainly to close the resisting eyes which glared horrible, turned the head towards the wall, so that the gaoler might, when he brought his evening meal, believe that he was asleep, as was his frequent custom; returned along the gallery, threw the bed against the wall, returned to the other cell, took from the hiding-place the needle and thread, flung off his rags that they might feel naked flesh only beneath the coarse sackcloth, and getting inside the sack, placed himself in the posture in which the dead body had been laid, and sewed up the mouth of the sack withinside.

The beating of his heart might have been heard if by any mischance the gaolers had entered at that moment.

Dantès might have waited until the evening visit was over, but he was afraid the governor might change his resolution, and order the dead body to be removed earlier.

In that case his last hope would have been destroyed.

Now his project was settled under any circumstances, and he hoped thus to carry it into effect.

If during the time he was being conveyed the grave-diggers should discover that they were conveying a live instead of a dead body. Dantès did not intend to give them time to recognise him, but with a sudden cut of the knife, he meant to open the sack from top to bottom, and, profiting by their alarm, escape; if they tried to catch him he would use his knife.

If they conducted him to the cemetery and laid him in the grave, he would allow himself to be covered with earth, and then, as it was night, the grave-diggers could scarcely have turned their backs, ere he would have worked his way through the soft soil and escape, hoping that the weight would not be too heavy for him to support.

If he was deceived in this and the earth proved too heavy, he would be stifled, and then, so much the better, all would be over.

Dantès had not eaten since the previous evening, but he had not thought of hunger or thirst, nor did he now think of it. His position was too precarious to allow him even time to reflect on any thought but one.

The first risk that Dantès ran was, that the gaoler when he brought him his supper at seven o'clock, might perceive the substitution he had effected; fortunately, twenty times at least, from misanthropy or fatigue, Dantès had received his gaoler in bed, and then the man placed his bread and soup on the table, and went away without saying a word.

This time the gaoler might not be as silent as usual, but speak to Dantès, and seeing that he received no reply, go to the bed, and thus discover all.

When seven o'clock came, Dantès' agony really commenced. His hand placed on his heart was unable to repress its throbbings, whilst, with the other, he wiped the perspiration from his temples. From time to time shudderings ran through his whole frame, and collapsed his heart as if it were frozen. Then he thought he was going to die. Yet the hours passed on without any stir in the Château, and Dantès felt he had escaped this first danger: it was a good augury. At length, about the hour the governor had appointed, footsteps were heard on the stairs. Edmond felt that the moment had arrived, and summoning up all his courage, held his breath, happy if at the same time he could have repressed in like manner the hasty pulsation of his arteries.

They stopped at the door—there were two steps, and Dantès guessed it was the two grave-diggers who had come to seek him —this idea was soon converted into certainty, when he heard the noise they made in putting down the hand-bier.

The door opened, and a dim light reached Dantès' eyes through the coarse sack that covered him; he saw two shadows approach his bed, a third remaining at the door with a torch in his hand. Each of these two men, approaching the ends of the bed, took the sack by its extremities.

" He's heavy though for an old and thin man," said one, as he raised the head.

" They say every year adds half a pound to the weight of the bones," said another, lifting the feet.

" Have you tied the knot? " inquired the first speaker.

" What would be the use of carrying so much more weight? " was the reply: " I can do that when we get there."

" Yes, you're right," replied the companion.

" What's the knot for? " thought Dantès.

They deposited the supposed corpse on the bier. Edmond stiffened himself in order to play his part of a dead man, and then the party, lighted by the man with the torch who went first, ascended the stairs.

Suddenly he felt the fresh and sharp night air, and Dantès recognised the *mistral*. It was a sudden sensation, at the same time replete with delight and agony.

The bearers advanced twenty paces, then stopped, putting their bier down on the ground.

One of them went away, and Dantès heard his shoes on the pavement.

" Where am I then? " he asked himself.

" Really, he is by no means a light load! " said the other bearer, sitting on the edge of the hand-barrow.

Dantès' first impulse was to escape, but fortunately he did not attempt it.

" Light me, you sir," said the other bearer, " or I shall not find what I am looking for."

The man with the torch complied, although not asked in the most polite terms.

" What can he be looking for? " thought Edmond. " The spade, perhaps."

An exclamation of satisfaction indicated that the grave-digger had found the object of his search.

" Here it is at last," he said, " not without some trouble though."

" Yes," was the answer, " but it has lost nothing by waiting."

As he said this, the man came towards Edmond, who heard a heavy and sounding substance laid down beside him, and the same moment a cord was fastened round his feet with sudden and painful violence.

" Well, have you tied the knot? " inquired the grave-digger, who was looking on.

"Yes, and pretty tight too, I can tell you," was the answer.
"Move on, then,"

And the bier was lifted once more, and they proceeded.

They advanced fifty paces farther, and then stopped to open a door, then went forward again. The noise of the waves dashing against the rocks, on which the Château is built, reached Dantès' ear distinctly as they progressed.

"Bad weather!" observed one of the bearers; "not a pleasant night for a dip in the sea."

"Why, yes, the abbé runs a chance of being wet." said the other; and then there was a burst of brutal laughter.

Dantès did not comprehend the jest, but his hair stood erect on his head.

"Well, here we are at last," said one of them. "A little farther—a little farther," said the other. "You know very well that the last was stopped on his way, dashed on the rocks, and the governor told us next day that we were careless fellows."

They ascended five or six more steps, and then Dantès felt that they took him, one by the head and the other by the heels, and swung him to and fro.

"One!" said the grave-diggers. "Two! Three, and away!"

And at the same instant Dantès felt himself flung into the air like a wounded bird, falling, falling with a rapidity that made his blood curdle. Although drawn downwards by the same heavy weight which hastened his rapid descent, it seemed to him as if the time were a century. At last, with a terrific dash, he entered the ice-cold water, and as he did so he uttered a shrill cry, stifled in a moment by his immersion beneath the waves.

Dantès had been flung into the sea, into whose depths he was dragged by a thirty-six pound shot tied to his feet.

The sea is the cemetery of Château d'If.

21

The Isle of Tiboulen

DANTÈS, although giddy and almost suffocated, had yet sufficient presence of mind to hold his breath; and as his right hand (prepared as he was for every chance) held his knife open, he rapidly ripped up the sack, extricated his arm, and then his body; but in spite of all his efforts to free himself from the bullet he felt it dragging him down still lower; ·he then bent his body, and by a desperate effort severed the cord that bound his legs at the moment he was suffocating. With a vigorous spring he rose to the surface of the sea, whilst the bullet bore to its depths the sack that had so nearly become his shroud.

Dantès merely paused to breathe, and then dived again in order to avoid being seen.

When he arose a second time he was fifty paces from where he had first sunk. He saw over head a black and tempestuous sky, over which the wind was driving the fleeting vapours that occasionally suffered a twinkling star to appear: before him was the vast expanse of waters, sombre and terrible, whose waves foamed and roared as if before the approach of a storm. Behind him, blacker than the sea, blacker than the sky, rose like a phantom the giant of granite, whose projecting crags seemed like arms extended to seize their prey; and on the highest rock was a torch that lighted two figures. He fancied these two forms were looking at the sea; doubtless these strange grave-diggers had heard his cry. Dantès dived again, and remained a long time beneath the water. This manœuvre was already familiar to him, and usually attracted a crowd of spectators in the bay before the lighthouse at Marseilles when he swam there, who, with one accord pronounced him the best swimmer in the port.

When he rose again the light had disappeared.

It was necessary to strike out to sea. Ratonneau and Pomègue are the nearest isles of all those that surround the Château d'If. But Ratonneau and Pomègue are inhabited, together with the islet of Daume; Tiboulen or Lemaire were the most secure. The isles of Tiboulen and Lemaire are a league from the Château d'If. Dantès, nevertheless, determined to make for them; but how could he find his way in the darkness of the night?

At this moment he saw before him, like a brilliant star, the lighthouse of Planier.

By leaving this light on the right, he kept the isle of Tiboulen a little on the left; by turning to the left, therefore, he would find it. But, as we have said, it was at least a league from the Château d'If to this island.

Often in prison Faria had said to him when he saw him idle and inactive:

" Dantès, you must not give way to this listlessness; you will be drowned, if you seek to escape; and your strength has not been properly exercised and prepared for exertion."

These words rang in Dantès' ears even beneath the waves: he hastened to cleave his way through them to see if he had not lost his strength; he found with pleasure that his captivity had taken away nothing of his power, and that he was still master of that element on whose bosom he had so often sported as a boy.

Fear, that relentless pursuer, clogged Dantès' efforts; he listened if any noise was audible; each time that he rose over the waves his looks scanned the horizon, and strove to penetrate the darkness; every wave seemed a boat in his pursuit, and he redoubled exertions that increased his distance from the Château, but the repetition of which weakened his strength. He swam on still, and already the terrible Château had disappeared in the darkness. He could not see it, but he *felt* its presence. An hour passed, during which Dantès, excited by the feeling of freedom, continued to cleave the waves.

" Let us see," said he, " I have swam above an hour; but as the wind is against me, that has retarded my speed; however, if I am not mistaken, I must be close to the isle of Tiboulen. But what if I were mistaken? "

A shudder passed over him. He sought to tread water in order to rest himself, but the sea was too violent, and he felt that he could not make use of this means of repose.

" Well," said he, " I will swim on until I am worn out, or the cramp seizes me, and then I shall sink; " and he struck out with the energy of despair.

Suddenly the sky seemed to him to become still darker and more dense, and compact clouds lowered towards him; at the same time he felt a violent pain in his knee. His imagination told him a ball had struck him, and that in a moment he would hear the report; but he heard nothing. Dantès put out his hand and felt resistance; he then extended his leg and felt the land, and in an instant guessed the nature of the object he had taken for a cloud.

Before him rose a mass of strangely formed rocks that resembled nothing so much as a vast fire petrified at the moment of its most fervent combustion. It was the isle of Tiboulen.

Dantès rose, advanced a few steps, and, with a fervent prayer of gratitude, stretched himself on the granite, which seemed to him softer than down. Then, in spite of the wind and rain, he fell into the deep sweet sleep of those worn out by fatigue.

At the expiration of an hour Edmond was awakened by the roar of the thunder. The tempest was unchained and let loose in all its fury; from time to time a flash of lightning stretched across the heavens like a fiery serpent lighting up the clouds that rolled on like the waves of an immense chaos.

Dantès had not been deceived—he had reached the first of the two isles, which was in reality Tiboulen. He knew that it was barren and without shelter; but when the sea became more calm, he resolved to plunge into its waves again, and swim to Lemaire, equally arid, but larger, and consequently better adapted for concealment.

An overhanging rock offered him a temporary shelter, and scarcely had he availed himself of it when the tempest burst forth in all its fury. Edmond felt the rock beneath which he lay tremble; the waves dashing themselves against the granite rock wetted him with their spray. In safety, as he was, he felt himself become giddy in the midst of this war of the elements and the dazzling brightness of the lightning. It seemed to him that the island trembled to its base, and that it would, like a vessel at anchor, break her moorings, and bear him off into the centre of the storm.

He then recollected that he had not eaten or drunk for four-and-twenty hours. He extended his hands and drank greedily of the rain-water that had lodged in a hollow of the rock.

As he rose, a flash of lightning, that seemed as if the whole of the heavens were opened, illumined the darkness. By its light, between the isle of Lemaire and Cape Croiselle, a quarter of a league distant, Dantès saw, like a spectre, a fishing-boat driven rapidly on by the force of the winds and waves. A second after he saw it again approaching nearer. Dantès cried at the top of his voice to warn them of their danger, but they saw it themselves. Another flash showed him four men clinging to the shattered mast and the rigging, while a fifth clung to the broken rudder.

The men he beheld saw him doubtless, for their cries were carried to his ears by the wind. Above the splintered mast a sail rent to tatters was waving; suddenly the ropes that still held it gave way, and it disappeared in the darkness of the night like a vast sea-bird. At the same moment a violent crash was heard, and cries of distress. Perched on the summit of the rock, Dantès saw by the lightning the vessel in pieces; and amongst the fragments were visible the agonised features of the unhappy sailors. Then all became dark again.

Dantès ran down the rocks at the risk of being himself dashed to pieces; he listened, he strove to examine, but he heard and saw nothing,—all human cries had ceased; and the tempest alone continued to rage.

By degrees the wind abated; vast gray clouds rolled towards the west; and the blue firmament appeared studded with bright stars. Soon a red streak became visible in the horizon; the waves whitened, a light played over them, and gilded their foaming crests with gold. It was day.

Dantès stood silent and motionless before this vast spectacle; for since his captivity he had forgotten it. He turned towards the fortress, and looked both at the sea and the land.

The gloomy building rose from the bosom of the ocean with that imposing majesty of inanimate objects that seems at once to watch and to command.

It was about five o'clock; the sea continued to grow calmer.

" In two or three hours," thought Dantès, " the turnkey will enter my chamber, find the body of my poor friend, recognise it, seek for me in vain, and give the alarm. Then the passage will be discovered; the men who cast me into the sea, and who must have heard the cry I uttered, will be questioned. Then boats filled with armed soldiers will pursue the wretched fugitive. The cannon will warn every one to refuse shelter to a man wandering about naked and famished. The police of Marseilles will be on the alert by land, whilst the governor pursues me by sea. I am cold, I am hungry. I have lost even the knife that saved me. Oh, my God! I have suffered enough surely. Have pity on me, and do for me what I am unable to do for myself."

As Dantès (his eyes turned in the direction of the Château d'If) uttered this prayer, he saw appear at the extremity of the isle of Pomègue, like a bird skimming over the sea, a small bark, that the eye of a sailor alone could recognise as a Genoese tartane.* She was coming out of Marseilles harbour, and was standing out to sea rapidly, her sharp prow cleaving through the waves.

" Oh! " cried Edmond, " to think that in half an hour I could join her, did I not fear being questioned, detected, and conveyed back to Marseilles. What can I do? What story can I invent? Under pretext of trading along the coast, these men, who are in reality smugglers, will prefer selling me to doing a good action. I must wait. But I cannot, I am starving. In a few hours my strength will be utterly exhausted; besides, perhaps, I have not been missed at the fortress. I can pass as one of the sailors wrecked last night. This story will pass current, for there is no one left to contradict me."

As he spoke, Dantès looked towards the spot where the fishing-vessel had been wrecked, and started. The red cap of one of the sailors hung to a point of the rock, and some beams that had formed a part of the vessel's keel, floated at the foot of the crags.

In an instant Dantès' plan was formed. He swam to the cap, placed it on his head, seized one of the beams, and struck out so as to cross the line the vessel was taking.

" I am saved," murmured he.

And this conviction restored his strength.

He soon perceived the vessel, which, having the wind right ahead, was tacking between the Château d'If and the tower of Planier. For an instant he feared lest the bark, instead of keeping in shore, should stand out to sea; but he soon saw by her man-oeuvres that she wished to pass, like most vessels bound for Italy, between the islands of Jaros and Calaseraigne. However, the vessel and the swimmer insensibly neared one another, and in one of its tacks the bark approached with in a quarter of a mile of him. He rose on the waves, making signs of distress; but no one on board perceived him, and the vessel stood on another tack. Dantès would have cried out, but he reflected that the wind would drown his voice.

It was then he rejoiced at his precaution in taking the beam, for without it he would have been unable, perhaps, to reach the vessel,—certainly to return to shore, should he be unsuccessful in attracting attention.

Dantès, although almost sure as to what course the bark would take, had yet watched it anxiously until it tacked and stood to-wards him. Then he advanced; but, before they had met, the vessel again changed her direction. By a violent effort, he rose half out of the water, waving his cap, and uttering a loud shout peculiar to sailors.

This time he was both seen and heard, and the tartane instantly steered towards him. At the same time, he saw they were about to lower the boat.

An instant after, the boat, rowed by two men, advanced rapidly towards him. Dantès abandoned the beam, which he thought now useless, and swam vigorously to meet them. But he had reckoned too much upon his strength, and then he felt how service-able the beam had been to him. His arms grew stiff, his legs had lost their flexibility, and he was almost breathless.

He uttered a second cry. The two sailors redoubled their efforts, and one of them cried in Italian, " Courage."

The word reached his ear as a wave, which he no longer had the strength to surmount, passed over is head. He rose again to the surface, supporting himself by one of those desperate efforts a drowning man makes, uttered a third cry, and felt himself sink again, as if the fatal bullet were again tied to his feet.

The water passed over his head, and the sky seemed livid. A violent effort again brought him to the surface. He felt as if something seized him by the hair; but he saw and heard nothing. He had fainted.

When he opened his eyes Dantès found himself on the deck of the tartanc. His first care was to see what direction they were pursuing. They were rapidly leaving the Château d'If behind. Dantès was so exhausted that the exclamation of joy he uttered was mistaken for a sigh.

As we have said, he was lying on the deck. A sailor was rubbing his limbs with a woollen cloth; another, whom he recognised as the one who had cried out " Courage! " held a gourd full of rum to his mouth; whilst the third, an old sailor, at once the pilot and captain, looked on with that egotistical pity men feel for a misfortune that they have escaped yesterday and which may overtake them to-morrow.

A few drops of the rum restored suspended animation, whilst the friction of his limbs restored their elasticity.

" Who are you? " said the pilot in bad French.

" I am," replied Dantès, in bad Italian, " a Maltese sailor. We were coming from Syracuse laden with grain. The storm of last night overtook us at Cape Morgion, and we were wrecked on these rocks."

" Where do you come from? "

" From these rocks, that I had the good luck to cling to whilst our captain and the rest of the crew were all lost. I saw your ship, and fearful of being left to perish on the desolate island, I swam off on a fragment of the vessel in order to try and gain your bark. You have saved my life, and I thank you," continued Dantès. " I was lost when one of your sailors caught hold of my hair."

" It was I," said a sailor, of a frank and manly appearance; " and it was time, for you were sinking."

" Yes," returned Dantès, holding out his hand, " I thank you again."

" I almost hesitated, though," replied the sailor; " you looked more like a brigand than an honest man, with your beard six inches and your hair a foot long."

Dantès recollected that his hair and beard had not been cut all the time he was at the Château d'If.

" Yes," said he, " in a moment of danger I made a vow to our Lady of the Grotto not to cut my hair or beard for ten years if I were saved; but to-day the vow expires."

" Now what are we to do with you? " said the captain.

" Alas! anything you please. My captain is dead; I have barely escaped; but I am a good sailor. Leave me at the first port you make; I shall be sure to find employment."

" Do you know the Mediterranean? "

" I have sailed over it since my childhood."

" You know the best harbours? "

" There are few ports that I could not enter or leave with my eyes blinded."

" I say, captain," said the sailor, who had cried " Courage! " to Dantès, " if what he says is true, what hinders his staying with us? "

" If he says true," said the captain doubtingly. " But in his present condition he will promise anything, and take his chance of keeping it afterwards."

" I will do more than I promise," said Dantès.

" We shall see," returned the other, smiling.

" Where are you going to? " asked Dantès.

" To Leghorn."

" Then why, instead of tacking so frequently, do you not sail nearer the wind? "

" Because we should run straight on to the island of Rion."

" You shall pass it by twenty fathoms."

" Take the helm, and let us see what you know."

The young man took the helm, ascertaining by a slight pressure if the vessel answered the rudder, and seeing that, without being a first-rate sailer, she yet was tolerably obedient,—

" To the braces," said he.

The four seamen, who composed the crew, obeyed, whilst the pilot looked on.

" Haul taut."

They obeyed.

" Belay."

This order was also executed, and the vessel passed, as Dantès had predicted, twenty fathoms to the right.

" Bravo! " said the captain.

" Bravo! " repeated the sailors.

And they all regarded with astonishment this man whose eye had recovered an intelligence, and his body a vigour they were far from suspecting.

" You see," said Dantès, quitting the helm, " I shall be

of some use to you, at least, during the voyage. If you do not want me at Leghorn, you can leave me there, and I will pay out of the first wages I get for my food and the clothes you lend me."

"Ah," said the captain, "we can agree very well, if you are reasonable."

"Give me what you give the others, and all will be arranged," returned Dantès.

"That's not fair," said the seaman who had saved Dantès; "for you know more than we do."

"What is that to you, Jacopo?" returned the captain. "Every one is free to ask what he pleases."

"That's true," replied Jacopo. "I only made a remark."

"Well, you would do much better to lend him a jacket and a pair of trousers, if you have them."

"No," said Jacopo; "but I have a shirt and a pair of trousers."

"That is all I want," interrupted Dantès.

Jacopo dived into the hold, and soon returned with what Edmond wanted.

"Now, then, do you wish for anything else?" said the patron.

"A piece of bread and another glass of the capital rum I tasted, for I have not eaten or drunk for a long time."

He had not tasted food for forty hours.

A piece of bread was brought, and Jacopo offered him the gourd.

"Larboard your helm," cried the captain to the steersman.

Dantès glanced to the same side as he lifted the gourd to his mouth; but his hand stopped.

"Halloa! what's the matter at the Château d'If?" said the captain.

A small white cloud, which had attracted Dantès' attention, crowned the summit of the bastion of the Château d'If.

At the same moment the faint report of a gun was heard. The sailors looked at one another.

"What is this?" asked the captain.

"A prisoner has escaped from the Château d'If, and they are firing the alarm gun," replied Dantès.

The captain glanced at him, but he had lifted the rum to his lips, and was drinking it with so much composure, that his suspicions, if he had any, died away.

"At any rate," murmured he, "if it be, so much the better, for I have made a rare acquisition."

Under pretence of being fatigued, Dantès asked to take the helm; the steersman, enchanted to be relieved, looked at the captain, and the latter by a sign indicated that he might abandon it to his new comrade. Dantès could thus keep his eyes on Marseilles.

"What is the day of the month?" asked he of Jacopo, who sat down beside him.

"The 28th of February!"

"In what year?"

"In what year—you ask me in what year?"

"Yes," replied the young man, "I ask you in what year!"

"You have forgotten then?"

"I got such a fright last night," replied Dantès, smiling, "that I have almost lost my memory, I ask you what year is it?"

"The year 1829," returned Jacopo.

It was fourteen years day for day since Dantès' arrest.

He was nineteen when he entered the Château d'If; he was thirty-three when he escaped.

A sorrowful smile passed over his face; he asked himself what had become of Mercédès, who must believe him dead.

Then his eyes lighted up with hatred as he thought of the three men who had caused him so long and wretched a captivity.

He renewed against Danglars, Fernand, and Villefort the oath of implacable vengeance he had made in his dungeon.

The oath was no longer a vain menace, for the fastest sailer in the Mediterranean would have been unable to overtake the little tartane, that with every stitch of canvas set was flying before the wind to Leghorn.

22

The Smugglers

DANTÈS had not been a day on board before he had an insight into the persons with whom he sailed. Without having been in the school of the Abbé Faria, the worthy master of *The Young Amelia* (the name of the Genoese tartane) knew a smattering of all the tongues spoken on the shores of that large lake called the Mediterranean, from the Arabic to the Provençal; and this, whilst it spared him interpreters, persons always troublesome and frequently indiscreet, gave him great facilities of communication, either with the vessels he met at sea, with the small barks sailing along the coast, or with those persons without name, country, or apparent calling, who are always seen on the quays of seaports, and who live by those hidden and mysterious means, which we must suppose come in a right line from Providence, as they have no visible means of existence. We may thus suppose that Dantès was on board a smuggling lugger.

In the first instance the master had received Dantès on board with a certain degree of mistrust. He was very well known to the custom-house officers of the coast, and as there was between these worthies and himself an exchange of the most cunning stratagems, he had at first thought that Dantès might be an emissary of these illustrious executors of rights and duties, who employed this ingenious means of penetrating some of the secrets of his trade. But the skilful manner in which Dantès had manœuvred the little bark had entirely reassured him, and then when he saw the light smoke floating like a plume above the bastion of the Château d'If, and heard the distant explosion, he was instantly struck with the idea that he had on board his vessel one for whom, like the goings in and comings out of kings, they accord salutes of cannons. This made him less uneasy, it must be owned, than if the new-comer had proved a custom-house officer, but this latter supposition also dispppeared like the first, when he beheld the perfect tranquillity of his recruit.

Edmond thus had the advantage of knowing what the owner was, without the owner knowing who he was; and, however the old sailor and his crew tried to " pump " him, they extracted nothing more from him; giving accurate descriptions of Naples and Malta, which he knew as well as Marseilles, and persisting stoutly in his first statement. Thus the Genoese, subtle as he was, was duped by Edmond, in whose favour his mild demeanour, his nautical skill, and his admirable dissimulation, pleaded. Moreover, it is possible that the Genoese was one of those shrewd persons who know nothing but what they should know, and believe nothing but what they should believe.

It was thus, in this reciprocal position, that they reached Leghorn.

Here Edmond was to undergo another trial; it was to see if he should recognise himself, never having beheld his own features for fourteen years. He had preserved a tolerably good remembrance of what the youth had been, and was now to find what the man had become. His comrades believed that his vow was fulfilled, as he had twenty times touched at Leghorn before he remembered a barber in the Rue Saint-Ferdinand: he went there to have his beard and hair cut.

The barber gazed in amaze at this man with the long hair and beard, thick and black as it was, and resembling one of Titian's glorious heads. At this period it was not the fashion to wear so large a beard and hair so long; now a barber would only be surprised if a man gifted with such advantages should consent voluntarily to deprive himself of them. The Leghorn barber went to work without a single observation.

When the operation was concluded, and Edmond felt his chin was completely smooth, and his hair reduced to its usual length, he requested a looking-glass in which he might see himself. He was now, as we have said, three-and-thirty years of age, and his fourteen years' imprisonment had produced a great change in his appearance.

Dantès had entered the Château d'If with the round, open, smiling face of a young and happy man, with whom the early paths of life have been smooth, and who relies on the future as a natural deduction of the past. This was now all changed.

His oval face was lengthened, his smiling mouth had assumed the firm and marked lines which betoken resolution; his eyebrows were arched beneath a large and thoughtful wrinkle; his eyes were full of melancholy, and from their depths occasionally sparkled gloomy fires of misanthropy and hatred; his complexion, so long kept from the sun, had now that pale colour which produces, when the features are encircled with black hair, the aristocratic beauty of the men of the north; the deep learning he had acquired had besides diffused over his features the rays of extreme intellect; and he had also acquired, although previously a tall man, that vigour which a frame possesses which has so long concentrated all its force within itself.

To the elegance of a nervous and slight form had succeeded the solidity of a rounded and muscular figure. As to his voice, prayers, sobs, and imprecations had changed it now into a soft and singularly touching tone, and now into a sound rude and almost hoarse. Moreover, being perpetually in twilight or darkness, his eyes had acquired that singular faculty of distinguishing objects in the night common to the hyena and the wolf.

Edmond smiled when he beheld himself: it was impossible that his best friend—if, indeed, he had any friend left—could recognise him; he could not recognise himself.

The master of *The Young Amelia*, who was very desirous of retaining amongst his crew a man of Edmond's value, had offered to him some advances out of his future profits, which Edmond had accepted. His next care on leaving the barber's who had achieved his first metamorphosis, was to enter a shop and buy a complete sailor's suit, a garb, as we all know, very simple, and consisting of white trousers, a striped shirt, and a cap.

It was in this costume, and bringing back to Jacopo the shirt and trousers he had lent him, that Edmond reappeared before the patron of *The Young Amelia*, who had made him tell his story over and over again before he could believe him, or recognise in the neat and trim sailor the man with thick and matted beard, his hair tangled with seaweed, and his body soaking in sea-brine, whom he had picked up naked and nearly drowned.

Attracted by his prepossessing appearance, he renewed his offers of an engagement to Dantès; but Dantès, who had his own projects, would not agree for a longer time than three months. *The Young Amelia* had a very active crew, very obedient to their captain, who lost as little time as possible. He had scarcely been a week at Leghorn before the hold of his vessel was filled with painted muslins, prohibited cottons, English powder, and tobacco on which the Crown had forgotten to put its mark. The master was to get all this out of Leghorn free of duties, and land it on the shores of Corsica, where certain speculators undertook to forward the cargo to France.

They sailed; Edmond was again cleaving the azure sea which had been the first horizon of his youth, and which he had so often dreamed of in prison. He left Gorgone on his right and La Pianosa on his left, and went towards the country of Paoli and Napoleon.

The next morning going on deck, which he always did at an early hour, the patron found Dantès leaning against the bulwarks gazing with intense earnestness at a pile of granite rocks, which the rising sun tinged with rosy light. It was the isle of Monte Cristo.

The Young Amelia left it three-quarters of a league to the larboard, and kept on for Corsica.

Dantès thought, as they passed thus closely the island whose name was so interesting to him, that he had only to leap into the sea and in half an hour he would be on the promised land. But then what could he do without instruments to discover his treasure, without arms to defend himself? Besides, what would the sailors say? What would the patron think? He must wait.

Fortunately, Dantès had learned how to wait; he had waited fourteen years for his liberty, and now he was free he could wait at least six months or a year for wealth.

Would he not have accepted liberty without riches if it had been offered to him?

Besides, were not these riches chimerical?—offspring of the brain of the poor Abbé Faria, had they not died with him?

It is true, this letter of the Cardinal Spada was singularly circumstantial, and Dantès repeated to himself, from one end to the other, the letter of which he had not forgotten a word.

The evening came on, and Edmond saw the island covered with every tint that twilight brings with it, and disappear in the darkness from all eyes; but he, with his gaze accustomed to the gloom of a prison, continued to see it after all the others, for he remained last upon deck.

The next morn broke off the coast of Aleria; all day they coasted, and in the evening saw the fires lighted on land; when they were extinguished, they no doubt recognised the signals for landing, for a ship's lantern was hung up at the mast-head instead of the streamer, and they neared the shore within gunshot.

Dantès remarked that at this time, too, the patron of *The Young Amelia* had, as he neared the land, mounted two small culverines, which, without making much noise, can throw a ball, of four to the pound, a thousand paces or so.

But on this occasion the precaution was superfluous, and everything proceeded with the utmost smoothness and politeness. Four shallops came off with very little noise alongside the bark, which, no doubt, in acknowledgment of the compliment, lowered her own shallop into the sea, and the five boats worked so well that by two o'clock in the morning all the cargo was out of *The Young Amelia* and on *terra firma*.

The same night, such a man of regularity was the patron of *The Young Amelia* that the profits were shared out, and each man had a hundred Tuscan livres, or about three guineas English.

But the voyage was not ended. They turned the bowsprit towards Sardinia, where they intended to take in a cargo which was to replace what had been discharged.

The second operation was as successful as the first, *The Young Amelia* was in luck.

This new cargo was destined for the coast of the Duchy of Lucca, and consisted almost entirely of Havana cigars, sherry, and Malaga wines.

There they had a bit of a skirmish in getting rid of the duties; the *gabelle**was, in truth, the everlasting enemy of the patron of *The Young Amelia*. A custom-house officer was laid low, and two sailors were wounded; Dantès was one of the latter, a ball having touched him in the left shoulder.

Dantès was almost glad of this affray and, almost pleased at being wounded, for they were rude lessons which taught him with what eye he could view danger, and with what endurance he could bear suffering. He had contemplated danger with a smile, and when wounded had exclaimed with the great philosopher, " Pain, thou art not an evil."

He had, moreover, looked upon the custom-house officer wounded to death; and, whether from heat of blood produced by the rencontre, or the chill of human sentiment, this sight had made but slight impression upon him; Dantès was on the way he desired to follow, and was moving towards the end he wished to achieve: his heart was in a fair way of petrifying in his bosom. Jacopo, seeing him fall, had believed him killed, and rushing towards him, raised him up, and then attended to him with all the kindness of an attached comrade.

This world was not then so good as Voltaire's Doctor Pangloss* believed it, neither was it so wicked as Dantès thought it, since this man who had nothing to expect from his comrade but the inheritance of his share of the prize-money, testified so much sorrow when he saw him fall.

Fortunately, as we have said, Edmond was only wounded, and with certain herbs gathered at certain seasons and sold to the smugglers by the old Sardinian women, the wound soon closed. Edmond then resolved to try Jacopo, and offered him in return for his attention a share of his prize-money, but Jacopo refused it indignantly.

It resulted, therefore, from this kind of sympathetic devotion which Jacopo had bestowed on Edmond from the first time he saw him, that Edmond felt for Jacopo a certain degree of affection. But this sufficed for Jacopo, who already instinctively felt that Edmond had a right to superiority of position—a superiority which Edmond had concealed from all others. And from this time the kindness which Edmond showed him was enough for the brave seaman.

Then in the long days on board ship, when the vessel, gliding on with security over the azure sea, required nothing, thanks to the favourable wind that swelled her sails, but the hand of the helmsman, Edmond, with a chart in his hand, became the instructor of Jacopo, as the poor Abbé Faria had been his tutor. He pointed out to him the bearings of the coast, explained to him the variations of the compass, and taught him to read in that vast book opened over our heads which they call heaven, and where God writes in azure with letters of diamonds. And when Jacopo inquired of him, " What is the use of teaching all these things to a poor sailor like me? " Edmond replied:

" Who knows? you may one day be the captain of a vessel; your fellow-countryman, Bonaparte, became Emperor."

We had forgotten to say that Jacopo was a Corsican.

Two months and a half elapsed in these trips, and Edmond had become as skilful a coaster as he had been a hardy seaman; he had formed an acquaintance with all the smugglers on the coast, and learned all the masonic signs by which these half pirates recognise each other. He had passed and repassed his isle of Monte Cristo twenty times, but not once had he found an opportunity of landing there.

He then formed a resolution. This was, as soon as his engagement with the patron of *The Young Amelia* ended, he would hire a small bark on his own account (for in his several voyages he had amassed a hundred piastres), and under some pretext land at the isle of Monte Cristo.

Then he would be free to make his researches, not perhaps entirely at liberty, for he would be doubtless watched by those who accompanied him. But in this world we must risk something.

Prison had made Edmond prudent, and he was desirous of running no risk whatever.

But in vain did he rack his imagination; fertile as it was, he could not devise any plan for reaching the wished-for isle without being accompanied thither.

Dantès was tossed about on these doubts and wishes, when the patron who had great confidence in him, and was very desirous of retaining him in his service, took him by the arm one evening and led him to a tavern on the Via del' Oglio, where the leading smugglers of Leghorn used to congregate.

It was here they discussed the affairs of the coast. Already Dantès had visited this maritime Bourse two or three times, and seeing all these hardy free-traders, who supplied the whole coast for nearly two hundred leagues in extent, he had asked himself what power might not that man attain who should give the impulse of his will to all these contrary and diverging links.

This time it was a great matter that was under discussion.

connected with a vessel laden with Turkey carpets, stuffs of the Levant, and cashmeres. It was requisite to find some neutral ground on which an exchange could be made, and then to try and land these goods on the coast of France.

If successful the profit would be enormous, there would be a gain of fifty or sixty piastres each for the crew.

The patron of *The Young Amelia* proposed as a place of landing the isle of Monte Cristo, which being completely deserted, and having neither soldiers nor revenue officers, seemed to have been placed in the midst of the ocean since the time of the heathen Olympus by Mercury, the god of merchants and robbers, classes which we in modern times have separated if not made distinct, but which antiquity appears to have included in the same category.

At the mention of Monte Cristo Dantès started with joy, he rose to conceal his emotion, and took a turn round the smoky tavern, where all the languages of the known world were jumbled in a *lingua franca*. When he again joined the two persons who had been discussing, it had been decided that they should touch at Monte Cristo, and set out on the following night.

Edmond, being consulted, was of opinion that the island offered every possible security, and that great enterprises to be well done, should be done quickly. Nothing then was altered in the plan arranged, and orders were given to get under weigh next night, and, wind and weather permitting, to gain the day after, the waters of the neutral isle.

23

The Isle of Monte Cristo

Thus at length, by one of those unexpected strokes of fortune which sometimes occur to those on whom an evil destiny has for a long time spent itself, Dantès was about to arrive at his wished-for opportunity by simple and natural means, and land in the island without incurring any suspicion. Only one night lay between him and his longed-for departure.

This night was one of the most feverish that Dantès had ever passed, and during its progress all the chances lucky and unlucky passed through his brain. If he closed his eyes, he saw the letters of Cardinal Spada written on the wall in characters of flame; if he slept for a moment, the wildest dreams haunted his brain. He descended into grottos paved with emeralds, with panels of rubies, and the roof glowing with diamond stalactites. Pearls fell drop by drop, as subterranean waters filter in their caves. Edmond, amazed, wonderstruck, filled his pockets with the radiant gems and then returned to daylight, when he discovered that his prizes were all converted into common pebbles. He then endeavoured to re-enter these marvellous grottos, but then beheld them only in the distance; and now the way serpentined into countless paths, and then the entrance became invisible, and in vain did he tax his memory for the magic and mysterious word which opened the splendid caverns of Ali Baba to the Arabian fisherman. All was useless, the treasure disappeared, and had again reverted to the genii from whom for a moment he had hoped to carry it off.

The day came at length, and was almost as feverish as the night had been; but it brought reason to aid his imagination, and Dantès was then enabled to arrange a plan which had hitherto been vague and unsettled in his brain.

Night came, and with it the preparation for departure, and these preparations served to conceal Dantès' agitation. He had by degrees assumed such authority over his companions that he was almost like a commander on board; and as his orders were always clear, distinct, and easy of execution, his comrades obeyed him with celerity and pleasure.

The old patron did not interfere, for he, too, had recognised the superiority of Dantès over the crew and himself. He saw in 'the young man his natural successor, and regretted that he had not a daughter that he might have bound Edmond to him by a distinguished alliance.

At seven o'clock in the evening all was ready, and at ten minutes past seven they doubled the lighthouse just as the beacon was kindled.

The sea was calm, and with a fresh breeze from the south-east they sailed beneath a bright blue sky, in which God also lighted up in turn his beacon lights, each of which is a world. Dantès told them that all hands might turn in and he would take the helm.

When the Maltese (for so they called Dantès) had said this it was sufficient, and all went to their cots contentedly. This frequently happened. Dantès, rejected by all the world, frequently experienced a desire for solitude, and what solitude is at the same time more complete, more poetical, than that of a bark floating isolated on the sea during the obscurity of the night, in the silence of immensity and under the eye of Heaven?

Now this solitude was peopled with his thoughts, the night lighted up by his illusions, and the silence animated by his anticipations. When the patron awoke, the vessel was hurrying on with every sail set, and every sail full with the breeze. They were making nearly ten knots an hour.

The isle of Monte Cristo loomed large in the horizon.

Edmond resigned the bark to the master's care, and went and lay down in his hammock, but in spite of a sleepless night he could not close his eyes for a moment.

Two hours afterwards he came on deck as the boat was about to double the isle of Elba. They were just abreast of Mareciana, and beyond the flat but verdant isle of La Pianosa. The peak of Monte Cristo, reddened by the burning sun, was seen against the azure sky.

Dantès desired the helmsman to put down his helm in order to leave La Pianosa on the right hand, as he knew that he should thus decrease the distance by two or three knots.

About five o'clock in the evening the island was quite distinct, and everything on it was plainly perceptible, owing to that clearness of the atmosphere which is peculiar to the light which the rays of the sun cast at its setting.

Edmond gazed most earnestly at the mass of rocks which gave out all the variety of twilight colours from the brightest pink to the deepest blue, and from time to time his cheeks flushed, his brow became purple, and a mist passed over his eyes.

Never did gamester whose whole fortune is staked on one cast of the die, experience the anguish which Edmond felt in his paroxysms of hope. Night came, and at ten o'clock p.m. they anchored. *The Young Amelia* was the first at the rendezvous.

In spite of his usual command over himself, Dantès could not restrain his impetuosity. He was the first who jumped on shore, and had he dared he would, like Lucius Brutus,* have " kissed his mother earth." It was dark, but at eleven o'clock the moon rose in the midst of the ocean, whose every wave she silvered, and then, " ascending high," played in floods of pale light on the rocky hills of this second Pelion.

The island was familiar to the crew of *The Young Amelia*; it was one of her halting-places. As to Dantès, he had passed it on his voyages to and from the Levant, but never touched at it.

He questioned Jacopo. " Where shall we pass the night? " he inquired.

" Why, on board the tartane," replied the sailor.

" Should we not be better in the grottos? "

" What grottos? "

" Why, the grottos—caves of the island."

" I do not know of any grottos," replied Jacopo.

A cold damp sprang to Dantès' brow.

" What! are there no grottos at Monte Cristo? " he asked.

" None."

For a moment Dantès was speechless, then he remembered that these caves might have been filled up by some accident, or even stopped up for the sake of greater security by Cardinal Spada.

The point was then to discover the lost opening. It was useless to search at night, and Dantès therefore delayed all investigation until the morning. Besides, a signal made half a league out at sea, and to which *The Young Amelia* also replied by a similar signal, indicated that the moment was arrived for business.

The boat that now arrived, assured by the answering signal that all was right, soon came in sight, white and silent as a phantom, and cast anchor within a cable's length of the shore.

Then the landing began. Dantès reflected, as he worked, on the shout of joy which with a single word he could produce from amongst all these men if he gave utterance to the one unchanging thought that pervaded his heart. But, far from disclosing this precious secret, he almost feared that he had already said too much, and by his restlessness and continual questions, his minute observations and evident preoccupation, had aroused suspicions. Fortunately, as regarded this circumstance, at least, with him the painful past reflected on his countenance an indelible sadness, and the glimmerings of gaiety seen beneath this cloud were indeed but transitory.

No one had the slightest suspicion; and when next day, taking a fowling-piece, powder, and shot, Dantès testified a desire to go and kill some of the wild goats that were seen springing from rock to rock, his wish was construed into a love of sport or a desire for solitude. However, Jacopo insisted on following him, and Dantès did not oppose this, fearing if he did so that he might incur distrust. Scarcely, however, had he gone a quarter of a league than, having killed a kid, he begged Jacopo to take it to his comrades and request them to cook it, and when ready to let him know by firing a gun. This, and some dried fruits, and a flask of the wine of Monte Pulciano, was the bill of fare.

Dantès went forwards, looking behind and round about him from time to time. Having reached the summit of a rock, he saw, a thousand feet beneath him, his companions, whom Jacopo had rejoined, and who were all busy preparing the repast, which Edmond's skill as a marksman had augmented with a capital dish.

Edmond looked at them for a moment with the sad and soft smile of a man superior to his fellows.

" In two hours' time," said he, " these persons will depart richer by fifty piastres each to go and risk their lives again by endeavouring to gain fifty more such pieces. Then they will return with a fortune of six hundred francs and waste this treasure in some city with the pride of sultans and the insolence of nabobs. At this moment Hope makes me despise their riches, which seem to me contemptible. Yet, perchance to-morrow deception will so act on me that I shall, on compulsion, consider such a contemptible possession as the utmost happiness. Oh, no! " exclaimed Edmond, " that will not be. The wise, unerring Faria could not be mistaken in this one thing. Besides it were better to die than to continue to lead this low and wretched life."

Thus Dantès, who but three months before had no desire but liberty, had now not liberty enough, and panted for wealth. The cause was not in Dantès but in Providence, who, whilst limiting the power of man, has filled him with boundless desires.

Meanwhile, by a way between two walls of rock, following a path worn by a torrent, and which, in all human probability, human foot had never before trod, Dantès approached the spot where he supposed the grottos must have existed. Keeping along the coast, and examining the smallest object with serious attention, he thought he could trace on certain rocks marks made by the hand of man.

Time, which encrusts all physical substances with its mossy mantle, as it invests all things moral with its mantle of forgetfulness, seemed to have respected these signs, traced with a certain regularity, and probably with the design of leaving traces. Occasion-, ally these marks disappeared beneath tufts of myrtle, which spread into large bushes laden with blossoms, or beneath parasitical lichen. It was thus requisite that Edmond should remove branches on one side or remove the mosses in order to retrace the indicating marks which were to be his guides in this labyrinth. These signs had renewed the best hopes in Edmond's mind. Why should not the cardinal have traced them, to serve as a guide to his nephew in the event of an unforeseen catastrophe? This solitary place was precisely suited for a man desirous of burying a treasure. Only, might not these betraying marks have attracted other eyes than those for whom they were made? and had the dark and wondrous isle indeed faithfully guarded its precious secret?

It seemed, however, to Edmond, who was hidden from his comrades by the inequalities of the ground, that at sixty paces from the harbour the marks ceased; nor did they terminate at any grotto. A large round rock, placed solidly on its base, was the only spot to which they seemed to lead. Edmond reflected that perhaps instead of having reached the end he might only have touched on the beginning, and he therefore turned round and retraced his steps.

During this time his comrades had prepared the repast, had got some water from a spring, spread out the fruit and bread, and cooked the kid. Just at the moment when they were taking the dainty animal from the spit, they saw Edmond, who, light and daring as a chamois, was springing from rock to rock, and they fired the signal agreed upon. The sportsman instantly changed his direction, and ran quickly towards them. But at the moment when they were all following with their eyes his agile bounds with a rashness which gave them alarm, Edmond's foot slipped, and they saw him stagger on the edge of a rock and disappear. They all rushed towards him, for all loved Edmond in spite of his superiority; yet Jacopo reached him first.

He found Edmond stretched bleeding and almost senseless. He had rolled down a height of twelve or fifteen feet. They poured some drops of rum down his throat, and this remedy, which had before been so beneficial to him, produced the same effect as formerly. Edmond opened his eyes, complained of great pain in his knee, a feeling of heaviness in his head, and severe pains in his loins. They wished to carry him to the shore, but when they touched him, although under Jacopo's directions, he declared, with heavy groans, that he could not bear to be moved.

It may be supposed that Dantès did not now think of his dinner; but he insisted that his comrades, who had not his reasons for fasting, should have their meal. As for himself, he declared that he had only need of a little rest, and that when they returned he should be easier. The sailors did not require much urging. They were hungry, and the smell of the roasted kid was very savoury, and your tars are not very ceremonious. An hour afterwards they returned. All that Edmond had been able to do was to drag himself about a dozen paces forward to lean against a moss-grown rock.

But, far from being easier, Dantès' pains had appeared to increase in violence. The old patron, who was obliged to sail in the morning in order to land his cargo on the frontiers of Piedmont and France, between Nice and Frejus, urged Dantès to try and rise. Edmond made great exertions in order to comply; but at each effort he fell back, moaning and turning pale.

" He has broken his ribs," said the commander, in a low voice. " No matter; he is an excellent fellow, and we must not leave him. We will try and carry him on board the tartane."

Dantès declared, however, that he would rather die where he was than undergo the agony caused by the slightest movement he made.

" Well," said the patron, " let what may happen, it shall never be said that we deserted a good comrade like you. We will not go till evening."

This very much astonished the sailors, although not one opposed it. The patron was so strict that this was the first time they had ever seen him give up an enterprise, or even delay an arrangement.

Dantès would not allow that any such infraction of regular and proper rules should be made in his favour.

" No, no," he said to the patron, " I was awkward, and it is just that I pay the penalty of my clumsiness. Leave me a small supply of biscuit, a gun, powder, and balls, to kill the kids or defend myself at need, and a pickaxe, to build me something like a shed if you delay in coming back for me."

" But you'll die of hunger," said the patron.

" I would rather do so," was Edmond's reply, " than suffer the inexpressible agonies which the slightest motion brings on."

The patron turned towards his vessel, which was undulating in the small harbour, and, with her sails partly set, was ready for sea when all her toilette should be completed.

" What are we to do, Maltese? " asked the captain. " We cannot leave you here so, and yet we cannot stay."

" Go, go! " exclaimed Dantès.

" We shall be absent at least a week," said the patron, " and then we must run out of our course to come here and take you up again."

"Why," said Dantès, "if in two or three days you hail any fishing-boats, desire them to come here to me. I will pay twenty-five piastres for my passage back to Leghorn. If you do not come across one, return for me."

The patron shook his head.

"Listen, Captain Baldi; there's one way of settling this," said Jacopo. "Do you go, and I will stay and take care of the wounded man."

"And give up your share of the venture," said Edmond, "to remain with me?"

"Yes," said Jacopo, "and without any hesitation."

"You are a good fellow and a kind-hearted mess-mate," replied Edmond, "and Heaven will recompense you for your generous intentions; but I do not wish any one to stay with me. A day or two's rest will set me up, and I hope I shall find amongst the rocks certain herbs most excellent for contusions."

A singular smile passed over Dantès' lips; he squeezed Jacopo's hand warmly; but nothing could shake his determination to remain—and remain alone.

The smugglers left with Edmond what he had requested, and set sail; but not without turning about several times, and each time making signs of a cordial leave-taking, to which Edmond replied with his hand only, as if he could not move the rest of his body.

Then, when they had disappeared, he said with a smile:

"'Tis strange that it should be amongst such men that we find proofs of friendship and devotion."

Then he dragged himself cautiously to the top of a rock, from which he had a full view of the sea, and thence he saw the tartane complete her preparations for sailing, weigh anchor, and, balancing herself as gracefully as a water-fowl ere it takes to the wing, set sail. At the end of an hour she was completely out of sight; at least, it was impossible for the wounded man to see her any longer from the spot where he was.

Then Dantès rose more agile and light than the kid amongst the myrtles and shrubs of these wild rocks, took his gun in one hand, his pickaxe in the other, and hastened towards the rock on which the marks he had noted terminated.

"And now," he exclaimed, remembering the tale of the Arabian fisherman, which Faria had related to him,—"now, open sesame!"

24

The Search

THE sun had nearly reached the meridian, and his scorching rays fell full on the rocks, which seemed themselves sensible of the heat. Thousands of grasshoppers, hidden in the bushes, chirped with a monotonous and dull note; the leaves of the myrtle and olive-trees waved and rustled in the wind. At every step that Edmond took he disturbed the lizards glittering with the hues of the emerald: afar off he saw the wild goats bounding from crag to crag. In a word, the isle was inhabited, yet Edmond felt himself alone, guided by the hand of God. He felt an indescribable sensation somewhat akin to dread,—that dread of the daylight which even in the desert makes us fear we are watched and observed.

This feeling was so strong, that at the moment when Edmond was about to commence his labour, he stopped, laid down his pickaxe, seized his gun, mounted to the summit of the highest rock, and from thence gazed round in every direction.

But it was not upon Corsica, the very houses of which he could distinguish; nor on Sardinia; nor on the isle of Elba, with its historical associations; nor upon the almost imperceptible line that to the experienced eye of a sailor alone revealed the coast of Genoa the proud, and Leghorn the commercial, that he gazed. It was at the brigantine that had left in the morning, and the tartane that had just set sail, that Edmond fixed his eyes. The first was just disappearing in the straits of Bonifacio; the other, following an opposite direction, was about to round the island of Corsica. This sight reassured him. He then looked at the objects near him. He saw himself on the highest point of the isle, a statue on this vast pedestal of granite, nothing human appearing in sight, whilst the blue ocean beat against the base of the island, and covered it with a fringe of foam. Then he descended with cautious and slow step, for he dreaded lest an accident similar to that he had so adroitly feigned should happen in reality.

Dantès, as we have said, had traced back the marks in the rock and he had noticed that they led to a small creek, hidden like the bath of some ancient nymph. This creek was sufficiently wide at its mouth, and deep in the centre, to admit of the entrance of a small vessel of the speronare class,* which would be perfectly concealed from observation.

Then following the clue that, in the hands of the Abbé Faria, had been so skilfully used to guide him through the Dædalian labyrinth of probabilities, he thought that the Cardinal Spada, anxious not to be watched, had entered the creek, concealed his little bark, followed the line marked by the notches in the rock, and at the end of it had buried his treasure. It was this idea that had brought Dantès back to the circular rock. One thing only perplexed Edmond, and destroyed his theory. How could this rock, which weighed several tons, have been lifted to this spot without the aid of many men? Suddenly an idea flashed across his mind. Instead of raising it, thought he, they have lowered it. And he sprang from the rock in order to inspect the base on which it had formerly stood.

He soon perceived that a slope had been formed; and the rock had slid along this until it stopped at the spot it now occupied. A large stone had served as a wedge; flints and pebbles had been inserted around it, so as to conceal the orifice: this species of masonry had been covered with earth, and grass and weeds had grown there: moss had clung to the stones, myrtle-bushes had taken root, and the old rock seemed fixed to the earth.

Dantès raised the earth carefully, and detected, or fancied he detected, the ingenious artifice. He attacked this wall, cemented by the hand of Time, with his pickaxe. After ten minutes' labour the wall gave way, and a hole large enough to insert the arm was opened. Dantès went and cut the strongest olive-tree he could find, stripped off its branches, inserted it in the hole, and used it as a lever. But the rock was too heavy, and too firmly wedged, to be moved by any one man, were he Hercules himself. Dantès reflected that he must attack this wedge. But how? He cast his eyes around and saw the horn full of powder, which his friend, Jacopo, had left him. He smiled; the infernal invention would serve him for this purpose. With the aid of his pickaxe, Dantès dug between the upper rock and the one that supported it a mine similar to those formed by pioneers when they wish to spare human labour, filled it with powder, then made a match by rolling his handkerchief in saltpetre. He lighted it and retired.

The explosion was instantaneous: the upper rock was lifted from its base by the terrific force of the powder; the lower one flew into pieces; thousands of insects escaped from the aperture Dantès had previously formed, and a huge snake, like the guardian demon of the treasure, rolled himself along with a sinuous motion, and disappeared.

Dantès approached the upper rock, which now, without any

support, leant towards the sea. The intrepid treasure-seeker walked round it, and selecting the spot from whence it appeared most easy to attack it, placed his lever in one of the crevices, and strained every nerve to move the mass.

The rock, already shaken by the explosion, tottered on its base. Dantès redoubled his efforts; he seemed like one of the ancient Titans, who uprooted the mountains to hurl against the father of the gods. The rock yielded, rolled, bounded, and finally disappeared in the ocean.

On the spot it had occupied, was visible a circular place, and which exposed an iron ring let into a square flagstone. Dantès uttered a cry of joy and surprise; never had a first attempt been crowned with more perfect success. He would fain have continued, but his knees trembled, his heart beat so violently, and his eyes became so dim, that he was forced to pause. This feeling lasted but for a moment. Edmond inserted his lever in the ring, and exerting all his strength, the flagstone yielded, and disclosed a kind of stair that descended until it was lost in the obscurity of a subterraneous grotto. Any one else would have rushed on with a cry of joy. Dantès turned pale, hesitated, and reflected.

"Come," said he to himself, "be a man. I am accustomed to adversity. I must not be cast down by the discovery that I have been deceived. What then, would be the use of all I have suffered? The heart breaks when, after having been elated by flattering hopes, it sees all these illusions destroyed. Faria has dreamed this; the Cardinal Spada buried no treasures here; perhaps he never came here, or if he did, Cæsar Borgia, the intrepid adventurer, the stealthy and indefatigable plunderer, has followed him, discovered his traces, pursued them as I have done, like me, raised the stone, and descending before me has left me nothing." He remained motionless and pensive, his eyes fixed on the sombre aperture that was open at his feet.

"Now that I expect nothing, now that I no longer entertain the slightest hopes, the end of this adventure becomes a simple matter of curiosity."

And he remained again motionless and thoughtful.

"Yes, yes, this is an adventure worthy of a place in the lights and shades of the life of this royal bandit. This fabulous event has formed but a link of a vast chain. Yes, Borgia has been here, a torch in one hand, a sword in the other, whilst within twenty paces, at the foot of this rock, perhaps, two guards kept watch on land and sea, whilst their masters descended as I am about to descend, dispelling the darkness before his terrible advance."

"But what was the fate of these guards who thus possessed his secret?" asked Dantès of himself.

"The fate," replied he, smiling, "of those who buried Alaric." *

"Yet, had he come," thought Dantès, "he would have found the treasure; and Borgia, he who compared Italy to an artichoke, which he could devour leaf by leaf, knew too well the value of time to waste it in replacing this rock."

"I will go down."

Then he descended; a smile on his lips, and murmuring that last word of human philosophy, "Perhaps!" But instead of the darkness, and the thick and mephitic atmosphere he had expected to find, Dantès saw a dim and bluish light, which, as well as the air, entered, not merely by the aperture he had just formed, but by the interstices and crevices of the rock which were visible from without, and through which he could distinguish the blue sky and the waving branches of the evergreen oaks, and the tendrils of the creepers that grew from the rocks.

After having stood a few minutes in the cavern, the atmosphere of which was rather warm than damp, Dantès' eye, habituated as it was to darkness, could pierce even to the remotest angles of the cavern, which was of granite that sparkled like diamonds.

"Alas!" said Edmond, smiling, "these are the treasures the cardinal has left; and the good abbé, seeing in a dream these glittering walls, has indulged in fallacious hopes."

But he called to mind the words of the will which he knew by heart: "In the farthest angle of the second opening," said the cardinal's will. He had only found the first grotto, he had now to seek the second.

Dantès commenced his search. He reflected that this second grotto must, doubtless, penetrate deeper into the isle; he examined the stones, and sounded one part of the wall where he fancied the opening existed, masked for precaution's sake.

The pickaxe sounded for a moment with a dull sound that covered Dantès' forehead with large drops of perspiration. At last it seemed to him that one part of the wall gave forth a more hollow and deeper echo; he eagerly advanced, and with the quickness of perception that no one but a prisoner possesses, saw that it was there, in all probability, the opening must be.

However, he, like Cæsar Borgia, knew the value of time; and, in order to avoid a fruitless toil, he sounded all the other walls with his pickaxe, struck the earth with the butt of his gun, and finding nothing that appeared suspicious, returned to that part of the wall whence issued the consoling sound he had before heard.

He again struck it, and with greater force.

Then a singular sight presented itself. As he struck the wall a species of stucco, similar to that used as the ground of arabesques, detached itself and fell to the ground in flakes, exposing a large white stone. The aperture of the rock had been closed with stones, then this stucco had been applied, and painted to imitate granite.

Dantès struck with the sharp end of his pickaxe, which entered some way between the interstices of the stone. It was there he must dig. But by some strange phenomenon of the human organisation, in proportion as the proofs that Faria had not been deceived became stronger, so did his heart give way, and a feeling of discouragement steal over him. This last proof, instead of giving him fresh strength, deprived him of it; the pickaxe descended, or rather fell; he placed it on the ground, passed his hand over his brow, and remounted the stairs, alleging to himself, as an excuse, a desire to be assured that no one was watching him, but in reality because he felt he was ready to faint. The isle was deserted, and the sun seemed to cover it with its fiery glance; afar off a few small fishing-boats studded the bosom of the blue ocean.

Dantès had tasted nothing, but he thought not of hunger at such a moment; he hastily swallowed a few drops of rum, and again entered the cavern. The pickaxe that had seemed so heavy, was now like a feather in his grasp; he seized it, and again attacked the wall. After several blows he perceived that the stones were not cemented, but merely placed one upon the other, and covered with stucco; he inserted the point of his pickaxe, and using the handle as a lever, soon saw with joy the stone turn as if on hinges, and fall at his feet. He had nothing more to do now, but with the iron tooth of the pickaxe to draw the stones towards him one by one. The first aperture was sufficiently large to enter, but by waiting, he could still cling to hope, and retard the certainty of deception.

At last after fresh hesitation, Dantès entered the second grotto. The second grotto was lower and more gloomy than the former; the air that could only enter by the newly-formed opening had that mephitic smell Dantès was surprised not to find in the first. He waited in order to allow pure air to displace the foul atmosphere, and then entered. At the left of the opening was a dark and deep angle. But to Dantès' eye there was no darkness. He glanced round this second grotto; it was, like the first, empty.

The treasure, if it existed, was buried in this corner. The time had at length arrived; two feet of earth removed, and Dantès' fate would be decided. He advanced towards the angle, and summoning all his resolution, attacked the ground with the pickaxe. At the fifth or sixth blow the pickaxe struck against an iron substance. Never did funeral knell, never did alarm-bell produce a greater effect on the hearer. Had Dantès found nothing, he could not have become more ghastly pale. He again struck his pickaxe into the earth, and encountered the same resistance, but not the same sound.

" It is a casket of wood bound with iron," thought he.

At this moment a shadow passed rapidly before the opening; Dantès seized his gun, sprang through the opening, and mounted the stair. A wild goat had passed before the mouth of the cave, and was feeding at a little distance.

This would have been a favourable occasion to secure his dinner; but Dantès feared lest the report of his gun should attract attention.

He reflected an instant, cut a branch of a resinous tree, lighted it at the fire at which the smugglers had prepared their breakfast, and descended with this torch. He wished to see all. He approached the hole he had formed with the torch, and saw that his pickaxe had in reality struck against iron and wood. He planted his torch in the ground and resumed his labour. In an instant a space three feet long by two feet broad was cleared, and Dantès could see an oaken coffer, bound with cut steel; in the midst of the lid he saw engraved on a silver plate which was still untarnished, the arms of the Spada family—viz., a sword, *pale*, on an oval shield, like all the Italian armorial bearings, and surmounted by a cardinal's hat; Dantès easily recognised them, Faria had so often drawn them for him. There was no longer any doubt the treasure was there; no one would have been at such pains to conceal an empty casket.

In an instant he had cleared every obstacle away, and he saw successively the lock, placed between two padlocks, and the two handles at each end, all carved as things were carved at that epoch, when art rendered the commonest metals precious. Dantès seized the handles, and strove to lift the coffer; it was impossible. He sought to open it; lock and padlock were closed; these faithful guardians seemed unwilling to surrender their trust. Dantès inserted the sharp end of the pickaxe between the coffer and the lid, and pressing with all his force on the handle, burst open the fastenings. The hinges yielded in their turn and fell, still holding in their grasp fragments of the planks, and all was open.

A vertigo seized Edmond; he cocked his gun and laid it beside him. He then closed his eyes as children do in order to perceive in shining night of their own imagination more stars than are visible in the firmament; then he reopened them, and stood motionless with amazement.

Three compartments divided the coffer. In the first, blazed piles of golden coin. In the second, bars of unpolished gold, which possessed nothing attractive save their value, were ranged. In the third, Edmond grasped handfuls of diamonds, pearls, and rubies, which, as they fell on one another, sounded like hail against glass.

After having touched, felt, examined these treasures, Edmond rushed through the caverns like a man seized with frenzy; he leapt on a rock, from whence he could behold the sea. He was alone. Alone with these countless, these unheard-of treasures! Was he awake, or was it but a dream?

He would fain have gazed upon his gold, and yet he had not strength enough; for an instant he leaned his head in his hands as if to prevent his senses from leaving him, and then rushed madly about the rocks of Monte Cristo, terrifying the wild goats and scaring the sea-fowls with his wild cries and gestures; then he returned, and still unable to believe the evidence of his senses, rushed into the grotto, and found himself before this mine of gold and jewels. This time he fell on his knees, and, clasping his hands convulsively, uttered a prayer intelligible to God alone. He soon felt himself calmer and more happy, for now only he began to credit his felicity.

He then set himself to work to count his fortune. There were a thousand ingots of gold, each weighing from two to three pounds; then he piled up twenty-five thousand crowns, each worth about four pounds sterling of our money, and bearing the effigies of Alexander VI and his predecessors; and he saw that the compartment was not half empty. And he measured ten double handfuls of precious stones, many of which, mounted by the most famous workmen, were valuable for their execution. Dantès saw the light gradually disappear; and fearing to be surprised in the cavern, left it, his gun in his hand. A piece of biscuit and a small quantity of rum formed his supper, and he snatched a few hours' sleep, lying over the mouth of the cave.

It was a night, at once joyous and terrible, such as this man of stupendous emotions had already experienced two or three times in his life.

25

At Marseilles again

DAYLIGHT, for which Dantès had so eagerly and impatiently
waited, again dawned upon the desert shores of Monte
Cristo. With the first dawn of day Dantès resumed his researches.
Again he climbed the rocky height he had ascended the previous
evening, and strained his view to catch every peculiarity of the
landscape; but it wore the same wild, barren aspect when seen
by the rays of the morning sun which it had done when surveyed
by the fading glimmer of eve. Returning to the entrance of the
cave, he raised the stone that covered it; and descending to the
place that contained the treasure, filled his pockets with precious
stones, put the box together as well and securely as he could,
sprinkled fresh sand over the spot from which it had been taken,
and then carefully trod down the ground to give it everywhere
a similar appearance; then quitting the grotto, he replaced the
stone, heaping on it broken masses of rocks and rough fragments
of crumbling granite, filling the interstices with earth, into which
was skilfully mingled a quantity of rapidly growing plants, such
as the wild myrtle and flowering thorn; then carefully watering
these new plantations, he scrupulously effaced every trace of
footmark, leaving the approach to the cavern as savage-looking
and untrodden as he had found it. This done he impatiently
awaited the return of his companions. To wait at Monte Cristo
for the purpose of watching over the almost incalculable riches
that had thus fallen into his possession satisfied not the cravings
of his heart, which yearned to return to dwell among mankind,
and to assume the rank, power, and influence unbounded wealth
alone can bestow.

On the sixth day the smugglers returned. From a distance
Dantès recognised the cut and manner of sailing of *The Young
Amelia*, and dragging himself with affected difficulty towards
the landing-place he met his companions with an assurance that,
although considerably better than when they quitted him, he
still suffered acutely from his late accident. He then inquired
how they had fared in their trip.

To this question the smugglers replied that, although successful
in landing their cargo in safety, they had scarcely done so, when
they received intelligence that a guardship had just quitted the

port of Toulon, and was crowding all sail towards them; this obliged them to make all the speed they could to evade the enemy; when they could but lament the absence of Dantès, whose superior skill in the management of a vessel would have availed them so materially. In fact, the chasing vessel had almost overtaken them, when, fortunately, night came on, and enabled them to double the Cape of Corsica, and so elude all further pursuit.

Upon the whole however, the trip had been sufficiently successful to satisfy all concerned; while the crew, and particularly Jacopo, expressed great regrets at Dantès not having been an equal sharer with themselves in the profits, amounting to no less a sum than fifty piastres each.

Edmond preserved the most admirable self-command, not suffering the faintest indication of a smile to escape him at the enumeration of all the benefits he would have reaped had he been able to quit the isle; but as *The Young Amelia* had merely come to Monte Cristo to fetch him away, he embarked that same evening, and proceeded with the captain to Leghorn. Arrived at Leghorn, he repaired to the house of a Jew, a dealer in precious stones, to whom he disposed of four of his smallest diamonds for five thousand francs each.

Dantès half feared that such valuable jewels in the hands of a poor sailor like himself might excite suspicion; but the cunning purchaser asked no troublesome questions concerning a bargain by which he gained at least four thousand francs.

The following day Dantès presented Jacopo with an entirely new vessel, accompanying the gift by a donation of one hundred piastres, that he might provide himself with a suitable crew and other requisites for his outfit, upon conditions of his going direct to Marseilles, for the purpose of inquiring after an old man named Louis Dantès, residing in the Allées de Meillan, and also a young female called Mercédès, an inhabitant of the Catalan village.

Jacopo could scarcely believe his senses at receiving this munificent present, which Dantès hastened to account for by saying that he had merely been a sailor from whim and a desire to spite his friends, who did not allow him as much money as he liked to spend; but that on his arrival at Leghorn, he had come into possession of a large fortune, left him by an uncle, whose sole heir he was. The superior education of Dantès gave an air of such extreme probability to this statement, that it never once occurred to Jacopo to doubt its accuracy.

The term for which Edmond had engaged to serve on board *The Young Amelia* having expired, Dantès took leave of the captain, who at first tried all his powers of persuasion to induce him to remain one of the crew, but having been told the history of the legacy he ceased to importune him further. The succeeding morning Jacopo set sail for Marseilles, with directions from Dantès to rejoin him at the island of Monte Cristo.

Having seen Jacopo fairly out of the harbour, Dantès proceeded to make his final adieus on board *The Young Amelia*. He distributed so liberal a gratuity among her crew as procured him unanimous good wishes and expressions of cordial interest in all that concerned him; to the captain he promised to write when he had made up his mind as to his future plans. This leave-taking over, Dantès departed for Genoa. At the moment of his arrival a small yacht was being tried in the bay; this yacht had been built by order of an Englishman, who, having heard that the Genoese excelled all other builders along the shores of the Mediterranean in the construction of fast-sailing vessels, was desirous of possessing a specimen of their skill. The price agreed upon between the Englishman and Genoese builder was forty thousand francs.

Dantès, struck with the beauty and capability of the little vessel, applied to its owner to transfer it to him, offering sixty thousand francs, upon condition of being allowed to take immediate possession of it. The proposal was too advantageous to be refused; the more so, as the person for whom the yacht was intended had gone upon a tour through Switzerland, and was not expected back in less than three weeks or a month, by which time the builder reckoned upon being able to complete another.

A bargain was therefore struck. Dantès led the owner of the yacht to the dwelling of a Jew; retired with the latter individual for a few minutes to a small back parlour, and upon their return the Jew counted out to the shipbuilder the sum of sixty thousand francs in bright golden money.

The delighted builder then offered his services in providing a suitable crew for the little vessel, but this Dantès declined, with many thanks; saying he was accustomed to cruise about quite alone, and his principal pleasure consisted in managing his yacht himself. The only thing the builder could oblige him in would be to contrive a sort of secret closet, in the cabin at his bed's head; the closet to contain three divisions, so constructed as to be concealed from all but himself. The builder cheerfully undertook the commission, and promised to have these secret places completed by the next day; Dantès furnishing the size and plan upon which he desired they should be arranged.

The following day Dantès sailed with his yacht from the port of Genoa, amid the gaze of an immense crowd drawn together by curiosity to see the rich Spanish nobleman who preferred managing his vessel himself; but their wonder was soon exchanged for admiration at the perfect skill with which Dantès handled the helm, and without quitting it, making his little vessel perform every movement he chose to direct. His bark seemed indeed animated with all but human intelligence, so promptly did it obey the slightest impulse given; and Dantès required but a short trial of his beautiful craft to acknowledge that it was not without truth the Genoese had attained their high reputation in the art of shipbuilding.

The spectators followed the little vessel with their eyes so long as it remained visible, they then turned their conjectures upon her probable destination; some insisted she was making for Corsica, others the Isle of Elba; bets were offered to any amount that she was bound for Spain; while Africa was positively reported by many persons as her intended course, but no one thought of Monte Cristo.

Yet, thither it was that Dantès guided his vessel, and at Monte Cristo he arrived at the close of the second day; his bark had proved herself a first-class sailer, and had come the distance from Genoa in thirty-five hours. Dantès had carefully noted the general appearance of the shore, and instead of landing at the usual place he dropped anchor in the little creek.

The isle was utterly deserted, nor did it seem as though human foot had trodden on it since he quitted it; his treasure was just as he had left it.

Early on the following morning he commenced the removal of his riches, and ere nightfall the whole of his immense wealth was safely deposited in the secret compartments of his hidden closet.

A week passed by. Dantès employed it in manœuvring his yacht round the island, studying it as a skilful horseman would the animal he destined for some important service, till at the end of that time he was perfectly conversant with its good and bad qualities. The former Dantès proposed to augment, the latter to remedy.

Upon the eighth day of his being on the island he discerned a small vessel crowding all sail towards Monte Cristo. As it neared, he recognised it as the bark he had given to Jacopo; he immediately signalled it; his signal was returned, and in two hours afterwards the bark lay at anchor beside the yacht.

A mournful answer awaited each of Edmond's eager inquiries as to the information Jacopo had obtained.

Old Dantès was dead, and Mercédès had disappeared.

Dantès listened to these melancholy tidings with outward calmness; but leaping lightly ashore, he signified his desire to be quite alone. In a couple of hours he returned. Two of the men from Jacopo's bark came on board the yacht to assist in navigating it, and he commanded she should be steered direct to Marseilles.

For his father's death he was in some manner prepared; but how to account for the mysterious disappearance of Mercédès he knew not.

Without divulging his secret, Dantès could not give sufficiently clear instructions to an agent—there were, besides, other particulars he was desirous of ascertaining, and those were of a nature he alone could investigate in a manner satisfactory to himself. His looking-glass had assured him during his stay at Leghorn that he ran no risk of recognition; added to which, he had now the means of adopting any disguise he thought proper. One fine morning, then, his yacht, followed by the little bark, boldly entered the port of Marseilles, and anchored exactly opposite the memorable spot, from whence, on the never-to-be-forgotten night of his departure for the Château d'If, he had been put on board the vessel destined to convey him thither.

Still Dantès could not view without a shudder the approach of a gendarme who accompanied the officers deputed to demand his bill of health, ere the yacht was permitted to hold communication with the shore; but with that perfect self-possession he had acquired during his acquaintance with Faria, Dantès coolly presented an English passport he had obtained from Leghorn, and with that prompt attention which all such English documents receive, he was informed there existed no obstacle to his immediate debarkation.

The first object that attracted the attention of Dantès as he landed on the Canebière was one of the crew belonging to the *Pharaon*. Edmond hailed the appearance of this man, who had served under himself, as a sure test of the safe and perfect change time had worked in his own appearance; going straight towards him, he commenced a variety of questions on different subjects, carefully watching the man's countenance as he did so. But not a word or look implied his having the slightest idea of ever having seen before the individual with whom he was then conversing.

Giving the sailor a piece of money in return for his civility, Dantès proceeded onwards; but ere he had gone many steps, he heard the man loudly calling him to stop. Dantès instantly turned to meet him.

" I beg your pardon, sir," said the honest fellow, in almost breathless haste; " but I believe you made a mistake; you intended to give me a two-franc piece, and see, you gave me a double Napoleon."

" Thank you, my good friend; I see that I made a trifling

mistake, as you say, but by way of rewarding your honest spirit, I give you another double Napoleon that you may drink to my health, and be able to ask your messmates to join you."

So extreme was the surprise of the sailor, that he was unable even to thank Edmond, whose receding figure he continued to gaze after in speechless astonishment; at length, when Dantès had wholly disappeared, he drew a deep breath, and with another look at his gold, he returned to the quay, saying to himself, " Ah! that's one of them nabob gentlemen from Ingy, no doubt: nobody else could afford to chuck gold about like that. Well! he said I was to drink to his health, and so I will with all my heart."

Dantès meanwhile continued his route; each step he trod oppressed his heart with fresh emotion. His first and most indelible recollections were there; not a tree, not a street that he passed but seemed filled with dear and cherished reminiscences. And thus he proceeded onwards till he arrived at the end of Rue de Noailles, whence a full view of the Allées de Meillan was obtained. At this spot, so pregnant with fond and filial remembrances, his heart beat almost to bursting, his knees tottered under him, a misty vapour floated over his sight, and had he not clung for support to one of the trees, he would inevitably have fallen to the ground, and been crushed beneath the many vehicles continually passing there. Recovering himself, however, he wiped the perspiration from his brows, and stopped not again till he found himself at the door of the house in which his father had lived.

The nasturtiums and other plants, which his parent had delighted to train before his window, had all disappeared from the upper part of the house. Leaning against a tree, he remained long gazing on those windows at which the busy hand of the active old man might be daily seen training and arranging his floral treasures. But Edmond remembered he had come thither for other reasons than to indulge a grief, now, alas! unavailing; and, stifling the deep sigh that rose to his lips, he advanced to the door and inquired whether there were any chambers to be let in the house; though answered in the negative, he begged so earnestly to be permitted to visit those on the fifth floor, that, in despite of the *concièrge's* oft-repeated assurance of their being occupied, Dantès succeeded in inducing the man to go up to the present possessors of these coveted rooms, and ask permission for a gentleman to be allowed to look at them. The tenants of the humble lodging, once the scene of all Dantès' early joys, consisted of a young couple who had been scarcely married a week, and the sight of a wedded happiness he was doomed never to experience, drove a bitter pang through his heart. Nothing in the two small chambers forming the apartments remained as it had been in the time of the elder Dantès; the very paper was different, while the articles of antiquated furniture with which the rooms had been filled in Edmond's time, had all disappeared. The four walls alone remained as he had left them. The bed belonging to the present occupants was placed as the former owner of the chamber had been accustomed to have his; and, spite of his efforts to prevent it, the eyes of Edmond were suffused in tears, as he reflected that on that spot his beloved parent had expired, vainly calling for his son. The young couple gazed with astonishment at the sight of their visitor's emotion, and wondered to see the large tears silently chase each other down his otherwise stern and immovable features; but they felt the sacredness of his grief, and kindly refrained from questioning him as to its cause, while, with instinctive delicacy, they left him to indulge his sorrow alone. When he withdrew from the scene of his painful recollections, they both accompanied him downstairs, reiterating their hope that he would come again whenever he pleased, and assuring him their poor dwelling should ever be open to him. As Edmond passed the door of similar rooms on the fourth floor, he paused to inquire whether Caderousse, the tailor, still dwelt there; but he received for reply, that the individual in question had got into difficulties, and at the present time kept a small inn on the route from Bellegarde to Beaucaire.

Having obtained the address of the person to whom the house in the Allées de Meillan belonged, Dantès next proceeded thither, and, under the name of Lord Wilmore (the same appellation as that contained in his passport), purchased the small dwelling for the sum of 25,000 francs, at least 10,000 more than it was worth; but had its owner asked ten times the sum he did, it would unhesitatingly have been given. The very same day the occupants of the apartments on the fifth floor of the house, now the property of Dantès, were duly informed by the notary who had arranged the necessary transfer of deeds, etc., that the new landlord gave them their choice of any of the rooms in the house without the least augmentation of rent, upon condition of their giving instant possession of the two small chambers they at present inhabited.

This strange event served to find food for wonder and curiosity in the neighbourhood of the Allées de Meillan, and a multitude of various conjectures were afloat as to the probable cause of the house being so suddenly and mysteriously disposed of; but each surmise seemed to wander farther and farther from the real truth.

But that which raised public astonishment to a climax, and set all speculations at defiance, was the circumstance of the same stranger who had in the morning visited the Allées de Meillan, being seen in the evening walking in the little village of the Catalans, and afterwards observed to enter a poor fisherman's hut, and to pass more than an hour in inquiring after persons who had either been dead, or gone away for more than fifteen or sixteen years. But on the following day, the family from whom all these particulars had been asked received a handsome present, consisting of an entirely new fishing-boat, with a full supply of excellent nets.

The delighted recipients of these munificent gifts would gladly have poured out their thanks to their generous benefactor; but they had seen him, upon quitting the hut, merely give some orders to a sailor, and then springing lightly on horseback, quit Marseilles by the Porte d'Aix.

26

The Inn of Pont du Gard

SUCH of my readers as have made a pedestrian excursion to the south of France* may perchance have noticed, midway between the town of Beaucaire and the village of Bellegarde a small roadside inn, from the front of which hung, creaking and flapping in the wind, a sheet of tin covered with a caricature resemblance of the Pont du Gard. This modern place of entertainment stood on the left-hand side of the grand route, turning its back upon the Rhone. It also boasted of what in Languedoc is styled a garden, consisting of a small plot of ground, a full view of which might be obtained from a door immediately opposite the grand portal by which travellers were ushered in to partake of the hospitality of mine host of the Pont du Gard. This plaisance or garden, scorched up beneath the ardent sun of a latitude of thirty degrees, permitted nothing to thrive or scarcely live in its arid soil; a few dingy olives and stunted fig-trees struggled hard for existence, but their withered, dusty foliage abundantly proved how unequal was the conflict. Between these sickly shrubs, grew a scanty supply of garlic, tomatoes, and eschalots, while, lone and solitary, like a forgotten sentinel, a tall pine raised its melancholy head in one of the corners of this unattractive spot, and displayed its flexible stem and fan-shaped summit dried and cracked by the withering influence of the *mistral*, that scourge of Province.

In the surrounding plain, which more resembled a dusty lake than solid ground, were scattered a few miserable stalks of wheat.

the effect, no doubt, of a curious desire on the part of the agriculturists of the country, to see whether such a thing as the raising of grain in those parched regions was practicable. The scanty produce, however, served to accommodate the numerous grasshoppers who follow the unfortunate invader of this bare soil with untiring persecution, resting themselves after their chase upon the stunted specimens of horticulture, while they fill the ear with their sharp, shrill cry.

For nearly the last eight years the small tavern we have just been describing had been kept by a man and his wife, with two servants, one a strong, sturdy wench, answering to the name of Trinette, officiated in the capacity of chambermaid, while the other, a shock-headed country lad, named Pacaud, undertook the management of the outer-door work, and contented himself with the title of *garçon d'écurie*, or ostler, as we should style it in England; but, alas! the occupation of each domestic was but nominal for, a canal recently made between Beaucaire and Aiguemortes had proved a most successful speculation, and had transferred the mode of sending merchandise and luggage from the heavy wagons to the towed barge, while travellers forsook the diligence to glide over the smooth waters by the more agreeable aid of the steamboat. And, as though to add to the daily misery which this prosperous canal inflicted on the unfortunate innkeeper, whose utter ruin it was fast accomplishing, it was situated not a hundred steps from the forsaken inn, of which we have given so faithful a description.

The innkeeper himself was a man of from forty to forty-five years of age, tall, strong, and bony, a perfect specimen of the natives of those southern latitudes. He had the dark, sparkling, and deep-set eye, curved nose, and teeth white as those of a carnivorous animal; his hair, which, spite of the light touch time had as yet left on it, seemed as though it refused to assume any other colour than its own, was like his beard, which he wore under his chin, thick and curly, and but slightly mingled with a few silvery threads. His naturally murky complexion had assumed a still further shade of brown from the habit the unfortunate man had acquired of stationing himself from early morn till latest eve at the threshold of his door, in eager hope that some traveller, either equestrian or pedestrian might bless his eyes, and give him the delight of once more seeing a guest enter his doors. But his patience and his expectations were alike useless. Yet there he stood, day after day, exposed to the meridianal rays of a burning sun, with no other protection for his head than a red handkerchief twisted around it, after the manner of the Spanish muleteers. This anxious, careworn innkeeper was no other than our old acquaintance, Caderousse. His wife, on the contrary, whose maiden name had been Madeleine Radelle, was pale, meagre, and sickly-looking. Born in the neighbourhood of Arles, she had shared in the beauty for which its females are proverbial; but that beauty had gradually withered beneath the devastating influence of one of those slow fevers so prevalent in the vicinity of the waters of Aiguemortes and the marshes of Camargue. She remained nearly always in her chamber, situated on the first floor; sitting shivering in her chair or extended languid and feeble on her bed, while her husband kept his daily watch at the door— a duty he performed with so much the greater willingness, as it saved him the necessity of listening to the endless plaints and murmurs of his helpmate, who never saw him without breaking out into bitter invectives against fate and the unmerited hardships she was called upon to endure; to all of which her husband would calmly return an unvarying reply, couched in these philosophic words:

"Cease to grieve about it, La Carconte. It is God's pleasure that you should suffer, and whether you like it or not you must bear it."

The sobriquet of La Carconte had been bestowed on Madeleine Radelle from the circumstance of her having been born in a village so called, situated between Salon and Lanbèse; and as a custom existed among the inhabitants of that part of France where Caderousse lived of styling every person by some particular and distinctive appellation, her husband had bestowed on her the name of La Carconte in place of her sweet and euphonious name of Madeleine, which, in all probability, his rude guttural language would not have enabled him to pronounce.

Still, let it not be supposed that amid this affected resignation to the will of Providence, the unfortunate innkeeper did not writhe under the double misery of seeing the hateful canal carry off alike his customers and profits, and the daily implication of his peevish partner's murmurs and lamentations.

Like other dwellers of the south, he was a man of sober habits and moderate desires, but fond of external show, vain, and addicted to display. During the days of his prosperity, not a *fête*, festivity, or ceremonial, took place without himself and wife being among the spectators. He dressed in the picturesque costume worn upon grand occasions by the inhabitants of the south of France, bearing equal resemblance to the style adopted both by the Catalans and Andalusians; while La Carconte displayed the charming fashion prevalent among the females of Arles, a mode of attire borrowed equally from Greece and Arabia. But, by degrees, watch-chains, necklaces, many-coloured scarfs, embroidered bodices, velvet vests, elegantly worked stockings, striped gaiters, and silver buckles for the shoes, all disappeared; and Gaspard Caderousse, unable to appear abroad in his pristine splendour, had given up any further participation in these pomps and vanities, both for himself or wife, although a bitter feeling of envious discontent filled his mind as the sound of mirth and merry music from the joyous revellers reached even the miserable hostelry to which he still clung, more for the shelter than the profit it afforded.

On the present day, Caderousse was, as usual, at his place of observation before the door, his eyes glancing listlessly from a piece of closely-shaven grass—on which some fowls were industriously, though fruitlessly, endeavouring to turn up some grain or insect suited to their palate—to the deserted road, the two extremities of which pointed respectively north and south, when he was roused from his daily speculations as to the possibility of the tavern of the Pont du Gard ever again being called upon to exercise its hospitable capabilities to any chance visitant by the shrill voice of his wife summoning him to her presence with all speed. Murmuring at the disagreeable interruption to his not very agreeable thoughts, he, however, proceeded to the floor in which was situated the chamber of his better half—taking care, however, preparatory to so doing, to set the entrance-door wide open, that, in the event of that *rara avis*, a traveller passing by, it should be made perfectly clear to his comprehension that no ceremony was requisite in entering.

At the moment Caderousse quitted his sentry-like watch before the door, the road on which he so eagerly strained his sight was void and lonely as a desert at midday. There it lay stretched out, one interminable line of dust and sand, with its sides bordered by tall, meagre trees, altogether presenting so uninviting an appearance, that no one in his senses could have imagined that any traveller, at liberty to regulate his hours for journeying, would choose to expose himself to the scorching heat of a meridian sun in such a formidable sahara. Nevertheless, had Caderousse but retained his post a few minutes longer, he might have caught a dim outline of something approaching from the direction of Bellegarde. As the moving object drew nearer, he would easily have perceived it consisted of a man and horse, between whom the kindest and most amiable understanding appeared to exist. The horse was of Hungarian breed, and ambled along with that easy pace peculiar to that race of animals. His rider was a priest, dressed in black, and wearing a three-cornered hat; and, spite of the ardent rays of a noonday sun, the pair came on at a tolerably smart trot.

Having arrived before the Pont du Gard, the horse stopped, but whether for his own pleasure or that of his rider would have been difficult to say. However that might have been, the measure appeared reciprocally agreeable, since no demur was observable in either. The priest, dismounting, led his steed by the bridle in search of some place to which he could secure him. Availing himself of a handle that projected from a half-fallen door, he tied the animal safely, patted him kindly, and, having drawn a red cotton handkerchief from his pocket, wiped away the perspiration that streamed from his brow; then, advancing to the door, struck thrice with the end of his iron-shod stick. At this unusual sound, a huge black dog came rushing to meet the daring assailant of his ordinarily tranquil abode, snarling and displaying his sharp, white teeth with a determined hostility that abundantly proved how little he was accustomed to society. At that moment a heavy footstep was heard descending the wooden staircase that led from the upper floor, and, with many bows and courteous smiles, mine host of the Pont du Gard welcomed the blessing Heaven had sent him in the shape of a weary traveller; while, retreating into the house with backward step, he besought his guest would honour him by entering also.

"You are welcome, sir, most welcome!" repeated the astonished Caderousse, in his blandest tones. "Now, then, Margontin," cried he, speaking to the dog, "will you be quiet? Pray don't heed him, sir!—he only barks, he never bites! I make no doubt a glass of good wine would be acceptable this dreadfully hot day!" Then perceiving for the first time the description of traveller he had to entertain, Caderousse hastily exclaimed, "A thousand pardons, your reverence! I really did not observe whom I had the honour to receive under my poor roof. What would you please to have, M. l'Abbé? What refreshment can I offer you? All I have is at your service."

The priest gazed on the individual addressing him with a long and searching gaze—there even seemed like a disposition on his part to court a similar scrutiny on the part of the innkeeper; then, remarking in the countenance of the latter no other expression than extreme surprise at his own want of attention to an inquiry so courteously worded, he deemed it as well to terminate this dumb show, and therefore said, speaking with a strong Italian accent:

"You are, I presume, M. Caderousse?"

"Your reverence is quite correct," answered the host, even more surprised at the question than he had been by the silence which had prefaced it; "I am Gaspard Caderousse, at your service."

"Gaspard Caderousse!" rejoined the priest. "Yes, that agrees both with the baptismal appellation and surname of the individual I allude to. You formerly lived, I believe, in the Allées de Meillan, on the fourth floor of a small house situated there?"

"I did."

"Where you followed the business of a tailor?"

"True, I was a tailor, till the trade fell off so as not to afford me a living. Then it is so very hot at Marseilles, that really I could bear it no longer; and it is my idea that all the respectable inhabitants will be obliged to follow my example and quit it. But talking of heat, is there nothing I can offer you by way of refreshment?"

"Yes; let me have a bottle of your best wine, and then, with your permission, we will resume our conversation from where we left off."

"As you please, M. l'Abbé," said Caderousse, who, anxious not to lose the present opportunity of finding a customer for one of the few bottles of vin de Cahors still remaining in his possession, hastily raised a trap-door in the floor of the apartment they were in, which served both as parlour and kitchen.

Upon his issuing forth from his subterranean retreat at the expiration of five minutes, he found the abbé seated on a species of stool, leaning his elbow on a table, while Margontin, whose animosity seemed appeased by the traveller having pronounced the unusual command for refreshments, had crept up to him, and had established himself very comfortably between his knees, his long, skinny neck resting on his lap, while his dim eye was fixed earnestly on the traveller's face.

"Are you quite alone?" inquired the guest, as Caderousse placed before him the bottle of wine and a glass.

"Quite, quite alone," replied the man,—"or, at least, all but so, M. l'Abbé; for my poor wife, who is the only person in the house besides myself, is laid up with illness, and unable to render me the least assistance, poor thing!"

"You are married, then?" said the priest, with a species of interest, glancing round as he spoke at the scanty style of the accommodations and humble fittings-up of the apartment.

"Ah, M. l'Abbé," said Caderousse, with a sigh, "it is easy to perceive I am not a rich man; but in this world a man does not thrive the better for being honest."

The abbé fixed on him a searching, penetrating glance.

"I can certainly say that much for myself," repeated the innkeeper, fairly sustaining the scrutiny of the abbé's gaze; "I can boast with truth of being an honest man; and," continued he significantly, shaking his head, " that is more than every one can say nowadays."

" So much the better for you, if what you assert be true," said the abbé: " for I am firmly persuaded that, sooner or later, the good will be rewarded, and the wicked punished."

" Such words as those belong to your profession, M. l'Abbé," answered Caderousse, " and you do well to repeat them; but," added he, with a bitter expression of countenance, " you cannot make people believe them in opposition to what passes before them every day, when the reverse takes place, and it is the wicked man who prospers, and the honest, deserving man who suffers."

" You are wrong to speak thus," said the abbé; " and, perhaps, I may, in my own person, be able to prove to you how completely you are in error in coming to so mischievous and dangerous a conclusion."

" What mean you? " inquired Caderousse, with a look of surprise.

" In the first place it is requisite I should be satisfied you are the person I am in search of! "

" What proofs do you require? "

" Did you in the year 1814 or 1815 know anything of a young sailor named Edmond Dantès? "

" Did I? I should think I did. Poor dear Edmond! Why, Edmond Dantès and myself were intimate friends! " exclaimed Caderousse, whose countenance assumed an almost purple hue, as he caught the penetrating gaze of the abbé fixed on him, while the clear, calm eye of the questioner seemed to cover him with confusion.

" You remind me," said the priest, " that the young man, concerning whom I asked you, was said to bear the name of Edmond."

" Said to bear the name! " repeated Caderousse, becoming excited and eager. " Why, he was so called as truly as I myself bore the appellation of Gaspard Caderousse; but, M. l'Abbé, tell me, I pray, what has become of poor Edmond. Did you know him? Is he alive and at liberty? Is he prosperous and happy? "

" He died a more wretched, hopeless, heart-broken prisoner than the felons who pay the penalty of their crimes at the galleys of Toulon."

A deadly paleness succeeded the deep suffusion which had before spread itself over the countenance of Caderousse, who turned away, but not so much so as to prevent the priest's observing him wiping away the tears from his eyes with a corner of the red handkerchief twisted round his head.

" Poor fellow! poor fellow! " murmured Caderousse. " Well,

there, M. l'Abbé, is another proof that good people are never rewarded on this earth, and that none but the wicked prosper. Ah," continued Caderousse, speaking in the highly-coloured language of the South, " the world grows worse and worse. Why does not God if he really hates the wicked, as he is said to do, send down brimstone and fire and consume them altogether? "

" You speak as though you had loved this young Dantès! " observed the abbé, without taking any notice of his companion's vehemence.

" And so I did," replied Caderousse; " though once, I confess I envied him his good fortune; but I swear to you, M. l'Abbé, I swear to you, by everything a man holds dear, I have since then deeply and sincerely lamented his unhappy fate."

There was a brief silence, during which the fixed, searching eye of the abbé was employed in scrutinising the agitated features of the innkeeper.

" You knew the poor lad, then? " continued Caderousse.

" Nay, I was merely called to see him when on his dying bed, that I might administer to him the consolations of religion."

" And of what did he die? " asked Caderousse, in a choking voice.

" Of what think you do young and strong men die in prison, when they have scarcely numbered their thirtieth year, unless it be of the horrors of that prison which has spread its stony walls against their breathing the air of heaven, or participating in the secret affections a gracious Creator permitted to find growth within the human breast? Edmond Dantès died in prison of sorrow and a broken heart."

Caderousse wiped away the large drops of perspiration that gathered on his brow.

" But the strangest part of the story is," resumed the abbé, " that Dantés, even in his dying moments, swore by his crucified Redeemer, that he was utterly ignorant of the cause of his imprisonment."

" And so he was! " murmured Caderousse. " How should he have been otherwise? Ah, M. l'Abbé, the poor fellow told you the truth."

" And for that reason he besought me to try and clear up a mystery he had never been able to penetrate, and to clear his memory should any foul spot or stain have fallen on it."

And here the look of the abbé, becoming more and more fixed, seemed to rest with ill-concealed satisfaction on the gloomy depression which seemed rapidly spreading over the countenance of Caderousse

" A rich Englishman," continued the abbé, " who had been

his companion in misfortune, but had been released from prison during the second restoration, was possessed of a diamond of immense value: this precious jewel he bestowed on Dantès upon himself quitting the prison, as a mark of his gratitude for the kindness and brotherly care with which Dantès had nursed him in a severe illness he underwent during his confinement. Instead of employing this diamond in attempting to bribe his gaolers, who might only have taken it and then betrayed him to the governor, Dantès carefully preserved it, that in the event of his getting out of prison he might have wherewithal to live, for the produce of such a diamond would have quite sufficed to make his fortune."

" Then, I suppose," asked Caderousse, with eager, glowing looks, " that it was a stone of immense value? "

" Why, everything is relative," answered the abbé. " To one in Edmond's position the diamond certainly was of great value. It was estimated at 50,000 francs."

" Bless me! " exclaimed Caderousse, " what a sum! 50,000 francs! Surely the diamond was as large as a nut to be worth all that! "

" No," replied the abbé, " it was not of such a size as that; but you shall judge for yourself. I have it with me."

The sharp gaze of Caderousse was instantly directed towards the priest's garments, as though hoping to discover the talked-of treasure.

Calmly drawing forth from his pocket a small box covered with black shagreen, the abbé opened it, and displayed to the delighted eyes of Caderousse the sparkling jewel it contained, set in a ring of admirable workmanship.

" And that diamond," cried Caderousse, almost breathless with eager admiration, " you say, is worth 50,000 francs? "

" It is, without the setting, which is also valuable." replied the abbé, as he closed the box, and returned it to his pocket, while its brilliant hues seemed still to dance before the eyes of the fascinated innkeeper.

" But how comes this diamond in your possession, M. l'Abbé? Did Edmond make you his heir? "

" No; merely his testamentary executor. When dying, the unfortunate youth said to me, ' I once possessed four dear and faithful friends, besides the maiden to whom I was betrothed; and I feel convinced they have all unfeignedly grieved over my loss. The name of one of the four friends I allude to is Caderousse.' "

The inkeeper shivered as though he felt the dead cold hand of the betrayed Edmond grasping his own.

" ' Another of the number,' " continued the abbé, without seeming to notice the emotion of Caderousse, " ' is called Danglars; and the third, spite of being my rival, entertained a very sincere affection for me.' "

A fiendish smile played over the features of Caderousse, who was about to break in upon the abbé's speech, when the latter waving his hand, said :

" Allow me to finish first, and then if you have any observations to make, you can do so afterwards."

" ' The third of my friends, although my rival, was much attached to me,—his name was Fernand: that of my betrothed was——' Stay, stay," continued the abbé, " I have forgotten what he called her."

" Mercédès! " cried Caderousse eagerly.

" True," said the abbé, with a stifled sigh. " Mercédès it was."

" Go on," urged Caderousse.

" Bring me a *carafe* of water," said the abbé.

Caderousse quickly performed the stranger's bidding; and after pouring some into a glass, and slowly swallowing its contents, the abbé, resuming his usual placidity of manner, said, as he placed his empty glass on the table:

" Where did we leave off? "

" Oh, that the betrothed of Edmond was called Mercédès! "

" To be sure. ' Well, then,' said Dantés—for you understand I repeat his words just as he uttered them—' you will go to Marseilles.' Do you understand? "

" Perfectly."

" ' For the purpose of selling this diamond; the produce of which you will divide into five equal parts, and give an equal portion to the only persons who have loved me upon earth.' "

" But why into five parts? " asked Caderousse; " you only mentioned four persons."

" Because the fifth is dead, as I hear. The fifth sharer in Edmond's bequest was his own father."

" Too true, too true! " ejaculated Caderousse, almost suffocated by the contending passions which assailed him, " the poor old man did die! "

" I learned so much at Marseilles," replied the abbé, making a strong effort to appear indifferent; " but from the length of time that has elapsed since the death of the elder Dantés, I was unable to obtain any particulars of his end. You possibly may be capable of furnishing me with such minute circumstances as may serve to substantiate the decease of the elder Dantés."

" I do not know who could if I could not," said Caderousse.

" Why, I lived almost on the same floor with the poor old man. Ah, yes! about a year after the disappearance of his son the old man died! "

" Of what did he die? "

" Why, the doctors called his complaint an internal inflammation, I believe; his acquaintances said he died of grief; but I, who saw him in his dying moments, I say he died of——"

" Of what? " asked the priest, anxiously and eagerly.

" Why, of downright starvation."

" Starvation! " exclaimed the abbé, springing from his seat. " Why, the vilest animals are not suffered to die by such a death as that. The very dogs that wander houseless and homeless in the streets, find some pitying hand to cast them a mouthful of bread; and that a man, a Christian, should be allowed to perish of hunger in the midst of other men equally Christian with himself, is too horrible for belief. Oh, it is impossible—utterly impossible! "

" What I have said, I have said," answered Caderousse.

" And you are a fool for having said anything about it," said a voice from the top of the stairs. " Why should you meddle with what does not concern you? "

The two male speakers turned round quickly, and perceived the sickly countenance of La Carconte leaning over the rail of the staircase; attracted by the sound of voices, she had feebly dragged herself down the stairs, and, seated on the lower step, she had listened to the foregoing conversation.

" Mind your own business, wife," replied Caderousse sharply. " This gentleman asks me for information, which common politeness will not permit me to refuse."

" Politeness, you simpleton! " retorted La Carconte. " What have you to do with politeness, I should like to know? Better study a little common prudence. How do you know the motives that person may have for trying to extract all he can from you? "

" I pledge you my sacred word, madame," said the abbé, " that my intentions are free from all thoughts of harm or injury to you or yours; and that your husband can incur no risk, provided he answers me candidly."

" Ah, that's all very fine," retorted the woman. " Nothing is easier than to begin with fair promises and assurances of nothing to fear; but when poor, silly folks like my husband there have been persuaded to tell all they know, the promises and assurances of safety are quickly forgotten; and at some moment when nobody is expecting it, behold trouble and misery, and all sorts of persecutions, are heaped on the unfortunate wretches, who cannot even see whence all their afflictions come."

" Nay, nay, my good woman, make yourself perfectly easy, I beg of you. Whatever evils may befall you, they will not be occasioned by my instrumentality, that I solemnly promise you."

Some inarticulate sounds escaped La Carconte, then letting her head, which she had raised during the excitement of conversation, again droop on to her lap, she commenced her usual aguish trembling, the result of her feverish attack, leaving the two speakers to resume the conversation, but still remaining herself so placed, as to be able to hear every word they uttered.

Again the abbé had been obliged to swallow a draught of water to calm the emotions that threatened to overpower him. When he had sufficiently recovered himself, he said:

" It appears, then, that the miserable old man you were telling me of was forsaken by every one. Surely, had not such been the case, he would not have perished by so dreadful a death as you described."

" Why, he was not altogether forsaken," continued Caderousse; " for Mercédès the Catalan and M. Morrel were very kind to him; but somehow the poor old man had contracted a profound hatred of Fernand—the very person," added Caderousse, with a bitter smile, " that you named just now as being one of Dantès' faithful and attached friends."

" And was he not so? " asked the abbé.

" Gaspard! Gaspard! " murmured the woman, from her seat on the stairs, " mind what you are saying! "

Caderousse made no reply to these words, though evidently irritated and annoyed by the interruption, but, addressing the abbé, said:

" Can a man be faithful to another whose wife he covets and desires for himself? But Dantès was so honourable and true in his own nature, that he believed everybody's professions of friendship. Poor Edmond! he was cruelly deceived; but it was a happy thing he never knew it, or he might have found it more difficult, when on his death-bed, to pardon his enemies. And, whatever people may say," continued Caderousse, in his native language, which was not altogether devoid of rude poetry, " I cannot help being more frightened at the idea of the malediction of the dead than the hatred of the living."

" Weak-minded coward! " exclaimed La Carconte.

" Do you then know in what manner Fernand injured Dantès? " inquired the abbé of Caderousse.

" Do I? No one better."

" Speak out, then; say what it was! "

" Gaspard! " cried La Carconte, " I cannot force you to do

otherwise than as you please, but, if you are guided by me, you
will have nothing to say on this subject."

"Well, well, wife," replied Caderousse, "I do not know but
what you are right! I shall follow your advice."

"Then you are determined not to reveal the circumstances
you alluded to?" said the abbé.

"Why, what good would it do?" asked Caderousse. "If the
poor lad were living, and came to me to beg I would candidly
tell which were his true and which his false friends, why, perhaps,
I should not hesitate. But you tell me he is no more, and therefore
can have nothing to do with hatred or revenge; so let all such
feelings be buried with him."

"You prefer, then," said the abbé, "allowing me to bestow on
men you say are false and treacherous, the reward intended for
faithful friendship?"

"That is true enough," returned Caderousse. "You say truly
the gift of poor Edmond was not meant for such traitors as Fernand
and Danglars; besides, what would it be to them? no more than
a drop of water in the ocean."

"And remember, husband," chimed in La Carconte, "that
to breathe one syllable against those two individuals would be to
raise up against yourself two formidable enemies, who at a word
could level you with the dust!"

"How so?" inquired the abbé. "Are these persons, then, so
rich and powerful?"

"Do you not know their history?"

"I do not. Pray relate it to me!"

Caderousse seemed to reflect for a few moments, then said:
"No, truly, it would take up too much time."

"Well, my good friend," returned the abbé, in a tone that
indicated utter indifference on his part, "you are at liberty either
to speak or be silent, just as you please; for my own part, I
respect your scruples and admire your sentiments. So let the
matter end. I shall do my duty as conscientiously as I can, and
fulfil my promise to the dying man. My first business will be to
dispose of this diamond."

So saying, the abbé again drew the small box from his pocket,
opened it, and contrived to hold it in such a light that a bright
flash of brilliant hues passed before the dazzled gaze of Caderousse.

"Wife, wife!" cried he, in a voice almost hoarse with eager
emotion, "come hither and behold this rich diamond!"

"Diamond!" exclaimed La Carconte, rising and descending
to the chamber with a tolerably firm step, "what diamond are
you talking about?"

" Why, did you not hear all we said? " inquired Caderousse.
" It is a beautiful diamond left by poor Edmond Dantès, to be
sold, and the money divided among his father, Mercédès, his
betrothed bride, Fernand, Danglars, and myself. The jewel is
worth, at least, 50,000 francs."

" Oh, what a splendid diamond! " cried the astonished woman.

" The fifth part of the produce of this stone belongs to us, then,
does it not? " asked Caderousse, still devouring the glittering
gem with his eyes.

" It does," replied the abbé; " with the addition of an equal
division of that part intended for the elder Dantès, which I conceive myself at liberty to share equally with the four surviving
persons."

" And wherefore among us four? " inquired Caderousse.

" As being the friends Edmond esteemed most faithful and
devoted to him."

" I don't call those friends who betray and ruin you," murmured the wife, in her turn, in a low, muttering voice.

" Of course not! " rejoined Caderousse quickly, " no more do
I; and that was what I was observing to this gentleman just now.
I said I looked upon it as a sacrilegious profanation to reward
treachery, perhaps crime."

" Remember," answered the abbé calmly, as he replaced the
jewel and its case in the pocket of his cassock, " it is your fault,
not mine, that I do so. You will have the goodness to furnish me
with the address of both Fernand and Danglars, in order that I
may execute Edmond's last wishes! "

The agitation of Caderousse became extreme, and large drops
of perspiration rolled from his heated brows. As he saw the abbé
rise from his seat and go towards the door, as though to ascertain
if his horse were sufficiently refreshed to continue his journey,
Caderousse and his wife exchanged looks of deep meaning with
each other.

" There you see, wife," said the former, " this splendid diamond
might be all ours if we chose! "

" Do you believe it? "

" Why, surely a man of his holy profession would not deceive
us! "

" Well," replied La Carconte, " do as you like. For my part I
wash my hands of the affair."

So saying, she once more climbed the staircase leading to her
chamber, her frame shuddering with aguish chills, and her teeth
rattling in her head, spite of the intense heat of the weather.
Arrived at the top stair, she turned round, and called out in a
warning tone to her husband:

" Gaspard, consider well what you are about to do! "

" I have both reflected and decided," answered he.

La Carconte then entered her chamber, the flooring of which creaked beneath her heavy, uncertain tread, as she proceeded towards her arm-chair, into which she fell as though exhausted.

" Well," asked the abbé, as he returned to the apartment below, " what have you made up your mind to do? "

" To tell you all I know," was the reply.

" I certainly think you act wisely in so doing," said the priest. " Not because I have the least desire to learn anything you may desire to conceal from me, but simply that if, through your assistance, I could distribute the legacy according to the wishes of the testator, why so much the better, that is all."

" I trust, indeed, such will be the case, and that poor Edmond's dying bequest will be given only to such as you shall be convinced are his faithful and attached friends," replied Caderousse, his eyes sparkling and his face flushed with the hope of obtaining all himself.

" Now, then, begin, if you please," said the abbé, " I am all attention."

" Stop a minute," answered Caderousse, " we might be interrupted in the most interesting part of my recital, which would be a pity, and it is as well that your visit hither should be made known only to ourselves."

With these words he went steathily to the door, which he closed, and by way of still greater precaution, bolted and barred it as he was accustomed to do at night. During this time the abbé had chosen his place for listening to the painful recital he expected Caderousse's would prove; he removed his seat into a corner of the room, where he himself would be in deep shadow, while the light would be fully thrown on the narrator; then, with head bent down and hands clasped or rather clenched together, he prepared to give his whole attention to Caderousse, who seated himself on the little stool, exactly opposite to him.

" Remember, I did not urge you to this," said the trembling voice of La Carconte, as though through the flooring of her chamber she viewed the scene that was enacting below.

" Enough, enough! " replied Caderousse, " say no more about it; I will take all the consequences upon myself."

He then commenced as follows.

27

The Tale

"Fɪʀsᴛ," said Caderousse, " sir, you must make me a promise."
"What is that? " inquired the abbé.

" Why, if you ever make use of the details I am about to give
you, that you will never let any one know that it was I who
supplied them, for the persons of whom I am about to talk are
rich and powerful, and if they only laid the tips of their fingers
on me, I should break to pieces like glass."

" Make yourself easy, my friend," replied the abbé; " I am a
priest, and confessions die in my breast; recollect our only desire
is to carry out in a fitting manner the last wishes of our friend.
Speak, then, without reserve as without hatred; tell the truth,
the whole truth; I do not know, never may know, the persons
of whom you are about to speak; besides, I am an Italian and
not a Frenchman, and belong to God and not to man, and I
retire to my convent, which I have only quitted to fulfil the last
wishes of a dying man."

This last assurance seemed to give Caderousse courage.

" Well, then, under these circumstances," said Caderousse,
" I will; indeed, I ought to undeceive you as to the friendship
which poor Edmond believed so sincere and unquestionable."

" Begin with his father, if you please," said the abbé; " Edmond
talked to me a great deal about the old man, for whom he had the
deepest love."

" The history is a sad one, sir," said Caderousse, shaking his
head; " perhaps you know all the earlier part of it? "

" Yes," answered the abbé, " Edmond related to me everything until the moment when he was arrested in a small cabaret
close to Marseilles."

" At La Réserve! oh, yes! I can see it all before me this moment."

" Was it not his betrothal feast? "

" It was; and the feast that began so gaily had a very sorrowful
ending: a commissary of police, followed by four soldiers, entered
and Dantès was arrested."

" Yes, and up to this point I know all," said the priest. " Dantès
himself only knew that which personally concerned him, for he
never beheld again the five persons I have named to you, nor
heard mention of any one of them."

" Well, when Dantès was arrested, M. Morrel hastened to obtain the particulars, and they were very sad. The old man returned alone to his home, folded up his wedding suit with tears in his eyes, and paced up and down his chamber the whole day, and would not go to bed at all, for I was underneath him and heard him walking the whole night; and for myself, I assure you I could not sleep either, for the grief of the poor father gave me great uneasiness, and every step he took went to my heart as really as if his foot had pressed against my breast.

" The next day, Mercédès came to implore the protection of M. de Villefort; she did not obtain it, however, and went to visit the old man; when she saw him so miserable and heart-broken, having passed a sleepless night, and not touched food since the previous day, she wished him to go with her that she might take care of him; but the old man would not consent.

" ' No,' was the old man's reply, ' I will not leave this house, for my poor dear boy loves me better than anything in the world; and if he gets out of prison he will come and see me the first thing, and what would he think if I did not wait here for him? '

" I heard all this from the window, for I was anxious that Mercédès should persuade the old man to accompany her, for his footsteps over my head night and day did not leave me a moment's repose."

" But did you not go upstairs and try to console the poor old man? " asked the abbé.

" Ah, sir! " replied Caderousse, " we cannot console those who will not be consoled, and he was one of these; besides, I know not why, but he seemed to dislike seeing me. One night, however, I heard his sobs, and I could not resist my desire to go up to him; but when I reached his door he was no longer weeping, but praying: I cannot now repeat to you, sir, all the eloquent words and imploring language he made use of; it was more than piety, it was more than grief: and I, who am no canter and hate the Jesuits, said then to myself, ' It is really well, and I am very glad that I have not any children, for if I were a father and felt such excessive grief as the old man does, and did not find in my memory or heart all he is now saying, I should throw myself into the sea at once, for I could not bear it.' "

" Poor father! " murmured the priest.

" From day to day he lived on alone, and more and more solitary. M. Morrel and Mercédès came to see him, but his door was closed; and although I was certain he was at home he would not make any answer. One day, when, contrary to his custom, he had admitted Mercédès, and the poor girl, in spite of her own grief and despair, endeavoured to console him, he said to her:

" ' Be assured, my dear daughter, he is dead; and instead of expecting him, it is he who is awaiting us; I am quite happy, for I am the oldest, and of course shall see him first.'

" However well disposed one may be, after a time one leaves off seeing people who are in sorrow; they make one melancholy: and so at last, old Dantès was left all to himself. I only saw from time to time strangers go up to him and come down again with some bundle they tried to hide; but I guessed what these bundles were, and he sold by degrees what he had to pay for his subsistence.

" At length, the poor old fellow reached the end of all he had; he owed three quarters' rent, and they threatened to turn him out; he begged for another week, which was granted to him. I know this, because the landlord came into my apartment when he left his. For the three first days I heard him walking about as usual, but on the fourth I heard him no longer. I then resolved to go up to him at all risks. The door was closed, but I looked through the keyhole, and saw him so pale and haggard, that believing him very ill I went and told M. Morrel, and then ran on to Mercédès. They both came immediately. M. Morrel brought a doctor, and the doctor said it was an affection of the stomach, and ordered him a limited diet. I was there, too, and I never shall forget the old man's smile at this prescription. From that time he opened his door; he had an excuse for not eating any more, as the doctor had put him on a diet."

The abbé uttered a kind of groan.

" The story interests you, does it not, sir? " inquired Caderousse.

" Yes," replied the abbé, " it is very affecting."

" Mercédès came again, and she found him so altered that she was even more anxious than before to have him taken to her own abode. This was M. Morrel's wish also, who would fain have conveyed the old man against his consent; but the old man resisted and cried so, that they were actually frightened. Mercédès remained, therefore, by his bedside, and M. Morrel went away, making a sign to the Catalan that he had left his purse on the chimney-piece. But availing himself of the doctor's order, the old man would not take any sustenance; at length (after nine day's despair and fasting), the old man died, cursing those who had caused his misery, and saying to Mercédès:

" ' If you ever see my Edmond again, tell him I die blessing him.' "

The abbé rose from his chair, made two turns round the chamber, and pressed his trembling hand against his parched throat.

" And you believe he died——"

" Of hunger, sir, of hunger," said Caderousse; " I am as certain of it as that we two are Christians."

The abbé with a shaking hand seized a glass of water that was standing by him half full, swallowed it at one gulp, and then resumed his seat with red eyes and pale cheeks.

" This was, indeed, a horrid event," said he, in a hoarse voice.

" The more so, sir, as it was men's and not God's doing."

" Tell me of those men," said the abbé, " and remember, too," he added, in a voice that was nearly menacing in its tone, " you have promised to tell me everything. Tell me, therefore, who are these men who have killed the son with despair, and the father with famine? "

" Two men jealous of him, sir; one from love, and the other ambition,—Fernand and Danglars."

" Say, how was this jealousy manifested? "

" They denounced Edmond as a Bonapartist agent."

" Which of the two denounced him? which was the real delinquent? "

" Both sir; one with a letter, and the other put it in the post."

" And where was this letter written? "

" At La Réserve, the day before the festival of the betrothing."

" 'Twas so, then—'twas so, then," murmured the abbé; " oh! Faria! Faria! how well did you judge men and things! "

" What did you please to say, sir? " asked Caderousse.

" Nothing, nothing," replied the priest, " go on."

" It was Danglars who wrote the denunciation with his left hand, that his writing might not be recognised, and Fernand who put it in the post."

" But," exclaimed the abbé suddenly, " you were there yourself."

" I! " said Caderousse, astonished; " who told you I was there? "

The abbé saw he had overshot the mark, and he added quickly.

" No one; but in order to have known everything so well, you must have been an eye-witness."

" True! true! " said Caderousse, in a choking voice, " I was there."

" And did you not remonstrate against such infamy? " asked the abbé; " if not, you were an accomplice."

" Sir," replied Caderousse, " they had made me drink to such an excess that I nearly lost all perception. I had only an indistinct understanding of what was passing around me. I said all that a man in such a state could say; but they both assured me that it was a jest they were carrying on, and perfectly harmless."

"Next day,—next day, sir, you must have seen plain enough what they had been doing, yet you said nothing, though you were present when Dantès was arrested."

"Yes, sir, I was there, and very anxious to speak; but Danglars restrained me."

"'If he should really be guilty,' said he, 'and did really put into the isle of Elba; if he is really charged with a letter for the Bonapartist committee at Paris, and if they find this letter upon him, those who have supported him will pass for his accomplice.'"

"I confess I had my fears in the state in which politics then were, and I held my tongue; it was cowardly, I confess, but it was not criminal."

"I comprehend—you allowed matters to take their course, that was all."

"Yes, sir," answered Caderousse, "and my remorse preys on me night and day. I often ask pardon of God, I swear to you, because this action, the only one with which I have seriously to reproach myself with in all my life, is no doubt the cause of my abject condition. I am expiating a moment of selfishness, and thus it is I always say to Carconte, when she complains, 'Hold your tongue, woman, it is the will of God.'"

And Caderousse bowed his head with every sign of real repentance.

"Well, sir," said the abbé, "you have spoken unreservedly, and thus to accuse yourself is to deserve pardon."

"Unfortunately Edmond is dead, and has not pardoned me."

"He was ignorant," said the abbé.

"But he knows it all now," interrupted Caderousse; "they say the dead know everything."

There was a brief silence; the abbé rose and paced up and down pensively, and then resumed his seat.

"You have two or three times mentioned a M. Morrel," he said; "who was he?"

"The owner of the *Pharaon* and patron of Dantès."

"And what part did he play in this sad drama?" inquired the abbé.

"The part of an honest man, full of courage and real regard. Twenty times he interceded for Edmond. When the emperor returned, he wrote, implored, threatened, and so energetically, that on the second restoration he was persecuted as a Bonapartist. Ten times, as I told you, he came to see Dantès' father, and offered to receive him in his own house; and the night or two before his death, as I have already said, he left his purse on the mantelpiece, with which they paid the old man's debts, and buried him decently, and then Edmond's father died as he had lived, without doing harm to any one. I have the purse still by me, a large one, made of red silk."

"And," asked the abbé, "is M. Morrel still alive?"

"Yes," replied Caderousse.

"In this case," replied the abbé, "he should be rich, happy." Caderousse smiled bitterly.

"Yes, happy as myself," said he.

"What! M. Morrel unhappy!" exclaimed the abbé.

"He is reduced almost to the last extremity,—nay, he is almost at the point of dishonour."

"How?"

"Yes," continued Caderousse, "and in this way: after five-and-twenty years of labour, after having acquired a most honourable name in the trade of Marseilles, M. Morrel is utterly ruined. He has lost five ships in two years, has suffered by the bankruptcy of three large houses, and his only hope now is in that very *Pharaon* which poor Dantès commanded, and which is expected from the Indies with a cargo of cochineal and indigo. If this ship founders like the others, he is a ruined man."

"And has the unfortunate man wife or children?" inquired the abbé.

"Yes, he has a wife, who in all this behaved like an angel; he has a daughter, who was about to marry the man she loved, but whose family now will not allow him to wed the daughter of a ruined man; he has besides a son, a lieutenant in the army, and, as you may suppose, all this, instead of soothing, doubles his grief. If he were alone in the world, he would blow out his brains, and there would be an end."

"Horrible!" ejaculated the priest.

"And it is thus Heaven recompenses virtue, sir," added Caderousse. "You see, I, who never did a bad action but that I have told you of, am in destitution: after having seen my poor wife die of a fever, unable to do anything in the world for her, I shall die of hunger as old Dantès did whilst Fernand and Danglars are rolling in wealth."

"How is that?"

"Because all their malpractices have turned to luck, while honest men have been reduced to misery."

"What has become of Danglars, the instigator, and therefore the most guilty?"

"What has become of him? why he left Marseilles, and was taken, on the recommendation of M. Morrel, who did not know his crime, as cashier into a Spanish bank. During the war with Spain, he was employed in the commissariat of the French army, and made a fortune; then with that money he speculated in the funds and trebled or quadrupled his capital; and, having first married his banker's daughter, who left him a widower, he has married a second time, a widow, a Madame de Nargonne, daughter of M. de Servieux, the king's chamberlain, who is in high favour at court. He is a millionaire, and they have made him a count, and now he is Le Comte Danglars, with a hotel in the Rue de Mont Blanc, with ten horses in his stables, six footmen in his antechamber, and I know not how many hundreds of thousands in his strong box."

" Ah! " said the abbé, with a peculiar tone, " he is happy."

" Happy! who can answer for that? Happiness or unhappiness is the secret known but to oneself, and the walls—walls have ears, but no tongue—but if a large fortune produces happiness, Danglars is happy."

" And Fernand? "

" Fernand! why that is another history."

" But how could a poor Catalan fisher-boy, without education and resources, make a fortune? I confess this staggers me."

" And it has staggered everybody; there must have been in his life some strange secret no one knows."

" But then, by what visible steps has he attained this high fortune or high position? "

" Both, sir; he has both fortune and position, both."

" This must be impossible."

" It would seem so, but listen and you will understand.

" Some days before the return of the emperor, Fernand was drawn in the conscription. The Bourbons left him quietly enough at the Catalans, but Napoleon returned, and extraordinary muster was determined on, and Fernand was compelled to join. I went, too, but as I was older than Fernand, and had just married my poor wife, I was only sent to the coast. Fernand was enrolled in the active troop, went to the frontier with his regiment, and was at the battle of Ligny. The night after that battle, he was sentry at the door of a general, who carried on a secret correspondence with the enemy. That same night the general was to go over to the English. He proposed to Fernand to accompany him; Fernand agreed to do so, deserted his post and followed the general.

" That which would have brought Fernand to a court-martial if Napoleon remained on the throne, served for his recommendation to the Bourbons. He returned to France with the epaulette of sub-lieutenant, and as the protection of the general, who is in the highest favour, was accorded to him, he was a captain in 1823 during the Spanish war, that is to say, at the time when Danglars made his early speculations. Fernand was a Spaniard, and being sent to Spain to ascertain the feeling of his fellow-countrymen, found Danglars there, became on very intimate terms with him, procured his general support from the royalists of the capital and the provinces, received promises and made pledges on his own part, guided his regiment by paths known to himself alone in gorges of the mountains kept by the royalists, and, in fact, rendered such services in this brief campaign, that after the taking of Trocadero he was made colonel, and received the title of count and the cross of an officer of the Legion of Honour."

" Destiny! destiny !" murmured the abbé.

" Yes, but listen, this was not all. The war with Spain being ended, Fernand's career was checked by the long peace which seemed likely to endure throughout Europe. Greece only had risen against Turkey, and had begun her war of independence; all eyes were turned towards Athens—it was the fashion to pity and support the Greeks.* The French government, without protecting them openly, as you know, tolerated partial migrations. Fernand sought and obtained leave to go and serve in Greece, still having his name kept in the ranks of the army. Some time after, it was stated that the Comte de Morcerf, this was the name he bore, had entered the service of Ali Pacha,* with the rank of instructor-general. Ali Pacha was killed, as you know, but before he died he recompensed the services of Fernand, by leaving him a considerable sum, with which he returned to France, when his rank of lieutenant-general was confirmed."

" So that now——" ? inquired the abbé.

" So that now," continued Caderousse, " he possesses a magnificent hotel, No. 27 Rue du Helder, Paris."

The abbé opened his mouth, remained for a moment like a man who hesitates, then making an effort over himself, he said:

" And Mercédès, they tell me that she has disappeared? "

" Disappeared," said Caderousse, " yes, as the sun disappears, to rise the next day with still more splendour."

" Has she made a fortune also? " inquired the abbé, with an ironical smile.

" Mercédès is at this moment one of the greatest ladies in Paris," replied Caderousse.

" Go on," said the abbé, " it seems as if I were hearing the recital of a dream. But I have seen things so extraordinary, that those you mention to me seem less astonishing."

" Mercédès was at first in the deepest despair at the blow which deprived her of Edmond. I have told you of her attempts to propitiate M. de Villefort, her devotion to the father of Dantès.

In the midst of her despair, a fresh trouble overtook her; this was the departure of Fernand, of Fernand whose crime she did not know, and whom she regarded as her brother. Fernand went, and Mercédès remained alone. Three months passed and found her all tears; no news of Edmond, no news of Fernand, nothing before her but an old man who was dying with despair. One evening, after having been seated, as was her custom, all day at the angle of two roads that lead to Marseilles from the Catalans, she returned to her home more depressed than ever; neither her lover nor her friend returned by either of these roads, and she had no intellignece of one or the other. Suddenly she heard a step she knew, turned round anxiously; the door opened, and Fernand, dressed in the uniform of a sub-lieutenant, stood before her. It was not the half of that she bewailed, but it was a portion of her past life that returned to her.

" Mercédès seized Fernand's hands with a transport, which he took for love, but which was only joy at being no longer alone in the world, and seeing at last a friend after long hours of solitary sorrow. And then, it must be confessed, Fernand had never been hated, he was only not precisely loved. Another possessed all Mercédès' heart; that other was absent, had disappeared, perhaps was dead. At this last idea Mercédès burst into a flood of tears, and wrung her hands in agony: but this idea, which she had always repelled before, when it was suggested to her by another, came now in full force upon her mind; and then too, old Dantès incessantly said to her, ' Our Edmond is dead; if he were not he would return to us.' The old man died, as I have told you; had he lived, Mercédès, perchance, had not become the wife of another, for he would have been there to reproach her infidelity. Fernand saw this, and when he learned the old man's death he returned. He was now a lieutenant. At his first coming he had not said a word of love to Mercédès, at the second he reminded her that he loved her. Mercédès begged for six months more to expect and bewail Edmond."

" So that," said the abbé, with a bitter smile, " that makes eighteen months in all; what more could the most devoted lover desire? "

Then he murmured the words of the English poet:

" ' Frailty, thy name is woman.' "*

" Six months afterwards," continued Caderousse, " the marriage took place in the church of Accoules."

" The very church in which she was to have married Edmond," murmured the priest; " there was only a change of bridegroom."

" Well, Mercédès was married," proceeded Caderousse, " but although in the eyes of the world she appeared calm, she nearly fainted as she passed La Réserve, where, eighteen months before, the betrothal had been celebrated with him whom she would have seen she still loved had she looked at the bottom of her heart. Fernand, more happy, but not more at his ease,—for I saw at this time he was in constant dread of Edmond's return,—Fernand was very anxious to get his wife away and to depart himself. There were too many dangers and recollections associated with the Catalans, and eight days after the wedding they left Marseilles."

"Did you ever see Mercédès again?" inquired the priest.

"Yes, during the war of Spain at Perpignan, where Fernand had left her; she was attending to the education of her son."

The abbé started.

"Her son?" said he.

"Yes," replied Caderousse, "little Albert."

"But, then, to be able to instruct her child," continued the abbé, "she must have received an education herself. I understood from Edmond that she was the daughter of a simple fisherman, beautiful but uneducated."

"Oh!" replied Caderousse, "did he know so little of his lovely betrothed? Mercédès might have been a queen, sir, if the crown were to be placed on the heads of the loveliest and most intelligent. Fernand's fortune already became greater, and she became greater with his growing fortune. She learned drawing, music, everything. Besides, I believe, between ourselves, she did this in order to distract her mind, that she might forget; and she only filled her head thus in order to alleviate the weight on her heart. But now everything must be told," continued Caderousse; "no doubt, fortune and honours have comforted her. She is rich, a countess, and yet——"

Caderousse paused.

"Yet what?" asked the abbé.

"Yet, I am sure, she is not happy," said Caderousse.

"What makes you believe this?"

"Why, when I found myself very wretched, I thought my old friends would, perhaps, assist me. So I went to Danglars, who would not even receive me. I called on Fernand, who sent me a hundred francs by his valet-de-chambre."

"Then you did not see either of them?"

"No; but Madame de Morcerf saw me."

"How was that?"

"As I went away, a purse fell at my feet—it contained five-and-twenty louis; I raised my head quickly, and saw Mercédès, who shut the blind directly."

"And M. de Villefort?" asked the abbé.

" Oh! he was never a friend of mine; I did not know him, and I had nothing to ask of him."

" Do you not know what became of him, and the share he had in Edmond's misfortunes? "

" No. I only know that some time after having arrested him, he married Mademoiselle de Saint-Méran, and soon after left Marseilles; no doubt but he has been as lucky as the rest; no doubt he is as rich as Danglars, as high in station as Fernand. I only, as you see, have remained poor, wretched, and forgotten."

" You are mistaken, my friend," replied the abbé; " God may seem sometimes to forget for a while, whilst his justice reposes, but there always comes a moment when he remembers—and behold! a proof."

As he spoke, the abbé took the diamond from his pocket, and giving it to Caderousse, said:

" Here, my friend, take this diamond, it is yours."

" What! for me only? " cried Caderousse; " ah, sir, do not jest with me! "

" This diamond was to have been shared amongst his friends. Edmond had one friend only, and thus it cannot be divided. Take the diamond then, and sell it: it is worth fifty thousand francs (£2000), and I repeat my wish that this sum may suffice to release you from your wretchedness."

" Oh, sir," said Caderousse, putting out one hand timidly, and with the other wiping away the perspiration which bedewed his brow,—" oh, sir, do not make a jest of the happiness or despair of a man."

" I know what happiness and what despair are, and I never make a jest of such feelings. Take it, then, but in exchange——"

Caderousse, who touched the diamond, withdrew his hand. The abbé smiled.

" In exchange," he continued, " give me the red silk purse that M. Morrel left on old Dantès' chimney-piece, and which you tell me is still in your hands."

Caderousse, more and more astonished, went towards a large oaken cupboard, opened it, and gave the abbé a long purse of faded red silk, round which were two copper runners that had once been gilt. The abbé took it, and in return gave Caderousse the diamond.

" Oh! you are a man of God, sir," cried Caderousse; " for no one knew that Edmond had given you this diamond, and you might have kept it."

" Which," said the abbé to himself, " you would have done." The abbé rose, took his hat and gloves.

"Well," he said, "all you have told me is perfectly true, then, and I may believe it in every particular."

"See, M. l'Abbé," replied Caderousse, "in this corner is a crucifix in holy wood—here on this shelf is the gospel of my wife; open this book, and I will swear upon it with my hand on the crucifix; I will swear to you by my soul's salvation, my faith as a Christian, I have told everything to you as it occurred, and as the angel of men will tell it to the ear of God at the day of the last judgment!"

"'Tis well," said the abbé, convinced by his manner and tone that Caderousse spoke the truth. "'Tis well, and may this money profit you! Adieu! I go far from men who thus so bitterly injure each other."

The abbé with difficulty got away from the enthusiastic thanks of Caderousse, opened the door himself, got out and mounted his horse, once more saluted the innkeeper, who kept uttering his loud farewells, and then returned by the road he had travelled in coming. When Caderousse turned round, he saw behind him La Carconte paler and trembling more than ever.

"Is, then, all that I have heard really true?" she inquired.

"What! that he has given the diamond to us only?" inquired Caderousse, half bewildered with joy.

"Yes!"

"Nothing more true! See! here it is."

The woman gazed at it a moment, and then said, in a gloomy voice, "Supposing it's false?"

Caderousse started, and turned pale.

"False!" he muttered. "False! why should that man give me a false diamond?"

"To possess your secret without paying for it, you blockhead!"

Caderousse remained for a moment aghast under the weight of such an idea.

"Oh!" he said, taking up his hat, which he placed on the red handkerchief tied round his head, "we will soon learn that."

"In what way?"

"Why, it is the fair of Beaucaire; there are always jewellers from Paris there, and I will show it to them. Take care of the house, wife, and I shall be back in two hours."

Caderousse left the house in haste, and ran rapidly in a direction contrary to that which the unknown had taken.

"Fifty thousand francs!" muttered La Carconte, when left alone; "it is a large sum of money, but it is not a fortune."

28

The Prison Registers

THE day after that on which the scene had passed on the road between Bellegarde and Beaucaire we have just related, a man of about thirty or two-and-thirty, dressed in a bright blue frock-coat, nankeen trousers, and a white waistcoat, having the appearance and accent of an Englishman, presented himself before the mayor of Marseilles.

"Sir," said he, "I am chief clerk of the house of Thomson and French, of Rome. We are, and have been these ten years, connected with the house of Morrel and Son, of Marseilles. We have a hundred thousand francs (£4000) or thereabouts engaged in speculation with them, and we are a little uneasy at reports that have reached us that the firm is on the eve of ruin. I have come, therefore, express from Rome, to ask you for information as to this house."

"Sir," replied the mayor, "I know very well that during the last four or five years, misfortune has seemed to pursue M. Morrel. He has lost four or five vessels and suffered by three or four bankruptcies; but it is not for me, although I am a creditor myself to the amount of ten thousand francs (£400), to give any information as to the state of his finances. Ask of me, as mayor, what is my opinion of M. Morrel, I shall say he is a man honourable to the last degree, and who has up to this time fulfilled every engagement with scrupulous punctuality. This is all I can say, sir. If you wish to learn more, address yourself to M. de Boville, the Inspector of Prisons, No. 15 Rue de Nouailles. He has, I believe, two hundred thousand francs placed in the hands of Morrel, and if there be any grounds for apprehension, as this is a greater amount than mine, you will most probably find him better informed than myself."

The Englishman seemed to appreciate this extreme delicacy, made his bow, and went away, walking with that step peculiar to the sons of Great Britain, towards the street mentioned. M. de Boville was in his private room, and the Englishman, on perceiving him, made a gesture of surprise, which seemed to indicate that it was not the first time he had been in his presence. As to M. de Boville, he was in such a state of despair, that it was evident all the faculties of his mind, absorbed in the thought which occupied him at the moment, did not allow either his memory or his imagination to stray to the past. The Englishman, with the coolness of his nation, addressed him in terms nearly similar to those with which he had accosted the mayor of Marseilles.

" Oh, sir," exclaimed M. de Boville, " your fears are unfortunately but too well founded, and you see before you a man in despair. I had two hundred thousand francs placed in the hands of Morrel and Son; these two hundred thousand francs were my daughter's dowry, who was to be married in a fortnight, and these two hundred thousand francs were payable, half on the 15th of this month, and the other half on the 15th of next month. I had informed M. Morrel of my desire to have these payments punctually, and he has been here within the last half-hour to tell me that if his ship, the *Pharaon*, did not come into port on the 15th, he would be wholly unable to make this payment."

" But," said the Englishman, " this looks very much like a suspension of payments! "

" Say, sir, that it resembles a bankruptcy! " exclaimed M. de Boville despairingly.

The Englishman appeared to reflect a moment, and then said:

" Thus, then, sir, this credit inspires you with considerable apprehensions! "

" To say truth, I consider it lost."

" Well, then, I will buy it of you."

" You? "

" Yes, I! "

" But at a tremendous discount, of course? "

" No; for two hundred thousand francs. Our house," added the Englishman, with a laugh, " does not do things in that way."

" And you will pay——"

" Ready money."

And the Englishman drew from his pocket a bundle of bank-notes, which might have been twice the sum M. de Boville feared to lose. A ray of joy passed across M. de Boville's countenance, yet he made an effort over himself, and said:

" Sir, I ought to tell you that, in all probability, you will not have six per cent. of this sum."

" That's no affair of mine," replied the Englishman, " that is the affair of the house of Thomson and French, in whose name I act. They have, perhaps, some motive to serve in hastening the ruin of a rival firm. But all I know, sir, is, that I am ready to hand you over this sum in exchange for your assignment of the debt. I only ask a brokerage."

" Of course, that is perfectly just," cried M. de Boville. " The commission is usually one and a half; will you have two—three—five per cent., or even more? Say! "

" Sir," replied the Englishman, laughing, " I am like my house, and do not do such things—no, the commission I ask is quite different."

" Name it, sir, I beg."

" You are the inspector of prisons? "

" I have been so these fourteen years."

" You keep the registers of entries and departures? "

" I do."

" To these registers there are added notes relative to the prisoners? "

" There are special reports on every prisoner."

" Well, sir, I was educated at Rome by a poor devil of an abbé, who disappeared suddenly. I have since learned that he was confined in the Château d'If, and I should like to learn some particulars of his death."

" What was his name? "

" The Abbé Faria."

" Oh, I recollect him, perfectly," cried M. de Boville; " he was crazy."

" So they said."

" Oh, he was, decidedly."

" Very possibly, but what sort of madness was it? "

" He pretended to know of an immense treasure, and offered vast sums to government if they would liberate him."

" Poor devil! and he is dead? "

" Yes, sir; five or six months ago, last February."

" You have a good memory, sir, to recollect dates so well! "

" I recollect this, because the poor devil's death was accompanied by a singular circumstance."

" May I ask what that was? " said the Englishman, with an expression of curiosity which a close observer would have been astonished at discovering in his phlegmatic countenance.

" Oh, dear, yes, sir; the abbé's dungeon was forty or fifty feet distant from that of an old agent of Bonaparte's—one of those who had the most contributed to the return of the usurper in 1815, a very resolute and very dangerous man."

" Indeed! " said the Englishman.

" Yes," replied M. de Boville; " I myself had occasion to see this man in 1816 or 1817, and we could only go into his dungeon with a file of soldiers: that man made a deep impression on me; I shall never forget his countenance! "

The Englishman smiled imperceptibly.

" And you say, sir," he said, " that the two dungeons——"

" Were separated by a distance of fifty feet; but it appears that this Edmond Dantès——"

" This dangerous man's name was——"

" Edmond Dantès. It appears, sir, that this Edmond Dantès had procured tools, or made them, for they found a passsage by which the prisoners communicated."

" This passage was formed, no doubt, with an intention of escape? "

" No doubt; but unfortunately for the prisoners, the Abbé Faria had an attack of catalepsy, and died."

" That must have cut short the projects of escape."

" For the dead man, yes," replied M. de Boville, " but not for the survivor: on the contrary, this Dantès saw a means of accelerating his escape. He, no doubt, thought that prisoners who died in the Château d'If were interred in a burial-ground as usual, and he conveyed the dead man into his own cell, assumed his place in the sack in which they had sewed up the defunct, and awaited the moment of interment."

" It was a bold step, and one that indicated some courage," remarked the Englishman.

" As I have already told you, sir, he was a very dangerous man; and fortunately, by his own act disembarrassed the government of the fears it had on his account."

" How was that? "

" How? do you not comprehend? "

" No."

" The Château d'If has no cemetery, and they simply throw the dead into the sea, after having fastened a thirty-six pound bullet to their feet."

" Well? " observed the Englishman, as if he were slow of comprehension.

" Well, they fastened a thirty-six pound bullet to his feet, and threw him into the sea."

" Really! " exclaimed the Englishman.

" Yes, sir," continued the inspector of prisons. " You may imagine the amazement of the fugitive when he found himself flung headlong beneath the rocks! I should like to have seen his face at that moment."

" That would have been difficult."

" No matter," replied De Boville, in supreme good-humour at the certainty of recovering his two hundred thousand francs,— " no matter, I can fancy it."

And he shouted with laughter.

" So can I," said the Englishman, and he laughed too; but he laughed as the English do, at the end of his teeth.

" And so," continued the Englishman, who first regained his composure, " he was drowned? "

" Unquestionably."

" So that the governor got rid of the fierce and crazy prisoner at the same time? "

" Precisely."

" But some official document was drawn up as to this affair, I suppose? " inquired the Englishman.

" Yes, yes, the mortuary deposition. You understand, Dantès' relations, if he had any, might have some interest in knowing if he were dead or alive."

" So that now, if there were anything to inherit from him, they may do so with easy conscience. He is dead, and no mistake about it? "

" Oh, yes; and they may have the fact attested whenever they please."

" So be it," said the Englishman. " But to return to these registers."

" True, this story has diverted our attention from them. Excuse me."

" Excuse you for what? for the story? By no means; it really seems to me very curious."

" Yes, indeed. So, sir, you wish to see all relating to the poor abbé, who really was gentleness itself? "

" Yes, you will much oblige me."

" Go into my study here, and I will show it to you."

And they both entered M. de Boville's study.

All was here arranged in perfect order; each register had its number, each file of paper its place, The inspector begged the Englishman to seat himself in an arm-chair, and placed before him the register and documents relative to the Château d'If, giving him all the time he desired to examine it, whilst De Boville seated himself in a corner, and began to read his newspaper.

The Englishman easily found the entries relative to the Abbé Faria; but it seemed that the history which the inspector had related interested him greatly, for after having perused the first documents he turned over the leaves until he reached the deposition respecting Edmond Dantès. There he found everything arranged in due order,—the denunciation, examination, Morrel's petition, M. de Villefort's marginal notes. He folded up the denunciation quietly, and put it as quietly in his pocket; read the examination, and saw that the name of Noirtier was not mentioned in it; perused, too, the application, dated 10th April 1815, in which Morrel, by the deputy-procureur's advice, exaggerated with the best intentions (for Napoleon was then on the throne) the services Dantès had rendered to the imperial cause,—services which Villefort's certificates rendered indispensable. Then he saw through all. This petition to Napoleon, kept back by Villefort, had become, under the second restoration, a terrible weapon against him in the hands of the procureur du roi. He was no longer astonished when he searched on to find in the register this note placed in a bracket against his name:—

EDMOND DANTÈS, { An inveterate Bonapartist; took an active part in the return from the Isle of Elba.
To be kept in complete solitary confinement, and to be strictly watched and guarded.

Beneath these lines was written, in another hand:

" See note above—nothing can be done."

He compared the writing in the bracket with the writing of the certificate placed beneath Morrel's petition, and discovered that the note in the bracket was the same writing as the certificate,—that is to say, were in Villefort's handwriting.

As to the note which accompanied this, the Englishman understood that it might have been added by some inspector, who had taken a momentary interest in Dantès situation, but who had, from the remarks we have quoted, found it impossible to give any effect to the interest he experienced.

As we have said, the inspector, from discretion, and that he might not disturb the Abbé Faria's pupil in his researches, had seated himself in a corner, and was reading *Le Drapeau Blanc*.*

He did not see the Englishman fold up and place in his pocket the denunciation written by Danglars under the arbour of La Réserve, and which had the postmark of Marseilles, 2nd March, delivery 6 o'clock P.M.

But it must be said that if he had seen it, he attached so small importance to this scrap of paper, and so great importance to his 200,000 francs, that he would not have opposed what the Englishman did, how incorrect soever it might be.

" Thanks! " said the latter, closing the register with a noise, " I have all I want; now it is for me to perform my promise. Give me a simple assignment of your debt; acknowledge therein the receipt of the cash, and I will hand you over the money."

He rose, gave his seat to M. de Boville, who took it without ceremony, quickly drew out the required assignment, whilst the Englishman was counting out the bank-notes on the other side of the desk.

29

The House of Morrel and Son

Anyone who had quitted Marseilles a few years previously well acquainted with the interior of Morrel's house, and had returned at this date, would have found a great change.

Instead of that air of life, of comfort, and of happiness that exhales from a flourishing and prosperous house,—instead of the merry faces seen at the windows, of the busy clerks hurrying to and fro in the long corridors—instead of the court filled with bales of goods, re-echoing the cries and the jokes of the porters, he would have at once perceived an air of sadness and gloom. In the deserted corridor and the empty office, out of all the numerous clerks that used to fill the office, but two remained. One was a young man of three or four-and-twenty who was in love with M. Morrel's daughter, and had remained with him, spite of the efforts of his friends to induce him to withdraw; the other was an old one-eyed cashier, named Coclès, a nickname given him by the young men who used to inhabit this vast beehive, now almost deserted, and which had so completely replaced his real name that he would not, in all probability, have replied to any one who addressed himself by it.

Coclès remained in M. Morrel's service, and a most singular change had taken place in his situation; he had at the same time risen to the rank of cashier, and sunk to the rank of a servant. He was, however, the same Coclès, good, patient, devoted, but inflexible on the subject of arithmetic, the only point on which he would have stood firm against the world, even against M. Morrel, and strong in the multiplication-table, which he had at his finger's ends, no matter what scheme or what trap was laid to catch him. In the midst of the distress of the house, Coclès was the only one unmoved. Coclès had seen all these numerous clerks go without thinking of inquiring the cause of their departure: everything was, as we have said, a question of arithmetic to Coclès, and during twenty years he had always seen all payments made with such exactitude, that it seemed as impossible to him that the house should stop payment, as it would to a miller that the river that so long turned his mill should cease to flow.

Nothing had as yet occurred to shake Coclès' belief; the last months' payment had been made with the most scrupulous exactitude; Coclès had detected an error of fourteen sous to the prejudice of Morrel, and the same evening he had brought them to M. Morrel, who, with a melancholy smile, threw them into an almost empty drawer, saying:

"Thanks, Coclès, you are the pearl of cashiers."

Coclès retired perfectly happy, for this eulogium of M. Morrel, himself the pearl of the honest men of Marseilles, flattered him more than a present of fifty pounds. But since the end of the month, M. Morrel had passed many an anxious hour. In order to meet the end of the month, he had collected all his resources, and, fearing lest the report of his distress should get bruited abroad at Marseilles when he was known to be reduced to such an extremity, he went to the fair of Beaucaire to sell his wife and daughter's jewels, and a portion of his plate. By this means the end of the month was passed, but his resources were now exhausted. Credit, owing to the reports afloat, was no longer to be had; and to meet the £4000 due on the 15th of the present month to M. de Boville, and the £4000 due on the 15th of the next month, M. Morrel had, in reality, no hope but the return of the *Pharaon*, whose departure he had learnt from a vessel which had weighed anchor at the same time, and which had already arrived in harbour.

But this vessel which, like the *Pharaon*, came from Calcutta had arrived a fortnight, whilst no intelligence had been received of the *Pharaon*.

Such was the state of things when, the day after his interview with M. de Boville, the confidential clerk of the house of Thomson and French, of Rome, presented himself at M. Morrel's. Emmanuel received him. Every fresh face alarmed the young man, for every fresh face meant a fresh creditor coming, in his uncertainty, to consult the head of the firm. The young man, wishing to spare his employer the pain of this interview, questioned the new-comer; but the stranger declared he had nothing to say to M. Emmanuel, and that his business was with M. Morrel in person.

Emmanuel sighed, and summoned Coclès. Coclès appeared, and the young man bade him conduct the stranger to M. Morrel's apartment. Coclès went first, and the stranger followed him. On the staircase they met a beautiful girl of sixteen or seventeen, who looked with anxiety at the stranger.

"M. Morrel is in his room, is he not, Mademoiselle Julie?" said the cashier.

"Yes; I think so, at least," said the young girl hesitatingly. "Go and see, Coclès, and, if my father is there, announce this gentleman."

"It will be useless to announce me, Mademoiselle," returned the Englishman. "M. Morrel does not know my name; this worthy gentleman has only to announce the confidential clerk of the house of Thomson and French, of Rome, with whom your father does business."

The young girl turned pale, and continued to descend, whilst the stranger and Coclès continued to mount the staircase. She entered the office where Emmanuel was, whilst Coclès, by the aid of a key he possessed, opened a door in the corner of a landing-place on the second staircase, conducted the stranger into an antechamber, opened a second door, which he closed behind him, and after having left the clerk of the house of Thomson and French alone, returned and signed to him that he could enter.

The Englishman entered, and found Morrel seated at a table, turning over the formidable columns of his ledger, which contained the list of his liabilities. At the sight of the stranger, M Morrel closed the ledger, rose, and offered a seat to the stranger, and when he had seen him seated, resumed his own chair.

Fourteen years had changed the worthy merchant, who, in his thirty-sixth year at the opening of this history, was now in his fiftieth. His hair had turned white, time and sorrow had ploughed deep furrows on his brow, and his look, once so firm and penetrating, was now irresolute and wandering, as if he feared being forced to fix his attention on an idea or a man. The Englishman looked at him with an air of curiosity, evidently mingled with interest.

"Monsieur," said Morrel, whose uneasiness was increased by this examination, "you wish to speak to me?"

"Yes, monsieur; you are aware from whom I come?"

"The house of Thomson and French; at least, so my cashier tells me."

"He has told you rightly. The house of Thomson and French had 300,000 or 400,000 francs (£12 to £16,000) to pay this month in France, and, knowing your strict punctuality, have collected all the bills bearing your signature, and charged me as they became due to present them, and to employ the money otherwise."

Morrel sighed deeply, and passed his hand over his forehead, which was covered with perspiration.

"So, then, sir," said Morrel "you hold bills of mine?"

"Yes, and for a considerable sum."

"What is the amount?" asked Morrel, with a voice he strove to render firm.

"Here is," said the Englishman, taking a quantity of papers from his pocket, "an assignment of 200,000 francs to our house by M. de Boville, the inspector of prisons, to whom they are due. You acknowledge, of course, you owe this sum to him? "

" Yes, he placed the money in my hands at four and a half per cent. nearly five years ago."

" When are you to pay? "

" Half the 15th of this month, half the 15th of next."

" Just so; and now here are 32,000 francs payable shortly; they are all signed by you, and assigned to our house by the holders."

" I recognise them," said Morrel, whose face was suffused as he thought that, for the first time in his life, he would be unable to honour his own signature. " Is this all? "

" No, I have for the end of the month these bills which have been assigned to us by the house of Pascal, and the house of Wild and Turner, of Marseilles, amounting to nearly 55,000 francs (£2200); in all, 287,500 francs (£11,500)."

It is impossible to describe what Morrel suffered during this enumeration.

" Two hundred and eighty-seven thousand five hundred francs," repeated he.

" Yes, sir," replied the Englishman.

" I will not," continued he, after a moment's silence, " conceal from you that whilst your probity and exactitude up to this moment are universally acknowledged, yet the report is current in Marseilles that you are not able to meet your engagements."

At this almost brutal speech Morrel turned deathly pale.

" Sir," said he, " up to this time—and it is now more than four-and-twenty years since I received the direction of this house from my father, who had himself conducted it for five-and thirty years —never has anything bearing the signature of Morrel and Son been dishonoured."

" I know that," replied the Englishman. " But as a man of honour should answer another, tell me fairly, shall you pay these with the same punctuality? "

Morrel shuddered, and looked at the man, who spoke with more assurance than he had hitherto shown.

" To questions frankly put," said he, " a straight-forward answer should be given. Yes, I shall pay, if, as I hope, my vessel arrives safely; for its arrival will again procure me the credit which the numerous accidents, of which I have been the victim, have deprived me; but if the *Pharaon* should be lost, and this last resource be gone——"

The poor man's eyes filled with tears.

" Well," said the other, " if this last resource fail you? "

" Well," returned Morrel, " it is a cruel thing to be forced to say, but, already used to misfortune, I must habituate myself to shame. I fear I shall be forced to suspend my payments."

" Have you no friends who could assist you? "

Morrel smiled mournfully.

" In business, sir," said he, " one has no friends, only correspondents."

" It is true," murmured the Englishman; " then you have but one hope."

" But one."

" The last? "

" The last."

" So that if this fail——"

" I am ruined,—completely ruined! "

" As I came here a vessel was entering the port."

" I know it, sir: a young man, who still adheres to my fallen fortunes, passes a part of his time in a belvedere at the top of the house, in hopes of being the first to announce good news to me: he has informed me of the entrance of this ship."

" And it is not yours? "

" No, it is a vessel of Bordeaux, *La Gironde*; it comes from India also; but it is not mine."

" Perhaps it has spoken the *Pharaon*, and brings you some tidings of it? "

" Shall I tell you plainly one thing, sir? I dread almost as much to receive any tidings of my vessel as to remain in doubt. Incertitude is still hope."

Then in a low voice Morrel added:

" This delay is not natural. The *Pharaon* left Calcutta the 5th of February; it ought to have been here a month ago."

" What is that? " said the Englishman. " What is the meaning of this noise? "

" Oh! oh! " cried Morrel, turning pale, " what is this? "

A loud noise was heard on the stairs of people moving hastily, and half-stifled sobs. Morrel rose and advanced to the door; but his strength failed him, and he sank into a chair. The two men remained opposite one another. Morrel trembling in every limb, the stranger gazing at him with an air of profound pity. The noise had ceased; but it seemed that Morrel expected something; something had occasioned the noise, and something must follow.

The stranger fancied he heard footsteps on the stairs, and that the steps, which were of those several persons, stopped at the door. A key was inserted in the lock of the first door, and the creaking of hinges was audible.

" There are only two persons who have the key of the door," murmured Morrel, " Coclès and Julie."

At this instant the second door opened, and the young girl, her eyes bathed with tears, appeared.

Morrel rose tremblingly, supporting himself by the arm of the chair. He would have spoken, but his voice failed him.

" Oh, father! " said she, clasping her hands, " forgive your child for being the messenger of ill."

Morrel again changed colour. Julie threw herself into his arms.

" Oh, father, father! " murmured she, " courage! "

" The *Pharaon* has then perished? " said Morrel, in a hoarse voice.

The young girl did not speak; but she made an affirmative sign with her head as she lay on her father's breast.

" And the crew? " asked Morrel.

" Saved," said the girl; " saved by the crew of the vessel that has just entered the harbour."

Morrel raised his two hands to heaven with an expression of resignation and sublime gratitude.

" Thanks, my God," said he, " at least you strike but me alone."

Spite of his phlegm a tear moistened the eye of the Englishman.

" Come in, come in," said Morrel, " for I presume you are all at the door."

Scarcely had he uttered these words than Madame Morrel entered, weeping bitterly, Emmanuel followed her, and in the antechamber were visible the rough faces of seven or eight half-naked sailors.

At the sight of these men the Englishman started and advanced a step; then restrained himself, and retired into the farthest and most obscure corner of the apartment.

Madame Morrel sat down by her husband and took one of his hands in hers, Julie still lay with her head on his shoulder, Emmanuel stood in the centre of the chamber, and seemed to form the link between Morrel's family and the sailors at the door.

" How did this happen? " said Morrel.

" Draw nearer, Penelon," said the young man, " and relate all."

An old seaman, bronzed by the tropical sun, advanced, twirling the remains of a hat between his hands.

" Good-day, M. Morrel," said he, as if he had just quitted Marseilles the previous evening, and had just returned from Aix to Toulon.

" Good-day, Penelon! " returned Morrel, who could not refrain from smiling through his tears, " where is the captain? "

" The captain, M. Morrel,—he has stayed behind sick at

Palma; but, please God, it won't be much, and you will see him in a few days all alive and hearty."

" Well, now tell your story, Penelon."

Penelon rolled his quid in his cheek, placed his hand before his mouth, turned his head, and sent a long jet of tobacco-juice into the antechamber, advanced his foot, and began:

" You see, M. Morrel," said he, " we were somewhere between Cape Blanc and Cape Bogador,* sailing with a fair breeze south-south-west after a week's calm, when Captain Gaumard comes up to me,—I was at the helm, I should tell you,—and says, ' Penelon, what do you think of those clouds that are arising there? '

" I was just then looking at them myself. ' What do I think, captain? why I think that they are rising faster than they have any business, and that they would not be so black if they did not mean mischief.'

" ' That's my opinion too,' said the captain, ' and I'll take precautions accordingly. We are carrying too much canvas. Holloa! all hands to slacken sail and lower the flying jib.'

" It was time; the squall was on us and the vessel began to heel.

" ' Ah,' said the captain, ' we have still too much canvas set; all hands to lower the mainsail! ' Five minutes after it was down, and we sailed under mizzen-topsails and topgallant-sails.

" ' Well, Penelon,' said the captain, ' what makes you shake your head? '

" ' Why,' I says, ' I don't think that we shall stop here.'

" ' I think you are right,' answered he; ' we shall have a gale.'

" ' A gale! more than that, we shall have a tempest, or I know nothing about it.'

" You could see the wind coming like the dust at Montredon:* luckily the captain understood his business.

" ' All hands take in two reefs in the topsails,' cried the captain; ' let go the bowlines, brace to, lower the topgallant-sails, haul out the reef-tackles on the yards.' "

" That was not enough for those latitudes," said the Englishman: " I should have taken four reefs in the topsails, and lowered the mizzen."

His firm, sonorous, and unexpected voice made every one start. Penelon put his hand over his eyes, and then stared at the man who thus criticised the manœuvres of his captain.

" We did better than that, sir," said the old sailor, with a certain respect; " we put the helm to the wind to run before the tempest; ten minutes after we struck our topsails and scudded under bare poles."

" The vessel was very old to risk that," said the Englishman.

"Eh, it was that that wrecked us; after having been tossed about for twelve hours, we sprung a leak. 'Penelon,' said the captain, 'I think we are sinking; give me the helm, and go down into the hold.'

"I gave him the helm, and descended; there was already three feet of water. I cried, 'All hands to the pumps!' but it was too late, and it seemed the more we pumped the more came in.

"'Ah!' said I, after four hours' work, 'since we are sinking, let us sink; we can die but once.'

"'That's the example you set, Penelon,' cries the captain, 'very well, wait a minute.'

"He went into his cabin, and came back with a brace of pistols.

"'I will blow the brains out of the first man who leaves the pump,' said he."

"Well done!" said the Englishman.

"There's nothing gives you so much courage as good reasons," continued the sailor; "and during that time the wind had abated, and the sea gone down, but the water kept rising; not much, only two inches an hour, but still it rose. Two inches an hour does not seem much, but in twelve hours that makes two feet, and three we had before, that makes five.

"'Come,' said the captain, 'we have done all in our power, and M. Morrel will have nothing to reproach us with; we have tried to save the ship, let us now save ourselves. To the boats, my lads, as quick as you can.'

"Now," continued Penelon, "you see, M. Morrel, a sailor is attached to his ship, but still more to his life: so we did not wait to be told twice; the more so, that the ship was sinking under us, and seemed to say, Get along, save yourselves.

"We soon launched the boat, and all eight of us got into it. The captain descended the last, or, rather, he did not descend, he would not quit the vessel; so I took him round the waist, and threw him into the boat, and then I jumped after him. It was time, for just as I jumped, the deck burst with a noise like the broadside of a man-of-war. Ten minutes after she pitched forward, then the other way, spun round and round, and then good-bye to the *Pharaon*. As for us, we were three days without anything to eat or drink, so that we began to think of drawing lots who should feed the rest, when we saw *La Gironde*; we made signals of distress, she perceived us, made for us, and took us all on board. There now, M. Morrel, that's the whole truth, on the honour of a sailor; is not it true, you fellows there?"

A general murmur of approbation showed that the narrator had faithfully detailed their misfortunes and sufferings.

"Well, well," said Morrel, " I know there was no one in fault but destiny, It was the will of God that this should happen, blessed be his name. What wages are due to you? "

"Oh, don't let us talk of that, M. Morrel."

"On the contrary, let us speak of it."

"Well, then, three months," said Penelon.

"Coclès, pay 200 francs to each of these good fellows," said Morrel. "At another time," added he, " I should have said, Give them, besides, 200 francs over as a present; but times are changed, and the little money that remains to me is not my own."

Penelon turned to his companions, and exchanged a few words with them.

"As for that, M. Morrel," said he, again turning his quid. " As for that——"

"As for what? "

"The money."

"Well——"

"Well, we all say that fifty francs will be enough for us at present, and that we will wait for the rest."

"Thanks, my friends, thanks! " cried Morrel gratefully; " take it—take it, and if you can find another employer, enter his service; you are free to do so."

These last words produced a prodigious effect on the seamen; Penelon nearly swallowed his quid; fortunately he recovered.

"What! M. Morrel," said he, in a low voice, " you send us away; you are then angry with us? "

"No, no," said M. Morrel, " I am not angry, on the contrary, I do not send you away; but I have no more ships, and therefore I do not want any sailors."

"No more ships! " returned Penelon; " well, then, you'll build some; we'll wait for you."

"I have no money to build ships with, Penelon," said the poor owner mournfully, " so I cannot accept your kind offer."

"No more money! then you must not pay us; we can go, like the *Pharaon*, under bare poles."

"Enough! enough! " cried Morrel, almost overpowered; " leave me, I pray you; we shall meet again in a happier time. Emmanuel, accompany them, and see that my orders are executed."

"At least, we shall see each other again, M. Morrel? " asked Penelon.

"Yes, I hope so, at least; now go."

He made a sign to Coclès, who marched first, the seamen followed him, and Emmanuel brought up the rear.

" Now," said the owner to his wife and daughter, " leave me;
I wish to speak with this gentleman."

And he glanced towards the clerk of Thomson and French,
who had remained ,motionless in the corner during this scene,
in which he had taken no part, except the few words we have
mentioned. The two females looked at this person, whose presence
they had entirely forgotten, and retired; but as she left the apartment, Julie gave the stranger a supplicating glance, to which he
replied by a smile, that an indifferent spectator would have
been surprised to see on his stern features.

The two men were left alone.

" Well, sir," said Morrel, sinking into a chair, " you have heard
all, and I have nothing further to tell you."

" I see," returned the Englishman, " that a fresh and unmerited
misfortune has overwhelmed you, and this only increases my desire
to serve you."

" Oh, sir! " cried Morrel.

" Let me see," continued the stranger, " I am one of your
largest creditors."

" Your bills, at least, are the first that will fall due."

" Do you wish for time to pay? "

" A delay would save my honour, and consequently my life."

" How long a delay do you wish for? "

Morrel reflected.

" Two months," said he.

" I will give you three," replied the stranger.

" But," asked Morrel, " will the house of Thomson and French
consent? "

" Oh, I take everything on myself. To-day is the 5th of June."

" Yes."

" Well, renew these bills up to the 5th of September, and on the
5th of September at eleven o'clock " (the hand of the clock pointed
to eleven), " I shall come to receive the money."

" I shall expect you," returned Morrel, " and I will pay you—
or I shall be dead."

These last words were uttered in so low a tone that the stranger
could not hear them. The bills were renewed, the old ones
destroyed, and the poor shipowner found himself with three
months before him to collect his resources. The Englishman
received his thanks with the phlegm peculiar to his nation, and
Morrel, overwhelming him with grateful blessings, conducted
him to the staircase.

The stranger met Julie on the stairs; she affected to be descending, but, in reality, she was waiting for him.

" Oh, sir——" said she, clasping her hands.

" Mademoiselle," said the stranger, " one day you will receive a letter, signed ' Sinbad the Sailor '; do exactly what the letter bids you, however strange it may appear."

" Yes, sir," returned Julie.

" Do you promise? "

" I swear to you I will."

" It is well. Adieu, mademoiselle!—remain as pure and virtuous as you are at present, and I have great hopes that Heaven will reward you by giving you Emmanuel for a husband."

Julie uttered a faint cry, blushed like a rose, and leaned against the baluster.

The stranger waved his hand, and continued to descend. In the court he found Penelon, who, with a rouleau of a hundred francs in either hand, seemed unable to make up his mind to retain them.

" Come with me, my friend," said the Englishman, " I wish to speak to you."

30

The Fifth of September

THE delay afforded by the agent of the house of Thomson and French, at the moment when Morrel expected it least, appeared to the poor shipowner one of those returns of good fortune which announce to a man that fate is at length weary of wasting her spite upon him. The same day he related to his wife, to Emmanuel, and his daughter, what had occurred to him, and a ray of hope, if not tranquillity, returned to the family. Unfortunately, however, Morrel had not only engagements with the house of Thomson and French, who had shown themselves so considerate towards him; and, as he had said, in business he had correspondents and not friends. When he reflected deeply, he could by no means account for this generous conduct on the part of Thomson and French towards him, and could only attribute it to the selfish reflection of the firm: " We had better support a man who owes us nearly 300,000 francs, and have that 300,000 francs at the end of three months than hasten his ruin, and have six or eight per cent. of capital."

Unfortunately, whether from hate or blindness, all Morrel's correspondents did not reflect similarly, and some made even a contrary reflection. The bills signed by Morrel were thus presented at his office with scrupulous exactitude, and, thanks to the delay granted by the Englishman, were paid by Coclès with equal punctuality. Coclès thus remained in his accustomed tranquillity. It was Morrel alone who remembered with alarm, that if he had to repay on the 15th the 100,000 francs of M. de Boville, and on the 30th the 32,500 francs of bills, for which (as well as the debt due to the inspector of prisons) he had time granted, he must be a ruined man.

The opinion of all the commercial men was, that under the reverses which had successively weighed down Morrel, it was impossible for him to stand against it. Great, therefore, was the astonishment when they saw the end of the month come, and he fulfilled all his engagements with his usual punctuality. Still confidence was not restored to all minds, and the general voice postponed only until the end of the month the complete ruin of the unfortunate shipowner. The month passed amidst unheard-of efforts on the part of Morrel to get in all his resources. Formerly, his paper at any date was taken with confidence, and was even in request. Morrel now tried to negotiate bills at ninety days days only, and found all the banks closed. Fortunately, Morrel had some moneys coming in on which he could rely, and as they reached him he found himself in a condition to meet his engagements when the end of July came.

The agent of Thomson and French had not been again seen at Marseilles: the day after, or two days after his visit to Morrel, he had disappeared, and as in that city he had had no intercourse but with the mayor, the inspector of prisons, and M. Morrel, his appearance left no other trace than the different remembrances of him which these three persons retained. As to the sailors of the *Pharaon*, it seemed that they must have found some engagement, for they had disappeared also.

Captain Gaumard, recovered from his illness, had returned from Palma. He hesitated to present himself at Morrel's, but the owner, hearing of his arrival, went to him. The worthy shipowner knew, from Penelon's recital, of the captain's brave conduct during the storm, and tried to console him. He brought him also the amount of his wages, which Captain Gaumard had not dared to apply for. As he descended the staircase, Morrel met Penelon, who was going up. Penelon had, it would seem, made good use of his money, for he was newly clad: when he saw his employer, the worthy tar seemed much embarrassed, drew on one side into the corner of the landing-place, passed his quid from one cheek to the other, stared stupidly with his great eyes, and only acknowledged the squeeze of the hand which Morrel as usual gave him by a slight pressure in return. Morrel attributed Penelon's embarrassment to the elegance of his attire: it was evident the good fellow had not gone to such an expense on his own account; he was no doubt engaged on board some other vessel, and thus his bashfulness arose from the fact of his not having, if we may so express ourselves, worn mourning for the *Pharaon* longer. Perhaps he had come to tell Captain Gaumard of his good luck, and to offer him employment from his new master.

" Worthy fellow! " said Morrel, as he went away, " may your new master love you as I loved you, and be more fortunate than I have been! "

August rolled by in unceasing efforts on the part of Morrel to renew his credit or revive the old. On the 20th of August it was known at Marseilles that he had taken a place in the mail-coach, and then it was said that it was at the end of the month the docket was to be struck, and Morrel had gone away before, that he might not be present at this cruel act; but had left his chief clerk Emmanuel, and his cashier Coclès to meet it. But, contrary, to all expectation, when the 31st of August came, the house opened as usual, and Coclès appeared behind the grating of the counter, examined all bills presented with the same scrutiny, and, from first to last, paid all with the same precision. There came in, moreover, two repayments which M. Morrel had anticipated, and which Coclès paid as punctually as those bills which the shipowner had accepted. All this was incomprehensible, and then, with the tenacity peculiar to prophets of bad news, the failure was put off until the end of September.

On the 1st, Morrel returned. He was awaited by his family with extreme anxiety, for from this journey to Paris they hoped a last means of safety would arrive. Morrel had thought of Danglars, who was now immensely rich, and had lain under great obligations to Morrel in former days, since to him it was owing that Danglars entered the service of the Spanish banker, with whom had commenced his vast wealth. It was said at this moment that Danglars was worth from £200,000 to £300,000, and had unlimited credit. Danglars then, without taking a crown from his pocket, could save Morrel; he had but to pass his word for a loan, and Morrel was saved. Morrel had long thought of Danglars, but there are those instinctive revoltings impossible to control, and Morrel had delayed as long as possible before he had recourse to this last resource. And Morrel was right, for he returned home borne down by all the humiliation of a refusal. Yet, on his arrival, Morrel did not utter a complaint, nor say one harsh word; he embraced his weeping wife and daughter, pressed Emmanuel's hand with friendly warmth, and then going to his private room on the second floor, had sent for Coclès.

"Then," said the two females to Emmanuel, "we are, indeed, ruined."

It was agreed in a brief council held amongst them, that Julie should write to her brother, who was in garrison at Nismes, to come to them as speedily as possible. The poor woman felt instinctively that they required all their strength to support the blow that impended. Besides, Maximilian Morrel, though hardly two-and-twenty, had great influence over his father. He was a strong-minded, upright young man. At the time when he decided on his profession his father had no desire to choose for him, but had consulted young Maximilian's taste. He had at once declared for a military life, and had in consequence studied hard, passed brilliantly through the Ecole Polytechnique,* and left it as sublieutenant of the 53rd of the line. For a year he had held this rank, and expected promotion on the first vacancy. In his regiment, Maximilian Morrel was noted as the most rigid observer, not only of the obligations imposed on a soldier, but also of the duties of a man, and he thus gained the name of "the stoic." We need hardly say, that many of those who gave him this epithet repeated it because they had heard it, and did not even know what it meant. This was the young man whom his mother and sister called to their aid to sustain them under the grave circumstances which they felt they would soon have to endure. They had not mistaken the gravity of this event, for the moment after Morrel had entered his cabinet with Coclès, Julie saw the latter leave it pale, trembling, and his features betraying the utmost consternation. She would have questioned him as he passed by her, but the worthy creature hastened down the staircase with unusual precipitation, and only raised his hands to heaven and exclaimed:

"Oh, mademoiselle! mademoiselle! what a dreadful misfortune! Who could ever have believed it?"

A moment afterwards Julie saw him go upstairs carrying two or three heavy ledgers, a pocket-book, and a bag of money.

Morrel examined the ledgers, opened the pocket-book, and counted the money. All his funds amounted to 6000 or 8000 francs, his expectancies up to the 5th to 4000 or 5000, which, making the best of everything, gave him 14,000 francs to meet bills amounting to 287,500 francs. He could not make such a proposal. However, when Morrel went down to his dinner, he appeared very composed. This calmness was more alarming to the two women than the deepest dejection would have been. After dinner Morrel usually went out, and used to take his coffee at the club of the Phocéens, and read the *Semaphore;** but this day he did not leave the house, but returned to his office.

As to Coclès, he seemed completely bewildered. For part of the day he went into the courtyard, seated himself on a stone with his head bare, and exposed to a sun of thirty degrees.

Emmanuel tried to comfort the females, but his eloquence faltered. The young man was too well acquainted with the business of the house, not to feel that a great catastrophe hung over the Morrel family.

Night came; the two women had watched, hoping that when he left his room Morrel would come to them, but they heard him pass before their door, and trying to conceal the noise of his footsteps. They listened; he went into his sleeping-room, and fastened the door inside. Madame Morrel sent her daughter to bed, and half an hour after Julie had retired, she rose, took off her shoes, and went stealthily along the passage, to see through the keyhole what her husband was doing. In the passage she saw a retreating shadow; it was Julie, who, uneasy herself, had anticipated her mother. The young lady went towards Madame Morrel.

" He is writing," she said.

They had understood each other without speaking. Madame Morrel looked again through the keyhole—Morrel was writing; but Madame Morrel remarked, what her daughter had not observed, that her husband was writing on stamped paper. The terrible idea that he was writing his will flashed across her; she shuddered, and yet had not strength to utter a word.

Next day M. Morrel seemed as calm as ever, went into his office as usual, came to his breakfast punctually, and then, after dinner, he placed his daughter beside him, took her head in his arms, and held her for a long time against his bosom. In the evening, Julie told her mother, that although so calm in appearance, she had remarked that her father's heart beat violently.

The two next days passed almost similarly. On the evening of the 4th of September, M. Morrel asked his daughter for the key of his cabinet. Julie trembled at this request, which seemed to her of bad omen. Why did her father ask for this key which she always kept, and which was only taken from her in childhood as a punishment? The young girl looked at Morrel.

" What have I done wrong, father," she said, " that you should take this key from me? "

" Nothing, my dear," replied the unhappy man, the tears starting to his eyes at this simple question,—" nothing, only I want it."

Julie made a pretence to feel for the key.

" I must have left it in my room," she said.

And she went out, but instead of going to her apartment she hastened to consult Emmanuel.

" Do not give this key to your father," said he, " and to-morrow morning, if possible, do not quit him for a moment."

She questioned Emmanuel, but he knew nothing, or would not say it if he did.

During the night, between the 4th and 5th of September, Madame Morrel remained listening for every sound, and, until three o'clock in the morning, she heard her husband pacing the room in great agitation. It was three o'clock when he threw himself on the bed. The mother and daughter passed the night together. They had expected Maximilian since the previous evening. At eight o'clock in the morning Morrel entered their chamber. He was calm; but the agitation of the night was legible in his pale and careworn visage. They did not dare to ask him how he had slept.

Morrel was kinder to his wife, more affectionate to his daughter, than he had ever been. He could not cease gazing at and kissing the sweet girl. Julie, mindful of Emmanuel's request, was following her father when he quitted the room, but he said to her quickly:

" Remain with your mother, dearest."

Julie wished to accompany him.

" I wish you to do so," he said.

This was the first time Morrel had ever so spoken, but he said it in a tone of paternal kindness, and Julie did not dare refuse compliance. She remained at the same spot, standing mute and motionless. An instant afterwards the door opened, she felt two arms encircle her, and a mouth pressed her forehead. She looked up, and uttered an exclamation of joy.

" Maximilian! my dearest brother! " she cried.

At these words Madame Morrel rose, and threw herself into her son's arms.

" Mother! " said the young man, looking alternately at Madame Morrel and her daughter, " what has occurred—what has happened? your letter has frightened me, and I have come hither with all speed."

" Julie," said Madame Morrel, making a sign to the young man, " go and tell your father that Maximilian has just arrived."

The young lady rushed out of the apartment, but on the first step of the staircase she found a man holding a letter in his hand.

" Are you not Mademoiselle Julie Morrel? " inquired the man with a strong Italian accent.

" Yes, sir," replied Julie, with hesitation; " what is your pleasure? I do not know you."

" Read this letter," he said, handing it to her.

Julie hesitated.

" It concerns the best interests of your father," said the messenger.

The young girl hastily took the letter from him. She opened it quickly and read:

" Go this moment to the Allées de Meillan, enter the house No. 15, ask the porter for the key of the room on the fifth floor, enter the apartment, take from the corner of the mantel-piece a purse netted in red silk, and give it to your father. It is important that he should receive it before eleven o'clock. You promised to obey me implicitly. Remember your oath.

"SINBAD THE SAILOR."

The young girl uttered a joyful cry, raised her eyes, looked round to question the messenger, but he had disappeared. She cast her eyes again over the note to peruse it a second time, and saw there was a postscript. She read:

" It is important that you should fulfil this mission in person and alone; if you go accompanied by any other person, or should any one else present themselves, the porter will reply that he does not know anything about it."

This postscript was a great check to the young girl's joy. Was there nothing to fear? was there not some snare laid for her? Her innocence had kept her in ignorance of the dangers that might assail a young girl of her age; but there is no need to know danger in order to fear it: indeed, it may be observed, that it is usually unknown perils that inspire the greatest terror.

Julie hesitated, and resolved to take counsel. Yet, by a singular feeling, it was neither to her mother nor her brother that she applied, but to Emmanuel.

She hastened down, and told him what had occurred on the day when the agent of the house of Thomson and French had come to her father's, related the scene on the staircase, repeated the promise she had made, and showed him the letter.

" You must go then, mademoiselle," said Emmanuel.

" Go there? " murmured Julie.

" Yes, I will accompany you."

" But did you not read that I must be alone? " said Julie.

" And you shall be alone," replied the young man. " I will await you at the corner of the Rue du Musée, and if you are so long absent as to make me uneasy, I will hasten to rejoin you, and woe to him of whom you shall have cause to complain to me! "

" Then, Emmanuel," said the young girl, with hesitation, " it is your opinion that I should obey this invitation? "

" Yes. Did not the messenger say your father's safety was in it? "

" But what danger threatens him, then, Emmanuel? " she asked.

Emmanuel hesitated a moment, but his desire to make Julie decide immediately, made him reply.

" Listen," he said, " to-day is the 5th of September—is it not? "

" Yes."

" To-day, then, at eleven o'clock, your father has nearly 300,000 francs to pay? "

" Yes, we know that."

" Well, then," continued Emmanuel, " we have not 15,000 francs in the house."

" What will happen then? "

" Why, if to-day before eleven o'clock your father has not found some one who will come to his aid he will be compelled at twelve o'clock to declare himself a bankrupt."

" Oh, come, then, come! " cried she, hastening away with the young man.

During this time, Madame Morrel had told her son everything. The young man knew quite well that after the succession of misfortunes which had befallen his father, great changes had taken place in the style of living and housekeeping, but he did not know that matters had reached such a point, He was thunderstruck. Then, rushing hastily out of the apartment, he ran upstairs, expecting to find his father in his cabinet, but he rapped there in vain. Whilst he was yet at the door of the cabinet he heard the bedroom door open, turned and saw his father. Instead of going direct to his cabinet, M. Morrel had returned to his bedchamber, which he was only this moment quitting.

Morrel uttered a cry of surprise at the sight of his son, of whose arrival he was ignorant. He remained motionless on the spot, pressing with his left hand something he had concealed under his coat. Maximilian sprung down the staircase and threw his arms round his father's neck; but suddenly he recoiled, and placed his hand on Morrel's breast.

" Father! " he exclaimed, turning pale as death, " what are you going to do with the brace of pistols under your coat? "

" Oh, this is what I feared! " said Morrel.

" Father, father! in Heaven's name," exclaimed the young man, " what are these weapons for? "

" Maximilian," replied Morrel, looking fixedly at his son,

" you are a man, and a man of honour. Come, and I will explain to you."

And with a firm step, Morrel went up to his cabinet, whilst Maximilian followed him, trembling as he went. Morrel opened the door and closed it behind his son; then crossing the anteroom, went to his desk, on which he placed the pistols, and pointed with his finger to an open ledger. In this ledger was made out an exact balance-sheet of affairs. Morrel had to pay, within half an hour, 287,500 francs. All he possessed was 15, 257 francs.

" Read! " said Morrel.

The young man was overwhelmed as he read. Morrel said not a word. What could he say? What need he add to such a desperate proof in figures?

" And have you done all that is possible, father, to meet this disastrous result? " asked the young man, after a moment's pause.

" I have," replied Morrel.

" You have no money coming in on which you can rely? "

" None."

" You have exhausted every resource? "

" All."

" And in half an hour," said Maximilian, in a gloomy voice, " our name is dishonoured! "

" Blood washes out dishonour," said Morrel.

" You are right, father; I understand you."

Then extending his hand towards one of the pistols, he said: " There is one for you and one for me—thanks! "

Morrel checked his hand.

" Your mother—your sister! Who will support them? "

A shudder ran through the young man's frame.

" Father," he said, " do you reflect that you are bidding me to live? "

" Yes, I do bid you," answered Morrel, " it is your duty. You have a calm, strong mind, Maximilian. Maximilian, you are no ordinary man: I desire nothing,—I command nothing. I only say to you, examine my position as if it were your own, and then judge for yourself."

The young man reflected an instant, then an expression of sublime resignation appeared in his eyes, and, with a slow and sad gesture, he took off his two epaulettes, the marks of his rank.

" Be it so, then, my father," he said, extending his hand to Morrel, " die in peace, my father; I will live."

Morrel was about to cast himself on his knees before his son, but Maximilian caught him in his arms, and those two noble hearts were pressed against each other for a moment.

" You know it is not my fault," said Morrel.

Maximilian smiled.

" I know, father, you are the most honourable man I have ever known."

" Good, my son, and now all is said; go now and rejoin your mother and sister."

" My father," said the young man, bending his knees, " bless me! "

Morrel took his head between his two hands, drew him towards him, and kissing his forehead several times, said, " Oh! yes, yes, I bless you in my own name, and in the name of three generations of irreproachable men, who say by my voice,—the edifice which misfortune has destroyed, Providence may build up again. On seeing me die such a death, the most inexorable will have pity on you; to you perhaps they will accord the time they have refused to me; try that the word of disgrace be never pronounced; go to work, labour, young man, struggle ardently and courageously: live yourself, your mother and sister, with the most rigid economy, so that from day to day the property of those whom I leave in your hands may augment and fructify. Reflect how glorious a day it will be, how grand, how solemn that day of complete restoration—on which you will say in this very office, ' My father died because he could not do what I have this day done; but he died calmly and peaceably, because in dying he knew what I should do."

" My father! my father! " cried the young man, " why should you not live? "

" If I live, all would be changed; if I live, interest would be converted into doubt, pity into hostility; if I live, I am only a man who has broken his word, failed in his engagements—in fact, only a bankrupt. If, on the contrary, I die, remember, Maximilian, my corpse is that of an honest but unfortunate man. Living, my best friends would avoid my house; dead all Marseilles, will follow me in tears to my last home. Living, you would feel shame at my name; dead, you may raise your head and say, ' I am the son of him you killed, because, for the first time, he has been compelled to fail in his word.' "

The young man uttered a groan, but appeared resigned.

" And, now" said Morrel, " leave me alone, and endeavour to keep your mother and sister away."

" Will you not see my sister once more? " asked Maximilian.

A last but final hope was concealed by the young man in the effect of this interview, and therefore he had suggested it.

Morrel shook his head.

" I saw her this morning, and bade her adieu."

"Have you no particular commands to leave with me, my father?" inquired Maximilian, in a faltering voice.

"Yes, my son, and a sacred command."

"Say it, my father."

"The house of Thomson and French is the only one, who, from humanity—or it may be selfishness—it is not for me to read men's hearts—have had any pity for me. His agent, who will in ten minutes present himself to receive the amount of a bill of 287,500 francs, I will not say granted, but offered me three months. Let this house be the first repaid, my son, and respect this man."

"Father, I will," said Maximilian.

"And now once more adieu," said Morrel; "go leave me, I would be alone; you will find my will in the secretaire in my bedroom."

The young man remained standing and motionless, having but the force of will, and not the power of execution.

"Hear me, Maximilian," said his father. "Suppose I were a soldier like you, and ordered to carry a certain redoubt, and you knew I must be killed in the assault, would you not say to me as you said just now, ' Go, father, for you are dishonoured by delay, and death is preferable to shame '? "

"Yes, yes! " said the young man—" yes; " and once again embracing his father with convulsive pressure, he said, " Be it so, my father."

And he rushed out of the cabinet.

When his son had left him, Morrel remained an instant standing, with his eyes fixed on the door—then putting forth his arm, he pulled the bell.

After a moment's interval, Coclès appeared.

It was no longer the same man—the fearful convictions of the three last days had crushed him. This thought—the house of Morrel is about to stop payment—bent him to the earth more than twenty years would otherwise have done.

"My worthy Coclès," said Morrel, in a tone impossible to describe, " do you remain in the antechamber; when the gentleman who came three months ago, the agent of the house of Thomson and French, arrives, announce his arrival to me."

Coclès made no reply: he made a sign with his head, went into the anteroom, and seated himself.

Morrel fell back in his chair, his eyes fixed on the clock; there were seven minutes left, that was all; the hand moved on with incredible rapidity; it seemed to him as if he saw it progress.

What then passed, at this final moment of time in the mind of this man, who, still young, had by a course of reasoning, false, perhaps, but at least specious, was about to separate himself from all he loved in the world, and quit life which possessed for him all domestic delights,—it is impossible to express:—to form the slightest idea of his feelings, he must have been seen with his brow bathed in perspiration, yet resigned; his eyes moistened with tears, and yet raised to heaven.

The clock hand moved on; the pistols were cocked he stretched forth his hand, took one up, and murmured his daughter's name.

Then he laid down the mortal weapon, took up his pen, and wrote a few words. It seemed to him as if he had not taken a sufficient farewell of his beloved daughter.

Then he turned again to the clock; he no longer counted by minutes, but by seconds. He took up the deadly weapon again, his mouth half opened and his eyes fixed on the clock, and then shuddered at the click of the trigger as he cocked the pistol.

At this moment of mortal agony, a damp colder than death passed over his brow, an agony stronger than death clutched at his heart-strings.

He heard the door of the staircase creak on its hinges. The clock gave its warning to strike eleven. The door of his cabinet opened—Morrel did not turn round, he expected these words of Coclès:

" The agent of Thomson and French."

He placed the muzzle of the pistol between his teeth. Suddenly he heard a cry,—it was his daughter's voice. He turned and saw Julie; the pistol fell from his hands.

" My father! " cried the young girl, out of breath and half dead with joy. " Saved!—you are saved! " And she threw herself into his arms, holding in her extended hand a red netted silk purse.

" Saved!—my child! " said Morrel; " what do you mean? "

" Yes, saved,—saved! see, see! " said the young girl.

Morrel took the purse, and started as he did so, for a vague remembrance reminded him that it once belonged to himself. At one end was the bill for the 287,500 francs *receipted*, at the other was a diamond as large as a hazel nut, with these words on a small slip of parchment:

" JULIE'S DOWRY."

Morrel passed his hand over his brow; it seemed to him a dream. At this moment the clock struck eleven. The sound vibrated as if each stroke of the hammer struck Morrel's heart.

" Explain, my child," he said; " explain—where did you find this purse? "

" In a house in the Allées de Meillan, No. 15, on the corner of a mantel-piece, in a small room on the fifth floor."

" But," cried Morrel, " this purse is not yours! "

Julie handed to her father the letter she had received in the morning.

" And did you go alone? " asked Morrel, after he had read it.

" Emmanuel accompanied me, father. He was to have waited for me at the corner of the Rue de Musée; but, strange to say, he was not there when I returned."

" Monsieur Morrel! " exclaimed a voice on the stairs. " Monsieur Morrel! "

" It is his voice! " said Julie.

At this moment Emmanuel entered, his countenance full of animation and joy.

" The *Pharaon*! " he cried; " the *Pharaon*! "

" What!—what! the *Pharaon*! Are you mad, Emmanuel? You know the vessel is lost."

" The *Pharaon*, sir—they signal the *Pharaon*! The *Pharaon* is entering the harbour! "

Morrel fell back in his chair, his strength was failing him; his understanding, weakened by such events, refused to comprehend such incredible, unheard-of, fabulous facts.

But his son came in.

" Father! " cried Maximilian, " how could you say the *Pharaon* was lost? The watch-tower has signalled her, and they say she is now coming into port."

" My dear friends! " said Morrel, " if this were so, it must be a miracle of Heaven! Impossible! impossible! "

But what was real and not less incredible was the purse he held in his hand; the acceptance receipted—the splendid diamond.

" Ah! sir," exclaimed Coclès, " what can it mean?—the *Pharaon*? "

" Come, my dear," said Morrel, rising from his seat, " let us go and see, and Heaven have pity upon us if it be false intelligence."

They all went out, and on the stairs met Madame Morrel, who had been afraid to go up into the cabinet. In an instant they were at the Cannebière. There was a crowd on the pier. All the crowd gave way before Morrel.

" The *Pharaon*! the *Pharaon*! " said every voice.

And, wonderful to say, in front of the tower of Saint-Jean, was a ship bearing on her stern these words, printed in white letters, " The *Pharaon*, Morrel and Son, of Marseilles." It was precisely resembling the other *Pharaon*, and loaded as that had been with cochineal and indigo. It cast anchor, brailed all sails, and on the deck was Captain Gaumard giving orders, and Maître Penelon making signals to M. Morrel.

To doubt any longer was impossible; there was the evidence of the senses, and ten thousand persons who came to corroborate the testimony.

As Morrel and his son embraced on the pier-head, in the presence and applause of the whole city witnessing this prodigy, a man with his face half covered by a black beard, and who, concealed behind the sentry-box, watched the scene with delight, uttered these words in a low tone: " Be happy, noble heart, be blessed for all the good thou hast done and wilt do hereafter, and let my gratitude rest in the shade with your kindness."

And with a smile in which joy and happiness were revealed, he left his hiding-place and, without being observed, descended one of those flights of steps which serve for debarkation, and hailing three times, shouted, " Jacopo! Jacopo! Jacopo! "

Then a shallop came to shore, took him on board, and conveyed him to a yacht splendidly fitted up, on whose deck he sprung with the activity of a sailor; thence he once again looked towards Morrel, who, weeping with joy, was shaking hands most cordially with all the crowd around him, and thanking with a look the unknown benefactor whom he seemed to be seeking in the skies.

" And now," said the unknown, " farewell kindness, humanity, and gratitude! Farewell to all the feelings that expand the heart! I have been Heaven's substitute to recompense the good—now the God of Vengeance yields to me his power to punish the wicked! "

At these words he gave a signal, and, as if only awaiting this signal, the yacht instantly put out to sea.

31

Italy: Sinbad the Sailor

TOWARDS the commencement of the year 1838, two young men belonging to the first society of Paris, the Viscount Albert de Morcerf and the Baron Franz d'Epinay, were at Florence. They had agreed to see the carnival at Rome that year, and that Franz, who for the last three of four years had inhabited Italy, should act as *cicerone* to Albert.

As it is no inconsiderable affair to spend the carnival at Rome, especially when you have no great desire to sleep on the Place du Peuple, or the Campo Vaccino, they wrote to Maître Pastrini, the proprietor of the Hôtel de Londres, Place d'Espagne, to reserve comfortable apartments for them. Maître Pastrini replied that he had only two rooms and a cabinet *al secondo piano*, which he offered at the low charge of a louis per diem. They accepted his offer; but wishing to make the best use of the time that was left, Albert started for Naples. As for Franz, he remained at Florence. After having passed several days here, during which time he promenaded in the Paradise called the Casines, and spent two or three evenings at the houses of the nobles of Florence, he took a fancy into his head, having already visited Corsica, the birthplace of Bonaparte, to visit Elba, the halting-place of Napoleon.

One evening he loosened a bark from the iron ring that secured it to the port of Leghorn, laid himself down, wrapped in his cloak, at the bottom, and said to the crew:

" To the isle of Elba."

The bark shot out of the harbour like a bird, and the next morning Franz disembarked at Porto-Ferrajo. He traversed the island, after having followed the traces which the footsteps of the giant have left and re-embarked for Marciana. Two hours after he again landed at Pianosa, where he was assured red partridges abounded. The sport was bad; Franz only succeeded in killing a few partridges, and, like every unsuccessful sportsman, he returned to the boat very much out of temper.

" Ah, if your excellency chose," said the captain, " you might have capital sport."

" Where? "

" Do you see that island? " continued the captain, pointing to a conical pile that rose from the sea.

" Well; what is this island? "

" The island of Monte Cristo."

" But I have no permission to shoot over this island."

" Your excellency does not require a permission, for the island is uninhabited."

" Ah, indeed! " said the young man. " A desert island in the midst of the Mediterranean must be a curiosity."

" It is very natural; this isle is a mass of rocks, and does not contain an acre of land capable of cultivation."

" To whom does this island belong? "

" To Tuscany."

" What game shall I find there? "

" Thousands of wild goats."

" Who live upon the stones, I suppose," said Franz, with an incredulous smile.

" No; but by browsing the shrubs and trees that grow out of the crevices of the rocks."

" Where can I sleep? "

" On shore in the grottos, or on board in your cloak; besides, if your excellency pleases, we can leave as soon as the chase is finished—we can sail as well by night as by day, and if the wind drops we can use our oars."

As Franz had sufficient time, and besides had no longer his apartments at Rome to seek after, he accepted the proposition. Upon his answer in the affirmative, the sailors exchanged a few words together in a low tone.

" Well? " asked he, " what, is there any difficulty to be surmounted? "

" No," replied the captain, " but we must warn your excellency that the island is contumacious."

" What do you mean? "

" That Monte Cristo, although uninhabited, yet serves occasionally as a refuge for the smugglers and pirates who come from Corsica, Sardinia, and Africa, and that if it becomes known that we have been there, we shall have to perform quarantine for six days on our return to Leghorn."

" The devil! that is quite another thing;—rather a long time too."

" But who will say your excellency has been to Monte Cristo? "

" Oh, I shall not," cried Franz.

" Nor I, nor I," chorused the sailors.

" Then steer for Monte Cristo."

The captain gave his orders, the helm was put up, and the bark was soon sailing in the direction of the island.

Franz waited until all was finished, and when the sail was filled, and the four sailors had taken their place—three forward, and one at the helm—he resumed the conversation.

"Gaetano," said he to the captain, "you tell me Monte Cristo serves as a refuge for pirates, who are, it seems to me, a very different kind of game from the goats."

"Yes, your excellency, and it is true."

"I knew there were smugglers, but I thought that since the capture of Algiers,* and the destruction of the regency, pirates only existed in the romances of Cooper and Captain Marryat."*

"Your excellency is mistaken; there are pirates like the bandits who were believed to have been exterminated by Pope Leo XII, and who yet every day rob travellers at the gates of Rome. Has not your excellency heard that the French *chargé d'affaires* was robbed six months ago within five hundred paces of Velletri?"

"Oh, yes, I heard that."

"Well, then, if like us, your excellency lived at Leghorn, you would hear, from time to time, that a little merchant-vessel, or an English yacht that was expected at Bastia, at Porto-Ferrajo or at Civita Vecchia, has not arrived. No one knows what has become of it, but, doubtless, it has struck on a rock and foundered. Now this rock it has met has been a long and narrow boat manned by six or eight men, who have surprised and plundered it some dark and stormy night, near some desert and gloomy isle, as bandits plunder a carriage at the corner of a wood."

"But," asked Franz, who lay wrapped in his cloak at the bottom of the bark, "why do not those who have been plundered complain to the French, Sardinian, or Tuscan governments?"

"Why?" said Gaetano with a smile.

"Yes, why?"

"Because, in the first place, they transfer from the vessel to their own boat whatever they think worth taking, then they bind the crew hand and foot, they attach to every one's neck a four-and-twenty pound ball, a large hole is pierced in the vessel's bottom, and then they leave her. At the end of ten minutes the vessel begins to roll, labour, and then sink; then one of the sides plunges, and then the other ; it rises and sinks again; suddenly a noise like the report of a cannon is heard—it is the air blowing up the deck; soon the water rushes out of the scupper-holes like a whale spouting, the vessel gives a last groan, spins round and round, and disappears, forming a vast whirlpool in the ocean, and then all is over; so that in five minutes nothing but the eye of God can see the vessel where she lies at the bottom of the sea. Do you understand now," said the captain, "why no complaints are made to the government, and why the vessel does not arrive at the port? "

It is probable that if Gaetano had related this previous to proposing the expedition, Franz would have hesitated ere he accepted it, but now that they had started, he thought it would be cowardly to draw back. He was one of those men who do not rashly court danger, but if danger present itself, combat it with the most unalterable *sang froid*; he was one of those calm and resolute men who look upon a danger as an adversary in a duel, who, calculating his movements, study his attacks; who retreat sufficiently to take breath, but not to appear cowardly; who, understanding all their advantages, kill at a single blow.

" Bah! " said he, " I have travelled through Sicily and Calabria, I have sailed two months in the Archipelago, and yet I never saw even the shadow of a bandit or a pirate."

" I did not tell your excellency this to deter you from your project," replied Gaetano, " but you questioned me, and I have answered; that's all."

" Yes, and your conversation is most interesting, and as I wish to enjoy it as long as possible, steer for Monte Cristo."

The wind blew strongly, the bark sailed six or seven knots an hour, and they were rapidly reaching the end of their voyage. As they approached, the isle became larger, and they could already distinguish the rocks heaped on one another, like bullets in an arsenal, in whose crevices they could see the green bushes and trees that were growing. As for the sailors, although they appeared perfectly tranquil, yet it was evident that they were on the alert, and that they carefully watched the glassy surface over which they were sailing, and on which a few fishing-boats, with their white sails, were alone visible. They were within fifteen miles of Monte Cristo when the sun began to set behind Corsica, whose mountains appeared against the sky, and showing their rugged peaks in bold relief. This mass of stones, like the giant Adamastor,* rose threateningly before the bark, from which it shaded the sun that gilded its lower parts. By degrees the shadow rose from the sea and seemed to drive before it the last rays of the expiring day. At last the reflection rested on the summit of the mountain, where it paused an instant, like the fiery crest of a volcano, then the shadow gradually covered the summit as it had covered the base, and the isle now only appeared to be a gray mountain that grew continually darker. Half an hour after and the night was quite dark.

Fortunately the mariners were used to these latitudes, and knew every rock in the Tuscan Archipelago; for in the midst of this obscurity Franz was not without uneasiness. Corsica had long since disappeared, and Monte Cristo itself was invisible, but the sailors seemed, like the lynx, to see in the dark, and the pilot, who steered, did not evince the slightest hesitation.

An hour had passed since the sun had set, when Franz fancied he saw, at a quarter of a mile to the left, a dark mass, but it was impossible to make out what it was, and fearing to excite the mirth of the sailors, by mistaking a floating cloud for land, he remained silent; suddenly, a great light appeared on the strand; land might resemble a cloud, but the fire was not a meteor.

" What is this light? " asked he.

" Silence! " said the captain. " It is a fire."

" But you told me the isle was uninhabited? "

" I said there were no fixed habitations on it; but I said also that it served sometimes as a harbour for smugglers."

" And for pirates? "

" And for pirates," returned Gaetano, repeating Franz's words. " It is for that reason I have given orders to pass the isle, for, as you see, the fire is behind us."

" But this fire? " continued Franz. " It seems to me rather to assure than alarm us: men who did not wish to be seen would not light a fire."

" Oh, that goes for nothing," said Gaetano. " If you can guess the position of the isle in the darkness, you will see that the fire cannot be seen from the side, or from Pianosa, but only from the sea."

" You think, then, that this fire announces unwelcome neighbours? "

" That is what we must ascertain," returned Gaetano, fixing his eyes on this terrestrial star.

" How can you ascertain? "

" You shall see."

Gaetano consulted with his companions, and after five minutes' discussion, a manœuvre was executed which caused the vessel to tack about, they returned the way they had come, and in a few minutes the fire disappeared, hidden by a rise in the land.

The pilot again changed the course of the little bark, which rapidly approached the isle, and was soon within fifty paces of it. Gaetano lowered the sail, and the bark remained stationary. All this was done in silence, and since their course had been changed, not a word was spoken.

Gaetano, who had proposed the expedition, had taken all the responsibility on himself; the four sailors fixed their eyes on him, whilst they prepared their oars and held themselves in readiness to row away, which, thanks to the darkness, would not be difficult. As for Franz, he examined his arms with the utmost coolness:

he had two double-barrelled guns and a rifle; he loaded them, looked at the locks, and waited quietly.

During this time the captain had thrown off his vest and shirt, and secured his trousers round his waist; his feet were naked, so he had no shoes and stockings to take off; after these preparations he placed his finger on his lips, and lowering himself noiselessly into the sea, swam towards the shore with such precaution that it was impossible to hear the slightest sound; he could only be traced by the phosphorescent line in his wake. This track soon disappeared; it was evident that he had touched the shore. Every one on board remained motionless during half an hour, when the same luminous track was again observed, and in two strokes he had regained the bark.

" Well! " exclaimed Franz and the sailors altogether.

" They are Spanish smugglers," said he; " they have with them two Corsican bandits."

" And what are these Corsican bandits doing here with Spanish smugglers? "

" Alas! " returned the captain, with an accent of the most profound pity, " we ought always to help one another. Very often the bandits are hard pressed by gendarmes or carbineers; well, they see a bark, and good fellows like us on board, they come and demand hospitality of us; you can't refuse help to a poor hunted devil; we receive them, and for greater security we stand out to sea. This costs us nothing, and saves the life, or at least the liberty, of a fellow-creature, who on the first occasion returns the service by pointing out some safe spot where we can land our goods without interruption."

" Ah! " said Franz, " then you are a smuggler occasionally, Gaetano? "

" Your excellency, we must live somehow," returned the other, smiling in a way impossible to describe.

" Then you know the men who are now on Monte Cristo? "

" Oh, yes, we sailors are like freemasons, and recognise each other by signs."

" And do you think we have nothing to fear if we land? "

" Nothing at all; smugglers are not thieves."

" But these two Corsican bandits? " said Franz, calculating the chances of peril.

" It is not their faults that they are bandits, but that of the authorities."

" How so? "

" Because they are pursued for having made a *peau*, as if it was not in a Corsican's nature to revenge himself."*

" What do you mean by having made a *peau*?—having assassin-ated a man? " said Franz, continuing his investigation.

" I mean that they have killed an enemy, which is a very differ-ent thing," returned the captain.

" Well," said the young man, " let us demand hospitality of these smugglers and bandits. Do you think they will grant it? "

" Without doubt."

" How many are they? "

" Four, and the two bandits make six."

" Just our number, so that if they prove troublesome, we shall be able to check them; so, for the last time, steer to Monte Cristo."

" Yes, but your excellency will permit us to take all due precautions."

" By all means, be as wise as Nestor and as prudent as Ulysses, —I do more than permit, I exhort you."

" Silence, then! " said Gaetano.

Every one obeyed.

For a man who, like Franz, viewed his position in its true light, it was a grave one. He was alone in the darkness with sailors whom he did not know, and who had no reason to be devoted to him; who knew that he had in his belt several thousand francs, and who had often examined his arms,—which were very beautiful,—if not with envy, at least with curiosity. On the other hand, he was about to land, without any other escort than these men, on an island whose name was religious, but which did not seem to Franz likely to afford him much hospitality, thanks to the smugglers and bandits. The history of the scuttled vessels which had appeared improbable during the day seemed very probable at night; placed as he was between two imaginary dangers, he did not quit the crew with his eyes, or his gun with his hand.

However, the sailors had again hoisted the sail, and the vessel was once more cleaving the waves. Through the darkness Franz, whose eyes were now more accustomed to it, distinguished the granite giant by which the bark was sailing, and then, turning an angle of the rock, he saw the fire more brilliant than ever, round which five or six persons were seated.

The blaze illumined the sea for a hundred paces round. Gaetano skirted the light, carefully keeping the bark out of its rays; then, when they were opposite the fire, he entered into the centre of the circle, singing a fishing song, of which his companions sung the chorus.

At the first words of the song, the men seated round the fire rose and approached the landing-place, their eyes fixed on the bark, of which they evidently sought to judge the force and divine the intention. They soon appeared satisfied, and returned (with the exception of one who remained at the shore) to their fire, at which a whole goat was roasting.

When the bark was within twenty paces of the shore, the man on the beach made with his carbine the movement of a sentinel who sees a patrol, and cried, " Who goes there? " in Sardinian. Franz coolly cocked both barrels. Gaetano then exchanged a few words with this man, which the traveller did not understand, but which evidently concerned him.

" Will your excellency give your name, or remain incognito? " asked the captain.

" My name must rest unknown,—merely say I am a Frenchman travelling for pleasure."

As soon as Gaetano had transmitted this answer, the sentinel gave an order to one of the men seated round the fire, who rose and disappeared among the rocks. Not a word was spoken, every one seemed occupied—Franz with his disembarkment, the sailors with their sails, the smugglers with their goat; but in the midst of all this carelessness it was evident that they mutually observed each other.

The man who had disappeared returned suddenly on the opposite side to that by which he had left; he made a sign with his head to the sentinel, who, turning to the bark, uttered these words, " S'accomodi." The Italian s'accomodi is untranslatable; it means at once, " Come, enter, you are welcome, make yourself at home, you are the master," It is like that Turkish phrase of Molière's that so astonished le bourgeois gentilhomme by the number of things it contained.

The sailors did not wait for a second invitation; four strokes of the oar brought them to the land; Gaetano sprang to shore, exchanged a few words with the sentinel, then his comrades descended, and lastly came Franz's turn. One of his guns was swung over his shoulder, Gaetano had the other, and a sailor held his rifle. His dress, half artist, half dandy, excited no suspicion, and consequently no disquietude. The bark was moored to the shore, and they advanced a few paces to find a comfortable bivouac; but, doubtless, the spot they chose did not suit the smuggler who filled the post of sentinel, for he cried out:

" Not that way, if you please."

Gaetano faltered an excuse, and advanced to the opposite side, whilst two sailors kindled torches at the fire to light them on their way. They advanced about thirty paces, and then stopped at a small esplanade, surrounded with rocks, in which seats had been cut, not unlike sentry-boxes. Around in the crevices of the rocks grew a few dwarf oaks and thick bushes of myrtles. Franz lowered a torch, and saw, by the light of a mass of cinders, that he was not the first to discover this retreat, which was, doubtless, one of the halting-places of the wandering visitors of Monte Cristo. As for his anticipation of events, once on *terra firma*, once that he had seen the indifferent, if not friendly, appearance of his hosts, his preoccupation had disappeared, or rather, at sight of the goat, had turned to appetite.

He mentioned this to Gaetano, who replied that nothing could be more easy than to prepare a supper when they had in their boat bread, wine, half a dozen partridges, and a good fire to roast them by.

" Besides," added he, " if the smell of their roast meat tempts you, I will go and offer them two of our birds for a slice."

" You seem born for negotiation," returned Franz; " go and try."

During this time the sailors had collected dried sticks and branches with which they made a fire.

Franz waited impatiently, smelling the odour of the goat, when the captain returned with a mysterious air.

" Well," said Franz, " anything new?—do they refuse? "

" On the contrary," returned Gaetano; " the chief, who was told you were a young Frenchman, invites you to sup with him."

" Well," observed Franz, " this chief is very polite, and I see no objection;—the more so, as I bring my share of the supper."

" Oh, it is not that,—he has plenty, and to spare, for supper; but he attaches a singular condition to your presentation at his house."

" His house! has he built one here, then? "

" No, but he has a very comfortable one all the same, so they say."

" You know this chief, then? "

" I have heard talk of him."

" Ill or well? "

" Both."

" The devil!—and what is this condition? "

" That you are blindfolded, and do not take off the bandage until he himself bids you."

Franz looked at Gaetano to see, if possible, what he thought of this proposal.

" Ah! " replied he, guessing Franz's thought, " I know this merits reflection."

" What should you do in my place? "

" I who have nothing to lose,—I should go."

" You would accept? "

" Yes, were it only out of curiosity."

" There is something very curious about this chief, then? "

" Listen," said Gaetano, lowering his voice, " I do not know if what they say is true——"

He stopped to look if any one was near.

" What do they say? "

" That this chief inhabits a cavern to which the Pitti Palace is nothing."

" What nonsense! " said Franz, reseating himself.

" It is no nonsense; it is quite true. Cama, the pilot of the *Saint Ferdinand*, went in once, and he came back amazed, vowing that such treasures were only to be heard of in fairy tales."

" Do you know," observed Franz, " that with such stories you would make me enter the enchanted cavern of Ali Baba? "

" I tell you what I have been told."

" Then you advise me to accept? "

" Oh, I don't say that; your excellency will do as you please; I should be sorry to advise you in the matter."

Franz reflected a few moments, felt that a man so rich could not have any intention of plundering him of what little he had; and seeing only the prospect of a good supper, he accepted. Gaetano departed with the reply. Franz was prudent, and wished to learn all he possibly could concerning his host; he turned towards the sailor, who, during this dialogue, had sat gravely plucking the partridges, with the air of a man proud of his office, and asked him how these men had landed, as no vessel of any kind was visible.

" Never mind that," returned the sailor, " I know their vessel."

" Is it a very beautiful vessel? "

" I would not wish for a better to sail round the world."

" Of what burden is she? "

" About a hundred tons; but she is built to stand any weather. She is what the English call a yacht."

" Where was she built? "

" I know not; but my own opinion is, she is a Genoese."

" And how did a leader of smugglers," continued Franz. " venture to build a vessel designed for such a purpose at Genoa? "

" I did not say that the owner was a smuggler," replied the sailor.

" No, but Gaetano did, I thought."

" Gaetano had only seen the vessel from a distance; he had not then spoken to any one."

" And if this person be not a smuggler, who is he? "

" A wealthy signor, who travels for his pleasure."

" Come," thought Franz, " he is still more mysterious, since the two accounts do not agree. What is his name? "

" If you ask him, he says, Sinbad the Sailor; but I doubt its being his real name."

" Sinbad the Sailor? "

" Yes."

" And where does he reside? "

" On the sea."

" What country does he come from? "

" I do not know."

" Have you ever seen him? "

" Sometimes."

" What sort of a man is he? "

" Your excellency will judge for yourself."

" Where will he receive me? "

" No doubt in the subterranean palace Gaetano told you of."

" Have you never had the curiosity, when you have landed and found this island deserted, to seek for this enchanted palace? "

" Oh, yes, more than once, but always in vain; we examined the grotto all over, but we never could find the slightest trace of any opening; they say that the door is not opened by a key, but a magical word."

" Decidedly," muttered Franz, " this is an adventure of the Arabian Nights."

" His excellency waits for you," said a voice, which he recognised as that of the sentinel.

He was accompanied by two of the yacht's crew. Franz drew his handkerchief from his pocket, and presented it to the man who had spoken to him. Without uttering a word they bandaged his eyes with a care that showed their apprehensions of his committing some indiscretion. Afterwards he was made to promise he would not make the least attempt to raise the bandage. He promised. Then his two guides took his arms, and he advanced, guided by them, and preceded by the sentinel. After advancing about thirty paces he smelt the appetising odour of the kid that was roasting, and knew thus that he was passing the bivouac. They then led him on about fifty paces farther, evidently advancing towards the shore, where they would not allow Gaetano to penetrate,—a refusal he could now comprehend. Presently, by a change in the atmosphere, he comprehended that they were entering a cave; after going on for a few seconds more he heard a crackling, and it seemed to him as though the atmosphere again changed, and became balmy and perfumed. At length his feet touched on a thick and soft carpet, and his guides let go their hold of him. There was a moment's silence, and then a voice, in excellent French, although with a foreign accent, said:

"Welcome, sir. I beg you will remove your bandage."

It may be supposed, then, Franz did not wait for a repetition of this permission, but took off the handkerchief, and found himself in the presence of a man from thirty-eight to forty years of age. This personage was dressed in a Tunisian costume, that is to say, a red cap with a long blue silk tassel, a vest of black cloth embroidered with gold, pantaloons of deep red, large and full gaiters of the same colour, embroidered with gold, like the vest, and yellow slippers; he had a splendid cashmere round his waist, and a small sharp and crooked cangiar was passed through his girdle. Although of a paleness that was almost livid, this man had a remarkably handsome face; his eyes were penetrating and sparkling; a nose, quite straight and projecting direct from the brow, gave out the Greek type in all its purity, whilst his teeth, as white as pearls, were set off to admiration by the black moustache that encircled them.

This pallor was so peculiar that it seemed as though it were that which would be exhibited by a man who had been inclosed for a long time in a tomb, and who was unable to resume the healthy glow and hue of the living. He was not particularly tall, but extremely well made, and, like the men of the south, had small hands and feet. But what astonished Franz, who had treated Gaetano's description as a fable, was the splendour of the apartment in which he found himself. The entire chamber was lined with crimson brocade, worked with flowers of gold. In a recess was a kind of divan, surmounted with a stand of Arabian swords in silver scabbards, and the handles resplendent with gems; from the ceiling hung a lamp of Venetian glass, of beautiful shape and colour, whilst the feet rested on a Turkey carpet, in which they sunk to the instep; tapestry hung before the door by which Franz had entered, and also in front of another door, leading into a second apartment, which seemed to be brilliantly lighted up. The host gave Franz time for his surprise, and, moreover, rendered him look for look, not even taking his eyes off him.

"Sir," he said, after some pause, "a thousand excuses for the precaution taken in your introduction hither; but as, during the greater portion of the year, this island is deserted, if the secret of this abode were discovered, I should, doubtless, find on my return my temporary retirement in a great state of disorder. That would be exceedingly annoying, not for the loss it occasioned me, but because I should not have the certainty I now possess of separating myself from all the rest of mankind at pleasure. Let me now endeavour to make you forget this temporary unpleasantness, and offer you what no doubt you did not expect to find here,—that is to say, a tolerable supper and pretty comfortable beds."

" *Ma foi!* my dear sir," replied Franz, " make no apologies. I have always observed that they bandage people's eyes who penetrate enchanted palaces, for instance those of Raoul in the *Huguenots,*＊ and really I have nothing to complain of, for what I see is a sequel to the wonders of the *Arabian Nights.*"

" Alas! I may say with Lucullus, if I could have anticipated the honour of your visit, I would have prepared for it. But such as is my hermitage, it is at your disposal; such as is my supper, it is yours to share, if you will. Ali, is the supper ready? "

At this moment the tapestry moved aside, and a Nubian, as black as ebony, and dressed in a plain white tunic, made a sign to his master that all was prepared in the *salle-à-manger.*

" Now," said the unknown to Franz, " I do not know if you are of my opinion, but I think nothing is more annoying than to remain two or three hours *tête-à-tête* without knowing by name or appellation how to address one another. Pray observe, that I too much respect the laws of hospitality to ask your name or title. I only request you to give me one by which I may have the pleasure of addressing you. As for myself, that I may put you at your ease, I tell you that I am generally called ' Sinbad the Sailor.' "

" And I," replied Franz, " will tell you, as I only require his wonderful lamp to make me precisely like Aladdin, that I see no reason why at this moment I should not be called Aladdin. That will keep us from going away from the East, whither I am tempted to think I have been conveyed by some good genius."

" Well, then, Signor Aladdin," replied the singular Amphitryon, " you heard our repast announced; will you now take the trouble to enter the *salle-à-manger,* your humble servant going first to show the way? "

At these words, moving aside the tapestry, Sinbad preceded his guest. Franz proceeded from one enchantment to another; the table was splendidly covered, and, once convinced of this important point, he cast his eyes around him. The *salle-à-manger* was scarcely less striking than the boudoir he had just left; it was entirely of marble, with antique bas-reliefs of priceless value; and at the four corners of this apartment, which was oblong, were four magnificent statues, having baskets on their heads. These baskets contained four pyramids of most splendid fruit; there were the pine-apples of Sicily, pomegranates from Malaga, oranges from the Balearic Isles, peaches from France, and dates from Tunis.

The supper consisted of a roast pheasant, garnished with Corsican blackbirds; a boar's ham *à la gelée*, a quarter of a kid *à la tartare*, a glorious turbot, and a gigantic lobster. Between these large dishes were smaller ones containing various dainties. The dishes were of silver, and the plates of Japanese china.

Franz rubbed his eyes in order to assure himself that this was not a dream. Ali alone was present to wait at table, and acquitted himself so admirably, that the guest complimented his host thereupon.

"Yes," replied he, whilst he did the honours of the supper with much ease and grace,—"yes, he is a poor devil who is much devoted to me, and does all he can to prove it. He remembers I saved his life, and as he has a regard for his head, he feels some gratitude towards me for having kept it on his shoulders."

Ali approached his master, took his hand and kissed it.

"Would it be impertinent, Signor Sinbad," said Franz, "to ask you the particulars of this kindness?"

"Oh! they are simple enough," replied the host. "It seems the fellow had been caught wandering nearer to the harem of the Bey of Tunis than etiquette permits to one of his colour, and he was condemned by the Bey to have his tongue cut out, and his hand and head cut off; the tongue the first day, the hand the second, and the head the third. I always had a desire to have a mute in my service, so learning the day his tongue was cut out, I went to the Bey, and proposed to give him for Ali a splendid double-barrelled gun, which I knew he was very desirious of having. He hesitated a moment, he was so very desirous to complete the poor devil's punishment. But when I added to the gun an English cutlass with which I had shivered his highness's yataghan to pieces, the Bey yielded, and agreed to forgive the hand and head, but on condition he never again set foot in Tunis. This was a useless clause in the bargain, for whenever the coward sees the first glimpse of the shores of Africa, he runs down below, and can only be induced to appear again when we are out of sight of that quarter of the globe."

Franz remained a moment mute and pensive, hardly knowing what to think of the half kindness, half cruelty, with which his host related the brief narrative.

"And like the celebrated sailor whose name you have assumed." he said, by way of changing the conversation, "you pass your life in travelling?"

"Yes. I made a vow at a time when I little thought I should ever be able to accomplish it," said the unknown, with a singular smile; "and I made some others also, which I hope I may fulfil in due season."

Although Sinbad pronounced these words with much calmness, his eyes darted gleams of singular ferocity.

" You have suffered a great deal, sir? " said Franz inquiringly.

Sinbad started and looked fixedly at him, as he replied, " What makes you suppose so? "

" Everything! " answered Franz,—" your voice, your look, your pallid complexion, and even the life you lead."

" I! I live the happiest life possible, the real life of a pacha. I am king of all creation. I am pleased with one place, and stay there; I get tired of it, and leave it; I am free as a bird and have wings like one; my attendants obey me at a signal. Sometimes I amuse myself by carrying off from human justice some bandit it is in quest of, some criminal whom it pursues. Then I have my mode of dispensing justice, silent and sure, without respite or appeal, which condemns or pardons, and which no one sees. Ah! if you had tasted my life, you would not desire any other, and would never return to the world unless you had some great project to accomplish there."

" A vengeance, for instance! " observed Franz.

The unknown fixed on the young man one of those looks which penetrate into the depth of the heart and thoughts.

" And why a vengeance? " he asked.

" Because," replied Franz, " you seem to me like a man who, persecuted by society, has a fearful account to settle with it."

" Ah! " responded Sinbad, laughing with his singular laugh which displayed his white and sharp teeth. " You have not guessed rightly! Such as you see me I am, a sort of philosopher, and one day perhaps I shall go to Paris to rival M. Appert, and the little man in the blue cloak."*

" And will that be the first time you ever took that journey? "

" Yes, it will! I must seem to you by no means curious, but I assure you that it is not my fault I have delayed it so long—it will happen one day or the other."

" And do you propose to make this journey very shortly? "

" I do not know; it depends on circumstances which depend on certain arrangements! "

" I should like to be there at the time you come, and I will endeavour to repay you as far as lies in my power for your liberal hospitality displayed to me at Monte Cristo."

" I should avail myself of your offer with pleasure," replied the host, " but, unfortunately, if I go there, it will be, in all probability, incognito."

The supper appeared to have been supplied solely for Franz, for the unknown scarcely touched one or two dishes of the splendid banquet to which his guest did ample justice. Then Ali brought

on the dessert, or rather took the baskets from the hands of the
statues and placed them on the table. Between the two baskets
he placed a small silver cup, closed with a lid of the same. The
care with which Ali placed this cup on the table roused Franz's
curiosity. He raised the lid and saw a kind of greenish paste,
something like preserved angelica, but which was perfectly
unknown to him. He replaced the lid, as ignorant of what the
cup contained as he was before he had looked at it, and then casting his eyes towards his host he saw him smile at his disappointment.

"You cannot guess," said he, "what there is in that small
vase, can you?"

"No, I really cannot!"

"Well, then, that kind of green preserve is nothing less than
the ambrosia which Hebe served at the table of Jupiter!"

"But," replied Franz, "this ambrosia, no doubt, in passing
through mortal hands, has lost its heavenly appellation and
assumed a human name; in vulgar phrase, what may you term
this composition, for which, to say the truth, I do not feel any
particular desire?"

"Ah! thus it is that our material origin is revealed," cried
Sinbad; "we frequently pass so near to happiness without seeing,
without regarding it, or if we do see and regard it, yet without
recognising it. Are you a man for the substantials, and is gold
your god? taste this, and the mines of Peru, Guserat, and Golconda are opened to you. Are you a man of imagination—a
poet? taste this, and the boundaries of possibility disappear;
the fields of infinite space open to you, you advance free in heart,
free in mind, into the boundless realms of unfettered reverie.
Are you ambitious, and do you seek after the greatnesses of the
earth? taste this, and in an hour you will be a king, not a king of
a petty kingdom hidden in some corner of Europe like France,
Spain, or England, but king of the world, king of the universe,
king of creation; without bowing at the feet of Satan, you will
be king and master of all the kingdoms of the earth. Is it not
tempting what I offer you, and is it not an easy thing, since it is
only to do thus? Look!"

At these words he uncovered the small cup which contained
the substance so lauded, took a teaspoonful of the magic sweet-
meat, raised it to his lips, and swallowed it slowly, with his eyes
half shut and his head bent backwards.

Franz did not disturb him whilst he absorbed his favourite
bonne bouche, but when he had finished, he inquired:

"What, then, is this precious stuff?"

" Did you ever hear," he replied, " of the Old Man of the Mountain who attempted to assassinate Philippe Augustus? "

" Of course I have! "

" Well, you know he reigned over a rich valley which was overhung by the mountain whence he derived his picturesque name. In this valley were magnificent gardens planted by Hassen-ben-Sabah,* and in these gardens isolated pavilions. Into these pavilions he admitted the elect; and there, says Marco Polo, gave them to eat a certain herb, which transported them to paradise, in the midst of ever-blooming shrubs, ever-ripe fruit, and ever-lovely virgins. But what these happy persons took for reality was but a dream; but it was a dream so soft, so voluptuous, so enthralling, that they sold themselves body and soul to him who gave it to them; and obedient to his orders as those of a deity, struck down the marked victim, died in torture without a murmur; believing that the death they underwent was but a quick transition to that life of delights of which the holy herb, now before you, had given them a slight foretaste."

" Then," cried Franz, " it is hatchis!* I know that—by name at least."

" That is it precisely, Signor Aladdin; it is hatchis—the purest and most unadulterated hatchis of Alexandria,—the hatchis of Abou-Gor, the celebrated maker, the only man, the man to whom there should be built a palace, inscribed with these words, ' A grateful world to the dealer in happiness.' "

" Do you know," said Franz, " I have a very great inclination to judge for myself of the truth or exaggeration of your eulogies! "

" Judge for yourself, Signor Aladdin—judge, but do not confine yourself to one trial. Like everything else, we must habituate the senses to a fresh impression, gentle or violent, sad or joyous. There is a struggle in nature against this divine substance,—in nature which is not made for joy and clings to pain. Nature subdued must yield in the combat, the dream must succeed to reality, and then the dream reigns supreme, then the dream becomes life, and life becomes the dream. But what changes occur! It is only by comparing the pains of actual being with the joys of the assumed existence, that you would desire to live no longer, but to dream thus for ever. When you return to this mundane sphere from your visionary world, you would seem to leave a Neapolitan spring for a Lapland winter—to quit paradise for earth—heaven for hell! Taste the hatchis, guest of mine— taste the hatchis! "

Franz's only reply was to take a teaspoonful of the marvellous preparation, about as much in quantity as his host had eaten, and lift it to his mouth.

" *Diable!* " he said, after having swallowed the divine preserve.
" I do not know if the result will be as agreeable as you describe,
but the thing does not appear to me as succulent as you say."

" Because your palate has not yet attained the sublimity of
the substances it flavours. Tell me, the first time you tasted oysters,
tea, porter, truffles, and sundry other dainties which you now
adore, did you like them? Could you comprehend how the
Romans stuffed their pheasants with assafœtida, and the Chinese
eat swallows' nests? Eh?. no! Well, it is the same with hatchis;
only eat for a week, and nothing in the world will seem to you to
equal the delicacy of its flavour, which now appears to you sleepy
and distasteful. Let us now go into the chamber beside you,
which is your apartment, and Ali will bring us coffee and pipes."

They both arose, and whilst he who called himself Sinbad,—
and whom we have occasionally named so, that we might, like
his guest, have some title by which to distinguish him,—gave
some orders to the servant, Franz entered the adjoining apartment. It was simply yet richly furnished. It was round, and a
large divan completely encircled it. Divan, walls, ceiling, floor,
were all covered with magnificent skins, as soft and downy as the
richest carpets; there were skins of the lions of Atlas, with their
large manes, skins of the Bengal tigers, with their striped hides;
skins of the panthers of the Cape spotted beautifully, like those
that appeared, to Dante; skins of the bears of Siberia, the foxes
of Norway, etc.; and all these skins were strewn in profusion one
on the other, so that it seemed like walking over the most mossy
turf, or reclining on the most luxurious bed.

Both laid themselves down on the divan: chibouques, with
jasmine tubes and amber mouthpieces, were within reach, and
all prepared so that there was no need to smoke the same pipe
twice. Each of them took one, which Ali lighted, and then retired
to prepare the coffee. There was a moment's silence, during which
Sinbad gave himself up to thoughts that seemed to occupy him
incessantly, even in the midst of his conversation; and Franz
abandoned himself to that mute reverie, into which we always
sink when smoking excellent tobacco, which seems to remove
with its fume all the troubles of the mind, and to give the smoker
in exchange all the visions of the soul. Ali brought in the coffee.

" How do you take it? " inquired the unknown, " *à la Française,*
or *à la Turque,* strong or weak, sugar or none, cool or boiling?
As you please, it is ready in all ways."

" I will take it *à la Turque,*" replied Franz.

" And you are right," said his host; " it shows you have a
tendency for an Oriental life. Ah! those Orientals! they are the
only men who know how to live. As for me," he added, with one

of those singular smiles which did not escape the young man,
" when I have completed my affairs in Paris, I shall go and die
in the East, and should you wish to see me again, you must seek
me at Cairo, Bagdad, or Ispahan."

" *Ma foi!* " said Franz, " it would be the easiest thing in the
world; for I feel eagle's wings springing out at my shoulders,
and with these wings I could make a tour of the world in four-
and-twenty hours."

" Ah! it is the hatchis that is operating. Well, unfurl your
wings and fly into superhuman regions; fear nothing, there is a
watch over you; and if your wings, like those of Icarus, melt
before the sun, we are here to receive you."

He then said some Arabian words to Ali, who made a sign of
obedience and withdrew, but not to any distance. As to Franz,
a strange transformation had taken place in him. All the bodily
fatigue of the day, all the preoccupation of mind which the events
of the evening had brought on, disappeared, as they would at
that first feeling of sleep, when we are still sufficiently conscious
to be aware of the coming of slumber. His body seemed to acquire
an airy lightness, his perception brightened in a remarkable manner, his senses seemed to redouble their power, the horizon
continued to expand; but it was not that gloomy horizon over
which a vague alarm prevails, and which he had seen before he
slept; but a blue, transparent, unbounded horizon, with all the
blue of the ocean, all the spangles of the sun, all the perfumes of
the summer breeze; then, in the midst of the songs of his sailors,
—songs so clear and sounding, that they would have made a
divine harmony had their notes been taken down,—he saw the
isle of Monte Cristo, no longer as a threatening rock in the midst
of the waves, but as an oasis lost in the desert: then, as the bark
approached, the songs became louder, for an enchanting and
mysterious harmony rose to heaven from this island, as if some
fay-like Lorelay,* or some enchanter like Amphion, had decreed
to attract thither a soul or build there a city.

At length the bark touched the shore, but without effort,
without shock, as lips touch lips, and he entered the grotto
amidst continued strains of most delicious melody. He descended,
or rather seemed to descend, several steps, inspiring the fresh
and balmy air, like that which may be supposed to reign around
the grotto of Circe, formed from such perfumes as set the mind
a-dreaming, and such fires as burn the very senses; and he saw
again all he had seen before his sleep, from Sinbad, his singular
host, to Ali, the mute attendant; then all seemed to fade away
and become confused before his eyes, like the last shadows of the
magic lantern before it is extinguished, and he was again in the

chamber of statues, lighted only by one of those pale and antique lamps which watch in the dead of the night over the sleep of pleasure. They were the same statues rich in form, in attraction, and poesy, with eyes of fascination, smiles of love, and bright and flowing hair. They were Phyne, Cleopatra, Messalina, those three celebrated courtesans; then amongst them glided like a pure ray, like a Christian angel in the midst of Olympus, one of those chaste figures, those calm shadows, those soft visions, which seemed to veil its virgin brow before these marble wantons. Then these three statues advanced towards him with looks of love, and approached the couch on which he was reposing, their feet hidden in their long tunics, their throats bare, hair flowing like waves, and assuming attitudes which the gods could not resist, but which saints withstood, and looks inflexible and ardent like the serpent's on the bird, and then he gave way before these looks as painful as a powerful grasp and as delightful as a kiss.

It seemed to Franz that he closed his eyes, and thought that in the last look he gave he saw the modest statue completely veiled, and then with his eyes closed upon all nature his senses awoke to impassable impressions, and he was under the painful yet delicious enthralment produced by the hatchis, whose enchantment had brought up this marvellous and thrilling vision.

32

The Awakening

WHEN Franz came to his senses, the objects around him seemed a second portion of his dream. He thought himself in a sepulchre, into which scarcely penetrated (and then like a look of pity) a ray of the sun. He stretched forth his hand and touched stone; he rose to his seat and found himself lying on his bournous in a bed of dry heather, very soft and odoriferous. The vision had entirely fled, and as if the statues had been but shadows coming from their tomb during his dream, they vanished at his waking.

He advanced several paces towards the point whence the light came, and to all the excitement of his dream succeeded the calmness of reality. He found that he was in a grotto, went towards the opening, and through a kind of fanlight saw a blue sea and an azure sky. The air and water were shining in the beams of the morning sun; on the shore the sailors were sitting chatting and laughing; and at ten yards from them the bark was at anchor.

undulating gracefully on the water. There for some time he enjoyed the fresh breeze which played on his brow, and listened to the dash of the waves on the beach, that left against the rocks a lace of foam as white as silver. He was for some time without reflection or thought for the divine charm which is in the things of nature, especially after a fantastic dream; then, gradually, this view of outward matters, so calm, so pure, so grand, reminded him of the illusiveness of a dream, and remembrance became busy again in his memory. He recalled his arrival on the island, his presentation to a smuggler chief, a subterranean palace full of splendour, an excellent supper, and a spoonful of hatchis. It seemed, however, even in the very face of open day, that at least a year had elapsed since all these things had passed, so deep was the impression made in his mind by the dream, and so strong a hold had it taken of his imagination. Also from time to time his fancy placed in the midst of the sailors, now crossing a rock, now hovering over the bark, one of those shadowy figures which had brightened his night by their sweet looks and their kisses. Otherwise his, head was perfectly clear and his limbs entirely reposed; he was free from the slightest headache; on the contrary, he felt a certain degree of lightness, a faculty of absorbing the pure air, and enjoying the bright sunshine more vividly than ever.

He went gaily up to the sailors, who rose as soon as they perceived him, and the patron accosting him, said:

" The Signor Sinbad has left his compliments for your excellency, and desired us to express the regret he feels at not being able to take his leave in person, but he trusts you will excuse him, as very important business calls him to Malaga."

" So then, Gaetano," said Franz, " this is then all reality. There exists a man who has received me in this isle, entertained me right royally, and has departed whilst I was asleep."

" He exists as certainly as that you may see his small yacht with all her sails spread; and if you will use your glass, you will, in all probability, recognise your host in the midst of his crew."

So saying, Gaetano pointed in a direction in which a small vessel was making sail towards the southern point of Corsica.

Frank adjusted his telescope and directed it toward the bark,

Gaetano was not mistaken. At the stern the mysterious stranger was standing up looking towards the shore, and holding a spyglass in his hand; he was attired as he had been on the previous evening, and waved his pocket-handkerchief to his guest in token of adieu.

Franz returned the salute by shaking his handkerchief as an exchange of signals.

After a second, a slight cloud of smoke was seen at the stern of the vessel, which rose gracefully as it expanded in the air, and then Franz heard a slight report.

" There! do you hear," observed Gaetano, " he is bidding you adieu! "

The young man took his carbine and fired it in the air, but without any idea that the noise could be heard at the distance which separated the yacht from the shore.

" What are your excellency's orders? " inquired Gaetano.

" In the first place, light me a torch."

" Ah, yes! I understand," replied the patron, " to find the entrance to the enchanted apartment. With much pleasure, your excellency, if it would amuse you, and I will get you the torch you ask for. But I, too, have had the idea you have, and two or three times the same fancy has come over me; but I have always given it up. Giovanni, light a torch," he added, " and give it to his excellency."

Giovanni obeyed; Franz took the lamp, and entered the subterranean grotto, followed by Gaetano. He recognised the place where he had awoke by the bed of heather that was there, but it was in vain that he carried his torch all round the exterior surface of the grotto; he saw nothing, unless that, by traces of smoke, others had before him attempted the same thing, and like him in vain. Yet he did not leave a foot of this granite wall, as impenetrable as futurity, without strict scrutiny; he did not see a fissure without introducing the blade of his hunting-sword in it, nor a projecting point on which he did not lean and press in the hopes it would give way: all was vain, and he lost two hours in his attempts, which were at last utterly useless.

At the end of this time he gave up his research, and Gaetano smiled.

When Franz appeared again on the shore, the yacht only seemed like a small white speck in the horizon; he looked again through his glass, but even then he could not distinguish anything. Gaetano reminded him that he had come for the purpose of shooting goats, which he had utterly forgotten. He took his fowling-piece and began to hunt over the isle with the air of a man who is fulfilling a duty rather than enjoying a pleasure, and at the end of a quarter of an hour he had killed a goat and two kids. These animals, though wild and agile as chamois, were too much like domestic goats, and Franz could not consider them as game.

Moreover, other ideas much more powerful occupied his mind. Since the evening before, he had really been the hero of one of the tales of the *Thousand and One Nights,* and he was irresistibly attracted towards the grotto. Then, in spite of the failure of his first search, he began a second, after having told Gaetano to roast one of the two kids. The second visit was a long one, and when he returned the kid was roasted and the repast ready.

Franz was sitting on the spot where he was on the previous evening when his mysterious host had invited him to supper, and he saw the little yacht, now like a sea-gull on the wave, continuing her flight towards Corsica.

"Why," he remarked to Gaetano, "you told me that Signor Sinbad was going to Malaga, whilst it seems he is in the direction of Porto-Vecchio."

"Don't you remember," said the patron, "I told you that amongst the crew there were two Corsican brigands?"

"True! and he is going to land them," added Franz.

"Precisely so," replied Gaetano. "Ah! he is an individual who fears neither God nor devil, they say, and would at any time run fifty leagues out of his course to do a poor devil a service."

"But such services as these might involve him with the authorities of the country in which he practises this kind of philanthropy," said Franz.

"And what cares he for that?" replied Gaetano, with a laugh, "or any authorities? He smiles at them. Let them try to pursue him—why, in the first place, his yacht is not a ship, but a bird, and he would beat any frigate three knots in every nine; and if he were to throw himself on the coast, why, isn't he certain of finding friends everywhere?"

It was perfectly clear that the Signor Sinbad, Franz's host, had the honour of being on excellent terms with the smugglers and bandits along the whole coast of the Mediterranean, which placed him in a position singular enough.

As to Franz, he had no longer any inducement to remain at Monte Cristo, for he had lost all hope of detecting the secret of the grotto. He therefore despatched his breakfast, and, his bark being ready, he hastened on board, and soon the vessel was under way.

At the moment the bark began her course they lost sight of the yacht, as it disappeared in the gulf of Porto-Vecchio. With it was effaced the last trace of the preceding night, and then supper, Sinbad, hatchis, statues, all became a dream for Franz. The bark went on all day and all night, and next morning, when the sun rose, they had lost sight of Monte Cristo.

When Franz had once again set foot on shore, he forgot, for the moment at least, the events which had just passed, whilst he finished his affairs of pleasure at Florence, and then thought of nothing but how he should rejoin his companion, who was awaiting him at Rome.

He set out, and on the Saturday evening reached the Place de la Douane by the mail-coach. An apartment, as we have said, had been retained beforehand, and thus he had but to go to the hotel of Maître Pastrini. This was not so easy a matter, however, for the streets were thronged with people, and Rome was already a prey to that low and feverish murmur which precedes all great events and at Rome there are four great events in every year—the Carnival, the Holy Week, the Fête Dieu, and the St. Peter. All the rest of the year the city is in that state of dull apathy, between life and death, which renders it similar to a kind of station between this world and the next: a sublime spot, a resting-place full of poetry and character, and at which Franz had already halted five or six times, and at each time found it more marvellous and striking. At last he made his way through this mob, which was continually increasing and more agitated, and reached the hotel. On his first inquiry, he was told, with the impertinence peculiar to hackney-coach-men who are hired and innkeepers with their houses full, that there was no room for him at the Hôtel de Londres. Then he sent his card to Maître Pastrini, and demanded Albert de Morcerf. This plan succeeded, and Maître Pastrini himself ran to him, excusing himself for having made his excellency wait, scolding the waiters, taking the candlestick in his hand from the cicerone, who was ready to pounce on the traveller, and was about to lead him to Albert when Morcerf himself appeared.

The apartment consisted of two small rooms and a closet. The two rooms looked on to the street, a fact which Maître Pastrini commented upon as an inappreciable advantage. The remainder of the story was hired by a very rich gentleman who was supposed to be a Sicilian or Maltese; but the host was unable to decide to which of the two nations the traveller belonged.

" Very good, Maître Pastrini," said Franz, " but we must have some supper instantly, and a carriage for to-morrow and the following days."

" As to supper," replied the landlord, " you shall be served immediately; but as for the carriage——"

" What as to the carriage? " exclaimed Albert; " come, come, Maître Pastrini, no joking; we must have a carriage."

" Sir," replied the host, " we will do all in our power to procure you one,—this is all I can say."

" And when shall we know? " inquired Franz.

" To-morrow morning," answered the innkeeper.

" Oh! the devil! then we shall pay the more, that's all, I see plainly enough. At Drake and Aaron's one pays twenty-five francs for common days, and thirty or thirty-five francs a day more for Sundays and fêtes, add five francs a day more for extras, that will make forty, and there's an end of it."

" I am afraid if we offer them double that, we shall not procure a carriage."

" Then they must put horses to mine; it is a little the worse for the journey, but that's no matter."

" There are no horses."

Albert looked at Franz like a man who hears a reply he does not understand.

" Do you understand that, my dear Franz? no horses! " he said; " but can't we have post-horses? "

" They have been all hired this fortnight, and there are none left, but those absolutely requisite for posting."

" What are we to say to this? " asked Franz.

" I say, that when a thing completely surpasses my comprehension, I am accustomed not to dwell on that thing, but to pass to another. Is supper ready, Maître Pastrini? "

" Yes, your excellency."

" Well, then, let us sup."

" But the carriage and horses? " said Franz.

" Be easy, my dear boy, they will come in due season; it is only a question of how much shall be charged for them."

Morcerf then, with that delightful philosophy which believes that nothing is impossible to a full purse and well-lined pocket-book, supped, went to bed, slept soundly, and dreamed he was racing all over Rome at Carnival time in a coach with six horses.

33

Roman Bandits

THE next morning Franz woke first, and instantly rang the bell. The sound had not yet died away when Maître Pastrini himself entered.

"Well, excellency," said the landlord triumphantly, and without waiting for Franz to question him, "I feared yesterday, when I would not promise you anything, that you were too late,—there is not a single carriage to be had,—that is, for the three last days."

"Yes," returned Franz, "the very three days it is most necessary."

"What is the matter?" said Albert, entering; "no carriage to be had?"

"Just so," returned Franz, "you have guessed it."

"Well! your Eternal City is a devilish nice city."

"That is to say, excellency," replied Pastrini, who was desirous to keep up the dignity of the capital of the Christian world in the eyes of his guests, "that there are no carriages to be had from Sunday to Tuesday evening, but from now till Sunday you can have fifty if you please."

"Ah! that is something," said Albert; "to-day is Thursday, and who knows what may arrive between this and Sunday?"

"Ten or twelve thousand travellers will arrive," replied Franz, "which will make it still more difficult."

"My friend," said Morcerf, "let us enjoy the present without gloomy forebodings for the future."

"At least we can have a window?"

"Where?"

"Looking on the Rue du Cours."

"Ah, a window!" exclaimed Maître Pastrini—"utterly impossible; there was only one left on the fifth floor of the Doria Palace, and that has been let to a Russian prince for twenty sequins a day."

The two young men looked at each other with an air of stupefacation.

"Well," said Franz to Albert, "do you know what is the best thing we can do? It is to pass the Carnival at Venice; there we are sure of obtaining gondolas if we cannot have carriages."

"Ah! the devil! no," cried Albert; "I came to Rome to see the Carnival, and I will, though I see it on stilts."

"Bravo! an excellent idea! we will disguise ourselves as monster pulchinellos or shepherds of the Landes,* and we shall have complete success."

"Do your excellencies still wish for a carriage from now to Sunday morning?"

"*Parbleu!*" said Albert, "do you think we are going to run about on foot in the streets of Rome, like lawyers' clerks?"

"I hasten to comply with your excellencies' wishes; only, I tell you before hand, the carriage will cost you six piastres a day."

"And, as I am not a millionaire, like the gentleman in the next apartments," said Franz, "I warn you, that as I have been four times before at Rome, I know the prices of all the carriages: we will give you twelve piastres for to-day, to-morrow, and the day after, and then you will make a good profit."

"But excellency——" said Pastrini, still striving to gain his point.

"Now go," returned Franz, "or I shall go myself and bargain with your *afflitatore*, who is mine also; he is an old friend of mine, who has plundered me pretty well already, and, in the hope of making more out of me, he will take a less price than the one I offer you; you will lose the preference, and that will be your fault."

"Do not give yourself the trouble, excellency," returned Maître Pastrini, with that smile of the Italian speculator who avows himself defeated; "I will do all I can, and I hope you will be satisfied."

"Ah, now we understand each other."

"When do you wish the carriage to be here?"

"In an hour."

"In an hour it will be at the door."

An hour after the vehicle was at the door; it was a hack conveyance, which was elevated to the rank of a private carriage in honour of the occasion; but, in spite of its humble exterior, the young men would have thought themselves happy to have secured it for the last three days of the Carnival.

"Excellency," cried the cicerone, seeing Franz approach the window, "shall I bring the carriage nearer the palace."

Accustomed as Franz was to the Italian phraseology, his first impulse was to look round him; but these words were addressed to him. Franz was the "excellency," the vehicle was the "carriage," and the Hôtel de Londres was the "palace."

Franz and Albert descended, the carriage approached the

palace, their excellencies stretched their legs along the seats, the cicerone sprang into the seat behind.

" Where do your excellencies wish to go? " asked he.

" To Saint Peter's first, and then to the Colosseum." returned Albert.

But Albert did not know that it takes a day to see Saint Peter's and a month to study it. The day was passed at Saint Peter's alone. Suddenly the daylight began to fade away; Franz took out his watch—it was half-past four. They returned to the hotel; at the door Franz ordered the coachman to be ready at eight. He wished to show Albert the Colosseum by moonlight, as he had shown him Saint Peter's by daylight. When we show a friend a city one has already visited, we feel the same pride as when we point out a woman whose lover we have been. He was to leave the city by the Porte del Popolo, skirt the outer wall, and re-enter by the Porte San Giovanni; thus they would behold the Colosseum without being in some measure prepared by the sight of the Capitol, the Forum, the Arch of Septimus Severus, the Temple of Antonius and Faustina, and the Via Sacra.

They sat down to dinner. Maître Pastrini had promised them a banquet; he gave them a tolerable repast. At the end of the dinner he entered in person. Franz concluded he came to hear his dinner praised, and began accordingly, but at the first words he interrupted him.

" Excellency," said he, " I am delighted to have your approbation, but it was not for that I came."

" Did you come to tell us you have procured a carriage? " asked Albert, lighting his cigar.

" No; and your excellencies will do well not to think of that any longer. At Rome things can or cannot be done: when you are told anything cannot be done, there is an end of it."

" It is much more convenient at Paris,—when anything cannot be done, you pay double, and it is done directly."

" That is what all the French say," returned Maître Pastrini, somewhat piqued; " for that reason I do not understand why they travel."

" But," said Albert, emitting a volume of smoke, and balancing his chair on its hind legs, " only madmen or blockheads, like we are, travel. Men in their senses do not quit their hotel in the Rue du Helder, their walk on the Boulevard de Gand, and the Café de Paris."

It is of course understood that Albert resided in the aforesaid *rue*, appeared every day on the fashionable walk, and dined frequently at the only *café* where you can really dine, that is, if you are on good terms with its frequenters.

Maître Pastrini remained silent a short time; it was evident that he was musing over this answer, which did not seem very clear.

" But," said Franz, in his turn interrupting his host's meditations, " you had some motive for coming here, may I beg to know what it was? "

" Ah, yes; you have ordered your carriage at eight o'clock precisely? "

" I have."

" You intend visiting *Il Colosseo*."

" You mean the Colosseum? "

" It is the same thing. You have told your coachman to leave the city by the Porto del Popolo, to drive round the walls, and re-enter by the Porte San Giovanni? "

" These are my words exactly."

" Well, this route is impossible."

" Impossible! "

" Very dangerous, to say the least."

" Dangerous! and why? "

" On account of the famous Luigi Vampa."

" Pray, who may this famous Luigi Vampa be? " inquired Albert; " he may be very famous at Rome, but I can assure you he is quite unknown at Paris."

" What! do you not know him? "

" I have not that honour."

" You have never heard his name? "

" Never."

" Well, then, he is a bandit, compared to whom the Decesaris and the Gasparones were mere children."

" Now then, Albert," cried Franz, " here is a bandit for you at last."

" I forewarn you, Maître Pastrini, that I shall not believe one word of what you are going to tell us; having told you this, begin."

" Once upon a time——"

" Well, go on."

Maître Pastrini turned round to Franz, who seemed to him the more reasonable of the two; we must do him justice,—he had had a great many Frenchmen in his house, but had never been able to comprehend them.

" Excellency," said he gravely, addressing Franz, " if you look upon me as a liar, it is useless for me to say anything; it was for your interest I——"

" Albert does not say you are a liar, Maître Pastrini," said

Franz; " but that he will not believe what you are going to tell us,—but I will believe all you say; so proceed."

" But if your excellency doubt my veracity——"

" Maître Pastrini," returned Franz, " you are more susceptible than Cassandra, who was a prophetess, and yet no one believed her, whilst you, at least, are sure of the credence of half your auditory. Come, sit down, and tell us all about M. Vampa."

" I had told your excellency he is the most famous bandit we have had since the days of Mastrilla."

" Well, what has this bandit to do with the order I have given the coachman, to leave the city by the Porte del Popolo, and to re-enter by the Porte San Giovanni? "

" This," replied Maître Pastrini; " that you will go out by one, but I very much doubt your returning by the other."

" Why? " asked Franz.

" Because after nightfall you are not safe fifty yards from the gates."

" On your honour, is that true? " cried Albert.

" M. le Comte," returned Maître Pastrini, hurt at Albert's repeated doubts of the truth of his assertions, " I do not say this to you, but to your companion, who knows Rome, and knows, too, that these things are not to be laughed at."

" My dear fellow," said Albert, turning to Franz, " here is an admirable adventure; we will fill our carriage with pistols, blunderbusses, and double-barrelled guns. Luigi Vampa comes to take us, and we take him—we bring him back to Rome, and present him to His Holiness the Pope, who asks how he can repay so great a service; then we merely ask for a carriage and a pair of horses, and we see the Carnival in the carriage, and doubtless the Roman people will crown us at the Capitol, and proclaim us, like Curtius and Horatius Cocles, the preservers of the country."

Whilst Albert proposed this scheme, Maître Pastrini's face assumed an expression impossible to describe.

" And pray," asked Franz, " where are these pistols, blunderbusses, and other deadly weapons with which you intend filling the carriage."

" Not out of my armoury, for at Terracina I was plundered even of my hunting-knife."

" I shared the same fate at Aquependente."

" Do you know, Maître Pastrini," said Albert, lighting a second cigar at the first, " that this practice is very convenient for robbers, and that it seems to have an arrangement between them."

Doubtless Maître Pastrini found this pleasantry compromising, for he only answered half the question, and then he spoke to Franz, as the only one likely to listen with attention.

"Your excellency knows that it is not customary to defend yourself when attacked by bandits."

"What!" cried Albert, whose courage revolted at the idea of being plundered tamely, "not make any resistance!"

"No, for it would be useless; what could you do against a dozen bandits who spring out of some pit, ruin, or aqueduct, and level their pieces at you?"

"Eh, *parbleu*!—they should kill me."

The innkeeper turned to Franz, with an air that seemed to say, "Your friend is decidedly mad."

"My dear Albert," returned Franz, "your answer is sublime, and worthy the '*Let him die*,' of Corneille, only, when Horace made that answer, the safety of Rome was concerned; but, as for us, it is only to gratify a whim, and it would be ridiculous to risk our lives for so foolish a motive."

Albert poured himself out a glass of *lacryma Christi*, which he sipped at intervals, muttering some unintelligible words.

"Well, Maître Pastrini," said Franz, "now that my companion is quieted, and you have seen how peaceful my intentions are, tell me who is this Luigi Vampa. Is he a shepherd or a nobleman? —young or old?—tall or short? Describe him, in order that, if we meet him by chance, like Jean Sbogar or Lara, we may recognise him."

"You could not apply to any one better able to inform you on all these points, for I knew him when he was a child; and one day that I fell into his hands going from Ferentino to Alatri, he, fortunately for me, recollected me, and set me free, not only without ransom, but made me a present of a very splendid watch and related his history to me."

"Let us see the watch," said Albert.

Maître Pastrini drew from his fob a magnificent Bréguet, bearing the name of its maker, of Parisian manufacture, and a count's coronet.

"Here it is," said he.

"*Peste!*" returned Albert, "I compliment you on it; I have its fellow:" he took his watch from his waistcoat pocket,—"and it cost me 3000 francs (£120)."

"Let us hear the history," said Franz, motioning Maître Pastrini to seat himself.

"Your excellencies permit it?" asked the host.

"*Pardieu!*" cried Albert, "you are not a preacher, to remain standing."

The host sat down after having made each of them a respectful bow, which meant to say he was ready to tell them all they wished to know concerning Luigi Vampa.

"You tell me," said Franz, at the moment Maître Pastrini was about to open his mouth, " that you knew Luigi Vampa when he was a child—he is still a young man, then? "

" A young man! he is only two-and-twenty;—he will gain himself a reputation."

" What do you think of that, Albert?—at two-and-twenty to be thus famous? "

" Yes, and at his age, Alexander, Cæsar, and Napoleon, who have all made some noise in the world, were not so advanced."

" So," continued Franz, " the hero of this history is only two-and-twenty? "

" Scarcely so much."

" Is he tall or short? "

" Of the middle height—about the same stature as his excellency," returned the host, pointing to Albert.

" Thanks for the comparison," said Albert, with a bow.

" Go on, Maître Pastrini," continued Franz, smiling at his friend's susceptibility. " To what class of society does he belong? "

" He was a shepherd-boy attached to the farm of the Comte de San-Felice, situated between Palestrina and the lake of Gabri He was born at Pampinara, and entered the count's service when he was five years old. His father was also a shepherd, who owned a small flock, and lived by the wool and the milk, which he sold at Rome. When quite a child, the little Vampa was of a most extraordinary disposition. One day, when he was seven years old, he came to the curé of Palestrina, and prayed him to teach him to read. It was somewhat difficult, for he could not quit his flock; but the good curé went every day to say mass at a little hamlet too poor to pay a priest, and which, having no other name, was called Borgo; he told Luigi that he might meet him on his return, and that then he would give him a lesson, warning him that it would be short, and that he must profit as much as possible by it. The child accepted joyfully.

" Every day Luigi led his flock to graze on the road that leads from Palestrina to Borgo; every day, at nine o'clock in the morning, the priest and the boy sat down on a bank by the way-side, and the little shepherd took his lesson out of the priest's breviary. At the end of three months he had learned to read. This was not enough—he must now learn to write.

" The priest had made, by a teacher of writing at Rome, three alphabets—one large, one middling, and one small, and pointed out to him, that by the help of a sharp instrument he could trace the letters on a slate, and thus learn to write.

" The same evening, when the flock was safe at the farm, the little Luigi hastened to the smith of Palestrina, took a large nail, forged it, sharpened it, and formed a sort of style. The next morning he had collected a quantity of slates and commenced. At the end of three months he had learned to write. The curé, astonished at his quickness and intelligence, made him a present of pens, paper, and a penknife. This was a fresh labour, but nothing compared to the first; at the end of a week he wrote as well with the pen as with the style.

" The curé related this anecdote to the Comte de San-Felice, who sent for the little shepherd, made him read and write before him, ordered his attendant to let him eat with the domestics, and to give him two piastres a month. With this, Luigi purchased books and pencils.

" He applied to everything his imitative powers, and, like Giotto, when young, he drew on his slate sheep, houses, and trees. Then, with his knife, he began to carve all sorts of objects in wood; it was thus that Pinelli, the famous sculptor, had commenced.

" A girl of six or seven—that is, a little younger than Vampa— tended sheep on a farm near Palestrina; she was an orphan, born at Valmontone, and was named Teresa.

" The two children met, sat down near each other, let their flocks mingle together, played, laughed, and conversed together; in the evening they separated the flock of the Comte de San-Felice from those of the Baron de Cervetri, and the children returned to their respective farms, promising to meet the next morning. The next day they kept their word, and thus grew up. Vampa was twelve, and Teresa eleven. And yet their natural disposition revealed itself.

" Besides his taste for the fine arts, which Luigi had carried as far as he could in his solitude, he was sad by fits, ardent by starts, angry by caprice, and always sarcastic. None of the lads of Pampinara, of Palestrina, or of Valmontone, had been able to gain any influence over him, or even to become his companion. His disposition (always inclined to exact concessions rather than to make them) kept him aloof from all friendships. Teresa alone ruled, by a look, a word, a gesture, this impetuous character, which yielded beneath the hand of a woman, and which beneath the hand of a man might have broken, but would never have bent or yielded.

" Teresa was, on the contrary, lively and gay, but coquettish to excess. The two piastres that Luigi received every month from the Comte de San-Felice's steward, and the price of all the little carvings in wood he sold at Rome, were expended in earrings, necklaces, and gold hairpins. So that, thanks to her friend's generosity, Teresa was the most beautiful and the best attired peasant near Rome.

" The two children grew up together, passing all their time with each other, and giving themselves up to the wild ideas of their different characters. Thus, in all their dreams, their wishes and their conversations, Vampa saw himself the captain of a vessel, general of an army, or governor of a province. Teresa saw herself rich, superbly attired, and attended by a train of liveried domestics. Then, when they had thus passed the day in building castles in the air, they separated their flocks, and descended from the elevation of their dreams to the reality of their humble position.

" One day the young shepherd told the count's steward he had seen a wolf come out of the Sabine mountains, and prowl around his flock. The steward gave him a gun; this was what Vampa longed for. This gun had an excellent barrel, made at Breschia, and carrying a ball with the precision of an English rifle; but one day the count broke the stock, and had then cast the gun aside. This, however, was nothing to a sculptor like Vampa; he examined the ancient stock, calculated what change it would require to adapt the gun to his shoulder, and made a fresh stock, so beautifully carved that it would have fetched fifteen or twenty piastres, had he chosen to sell it. But nothing could be farther from his thoughts. For a long time a gun had been the young man's greatest ambition. In every country where independence has taken the place of liberty, the first desire of a manly heart is to possess a weapon which at once renders him capable of defence or attack, and, by rendering its owner terrible, makes him often redoubted.

" From this moment Vampa devoted all his leisure time in perfecting himself in the use of this precious weapon; he purchased powder and ball, and everything served him for a mark —the trunk of some old and moss-grown olive-tree, that grew on the Sabine mountains; the fox, as he quitted his earth on some marauding excursion; the eagle that soared above their heads; and thus he soon became so expert, that Teresa overcame the terror she at first felt at the report, and amused herself by watching him direct the ball wherever he pleased, with as much accuracy as if placed by the hand.

" One evening a wolf emerged from a pine-wood near which they were usually stationed, but the wolf had scarcely advanced ten yards ere he was dead. Proud of this exploit, Vampa took the dead animal on his shoulders, and carried him to the farm.

" All these circumstances had gained Luigi considerable reputation. The man of superior abilities always finds admirers, go where he will. He was spoken of as the most adroit, the strongest, and the most courageous *contadino* for ten leagues round; and although Teresa was universally allowed to be the most beautiful girl of the Sabines, no one had ever spoken to her of love, because it was known that she was beloved by Vampa. And yet the two young people had never declared their affection; they had grown together like two trees whose roots are mingled, whose branches intertwine, and whose perfume rises together to the heavens. Only their wish to see each other had become a necessity, and they would have preferred death to a day's separation. Teresa was sixteen and Vampa eighteen.

" About this time, a band of brigands, that had established itself in the Lepini mountains, began to be much spoken of. The brigands have never been really extirpated from the neighbourhood of Rome. Sometimes it wants a chief, but when a chief presents himself he rarely wants a band.

" The celebrated Cucumetto, pursued in the Abruzzo, driven out of the kingdom of Naples, where he had carried on a regular war, had crossed the Garigliano, like Manfred,* and had come between Sonnino and Juperno, to take refuge on the banks of the Amasine. He it was who strove to reorganise a band, and who followed the footsteps of Decesaris and Gasperone, whom he hoped to surpass. Many young men of Palestrina, Frascati, and Pampinara disappeared. Their disappearance, at first, caused much disquietude; but it was soon known they had joined the band of Cucumetto. After some time Cucumetto became the object of universal attention; the most extraordinary traits of ferocious daring and brutality were related of him. One day he carried off a young girl, the daughter of a surveyor of Frosinone. The bandits' laws are positive; a young girl belongs first to him who carries her off, then the rest draw lots for her, and she is abandoned to their brutality until death relieves her sufferings. When their parents are sufficiently rich to pay a ransom, a messenger is sent to treat concerning it; the prisoner is hostage for the security of the messenger; should the ransom be refused, the prisoner is irrecoverably lost. The young girl's lover was in Cucumetto's troop; his name was Carlini. When she recognised her lover, the poor girl extended her arms to him, and believed herself safe; but Carlini felt his heart sink, for he but too well knew the fate that awaited her. However, as he was a favourite with Cucumetto, as he had for three years faithfully served him, and as he had saved his life by shooting a dragoon who was about to cut him down, he hoped he would have pity on him. He took him apart, whilst the young girl, seated at the foot of a huge pine that stood in the centre of the forest, formed with her picturesque head-dress a veil to hide her face from the lascivious gaze of the bandits. There he told him all, his affection for the prisoner, their promises of mutual fidelity, and how every night, since he had been near, they had met in a ruin.

"It so happened that night that Cucumetto had sent Carlini to a neighbouring village, so that he had been unable to go to the place of meeting. Cucumetto had been there, however, by accident, as he said, and had carried the maiden off.

"Carlini besought his chief to make an exception in Rita's favour, as her father was rich and could pay a large ransom. Cucumetto seemed to yield to his friend's entreaties, and bade him find a shepherd to send to Rita's father at Frosinone. Carlini flew joyfully to Rita, telling her she was saved, and bidding her write to her father to inform him what had occurred and that her ransom was fixed at three hundred piastres. Twelve hours' delay was all that was granted—that is, until nine the next morning.

"The instant the letter was written, Carlini seized it, and hastened to the plain to find a messenger. He found a young shepherd watching his flock. The natural messengers of the bandits are the shepherds, who live between the city and the mountains, between civilised and savage life. The boy undertook the commission, promising to be at Frosinone in less than an hour. Carlini returned, anxious to see his mistress, and announce the joyful intelligence. He found the troop in the glade, supping off the provisions exacted as contributions from the peasants; but his eye vainly sought Rita and Cucumetto amongst them. He inquired where they were, and was answered by a burst of laughter. A cold perspiration burst from every pore, and his hair stood on end. He repeated his question. One of the bandits rose, and offered him a glass filled with wine of Orvietto, saying: "'To the health of the brave Cucumetto and the fair Rita.'

"At this moment Carlini heard the cry of a woman; he divined the truth, seized the glass, broke it across the face of him who presented it, and rushed towards the spot whence the cry came. After a hundred yards he turned the corner of a thicket, he found Rita senseless in the arms of Cucumetto. At the sight of Carlini Cucumetto rose, a pistol in each hand. The two brigands looked at each other for a moment; the one with a smile of lasciviousness on his lips, the other with the pallor of death on his brow. It seemed that something terrible was about to pass between these two men, but by degrees Carlini's features relaxed, his hand which had grasped one of the pistols in his belt fell to his side. Rita lay between them. The moon lighted the group.

"'Well,' said Cucumetto, 'have you executed your commission?'

" ' Yes, captain,' returned Carlini. ' At nine o'clock to-morrow Rita's father will be here with the money.'

" ' It is well; in the meantime we will have a merry night; this young girl is charming, and does credit to your taste. Now, as I am not egotistical, we will return to our comrades and draw lots for her."

" ' You have determined, then, to abandon her to the common law? ' said Carlini.

" ' Why should an exception be made in her favour? '

" ' I thought that my entreaties——'

" ' What right have you, any more than the rest, to ask for an exception? '

" ' It is true.'

" ' But never mind,' continued Cucumetto, laughing, " sooner or later your turn will come.'

" Carlini's teeth clenched convulsively.

" ' Now then,' said Cucumetto, advancing towards the other bandits, ' are you coming? '

" ' I follow you.'

" Cucumetto departed without losing sight of Carlini, for, doubtless, he feared lest he should strike him unawares; but nothing betrayed a hostile design on Carlini's part. He was standing, his arms folded, near Rita, who still was insensible. Cucumetto fancied for a moment the young man was about to take her in his arms and fly; but this mattered little to him now, Rita had been his, and as for the money, three hundred piastres distributed amongst the band was so small a sum that he cared little about it. He continued to follow the path to the glade; but, to his great surprise, Carlini arrived almost as soon as himself.

" ' Let us draw lots!—let us draw lots! ' cried all the brigands, when they saw the chief.

" Their demand was fair, and the chief inclined his head in sign of acquiescence. The eyes of all shone fiercely as they made their demand, and the red light of the fire made them look like demons. The names of all, including Carlini, were placed in a hat, and the youngest of the band drew forth a ticket; the ticket bore the name of Diavolaccio. He was the man who had proposed to Carlini the health of their chief, and to whom Carlini replied by breaking the glass across his face. A large wound, extending from the temple to the mouth, was bleeding profusely. Diavolaccio, seeing himself thus favoured by fortune, burst into a loud laugh.

" ' Captain,' said he, ' just now Carlini would not drink your health when I proposed it to him; propose mine to him, and let us see if he will be more condescending to you than to me.'

" Every one expected an explosion on Carlini's part; but to their great surprise he took a glass in one hand and a flask in the other, and filling it,—

" ' Your health, Diavolaccio,' said he calmly, and he drank it off without his hand trembling in the least. Then sitting down by the fire, ' My supper,' said he, ' my expedition has given me an appetite.'

" ' Well done, Carlini,' cried the brigands. ' That is acting like a good fellow; ' and they all formed a circle round the fire, while Diavolaccio disappeared.

" Carlini ate and drank as if nothing had happened. The bandits looked on with astonishment at this singular conduct until they heard footsteps. They turned round, and saw Diavolaccio bearing the young girl in his arms. Her head hung back, and her long hair swept the ground. As they entered the circle, the bandits could perceive, by the firelight, the unearthly pallor of the young girl and of Diavolaccio. This apparition was so strange and so solemn, that every one rose, with the exception of Carlini, who remained seated, and ate and drank calmly. Diavolaccio advanced amidst the most profound silence and laid Rita at the captain's feet. Then every one could understand the cause of the unearthly pallor of the young girl and the bandit. A knife was plunged up to the hilt in Rita's left breast. Every one looked at Carlini, the sheath at his belt was empty.

" ' Ah! ' said the chief, ' I now understand why Carlini stayed behind.'

" All savage natures appreciate a desperate deed. No other of the bandits would, perhaps, have done the same, but they all understood what Carlini had done.

" ' Now, then,' cried Carlini, rising in his turn, and approaching the corpse, his hand on the butt of one of his pistols, ' does anyone dispute the possession of this woman with me? '

" ' No,' returned the chief, ' she is thine.'

" Carlini raised her in his arms and carried her out of the circle of light caused by the fire. Cucumetto placed his sentinels for the night, and the bandits wrapped themselves in their cloaks and lay down before the fire.

" At midnight the sentinel gave the alarm, and in an instant all were on the alert. It was Rita's father, who brought his daughter's ransom in person.

" ' Here! ' said he, to Cucumetto,—' here are three hundred piastres; give me back my child.'

" But the chief, without taking the money, made a sign to him to follow him. The old man obeyed, they both advanced beneath the trees, through whose branches streamed the moonlight;

Cucumetto stopped at last, and pointed to two persons grouped at the foot of a tree.

"'There!' said he, 'demand thy child of Carlini; he will tell thee what has become of her;' and he returned to his companions.

"The old man remained motionless; he felt that some great and unforeseen misfortune hung over his head. At length he advanced towards the group, which he could not comprehend. As he approached, Carlini raised his head, and the forms of two persons became visible to the old man's eyes. A female lay on the ground, her head resting on the knees of a man, who was seated by her; as he raised his head the female's face became visible. The old man recognised his child, and Carlini recognised the old man.

"'I expected thee,' said the bandit to Rita's father.

"'Wretch!' returned the old man, 'what hast thou done?' and he gazed with terror on Rita, pale and bloody, a knife buried in her bosom. A ray of moonlight poured through the trees, and lighted up the face of the dead.

"'Cucumetto had violated thy daughter,' said the bandit, 'I loved her, therefore I slew her; for she would have served as the sport of the whole band.'

"The old man spoke not, and grew pale as death.

"'Now,' continued Carlini, 'if I have done wrongly, avenge her;' and withdrawing the knife from the wound in Rita's bosom, he held it out to the old man with one hand, whilst with the other he tore open his vest.

"'Thou hast done well!' returned the old man, in a hoarse voice; 'embrace me, my son!'

"Carlini threw himself, sobbing like a child, into the arms of his mistress's father. These were the first tears the man of blood had ever wept.

"'Now,' said the old man 'aid me to bury my child.'

"Carlini fetched two pickaxes; and the father and the lover began to dig at the foot of a huge oak, beneath which the young girl was to repose. When the grave was formed, the father embraced her first and then the lover; afterwards one taking the head, the other the feet, they placed her in the grave. Then they knelt on each side of the grave, and said the prayers of the dead. Then, when they had finished, they cast the earth over the corpse, until the grave was filled. Then extending his hand, the old man said:

"'I thank you, my son; and now leave me alone.'

"'Yet——' replied Carlini.

"'Leave me, I command you!'

" Carlini obeyed, rejoined his comrades, folded himself in his cloak, and soon appeared as deep asleep as the rest. It had been resolved the night before to change their encampment. An hour before daybreak, Cucumetto aroused his men, and gave the word to march. But Carlini would not quit the forest without knowing what had become of Rita's father. He went towards the place where he had left him. He found the old man suspended from one of the branches of the oak which shaded his daughter's grave. He then took an oath of bitter vengeance over the dead body of the one and the tomb of the other. But he was unable to complete this oath, for two days afterwards, in a rencontre with the Roman carbineers, Carlini was killed. There was some surprise, however, that, as he was with his face to the enemy, he should have received a ball between the shoulders. That astonishment ceased when one of the brigands remarked to his comrades that Cucumetto was stationed ten paces in Carlini's rear when he fell.

" On the morning of the departure from the forest of Frosinone he had followed Carlini in the darkness, had heard his oath of vengeance, and, like a wise man, anticipated it. They told ten other stories of this bandit chief, each more singular than the other. Thus, from Fondi to Perouse, every one trembles at the name of Cucumetto. These narratives were frequently the themes of conversation between Luigi and Teresa. The young girl trembled very much at all these tales; but Vampa reassured her with a smile, tapping the butt of his good fowling-piece, which threw its ball so well, and if that did not restore her courage, he pointed to a crow perched on some dead branch, took an aim, touched the trigger, and the bird fell dead at the foot of the tree.

" Time passed on, and the two young people had settled to be married when Vampa should be twenty and Teresa nineteen years of age. They were both orphans, and had only their employers' leave to ask, which had been already sought and obtained. One day when they were talking over their plans for the future, they heard two or three reports of firearms, and then suddenly a man came out of the wood, near which the two young persons used to graze their flocks, and hurried towards them. When he came within hearing he exclaimed:

" ' I am pursued; can you conceal me? '

" They knew full well that this fugitive must be a bandit; but there is an innate sympathy between the Roman brigand and the Roman peasant, and the latter is always ready to aid the former. Vampa, without saying a word, hastened to the stone that closed up the entrance to their grotto, drew it away, made a sign to the fugitive to take refuge there, in a retreat unknown to every one, closed the stone upon him, and then went and resumed his seat by Teresa. Instantly afterwards four carbineers, on horseback, appeared on the edge of the wood; three of them appeared to be looking for the fugitive, whilst the fourth dragged a brigand prisoner by the neck. The three carbineers scrutinised on all sides, saw the young peasants, and, galloping up, interrogated them. They had seen no one.

" ' That is very annoying,' said the brigadier, ' for the man we are looking for is the chief.'

" ' Cucumetto? ' cried Luigi and Teresa at the same moment.

" ' Yes,' replied the brigadier.

" ' And, as his head is valued at a thousand Roman crowns, there would have been five hundred for you if you had helped us to catch him.'

" The two young persons exchanged looks. The brigadier had a moment's hope. Five hundred Roman crowns are three thousand francs, and three thousand francs are a fortune for two poor orphans who are going to be married.

" ' Yes, it is very annoying,' said Vampa; ' but we have not seen him.'

" Then the carbineers scoured the country in different directions, but in vain; then, after a time, they disappeared. Vampa then removed the stone, and Cucumetto came out. He had seen through the crevices in the granite the two young peasants talking with the carbineers, and guessed the subject of their parley. He had read in the countenances of Luigi and Teresa their steadfast resolution not to surrender him, and he drew from his pocket a purse full of gold, which he offered to them. But Vampa raised his head proudly; as to Teresa, her eyes sparkled when she thought of all the fine gowns and gay jewellery she could buy with this purse of gold.

" Cucumetto was a cunning fiend, and had assumed the form of a brigand instead of a serpent, and this look of Teresa revealed to him that she was a worthy daughter of Eve. He returned to the forest, pausing several times on his way, under the pretext of saluting his protectors. Several days elapsed, and they neither saw nor heard of Cucumetto."

34

Vampa

" THE time of the Carnival was at hand. The Comte de San-Felice announced a grand masqued ball, to which all that were distinguished in Rome were invited.

" Teresa had a great desire to see this ball. Luigi asked permission of his protector, the steward, that she and he might be present amongst the servants of the house. This was granted.

" The ball was given by the count for the particular pleasure of his daughter Carmela, whom he adored. Carmela was precisely the age and figure of Teresa, and Teresa was as handsome as Carmela. On the evening of the ball Teresa was attired in her best, her most brilliant hair ornaments, and gayest glass beads— she was in the costume of the women of Frescati. Luigi wore the very picturesque garb of the Roman peasant at holiday time. They both mixed, as they had leave to do, with the servants and peasants.

" The fête was magnificent. Not only was the villa brilliantly illuminated, but thousands of coloured lanterns were suspended from the trees in the garden; and very soon the palace over-flowed to the terraces, and the terraces to the garden-walks. At each crosspath was an orchestra, and tables spread with refresh-ments; the guests stopped, formed quadrilles, and danced in every part of the grounds they pleased.

" Carmela was attired like a woman of Sonnino. Her cap was embroidered with pearls, the pins in her hair were of gold and diamonds, her girdle was of Turkey silk, with large embroidered flowers, her bodice and skirt were of cashmere, her apron of Indian muslin, and the buttons of her corset were of jewels.

" Two of her companions were dressed, the one as a woman of Nettuno, and the other as a woman of La Riccia. Four young men of the richest and noblest families of Rome accompanied them with that Italian freedom which has not its parallel in any other country of the world. They were attired as peasants of Albano, Velletri, Civita-Castellana, and Sora. We need hardly add that these peasant costumes, like those of the females, were brilliant with gold and jewels.

" Carmela wished to make a uniform quadrille, but there was one lady wanting. Carmela looked all around her, but not one of the guests had a costume similar to her own, or those of her companions.

" The Comte de San-Felice pointed out to her, in the group of peasants, Teresa, who was hanging on Luigi's arm.

" ' Will you allow me, father? ' said Carmela.

" ' Certainly,' replied the count, ' are we not in Carnival time? '

" Carmela turned towards the young man who was talking with her, and saying a few words to him, pointed with her finger to Teresa. The young man followed with his eyes the lovely hand which made this indication, bowed in obedience, and then went to Teresa, and invited her to dance in a quadrille, directed by the count's daughter. Teresa felt something like a flame pass over her face, she looked at Luigi, who could not refuse his assent. Luigi slowly relinquished Teresa's arm, which he had held beneath his own, and Teresa, accompanied by her elegant cavalier, took her appointed place with much agitation in the aristocratic quadrille.

" Certainly, in the eyes of an artist, the exact and strict costume of Teresa had a very different character from that of Carmela and her companions; and Teresa was frivolous and coquettish, and thus the embroidery and muslins, the cashmere waist-girdles, all dazzled her, and the reflection of sapphires and diamonds almost turned her giddy brain.

" Luigi felt a sensation hitherto unknown arising in his mind. It was like an acute pain which gnawed at his heart, and then passed thrillingly throughout his frame, chasing through his veins and pervading his entire body. He followed with his eye each movement of Teresa and her cavalier; when their hands touched, he felt as though he should swoon; every pulse beat with violence, and it seemed as though a bell were ringing in his ears. When they spoke, although Teresa listened timidly and with downcast eyes to the conversation of her cavalier, as Luigi could read in the ardent looks of the good-looking young man that his language was that of praise, it seemed as if the whole world was turning round him, and all the voices of hell were whispering in his ears ideas of murder and assassination. Then fearing that his paroxysm might get the better of him, he clutched with one hand the branch of a tree against which he was leaning, and with the other convulsively grasped the dagger with a carved handle, which was in his belt, and which, unwittingly, he drew from the scabbard from time to time.

" Luigi was jealous! He felt that, influenced by her ambition and coquettish disposition, Teresa might escape him.

" The young peasant girl, at first timid and scared, soon recovered herself. We have said that Teresa was handsome, but this is not all; Teresa was replete with all those wild graces which are so much more potent than our affected and studied elegances. She had almost all the honours of the quadrille, and if she were envious of the Comte de San-Felice's daughter, we will not undertake to say that Carmela was not jealous of her. And with overpowering compliments, her handsome cavalier led her back to the place whence he had taken her and where Luigi awaited her.

" Twice or thrice during the dance the young girl had glanced at Luigi, and each time she saw he was pale, and his features agitated. Once even the blade of his knife, half drawn from its sheath, had dazzled her eyes with its sinister glare. Thus, it was almost trembling that she resumed her lover's arm.

" The quadrille had been most perfect, and it was evident there was a great demand for a second edition, Carmela alone objecting to it; but the Comte de San-Felice begged his daughter so earnestly that she acceded to it. One of the cavaliers then hastened to invite Teresa, without whom it was impossible the quadrille could be formed, but the young girl had disappeared.

" The truth was, that Luigi had not felt the strength to support another such trial, and, half by persuasion and half by force, he had removed Teresa towards another part of the garden. Teresa had yielded in spite of herself, but when she looked at the agitated countenance of the young man, she understood by his silence and trembling voice that something strange was passing within him. She herself was not exempt from internal emotion, and without having done anything wrong, yet fully comprehended that Luigi was right in reproaching her. Why, she did not know; but yet she did not the less feel that these reproaches were merited. However, to Teresa's great astonishment, Luigi remained mute, and not a word escaped his lips the rest of the evening. When the chill of the night had driven away the guests from the gardens, and the gates of the villa were closed on them for the fête indoors, he took Teresa quite away, and as he left her at her home, he said,—

" ' Teresa, what were you thinking of as you danced opposite the young Comtesse de San-Felice? '

" ' I thought,' replied the young girl, with all the frankness of her nature, ' that I would give half my life for a costume such as she wore.'

" ' And what said your cavalier to you? '

" ' He said it only depended on myself to have it, and I had only one word to say.'

" ' He was right,' said Luigi. ' Do you desire it as ardently as you say? '

" ' Yes.'

" ' Well, then, you shall have it! '

" The young girl, much astonished, raised her head to look at him, but his face was so gloomy and terrible that her words froze to her lips.

" As Luigi spoke thus, he left her. Teresa followed him with her eyes into the darkness as long as she could, and when he had quite disappeared, she entered her apartment with a sigh.

" That night a great accident happened—no doubt from the imprudence of some servant who had neglected to extinguish the lights. The Villa de San-Felice took fire in the rooms adjoining the very apartment of the lovely Carmela. Awoke in the night by the light of the flames, she had sprung out of bed, wrapped herself in a dressing-gown, and attempted to escape by the door, but the corridor by which she hoped to fly was already a prey to the flames. She had then returned to her room, calling for help as loudly as she could, when suddenly, her window, which was twenty feet from the ground, was opened, a young peasant jumped into the chamber, seized her in his arms, and with superhuman skill and strength, conveyed her to the turf of the grass-plot, where she fainted. When she recovered, her father was by her side. All the servants surrounded her, offering her assistance. An entire wing of the villa was burnt down; but what was that as Carmela was safe and uninjured? Her preserver was everywhere sought for, but her deliverer did not appear; he was inquired for everywhere, but no one had seen him. Carmela was greatly troubled that she had not recognised him.

" As the count was immensely rich, excepting the danger Carmela had run, and, as appeared to him, the marvellous manner in which she had escaped, which was rather a favour of Providence than a real misfortune, the loss occasioned by the conflagration was to him but a trifle.

" The next day, at the usual hour, the two young peasants were on the borders of the forest. Luigi arrived first. He came towards Teresa in high spirits, and seemed to have completely forgotten the events of the previous evening. The young girl was very pensive, but seeing Luigi so cheerful, she on her part, assumed a smiling air, which was natural to her when no excitement of passion came to disturb her.

" Luigi took her arm beneath his own, and led her to the door of the grotto. Then he paused. The young girl, perceiving that there was something extraordinary, looked at him steadfastly.

" ' Teresa,' said Luigi, ' yesterday evening you told me you would give all the world to have a costume similar to that of the count's daughter.'

" ' Yes,' replied Teresa, with astonishment; ' but I was mad to utter such a wish.'

" ' And I replied, ' Very well, you shall have it.'

" ' Yes,' replied the young girl, whose astonishment increased at every word uttered by Luigi, ' but of course your reply was only to please me.'

" ' I have promised no more than I have given you, Teresa,' said Luigi proudly. ' Go into the grotto and dress yourself.'

" At these words he drew away the stone, and showed Teresa the grotto, lighted up by two waxlights, which burnt on each side of a splendid mirror; on a rustic table made by Luigi, were spread out the pearl necklace and the diamond pins, and on a chair at the side was laid the rest of the costume.

" Teresa uttered a cry of joy, and, without inquiring whence this attire came, or even thanking Luigi, darted into the grotto transformed into a dressing-room.

" Luigi pushed the stone behind her, for he saw on the crest of a small adjacent hill which prevented him from seeing Palestrina from where he was, a traveller on horseback, who stopped a moment, as if uncertain of his road, and thus presented, in the blue sky, that perfect outline peculiar to the distances of southern climes.

" When he saw Luigi, he put his horse into a gallop and advanced towards him. Luigi was not mistaken. The traveller, who was going from Palestrina to Tivoli, had mistaken his way: the young man directed him; but as at a quarter of a mile distance the road again divided into three ways, and on reaching these the traveller might again stray from his route, he begged Luigi to be his guide. Luigi threw his cloak on the ground, placed his carbine on his shoulder, and freed from his heavy covering, preceded the traveller with the rapid step of a mountaineer, which a horse can scarcely keep up with. In ten minutes Luigi and the traveller reached the crossroads alluded to by the young shepherd. On arriving there, with an air as majestic as that of an emperor, he stretched his hand towards that one of the roads which the traveller was to follow.

" ' That is your road, excellency, and now you cannot again mistake.'

" ' And here is your recompense,' said the traveller, offering the young herdsman some pieces of small money.

" ' Thank you,' said Luigi, drawing back his hand; ' I render a service, I do not sell it.'

" ' Well,' replied the traveller, who seemed used to this difference between the servility of a man of the cities and the pride of the mountaineer, 'if you refuse pay, you will, perhaps, accept of a present.'

" 'Ah, yes, that is another thing.'

" 'Then,' said the traveller, ' take these two Venice sequins and give them to your bride, to make herself a pair of earrings.'

" 'And then do you take this poniard,' said the young herdsman; ' you will not find one better carved between Albana and Civita-Castellana.'

" ' I accept it,' answered the traveller, ' but then the obligation will be on my side, for this poniard is worth more than two sequins.'

" ' For a dealer, perhaps; but for me, who engraved it myself, it is hardly worth a piastre.'

" ' What is your name? ' inquired the traveller.

" ' Luigi Vampa,' replied the shepherd, with the same air as he would have replied, Alexander, King of Macedon.

" ' And yours? '

" ' I,' said the traveller, ' am called Sinbad the Sailor.' "

Franz d'Epina started with surprise.

" Sinbad the Sailor? " he said.

" Yes," replied the narrator; " that was the name which the traveller gave to Vampa as his own."

" Well, and what have you to say against this name? " inquired Albert; " it is a very pretty name, and the adventures of the gentleman of that name amused me very much in my youth, I must confess."

Franz said no more. The name of Sinbad the Sailor, as may be well supposed, awakened in him a world of recollections, as had the name of the Count of Monte Cristo on the previous evening.

" Proceed! " said he to the host.

" Vampa put the two sequins haughtily into his pocket, and slowly returned by the way he had gone. As he came within two or three hundred paces of the grotto, he thought he heard a cry. He listened to know whence this sound could proceed. A moment afterwards and he heard his own name pronounced distinctly. The cry proceeded from the grotto. He bounded like a chamois, cocking his carbine as he went, and in a moment reached the summit of a hill opposite to that on which he had perceived the traveller. Thence cries of help came more distinctly on his ear. He cast his eyes around him, and saw a man carrying off Teresa, as did the Centaur Nessus, Dejanira. This man, who was hastening towards the wood, was already three-quarters of the way on the road from the grotto to the forest. Vampa measured the distance, the man was at least two hundred paces in advance

of him, and there was not a chance of overtaking him. The young
shepherd stopped, as if his feet had been rooted to the ground;
then he put the butt of his carbine to his shoulder, took aim at
the ravisher, followed him for a second on his track, and then,
fired. The ravisher stopped suddenly, his knees bent under him,
and he fell with Teresa in his arms. The young girl rose instantly
but the man lay on the earth struggling in the agonies of death.
Vampa then rushed towards Teresa; for at ten paces from the
dying man, her legs had failed her, and she had dropped on her
knees, so that the young man feared the ball that had brought
down his enemy, had also wounded his betrothed. Fortunately,
she was unscathed, and it was fright alone that had overcome
Teresa. When Luigi had assured himself that she was safe and
unharmed, he turned towards the wounded man. He had just
expired, with clenched hands, his mouth in a spasm of agony,
and his hair on end in the sweat of death. His eyes remained
open and menacing. Vampa approached the carcass and
recognised Cucumetto. From the day on which the bandit had
been saved by the two young peasants he had been enamoured
of Teresa, and had sworn she should be his. From that time
he had watched them, and profiting by the moment when her
lover had left her alone, whilst he guided the traveller on his
way, had carried her off, and believed he at length had her in his
power, when the ball, directed by the unerring skill of the young
herdsman, had pierced his heart. Vampa gazed on him for a
moment without betraying the slightest emotion; whilst, on the
contrary, Teresa, shuddering in every limb, dared not approach
the slain ruffian but by degrees, and threw a hesitating glance at
the dead body over the shoulder of her lover. Suddenly Vampa
turned towards his mistress:

" ' Ah! ah! ' said he; ' good, good, you are attired, it is now
my turn to dress myself.'

" Teresa was clothed from head to foot in the garb of the
Comte de San-Felice's daughter. Vampa took Cucumetto's
body in his arms and conveyed it to the grotto, whilst in her turn
Teresa remained outside. If a second traveller had passed, he
would have seen a strange thing; a shepherdess watching her
flock, clad in a cashmere gown, with earrings and necklace of
pearls, diamond pins and buttons of sapphires, emeralds and,
rubies. He would, no doubt, have believed that he had returned
to the times of Florian,* and would have declared, on reaching
Paris, that he had met a shepherdess of the Alps seated at the foot
of the Sabine Hill. At the end of a quarter of an hour Vampa
quitted the grotto: his costume was no less elegant than that of
Teresa. He wore a vest of garnet-coloured velvet, with buttons

of cut gold; a silk waistcoat covered with embroidery; a Roman scarf tied round his neck; a cartouche-box worked with gold, and red and green silk; sky-blue velvet breeches, fastened above the knee with diamond buckles; garters of deer-skin, worked with a thousand arabesques, and a hat whereon hung ribands of all colours; two watches hung from his girdle, and a splendid poniard was in his belt. Teresa uttered a cry of admiration. Vampa in this attire resembled a painting by Leopold Robert or Schnetz. He had assumed the entire costume of Cucumetto. The young man saw the effect produced on his betrothed, and a smile of pride passed over his lips.

" ' Now,' he said to Teresa, ' are you ready to share my fortune, whatever it may be? '

" ' Oh, yes! ' exclaimed the young girl enthusiastically.

" ' And follow me wherever I go? '

" ' To the world's end.'

" ' Then take my arm and let us on; we have no time to lose.'

" The young girl did so without questioning her lover as to where he was conducting her, for he appeared to her at this moment as handsome, proud, and powerful, as a god. They went towards the forest, and soon entered it. We need scarcely say that all the paths of the mountain were known to Vampa; he therefore went forward without a moment's hesitation, although there was no beaten track; but he knew his path by looking at the trees and bushes; and thus they kept on advancing for nearly an hour and a half. At the end of this time they had reached the thickest of the forest. A torrent, whose bed was dry, led into a deep gorge. Vampa took this wild road which enclosed between two ridges, and shadowed by the tufted umbrage of the pines, seemed, but for the difficulties of its descent, that path to Avernus of which Virgil speaks. Teresa had become alarmed at the wild and deserted look of the plain around her, and pressed closely against her guide, not uttering a syllable; but as she saw him advance with even step and composed countenance, she endeavoured to repress her emotion. Suddenly, about ten paces from them, a man advanced from behind a tree and aimed at Vampa.

" ' Not another step,' he said, ' or you are a dead man.'

" ' What then? ' said Vampa, raising his hand with a gesture of disdain, whilst Teresa, no longer able to restrain her alarm, clung closely to him; ' do wolves rend each other? '

" ' Who are you? ' inquired the sentinel.

" ' I am Luigi Vampa, shepherd of the farm of San-Felice.'

" ' What do you want? '

" ' I would speak with your companions who are in the recess at Rocca Bianca.'

" ' Follow me, then,' said the sentinel: ' or, as you know your way, go first.'

" Vampa smiled disdainfully at this precaution of the bandit, went before Teresa, and continued to advance with the same firm and easy step as before. At the end of ten minutes the bandit made them a sign to stop. The two young persons obeyed. Then the bandit thrice imitated the cry of a crow; a croak answered this signal.

" ' Good! ' said the sentry; ' you may now advance.'

" Luigi and Teresa again set forward; as they advanced, Teresa clung tremblingly to her lover, as she saw through the trees arms appear and the barrels of carbines shine. The retreat of Rocca Bianca was at the top of a small mountain, which no doubt in former days had been a volcano,—an extinct volcano before the days when Remus and Romulus had deserted Alba to come and found the city of Rome. Teresa and Luigi reached the summit, and all at once found themselves in the presence of twenty bandits.

" ' Here is a young man who seeks and wishes to speak to you,' said the sentinel.

" ' What has he to say? ' inquired the man who was in command in the chief's absence.

" ' I wish to say, that I am tired of a shepherd's life,' was Vampa's reply.

" ' Ah, I understand,' said the lieutenant; ' and you seek admittance into our ranks? '

" ' Welcome! ' cried several bandits of Ferrusino, Pampinara, and Anagni, who had recognised Luigi Vampa.

" ' Yes, but I come to ask something more than to be your companion.'

" ' And what may that be? ' inquired the bandits, with astonishment.

" ' I come to ask to be your captain,' said the young man.

" The bandits shouted with laughter.

" ' And what have you done to aspire to this honour? ' demanded the lieutenant.

" ' I have killed your chief, Cucumetto, whose dress I now wear; and I set fire to the Villa San-Felice to procure a wedding-dress for my betrothed.'

" An hour afterwards Luigi Vampa was chosen captain, *vice* Cucumetto deceased."

" Well, my dear Albert," said Franz, turning towards his friend, " what think you of citizen Luigi Vampa? "

" I say he is a myth," replied Albert, " and never had an existence."

" And what may a myth be? " inquired Pastrini.

" The explanation would be too long, my dear landlord," replied Franz.

" And you say that Maître Vampa exercises his profession at this moment in the environs of Rome? "

" And with a boldness of which no bandit before him ever gave an example."

" Then the police have vainly tried to lay hands on him? "

" Why, you see, he has a good understanding with the shepherds in the plains, the fishermen of the Tiber, and the smugglers of the coast. They seek for him in the mountains, and he is on the waters; they follow him on the waters, and he is on the open sea; then they pursue him and he has suddenly taken refuge in the isle of Giglio, of Guanouti, or Monte Cristo; and when they hunt for him there he reappears suddenly at Albano, Tivoli, or La Riccia."

" And how does he behave towards travellers? "

" Alas! his plan is very simple. It depends on the distance he may be from the city, whether he gives eight hours, twelve hours, or a day wherein to pay their ransom; and when that time has elapsed he allows another hour's grace. At the sixtieth minute of this hour, if the money is not forthcoming, he blows out the prisoner's brains with a pistol-shot, or plants his dagger in his heart, and that settles the account."

" Well, Albert," inquired Franz of his companion, " are you still disposed to go to the Colosseum by the outer Boulevards? "

" Perfectly," said Albert, " if the way be picturesque."

The clock struck nine as the door opened, and a coachman appeared.

" Excellencies," said he, " the coach is ready."

" Well, then," said Franz, " let us to the Colosseum."

" By the Porto del Popolo or by the streets, your excellencies? "

" By the streets, morbleu! by the streets," cried Franz.

" Ah, my dear fellow! " said Albert, rising, and lighting his third cigar; " really, I thought you had more courage."

So saying, the two young men went down the staircase, and got into the carriage.

35

The Colosseum

Franz had so managed his route, that during the ride to the Colosseum they passed not a single ancient ruin, so that no gradual preparation was made on the mind for the colossal proportions of the gigantic building they came to admire. This itinerary possessed another great advantage, that of leaving Franz at full liberty to indulge his deep reverie upon the subject of the story recounted by Maître Pastrini, in which his mysterious host of the isle of Monte Cristo was so strangely mixed up. Seated with folded arms in a corner of the carriage, he continued to ponder over the singular history he had so lately listened to, and to ask himself an interminable number of questions touching its various circumstances, without, however, arriving at a satisfactory reply to any of them. One fact more than the rest brought his friend " Sinbad the Sailor " back to his recollection, and that was the mysterious sort of intimacy that seemed to exist between the brigands and sailors; and Pastrini's account of Vampa's having found refuge on board the vessels of smugglers and fishermen, reminded Franz of the two Corsican bandits he had found supping so amicably with the crew of the little yacht which had even deviated from its course and touched at Porto-Vecchio for the sole purpose of landing them. The very name assumed by his host of Monte Cristo, and again repeated by the landlord of the Hôtel de Londres, abundantly proved to him, that his island friend was playing his philanthropic part equally on the shores of Piombino, Civita Vecchia, Ostia, and Gaëta, as on those of Corsica, Tuscany, and Spain; and further, Franz bethought him of having heard his singular entertainer speak both of Tunis and Palermo, proving thereby how largely his circle of acquaintances extended.

But however the mind of the young man might be absorbed in these reflections, they were at once dispersed at the sight of the dark frowning ruins of the stupendous Colosseum, through the various openings of which the pale moonlight played and flickered like the unearthly gleam from the eyes of the wandering dead. The carriage stopped near the Meta Sudans, the door was opened, and the young men eagerly alighting, found themselves opposite a cicerone, who appeared to have sprung up from the ground, so unexpected was his appearance.

The usual guide from the hotel having followed them, they had paid two conductors. Nor is it possible, at Rome, to avoid this abundant supply of guides. Besides the ordinary cicerone who seizes upon you directly you set foot in your hotel, and never quits you while you remain in the city, there is also a special cicerone belonging to each monument,—nay, almost to each part of a monument.

As for Albert and Franz, they essayed not to escape from their ciceronian tyrants. And, indeed, it would have been so much the more difficult to break their bondage, as the guides alone are permitted to visit these monuments with torches in their hands; thus, then, the young men made no attempt at resistance, but blindly and confidingly surrendered themselves into the care and custody of their conductors. Albert had already made seven or eight similar excursions to the Colosseum, while his less favoured companion trod for the first time in his life the classic ground forming the monument of Flavius Vespasian, and to his credit be it spoken, his mind, even amid the glib loquacity of the guides was duly and deeply touched with awe and enthusiastic admiration of all he saw. Certainly no adequate notion of these stupendous ruins can be formed save by such as have visited them, and more especially by moonlight. Then the vast proportions of the building appear twice as large as when viewed by the mysterious beams of a southern moonlit sky, whose rays are sufficiently clear and vivid to gild the horizon with a glow equal to the soft twilight of an eastern clime. Scarcely, therefore, had the reflective Franz walked a hundred steps beneath the interior porticoes of the ruin, than, abandoning Albert to the guides, Franz ascended a half-dilapidated staircase; and leaving them to follow their monotonous round, seated himself at the foot of a column, and immediately opposite a large chasm, which permitted him to enjoy a full and undisturbed view of the gigantic dimensions of this majestic ruin.

Franz had remained for nearly a quarter of an hour perfectly hidden by the shadow of the vast column at whose base he had found a resting-place, and from whence his eyes followed the motions of Albert and his guides, when all at once his ear caught a sound resembling that of a stone rolling down the staircase opposite the one by which he had himself ascended. There was nothing remarkable in the circumstance of a morsel of granite giving way and falling heavily below; but it seemed to him that the substance that fell gave way beneath the pressure of a foot; and also that some one, who endeavoured as much as possible to prevent his footsteps from being heard, was approaching the spot where he sat. Conjecture soon became certainty, for the figure of a man was distinctly visible to Franz, gradually emerging from the staircase opposite, upon which the moon was at that moment pouring a full tide of silvery brightness.

The stranger thus presenting himself was probably a person who, like Franz, preferred the enjoyment of solitude and his own thoughts to the frivolous gabble of the guides, and his appearance had nothing extraordinary in it; but the hesitation with which he proceeded onwards, stopping and listening with anxious attention at every step he took, convinced Franz he expected the arrival of some person. By a sort of instinctive impulse, Franz withdrew as much as possible behind his pillar. About ten feet from the spot where himself and the stranger were placed, the roof had given way, leaving a large round aperture, through which might be seen the blue vault of heaven thickly studded with stars. Around this opening which had, possibly for ages, permitted a free entrance to the brilliant moonbeams that now illumined the vast pile, grew a quantity of creeping plants, whose delicate green branches stood out in bold relief against the clear azure of the firmament, while large masses of thick strong fibrous shoots forced their way through the chasm and hung floating to and fro like so many waving strings.

The person, whose mysterious arrival had attracted the attention of Franz, stood in a kind of half-light, that rendered it impossible to distinguish his features, although his dress was easily made out. He wore a large brown mantle, one fold of which thrown over his left shoulder served likewise to mask the lower part of his countenance, while the upper part was completely hidden by his broad-brimmed hat; the lower part of his dress was more distinctly visible by the bright rays of the moon, which entering through the broken ceiling shed their refulgent beams on feet cased in elegantly made boots of polished leather, over which descended fashionably cut trousers of black cloth.

From the imperfect means Franz had of judging, he could only come to one conclusion,—that the individual whom he was thus watching certainly belonged to no inferior station in life. Some few minutes had elapsed, and the stranger began to show manifest signs of impatience, when a slight noise was heard outside the aperture in the roof, and almost immediately a dark shadow seemed to obstruct the flood of light that had entered from it, and the figure of a man was clearly seen gazing with eager scrutiny on the immense space beneath him; then as his eye caught sight of the individual in the mantle, he grasped a floating mass of thickly matted boughs, and glided down by their help to within three or four feet of the ground, and then leaped lightly on his feet. The man who had performed this daring act with so much indifference wore the costume of Transtevere.

" I beg your excellency's pardon for keeping you waiting,"
said the man, in the Roman dialect, " but I don't think I'm many
minutes after my time; ten o'clock has just struck by the clock
of Saint-Jean-de-Latran."

" Say not a word about being late," replied the stranger, in
purest Tuscan; " 'tis I who am too soon; but even if you had
caused me to wait a little while, I should have felt quite sure that
the delay was not occasioned by any fault of yours."

" Your excellency is perfectly right in so thinking," said the
man; " I came here direct from the Château Saint-Ange."

" And what news did you glean? "

" That two executions of considerable interest will take place
the day after to-morrow at two o'clock, as is customary at Rome
at the commencement of all great festivals; one of the culprits
will be *mazzolato*;* he is an atrocious villain, who murdered the
priest who brought him up, and deserves not the smallest pity;
the other sufferer is sentenced to be *decapitato*; and he, your
excellency, is poor Peppino."

" The fact is that you have inspired not only the pontifical
government, but also the neighbouring states, with such extreme
fear, that they are glad of an opportunity of making an example."

" But Peppino did not even belong to my band; he was merely
a poor shepherd, whose only crime consisted in furnishing us with
provisions."

" Which makes him your accomplice to all intents and purposes.
But mark the distinction with which he is treated; instead of being
knocked on the head as you would be if once they caught hold of
you, he is simply sentenced to be guillotined, by which means,
too, the amusements of the day are diversified, and there is a
spectacle to please every spectator."

" Without reckoning the wholly unexpected one I am preparing
to surprise them with."

" My good friend," said the man in the cloak," excuse me for
saying that you seem to me precisely in the mood to commit
some wild or extravagant act."

" Perhaps I am; but one thing I have resolved on, and that is,
to stop at nothing to restore a poor devil to liberty, who has got
into this scrape solely from having served me. I should hate and
despise myself as a coward, did I desert the brave fellow in his
present extremity."

" And what do you mean to do ? "

" To surround the scaffold with twenty of my best men, who,
at a signal from me, will rush forward directly Peppino is brought
for execution, and, by the assistance of their stilettos, drive back
the guard and carry off the prisoner."

" That seems to me as hazardous as uncertain, and convinces me my scheme is far better than yours."

" And what is your excellency's project? "

" Just this! I will so advantageously bestow 2000 piastres, that the person receiving them shall obtain a respite till next year for Peppino; and during that year, another skilfully placed 1000 piastres shall afford him the means of escaping from his prison. I can do more single-handed by the means of gold, than you and all your troop could effect with stilettos, pistols, carbines, and blunderbusses included. Leave me then to act, and have no fears for the result."

" At least there can be no harm in myself and party being in readiness, in case your excellency should fail."

" None whatever; take what precautions you please, if it is any satisfaction to you to do so; but rely upon my obtaining the reprieve I seek."

" Remember, the execution is fixed for the day after to-morrow, and that you have but one day to work in."

" And what then? is not a day divided into twenty-four hours, each hour into sixty minutes, and every minute subdivided into sixty seconds? Now in 86,400 seconds very many things can be done."

" And how shall I know whether your excellency has succeeded or not? "

" Oh! that is very easily arranged. I have engaged the three lower windows at the Café Rospoli; should I have obtained the requisite pardon for Peppino, the two outside windows will be hung with yellow damasks, and the centre with white, having a large cross in red marked on it."

" And whom will you employ to carry the reprieve to the officer directing the execution? "

" Send one of your men disguised as a penitent friar, and I will give it to him: his dress will procure him the means of approaching the scaffold itself, and will deliver the official order to the officer, who in his turn will hand it to the executioner; in the meantime, it will be as well to acquaint Peppino with what we have determined on, if it be only to prevent his dying of fear or losing his senses, because in either case a very useless expense will have been incurred."

" Your excellency," said the man, " you are fully persuaded of my entire devotion to you, are you not? "

" Nay, I flatter myself that there can be no doubt of it," replied the cavalier in the cloak.

" Well, then, only fulfil your promise of rescuing Peppino, and henceforward you shall receive not only devotedness, but the most absolute obedience from myself and those under me that one human being can render to another."

" Have a care how far you pledge yourself, my good friend, for I may remind you of your promises at some, perhaps not very distant, period, when I, in my turn, may require your aid and influence."

" Let that day come soon or late, your excellency will find me what I have found you in this my heavy trouble; and if from the other end of the world you but write me word to do such or such a thing, conclude it done, for done it shall be, on the word and faith of——"

" Hush! " interrupted the stranger; " I hear a noise."

" 'Tis some travellers, who are visiting the Colosseum by torchlight."

" 'Twere better we should not be seen together; those guides are nothing but spies, and might possibly recognise you; and however I may be honoured by your friendship, my worthy friend, if once the extent of our intimacy were known, I am sadly afraid both my reputation and credit would suffer thereby. "

" Well, then, if you obtain the reprieve? "

" The middle window at the Café Rospoli will be hung with white damask bearing on it a red cross."

" And if you fail? "

" Then all three windows will have yellow draperies."

" And then? "

" And then, my good fellow, use your daggers in any way you please; and I further promise you to be there as a spectator of your prowess."

" All is then understood between us. Adieu, your excellency, depend upon me as firmly as I do upon you."

Saying these words, the Transtevere disappeared down the staircase, while his companion, muffling his features more closely than before in the folds of his mantle, passed almost close to Franz, and descended to the arena by an outward flight of steps. The next minute Franz heard himself called by Albert, who made the lofty building re-echo with the sound of his friend's name. Franz, however, did not obey the summons till he had satisfied himself the two individuals, whose conversation he had thus surprised, were at a sufficient distance to prevent his encountering them in his descent, not wishing that they should suspect having had a witness to their discourse, who, if unable to recognise their faces, had at least heard every word that passed. In ten minutes from the parting of the strangers, Franz was on the road to the Hôtel d'Espagne.

One of the two men whose mysterious rendezvous in the

Colosseum he had so unintentionally witnessed was an entire stranger to him, but not so the other; and though Franz had been unable to distinguish his features, from his being either wrapped in his mantle or obscured by the shadow, the tones of his voice had made too powerful an impression on him the first time he heard them for him ever again to forget them, hear them when or where he might. It was more especially when speaking in a manner half jesting, half bitter, that Franz's ear recalled most vividly the deep sonorous, yet well-pitched voice, that had spoken to him in the grotto of Monte Cristo, and which he heard for the second time amid the darkness and ruined grandeur of the Colosseum. And the more he thought, the more entire was his conviction, that the individual in the mantle was no other than his former host and entertainer, " Sinbad the Sailor."

Under any other circumstances, Franz would have found it impossible to resist his extreme curiosity to know more of so singular a personage, and with that intent have sought to renew their short acquaintance; but in the present instance, the confidential nature of the conversation he had overheard made him, with propriety, judge that his appearance at such a time would be anything but agreeable. As we have seen, therefore, he permitted his former host to retire without attempting a recognition; but fully promising himself a rich indemnity for his present forbearance should chance afford him another opportunity.

In vain did Franz endeavour to forget the many perplexing thoughts which assailed him; in vain did he court the refreshment of sleep. Worn out at length, he fell asleep at daybreak, and did not awake till late. Like a genuine Frenchman, Albert had employed his time in arranging for the evening's diversion; he had sent to engage a box at the Teatro Argentino; and Franz having a number of letters to write, relinquished the carriage to Albert for the whole of the day.

At five o'clock Albert returned, delighted with his day's work. He had been occupied in leaving his letters of introduction, and had received in return more invitations to balls and soirées than it would be possible for him to fulfil; besides this, he had seen (as he called it) all the remarkable sights at Rome. Yes, in a single day he had accomplished what his more reflective companion would have taken weeks to effect. Neither had he neglected to ascertain the name of the piece to be played that night at the Teatro Argentino, and also what performers appeared in it.

The opera of *Parisina** was announced for representation, and the principal actors were Coselli, Moriani, and La Spech. The young men, therefore, had reason to consider themselves fortunate in having the opportunity of hearing one of the best works by the composer of *Lucia di Lammermoor*, supported by three of the most renowned vocalists of Italy. Albert had never been able to endure the Italian theatres, with their orchestras from which it is impossible to see, and the absence of balconies or open boxes; all these defects pressed hard on a man who had had his stall at the Opera buffa, and his share in the omnibus box at the Italian Opera.* Still, in despite of this, Albert displayed his most dazzling and effective costume each time he visited the theatres; but alas,! his *recherchée* toilette was wholly thrown away; and one of the most worthy representatives of Parisian fashion had to carry with him the mortifying reflection of having nearly overrun Italy without meeting with a single adventure.

Sometimes Albert would affect to make a joke of his want of success, but internally he was deeply wounded, and his self-love immensely piqued to think that Albert de Morcerf, the most admired and most sought after of any young person of his day, should thus be passed over, and merely have his labour for his pains. And the thing was so much the more annoying, as, according to the characteristic modesty of a Frenchman, Albert had quitted Paris with the full conviction that he had only to show himself in Italy to carry all before him, and that upon his return he should astonish the Parisian world with the recital of his numerous love-affairs.

Alas! poor Albert, none of those interesting adventures fell in his way; the lovely Genoese, Florentine, and Neapolitan females were all faithful, if not to their husbands, at least to their lovers, and thought not of changing even for the splendid appearance of Albert de Morcerf; and all he gained was the painful conviction that the ladies of Italy have this advantage over those of France, that they are faithful even in their infidelity. Yet he could not restrain a hope that in Italy, as elsewhere, there might be an exception to the general rule. Albert, besides being an elegant, well-looking young man, was also possessed of considerable talent and ability. Moreover, he was a viscount—a recently created one certainly; but in the present day it is not necessary to go as far back as Noah in tracing a descent, and a genealogical tree is equally estimated, whether dated from 1399 or merely 1815. To crown all these advantages, Albert de Morcerf commanded an income of 50,000 livres (£2000), a more than sufficient sum to render him a personage of considerable importance in Paris. Albert, however, hoped to indemnify himself for all these slights and indifferences during the Carnival, knowing full well that among the different states and kingdoms in which this festivity is celebrated, Rome is the spot where even the wisest and gravest throw off the usual rigidity of their lives, and deign to mingle in the follies of this time of liberty and relaxation.

The Carnival was to commence on the morrow; therefore Albert had not an instant to lose in setting forth the programme of his hopes, expectations, and claims to notice. With this design, he had engaged a box in the most conspicuous part of the theatre, and exerted himself to set off his personal attractions by the aid of the most *recherchée* and elaborate toilette. The box taken by Albert was in the first circle. Although each of the three tiers of boxes is deemed equally aristocratic, and is, for this reason, generally styled the " nobility's boxes," and although the box engaged for the two friends was sufficiently capacious to contain at least a dozen persons, it had cost less than would be paid at some of the French theatres for one admitting merely four occupants.

Another motive had influenced Albert's selection of his seat:— who knew but that thus advantageously placed, he could not fail to attract the notice of some fair Roman; and an introduction might ensue that would procure him the offer of a seat in a carriage, or a place in a princely balcony, from which he might behold the gaieties of the Carnival?

These united considerations made Albert more lively and anxious to please than he had hitherto been. Totally disregarding the business of the stage, he leaned from his box and began attentively scrutinising the beauty of each pretty woman, aided by a powerful lorgnette; but, alas! this attempt to attract similar notice wholly failed; not even curiosity had been excited; and it was but too apparent that the lovely creatures, into whose good graces he was desirous of stealing, were all so much engrossed with themselves, their lovers, or their own thoughts, that they had not so much as remarked him or the pointing of his glass.

Towards the close of the first act, the door of a box which had been hitherto vacant was opened; a lady entered to whom Franz had been introduced in Paris, where, indeed, he had imagined she still was. The quick eye of Albert caught the involuntary start with which his friend beheld the new arrival, and turning to him, he said hastily:

" Do you know the female who has just entered the box? "

" Yes; what do you think of her? "

" Oh, she is perfectly lovely—what a complexion? And such magnificent hair! Is she French? "

" No; a Venetian."

" And her name is——"

" Countess G——"*

"Ah! I know her by name," exclaimed Albert; "she is said to possess as much wit and cleverness as beauty! I was to have been presented to her when I met her at Madame Villefort's ball."

"Shall I assist you in repairing your negligence?" asked Franz.

"My dear fellow, are you really on such good terms with her as to venture to take me to her box?"

"Why, I have only had the honour of being in her society and conversing with her three or four times in my life; but you know that even such an acquaintance as that might warrant my doing what you ask."

At this instant the countess perceived Franz, and graciously waved her hand to him, to which he replied by a respectful inclination of the head.

"Upon my word," said Albert, "you seem to be on excellent terms with the beautiful countess!"

"You are mistaken in thinking so," returned Franz calmly; "but you merely fall into the same error which leads so many of our countrymen to commit the most egregious blunders,—I mean that of judging the habits and customs of Italy and Spain by our Parisian notions."

"Well, be it so," said Albert; "but the question for the present is—are you going to keep your promise of introducing me to the fair subject of our remarks?"

"Certainly, directly the curtains falls on the stage!"

"What a confounded time this first act is about! I believe, on my soul, that they never mean to finish it!"

The curtain at length fell on the performances, to the infinite satisfaction of the Vicomte de Morcerf, who seized his hat, rapidly passed his fingers through his hair, arranged his cravat and wristbands, and signified to Franz that he was waiting for him to lead the way.

Franz, who had mutely interrogated the countess, and received from her a gracious smile in token that he would be welcome, sought not to retard the gratification of Albert's eager impatience, but commenced at once the tour of the house, closely followed by Albert. They arrived at the countess's box, and at the knock the door was immediately opened, and the young man, who was seated beside the countess in the front of the *loge*, in obedience to the Italian custom, instantly rose and surrendered his place to the strangers, who, in turn, would be expected to retire upon the arrival of other visitors.

Franz presented Albert as one of the most distinguished young men of the day, both as regarded his position in society and extraordinary talents: nor did he say more than the truth, for in Paris and the circle in which the viscount moved, he was looked upon and cited as a model of perfection. Franz added that his companion, deeply grieved at having been prevented the honour of being presented to the countess during her sojourn in Paris, was most anxious to make up for it, and had requested him (Franz) to remedy the past misfortune by conducting him to her box, and concluded by asking pardon for his presumption in having taken upon himself to do so. The countess in reply bowed gracefully to Albert, and extended her hand with cordial kindness to Franz; then, inviting Albert to take the vacant seat beside her, she recommended Franz to take the next best, if he wished to view the ballet, and pointed to the one behind her own chair. Albert was soon deeply engrossed in discoursing upon Paris and Paris matters, speaking to the countess of the various persons they both knew there. Franz perceived how completely he was in his element; and, unwilling to interfere with the pleasure he so evidently felt, took up Albert's enormous lorgnette, and began in his turn to survey the audience. Sitting alone, in the front of a box immediately opposite, but situated on the third row, was a female of exquisite beauty, dressed in a Greek costume, which it was evident, from the ease and grace with which she wore it, was her national attire, Behind her, but in deep shadow, was the outline of a male figure; but the features of this latter personage it was not possible to distinguish. Franz could not forbear breaking in upon the apparently interesting conversation passing between the countess and Albert, to inquire of the former if she knew who was the fair Albanaise opposite, since beauty such as hers was well worthy of being remarked by either sex.

" All I can tell you about her," replied the countess, " is, that she has been at Rome since the beginning of the season; for I saw her where she now sits the very first night of the theatre's opening, and since then she has never missed a performance. Sometimes accompanied by the individual who is with her, and at others merely attended by a black servant."

" And what do you think of her personal appearance? "

" Oh, I consider her perfectly lovely,—she is just my idea of what Medora* must have been."

Franz and the countess exchanged a smile, and then the latter resumed her conversation with Albert, while Franz returned to his previous survey of the house and company. The curtain rose on the ballet, which was one of those excellent specimens of the Italian school, admirably arranged and put on the stage by Henri,* who has established for himself a great reputation throughout Italy for his taste and skill in the chorographic art. However much the ballet might have claimed his attention, Franz was too deeply occupied with the beautiful Greek to take any note of it, while she seemed to experience an almost childlike delight in watching it; her eager, animated looks, contrasting strongly with the utter indifference of her companion, who, during the whole time the piece lasted, never even moved, spite of the furious crashing din produced by the trumpets, cymbals, and Chinese bells, made to produce their loudest sound from the orchestra. The apathetic companion of the fair Greek took no heed of the deafening sounds that prevailed; but was, as far as appearances might be trusted, enjoying soft repose and bright celestial dreams. The ballet at length came to a close, and the curtain fell amidst the loud unanimous plaudits of an enthusiastic and delighted audience.

Owing to the very judicious plan of dividing the two acts of the opera with a ballet, the pauses between the performances are very short; the singers in the opera having time to repose themselves and change their costume, when necessary, while the dancers are executing their pirouettes, and exhibiting their graceful steps. The overture to the second act began; and at the first sound of the leader's bow across his violin, Franz observed the sleeper slowly arise and approach the Greek girl, who turned round to say a few words to him, and then leaning forward again on her box, she became as absorbed as before in what was going on. The countenance of the person who had addressed her remained so completely in the shade, that though Franz tried his utmost, he could not distinguish a single feature. The curtain drew up, and the attention of Franz was attracted by the actors, and his eyes quitted their gaze at the box containing the Greek girl and her strange companion to watch the business of the stage.

Most of my readers are aware that the second act of *Parisina* opens with the celebrated and effective duet, in which Parisina, while sleeping, betrays to Azzo the secret of her love for Ugo. The injured husband goes through all the workings of jealousy, until conviction seizes on his mind, and then, in a frenzy of his rage and indignation, he awakens his guilty wife to tell her he knows her guilt, and to threaten her with his vengeance. This duet is one of the finest conceptions that has ever emanated from the fruitful pen of Donizetti. Franz now listened to it for the third time, yet its notes, so tenderly expressive and fearfully grand, as the wretched husband and wife give vent to their different griefs and passions, thrilled through the soul of Franz with an effect equal to his first emotions upon hearing it. Excited beyond his usual calm demeanour, Franz rose with the audience, and was about to join the loud enthusiastic applause that followed, but suddenly his purpose was arrested, his hands fell by his sides, and the half-uttered " bravos " expired on his lips.

The occupant of the box in which the Greek girl sat appeared to share the universal animation that prevailed, for he left his seat to stand up in the front, so that his countenance being fully revealed, Franz had no difficulty in recognising him as the mysterious inhabitant of Monte Cristo, and the very same individual he had encountered the preceding evening in the ruins of the Colosseum, and whose voice and figure had seemed so familiar to him. All doubt of his identity was now at an end; his singular host evidently resided at Rome. The surprise and agitation occasioned by this full confirmation of Franz's former suspicion had, no doubt, imparted a corresponding expression to his features; for the countess, after gazing with a puzzled look on his speaking countenance, burst into a fit of laughter, and begged to know what had happened.

" Madame la Comtesse," returned Franz, totally unheeding her raillery, " I asked you a short time since if you knew any particulars respecting the Albanian lady opposite; I must now beseech you to inform me who and what is her husband? "

" Nay," answered the countess, " I know no more of him than yourself."

" Perhaps you never before remarked him? "

" What a question! so truly French! Do you not know that we Italians have eyes only for the man we love? "

" True," replied Franz.

" All I can say," continued the countess, taking up the lorgnette, and directing it to the box in question, " is that the gentleman, whose history I am unable to furnish, seems to me as though he had just been dug up; he looks more like a corpse permitted by some friendly grave-digger to quit his tomb for a while, and revisit this earth of ours, than anything human. How ghastly pale he is! "

" Oh, he is always as colourless as you now see him," said Franz.

" Then you know him? " almost screamed the countess. " Oh! pray do, for Heaven's sake, tell us all about——is he a vampire or a resuscitated corpse, or what? "

" I fancy I have seen him before; and I even think he recognises me."

" And I can well understand," said the countess, shrugging up her beautiful shoulders, as though an involuntary shudder passed through her veins, " that those who have once seen that man will never be likely to forget him."

The sensation experienced by Franz was evidently not peculiar to himself,—another, and wholly uninterested person, felt the same unaccountable awe and misgiving.

"Well," inquired Franz, after the countess had a second time directed her lorgnette at the *loge* of their mysterious *vis-à-vis*, "what do you think of our opposite neighbour?"

"Why, that he is no other than Lord Ruthven* himself in a living form."

This fresh allusion to Byron drew a smile to Franz's countenance; although he could but allow that if anything was likely to induce belief in the existence of vampires, it would be the presence of such a man as the mysterious personage before him.

"I must positively find out who and what he is," said Franz, rising from his seat.

"No, no!" cried the countess, "you must not leave me. I depend upon you to escort me home. Oh, indeed, I cannot permit you to go."

"Is it possible," whispered Franz, "that you entertain any fear?"

"I'll tell you," answered the countess. "Byron had the most perfect belief in the existence of vampires, and even assured me he had seen some. The description he gave me perfectly corresponds with the features and character of the man before us. Oh! it is the exact personification of what I have been led to expect. The coal-black hair, large bright, glittering eyes, in which a wild, unearthly fire seems burning—the same ghastly paleness. Then observe, too, that the very female he has with him is altogether unlike all others of her sex. She is a foreigner—a stranger. Nobody knows who she is, or where she comes from. No doubt she belongs to the same horrible race he does, and is, like himself, a dealer in magical arts. I entreat you not to go near him—at least to-night: and if to-morrow your curiosity still continues as great, pursue your researches if you will; but to-night you neither can or shall. For that purpose I mean to keep you all to myself."

Franz protested he could not defer his pursuit till the following day, for many reasons.

"Listen to me," said the countess, "and do not be so very headstrong. I am going home. I have a party at my house to-night, and therefore cannot possibly remain till the conclusion of the opera. Now, I cannot for one instant believe you so devoid of gallantry as to refuse a lady your escort when she even condescends to ask you for it."

There was nothing else left for Franz to do but to take up his hat, open the door of the *loge*, and offer the countess his arm.

It was quite evident, by the countess's manner, that her uneasiness was not feigned; and Franz himself could not resist a species of superstitious dread—so much the stronger in him, as it arose from a variety of corroborating recollections, while the terror of the countess sprung from an instinctive feeling, originally created in her mind by the wild tales she had listened to till she believed them truths. Franz could even feel her arm tremble as he assisted her into the carriage.

Upon arriving at her hotel, Franz perceived that she had deceived him when she spoke of expecting company; on the contrary, her own return before the appointed hour seemed greatly to astonish the domestics.

"Excuse my little subterfuge," said the countess, in reply to her companion's half-reproachful observation on the subject; "but that horrid man had made me feel quite uncomfortable, and I longed to be alone that I might compose my startled mind."

Franz essayed to smile.

"Nay," said she, "smile not; it ill accords with the expression of your countenance, and I am sure it springs not from your heart. However, promise me one thing."

"What is it?"

"Promise me, I say."

"I will do anything you desire, except relinquish my determination of finding out who this man is. I have more reason than you can imagine for desiring to know who he is, from whence he came, and whither he is going."

"Where he comes from I am ignorant; but I can readily tell you where he is going to, and that is down below without the least doubt."

"Let us only speak of the promise you wished me to make," said Franz.

"Well, then, you must give me your word to return immediately to your hotel; and make no attempt to follow this man to-night. There are certain affinities between the persons we quit and those we meet afterwards. For Heaven's sake do not serve as a conductor between that man and me. Pursue your chase after him to-morrow as eagerly as you please; but never bring him near me if you would not see me die of terror. And now, good-night; retire to your apartments, and try to sleep away all recollections of this evening. For my own part, I am quite sure I shall not be able to close my eyes." So saying, the countess quitted Franz, leaving him unable to decide whether she were merely amusing herself at his expense, or that her fears and agitations were genuine.

Upon his return to the hotel, Franz found Albert in his dressing-gown and slippers, listlessly extended on a sofa, smoking a cigar.

" My dear fellow," cried he, springing up, " is it really you? Why, I did not expect to see you before to-morrow."

" My dear Albert," replied Franz, " I am glad of this opportunity to tell you once and for ever that you entertain a most erroneous notion concerning Italian females. I should have thought the continual failures you have met with in all your own love-affairs might have taught you better by this time."

" Upon my soul! these women would puzzle the very devil to read them aright. Why, here—they give you their hand— they press yours in return—they keep up a whispering conversation—permit you to accompany them home! Why if a Parisian were to indulge in a quarter of these marks of flattering attention, her reputation would be gone for ever."

" And the very reason why the females of this fine country put so little restraint on their words and actions, is because they live so much in public, and have really nothing to conceal. Besides, you must have perceived that the countess was really alarmed."

" At what? At the sight of that respectable gentleman sitting opposite to us in the same *loge* as the lovely Greek girl? Now, for my part, I met them in the lobby after the conclusion of the piece; and, hang me, if I can guess where you took your notions of the other world from! I can assure you that this hob-goblin of yours is a deuced fine-looking fellow—admirably dressed; indeed, I feel quite sure, from the cut of his clothes, they are made by a first-rate Paris tailor—probably Blin or Humann.* He was rather too pale, certainly; but, then, you know, paleness is always looked upon as a strong proof of aristocratical descent and distinguished breeding."

Franz smiled; for he well remembered that Albert particularly prided himself on the entire absence of colour in his own complexion.

" Well, that tends to confirm my own ideas," said Franz, " that the countess's suspicions were destitute alike of sense and reason. Did he speak in your hearing? and did you catch any of his words? "

" I did; but they were uttered in the Romaic dialect. I knew that from the mixture of Greek words. I don't know whether I ever told you that when I was at college I was rather strong in Greek."

" He spoke the Romaic language, did he? "

" I think so."

" That settles it," murmured Franz. " 'Tis he, past all doubt."

" What do you say? "

" Nothing, nothing. But tell me, what were you thinking about when I came in? "

" Oh, I was arranging a little surprise for you."

" Indeed! Of what nature? "

" Why, you know, it is quite impossible to procure a carriage."

" Certainly; and I also know that we have done all that human means afforded to endeavour to get one."

" Now, then, in this difficulty, a bright idea has flashed across my brain."

Franz looked at Albert as though he had not much confidence in the suggestions of his imagination.

" Well, now, what do you say to a cart? I dare say such a thing might be had."

" Very possibly."

" And a pair of oxen? "

" As easily found as the cart."

" Then you see, my good fellow, with a cart and couple of oxen our business can be managed. The cart must be tastefully ornamented; and if you and I dress ourselves as Neapolitan reapers, we may get up a striking tableau, after the manner of that splendid picture by Leopold Robert. It would add greatly to the effect if the countess would join us in the costume of a peasant from Puzzoli or Sorento. Our group would then be quite complete, more especially as the countess is quite beautiful enough to represent the mother with child."

" Well," said Franz, " this time, M. Albert, I am bound to give you credit for having hit upon a most capital idea."

" And quite a national one, too," replied Albert, with gratified pride. " A mere masque borrowed from our own festivities. Ha! ha! Messieurs les Romains! you thought to make us unhappy strangers trot at the heels of your processions, like so many lazzaroni, because no carriages or horses are to be had in your beggarly city. But you don't know us; when we can't have one thing we invent another."

" And have you communicated your triumphant idea to any person? "

" Only to our host. Upon my return home I sent to desire he would come to me, and I then explained to him what I wished to procure. He assured me that nothing would be easier than to furnish all I desired. One thing I was sorry for: when I bade him have the horns of the oxen gilded, he told me there would not be time, as it would require three days to effect that; so you see we must do without this little superfluity."

" And where is he now? "

" Who? "

" Our host."

" Gone out in search of our equipage: by to-morrow it might be too late."

" Then he will be able to give us an answer to-night? "

" Oh, I expect him every minute."

At this instant the door opened, and the head of Maître Pastrini appeared.

" *Permesso?* " inquired he.

" Certainly—certainly," cried Franz. " Come in, mine host."

" Now, then," asked Albert eagerly, " have you found the desired cart and oxen? "

" Better than that! " replied the Maître Pastrini, with the air of a man perfectly well satisfied with himself.

" Take care, my worthy host," said Albert, " *better* is a sure enemy to *well*."

" Let your excellencies only leave the matter to me," returned Maître Pastrini, in a tone indicative of unbounded self-confidence.

" But what *have* you done? " asked Franz. " Speak out, there's a worthy fellow."

" Your excellencies are aware," responded the landlord, swelling with importance, " that the Count of Monte Cristo is living on the same floor with yourselves! "

" I should think we did know it," exclaimed Albert, " since it is owing to that circumstance that we are packed into these small rooms, like two poor students in the back streets of Paris."

" Well, then, the Count of Monte Cristo, hearing of the dilemma in which you are placed, has sent to offer you seats in his carriage and two places at his windows in the Palace Rospoli."

The friends looked at each other with unutterable surprise.

" But do you think," asked Franz, " that we ought to accept such offers from a perfect stranger? "

" What sort of person is this Count of Monte Cristo? " asked Franz of his host.

" A very great nobleman, but whether Maltese or Sicilian I cannot exactly say; but this I know, that he is noble as a Borghese and rich as a gold-mine."

" It seems to me," said Franz, speaking in an undertone to Albert, " that if this individual merited the high panegyrics of our landlord, he would have conveyed his invitation through another channel, and not permitted it to be brought to us in this unceremonious way. He would have written—or——"

At this instant some one knocked at the door.

" Come in! " said Franz.

A servant, wearing a livery of considerable style and richness, appeared at the threshold, and placing two cards in the landlord's hands, who forthwith presented them to the two young men, he said, " Please to deliver these, from M. le Comte de Monte Cristo, to M. le Vicomte Albert de Morcerf and M. Franz Epinay. M. le Comte de Monte Cristo," continued the servant, " begs these gentlemen's permission to wait upon them as their neighbour, and he will be honoured by an intimation of what time they will please to receive him."

" Faith, Franz," whispered Albert, " there is not much to find fault with here."

" Tell the count," replied Franz, " that we will do ourselves the pleasure of calling on him."

The servant bowed and retired.

" That is what I call an elegant mode of attack," said Albert. " You were quite correct in what you stated, Maître Pastrini. The Count of Monte Cristo is unquestionably a man of first-rate breeding and knowledge of the world."

" Then you accept his offer? " said the host.

" Of course we do," replied Albert. " Still I must own I am sorry to be obliged to give up the cart and the group of reapers— it would have produced such an effect! And were it not for the windows at the Palace Rospoli, by way of recompense for the loss of our beautiful scheme, I don't know but what I should have held on by my original plan. What say you, Franz? "

" Oh, I agree with you; the windows in the Palace Rospoli alone decided me."

The truth was, that the mention of two places in the Palace Rospoli had recalled to Franz's mind the conversation he had overheard the preceding evening in the ruins of the Colosseum between the mysterious unknown and the Transtevere, in which the stranger in the cloak had undertaken to obtain the freedom of a condemned criminal; and if this muffled-up individual proved (as Franz felt sure he would) the same as the person he had just seen in the Teatro Argentino, then he should be able to establish his identity, and also to prosecute his researches respecting him with perfect facility and freedom. The next day must clear up every doubt, and unless his near neighbour and would-be friend, the Count of Monte Cristo, possessed the ring of Gyges,* and by its power were able to render himself invisible, it was very certain he could not escape this time. Eight o'clock found Franz up and dressed, while Albert, who had not the same motives for early rising, was still profoundly asleep. The first act of Franz was to summon his landlord, who presented himself with his accustomed obsequiousness.

" Pray, Maître Pastrini," asked Franz, " is not some execution appointed to take place to-day? "

" Yes, your excellence; but if your reason for inquiry is, that you may procure a window to view it from, you are much too late."

" Oh, no! " answered Franz; " I had no such intention; and even if I had felt a wish to witness the spectacle, I might have done so from Monte Pincio,—could I not? "

" Ah! " exclaimed mine host; " I did not think it likely your excellence would have chosen to mingle with such a rabble as are always collected on that hill, which, indeed, they consider as exclusively belonging to themselves."

" Very possibly I may not go," answered Franz; " but in case I feel disposed, give me some particulars of to-day's executions."

" That happens just lucky, your excellence! Only a few minutes ago they brought me the *tavolettas*."

" What are they? "

" Sort of wooden tablets hung up at the corners of streets the evening before an execution, on which is pasted up a paper containing the names of the condemned persons, their crimes, and mode of punishment. The reason for so publicly announcing all this, is that all good and faithful Catholics may offer up their prayers for the unfortunate culprits, and, above all, beseech of Heaven to grant them a sincere repentance."

" And these tablets are brought to you, that you may add your prayers to those of the faithful, are they? " asked Franz, somewhat incredulously.

" Oh dear, no, your excellence; I have not time for anybody's affairs but my own and those of my honourable guests; but I make an agreement with the man who pastes up the papers, and he brings them to me as he would the play-bills, that in case any person staying at my hotel should like to witness an execution, he may obtain every requisite information concerning the time and place, etc."

" Upon my word, that is most delicate attention on your part, Maître Pastrini," cried Franz.

"Why, your excellence," returned the landlord, chuckling and rubbing his hands with infinite complacency, " I think I may take upon myself to say I neglect nothing to deserve the support and patronage of the noble visitors to this poor hotel."

" I see that plainly enough, my most excellent host, and you may rely upon my repeating so striking a proof of your attention to your guests wherever I go. Meanwhile, oblige me by a sight of one of these *tavolettas*."

" Nothing can be easier than to comply with your excellence's wish," said the landlord, opening the door of the chamber; " I have caused one to be placed on the landing, close by your apartment." Then taking the tablet from the wall, he handed it to Franz, who read as follows:—

" ' The public is informed, that on Wednesday, February 23rd, being the first day of the Carnival, two executions will take place in the Place del Popolo, by order of the Tribunal de la Rota, of two individuals, named Andrea Rondola and Peppino otherwise called Rocca Priori; the former found guilty of the murder of a venerable and exemplary priest, named Don César Torlini, canon of the church of Saint-Jean-de-Latran; and the latter, convicted of being an accomplice of the atrocious and sanguinary bandit Luigi Vampa and his troop. The first-named malefactor will be *mazzolato*, the second culprit, *decapitato*. The prayers of all good Christians are entreated for these unfortunate men, that it may please God to awaken them to a sense of their guilt, and to grant them a hearty and sincere repentance for their crimes.' "

This was precisely what Franz had heard the evening before in the ruins of the Colosseum. No part of the programme differed —the names of the condemned persons—their crimes and mode of punishment—all agreed with his previous information. In all probability, therefore, the Transtevere was no other than the bandit Luigi Vampa himself, and the man shrouded in the mantle the same he had known as " Sinbad the Sailor," but who, no doubt, was still pursuing his philanthropic expedition in Rome, as he had already done at Porto-Vecchio and Tunis. Time was getting on, however, and Franz deemed it advisable to awaken Albert; but at the moment he prepared to proceed to his chamber, his friend entered the saloon in perfect costume for the day. The anticipated delights of the Carnival had so run in his head as to make him leave his pillow long before his usual hour.

" Now, my excellent Maître Pastrini," said Franz, addressing his landlord, " since we are both ready, do you think we may proceed at once to visit the Count of Monte Cristo? "

" Most assuredly," replied he. " The Count of Monte Cristo is always an early riser; and I can answer for his having been up these two hours."

" Well, then, if it be so; are you ready, Albert? "

" Perfectly! "

" Let us go and return our best thanks for his courtesy."

The landlord preceded the friends across the landing which was all that separated them from the apartments of the count, rang at a bell, and upon the door being opened by a servant, said:

" *I Signori Francesi.*"

The domestic bowed respectfully, and invited them to enter. They passed through two rooms, furnished with a style and luxury they had not calculated on finding under the roof of Maître Pastrini, and were shown into an elegantly fitted-up saloon. The richest Turkey carpets covered the floor, and the softest and most inviting couches, *bergères*, and sofas, offered their high-piled and yielding cushions to such as desired repose or refreshment. Splendid paintings by the first masters were ranged against the walls, intermingled with magnificent trophies of war, while heavy curtains of costly tapestry were suspended before the different doors of the room.

" If your excellencies will please to be seated," said the man, " I will let M. le Comte know you are here."

And with these words he disappeared behind one of the tapestried *portières*. As the door opened, the sound of a *guzla** reached the ears of the young men, but was almost immediately lost, for the rapid closing of the door merely allowed one rich swell of harmony to enter the saloon. Franz and Albert looked inquiringly at each other, then at the gorgeous fittings-up of the apartment. All seemed even more splendid at a second view than it had done at their first rapid survey.

" Well," said Franz to his friend, " what think you of all this? "

" Why, upon my soul, my dear fellow, it strikes me our elegant and attentive neighbour must either be some successful stock-jobber who has speculated in the fall of the Spanish funds, or some prince travelling *incog.*"

" Hush! hush! " replied Franz, " we shall ascertain who and what he is—he comes! "

As Franz spoke he heard the sound of a door turning on its hinges, and almost immediately afterwards the tapestry was drawn aside, and the owner of all these riches stood before the two young men. Albert instantly rose to meet him, but Franz remained, in a manner spell-bound on his chair, for in the person of him who had just entered he recognised not only the mysterious visitant to the Colosseum, and the occupant of the *loge* at the Salle Argentino, but also his singular host of Monte Cristo.

36

La Mazzolata

" GENTLEMEN," said the Count of Monte Cristo as he entered, " I pray you excuse me for suffering my visit to be anticipated; but I feared to disturb you by presenting myself earlier at your apartments; besides, you sent me word you would come to me, and I have held myself at your disposal."

" Franz and I have to thank you a thousand times, M. le Comte," returned Albert. " You extricated us from a great dilemma, and we were on the point of inventing some very fantastic vehicle when your friendly invitation reached us."

" Indeed! " returned the count, motioning the two young men to sit down. " It was the fault of that blockhead Pastrini, that I did not sooner assist you in your distress. He did not mention a syllable of your embarrassment to me, although he knows that, alone and isolated as I am, I seek every opportunity of making the acquaintance of my neighbours. As soon as I learned I could in any way assist you, I most eagerly seized the opportunity of offering my services."

The two young men bowed. Franz had, as yet, found nothing to say. He had adopted no determination; and as nothing in the count's manner manifested the wish that he should recognise him, he did not know whether to make any allusion to the past, or wait until he had more proof. Besides, although sure it was he who had been in the box the previous evening, he could not be equally positive that he was the man he had seen at the Colosseum. He resolved, therefore, to let things take their course without making any direct overture to the count. Besides, he had this advantage over him, that he was master of the count's secret, whilst the count had no hold on Franz, who had nothing to conceal.

However, he resolved to lead the conversation to a subject which might possibly clear up his doubts.

" M. le Comte," said he, " you have offered us places in your carriage, and at your windows of the Rospoli Palace. Can you tell us where we can obtain a sight of the Place del Popolo? "

" Ah," said the count negligently, looking attentively at Morcerf, " is there not something like an execution upon the Place del Popolo? "

" Yes," returned Franz, finding that the count was coming to the point he wished.

" Stay, I think I told my steward yesterday to attend to this; perhaps I can render you this slight service also."

He extended his hand, and rang the bell thrice.

" Did you ever occupy yourself," said he to Franz, " with the employment of time and the means of simplifying the summoning your servants? I have:—when I ring once, it is for my valet; twice, for my maître d'hôtel; thrice, for my steward. Thus I do not waste a minute or a word. Here he is! " A man of about five-and-forty to fifty entered, exactly resembling the smuggler who had introduced Franz into the cavern, but he did not appear to recognise him. It was evident he had his orders.

" M. Bertuccio," said the count, " have you procured me windows looking on the Place del Popolo, as I ordered you yesterday? "

" Yes, excellency," returned the steward, " but it was very late."

" Did I not tell you I wish for one? " replied the count, frowning.

" And your excellency has one, which was let to Prince Lobanieff, but I was obliged to pay a hundred——"

" That will do—that will do, Monsieur Bertuccio, spare these gentleman all such domestic arrangements. You have the window, that is sufficient. Give orders to the coachman, and be in readiness on the stairs to conduct us to it."

The steward bowed, and was about to quit the room.

" Ah! " continued the count, " be good enough to ask Pastrini if he has received the *tavoletta*, and if he can send us an account of the execution."

" There is no need to do that," said Franz, taking out his tablets, " for I saw the account, and copied it down."

" Very well, you can retire, Maître Bertuccio; let us know when breakfast is ready. These gentlemen," added he, turning to the two friends, " will, I trust, do me the honour to breakfast? "

" But, M. le Comte," said Albert, " we shall abuse your kindness."

" Not at all; on the contrary, you will give me great pleasure. You will, one or other of you, perhaps both, return it to me at Paris. Maître Bertuccio, lay covers for three."

He took Franz's tablets out of his hand.

" ' We announce,' he read, in the same tone with which he would have read a newspaper, ' that to-day, the 23rd of February, will be executed Andrea Rondolo, guilty of murder on the person of the respectable and venerated Don César Torlini, canon of the

Church Saint-Jean-de-Latran, and Peppino, called Rocca
Priori, convicted of complicity with the detestable bandit Luigi
Vampa and the men of his troop.' Hum! 'The first will be
mazzolato, the second *decapitato*.' Yes," continued the count,
" it was at first arranged in this way, but I think since yesterday
some change has taken place in the order of the ceremony."

" Really! " said Franz.

" Yes, I passed the evening at the Cardinal Rospigliosi's, and
there mention was made of something like a pardon for one of
the two men."

" For Andrea Rondolo? " asked Franz.

" No," replied the count carelessly, " for the other " (he glanced
at the tablets as if to recall the name), " for Peppino, called Rocca
Priori. You are thus deprived of seeing a man guillotined, but
the *mazzolato* still remains, which is a very curious punishment
when seen for the first time, and even the second, whilst the other,
as you must know, is very simple. The *mandaïa* never fails, never
trembles, never strikes thirty times ineffectually, like the soldier
who beheaded the Comte de Chalais,* and to whose tender mercy
Richelieu had doubtless recommended the sufferer. Ah! "
added the count, in a contemptuous tone, " do not tell me of
European punishments, they are in the infancy, or rather the
old age, of cruelty."

" Really, M. le Comte," replied Franz, " one would think
that you had studied the different tortures of all the nations of the
world."

" There are, at least, few that I have not seen," said the count
coldly.

" And you took pleasure in beholding these dreadful spectacles? "

" My first sentiment was horror, the second indifference, the
third curiosity."

" Curiosity! that is a terrible word."

" Why so? In life, our greatest preoccupation is death; is it
not, then, curious to study the different ways by which the soul
and body can part, and how, according to their different characters, temperaments, and even the different customs of their
countries, individuals bear the transition from life to death, from
existence to annihilation? As for myself, I can assure you of one
thing, the more men you see die, the easier it becomes to die;
and in my opinion, death may be a torture, but it is not an
expiation."

" I do not quite understand you," replied Franz; " pray
explain your meaning, for you excite my curiosity to the highest
pitch."

"Listen," said the count, and deep hatred mounted to his face, as the blood would to the face of any other. "If a man had by unheard-of and excruciating tortures destroyed your father, your mother, your mistress, in a word, one of those beings, who when they are torn from you leave a desolation, a wound that never closes, in your breast, do you think the reparation that society gives you sufficient by causing the knife of the guillotine to pass between the base of the occiput and the trapezal muscles of the murderer—because he who has caused us years of moral sufferings undergoes a few moments of physical pain?"

"Yes, I know," said Franz, "that human justice is insufficient to console us. She can give blood in return for blood, that is all; but you must demand from her only what it is in her power to grant."

"I will put another case to you," continued the count; "that where society, attacked by the death of a person, avenges death by death. But are there not a thousand tortures by which a man may be made to suffer without society taking the least cognisance of them, or offering him even the insufficient means of vengeance of which we have just spoken? Are there not crimes for which the empalement of the Turks, the augers of the Persians, the stake and the brand of the Iroquois Indians, are inadequate tortures, and which are unpunished by society? Answer me, do not these crimes exist?"

"Yes," answered Franz, "and it is to punish them that duelling is tolerated."

"Ah, duelling!" cried the count; "a pleasant manner, upon my soul, of arriving at your end when that end is vengeance! A man has carried off your mistress, a man has seduced your wife, a man has dishonoured your daughter; he has rendered the whole life of one who had the right to expect from Heaven that portion of happiness God has promised to every one of his creatures, an existence of misery and infamy; and you think you are avenged because you send a ball through the head, or pass a sword through the breast, of that man who has planted madness in your brain, and despair in your heart. Without recollecting that it is often he who comes off victorious from the strife, absolved of all crime in the eyes of the world! No, no," continued the count, "had I to avenge myself, it is not thus I would take revenge."

"Then you disapprove of duelling! you would not fight a duel?" asked Albert in his turn, astonished at this strange theory.

"Oh, yes," replied the count; "understand me, I would fight a duel for a trifle, for an insult, for a blow; and the more so, that, thanks to my skill in all bodily exercises, and the indifference to danger I have gradually acquired, I should be almost certain to kill my man. Oh! I would fight for such a cause, but in return for a slow, profound, eternal torture, I would give back the same were it possible: an eye for an eye, a tooth for a tooth, as the Orientalists say;—our masters in everything; those favoured creatures who have formed for themselves a life of dreams and a paradise of realities."

"But," said Franz to the count, "with this theory, which renders you at once judge and executioner of your own cause, it would be difficult to adopt a course that would for ever prevent your falling under the power of the law. Hatred is blind; rage carries you away; and he who pours out vengeance runs the risk of tasting a bitter draught."

"Yes, if he be poor and inexperienced, not if he be rich and skilful. Besides, the worst that could happen to him would be the punishment of which we have already spoken, and which the philanthropic French Revolution has substituted for being torn to pieces by horses or broken on the wheel.* What matters this punishment as long as he is avenged? On my word, I almost regret that in all probability this miserable Peppino will not be *decapitato*, as you might have had an opportunity then of seeing how short a time the punishment lasts, and whether it is worth even mentioning. But, really, this is a most singular conversation for the Carnival, gentlemen; how did it arise? Ah! I recollect, you asked for a place at my window; you shall have it; but let us first sit down to table, for here comes the servant to inform us breakfast is ready."

As he spoke, a servant opened one of the four doors of the salon, saying:

" *Al suo commodo!* "

The two young men rose and entered the breakfast-room.

During the meal, which was excellent and admirably served, Franz looked repeatedly at Albert in order to remark the impression which he doubted not had been made on him by the words of their entertainer, but whether with his usual carelessness he had paid but little attention to him, whether the explanation of the Count of Monte Cristo with regard to duelling had satisfied him, or whether the events which Franz knew of had a double effect on him alone, he remarked that his companion did not pay the least regard to them, but on the contrary ate like a man who for the last four or five months had been condemned to partake of Italian cookery—that is, the worst in the world. As for the count, he just touched the dishes; he seemed as if he fulfilled the duties of an entertainer by sitting down with his guests, and awaited their departure to be served with some strange or more delicate food. This brought back to Franz, in spite of himself, the recollection of the terror with which the count had inspired the Countess G——, and her firm conviction that the man in the opposite box was a vampire.

At the end of the breakfast Franz took out his watch.

" Well," said the count, " what are you doing? "

" You must excuse us, M. le Comte," returned Franz, " but we have still much to do."

" What may that be? "

" We have no disguises, and it is absolutely necessary to procure them."

" Do not concern yourself about that; we have, I think, a private room in the Place del Popolo; I will have whatever costumes you choose brought to us, and you can dress there."

" After the execution? " cried Franz.

" Before or after, which you please."

" Opposite the scaffold? "

" The scaffold forms part of the fête."

" M. le Comte, I have reflected on the matter," said Franz. " I thank you for your courtesy, but I shall content myself with accepting a place in your carriage and at your window at the Rospoli Palace, and I leave you at liberty to dispose of my place at the Place del Popolo."

" But I warn you, you will lose a very curious sight," returned the count.

" You will relate it to me," replied Franz, " and the recital from your lips will make as great an impression on me as if I had witnessed it. I have more than once intended witnessing an execution, but I have never been able to make up my mind; and you, Albert? "

" I," replied the viscount—" I saw Castaing executed, but I think I was rather intoxicated that day, for I had quitted college the same morning, and we had passed the previous night at a tavern."

" Besides, it is no reason because you have not seen an execution at Paris, that you should not see one anywhere else; when you travel, it is to see everything. Think what a figure you will make when you are asked, ' How do they execute at Rome? ' and you reply, ' I do not know! ' And, besides, they say that the culprit is an infamous scoundrel, who killed with a log of wood a worthy canon who had brought him up like his own son. Diable! when a churchman is killed, it should be with a different weapon than a log, especially when he has behaved like a father. If you went to Spain, would you not see the bull-fights? Well, suppose it is a bull-fight you are going to see? Recollect the ancient Romans of the Circus, and the sports where they killed three hundred lions and a hundred men. Think of the eighty thousand applauding spectators, the sage matrons who took their daughters, and the charming Vestals who made with the thumb of their white hands the fatal sign that said, ' Come, despatch this man already nearly dead.' "

" Shall you go, then, Albert? " asked Franz.

" *Ma foi!* yes; like you I hesitated, but the count's eloquence decides me! "

" Let us go, then," said Franz, " since you wish it, but on our way to the Place del Popolo I wish to pass through the Rue de Cours. Is this possible, M. le Comte? "

" On foot, yes; in a carriage, no."

" I will go on foot, then."

" Is it important that you should pass through this street? "

" Yes, there is something I wish to see."

" Well, we will pass by the Rue de Cours. We will send the carriage to wait for us on the Piazza del Popolo, by the Strada del Babuino, for I shall be glad to pass, myself, through the Rue de Cours, to see if some orders I have given have been executed."

" Excellency," said a servant, opening the door, " a man in the dress of a penitent wishes to speak to you."

" Ah, yes! " returned the count, " I know who he is, gentlemen; will you return to the salon? you will find on the centre table some excellent Havana cigars. I will be with you directly."

The young men rose and returned into the salon, whilst the count, again apologising, left by another door. Albert, who was a great smoker, and who had considered it no small sacrifice to be deprived of the cigars of the Café de Paris, approached the table, and uttered a cry of joy at perceiving some veritable *pueros.*

" Well," asked Franz, " what think you of the Count of Monte Cristo? "

" What do I think? " said Albert, evidently surprised at such a question from his companion; " I think that he is a delightful fellow, who does the honours of his table admirably; who has travelled much, read much, is, like Brutus, of the Stoic school, and moreover," added he, sending a volume of smoke up towards the ceiling, " that he has excellent cigars."

Such was Albert's opinion of the count, and as Franz well knew that Albert professed never to form an opinion except upon long reflection, he made no attempt to change it.

" But," said he, " did you remark one very singular thing? "

" What? "

" How attentively he looked at you."

" At me? "

" Yes."

Albert reflected.

" Ah! " replied he, sighing, " that is not very surprising; I have been more than a year absent from Paris, and my clothes are of a most antiquated cut; the count takes me for a provincial. The first opportunity you have, undeceive him, I beg, and tell him I am nothing of the kind."

Franz smiled: an instant after, the count entered.

" I am now quite at your service, gentlemen," said he. " The carriage is going one way to the Place del Popolo, and we will go another; and if you please, by the Rue du Cours. Take some more of these cigars, M. de Morcerf."

" With all my heart," returned Albert; " these Italian cigars are horrible. When you come to Paris, I will return all this."

" I will not refuse. I intend going there soon, and since you allow me, I will pay you a visit. Come! let us set off! "

All three descended: the coachman received his master's orders and drove down the Via del Babuino. Whilst the three gentlemen walked towards the Place d'Espagne and the Via Frattina, which led directly between the Fiano and Rospoli Palaces, all Franz's attention was directed towards the windows of that last palace, for he had not forgotten the signal agreed upon between the man in the mantle and the Transtevere peasant.

" Which are your windows? " asked he of the count, with as much indifference as he could assume.

" The three last," returned he, with a negligence evidently unaffected; for he could not imagine with what intention the question was put.

Franz glanced rapidly towards the three windows. The side windows were hung with yellow damask, and the centre one with white damask and a red cross. The man in the mantle had kept his promise to the Transtevere, and there could now be no doubt that he was the Count. The three windows were still untenanted. Preparations were making on every side; chairs were placed, scaffolds were raised, and windows were hung with flags. The masks could not appear; the carriages could not move about; but the masks were visible behind the windows, the carriages, and the doors.

Franz, Albert, and the count continued to descend the Rue du Cours. As they approached the Place del Popolo, the crowd became more dense, and above the heads of the multitude two objects were visible; the obelisk surmounted by a cross, which marks the centre of the place, and before the obelisk, at the point where the three streets, del Babuino, del Corso, and di Ripetta meet, the two uprights of the scaffold, between which glittered the curved knife of the *mandaïa*. At the corner of the street they met the count's steward, who was awaiting his master.

The window, let at an exorbitant price which the count had doubtless wished to conceal from his guests, was on the second floor of the great palace situated between the Rue del Babuino and the Monte-Pincio. It consisted, as we have said, of a small dressing-room opening into a bedroom, and when the door of communication was shut, the inmates were quite alone. On two chairs were laid as many elegant costumes of *paillasse*, in blue and white satin.

" As you left the choice of your costumes to me," said the count to the two friends, " I have had these brought, as they will be the most worn this year; and they are most suitable on account of the *confetti* (sweetmeats), as they do not show the flour."

Franz heard the words of the count but imperfectly, and he perhaps did not fully appreciate this new attention to their wishes; for he was wholly absorbed by the spectacle that the Piazza del Popolo presented, and by the terrible instrument that was in the centre. It was the first time Franz had ever seen a guillotine,— we say guillotine, because the Roman *mandaïa* is formed on almost the same model as the French instrument: the knife, which is shaped like a crescent, that cuts with the convex side, falls from a less height, and that is all the difference. The prisoners, transported the previous evening from the Carceri Nuovo to the little church of Santa Maria del Popolo, had passed the night each accompanied by two priests, in a chapel closed by a grating, before which were two sentinels, relieved at intervals. A double line of carbineers, placed on each side of the door of the church, reached to the scaffold, and formed a circle round it, leaving a path about ten feet wide, and around the guillotine a space of nearly a hundred feet. All the rest of the place was paved with heads. Many women held their infants on their shoulders, and thus the children had the best view. The Monte-Pincio seemed a vast amphitheatre filled with spectators: the balconies of the two churches at the corner of the Rue del Babuino and the Rue di Rippeta were crammed: the steps even seemed a parti-coloured sea, that was impelled towards the portico: every niche in the wall held its living statue. What the count said was true,— the most curious spectacle in life is that of death. And yet, instead of the silence and the solemnity demanded by the occasion, a noise of laughter and jest arose from the crowd: it was evident that this execution was, in the eyes of the people, only the commence-ment of the Carnival. Suddenly the tumult ceased, as if by magic:

the doors of the church opened. A brotherhood of penitents, clothed from head to foot in robes of gray sackcloth with holes for the eyes alone, and holding in their hand a lighted taper, appeared first: the chief marched at the head. Behind the penitents came a man of vast stature and proportions. He was naked, with the exception of cloth drawers, at the left side of which hung a large knife in a sheaf, and he bore on his right shoulder a heavy mace. This man was the executioner. He had, moreover, sandals bound on his feet by cords. Behind the executioner came, in the order in which they were to die, first Peppino, and then Andrea. Each was accompanied by two priests. Neither had their eyes bandaged. Peppino walked with a firm step, doubtless aware of what awaited him. Andrea was supported by two priests. Each of them kissed, from time to time, the crucifix a confessor held out to them. At this sight alone Franz felt his legs tremble under him: he looked at Albert,—he was as white as his shirt, and mechanically cast away his cigar, although he had not half smoked it. The count alone seemed unmoved,—nay, more, a slight colour seemed striving to rise in his pale cheeks. His nostril dilated like a wild beast that scents its prey, and his lips, half opened, disclosed his white teeth, small and sharp like those of a jackal. And yet his features wore an expression of smiling tendernêss, such as Franz had never before witnessed in them; his black eyes especially were full of kindness and pity. However, the two culprits advanced, and as they approached, their faces became visible. Peppino was a handsome young man of four or five and twenty, bronzed by the sun: he carried his head erect, and seemed to look on which side his liberator would appear. Andrea was short and fat. His visage, marked with brutal cruelty, did not indicate age: he might be thirty. In prison he had suffered his beard to grow,—his head fell on his shoulder,—his legs bent beneath him, and he seemed to obey a mechanical movement, of which he was unconscious.

" I thought," said Franz to the count, " that you told me there would be but one execution? "

" I told you true," replied he coldly.

" However, here are two culprits."

" Yes; but only one of these two is about to die!—the other has long years to live."

" If the pardon is to come, there is no time to lose."

" And, see, here it is," said the count.

At the moment when Peppino arrived at the foot of the *mandaïa*, a penitent, who seemed to arrive late, forced his way through the soldiers, and, advancing to the chief of the brotherhood, gave him a folded paper.

The piercing eye of Peppino had noticed all. The chief took the paper, unfolded it, and, raising his hands, " Heaven be praised! and his Holiness also! " said he, in a loud voice. " Here is a pardon for one of the prisoners."

" A pardon! " cried the people with one voice. " A pardon! " At this cry, Andrea raised his head.

" Pardon for whom? " cried he.

Peppino remained breathless.

" A pardon for Peppino, called Rocca Priori," said the principal friar. And he passed the paper to the officer commanding the carbineers, who read and returned it to him.

" For Peppino! " cried Andrea, who seemed aroused from the torpor in which he had been plunged. " Why for him and not for me? We ought to die together. I was promised he should die with me. You have no right to put me to death alone. I will not, die alone,—I will not! " And he broke from the priests, struggling and raving like a wild beast, and striving desperately to break the cords that bound his hands.

The executioner made a sign, and his assistant leaped from the scaffold and seized him. A dreadful struggle ensued, Andrea exclaiming, " He ought to die!—he shall die!—I will not die alone! " The people all took part against Andrea, and twenty thousand voices cried, " Put him to death!—put him to death! "

Franz sprang back; but the count seized his arm, and held him before the window.

" What are you doing? " said he. " Do you pity him? If you heard the cry of ' Mad dog! ' you would take your gun,—you would, unhesitatingly, shoot the poor beast, who, after all, was only guilty of having been bitten by another dog. And yet you pity a man who, without being bitten by one of his race, has yet murdered his benefactor; and who, now unable to kill any one, because his hands are bound, wishes to see his companion in captivity perish. No,—no: look!—look! "

This recommendation was needless; Franz was fascinated by the horrible spectacle. The two assistants had borne Andrea to the scaffold; and there, spite of his struggles, his bites, and his cries, had forced him to his knees. During this time the executioner had raised his mace, and signed to them to get out of the way: the criminal strove to rise, but, ere he had time, the mace fell on his left temple. A dull and heavy sound was heard, and the man dropped like an ox on his face, and then turned over on his back. The executioner let fall his mace, drew his knife, and with one stroke opened his throat; and, mounting on his stomach, stamped violently on it with his feet. At every stroke a jet of blood sprang from the wound.

This time Franz could sustain himself no longer, but sank, half fainting, into a seat. Albert, with his eyes closed, was standing grasping the window curtains. The count was erect and triumphant, like the Avenging Angel!

37

The Carnival at Rome

WHEN Franz recovered his senses, he saw Albert drinking a glass of water, of which his paleness showed he stood in great need; and the count, who was assuming his costume of *paillasse.** He glanced mechanically towards the place; all had disappeared,—scaffold, executioners, victims. Nought remained but the people, full of noise and excitement. The bell of Monte-Citorio, which only sounds on the pope's decease and the opening of the Carnival, was ringing a joyous peal.

" Well," asked he of the count; " what has then happened? "

" Nothing," replied the count; " only, as you see, the Carnival has commenced. Make haste and dress yourself."

" In reality," said Franz, " this horrible scene has passed away like a dream."

" It is but a dream,—the nightmare, that has disturbed you."

" Yes, that I have suffered. But the culprit? "

" That is a dream also; only he has remained asleep, whilst you have awoke; and who knows which of you is the most fortunate? "

" But Peppino, what has become of him? "

" Peppino is a lad of sense, who, unlike most men who are furious if they pass unnoticed, was delighted to see that the general attention was directed towards his companion. He profited by this distraction to slip away amongst the crowd, without even thanking the worthy priests who accompanied him. Decidedly man is an ungrateful and egotistical animal. But dress yourself; see, M. de Morcerf sets you the example."

Albert was, in reality, drawing on the satin pantaloon over his black trousers and varnished boots.

" Well, Albert," said Franz; " do you feel much inclined to join the revels? Come, answer frankly! "

" *Ma foi!* no," returned Albert. " But I am really glad to have seen such a sight; and I understand what M. le Comte said, that when you have once habituated yourself to a similar spectacle, it is the only one that causes you any emotion."

" Without reflecting that this is the only moment in which you can study characters," said the count, " on the steps of the scaffold death tears off the mask that has been worn through life, and the real visage is disclosed. It must be allowed Andrea was not very handsome,—the hideous scoundrel! Come, dress yourselves, gentlemen,—dress yourselves."

Franz felt it would be ridiculous not to follow his two companions' example. He assumed his costume, and fastened on his mask, that scarcely equalled the pallor of his own face. Their toilette finished, they descended; the carriage awaited them at the door, filled with sweetmeats and bouquets. They fell into the line of carriages.

It is difficult to form an idea of the perfect change that had taken place. Instead of the spectacle of gloomy and silent death, the Place del Popolo presented a spectacle of gay and noisy mirth and revelry. A crowd of masks flowed in from all sides, escaping from the doors, descending from the windows. From every street and every turn drove carriages filled with pierrots, harlequins, dominoes, marquises, Transteveres, knights, and peasants,—screaming, fighting, gesticulating, whirling eggs filled with flour, confetti, nosegays,—attacking, with their sarcasms and their missiles, friends and foes, companions and strangers, indiscriminately, without any one taking offence, or doing anything else than laugh. Franz and Albert were like men who, to drive away a violent sorrow, have recourse to wine, and who, as they drink and become intoxicated, feel a thick veil drawn between the past and the present. They saw, or rather continued to see, the image of what they had witnessed; but, little by little, the general vertigo seized them, and they felt themselves obliged to take a part in the noise and confusion. A handful of confetti that came from a neighbouring carriage, and which, whilst it covered Morcerf and his two companions with dust, pricked his neck and that portion of his face uncovered by his mask like a hundred pins, plunged him into the general combat in which all the masks around him were engaged. He rose in his turn, and seizing handfuls of confetti and sweetmeats, with which the carriage was filled, cast them with all the force and address he was master of.

The strife had fairly commenced, and the recollection of what they had seen half an hour before was gradually effaced from the young men's minds, so much were they occupied by the gay and glittering procession they now beheld. As for the Count of Monte Cristo, he had never for an instant showed any appearance of having been moved. Imagine the large and splendid Rue du Cours, bordered from one end to the other with lofty palaces, with their balconies hung with carpets, and their windows with flags; at these balconies three hundred thousand spectators— Romans, Italians, strangers from all parts of the world. The united aristocracy of birth, wealth, and genius; lovely women who, yielding to the influence of the scene, bend over their balconies, or lean from their windows, and shower down confetti, which are returned by bouquets. The air seems darkened with confetti that fall, and flowers that mount. In the streets the lively crowd, dressed in the most fantastic costumes, Gigantic cabbages walked gravely about,—buffalo's heads bellowed from men's shoulders,—dogs who walked on their hind-legs. In the midst of all this a mask is lifted, and, as in Callot's Temptation of St. Anthony,* a lovely face is exhibited, which we would fain follow, but from which we are separated by troops of fiends—and this will give a faint idea of the Carnival at Rome.

At the second turn the count stopped the carriage, and requested permission to quit them, leaving the vehicle at their disposal. Franz looked up; they were opposite the Rospoli Palace. At the centre window, the one hung with white damask with a red cross, was a blue domino, beneath which Franz's imagination easily pictured the beautiful Greek of the Argentina.

" Gentlemen," said the count, springing out, " when you are tired of being actors, and wish to become spectators of this scene, you know you have places at my windows. In the meantime, dispose of my coachman, my carriage, and my servants."

We have forgotten to mention that the count's coachman was attired in a bear-skin, exactly resembling Odry's in *The Bear and the Pacha*;* and the two footmen behind were dressed up as green monkeys, with spring masks, with which they made grimaces at every one who passed.

Franz thanked the count for his attention. As for Albert, he was busily occupied throwing bouquets at a carriage full of Roman peasants that was passing near him. Unfortunately for him, the line of carriages moved on again, and whilst he descended the Place del Popolo, the other ascended towards the Palais de Vénise.

" Ah! my dear fellow! " said he to Franz; " you did not see? "
" What? "
" There,—that calèche filled with Roman peasants."
" No."
" Well, I am convinced they were all charming women."
" How unfortunate you were masked, Albert! " said Franz; " here was an opportunity of making up for past disappointments."

" Oh! " replied he, half laughing, half serious, " I hope the Carnival will not pass without some amends in one shape or another."

But, in spite of Albert's hope, the day passed unmarked by any incident, except meeting two or three times the calèche with the Roman peasants. At one of these encounters, accidentally or purposely, Albert's mask fell off. He instantly rose and cast the remainder of the bouquets into the carriage. Doubtless one of the charming females Albert had divined beneath their coquettish disguise was touched by his gallantry; for, in her turn, as the carriage of the two friends passed her, she threw a bunch of violets into it. Albert seized it, and as Franz had no reason to suppose it was addressed to him, he suffered Albert to retain it. Albert placed it in his button-hole, and the carriage went triumphantly on.

" Well," said Franz to him, " here is the commencement of an adventure."

" Laugh if you please. I really think so. So I will not abandon this bouquet.".

" *Pardieu!* " returned Franz laughing, " in token of your gratitude."

The jest, however, soon appeared to become earnest; for when Albert and Franz again encountered the carriage with the *contadini*, the one who had thrown the violets to Albert clapped her hands when she beheld them in his button-hole.

" Bravo! bravo! " said Franz; " things go wonderfully. Shall I leave you? Perhaps you would prefer being alone? "

" No," replied he; " I will not be caught like a fool at a first demonstration by a rendezvous beneath the clock, as they say at the opera balls. If the fair peasant wishes to carry matters any further, we shall find her, or rather she will find us to-morrow: then she will give me some sign or other, and I shall know what I have to do."

" On my word," said Franz, " you are wise as Nestor and prudent as Ulysses, and your fair Circe must be very skilful or very powerful if she succeed in changing you into a beast of any kind."

Albert was right; the fair unknown had resolved, doubtless, to carry the intrigue no further; for although the young men made several more turns, they did not again see the calèche, which had turned up one of the neighbouring streets. Then they returned to the Rospoli Palace; but the count and the blue domino had also disappeared; the two windows, hung with yellow damask, were still occupied by the persons whom the count had invited. At this moment, the same bell that had proclaimed the commencement of the mascherata sounded the retreat. The file on the Corso broke the line, and in a second all the carriages had disappeared. Franz and Albert were opposite the Via delle Maratte; the coachman, without saying a word, drove up it, passed along the Place d'Espagne and the Rospoli Palace, and stopped at the door of the hotel.

Maître Pastrini came to the door to receive his guests.

Franz's first care was to inquire after the count, and to express his regret he had not returned in sufficient time to take him up; but Pastrini reassured him by saying, that the Count of Monte Cristo had ordered a second carriage for himself, and that it had gone at four o'clock to fetch him from the Rospoli Palace. The count had, moreover, charged him to offer the two friends the key of his box at the Argentina. Franz questioned Albert as to his intentions; but Albert had great projects to put into execution before going to the theatre; and instead of making any answer, he inquired if Maître Pastrini could procure him a tailor.

" A tailor! " said the host; " and for what? "

" To make us between now and to-morrow two costumes of Roman peasants," returned Albert.

The host shook his head. " To make you two costumes between now and to-morrow? I ask your excellencies' pardon, but this is a demand quite French; for the next week you will not find a single tailor who would consent to sew six buttons on a waistcoat if you paid him a crown a piece for each button."

" Then I must give up the idea? "

" No; we have them ready-made. Leave all to me; and, to-morrow, when you wake, you shall find a collection of costumes with which you will be satisfied."

" My dear Albert," said Franz, " leave all to our host; he has already proved himself full of resources; let us dine quietly, and afterwards go and see *l'Italienne à Alger!* "*

" Agreed," returned Albert; " but recollect, Maître Pastrini, that both my friend and myself attach the greatest importance to having to-morrow the costumes we have asked for."

The host again assured them they might rely on him, and that their wishes should be attended to; upon which Franz and Albert mounted to their apartments, and proceeded to disencumber themselves of their costume. Albert, as he took off his dress, carefully preserved the bunch of violets; it was his sign of recognition for the morrow. The two friends sat down to table; but they could not refrain from remarking the difference between the table of the Count of Monte Cristo and that of Maître Pastrini. Truth compelled Franz, spite of the dislike he seemed to have taken to the count, to confess that the advantage was not on Pastrini's side.

During dessert the servant inquired at what time they wished for the carriage. Albert and Franz looked at each other, fearing really to abuse the count's kindness. The servant understood them.

" His excellency the Count of Monte Cristo had," he said, " given positive orders that the carriage was to remain at their lordships' orders all the day, and they could, therefore, dispose of it without fear of indiscretion."

They resolved to profit by the count's courtesy, and ordered the horses to be harnessed, whilst they substituted an evening costume for that which they had on, and which was somewhat the worse for the numerous combats they had sustained. This precaution taken, they went to the theatre, and installed themselves in the count's box. During the first act, the Countess G—— entered hers. Her first look was at the *loge* where she had seen the count the previous evening, so that she perceived Franz and Albert in the box of the very person concerning whom she had expressed so strange an opinion to Franz. Her opera-glass was so fixedly directed towards them, that Franz saw it would be cruel not to satisfy her curiosity; and, availing himself on one of the privileges of the spectators of the Italian theatres, which consists in using their boxes as their drawing-room, the two friends quitted their box to pay their respects to the countess. Scarcely had they entered the *loge*, than she motioned to Franz to assume the seat of honour. Albert, in his turn, sat behind.

" Well," said she, hardly giving Franz time to sit down, " it seems you have nothing better to do than to make the acquaintance of this new Lord Ruthven, and you are the best friends in the world."

" Without being so far advanced as that, Madame la Comtesse," returned Franz, " I cannot deny we have abused his good-nature all day."

" All day? "

" Yes; this morning we breakfasted with him; we rode in his carriage all day, and now we have taken possession of his box."

" You know him, then? "

" Yes, and no."

" How so? "

" It is a long story."

" Relate it to me."

" It would frighten you too much."

" Another reason."

" At least wait until the story has a conclusion."

"Very well; I prefer complete histories; but tell me how you made his acquaintance. Did any one introduce you to him?"

"No; it was he who introduced himself to us."

"When?"

"Last night, after we left you."

"Through what medium?"

"The very prosaic one of our landlord."

"He is staying then at the Hôtel de Londres with you?"

"Not only in the same hotel, but on the same floor."

"What is his name: for, of course, you know?"

"The Count of Monte Cristo."

"That is not a family name?"

"No, it is the name of the isle he has purchased."

"And he is a count?"

"A Tuscan count."

"Well, we must put up with that," said the countess, who was herself of one of the oldest families of Venice. "What sort of a man is he?"

"Ask the Vicomte de Morcerf."

"You hear, M. de Morcerf, I am referred to you," said the countess.

"We should be very hard to please, madame," returned Albert, "did we not think him delightful; a friend of ten years' standing could not have done more for us, or with a more perfect courtesy."

"Come," observed the countess, smiling; "I see my vampire is only some millionaire, who has taken the appearance of Lara in order to avoid being confounded with M. de Rothschild; and have you seen her?"

"Her?"

"The beautiful Greek of yesterday.'

"No; we heard, I think, the sound of her *guzla*, but she remained perfectly invisible."

"When you say invisible," interrupted Albert, "it is only to keep up the mystery; for whom do you take the blue domino at the window with the white curtains?"

"Where was this window with white hangings?" said the countess.

"At the Rospoli Palace."

"The count had three windows of the Rospoli Palace?"

"Yes. Did you pass through the Rue du Cours?"

"Yes."

"Well, did you remark two windows hung with yellow damask, and one with white damask with a red cross? Those were the count's windows."

" Why, he must be a nabob! Do you know what those three windows were worth? "

" Two or three hundred Roman crowns? "

" Two or three thousand! "

" The devil! "

" Does his isle produce him such a revenue? "

" It does not bring him a bajocco."*

" Then why did he purchase it? "

" For a whim."

" He is an original, then? "

" In reality," observed Albert, " he seemed to me somewhat eccentric; were he at Paris, and a frequenter of the theatres, I should say he was a poor devil, literally mad. This morning he made two or three exits worthy of Didier or Anthony."*

At this moment a fresh visitor entered, and, according to custom, Franz gave up his seat to him. This circumstance had, moreover, the effect of changing the conversation; an hour afterwards the two friends returned to their hotel. Maître Pastrini had already set about procuring their disguises for the morrow; and he assured them they would be perfectly satisfied. The next morning, at nine o'clock, he entered Franz's room, followed by a tailor, who had eight or ten costumes of Roman peasants on his arm; they selected two exactly alike, and charged the tailor to sew on each of their hats about twenty yards of riband, and to procure them two of those long silken sashes of different colours with which the lower orders decorate themselves on fête-days. Albert was impatient to see how he looked in his new dress: it was a jacket and breeches of blue velvet, silk stockings with clocks, shoes with buckles, and a silk waistcoat. This picturesque attire set him off to great advantage; and when he had bound the scarf around his waist, and when his hat placed coquettishly on one side, let fall on his shoulder a stream of ribands, Franz was forced to confess that costume has much to do with the physical superiority we accord to certain nations. Franz complimented Albert, who looked at himself in the glass with an unequivocal smile of satisfaction. They were thus engaged when the Count of Monte Cristo entered.

" Gentlemen," said he, " although a companion is agreeable, perfect freedom is sometimes still more agreeable. I come to say that to-day, and the remainder of the Carnival, I leave the carriage entirely at your disposal. The host will tell you I have three or four more, so that you do not deprive me in any way of it. Employ it, I pray you, for your pleasure or your business."

The young men wished to decline; but they could find no good reason for refusing an offer which was so agreeable to them. The

Count of Monte Cristo remained a quarter of an hour with them, conversing on all subjects with the greatest ease. He was, as we have already said, perfectly well acquainted with the literature of all countries. A glance at the walls of his salon proved to Franz and Albert that he was no amateur of pictures. A few words he let fall showed them he was no stranger to the sciences, and he seemed much occupied with chemistry. The two friends did not venture to return the count the breakfast he had given them: it would have been too absurd to offer him in exchange for his excellent table the very inferior one of Maître Pastrini. They told him so frankly, and he received their excuses with the air of a man who appreciated their delicacy. Albert was charmed with the count's manners, and he was only prevented from recognising him for a veritable gentleman by his science. The permission to do what he liked with the carriage pleased him above all; for the fair peasants had appeared in a most elegant carriage the preceding evening, and Albert was not sorry to be upon an equal footing with them. At half-past one they descended; the coachman and footman had put on their livery over their disguises, which gave them a more ridiculous appearance than ever; and which gained them the applause of Franz and Albert. Albert had fastened the faded bunch of violets to his button-hole. At the first sound of the bell they hastened into the Rue du Cours by the Via Vittoria.

At the second turn, a bunch of fresh violets, thrown from a carriage filled with *paillassines*, indicated to Albert that, like himself and his friend, the peasants had changed their costume also; and whether it was the result of chance, or whether a similar feeling had possessed them both, whilst he had changed his costume they had assumed his.

Albert placed the fresh bouquet in his button-hole; but he kept the faded one in his hand; and when he again met the calèche, he raised it to his lips, an action which seemed greatly to amuse not only the fair lady who had thrown it, but her joyous companions also. The day was as gay as the preceding one, perhaps even more animated and noisy; the count appeared for an instant at his window, but when they again repassed, he had disappeared. It is almost needless to say that the flirtation between Albert and the fair peasant continued all day. The evening on his return Franz found a letter from the embassy to inform him he would have the honour of being received by his Holiness the next day. At each previous visit he had made to Rome, he had solicited and obtained the same favour; and incited as much by a religious feeling as by gratitude, he was unwilling to quit the capital of the Christian world without laying his respectful homage at the feet of one of St. Peter's successors, who has set the rare example of all virtues. He did not then think of the Carnival; for in spite of his condescension and touching kindness, one cannot incline oneself without awe before the venerable and noble old man called Gregory XVI: On his return from the Vatican, Franz carefully avoided the Rue du Cours; he brought away with him a treasure of pious thoughts, to which the mad gaiety of the *mascherata* would have been profanation.

At ten minutes past five Albert entered overjoyed. The *paillassine* had resumed her peasant's costume, and as she passed had raised her mask. She was charming.

Franz congratulated Albert, who received his congratulations with the air of a man conscious they are merited. He had recognised, by certain unmistakable signs, that his fair *incognita* belonged to the aristocracy. He had made up his mind to write to her the next day.

Franz remarked whilst he gave these details, that Albert seemed to have something to ask of him, but that he was unwilling to ask it. He insisted upon it, declaring beforehand that he was willing to make any sacrifice he required. Albert let himself be pressed just as long as friendship required, and then avowed to Franz that he would do him a great favour by suffering him to occupy the carriage alone the next day.

Albert attributed to Franz's absence the extreme kindness of the fair peasant in raising her mask.

Franz was not sufficiently egotistical to stop Albert in the middle of an adventure that promised to prove so agreeable to his curiosity and so flattering to his vanity. He felt assured that the perfect indiscretion of his friend would duly inform him of all that happened; and as during three years that he had travelled all over Italy, a similar piece of good fortune had never fallen to his share, Franz was by no means sorry to learn how to act on such an occasion. He therefore promised Albert that he would content himself the morrow with witnessing the Carnival from the windows of Rospoli Palace.

The next morning he saw Albert pass and repass. He held an enormous bouquet, which he, doubtless, meant to make the bearer of his amorous epistle. This belief was changed into certainty when Franz saw the bouquet (remarkable by a circle of white camellias) in the hand of a charming *paillassine* dressed in rose-coloured satin.

The evening was no longer joy but delirium. Albert nothing doubted but that the fair unknown would reply in the same manner. Franz anticipated his wishes by telling him the noise.

fatigued him, and that he should pass the next day in writing and looking over his journal.

Albert was not deceived; for the next evening Franz saw him enter, shaking triumphantly a folded paper he held by one corner.

" Well," said he, " was I mistaken? "

" She has answered you! " cried Franz.

" Read! "

This word was pronounced in a manner impossible to describe. Franz took the letter and read:

" Tuesday evening, at seven o'clock, descend from your carriage opposite the Via dei Pontefici, and follow the Roman peasant who snatches your *moccoletto* from you. When you arrive at the first step of the church of San Giacomo, be sure to fasten a knot of rose-coloured ribands to the shoulder of your costume of *paillasse*, in order that you may be recognised. Until then you will not see me.

CONSTANCY AND DISCRETION."

" Well," asked he, when Franz had finished, " what do you think of that? "

" I think that the adventure is assuming a very agreeable appearance."

" I think so, also," replied Albert; " and I very much fear you will go alone to the Duke of Bracciano's ball."

Franz and Albert had received that morning an invitation from the celebrated Roman banker.

" Take care, Albert," said Franz. " All the nobility of Rome will be present; and if your fair *incognita* belongs to the higher class of society she must go there,"

" Laugh as much as you will," replied Albert, " I am in love."

" You alarm me," cried Franz. " I see that I shall not only go alone to the Duke of Bracciano's, but also return to Florence alone."

" If my unknown be as amiable as she is beautiful," said Albert, " I shall fix myself at Rome for six weeks at least. I adore Rome, and I have always had a great taste for archæology."

" Come, two or three more such adventures, and I do not despair of seeing you a member of the Academy."

Doubtless Albert was about to discuss seriously his right to the academic chair, when they were informed dinner was ready. Albert's love had not taken away his appetite. He hastened with Franz to seat himself, free to recommence the discussion after dinner.

After dinner, the Count of Monte Cristo was announced. They had not seen him for two days. Maître Pastrini informed them that business had called him to Civita Vecchia. He had started the previous evening, and had only returned an hour since. He was charming. Whether he kept a watch over himself, or whether accident did not sound the acrimonious chords that certain circumstances had already touched, he was like everybody else. This man was an enigma to Franz. The count must feel sure he recognised him; and yet he had not let fall a single word that indicated he had seen him anywhere. On his side, however great Franz's desire was to allude to their former interview, the fear of its being disagreeable to the man who had loaded himself and his friend with kindness prevented him from mentioning it. The count had learned the two friends had sent to secure a box at the Argentina Theatre, and were told they were all let. In consequence, he brought them the key of his own—at least such was the apparent motive of his visit. Franz and Albert made some difficulty, alleging their fear of depriving him of it; but the count replied that, as he was going to the Palli Theatre, the box at the Argentina Theatre would be lost if they did not profit by it. This assurance determined the two friends to accept it.

Franz had become by degrees accustomed to the count's paleness, which had so forcibly struck him the first time he saw him. He could not refrain from admiring the severe beauty of his features, the only defect, or rather the principal quality of which was the pallor. Veritable hero of Byron! The count was no longer young. He was at least forty; and yet it was easy to understand he was formed to rule the young men with whom he associated at present. In reality, to complete his resemblance with the fantastic heroes of the English poet, the count seemed to have the power of fascination. Albert was constantly expatiating on their good fortune in meeting such a man. Franz was less enthusiastic; but the count exercised over him also the ascendancy a strong mind always acquires. He thought several times of the project the count had of visiting Paris; and he had no doubt but that with his eccentric character, his characteristic face, and his colossal fortune, he would produce a great effect there. And yet he did not wish to be at Paris when the count was there.

The evening passed as evenings mostly pass at Italian theatres: that is, not in listening to the music, but in paying visits and conversing. The Countess G—— wished to revive the subject of the count, but Franz announced he had something far newer to tell her; and, in spite of Albert's demonstrations of false modesty, he informed the countess of the great event which had preoccupied them for the last three days. As similar intrigues are not uncommon in Italy, if we may credit travellers, the countess did not manifest the least incredulity, but congratulated Albert on his success. They promised, upon separating, to meet at the Duke of Bracciano's ball, to which all Rome was invited. The heroine of the bouquet kept her word; she gave Albert no sign of her existence the morrow and day after.

At length arrived the Tuesday, the last and most tumultuous day of the Carnival. The Tuesday the theatres open at ten o'clock in the morning, as Lent begins after eight at night; the Tuesday all those who, through want of money, time, or enthusiasm, have not been to see the Carnival before, mingle in the gaiety and contribute to the noise of excitement. From two o'clock till five Franz and Albert followed in the fête, exchanging handfuls of confetti with the other carriages and the pedestrians, who crowded amongst the horses' feet and the carriage-wheels without a single accident, a single dispute, or a single fight.

Albert was triumphant in his costume of *paillasse*. A knot of rose-coloured ribands fell from his shoulder almost to the ground. In order that there might be no confusion, Franz wore his peasant's costume. As the day advanced the tumult became greater. There was not on the pavement, in the carriages, at the windows, a single tongue that was silent, a single arm that did not move. It was a human storm composed of a thunder of cries, and a hail of sweetmeats, flowers, eggs, oranges, and nosegays. At three o'clock the sound of fireworks, let off on the Place del Popolo and the Palais de Vénise (heard with difficulty amid the din and confusion), announced that the races were about to begin. The races, like the *moccoli*, are one of the episodes peculiar to the last days of the Carnival. At the sound of the fireworks the carriages instantly broke the ranks and retired by the adjacent streets. All these evolutions are executed with an inconceivable address and marvellous rapidity, without the police interfering in the matter.

The pedestrians ranged themselves against the walls; then the trampling of horses and the clashing of steel were heard. A detachment of carbineers, fifteen abreast, galloped up the Rue du Cours in order to clear it for the *barberi.** When the detachment arrived at the Palais de Vénise, a second volley of fireworks was again discharged to announce that the street was clear. Almost instantly, in the midst of a tremendous and general outcry, seven or eight horses, excited by the shouts of three hundred thousand spectators, passed by like lightning. Then the Castle of Saint Angelo fired three cannons to indicate that number three had won. Immediately, without any other signal, the carriages moved on, flowing on towards the Corso, down all the streets,

like torrents pent up for a while, which again flow into the parent
river; and the immense stream again continued its course between
its two banks of granite.

A new source of noise and movement was added to the crowd.
The sellers of *moccoletti* entered on the scene. The *moccoli*, or
moccoletti, are candles which vary in size from the pascal taper to
the rushlight, and which cause the actors on the great scene
which terminates the Carnival two different sources of thought:
1st. How to preserve their *moccoletti* alight; 2nd. How to extinguish the *moccoletti* of others. The *moccoletti* is like life: man has
found but one means of transmitting it, and that one comes from
God. But he has discovered a thousand means of taking it away,
although the devil has somewhat aided him. The *moccoletti* is
kindled by approaching it to a light. But who can describe the
thousand means of extinguishing the *moccoletti*?—the gigantic
bellows, the monstrous extinguishers, the superhuman fans.
Every one hastened to purchase *moccoletti*—Franz and Albert
among the rest.

The night was rapidly approaching; and already at the cry
of " *moccoletti!* " repeated by the shrill voices of a thousand venders,
two or three stars began to burn among the crowd. It was a
signal. At the end of ten minutes fifty thousand lights glittered,
descending from the Palais de Vénise to the Place del Popolo,
and mounting from the Place del Popolo to the Palais de Vénise.
It seemed the fête of Jack-o'-lanterns. It is impossible to form any
idea of it, without having seeen it. Suppose all the stars had
descended from the sky and mingled in a wild dance on the face
of the earth; the whole accompanied by cries that were never
heard in any other part of the world. The *facchino* follows the
prince, the Transtevere the citizen, every one blowing, extinguishing, relighting. Had old Æolus appeared at this moment, he
would have been proclaimed king of the *moccoli*, and Aquilo the
heir-presumptive to the throne.

This flaming race continued for two hours; the Rue du Cours
was light as day; the features of the spectators on the third and
fourth stories were visible. Every five minutes Albert took out his
watch; at length it pointed to seven. The two friends were in
the Via dei Pontefici. Albert sprang out, bearing his *moccoletto*
in his hand. Two or three masks strove to knock his *moccoletto* out
of his hand; but Albert, a first-rate pugilist, sent them rolling in
the street, one after the other, and continued his course towards
the church of San Giacomo. The steps were crowded with masks,
who strove to snatch each other's flambeau. Franz followed
Albert with his eyes, and saw him mount the first step. Instantly
a mask, wearing the well-known costume of a female peasant,

snatched his *moccoletto* from him without his offering any resistance. Franz was too far off to hear what they said, but without doubt nothing hostile passed, for he saw Albert disappear arm-in-arm with the peasant girl.

He watched them pass through the crowd some time, but at length he lost sight of them in the Via Macello. Suddenly the bell that gives the signal for the Carnival sounded, and at the same instant all the *moccoletti* were extinguished as if by enchantment. It seemed as though one immense blast of the wind had extinguished every one. Franz found himself in utter darkness. No sound was audible save that of the carriages that conveyed the masks home; nothing was visible save a few lights that burnt behind the windows.

The Carnival was finished.

38

The Catacombs of Saint Sebastian

DINNER was waiting when Franz, after a ten minutes' drive, arrived at the Hôtel de Londres. Albert had told him that he should not return so soon, and Franz sat down without him. Maître Pastrini, who had been accustomed to see them dine together, inquired into the cause of his absence, but Franz merely replied that Albert had received on the previous evening an invitation which he had accepted. Franz resolved to wait for Albert as late as possible. He ordered the carriage, therefore, for eleven o'clock, desiring Maître Pastrini to inform him the moment Albert returned to the hotel. At eleven o'clock Albert had not come back. Franz dressed himself and went out, telling his host that he was going to pass the night at the Duke of Bracciano's. The house of the Duke of Bracciano is one of the most delightful in Rome; his lady, one of the last heiresses of the Colonnas, does its honours with the most consummate grace, and thus their fêtes have a European celebrity. Franz and Albert had brought to Rome letters of introduction to them; and the count's first question on Franz's arrival was to ask him where was his travelling companion. Franz replied that he had left him at the moment they were about to extinguish the *moccoli*, and that he had lost sight of him in the Via Macello.

" Then he has not returned? " said the duke.

" I waited for him until this hour," replied Franz.

" And do you know whither he went? "

" No, not precisely: however, I think it was something very like an assignation."

" Diavolo! " said the duke, " this is a bad day, or rather a bad night, to be out late ; is it not, countess? "

These words were addressed to the Countess G——, who had just arrived, and was leaning on the arm of Signor Torlonia, the duke's brother.

" I think, on the contrary, that it is a charming night," replied the countess, " and those who are here will not complain but of one thing, that of its too rapid flight."

" I am not speaking," said the duke, with a smile, " of the persons who are here: the men run no other danger than that of falling in love with you, and the women of falling ill of jealousy at seeing you so lovely; I alluded to persons who were out in the streets of Rome."

" Ah! " asked the countess, " who is out in the streets of Rome at this hour, unless it be to go to a ball? "

" Our friend, Albert de Morcerf, countess, whom I left in pursuit of his unknown about seven o'clock this evening," said Franz, " and whom I have not since seen."

" And don't you know where he is? "

" Not at all."

" Is he armed? "

" He is *en paillasse*."

" You should not have allowed him to go," said the duke to Franz; " you who know Rome better than he does."

" You might as well have tried to stop number three of the *barberi*, who gained the prize in the race to-day," replied Franz; " and then, moreover, what could happen to him? "

" Who can tell? The night is gloomy, and the Tiber is very near the Via Macello."

Franz felt a shudder run through his veins at observing the feeling of the duke and the countess so much in unison with his own personal disquietude.

" I informed them at the hotel that I had the honour of passing the night here, duke," said Franz; " and desired them to come and inform me of his return."

" Ah! " replied the duke, " here, I think, is one of my servants who is seeking you."

The duke was not mistaken; when he saw Franz, the servant came up to him.

" Your excellency," he said, " the master of the Hôtel de Londres has sent to let you know that a man is waiting for you with a letter from the Vicomte de Morcerf."

" A letter from the viscount! " exclaimed Franz. " And where is the messenger? "

" He went away directly he saw me enter the ballroom to find you."

" Oh! " said the countess to Franz; " go with all speed,—poor young man! perhaps some accident has happened to him."

" I will hasten," replied Franz.

" Shall we see you again to give us any information? " inquired the countess.

" Yes, if it is not any serious affair, otherwise I cannot answer as to what I may do myself."

Franz took his hat and went away in haste. He had sent away his carriage with orders for it to fetch him at two o'clock: fortunately the Plazzo Bracciano, which is on one side in the Rue du Cours and on the other in the Place des Saints Apôtres, is hardly ten minutes' walk from the Hôtel de Londres. As he came near the hotel, Franz saw a man in the centre of the street. He had no doubt that it was the messenger from Albert. The man was wrapped up in a large cloak. He went up to him, but to his extreme astonishment this individual first addressed him.

" What wants your excellency of me? " inquired the man, retreating a step or two as if to keep on his guard.

" Are not you the person who brought me a letter," inquired Franz, " from the Vicomte de Morcerf? "

" Your excellency's name—— "

" Is the Baron Franz d'Epinay."

" Then it is to your excellency that this letter is addressed."

" Is there any answer? " inquired Franz, taking the letter from him.

" Yes,—your friend, at least, hopes so."

" Come upstairs with me, and I will give it to you."

" I prefer waiting here," said the messenger, with a smile.

" And why? "

" Your excellency will know when you have read the letter."

" Shall I find you, then, here? "

" Certainly."

Franz entered the hotel. On the staircase he met Maître Pastrini.

" Well? " said the landlord.

" Well—what? " responded Franz.

" You have seen the man who desired to speak with you from your friend? " he asked of Franz.

" Yes, I have seen him," he replied, " and he has handed this letter to me. Light the candle in my apartment, if you please."

The innkeeper gave orders to a servant to go before Franz with a bougie. The young man had found Maître Pastrini looking very much alarmed, and this had only made him the more anxious to read Albert's letter, and thus he went instantly towards the waxlight and únfolded the letter. It was written and signed by Albert. Franz read it twice before he could comprehend what it contained. It was thus worded:—

" My DEAR FELLOW,—The moment you have received this, have the kindness to take from my pocket-book, which you will find in the square drawer of the secretaire, the letter of credit; add your own to it, if it be not sufficient. Run to Torlonia, draw from him instantly four thousand piastres, and give them to the bearer. It is urgent that I should have this money without delay.

" I do not say more, relying on you as you may rely on me."
" Your friend,
" ALBERT DE MORCERF.

" P.S.—I now believe in Italian banditti."

Below these lines were written, in a strange hand, the following in Italian:—

" Se alle sei della mattina le quattro mile piastre non sono nelle mie mani, alle sette il Conte Alberto avrà cessato di vivere.
" LUIGI VAMPA."

" *If by six in the morning the four thousand piastres are not in my hands, by seven o'clock the Count Albert will have ceased to live.*"

This second signature explained all to Franz, who now understood the objection of the messenger to coming up into the apartment; the street was safer for him. Albert, then, had fallen into the hands of the famous chief of banditti, in whose existence he had for so long a time refused to believe. There was no time to lose. He hastened to open the secretaire, and found the pocketbook in the drawer, and in it the letter of credit; there was in all six thousand piastres, but of these six thousand Albert had already expended three thousand. As to Franz, he had no letter of credit as he lived at Florence, and had only come to Rome to pass seven or eight days; he had brought but a hundred louis and, of these he had not more than fifty left. Thus seven or eight hundred piastres were wanting to them both to make up the sum that Albert required. True, he might in such a case rely on the kindness of M. Torlonia. He was, therefore, about to return to the Palazzo Bracciano without loss of time when suddenly a luminous idea crossed his mind. He remembered the Count of Monte Cristo. Franz was about to ring for Maître Pastrini, when that worthy presented himself.

" My dear sir," he said hastily, " do you know if the count is within? "

" Yes, your excellency; he has this moment returned."

" Then ring at his door, if you please, and request him to be so kind as to give me an audience."

Maître Pastrini did as he was desired, and returning five minutes after, he said:

" The count awaits your excellency."

Franz went along the corridor, and a servant introduced him to the count. He was in a small cabinet which Franz had not yet seen, and which was surrounded with divans. The count came towards him.

" Well, what good wind blows you hither at this hour? " said he; " have you come to sup with me? it would be very kind of you."

" No; I have come to speak to you of a very serious matter."

" A serious matter! " said the count, looking at Franz with the earnestness usual to him; " and what may it be? "

" Are we alone? "

" Yes," replied the count, going to the door and returning. Franz gave him Albert's letter.

" Read that," he said.

The count read it.

" Ah! ah! " said he.

" Did you see the postscript? "

" I did indeed."

" What think you of it? " inquired Franz.

" Have you the money he demands? "

" Yes, all but eight hundred piastres."

The count went to his secretaire, opened it, and pulling out a drawer filled with gold, said to Franz:

" I hope you will not offend me by applying to any one but myself."

" You see, on the contrary, I come to you first and instantly," replied Franz.

" And I thank you; have what you will; " and he made a sign to Franz to take what he pleased.

" Is it absolutely necessary, then, to send the money to Luigi Vampa? " asked the young man, looking fixedly in his turn at the count.

"Judge yourself," replied he. "The postscript is explicit."

"I think that if you would take the trouble of reflecting, you could find a way of simplifying the negotiation," said Franz.

"How so?" returned the count, with surprise.

"If we were to go together to Luigi Vampa, I am sure he would not refuse you Albert's freedom."

"What influence can I possibly have over a bandit?"

"Have you not just rendered him one of those services that are never forgotten?"

"What is that?"

"Have you not saved Peppino's life?"

"Ah! ah!" said the count, "who told you that?"

"No matter; I know it."

The count knit his brows, and remained silent an instant.

"And if I went to seek Vampa, would you accompany me?"

"If my society would not be disagreeable."

"Be it so. Where is the man who brought the letter?"

"In the street."

"He awaits the answer?"

"Yes."

"I must learn where we are going. I will summon him hither."

"It is useless; he would not come up."

"To your apartments, perhaps; but he will not make any difficulty in entering mine."

The count went to the window of the apartment that looked on to the street, and whistled in a peculiar manner. The man in the mantle quitted the wall, and advanced into the centre of the street.

"*Salite!*" said the count, in the same tone in which he would have given an order to his servant. The messenger obeyed without the least hesitation, but rather with alacrity, and mounting the steps of the passage at a bound, entered the hotel; five seconds afterwards he was at the door of the cabinet.

"Ah! it is you, Peppino," said the count.

But Peppino, instead of answering, threw himself on his knees, seized the count's hand, and covered it with kisses.

"Ah!" said the count, "you have, then, not forgotten that I saved your life; that is strange, for it is a week ago"

"No, excellency; and I never shall forget it," returned Peppino, with an accent of profound gratitude.

"Never! that is a long time; but it is something that you believe so. Rise and answer."

Peppino glanced anxiously at Franz.

"Oh, you may speak before his excellency," said he. "He is one of my friends—You allow me to give you this title," continued the count in French; " it is necessary to excite this man's confidence."

" You can speak before me," said Franz. " I am a friend of the count's."

" Good," returned Peppino; " I am ready to answer any questions your excellency may address to me."

" How did the Viscount Albert fall into Luigi's hands? "

" Excellency, the Frenchman's carriage passed several times the one in which was Teresa."

" The chief's mistress? "

" Yes; the Frenchman threw her a bouquet; Teresa returned it—all this with the consent of the chief, who was in the carriage."

" What! " cried Franz, " was Luigi Vampa in the carriage with the Roman peasants? "

" It was he who drove, disguised as the coachman," replied Peppino.

" Well? " said the count.

" Well, then the Frenchman took off his mask; Teresa, with the chief's consent, did the same. The Frenchman asked for a rendezvous; Teresa gave him one—only, instead of Teresa, it was Beppo who was on the steps of the church of San Giacomo."

" What! " exclaimed Franz, " the peasant girl who snatched his *moccoletto* from him——"

" Was a lad of fifteen," replied Peppino; " but it was no disgrace to your friend to have been decieved. Beppo has taken in plenty of others."

" And Beppo led him outside the walls? " said the count.

" Exactly so; a carriage was waiting at the end of Via Macello. Beppo got in, inviting the Frenchman to follow him, and he did not wait to be asked twice. Beppo told him he was going to take him to a villa, a league from Rome; the Frenchman assured him he would follow him to the end of the world. The coachman went up the Via di Ripetta and the Porta San Paola; and when they were two hundred yards outside, as the Frenchman became somewhat too forward, Beppo put a brace of pistols to his head, the coachman pulled up and did the same. At the same time, four of the band, who were concealed on the banks of the Almo, surrounded the carriage. The Frenchman made some resistance, and nearly strangled Beppo; but he could not resist five armed men, and was forced to yield. They made him get out, walk along the banks of the river, and then brought him to Teresa and Luigi, who were waiting for him in the catacombs of Saint Sebastian."

" Well," said the count, turning towards Franz, " it seems to me that this is a very likely story. What do you say to it? "

"Why, that I should think it very amusing," replied Franz, "if it had happened to any one but poor Albert."

"And, in truth, if you had not found me here," said the count, "it might have proved a gallant adventure. which would have cost your friend dear; but now be assured, his alarm will be the only serious consequence."

"And shall we go and find him?" inquired Franz.

"Oh, decidedly, sir; he is in a very picturesque place. Do you know the catacombs of Saint Sebastian?"

"I was never in them, but I have often resolved to visit them."

"Well, here is an opportunity made to your hand, and it would be difficult to contrive a better. Have you a carriage?"

"No."

The count rang, and a footman appeared.

"Order out the carriage," he said, "and remove the pistols which are in the holsters. You need not awaken the coachman. Ali will drive."

In a very short time the noise of wheels was heard, and the carriage stopped at the door. The count took out his watch.

"Half-past twelve," he said; "we might start at five o'clock and be in time, but the delay may cause your friend to pass an uneasy night; and, therefore, we had better go with all speed to extricate him from the hands of the infidels. Are you still resolved to accompany me?"

"More determined than ever."

"Well, then, come along."

Franz and the count went downstairs, accompanied by Peppino. At the door they found the carriage. Ali was on the box, in whom Franz recognised the dumb slave of the grotto of Monte Cristo. Franz and the count got into the carriage. Peppino placed himself beside Ali, and they set off at a rapid pace. After quitting the city, the road which the carriage traversed was the ancient Appian Way, which is bordered with tombs. From time to time, by the light of the moon which began to rise, Franz imagined that he saw something like a sentinel appear from various points of the ruin, and suddenly retreat into the darkness on a signal from Peppino.

A short time before they reached the Circus of Caracalla the carriage stopped; Peppino opened the door, and the count and Franz alighted.

"In ten minutes," said the count to his companion, "we shall arrive there."

He then took Peppino aside, gave him some order in a low voice, and Peppino went away, taking with him a torch, brought with them in the carriage. Five minutes elapsed, during which

Franz saw the shepherd advance along a narrow path in the midst of the irregular ground which forms the irregular and broken surface of the Campagna, and disappear in the midst of the high red herbage, which seemed like the bristling mane of some enormous lion.

" Now," said the count, " let us follow him."

They came to an opening behind a clump of bushes, and in the midst of a pile of rocks by which a man could scarcely pass. Peppino glided first into this crevice, but after advancing a few paces the passage widened. Then he paused, lighted his torch, and turned round to see if they came after him. The count first reached a kind of square space, and Franz followed him closely. The earth sloped in a gentle descent, enlarging as they proceeded; still, Franz and the count were compelled to advance, stooping, and scarcely able to proceed two abreast. They went on a hundred and fifty paces thus, and then were stopped by " Who goes there? "

At the same time they saw the reflection of a torch on the barrel of a carbine.

" A friend! " responded Peppino; and, advancing alone towards the sentry, he said a few words to him in a low tone; and then he, like the first, saluted the nocturnal visitors, making a sign that they might proceed.

Behind the sentinel was a staircase with twenty steps. Franz and the count descended these, and found themselves in a kind of cross-roads, forming a burial-ground. Five roads diverged like the rays of a star, and the walls, dug into niches, placed one above the other in the shape of coffins, showed that they were at last in the catacombs. In one of the cavities, whose extent it was impossible to determine, some rays of light were visible. The count laid his hand on Franz's shoulder:

" Would you like to see a camp of bandits in repose? " he inquired.

" Exceedingly," replied Franz.

" Come with me, then. Peppino, extinguish the torch."

Peppino obeyed, and Franz and the count were suddenly in utter darkness, only that fifty paces in advance of them there played along the wall some reddish beams of light, more visible since Peppino had put out his torch. They advanced silently, the count guiding Franz as if he had the singular faculty of seeing in the dark. Franz himself, however, distinguished his way more plainly in proportion as he advanced towards the rays of light which served them for guides,—three arcades, of which the middle served as the door, offered themselves. These arcades opened on one side to the corridor, in which were the count and

Franz, and on the other to a large square chamber, entirely surrounded by niches similar to those of which we have spoken. In the midst of this chamber were four stones, which had formerly served as an altar, as was evident from the cross which still surmounted them. A lamp, placed at the base of a pillar, lighted up with its pale and flickering flame the singular scene which presented itself to the eyes of the two visitors concealed in the shadow. A man was seated with his elbow leaning on the column, and was reading with his back turned to the arcades, through the openings of which the new-comers contemplated him. This was the chief of the band, Luigi Vampa. Around him, and in groups, according to their fancy, lying in their mantles, or with their backs against a kind of stone bench, which went all round the Columbarium, were to be seen twenty brigands or more, each having his carbine within reach. At the bottom, silent, scarcely visible, and like a shadow, was a sentinel, who was walking up and down before a kind of opening, which was only distinguishable because in that spot the darkness seemed thicker. When the count thought Franz had gazed sufficiently on this picturesque tableau, he raised his finger to his lips, to warn him to be silent, and ascending the three steps which led to the corridor of the Columbarium, entered the chamber by the centre arcade, and advanced towards Vampa, who was so intent on the book before him that he did not hear the noise of his footsteps.

" Who goes there? " cried the sentinel, less occupied, and who saw by the lamp's light a shadow which approached his chief.

At this sound, Vampa rose quickly, drawing at the same moment a pistol from his girdle. In a moment all the bandits were on their feet, and twenty carbines were levelled at the count.

" Well," said he, in a voice perfectly calm, and no muscle of his countenance disturbed, " well, my dear Vampa, it appears to me that you receive a friend with a great deal of ceremony! "

" Ground arms! " exclaimed the chief, with an imperative sign of the hand, whilst with the other he took off his hat respectfully; then, turning to the singular personage who had caused this scene, he said: " Your pardon, M. le Comte, but I was so far from expecting the honour of a visit, that I did not really recognise you."

" It seems that your memory is equally short in everything, Vampa," said the count; " and that not only do you forget people's faces, but also the conditions you make with them."

" What conditions have I forgotten, M. le Comte? " inquired the bandit, with the air of a man who, having committed an error, is anxious to repair it.

"Was it not agreed," asked the count, "that not only my person, but also that of my friends, should be respected by you?"

"And how have I broken that treaty, your excellency?"

"You have this evening carried off and conveyed hither the Vicomte Albert de Morcerf. Well," continued the count, in a tone that made Franz shudder, "this young gentleman is one of *my friends*,—this young gentleman lodges in the same hotel as myself,—this young gentleman has been up and down the Corso for eight hours, in my private carriage and yet, I repeat to you, you have carried him off, and conveyed him hither, and," added the count, taking the letter from his pocket, "you have set a ransom on him as if he were an indifferent person."

"Why did you not tell me all this, you?" inquired the brigand chief, turning towards his men, who all retreated before his look. "Why have you exposed me thus to fail in my word towards a gentleman like the count, who has all our lives in his hands? By heavens, if I thought one of you knew that the young gentleman was the friend of his excellency, I would blow his brains out with my own hands!"

"Well," said the count, turning towards Franz, "I told you there was some mistake in this,"

"Are you not alone?" asked Vampa, with uneasiness.

"I am with the person to whom this letter was addressed, and to whom I desired to prove that Luigi Vampa was a man of his word.—Come, your excellency, here is Luigi Vampa, who will himself express to you his deep regret at the mistake he has committed."

Franz approached, the chief advancing several steps to meet him.

"Welcome amongst us, your excellency," he said to him; "you heard what the count just said, and also my reply; let me add that I would not for the four thousand piastres at which I had fixed your friend's ransom that this had happened."

"But," said Franz, looking around him uneasily, "where is the viscount?—I do not see him."

"Nothing has happened to him, I hope?" said the count frowningly.

"The prisoner is there," replied Vampa, pointing to the hollow place in front of which the bandit was on guard, "and I will go myself and tell him he is free."

The chief went towards the place he had pointed out as Albert's prison, and Franz and the count followed him.

"What is the prisoner doing?" inquired Vampa of the sentinel.

"*Ma foi*, captain," replied the sentry, "I do not know, for the last hour I have not heard him stir."

"Come in, your excellency," said Vampa.

The count and Franz ascended seven or eight steps after the chief, who drew back a bolt, and opened a door. Then by the gleam of a lamp, similar to that which lighted the Columbarium, Albert was to be seen wrapped up in a cloak which one of the bandits had lent him, lying in a corner in profound slumber.

"Come!" said the count, smiling with his own peculiar smile, "not so bad for a man who is to be shot at seven o'clock to-morrow morning!"

Vampa looked at Albert with a kind of admiration; he was not insensible to such a proof of courage.

"You are right, M. le Comte," he said; "this must be one of your friends."

Then going to Albert, he touched him on the shoulder, saying:

"Will your excellency please to awaken?"

Albert stretched out his arms, rubbed his eyelids, and opened his eyes.

"Ah! ah!" said he, "is it you, captain. You should have allowed me to have slept. I had such a delightful dream: I was dancing the galop at Torlonia's with the Countess G——."

Then he drew from his pocket his watch, which he had preserved that he might see how time sped.

"Half-past one only," said he. "Why the devil do you rouse me at this hour?"

"To tell you that you are free, your excellency."

"My dear fellow," replied Albert, with perfect ease of mind, "remember, for the future, Napoleon's maxim, 'Never awaken me but for bad news'; if you had let me sleep on, I should have finished my galop, and have been grateful to you all my life. So then, they have paid my ransom?"

"No, your excellency!"

"Well, then, how am I free?"

"A person to whom I can refuse nothing has come to demand you."

Albert looked round, and perceived Franz.

"What!" said he, "is it you, my dear Franz, whose devotion and friendship are thus displayed?"

"No, not I," replied Franz, "but our neighbour, the Count of Monte Cristo."

"Ah! ah! M. le Comte," said Albert gaily, and arranging his cravat and waistbands, "you are really most kind, and I hope you will consider me as eternally obliged to you, in the first place for the carriage, and in the next for this!" and he put out his hand to the count, who shuddered as he gave his own, but who neverthe-less did give it.

The bandit gazed on this scene with amazement; he was evidently accustomed to see his prisoners tremble before him, and yet here was one whose gay temperament was not for a moment altered; as for Franz, he was enchanted at the way in which Albert had sustained the national honour in the presence of the bandit.

" My dear Albert," he said, " if you will make haste, we shall yet have time to finish the night at Torlonia's. You may conclude your interrupted galop, so that you will owe no ill-will to Signor Luigi who has, indeed, throughout this whole affair acted like a gentleman."

" You are decidedly right; and we may reach the Palazzo at two o'clock. Signor Luigi," continued Albert, " is there any formality to fulfil before I take leave of your excellency? "

" None, sir," replied the bandit; " you are as free as air."

" Well, then, a happy and merry life to you. Come, gentlemen, come! "

And Albert, followed by Franz and the count, descended the staircase, crossed the square chamber, where stood all the bandits, hat in hand.

" Peppino," said the brigand chief, " give me the torch."

" What are you going to do, then? " inquired the Count.

" I will show you the way back myself," said the captain; " that is the least honour I can testify to your excellency."

And taking the lighted torch from the hand of the herdsman, he preceded his guests, not as a servant who performs an act of servility, but like a king who precedes ambassadors. On reaching the door, he bowed.

" And now, M. le Comte," added he, " allow me to repeat my apologies, and I hope you will not entertain any resentment at what has occurred."

" No, my dear Vampa," replied the count; " besides, you compensate for your mistakes in so gentlemanly a way, that one almost feels obliged to you for having committed them."

" Gentlemen! " added the chief, turning towards the young men, " perhaps the offer may not appear very tempting to you, but if you should ever feel inclined to pay me a second visit, wherever I may be, you shall be welcome."

Franz and Albert bowed.

The count went out first, then Albert; Franz paused for a moment.

" Has your excellency anything to ask me? " said Vampa, with a smile.

" Yes, I have," replied Franz. " I am curious to know what work you were perusing with so much attention as we entered."

" Cæsar's *Commentaries*," said the bandit; " it is my favourite work."

" Well, are you coming? " asked Albert.

" Yes," replied Franz, " here I am! " and he in his turn, left the caves.

They advanced to the plain.

" Now, M. le Comte," Albert said, " let us on with all the speed we may. I am enormously anxious to finish my night at the Duke of Bracciano's."

They found the carriage where they had left it. The count said a word in Arabic to Ali, and the horses went off at great speed. It was just two o'clock by Albert's watch, when the two friends entered into the dancing-room.

Their return was quite an event, but as they entered together, all uneasiness on Albert's account ceased instantly.

" Madame," said the Viscount Morcerf, advancing towards the countess, " yesterday you were so condescending as to promise me a galop; I am rather late in claiming this gracious promise, but here is my friend, whose character for veracity you well know, and he will assure you the delay arose from no fault of mine."

And as at this moment the music gave the warning for the waltz, Albert put his arm round the waist of the countess, and disappeared with her in the whirl of dancers. In the meantime Franz was considering the singular shudder that had pervaded the Count of Monte Cristo's frame at the moment when he had been, in some sort, forced to give his hand to Albert.

39

The Rendezvous

ALBERT'S first words to his friend, on the following morning, contained a request that Franz would accompany him to visit the count; true, he had warmly and energetically thanked him the previous evening, but services such as he had rendered could never be too often acknowledged. The count joined them in the saloon.

" M. le Comte," said Albert, advancing to meet him, " permit me to repeat the poor thanks I offered last night, and to assure you that the remembrance of all I owe you will never be effaced from my memory; believe me, while I have life I shall never cease to dwell with grateful recollection on the prompt and im portant service you rendered me; as also to remember that to you I am indebted even for my life."

" My very good friend and excellent neighbour," replied the count with, a smile, " you really exaggerate my trifling exertions. You owe me nothing but some trifle of 20,000 francs, which you have been saved out of your travelling expenses, so that there is not much of a score between us;—but you must really permit me to congratulate you on the ease and unconcern with which you resigned yourself to your fate, and the perfect indifference you manifested as to the turn events might take."

" Upon my word," said Albert, " I deserve no credit for what I could not help, namely, a determination to take everything as I found it, and to let those bandits see, that although men get into troublesome scrapes all over the world, there is no nation but the French can smile even in the face of grim Death himself. All that, however, has nothing to do with my obligations to you, and I now come to ask you, whether, in my own person, my family, or connections, I can, in any way, serve you? My father, the Comte de Morcerf, although of Spanish origin, possesses considerable influence, both at the court of France and Madrid, and I unhesitatingly place the best services of myself, and all to whom my life is dear, at your disposal."

" M. de Morcerf," replied the count, " your offer, far from surprising me, is precisely what I expected from you, and I accept it in the same spirit of hearty sincerity with which it is made; —nay, I will go still further and say that I had previously made up my mind to ask a great favour at your hands."

" Oh, pray name it."

" I am wholly a stranger to Paris—it is a city I have never yet seen."

" Is it possible," exclaimed Albert, " that you have reached your present age without visiting the finest capital in the world? I can scarcely credit it."

" Nevertheless, it is quite true; still, I agree with you in thinking that my present ignorance of the first city in Europe is a reproach to me in every way, and calls for immediate correction; but, in all probability, I should have performed so important, so necessary a duty, as that of making myself acquainted with the wonders and beauties of your justly celebrated capital, had I known any person who would have introduced me into the fashionable world, but unfortunately I possessed no acquaintance there, and, of necessity, was compelled to abandon the idea."

" So distinguished an individual as yourself," cried Albert, " could scarcely have required an introduction."

" You are, most kind; but as regards myself, I can find no merit I possess, save that, as a millionaire, I might have become a partner in the speculations of M. Aguado and M. Rothschild; * but as my motive in travelling to your capital would not have been for the pleasure of dabbling in the funds, I stayed away till some favourable chance should present itself of carrying my wish into execution: your offer, however, smooths all difficulties, and I have only to ask you, my dear M. de Morcerf " (these words were accompanied by a most peculiar smile), " whether you undertake, upon my arrival in France, to open to me the doors of that fashionable world, of which I know no more than a Huron or native of Cochin-China? "

" Oh, that I do, and with infinite pleasure! " answered Albert; " and so much the more readily, as a letter received this morning from my father summons me to Paris in consequence of a treaty of marriage (my dear Franz, do not smile, I beg of you) with a family of high standing, and connected with the very *élite* of Parisian society."

" Connected by marriage, you mean," said Franz laughingly.

" Well, never mind how it is," answered Albert, " it comes to the same thing in the end. Perhaps by the time you return to Paris, I shall be quite a sober, staid father of a family! A most edifying representative I shall make of all the domestic virtues— don't you think so? But as regards your wish to visit our fine city, my dear count, I can only say, that you may command me and mine to any extent you please."

" Then it is a settled affair," said the count; " and I give you my solemn assurance that I only waited an opportunity like the present to realise schemes I have long meditated."

Franz doubted not that these schemes were the same concerning which he had dropped some words in the grotto of Monte Cristo; and while the count gave utterance to the expression, the young man closely examined his features in the hopes that some powerful emotion might render the nature of these projects easily traced upon his expressive countenance; but it was altogether impossible to read the thoughts of the mysterious individual before him, especially when he employed one of those bewildering smiles he so well knew how to call up.

" But tell me now, count," exclaimed Albert, delighted at the idea of having to chaperon so distinguished a person as Monte Cristo; " tell me truly whether you are in earnest, or if this project of visiting Paris is merely one of those chimerical and uncertain things of which we make so many in the course of our lives, but which, like a house built on the sand, is liable to be blown over by the first puff of wind? "

" I pledge you my honour," returned the count, " that I mean to do as I have said; both inclination and positive necessity compel me to visit Paris."

" When do you propose going thither? "

" Have you made up your mind when you shall be there yourself? "

" Certainly I have; in a fortnight or three weeks' time: that is to say, as fast as I can get there! "

" Nay," said the count; " I will give you three months ere I join you; you see I make an ample allowance for all delays and difficulties."

" And in three months' time," said Albert, " you will be at my house? "

" Shall we make a positive appointment for a particular day and hour? " inquired the count; " only let me warn you that I am proverbial for my punctilious exactitude in keeping my engagements."

" The very thing! " exclaimed Albert; " yes, by all means let us have this rendezvous duly drawn up and attested."

" So be it, then," replied the count, and extending his hand towards an almanac, suspended near the chimney-piece, he said, " to-day is the 21st of February," and drawing out his watch, added, " it is exactly half-past ten o'clock. Now promise me to remember this, and expect me the 21st of May at the same hour in the forenoon."

" Capital! " exclaimed Albert; " and you shall find everything and everybody ready to receive you. I take upon myself to promise that your breakfast shall be smoking hot awaiting your arrival."

" Where do you live? "

" No, 27 Rue du Helder."

" Have you bachelor's apartments there? I hope my coming will not put you to any inconvenience."

" I reside in my father's hotel, but occupy a pavilion at the farther side of the courtyard, entirely separated from the main building."

" Quite sufficient," replied the count, as taking out his tablets he wrote down " No. 27 Rue du Helder, 21st May, half-past ten in the morning." " Now then," said the count, returning his tablets to his pocket, " make yourself perfectly easy, the hand of your timepiece will not be more accurate in marking the time than myself."

" Shall I see you again ere my departure? " asked Albert.

" That will be according to circumstances; but when do you set off? "

" To-morrow evening, at five o'clock."

" In that case I must say adieu to you, as I am compelled to go to Naples, and shall not return hither before Saturday evening or Sunday morning. And you, M. le Baron," pursued the count, addressing Franz, " do you also depart to-morrow? "

" Yes, I go also."

" And whither do you wend your way? to Paris? "

" No, to Venice; I shall remain in Italy for another year or two."

" Then we shall not meet in Paris? "

" I fear I shall not have that honour."

" Well, since we must part," said the count, holding out a hand to each of the young men, " allow me to wish you a safe and pleasant journey."

It was the first time the hand of Franz had come in contact with that of the mysterious individual before him, and unconsciously he shuddered at its touch, for it felt cold and icy as that of a corpse.

" Let us understand each other," said Albert; " it is agreed—is it not?—that you are to be in the Rue du Helder, on the 21st of May, at half-past ten in the morning, and your word of honour passed for your punctuality? "

" All that is settled and arranged upon honour," replied the count; " rely upon seeing me at the time and place agreed on."

The young men then rose, and courteously bowing to their singular acquaintance, quitted the room.

" What is the matter? " asked Albert of Franz, when they had returned to their own apartments; " you seem more than commonly thoughtful."

" I will confess to you, Albert," replied Franz, " that I am deeply puzzled to unravel the real character of this strange count; and the appointment you have made to meet him in Paris fills me with a thousand apprehensions."

" My dear fellow," exclaimed Albert, " what can there possibly be in that to excite uneasiness? Why, you must have lost your senses to imagine either harm or danger can spring from it."

" Whether I am in my senses or not," answered Franz, " such is my view of the evil effects that may arise from a second meeting with this incomprehensible count, that I would give much you had not crossed his path."

" Listen to me, Franz," said Albert; " I am not sorry that our present conversation gives me an opportunity of remarking to you how much I have been struck with the difference of your manner towards the count to that with which you treat your friends in general: to him you are frigid and polite, while to myself, for instance, you are warm and cordial as a friend should be; have you any private reasons for so acting? "

" Possibly."

" Did you ever meet him previous to coming hither? "

" I have."

" And where? "

" Will you promise me not to repeat a single word of what I am about to tell you? "

" I promise you to observe the utmost secrecy."

" And you pledge me your honour that nothing shall induce you to divulge it? "

" I pledge my honour."

" Then listen to me."

Franz then related to his friend the history of his excursion to the isle of Monte Cristo, and of his finding a party of smugglers there, with whom were two Corsican bandits: he dwelt with considerable force and energy on the almost magical hospitality he had received from the count, and the magnificence of his entertainment in the grotto of the *Thousand and One Nights*; he recounted with circumstantial exactitude all particulars of the supper; the hatchis, the statues, the dream, and reality, and how at his awakening, there remained no proof or trace of all these events, save the small yacht, seen in the distant horizon hastening with spread sails towards Porto-Vecchio. Then he detailed the conversation overheard by him at the Colosseum, between the mysterious visitant Vampa, in which the count had promised to obtain the release of the bandit Peppino—an engagement which, as our readers are aware, he most faithfully fulfilled.

At last he arrived at the adventure of the preceding night; and the embarrassment in which he found himself placed, by not having sufficient cash to complete the sum of six or seven hundred piastres, with the circumstance of his having applied to the count to furnish the money in which he was deficient, an impulse which had led to results so picturesque and satisfactory. Albert listened with the most profound attention.

"Well!" said he, when Franz had concluded, "what do you find to object to in all you have related? The count is fond of travelling, and being rich, possesses a vessel of his own. Go but to Portsmouth or Southampton, and you will find the harbours crowded with the yachts belonging to such of the English as can afford the expense, and have the same liking for this amusement as your mysterious acquaintance of the isle of Monte Cristo. Now, by way of having a resting-place during his excursions, avoiding the wretched cookery which has been trying its best to poison me during the last four months, while you have manfully resisted its effects for as many years, and obtaining a bed, on which it is impossible to slumber, Monte Cristo has furnished for himself a temporary abode, where you first found him; but, to prevent the possibility of the Tuscan government taking a fancy to his enchanted palace, and thereby depriving him of the advantages naturally expected from so large an outlay of capital, he has wisely enough purchased the island, and assumed the title of its count. Just ask yourself, my good fellow, whether there are not many persons of our acquaintance who assume the names of lands and properties they never in their lives were master of?"

"But," said Franz, "how do you account for the circumstance of the Corsican bandits being among the crew of his vessel?"

"Why, really, the thing seems to me simple enough. Nobody knows better than yourself that the bandits of Corsica are not rogues or thieves, but purely and simply fugitives, driven by some sinister motive from their native town or village, and that their fellowship involves no disgrace or stigma. For my own part, I protest that should I ever visit Corsica, my first visit, ere even I presented myself to the mayor or *préfet*, should be to the bandits of Colomba,* if I could only manage to find them; for, on my conscience, they are a race of men I admire greatly."

"Still," persisted Franz, "I suppose you will allow that such men as Vampa and his band are regular villains, who have no other motive than plunder when they seize your person. How do you explain the influence the count evidently possessed over those ruffians? "

" My good friend, as in all probability I owe my present safety to that influence, it would ill become me to search too closely into its source; therefore, instead of condemning him for his intimacy with outlaws, you must give me leave to excuse any little irregularity there may be in such a connection. Not altogether for preserving my life, for my own idea is, that it never was in much danger; but certainly, for saving me 4000 piastres, which, being translated, means neither more nor less than 24,000 livres of our money."

" Can you tell me," replied Franz, " what country produced this mysterious person, what is his native tongue, his means of existence, and from whence does he derive his immense fortune, and what were those events of hi : early life,—a life as marvellous as unknown,—that have tinctured his succeeding years with so dark and gloomy a misanthropy? Certainly these are questions that, in your place, I should like to have answered."

" My dear Franz," replied Albert, " when, upon receipt of my letter, you found the necessity of asking the count's assistance, you promptly went to him, saying ' My friend, Albert de Morcerf, is in danger; help me to deliver him.' Was not that nearly what you said? "

" It was."

" Well, then, did he ask you, ' Who is M. Albert de Morcerf? how does he come by his name—his fortune? what are his means of existence? what is his birthplace? of what country is he a native? ' Tell me, did he put all these questions to you? "

" I confess he asked me none."

" No; he merely came and freed me from the hands of Signor Vampa, where I can assure you, spite of all my outward appearance of ease and unconcern, I did not very particularly care to remain. Now then, Franz, when, in return for services so promptly and unhesitatingly rendered, he but asks me in return to do for him what is done daily for any Russian prince or Italian noble who may pass through Paris, merely to introduce him into society, —would you have me refuse? My good fellow, you must have lost your senses to think it possible I could act with such cold-blooded policy."

And this time it must be confessed, that in direct opposition to the ordinary discussion between the young men, all the good and powerful reasons were on Albert's side.

The following afternoon, at half-past five o'clock, the young men parted, Albert de Morcerf to return to Paris, and Franz d'Epinay to pass a fortnight at Venice. But ere he entered his travelling carriage, Albert, in the fear of his expected guest forgetting the engagement he had entered into, placed in the care of the waiter of the hotel a card to be delivered to the Count of Monte Cristo, on which, beneath the name of Albert de Morcerf, he had written in pencil:

" 27 Rue du Helder, on the 21st May, half-past 10 A.M."

40

The Guests

In the house in the Rue du Helder, where Albert had invited the Count of Monte Cristo, everything was being prepared on the morning of the 21st of May to fulfil the engagement.

Albert de Morcerf inhabited a pavilion situated at the corner of a large court, and directly opposite another building, in which were the servants' apartments. Two windows only of the pavilion faced the street; three other windows looked into the court, and two at the back into the garden. Between the court and the garden, built in the heavy style of the imperial architecture, was the large and fashionable dwelling of the Comte and Comtesse de Morcerf. A high wall surrounded the whole of the hotel, surmounted at intervals by vases filled with flowers, and broken in the centre by a large gate of gilt iron, which served as the carriage entrance. A small door, close to the lodge of the concierge, gave ingress and egress to the servants and masters when they were on foot.

It was easy to discover that the delicate care of a mother, unwilling to part from her son, and yet aware he required the full exercise of his liberty, had chosen this habitation for Albert. On the other hand was visible the intelligent independence of youth, enchanted with the free and idle life of a young man. By means of these two windows, looking into the street, Albert could see all that passed; the sight of what is going on is so necessary to young men, who wish always to see the world traverse their horizon, be that horizon but the street only. Then, should anything appear to merit a more minute examination, Albert de Morcerf could follow up his researches by means of a small gate, similar to that close to the concierge's door, and which merits a particular description. It was a little entrance that seemed never to have been opened since the house was built, so entirely was it covered with dust and dirt; but the well-oiled hinges and lock announced a frequent and mysterious employment. This door laughed at the concierge, from whose vigilance and jurisdiction it escaped, opening, like the door in the *Arabian Nights*, the " *open Sesame* " of Ali Baba, by a cabalistic word or a concerted tap without from the sweetest voices or whitest fingers in the world. At the end of a long corridor, with which the door communicated, and which formed the antechamber, was, on the right, Albert's breakfast-room, looking into the court, and on the left the saloon, looking into the garden. Shrubs and creeping plants covered the windows, and hid from the garden and court these two apartments, the only rooms into which, as they were on the ground-floor, the prying eyes of the curious could penetrate. On the first floor were the same rooms with the addition of a third, formed out of the antechamber; these three rooms were a salon, a boudoir, and a bedroom. The salon downstairs was only an Algerian divan, for the use of smokers. The boudoir upstairs communicated with the bedchamber by an invisible door on the staircase;—it was evident every precaution had been taken. Above this floor was a large *atelier*, which had been increased in size by pulling down the partitions: a pandemonium, in which the artist and the dandy strove for pre-eminence. There were collected and piled up all Albert's successive caprices, hunting-horns, bass-viols, flutes—a whole orchestra, for Albert had had not a taste but a fancy for music; easels, palettes, brushes, pencils —for music had been succeeded by painting; foils, boxing-gloves, broadswords, and singlesticks—for, following the example of the fashionable young men of the time, Albert de Morcerf cultivated with far more perseverance than music and drawing, the three arts that complete a dandy's education, *i.e.* fencing, boxing, and single-stick; and it was in this apartment that he received Grisier, Cook, and Charles Lecour.* The rest of the furniture of this privileged apartment consisted of old cabinets of the time of Francis I, filled with china and Japan vases, earthenware from Lucca or Robbia, plates of Bernard de Palissy;* of old arm-chairs, in which had perhaps reposed themselves Henri IV or Sully, Louis XIII or Richelieu, for two of these arm-chairs, adorned with a carved shield on which were engraved the fleur-de-lis of France on an azure field, evidently came from the Louvre, or, at least, some royal residence. On these dark and sombre chairs were thrown splendid stuffs, dyed beneath Persia's sun, or woven by the fingers of the women of Calcutta or of Chandernagor. What these stuffs did there, it was impossible to say; they awaited, whilst gratifying the eyes, a destination unknown to their owner himself; in the meantime they filled the room with their golden and silky reflections. In the centre of the room was a piano of rosewood, of Roller and Blanchet,* of small dimensions, but containing an orchestra in its narrow and sonorous cavity, and groaning beneath the weight of the chefs-d'œuvres of Beethoven, Weber, Mozart, Haydn, Grétry, and Porpora.*

On the walls, over the doors, on the ceiling, were swords, daggers, Malay creeses, maces, battle-axes, suits of armour, gilded, damasked, and inlaid, dried plants, minerals, and stuffed birds, opening their flame-coloured wings as if for flight, and their beaks that never close. This was the favourite sitting-room of Albert.

However, the morning of the appointment, the young man had established himself in the small salon downstairs. There, on a table, surrounded at some distance by a large and luxurious divan, every species of tobacco known, from the yellow tobacco of Petersburgh, to the black tobacco of Sinai, the Maryland, the Porto-Rico, and the Latakieh, was exposed in those pots of crackled earthenware of which the Dutch are so fond; beside them, in boxes of fragrant wood, were ranged, according to their size and quality, pueros, regalias, havanas, and manillas; and, in an open cabinet, a collection of German pipes, of chibouques, with their amber mouth-pieces ornamented with coral, and of narghiles, with their long tubes of morocco, awaited the caprice or the sympathy of the smokers. Albert had himself presided at the arrangement, or, rather the symmetrical derangement which, after coffee, the guests at a breakfast of modern days love to contemplate through the vapour that escapes from their mouth, and ascends in long and fanciful wreaths to the ceiling.

At a quarter to ten, a valet entered; he composed, with a little groom named John, and who only spoke English, all Albert's establishment, although the cook of the hotel was always at his service, and on great occasions the count's chasseur also. This valet, whose name was Germain, and who enjoyed the entire confidence of his young master, held in one hand a number of papers, and in the other a packet of letters, which he gave to Albert. Albert glanced carelessly at the different missives, selected two written in a small and delicate hand, and enclosed in scented envelopes, opened them, and perused their contents with some attention.

" How did these letters come? " said he.

" One by the post; Madame Danglars' footman left the other."

" Let Madame Danglars know that I accept the place she offers me in her box. Wait: then, during the day, tell Rosa that when I leave the Opera I will sup with her, as she wishes. Take her six bottles of different wine, Cyprus, sherry, and Malaga, and a barrel of Ostend oysters; get them at Borel's,* and be sure you say they are for me."

" At what o'clock, sir, do you breakfast? "

" What time is it now? "

" A quarter to ten."

" Very well, at half-past ten. Debray will, perhaps, be obliged to go to the minister,—and besides " (Albert looked at his tablets), " it is the hour I told the count, 21st May, at half-past ten; and though I do not much rely upon his promise, I wish to be punctual. Is Madame la Comtesse up yet? "

" If M. le Vicomte wishes I will inquire? "

" Yes, ask her for one of her liqueur cellarets, mine is incomplete; and tell her I shall have the honour of seeing her about three o'clock, and that I request permission to introduce some one to her."

The valet left the room. Albert threw himself on the divan, tore off the cover of two or three of the papers, looked at the playbills, made a face at perceiving they played an opera, and not a ballet; hunted vainly amongst the advertisements for a new tooth-powder of which he had heard, and threw down, one after the other, the three leading papers of Paris, muttering:

" These papers become more and more stupid every day."

A moment after, a carriage stopped before the door, and the servant announced M. Lucien Debray. A tall young man, with light hair, clear gray eyes, and thin and compressed lips, dressed in a blue coat with buttons of gold, beautifully carved, a white neckcloth, and a tortoise-shell eyeglass suspended by a silken thread, and which, by an effort of the superciliary and zygomatic nerves, he fixed in his eye, entered, with a half-official air, without smiling or speaking.

" Good-morning, Lucien! good-morning! " said Albert; " your punctuality really alarms me. What do I say? punctuality! You, whom I expected last, you arrive at five minutes to ten, when the time fixed was half-past! Have ministers resigned? "

" No, my dear fellow," returned the young man, seating himself on the divan; " reassure yourself: we are tottering always, but we never fall; and I begin to believe that we shall pass into a state of immobility, and then the affairs of the Peninsula* will completely consolidate us."

" Ah, true! you drive Don Carlos out of Spain."

" No, no, my dear fellow, do not confound our plans. We take him to the other side of the French frontier, and offer him hospitality at Bourges."

" At Bourges? "

" Yes, he has not much to complain of; Bourges is the capital of

Charles VII. Do you not know that all Paris knew it yesterday, and the day before it had already transpired on the Bourse, and M. Danglars (I do not know by what means that man contrives to obtain intelligence as soon as we do) made a million (£40,000)? "

" And you another order, for I see you have a blue riband at your button-hole."

" Yes, they sent me the order of Charles III," returned Debray carelessly.

" Come, do not affect indifference, but confess you were pleased to have it."

" Oh, it is very well as a finish to the toilette. It looks very neat on a black coat buttoned up."

" Well, I am going to amuse you by introducing to you a new acquaintance."

" A man or a woman? "

" A man."

" I know so many already."

" But you do not know this man."

" Where does he come from—the end of the world? "

" Farther still, perhaps."

" The devil! I hope he does not bring our breakfast with him."

" Oh, no; our breakfast comes from my father's kitchen. Are you hungry? "

" Humiliating as such a confession is, I am. But I dined at M. de Villefort's, and lawyers always give you very bad dinners. You would think they felt some remorse; did you ever remark that? "

" Ah, depreciate other persons' dinners; you ministers give such splendid ones."

" Yes; but we do not invite people of fashion. If we were not forced to entertain a parcel of country boobies because they think and vote with us, we should never dream of dining at home. I assure you."

" Well, take a glass of sherry and a biscuit."

" Willingly. Your Spanish wine is excellent. You see we were quite right to pacify that country."

" Yes; but Don Carlos? "

" Well, Don Carlos will drink Bordeaux, and in ten years we will marry his son to the little queen."

" You will then obtain the Golden Fleece, if you are still in the ministry."

" I think, Albert, you have adopted the system of feeding me on smoke this morning."

" Well, you must allow it is the best thing for the stomach:'

but I hear Beauchamp in the next room; you can dispute together, and that will pass away the time."

" About what? "

" About the papers."

" My dear friend," said Lucien, with an air of sovereign contempt, " do I ever read the papers? "

" Then you will dispute the more."

" M. Beauchamp," announced the servant.

" Enter, enter," said Albert, rising and advancing to meet the young man.

" Here is Debray, who detests you without reading you, so he says."

" He is quite right," returned Beauchamp, " for I criticise him without knowing what he does. Good-day, Commander! "

" Ah, you know that already," said the private secretary, smiling and shaking hands with him. " And what do they say of it in the world? "

" They say that it is quite fair, and that you sow so much red, that you must reap a little blue."

" Come, come! that is not bad! " said Lucien. " Why do you not join our party, my dear Beauchamp? With your talents you would make your fortune in three or four years."

" I only await one thing before following your advice, that is, a minister who will hold office for six months. My dear Albert, one word, for I must get poor Lucien a respite. Do we breakfast or dine? I must go to the Chamber, for our life is not an idle one."

" You only breakfast: I await two persons, and the instant they arrive we shall sit down to table."

41

The Breakfast

" AND what sort of persons do you expect to breakfast? " said Beauchamp.

" A gentleman, and a diplomatist."

" Then we shall have to wait two hours for the gentleman, and three for the diplomatist. I shall come back to dessert; keep me some strawberries, coffee, and cigars. I shall take a cutlet on my way to the Chambers."

" Do not do anything of the sort, for were the gentleman a Montmorency, and the diplomatist a Metternich, we will breakfast at eleven; in the meantime, follow Debray's example, and take a glass of sherry and a biscuit."

" Be it so, I will stay. I must do something to distract my thoughts."

" You are like Debray; and yet it seems to me that when the minister is out of spirits, the opposition ought to be joyous."

" Ah, you do not know with what I am threatened, I shall hear this morning M. Danglars make a speech at the Chamber of Deputies, and at his wife's this evening I shall hear the tragedy of a peer of France. The devil take the constitutional government! and since we had our choice, as they say at least, how could we choose that? "

" I understand; you must lay in a stock of hilarity."

" Do not run down M. Danglars' speeches," said Debray; " he votes for you, for he belongs to the opposition."

" *Pardieu!* that is exactly the worst of all: I am waiting until you send him to speak of the Luxembourg to laugh at my ease."

" My dear friend," said Albert to Beauchamp, " it is plain the affairs of Spain are settled, for you are most desperately out of humour this morning. Recollect that Parisian gossip has spoken of a marriage between myself and Mlle. Eugénie Danglars; I cannot, in conscience, therefore, let you run down the speeches of a man who will one day say to me, ' M. le Vicomte, you know I give my daughter eighty thousand pounds.' "

" Ah, this marriage will never take place," said Beauchamp. " The king has made him a baron, and can make him a peer, but he cannot make him a gentleman; and the Comte de Morcerf is too aristocratic to consent, for the paltry sum of eighty thousand pounds, to a *mésalliance*. The Vicomte de Morcerf can only wed a marchioness."

"But eighty thousand pounds is a nice little sum," replied Morcerf.

"M. de Château-Renaud! M. Maximilian Morrel!" said the servant, announcing two fresh guests.

"Now, then, to breakfast," said Beauchamp; "for if I remember, you told me you only expected two persons, Albert."

"Morrel!" muttered Albert, "Morrel! who is he?"

But before he had finished, M. de Château-Renaud, a handsome young man of thirty, gentleman all over, that is, with the figure of a Guiche and the wit of a Mortemart, took Albert's hand.

"My dear Albert," said he, "let me introduce to you M. Maximilian Morrel, captain of Spahis, my friend, and what is more—however the man speaks for himself—my preserver. Salute my hero, viscount."

And he stepped on one side, exhibiting the large and open brow, the piercing eyes, and black moustache of the fine and noble young man, whom our readers have already seen at Marseilles, under circumstances sufficiently dramatic not to be forgotten. A rich uniform, half French, half Oriental, set off his broad chest, decorated with the order of the Legion of Honour, and his graceful and stalwart figure.

The young officer bowed with easy and elegant politeness.

"Monsieur," said Albert, with affectionate courtesy, "M. le Comte de Château-Renaud knew how much pleasure this introduction would give me; you are his friend, be ours also."

"Well said!" interrupted Château-Renaud; "and pray that, if you should ever be in a similar predicament, he may do as much for you as he did for me."

"What has he done?" asked Albert.

"Oh, nothing worth speaking of," said Morrel; "M. de Château-Renaud exaggerates."

"Not worth speaking of?" cried Château-Renaud; "life is not worth speaking of!—that is rather too philosophical, on my word, Morrel. It is very well for you, who risk your life every day; but for me who only did so once——"

"What is evident in all this, baron, is, that M. le Capitaine Morrel saved your life."

"Exactly so!"

"On what occasion?" asked Beauchamp.

"Beauchamp, my good fellow, you know I am starving," said Debray, "do not set him off on some long story."

" Well, I do not prevent your sitting down to table," replied Beauchamp; " Château-Renaud can tell us whilst we eat our breakfast."

" Gentlemen," said Morcerf, " it is only a quarter past ten, and I expect some one else."

" Ah, true! a diplomatist! " observed Debray.

" I know not whether he be or not; I only know that I gave him a mission which he terminated so entirely to my satisfaction, that had I been king, I should have instantly created him knight of all my orders, even had I been able to offer him the Golden Fleece and the Garter."

" Well, since we are not to sit down to table," said Debray, " take a glass of sherry and tell us all about it."

" You all know that I had the fancy of going to Africa."

" It is a road your ancestors have traced for you," said Albert gallantly.

" Yes, but I doubt that your object was like theirs—to rescue the Holy Sepulchre."

" You are quite right, Beauchamp," observed the young aristocrat. " It was only to fight as an amateur. I cannot bear duelling ever since two seconds, whom I had chosen to accommodate a quarrel, forced me to break the arm of one of my best friends, one whom you all know—poor Franz d'Epinay."

" Ah, true! " said Debray, " you did fight some time ago;— about what? "

" The devil take me, if I remember! " returned Château-Renaud. " But I recollect perfectly one thing: that, being unwilling to let such talents as mine sleep, I wished to try upon the Arabs the new pistols that had been given to me. In consequence, I embarked for Oran, and went from thence to Constantine, where I arrived just in time to witness the raising of the siege. I retreated with the rest, during eight-and-forty hours. I endured the rain during the day and the cold during the night, tolerably well, but the third morning my horse died of cold. Poor brute accustomed to be covered up and to have a stove in the stable, an Arabian finds himself unable to bear ten degrees of cold in Arabia."

" That's why you want to purchase my English horse," said Debray; " you think he will bear the cold better."

" You are mistaken, for I have made a vow never to return to Africa."

" You were very much frightened then? " asked Beauchamp.

" I confess it, and I had good reason to be so," replied Château-Renaud. " I was retreating on foot, for my horse was dead. Six Arabs came up full gallop to cut off my head. I shot two with my double-barrelled gun, and two more with my pistols, but I was then disarmed, and two were still left; one seized me by the hair (that is why I now wear it so short, for no one knows what may happen), the other encircled my neck with the yataghan, when this gentleman whom you see here charged them, shot the one who held me by the hair with a pistol, and cleft the skull of the other with his sabre. He had assigned himself the task of saving the life of a man that day; chance caused that man to be myself. When I am rich, I will order a statue of Chance from Klugmann or Marochetti."*

"Yes," said Morrel, smiling, "it was the 5th of September, the anniversary of the day on which my father was miraculously preserved; therefore, as far as it lies in my power, I endeavour to celebrate it by some——"

"Heroic action," interrupted Château-Renaud. "I was chosen. But this is not all: after rescuing me from the sword, he rescued me from the cold, not by sharing his cloak with me, like St. Martin, but by giving me it all; then, from hunger, by sharing with me—guess what?"

"A Strasbourg pie?" asked Beauchamp.

"No, his horse; of which we each of us ate a slice with a hearty appetite: it was very hard."

"The horse?" said Morcerf, laughing.

"No, the sacrifice," returned Château-Renaud; "ask Debray if he would sacrifice his English steed for a stranger?"

"Not for a stranger," said Debray, "but for a friend, I might, perhaps."

"I divined that you would become mine, M. le Comte," replied Morrel; "besides, as I had the honour to tell you, heroism or not, sacrifice or not, that day I owed an offering to bad fortune in recompense for the favours good fortune had on other days granted to us."

"The history to which M. Morrel alludes," continued Château-Renaud, "is an admirable one, which he will tell you some day when you are better acquainted with him. To-day let us fill our stomachs, and not our memories. What time do you breakfast, Albert?"

"At half-past ten."

"Precisely?" asked Debray, taking out his watch.

"Oh, you will give me five minutes' grace," replied Morcerf, "for I also expect a preserver."

"And where does he come from?" asked Debray. "You have already answered the question once, but so vaguely, that I venture to put it a second time."

"Really," said Albert, "I do not know; when I invited him

three months ago, he was then at Rome, but since that time who knows where he may have gone? "

" And you think him capable of being exact? " demanded Debray.

" I think him capable of everything."

" Well, with the five minutes' grace, we have only ten left."

" I will profit by them to tell you something about my guest."

" I beg pardon! " interrupted Beauchamp; " are there any materials for an article in what you are going to tell us? "

" Yes; and for a most curious one."

" Go on, then, for I see I shall not get to the Chamber this morning, and I must make up for it."

" I was at Rome the last Carnival."

" We know that," said Beauchamp.

" Yes, but what you do not know is that I was carried off by bandits."

" There are no bandits," cried Debray.

" Yes, there are and most hideous, or rather most admirable ones, for I found them ugly enough to frighten me. I was informed I was a prisoner until I paid the sum of 4000 Roman crowns— about 24,000 francs (£960). Unfortunately, I had not above 1500. I was at the end of my journey and of my credit. I wrote to Franz—and were he here he would confirm every word—I wrote then to Franz, that if he did not come with the four thousand crowns before six, at ten minutes past I should have gone to join the blessed saints and glorious martyrs, in whose company I had the honour of being; and Sig. Luigi Vampa, such was the name of the chief of these bandits, would have scrupulously kept his word."

" But Franz did come with the four thousand crowns," said Château-Renaud. " A man whose name is Franz d'Epinay or Albert de Morcerf has not much difficulty in procuring them."

" No; he arrived accompanied simply by the guest I am going to present to you."

" Ah! this gentleman is a Hercules killing Cacus, a Perseus freeing Andromeda! "

" No, he is a man about my own size! "

" Armed to the teeth? "

" He had not even a knitting-needle."

" But he paid your ransom? "

" He said two words to the chief, and I was free."

" And they apologised to him for having carried you off? " said Beauchamp.

" Just so."

" Why, he is a second Ariosto."

" No; his name is the Count of Monte Cristo."

" There is not a Count of Monte Cristo," said Debray.

" I do not think so," added Château-Renaud, with the air of a man who knows the whole of the European nobility perfectly.

" Does any one know anything of a Count of Monte Cristo? "

" He comes possibly from the Holy Land, and one of his ancestors possessed Calvary as the Mortemarts did the Dead Sea."

" I think I can assist your researches," said Maximilian. " Monte Cristo is a little island I have often heard spoken of by the old sailors my father employed. A grain of sand in the centre of the Mediterranean, an atom in the infinite."

" Precisely! " cried Albert. " Well, he of whom I speak is the lord and master of this grain of sand, of this atom; he has purchased the title of count somewhere in Tuscany."

" He is rich, then? "

" I believe so."

" But that ought to be visible."

" That is what deceives you, Debray."

" I do not understand you."

" Have you read the *Arabian Nights*? "

" What a question! "

" Well, do you know if the persons you see there are rich or poor, if their sacks of wheat are not rubies or diamonds? They seem like poor fishermen, and suddenly they open some mysterious cavern filled with the wealth of the Indies."

" Afterwards? "

" My Count of Monte Cristo is one of those fishermen. He has even a name taken from the book, since he calls himself Sinbad the Sailor, and has a cave filled with gold."

" And you have seen this cavern, Morcerf? " asked Beauchamp.

" No; but Franz has: for Heaven's sake not a word of this before him. Franz went in with his eyes blindfolded, and was served by mutes and women, to whom Cleopatra was nothing. Only he is not quite sure about the women, for they did not come in until after he had taken some hatchis, so that what he took for women might have been simply a row of statues."

The two young men looked at Morcerf as if to say;

" Are you mad, or are you laughing at us? "

" And I, also," said Morrel thoughtfully, " have heard something like this from an old sailor named Penelon."

" Ah! " cried Albert, " it is very lucky that M. Morrel comes to aid me; you are vexed, are you not, that he thus gives a clue to the labyrinth? "

" My dear Albert," said Debray, " what you tell us is so extraordinary."

"Ah! because your ambassadors and your consuls do not tell you of them—they have no time. They must not molest their countrymen who travel."

"Now you get angry and attack our poor agents. How will you have them protect you? The Chamber cuts down their salaries every day, so that now they have scarcely any. Will you be ambassador, Albert? I will send you to Constantinople."

"No; lest on the first demonstration I make in favour of Mehemet Ali,* the Sultan send me the bowstring, and make my secretaries strangle me."

"There, now!" said Debray.

"Yes, but this does not prevent the Count of Monte Cristo from existing."

"Pardieu! every one exists."

"Doubtless, but not in the same way; every one has not black slaves, superb galleys, arms like those at La Cassauba, Arabian horses, and Greek mistresses."

"Have you seen his Greek?"

"I have both seen and heard her. I saw her at the theatre, and heard her one morning when I breakfasted with the count."

"He eats, then?"

"Yes, but so little it can hardly be called eating."

"He must be a vampire."

"Laugh if you will: the Countess G——, who had known Lord Ruthven, declared the count was a vampire."

"Ah, capital!" said Beauchamp. "For a man not connected with newspapers here is the pendant to the famous sea serpent of the *Constitutionnel*."*

"Wild eyes, the iris of which contracts or dilates at pleasure," said Debray; "facial angle strongly developed, magnificent forehead, livid complexion, black beard, sharp and white teeth, politeness unexceptionable."

"Just so, Lucien," returned Morcerf. "You have described him feature for feature. Yes, keen and cutting politeness. This man has often made me shudder; and one day that we were viewing an execution I thought I should faint, more from hearing the cold and calm manner in which he spoke of every description of torture, than from the sight of the executioner and the culprit."

"At the same time," added Château-Renaud, "your Count of Monte Cristo is a very fine fellow, always excepting his little arrangements with the Italian banditti."

"There are no Italian banditti!" said Debray. "No Count of Monte Cristo! There is half-past ten striking, Albert!"

"Confess you have dreamed this, and let us sit down to breakfast," continued Beauchamp.

But the sound of the clock had not died away when Germain announced:

" His Excellency the Count of Monte-Cristo."

The involuntary start every one gave, proved how much Morcerf's narrative had impressed them, and Albert himself could not prevent himself from feeling a sudden emotion. He had not heard a carriage stop in the street, or steps in the antechamber; the door had itself opened noiselessly.

The count appeared, dressed with the greatest simplicity, but the most fastidious dandy could have found nothing to cavil at in his toilette, every article of dress, hat, coat, gloves, and boots, were from the first makers. He seemed scarcely five-and-thirty; but what struck everybody was his extreme resemblance with the portrait Debray had drawn.

The count advanced smiling into the centre of the room and approached Albert, who hastened towards him holding out his hand.

" Punctuality," said Monte Cristo, " is the politeness of kings —according to one of your sovereigns, I think; but it is not the same with travellers. However, I hope you will excuse the two or three seconds I am behindhand; five hundred leagues are not to be accomplished without some trouble, and especially in France, where it seems it is forbidden to beat the postilions."

" M. le Comte," replied Albert, " I was announcing your visit to some of my friends, whom I had invited in consequence of the promise you did me the honour to make, and whom I now present to you. They are M. le Comte de Château-Renaud, whose nobility goes back to the twelve peers, and whose ancestors had a place at the Round Table; M. Lucien Debray, private secretary to the Ministre de l'Intèrieur; M. Beauchamp, an editor of a paper, and the terror of the French government, but of whom, in spite of his celebrity, you have not heard of in Italy, since his paper is prohibited there; and M. Maximilian Morrel, captain of Spahis."

At this name the count, who had hitherto saluted every one with courtesy, but at the same time with coldness and formality, stepped a pace forward, and a slight tinge of red coloured his pale cheeks.

" You wear the uniform of the new French conquerors, monsieur," said he. " It is a handsome uniform."

No one could have said what caused the count's voice to vibrate so deeply, and what made his eye flash, which was in general so clear, lustrous, and limpid when he pleased.

" You have never seen our Africans, M. le Comte? " said Albert.

"Never," replied the count, who was by this time perfectly master of himself again.

"Well, beneath this uniform beats one of the bravest and noblest hearts in the whole army."

"Oh, M. de Morcerf!" interrupted Morrel.

"Let me go on, captain! And we have just heard," continued Albert, "of a fresh action of monsieur, and so heroic a one, that, although I have seen him to-day for the first time, I request you to allow me to introduce him as my friend."

At these words it was still possible to remark in Monte Cristo that fixed gaze, that passing colour, and that slight trembling of the eyelid, that showed his emotion.

"Ah, you have a noble heart!" said the count; "so much the better."

This exclamation, which corresponded to the count's own thought rather than to what Albert was saying, surprised everybody, and especially Morrel, who looked at Monte Cristo with surprise. But, at the same time, the intonation was so soft, that, however strange the exclamation might seem, it was impossible to be offended at it.

"Gentlemen," said Albert, "Germain informs me breakfast is ready. My dear count, allow me to show you the way."

They passed silently into the breakfast-room; every one took his place.

"Gentlemen," said the count, seating himself, "permit me to make a confession which must form my excuse for any *inconvènances* I may commit. I am a stranger, and a stranger to such a degree, that this is the first time I have ever been at Paris. The French way of living is utterly unknown to me, and up to the present time I have followed the Eastern customs, which are entirely in contrast to the Parisian. I beg you, therefore, to excuse if you find anything in me too Turkish, too Italian, or too Arabian. Now, then, let us breakfast."

"With what an air he says all this!" muttered Beauchamp; "decidedly he is a great man."

"A great man in his country," added Debray.

"A great man in every country, M. Debray," said Château-Renaud.

The count was, it may be remembered, a most temperate guest. Albert remarked this, expressing his fears lest, at the outset, the Parisian mode of life should displease the traveller in the most essential point.

"My dear count," said he, "I fear one thing, and that is, that the fare of the Rue du Helder is not so much to your taste as that of the Place d'Espagne. I ought to have consulted you on the point, and have had some dishes prepared expressly."

" Did you know me better," returned the count, smiling, " you would not give one thought of such a thing for a traveller like myself, who has successively lived on maccaroni at Naples, polenta at Milan, olla podrida at Valencia, pilau at Constantinople, karrick in India, and swallow's nests in China. I eat everywhere, and of everything, only I eat but little; and to-day, that you reproach me with my want of appetite, is my day of appetite, for I have not eaten since yesterday morning."

" What! " cried all the guests, " you have not eaten for four-and-twenty hours? "

" No," replied the count; " I was forced to go out of my road to obtain some information near Nîmes, so that I was somewhat late, and therefore I did not choose to stop."

" And you ate in your carriage? " asked Morcerf.

" No; I slept, as I generally do when I am weary without having the courage to amuse myself, or when I am hungry without feeling inclined to eat."

" But you can sleep when you please, monsieur? " said Morrel.

" Yes,"

" You have a recipe for it? "

" An infallible one."

" May we inquire what is this recipe? " asked Debray.

" Oh, yes," returned Monte Cristo, " I make no secret of it; it is a mixture of excellent opium, which I fetched myself from Canton in order to have it pure, and the best hatchis which grows in the East, that is, between the Tigris and Euphrates. These two ingredients are mixed in equal proportions, and formed into pills. Ten minutes after one is taken the effect is produced. Ask M. le Baron Franz d'Epinay; I think he tasted them one day."

" Yes," replied Morcerf; " he said something about it to me."

" But," said Beauchamp, who, in his capacity of journalist, was very incredulous, " you always carry this drug about you?

" Always."

" Would it be an indiscretion to ask to see those precious pills? " continued Beauchamp, hoping to take him at a disadvantage.

" No, monsieur," returned the count; and he drew from his pocket a marvellous *bonbonnière*, formed out of a single emerald, and closed by a golden lid, which unscrewed and gave passage to a small ball of a greenish colour, and about the size of a pea. This ball had an acrid and penetrating odour. There were four or five more in the emerald, which would contain about a dozen.

The *bonbonnière* passed round the table, but it was more to examine the admirable emerald than to see the pills that it passed from hand to hand.

"And is it your cook who prepares these pills?" asked Beauchamp.

"Oh, no, monsieur," replied Monte Cristo; "I do not thus betray my enjoyments to the vulgar; I am a tolerable chemist, and prepare my pills myself."

"This is a magnificent emerald, and the largest I have ever seen," said Château-Renaud, "although my mother has some remarkable family jewels."

"I had three similar ones," returned Monte Cristo; "I gave one to the Grand Signior, who mounted it in his sabre; another to our holy father the Pope, who had it set in his tiara, opposite to nearly as large, though not so fine a one, given by the Emperor Napoleon to his predecessor Pius VII. I kept the third for myself, and I had it hollowed out, which reduced its value, but rendered it more commodious for the purpose I intended it for."

Every one looked at Monte Cristo with astonishment; he spoke with so much simplicity that it was evident he spoke the truth, or that he was mad. However, the sight of the emerald made them naturally incline to the former belief.

"And what did these two sovereigns give you in exchange for these magnificent presents?" asked Debray.

"The Grand Signior, the liberty of a woman," replied the count; "the Pope, the life of a man; so that once in my life I have been as powerful as if Heaven had made me come into the world on the steps of a throne."

"And it was Peppino you saved, was it not?" cried Morcerf, —"it was for him that you obtained pardon."

"Perhaps," returned the count, smiling.

"Monsieur le Comte, you have no idea what pleasure it gives me to hear you speak thus," said Morcerf. "I had announced you beforehand to my friends as an enchanter of the *Arabian Nights*, a wizard of the Middle Ages; but the Parisians are people so subtle in paradoxes, that they mistake for caprices of the imagination the most incontestable truths, when these truths do not form part of their daily existence. For example, here is Debray who reads, and Beauchamp who prints, every day, —' A member of the Jockey Club has been stopped and robbed on the Boulevard; that four persons have been assassinated in the Rue St. Denis or the Faubourg Saint-Germain; that ten, fifteen or, twenty thieves have been arrested in a café on the Boulevard du Temple, or in the Thermes de Julien,' and who yet contest the existence of the bandits of the Maremna, of the Campagna di Romana, or the Pontine Marshes. Tell them yourself that I was taken by bandits, and that without your generous intercession I should now have been sleeping in the Catacombs of St. Sebastian, instead of receiving them in my humble abode in the Rue du Helder."

" Ah," said Monte Cristo, " you promised me never to mention that circumstance."

" It was not I who made that promise," cried Morcerf; " it must have been some one else whom you have rescued in the same manner, and whom you have forgotten. Pray speak of it, for I shall not only, I trust, relate the little I do know, but also a great deal I do not know."

" It seems to me," returned the count, smiling, " that you played a sufficiently important part to know as well as myself what happened."

" Well, you promise me, if I tell all I know, to relate, in your turn, all that I do not know."

" That is but fair," replied Monte Cristo.

" Well," said Morcerf, " for three days I believed myself the object of the attentions of a mask, whom I took for a descendant of Tullia or Poppœa, whilst I was simply the object of the attentions of a *contadina*, and I say *contadina* to avoid saying peasant. What I know is, that, like a fool, a greater fool than he of whom I spoke just now, I mistook for this peasant girl a young bandit of fifteen or sixteen, with a beardless chin and slim waist, and who, just as I was about to imprint a chaste salute on his lips, placed a pistol to my head, and, aided by seven or eight others, led, or rather dragged me to the Catacombs of St. Sebastian, where I found a highly educated chief of brigands perusing Cæsar's *Commentaries*, and who deigned to leave off reading to inform me, that unless the next morning, before six o'clock, four thousand piastres were paid in to his account at his banker's, at a quarter past six I should have ceased to exist. The letter is still to be seen, for it is in Franz d'Epinay's possession, signed by me, and with a postscript of M. Luigi Vampa. This is all I know; but I know not, M. le Comte, how you contrived to inspire with such respect the bandits of Rome, who have so little respect for anything; I assure you Franz and I were lost in admiration."

" Nothing more simple," returned the count. " I had known the famous Vampa for more than ten years. When he was quite a child, and only a shepherd, I gave him, for having shown me the way to a place, some pieces of gold; he, in order to repay me, gave me a poniard, the hilt of which he had carved with his own hand, and which you may have seen in my collections of arms. In after years, whether he had forgotten this interchange of presents, which ought to have cemented our friendship, or whether he did not recollect me, he sought to take me, but, on the contrary, it was I who captured him, and a dozen of his band. I might have handed him over to Roman justice, which is somewhat expeditious, and which would have been still more so with him; but I did nothing of the sort—I suffered him and his band to depart."

"With the condition that they should sin no more," said Beauchamp, laughing. " I see they kept their promise."

"No, monsieur," returned Monte Cristo; "upon the simple condition that they should respect myself and my friends. Perhaps what I am about to say may seem strange to you, who are socialists, and vaunt humanity and your duty to your neighbour, but I never seek to protect society who does not protect me, and whom I will even say, in general, occupies itself about me only to injure me; and thus giving them a low place in my esteem, and preserving a neutrality towards them, it is society and my neighbour who are indebted to me."

"Bravo! " cried Château-Renaud; " you are the first man I ever met sufficiently courageous to preach egotism. Bravo, M. le Comte, bravo! "

"It is frank, at least," said Morrel. " But I am sure that M. le Comte does not regret having once deviated from the principles he has so boldly avowed."

"How have I deviated from those principles, monsieur? " asked Monte Cristo, who could not help looking at Morrel with so much intensity, that two or three times the young man had been unable to sustain the clear and piercing eye of the count.

"Why, it seems to me," replied Morrel, " that, in delivering M. de Morcerf, whom you did not know, you did good to your neighbour and to society."

"Of which he is the brightest ornament," said Beauchamp, drinking off a glass of champagne.

"Monsieur le Comte," cried Morcerf, " you are at fault; you, one of the most formidable logicians I know—and you must see it clearly proved, that instead of being an egotist, you are a philanthropist. Ah! you call yourself Oriental, a Levantine, Maltese, Indian, Chinese; your family name is Monte Cristo; Sinbad the Sailor is your baptismal appellation, and yet the first day you set foot in Paris, you instinctively possess the greatest virtue, or rather the chief defect, of us eccentric Parisians,—that is you assume the vices you have not, and conceal the virtues you possess."

"My dear vicomte," returned Monte Cristo, " I do not see, in all I have done, anything that merits, either from you or these gentlemen, the pretended eulogies I have received. You are no stranger to me, for I knew you since I had given up two rooms to you—since I had invited you to breakfast with me—since I had lent you one of my carriages—since we had witnessed the Carnival together, and since we had also seen from a window of the Place del Popolo the execution that affected you so much that you nearly fainted. I will appeal to any of these gentlemen, could I leave my guest in the hands of a hideous bandit, as you term him? Besides, you know, I had the idea that you could introduce me into some of the Paris salons when I came to France. You might, some time ago, have looked upon this resolution as a vague project, but to-day you see it was a reality, and you must submit to it under penalty of breaking your word."

" I will keep it," returned Morcerf; " but I fear that you will be much disappointed, accustomed as you are to picturesque events and to fantastic horizons. Amongst us you will not meet with any of those episodes with which your adventurous existence has so familiarised you. There is but one service I can render you, and for that I place myself entirely at your orders; that is, to present, or make my friends present, you everywhere: besides, you have no need of any one to introduce you—with your name, and your fortune, and your talent " (Monte Cristo bowed with a somewhat ironical smile), " you can present yourself everywhere, and be well received; I can be useful in one way only—if knowledge of Parisian habits, of the means of rendering yourself comfortable, or of the bazaars, can assist, you may dispose of me to find you a fitting dwelling here. I do not dare offer to share my apartments with you, as I shared yours at Rome—I, who do not possess egotism, but am yet egotistical *par excellence*; for, except myself, these rooms would not contain a shadow, unless it were the shadow of a female."

" Ah," said the count, " that is a most conjugal reservation; I recollect that at Rome you said something of a projected marriage. May I congratulate you? "

" The affair is still in projection."

" And he who says ' in projection,' means already decided," said Debray.

" No," replied Morcerf, " my father is most anxious about it; and I hope, ere long, to introduce you, if not to my wife, at least to my intended—Mademoiselle Eugénie Danglars."

" Eugénie Danglars! " said Monte Cristo; " tell me, is not her father M. le Baron Danglars? "

" Yes," returned Morcerf; " a baron of a new creation."

" What matter," said Monte Cristo, " if he has rendered the State services which merit this distinction? "

" Enormous ones," answered Beauchamp. " Although in reality a liberal, he negotiated a loan of six millions (£240,000) for Charles X, in 1829, who made him a baron and chevalier de la Légion d'Honneur; so that he wears the riband, not, as you would think, in his waistcoat pocket, but at his button-hole."

"Ah," interrupted Morcerf, laughing, "Beauchamp, Beauchamp, keep that for the *Charivari*,* but spare my future father-in-law before me." Then, turning to Monte Cristo, "You just now pronounced his name as if you knew the baron?"

"I do not know him," returned Monte Cristo; "but I shall probably soon make his acquaintance, for I have a credit opened with him by the house of Richard and Blount of London, Arstein and Eskeles of Vienna, and Thomson and French of Rome."

As he pronounced the two last names, the count glanced at Maximilian Morrel.

If the stranger expected to produce an effect on Morrel, he was not mistaken—Maximilian started as if he had been electrified.

"Thomson and French!" said he; "do you know this house, monsieur?"

"They are my bankers in the capital of the Christian world," returned the count quietly. "Can my influence with them be of any service to you?"

"Oh, M. le Comte, you could assist me, perhaps, in researches which have been, up to the present, fruitless. This house, in past years, did ours a great service, and has, I know not for what reason, always denied having rendered us this service."

"I shall be at your orders," said Monte Cristo, inclining himself.

"But," continued Morcerf, "*à propos* of Danglars,—we have strangely wandered from the subject. We were speaking of a suitable habitation for the Count of Monte Cristo. Come, gentlemen, let us all propose some place; where shall we lodge this new guest in our great capital?"

"Faubourg Saint-Germain,"* said Château-Renaud. The count will find there a charming hotel, with a court and garden."

"Bah! Château-Renaud," returned Debray, "you only know your dull and gloomy Faubourg Saint-Germain; do not pay any attention to him, M. le Comte—live in the Chaussée d'Antin, that's the real centre of Paris."

"Boulevard de l'Opéra," said Beauchamp; "on the first floor—a house with a balcony. M. le Comte will have his cushions of silver cloth brought there, and as he smokes his chibouque* see all Paris pass before him."

"You have no idea, then, Morrel?" asked Château-Renaud; "you do not propose anything?"

"Oh, yes," returned the young man, smiling; "on the contrary, I have one; but I expected the count would be tempted by one of the brilliant proposals made him; yet as he has not replied to any of them, I will venture to offer him a suite of apartments in a charming hotel, in the Pompadour style, that my sister has inhabited for a year, in the Rue Meslay."

" You have a sister? " asked the count.

" Yes, monsieur, a most excellent sister."

" Married? "

" Nearly nine years."

" Happy? " asked the count, again.

" As happy as it is permitted to a human creature to be." replied Maximilian. " She married the man she loved, who remained faithful to us in our fallen fortunes—Emmanuel Herbaut."

Monte Cristo smiled imperceptibly.

" I live there during my leave of absence," continued Maximilian; " and I shall be, together with my brother-in-law, Emmanuel, at the disposition of M. le Comte, whenever he thinks fit to honour us."

" One minute! " cried Albert, without giving Monte Cristo the time to reply. " Take care, you are going to immure a traveller, Sinbad the Sailor, a man who comes to see Paris; you are going to make a patriarch of him."

" Oh, no," said Morrel; " my sister is five-and-twenty, my brother-in-law is thirty; they are gay, young, and happy; besides, M. le Comte will be in his own house, and only see them when he thinks fit to do so."

" Thanks, monsieur," said Monte Cristo, " I shall content myself with being presented to your sister and her husband, if you will do me the honour to introduce me; but I cannot accept the offer of any one of these gentlemen, since my habitation is already prepared."

" What! " cried Morcerf, " you are, then, going to an hotel— that will be very dull for you."

" Was I so badly lodged at Rome? " said Monte Cristo, smiling.

" *Parbleu!*—at Rome you spent fifty thousand piastres in furnishing your apartments, but I presume that you are not disposed to spend a similar sum every day."

" It is not that which deterred me," replied Monte Cristo; " but as I determined to have a house to myself, I sent on my valet-de-chambre, and he ought, by this time, to have bought the house and furnished it."

" But you have, then, a valet-de-chambre who knows Paris? " said Beauchamp.

" It is the first time he has ever been in Paris. He is black and cannot speak," returned Monte Cristo.

" It is Ali! " cried Albert, in the midst of the general surprise.

" Yes, Ali himself, my Nubian mute, whom you saw, I think, at Rome."

" Certainly," said Morcerf; " I recollect him perfectly. But how could you charge a Nubian to purchase a house, and a mute to furnish it? he will do everything wrong."

" Undeceive yourself, monsieur," replied Monte Cristo; " I am quite sure that, on the contrary, he will choose everything as I wish. He knows my tastes, my caprices, my wants; he has been here a week, with the instinct of a hound, hunting by himself; he will organise everything for me. He knew I should arrive to-day at ten o'clock; since nine he awaited me at the Barrière de Fontainbleau. He gave me this paper; it contains the number of my new abode; read it yourself," and Monte Cristo passed a paper to Albert.

" Ah, that is really original," said Beauchamp.

" And very princely," added Château-Renaud.

" What! do you not know your house? " asked Debray.

" No," said Monte Cristo; " I told you I did not wish to be behind my time; I dressed myself in the carriage, and descended at the vicomte's door."

The young men looked at each other; they did not know if it was a comedy Monte Cristo was playing; but every word he uttered had such an air of simplicity, that it was impossible to suppose what he said was false: besides, why should he tell a falsehood?

" We must content ourselves, then," said Beauchamp, " with rendering M. le Comte all the little services in our power. I, in my quality of journalist, open all the theatres to him."

" Thanks, monsieur," returned Monte Cristo; " my steward has orders to take a box at each theatre."

" Is your steward also a Nubian? " asked Debray.

" No, he is a countryman of yours, if a Corsican is a countryman of any one's. But you know him, M. de Morcerf."

" Is it that excellent M. Bertuccio, who understands hiring windows so well? "

" Yes, you saw him the day I had the honour of receiving you; he has been a soldier, a smuggler—in fact, everything. I would not be quite sure that he has not been mixed up with the police for some trifle—a stab with a knife, for instance."

" And you have chosen this honest citizen for your steward? " said Debray. " Of how much does he rob you every year?"

" On my word," replied the count, " not more than another. I am sure he answers my purpose, knows no impossibility, and so I keep him."

" Then," continued Château-Renaud, " since you have an

establishment, a steward, and an hotel in the Champs Elysées, you only want a mistress."

Albert smiled. He thought of the fair Greek he had seen in the count's box at the Argentina and Valle theatres.

"I have something better than that," said Monte Cristo; "I have a slave. You procure your mistresses from the Opera, the Vaudeville, or the Variétés; I purchased mine at Constantinople; it cost me more, but I have nothing to fear."

They had long since passed to dessert and cigars.

"My dear Albert," said Debray, rising, "it is half-past two. Your guest is charming: but you leave the best company to go into the worst sometimes. I must return to the minister's. I will tell him of the count, and we shall soon know who he is."

"Take care," returned Albert; "no one has been able to accomplish that."

"Oh, we have three millions for our police; it is true they are almost always spent beforehand; but no matter, we shall still have fifty thousand francs to spend for this purpose."

"And when you know, will you tell me?"

"I promise you. Au revoir, Albert. Gentlemen, good-morning."

As he left the room, Debray called out loudly:

"My carriage."

"Bravo!" said Beauchamp to Albert; "I do not go to the Chamber, but I have something better to offer my readers than a speech of M. Danglars."

"For Heaven's sake, Beauchamp!" returned Morcerf, "do not deprive me of the merit of introducing him everywhere. Is he not peculiar?"

"He is more than that," replied Château-Renaud; "he is one of the most extraordinary men I ever saw in my life. Are you coming, Morrel?"

"Directly I have given my card to M. le Comte, who has promised to pay us a visit at Rue Meslay, No. 14."

"Be sure I shall not fail to do so," returned the count, bowing.

And Maximilian Morrel left the room with the Baron de Château-Renaud, leaving Monte Cristo alone with Morcerf

The Presentation

WHEN Albert found himself alone with Monte Cristo, "M. le Comte," said he, "allow me to commence my ciceroneship by showing you a specimen of a bachelor's apartment. You, who are accustomed to the palaces of Italy, can amuse yourself by calculating in how many square feet a young man who is not the worst lodged in Paris can live."

Monte Cristo had already seen the breakfast-room and the salon on the ground-floor. Albert led him first to his *atelier*, which was, as we have said, his favourite apartment. Monte Cristo was a worthy appreciator of all that Albert had collected here,—old cabinets, Japan porcelain, Oriental stuffs, Venetian glass, arms from all parts of the world,—everything was familiar to him; and at the first glance he recognised their date, their country, and their origin. Morcerf had expected he should be the guide; on the contrary, it was he who, under the count's guidance, followed a course of archæology, mineralogy, and natural history. They descended to the first floor; Albert led his guest into the salon. The salon was filled with the works of modern artists; there were landscapes of Dupré, with their long reeds and tall trees, their lowing oxen and marvellous skies; Delacroix' Arabian cavaliers, with their long white burnous, their shining belts, their damasked arms, their horses, who tore each other with their teeth whilst their riders contended fiercely with their maces; *aquarelles* of Boulanter, representing Nôtre Dame de Paris with that vigour that makes the artist the rival of the poet; there were paintings by Dias, who makes his flowers more beautiful than flowers, his suns more brilliant than the sun; designs of Decamp, as vividly coloured as those of Salvator Rosa, but more poetic; *pastels* of Giraud and Müller, representing children like angels and women with the features of a virgin; sketches torn from the album of Dauzats' "Travels in the East," that had been made in a few seconds on the saddle of a camel or beneath the dome of a mosque: in a word, all that modern art* can give in exchange and as recompense for the art lost and gone with ages long since past.

Albert expected to have something new this time to show to the traveller, but, to his great surprise, the latter, without seeking for the signatures, many of which, indeed, were only initials, named instantly the author of every picture in such a manner that it was easy to see that each name was not only known to him, but that each of their styles had been appreciated and studied by him.

From the salon they passed into the bedchamber; it was a model of taste and simple elegance. A single portrait, signed Leopold Robert, shone in its carved and gilded frame.

This portrait attracted the Count of Monte Cristo's attention, for he made three rapid steps in the chamber, and stopped suddenly before it. It was the portrait of a young woman of five or six and twenty, with a dark complexion, and light and lustrous eyes veiled beneath their long lashes. She wore the picturesque costume of the Catalan fisherwomen, a red and black bodice, and the golden pins in her hair. She was looking at the sea, and her shadow was defined on the blue ocean and sky.

The light was so faint in the room, that Albert did not perceive the paleness that spread itself over the count's visage, or the nervous heaving of his chest and shoulders. Silence prevailed for an instant, during which Monte Cristo gazed intently on the picture.

"You have there a most charming mistress, viscount," said the count, in a perfectly calm tone; "and this costume—a ball costume, doubtless, becomes her admirably."

"Ah, monsieur!" returned Albert, "I would never forgive you this mistake if you had seen another picture beside this. You do not know my mother; she it is whom you see here: she had her portrait painted thus six or eight years ago. This costume is a fancy one it appears, and the resemblance is so great that I think I still see my mother the same as she was in 1830. The countess had this portrait painted during the count's absence. She doubtless intended giving him an agreeable surprise, but, strange to say, this portrait seemed to displease my father, and the value of the picture, which is, as you see, one of the best works of Leopold Robert, could not overcome his dislike to it. It is true, between ourselves, that M. de Morcerf is one of the most assiduous peers at the Luxembourg, a general renowned for theory, but a most mediocre amateur of art. It is different with my mother, who paints exceedingly well, and who, unwilling to part with so valuable a picture, gave it to me to put here, where it would be less likely to displease M. de Morcerf, whose portrait by Gros I will also show you. Excuse my talking of family matters, but as I shall have the honour of introducing you to the count, I tell you this to prevent you making any allusions to this picture. The picture seems to have a malign influence, for my mother rarely comes here without looking at it, and still more rarely does she look at it without weeping. This disagreement is the only one that has ever taken place between the count and countess, who are still as much united, although married more than twenty years, as the first day of their wedding."

Monte Cristo glanced rapidly at Albert, as if to seek a hidden meaning in his words, but it was evident the young man uttered them in the simplicity of his heart.

"Now," said Albert, " that you have seen all my treasures, allow me to offer them to you, unworthy as they are. Consider yourself as in your own house, and to put yourself still more at your ease, pray accompany me to the apartments of M. de Morcerf, to whom I wrote from Rome an account of the services you rendered me, and to whom I announced your promised visit, and I may say that both the count and countess anxiously desire to thank you in person.

Monte Cristo bowed without making any answer; he accepted the offer without enthusiasm and without regret, as one of those conventions of society which every gentleman looks upon as a duty. Albert summoned his servant, and ordered him to acquaint M. and Madame de Morcerf of the arrival of the Count of Monte Cristo.

Albert followed him with the count. When they arrived at the antechamber, above the door was visible a shield, which, by its rich ornaments and its harmony with the rest of the furniture, indicated the importance the owner attached to this blazon: Monte Cristo stopped and examined it attentively.

"Azure seven merlets, or, placed bender," said he. " These are, doubtless, your family arms? Except the knowledge of blazons that enable me to decipher them, I am very ignorant of heraldry,—I, a count of a fresh creation, fabricated in Tuscany by the aid of a commandery of St. Stephen; and who would not have taken the trouble had I not been told that when you travel much it is necessary. Besides, you must have something on the panels of your carriage, to escape being searched by the custom-house officers. Excuse my putting such a question to you."

"It is not indiscreet," returned Morcerf, with the simplicity of conviction. " You have guessed rightly. These are our arms; that is, those of my father; but they are, as you see, joined to another shield, which has gules, a silver tower, which are my mother's. By her side I am Spanish, but the family of Morcerf is French, and, I have heard, one of the oldest of the south of France."

"Yes," replied Monte Cristo, " these blazons prove that. Almost all the armed pilgrims that went to the Holy Land took for their arms either a cross, in honour of their mission, or birds of passage, in sign of the long voyage they were about to undertake, and which they hoped to accomplish on the wings of faith. One of your ancestors had joined that Crusades; and supposing it to be only that of St. Louis, that makes you mount to the thirteenth century, which is tolerably ancient."

"It is possible," said Morcerf, "my father has in his study a genealogical tree which will tell you all that, and on which I made commentaries that would have greatly edified Hozier and Jaucourt.* At present I no longer think of it; and yet I must tell you that we are beginning to occupy ourselves greatly with these things under our popular government."

Morcerf then opened the door above which were his arms, and which, as we have said, opened into the salon. In the most conspicuous part of the salon was another portrait. It was that of a man from five to eight and thirty, in the uniform of a general officer, wearing the double epaulette *en torsade*, that indicates superior rank; the riband of the Legion of Honour round his neck, which showed he was a commander; and on the breast, on the right, the star of a grand officer of the order of the Saviour, and on the left that of the grand cross of Charles III, which proved that the person represented by the picture had served in the wars of Greece and Spain, or, what was just the same thing as regarded decorations, had fulfilled some diplomatic mission in the two countries.

Monte Cristo was engaged in examining this portrait with no less care than he had bestowed upon the other, when another door opened, and he found himself opposite to the Comte de Morcerf himself. He was a man of forty to forty-five years but he seemed at least fifty, and his black moustache and eyebrows contrasted strangely with his almost white hair, which was cut short, in the military fashion. He was dressed in plain clothes, and wore at his button-hole the ribands of the different orders to which he belonged. This man entered with a tolerably dignified step, and with a species of haste. Monte Cristo saw him advance towards him without making a single step. It seemed as if his feet were rooted to the ground, and his eyes on the Comte de Morcerf.

"Father," said the young man, "I have the honour of presenting to you M. le Comte de Monte Cristo, the generous friend whom I had the good fortune to meet in the critical juncture of which I have told you."

"You are most welcome, monsieur," said the Comte de Morcerf, saluting Monte Cristo with a smile. "And monsieur has rendered our house, in preserving its only heir, a service which ensures him our eternal gratitude."

As he said these words, the Comte de Morcerf pointed to a

chair, whilst he seated himself in another opposite the window.

Monte Cristo, whilst he took the seat Morcerf offered him, placed himself in such a manner as to remain concealed in the shadow of the large velvet curtains, and read on the careworn and livid features of the count a whole history of secret grief written in each wrinkle time had planted there.

"Madame la Vicomtesse," said Morcerf, "was at her toilette when she was informed of the visit she was about to receive. She will, however, be in the salon in ten minutes."

"It is a great honour for me," returned Monte Cristo, "to be thus, on the first day of my arrival in Paris, brought in contact with a man whose merit equals his reputation, and to whom fortune has for once been equitable, but has she not still on the plains of Mitidja, or in the mountains of Atlas, a marshal's staff to offer you?"

"Oh," replied Morcerf, reddening slightly, "I have left the service, monsieur. Made a peer at the Restoration, I served through the first campaign under the orders of Marshall Bourmont: I could, therefore, expect a higher rank, and who knows what might have happened had the elder branch remained on the throne? But the Revolution of July was, it seems, sufficiently glorious to allow itself to be ungrateful, and it was so for all services that did not date from the imperial period. I tendered my resignation, for when you have gained your epaulettes on the battlefield, you do not know how to manœuvre on the slippery ground of the salons. I have hung up my sword, and cast myself into politics. I have devoted myself to industry; I study the useful arts. During the twenty years I served, I often wished to do so, but I had not the time."

"These are the ideas that render your nation superior to any other," returned Monte Cristo. "A gentleman of high birth, possessor of an ample fortune, you have consented to gain your promotion as an obscure soldier, step by step—this is uncommon; then become general, peer of France, commander of the Legion of Honour, you consent to again commence a second apprenticeship, without any other hope or any other desire than that of one day becoming useful to your fellow-creatures; this, indeed, is praiseworthy,—nay, more, it is sublime."

Albert looked on and listened with astonishment; he was not used to see Monte Cristo give vent to such bursts of enthusiasm.

"Alas!" continued the stranger, doubtless to dispel the slight cloud that covered Morcerf's brow, "we do not act thus in Italy; we grow according to our race and our species, and we pursue the same lines, and often the same uselessness, all our lives."

"But, monsieur," said the Comte de Morcerf, "for a man of

your merit, Italy is not a country, and France opens her arms to receive you; respond to her call. France will not, perhaps, be always ungrateful! She treats her children ill, but she always welcomes strangers."

" Ah, father! " said Albert, with a smile, " it is evident you do not know M. le Comte de Monte Cristo; he despises all honours, and contents himself with those that are written on his passport."

" That is the most just remark," replied the stranger; " I ever heard made concerning myself! "

" You have been free to choose your career," observed the Comte de Morcerf, with a sigh; " and you have chosen the path strewed with flowers."

" Precisely, monsieur," replied Monte Cristo, with one of those smiles that a painter could never represent or a physiologist analyse.

" If I did not fear to fatigue you," said the general, evidently charmed with the count's manners, " I would have taken you to the Chamber ; there is a debate very curious to those who are strangers to our modern senators."

" I shall be most grateful, monsieur, if you will, at some future time, renew your offer; but I have been flattered with the hope of being introduced to the countess, and I will therefore wait."

" Ah! here is my mother," cried the viscount.

Monte Cristo turned round hastily, and saw Madame de Morcerf at the entrance of the salon, at the door opposite to that by which her husband had entered, pale and motionless; when Monte Cristo turned round, she let fall her arm, which for some unknown reason had been resting on the gilded door-post. She had been there some moments, and had overheard the last words of the visitor. The latter rose and bowed to the countess, who inclined herself without speaking.

" Ah! good heavens, madame! " said the count, " are you unwell, or is it the heat of the room that affects you? "

" Are you ill, mother? " cried the viscount, springing towards her.

She thanked them both with a smile.

" No," returned she, " but I feel some emotion on seeing, for the first time, the man without whose intervention we should have been in tears and desolation. Monsieur," continued the countess, advancing with the majesty of a queen, " I owe to you the life of my son, and for this I bless you. Now I thank you for the pleasure you give me in thus affording me the opportunity of thanking you as I have blessed you, from the bottom of my heart."

The count bowed again, but lower than before; he was even paler than Mercédès.

" Madame," said he, " M. le Comte and yourself recompense too generously a simple action. To save a man, to spare a father's feeling or a mother's sensibility, is not to do a good action, but a simple deed of humanity."

At these words, uttered with. the most exquisite sweetness and politeness, Madame de Morcerf replied:

" It is very fortunate for my son, monsieur, that he found such a friend, and I thank God that things are thus."

And Mercédès raised her fine eyes to heaven with so fervent an expression of gratitude that the count fancied he saw tears in them.

M. de Morcerf approached her.

" Madame," said he, " I have already made my excuses to M. le Comte for quitting him, and I pray you to do so also. The sitting commences at two; it is now three, and I am to speak."

" Go, then, and monsieur and I will strive our best to forget your absence! " replied the countess, with the same tone of deep feeling. " M. le Comte," continued she, turning to Monte Cristo, " will you do us the honour of passing the rest of the day with us? "

" Believe me, madame, I feel most grateful for your kindness, but I got out of my travelling carriage at your door this morning, and I am ignorant how I am installed in Paris, which I scarcely know; this is but a trifling inquietude, I know, but one that may be appreciated."

" We shall have this pleasure another time! " said the countess; " you promise that? "

Monte Cristo inclined himself without answering, but the gesture might pass for assent.

" I will not detain you, monsieur," continued the countess; " I would not have our gratitude become indiscreet or importunate."

" My dear count," said Albert, " I will endeavour to return your politeness at Rome, and place my coupé at your disposal until your own be ready."

" A thousand thanks for your kindness, viscount," returned the Count of Monte Cristo, " but I suppose that M. Bertuccio has suitably employed the four hours and a half I have given him, and that I shall find a carriage of some sort ready at the door."

Monte Cristo was not deceived; as soon as he appeared in the Comte de Morcerf's antechamber, a footman, the same who at Rome had brought the count's card to the two young men, and announced his visit, sprang into the vestibule, and when he arrived at the door the illustrious traveller found his carriage awaiting him.

It was a coupé of Koller's building, and with horses and harness, for which Drake had, to the knowledge of all the lions of Paris, refused on the previous day seven hundred guineas.

" Monsieur," said the count to Albert, " I do not ask you to accompany me to my house, as I can only show you a habitation fitted up in a hurry, and I have, as you know, a reputation to keep up as regards not being taken by surprise. Give me, therefore, one more day before I invite you; I shall then be certain not to fail in my hospitality."

" If you ask me for a day, count, I know what to anticipate; it will not be a house I shall see, but a palace. You have decidedly some *génie* at your control."

As Monte Cristo sprang into the vehicle, the door was closed, but not so rapidly, that he failed to perceive the almost imperceptible movement which stirred the curtains of the apartment in which he had left Madame de Morcerf.

When Albert returned to his mother, he found her in the boudoir, reclining in a large velvet arm-chair; the whole room so obscure that only the shining spangle, fastened here and there to the drapery, and the angles of the gilded frames of the pictures, gave a kind of light to the room. Albert could not see the countenance of the countess, which was lost in a thin veil she had put on her head, and which descended around her features like a cloud of vapour, but it seemed to him as though her voice had altered. He could distinguish amidst the perfumes of the roses and heliotropes in the flower-stands the sharp and fragrant odour of volatile salts, and he noticed in one of the chased cups on the mantelpiece the countess's smelling-bottle, taken from its shagreen case, and exclaimed in a tone of uneasiness, as he entered :

" My dear mother, have you been unwell during my absence? "

" No, no, Albert! but you know these roses, tuberoses, and orange-flowers, throw out at first, before one is used to them, such violent perfumes."

" Then, my dear mother," said Albert, putting his hand to the bell, " they must be taken into the antechamber. You are really unwell, and just now were so pale as you came into the room——"

" Was I pale, Albert? "

" Yes; a paleness that suits you admirably, mother; but which did not the less alarm my father and myself."

" Did your father speak of it? " inquired Mercédès eagerly.

" No, madame; but do you not remember that he remarked the fact to you? "

" Yes; I do remember!, " replied the countess.

A servant entered, summoned by Albert's ring of the bell.

"Take these flowers into the anteroom or dressing-room," said the viscount; "they make the countess unwell."

The footman obeyed his orders. A long pause ensued, which lasted until all the flowers were removed.

"What is this name of Monte Cristo?" inquired the countess, when the servant had taken away the last vase of flowers; "is it a family name, or the name of the estate, or a simple title?"

"I believe, mother, it is merely a simple title. The count purchased an island in the Tuscan Archipelago, and, as he told you to-day, has founded a commandery. You know the same thing was done for Saint Stephen of Florence, Saint George, Constantinian of Parma, and even for the Order of Malta. Except this, he has no pretension to nobility, and calls himself a chance count, although the general opinion at Rome is, that the count is a man of very high distinction."

"His manners are admirable!" said the countess; "at least, as far as I could judge in the few moments he remained here."

"They are perfect, mother—so perfect that they surpass by far all I have known in the leading aristocracy of the three proudest *noblesses* of Europe—the English aristocracy, Spanish aristocracy, and German aristocracy."

The countess paused a moment; then, after a slight hesitation, she resumed:

"You have seen, my dear Albert—I ask the question as a mother—you have seen M. de Monte Cristo in his house; you are quick-sighted, have much knowledge of the world, more tact than is usual at your age; do you think the count is really what he appears to be?"

"What does he appear to be?"

"Why, you have just said,—a man of high distinction."

"I told you, my dear mother, he was esteemed such."

"But what is your own opinion, Albert?"

"I must tell you that I have not come to any decided opinion respecting him, but I think him a Maltese."

"I do not ask you of his origin, but what he is."

"Ah! what he is; that is quite another thing. I have seen so many remarkable things of him that if you would have me really say what I think, I shall reply that I really do look upon him as one of Byron's heroes* whom Misery has marked with a fatal brand;—some Manfred, some Lara, some Werner, one of those wrecks, as it were, of some ancient family, who, disinherited of their patrimony, have achieved one by the force of their adventurous genius which has placed them above the laws of society."

"You say——"

" I say that Monte Cristo is an island in the midst of the Mediterranean, without inhabitants or garrison, the resort of smugglers of all nations, and pirates of every flag. Who knows whether or not these industrious worthies do not pay to their feudal lord some dues for his protection? "

" That is possible," said the countess, reflecting.

" Never mind," continued the young man, " smuggler or not, you must agree, mother dear, as you have seen him, that the Count of Monte Cristo is a remarkable man, who will have the greatest success in the salons of Paris. Why, this very morning, at my abode, he made his *entrée* amongst us by striking every man of us with amazement, not even excepting Château-Renaud."

" And what do you suppose is the count's age? " inquired Mercédès, evidently attaching great importance to this question.

" Thirty-five or thirty-six, mother."

" So young! it is impossible," said Mercédès, replying at the same time to what Albert said as well as to her own private reflection.

" It is the truth, however. Three or four times he has said to me, and certainly without the slightest premeditation, ' at such a period I was five years old, at another ten years old, at another twelve,' and I, induced by curiosity, which kept me alive to these details, have compared the dates, and never found him inaccurate. The age of this singular man, who is of no age, is then, I am certain, thirty-five. Besides, mother, remark how vivid his eye, how raven-black his hair, and his brow, though so pale, is free from wrinkles, —he is not vigorous, but also young."

The countess bent her head as if beneath a heavy wave of bitter thoughts.

" And has this man displayed a friendship for you, Albert? " she asked with a nervous shudder.

" I am inclined to think so."

" And—do—you—like—him? "

" Why, he pleases me in spite of Franz d'Epinay, who tries to convince me that he is a being returned from the other world."

The countess shuddered.

" Albert," she said, in a voice which was altered by emotion, " I have always put you on your guard against new acquaintances. Now you are a man, and are able to give me advice; yet, I repeat to you, Albert, be prudent."

" Why, my dear mother, it is necessary, in order to make your advice turn to account, that I should know beforehand what I have to distrust. The count never plays, he only drinks pure water tinged with a little sherry, and is so rich that he cannot, without intending to laugh at me, try to borrow money. What, then, have I to fear from him? "

" You are right," said the countess, " and my fears are weakness, especially when directed against a man who has saved your life How did your father receive him, Albert? It is necessary that we should be more than complaisant to the count. M. de Morcerf is sometimes occupied; his business makes him reflective; and he might, without intending it——"

" Nothing could be in better taste than my father's demeanour, madame," said Albert; " nay, more, he seemed greatly flattered at two or three compliments which the count very skilfully and agreeably paid him with as much ease as if he had known him these thirty years. Each of these little tickling arrows must have pleased my father," added Albert, with a laugh. " And thus they parted the best possible friends; and M. de Morcerf even wished to take him to the Chamber to hear the speakers."

The countess made no reply. She fell into so deep a reverie that her eyes gradually closed. The young man, standing up before her, gazed upon her with that filial affection which is so tender and endearing with children whose mothers are still young and handsome. Then, after seeing her eyes closed, and hearing her breathe gently, he believed she had dropped asleep, and left the apartment on tiptoe, closing the door after him with the utmost precaution.

" This devil of a fellow," he muttered, shaking his head. " I said at the time he would create a sensation here, and I measure his effect by an infallible thermometer. My mother has noticed him, and he must therefore, perforce, be remarkable."

43

Monsieur Bertuccio

DURING this time the count had arrived at his house; it had taken him six minutes to perform the distance, but these six minutes were sufficient to induce twenty young men who knew the price of the equipage they had been unable to purchase themselves, to put their horses into a gallop in order to see the rich foreigner who could afford to give 20,000 francs apiece for his horses.

The house Ali had chosen, and which was to serve as a town residence to Monte Cristo, was situated on the right hand as you ascended the Champs Elysées. A thick clump of trees and shrubs rose in the centre, and masked a portion of the front; around this shrubbery two alleys, like two arms, extended right and left, and formed a carriage-drive from the iron gates to a double portico, on every step of which stood a porcelain vase, filled with flowers. This house, isolated from the rest, had, besides the main entrance, another in the Rue Ponthieu. Even before the coachman had hailed the concierge, the massy gates rolled on their hinges;— they had seen the count coming, and at Paris, as everywhere else, he was served with the rapidity of lightning. The coachman entered, and traversed the half-circle without slackening his speed, the gates were closed ere the wheels had ceased to sound on the gravel. The carriage stopped at the left side of the portico, two men presented themselves at the carriage window; the one was Ali, who, smiling with an expression of the most sincere joy, seemed amply repaid by a mere look from Monte Cristo. The other bowed respectfully, and offered his arm to assist the count in descending.

"Thanks, Monsieur Bertuccio," said the count, springing lightly up the three steps of the portico; " and the notary? "

" He is in the small salon, excellency," returned Bertuccio.

" And the cards I ordered to have engraved as soon as you knew the number of the house? "

" M. le Comte, it is done already. I have been myself to the best engraver of the Palais Royal, who did the plate in my presence. The first card struck off was taken, according to your orders, to M. le Baron Danglars, Rue de la Chaussée d'Antin, No. 7; the others are on the mantelpiece of your excellency's bedroom.".

" Good; what o'clock is it? "

" Four o'clock."

Monte Cristo gave his hat, cane, and gloves, to the same French footman, who had called his carriage at the Comte de Morcerf's, and then he passed into the small salon, preceded by Bertuccio, who showed him the way.

" These are but indifferent marbles in this antechamber." said Monte Cristo. " I trust all this will soon be taken away."

Bertuccio bowed. As the steward had said, the notary awaited him in the small salon. He was a simple-looking lawyer's clerk, elevated to the extraordinary dignity of a provincial scrivener.

" You are the notary empowered to sell the country-house that I wish to purchase, monsieur? " asked Monte Cristo.

" Yes, M. le Comte," returned the notary.

" Is the deed of sale ready? "

" Yes, M. le Comte. Here it is."

" Very well; and where is this house that I purchase? " asked the count carelessly, addressing himself half to Bertuccio, half to the notary.

The steward made a gesture that signified, " I do not know."

The notary looked at the count with astonishment.

" What! " said he, " does not M. le Comte know where the house he purchases is situated? "

" How should I know it? I have arrived from Cadiz this morning. I have never before been at Paris; and it is the first time I have ever even set my foot in France."

" Ah! that is different; the house you purchase is situated at Auteuil."

At these words Bertuccio turned pale.

" And where is Auteuil? " asked the count.

" Close by here, monsieur," replied the notary, " a little beyond Passy; a charming situation in the heart of the Bois de Boulogne."

" So near as that? " said the count; " but that is not in the country. What made you choose a house at the gates of Paris, Monsieur Bertuccio? "

" I! " cried the steward, with a strange expression. " M. le Comte did not charge me to purchase this house. If M. le Comte will recollect—if he will think——"

" Ah, true," observed Monte Cristo; " I recollect now. I read the advertisement in one of the papers, and was tempted by the false title, ' a country-house.' "

" It is not yet too late," cried Bertuccio eagerly; "and if your excellency will entrust me with the commission, I will find you a better at Enghien, at Fontenay-aux-Roses, or at Bellevue."

" Oh no," returned Monte Cristo negligently; " since I have this, I will keep it."

" And you are quite right," said the notary, who feared to lose his fee. " It is a charming place, well supplied with spring water and fine trees; a comfortable habitation, although abandoned for a long time, without reckoning the furniture, which, although old, is yet valuable, now that old things are so much sought after. I suppose M. le Comte has the tastes of the day? "

" To be sure," returned Monte Cristo, " it is very convenient, then? "

" It is more—it is magnificent."

" *Peste!* let us not lose such an opportunity," returned Monte Cristo. " The deed, if you please, M. le Notaire." And he signed it rapidly, after having first ran his eye over that part of the deed in which were specified the situation of the house and the names of the proprietors.

" Bertuccio," said he, " give 55,000 francs to monsieur."

The steward left the room with a faltering step, and returned with a bundle of bank-notes, which the notary counted like a man who never gives a receipt for money until after legal examination.

" And now," demanded the count, " are all the forms complied with? "

" All, M. le Comte."

" Have you the keys? "

" They are in the hands of the concierge, who takes care of the house; but here is the order I have given him to instal Monsieur le Comte in his new possession."

" Very well; " and Monte Cristo made a sign with his hand to the notary, which said, " I have no further need of you; you may go."

" But," observed the honest notary, " you are mistaken, I think, M. le Comte; it is only 50,000 francs, everything included."

" And your fee? "

" Is included in this sum."

" But have you not come from Auteuil here? "

" Yes, certainly."

" Well, then, it is but fair that you should be paid for your loss of time and trouble," said the count, and he made a gesture of polite dismissal.

The notary left the room backwards, and bowing down to the ground; it was the first time he had ever met a similar client.

" See this gentleman out," said the count to Bertuccio.

And the steward followed the notary out of the room.

Scarcely was the count alone, when he drew from his pocket a book closed with a lock, and opened it with a key which he wore round his neck, and which never left him. After having sought for a few minutes, he stopped at a leaf which had several notes, and compared them with the deed of sale which lay on the table, and recalling his *souvenirs*:—

"'Auteuil, Rue de la Fontaine, No. 28;' it is indeed the same," said he; "and now, am I to rely upon an avowal extorted by religious or physical terror? However, in an hour I shall know all."

"Bertuccio!" cried he, striking a light hammer with a pliant handle on a small gong. "Bertuccio!"

The steward appeared at the door.

"Monsieur Bertuccio," said the count "did you never tell me that you had travelled in France?"

"In some parts of France,—yes, excellency."

"You know the environs of Paris, then?"

"No, excellency, no," returned the steward, with a sort of nervous trembling, which Monte Cristo, a connoisseur in all emotions, rightly attributed to great disquietude.

"It is unfortunate," returned he, "that you have never visited the environs, for I wish to see my new property this evening, and had you gone with me, you could have given me some useful information."

"To Auteuil!" cried Bertuccio, whose copper complexion became livid. "I go to Auteuil!"

"Well, what is there surprising in that? When I live at Auteuil, you must come there, as you belong to my service."

Bertuccio hung down his head before the imperious look of his master, and remained motionless, without making any answer.

"Why, what has happened to you?—are you going to make me ring a second time for the carriage?" asked Monte Cristo, in the same tone that Louis XIV pronounced the famous "I have been almost obliged to wait."*

Bertuccio made but one bound to the antechamber, and cried in a hoarse voice:

"His excellency's horses!"

Monte Cristo wrote two or three notes, and as he sealed the last, the steward appeared.

"Your excellency's carriage is at the door," said he.

"Well, take your hat and gloves," returned Monte Cristo.

"Am I to accompany you, M. le Comte?" cried Bertuccio.

"Certainly, you must give your orders, for I intend residing at the house."

It was unexampled for a servant of the count's to dare to dispute an order of his, so the steward, without saying a word, followed his master, who got into the carriage, and signed him to follow, which he did, seating himself respectfully on the front seat.

44

The House at Auteuil

MONTE CRISTO had remarked that, as they descended the staircase, Bertuccio signed himself in the Corsican manner —that is, had formed the sign of the cross in the air with his thumb—and as he seated himself in the carriage, muttered a short prayer.

Any one but a curious man would have had pity on seeing the steward's extraordinary repugnance for the count's projected drive *extra muros*; but it seemed the count was too curious to excuse Bertuccio this little journey. In twenty minutes they were at Auteuil; the steward's emotion had continued to augment as they entered the village. Bertuccio, crouched in a corner of the carriage, began to examine with a feverish anxiety every house they passed.

"Tell them to stop at Rue de la Fontaine, No. 28," said the count, fixing his eyes on the steward, to whom he gave this order.

Bertuccio's forehead was covered with perspiration, but, however, he obeyed, and, leaning out of the window, he cried to the coachman:

"Rue de la Fontaine, No. 28."

No. 28 was situated at the extremity of the village; during the drive night had set in, and a black cloud, charged with electricity, gave to these surroundings the appearance and solemnity of a dramatic episode. The carriage stopped, the footman sprang off the box, and opened the door.

"Well," said the count, "you do not get out, M. Bertuccio— you are going to stay in the carriage, then? What are you thinking of this evening?"

Bertuccio sprang out, and offered his shoulder to the count, who, this time, leaned upon it as he descended the three steps of the carriage.

"Knock," said the count, "and announce me."

Bertuccio knocked, the door opened, and the concierge appeared.

"What is it?" asked he..

"It is your new master, my good fellow," said the footman. And he held out to the concierge the notary's order.

"The house is sold, then?" demanded the concierge; "and this gentleman is coming to live here?"

"Yes, my friend," returned the count; "and I will endeavour to give you no cause to regret your old master."

"Oh, monsieur," said the concierge, "I shall not have much cause to regret him, for he came here but seldom; it is five years since he was here last, and he did well to sell the house, for it did not bring him in anything at all."

"What was the name of your old master?" said Monte Cristo.

"M. le Marquis de Saint-Méran. Ah, I am sure he has not sold the house for what he gave for it."

"The Marquis de Saint-Méran!" returned the count. "The name is not unknown to me; the Marquis de Saint-Méran!" and he appeared to meditate.

"An old gentleman," continued the concierge, "a staunch follower of the Bourbons; he had an only daughter, who married M. de Villefort, who had been the procureur du roi at Nîmes, and afterwards at Versailles."

Monte Cristo glanced at Bertuccio, who became whiter than the wall against which he leaned to prevent himself from falling.

"And is not this daughter dead?" demanded Monte-Cristo; "I fancy I have heard so."

"Yes, monsieur, one-and-twenty years ago; and since then we have not seen the poor marquis three times."

"Thanks, thanks," said Monte Cristo, judging from the steward's utter prostration that he could not stretch the cords further without danger of breaking it. "Give me a light."

"Shall I accompany you, monsieur?"

"No, it is unnecessary; Bertuccio will show me a light." And Monte Cristo accompanied these words by the gift of two pieces of gold, which produced a torrent of thanks and blessings from the concierge.

"Ah, monsieur," said he, after having vainly searched on the mantelpiece and the shelves, "I have not got any candles."

"Take one of the carriage-lamps, Bertuccio," said the count, "and show me the apartments."

The steward obeyed in silence; but it was easy to see from the manner in which the hand that held the light trembled, how much it cost him to obey. They went over a tolerably large ground-floor, a first floor consisting of a salon, a bathroom, and two bedrooms; by one of these bedrooms they arrived at a winding-staircase that opened on to the garden.

"Ah! here is a private staircase," said the count; "that is convenient. Light me, M. Bertuccio, and go first; we will see where it leads to."

"Monsieur," replied Bertuccio, "it leads to the garden."

"And, pray, how do you know that?"

" It ought to do so, at least."

" Well, let us be sure of that."

Bertuccio sighed, and went on first; the stairs led, in reality, to the garden. At the outer door the steward paused.

" Go on, Monsieur Bertuccio," said the count.

But he to whom he spoke was stupefied, bewildered, stunned; his haggard eyes glanced around, as if in search of the traces of some terrible event, and with his clenched hands he seemed striving to shut out some horrible recollections.

" Well! " insisted the count.

" No, no," cried Bertuccio, setting down the lantern at the angle of the interior wall. " No, monsieur, it is impossible ; I can go no further."

" What does this mean? " demanded the irresistible voice of Monte Cristo.

" Why, you must see, M. le Comte," cried the steward, " that this is not natural; that, having a house to purchase, you purchase it exactly at Auteuil, and that, purchasing it at Auteuil, this house should be No. 28 Rue de la Fontaine. Oh! why did I not tell you all? I am sure you would not have forced me to come. I hoped your house would have been some other one than this; as if there was not another house at Auteuil than that of the assassination! "

" Ah! ah! " cried Monte Cristo, stopping suddenly, " what words did you utter? Devil of a man, Corsican that you are— always mysteries or superstitions. Come, take the lantern, and let us visit the garden; you are not afraid of ghosts with me, I hope? "

Bertuccio raised the lantern, and obeyed. The door, as it opened, disclosed a gloomy sky, in which the moon strove vainly to struggle through a sea of clouds that covered her with their sombre wave that she illumined for an instant, and was then lost in the darkness. The steward wished to turn to the left.

" No, no, monsieur," said Monte Cristo. " What is the use of following the alleys? Here is a beautiful lawn, let us go on straight forward."

Bertuccio wiped the perspiration from his brow, but obeyed ; however, he continued to take the left hand. Monte Cristo, on the contrary, took the right hand; arriving near a clump of trees, he stopped. The steward could not restrain himself.

" Move, monsieur,—move away, I entreat you; you are exactly in the spot! "

" What spot? "

" Where he fell."

" My dear Monsieur Bertuccio," said Monte Cristo, laughing,

" recover yourself; we are no longer at Sartène or at Corte. This is not a *mâquis*, but an English garden; badly kept, I own, but still you must not calumniate it for that."

" Monsieur, I implore you do not stay there! "

" I think you are going mad, Bertuccio," said the count coldly. " If that is the case, I warn you, I shall have you put in a lunatic asylum."

" Alas! excellency," returned Bertuccio, joining his hands, and shaking his head in a manner that would have excited the count's laughter, had not thoughts of a superior interest occupied him, and rendered him attentive to the least revelation of this timorous conscience. " Alas! excellency, the evil has arrived! "

" M. Bertuccio," said the count, " I knew you were a Corsican. I knew you were gloomy, and always brooding over some old history of the vendetta; and I overlooked that in Italy, because in Italy those things are thought nothing of. But in France they are considered in very bad taste; there are gendarmes who occupy themselves with such affairs, judges who condemn, and scaffolds which avenge."

Bertuccio clasped his hands, and as, in all these evolutions, he did not let fall the lantern, the light showed his pale and altered countenance. Monte Cristo examined him with the same look that, at Rome, had viewed the execution of Andrea, and then, in a tone that made a shudder pass through the veins of the poor steward,—

" The Abbé Busoni, then, told me an untruth," said he, " when, after his journey in France, in 1829, he sent you to me, with a letter of recommendation, in which he enumerated all your valuable qualities. Well, I shall write to the abbé; I shall render him responsible for his protégé's misconduct, and I shall soon know all about this assassination. Only I warn you, that when I reside in a country, I conform to all its code, and I have no wish to put myself within the compass of the French laws for your sake."

" Oh, do not do that, excellency; I have always served you faithfully," cried Bertuccio, in despair. " I have always been an honest man, and, as far as lay in my power, I have done good."

" I do not deny it," returned the count; " but why are you thus agitated? It is a bad sign; a quiet conscience does not occasion such paleness in the cheeks, and such fear in the hands of a man."

" But, M. le Comte," replied Bertuccio hesitatingly, " did not M. l'Abbé Busoni, who heard my confession in the prison at Nîmes, tell you I had a heavy reproach to make against myself? "

" Yes; but as he said you would make an excellent steward, I concluded you had stolen—that was all."

"Oh, Monsieur le Comte!" returned Bertuccio contemptuously.

"Or, as you are a Corsican, that you had been unable to resist the desire of making a *peau*, as you call it."

"Yes, my good master," cried Bertuccio, casting himself at the count's feet, "it was simply a vengeance,—nothing else."

"I understand that; but I do not understand what it is that galvanises you in this manner."

"But, monsieur, it is very natural," returned Bertuccio, "since it was in this house that my vengeance was accomplished."

"What had you to revenge on the Marquis de Saint-Méran?"

"Oh, it was not on him, monsieur; it was on another."

"This is strange," returned Monte Cristo, seeming to yield to his reflections, "that you should find yourself without any preparation in a house where the event happened that causes you so much remorse."

"Monsieur," said the steward, "it is fatality, I am sure. First, you purchase a house at Auteuil—this house is the one where I have committed an assassination; you descend to the garden by the same staircase by which he descended; you stop at the spot where he received the blow; and two paces farther is the grave in which he had just buried his child. This is not chance; for chance, in this case, resembles Providence too much."

"Well, M. le Corse, let us suppose it is Providence. I always suppose anything people please; and, besides, you must concede something to diseased minds. Come, collect yourself, and tell me all."

"I have related it but once, and that was to the Abbé Busoni. Such things," continued Bertuccio, shaking his head, "are only related under the seal of confession."

"Then," said the count, "I refer you to your confessor: turn Chartreux or Trappist, and relate your secrets; but as for me, I do not like any one who is alarmed by such phantasms, and I do not choose that my servants should be afraid to walk in the garden of an evening. I confess I am not very desirous of a visit from the commissaire de police; for, in Italy, justice is only paid when silent, in France she is paid only when she speaks. *Peste!* I thought you somewhat Corsican, a great smuggler, and an excellent steward; but I see you have other strings to your bow. You are no longer in my service, Monsieur Bertuccio."

"Oh, M. le Comte! M. le Comte!" cried the steward, struck with terror at this threat, "if that is the only reason I cannot remain in your service, I will tell all; for if I quit you, it will only be to go to the scaffold."

"That is different," replied Monte Cristo; "but if you intend to tell an untruth, reflect it were better not to speak at all."

"No, monsieur, I swear to you, by my hopes of salvation, I will tell you all for the Abbé Busoni himself only knew a part of my secret; but, I pray you, go away from that plane-tree; the moon is just bursting through the clouds, and there, standing where you do, and wrapped in that cloak that conceals your figure, you remind me of M. de Villefort."

"What!" cried Monte Cristo, "it was M. de Villefort?"

"Your excellency knows him?"

"The former procureur du roi at Nîmes?"

"Yes."

"Who married the Comte de Saint-Méran's daughter?"

"Yes."

"Who enjoyed the reputation of being the most severe, the most upright, the most rigid magistrate on the bench?"

"Well, monsieur," said Bertuccio, "this man with this spotless reputation——"

"Well?"

"Was a villain."

"Bah!" replied Monte Cristo; "impossible!"

"It is as I tell you,"

"Ah! really," said Monte Cristo. "Have you the proof of this?"

"I had it."

"And you have lost it. How stupid!"

"Yes; but by careful search it might be recovered."

"Really," returned the count; "relate it to me, for it begins to interest me."

And the count, humming an air from *Lucia di Lammermoor*, went to sit down on a bench, whilst Bertuccio followed him, collecting his thoughts. Bertuccio remained standing before him.

45

The Vendetta

"FROM what point shall I commence my story, M. le Comte?" asked Bertuccio.

"From where you please," returned Monte Cristo, "since I know nothing at all of it."

"I thought M. l'Abbé Busoni had told your excellency."

"Some particulars, doubtless; but that is seven or eight years ago, and I have forgotten them."

"Then I can speak without fear of tiring your excellency."

"Go on, M. Bertuccio; you will supply the want of the evening papers."

"The story begins in 1815."

"Ah!" said Monte Cristo, "1815 is not yesterday."

"No, monsieur; and yet I recollect all things as clearly as if they had happened but then. I had a brother, an elder brother, who was in the service of the emperor; he had become lieutenant in a regiment composed entirely of Corsicans. This brother was my only friend; we became orphans—I at five, he at eighteen. He brought me up as if I had been his son; and, in 1814, he married. When the emperor returned from the Island of Elba, my brother instantly joined the army, was slightly wounded at Waterloo, and retired with the army behind the Loire."

"But that is the history of the Hundred Days, M. Bertuccio," said the count; "unless I am mistaken, it has been already written."

"Excuse me, excellency, but these details are necessary, and you promised to be patient."

"Go on; I will keep my word."

"One day we received a letter. I should tell you that we lived in the little village of Rogliano, at the extremity of Cape Corso. This letter was from my brother. He told us that the army was disbanded, and that he should return by Châteauroux, Clermont-Ferrand, le Puy, and Nîmes; and, if I had any money, he prayed me to leave it for him at Nîmes, with an innkeeper with whom I had dealings."

"In the smuggling line?" said Monte Cristo.

"Eh, M. le Comte, every one must live."

"Certainly; continue."

" I loved my brother tenderly, as I told your excellency, and I resolved not to send the money, but to take it to him myself. I possessed a thousand francs (£40). I left five hundred with Assunta, my sister-in-law, and with the other five hundred I set off for Nîmes. It was easy to do so; and as I had my boat and a lading to take in at sea, everything favoured my project.

" But, after we had taken in our cargo, the wind became contrary, so that we were four or five days without being able to enter the Rhone. At last, however, we succeeded, and worked up to Arles. I left the boat between Bellegarde and Beaucaire, and took the road to Nîmes."

" We are getting to the story now? "

" Yes, your excellency; excuse me, but, as you will see, I only tell you what is absolutely necessary. Just at this time, the famous massacres of the South of France took place. Two or three brigands called Trestaillon, Truphemy, and Graffan, publicly assassinated everybody whom they suspected of Bonapartism. You have, doubtless, heard of these massacres, M. le Comte? "

" Vaguely; I was far from France at that period. Go on."

" As I entered Nîmes, I literally waded in blood; at every step you encountered dead bodies and bands of the murderers, who killed, plundered, and burned. At the sight of this slaughter and devastation I became terrified, not for myself,—for I, a simple Corsican fisherman, had nothing to fear; on the contrary, that time was most favourable for us smugglers,—but for my brother, a soldier of the empire, returning from the army of the Loire, with his uniform and his epaulettes, there was everything to apprehend.

" I hastened to the innkeeper. My presages had been but too true; my brother had arrived the previous evening at Nîmes and, at the very door of the house where he was about to demand hospitality, he had been assassinated.

" I did all in my power to discover the murderers, but no one durst tell me their names, so much were they dreaded. I then thought of that French justice of which I had heard so much, and which feared nothing, and I went to the procureur du roi."

" And this procureur du roi was named Villefort? " asked Monte Cristo carelessly.

" Yes, your excellency; he came from Marseilles, where he had been deputy-procureur. His zeal had procured him advancement, and he was said to be one of the first who had informed the government of the departure from the Island of Elba."

" Then," said Monte Cristo, " you went to him? "

" ' Monsieur,' I said, ' my brother was assassinated yesterday in the streets of Nîmes, I know not by whom, but it is your duty to find out. You are the head of justice here; and it is for justice to avenge those she has been unable to protect.'

"'Who was your brother?' asked he.

"'A lieutenant in the Corsican battalion.'

"'A soldier of the usurper, then?'

"'A soldier of the French army.'

"'Well,' replied he, 'he has smitten with the sword, and has perished with the sword.'

"'You are mistaken, monsieur,' I replied; 'he has perished by the poniard.'

"'What do you want me to do?' asked the magistrate.

"'I have already told you: avenge him.'

"'On whom?'

"'On his murderers.'

"'How should I know who they are?'

"'Order them to be sought for.'

"'Why, your brother has been involved in a quarrel, and killed in a duel. All these old soldiers commit excesses which were tolerated in the time of the emperor, but which are not suffered now: for the people here do not like soldiers of such disorderly conduct.'

"'Monsieur,' I replied, 'it is not for myself that I entreat your interference,—I should grieve for him or avenge him; but my poor brother had a wife, and, were anything to happen to me, the poor creature would perish from want: for my brother's pay alone kept her. Pray try and obtain a small government pension for her.'

"'Every revolution has its catastrophes,' returned M. de Villefort. 'Your brother has been the victim of this; it is a misfortune, and government owes nothing to his family. If we are to judge by all the vengeance that the followers of the usurper exercised on the partisans of the king, when, in their turn, they were in power, your brother would be to-day, in all probability, condemned to death. What has happened is quite natural, and is only the law of reprisals.'

"'What!' cried I, 'do you, a magistrate, speak thus to me?'

"'All these Corsicans are mad, on my honour,' replied M. de Villefort; 'they fancy that their countryman is still emperor. You have mistaken the time; you should have told me this two months ago; it is too late now. Depart instantly, or I will compel you to do so.'

"I looked at him an instant to see if, by renewed entreaties, there was anything to hope.

"But this man was of stone. I approached him, and said, in a low voice:

"'Well, since you know the Corsicans so well, you know that they always keep their word. You think that it was a good deed to kill my brother, who was a Bonapartist, because you are a royalist! Well, I, who am a Bonapartist also, declare one thing to you, which is, that I will kill you; from this moment I declare the vendetta against you: so protect yourself as well as you can, for the next time we meet your last hour has come.'

"And before he had recovered from his surprise, I opened the door and left the room."

"Ah! ah!" said Monte Cristo. "With your innocent appearance you do those things, M. Bertuccio; and to a procureur du roi! Moreover, did he know what was meant by this terrible word 'vendetta'?"

"He knew so well, that from this moment he shut himself in his house, and never went out unattended, seeking me high and low. Fortunately, I was so well concealed that he could not find me.

"Then he became alarmed, and dared not reside any longer at Nîmes, so he solicited a change of residence, and as he was in reality very influential, he was nominated to Versailles. But, as you know, a Corsican who has sworn to avenge himself cares not for distance; so his carriage, fast as it went, was never above half a day's journey before me, who followed him on foot.

"The most important thing was, not to kill him only, for I had an opportunity of doing so a hundred times, but to kill him without being discovered—at least, without being arrested.

"I no longer belonged to myself, for I had my sister-in-law to protect and provide for. During three months I watched M. de Villefort; for three months he took not a step out of doors without my following him. At length, I discovered that he went mysteriously to Auteuil. I followed him thither, and I saw him enter the house where we now are; only, instead of entering by the great door that looks into the street, he came on horseback, or in his carriage, left the one or the other at the little inn, and entered by the gate you see there."

Monte Cristo made a sign with his head that he could discern amid the darkness the door to which Bertuccio alluded.

"As I had nothing more to do at Versailles, I went to Auteuil, and gained all the information I could. If I wished to surprise him, it was evident this was the spot to lie in wait for him. The house belonged, as the concierge informed your excellency, to M. de Saint-Méran, Villefort's father-in-law; M. de Saint-Méran lived at Marseilles, so that this country-house was useless to him, and it was reported to be let to a young widow, known only by the name of the baroness.

" One evening, as I was looking over the wall, I saw a young and handsome woman, who was walking alone in that garden, which was not overlooked by any windows, and I guessed that she was awaiting M. de Villefort. When she was sufficiently near to distinguish her features, I saw she was from eighteen to nineteen, tall and very fair. As she had a loose muslin dress on, and as nothing concealed her figure, I saw she would ere long become a mother. A few moments after, the little door was opened and a man entered. The young female hastened to meet him; they threw themselves into each other's arms, embraced tenderly, and returned together to the house. This man was M. de Villefort; I fully believed that when he went out in the night he would be forced to traverse the whole of the garden alone."

" And," asked the count, " did you ever know the name of this woman? "

" No, excellency," returned Bertuccio; " you will see I had not time to learn it."

" Go on."

" That evening," continued Bertuccio, " I could have killed the procureur du roi; but as I was not sufficiently master of the localities, I was fearful of not killing him on the spot, and that should his cries give the alarm, I could not escape. I put it off until the next occasion, and in order that nothing should escape me, I took a chamber looking into the street along which ran the wall of the garden.

" Three days after, about seven o'clock in the evening, I saw a servant on horseback leave the house at full gallop, and take the road that led to Sèvres. I conjectured he was going to Versailles, and I was not deceived. Three hours after, the man returned covered with dust, his errand was performed and ten minutes after, another man on foot, muffled in a mantle, opened the little door of the garden, which he closed after him. I descended rapidly; although I had not seen Villefort's face, I recognised him by the beating of my heart. I crossed the street, and stopped at a post placed at the angle of the wall, and by means of which I had once before looked into the garden. This time I did not content myself with looking, but I took my knife out of my pocket, felt that the point was sharp, and sprang over the wall. My first care was to run to the door; he had left the key in it, taking the simple precaution of turning it twice in the lock. Nothing, then, preventing my escape by this means, I examined the localities. The garden formed a long square, a terrace of smooth turf extended in the middle, and at the corners were tufts of trees with thick and massy foliage, that mingled with the shrubs and flowers.

" In order to go from the door to the house, or from the house to the door, M. de Villefort was compelled to pass by one of these clumps.

" It was the end of September; the wind blew violently. The faint glimpses of the pale moon, hidden at every instant by the masses of dark clouds that were sweeping across the sky, whitened the gravelled walks that led to the house, but were unable to pierce the obscurity of the thick shrubberies, in which a man could conceal himself without any fear of discovery. I hid myself in the one nearest to the path Villefort must take, and scarcely was I there when, amidst the gusts of wind, I fancied I heard groans; but you know, or rather you do not know, M. le Comte, that he who is about to commit an assassination fancies he hears low cries perpetually ringing in his ears. Two hours passed thus, during which I imagined I heard these moans repeated. Midnight struck. As the last stroke died away, I saw a faint light shine through the windows of the private staircase by which we have just descended. The door opened, and the man in the mantle reappeared. The terrible moment had come, but I had so long been prepared for it that my heart did not fail in the least. I drew my knife from my pocket again, opened it, and prepared myself to strike. The man in the mantle advanced towards me, but as he drew near I saw he had a weapon in his hand. I was afraid, not of a struggle, but of a failure. When he was only a few paces from me, I saw that what I had taken for a weapon was only a spade. I was still unable to divine for what reason M. de Villefort had this spade in his hands, when he stopped close to the clump, glanced round, and began to dig a hole in the earth. I then perceived that he hid something beneath his mantle, which he laid on the grass in order to dig more freely. Then, I confess, curiosity became mixed with my hatred; I wished to see what Villefort was going to do there, and I remained motionless and holding my breath. Then an idea crossed my mind, which was confirmed when I saw the procureur du roi lift from under his mantle a box, two feet long, and six or eight inches deep. I let him place the box in the hole he had made, then, whilst he stamped with his feet to remove all traces of his occupation, I rushed on him and plunged my knife into his breast, exclaiming:

" ' I am Giovanni Bertuccio; thy death for my brother's; thy treasure for his widow; thou seest that my vengeance is more complete than I had hoped.'

" I know not if he heard these words; I think he did not, for he fell without a cry. I felt his blood gush over my face, but I was intoxicated, I was delirious, and the blood refreshed, instead of burning me. In a second I had disinterred the box; then, that it might not be known I had done so, I filled up the hole, threw the spade over the wall, and rushed through the door, which I double-locked, carrying off the key."

"Ah!" said Monte Cristo, "it seems to me this was only a murder and robbery."

"No, your excellency," returned Bertuccio; "it was a vendetta followed by a restitution."

"And was the sum a large one?"

"It was not money!"

"Ah! I recollect," replied the count; "did you not say something of an infant?"

"Yes, excellency; I hastened to the river, sat down on the bank, and with my knife forced open the lock of the box. In a fine linen cloth was wrapped a new-born child. Its purple visage, and its violet-coloured hands, showed it had perished from suffocation; but as it was not yet cold, I hesitated to throw it into the water that ran at my feet. In reality, at the end of an instant I fancied I felt a slight pulsation of the heart; and as I had been assistant at the hospital at Bastia, I did what a doctor would have done— I inflated the lungs by blowing air into them, and at the expiration of a quarter of an hour, I saw the breathing commence, and a feeble cry was heard. In my turn I uttered a cry, but a cry of joy. 'God has not cursed me then,' I cried; 'since he permits me to save the life of a human creature, in exchange for the life I have taken away!'"

"And what did you do with the child?" asked Monte Cristo. "It was an embarrassing load for a man seeking to escape."

"I had not for a moment the idea of keeping it, but I knew that at Paris there was an hospital where they receive these poor creatures. As I passed the barrier, I declared I had found this child on the road, and I inquired where the hospital was; the box confirmed my statement, the linen proved it belonged to wealthy parents, the blood with which I was covered might have proceeded from the child as well as from any one else. No objection was raised, but they pointed out to me the hospital, which was situated at the upper end of the Rue d'Enfer; and after having taken the precaution of cutting the linen in two pieces, so that one of the two letters which marked it was wrapped round the child, whilst the other remained in my possession, I rang the bell, and fled with all speed. A fortnight after I was at Rogliano, and I said to Assunta:

"'Console thyself, sister; Israel is dead, but he is avenged.'

"She demanded what I meant, and when I had recounted all to her,—

"'Giovanni,' said Assunta, 'you should have brought this child with you; we would have replaced the parents it has lost, 'have called it Benedetto, and then, in consequence of this good action, God would have blessed us.'

" In reply I gave her the half of the linen I had kept in order to reclaim him if we became rich."

" What letters were marked on the linen? " said Monte Cristo.

" An H and an N, surmounted by a baron's coronet."

" By heaven, M. Bertuccio, you make use of heraldic terms where did you study heraldry? "

" In your service, excellency, where everything is learned."

" Go on; I am curious to know two things."

" What are they, monseigneur? "

" What became of this little boy? for I think you told me it was a boy, Monsieur Bertuccio."

" No, excellency, I do not recollect telling you that! "

" I thought you did; I must have been mistaken! "

" No, you were not, for it was in reality a little boy. But your excellency wished to know two things; what was the second? "

" The second was the crime of which you were accused when you asked for a confessor, and the Abbé Busoni came to visit you at your request in the prison at Nîmes."

" The story will be very long, excellency."

" What matter? you know I take but little sleep, and I do not suppose you are very much inclined for it, either."

Bertuccio bowed, and resumed his story.

" Partly to drown the recollections of the past that haunted me, partly to supply the wants of the poor widow, I eagerly returned to my trade of smuggler, which had become more easy since that relaxation of the laws which always follows a revolution. The southern districts were ill watched in particular, in consequence of the disturbances that were perpetually breaking out in Avignon, Nîmes, or Uzés. We profited by the kind of respite government gave us to make friends everywhere. Since my brother's assassination in the streets of Nîmes, I had never entered the town. The result was, the innkeeper with whom we were connected, seeing we would no longer come to him, was forced to come to us, and had established a branch to his inn, on the road from Bellegarde to Beaucaire, at the sign of the Pont du Gard. We had thus, both on the side of Aigues-Mortes, Martigues, or at Bouc, a dozen places where we left our goods, and where, in case of necessity, we concealed ourselves from the gendarmes and custom-house officers. Smuggling is a profitable trade, when a certain degree of vigour and intelligence is employed; as for myself, brought up in the mountains, I had a double motive for fearing the gendarmes and custom-house officers, as my appearance before the judges would cause an inquiry, and an inquiry always looks back into the past. And in my past life they might find something far more grave than the selling of smuggled cigars, or barrels of brandy without a permit. So, preferring death to capture, I accomplished the most astonishing deeds and which, more than once, showed me that the too great care we take of our bodies is the only obstacle to the success of those projects which require a rapid decision and vigorous and determined execution. In reality, when you have once devoted your life, you are no longer the equal of other men, or, rather, other men are no longer your equals; and whosoever has taken this resolution feels his strength and resources doubled."

" Philosophy, Monsieur Bertuccio," interrupted the count; " you have done a little of everything in your life."

" Oh, excellency."

" No, no, but philosophy at half-past ten at night is somewhat late; yet I have no other observation to make, for what you say is correct, which is more than can be said for all philosophy."

" My journeys became more and more extensive and more productive. Assunta took care of all, and our little fortune increased. One day as I was setting off on an expedition, ' Go ' said she; ' at your return I will give you a surprise.' I questioned her, but in vain; she would tell me nothing, and I departed.

" Our expedition lasted nearly six weeks; we had been to Lucca to take in oil, to Leghorn for English cottons, and we ran our cargo without opposition, and returned home full of joy.

" When I entered the house, the first thing I beheld in the centre of Assunta's chamber was a cradle that might be called sumptuous compared with the rest of the furniture, and in it a baby of seven or eight months old. I uttered a cry of joy; the only moments of sadness I had known since the assassination of the procureur du roi were caused by the recollection that I had abandoned this child. For the assassination itself I had never felt any remorse.

" Poor Assunta had guessed all. She had profited by my absence, and furnished with the half of the linen, and having written down the day and hour at which I had deposited the child at the hospital, had set off for Paris, and had reclaimed it. No objection was raised, and the infant was given up to her. Ah, I confess, M. le Comte, when I saw this poor creature sleeping peacefully in its cradle, I felt my eyes filled with tears.

" ' Ah, Assunta,' cried I, ' you are an excellent woman, and Heaven will bless you.' "

" This," said Monte Cristo, " is less correct than your philosophy ; it is only faith."

" Alas! your excellency is right," replied Bertuccio, " and God made this infant the instrument of our punishment. Never did a perverse nature declare itself more prematurely; and yet it was not owing to any fault in his bringing up. He was a most lovely child, with large blue eyes, of that deep colour that harmonises so well with the general fairness of the complexion; only his hair, which was too light, gave his face a most singular expression, which redoubled the vivacity of his look and the malice of his smile. Unfortunately, there is a proverb that says, that ' red is either altogether good or altogether bad.' The proverb was but too correct as regarded Benedetto, and even in his infancy he manifested the worst disposition. It is true that the indulgencies of his mother encouraged him. This child, for whom my poor sister would go to the town, five or six leagues off, to purchase the earliest fruits and the most tempting sweetmeats, preferred to the grapes of Palma, or the preserves of Genoa, the chestnuts stolen from a neighbour's orchard, or the dried apples in his loft, when he could eat as well of the nuts and apples that grew in my garden.

" One day, when Benedetto was about five or six, our neighbour Wasilio, who, according to the custom of the country, never locked up his purse or his valuables,—for, as your excellency knows, there are no thieves in Corsica, —complained that he had lost a louis out of his purse. We thought he must have made a mistake in counting his money, but he persisted in the accuracy of his statement. One day, Benedetto, who had been gone from the house since morning, to our great anxiety, did not return until late in the evening, dragging a monkey after him, which he said he had found chained to the foot of a tree. For more than a month past, the mischievous child who knew not what to wish for, had taken it into his head to have a monkey. A boatman, who had passed by Rogliano, and who had several of these animals, whose tricks had greatly diverted him, had, doubtless, suggested this idea to him.

" ' Monkeys are not found in our woods chained to trees,' said I; ' confess how you obtained this animal.'

" Benedetto maintained the truth of what he had said, and accompanied it with details that did more to his imagination than to his veracity. I became angry; he began to laugh; I threatened to strike him, and he made two steps backwards.

" ' You cannot beat me,' said he; ' you have no right, for you are not my father.'

" We never knew who had revealed this fatal secret, which we had so carefully concealed from him; however, it was this answer, in which the child's whole character revealed itself, that almost terrified me, and my arm fell without touching him. The boy triumphed, and this victory rendered him so audacious that all the money of Assunta, whose affection for him seemed to increase as he became more unworthy of it, was spent in prices she knew not how to contend against, and follies she had not the courage to prevent. When I was at Rogliano everything went on properly, but no sooner was my back turned than Benedetto became master, and everything went ill. When he was only eleven, he chose his companions from among the young men of eighteen or twenty, the worst characters in Bastia, or, indeed, in Corsica, and they had already, for some pieces of mischief, been several times threatened with a prosecution.

" I became alarmed, as any prosecution might be attended with serious consequences. I was compelled, at this period, to leave Corsica on an important expedition; I reflected for a long time, and with the hope of averting some impending misfortune, I resolved that Benedetto should accompany me. I hoped that the active and laborious life of a smuggler, with the severe discipline on board, would have a salutary effect on his character, well-nigh, if not quite, corrupt.

" I spoke to Benedetto alone, and proposed to him to accompany me, endeavouring to tempt him by all the promises most likely to dazzle the imagination of a child of twelve years old.

" He heard me patiently, and when I had finished, burst out laughing.

"' Are you mad, uncle?' (he called me by this name when he was in a good humour); ' do you think I am going to change the life I lead for your mode of existence, my agreeable indolence for the hard and precarious toil you impose on yourself? exposed to the bitter frost at night, and the scorching heat by day, compelled to conceal yourself, and when you are perceived, receive a volley of balls, and all to earn a paltry sum? Why, I have as much money as I want; mother Assunta always furnishes me when I ask for it! You see that I should be a fool to accept your offer.'

" The arguments, and this audacity, perfectly stupefied me. Benedetto rejoined his associates, and I saw him from a distance point me out to them as a fool."

" Sweet child! " murmured Monte Cristo.

" Oh! had he been my own son," replied Bertuccio, " or even my nephew, I would have brought him back to the right road, for the knowledge that you are doing your duty gives you strength; but the idea that I was striking a child whose father I had killed, made it impossible for me to punish him. I gave my sister, who constantly defended the unfortunate boy, good advice;

and as she confessed that she had several times missed money to a considerable amount, I showed her a safe place in which to conceal our little treasure for the future. My mind was already made up. Benedetto could read, write, and cipher perfectly, for when the fit seized him, he learned more in a day than others in a week. My intention was to enter him as clerk in some ship, and without letting him know anything of my plan, to convey him some morning on board: by this means his future treatment would depend upon his own conduct.

" I set off for France after having fixed upon this plan.

" All our cargo was to be landed in the Gulf of Lions, and this was the more difficult, because it was then the year 1829. The most perfect tranquillity was restored, and the vigilance of the custom-house officers was redoubled, and this strictness was increased at this time, in consequence of the fair of Beaucaire.

" Our expedition commenced favourably. We anchored our bark, which had a double hold, where our goods were concealed, amidst a number of other vessels that bordered the banks of the Rhone from Beaucaire to Arles. On our arrival there we began to discharge our cargo in the night, and to convey it into the town, by help of the innkeeper with whom we were connected. Whether success rendered us imprudent, or whether we were betrayed, I know not; but one evening, about five o'clock, our little cabin-boy hastened, breathless, to inform us that he had seen a detachment of custom-house officers advancing in our direction. It was not their proximity that alarmed us, for detachments were constantly patrolling along the banks of the Rhone, but the care, according to the boy's account, they took to avoid being seen. In an instant we were on the alert, but it was too late; our vessel was surrounded, and amongst the custom-house officers I observed several gendarmes, and, as terrified at the sight of their uniforms as I was brave at the sight of any other, I sprang into the hold, opened a port, and dropped into the river, dived, and only rose at intervals to breathe, until I reached a cutting that led from the Rhone to the canal that runs from Beaucaire to Aigues-Mortes. I was now safe, for I could swim along the cutting without being seen, and I reached the canal in safety. I had designedly taken this direction. I have already told your excellency of an innkeeper of Nîmes who had set up a little inn on the road from Bellegarde to Beaucaire."

" Yes," said Monte Cristo, " I perfectly recollect him; I think he was your colleague."

" Precisely," answered Bertuccio; " but he had, seven or eight years before this period, sold his establishment to a tailor at Marseilles, who having almost ruined himself in his old trade, wished to make his fortune in another. Of course, we made the same arrangements with the new landlord that we had with the old; and it was of this man that I intended to ask shelter."

" What was his name? " inquired the count, who seemed to become somewhat interested in Bertuccio's story.

" Gaspard Caderousse; he had married a woman from the village of Carconte, and whom we did not know by any other name than that of her village. She was suffering from the marsh-fever, and seemed dying by inches. As for her husband, he was a strapping fellow of forty, or forty-and-five, who had more than once, in time of danger, given ample proof of his presence of mind and courage."

" And you say," interrupted Monte Cristo, " that this took place towards the year——"

" 1829, M. le Comte."

" In what month? "

" June."

" The beginning or the end? "

" The evening of the 3rd."

" Ah," said Monte Cristo, " the evening of the 3rd of June, 1829. Go on."

" It was from Caderousse that I intended demanding shelter; and as we never entered by the door that opened on to the road, I resolved not to break through the rule, and climbing over the garden-hedge, I crept amongst the olive and wild fig trees, and fearing that Caderousse might have some one there, I entered a kind of shed in which I had often passed the night, and which was only separated from the inn by a partition, in which holes had been made in order to enable us to watch an opportunity of announcing our presence. My intention was, if Caderousse was alone, to acquaint him with my presence, finish the meal the custom-house officers had interrupted, and profit by the threatened storm to return to the Rhone, and ascertain the state of our vessel and its crew. I stepped into the shed, and it was fortunate I did so, for at that moment Caderousse entered with a stranger.

" I waited patiently—not to overhear what they said, but because I could do nothing else; besides, the same thing had occurred often before. The man who was with Caderousse was evidently a stranger to the South of France. He was one of those merchants who come to sell jewellery at the fair of Beaucaire, and who, during the month the fair lasts, and during which there is so great an influx of merchants and customers from all parts of Europe, often have dealings to the amount of 100,000 to 150,000 francs (£4000 to £6000).

" Caderousse entered hastily.

" Then seeing that the room was, as usual, empty, and only guarded by the dog, he called to his wife:

" ' Hilloa! Carconte! ' said he, ' the worthy priest has not deceived us; the diamond is real.'

" An exclamation of joy was heard, and the staircase creaked beneath a feeble step.

" ' What do you say? ' asked is wife, pale as death.

" ' I say that the diamond is real, and that this gentleman, one of the first jewellers of Paris, will give us 50,000 francs for it (£2000). Only in order to satisfy himself it really belongs to us, he wishes you to relate to him, as I have done already, the miraculous manner in which the diamond came into our possession. In the meantime, please to sit down, monsieur, and I will fetch you some refreshment.'

" The jeweller examined attentively the interior of the inn and the visible poverty of the persons who were about to sell him a diamond that seemed to have come from the casket of a prince.

" ' Relate your story, madame,' said he, wishing, no doubt, to profit by the absence of the husband, so that the latter could not influence the wife's story, to see if the two recitals tallied.

" ' Oh! ' returned she, ' it was a gift of Heaven! My husband was a great friend, in 1814 or 1815, of a sailor named Edmond Dantès. This poor fellow, whom Caderousse had forgotten, had not forgotten him, and at his death bequeathed this diamond to him.'

" ' But how did he obtain it? ' asked the jeweller; ' had he it before he was imprisoned? '

" ' No, monsieur; but it appears that in prison he made the acquaintance of a rich Englishman; and as in prison he fell sick, and Dantès took the same care of him as if he had been his brother, the Englishman, when he was set free, gave this stone to Dantès, who, less fortunate, died, and, in his turn, left it us, and charged the excellent abbé, who was here this morning, to deliver it.'

" ' The same story! ' muttered the jeweller; ' and, improbable as it seems at first, the history may be true: there's only the price we are not agreed about.'

" ' How not agreed about? ' said Caderousse; ' I thought we agreed for the price I asked.'

" ' That is,' replied the jeweller, ' I offered 40,000 francs.'

" ' Forty thousand! ' cried La Carconte; ' we will not part with it for that sum; the abbé told us it was worth 50,000 without the setting.'

" ' What was the abbé's name? ' asked the indefatigable questioner.

" ' The Abbé Busoni,' said La Carconte.

" ' He was a foreigner? '

" ' An Italian from the neighbourhood of Mantua, I believe.'

" ' Let me see this diamond again,' replied the jeweller; ' the first time you are often mistaken as to the value of a stone.'

" Caderousse took from his pocket a small case of black shagreen, opened, and gave it to the jeweller. At the sight of the diamond, which was as large as a hazel-nut, La Carconte's eyes sparkled with cupidity."

" And what did you think of this fine story, eavesdropper? " said Monte Cristo; " did you credit it? "

" Yes, your excellency. I did not look on Caderousse as a bad man, and I thought him incapable of committing a crime, or even a theft."

" That did more honour to your heart than to your experience, M. Bertuccio. Had you known this Edmond Dantès, of whom they spoke? "

" No, your excellency, I had never heard of him before, and never but once afterwards, and that was from the Abbé Busoni himself, when I saw him in the prison at Nîmes."

" Go on."

" The jeweller took the ring, and drawing from his pocket a pair of steel pliers and a small set of copper scales, he took the stone out of its setting, and weighed it carefully.

" ' I will give you 45,000,' said he, ' but not a halfpenny more; besides, as that is the exact value of the stone, I brought just that sum with me.'

" ' Oh, that's no matter,' replied Caderousse, ' I will go back with you to fetch the other 5000 francs.'

" ' No,' returned the jeweller, giving back the diamond and the ring to Caderousse; ' no, it is worth no more, and I am sorry I offered so much, for the stone has a flaw in it, which I had not seen. However, I will not go from my word, and I will give 45,000.'

" ' At least, replace the diamond in the ring,' said Carconte sharply.'

" ' Ah, true,' replied the jeweller, and he reset the stone.

" ' No matter,' observed Caderousse, replacing the box in his pocket, ' some one else will purchase it.'

" ' Yes,' continued the jeweller; ' but some one else will not be so easy as I am, or content himself with the same story. It is not natural that a man like you should possess such a diamond. He will inform against you. You will have to find the Abbé Busoni, and abbés who give diamonds worth two thousand louis are rare. Justice will seize it, and put you in prison. If at the end of three or four months you are set at liberty, the ring will be lost,

or a false stone worth three francs will be given you instead of a
diamond worth 50,000 or perhaps 55,000 francs, but which you
must allow one runs considerable risk in purchasing.'

"Caderousse and his wife looked eagerly at each other.

"'No,' said Caderousse, 'we are not rich enough to lose
500 francs.'

"'As you please my dear sir,' said the jeweller; 'I had,
however, as you see, brought you the money in bright coin.'

"And he drew from his pocket a handful of gold, which he
made to sparkle in the dazzled eyes of the innkeeper, and in the
other hand he held a packet of bank-notes.

"There was evidently a severe struggle in the mind of Caderousse; it was evident that the small shagreen case, which he
turned and re-turned in his hand, did not seem to him commen-
surate in value to the enormous sum which fascinated his gaze.

"He turned towards his wife.

"'What do you think of this?' he asked, in a low voice.

"'Let him have it,—let him have it,' she said. 'If he returns
to Beaucaire without the diamond, he will inform against us;
and, as he says, who knows if we shall ever again see the Abbé
Busoni? In all probability we shall never see him.'

"'Well, then, so I will!' said Caderousse; 'so you may have
the diamond for 45,000 francs. But my wife wants a gold chain,
and I want a pair of silver buckles.'

"The jeweller drew from his pocket a long flat box, which
contained several samples of the articles demanded.

"'Here,' he said, 'I am very plain in my dealings,—take your
choice.'

"The woman selected a gold chain worth about five louis,
and the husband a pair of buckles, worth, perhaps, fifteen francs.

"'I hope you will not complain now?' said the jeweller.

"'The abbé told me it was worth 50,000 francs' muttered
Caderousse.

"'Come, come—give it to me! What a strange fellow you
are!' said the jeweller, taking the diamond from his hand. 'I
gave you 45,000 francs,—that is, 2500 livres of income,—a fortune
such as I wish I had myself, and you are not satisfied!'

"'And the five-and-forty thousand francs,' inquired Caderousse
in a hoarse voice, 'where are they? Come,—let us see them!'

"'Here they are,' replied the jeweller; and he counted out
upon the table 15,000 francs in gold, and 30,000 francs in bank-
notes.

"'Wait whilst I light the lamp,' said La Carconte; 'it is
growing dark, and there may be some mistake.'

"In fact, night had come on during this conversation, and with night the storm which had been threatening for the last half-hour. The thunder was heard growling in the distance; but neither the jeweller, nor Caderousse, nor La Carconte seemed to heed it, absorbed as they were all three with the demon of gain. I myself felt a strange kind of fascination at the sight of all this gold and all these bank-notes; it seemed to me that I was in a dream; and, as it always happens in a dream, I felt myself riveted to the spot. Caderousse counted and again counted the gold and the notes, then handed them to his wife who counted and counted then again in her turn. During this time, the jeweller made the diamond play and sparkle beneath the ray of the lamp, and the gem threw out jets of light which made him unmindful of those which—precursors of the storm—began to play in at the windows.

" ' Well,' inquired the jeweller; ' is the cash all right? '

" ' Yes,' said Caderousse. ' Give me the pocket-book, La Carconte, and find a bag somewhere.'

" La Carconte went to a cupboard, and returned with an old leathern pocket-book, from which she took some greasy letters, and put in their place the bank-notes, and a bag, in which were at the moment two or three crowns of six livres each, and which, in all probability, formed the entire fortune of the miserable couple.

" ' There,' said Caderousse; ' and now, although you have wronged us of perhaps 10,000 francs, will you have your supper with us? I invite you with goodwill.'

" ' Thank you,' replied the jeweller; ' it must be getting late, and I must return to Beaucaire,—my wife will be getting uneasy.' He drew out his watch, and exclaimed, ' *Morbleu!* nearly nine o'clock!—why, I shall not get back to Beaucaire before midnight! Good-night, my dears. If the Abbé Busoni should by any accident return, think of me.'

" ' In another week you will have left Beaucaire,' remarked Caderousse, ' for the fair finishes in a few days.'

" ' True; but that is no consequence. Write to me at Paris, to M. Joannes, in the Palais Royal, Stone Gallery, No. 45; I will make the journey on purpose to see him, if it is worth while.'

" At this moment there was a tremendous clap of thunder, accompanied by a flash of lightning so vivid, that it quite eclipsed the light of the lamp.

" ' Oh dear! ' exclaimed Caderousse. ' You cannot think of going out in such weather as this! '

" ' Oh, I am not afraid of thunder! ' said the jeweller.

" ' And then there are robbers,' said La Carconte. ' The road is never very safe during fair time.'

" ' Oh, as to the robbers,' said Joannes, ' here is something for them;' and he drew from his pocket a pair of small pistols, loaded to the muzzle. 'Here,' said he, 'are dogs who bark and bite at the same time: they are for the two first who shall have a longing for your diamond, Daddy Caderousse.'

"Caderousse and his wife again interchanged a meaning look. It seemed as though they were both inspired at the same time with some horrible thought.

"'Well, then, a good journey to you!' said Caderousse.

"'Thank ye,' replied the jeweller. He then took his cane, which he had placed against an old cupboard, and went out. At the moment when he opened the door, such a gust of wind came in that the lamp was nearly extinguished. 'Oh,' said he, 'this is very nice weather; and two leagues to go in such a storm!'

"'Remain,' said Caderousse. 'You can sleep here.'

"'Yes—do stay,' added La Carconte, in a tremulous voice; 'we will take every care of you.'

"'No; I must sleep at Beaucaire. So, once more, good-night!'

"Caderousse followed him slowly to the threshold.

"'I can neither see heaven nor earth!' said the jeweller, who was outside the door. 'Do I turn to the right or left hand?'

"'To the right,' said Caderousse. 'You cannot go wrong,— the road is bordered by trees on both sides.'

"'Good,—all right!' said a voice almost lost in the distance.

"'Close the door!' said La Carconte; 'I do not like open doors when it thunders!'

"'Particularly when there is money in the house, eh?' answered Caderousse, double-locking the door.

"He came into the room, went to the cupboard, took out the bag and pocket-book, and both began, for the third time, to count their gold and bank-notes. I never saw such an expression of cupidity as the flickering lamp revealed in the two countenances. The woman, especially, was hideous; the feverish tremulousness she usually had was redoubled; her countenance had become livid, and her eyes resembled burning coals.

"'Why,' she inquired, in a hoarse voice, 'did you invite him to sleep here to-night?'

"'Why?' said Caderousse, with a shudder; 'why, that he might not have the trouble of returning to Beaucaire.'

"'Ah!' responded the woman, with an expression impossible to render; 'I thought it was for something else.'

"'Woman, woman,—why do you have such ideas?' cried Caderousse; 'or if you have them, why don't you keep them to yourself?'

"'Well!' said La Carconte, after a moment's pause; 'you are not a man!'

" ' What do you mean? ' added Caderousse.

" ' If you had been a man, you would not have let him go from here.'

" ' Woman! '

" 'Or else he should not have reached Beaucaire.'

" ' Woman! '

" ' The road takes a turn,—he is obliged to follow it,—whilst alongside the canal there is a shorter road.'

" ' Woman!—you offend the *bon Dieu*! There!—listen! ' And at this moment there was heard a tremendous peal of thunder, whilst the livid lightning illumined the room; and the thunder then rolling away to a distance, seemed as though it left the cursed abode lingeringly.

" ' Mercy! ' said Caderousse, crossing himself.

" At the same moment, and in the midst of the silence so full of terror which usually follows claps of thunder, they heard a knocking at the door. Caderousse and his wife started and looked aghast at each other!

" ' Who's there? ' cried Caderousse, rising, and drawing up in a heap the gold and notes scattered over the table, and which he covered with his two hands.

" ' It is I! ' shouted a voice.

" ' And who are you? '

" ' Eh, *pardieu!* Joannes, the jeweller! '

" ' Well, and you said I offended the *bon Dieu*,' said Carconte, with a horrid smile. ' Why, it is the *bon Dieu* who sends him back again.'

" Caderousse fell back, pale and breathless, in his chair.

" La Carconte, on the contrary, rose, and going with a firm step towards the door, opened it, saying, as she did so:

" ' Come in, dear M. Joannes.'

" ' *Ma foi!* ' said the jeweller, drenched with rain, ' it seems as if I was not to return to Beaucaire to-night. The shortest follies are best, my dear Caderousse. You offered me hospitality, and I accept it, and have returned to sleep beneath your friendly roof.'

" Caderousse stammered out some words, whilst he wiped away the damp that started to his brow. La Carconte double-locked the door behind the jeweller.

46

The Rain of Blood

"As the jeweller returned to the apartment, he cast around him a scrutinising glance—but there was nothing to excite suspicion, if it existed not, or to confirm it, if already awakened. Caderousse's hands still grasped his gold and bank-notes, and La Carconte called up her sweetest smiles while welcoming the reappearance of their guest.

" ' Heyday! ' said the jeweller, ' you seem, my good friends, to have had some fears respecting the accuracy of your money, by counting it over so carefully directly I was gone.'

" ' No, no,' answered Caderousse, ' that was not my reason, I can assure you; but the circumstances by which we have become possessed of this wealth are so unexpected, as to make us scarcely credit our good fortune, and it is only by placing the actual proof of our riches before our eyes that we can persuade ourselves the whole affair is not a dream.'

" The jeweller smiled.

" ' Have you any other guests in your house? ' inquired he.

" ' Nobody but ourselves,' replied Caderousse; 'the fact is, we do not lodge travellers—indeed, our tavern is so near to the town, that nobody would think of stopping here.'

" ' Then I am afraid I shall very much inconvenience you! '

" ' Oh, dear me, no!—indeed, good sir, you will not,' said La Carconte, in her most gracious manner. ' I vow and protest your passing the night under shelter of our poor roof will not make the slightest difference in the world to us.'

" ' But where will you manage to stow me? '

" ' In the chamber overhead.'

" ' Surely that is where you yourselves sleep? '

" 'Never mind that, we have a second bed in the adjoining room.'

" Caderousse stared at his wife with much astonishment.

" The jeweller, meanwhile, was humming a song as he stood warming himself by the bright, cheering blaze of a large fagot kindled by the attentive Carconte, to dry the wet garments of her guest; and this done, she next occupied herself in arranging his supper, by spreading a napkin at the end of the table, and placing on it the slender remains of their dinner, to which she added three or four fresh-laid eggs.

"Caderousse had once more parted with his treasures—the bank-notes were replaced in the pocket-book, the gold put back into the bag, and the whole carefully locked in the *armoire*, which formed his stronghold; he then commenced pacing the room with a pensive and gloomy air, glancing from time to time at the jeweller, who stood reeking with the steam from his wet clothes, and merely changing his place on the warm hearth to enable the whole of the garments to be in turns dried by the genial heat that issued from it.

" ' Now then, my dear sir,' said La Carconte, as she placed a bottle of wine on the table, ' supper is ready whenever you are inclined to partake of it.'

" ' But you are going to sit down with me, are you not? ' asked Joannes.

" ' I shall not take any supper to-night,' said Caderousse.

" ' We dined so very late,' hastily interposed La Carconte

" ' Then it seems I am to eat alone,' remarked the jeweller.

" ' Oh, we shall have the pleasure of waiting upon you,' answered La Carconte, with an eager attention she was not accustomed to manifest even to guests who paid for what they took.

" From one minute to another, Caderousse darted on his wife keen, searching glances, but rapid as the lightning-flash.

" The storm still continued.

" ' There! there! ' said La Carconte; ' do you hear that! Upon my word, you did well to return hither.'

" ' Nevertheless,' replied the jeweller, ' if by the time I have finished my supper, the tempest has at all abated, I shall make another attempt to complete my journey.'

" ' Oh,' said Caderousse, shaking his head, ' there is not the slightest chance of its abating—it is the mistral, and that will be sure to last till to-morrow morning.' He then sighed heavily.

" ' Well,' said the jeweller, as he placed himself at table, ' all I can say is, so much the worse for those who are abroad and cannot obtain a shelter.'

" ' Ah! ' chimed in La Carconte, ' they will have a wretched night of it, be they who they may.'

" The jeweller commenced eating his supper, and the woman, who was ordinarily so querulous and indifferent to all who approached her, was suddenly transformed into the most smiling and attentive hostess. Had the unhappy man on whom she lavished her assiduities been previously acquainted with her, so sudden an alteration might well have excited suspicion in his mind, or at least have greatly astonished him. Caderousse, meanwhile, continued in gloomy silence to pace the room, sedulously avoiding the sight of his guest but as soon as the stranger had completed his repast, the agitated innkeeper went eagerly to the door and opened it.

" ' The storm seems over,' said he.

" But as if to contradict his statement, at that instant a violent clap of thunder seemed to shake the house to its very foundation, while a sudden gust of wind, mingled with rain, extinguished the lamp he held in his hand. Trembling and awestruck, Caderousse hastily shut the door and returned to his guest, while La Carconte lighted a candle by the smouldering ashes that glimmered on the hearth.

" ' You must be tired,' said she to the jeweller; ' I have spread a pair of my finest and whitest sheets on your bed, so you have nothing to do but to sleep as soundly as I wish you may—you can easily find your room, it is exactly over this.'

" Joannes remained a short time listening whether the storm seemed to abate in its fury, but a brief space of time sufficed to assure him that, far from diminishing, the violence of the rain and thunder momentarily increased; resigning himself, therefore, to what seemed inevitable, he bade his host good-night, and mounted to his sleeping apartment. As he passed over my head, the flooring seemed to creak beneath his tread, proving how slight must be the division between us. The quick eager, glance of La Carconte followed him as he ascended the staircase, while Caderousse, on the contrary, turned his back, and seemed most anxiously to avoid even glancing at him.

" All these particulars did not strike me as painfully at the time as they have since done. In fact, all that had happened (with the exception of the story of the diamond, which certainly did wear an air of improbability) appeared natural enough, and called for neither apprehension nor mistrust. But, worn-out as I was with fatigue, and fully purposing to proceed onwards directly the tempest abated, I determined to take advantage of the comparative silence and tranquillity that prevailed to obtain the refreshment of a few hours' sleep. Overhead I could accurately distinguish every movement of the jeweller, who, after making the best arrangements in his power for passing a comfortable night, threw himself on his bed, and I could hear it creak and groan beneath his weight. Insensibly my eyelids grew heavy, deep sleep stole over me, and having no suspicion of anything wrong, I sought not to shake it off. For the last time I looked in upon the room where Caderousse and his wife were sitting; the former was seated upon one of those low wooden stools which, in country places, are frequently used instead of chairs; his back being turned towards me, prevented me from seeing the expression of his countenance—neither should I have been able to do so had he been placed differently, as his head was buried between his two hands. La Carconte continued to gaze on him for some time in contemptuous silence, then, shrugging up her shoulders, she took her seat immediately opposite to him. At this moment the expiring embers threw up a fresh flame from the kindling of a piece of wood that lay near, and a bright gleam was thrown on the scene and the actors in it. La Carconte still kept her eyes fixed on her husband, but as he made no sign of changing his position, she extended her hard, bony hand, and touched him on the forehead.

" Caderousse shuddered!—the woman's lips seemed to move, as though she were talking!—but whether she merely spoke in a undertone, or that my senses were dulled by sleep, I did not catch a word she uttered. Confused sights and sounds seemed to float before me, and gradually I fell into a deep, heavy sleep. How long I had been in this unconscious state I know not, when I was suddenly aroused by the report of a pistol, followed by a fearful cry. Weak and tottering footsteps resounded across the chamber above me, and the next instant a dull, heavy weight seemed to fall powerless on the staircase. I had not yet fully recovered my recollection, when again I heard groans, mingled with half-stifled cries, as if from persons engaged in a deadly struggle. These evidences of the perpetration of some violent deed effectually roused me from my drowsy lethargy. Hastily raising myself on one arm, I looked around, but all was dark; and it seemed to me as if the rain must have penetrated through the flooring of the room above, for some kind of moisture appeared to fall, drop by drop, upon my forehead, and when I passed my hand across my brow, I felt it wet and clammy.

" To the fearful noises that had awakened me had succeeded the most perfect silence,—unbroken, save by the footsteps of a man walking about in the chamber above. By the creaking of the staircase, I judged the individual, whoever he was, was proceeding to the lower apartment. In another minute I heard some person moving there; and, looking through, I saw a man stooping towards the fire to light a candle he held in his hand. As he turned round, I recognised the features of Caderousse,—pale, ghastly, and convulsed,—while the front and sleeves of his dress were covered with blood. Having obtained the light he had evidently descended to seek, he hurried upstairs again and once more I heard his rapid and uneasy step in the chamber above. Ere long he came below, holding in his hand the small shagreen case, which he opened, to assure himself it contained the diamond, —seemed to hesitate as to which pocket he should put it in; then, as if dissatisfied with the security of either pocket, he deposited it in his red handkerchief, which he carefully rolled round his head. After this he took from his cupboard the bank-notes and gold he had put there, thrust the one in the pocket of his trousers, and the other into that of his waistcoat,—hastily tied up a small bundle of linen, and rushing towards the door, disappeared in the darkness of the night.

" Then all became clear and manifest to me; and I reproached myself with what had happened, as though I myself had done the guilty deed. I fancied that I still heard faint moans, and imagining that the unfortunate jeweller might not be quite dead, I determined to go to his relief, by way of atoning in some slight degree, not for the crime I had committed, but for that which I had not endeavoured to prevent. For this purpose I applied all the strength I possessed to force an entrance from the cramped spot in which I lay, to the adjoining room. The badly arranged planks which alone divided me from it, yielded to my efforts, and I found myself in the house. Hastily snatching up the lighted candle, I hurried to the staircase. Towards the middle of it I stumbled over a human body lying quite across the stairs. As I stooped to raise it, I discovered in the agonised features those of La Carconte. The pistol I had heard had doubtless been discharged at the unfortunate woman, whose throat it had frightfully lacerated, leaving a gaping wound, from which, as well at the mouth, the blood was welling in sanguinary streams.

" Finding the miserable creature past all human aid, I strode past her and ascended to the sleeping chamber, which presented an appearance of the wildest disorder. The furniture had been knocked over in the deadly struggle that had taken place there, and the sheets, to which the unfortunate jeweller had doubtless clung, were dragged across the room. The murdered man lay on the ground, his head leaning against the wall, weltering in a gory stream, poured forth from three large wounds in his breast; there was a fourth gash, but the blood was prevented escaping in consequence of the weapon (a large table-knife) still sticking in it.

" I stumbled over some object; I stooped to examine—it was the second pistol, which had not gone off, probably from the powder being wet. I approached the jeweller, who was not quite dead, and at the sound of my footsteps, causing as they did the creaking of the floor, he opened his eyes, fixed them on me with an anxious and inquiring gaze, moved his lips as though trying to speak, then, overcome by the effort, fell back and expired.

" This appalling sight almost bereft me of my senses and finding that I could no longer be of service to any one in the house, my only desire was to fly from such an accumulation of horrors as quickly as I could. Almost distracted, I rushed towards the staircase, clasping my burning temples with both hands, and uttering cries of horror.

" Upon reaching the room below, I found five or six custom-house officers, accompanied by an armed troop of soldiery, who immediately seized me, ere, indeed, I had sufficiently collected my ideas to offer any resistance; in truth, my senses seemed to have wholly forsaken me and when I strove to speak, a few inarticulate sounds alone escaped my lips.

" As I noticed the significant manner in which the whole party pointed to my blood-stained garments, I involuntarily surveyed myself, and then I discovered that the thick warm drops that had so bedewed me as I lay beneath the staircase, must have been the blood of La Carconte. Paralysed with horror, I could barely indicate by a movement of my hand the spot where I had concealed myself.

" ' What does he mean? ' asked a gendarme.

" One of the officers went to the place I directed.

" ' He means,' replied the man upon his return, ' that he effected his entrance by means of this hole; ' showing the place where I had broken my way through the planks into the house.

" Then, and not before, the true nature of my situation flashed on me, and I saw that I was considered the guilty author of all that had occurred. With this frightful conviction of my danger, I recovered force and energy enough to free myself from the hands of those who held me, while I managed to stammer forth:

" ' I did not do it! Indeed, indeed, I did not! '

" A couple of gendarmes held the muzzles of their carbines against my breast.

" ' Stir but a step,' said they, ' and you are a dead man! '

" ' Why should you threaten me with death,' cried I, ' when I have already declared my innocence? '

" ' Tush! tush! ' cried the men; ' keep your innocent stories to tell to the judge at Nîmes. Meanwhile, come along with us, and the best advice we can give you is to do so unresistingly.'

" Alas! resistance was far from my thoughts, I was utterly overpowered by surprise and terror; and without a word I suffered myself to be handcuffed and tied to a horse's tail, in which disgraceful plight I arrived at Nîmes.

" It seems I had been tracked by an officer, who had lost sight of me near the tavern. Feeling assured that I intended to pass the night there, he had returned to summon his comrades, who just arrived in time to hear the report of the pistol, and to take me in the midst of such circumstantial proofs of my guilt as rendered all hopes of proving my innocence utterly at an end. One only chance was left me, that of beseeching the magistrate before whom I was taken to cause every inquiry to be made for an individual named the Abbé Busoni, who had stopped at the inn of the Pont du Gard, on the morning previous to the murder. If, indeed, Caderousse had not invented the story relative to the diamond, and that there existed no such person as the Abbé Busoni, in which case I was lost past redemption, or, at least, my life hung upon the feeble chance of Caderousse himself being apprehended and confessing the whole truth.

" Two months passed away in hopeless expectation on my part, while I must do the magistrate justice by declaring he used every means to obtain information of the person I declared could exculpate me if he would. Caderousse still evaded all pursuit, and I had resigned myself to what seemed my inevitable fate. My trial was to come on at the approaching sessions; when on the 8th of September, that is to say, precisely three months and five days after the events which had perilled my life, the Abbé Busoni, whom I never ventured to believe I should see, presented himself at the prison doors, saying he understood one of the prisoners wished to speak to him; he added, that having learned the particulars of my imprisonment, he hastened to comply with my desire. You may easily imagine with what eagerness I welcomed him, and how minutely I related the whole of what I had seen and heard. I felt some degree of nervousness as I entered upon the history of the diamond; but to my inexpressible astonishment, he confirmed it in every particular, and to my equal surprise, he seeked to place entire belief in all I stated. And then it was, that won by his mild charity, perceiving him acquainted with all the habits and customs of my own country, and considering also that pardon for the only crime of which I was really guilty might come with a double power from lips so benevolent and kind, I besought him to receive my confession, under the seal of which I recounted the affair of Auteuil, in all its details, as well as every other transaction of my life. That which I had done by the impulse of my best feelings, produced the same effect as though it had been the result of calculation. My voluntary confession of the assassination at Auteuil, proved to him that I had not committed that with which I stood accused. When he quitted me, he] bade me be of good courage, and rely upon his doing all in his power to convince my judges of my innocence.

" I had speedy proofs that the excellent abbé was engaged in my behalf, for the rigours of my imprisonment were alleviated by .

many trifling though acceptable indulgences; and I was told that my trial was to be postponed to the assizes following those now being held.

" In the interim it pleased Providence to cause the apprehension of Caderousse, who was discovered in some distant country, and brought back to France, where he made a full confession, refusing to make the fact of his wife's having suggested and arranged the murder any excuse for his own guilt. The wretched man was sentenced to the galleys for life, and I immediately set at liberty."

" And then it was, I presume," said Monte Cristo, " that you came to me as the bearer of a letter from the Abbé Busoni? "

" It was, your excellency; the benevolent abbé took an evident interest in all that concerned me.

" ' Your mode of life as a smuggler,' said he to me one day, ' will be the ruin of you if you persist in it; let me advise you when you get out of prison to choose something more safe as well as respectable.'

" ' But how,' inquired I, ' am I to maintain myself and my poor sister? '

" ' A person, whose confessor I am,' replied he, ' and who entertains a high regard for me, applied to me a short time since to procure him a confidential servant. Would you like such a post? If so, I will give you a letter of introduction to the friend I allude to.'

" ' With thankfulness shall I profit by your permitting me to wait upon the gentleman you speak of.'

" ' One thing you must do; swear solemnly that I shall never have reason to repent my recommendation.'

" I extended my hand, and was about to pledge myself by any promise he would dictate, but he stopped me.

" ' It is unnecessary for you to bind yourself by any vow,' said he; ' I know and admire the Corsican nature too well to fear you! Here, take this,' continued he, after rapidly writing the few lines I brought to your excellency, and upon receipt of which you deigned to receive me into your service, and I venture most respectfully, and humbly, to ask whether your excellency has ever had cause to repent having done so? "

" On the contrary, Bertuccio, I have ever found you faithful, honest, and deserving. One fault I find with you, and that is, your not having placed sufficient confidence in me."

" Indeed, your excellency, I know not what you mean! "

" Simply this: how comes it, that having both a sister and an adopted son, you have never spoken to me of either? "

" Alas! I have still to recount the most distressing period of my life. Anxious as you may suppose I was to behold and comfort my dear sister, I lost no time in hastening to Corsica, but when I arrived at Rogliano, I found a house of mourning and of desolation, the consequences of a scene so horrible that the neighbours remember and speak of it to this day. Acting by my advice, my poor sister had refused to comply with the unreasonable demands of Benedetto, who was continually tormenting her for money, as long as he believed there was a sou left in her possession. One morning that he had demanded money, threatening her with the severest consequences if she did not supply him with what he desired, he disappeared throughout the whole of the day, leaving the kind-hearted Assunta, who loved him as if he were her own child, to weep over his conduct and bewail his absence. Evening came, and still with all the patient solicitude of a mother she watched for his return.

" As the eleventh hour struck, he entered with a swaggering air, attended by two of the most dissolute and reckless of his ordinary companions. As poor Assunta rose to clasp her truant in her arms, forgetting all but the happiness of seeing him again, she was seized upon by the three ruffians, while the unnatural Benedetto exclaimed:

" ' Come, if the old girl refuses to tell us where she keeps her money, let us just give her a taste of the torture; that will make her find her tongue, I'll engage.'

" It unfortunately happened that our neighbour, Wasilio, was at Bastia, leaving no person in his house but his wife; no human creature except she could hear or see anything that took place within our dwelling. Two of the brutal companions of Benedetto held poor Assunta, who, unable to conceive that any harm was intended to her, smiled innocently and kindly in the face of those who were soon to become her executioners, while the third ruffian proceeded to barricade the doors and windows, then returning to his infamous accomplices, the three united in stifling the cries uttered by the poor victim at the sight of these alarming preparations; this effected, they dragged the unoffend-ing object of their barbarity towards the fire, on which they forcibly held her feet, expecting by this diabolical expedient to wring from her where her supposed treasure was secreted. In the struggles made by my poor sister, her clothes caught fire, and her fiendish and cowardly tormentors were compelled to let go their hold in order to preserve themselves from sharing the same fate. Covered with flames, Assunta rushed wildly to the door, but it was fastened. Tortured by the agony she endured, the unfortunate sufferer flew to the windows, but they were also strongly barricaded. Then her cries and shrieks of anguish filled the place; to these succeeded convulsive sobs and deep groans, which, subsiding in faint moans, at length died away, and all was still as the grave.

"Next morning, as soon as the wife of Wasilio could muster up courage to venture abroad, she caused the door of our dwelling to be opened by the public authorities, when Assunta, though dreadfully burnt, was found still breathing. Every drawer and closet in the house had been forced open, and everything worth carrying off stolen from them.

"Benedetto never again appeared at Rogliano, neither have I since that day either seen or heard anything concerning him.

"It was subsequently to these dreadful events that I waited on your excellency, to whom it would have been folly to have mentioned Benedetto, since all trace of him seemed entirely lost, or of my sister, since she was dead."

"And in what light did you view the tragical occurrence?" inquired Monte Cristo.

"As a punishment for the crime I had committed," answered Bertuccio. "Oh, those Villeforts are an accursed race!"

"Truly they are," murmured the count, with a most singular expression of countenance.

"And now," resumed Bertuccio, "your excellency may, perhaps, be able to comprehend that this place, which I revisit for the first time,—this garden, the actual scene of my crime,— must have given rise to reflections of no very agreeable nature, and produced that gloom and depression of spirits which excited the notice of your excellency, who was pleased to express a desire to know the cause. At this instant, a shudder passes over me as I reflect that possibly I am now standing on the very grave in which lies M. de Villefort, by whose hand the ground was dug to receive the corpse of his child."

"It may be so," said Monte Cristo, rising from the bench on which he had been sitting: "but," added he, in a lower tone, "whether the procureur du roi be dead or not, the Abbé Busoni did right to send you to me, and you have also acted extremely properly in relating to me the whole of your history, as it will prevent my forming any erroneous opinions concerning you in future. As for that Benedetto, who so grossly belied his name, have you never made any effort to trace out whither he has gone, or what has become of him?"

"No; far from wishing to learn whither he had betaken himself, I should have shunned the possibility of meeting him, as I would a wild beast or a savage monster. Thank God, I have never heard his name mentioned by any person, and I hope and believe he is dead."

"Flatter not yourself that such is the case," replied the count;

" an all-wise Providence permits not sinners to escape thus easily from the punishment they have merited on earth, but reserves them to aid his own designs, using them as instruments whereby to work his vengeance on the guilty."

" I am content to have him live,"continued Bertuccio, " so that he spares me the misery of ever again beholding him. And now, M. le Comte," added the steward, bending humbly forward, " you know every secret of my life."

Bertuccio hid his face in his hands as he uttered these words, while Monte Cristo fixed on him a long and indescribable gaze.

After a brief silence, rendered still more solemn by the time and place, the count said, in a tone of melancholy wholly unlike his usual manner:

" In order to bring this conversation to a fitting termination (as I promise you never again to revert to it), I will repeat to you some words I have heard from the lips of the Abbé Busoni himself, and which I recommend you to treasure up for your consolation—that all earthly ills yield to two all-potent remedies, time and silence. And now leave me, I would enjoy the cool solitude of this place. The very circumstances which inflict on you as a principal in the tragic scene enacted here such painful emotions, are to me, on the contrary, a source of extreme delight, and serve but to enhance the value of this dwelling in my estimation. Retire within, Bertuccio, and tranquillise your mind: should your confessor be less indulgent to you in your dying moments than you found the Abbé Busoni, send for me, if I am still on earth, and I will soothe your ear with words that shall effectually calm and soothe your parting soul."

Bertuccio bowed lowly and respectfully, and turned away, sighing heavily as he quitted his patron.

When he had quite disappeared, Monte Cristo arose, and taking three or four steps onwards, he murmured:

" Here, beneath this plane-tree must have been where the infant's grave was dug. There is the little door opening into the garden. At this corner is the private staircase communicating with the sleeping apartment. There will be no necessity for me to make a note of these particulars, for there, before my eyes, beneath my feet all, around me, I have the plan sketched with all the living reality of truth."

After making the tour of the garden a second time, the count regained the house and re-entered his carriage; while Bertuccio, who perceived the thoughtful expression of his master's features, took his seat beside the driver without uttering a word. The carriage proceeded rapidly towards Paris.

That same evening, upon reaching his abode in the Champs

Elysées, the Count of Monte Cristo went over the whole building with the air of one long acquainted with each nook or corner. Nor, although preceding the party, did he once mistake one door for another, or commit the smallest error when choosing any particular corridor or staircase to conduct him to a place or suite of rooms he desired to visit. Ali was his principal attendant during the somewhat late hour of his survey. Having given various orders to Bertuccio relative to the improvements and alterations he desired to make in the house, the count, drawing out his watch, said to the attentive Nubian:

" It is half-past eleven o'clock; Haydée will not be long ere she arrives. Have the French attendants been summoned to await her coming? "

Ali extended his hands towards the apartments destined for the fair Greek, which were at a distance from the habitable part of the dwelling, and so effectually concealed by means of a tapestried entrance, that it would have puzzled the most curious to have divined that beyond that spot lay hid a suite of rooms, fitted up with a rich magnificence worthy of the lovely being who was to tenant them. Ali having pointed to the apartments counted three on the fingers of his right hand, and then, placing it beneath his head, shut his eyes, and feigned to sleep.

" I understand," said Monte Cristo, well-acquainted with Ali's pantomime; " you mean to tell me that three female attendants await their new mistress in her sleeping chamber."

Ali, with considerable animation, made a sign in the affirmative.

" The young lady must needs be fatigued with her journey," continued Monte Cristo, " and will, no doubt, wish to retire to rest immediately upon her arrival. Desire the French attendants not to weary her with questions, but merely to pay their respectful duty and retire. You will also see that the Greek servant holds no communication with those of this country."

Ali bowed obediently and reverentially.

Just at that moment voices were heard hailing the concierge. The gate opened, a carriage rolled down the avenue, and stopped at the flight of steps leading to the house. The count hastily descended, and presented himself at the already opened carriage-door to assist a young female, completely enveloped in a mantle of green and gold, to alight. The female raised the hand extended towards her to her lips, and kissed it with a mixture of love and respect. Some few words passed between them in that sonorous language in which Homer makes his gods converse. The female spoke with an expression of deep tenderness, while the count replied with an air of gentle gravity. Preceded by Ali, who carried a rose-coloured flambeau in his hand, the female, who was no other than the lovely Greek, who had been Monte Cristo's companion in Italy, was conducted to her apartments, while the count retired to the pavilion reserved for himself. In another hour every light in the house was extinguished.

47

Unlimited Credit

ABOUT two o'clock the following day a calèche, drawn by a pair of magnificent English horses, stopped at the door of Monte Cristo, and a person dressed in a blue coat, with buttons of a similar colour, a white waistcoat, over which was displayed a massive gold chain, brown trousers, and a quantity of black hair descending so low over his eyebrows as to leave it doubtful whether it were not artificial, so little did its jetty glossiness assimilate with the deep wrinkles stamped on his features, bent forwards from the carriage-door, on the panels of which were emblazoned the armorial bearings of a baron, and directed his groom to inquire at the porter's lodge whether the Count of Monte Cristo resided there, and if he were within. While waiting, the occupant of the carriage surveyed the house, the garden, so far as he could distinguish it, and the livery of the servants who passed to and fro, with an attention so close as to be somewhat impertinent.

The groom, in obedience to his orders, tapped at the window of the porter's lodge, saying:

" Pray, does not the Count of Monte Cristo live here? "

" His excellency does reside here," replied the concierge, " but——" added he, glancing an inquiring look at Ali.

Ali returned a sign in the negative.

" But what? " asked the groom.

" His excellency does not receive visitors to-day."

" Then take my master's card. You'll see who master is— M. le Baron Danglars! Be sure to give the card to the count, and say that, although in haste to attend the Chamber, my master came out of his way to have the honour of calling upon him."

" I never speak to his excellency," replied the concierge; " the valet-de-chambre will carry your message."

The groom returned to the carriage.

" Well? " asked Danglars.

The man, somewhat crestfallen by the rebuke he had received, detailed to his master all that had passed between himself and the concierge.

" Bless me! " murmured M. le Baron Danglars; " this must surely be a prince instead of a count by their styling him ' excellency,' and only venturing to address him by the medium of his valet-de-chambre. However, it does not signify; he has a letter of credit on me, so I must see him when he requires his money."

Then throwing, himself back in his carriage, Danglars called out to his coachman, in a voice that might be heard across the road:

" To the Chamber of Deputies."

Apprised in time of the visit paid him, Monte Cristo had, from behind the blinds of his pavilion, as minutely observed the baron by means of an excellent lorgnette as Danglars himself had scrutinised the house, garden, and servants.

" That fellow has a decidedly bad countenance," said the count, in a tone of disgust, as he shut up his glass into its ivory case. " Ali! " cried he, striking at the same time on the brazen gong. Ali appeared.

" Summon Bertuccio! " said the count.

Almost immediately Bertuccio entered the apartment.

" Did your excellency desire to see me? " inquired he.

" I did," replied the count. " You no doubt observed the horses standing a few minutes since at the door? "

" Certainly, your excellency: I noticed them for their remarkable beauty."

" Then, how comes it," said Monte Cristo, with a frown, " that, when I desired you to purchase for me the finest pair of horses to be found in Paris, you permitted so splendid a couple as those I allude to, to be in the possession of any one but myself? "

At the look of displeasure, added to the angry tone in which the count spoke, Ali turned pale and held down his head.

" It is not your fault, my good Ali," said the count in the Arabic language, and in a tone of such gentleness as none would have given him credit for being capable of showing, " it is not your fault. You do not profess to understand the choice of English horses."

The countenance of poor Ali recovered its serenity.

" Permit me to assure your excellency," said Bertuccio, " that the horses you speak of were not to be sold when I purchased yours."

Monte Cristo shrugged his shoulders.

" It seems, M. l'Intendant," said he, " that you have yet to learn that all things are to be sold to such as care to pay the price."

"M. le Comte is not, perhaps, aware that M. Danglars gave 16,000 francs for his horses?"

"Very well! then offer him double that sum; a banker never loses an opportunity of doubling his capital."

"Is your excellency really in earnest?" inquired the steward.

Monte Cristo regarded the person who durst presume to doubt his words with the look of one equally surprised and displeased.

"I have to pay a visit this evening," replied he. "I desire that these horses, with completely new harness, may be at the door with my carriage."

Bertuccio bowed, and was about to retire; but when he reached the door, he paused, and then said:

"At what o'clock does your excellency wish the carriage and horses ready?"

"At five o'clock," replied the count.

"I beg your excellency's pardon," interposed the steward, in a deprecating manner, "for venturing to observe that it is already two o'clock."

"I am perfectly aware of that fact," answered Monte Cristo calmly. Then, turning towards Ali, he said, "Let all the horses in my stables be led before the windows of your young lady, that she may select those she prefers for her carriage. Request her, also, to oblige me by saying whether it is her pleasure to dine with me; if so, let dinner be served in her apartments."

The count then motioned to Ali to follow him into his study, where they conversed long and earnestly together.

As the hand of the clock pointed to five o'clock the count struck thrice upon his gong. When Ali was wanted one stroke was given, two summoned Baptistin, and three Bertuccio.

The steward entered.

"My horses!" said Monte Cristo.

"They are at the door harnessed to the carriage as your excellency desired. Does M. le Comte wish me to accompany him?"

"No, the coachman, Ali, and Baptistin will be sufficient without you."

The count descended to the door of his mansion, and beheld his carriage drawn by the very pair of horses he had so much admired in the morning as the property of Danglars. As he passed them, he said:

"They are extremely handsome certainly, and you have done well to purchase them, although you were somewhat remiss not to have procured them sooner."

"Indeed, your excellency, I had very considerable difficulty in obtaining them, and, as it is, they have cost an enormous price."

" Does the sum you gave for them make the animals less beautiful? " inquired the count, shrugging his shoulders.

" Nay, if your excellency is satisfied, all is as I could wish it. Whither does M. le Comte desire to be driven? "

" To the residence of M. le Baron Danglars, Rue de la Chaussée d'Antin."

This conversation had passed as they stood upon the terrace from which a flight of stone steps led to the carriage-drive. As Bertuccio, with a respectful bow, was moving away, the count called him back.

" I have another commission for you, M. Bertuccio," said he; " I am desirous of having an estate by the seaside in Normandy, for instance between Havre and Boulogne. You see I give you a wide range. It will be absolutely necessary that the place you may select have a small harbour, creek, or bay, into which my vessel can enter and remain at anchor. She merely draws fifteen feet water. She must be kept in constant readiness to sail immediately I think proper to give the signal. Make the requisite inquiries for a place of this description, and when you have met with an eligible spot, visit it, and if it possess the advantages desired, purchase it at once in your own name. The corvette must now, I think, be on her way to Fécamp, must she not? "

" Certainly, your excellency; I saw her put to sea the same evening we quitted Marseilles."

" And the yacht? "

" Was ordered to remain at Martigues."

" 'Tis well! I wish you to write from time to time to the captains in charge of the two vessels, so as to keep them on the alert."

" And the steamboat? Has your excellency any orders to give respecting her? "

" She is at Chalons, is she not? "

" She is, my lord."

" The directions I gave you for the other two vessels may suffice for the steamboat also."

" I understand, my lord, and will punctually fulfil your commands."

" When you have purchased the estate I desire, I mean to establish constant relays of horses at ten leagues' distance one from the other along the northern and southern road."

" Your excellency may fully depend upon my zeal and fidelity in all things."

The count gave an approving smile, descended the terrace

steps, and sprang into his carriage, which, drawn by the beautiful animals so expensively purchased, was whirled along with incredible swiftness, and stopped only before the house of the banker.

Danglars was engaged at that moment presiding over a railroad committee. But the meeting was nearly concluded when the name of his visitor was announced. As the count's title sounded on his ear he rose, and addressing his colleagues, many of whom were members of either Chamber, he said:

" Gentlemen, I must pray you to excuse my quitting you thus; but a most ridiculous circumstance has occurred, which is this,— Thomson and French, the bankers at Rome, have sent to me a certain individual calling himself the Count of Monte Cristo, who is desirous of opening an account with me to any amount he pleases. I confess this is the drollest thing I have ever met with in the course of my extensive foreign transactions and you may readily suppose it has greatly roused my curiosity; indeed, so much did I long to see the bearer of so unprecedented an order for an unlimited credit, that I took the trouble this morning to call on the pretended count, for his title is a mere fiction—of that I am persuaded. We all know counts nowadays are not famous for their riches. But would you believe, upon arriving at the residence of the *soi-disant* Count of Monte Cristo, I was very coolly informed, ' He did not receive visitors that day! ' Upon my word, such airs are ridiculous, and befitting only some great millionaire or a capricious beauty. I made inquiries, and found that the house where the said count resides in the Champs Elysées is his own property, and certainly it was very decently kept up and arranged as far as I could judge from the gardens and exterior of the house. But," pursued Danglars, with one of his sinister smiles, " an order for unlimited credit calls for something like caution on the part of the banker on whom that order is given. These facts stated, I will freely confess I am very anxious to see the individual just now announced. I suspect a hoax is intended, but the good folks who thought fit to play it off on me knew but little whom they had to deal with."

Having delivered himself of this pompous address, uttered with a degree of energy that left the baron almost out of breath, he bowed to the assembled party and withdrew to his drawing-room, whose sumptuous fittings-up of white and gold had caused a great and admiring sensation in the Chaussée d'Antin.

It was to this apartment he had desired his guest to be shown, fully reckoning upon the overwhelming effect so dazzling a *coup d'œil* would produce.

He found the count standing before some copies of Albano and

Fattore that had been passed off to the bankers as originals; but which, copies of the paintings of those great masters as they were, seemed to feel their degradation in being brought into juxtaposition with the gaudy gilding that covered the ceiling.

The count turned round as he heard the entrance of Danglars into the room.

With a slight inclination of the head, Danglars signed to the count to be seated, pointing significantly to a gilded arm-chair, covered with white satin embroidered with gold.

The count obeyed.

" I have the honour, I presume, of addressing M. de Monte Cristo."

The count bowed.

" And I of speaking to Baron Danglars, Chevalier de la Légion d'Honneur, and Member of the Chamber of Deputies? "

With an air of extreme gravity Monte Cristo slowly enumerated the various titles engraved on the card left at his house by the baron.

Danglars felt all the irony contained in the address of his visitor. For a minute or two he compressed his lips as though seeking to conquer his rage ere he trusted himself to speak. Then, turning to his visitor, he said:

" You will, I trust, excuse my not having called you by your title when I first addressed you, but you are aware we are living under a popular form of government, and that I am, myself, a representative of the liberties of the people."

" So much so," replied Monte Cristo, " that while preserving the habit of styling yourself baron, you have deemed it advisable to lay aside that of calling others by their titles."

" Upon my word," said Danglars, with affected carelessness, " I attach no sort of value to such empty distinctions, but the fact, is, I was made Baron, and also Chevalier de la Légion d'Honneur, in consequence of some services I had rendered government, but——"

" You have abdicated your titles after the example set you by Messrs. de Montmorency and Lafayette?* Well, you cannot possibly choose more noble models for your conduct! "

" Why," replied Danglars, " I do not mean to say I have altogether laid aside my titles; with the servants, for instance— there I think it right to preserve my rank with all its outward forms."

" I see; to your domestics you are, ' My lord! ' ' M. le Baron! ' the journalists of the day style you ' Monsieur! ' while your constituents term you ' Citizen! ' "

Again Danglars bit his lips with baffled spite, he saw well

enough that he was no match for Monte Cristo in an argument of this sort, and he therefore hastened to turn to subjects more familiar to him, and calculated on having all the advantages on his side.

" Permit me to inform you, M. le Comte," said he, bowing, " that I have received a letter of advice from Thomson and French of Rome."

" I am glad to hear it, M. le Baron, for I must claim the privilege of so addressing you as well as your servants. I have acquired the bad habit of calling persons by their style and title from living in a country where barons are still met with, simply because persons are never suddenly elevated to a rank which is possessed only in right of ancestry. But as regards the letter of advice, I am charmed to find it has reached you; that will spare me the troublesome and disagreeable task of coming to you for money myself. You have received a regular letter of advice, therefore my cheques will be duly honoured, and we shall neither of us have to go out of our way in the transaction."

" There is one slight difficulty," said Danglars, " and that consists in my precisely comprehending the letter itself! "

" Indeed? "

" And for that reason I did myself the honour of calling upon you, in order to beg you would explain some part of it to me."

" With much pleasure! Pray, now I am here, let me know what it was that baffled your powers of comprehension! "

" Why," said Danglars, " in the letter—I believe I have it about me—(here he felt in his breast-pocket)—yes, here it is! Well, this letter gives M. le Comte de Monte Cristo unlimited credit on our house."

" And what is there that requires explaining in that simple fact, may I ask, M. le Baron? "

" Merely the term *unlimited*; nothing else, certainly."

" Is not that word known in France? Perhaps, indeed, it does not belong to the language; for the persons from whom you received your letter of advice are a species of Anglo-Germans, and very probably do not write very choice or accurate French."

" Oh, as for the composition of the letter, there is not the smallest error in it; but as regards the competency of the document, I certainly have doubts."

" Is it possible? " asked the count, assuming an air and tone of the utmost simplicity and candour. " Is it possible that Thomson and French are not looked upon as safe and solvent bankers? Pray tell me what you think, M. le Baron, for I feel uneasy, I can assure you, having some considerable property in their hands."

" Thomson and French are bankers of the highest repute," replied Danglars, with an almost mocking smile; " and it was not of their solvency or capability I spoke, but of the word *unlimited*, which, in financial affairs, is so extremely vague a term,—that—that——"

"In fact," said Monte Cristo, "that its sense is also without limitation."

"Precisely what I was about to say," cried Danglars. "Now, what is vague is doubtful; and, says the wise man, 'where there is doubt there is danger!'"

"Meaning to say," rejoined Monte Cristo, "that however Thomson and French may be inclined to commit acts of imprudence and folly, M. le Baron Danglars is not disposed to follow their example."

"How so, M. le Comte?"

"Simply thus; the banking-house of Thomson and French set no bounds to their engagements, while that of M. Danglars has its limits; truly he is wise as the sage whose prudent apophthegm he quoted but just now."

"Monsieur!" replied the banker, drawing himself up with a haughty air, "the amount of my capital, or the extent and solvency of my engagements, have never yet been questioned."

"It seems, then, reserved for me," said Monte Cristo coldly, "to be the first to do so."

"And by what right, sir?"

"By right of the objections you have raised, and the explanations you have demanded, which certainly imply considerable distrust on your part, either of yourself or me—the former, most probably."

"Well, sir," resumed Danglars, after a brief silence, "I will endeavour to make myself understood, by requesting you to inform me for what sum you propose to draw upon me?"

"Why, truly," replied Monte Cristo, determined not to lose an inch of the ground he had gained, "my reason for desiring an 'unlimited' credit was precisely because I did not know what money I might expend."

The banker now thought it his turn to show off, and make a display of wealth and consequence; flinging himself back therefore in his arm-chair, he said, with an arrogant and purse-proud air:

"Let me beg of you not to hesitate in naming your wishes; you will then be convinced that the resources of the house of Danglars, however limited, are still equal to meeting the largest demands; and were you even to require a million——"

"I beg your pardon!" interposed Monte Cristo.

"I observed," replied Danglars, with a patronising and pompous air, "that should you be hard pressed, the concern, of which I am the head, would not scruple to accommodate you to the amount of a million."

"A million?" retorted the count; "and what use can you possibly suppose so pitiful a sum would be to me? My dear sir, if a trifle like that could suffice me, I should never have given myself the trouble of opening an account for so contemptible an amount. A million! Excuse my smiling when you speak of a sum I am in the habit of carrying in my pocket-book or dressing-case."

And with these words Monte Cristo took from his pocket a small case containing his visiting-cards, and drew forth two orders on the treasury for 500,000 francs each, payable at sight to the bearer.

A man like Danglars was wholly inaccessible to any gentler method of correction. His upstart arrogance, his ostentatious vulgarity, were only assailable by blows dealt with the force and vigour of the present *coup*. Its effect on the banker was perfectly stunning; and as though scarcely venturing to credit his senses, he continued gazing from the paper to the count with a confused and mystified air.

"Come, come," said Monte Cristo, "confess honestly that you have not perfect confidence in the responsibility of the house of Thomson and French: there is nothing very strange in your exercising what seems to you a necessary caution; however, foreseeing that such might be the case, I determined, spite of my ignorance in such matters, to be provided with the means of banishing all scruples from your mind, and at the same time leaving you quite at liberty to act as you pleased in the affair. See, here are two similar letters to that you have yourself received; the one from the house of Arstein and Eskeles of Vienna to Baron de Rothschild, the other drawn from Baring of London to M. Laffitte. Now, sir, you have but to say the word, and I will spare you all uneasiness and alarm on the subject, by presenting my letter of credit at one or other of the establishments I have named."

The blow had struck home, and Danglars was entirely vanquished. With a trembling hand he took the two letters from Vienna and London from the count, who held them carelessly between his finger and thumb, as though to him they were mere everyday matters to which he attached but very little interest. Having carefully perused the documents in question, the banker proceeded to ascertain the genuineness of the signatures, and this he did with a scrutiny so severe as might have appeared insulting to the count, had it not suited his present purpose to mislead the banker in every respect.

" Well, sir," said Danglars, rising, after he had well convinced himself of the authenticity of the documents he held, and bowing, as though in adoration of a man, the thrice happy possessor of as many orders for unlimited credit on the three principal banks of Paris, " you have there signatures worth untold wealth; although your conversation and vouchers put an end to all mistrust in the affair, you must pardon me, M. le Comte, for confessing the most extreme astonishment."

" Nay, nay," answered Monte Cristo, with the easiest and most gentlemanly air imaginable, " 'tis not for such trifling sums as these to startle or astonish the banking-house of M. le Baron Danglars. Then, as all is settled as to forms between us, I will thank you to send a supply of money to me to-morrow."

" By all means, M. le Comte! What sum do you want? "

" Why," replied Monte Cristo, " since we mutually understand each other, we may as well fix a sum as the probable expenditure of the first year:—suppose we say six millions to——"

" Six millions! " gasped out Danglars,—" certainly, whatever you please."

" Then if I should require more," continued Monte Cristo, in a careless and indifferent manner, " why, of course, I should draw upon you; but my present intention is not to remain in France more than a year, and during that period I scarcely think I shall exceed the sum I mentioned. However, we shall see."

" The money you desire shall be at your house by ten o'clock to-morrow morning, M. le Comte," replied Danglars. " How would you like to have it? in gold, silver, or notes? "

" Half in gold, and the other half in bank-notes, if you please," said the count, rising from his seat.

" I must confess to you, M. le Comte," said Danglars, " that I have hitherto imagined myself acquainted with the degree of fortune possessed by all the rich individuals of Europe, and still wealth such as yours has been wholly unknown to me. May I presume to ask whether you have long possessed it? "

" It has been in the family a very long while," returned Monte Cristo, " a sort of treasure expressly forbidden to be touched for a certain period of years, during which the accumulated interest has doubled the capital. The period appointed by the testator for the disposal of these riches occurred only a short time ago; and they have only been employed by me within the last few years. Your ignorance on the subject, therefore, is easily accounted for. However, you will be better informed as to me and my possessions ere long."

And the count, while pronouncing these latter words, accompanied them with one of those ghastly smiles that used to strike terror into poor Franz d'Epinay.

"With your tastes and means of gratifying them," continued Danglars, "you will exhibit a splendour that must effectually put us poor miserable millionaires quite in the background. If perfectly agreeable to you, I shall do myself the honour of introducing you to Madame la Baronne Danglars. Excuse my impatience, M. le Comte, but a person of your wealth and influence cannot receive too much attention."

Monte Cristo bowed in sign that he accepted the proffered honour, and the financier immediately rang a small bell, which was answered by a servant in a showy livery.

"Is Madame la Baronne at home?" inquired Danglars.

"Yes, M. le Baron," answered the man.

"And alone?"

"No, M. le Baron, madame has visitors."

"Have you any objection to meet any persons who may be with madame, or do you desire to preserve a strict incognito?"

"No, indeed," replied Monte Cristo, with a smile; "I do not arrogate to myself the right of so doing."

"And who is with madame? M. Debray?" inquired Danglars, with an air of indulgence and good nature that made Monte Cristo smile, acquainted as he was with the secrets of the banker's domestic life.

"Yes, M. le Baron," replied the servant, "M. Debray is with madame."

Danglars nodded his head; then, turning to Monte Cristo, said, "M. Lucien Debray is an old friend of ours, and private secretary to the Ministre de l'Intérieur. As for my wife, I must tell you, she lowered herself by marrying me, for she belongs to one of the most ancient families in France. Her maiden name was De Servières, and her first husband was M. le Colonel Marquis de Nargonne."

"I have not the honour of knowing Madame Danglars, but I have already met M. Lucien Debray."

"Ah, indeed!" said Danglars, "and where was that?"

"At the house of M. de Morcerf."

"Oh! what! you are acquainted with the young viscount, are you?"

"We were together a good deal during the Carnival at Rome."

"True, true!" cried Danglars; "let me see—have I not heard talk of some strange adventure with bandits or thieves hid in ruins, and of his having had a miraculous escape?—I forget how, but I know he used to amuse my wife and daughter by telling them about it after his return from Italy."

" Madame la Baronne is waiting to receive you, gentlemen,"
said the servant, who had gone to inquire the pleasure of his
mistress.

" With your permission," said Danglars, bowing, " I will
precede you to show you the way."

" By all means," replied Monte Cristo; " I follow you."

48

The Dappled Grays

THE baron, followed by the count, traversed a long suite of
apartments, in which the prevailing characteristics were
heavy magnificence and the gaudiness of ostentatious wealth,
until he reached the boudoir of Madame Danglars, a small
octagonal-shaped room, hung with pink satin, covered with
white Indian muslin. The chairs were of ancient workmanship
and materials; over the doors were painted sketches of shepherds
and shepherdesses after the style and manner of Boucher;
and at each side pretty medallions in crayons, harmonising well
with the fittings-up of this charming apartment, the only one
throughout the vast mansion in which any distinctive taste prevailed. The truth was, it had been entirely overlooked in the
plan arranged and followed out by M. Danglars and his
architect, who had been selected to aid the baron in the great
work of improvement he meditated, solely because he was the
most fashionable and celebrated decorator of the day. The
ornamental part of the fittings-up of Madame Danglars' boudoir
had then been left entirely to herself and Lucien Debray. M.
Danglars, however, while possessing a great admiration for the
antique, as it was understood during the time of the Directory,
entertained the most sovereign contempt for the simple elegance
of his wife's favourite sitting-room—where, by the way, he was
never permitted to intrude, unless, indeed, he excused his own
appearance by ushering in some more agreeable visitor than
himself; and even then he had rather the air and manner of a
person who was himself introduced, than as being the presenter
of another, his reception being either cordial or frigid, in proportion as the individual who accompanied him chanced to please
or displease his lady wife.

As Danglars now entered he found Madame la Baronne
(who, although past the first bloom of youth, was still strikingly

handsome) seated at the piano, a most elaborate piece of cabinet and inlaid work, while Lucien Debray, standing before a small work-table, was turning over the pages of an album. Lucien had found time, preparatory to the count's arrival, to relate many particulars respecting him to Madame Danglars. It will be remembered that Monte Cristo had made a lively impression on the minds of all the party assembled at the breakfast given by Albert de Morcerf; and although Debray was not in the habit of yielding to such feelings, he had never been able to shake off the powerful influence excited in his mind by the impressive look and manner of the count. Consequently the description given by Lucien to the baroness bore the highly-coloured tinge of his own heated imagination. Already excited by the wonderful stories related of the count by De Morcerf, it is no wonder that Madame Danglars eagerly listened to, and fully credited, all the additional circumstances detailed by Debray. The sound of approaching footsteps compelled the animated pair to assume an appearance of calm indifference and worldly ease; the lady flew to her piano, and her companion snatched up an album which fortunately lay near, and seemed as though really interested in its contents. A most gracious welcome and unusual smile were bestowed on M. Danglars; the count, in return for his gentlemanly bow, received a formal though graceful curtsey; while Lucien exchanged with the count a sort of distant recognition, and with Danglars a free and easy nod.

" Baroness," said Danglars, " give me leave to present to you the Count of Monte Cristo, who has been most warmly recommended to me by my correspondents at Rome. I need but mention one fact to make all the ladies in Paris court his notice, and that is, that the noble individual before you has come to take up his abode in our fine capital for one year, during which brief period he proposes to spend six millions of money,—think of that! It sounds very much like an announcement of balls, fêtes, dinners, and picnic parties, in all of which I trust M. le Comte will remember us, as he may depend upon it we shall remember him in all the entertainments we may give, be they great or small."

In spite of the gross flattery and coarseness of this address, Madame Danglars could not forbear gazing with considerable interest on a man capable of expending six millions in twelve months, and who had selected Paris, for the scene of his princely extravagance.

" And when did you arrive here? " inquired she.

" Yesterday morning, madame."

" Coming as usual, I presume, from the extreme end of the

globe? Pardon me—at least such I have heard is your custom."

"Nay, madame! this time I have merely proceeded from Cadiz hither."

"You have selected a most unfavourable moment for your first visit to our city. Paris is a horrible place in summer! Balls, parties, and fêtes are over; the Italian opera is in London, the French opera everywhere except at Paris. As for the Théâtre Français, you know, of course, that it is nowhere;* the only amusement left us are the indifferent races held in the Champ de Mars and Satory.* Do you propose entering any horses at either of these races, M. le Comte?"

"I assure you, madame," replied Monte Cristo, "my present intentions are, to do whatever will tend to render my sojourn in Paris most agreeable to myself and others. I only pray I may find some kind, pitying friend who will commiserate my lamentable ignorance of such matters, and instruct me rightly to understand the habits and etiquette of this polished city."

"Are you fond of horses, Monsieur le Comte?"

"I have passed a considerable part of my life in the East, madame; and you are, doubtless, aware that the inhabitants of those climes value only two things—the fine breeding of their horses and the beauty of their females."

"Nay, M. le Comte!" said the baroness, "it would have been somewhat more gallant to have placed the ladies before the animals"

"You see, madame, how rightly I spoke when I said I required a preceptor to guide me in all my sayings and doings here."

At this instant the favourite attendant of Madame Danglars entered the boudoir; approaching her mistress, she spoke some words in an undertone. Madame Danglars turned very pale, then exclaimed:

"I cannot believe it; the thing is impossible!"

"I assure you, madame," replied the woman, "it is even as I have said."

Turning impatiently towards her husband, Madame Danglars demanded:

"Is this true?"

"Is what true, madame?" inquired Danglars, visibly agitated.

"That when my coachman was about to prepare my carriage, he discovered that the horses had been removed from the stables without his knowledge. I desire to know what is the meaning of this?"

"Be kind enough, madame, to listen to me," said Danglars.

"Fear not my listening,—ay, and attentively, too; for, in truth, I am most curious to hear what explanation you purpose offering for conduct so unparalleled. These two gentlemen shall decide between us; but, first, I will state the case to them. Gentlemen," continued the baroness, " among the ten horses in the stables of M. le Baron Danglars, are two that belong exclusively to me— a pair of the handsomest and most spirited creatures to be found in Paris. But to you, at least, M. Debray, I need not give a further description, because to you my beautiful pair of dappled grays were well known. Well! I had promised Madame de Villefort the loan of my carriage to drive to-morrow to the Bois de Boulogne; but when my coachman goes to fetch the grays from the stables, they are gone,—positively gone. No doubt, M. Danglars has sacrificed them to the selfish consideration of gaining some thousands of paltry francs. Oh! how I hate and detest that money-grasping nature! Heaven defend me from all the race of mercenary speculators! "

" Madame," replied Danglars, " the horses were not sufficiently quiet for you: they were scarcely four years old, and they made me extremely uneasy on your account."

" Nonsense! " retorted the baroness; " you could not have entertained any alarm on the subject, because you are perfectly well aware that I have recently engaged a coachman who is said to be the best in Paris. But, perhaps, you have disposed of the coachman as well as the horses? "

" My dear love! pray do not say any more about them, and I promise you another pair exactly like them in appearance, only more quiet and steady."

The baroness shrugged up her shoulders with an air of ineffable contempt, while her husband, affecting not to observe it, turned towards Monte Cristo, and said:

" Upon my word, M. le Comte I am quite sorry I was not sooner aware of your establishing yourself in Paris."

" And wherefore? " asked the count.

" Because I should have liked to have made you the offer of these horses. I have almost given them away, as it is; but, as I before said, I was anxious to get rid of them upon any terms. They were only fit for a young man; not at all calculated for a person at my time of life."

" I am much obliged by your kind intentions towards me," said Monte Cristo; " but this morning I purchased a very excellent pair of carriage-horses, and I do not think they were dear. There they are! Come M. Debray, you are a connoisseur, I believe, let me have your opinion upon them."

As Debray walked towards the window, Danglars approached his wife.

" I could not tell you before others," said he, in a low tone,

" the reason of my parting with the horses; but a most enormous price was offered me this morning for them. Some madman or fool, bent upon ruining himself as fast as he can, actually sent his steward to me to purchase them at any cost; and the fact is, I have gained 16,000 francs by the sale of them. Come, don't look so angry, and you shall have 4000 francs of the money to do what you like with, and Eugénie shall have 2000. There! what do you think now of the affair? Wasn't I right to part with the horses? "

Madame Danglars surveyed her husband with a look of withering contempt.

" What do I see? " suddenly exclaimed Debray.

" Where? " asked the baroness.

" I cannot be mistaken; there are your horses! The very animals we were speaking of harnessed to the count's carriage! "

" My dear, beautiful dappled grays? " demanded the baroness, springing to the window. " 'Tis indeed they! " said she.

Danglars looked absolutely stultified.

" How very singular! " cried Monte Cristo, with well-feigned astonishment.

Madame Danglars whispered a few words in the ear of Debray, who approached Monte Cristo, saying, " The baroness wishes to know what you paid her husband for the horses."

" I scarcely know," replied the count; " it was a little surprise prepared for me by my steward; he knew how desirous I was of meeting with precisely such a pair of horses,—and—so he bought them. I think, if I remember rightly, he hinted that he had given somewhere about 30,000 francs."

Debray conveyed the count's reply to the baroness.

Poor Danglars looked so crestfallen and discomfited that Monte Cristo assumed a pitying air towards him.

" See," said the count, " how very ungrateful women are! Your kind attention, in providing for the safety of the baroness by disposing of the horses, does not seem to have made the least impression on her. But so it is; a woman will often, from mere wilfulness, prefer that which is dangerous to that which is safe. Therefore, in my opinion, my dear baron, the best and easiest, way is to leave them to their fancies, and allow them to act as they please; and then, if any mischief follows, why, at least, they have no one to blame but themselves."

Danglars made no reply; he was occupied in anticipations of the coming scene between himself and the baroness, whose threatening looks and frowning brow, like that of Olympic Jove, predicted a fearful storm.

Debray, who perceived the gathering clouds, and felt no desire to witness the explosion of Madame Danglars' rage, suddenly recollected an appointment, which compelled him to take his leave; while Monte Cristo, unwilling to destroy the advantages he hoped to obtain by prolonging his stay, made a farewell bow and departed, leaving Danglars to endure the angry reproaches of his wife.

" Excellent! " murmured Monte Cristo to himself, as he retraced the way to his carriage. " All has gone according to my wishes. The domestic peace of this family is henceforth in my hands. Now, then, to play another, master-stroke by which I shall gain the heart of both husband and wife—delightful! Still," added he, " amid all this, I have not yet been presented to Mademoiselle Eugénie Danglars, whose acquaintance I should have been glad to make. But never mind," pursued he, with that peculiar smile that at times lighted up his countenance, " it matters not for the present. I am on the spot, and have plenty of time before me—by and by will do for that part of my scheme."

The count's further meditations were interrupted by his arrival at his own abode. Two hours afterwards, Madame Danglars received a most flattering epistle from the count, in which he entreated her to receive back her favourite " dappled grays "; protesting that he could not endure the idea of making his *début* in the Parisian world of fashion with the knowledge that his splendid equipage had been obtained at the price of a lovely woman's regrets. The horses were sent back wearing the same harness they had done in the morning; the only difference consisted in the rosettes worn on the heads of the animals being adorned with a large diamond placed in the centre of each, by order of the count. To Danglars Monte Cristo also wrote, requesting him to excuse the whimsical gift of a capricious millionaire, and to beg of Madame la Baronne to pardon the Eastern fashion adopted in the return of the horses.

During the evening Monte Cristo quitted Paris for Auteuil, accompanied by Ali. The following day about three o'clock, a single blow struck on the gong, summoned Ali to the presence of the count.

" Ali," observed his master, as the Nubian entered the chamber, " you have frequently explained to me how more than commonly skilful you are in throwing the lasso, have you not? "

Ali drew himself up proudly, and then returned a sign in the affirmative.

" I thought I did not mistake. With your lasso you could stop an ox? "

Again Ali repeated his affirmative gesture.

" Or a tiger? "

Ali bowed his head in token of assent.

" A lion, even? "

Ali sprung forwards, imitating the action of one throwing the lasso; then of a strangled lion.

" I understand," said Monte Cristo; " you wish to tell me you have hunted the lion? "

Ali smiled, with triumphant pride, as he signified that he had indeed both chased and captured many lions.

" But do you believe you could arrest the progress of two horses rushing forwards with ungovernable fury? "

The Nubian smiled.

" It is well," said Monte Cristo; " then listen to me. Ere long a carriage will dash past here, drawn by the pair of dappled gray horses you saw me with yesterday; now, at the risk of your own life, you must manage to stop those horses before my door."

Ali descended to the street, and marked a straight line on the pavement immediately at the entrance of the house, and then pointed out the line he had traced to the count, who was watching him. The count patted him gently on the back—his usual mode of praising Ali—who, pleased and gratified with the commission assigned him, walked calmly towards a projecting stone forming the angle of the street and house, and, seating himself thereon, began to smoke his chibouque, while Monte Cristo re-entered his dwelling, perfectly assured of the success of his plan. Still, as five o'clock approached, and the carriage was momentarily expected by the count, the indication of more than common impatience and uneasiness might be observed in his manner. He stationed himself in a room commanding a view of the street, pacing the chamber with restless steps, stopping merely to listen from time to time for the sound of approaching wheels, then to cast an anxious glance on Ali: but the regularity with which the Nubian puffed forth the smoke of his chibouque, proved that he at least was wholly absorbed in the enjoyment of his favourite occupation. Suddenly a distant sound of rapidly advancing wheels was heard, and almost immediately a carriage appeared, drawn by a pair of wild ungovernable horses, who rushed forward as though urged by the fiend himself, while the terrified coachman strove in vain to restrain their furious speed.

In the vehicle was a female, apparently young, and a child of about seven or eight years of age. Terror seemed to have deprived them even of the power of uttering a cry, and both were clasped in each other's arms, as though determined not to be parted by death itself. The carriage creaked and rattled as it flew over the rough stones; and had it encountered the slightest impediment to its progress it must inevitably have upset; but it still flew on,

and the cries of the affrighted spectators testified the universal
sense of the imminent peril its occupants were threatened with.

Then Ali knew the right moment was come; and, throwing
down his chibouque, he drew the lasso from his pocket—threw
it so skilfully as to catch the forelegs of the near horse in its triple
fold—suffered himself to be dragged on for a few steps, by which
time the tightening of the well-cast lasso had so completely
hampered the furious animal as to bring it to the ground, and
falling on the pole, it snapped, and therefore prevented the other
animal from pursuing its headlong way. Gladly availing himself
of this opportunity, the coachman leaped from his box; but Ali
had promptly seized the nostrils of the second horse, and held
them in his iron grasp, till the maddened beast, snorting with
pain, sunk beside his companion. All this was achieved in much
less time than is occupied in the recital. The brief space had,
however, been sufficient for an individual, followed by a number
of servants, to rush from the house before which the accident had
occurred, and, as the coachman opened the door of the carriage,
to take from it a lady who was convulsively grasping the cushions
with one hand, while with the other she pressed to her bosom her
young companion, who had lost all consciousness of what was
passing.

Monte Cristo carried them both to the salon, and deposited
them on a sofa.

"Compose yourself, madame," said he; "all danger is over."

The female looked up at these words, and, with a glance far
more expressive than any entreaties could have been, pointed to
her child, who still continued insensible.

"I understand the nature of your alarms, madame," said the
count, carefully examining the child, "but I assure you there is
not the slightest occasion for uneasiness; your little charge has
not received the least injury,—his insensibility is merely the effects
of terror, and will soon cease."

"Are you quite sure you do not say so to tranquillise my fears?
See how deadly pale he is! My child! my darling Edward!
speak to your mother; open your dear eyes and look on me once
again!—Oh, sir, in pity send for help! my whole fortune shall
not be thought too much for the recovery of my blessed boy."

With a calm smile and gentle wave of the hand, Monte Cristo
signed to the distracted mother to lay aside her apprehensions;
then opening a casket that stood near, he drew forth a phial
composed of Bohemian glass, containing a liquid of the colour
of blood, of which he let fall a single drop on the child's lips.
Scarcely had it reached them, ere the boy, though still pale as
marble, opened his eyes, and eagerly gazed around him.

At this unhoped-for sight, the wild delight of the mother equalled her former despair.

" Where am I? " exclaimed she, when her first raptures at her son's recovery were past, " and to whom am I indebted for so happy a termination to my late dreadful alarm? "

" Madame," answered the count, " you are under the roof of one who esteems himself most fortunate in having been able to save you from a further continuance of your sufferings."

" My wretched curiosity has brought all this about," pursued the lady. " All Paris rung with the praises of Madame Danglars' beautiful horses, and I had the folly to desire to know whether they really merited the high character given of them."

" Is it possible," exclaimed the count, with well-feigned astonishment, " that these horses belong to Madame la Baronne? "

" They do, indeed. May I inquire if you are acquainted with Madame Danglars? "

" I have that honour; and my happiness at your escape from the danger that threatened you is redoubled by the consciousness that I have been the unwilling and unintentional cause of all the peril you have incurred. I yesterday purchased these horses of the baron; but as the baroness evidently regretted parting with them, I ventured to send them back to her, with a request that she would gratify me by accepting them from my hands."

" You are then, doubtless, the Count of Monte Cristo of whom Hermine has talked to me so much? "

" You have rightly guessed, madame," replied the count.

" And I am Madame Héloïse de Villefort."

The count bowed with the air of a person who hears a name for the first time.

" How grateful will M. de Villefort be for all your goodness! how thankfully will he acknowledge that to you alone it is owing that his wife and child exist! Most certainly but for the prompt assistance of your intrepid servant, this dear child and myself must both have perished."

" Indeed, I still shudder at the recollection of the fearful danger you were placed in, as well as your interesting child."

" I trust you will not object to my offering a recompense to your noble-hearted servant, proportionate to the service he has rendered me and mine."

" I beseech you, madame," replied Monte Cristo, " not to spoil Ali, either by too great praise or rewards. I cannot allow him to acquire the habit of expecting to be recompensed for every trifling service he may render. Ali is my slave, and in saving your life he was but discharging his duty to me."

" Nay," interposed Madame de Villefort, on whom the authori-

tative style adopted by the count made a deep impression,—
" nay, but, consider that to preserve my life he has risked his own."

" His life, madame, belongs not to him; it is mine, in return
for my having myself saved him from death."

Madame de Villefort made no further reply: her mind was
utterly absorbed in the contemplation of the singular individual,
who, from the first instant of her beholding him, had made so
powerful an impression on her.

During the evident preoccupation of Madame de Villefort,
Monte Cristo scrutinised the features and appearance of the boy
she kept folded in her arms, lavishing on him the most tender
endearments. The child was small for his age, and unnaturally
pale. A mass of straight black hair, defying all attempts to train
or curl it, fell over his projecting forehead, and hung down to his
shoulders, giving increased vivacity to eyes already sparkling with
a youthful love of mischief and fondness for every forbidden
enjoyment. His mouth was large, and the lips, which had not
yet regained their colour, were particularly thin; in fact, the
deep and crafty look, forming the principal character of the
child's face, belonged rather to a boy of twelve or fourteen years
of age, than to one so young. His first movement was to free
himself by a violent push from the encircling arms of his mother,
and to rush forwards to the casket from whence the count had
taken the phial of elixir, then, without asking permission of any
one, he proceeded, in all the wilfulness of a spoiled child unaccustomed to restrain either whims or caprices, to pull the corks
out of all the bottles in the casket.

" Touch nothing, my little friend," cried the count eagerly;
" some of those liquids are not only dangerous to taste, but even
to smell."

Madame de Villefort became very pale, and, seizing her son's
arm, drew him anxiously towards her; but once satisfied of his
safety, she also cast a brief but expressive glance on the casket,
which was not lost upon the count. At this moment Ali entered.
At sight of him, Madame de Villefort uttered an expression of
pleasure, and holding the child still closer towards her, she said:

" Edward, dearest! do you see that good man? He has shown
very great courage and resolution, for he exposed his own life
to stop the horses that were running away with us, and would
certainly have dashed the carriage to pieces ere long. Thank
him, then, my child, in your very best manner, for had he not come
to our aid, neither you nor I would have been alive to speak our
thanks."

This address, however, excited no similar feeling of gratitude
on the part of the child, who, instead of obeying his mother's

directions, stuck out his lips and turned away his head in a disdainful and contemptuous manner, saying:

" I don't like him—he's too ugly for me! "

The count witnessed all this with internal satisfaction, and a smile stole over his features as he thought that such a child bade fair to realise one part of his hopes; while Madame de Villefort reprimanded her son with a gentleness and moderation very far from conveying the least idea of a fault having been committed.

" This lady," said the count, speaking to Ali in the Arabic language, " is desirous that her son should thank you for saving both their lives, but the boy refuses, saying, ' You are too ugly! ' "

Ali turned his intelligent countenance towards the boy, on whom he gazed without any apparent emotion, but the sort of spasmodic working of the nostrils showed to the practised eye of Monte Cristo how deeply the Arab was wounded by the unfeeling remark.

" Will you permit me to inquire," said Madame de Villefort, as she rose to take her leave, " whether you usually reside here? "

" No, I do not," replied Monte-Cristo; " it is a small place I have purchased quite lately. My place of abode is No. 30 Avenue des Champs-Elysées; but I am delighted to see your countenance seems expressive of a perfect return to tranquillity. You have quite recovered from your fright, and are, no doubt, desirous of returning home. Anticipating your wishes, I have desired the same horses you came with to be put to one of my carriages, and Ali, he whom you think so very ugly," continued he, addressing the boy with a smiling air, " will have the honour of driving you home, while your coachman remains here to attend to the necessary repairs of your calèche. Directly that important business is concluded, I will have a couple of my own horses harnessed to convey it direct to Madame Danglars."

" I dare not return with those dreadful horses," said Madame de Villefort.

" You will see," replied Monte Cristo, " that they will be as different as possible in the hands of Ali. With him they will be gentle and docile as lambs."

Ali had, indeed, given proof of this; for, approaching the animals, who had been got upon their legs with considerable difficulty, he rubbed their foreheads and nostrils with a sponge soaked in aromatic vinegar, and wiped off the sweat and foam that covered their mouths. Then, commencing a loud whistling noise, he rubbed them well all over their bodies for several minutes; and, undisturbed by the noisy crowd collected round the broken carriage, Ali quietly harnessed the pacified animals to the count's chariot, took the reins in his hands, and mounted the box, when, lo! to the utter astonishment of those who had witnessed the ungovernable spirit and maddened velocity of the same horses, he was actually compelled to apply his whip in no very gentle manner ere he could induce them to start and even then all that could be obtained from the celebrated "dappled grays," now changed into a couple of as dull, sluggish, stupid brutes as "the most timid driver" would desire to meet with, was a slow, pottering pace, kept up with so much difficulty that Madame de Villefort was more than a couple of hours returning to her residence in the Faubourg Saint-Honoré.

Scarcely had the first congratulations upon her miraculous escape been gone through, than she retired to her room, ostensibly for the purpose of seeking a little repose, but in reality to write the following letter to Madame Danglars:

"DEAR HERMINE,—I have just had a wonderful escape from the most imminent danger, and I owe my safety to the very Count of Monte Cristo we were talking about yesterday, but whom I little expected to see to-day. I remember how unmercifully I laughed at what I considered your eulogistic and exaggerated praises of him, but I have now ample cause to admit that your enthusiastic description of this wonderful man fell far short of his merits. But I must endeavour to render the account of my adventures somewhat more intelligible. You must know, then, my dear friend, that when I had proceeded with your horses as far as Ranelagh, they darted forwards like mad things, and galloped away at so fearful a rate, that there seemed no other prospect for myself and my poor Edward but that of being dashed to pieces against the first object that impeded their progress, when a strange-looking man, an Arab or a Nubian, at least a black of some nation or other, at a signal from the count, whose domestic he is, suddenly seized and stopped the infuriated animals, even at the risk of being trampled to death himself; and certainly he must have had a most wonderful escape. The count then hastened to us, and carried myself and son into his house, where, by some skilful application, he speedily recalled my poor Edward (who was quite insensible from terror) to life. When we were sufficiently recovered, he sent us home in his own carriage. Yours will be returned to you to-morrow. I am fearful you will not be able to use your horses for some days; they seem thoroughly stupefied, as if sulky and vexed at having allowed this black servant to conquer them after all. The count, however, has commissioned me to assure you that two or three days' rest, with plenty of barley for their sole food during that time, will bring them back to their former fine condition, which means I suppose, that they, will be ready to run off with the carriage again, and play their wild pranks with as much headstrong fury as they evinced yesterday. Do not let them endanger your life, dear Hermine, as they did mine; for Providence may not send a Monte Cristo, or his Nubian servant, to preserve you from destruction, as it did me. Adieu! I cannot return you many thanks for the drive of yesterday; but after all, I ought not to blame you for the misconduct of your horses, more especially as it procured me the pleasure of an introduction to the Count of Monte Cristo,—and certainly that illustrious individual, apart from the millions he is said to be so very anxious to dispose of seemed to me one of those curiously interesting problems which I, for one, delight in solving at any risk or danger. Nay, so bent am I on following up my acquaintance with this remarkable personage, that if all other means fail, I really believe I shall have to borrow your horses again and make another excursion to the Bois de Boulogne. My sweet Edward endured the accident with admirable courage—he did not utter a single cry, but fell lifeless into my arms, nor did a tear fall from his eyes after it was over. I doubt not you will consider these praises the result of blind maternal affection; but the delicate fragile form of my beloved child contains a mind of no ordinary strength with the heroic firmness of a Spartan boy. Valentine sends many affectionate remembrances to your dear Eugénie—and with best love to her and yourself.

" I remain,

" Ever yours truly,

" HÉLOISE DE VILLEFORT.

" P.S.—Do pray contrive some means for my meeting the Count of Monte Cristo at your house. I must and will see him again. I have just made M. de Villefort promise to call on him, in order to acknowledge the signal service he has rendered our family in preserving our child, if my unworthy self goes for nothing and I flatter myself my husband's visit will be returned by the count."

Nothing was talked of throughout the evening but the adventure at Auteuil. Albert related it to his mother, Château-Renaud recounted it at the Jockey Club, and Debray detailed it at length in the salons of the minister; even Beauchamp accorded twenty lines in his journal to the relation of the count's courage and gallantry, thereby placing him as the greatest hero of the day before the eyes of all the fair members of the aristocracy of France. Vast was the crowd of visitors and inquiring friends, who left their names at the hotel of Madame de Villefort, with the design of renewing their visit at the right moment, of hearing from her lips all the interesting circumstances of this most romantic adventure. As Héloïse had stated, M. de Villefort donned his best black suit, drew on a pair of new white kid gloves, ordered the servants to attend the carriage dressed in their full livery, and forthwith drove to the hotel of the count, situated, as the reader is already informed, in the Avenue des Champs-Elysées.

49

Ideology

IF the Count of Monte Cristo had lived for a very long time in Parisian society, he would have fully appreciated the value of the step which M. de Villefort had taken. Standing well at court, whether the king regnant was of the elder or younger branch, whether the government was doctrinaire, liberal, or conservative: esteemed clever by all, just as we generally esteem those clever who have never experienced a political check; hated by many, but warmly protected by others, without being really liked by anybody, M. de Villefort held a high position in the magistracy, and maintained his eminence like a Harlay or a Molé.* His drawing-room regenerated by a young wife, and a daughter by his first marriage scarcely eighteen, was still one of those well-regulated Paris salons where the worship of traditional customs, and the observance of rigid etiquette, were carefully maintained. A freezing politeness, a strict fidelity to government principles, a profound contempt for theories and theorists, a deep-seated hatred of ideality—these were the elements of private and public life displayed by M. de Villefort.

M. de Villefort was not only a magistrate, he was almost a diplomatist. His relations with the ancient court, of which he always spoke with dignity and respect, made him respected by the new one, and he knew so many things, that not only was he always carefully considered, but sometimes consulted. Perhaps this would not have been so had it been possible to get rid of M. de Villefort; but, like the feudal barons who rebelled against their sovereign, he dwelt in an impregnable fortress. This fortress was his post as procureur du roi, all the advantages of which he worked out marvellously, and which he would not have resigned, but to be made deputy, and thus have converted neutrality into opposition. M. de Villefort made and returned very few visits. For his friends, M. de Villefort was a powerful protector; for his enemies, he was a silent, but bitter enemy; for those who were neither the one nor the other, he was a statue of the law-made man. Haughty air, immovable countenance, look steady and impenetrable, or else insultingly piercing and inquiring, such was the man for whom four revolutions, skilfully piled one on the other, had first constructed and afterwards cemented the pedestal on which his fortune was elevated.

M. de Villefort had the reputation of being the least curious and least wearisome man in France. He gave a ball every year, at which he appeared for a quarter of an hour only,—that is to say, five-and-forty minutes less than the king is visible at his balls. He was never seen at the theatres, at concerts, or in any place of public resort. Occasionally, but seldom, he played at whist, and then care was taken to select partners worthy of him—sometimes they were ambassadors, sometimes archbishops, or sometimes a prince, or a president, or some dowager duchess. Such was the man whose carriage had just now stopped before the Count of Monte Cristo's door.

The valet-de-chambre announced M. de Villefort at the moment when the count, leaning over a large table, was tracing on a map the route from St. Petersburgh to China.

The procureur du roi entered with the same grave and measured step he would have employed in entering a court of justice. He was the same man, or rather the completion of the same man, whom we have heretofore seen as *substitut* at Marseilles. Nature, following up its principles, had changed nothing for him in the course he had chalked out for himself. From slender he had become meagre; from pale, yellow; his deep-set eyes were now hollow, and gold spectacles, as they shielded his eyes, seemed to make a portion of his face. All his costume was black, with the exception of his white cravat, and this funereal appearance was only broken in upon by the slight line of red riband which passed almost imperceptibly through his button-hole, and which appeared like a streak of blood traced with a pencil.

Although master of himself, Monte Cristo scrutinised with irrepressible curiosity the magistrate, whose salute he returned, and who, distrustful by habit, and especially incredulous as to social marvels, was much more disposed to see in the noble stranger, as Monte Cristo was already called, a *chevalier d'industrie*, who had come to try new ground, or some malefactor who had broken his prescribed limits, than a prince of the Holy See, or a sultan of the Arabian Nights.

" Sir," said Villefort, in the tone assumed by magistrates in their oratorical periods, and of which they cannot, or will not, divest themselves in society,—" sir, the signal service which you yesterday rendered to my wife and son has made it a duty in me to offer you my thanks. Allow me, therefore, to discharge this duty, and express to you all my gratitude."

And as he said this, the " eye severe " of the magistrate had lost nothing of its habitual arrogance. These words he articulated in the voice of a procureur-genéral, with the rigid inflexibility of neck and shoulders, which caused his flatterers to say (as we have said before) that he was the living statue of the law.

" Monsieur," replied the count, with a chilling air, " I am very happy to have been the means of preserving a son to his mother, for they say that the sentiment of maternity is the most holy of all; and the good fortune which occurred to me, monsieur, might have enabled you to dispense with a duty which, in its discharge, confers an undoubtedly great honour; for I am aware that M. de Villefort is not lavish of the favour he bestows on me, but which, however estimable, is unequal to the satisfaction which I internally experience."

Villefort, astonished at this reply, which he by no means expected, started like a soldier who feels the blow levelled at him over the armour he wears, and a curl of his disdainful lip indicated that from that moment he noted in the tablets of his brain that the Count of Monte Cristo was by no means a highly bred gentleman. He glanced round, in order to seize on something on which the conversation might turn, and seem to fall easily. He saw the map which Monte Cristo had been examining when he entered, and said:

" You seem geographically engaged, sir? It is a rich study for you who, as I learn, have seen as many lands as are delineated on this map."

" Yes, sir," replied the count; " I have sought to make on the human race, taken as a mass, what you practice everyday on individuals—a physiological study. I have believed it was much easier to descend from the whole to a part than to ascend from a part to the whole. It is an algebraic axiom, which makes us proceed from a known to an unknown quantity, and not from an unknown to a known; but sit down, sir, I beg of you."

Monte Cristo pointed to a chair, which the procureur du roi was obliged to take the trouble to move forwards himself, whilst the count merely fell back into his own, on which he had been kneeling when M. Villefort entered. Thus the count was half-way turned towards his visitor, having his back towards the window, his elbow resting on the geographical chart which afforded the conversation for the moment, a conversation which assumed, as had done those with Danglars and Morcerf, a turn analogous to the persons, if not to the situation.

"Ah, you philosophise," replied Villefort, after a moment's silence, during which, like a wrestler, who encounters a powerful opponent, he took breath; "well, sir, really, if, like you, I had nothing else to do, I should seek a more amusing occupation."

"Why, in truth, sir," was Monte Cristo's reply, "man is but an ugly caterpillar for him who studies him through a solar microscope; but you said, I think, that I had nothing else to do. Now, really, let me ask, sir, have you?—do you believe you have anything to do? or, to speak in plain terms, do you really think that what you do deserves being called anything?"

Villefort's astonishment redoubled at this second thrust so forcibly made by his strange adversary. It was a long time since the magistrate had heard a paradox so strong, or rather, to say the truth more exactly, it was the first time he had ever heard it. The procureur du roi exerted himself to reply.

"Sir," he responded, "you are a stranger, and I believe you say yourself that a portion of your life has been spent in Oriental countries: thus, then, you are not aware how human justice, so expeditious in barbarous countries, takes with us a prudent and well-studied course."

"Oh, yes,—yes, I do, sir; it is the *pede claudo* of the ancients. I know all that, for it is with the justice of all countries especially that I have occupied myself—it is with the criminal procedure of all nations that I have compared natural justice, and I must say, sir, that it is the law of primitive nations; that is, the law of retaliation that I have most frequently found to be according to the law of God."

"If this law were adopted, sir," said the procureur du roi, "it would greatly simplify our legal codes and in that case the magistrates would not (as you have just observed) have much to do."

"It may, perhaps, come to this in time," observed Monte Cristo; "you know that human inventions march from the complex to the simple, and simplicity is always perfection."

"In the meanwhile," continued the magistrate, "our codes are in full force with all their contradictory enactments derived from Gallic customs, Roman laws, and Frank usages; the knowledge of all which, you will agree, is not to be acquired without lengthened labour, and it requires a tedious study to acquire this knowledge, and when that is acquired, a strong power of brain is necessary in order to retain it."

"I agree with you entirely, sir; but all that even you know with respect to the French code; I know not only in reference to that code, but as regards the codes of all nations—the English, Turkish, Japanese, Hindoo laws, are as familiar to me as the French laws, and thus I was right, when I said to you, that relatively (you know that everything is relative, sir)—that relatively to what I have done, you have very little to do; but that relatively to all I have learned, you have yet a great deal to learn."

" But with what motive have you learned all this? " inquired Villefort, astonished.

Monte Cristo smiled.

" Really, sir," he observed, " I see that in spite of the reputation which you have acquired as a superior man, you contemplate everything in the material and vulgar view of society, beginning with man, and ending with man—that is to say, in the most restricted, most narrow view which it is possible for human understanding to embrace."

" Pray, sir, explain yourself," said Villefort, more and more astonished, " I really do—not—understand you—perfectly."

" I say, sir, that with the eyes fixed on the social organisation of nations, you see only the springs of the machine, and lose sight of the sublime workman who makes them act: I say that you do not recognise before you and around you any but those placemen whose brevets have been signed by the minister or the king; and that the men whom God has put above those titulars, ministers, and kings, by giving them a mission to follow out, instead of a post to fill—I say that they escape your narrow, limited ken. It is thus that human weakness fails from its debilitated and imperfect organs. Tobias took the angel who restored him to light for an ordinary young man. The nations took Attila, who was doomed to destroy them, for a conqueror merely similar to other conquerors, and it was necessary for both to reveal their missions, that they might be known and acknowledged; one was compelled to say, ' I am the angel of the Lord; ' and the other, ' I am the hammer of God,' in order that the Divine essence in both might be revealed."

" Then," said Villefort more and more amazed and really supposing he was speaking to a mystic or a madman, " you consider yourself as one of those extraordinary beings whom you have mentioned? "

" And why not? " said Monte Cristo coldly.

" Your pardon, sir," replied Villefort, quite astounded, " but you will excuse me if, when I presented myself to you, I was unaware that I should meet with a person whose knowledge and understanding so far surpass the usual knowledge and understanding of men. It is not usual with us, corrupted wretches of civilisation, to find gentlemen like yourself, possessors, as you are, of immense fortune—at least, so it is said—and I beg you to observe that I do not inquire, I merely repeat;—it is not usual, I say, for such privileged and wealthy beings to waste their time in speculations on the state of society, in philosophical reveries, intended at best to console those whom fate has disinherited from the goods of this world."

"Really, sir," retorted the count, "have you attained the eminent situation in which you are without having admitted or even without having met with exceptions? and do you never use your eyes, which must have acquired so much finesse and certainty, to divine, at a glance, the kind of man who has come before you? Should not a magistrate be not merely the best administrator of the law, but the most crafty expounder of the chicanery of his profession, a steel probe to search hearts, a touchstone to try the gold which in each soul is mingled with more or less of alloy?"

"Sir," said Villefort, "upon my word you overcome me. I really never heard a person speak as you do."

"Because you remain eternally encircled in a round of general conditions, and have never dared to raise your wing into those upper spheres which God has peopled with invisible or marked beings."

"And you allow then, sir, that spheres exist, and that these marked and invisible beings mingle amongst us?"

"Why should they not? Can you see the air you breathe, and yet without which you could not for a moment exist?"

"Then we do not see those beings to whom you allude?"

"Yes, we do;—you see them whenever God pleases to allow them to assume a material form: you touch them, come in contact with them, speak to them, and they reply to you."

"Ah," said Villefort, smiling, "I confess I should like to be warned when one of these beings is in contact with me."

"You have been served as you desire, monsieur, for you have been warned just now, and I now again warn you."

"Then you yourself are one of these marked beings?"

"Yes, monsieur, I believe so; for until now, no man has found himself in a position similiar to mine. The dominions of kings are limited, either by mountains or rivers, or a change of manners, or an alteration of language. My kingdom is bounded only by the world, for I am neither an Italian, nor a Frenchman, nor a Hindoo, nor an American, nor a Spaniard. I am a cosmopolite. No country can say it saw my birth. God alone knows what country will see me die. I adopt all customs, speak all languages. You believe me to be a Frenchman, for I speak French with the same facility and purity as yourself. Well, Ali, my Nubian, believes me to be an Arab; Bertuccio, my steward, takes me for a Roman; Haydée, my slave, thinks me a Greek. You may, therefore, comprehend, that being of no country, asking no protection from any government, acknowledging no man as my brother, not one of the scruples that arrest the powerful, or the obstacles which paralyse the weak, paralyse or arrest me. I have only two adversaries—I will not say two conquerors, for with perseverance I subdue even them, though they are time and distance. There is a third, and the most terrible—that is my condition as a mortal being. This alone can stop me in my onward career, and before I have attained the goal at which I aim, for all the rest I have calculated. What men call the chances of fate, namely, ruin, change, circumstances—I have anticipated them all, and if any of these should overtake me, yet they will not overwhelm me. Unless I die, I shall always be what I am, and therefore it is that I utter the things you have never heard, even from the mouths of kings—for kings have need, and other persons have fear of you. For who is there who does not say to himself, in society as incongruously organised as ours, ' Perhaps some day I shall have to do with the procureur du roi '? "

" But can you not say that, sir? for the moment you become an inhabitant of France you are naturally subjected to the French laws."

" I know it, sir," replied Monte Cristo; " but when I visit a country I begin to study, by all the means which are available, the men from whom I may have anything to hope or to fear, until I know them as well, perhaps better, than they know themselves. It follows from this, that the procureur du roi, be he who he may, with whom I should have to deal would assuredly be more embarrassed than I should."

" That is to say," replied Villefort, with hesitation, " that human nature being weak, every man according to your creed, has committed faults."

" Faults or crimes," responded Monte Cristo, with a negligent air.

" And that you alone, amongst the men whom you do not recognise as your brothers—for you have said so," observed Villefort, in a tone that faltered somewhat, " you alone are perfect? "

" No, not perfect," was the count's reply; " only impenetrable, that's all. But let us leave off this strain, sir, if the tone of it is displeasing to you: I am no more disturbed by your justice than you are by my second sight."

" No, no—by no means," said Villefort, who was afraid of seeming to abandon his ground. " No; by your brilliant and almost sublime conversation you have elevated me above the ordinary level; we no longer talk—we rise to dissertation. But you know how the theologians in their collegiate chairs, and philosophers in their controversies, occasionally say cruel truths; let us suppose for the moment that we are theologising in a social way, or even philosophically, and I will say to you, rude as it may seem, ' My brother, you sacrifice greatly to pride; you may be above others, but above you there is God.' "

" Above us all, sir," was Monte Cristo's response, in a tone and with an emphasis so deep, that Villefort involuntarily shuddered. " I have my pride for men—serpents always ready to erect themselves against every one who may pass without crushing them. But I lay aside that pride before God, who has taken me from nothing to make me what I am."

" Then, *M. le Comte*, I admire you," said Villefort, who, for the first time in this strange conversation, used the aristocratical form to the unknown personage whom, until now, he had only called *monsieur*. " Yes, and I say to you, if you are really strong, really superior, really pious, or impenetrable, which you were right in saying amounts to the same thing—yet be proud sir, that is the characteristic of predominance—yet you have unquestionably some ambition."

" I have, sir."

" And what may it be? "

" I, too, as happens to every man once in his life, have been taken by Satan into the highest mountain in the earth, and when there he showed me all the kingdoms of the earth, and as he said before, so said he to me, ' Child of earth, what wouldst thou have to make thee adore me? ' I reflected long, for a gnawing ambition had long preyed upon me, and then I replied, ' Listen,—I have always heard tell of Providence, and yet I have never seen him, nor anything that resembles him, or which can make me believe that he exists. I wish to be Providence myself, for I feel that the most beautiful, noblest, most sublime thing in the world, is to recompense and punish.' Satan bowed his head and groaned. ' You mistake,' he said; ' Providence does exist, only you have never seen him, because the child of God is as invisible as the parent. You have seen nothing that resembles him, because he works by secret springs and moves by hidden ways. All I can do for you is to make you one of the agents of that Providence.' The bargain was concluded. I may sacrifice my soul, but what matters it? " added Monte Cristo. " If the thing were to do again, I would again do it."

Villefort looked at Monte Cristo with extreme amazement. " Monsieur le Comte," he inquired, " have you any relations? "

" No, sir, I am alone in the world."

" So much the worse."

" Why? " asked Monte Cristo.

" Because then you might witness a spectacle calculated to break down your pride. You say you fear nothing but death? "

"I did not say that I feared it; I only said that that alone could check me."

" And old age? "

" My end will be achieved before I grow old."

" And madness? "

" I have been nearly mad; and you know the axiom—*non bis in idem*.* It is an axiom of criminal law, and, consequently, you understand its full application."

" Sir," continued Villefort, "there is something to fear besides death, old age, and madness. For instance, there is apoplexy—that lightning-stroke which strikes but does not destroy you, and yet after which all is ended. You are still yourself as now, and yet you are yourself no longer; you who, like Ariel, touch on the angelic, are but an inert mass, which, like Caliban, touches on the brutal; and this is called in human tongue, as I tell you, neither more nor less than apoplexy. Come, if so you will, M. le Comte, and continue this conversation at my house, any day you may be willing to see an adversary capable of understanding and anxious to refute you, and I will show you my father, M. Noirtier de Villefort, one of the most fiery Jacobins of the French Revolution; that is to say, the most remarkable audacity, seconded by a most powerful organisation,—a man who, perhaps, has not, like yourself, seen all the kingdoms of the earth, but who has helped to overturn one of the most powerful; in fact, a man who, like you, believed himself one of the envoys—not of God, but of a Supreme Being; not of Providence, but of Fate. Well, sir, the rupture of a blood-vessel on a lobe of the brain has destroyed all this—not in a day, not in an hour—but in a second. M. Noirtier, who on the previous night was the old Jacobin, the old senator, the old Carbonaro, laughing at the guillotine, laughing at the cannon, laughing at the dagger,—M. Noirtier, playing with revolutions,—M. Noirtier, for whom France was a vast chess-board, from which pawns, rooks, knights, and queens, were to disappear, so that the king was checkmated,—M. Noirtier, so redoubted, was the next morning *poor M. Noirtier*, the helpless old man, at the tender mercies of the weakest creature in the household, that is, his grandchild, Valentine; a dumb and frozen carcase, in fact, who only lives without suffering, that time may be given to his frame to decompose without his consciousness of his decay."

" Alas, sir," said Monte Cristo, " this spectacle is neither strange to my eye nor my thought. I am something of a physician, and have, like my fellows, sought more than once for the soul in living, and in dead matter; yet like Providence, it has remained invisible to my eyes, although present to my heart. A hundred writers since Socrates, Seneca, St. Augustine, and Gall, have made, in verse and prose, the comparison you have made, and yet I can well understand that a father's sufferings may effect great changes in the mind of a son. I will call on you, sir, since you bid me contemplate, for the advantage of my pride, this terrible spectacle, which must spread so much sorrow throughout your house."

" It would have done so unquestionably, had not God given me so large a compensation. In presence of the old man, who is dragging his way to the tomb, are two children just entering into life—Valentine, the daughter by my first wife Mademoiselle Renée de Saint-Méran, and Edward, the boy whose life you have this day saved."

" And what is your deduction from this compensation, sir? " inquired Monte Cristo.

" My deduction is," replied Villefort, " that my father, led away by his passions, has committed some fault unknown to human justice, but marked by the justice of God! That God, desirous in his mercy to punish but one person, has visited this justice on him alone."

Monte Cristo, with a smile on his lips, had yet a groan at his heart, which would have made Villefort fly had he but heard it.

" Adieu, sir," said the magistrate, who had risen from his seat; " I leave you, bearing a remembrance of you—a remembrance of esteem, which I hope will not be disagreeable to you when you know me better; for I am not a man to bore my friends, as you will learn. Besides, you have made an eternal friend of Madame de Villefort."

The count bowed, and contented himself with seeing Villefort to the door of his cabinet, the procureur being escorted to his carriage by two footmen, who, on a signal from their master, followed him with every mark of attention. When he had gone, Monte Cristo drew a hard breath from his oppressed bosom, and said:

" Enough of this poison, let me now seek the antidote." Then sounding his bell, he said to Ali, who entered. " I am going to madame's chamber—have the carriage ready at one o'clock."

50

Haydée

IT will be remembered that the new, or rather old acquaintances of the Count of Monte Cristo, residing in the Rue Meslay, were no other than Maximilian, Julie, and Emmanuel.

The very anticipations of delight to be enjoyed in his forth-coming visits—the bright, pure gleam of heavenly happiness it diffused over the almost deadly warfare in which he had volun-tarily engaged, illumined his whole countenance with a look of ineffable joy and calmness, as, immediately after the departure of Villefort, his thoughts flew back to the cheering prospect before him, of tasting, at least, a brief respite from the fierce and stormy passions of his mind.

It was the hour of noon, and Monte Cristo had set apart one hour to be passed in the apartments of Haydée; as though his so-long crushed spirit could not all at once admit the feeling of pure and unmixed joy, but required a gradual succession of calm and gentle emotions to prepare his mind to receive full and perfect happiness, in the same manner as ordinary natures demand to be inured by degrees to the reception of strong or violent sensations.

The young Greek, as we have already stated, occupied apart-ments wholly unconnected with those of the count. The rooms had been fitted up in strict accordance with the Eastern style, that is to say, the floors were covered with the richest carpets Turkey could produce; the walls hung with brocaded silk of the most magnificent designs and texture; while around each chamber, luxurious divans were placed, with piles of soft and yielding cushions, that needed only to be arranged at the pleasure or convenience of such as sought repose.

Haydée's female establishment consisted of three French attendants, and a fourth who was, like herself, a native of the climes of Greece. The three first remained constantly in a small waiting-room, ready to obey the first sound of a small golden bell, or to receive the orders of the Romaic slave, who just knew sufficient French to be enabled to transmit her mistress's orders to the three other waiting-women, who had received most peremptory instructions from Monte Cristo to treat Haydée with all the respect and deference they would observe to a queen.

· The fair Greek herself generally passed her time in the apartment forming the extremity of the suite of rooms assigned to her. It was a species of boudoir, circular, and lighted only from the top, which consisted of pale pink glass. Haydée was reclining upon soft downy cushions, covered with blue satin spotted with silver; her head, supported by one of her exquisitely moulded arms, rested on the divan immediately behind her, while the other was employed in adjusting to her lips the coral tube of a rich narghile, whose flexible pipe, placed amid the coolest and most fragrant essences, permitted not the perfumed vapour to ascend until fully impregnated with the rich odours of the most delicious flowers. Her attitude, though perfectly natural for an Eastern female, would have been deemed too full of coquettish straining after effect in a European. Her dress, which was that of the women of Epirus, consisted of a pair of white satin trousers, embroidered with pink roses, displaying feet so exquisitely formed and so delicately fair, that they might well have been taken for Parian marble, had not the eye been undeceived by their constantly shifting in and out of the fairy-like slippers in which they were encased; these tiny coverings were beautifully ornamented with gold and pearls, and turned up at the point; a blue and white striped vest, with long open sleeves, trimmed with silver loops and buttons of pearls. She also wore a species of bodice, which, closing only from the centre to the waist, exhibited the whole of the ivory throat and upper part of the bosom; three magnificent diamond clasps fastened it where requisite. The junction of the bodice and drawers was entirely concealed by one of those many-coloured scarfs, whose brilliant hues and rich silken fringe have rendered them so precious in the eyes of Parisian belles. A small cap of gold, embroidered with pearls, was placed with tasteful elegance on one side of the fair Greek's head while on the other, a natural rose, of that dark crimson almost inclining to purple, mingled its glowing colours with the luxuriant masses of her hair, which, for jetty lustre, outrivalled the raven's wing.

The extreme beauty of the countenance, that shone forth in loveliness that mocked the vain attempts of dress to augment it, was peculiarly and purely Grecian—there were the large dark melting eyes, the finely formed nose, the coral lips, and pearly teeth, that belonged to her race and country. And to complete the whole, Haydée was in the very springtide and fulness of youthful charms—she had not yet numbered more than eighteen summers.

Upon Monte Cristo entering the apartments of the fair girl, he summoned her Greek attendant, and bade her inquire whether it would be agreeable to her mistress to receive his visit.

Haydée's only reply was to direct her servant, by a sign, to withdraw the tapestried curtain that hung before the door of her boudoir, the frame-work of the opening thus made serving as a sort of border to the graceful tableau presented by the picturesque attitude and appearance of Haydée.

As Monte Cristo approached, she leaned upon the elbow of the arm that held the narghile, and extending to him her other hand, said, with a smile of captivating sweetness, in the sonorous language spoken by the females of Athens and Sparta, " Why demand permission ere you enter? Are you no longer my master; or have I ceased to be your slave? "

Monte Cristo returned his smile. " Haydée," said he, " you well know."

" Why do you address me so coldly—so distantly? " asked the fair Greek. " Have I by any means displeased you? Oh, if so, punish me as you will; but do not—do not speak to me in tones and manner so formal and constrained! "

" Listen to me, Haydée," replied the count. " I was about to remind you of a circumstance you are perfectly acquainted with; namely, that we are now in France, and that you are consequently free! "

" Free! " repeated the fair girl. " Of what use would freedom be to me? "

" It would enable you to quit me! "

" Quit you! Wherefore should I do so? "

" That is not for me to say; but we are now about to mix in society—to visit and be visited."

" I desire to see no one but yourself."

" Nay, but hear me, Haydée. You cannot remain in seclusion in the midst of this gay capital; and should you see one whom you could prefer, think not I would be so selfish or unjust as to——"

" No, no! " answered Haydée, with energetic warmth, " that can never be. No man could appear charming in my eyes but yourself. None save yourself and my father have ever possessed my affection; nor will it be bestowed upon any other."

" My poor child," replied Monte Cristo, " that is merely because your father and myself are the only men with whom you have ever conversed."

" And what care I for all others in the world! My father called me *his joy*—you style me your *love*,—and both of you bestowed on me the endearing appellation of *your child*! "

" Do you remember your father, Haydée? "

The young Greek smiled. " He is here, and here," said she, touching her eyes and her heart.

" And where am I? " inquired Monte Cristo laughingly.

"You?" cried she, with tones of thrilling tenderness, "you are everywhere!"

Monte Cristo took the delicate hand of the young girl in his, and was about to raise it to his lips, when the simple child of nature hastily withdrew it, and presented her fair cheek instead.

"You now understand, Haydée," said the count, "that from this moment you are absolutely free; that here you exercise unlimited sway, and are at liberty to lay aside or continue the costume of your country, as it may suit your inclination. Within this mansion you are absolute mistress of your actions, and may go abroad or remain in your apartments, as may seem most agreeable to you. A carriage waits your orders, and Ali and Myrta will accompany you, whithersoever you desire to go. There is but one favour I would entreat of you."

"Oh, speak!"

"Preserve most carefully the secret of your birth. Make no allusion to the past; nor upon any occasion be induced to pronounce the names of your illustrious father or ill-fated mother."

"I have already told my lord, it is not my intention to hold converse with any one save himself."

"It is possible, Haydée, that so perfect a seclusion, though conformable with the habits and customs of the East, may not be practicable in Paris. Endeavour, then, to accustom yourself to our manner of living in these northern climes, as you did to those of Rome, Florence, Milan, and Madrid; it may be useful to you, one of these days, whether you remain here or return to the East."

The fair girl raised her tearful eyes towards Monte Cristo, as she said, with touching earnestness, "My lord would mean whether *we* return to the East or continue here, would he not?"

"My child," returned Monte Cristo, "you know full well, that whenever we part, it will be by no fault or wish of mine: the tree forsakes not the blossom that embellishes it—it is the flower that falls from the tree on which it grew."

"My lord," replied Haydée, "never will I quit you, for sure I am I could not exist if banished your presence; alas! what would life be worth then?"

"My poor girl, you forget that ten years will effect an essentially different change in both of us; to you that space of time will bring but the perfection of womanly graces, while it will wrinkle my brows and change my hair to gray."

"My father had numbered sixty years, and the snows of age were on his head; but I admired and loved him far better than all the gay, handsome youths I saw about his court."

"Then tell me, Haydée, do you believe you shall be able to accustom yourself to our present mode of life?"

" Shall I see you? "

" Every day."

" Then what does my lord apprehend for me? "

" I fear your growing weary."

" Nay, my lord! that cannot be. In the morning I shall rejoice in the prospect of your coming, and in the evening dwell with delight on the happiness I have enjoyed in your presence. Oh, believe me that when three great passions, such as sorrow, love, and gratitude fill the heart, *ennui* can find no place."

" You are a worthy daughter of Epirus, Haydée, and your charming and poetical ideas prove well your descent from that race of goddesses who claim your country as their birthplace. Depend on my care, to see that your youth is not blighted, or suffered to pass away in ungenial solitude; and of this be well assured, that if you love me as a father, I, in my turn, feel for you all the affection of the fondest parent."

" Let not my lord be deceived, the love I bear you resembles in no degree my feelings towards my father; I survived *his* death; but were any evil to befall you, the moment in which I learned the fatal tidings would be the last of my life."

The count, with a look of indescribable tenderness, extended his hand to the animated speaker, who carried it reverentially and affectionately to her lips. The carriage was prepared according to orders, and stepping lightly into it, the count drove off at his usual rapid pace.

51

The Morrel Family

IN a very few minutes the count reached No. 7 in the Rue Meslay. The house was of white stone, and in a small court before it were two small beds full of beautiful flowers. In the concierge that opened the gate the count recognised Coclès; but as he had but one eye, and that eye had considerably weakened in the course of nine years, Coclès did not so readily recognise the count. The carriages that drove up to the door were compelled to turn, to avoid a fountain that played in a basin of rockwork, in which sported a quantity of gold and silver fishes, an ornament that had excited the jealousy of the whole quarter, and had gained for the house the appellation of " *le Petit Versailles.*"

The house, raised above the kitchens and cellars, had, besides the ground-floor, two stories and attics. The whole of the property, consisting of an immense workshop, two pavilions at the bottom of the garden, and the garden itself, had been purchased by Emmanuel, who had seen at a glance that he could make a profitable speculation of it. He had reserved the house and half the garden, and building a wall between the garden and the workshops, had let them upon lease with the pavilions at the bottom of the garden. So that for a trifling sum he was as well lodged, and as perfectly shut out from observation, as the inhabitant of the finest hotel in the Faubourg St. Germain.

The breakfast-room was of oak; the salon of mahogany and blue velvet; the bedroom of citronwood and green damask; there was a study for Emmanuel who never studied, and a music-room for Julie who never played. The whole of the second story was set apart for Maximilian; it was precisely the same as his sister's apartments, except that the breakfast-parlour was changed into a billiard-room, where he received his friends. He was superintending the dressing of his horse and smoking his cigar at the entrance to the garden when the count's carriage stopped at the door.

Coclès opened the gate, and Baptistin, springing from the box, inquired whether Monsieur and Madame Herbault and Monsieur Maximilian Morrel would see M. le Comte de Monte Cristo.

" M. le Comte de Monte Cristo? " cried Morrel, throwing away his cigar and hastening to the carriage; " I should think we would see him. Ah! a thousand thanks, M. le Comte, for not having forgotten your promise."

And the young officer shook the count's hand so warmly that the latter could not be mistaken as to the sincerity of his joy, and he saw that he had been expected with impatience, and was received with pleasure.

" Come, come! " said Maximilian, " I will serve as your guide; such a man as you are ought not to be introduced by a servant. My sister is in the garden, plucking the dead roses; my brother reading his two papers, *la Presse* and *les Débats*,* within five steps of her, for wherever you see Madame Herbault, you have only to look within a circle of four yards and you will find M. Emmanuel, and ' reciprocally,' as they say at the École Polytechnique."

At the sound of their steps, a young woman of twenty to five-and-twenty, dressed in a silk robe de chambre, and busily engaged plucking the dead leaves off a splendid rose-tree, raised her head.

This female was Julie, who had become, as the clerk of the house of Thomson and French had predicted, Madame Emmanuel Herbault.

She uttered a cry of surprise at the sight of a stranger, and Maximilian began to laugh.

"Don't disturb yourself, Julie," said he.

"M. le Comte has only been two or three days in Paris, but he already knows what a woman of fashion, of the Marais is and if he does not, you will show him."

"Ah, monsieur," returned Julie, "it is treason in my brother to bring you thus, but he never has any regard for his poor sister. Penelon, Penelon!"

An old man who was digging busily at one of the beds of roses, stuck his spade in the earth, and approached cap in hand, and striving to conceal a quid of tobacco he had just thrust into his cheek. A few locks of gray mingled with his hair, which was still thick and matted, whilst his bronzed features and determined glance announced the old sailor who had braved the heat of the equator and the storms of the tropics.

"I think you hailed me, Mademoiselle Julie?" said he.

Penelon had still preserved the habit of calling his master's daughter "Mademoiselle Julie," and had never been able to change the name to Madame Herbault.

"Penelon," replied Julie, "go and inform M. Emmanuel of this gentleman's visit, and Maximilian will conduct him to the salon."

Then, turning to Monte Cristo,—

"I hope you will permit me to leave you for a few minutes," continued she; and without awaiting any reply, disappeared behind a clump of trees, and entered the house by a lateral alley.

"I am sorry to see," observed Monte Cristo to Morrel, "that I cause no small disturbance in your house."

"Look there," said Maximilian laughing; "there is her husband changing his jacket for a coat. I assure you, you are well known in the Rue Meslay."

"Your family appears to me a very happy one." said the count, as if speaking to himself.

"Oh, yes, I assure you, M. le Comte, they want nothing that can render them happy; they are young and cheerful, they are tenderly attached to each other, and with twenty-five thousand francs a year, they fancy themselves as rich as Rothschild."

"Five-and-twenty thousand francs is not a large sum, however," replied Monte Cristo, with a tone so sweet and gentle, that it went to Maximilian's heart like the voice of a father; "but they will not be content with that. Your brother-in-law is a barrister? a doctor?"

"He was a merchant, M. le Comte, and had succeeded to the

business of my poor father. M. Morrel, at his death, left 500,000 francs (£20,000), which were divided between my sister and myself, for we were his only children. Her husband, who, when he married her, had no other patrimony than his noble probity, his first-rate ability, and his spotless reputation, wished to possess as much as his wife. He laboured and toiled until he had amassed 250,000 francs; six years sufficed to achieve this object. Oh, I assure you, M. le Comte it was a touching spectacle to see these young creatures, destined by their talents for higher stations, toiling together, and who, unwilling to change any of the customs of their paternal house, took six years to accomplish that which innovators would have effected in two or three. Marseilles resounded with their well-earned praises. At last, one day, Emmanuel came to his wife who had just finished making up the accounts.

" ' Julie,' said he to her, ' Coclès has just given me the last rouleau of a hundred francs; that completes the 250,000 francs we had fixed as the limits of our gains. Can you content yourself with the small fortune which we shall possess for the future? Listen to me. Our house transacts business to the amount of a million a year, from which we derive an income of 40,000 francs. We can dispose of the business if we please, in an hour, for I have received a letter from M. Delaunay, in which he offers to purchase the goodwill of the house, to unite with his own, for 300,000 francs. Advise me what I had better do.'

" ' Emmanuel,' returned my sister, ' the house of Morrel can only be carried on by a Morrel. Is it not worth 300,000 francs to save our father's name from the chances of evil fortune and failure? '

" ' I thought so,' replied Emmanuel; ' but I wished to have your advice.'

" ' This is my counsel:—Our accounts are made up and our bills paid; all we have to do is to stop the issue of any more, and close our office.'

" This was done instantly. It was three o'clock; at a quarter past, a merchant presented himself to insure two ships; it was a clear profit of 15,000 francs.

" ' Monsieur,' said Emmanuel, ' have the goodness to address yourself to M. Delaunay. We have quitted business.'

" ' How long? ' inquired the astonished merchant.

" ' A quarter of an hour,' was the reply.

" And this is the reason, monsieur," continued Maximilian, " of my sister and brother-in-law having only 25,000 francs a year."

Maximilian had scarcely finished her story, during which the count's heart had seemed ready to burst, when Emmanuel entered, clad in a hat and coat. He saluted the count with the air of a man who is aware of the rank of his guest; then, after having led Monte Cristo round the little garden, he returned to the house.

A large vase of Japan porcelain filled with flowers, that impregnated the air with their perfume, stood in the salon. Julie, suitably dressed, and her hair arranged (she had accomplished this feat in less than ten minutes), received the count on his entrance.

The songs of the birds were heard in an aviary hard by—the branches of false ebony-trees and rose acacias forming the border of the blue velvet curtains. Everything in this charming retreat, from the warble of the birds to the smile of the mistress, breathed tranquillity and repose.

The count had felt, from the moment he entered the house, the influence of this happiness, and he remained silent and pensive, forgetting that he was expected to recommence the conversation, which had ceased after the first salutations had been exchanged. He perceived the pause, and, by a violent effort, tearing himself, from his pleasing reverie,—

" Madame," said he at length, " I pray you to excuse my emotion, which must astonish you who are only accustomed to the happiness I meet here; but satisfaction is so new a sight to me, that I could never be weary of looking at yourself and your husband."

" We are very happy, monsieur," replied Julie; "but we have also known unhappiness, and few have ever undergone more bitter sufferings than ourselves."

The count's features displayed an expression of the most intense curiosity.

" Oh, all this a family history, as Château-Renaud told you the other day," observed Maximilian. " This humble picture would have but little interest for you, accustomed as you are to behold the pleasures and the misfortunes of the wealthy and illustrious; but such as we are, we have experienced bitter sorrows."

" And God has poured balm into your wounds as he does to all those who are in affliction? " said Monte Cristo inquiringly.

" Yes, M. le Comte," returned Julie, " we may indeed say he has; for he has done for us what he grants only to his chosen; he sent us one of his angels."

The count's cheeks became scarlet, and he coughed, in order to have an excuse for putting his handkerchief to his mouth.

" Those born to wealth, and who have the means of gratifying every wish," said Emmanuel, " know not what is the real happiness of life; just as those who have been tossed on the stormy waters of the ocean on a few frail planks can alone estimate the value of a clear and serene sky."

Monte Cristo rose, and, without making any answer (for the tremulousness of his voice would have betrayed his emotion), walked up and down the apartment with a slow step.

" Our magnificence makes you smile, M. le Comte? " said Maximilian, who had followed him with his eyes.

" No, no," returned Monte Cristo, pale as death, pressing one hand on his heart to still its throbbings whilst with the other he pointed to a crystal cover, beneath which a silken purse lay on a black velvet cushion. " I was wondering what could be the use of this purse, which contains a paper at one end and at the other a large diamond."

" M. le Comte," replied Maximilian, with an air of gravity, " those are our most precious family treasures."

" The stone seems very brilliant," answered the count.

" Oh, my brother does not allude to its value, although it has been estimated at 100,000 francs (£4000); he means, that the articles contained in this purse are the relics of the angel I spoke of just now."

" This I do not comprehend; and yet I may not ask for an explanation, madame," replied Monte Cristo, bowing. " Pardon me, I had no intention of committing an indiscretion."

" Indiscretion!—oh, you make us happy by giving us an occasion of expatiating on this subject. Did we intend to conceal the noble action this purse commemorates, we should not expose it thus. Oh, would we could relate it everywhere, and to every one, so that the emotion of our unknown benefactor might reveal his presence."

" Ah, really," said Monte Cristo, in a half-stifled voice.

" Monsieur," returned Maximilian, raising the glass cover and respectfully kissing the silken purse, " this has touched the hand of a man who saved my father from suicide, us from ruin, and our name from shame and disgrace,—a man by whose matchless benevolence we, poor children, doomed to want and wretchedness, can at present hear every one envying our happy lot. This letter," (as he spoke, Maximilian drew a letter from the purse and gave it to the count)—" this letter was written by him the day that my father had taken a desperate resolution, and this diamond was given by the generous unknown to my sister as her dowry."

Monte Cristo opened the letter, and read it with an indescribable feeling of delight. It was the letter, written (as our readers know) to Julie, and signed " Sinbad the Sailor."

"Unknown, you say, is the man who rendered you this service—unknown to you?"

"Yes; we have never had the happiness of pressing his hand," continued Maximilian. "We have supplicated Heaven in vain to grant us this favour, but all the affair has had a mysterious direction we cannot comprehend; all has been guided by a hand invisible, but powerful as that of an enchanter."

"Oh," cried Julie, "I have not lost all hope of some day kissing that hand, as I now kiss the purse which he has touched. Four years ago, Penelon was at Trieste,—Penelon, M. le Comte, is the old sailor you saw in the garden, and who, from quartermaster, has become gardener,—Penelon, when he was at Trieste, saw on the quay an Englishman, who was on the point of embarking on board a yacht, and he recognised him as the person who called on my father the 5th of June, 1829, and who wrote me this letter the 5th of September. He felt quite convinced of his identity, but he did not venture to address him."

"An Englishman!" said Monte Cristo, who grew uneasy at the attention with which Julie looked at him. "An Englishman, you say?"

"Yes," replied Maximilian, "an Englishman, who represented himself as the confidential clerk of the house of Thomson and French at Rome. It was this that made me start when you said the other day, at M. de Morcerf's, that Messrs. Thomson and French were your bankers. That happened, as I told you, in 1829. For God's sake, tell me, did you know this Englishman?"

"But you tell me, also, that the house of Thomson and French have constantly denied having rendered you this service?"

"Yes."

"Then is it not probable that this Englishman may be some one, who, grateful for a kindness your father had shown him, and which he himself had forgotten, has taken this method of requiting the obligation?"

"Everything is possible on such an occasion, even a miracle."

"What was his name?" asked Monte Cristo.

"He gave no other name," answered Julie, looking earnestly at the count, "than that at the end of his letter—'Sinbad the Sailor.'"

"Which is evidently not his real name, but a fictitious one."

Then, noticing that Julie was struck with the sound of his voice,—

"Tell me," continued he, "was he not about my height, perhaps a little taller; his chin imprisoned, to use the word, in a high cravat; his coat closely buttoned up, and constantly taking out his pencil?"

"Oh, do you then know him?" cried Julie, whose eyes sparkled with joy.

"No," returned Monte Cristo, "I only guessed. I knew a Lord Wilmore, who was constantly doing actions of this kind."

"Without revealing himself?"

"He was an eccentric being, and did not believe in the existence of gratitude."

"O Heaven!" exclaimed Julie, clasping her hands. "In what did he believe, then?"

"He did not credit it at the period when I knew him," said Monte Cristo, touched to the heart by the accent of Julie's voice; "but, perhaps, since then he has had proofs that gratitude does exist."

"And do you know this gentleman, monsieur?" inquired Emmanuel.

"Oh, if you do know him," cried Julie, "can you tell us where he is—where we can find him? Maximilian—Emmanuel—if we do but discover him, he must believe in the gratitude of the heart!"

Monte Cristo felt tears start into his eyes, and he again walked hastily up and down the room.

"In the name of Heaven," said Maximilian, "if you know anything of him, tell us what it is."

"Alas," replied Monte Cristo, striving to repress his emotion, "if Lord Wilmore was your unknown benefactor, I fear you will never again see him. I parted from him, two years ago, at Palermo, and he was then on the point of setting out for the most remote regions; so that I fear he will never return."

"Oh, monsieur, this is cruel of you," said Julie, much affected; and the young lady's eyes swam with tears.

"Madame," replied Monte Cristo gravely, and gazing earnestly on the two liquid pearls that trickled down Julie's cheeks, "had Lord Wilmore seen what I now see, he would become attached to life, for the tears you shed would reconcile him to mankind;" and he held out his hand to Julie, who gave him hers, carried away by the look and accent of the count.

"But," continued she, "Lord Wilmore had a family or friends, he must have known some one, can we not——"

"Oh, it is useless to inquire," returned the count; "he was not the man you seek for, he was my friend; he had no secrets from me, and he would have confided this also to me."

"And he told you nothing?"

"Not a word."

"And yet you instantly named him."

"Ah, in such a case one supposes——"

"Sister, sister," said Maximilian, coming to the count's aid, "monsieur is quite right. Recollect what our excellent father so often told us, ' It was no Englishman that thus saved us.' "

Monte Cristo started.

"What did your father tell you, M. Morrel? " said he eagerly.

"My father thought that this action had been miraculously performed,—he believed that a benefactor had arisen from the grave to serve us. Oh, it was a touching superstition, monsieur, and although I did not myself believe it, I would not for the world have destroyed my father's faith in it. How often did he muse over it and pronounce the name of a dear friend—a friend lost to him for ever; and on his death-bed, when the near approach of eternity seemed to have illumined his mind with supernatural light, this thought, which had until then been but a doubt, became a conviction, and his last words were, ' Maximilian, it was Edmond Dantès! ' "

At these words the count's paleness, which had for some time been increasing, became alarming; he could not speak; he looked at his watch like a man who had forgotten the time, said a few hurried words to Madame Herbault, and pressing the hands of Emmanuel and Maximilian,—

"Madame," said he, " I trust you will allow me to visit you from time to time; I value your friendship, and feel grateful to you for your welcome, for this is the first time for many years that I have thus yielded to my feelings; " and he hastily quitted the apartment.

"This Count of Monte Cristo is a singular man," said Emmanuel.

"Yes," answered Maximilian; "but I feel sure he has an excellent heart, and that he likes us."

"His voice went to my heart," observed Julie; "and two or three times I fancied I had heard it before."

52

Pyramus and Thisbe

ABOUT the centre of the Faubourg Saint-Honoré, and at the back of one of the most distinguished-looking mansions in this rich neighbourhood, where the various hotels vie with each other for elegance of design and magnificence of construction, extended a large garden, whose widely spreading chestnut-trees raised their heads above the walls high and solid as those of a rampart, scattering, each spring, a shower of delicate pink and white blossoms into the large stone vases placed at equal distances upon the two square pilasters, supporting an iron gate, curiously wrought, after the style and manner of the reign of Louis XIV. This noble entrance, however, in spite of its striking appearance and the graceful effect of the geraniums planted in the two vases, as they waved their variegated leaves in the wind, and charmed the eye with their scarlet bloom, had fallen into utter disuse, from the period when the proprietors of the hotel (and many years had elapsed since then) had confined themselves to the possession of the hotel with its thickly planted courtyard, opening into the Faubourg Saint-Honoré, and the garden shut in by this gate, which formerly communicated with a fine kitchen-garden of about an acre in extent. But the demon of speculation having drawn a line, or in other words projected a street, at the extremity of this kitchen-garden, and even before the foundations of the said street were dug, its name being duly affixed upon an iron plate at the corner of the situation chosen, it occurred to the then possessor of the hotel we are describing that a handsome sum might be obtained for the ground now devoted to fruits and vegetables, for the purpose of adding it to the projected street intended to form a great branch of communication with the Faubourg Saint-Honoré itself, one of the most important thoroughfares in the city of Paris.

In matters of speculation, however, though " man proposes," yet money " disposes." From some such difficulty the newly named street died almost in birth, and the purchaser of the " kitchen-garden," having paid a high price for it, and being quite unable to find any one willing to take his bargain off his hands without a considerable loss, yet still clinging to the belief that at some future day he should obtain a sum for it that would repay him, not only for his past outlay, but also the interest upon the capital locked up in his new acquisition, contented himself with letting the ground temporarily to some market-gardeners, at a yearly rent of 500 francs.

Thus, then, as already stated, the iron gate leading into the kitchen-garden had been closed up and left to the rust, which bade fair to destroy its hinges ere long, while to prevent the ignoble glances of the diggers and delvers of the ground from presuming to sully the aristocratical enclosure belonging to the hotel, the gate in question had been boarded up to a height of six feet. True, the planks were not so closely adjusted but that a hasty peep might be obtained between their interstices; but the strict decorum and rigid propriety of the inhabitants of the hotel left no grounds for apprehending that advantage would be taken of that circumstance.

Horticulture seemed, however, to have been abandoned in the deserted kitchen-garden, and where the most choice and delicate of fruits and vegetables once reared their heads, a scanty crop of lucerne alone bore evidence of its being deemed worthy of cultivation. A small, low door gave egress from the walled space we have been describing into the projected street, the ground having been abandoned as unproductive by its various renters, and had now fallen so completely in general estimation as to return not even a fraction of the poor ten shillings per cent. it had originally paid.

Towards the hotel the chestnut-trees we have before mentioned rose high above the wall, without in any way affecting the growth of other luxuriant shrubs and flowers that eagerly pressed forward to fill up the vacant spaces, as though asserting their right to enjoy the boon of light, and air also. At one corner where the foliage became so thick as almost to shut out day, a large stone bench and sundry rustic seats indicated that this sheltered spot was either in general favour or particular use by some inhabitant of the hotel, which was faintly discernible through the dense mass of verdure that partially concealed it, though situated but a hundred paces off.

Whoever had selected this retired portion of the grounds as the boundary of their walks or scene of their meditative musings, was abundantly justified in their choice by the absence of all glare, the cool, refreshing shade, the screen it afforded from the scorching rays of the sun that found no entrance there even during the burning days of hottest summer, the incessant and melodious warbling of birds, and the entire removal from either the noise of the street or the bustle of the hotel.

On the evening of one of the warmest days spring had yet bestowed on the inhabitants of Paris, might be seen, negligently thrown upon the stone bench, a book, a parasol, and a work-basket, from which hung a partly-embroidered cambric handkerchief, while, at a little distance from these articles, was a young female, standing close to the iron gate, endeavouring to discern something on the other side by means of the openings in the planks, whilst the earnestness of her attitude and the fixed gaze with which she seemed to seek the object of her wishes, proved how much her feelings were interested in the matter.

At that instant the little side-door leading from the waste ground to the street was noiselessly opened, and a tall, powerful young man, dressed in a common gray blouse and velvet cap, but whose carefully-arranged hair, beard, and moustaches, all of the richest and glossiest black, ill-accorded with his plebeian attire, and after casting a rapid glance around him, in order to assure himself he was unobserved, entered by this door, and carefully closing and securing it after him, proceeded with a hurried step towards the iron gate.

At the sight of him she expected, though probably not under such a costume, the female we have before mentioned started in terror, and was about to make a hasty retreat. But the eye of love had already seen the movement of the white robe, and observed the fluttering of the blue sash fastened around the slender waist of his fair neighbour. Pressing his lips close to the envious planks that prevented his further progress, he exclaimed, " Fear nothing, Valentine—it is I! "

Again the timid girl found courage to return to the gate, saying, as she did so, " And wherefore come you so late to-day? It is almost the dinner-hour, and I have been compelled to exercise my utmost skill to get rid of the incessant watchfulness of my stepmother, as well as the espionage of my maid, who, no doubt, is employed to report all I do and say. Nor has it cost me a little trouble to free myself from the troublesome society of my brother, under pretence of coming hither to work undisturbed at my embroidery, which, by the way, I am in no hurry to finish. So pray excuse yourself as well as you can for having made me wait, and, after that, tell me why I see you in so singular a dress, that at first I did not recognise you."

" Dearest Valentine," said the young man, " the difference between our respective stations makes me fear to offend you by speaking of my love, but yet I cannot find myself in your presence without longing to pour forth my soul and to tell you how fondly I adore you. If it be but to carry away with me the recollection of such sweet moments, I could even bless—thank you for chiding me, for it leaves me a gleam of hope, that if not expecting me (and that indeed would be worse than vanity of me to suppose), at least I was in your thoughts. You asked me the cause of my being late, as also why I come thus disguised. I will candidly explain the reason of both, and I trust to your goodness to pardon me. But first, let me tell you I have chosen a trade."

" A trade! Oh, Maximilian, how can you jest at a time when we have such deep cause for uneasiness? "

" Heaven keep me from jesting with that which is far dearer to me than life itself! But listen to me, Valentine, and I will tell you all about it. Tired out with ranging fields and scaling walls, and seriously alarmed at the idea suggested by yourself, that if caught hovering about here your father would very likely have me sent to prison as a thief, a sort of thing not very desirable for an officer in the French army, whose continual presence in a place where no warlike projects could be supposed to account for it, might well create surprise; so from a captain of Spahis, I have become a gardener, and consequently adopted the costume of my calling."

" What excessive nonsense you talk, Maximilian! "

" Nonsense! Pray do not call what I consider the wisest action of my life by such a name. Consider, by becoming a gardener I effectually screen our meetings from all suspicion or danger."

" I beseech of you, Maximilian, to cease trifling, and tell me what you really mean."

" Simply, that having ascertained that the piece of ground on which I stand was to let, I made application for it, was readily accepted by the proprietor, and am now master of this fine crop of lucerne! Think of that, Valentine! There is nothing now to prevent my building myself a little hut on my plantation, and residing not twenty yards from you. Only imagine what happiness that would afford me. I can scarcely contain myself at the bare idea. Such felicity seems above all price—as a thing impossible and unattainable. But would you believe that I purchase all this delight, joy, and happiness, for which I would cheerfully have surrendered ten years of my life, at the small cost of 500 francs per annum, paid quarterly! Henceforth we have nothing to fear. I am on my own ground, and have an undoubted right to place a ladder against the wall, and to look over when I please, without having any apprehensions of being taken off by the police as a suspicious character. I may also enjoy the precious privilege of assuring you of my fond, faithful, and unalterable affection, whenever you visit your favourite bower; unless, indeed, it offends your pride to listen to professions of love from the lips of a poor working man, clad in a blouse and cap."

A faint cry of mingled pleasure and surprise escaped from the lips of Valentine, who almost instantly said, in a saddened tone, as though some envious cloud darkened the joy which illumined her heart:

" Alas! No, Maximilian, this must not be for many reasons! We should presume too much on our own strength, and, like others, perhaps, be led astray by our blind confidence in each other's prudence."

" How can you for an instant entertain so unworthy a thought, dear Valentine? Have I not, from the first blessed hour of our acquaintance, schooled all my words and actions to your sentiments and ideas? And you have, I am sure, the fullest confidence in my honour. When you spoke to me of your experiencing a vague and indefinite sense of coming danger, I placed myself blindly and devotedly at your service, asking no other reward than the pleasure of being useful to you; and have I ever since, by word or look, given you cause of regret for having selected me from the numbers that would willingly have sacrificed their lives for you? You told me, my dear Valentine, that you were engaged to M. d'Epinay, and that your father was resolved upon completing the match, and that from his will there was no appeal, as M. de Villefort was never known to change a determination once formed. I kept in the background as you wished, waiting not the decision of your heart or my own; but hoping Providence would graciously interpose in our behalf, and order events in our favour. But what cared I for delays or difficulties so long as my sweet Valentine confessed she loved me, and accepted my fervent vows of unfailing constancy? Blessed avowal! the very recollection of which can at all times raise me even from despair itself. To hear you repeat those enrapturing words from time to time is all I ask, and to obtain that privilege I would cheerfully endure even double my present disquietudes."

" Ah, Maximilian, that is the very thing that makes you so bold, and which renders me at once so happy and unhappy, that I frequently ask myself whether it is better for me to endure the harshness of my stepmother, and her blind preference for her own child, or to be, as I now am, insensible to my pleasure save such as I find in these our meetings, so fraught with danger to both."

" I will not admit that word," returned the young man; " it is at once cruel and unjust. Is it possible to find a more submissive slave than myself? You have permitted me to converse with you from time to time, Valentine, but forbidden my ever following you in your walks or elsewhere—have I not obeyed? And since I found means to enter this enclosure to exchange a few words with you through this door—to be close to you without being enabled to obtain a view of your dear features, have I even solicited to touch the tip of your glove through the small openings of the palisades? Think you that at my age, and with my strength, this wall that now parts us would keep me from your side one instant were it not that my respect for your wishes presents an impassable barrier? Never has a complaint or a murmur of your rigour escaped me. I have been bound by my promises as rigidly as any knight of olden times. Come, come, dearest Valentine, confess that what I say is true, lest I be tempted to call you unjust."

" It is, indeed, most true! " said Valentine, as she passed the end of her slender fingers through a small opening in the planks, thus permitting her lover to press his lips to the taper fingers that almost instantly disappeared, " and you are a true and faithful friend; but still you acted from motives of self-interest, my dear

Maximilian, for you well knew that from the moment in which you had manifested an opposite spirit all would have been ended between us. You promised to bestow on me the friendly affection of a brother. I who have no friend but yourself upon earth, who am neglected and forgotten by my father, harassed and persecuted by my stepmother, and left to the sole companionship of a paralysed and speechless old man, whose withered hand can no longer press mine, and whose eye alone converses with me, while, doubtless, however fixed, chilled his frame, there still lingers in his heart the warmest tenderness for his poor grandchild. Oh, how bitter a fate is mine to serve either as a victim or an enemy to all who are stronger than myself, while my only friend and supporter is but a living corpse! Indeed, indeed, Maximilian, I am very miserable, and you are right to love me for myself alone."

"Dear Valentine," replied the young man, deeply affected, "I will not say you are all I love in the world, for I dearly prize my sister and brother-in-law; but my affection for them is calm and tranquil, in no manner resembling that I feel for you. At the mere thoughts of you my heart beats more quickly, my blood flows with increased rapidity through my veins, and my breast heaves with tumultuous emotions; but I solemnly promise you to restrain all this ardour, this fervour and intensity of feeling, until you yourself shall require me to render them available in serving or assisting you. M. Franz is not expected to return home for a year to come, I am told; in that time many favourable and unforeseen chances may befriend us. Let us then hope for the best,—hope is so sweet a comforter! Meanwhile, Valentine, while reproaching me with selfishness, think a little what you have been to me—the beautiful but cold resemblance of a marble Venus. What promise of future reward have you made me for all the submission and obedience I have evinced?—none whatever! What granted me?—scarcely more! You tell me of M. Franz d'Epinay, your betrothed lover, and you shrink from the idea of being his wife; but tell me, Valentine, is there no other sorrow in your heart? You see me devoted to you body and soul, my life and each warm drop that circles round my heart are consecrated to your service; you know full well that my existence is bound up in yours, that were I to lose you I would not outlive the hour of such crushing misery; yet you speak with calmness of the prospect of your being the wife of another! Oh, Valentine, were I in your place, and did I feel conscious, as you do, of being worshipped, adored, with such a love as mine, a hundred times at least should I have passed my hand between these iron bars, and said to poor Maximilian, 'Take this hand, dearest Maximilian, and believe that, living or dead, I am yours,—yours only, and for ever!'"

The poor girl made no reply, but her lover could plainly hear her sobs. A rapid change took place in the young man's feelings.

"Dearest, dearest Valentine," exclaimed he, "forgive me if I have offended you, and forget the words I spoke if they have unwittingly caused you pain."

"No, Maximilian, I am not offended," answered she; "but do you not see what a poor, helpless being I am, almost a stranger and an outcast in my father's house, where even he is seldom seen; whose will has been thwarted, and spirits broken, from the age of ten years, beneath the iron rod so sternly exercised over me; oppressed, mortified, and persecuted, day by day, hour by hour, minute by minute; no person has cared for, even observed my sufferings, nor have I ever breathed one word on the subject, save to yourself. Outwardly, and in the eyes of the world, I am surrounded by kindness and affection; but the reverse is the case. The general remark is, ' Oh, it cannot be expected that one of so stern a character as M. Villefort could lavish the tenderness some fathers do on their daughters! What, though she has lost her own mother at a tender age, she has had the happiness to find a second mother in Madame de Villefort.' The world, however, is mistaken; my father abandons me from utter indifference, while my stepmother detests me with a hatred so much the more terrible as it is veiled beneath a continual smile."

"Hate you, sweet Valentine!" exclaimed the young man; "how is it possible for any one to do that?"

"Alas," replied the weeping girl, "I am obliged to own that my stepmother's aversion to me arises from a very natural source —her overweening love for her own child, my brother Edward."

"But why should it?"

"Nay! I know not; but, though unwilling to introduce money matters into our present conversation, I will just say this much, that her extreme dislike to me has its origin in mercenary motives; and I much fear she envies me the fortune I already enjoy in right of my mother, and which will be more than doubled at the death of M. and Madame de Saint-Méran whose sole heiress I am. Madame de Villefort has nothing of her own, and, hates me for being so richly endowed. Alas, how gladly would I exchange the half of this wealth for the happiness of at least sharing my father's love! God knows, I would prefer sacrificing the whole, so that it would obtain me a happy and affectionate home."

"Poor Valentine!"

"I seem to myself as though living a life of bondage, yet at the same time am so conscious of my own weakness, that I fear to break the restraint in which I am held, lest I fall utterly powerless and helpless. Then, too, my father is not a person whose orders may be infringed with impunity: protected as he is by his high position, and firmly established reputation for talent and unswerving integrity, no one could oppose him; he is all-powerful with even his king: you he would crush at a word, and myself he would cause to expire of terror at his feet. Dear Maximilian, believe me when I assure you that I attempt not to resist my father's commands, more on your account than my own; for, though I could willingly sacrifice myself, I would not peril your safety."

" But wherefore, my sweet Valentine, do you persist in anticipating the worst, and in viewing everything through so gloomy a medium—why picture the future so fraught with evil? "

" Because I judge it from the past."

" Still, consider that although I may not be, strictly speaking, what is termed an illustrious match for you, I am for many reasons not altogether so much beneath your alliance. The days when such distinctions were so nicely weighed and considered no longer exist in France, and the first families of the monarchy have intermarried with those of the empire. The aristocracy of the lance has allied itself with the nobility of the cannon.* Now I belong to this last-named class; and certainly my prospects of military preferment are most encouraging as well as certain. My fortune, though small, is free and unfettered, and the memory of my late father respected in our country, Valentine, as that of the most upright and honourable merchant of the city;—I say our country, because you were born nor far from Marseilles."

" Name not Marseilles, I beseech you, Maximilian; that one word brings back my mother to my recollection,—my angel mother, who died too soon for myself and all who knew her; but who, after watching over her child, during the brief period allotted to her in this world, now I fondly hope, and fully believe, contemplates her with pitying tenderness from those realms of bliss to which her pure spirit has flown. Ah, were she still living, we need fear nothing, Maximilian, for I would confide our love to her, and she would aid and protect us."

" I fear, Valentine," replied the lover, " that were she living I should never have had the happiness of knowing you; you would then have been too happy to have stooped from your grandeur to bestow a thought on a humble, obscure individual like myself."

" It is you who are unkind, ay, and unjust to, now, Maximilian." cried Valentine; " but there is one thing I wish to know."

"And what is that?" inquired the young man, perceiving that Valentine hesitated and seemed at a loss how to proceed.

"Tell me, truly, Maximilian, whether in former days, when our fathers dwelt at Marseilles, there ever existed any misunderstanding between them?"

"Not that I am at all aware of," replied the young man, "unless, indeed, any ill-feeling might have arisen from their being of opposite parties; your father being, as you know, a zealous partisan of the Bourbons, while mine was wholly devoted to the emperor—there could not possibly be any other difference between them; but now, that I have answered your question to the best of my power and knowledge, tell me, dearest, why you ask?"

"I will," replied his fair companion, "for it is but right you should know all. Then, I must begin by referring to the day when your being made an officer of the Legion of Honour was publicly announced in the papers. We were all sitting in the apartments of my grandfather, M. Noirtier; M. Danglars was there also,—you recollect M. Danglars, do you not, Maximilian, the banker, whose horses ran away with my stepmother and little brother, and very nearly killed them? While the rest of the company were discussing the approaching marriage of Mademoiselle Danglars, I was occupied in reading the paper aloud to my grandfather; but when I came to the paragraph concerning you, although I had done nothing else but read it over to myself all the morning (you know you had told me all about it the previous evening), I felt so happy, and yet so nervous, at the idea of pronouncing your beloved name aloud, and before so many people, that I really think I should have passed it over, but for the fear that my so doing might create suspicions as to the cause of my silence, so I summoned up all my courage, and read it as firmly and steadily as I could."

"Dear Valentine!"

"Well, would you believe it, directly my father caught the sound of your name, he turned round quite hastily, and, like a poor silly thing, I was so persuaded that every one must be as much affected as myself, by the utterance of your name, that I was not surprised to see my father start, and almost tremble; but I even thought (though that surely must have been a mistake) that M. Danglars underwent a similar emotion.

"'Morrel, Morrel!' cried my father, 'stop a bit;' then knitting his brows into a deep frown, he added, 'Surely this cannot be one of the Morrel family who lived at Marseilles, and gave us so much trouble from their being such violent Bonapartists —I mean about the year 1815.'

" ' I fancy,' replied M. Danglars, '.that the individual alluded
to in the journal mademoiselle is reading is the son of the large
shipowner there.' "

" Indeed," answered Maximilian; " and what said your father
then, Valentine? "

" Oh, such a dreadful thing, I dare not repeat it."

" Nay, dearest," said the young man, " be not afraid to tell
me—say, what was it? "

" ' Ah,' continued my father, still frowning severely, ' their
idolised emperor treated these madmen as they deserved; he
called them ' *food for cannon*,' which was precisely all they were
good for; and I am delighted to see the present government have
adopted this salutary principle with all its pristine vigour; if
Algiers* were good for nothing but to furnish out the means of
carrying so admirable an idea into practice, it would be an
acquisition well worthy of struggling to obtain. Though it
certainly does cost France somewhat dear to assert its rights in
that uncivilised country.' "

" The sentiments expressed were somewhat unfeeling, I must
confess," said Maximilian; " but do not let that tinge your fair
cheek with the blush of shame my gentle Valentine; for I can
assure you, that although in a different way, my father was not a
jot or tittle behind yours in the heat of his political expressions:
' Why,' said he, ' does not the emperor, who has devised so many
clever and efficient modes of improving the art of war, not form
a regiment of lawyers, judges, and legal practioners, sending them
in the hottest fire the enemy could maintain, and using them to
save better men? ' You see, my sweet Valentine, that for mildness
of expression and imaginative benefits, there is not much to choose
between the language of either Royalist or Bonapartist. But
what said M. Danglars to this burst of party spirit on the part of
the procureur du roi? "

" Oh, he laughed, and in that singular manner so peculiar
to himself—half malicious, half ferocious; his smile, even, has
always made me shudder, it has so very unnatural a look—he
almost immediately rose and took his leave; then, for the first
time, I observed the agitation of my grandfather, and I must tell
you, Maximilian, that I am the only person capable of discerning
emotion in the paralysed frame of my poor afflicted relative. And
I suspected that the conversation that had been carried on in his
presence (for no one ever cares to refrain from saying and doing
what they like before the dear old man, without the smallest
regard to his feelings) had made a strong impression on his mind;
for, naturally enough, it must have pained him to hear the

emperor he so devotedly loved and served spoken of in that depreciating manner."

"The name of M. Noirtier," interposed Maximilian, "is celebrated throughout Europe; he was a statesman of high standing, and I know not whether you are aware, Valentine, that he took a leading part in every Bonapartean conspiracy set on foot during the restoration of the Bourbons."

"Oh, I have often heard whispers of things that seem to me most strange—the father a Bonapartist, the son a Royalist; what can have been the reason of so singular a difference in parties and politics? But to resume my story; I turned towards my grandfather, as though to question him as to the cause of his emotion; he looked expressively at the newspaper I had been reading.

"'What is the matter, dear grandfather?' said I, 'are you pleased?'

"He gave me a sign in the affirmative.

"'With what my father said just now?'

"He returned a sign in the negative.

"'Perhaps you liked what M. Danglars remarked?'

"Another sign in the negative.

"'Oh, then, you were glad to hear that M. Morrel (I durst not pronounce the dear name of Maximilian) had been made an officer of the Legion of Honour, was that it, dear grandpapa?'

"He signified assent in a way that convinced me he was more than glad—that he was delighted; only think of the poor old man's being so pleased to think that you, who were a perfect stranger to him, had been made an officer of the Legion of Honour! Perhaps, though, it was a mere whim on his part, for he is almost falling into a second childhood; but for all that I love him dearly, and pray that he may long be spared to me."

"How singular," murmured Maximilian, "that your father should apparently hate the very mention of my name, while your grandfather on the contrary——Well, well, it is no use to endeavour to find a reason for these things; strange, indeed, are the feelings brought into play by the action of party likes or dislikes."

"Hush!" cried Valentine suddenly, "conceal yourself!—Go, go! Some one comes!" Maximilian leaped at one bound into his crop of lucerne, which he commenced pulling up in the most pitiless manner, under the pretext of being occupied in weeding it.

"Mademoiselle, mademoiselle!" exclaimed a voice from behind the trees. "Madame is searching for you everywhere; there are visitors in the drawing-room."

" Who is it? " inquired Valentine, much agitated, " are they ladies? "

" Oh, no, mademoiselle! I believe it is some grand prince, or a duke, or a king, perhaps; stay, now I remember, they said he was the Count of Monte Cristo, and that he wished particularly to see you."

" I will come directly," said Valentine aloud.

The name caused an electric shock to the individual on the other side of the iron gate, on whose ear the " *I will come!* " of Valentine, sounded the usual parting knell of all their interviews.

" Now, then," said Maximilian, as, tired with his unusual employment, he stopped to rest himself, by leaning on the handle of a spade he had taken care to furnish himself with, " would I give much to know how it comes about that the Count of Monte Cristo is acquainted with M. de Villefort.".

53

Toxicology

IT was really the Count of Monte Cristo who had just arrived at Madame de Villefort's for the purpose of returning the visit of the procureur du roi, and at this name, as may be easily imagined, the whole house was in confusion. Madame de Villefort, who was alone in her drawing-room when the count was announced, desired that her son might be brought thither instantly to renew his thanks to the count; and Edward, who heard nothing and nobody talked of for two whole days but this great personage, made all possible haste to come to him, not from obedience to his mother, not from any feeling of gratitude to the count, but from sheer curiosity, and that he might make some remark, by help of which he might find an opportunity for saying one of those small pertnesses which made his mother say:

" Oh, that sad child! but pray excuse him, he is really *so* clever."

After the first and usual civilities, the count inquired after M. de Villefort.

" My husband dines with the chancellor," replied the young wife; " he has just gone, and I'm sure he'll be exceedingly sorry not to have had the pleasure of seeing you before he went."

Two visitors who were there when the count arrived, having

gazed at him with all their eyes, retired after that reasonable delay which politeness admits and curiosity requires.

" Ah! what is your sister Valentine doing? " inquired Madame de Villefort of Edward: " tell some one to bid her come here, that I may have the honour of introducing her to the count."

" You have a daughter, then, madame? " inquired the count; " very young, I presume? "

" The daughter of M. de Villefort," replied the young wife, by his first marriage; a fine well-grown girl."

" But melancholy," interrupted Master Edward, snatching the feathers out of the tail of a splendid parroquet, that was screaming on its gilded perch, in order to make a plume for his hat.

Madame de Villefort merely cried.

" Silence, Edward! "

She then added:

" This young madcap is, however, very nearly right, and merely re-echoes what he has heard me say with pain a hundred times; for Mademoiselle de Villefort is, in spite of all we can do to rouse her, of a melancholy disposition and taciturn habit, which frequently injure the effect of her beauty. But what detains her? Go, Edward, and see."

" Because they are looking for her where she is not to be found."

" And where are they looking for her? "

" With grandpapa Noirtier."

" And do you think she is not there? "

" No, no, no, no, no, she is not there! " replied Edward, singing his words.

" And where is she, then? if you know, why don't you tell? "

" She is under the great chestnut-tree," replied the spoiled brat, as he gave, in spite of his mother's cries, live flies to the parrot, who appeared to relish such " small deer " exclusively.

Madame de Villefort stretched out her hand to ring, intending to direct her waiting-maid to the spot where she would find Valentine, when the young lady herself entered the apartment. She appeared much dejected; and any person who considered her attentively might have observed the traces of recent tears in her eyes. Valentine, whom we have in the rapid march of our narrative presented to our readers, without formally introducing her, was a tall and graceful girl of nineteen years of age, with bright chestnut hair, deep blue eyes, and that languishing air so full of distinction which characterised her mother. Her white and slender fingers, her pearly neck, her cheeks tinted with varying hues, gave her at the first view the aspect of one of these lovely Englishwomen who have been so poetically compared in their manner to a swan admiring itself. She entered the apartment, and seeing near her stepmother the stranger of whom she had already heard so much, saluted him without any girlish awkwardness, or even lowering her eyes, and with an elegance that redoubled the count's attention. He rose to return the salutation.

"Mademoiselle de Villefort, my stepdaughter," said Madame de Villefort to Monte Cristo, leaning back on her sofa and motioning towards Valentine with her hand.

"And M. de Monte Cristo, king of China, emperor of Cochin-China," said the young imp, looking slyly towards his sister.

Madame de Villefort at this really did turn pale, and was very nearly angry with this houshold plague who answered to the name of Edward; but the count, on the contrary, smiled, and appeared to look at the boy complacently, which caused the maternal heart to bound again with joy and enthusiasm.

"But, madame," replied the count, continuing the conversation, and looking by turns at Madame de Villefort and Valentine, "have I not already had the honour of meeting yourself and mademoiselle before? I could not help thinking so just now; the idea came over my mind, and as mademoiselle entered, the sight of her was an additional ray of light thrown on a confused remembrance; excuse me the remark."

"I do not think it likely, sir; Mademoiselle de Villefort is not very fond of society, and we very seldom go out," said the lady.

"Then it was not in society that I met with mademoiselle or yourself, madame, or this charming little merry boy? Besides, the Parisian world is entirely unknown to me, for, as I believe I told you, I have been in Paris but very few days. No—but, perhaps, you will permit me to call to mind—stay!"

The count placed his hand on his brow as if to collect his thoughts.

"No—it was somewhere—away from here—it was—I do not know—but it appears that this recollection is connected with a lovely sky and some religious fête; mademoiselle was holding flowers in her hand, the interesting boy was chasing a beautiful peacock in a garden, and you, madame, were under the trellis of some arbour. Pray come to my aid, madame; do not these circumstances bring to your mind some reminiscences?"

"No, indeed," replied Madame de Villefort; "and yet it appears to me, sir, that if I had met you anywhere, the recollection of you must have been imprinted on my memory."

"Perhaps M. le Comte saw us in Italy," said Valentine timidly.

"Yes, in Italy; it was in Italy most probably," replied Monte Cristo; "you have travelled then in Italy, mademoiselle?"

"Yes; madame and I were there two years ago. The doctors

were afraid of my lungs, and prescribed the air of Naples. We went by Bologna, Perusa, and Rome."

"Ah, yes—true mademoiselle," exclaimed Monte Cristo, as if this simple indication was sufficient to determine his recollections. "It was at Perusa, on the day of the Fête-Dieu in the garden of the Hôtel des Postes, when chance brought us together: you, Madame de Villefort, and your son, I now remember having had the honour of meeting you."

"I perfectly well remember Perusa, sir, and the Hôtel des Postes, and the fête to which you allude," said Madame de Villefort, "but in vain do I tax my memory, of whose treachery I am ashamed, for I really do not recall to mind that I ever had the pleasure of seeing you before."

"It is strange, but neither do I recollect meeting with you," observed Valentine, raising her beautiful eyes to the count.

"But I remember it perfectly," interposed the darling Edward.

"I will assist your memory, madame," continued the count; "the day had been burning hot: you were waiting for horses, which were delayed in consequence of the festival. Mademoiselle was walking in the shade of the garden, and your son disappeared in pursuit of the bird."

"And I caught it, mamma, don't you remember?" interposed Edward, "and I pulled three such beautiful feathers out of his tail."

"You, madame, remained under the arbour formed by the vine; do you not remember, that whilst you were seated on a stone-bench, and whilst, as I told you, Mademoiselle de Villefort and your young son were absent, you conversed for a considerable time with somebody?"

"Yes, in truth, yes," answered the lady, turning very red, "I do remember conversing with an individual wrapped in a long woollen mantle; he was a medical man, I think."

"Precisely so, madame; that man was myself. For a fortnight I had been at that hotel, during which period I had cured my valet-de-chambre of a fever, and my landlord of the jaundice, so that I really acquired a reputation as a skilful physician. We discoursed a long time, madame, on different subjects;* of Perugino, of Raffaelle, of manners, customs, of the famous *aqua-tofana* of which they had told you, I think you said, that certain individuals in Perusa had preserved the secret."

"Yes, true," replied Madame de Villefort, with a kind of uneasiness, "I remember now."

"I do not recollect now all the various subjects of which we discoursed, madame," continued the count, with perfect calmness; "but I perfectly remember that, falling into the error which others had entertained respecting me, you consulted me as to the health of Mademoiselle de Villefort."

" Yes, really, sir, you were in fact a medical man," said Madame de Villefort, " since you had cured the sick."

" Molière or Beaumarchais would reply to you, madame, that it was precisely because I was not, that I had cured my patients. For myself, I am content to say to you that I have studied chemistry and the natural sciences somewhat deeply, but still only as an amateur, you understand."

At this moment the clock struck six.

" It is six o'clock," said Madame de Villefort, evidently agitated. " Valentine, will you not go and see if your grandpapa will have his dinner? "

Valentine rose, and saluting the count, left the apartment without replying a single word.

" Oh, madame," said the count, when Valentine had left the room, " was it on my account that you sent Mademoiselle de Villefort away? "

" By no means," replied the lady quickly; " but this is the hour when we give to M. Noirtier the sad repast which supports his sad existence. You are aware, sir, of the deplorable condition of my husband's father? "

" Yes, madame, M. de Villefort spoke of it to me—a paralysis, I think."

" Alas, yes! there is an entire want of movement in the frame of the poor old gentleman; the mind alone is still active in this human machine, and that is faint and flickering, like the light of a lamp about to expire. But excuse me, sir, for talking of our domestic misfortunes; I interrupted you at the moment when you were telling me that you were a skilful chemist."

" No, madame, I did not say so much as that," replied the count, with a smile; "quite the contrary. I have studied chemistry, because, having determined to live in eastern climates, I have been desirous of following the example of King Mithridates."

" *Mithridates, rex Ponticus*,"* said the young scamp, as he tore some beautiful portraits out of a splendid album, " the individual who breakfasted every morning with a cup of poison *à la crême*."

" Edward, you naughty boy! " exclaimed Madame de Villefort, snatching the mutilated book from the urchin's grasp; " you are positively past bearing; you really disturb the conversation: go, leave us, and join your sister Valentine in dear grandpapa Noirtier's room."

" The album," said Edward sulkily.

" What do you mean?—the album! "

" I want the album."

" How dare you tear out the drawings? "

" Oh, it amuses me."

" Go—go directly."

" I won't go unless you give me the album." said the boy, seating himself doggedly in an arm-chair, according to his habit of never giving way.

" Take it, then, and pray disturb us no longer," said Madame de Villefort, giving the album to Edward, who then went towards the door, led by his mother.

The count followed her with his eyes.

" Let us see if she shuts the door after him," he muttered.

Madame de Villefort closed the door carefully after the child, the count appearing not to notice her; then casting a scrutinising glance around the chamber, the young wife returned to her chair, in which she seated herself.

" Allow me to observe, madame," said the count, with that kind tone he could assume so well, " you are really very severe with that dear clever child."

" Oh, sometimes severity is quite necessary," replied Madame de Villefort, with all a mother's real firmness.

" It was his Cornelius Nepos that Master Edward was repeating when he referred to King Mithridates," continued the count, " and you interrupted him in a quotation, which proves that his tutor has by no means neglected him, for your son is really advanced for his years."

" The fact is, M. le Comte," answered the mother, agreeably flattered, " he has great aptitude, and learns all that is set before him. He has but one fault, he is somewhat wilful; but really, on referring for the moment to what he said, do you truly believe that Mithridates used these precautions, and that these precautions were efficacious? "

" I think so, madame, because I—I who now address you, have made use of them, that I might not be poisoned at Naples, at Palermo, and at Smyrna—that is to say, in three several occasions of my life, when, but for these precautions, I must have lost my life."

" And your precautions were successful? "

" Completely so."

" Yes, I remember now your mentioning to me at Perusa something of this sort."

" Indeed, did I? " said the count, with an air of surprise remarkably well counterfeited; " I really did not remember it."

" I inquired of you if poisons acted equally and with the same effect, on men of the north as on men of the south; and you answered me that the cold and sluggish habits of the north did not present the same aptitude as the rich and energetic temperaments of the natives of the south."

" And that is the case," observed Monte Cristo. " I have seen Russians devour, without being visibly inconvenienced, vegetable substances which would infallibly have killed a Neapolitan or an Arab."

" And you really believe the result would be still more sure with us than in the East, and in the midst of our fogs and rains a man would habituate himself more easily than in a warm latitude to this progressive absorption of poison."

" Certainly; it being at the same time perfectly understood that he should have been duly fortified against the poison to which he had not been accustomed."

" Yes, I understand that; and how would you habituate yourself, for instance, or rather, how did you habituate yourself to it? "

" Oh, very easily. Suppose you knew beforehand the poison that would be made use of against you; suppose the poison, was for instance, brucine——"

" Brucine is extracted from the *Bruœa ferruginea*, is it not? " inquired Madame de Villefort.

" Precisely, madame," replied Monte Cristo; " but I perceive I have not much to teach you. Allow me to compliment you on your knowledge; such learning is very rare amongst ladies."

" Oh, I am aware of that," said Madame de Villefort; " but I have a passion for the occult sciences, which speak to the imagination like poetry, and are reducible to figures, like an algebraic equation; but go on, I pray of you; what you say interests me to the greatest degree."

" Well," replied Monte Cristo, " suppose, then, that this poison was brucine, and you were to take a milligramme the first day, two milligrammes the second day, and so on. Well, at the end of ten days, you would have taken a centigramme; at the end of twenty days increasing another milligramme, you would have taken three hundred centigrammes; that is to say, a dose which you would support without inconvenience, and which would be very dangerous for any other person who had not taken the same precautions as yourself. Well, then, at the end of a month, when drinking water from the same *carafe*, you would kill the person who drank this water as well as yourself, without your perceiving, otherwise than from slight inconvenience, that there was any poisonous substance mingled with this water."

" Do you know any other counter-poison? "

" I do not."

" I have often read and read again the history of Mithridates," said Madame de Villefort, in a tone of reflection, " and had always considered it as a fable."

" No, madame, contrary to most history, it is a truth; but what you tell me, madame, what you inquire of me, is not the result of a chance question, for two years since you asked me the same questions, and said, too, that for a very long time this history of Mithridates occupied your mind."

" True, sir. The two favourite studies of my youth were botany and mineralogy, and subsequently, when I learned that the use of simples frequently explained the whole history of a people, and the entire life of individuals in the East, as flowers betoken and symbolise a love affair, I have regretted I was not a man, that I might have been a Flamel, a Fontana, or a Cabanis.""

" And the more, madame," said Monte Cristo, " as the Orientals do not confine themselves, as did Mithridates, to make a cuirass of his poisons, but they also make them a dagger. Science becomes, in their hands, not only a defensive weapon, but still more frequently an offensive one; the one serves against all their physical sufferings, the other against all their enemies; with opium, with belladonna, with brucæa, snake-wood, the cherry-laurel, they put to sleep all those who would arouse them. There is not one of those women, Egyptian, Turk, or Greek, whom here you call ' good women,' who do not know how, by means of chemistry, to stupefy a doctor, and in psychology to amaze a confessor."

" Really! " said Madame de Villefort, whose eyes sparkled with strange fire at this conversation.

" Eh, indeed! Yes, madame," continued Monte Cristo, " the secret dramas of the East begin and end thus, from the plant which can create love to the plant that can cause death; from the draught which opens heaven before your eyes to that which plunges a man in hell! There are as many shades of every kind as there are caprices and peculiarities in human, physical and moral nature; and I will say further, the art of these chemists knows excellently well how to accommodate and proportion the remedy and the ill to its yearnings of love or its desires for vengeance."

" But, sir," remarked the lady, " these eastern societies, in the midst of which you have passed a portion of your existence, are as wild and visionary as the tales that come from their strange land—a man can easily be put out of the way there then: it is, indeed, the Baghdad and Bassora of M. Galland.* The sultans and viziers, who rule over such society, and who constitute what in France we call the government, are, in fact, really these Haroun-al-Raschids and Giaffars, who not only pardon a poisoner, but even make him a prime minister if his crime has been an ingenious one, and who, under such circumstances, have the whole story written in letters of gold to divert their hours of idleness and ennui."

"By no means, madame; the fanciful exists no longer in the East. There are there now, disguised under other names, and concealed under other costumes, agents of police, magistrates, attorney-generals, and bailiffs. They hang, behead, and impale their criminals in the most agreeable possible manner; but some of these, like clever rogues, have contrived to escape human justice, and succeed in their fraudulent enterprises by cunning stratagems. Amongst us a simpleton, possessed by the demon of hate or cupidity, who has an enemy to destroy, or some near relation to dispose of, goes straight to the grocer's or druggist's, gives a false name, which leads more easily to his detection than his real one, and purchases, under a pretext that the rats prevent him from sleeping, five or sixpennyworth of arsenic—if he is really a cunning fellow he goes to five or six different druggists or grocers, and thereby becomes only five or six times more easily traced—then, when he has acquired his specific, he adminsiters duly to his enemy, or near kinsman, a dose of arsenic which would make a mammoth or mastodon burst, and which, without rhyme or reason, makes his victim utter groans which alarm the entire neighbourhood. Then arrive a crowd of policemen and constables. They fetch a doctor, who opens the dead body, and collects from the entrails and stomach a quantity of arsenic in a spoon. Next day, a hundred newspapers relate the fact, with the names of the victim and the murderer. The same evening, the grocer or grocers, druggist or druggists, come and say, 'It was I who sold the arsenic to the gentleman accused;' and rather than not recognise the guilty purchaser, they will recognise twenty. Then the foolish criminal is taken imprisoned, interrogated, confronted, confounded, condemned, and cut off by hemp or steel; or, if she be a woman of any consideration, they lock her up for life. This is the way in which you northerns understand chemistry, madame. Desrues was, however, I must confess, more skilful."

"What would you have, sir?" said the lady, laughing; "we do what we can. All the world has not the secert of the Medicis or the Borgias."

"Now," replied the count, shrugging his shoulders, "shall I tell you the cause of all these stupidities? It is because, at your theatres, by what at least I could judge by reading the pieces they play, they see persons swallow the contents of a phial, or suck the button of a ring, and fall dead instantly. Five minutes afterwards, the curtain falls, and the spectators depart. They are ignorant of the consequences of the murder; they see neither the commissary of police with his badge of office, nor the corporal with his four men; and that is an authority for weak brains to believe that this is the way that things pass. But go a little way from France—go either to Aleppo or Cairo, or only to Naples or Rome, and you will see people passing by you in the streets,—people erect, smiling, and fresh-coloured, of whom Asmodeus,* if you were holding on by the skirt of his mantle, would say. ' That man was poisoned three weeks ago; he will be a dead man in a month.' "

" Then," remarked Madame de Villefort, " they have again discovered the secret of the famous *aqua-tofana* that they said was lost at Perusa."

" Eh, indeed, does mankind ever lose anything? The arts are removed, and make a tour of the world! things change their names, and the vulgar do not follow them—that is all; but there is always the same result. Poison acts particularly on one organ or the other; one on the stomach, another on the brain, another on the intestines. Well, the poison brings on a cough, the cough an inflammation of the lungs, or some other complaint catalogued in the book of science, which, however, by no means precludes it from being decidedly mortal; and if it were not, would be sure to become so, thanks to the remedies applied by foolish doctors, who are generally bad chemists, and which will act in favour of or against the malady as you please; and then there is a human being killed according to all the rules of art and skill, and of whom justice learns nothing, as was said by a terrible chemist of my acquaintance, the worthy Abbé Adelmonte de Taormine,* in Sicily, who had studied these national phenomena very profoundly."

" It is quite frightful, but deeply interesting," said the lady, motionless with attention. " I thought I, must confess, that these tales were inventions of the Middle Ages."

" Yes, no doubt, but improved upon by ours. What is the use of time, encouragements, medals, crosses, Monthyon prizes,* etc., etc., if they do not lead society towards more complete perfection? Yet man will never be perfect until he learns to create and destroy; he does know how to destroy, and that is half way on the road."

" So," added Madame de Villefort, constantly returning to her object, " the poisons of the Borgias, the Medicis, the Renés, the Ruggieris, and later, probably, that of Baron de Trenck,* whose story has been so misused by modern drama and romance——"

" Were objects of art, madame, and nothing more," replied the count. " Do you suppose that the real *savant* addresses himself stupidly to the mere individual? By no means, Science loves eccentricities, leaps and bounds, trials of strength, fancies, if I may be allowed so to term them. Thus, for instance, the excellent Abbé Adelmonte, of whom I spoke to you just now, made in this way some marvellous experiments."

" Really! "

" Yes; I will mention one to you. He had a remarkably fine garden, full of vegetables, flowers, and fruit. From amongst these vegetables he selected the most simple—a cabbage, for instance. For three days he watered this cabbage with a distillation of arsenic; on the third, the cabbage began to droop and turn yellow. At that moment he cut it. In the eyes of everybody it seemed fit for table, and preserved its wholesome appearance. It was only poisoned to the Abbé Adelmonte. He then took the cabbage to the room where he had rabbits, for the Abbé Adelmonte had a collection of rabbits, cats, and guinea-pigs, equally fine as his collection of vegetables, flowers, and fruit. Well, the Abbé Adelmonte took a rabbit, and made it eat a leaf of the cabbage. The rabbit died. What magistrate would find, or even venture to insinuate anything against this? What procureur du roi has ever ventured to draw up an accusation against M. Magendie or M. Flourens,* in consequence of the rabbits, cats, and guinea-pigs they have killed?—not one. So, then, the rabbit dies, and justice takes no notice. This rabbit dead, the Abbé Adelmonte has its entrails taken out by his cook and thrown on the dunghill; on this dunghill was a hen, who, pecking these intestines, was, in her turn, taken ill, and dies next day. At the moment when she was struggling in the convulsions of death, a vulture was flying by (there are a good many vultures in Adelmonte's country); this bird darts on the dead bird and carries it away to a rock, where he dines off his prey. Three days afterwards, this poor vulture, who has been very much indisposed since that dinner, feels very giddy, suddenly, whilst flying aloft in the clouds, and falls heavily into a fish-pond. The pike, eels, and carp eat greedily always, as everybody knows—well, they feast on the vulture. Well, suppose, the next day, one of these eels, or pike, or carp is served at your table, poisoned as they are to the third generation. Well, then, your guest will be poisoned in the fifth generation, and die, at the end of eight or ten days, of pains in the intestines, sickness, or abscess of the pylorus. The doctors open the body and say, with an air of profound learning, ' The subject has died of a tumour on the liver, or typhoid fever! ' "

" But," remarked Madame de Villefort, " all these circumstances which you link thus one to another may be broken by the least accident; the vulture may not pass at the precise moment, or may fall a hundred yards from the fish-pond."

" Ah, this it is which is art. To be a great chemist in the East, we must direct chance; and this is to be achieved."

Madame de Villefort was deep in thought, yet listened attentively.

" But," she exclaimed suddenly, " arsenic is indelible, indestructible; in what way soever it is absorbed, it will be found again in the body of the creature from the moment when it has been taken in sufficient quantity to cause death."

" Precisely so," cried Monte Cristo,—" precisely so; and this is what I said to my worthy Adelmonte. He reflected, smiled, and replied to me by a Sicilian proverb, which I believe is also a French proverb. ' My son, the world was not made in a day—but in seven. Return on Sunday.' On the Sunday following I did return to him. Instead of having watered his cabbage with arsenic, he had watered it this time with a solution of salts, having their bases in strychnine, *strychnos colubrina*, as the learned term it. Now, the cabbage had not the slightest appearance of disease in the world, and the rabbit had not the smallest distrust; yet five minutes afterwards, the rabbit was dead. The fowl pecked at the rabbit, and next day was a dead hen. This time we were the vultures, so we opened the bird, and this time all particular symptoms had disappeared, there were only general symptoms. There was no peculiar indication in any organ—an excitement of the nervous system—that was it;—a case of cerebral congestion— nothing more. The fowl had not been poisoned—she had died of apoplexy. Apoplexy is a rare disease amongst fowls, I believe, but very common amongst men."

Madame de Villefort appeared more and more reflective.

" It is very fortunate," she observed, " that such substances could only be prepared by chemists; for else, really, all the world would be poisoning each other."

" By chemists and persons who have a taste for chemistry." said Monte Cristo carelessly.

" And then," said Madame de Villefort, endeavouring by a struggle, and with effort, to get away from her thoughts, " however skilfully it is prepared, crime is always crime, and if it avoid human scrutiny, it does not escape the eye of God. The Orientals are stronger than we are in cases of conscience, and very prudently have no hell—that is the point."

" Really, madame, this is a scruple which naturally must occur to a pure mind like yours, but which would easily yield before sound reasoning. The bad side of human thought will always be defined by the paradox of Jean Jacques Rousseau,—you know, —the mandarin, who is killed at 500 leagues' distance by raising the tip of the finger.* Man's whole life passes in doing these things, and his intellect is exhausted by reflecting on them. You will find very few persons who will go and brutally thrust a knife in the heart of a fellow-creature, or will administer to him, in order to remove him from that surface of the globe on which we move with life and animation, that quantity of arsenic of which we just now talked. Such a thing is really out of rule— eccentric or stupid. To attain such a point, the blood must be warmed to thirty-six degrees, the pulse be, at least, at ninety, and the feelings excited beyond the ordinary limit. But if passing, as we do in philology, from the word itself to its softened synonym, you make an elimination—a simple change of words: instead of committing an ignoble assassination, if you merely and simply remove from your path the individual who is in your way, and that without shock or violence, without the display of those sufferings which, becoming a punishment, make a martyr of the victim, and of him who inflicts them a butcher, in every sense of the word; if there be no blood, no groans, no convulsions, and, above all, that horrid and compromising moment of accomplishing the act, then one escapes the clutch of the human law, which says to you, ' Do not disturb society! ' This is the mode in which they manage these things, and succeed, in Eastern climes, where there are grave and phlegmatic persons who care very little for the questions of time in conjunctures of importance."

" Yet conscience remains," remarked Madame de Villefort, in an agitated voice, and with a stifled sigh.

" Yes," answered Monte Cristo,—" happily, yes, conscience does remain, and if it did not, how wretched we should be! After every action requiring exertion, it is conscience that saves us, for it supplies us with a thousand good excuses, of which we alone are judges; and these reasons, how excellent ocver in producing sleep, would avail us but very little before a tribunal when we were tried for our lives. Thus, Richard III, for instance, was marvellously served by his conscience after putting away of the two children of Edward IV; in fact, he could say, ' These two children of a cruel and persecuting king, who have inherited the vices of their father, which I alone could perceive in their juvenile propensities,—these two children are impediments in my way of promoting the happiness of the English people, whose unhappiness they (the children) would infallibly have caused.' Thus was Lady Macbeth served by her conscience when she sought to give her son and not her husband (whatever Shakespeare may say) a throne! Ah, maternal love is a great virtue, a powerful motive, so powerful that it excuses a multitude of things, even if after Duncan's death, Lady Macbeth had been at all pricked by her conscience."

Madame de Villefort listened with avidity to these appalling maxims and horrible paradoxes, delivered by the count with that ironical simplicity which was peculiar to him.

After a moment's silence, the lady inquired:

" Do you know," she said, " M. le Comte, that you are a very terrible reasoner, and that you look at the world through a somewhat distempered medium? Have you really measured the world by scrutinies, or through alembics and crucibles? For, truth to say, you are a great chemist, and the elixir you administered to my son, which recalled him to life almost instantaneously——"

" Oh, do not place any reliance on that, madame; *one* drop of that elixir sufficed to recall life to a dying child, but three drops would have impelled the blood into his lungs in such a way as to have produced most violent palpitations; six would have suspended his respiration and caused syncope more serious than that in which he was; ten would have destroyed him. You know, madame, how suddenly I snatched him from those phials which he so imprudently touched? "

" Is it, then, so terrible a poison? "

" Oh, no. In the first place, let us agree that the word poison does not exist, because in medicine use is made of the most violent poisons, which become, according as they are made use of, most salutary remedies."

" What, then, is it? "

" A skilful preparation of my friend's, the worthy Abbé Adelmonte, who taught me the use of it."

" Oh! " observed Madame de Villefort; " it must be an admirable anti-spasmodic."

" Perfect, madame, as you have seen," replied the count; "and I frequently make use of it, with all possible prudence though, be it observed," he added, with a smile of intelligence.

" Most assuredly," responded Madame de Villefort, in the same tone; " as for me, so nervous, and so subject to fainting-fits, I should require a Doctor Adelmonte to invent for me some means of breathing freely, and tranquillising my mind, in the fear I have of dying some fine day of suffocation. In the meanwhile, as the thing is difficult to find in France, and your abbé is not probably disposed to make a journey to Paris on my account, I must continue to use the anti-spasmodics of M. Planché; and mint and Hoffmann's drops are amongst my favourite remedies. Here are some lozenges which I have made up on purpose; they are compounded doubly strong."

Monte Cristo opened the tortoise-shell box which the lady presented to him and imbibed the odour of the pastilles with the air of an amateur who thoroughly appreciated their composition.

"They are, indeed, exquisite," he said; "but as they are necessarily submitted to the process of deglutition—a function which it is frequently impossible for a fainting person to accomplish, I prefer my own specific."

"Undoubtedly, and so should I prefer it, after the effects I have seen produced; but of course it is a secret, and I am not so indiscreet as to ask it of you."

"But I," said Monte Cristo, rising as he spoke,—" I am gallant enough to offer it you. Only remember one thing, a small dose is a remedy, a large one is poison. One drop will restore life as you have witnessed; five or six will inevitably kill, and in a way the more terrible, inasmuch as, poured into a glass of wine, it would not in the slightest degree affect its flavour. But I say no more, madame; it is really as if I were advising you."

The clock struck half-past six, and a lady was announced, a friend of Madame de Villefort, who came to dine with her.

"If I had had the honour of seeing you for the third or fourth time, M. le Comte, instead of only for the second," said Madame de Villefort,—" if I had had the honour of being your friend, instead of only having the happiness of lying under an obligation to you, I should insist on detaining you to dinner, and not allow myself to be daunted by a first refusal."

"A thousand thanks," replied Monte Cristo, "but I have an engagement which I cannot break. I have promised to escort to the Académie a Greek princess of my acquaintance who has never seen your grand Opera, and who relies on me to conduct her thither."

"Adieu, then, sir! and do not forget my recipe."

"Ah, in truth, madame, to do that, I must forget the hour's conversation I have had with you, which is indeed impossible."

Monte Cristo bowed, and left the house.

Madame de Villefort remained immersed in thought.

"He is a very strange man," she said, "and in my opinion is himself the Adelmonte he talks about."

As to Monte Cristo, the result had surpassed his utmost expectations.

"Good," said he, as he went away; "this is a fruitful soil, and I feel certain that the seed sown will not be cast on barren ground."

Next morning, faithful to his promise, he sent the prescription requested.

54

*Robert le Diable**

THE pretext of an Opera engagement was so much the more feasible, as there chanced to be on that very night a more than ordinary attraction at the Académie Royale. Levasseur, who had been suffering under severe illness, made his reappearance in the character of Bertram, and, as usual, the announcement of the most admired production of the favourite composer of the day had attracted an audience consisting of the very *élite* of Parisian fashion. Morcerf, like most other young men of rank and fortune, had his orchestral stall, with the certainty of always finding a seat in at least a dozen of the principal boxes occupied by persons of his acquaintance; he had moreover his right of entry into the omnibus box. Château-Renaud rented a stall beside his own; while Beauchamp, in his editorial capacity, had unlimited range all over the theatre.

It happened that on that particular night the minister's box was placed at the disposal of Lucien Debray, who offered it to the Comte de Morcerf, who again, upon his mother's rejection of it, sent it to Danglars, with an intimation that he should probably do himself the honour of joining the baroness and her daughter during the evening in the event of their accepting the box in question. The ladies received the offer with too much pleasure to dream of a refusal. To no class of persons is the presentation of a gratuitous opera-box more acceptable than to the wealthy millionaire, who still hugs economy while boasting of carrying a king's ransom in his waist-coat-pocket.

Danglars had, however, protested against showing himself in a ministerial box, declaring that his political principles, as well as being a member of the opposition party, would not permit him so to commit himself; the baroness had, therefore, despatched a note to Lucien Debray, bidding him call for them, it being wholly impossible for her to go alone with her daughter to the Opera. There is no gainsaying the plain fact, that a very unfavourable construction would have been put upon the circumstance of two females going together to a public place, while the addition of a third, in the person of her mother's admitted lover, enabled Mademoiselle Danglars to defy malice and ill-nature while visiting so celebrated a place of amusement. Thus, then, we perceive that for a mother, however innocent and pure-minded, to conduct her child alone to operas or spectacles, would be deemed a breach of decorum; but to go thither under the guidance of one who, if not actually her seducer, might in time become so, made all right, and set the world at defiance: let others reconcile these strange inconsistencies if they will, we confess it above our powers!

The curtain rose as usual to an almost empty house, it being one of the absurdities of Parisian fashion never to appear at the Opera until after the commencement of the performances, so that the first act is generally played without the slightest attention being paid to it, that part of the audience already assembled being too much occupied in observing the fresh arrivals, and noting each batch of *élégantes* as they take possession of their boxes, to have eyes or ears for the business of the stage; while the noise of opening and shutting doors, with the mingled buzz of many conversations, effectually prevents even those few who would listen to the orchestra from being able to do so.

" Surely! " said Albert, as the door of a box on the first circle opened, and a lady entered, resplendent with beauty and jewels, " that must be the Countess G——"

" And who may she be, pray? " inquired Château-Renaud carelessly.

" What a question! Now, do you know, baron, I have a great mind to pick a quarrel with you for asking it, as if all the world did not know who the Countess G—— was."

" Ah, to be sure," replied Château-Renaud, " I remember now—your lovely Venetian, is it not? "

" Herself! "

At this moment the countess perceived Albert, and returned his salutation with a graceful smile.

" You are acquainted with her, it seems? " said Château-Renaud.

" Franz introduced me to her at Rome," replied Albert.

" Well, then, will you do as much for me in Paris as he did for you in the ' Queen of Cities '? "

" With much pleasure."

" Silence! " exclaimed the audience.

This manifestation on the part of the spectators of their wish to be allowed to enjoy the rich music then issuing from the stage and orchestra produced not the slightest effect on the two young men, who continued talking as though they had not even heard it.

" The countess was present at the races in the Champ-de-Mars." said Château-Renaud.

" To-day? "

" Yes."

" Bless me! I quite forgot the races—did you bet? "

" Oh, merely a paltry fifty louis."

" And who was the winner? "

" Nautilus. I betted on him."

" But there were three races, were there not? "

" Yes; there was the prize given by the Jockey Club—a gold cup, you know—and a very singular circumstance occurred about that race."

" What was it? "

" Silence! " again vociferated the music-loving part of the audience.

" Why, that it was gained by a horse and rider utterly unknown on the course."

" Is that possible? "

" True as day; the fact was, nobody had observed a horse entered by the name of Vampa, or that of a jockey styled Job, when at the last moment a splendid roan, mounted by a jockey about as big as your fist, presented themselves at the starting-post. They were obliged to stuff at least twenty pounds' weight of shot in the small rider's pockets to make him weight; but with all that he outstripped Ariel and Barbaro, against whom he ran, by at least three whole lengths."

" And was it not found out at last to whom the horse and jockey belonged? "

" No."

" You say that the horse was entered under the name of Vampa? "

" Exactly; that was the title."

" Then," answered Albert, " I am better informed than you are, and know who the owner of that horse was."

" Silence there! " cried the whole collective force of the *parterre* (or pit). And this time the tone and manner in which the command was given betokened such growing hostility, that the two young men perceived, for the first time, that the mandate was addressed to them. Leisurely turning round, they calmly scrutinised the various countenances around them, as though demanding some one person who would take upon himself the responsibility of what they deemed excessive impertinence; but as no one responded to the challenge, the friends turned again to the front of the theatre, and affected to busy themselves with the stage.

At this moment the door of the minister's box opened, and Madame Danglars, accompanied by her daughter, entered, escorted by Lucien Debray, who assiduously conducted them to their seats.

" Ha, ha!" said Château-Renaud, "here come some friends of yours, viscount!—What are you looking at there? don't you see they are trying to catch your eye?"

Albert turned round, just in time to receive a gracious wave of the fan from Madame la Baronne; as for Mademoiselle Eugénie, she scarcely vouchsafed to waste the glances of her large black eyes even upon the business of the stage.

" I tell you what, my dear fellow," said Château-Renaud, " I cannot imagine what objection you can possibly have to Mademoiselle Danglars—that is, setting aside her want of ancestry and somewhat inferior rank, which, by the way, I don't think you care very much about. Now, barring all that, I mean to say she is a deuced fine girl!"

" Handsome, certainly," replied Albert, " but not to my taste, which, I confess, inclines to a softer, gentler, and more feminine style than that possessed by the young lady in question."

" Bless my heart!" exclaimed Château-Renaud, who, because he had seen his thirtieth summer, fancied himself duly warranted in assuming a sort of paternal air with his more youthful friend, " you young people are never satisfied; why, what would you have more? your parents have chosen you a bride who might serve as the living model of the ' Hunting Diana,' and yet you are not content."

" No, for that very resemblance affrights me; I should have liked something more in the manner of the Venus of Milo or Capua; but this chase-loving Diana, continually surrounded by her nymphs, gives me a sort of alarm, lest she should some day entail on me the fate of Actæon."

And, indeed, it required but one glace of Mademoiselle Danglars to comprehend the nature, as well as justness, of Morcerf's remark: " she was certainly handsome," but her beauty was of too marked and decided a character to please a fastidious taste; her hair was raven black, but amid its natural waves might be seen a species of rebellion to the hand that sought to band and braid it; her eyes, of the same colour as her hair, were richly fringed and surmounted by well-arched brows, whose great defect, however, consisted in an almost habitual frown; while her whole physiognomy wore that expression of firmness and decision so little in accordance with the gentler attributes of her sex—her nose was precisely what a statuary would have chosen for a chiselled Juno. Her mouth, which might have been found fault with as too large, displayed teeth of pearly whiteness, rendered still more conspicuous by the over-redness of her lips, beside which her naturally pale complexion seemed even more colourless. But that which completed the almost masculine look Morcerf found so little to his taste, was a dark mole, of much larger dimensions than these freaks of nature generally are placed just at the corner of her mouth; and the effect tended to increase the expression of unbending resolution and self-dependence that formed the characteristics of her countenance. The rest of Mademoiselle Eugénie's person was in perfect keeping with the head just described; she, indeed, reminded you of the Hunting Diana, as Château-Renaud observed, but with a more haughty and resolute air than statuaries have bestowed on the " Chaste Goddess of the silver bow." As regarded her attainments, the only fault to be found with them was the same that a fastidious connoisseur might have found with her beauty, that they were somewhat too erudite and masculine for so young a person: she was a perfect linguist; a first-rate artist; wrote poetry, and composed music; to the study of the latter she professed to be entirely devoted, studying it with indefatigable perseverance, assisted by a schoolfellow who, having been educated with a view of turning her talents to account, was now busily engaged in improving her vocal powers, in order to take (what she was assured by her friends she would infallibly attain) a leading position at the Academy of Music. It was rumoured that she was an object of almost paternal interest to one of the principal composers of the day, who excited her to spare no pains in the cultivation of her voice, which might hereafter prove a source of wealth and independence. But this counsel effectually decided Mademoiselle Danglars never to commit herself by being seen in public with one destined for a theatrical life; and acting upon this principle, the banker's daughter, though perfectly willing to allow Mademoiselle Louise d'Armilly (for so was the future *débutante* named) to practise with her through the day, took especial care not to compromise herself by being seen in her company. Still, though not actually received at the Hôtel Danglars in the light of an acknowledged friend, Louise was treated with far more kindness and consideration than is usually bestowed on that most unfortunate class of deserving females styled governesses.

The curtain fell almost immediately after the entrance of Madame Danglars into her box, the band quitted the orchestra for the accustomed half-hour's interval allowed between the acts, and the audience were left at liberty to promenade the salon or lobbies, or to pay and receive visits in their respective boxes. Morcerf and Château-Renaud were amongst the first to avail themselves of this permission. For an instant the idea struck Madame Danglars that this eagerness on the part of the young viscount arose from his impatience to join her party, and she whispered her expectations to her daughter that Albert was hurrying to pay his respects to them. Mademoiselle Eugénie, however, merely returned a dissenting movement of the head, while, with a cold smile, she directed the attention of her mother to an opposite *loge* situated on the first circle, in which sat the Countess G——, and where Morcerf had just made his appearance.

" So we meet again, my travelling friend, do we? " cried the countess, extending her hand to him with all the warmth and cordiality of an old acquaintance; " it was really very good of you to recognise me so quickly, and still more so to bestow your first visit on me."

" Be assured," replied Albert, " that if I had been aware of your arrival in Paris, and had known your address, I should have paid my respects to you long ere this. Allow me to introduce my friend, Baron de Château-Renaud, one of the rare specimens of real gentlemen now to be found in France, and from whom I have just learned that you were a spectator of the races in the Champ-de-Mars yesterday."

Château-Renaud bowed to the countess.

" Were you at the races, then, M. le Baron? " inquired the countess eagerly.

" I was."

" Well, then," pursued Madame G——, with considerable animation, " you can probably tell me to whom belonged the winner of the Jockey Club stakes? "

" I am sorry to say I cannot," replied the baron; " and I was just asking the same question of my friend Albert."

" Are you very anxious to know, Madame la Comtesse? " asked Albert.

" To know what? "

" The name of the owner of the winning horse? "

" Excessively: only imagine—but do tell me, M. le Vicomte, whether you really are acquainted with it or no? "

" I beg your pardon, madame, but you were about to relate some story, were you not? You said, ' Only imagine,'—and then paused. Pray continue."

" Well, then, listen! You must know I felt so interested for the splendid roan horse, with his elegant little rider so tastefully dressed in a pink satin jacket and cap, that I could not help praying for their success with as much earnestness as though the half of my fortune were at stake; and when I saw them outstrip all the others, and come to the winning-post in such gallant style, I actually clapped my hands with joy. Imagine my surprise, when, upon returning home, the first object I met on the staircase was the identical jockey in the pink jacket! I concluded that, by some singular chance, the owner of the winning horse must live in the same hotel as myself; but lo! as I entered my apartments I beheld the very gold cup awarded as a prize to the unknown horse and rider. Inside the cup was a small piece of paper, on which were written these words 'From Lord Ruthven to Countess G——' "

"Precisely; I was sure of it," said Morcerf.

"Sure of what?"

"That the owner of the horse was Lord Ruthven himself."

"What Lord Ruthven do you mean?"

"Why, our Lord Ruthven—the Vampire of the Salle Argentino!"

"Mercy upon me!" exclaimed the countess; "is he here, too?"

"To be sure,—why not?"

"And you visit him?—meet him at your own house and elsewhere?"

"I assure you he is my most intimate friend, and M. de. Château-Renaud has also the honour of his acquaintance."

"But what makes you so convinced of his being the winner of the Jockey Club prize?"

"Was not the winning horse entered by the name of Vampa?"

"What of that?"

"Why, do you not recollect it was the appellation of the celebrated bandit by whom I was made prisoner?"

"True."

"And from whose hands the count extricated me in so wonderful a manner?"

"To be sure, I remember it all now."

"Now I argue from the circumstance of the horse and bandit bearing the same singular name, that the count was the person to whom the unknown horse belonged."

"But what could have been his motive for sending the cup to me?"

"In the first place, because I had spoken much of you to him, as you may believe; and in the second, because he delighted to see a countrywoman take so lively an interest in his success."

"I trust and hope you never repeated to the count all the foolish remarks we used to make about him?"

"I should not like to affirm upon oath that I have not. Besides his presenting you the cup under the name of Lord Ruthven proves his knowledge of the comparison instituted between himself and that individual."

"Oh, but that is dreadful! Why, the man must owe me a fearful grudge for so doing."

" Does his offering you the fruits of his victory seem like the conduct of one who felt ill-will towards you? "

" No, certainly not! "

" Well then——"

" And so this singular being is in Paris? "

" He is."

" And what effect does he produce? "

" Why," said Albert, " certainly, during the first week of his arrival here, he was the great lion of the day; nothing else was thought of or talked about but the wonderful Count of Monte Cristo and his extraordinary actions; then the coronation of the Queen of England took place, followed almost immediately afterwards by the robbery of Mademoiselle Mars' diamonds and two such interesting events turned public attention into other channels."

" My good fellow," said Château-Renaud, " the count happens to be so great a favourite of yours, that you treat him as carefully and delicately as though he were your best and most intimate friend. Do not believe what Albert is telling you, Madame la Comtesse; so far from the sensation excited in the Parisian circles by the appearance of the Count of Monte Cristo having abated, I take upon myself to declare that it is as strong as ever. His first astounding act upon coming amongst us was to present a pair of horses, worth 32,000 francs to Madame Danglars; his second, the almost miraculous preservation of Madame de Villefort's life; now it seems that he has carried off the prize awarded by the Jockey Club! I, therefore, assert and maintain, in spite of whatever Morcerf may advance, that not only is the count the object of universal remark, interest, and curiosity, at this present moment, but also that he will continue to be so while he pleases to exhibit an eccentricity of conduct and action which, after all, may be his ordinary mode of amusing himself as well as the world."

" Perhaps you are right," said Morcerf, " but just cast your eyes towards the box formerly belonging to the Russian ambassador, and tell me, if you can, who is the present occupant of it? "

" Which box do you mean? "

" The one between the pillars on the first tier—it seems to have been fitted up entirely afresh."

" Did you observe any one during the first act? "

" Where? "

" In that box."

" No," replied the countess; " it was certainly empty during the first act," then, resuming the subject of their previous conversation, she said, " And so you really believe it was your mysterious Count of Monte Cristo that gained the prize? "

" I am sure of it."

" And who afterwards sent the golden cup to me? "

" Undoubtedly! "

" Then, do you know," said the countess, " I have a strong inclination to return it! I cannot understand receiving such presents from a person wholly unknown to you."

" Do no such thing, I beg of you; it would only produce a second goblet, formed of a magnificent sapphire, or hollowed out of a gigantic ruby. It is his manner of acting, and you must take him as you find him."

At this moment the bell rang to announce the drawing up of the curtain for the second act. Albert rose to return to his place.

" Shall I see you again? " asked the countess.

" If you will permit me to make a second visit between the next pause in the opera, I will do myself the honour of coming to inquire whether there is anything in which I can be useful to you in Paris? "

" Pray take notice," said the countess, " that my present residence is 22 Rue de Rivoli, and that I am at home to my friends every Saturday evening. So now, you gentlemen cannot plead ignorance both of when and where you may see me, if so inclined."

The young men bowed, and quitted the box. Upon reaching their stalls, they found the whole of the audience in the parterre standing up and directing their gaze towards the box formerly possessed by the ambassador of Russia. Following the universal example, the friends perceived that an individual of from thirty-five to forty years of age, dressed in deep black, had just entered, accompanied by a female dressed after the Eastern style. The lady was young and surpassingly beautiful, while the rich magnificence of her attire drew all eyes upon her.

" By heavens! " said Albert, " it is Monte Cristo himself with his fair Greek! "

The strangers were, indeed, no other than the count and Haydée. The sensation excited by the beauty and dazzling appearance of the latter soon communicated itself to every part of the theatre, and even ladies leaned forwards from the boxes to admire the many-coloured coruscations that darted their sparkling beams whenever the superb diamonds worn by the young Greek played and glittered among the cut-glass lustres with their waxen lights.

The second act passed away during one continued buzz of voices, one deep whisper, intimating that some great and universally interesting event had occurred; all eyes, all thoughts were occupied with the young and beautiful female, whose gorgeous apparel and splendid jewels threw an air of insignificance upon all the fair visitants of the theatre; the business of the stage was utterly neglected—all seemed to consider the contemplation of so much loveliness far more deserving attention.

Upon this occasion an unmistakable sign from Madame Danglars intimated her desire to see Albert in her box directly the curtain fell on the second act, and neither the politeness nor good taste of Morcerf would permit his neglecting an invitation so unequivocally given. At the close of the act he therefore proceeded to the baroness's *loge*. Having bowed to the two ladies, he extended his hand to Debray. By the baroness he was most graciously welcomed, while Eugénie received him with her accustomed coldness.

" My dear fellow," said Debray, " you have just come in the very nick of time to help a fellow-creature regularly beaten and at a standstill. There is madame overwhelming me with questions respecting the count; she insists upon it that I can tell her his birth, education, and parentage, where he came from and whither he is going. Being no disciple of Cagliostro,* I was wholly unable to do this; so, by way of getting out of the scrape, I said, ' Ask Morcerf, he has got the whole history of his beloved Monte Cristo at his fingers' ends; ' whereupon the baroness made you a sign to come hither, and now I leave the solution of her questions in your hands."

" Is it not almost incredible," said Madame Danglars, " that a person having at least half a million of secret service money at his command, should possess so little information upon so everyday a matter as the present? "

" Let me assure you, madame," said Lucien, " that had I really the sum you mention at my disposal, I would employ it more profitably than in troubling myself to obtain particulars respecting the Count of Monte Cristo, whose only merit in my eyes consists in his being twice as rich as a nabob. However, I have turned the business over to Morcerf, so pray settle it with him as may be most agreeable to you; for my own part, I care nothing about the count or his mysterious doings."

" I am very sure no nabob of our time would have sent me a pair of horses worth 32,000 francs, wearing on their heads four diamonds valued at 5000 francs each."

" He seems to have a mania for diamonds," said Morcerf, smiling; " and I verily believe that, like Potemkin,* he keeps his pockets filled for the sake of strewing them along the road, as little Thumb* did his flint-stones."

" Perhaps he has discovered some mine," said Madame Danglars. " I suppose you know he has an order for unlimited credit on the baron's banking establishment? "

" I was not aware of it," replied Albert, " but I can readily believe it."

" And, further, that he stated to M. Danglars his intention of only staying a year in Paris, during which time he proposed to spend six millions. He must be the Shah of Persia travelling *incog*."

" Have you remarked the extreme beauty of that young female by whom he is accompanied, M. Lucien? " inquired Eugénie.

" I really never met with one woman so ready to do justice to the charms of another as yourself; let us see how far she merits your praises," continued Lucien, raising his lorgnette to his eye. " A most lovely creature, upon my soul! " cried he, after a long and searching scrutiny.

" Who is this young person, M. Morcerf," inquired Eugénie; " does anybody know? "

" Allow me to state," said Albert, replying to this direct appeal, " that I can give you very tolerable information on that subject as well as on most points relative to the singular person of whom we are now conversing—the young female is a Greek."

" So I should presume by her dress; if, therefore, you know no more than that one self-evident fact, the whole of the spectators in the theatre are as well informed as yourself."

" I am extremely sorry you find me so ignorant a cicerone," replied Morcerf, " but I am reluctantly obliged to confess, I have nothing further to communicate—yes, stay, I do know one thing more, namely, that she is a musician, for one day that I chanced to be breakfasting with the count, I heard the sound of a guzla—it is impossible it could have been touched by any finger than her own."

" Then your count entertains visitors, does he? " asked Madame Danglars.

" Indeed he does, and in a most noble manner, I can assure you."

" I must try and persuade M. Danglars to invite him to a ball or dinner, or something of the sort, that he may be compelled to ask us in return."

" What! " said Debray, laughing; " do you really mean you would go to his house? "

" Why not? my husband could accompany me."

" But do you know this mysterious count is a bachelor? "

" You have ample proof to the contrary if you look opposite," said the baroness, as she laughingly pointed to the beautiful Greek.

" No, no! " exclaimed Debray; " that female is not his wife, he told us himself she was his slave; do you not recollect, Morcerf, his telling us so at your breakfast? "

" Well, then," said the baroness, " if slave she be, she has all the air and manners of a princess."

" Of the *Arabian Nights*? "

" If you like; but tell me, my good Lucien, what is it that constitutes a princess? gold, silver, and jewels, and our Greek beauty there is one blaze of diamonds; I doubt if any queen's could equal them."

" To me she seems overloaded," observed Eugénie, " she would look far better if she wore fewer, and we should then be able to see her finely formed throat and wrists."

" See, how the artist peeps out! " exclaimed Madame Danglars; " my poor Eugénie; you must conceal your passion for the fine arts."

" I admire all that is beautiful in art or nature," returned the young lady.

" What do you think of the count? " inquired Debray; " he is not much amiss, according to my ideas of good looks."

" The count? " repeated Eugénie, as though it had not occurred to her to observe him sooner, " the count? oh!—he is so dreadfully pale."

" I quite agree with you," said Morcerf; " and it is in that very paleness that consists the secret we want to find out. The Countess G—— insists upon it he is a vampire."

" Then the Countess G—— has returned to Paris, has she? " inquired the baroness.

" Is that she, mamma? " asked Eugénie; " almost opposite to us, with that profusion of beautiful light hair? "

" Yes, yes, there she is! " cried Madame Danglars. " Shall I tell you what you ought to do, Morcerf? "

" Command me, madame, I am all attention."

" Well, then, you should go and bring your Count of Monte Cristo to us."

" What for? " asked Eugénie.

" What for? why, to converse with him, of course; if you have no curiosity to hear whether he expresses himself like other people I can assure you I have. Have you really no desire to be introduced, to this singular being? "

" None whatever," replied Eugénie.

" Strange girl! " murmured the baroness.

" He will very probably come of his own accord," said Morcerf. " There! do you see, madame, he recognises you, and bows."

The baroness returned the salute in the most smiling and graceful manner.

" Well," said Morcerf, " I may as well be magnanimous and tear myself away to forward your wishes. Adieu; I will go and, try if there are any means of speaking to him."

" Go straight to his box; that will be the simplest plan."

" But I have never been presented."

" Presented to whom? "

" To the beautiful Greek."

" You say she is only a slave? "

" While you assert that she is a queen, or at least a princess. No, no, I cannot venture to enter his box; but I hope that when he observes me leave you, he will come and take my place."

" We shall see; it is just probable, therefore go at once."

" Adieu! I sacrifice myself, remember that," said Albert, as he made his parting bow.

As he had predicted, just as he was passing the count's box, the door opened, and Monte Cristo came forth. After giving some directions to Ali, who stood in the lobby, the count observed Albert, and, taking his arm, walked onwards with him. Carefully closing the box-door, Ali placed himself before it, while a crowd of wondering spectators assembled round the unconscious Nubian.

" Upon my word," said Monte Cristo, " Paris is a strange city, and the Parisians a very singular people. Do pray observe that cluster of persons collected round poor Ali, who is as much astonished as themselves; really one might suppose he was the only Nubian they had ever beheld. Now I will pledge myself that a Frenchman might show himself in public, either in Tunis, Constantinople, Bagdad, or Cairo, without drawing a circle of gazers around him."

" That shows that the Eastern nations have too much good sense to waste their time and attention on objects undeserving of either. However, as far as Ali is concerned, I can assure you, the interest he excites is merely from the circumstance of his being your attendant: you who are at this moment the most celebrated and fashionable person in Paris."

" Really? and what has procured me so flattering a distinction? "

" What? why, yourself, to be sure! You give away horses worth a thousand guineas; you save the lives of ladies of high rank and beauty; you send thoroughbred racers to contest the prize of the Jockey Club, the horses being rode by tiny urchins not larger than marmots; then, when you have carried off the golden trophy of victory, instead of setting any value on it, you give it to the first handsome woman you think of! "

" And who has filled your head with all this nonsense? "

" Why, in the first place, I heard it from Madame Danglars, who, by the bye is, dying to see you in her box, or to have you seen there by others; secondly, I learned it from Beauchamp's journal; and thirdly from my own imagination. Why, if you sought concealment, did you call your horse Vampa? "

" That was an oversight, certainly," replied the count; " but tell me, does the Comte de Morcerf never visit the Opera? I have been looking for him, but without success."

" He will be here to-night."

" In what part of the house? "

" In the baroness's *loge*, I believe."

" Is the charming young female with her—her daughter? "

" Yes."

" Indeed! then I congratulate you."

Morcerf smiled. " We will discuss that subject at length some future time," said he. " But what think you of the music? "

" What music? "

" That which you have just heard."

" Oh, it is admirable as the production of a human composer, sung by a party of bipeds without feathers, as Diogenes styled mankind."

" Why, my dear, count would you have me understand that you undervalue our terrestrial harmony, because you can at pleasure enjoy the seraphic strains that proceed from the seven choirs of paradise? "

" You are right, in some degree; but when I wish to listen to sounds so exquisitely attuned to melody as mortal ear never yet listened to, I go to sleep."

" Then why not indulge yourself at once? Sleep, by all means, if such be your means of procuring the concord of celestial sounds. Pray do not hesitate; you will find every incentive to slumber, and for what else but to send people to sleep, was the opera invented? "

" No thank, you. Your orchestra is rather too noisy to admit the soft wooing of the drowsy god. The sleep, after the manner I have mentioned, and to produce the desired effects, absolute calm and silence are necessary, and a certain preparation must also be called in aid."

" I know—the famous hatchis! "

" Precisely. Now you know my secret, let me recommend you, my dear viscount, to come and sup with me whenever you wish to be regaled with music really worth listening to."

" I have already enjoyed that treat when breakfasting with you," said Morcerf.

" Do you mean at Rome? "

" I do."

" Ah, then, I suppose you heard Haydée's guzla; the poor exile frequently beguiles a weary hour in playing over to me the airs of her native land."

Morcerf did not pursue the subject, and Monte Cristo himself fell into a silent reverie.

The bell rang at this moment for the rising of the curtain.

"You will excuse my leaving you," said the count, turning in the direction of his *loge.*

"What! Are you going?"

"Pray, say everything that is kind to Countess G—— on the part of her friend the Vampire."

"And what message shall I convey to the baroness"

"That, with her permission, I propose doing myself the honour of paying my respects in the course of the evening."

The third act had now commenced; and during its progress the Comte de Morcerf, according to promise, made his appearance in the box of Madame Danglars. The Comte de Morcerf was not one of those persons whose aspect would create either interest or curiosity in a place of public amusement; his presence, therefore, was wholly unnoticed, save by the occupants of the box in which he had just seated himself. The quick eye of Monte Cristo, however, marked his coming; and a slight though meaning smile passed over his lips as he did so. Haydée, whose soul seemed centred in the business of the stage, like all unsophisticated natures, delighted in whatever addressed itself to the eye or ear. The third act passed off as usual. Mesdemoiselles Noblet, Julie, and Leroux* executed the customary quantity of pirouettes; Robert duly challenged the Prince of Grenada; and the royal parent of the Princess Isabella, taking his daughter by the hand, swept round the stage with majestic strides, the better to display the rich folds of his velvet robe and mantle. After which the curtain again fell, and the spectators poured forth from the theatre into the lobbies and salon. The count, quitting his box, proceeded at once to the box of Madame Danglars, who could scarcely restrain a cry of mingled pleasure and surprise.

"Welcome, M. le Comte!" exclaimed she, as he entered. "I have been most anxious to see you that I might repeat verbally those thanks writing can so ill express."

"Surely so trifling a circumstance cannot deserve a place in your remembrance. Believe me, madame, I had entirely forgotten it!"

"But it is not so easy to forget, M. le Comte, that the very day following the one in which you kindly prevented my disappointment respecting the horses, you saved the life of my dear friend Madame de Villefort, which I had placed in danger by lending her the very animals your generosity restored to me."

"This time, at least, I cannot accept of your flattering acknowledgments. In the latter affair you owe me nothing. Ali, my Nubian slave, was the fortunate individual who enjoyed the privilege of rendering to your friend the trifling assistance you allude to."

" Was it Ali," asked the Comte de Morcerf, " who rescued my son from the hands of bandits? "

" No, M. le Comte," replied Monte Cristo, pressing with friendly warmth the hand held out to him by the general; " in this instance I may fairly and freely accept your thanks; but you have already tendered them, and fully discharged your debt—if, indeed, there existed one—and I feel almost mortified to find you still revert to the trifling aid I was able to render your son."

" May I beg of you, Madame la Baronne, to honour me with an introduction to your charming daughter? "

" Oh, you are no stranger—at least not by name," replied Madame Danglars, " and the last two or three days we have really talked of nothing else but yourself. Eugénie," continued the baroness, turning towards her daughter, " M. le Comte de Monte Cristo."

The count bowed, while Mademoiselle Danglars returned a slight inclination of the head.

" You have a charming young person with you to-night, M. le Comte," said Eugénie. " Your daughter, I presume? "

" No, indeed," said Monte Cristo, astonished at the coolness and freedom of the question. " The female you allude to is a poor unfortunate Greek left under my care."

" And what is her name? "

" Haydée," replied Monte Cristo.

" A Greek? " murmured the Comte de Morcerf.

" Yes, indeed, count," said Madame Danglars; " and tell me, did you ever see at the court of Ali Tebelen,* whom you so gloriously and valiantly served, a more exquisite beauty or richer costume than is displayed in the fair Greek before us? "

" Did I hear rightly, M. le Comte," said Monte Cristo, " that you served at Yanina? "

" I was inspector-general of the pacha's troops," replied Morcerf; " and I seek not to conceal that I owe my fortune, such as it is, to the liberality of the illustrious Albanese chief."

" But look! pray look," exclaimed Madame Danglars.

" Where? " stammered out Morcerf.

"There, there!" said Monte Cristo, as, wrapping his arms around the count, he leaned with him over the front of the box, just as Haydée, whose eyes were occupied in examining the theatre in search of the count, perceived his pale marble features close to the countenance of Morcerf, whom he was holding in his arms. This sight produced on the astonished girl an effect similar to that of the fabulous head of Medusa. She bent forwards as though to assure herself of the reality of what she beheld, then uttering a faint cry, threw herself back in her seat. The sound that burst from the agitated Greek quickly reached the ear of the watchful Ali, who instantly opened the box-door to ascertain the cause.

" Bless me! " exclaimed Eugénie, " what has happened to your ward, M. le Comte? she seems taken suddenly ill! "

" Very probably! " answered the count. " But do not be alarmed on her account! Haydée's nervous system is delicately organised, and she is peculiarly susceptible of the odours even of flowers—nay, there are some which cause her to faint if brought into her presence. However," continued Monte Cristo, drawing a small phial from his pocket, " I have an infallible remedy for such attacks."

So saying, he bowed to the baroness and her daughter, exchanged a parting shake of the hand with Debray and the count, and quitted the box. Upon his return to Haydée, he found her extremely pale and much agitated. Directly she saw him she seized his hand, while the icy coldness of her own made Monte Cristo start.

" With whom was my lord conversing a few minutes since? " asked she, in a trembling voice.

" With the Comte de Morcerf," answered Monte Cristo. " He tells me he served your illustrious father, and that he owes his fortune to him! "

" Base, cowardly traitor that he is! " exclaimed Haydée, her eyes flashing with rage, " he it was who sold my beloved parent to the Turks, and the fortune he boasts of was the price of his treachery! Knowest thou not that, my dear lord? "

" Something of this I heard in Epirus," said Monte Cristo; " but the particulars are still unknown to me. You shall relate them to me, my child. They are, no doubt, both curious and interesting."

" Yes, yes! but let us go hence, I beseech you. I feel as though it would kill me to remain longer near that dreadful man."

So saying, Haydée arose, and wrapping herself in her burnous of white cashmere embroidered with pearls and coral, she hastily quitted the box at the moment when the curtain was rising upon the fourth act.

" Do you observe," said the Countess G—— to Albert, who had returned to her side, " that man does nothing like other people; he listens most devoutly to the third act of *Robert le Diable*, and when the fourth begins, makes a precipitate retreat."

55

A Talk about Stocks

SOME days after this meeting, Albert de Morcerf visited the Count of Monte Cristo at his house in the Champs Elysées, which had already assumed that palace-like appearance which the count's princely fortune enabled him to give even to his most temporary residences. He came to renew the thanks of Madame Danglars which had been already conveyed to the count through the medium of a letter, signed " Baronne Danglars, née Hermine de Servieux." Albert was accompanied by Lucien Debray, who, joining in his friend's conversation, added some passing compliments, the source of which the count's talent for finesse easily enabled him to guess. He was convinced that Lucien's visit to him was to be attributed to a double feeling of curiosity, the larger half of which sentiment emanated from the Rue de la Chausée d'Antin. In short, Madame Danglars, not being able personally to examine in detail the domestic economy and household arrangements of a man who gave away horses worth 30,000 francs, and who went to the Opera with a Greek slave wearing diamonds to the amount of a million of money, had deputed those eyes, by which she was accustomed to see, to give her a faithful account of the mode of life of this incomprehensible individual. But the count did not appear to suspect there could be the slightest connection between Lucien's visit and the baroness's curiosity.

" You are in constant communication, then, with the Baron Danglars? " inquired the count of Albert de Morcerf.

" Yes, count, you know what I told you? "

" All remains the same, then, in that quarter? "

" It is more than ever a settled thing," said Lucien; and, considering this remark was all that he was at that time called upon to make, he adjusted the glass to his eye, and biting the top of his gold-headed cane, began to make the tour of the apartment, examining the arms and the pictures.

" Ah," said Monte Cristo, " I did not expect the affair would have been so promptly concluded."

" Oh, things take their course without our assistance. Whilst we are forgetting them, they are falling into their appointed order; and when, again, our attention is directed to them, we are surprised at the progress they have made towards the proposed end. My father and M. Danglars served together in Spain, my father in the army and M. Danglars in the commissariat department. It was there that my father, ruined by the revolution, and M. Danglars, who never had possessed any patrimony, both laid the foundation of their different fortunes."

"Yes," said Monte Cristo, " I think M. Danglars mentioned that in a visit which I paid him; and," continued he, casting a side-glance at Lucien, who was turning over the leaves of an album, "is Mademoiselle Eugénie pretty—for I, think, I remember that to be her name? "

"Very pretty, or rather, very beautiful," replied Albert, " but of that style of beauty, which I do not appreciate; I am an ungrateful fellow."

"You speak as if you were already her husband."

"Ah!" returned Albert, in his turn looking round to see what Lucien was doing.

"Really," said Monte Cristo, lowering his voice, " you do not appear to me to be very enthusiastic on the subject of this marriage."

"Mademoiselle Danglars is too rich for me," replied Morcerf, " and that frightens me."

"Bah!" exclaimed Monte Cristo, " that's a fine reason to give. Are you not rich yourself? "

"My father's income is about 50,000 francs per annum; and he will give me, perhaps, ten or twelve thousand when I marry."

"That, perhaps, might not be considered a large sum, in Paris especially," said the count; " but everything does not depend on wealth, and it is a fine thing to have a good name, and to occupy a high station in society. Your name is celebrated, your position magnificent; and then the Comte de Morcerf is a soldier, and it is pleasing to see the integrity of a Bayard united to the poverty of a Duguesclin: disinterestedness is the brightest ray in which a noble sword can shine. As for me, I consider the union with Mademoiselle Danglars a most suitable one; she will enrich you, and you will ennoble her."

Albert shook his head, and looked thoughtful.

"There is still something else," said he.

"I confess," observed Monte Cristo, " that I have some difficulty in comprehending your objection to a young lady who is both rich and beautiful."

"Oh," said Morcerf, " this repugnance, if repugnance, it may be called, is not all on my side."

"Whence can it arise then? for you told me your father desired the marriage."

"My mother's is the dissenting voice; she has a clear and penetrating judgment, and does not smile on the proposed union.

I cannot account for it, but she seems to entertain some prejudice against the Danglars."

"Ah," said the count, in a somewhat forced tone, "that may be easily explained; Madame la Comtesse de Morcerf, who is aristocracy and refinement itself, does not relish the idea of being allied by your marriage with one of ignoble birth; that is natural enough."

"I do not know if that is her reason," said Albert; "but one thing I do know, that if this marriage be consummated, it will render her quite miserable. There was to have been a meeting six weeks ago in order to talk over and settle the affair; but I had such a sudden attack of indisposition——"

"Real?" interrupted the count, smiling.

"Oh, real enough, from anxiety doubtless, that they postponed the rendezvous for two months longer. There is no hurry, you know, I am not yet twenty-one, and Eugénie is only seventeen years of age; but the two months expire next week. It must be done. My dear count, you cannot imagine how my mind is harassed. How happy you are in being exempted from all this!"

"Well, and why should not you be free too? What prevents you from being so?"

"Oh, it will be too great a disappointment to my father if I do not marry Mademoiselle Danglars."

"Marry her then," said the count, with a significant shrug of the shoulders.

"Yes," replied Morcerf, "but that will plunge my mother into positive grief."

"Then do not marry her," said the count.

"Well, I shall see. I will try and think over what is the best thing to be done; you will give me your advice, will you not? and if possible extricate me from my unpleasant position? I think, rather than give pain to my excellent mother, I would run the risk of offending the count."

Monte Cristo turned away; he seemed moved by this last remark.

"Ah," said he to Debray, who had thrown himself into an easy-chair at the farthest extremity of the salon, and who held a pencil in his right hand and an account-book in his left, "what are you doing there? are you making a sketch after Poussin?"

"No, no; I am doing something of a very opposite nature to painting. I am engaged with arithmetic."

"Arithmetic!"

"Yes; I am calculating—by the way, Morcerf, that indirectly concerns you—I am calculating what the house of Danglars must have gained by the last rise in Haïti stock: from 206 they have risen to 409 in three days, and the prudent banker had purchased at 206, therefore he must have made 300,000 livres."

"That is not his best stroke of policy," said Morcerf; "did he not gain a million from the Spaniards this last year?"

"My dear fellow," said Lucien, "here is the Count of Monte Cristo, who will say to you as the Italians do:

> " Danaro e santia,
> Metà della metà.*

When they tell me such things I only shrug my shoulders and say nothing."

"But you were speaking of Haïti?" said Monte Cristo

"Ah, Haïti!—that is quite another thing! Haïti is the écarté* of French stock-jobbing. They may like la bouillotte, delight in whist, be enraptured with le boston, and yet grow tired of all; but they always come back to écarté—that is the game, *par excellence*. M. Danglars sold yesterday at 405, and pockets 300,000 francs. Had he but waited till to-day, the stocks would have fallen to 205, and instead of gaining 300,000 francs, he would have lost 20 or 25,000."

"And what has caused the sudden fall from 409 to 206?" asked Monte Cristo; "I am profoundly ignorant of all these stock-jobbing intrigues."

"Because," said Albert, laughing, "one piece of news follows another, and there is often great dissimilarity between them."

"Ah," said the count, "I see that M. Danglars is accustomed to play at gaining or losing 300,000 francs in a day; he must be enormously rich!"

"It is not he who plays," exclaimed Lucien, "it is Madame Danglars; she is indeed daring."

"But you who are a reasonable being, Lucien, and who know how little dependence is to be placed on the news, since you are at the fountain-head, surely you ought to prevent it," said Morcerf, with a smile.

"How can I, if her husband fails in controlling her?" asked Lucien; "you know the character of the baroness—no one has any influence with her, and she does precisely what she pleases."

"Ah, if I were in your place——" said Albert.

"Well?"

"I would reform her; it would be rendering a service to her future son-in-law."

"How would you set about it?"

"Ah, that would be easy enough—I would give her a lesson."

"A lesson?"

"Yes. Your position as secretary to the minister renders your authority on the subject of political news; you never open your mouth but the stockbrokers immediately stenograph your words. Cause her to lose 2 or 300,000 francs in a short space of time, and that would teach her prudence."

"I do not understand," stammered Lucien.

"It is very clear, notwithstanding," replied the young man, with a *naïveté* totally free from all affectation; "tell her some fine morning an unheard-of piece of intelligence—some telegraphic despatch, of which you alone are in possession: for instance, that Henri IV was seen yesterday at the house of Gabrielle; that will cause the funds to rise, she will lay her plans accordingly, and she will certainly lose when Beauchamp announces the following day in his gazette, ' The report which has been circulated by some individuals, stating the king to have been seen yesterday at Gabrielle's house, is totally without foundation. We can positively assert that his majesty did not quit the Pont-Neuf.' "

Lucien half smiled. Monte Cristo, although apparently indifferent, had not lost one word of this conversation, and his penetrating eye had even read a hidden secret in the embarrassed manner of the secretary. This embarrassment had completely escaped Albert, but it caused Lucien to shorten his visit; he was evidently ill at ease. The count, in taking leave of him, said something in a low voice, to which he answered, "Willingly, M. le Comte; I accept your proposal." The count returned to young De Morcerf.

"Do you not think on reflection," said he to him, "that you have done wrong in thus speaking of your mother-in-law in the presence of M. Debray? "

"M. le Comte," said Morcerf, "I beg of you not to apply that title so prematurely."

"Now, speaking without any exaggeration, is your mother really so very much averse to this marriage? "

"So much so, that the baroness very rarely comes to the house, and my mother has not, I think, visited Madame Danglars twice in her whole life."

"Then," said the count, "I am emboldened to speak openly to you. M. Danglars is my banker; M. de Villefort has overwhelmed me with politeness in return for a service which a casual piece of good fortune enabled me to render him. I predict from all this an avalanche of dinners and routs. Now, in order not to appear to expect such a proceeding, and also to be beforehand with them, if you like it, I have thought of inviting M. and Madame Danglars, and M. and Madame de Villefort, to my country-house at Auteuil. If I were to invite you and the Comte and Comtesse de Morcerf to this dinner, it would give it the air of a matrimonial rendezvous, or at least, Madame de Morcerf would look upon the affair in that light, especially if M. le Baron Danglars did me the honour to bring his daughter. In that case your mother would hold me in aversion, and I do not at all wish that; on the contrary, I desire to occupy a prominent place in her esteem."

"Indeed, count," said Morcerf, "I thank you sincerely for having used so much candour towards me, and I gratefully accept the exclusion which you propose to me. You say you desire my mother's good opinion; I assure you, it is already yours to a very unusual extent."

"Do you think so?" said Monte Cristo, with interest.

"Oh, I am sure of it; we talked of you an hour after you left us the other day. But to return to what we were saying. If my mother could know of this attention on your part, and I will venture to tell her, I am sure that she will be most grateful to you; it is true that my father will be equally angry."

The count laughed.

"Well," said he to Morcerf, "but I think your father will not be the only angry one; M. and Madame Danglars will think me a very ill-mannered person. They know that I am intimate with you—that you are, in fact, one of the oldest of my Parisian acquaintances, and they will not find you at my house; they will certainly ask me why I did not invite you. Be sure to provide yourself with some previous engagement which shall have a semblance of probability, and communicate the fact to me by a line in writing. You know that with bankers nothing but a written document will be valid."

"I will do better than that," said Albert; "my mother is wishing to go to the seaside—what day is fixed for your dinner?"

"Saturday."

"This is Tuesday—well, to-morrow evening we leave, and the day after we shall be at Tréport. Really, M. le Comte, you are a charming person to set people at their ease."

"Indeed, you give me more credit than I deserve; I only wish to do what will be agreeable to you, that is all."

"When shall you send your invitations?"

"This very day."

"Well, I will immediately call on M. Danglars, and tell him that my mother and myself leave Paris to-morrow. I have not seen you, consequently I know nothing of your dinner."

"How foolish you are!—have you forgotten that M. Debray has just seen you at my house?"

"Ah, true!"

"On the contrary, I have seen you, and invited you without

any ceremony, when you instantly answered that it would be impossible for you to be amongst the number of my guests as you were going to Tréport."

"Well, then, that is settled; but you will come and call on my mother before to-morrow."

"Before to-morrow?—that will be a difficult matter to arrange, besides I shall just be in the way of all the preparations for departure."

"You were only a charming man before, but if you accede to my proposal, you will be adorable."

"What must I do to attain such a height?"

"You are to-day free as air—come and dine with me; we shall be a small party—only yourself, my mother, and I. You have scarcely seen my mother, you shall have an opportunity of observing her more closely. She is a remarkable woman, and I only regret that there does not exist another who resembles her about twenty years younger; in that case, I assure you, there would very soon be a Comtesse and Vicomtesse de Morcerf. As to my father, you will not see him; he is officially engaged, and dines with M. le Grand Référendaire.* We will talk over our travels; and you, who have seen the whole world, will relate your adventures—you shall tell us the history of the beautiful Greek who was with you the other night at the Opera, and whom you call your slave, and yet treat like a princess. We will talk Italian and Spanish. Come, accept my invitation, and my mother will thank you."

"A thousand thanks," said the count,—"your invitation is most gracious, and I regret exceedingly that it is not in my power to accept it. I am not so much at liberty as you supposed; on the contrary, I have a most important engagement."

"Ah, take care, you were teaching me just now how, in case of an invitation to dinner, one might creditably make an excuse. I require the proof of a pre-engagement. I am not a banker like M. Danglars, but I am quite as incredulous as he is."

"I am going to give you a proof," replied the count, and he rang the bell.

"Humph!" said Morcerf, "this is the second time you have refused to dine with my mother; it is evident you wish to avoid her."

Monte Cristo started.

"Oh, you do not mean that," said he; "besides, here comes the confirmation of my assertion."

Baptistin entered, and remained standing at the door.

"I had no previous knowledge of your visit, had I?"

"Indeed, you are such an extraordinary person, that I would not answer for it."

" At all events, I could not guess that you would invite me to dinner? "

" Probably not."

" Well, listen; Baptistin, what did I tell you this morning when I called you into my laboratory? "

" To close the door against visitors as soon as the clock struck five." replied the valet.

" What then? "

" Ah, M. le Comte——" said Albert.

" No, no, I wish to do away with that mysterious reputation that you have given me, my dear viscount; it is tiresome to be always acting Manfred. I wish my life to be free and open. Go on, Baptistin."

" Then to admit no one except M. le Major Bartolomeo Cavalcanti and his son."

" You hear: Major Bartolomeo Cavalcanti; a man who ranks amongst the most ancient nobility of Italy whose name Dante has celebrated in the tenth canto of *L'Inferno;** you remember it do you not? Then there is his son, a charming young man, about your own age, viscount, bearing the same title as yourself, and who is making his *entrée* into the Parisian world, aided by his father's millions. The major will bring his son with him this evening, the *contino*, as we say in Italy; he confides him to my care. If he prove himself worthy of it, I will do what I can to advance his interests; you will assist me in the work, will you not? "

" Most undoubtedly! This Major Cavalcanti is an old friend of yours, then? "

" By no means, he is a perfect nobleman, very polite, modest, and agreeable, such as may be found constantly in Italy, descendants of very ancient families. I have met him several times at Florence, Bologna, and Lucca, and he has now communicated to me the fact of his arrival in this place. The acquaintances one makes in travelling have a sort of claim on one; they everywhere expect to receive the same attention which you once paid them by chance; as though the civilities of a passing hour were likely to awaken any lasting interest in favour of the man in whose society you may happen to be thrown in the course of your journey. This good Major Cavalcanti is come to take a second view of Paris, which he only saw in passing through in the time of the Empire, when he was on his way to Moscow. I shall give him a good dinner: he will confide his son to my care; I will promise to watch over him; I shall let him follow in whatever path his folly may lead him, and then I shall have done my part."

" Certainly; I see you are a precious Mentor," said Albert.

" Good-bye, we shall return on Sunday. By the way, I have received news of Franz."

" Have you? Is he still amusing himself in Italy? "

" I believe so; however, he regrets your absence extremely. He says you were the sun of Rome, and that without you all appears dark and cloudy; I do not know if he does not even go so far as to say that it rains."

" His opinion of me is altered for the better then? "

" No, he still persists in looking upon you as the most incomprehensible and mysterious of beings."

" He is a charming young man," said Monte Cristo, " and I felt a lively interest in him the very first evening of my introduction, when I met him in search of a supper, and prevailed upon him to accept a portion of mine. He is, I think, the son of General d'Epinay? "

" He is."

" The same who was so shamefully assassinated in 1815? "

" By the Bonapartists."

" Yes!—really I like him extremely; is there not also a matrimonial engagement contemplated for him? "

" Yes, he is to marry Mademoiselle de Villefort."

" Indeed! "

" And you know I am to marry Mademoiselle Danglars," said Albert, laughing.

" You smile? "

" Yes."

" Why do you do so? "

" I smile because there appears to me to be about as much inclination for the consummation of the engagement in question as there is for my own. But really, my dear count, we are talking as much of women as they do of us; it is unpardonable! "

Albert rose.

" Are you going? "

" Really that is a good idea of yours!—two hours have I been boring you to death with my company, and then you, with the greatest politeness, ask me if I am going. Indeed, count, you are the most polished man in the world! And your servants, too, how very well behaved they are; there is quite a style about them. M. Baptistin especially; I could never get such a man as that. My servants seem to imitate those you sometimes see in a play, who, because they have only a word or two to say, acquit themselves in the most awkward manner possible. Therefore, if you part with M. Baptistin, give me the refusal of him."

" Agreed, viscount."

" That is not all; give my compliments to your illustrious

visitor, Cavalcante of the Cavalcanti; and if by any chance he should be wishing to establish his son, find him a wife very rich, very noble on her mother's side at least, and a baroness in right of her father, I will help you in the search."

" Oh! oh! you will do as much as that, will you? "

" Yes."

" Well, really, nothing is certain in this world."

" Oh, count, what a service you might render me! I should like you a hundred times better, if, by your intervention, I could manage to remain a bachelor, even were it only for ten years."

" Nothing is impossible," gravely replied Monte Cristo; and, taking leave of Albert, he returned into the house, and struck the gong three times.

Bertuccio appeared.

" M. Bertuccio, you understand that I intend entertaining company on Saturday at Auteuil."

Bertuccio slightly started.

" I shall require your services to see that all be properly arranged. It is a beautiful house, or at all events may be made so."

" There must be a good deal done before it can deserve that title, M. le Comte, for the tapestried hangings are very old."

" Let them all be taken away and changed then, with the exception of the sleeping-chamber, which is hung with red damask; you will leave that exactly as it is."

Bertuccio bowed.

" You will not touch the garden either; as to the yard, you may do what you please with it; I should prefer that being altered beyond all recognition."

" I will do everything in my power to carry out your wishes, M. le Comte. I should be glad, however, to receive your excellency's commands concerning the dinner."

" Really, my dear M. Bertuccio," said the count, " since you have been in Paris, you have become quite nervous, and apparently out of your element; you no longer seem to understand me."

" But surely your excellency will be so good as to inform me whom you are expecting to receive? "

" I do not yet know myself, neither is it necessary that you should do so. ' Lucullus dines with Lucullus.'" that is quite sufficient."

Bertuccio bowed, and left the room.

56

Major Cavalcanti

BOTH the count and Baptistin had told the truth when they announced to Morcerf the proposed visit of the major, which had served Monte Cristo as a pretext for declining the invitation which he had received from Albert.

Seven o'clock had just struck, and M. Bertuccio, according to the command which had been given him, had two hours before he left for Auteuil, when a *fiacre* stopped at the door of the hotel, and after depositing its occupant at the gate, immediately hurried away, as if ashamed of its employment. The individual who alighted from the vehicle was about fifty-two years of age, dressed in one of those green surtouts, ornamented with black frogs, which have so long maintained their popularity all over Europe. He wore trousers of blue cloth, boots tolerably clean, but not of the brightest polish, and a little too thick in the soles, buckskin gloves, a hat somewhat resembling in shape those usually worn by the gendarmes, and a black cravat striped with white, which, if the proprietor had not worn it of his own free will, might have passed for a halter, so much did it resemble one. Such was the picturesque costume of the person who rang at the gate, and demanded if it was not No. 30 in the Avenue des Champs-Elysées that M. le Comte de Monte Cristo inhabited, and who, being answered by the porter in the affirmative, entered, closed the gate after him, and began to ascend the steps of the house.

The small and angular head of the individual in question, his white hair, and thick gray moustache, caused him to be easily recognised by Baptistin, who had received an exact description of the expected visitor, and who was awaiting him in the hall. Therefore, scarcely had the stranger time to pronounce his name before the count was apprised of his arrival. He was ushered into a simple and elegant drawing-room, and the count rose to meet him with a smiling air.

"Ah, my dear sir, you are most welcome; I was expecting you."

"Indeed!" said the Italian; "was your excellency then aware of my visit?"

"Yes; I had been told that I should see you to-day at seven o'clock."

"Then you have received full information concerning my arrival?"

"Decidedly."

"But you are sure you are not mistaken?"

"I am *quite* sure of it."

"It really was I whom your excellency expected at seven o'clock this evening?"

"I will prove it to you beyond a doubt."

"Oh, no, never mind that," said the Italian; "it is not worth the trouble."

"Yes, yes," said Monte Cristo.

His visitor appeared slightly uneasy.

"Let me see," said the count; "are you not M. le Marquis Bartolomeo Cavalcanti?"

"Bartolomeo Cavalcanti," joyfully replied the Italian; "yes, I am really he."

"Ex-major in the Austrian service?"

"Was I a major?" timidly asked the old soldier.

"Yes," said Monte Cristo, "you were a major; that is the title the French give to the post which you filled in Italy."

"Very good," said the major; "I do not demand more, you understand——"

"Your visit here to-day is not of your own suggestion, is it?" said Monte Cristo.

"No; certainly not."

"You were sent by some other person?"

"Yes."

"By the excellent Abbé Busoni?"

"Exactly so," said the delighted major.

"And you have a letter?"

"Yes; there it is."

"Give it me, then;" and Monte Cristo took the letter, which he opened and read.

"Yes, yes, I see. 'Major Cavalcanti, a worthy patrician of Lucca, a descendant of the Cavalcanti, of Florence,'" continued Monte Cristo, reading aloud, "possessing an income of half a million.'"

"Half a million, is it?" said the major.

"Yes, in so many words; and it must be so, for the abbé knows correctly the amount of all the largest fortunes in Europe."

"Be it half a million, then; but, on my word of honour, I had no idea that it was so much."

"Because you are robbed by your steward; you must make some reformation in that quarter."

" You have opened my eyes," said the Italian gravely, " I will show the gentleman the door."

Monte Cristo resumed the perusal of the letter:

" ' And who only needs one thing more to make him happy.' "

" Yes, indeed! but one! " said the major, with a sigh.

" ' Which is to recover a lost and adored son.' "

" A lost and adored son! "

" ' Stolen away in his infancy, either by an enemy of his noble family or by the gipsies.' "

" At the age of five years, sir," said the major, with a deep sigh, and raising his eyes to heaven.

" Unhappy father! " said Monte Cristo.

The count continued:

" ' I have given him renewed life and hope, in the assurance that you have the power of restoring the son whom he has vainly sought for fifteen years.' "

The major looked at the count with an indescribable expression of anxiety.

" I have the power of so doing," said Monte Cristo.

The major recovered his self-possession.

" Ah! ah! " said he, " the letter was true then to the end? "

" Did you doubt it, M. Bartolomeo? "

" No, indeed! certainly not; a good man, a man holding a religious office, as does the Abbé Busoni, could not condescend to deceive or play off a joke; but your excellency has not read all."

" Ah! true! " said Monte Cristo, " there is a postscript."

" Yes," repeated the major, " yes—there—is—a—postscript."

" ' In order to save Major Cavalcanti the trouble of drawing on his banker, I send him a draft for 2000 francs to defray his travelling expenses, and credit on you for the further sum of 48,000, which you still owe me.' "

The major awaited the conclusion of the postscript, apparently with great anxiety.

" Very good," said the count.

" He said ' very good,' " muttered the major; " then—sir——" replied he.

" Then what? " asked Monte Cristo.

" Then the postscript——"

" Well! what of the postscript? "

" Then the postscript is as favourably received by you as the rest of the letter? "

" Certainly; you attached great importance then to this postscript, my dear M. Cavalcanti? Is it possible, that a man of your standing should be embarrassed anywhere? " said Monte Cristo.

" Why, really I know no one," said the major.

" But then you yourself are known to others? "

" Yes, I am known; so that——"

" Proceed, my dear M. Cavalcanti! "

" So that you will remit to me these 48,000 francs? "

" Certainly, at your first request."

The major's eyes dilated with pleasing astonishment.

" But sit down," said Monte Cristo; " really I do not know what I have been thinking of—I have positively kept you standing for the last quarter of an hour."

" Don't mention it." The major drew an arm-chair towards him, and proceeded to seat himself.

" Now," said the count, " what will you take? a glass of port, sherry, or vin d'Alicant? "

" Vin d'Alicant, if you please; it is my favourite wine."

" I have some which is excellent; you will take a biscuit with it, will you not? "

" Yes, I will take a biscuit, as you are so obliging."

Monte Cristo rang; Baptistin appeared. The count advanced to meet him.

" Well? " said he, in a low voice.

" The young man is here," said the valet-de-chambre, in the same tone.

" Into what room did you take him? "

" Into the blue drawing-room, according to your excellency's orders."

" That's right; now bring the vin d'Alicant and some biscuits."

Baptistin left the room.

" Really," said the major, " I am quite ashamed of the trouble I am giving you."

" Pray don't mention such a thing," said the count.

Baptistin re-entered with glasses, wine and biscuits. The count filled one glass, but in the other he only poured a few drops of the ruby-coloured liquid. The bottle was covered with spiders' webs, and all the other signs which indicate the age of wine more truly than do wrinkles on the face of a man. The major made a wise choice; he took the full glass and a biscuit.

The count told Baptistin to leave the plate within reach of his guest, who began by sipping the Alicant with an expression of great satisfaction, and then delicately steeped his biscuit in the wine.

" So, sir, you inhabited Lucca, did you? You were rich, noble, held in great esteem, had all that could render a man happy? "

" All," said the major, hastily swallowing his biscuit, " positively all."

" And yet there was one thing wanting in order to complete your happiness? " ʲ

" Only one thing," said the Italian.

" And that one thing, your lost child! "

" Ah! " said the major, taking a second biscuit, " that consummation of my happiness was indeed wanting." The worthy major raised his eyes to heaven and sighed.

" Let me hear then," said the count, " who this deeply regretted son was; for I always understood you were a bachelor." '

" That was the general opinion, sir," said the major, " and I——"

" Yes," replied the count, " and you confirmed the report. A youthful indiscretion, I suppose, which you were anxious to conceal from the world at large? "

The major recovered himself, and resumed his usual calm manner; at the same time casting his eyes down, either to give himself time to compose his countenance, or to assist his imagination, all the while giving an under-look at the count, the protracted smile on whose lips still announced the same polite curiosity.

" Yes," said the major, " I did wish this fault to be hidden from every eye."

" Not on your account, surely," replied Monte Cristo, " for a man is above all these things? "

" Oh, no, certainly not on my own account," said the major, with a smile and a shake of the head.

" But for the sake of the mother? " said the count.

" Yes, for the mother's sake—his poor mother! " cried the major, taking a third biscuit.

" She belonged to one of the first families in Italy, I think, did she not? "

" She was of a noble family of Fiesole, M. le Comte."

" And her name was——"

" Do you desire to know her name? "

" Oh! " said Monte Cristo, " it would be quite superfluous for you to tell me, for I already know it. Oliva Corsinari, was it not? "

" Oliva Corsinari! "

" A marchioness? "

" A marchioness! "

" And you married her at last, notwithstanding the opposition of her family? "

" Yes, I did so."

"And you have doubtless brought all your papers with you?" said Monte Cristo.

"What papers?"

"The certificate of your marriage with Oliva Corsinari, and the register of your child's birth?"

"The register of my child's birth?"

"The register of the birth of Andrea Cavalcanti—of your son; is not his name Andrea?"

"I believe so," said the major.

"What! you are not sure that is his name?"

"I dare not positively assert it, as he has been lost for so long a time."

"Well, then," said Monte Cristo, "you have all the documents with you?"

"M. le Comte, I regret to say, that not knowing it was necessary to come provided with these papers, I neglected to bring them with me."

"That is unfortunate," returned Monte Cristo.

"Were they then so necessary?"

"They were indispensable."

The major passed his hand across his brow.

"Ah! *per Bacco*, indispensable, were they?"

"Certainly they were; supposing there were to be doubts raised as to the validity of your marriage or the legitimacy of your child?"

"True," said the major, "there might be doubts raised."

"In that case your son would be very unpleasantly situated."

"It would be fatal to his interests."

"It might cause him to fail in some desirable matrimonial speculation."

"*O peccato!*"

"You must know that in France they are very particular on these points; it is not sufficient, as in Italy, to go to the priest, and say, 'We love each other, and want you to marry us.' Marriage is a civil affair in France, and in order to marry in an orthodox manner, you must have papers which undeniably establish your identity."

"That is the misfortune! you see I have not these necessary papers."

"Fortunately I have them, though," said Monte Cristo.

"Ah, indeed!" said the major, who seeing the object of his journey frustrated by the absence of the papers, feared also that his forgetfulness might give rise to some difficulty concerning the 48,000 francs. "Ah, indeed, that is a fortunate circumstance.

Yes, that really is lucky, for it never occurred to me to bring them."

"I do not at all wonder at it—one cannot think of everything; but happily the Abbé Busoni thought for you."

"He is an admirable man," said the major; "and he sent them to you?"

"Here they are."

The major clasped his hands in token of admiration.

"You married Oliva Corsinari in the church of San Paolo del Monte-Cattini; here is the priest's certificate."

"Yes, indeed, there it is truly," said the Italian, looking on with astonishment.

"And here is Andrea Cavalcanti's baptismal register, given by the curé of Saravezza."

"All quite correct."

"Take these documents, then; they do not concern me. You will give them to your son, who will of course take great care of them."

"I should think so, indeed! If he were to lose them, it would be necessary to write to the curé for duplicates, and it would be some time before they could be obtained."

"It would be a difficult matter to arrange," said Monte Cristo.

"Almost an impossibility," replied the major.

"I am very glad to see that you understand the value of these papers."

"I regard them as invaluable."

"Now," said Monte Cristo, "as to the mother of the young man——"

"As to the mother of the young man——" repeated the Italian, with anxiety.

"As regards la Marquise Corsinari——"

"Really," said the major, "difficulties seem to thicken upon us; will she be wanted in any way?"

"No, sir," replied Monte Cristo; "besides, has she not——"

"Yes, yes," said the major, "she has——"

"Paid the last debt of nature?"

"Alas, yes," returned the Italian.

"I knew that," said Monte Cristo; "she has been dead these ten years."

"And I am still mourning her loss," exclaimed the major, drawing from his pocket a checked handkerchief, and alternately wiping first the right and then the left eye.

"What would you have?" said Monte Cristo, "we are all mortal. Now, you understand, my dear M. Cavalcanti, that it

is useless for you to tell people in France that you have been
separated from your son for fifteen years. Stories of gipsies, who
steal children, are not at all in vogue in this part of the world,
and would not be believed. You sent him for his education to
a college in one of the provinces, and now you wish him to complete his education in the Parisian world. That is the reason
which has induced you to leave Via Reggio, where you have lived
since the death of your wife. That will be sufficient."

" Very well, then."

" If they should hear of the separation———"

" Ah, yes; what could I say? "

" That an unfaithful tutor, bought over by the enemies of
your family———"

" By the Corsinari? "

" Precisely. Had stolen away this child in order that your
name might become extinct."

" That will do well, since he is an only son."

" Well, now that all is arranged, do not let these newly
awakened remembrances be forgotten. You have, doubtless,
already guessed that I was preparing a surprise for you. Someone
has told you the secret, or, perhaps, you guessed that he was
here."

" That who was here? "

" Your child—your son—your Andrea."

" I did guess it," replied the major, with the greatest *sang froid*
possible. " Then he is here? "

" He is," said Monte Cristo; " when the valet-de-chambre
came in just now, he told me of his arrival."

" Ah, very well! very well! " said the major, clutching the
buttons of his coat at each exclamation which he made.

" My dear sir," said Monte Cristo, " I understand all your
emotion; you must have time to recover yourself. I will, in the
meantime, go and prepare the young man for this much-desired
interview, for I presume that he is not less impatient for it than
yourself."

" I should quite imagine that to be the case," said Cavalcanti.

" Well, in a quarter of an hour he shall be with you."

" You will bring him, then; you carry your goodness so far
as even to present him to me yourself? "

" No, I do not wish to come between a father and son. Your
interview will be private. But do not be uneasy; even if the
powerful voice of nature should be silent, you cannot well mistake
him; he will enter by this door. He is a fine young man, of fair
complexion, a little too fair, perhaps, pleasing manners—but you
will see and judge for yourself."

"By the way," said the major, "you know I have only the 2000 francs which the Abbé Busoni sent me; this sum I have expended upon travelling expenses, and——"

"And you want money—that is a matter of course, my dear M. Cavalcanti. Well, here are 8000 francs on account."

The major's eyes sparkled brilliantly.

"It is 40,000 francs which I now owe you," said Monte Cristo.

"Does your excellency wish for a receipt?" said the major, at the same time slipping the money into the inner pocket of his coat.

"For what?" said the count.

"I thought you might want it to show the Abbé Busoni."

"Well, when you receive the remaining 40,000, you shall give me a receipt in full. Between honest men such excessive precaution is, I think, quite unnecessary."

"Yes, so it is between perfectly upright people."

"One word more," said Monte Cristo.

"Say on."

"You will permit me to make one remark?"

"Certainly; pray do so."

"Then I should advise you to leave off wearing that style of dress."

"Indeed!" said the major, regarding himself with an air of complete satisfaction.

"Yes, it may be worn at Via Reggio; but that costume, however elegant in itself, has long been out of fashion in Paris."

"That's unfortunate."

"Oh, if you really are attached to your old mode of dress, you can easily resume it when you leave Paris."

"But what shall I wear?"

"What you find in your trunks."

"In my trunks? I have but one portmanteau."

"I dare say you have nothing else with you. What is the use of boring oneself with so many things? Besides, an old soldier always likes to march with as little baggage as possible."

"That is just the case, precisely so!"

"But you are a man of foresight and prudence, therefore you sent your luggage on before you. It has arrived at the Hôtel des Princes, Rue de Richelieu. It is there you are to take up your quarters."

"Then, in these trunks——"

"I presume you have given orders to your valet-de-chambre to put in all you are likely to need,—your plain clothes and your uniform. On grand occasions you must wear your uniform; that will look very well. Do not forget your crosses. They still laugh at them in France, and yet always wear them, for all that."

" Very well! very well! " said the major, who was in ecstasy at the attention paid him by the count.

" Now," said Monte Cristo, " that you have fortified yourself against all painful excitement, prepare yourself, my dear M. Cavalcanti, to meet your lost Andrea."

Saying which, Monte Cristo bowed, and disappeared behind the tapestry, leaving the major fascinated beyond expression with the delightful reception which the count had given him.

57

Andrea Cavalcanti

THE Count of Monte Cristo entered the adjoining room which Baptistin had designated as the blue drawing-room, and found there a young man of graceful demeanour and elegant appearance, who had arrived in a *fiacre* about half an hour previously. Baptistin had not found any difficulty in recognising the individual who presented himself at the door for admittance. He was certainly the tall young man with light hair, red beard, black eyes, and brilliant complexion, whom his master had so particularly described to him.

When the count entered the room the young man was carelessly stretched on a sofa, tapping his boot with the gold-headed cane which he held in his hand. On perceiving the count he rose quickly.

" The Count of Monte Cristo, I believe? " said he.

" Yes, sir, and I think I have the honour of addressing Count Andrea Cavalcanti? "

" Count Andrea Cavalcanti," repeated the young man, accompanying his words with a bow.

" You are charged with a letter of introduction addressed to me, are you not? " said the count.

" I did not mention that, because the signature seemed to me so strange."

" The letter is signed ' Sinbad the Sailor,' is it not? "

" Exactly so. Now, as I have never known any Sinbad, with the exception of the one celebrated in the *Thousand and One Nights*——"

" Well, it is one of his descendants, and a great friend of mine;

he is a very rich Englishman, eccentric almost to insanity, and his real name is Lord Wilmore."

"Ah, indeed! then that explains everything," said Andrea, "that is extraordinary. He is, then, the same Englishman whom I met—at—yes, very well! M. le Comte, I am at your service."

"If what you say be true," replied the count, smiling, "perhaps you will be kind enough to give me some account of yourself and your family?"

"Certainly, I will do so," said the young man, with a quickness which gave proof of his ready invention. "I am (as you have said) the Count Andrea Cavalcanti, son of Major Bartolomeo Cavalcanti, a descendant of the Cavalcanti whose names are inscribed in the golden book of Florence. Our family, although still rich (for my father's income amounts to half a million), has experienced many misfortunes, and I myself was, at the age of five years, taken away by the treachery of my tutor, so that for fifteen years I have not seen the author of my existence. Since I have arrived at years of discretion and become my own master, I have been constantly seeking him, but all in vain. At length I received this letter from your friend, which states that my father is in Paris, and authorises me to address myself to you for information respecting him."

"Really, all you have related to me is exceedingly interesting," said Monte Cristo, observing the young man with a gloomy satisfaction; "and you have done well to conform in everything to the wishes of my friend Sinbad; for your father is indeed here, and is seeking you."

The count, from the moment of his first entering the drawing-room, had not once lost sight of the expression of the young man's countenance; he had admired the assurance of his look and the firmness of his voice; but at these words, so natural in themselves, "Your father is indeed here, and is seeking you," young Andrea started, and exclaimed:

"My father!—is my father here?"

"Most undoubtedly," replied Monte Cristo; "your father, the Major Bartolomeo Cavalcanti."

The expression of terror, which for the moment had overspread the features of the young man, had now disappeared.

"Ah, yes, that is the name, certainly, Major Bartolomeo Cavalcanti. And you really mean to say, M. le Comte, that my dear father is here?"

"Yes, sir; and I can even add that I have only just left his company. The history which he related to me of his lost son touched me to the quick; indeed his griefs, hopes and fears, on that subject, might furnish material for a most touching and pathetic poem. At length, he one day received a letter, stating that the parties who had deprived him of his son now offered to restore him, or at least to give notice where he might be found, on condition of receiving a large sum of money, by way of ransom. Your father did not hesitate an instant, and the sum was sent to the frontier of Piedmont, with a passport signed for Italy. You were in the south of France, I think? "

" Yes," replied Andrea, with an embarrassed air, " I was in the south of France."

" A carriage was to await you at Nice? "

" Precisely so; and it conveyed me from Nice to Genoa, from Genoa to Turin, from Turin to Chambéry, from Chambéry to Pont-de-Beauvoisin, and from Pont-de-Beauvoisin to Paris."

" Capital! He always hoped to meet you on the road, for that was the route he himself followed; that is why your journey had been planned thus."

" But," said Andrea, " if my father had met me, I doubt if he would have recognised me; I must be somewhat altered since he last saw me."

" Oh! the voice of nature," said Monte Cristo.

" True," interrupted the young man, " I had not looked upon it in that point of view."

" Now," replied Monte Cristo, " there is only one source of uneasiness left in your father's mind, which is this—he is anxious to know how you have been employed during your long absence from him, how you have been treated by your persecutors, and if they have conducted themselves towards you with all the deference due to your rank. Finally, he is anxious to see if you have been fortunate enough to escape the bad moral influence to which you have been exposed, and which is infinitely more to be dreaded than any physical suffering; he wishes to discover if the fine abilities with which nature had endowed you have been weakened by want of culture; and, in short, whether you consider yourself capable of resuming and retaining in the world the high position to which your rank entitles you."

" Sir," exclaimed the young man, quite astounded; " I hope no false report——"

" As for myself I first heard you spoken of by my friend Wilmore, the philanthropist. I believe he found you in some unpleasant position, but do not know of what nature, for I did not ask, not being inquisitive. Your misfortunes engaged his sympathies; so you see you must have been interesting. He told me that he was anxious to restore you to the position which you had lost, and that he would seek your father until he found him.

He did seek, and has found him apparently, since he is here now; and, finally, my friend apprised me of your coming, and gave me a few other instructions relative to your future fortune. I am quite aware that my friend Wilmore is an original, but he is sincere, and as rich as a gold mine, consequently he may indulge his eccentricities without any fear of their ruining him, and I have promised to adhere to his instructions. Now, sir, pray do not be offended at the question I am about to put to you, as it comes in the way of my duty as your patron. I would wish to know if the misfortunes which have happened to you—misfortunes entirely beyond your control, and which in no degree diminish my regard for you,—I would wish to know if they have not, in some measure, contributed to render you a stranger to the world in which your fortune and your name entitle you to make a conspicuous figure ? "

" Sir," returned the young man, with a reassurance of manner, " make your mind easy on this score. Those who took me from my father, and who always intended, sooner or later, to sell me again to my original proprietor, as they have now done, calculated that, in order to make the most of their bargain, it would be politic to leave me in possession of all my personal and hereditary worth, and even to increase the value if possible. I have, therefore, received a very good education, and have been treated by these kidnappers very much as the slaves were treated in Asia Minor, whose masters made them grammarians, doctors and philosophers, in order that they might fetch a higher price in the Roman market."

Monte Cristo smiled with satisfaction; it appeared as if he had not expected so much from M. Andrea Cavalcanti.

" Besides," continued the young man, " if there did appear some defect in education, or offence against the established forms of etiquette, I suppose they would be excused in consideration of the misfortunes which accompanied my birth and followed me through my youth."

" Well," said Monte Cristo, in an indifferent tone, " you will do as you please, count, for you are the master of your own actions, and are the person most concerned in the matter; but if I were you, I would not divulge a word of all these adventures. Your history is quite a romance, and the world, which delights in romances contained in two covers of yellow paper, strangely mistrusts those which are bound in living parchment, even though they be gilded like yourself. This is the kind of difficulty which I wished to represent to you, M. le Comte. You would hardly have recited your touching history than it would go forth to the world, and be deemed unlikely and unnatural. You would be no longer a lost child found, but you would be looked upon as an upstart, who had sprung up like a mushroom in the night. You might excite a little curiosity, but it is not everyone who likes to be made the centre of observation and the subject of unpleasant remark."

" I agree with you, M. le Comte," said the young man, turning pale, and in spite of himself trembling beneath the scrutinising look of his companion, " such consequences would be extremely unpleasant."

" Nevertheless, you must not exaggerate the evil," said Monte Cristo, " or by endeavouring to avoid one fault you will fall into another. You must resolve upon one simple and single line of conduct, and for a man of your intelligence this plan is as easy as it is necessary; you must form honourable friendships, and by that means counteract the prejudice which may attach to the obscurity of your former life."

Andrea visibly changed countenance.

" I would offer myself as your surety and friendly adviser," said Monte Cristo, " did I not possess a moral distrust of my best friends, and a sort of inclination to lead others to doubt them too; therefore, in departing from this rule, I should (as the actors say) be playing a part quite out of my line, and should therefore run the risk of being hissed, which would be an act of folly."

" However, M. le Comte," said Andrea, " in consideration of Lord Wilmore, by whom I was recommended to you——"

" Yes, certainly," interrupted Monte Cristo; " but Lord Wilmore did not omit to inform me, my dear M. Andrea, that the season of your youth was rather a stormy one. Ah! " said the count, watching Andrea's countenance, " I do not demand any confession from you; it is precisely to avoid that necessity that your father was sent for from Lucca. You shall soon see him; he is a little stiff and pompous in his manner, and he is disfigured by his uniform; but when it becomes known that he is in the Austrian service, all that will be pardoned. We are not generally very severe with the Austrians. In short, you will find your father a very presentable person, I assure you."

" Ah, sir, you have given me confidence; it is so long since we were separated, that I have not the least remembrance of him; and, besides, you know that in the eyes of the world a large fortune covers all defects."

" He is a millionaire—his income is 500,000 francs."

" Then," said the young man, with anxiety, " I shall be sure to be placed in an agreeable position? "

" One of the most agreeable possible, my dear sir; he will

allow you an income of 50,000 livres per annum during the whole time of your stay in Paris."

" Then in that case I shall always choose to remain there."

" You cannot control circumstances, my dear sir: ' man proposes, and God disposes.' "

Andrea sighed.

" But," said he, " so long as I do remain in Paris and nothing forces me to quit it, do you mean to tell me that I may rely on receiving the sum you just now mentioned to me? "

" You may."

" Shall I receive it from my father? " asked Andrea, with some uneasiness.

" Yes, you will receive it from your father personally, but Lord Wilmore will be the security for the money; he has, at the request of your father, opened an account of 5000 francs a month at M. Danglars', which is one of the safest banks in Paris."

" And does my father mean to remain long in Paris? " asked Andrea.

" Only a few days," replied Monte Cristo. " His service does not allow him to absent himself more than two or three weeks together."

" Ah, my dear father! " exclaimed Andrea, evidently charmed with the idea of his speedy departure.

" Therefore," said Monte Cristo, feigning to mistake his meaning—" therefore I will not, for another instant, retard the pleasure of your meeting. Are you prepared to embrace your worthy father? "

" I hope you do not doubt it."

" Go, then, into the drawing-room, my young friend, where you will find your father awaiting you."

Andrea made a low bow to the count, and entered the adjoining room.

Monte Cristo watched him till he disappeared, and then touched a spring made to look like a picture, which, in sliding partially from the frame, discovered to view a small interstice, which was so cleverly contrived that it revealed all that was passing in the drawing-room now occupied by Cavalcanti and Andrea.

The young man closed the door behind him, and advanced towards the major, who had risen when he heard steps approaching him.

" Ah, my dear father! " said Andrea, in a loud voice, in order that the count might hear him in the next room, " is it really you? "

" How do you do, my dear son? " said the major gravely.

"After so many years of painful separation," said Andrea, in the same tone of voice, and glancing towards the door, "what a happiness it is to meet again!"

"Indeed it is, after so long a separation."

"Will you not embrace me, sir?" said Andrea.

"If you wish it, my son," said the major, and the two men embraced each other after the fashion of actors on the stage; that is to say, each rested his head on the other's shoulder.

"Then we are once more reunited?" said Andrea.

"Once more," replied the major.

"Never more to be separated?"

"Why, as to that—I think, my dear son. you must be by this time so accustomed to France as to look upon it almost as a second country."

"The fact is," said the young man, "that I should be exceedingly grieved to leave it."

"As for me, you must know I cannot possibly live out of Lucca; therefore I shall return to Italy as soon as I can."

"But before you leave France, my dear father, I hope you will put me in possession of the documents which will be necessary to prove my descent."

"Certainly, I am come expressly on that account. It has cost me much trouble to find you, but I had resolved on giving them into your hands; and if I had to recommence my search, it would occupy all the few remaining years of my life."

"Where are these papers, then?"

"Here they are."

Andrea seized the certificate of his father's marriage and his own baptismal register, and after having opened them with all the eagerness which might be expected under the circumstances, he read them with a facility which proved that he was accustomed to similar documents, and with an expression which plainly denoted an unusual interest in the contents. When he had perused the documents, an indefinable expression of pleasure lighted up his countenance, and looking at the major with a most peculiar smile. he said, in very excellent Tuscan:

"Then there is no longer any such thing in Italy as being condemned to the galleys?"

The major drew himself up to his full height.

"Why?—what do you mean by that question?"

"I mean that if there were, it would be impossible to draw up with impunity two such deeds as these. In France, my dear sir, half such a piece of effrontery as that would cause you to be quickly despatched to Toulon for five years, for change of air."

"Will you be good enough to explain your meaning?" said

the major, endeavouring as much as possible to assume an air of the greatest majesty.

"My dear M. Cavalcanti," said Andrea, taking the major by the arm in a confidential manner, "how much are you paid for being my father?"

The major was about to speak, when Andrea continued, in a low voice:

"Nonsense! I am going to set you an example of confidence; they give me 50,000 francs a year to be your son; consequently, you can understand that it is not at all likely I shall ever deny my parent."

The major looked anxiously around him.

"Make yourself easy, we are quite alone," said Andrea; "besides, we are conversing in Italian."

"Well, then," replied the major, "they paid me 50,000 francs down."

"Monsieur Cavalcanti," said Andrea, "do you believe in fairy-tales?"

"I used not to do so, but I really feel now almost obliged to have faith in them."

"You have then been induced to alter your opinion; you have had some proofs of their truth?"

The major drew from his pocket a handful of gold.

"Most palpable proofs," said he, "as you may perceive."

"You think, then, that I may rely on the count's promises?"

"Certainly I do."

"You are sure he will keep his word with me?"

"To the letter; but at the same time, remember, we must continue to play our respective parts. I, as a tender father——"

"And I as a dutiful son, as they choose that I shall be descended from you."

"Whom do you mean by they?"

"*Ma foi!* I can hardly tell, but I was alluding to those who wrote the letter; you received one, did you not?"

"Yes."

"From whom?"

"From a certain Abbé Busoni."

"Have you any knowledge of him?"

"No, I have never seen him."

"What did he say in the letter?"

"You will promise not to betray me?"

"Rest assured of that; you well know that our interests are the same."

"Then read for yourself"; and the major gave a letter into the young man's hand.

Andrea read in a low voice:—

"You are poor; a miserable old age awaits you. Would you like to become rich, or at least independent? Set out immediately for Paris, and demand of the Count of Monte Cristo, Avenue des Champs-Elysées, No. 30, the son whom you had by the Marquise Corsinari, and who was taken from you at five years of age. This son is named Andrea Cavalcanti. In order that you may not doubt the kind intention of the writer of this letter, you will find enclosed an order for 2400 francs, payable in Florence at the house of M. Gozzi, also a letter of introduction to M. le Comte de Monte Cristo, on whom I give you a draft for 48,000 francs. Remember to go to the count on the 26th of May, at seven o'clock in the evening.

(Signed)   "Abbé Busoni."

"It is the same."

"What do you mean?" said the major.

"I was going to say that I received a letter almost to the same effect."

"From the Abbé Busoni?"

"No; from an Englishman, called Lord Wilmore, who takes the name of Sinbad the Sailor."

"And of whom you have no more knowledge than I of the Abbé Busoni?"

"You are mistaken! there I am in advance of you."

"You have seen him then?"

"Yes, once."

"Where?"

"Ah! that is just what I cannot tell you; if I did, I should make you as wise as myself, which it is not my intention to do."

"And what did the letter contain?"

"Read it."

"'You are poor, and your future prospects are dark and gloomy. Do you wish for a name? should you like to be rich, and your own master?'"

"*Ma foi!*" said the young man; "was it possible there could be two answers to such a question?"

"Take the post-chaise which you will find waiting at the Porte de Gênes, as you enter Nice; pass through Turin, Chambéry, and Pont-de-Beauvoisin. Go up to the Count of Monte Cristo,

Avenue des Champs-Elysées, on the 26th of May, at seven o'clock in the evening, and demand of him your father. You are the son of the Marquis Cavalcanti and the Marquise Oliva Corsinari. The marquis will give you some papers which will certify this fact, and authorise you to appear under that name in the Parisian world. As to your rank, an annual income of 50,000 livres will enable you to support it admirably. I enclose a draft for 5000 livres, payable on M. Ferrea, banker at Nice, and also a letter of introduction to the Count of Monte Cristo, whom I have directed to supply all your wants.

" SINBAD THE SAILOR."

" Humph! " said the major; " very good! You have seen the count, you say? "

" I have only just left him."

" And has he conformed to all which the letter specified? "

" He has."

" Do you understand it? "

" Not in the least."

" There is a dupe somewhere."

" At all events, it is neither you nor I."

" Certainly not."

" Well, then——"

" Why, it does not much concern us; do you think it does? "

" No; I agree with you there; we must play the game to the end, and consent to be blindfold."

Monte Cristo chose this moment for re-entering the drawing-room. On hearing the sound of his footsteps, the two men threw themselves in each other's arms, and in the midst of this embrace, the count entered.

" Well, marquis," said Monte Cristo, " you appear to be in no way disappointed in the son whom your good fortune has restored to you."

" Ah! M. le Comte, I am overwhelmed with delight. There is only one thing which grieves me," observed the major, " and that is the necessity there is for my leaving Paris so soon."

" Ah! my dear M. Cavalcanti, I trust you will not leave before I have had the honour of presenting you to some of my friends."

" I am at your service, sir," replied the major.

" Now, sir," said Monte Cristo, addressing Andrea, " make your confession."

" To whom? "

" Tell M. Cavalcanti something of the state of your finances."

" *Ma foi!* M. le Comte, you have touched upon a tender chord."

" Do you hear what he says, major? "

" Certainly I do; but what would you have me do? " said the major.

" You should furnish him with some money, of course," replied Monte Cristo.

" I? "

" Yes, you! " said the count, at the same time advancing towards Andrea, and slipping a packet of bank-notes into the young man's hand.

" What is this? "

" It is from your father. He deputes me to give you this."

" Am I to consider this as part of my income on account? "

" No, it is for the first expenses of your settling in Paris."

" Ah, how good my dear father is! "

" Silence! " said Monte Cristo; " he does not wish you to know that it comes from him."

" I fully appreciate his delicacy," said Andrea.

" And now, gentlemen, I wish you good morning," said Monte Cristo.

" And when shall we have the honour of seeing you again, M. le Comte? " asked Cavalcanti.

" Ah! " said Andrea, " when may we hope for that pleasure? "

" On Saturday, if you will—yes.—Let me see—Saturday— I am to dine at my country-house, at Auteuil, on that day, Rue la Fontaine, No. 28. Several persons are invited, and amongst others, M. Danglars, your banker. I will introduce you to him; for it will be necessary he should know you, as he is to pay your money."

" Full dress? " said the major, half aloud.

" Oh, yes, certainly," said the count; " uniform, cross, etc., etc."

" And how shall I be dressed? " demanded Andrea.

" Oh, very simply; black trousers, polished boots, white waistcoat, either a black or blue coat, and a long cravat. Go to Blin or Veronique for your dress. Baptistin will tell you where they live, if you do not know where to address them. The less pretension there is in your dress, the better will be the effect, as you are a rich man. If you mean to buy any horses, get them of Devedeux; and if you purchase a phaeton, go to Baptiste for it."

" At what hour shall we come? " asked the young man.

" About half-past six."

" We will be with you at that time," said the major.

The two Cavalcanti bowed to the count, and left the house. Monte Cristo went to the window, and saw them crossing the street, arm in arm.

" There go two miscreants! " said he. " It is a pity they are not really related! " then, after an instant of gloomy reflection, " Come, I will go to see the Morrels! " said he; " I think that disgust is even more sickening than hatred."

58

At the Gate

OUR readers must now allow us to transport them again to the enclosure surrounding M. de Villefort's house, and, behind the gate, half screened from view by the large chestnut-trees, which on all sides spread their luxuriant branches, we shall find some persons of our acquaintance.

This time Maximilian was the first to arrive. He was intently watching for a shadow to appear amongst the trees, and awaiting with anxiety the sound of a light step on the gravel-walk. At length, the long-desired sound was heard, and instead of one figure, as he had expected, he perceived that two were approaching him.

The delay had been occasioned by a visit from Madame Danglars and Eugénie, which had been prolonged beyond the time at which Valentine was expected. That she might not appear to fail in her promise to Maximilian, she proposed to Mademoiselle Danglars that they should take a walk in the garden, being anxious to show that the delay, which was doubt-less a cause of vexation to him, was not occasioned by any neglect on her part. The young man, with the intuitive perception of a lover, quickly understood the circumstances in which she was involuntarily placed, and he was comforted. Besides, although she avoided coming within speaking distance, Valentine arranged so that Maximilian could see her pass and re-pass; and each time she did so, she managed, unperceived by her companion, to cast an expressive look at the young man, which seemed to say, " Have patience! You see it is not my fault." In the space of about half an hour the ladies retired, and Maximilian under-stood that Mademoiselle Danglars' visit had at last come to a conclusion. In a few minutes Valentine re-entered the garden alone. For fear that anyone should be observing her return, she walked slowly; and, instead of immediately directing her steps towards the gate, she seated herself on a bank, and carefully casting her eyes around to convince herself that she was not watched, she presently rose, and proceeded quickly to join Maximilian.

" Good evening, Valentine," said a well-known voice.

" Good evening, Maximilian; I know I have kept you waiting, but you saw the cause of my delay."

" Yes, I recognised Mademoiselle Danglers. I was not aware that you were so intimate with her."

" Who told you we were intimate, Maximilian? "

" No one, but you appeared to be so; from the manner in which you walked and talked together, one would have thought you were two schoolgirls telling your secrets to each other."

" We were having a confidential conversation," returned Valentine; " she was owning to me her repugnance to the marriage with M. de Morcerf, and I, on the other hand, was confessing to her how wretched it made me to think of marrying M. d'Epinay."

" Dear Valentine! "

" That will account to you for the unreserved manner which you observed between me and Eugénie; as in speaking of the man whom I could not love, my thoughts involuntarily reverted to him on whom my affections were fixed."

" Ah, how good you are to say so, Valentine! You possess a quality which can never belong to Mademoiselle Danglars! It is that indefinable charm, which is to a woman what perfume is to the flower and flavour to the fruit; for the beauty of either is not the only quality we seek."

" It is your love which makes you look upon everything in that light."

" No, Valentine, I assure you such is not the case. I was observing you both when you were walking in the garden, and, on my honour, without at all wishing to depreciate the beauty of Mademoiselle Danglars, I cannot understand how any man can really love her."

" The fact is, Maximilian, that I was there, and my presence had the effect of rendering you unjust in your comparison."

" No; but tell me—it is a question of simple curiosity—does Mademoiselle Danglars object to this marriage with M. de Morcerf on account of loving another? "

" I told you I was not on terms of strict intimacy with Eugénie."

" Yes, but girls tell each other secrets without being particularly intimate: own, now, that you did question her on the subject. Ah! I see you are smiling."

"If you are already aware of the conversation that passed, the wooden partition which interposed between us and you has proved but a slight security."

"Come, what did she say?"

"She told me that she loved no one," said Valentine; "that she disliked the idea of being married; that she would infinitely prefer leading an independent and unfettered life; and that she almost wished her father might lose his fortune, that she might become an artist, like her friend, Mademoiselle Louise d'Armilly."

"Ah, you see——"

"Well, what does that prove?" asked Valentine.

"Nothing," replied Maximilian.

"Then why did you smile?"

"Why, you yourself had your eyes fixed on me."

"Do you wish me to go?"

"Ah, no, no! But do not let us lose time; you are the subject on which I would wish to speak."

"True, we must be quick, for we have scarcely ten minutes more to pass together."

"*Ma foi!*" said Maximilian, in consternation.

"Yes, you are right; I am but a poor friend to you. What a life I cause you to lead, poor Maximilian, you who are so formed for happiness! I bitterly reproach myself, I assure you."

"Well! what does it signify, Valentine, so long as I am satisfied, and feel that even this long and painful suspense is amply repaid by five minutes of your society, or two words from your mouth? And I have also a deep conviction that Heaven would not have created two hearts, harmonising as ours do, and restored us to each other, almost miraculously, at last to separate us."

"Thank you for your kind and cheering words. You must hope for us both, Maximilian, for I am almost incapable of realising the feeling."

"But why must you leave me so soon?"

"I do not know particulars. I can only tell you that Madame de Villefort sent to request my presence, as she had a communication to make on which a part of my fortune depended. Let them take my fortune, I am already too rich; and, perhaps, when they have taken it, they will leave me in peace and quietness. You would love me as much if I were poor, would you not, Maximilian?"

"Oh, I shall always love you. What should I care for either riches or poverty, if my Valentine was near me, and I felt certain that no one could deprive me of her? But do you not fear that this communication may relate to your marriage?"

"I do not think that is the case."

"However it may be, Valentine, I protest to you that I will never love another!"

"And do you think it makes me happy to hear such a protestation?"

"Pardon me, I did not mean to grieve you."

"But I was going to tell you that I met M. de Morcerf the other day, and he told me he had received a letter from Franz, announcing his immediate return."

Valentine turned pale, and leaned against the gate for support.

"Can it really be true, and is that why Madame de Villefort has sent for me? No, that cannot be the case, for the communication would not be likely to come through her instrumentality."

"Why not?"

"Because—I scarcely know why—but it has appeared as if Madame de Villefort secretly objected to the marriage, although she did not choose openly to oppose it."

"Is it so? Then I feel as if I could adore Madame de Villefort."

"Do not be in such a hurry to do that," said Valentine, with a sad smile.

"If she objects to your marrying M. d'Epinay, she would be all the more likely to listen to any other proposition."

"No, Maximilian, it is not suitors to which Madame de Villefort objects, it is marriage itself."

"Marriage! If she dislikes that so much, why did she ever marry herself?"

"You do not understand me, Maximilian. About a year ago, I talked of retiring to a convent; Madame de Villefort, in spite of all the remarks which she considered it her duty to make, secretly approved of the proposition; my father consented to it at her instigation, and it was only on account of my poor grandfather that I finally abandoned the project. You can form no idea of the expression of that old man's eye when he looks at me, the only person in the world whom he loves, and, I had almost said, by whom he is beloved in return. When he learned my resolution, I shall never forget the reproachful look which he cast on me, and the tears of utter despair which chased each other down his lifeless cheeks. Ah, Maximilian, I experienced, at that moment, such remorse for my intention, that, throwing myself at his feet, I exclaimed, ' Forgive me, pray forgive me, my dear grandfather; they may do what they will with me, I will never leave you.' When I had ceased speaking, he thankfully raised his eyes to heaven, but without uttering a word. Ah, Maximilian, I may have much to suffer, but I feel as if my grandfather's look at that moment would more than compensate for all."

" Dear Valentine, you are a perfect angel; and I am sure I do not know what I can have done to merit your being revealed to me. But tell me what interest Madame de Villefort can have in your remaining unmarried? "

" Did I not tell you just now that I was rich, Maximilian— too rich? I possess nearly 50,000 livres in right of my mother; my grandfather and my grandmother, the Marquis and Marquise de Saint-Méran will leave me as much more; and M. Noirtier evidently intends making me his heir. My brother Edward, who inherits nothing from his mother, will therefore be poor in comparison with me. Now, if I had taken the veil, all this fortune would have descended to my father, and, in reversion, to his son."

" Ah, how strange it seems that such a young and beautiful woman should be so avaricious! "

" It is not for herself that she is so, but for her son; and what you regard as a vice becomes almost a virtue when looked at in the light of maternal love."

" But could you not compromise matters, and give up a portion of your fortune to her son? "

" How could I make such a proposition, especially to a woman who always professes to be so entirely disinterested? "

" Valentine, I have always regarded our love in the light of something sacred; consequently, I have covered it with the veil of respect, and hid it in the inmost recesses of my soul; no human being, not even my sister, is aware of its existence. Valentine, will you permit me to make a confidant of a friend, and reveal to him the love I bear you? "

Valentine started.

" A friend, Maximilian; and who is this friend? I tremble to give my permission."

" Listen, Valentine. Have you never experienced for anyone that sudden and irresistible sympathy which made you feel as if the object of it had been your old and familiar friend, though, in reality, it was the first time you had ever met? Nay, further, have you never endeavoured to recall the time, place, and circumstances of your former intercourse; and failing in this attempt, have almost believed that your spirits must have held converse with each other in some state of being anterior to the present, and that you are only now occupied in a reminiscence of the past? "

" Yes."

" Well! that is precisely the feeling which I experienced when I first saw that extraordinary man."

" Extraordinary, did you say? "

" Yes."

" You have known him for some time, then? "

" Scarcely longer than eight or ten days."

" And do you call a man your friend whom you have only known for eight or ten days? Ah, Maximilian, I had hoped you set a higher value on the title of friend."

" Your logic is most powerful, Valentine, but say what you will, I can never renounce the sentiment which has instinctively taken possession of my mind. I feel as if it was ordained that this man should be associated with all the good which the future may have in store for me. And sometimes it really seems as if his eye was able to see what was to come, and his hand endowed with the power of directing events according to his own will."

" He must be a prophet then," said Valentine, smiling.

" Indeed! " said Maximilian, " I have often been almost tempted to attribute to him the gift of prophecy; at all events he has a wonderful power of foretelling any future good."

" Ah," said Valentine, in a mournful tone, " do let me see this man, Maximilian; he may tell me whether I shall ever be loved sufficiently to make amends for all I have suffered."

" My poor girl! you know him already."

" I know him? "

" Yes; it was he who saved the life of your stepmother and her son."

" The Count of Monte Cristo? "

" The same."

" Ah," cried Valentine, " he is too much the friend of Madame de Villefort ever to be mine."

" The friend of Madame de Villefort! It cannot be; surely, Valentine, you are mistaken? "

" No, indeed, I am not, for I assure you, his power over our household is almost unlimited. Courted by my stepmother, who regards him as the epitome of human wisdom; admired by my father, who says he has never before heard such sublime ideas so eloquently expressed; idolised by Edward, who, notwithstanding his fear of the count's large black eyes, runs to meet him the moment he arrives, and opens his hand, in which he is sure to find some delightful present. M. de Monte Cristo appears to exert a mysterious and almost uncontrollable influence over all the members of our family."

" If such be the case, my dear Valentine, you must yourself have felt, or at all events will soon feel, the effects of his presence. He meets Albert de Morcerf in Italy—it is to rescue him from the hands of the banditti; he introduces himself to Madame Danglars—it is that he may give her a royal present; your stepmother and her son pass before his door,—it is that his Nubian may save them from destruction. This man evidently possesses the power of influencing events both as regards men and things. I never saw more simple tastes united to greater magnificence. His smile is so sweet when he addresses me, that I forget it can ever be bitter to others. Ah, Valentine, tell me, if he ever looked on you with one of those sweet smiles? if so, depend on it, you will be happy."

" Me! " said the young girl, " he never even glances at me; on the contrary, if I accidentally cross his path, he appears rather to avoid me. Ah! he is not generous, neither does he possess that supernatural penetration which you attribute to him; for if he had, he would have perceived that I was unhappy; and if he had been generous, seeing me sad and solitary, he would have used his influence to my advantage; and since, as you say, he resembles the sun, he would have warmed my heart with one of his life-giving rays. You say he loves you, Maximilian: how do you know that he does? All would pay deference to an officer like you, with a fierce moustache and a long sabre; but they think they may crush a poor weeping girl with impunity."

" Ah, Valentine, I assure you, you are mistaken."

" If it were otherwise; if he treated me diplomatically—that is to say, like a man who wishes, by some means or other, to obtain a footing in the house, so that he may ultimately gain the power of dictating to its occupants—he would, if it had been but once, have honoured me with the smile which you extol so loudly; but no, he saw that I was unhappy, he understood that I could be of no use to him, and therefore paid me no regard whatever. Who knows, but that in order to please Madame de Villefort and my father, he may not persecute me by every means in his power? It is not just that he should despise me thus without any reason for so doing. Ah! forgive me," said Valentine, perceiving the effect which her words were producing on Maximilian; " I have done wrong, for I have given utterance to thoughts concerning that man which I did not even know existed in my heart. I do not deny the influence of which you speak, or that I have not myself experienced it, but with me it has been productive of evil rather than good."

" Well, Valentine," said Morrel, with a sigh, " we will not discuss the matter further; I will not make a confidant of him."

" Alas! " said Valentine, " I see that I have given you pain. I can only say how sincerely I ask pardon for having grieved you. But indeed, I am not prejudiced beyond the power of conviction; tell me what this Count of Monte Cristo has done for you."

" I own that your question embarrasses me, Valentine, for I

cannot say that the count has rendered me any ostensible service. Still, as I have already told you, I have an instinctive affection for him, the source of which I cannot explain to you. Has the sun done anything for me?—No; he warms me with his rays, and it is by his light that I see you, nothing more. Has such and such a perfume done anything for me?—No; its odour charms one of my senses; that is all I can say when I am asked why I praise it. My friendship for him is as strange and unaccountable as his for me. A secret voice seems to whisper to me that there must be something more than chance in this unexpected reciprocity of friendship. In his most simple actions, as well as in his most secret thoughts, I find a relation to my own. You will, perhaps, smile at me, when I tell you that ever since I have known this man, I have involuntarily entertained the idea that all the good fortune which has befallen me originated from him. However, I have managed to live thirty years without this protection, you will say; but I will endeavour a little to illustrate my meaning. He invited me to dine with him on Saturday, which was a very natural thing for him to do. Well! what have I learnt since? That your mother and M. de Villefort are both coming to this dinner. I shall meet them there, and who knows what future advantages may result from the interview? This may appear to you to be no unusual combination of circumstances; nevertheless, I perceive some hidden plot in the arrangement, something, in fact, more than is apparent on a casual view of the subject. I believe that this singular man, who appears to fathom the motives of everyone, has purposely arranged for me to meet M. and Madame de Villefort; and sometimes, I confess, I have gone so far as to try to read in his eyes whether he was in possession of the secret of our love."

" My good friend," said Valentine, " I should take you for a visionary, and should tremble for your reason, if I were always to hear you talk in a strain similar to this. Is it possible that you can see anything more than the merest chance in this meeting? Pray reflect a little. My father, who never goes out, has several times been on the point of refusing this invitation; Madame de Villefort, on the contrary, is burning with the desire of seeing this extraordinary nabob in his own house, therefore she has, with great difficulty, prevailed on my father to accompany her. No, no; it is as I have said, Maximilian; there is no one in the world of whom I can ask help but yourself, and my grandfather, who is little better than a corpse."

" I see that you are right, logically speaking," said Maximilian; " but the gentle voice which usually has such power over me fails to convince me to-day."

" I feel the same as regards yourself," said Valentine; " and I own, that if you have no stronger proof to give me——"

" I have another," replied Maximilian; " but I fear you will deem it even more absurd than the first."

" So much the worse," said Valentine, smiling.

" It is, nevertheless, conclusive to my mind: my ten years of service have also confirmed my ideas on the subject of sudden inspirations, for I have several times owed my life to one of those mysterious impulses which directed me to move at once either to the right or to the left, in order to escape the ball which killed the comrade fighting by my side, whilst it left me unharmed."

" Dear Maximilian, why not attribute your escape to my constant prayers for your safety? When you are away, I no longer pray for myself, but for you."

" Yes, since you have known me," said Morrel, smiling; " but that cannot apply to the time previous to our acquaintance, Valentine."

" You are very provoking, and will not give me credit for anything; but let me hear this second example, which you yourself own to be absurd."

" Well, look through this opening, and you will see the beautiful new horse which I rode here."

" Ah, what a beautiful creature! " cried Valentine; " why did you not bring it close to the gate, that I might talk to it and pat it? "

" It is as you say, a very valuable animal," said Maximilian; " you know that my means are limited, and that I am what would be designated a man of moderate pretensions. Well, I went to a horse-dealer's where I saw this magnificent horse, which I have named Medea. I asked the price of it; they told me it was 4500 francs. I was therefore obliged to give it up, as you may imagine, but I own I went away with rather a heavy heart, for the horse had looked at me affectionately, had rubbed its head against me, and when I mounted it had pranced in the most coquettish way imaginable, so that I was altogether fascinated with it. That same evening some friends of mine visited me, M. de Château-Renaud, M. Debray, and five or six other choice spirits, whom you do not know even by name. They proposed *la bouillotte*. I never play, for I am not rich enough to afford to lose, nor sufficiently poor to desire to gain. But I was at my own house, you understand, so there was nothing to be done but to send for the cards, which I did. Just as they were sitting down to table, M. de Monte Cristo arrived. He took his seat amongst them, they played, and I won. I am almost ashamed to say that

my gains amounted to 5000 francs. We separated at midnight.
I could not defer my pleasure, so I took a cabriolet and drove
to the horse-dealer's. Feverish and excited, I rang at the door.
The person who opened it must have taken me for a madman,
for I rushed at once to the stable. Medea was standing at the
rack eating her hay. I immediately put on the saddle and bridle,
to which operation she lent herself with the best grace possible;
then putting the 4500 francs into the hands of the astonished
dealer, I proceeded to fulfil my intention of passing the night
in riding in the Champs Elysées. As I rode by the count's house,
I perceived a light in one of the windows, and fancied I saw the
shadow of his figure moving behind the curtain. Now, Valentine,
I firmly believe that he knew of my wish to possess this horse,
and that he lost expressly to give me the means of procuring it."

" My dear Maximilian, you are really too fanciful; you will
not love even me long. A man who accustoms himself to live
in such a world of poetry and imagination must find far too little
excitement in a common, everyday sort of attachment such as
ours. But they are calling me.—Do you hear? "

" Ah, Valentine! " said Maximilian, " give me but one finger
through this opening in the grating, that I may have the happiness
of kissing it."

" Maximilian, we said we would be to each other as two voices,
two shadows."

" As you will, Valentine."

" Shall you be happy if I do what you wish? "

" Oh, yes."

Valentine mounted the bank, and passed not only her finger
but her whole hand through the opening. Maximilian uttered
a cry of delight, and, springing forward, seized the hand extended
towards him, and imprinted on it a fervent and impassioned kiss.
The little hand was then immediately withdrawn, and the young
man saw Valentine hurrying towards the house, as though she
were almost terrified at her own sensations.

59

M. Noirtier de Villefort

WE will now relate what was passing in the house of the procureur du roi after the departure of Madame Danglars and her daughter, and during the time of the conversation between Maximilian and Valentine, which we have just detailed. M. de Villefort entered his father's room, followed by Madame de Villefort. Both of the visitors, after saluting the old man and speaking to Barrois, a faithful servant, who had been twenty-five years in his service, took their places on either side of the paralytic.

M. Noirtier was sitting in an arm-chair, which moved upon castors, in which he was wheeled into the room in the morning, and in the same way drawn out again at night. He was placed before a large glass, which reflected the whole apartment, and permitted him to see, without any attempt to move, which would have been impossible, all who entered the room, and everything which was going on around him. M. Noirtier, although almost as immovable and helpless as a corpse, looked at the new-comers with a quick and intelligent expression, perceiving at once, by their ceremonious courtesy, that they were come on business of an unexpected and official character. Sight and hearing were the only senses remaining, and they appeared left, like two solitary sparks, to animate the miserable body which seemed fit for nothing but the grave; it was only, however, by means of one of these senses that he could reveal the thoughts and feelings which still worked in his mind, and the look by which he gave expression to this inner life resembled one of those distant lights which are sometimes seen in perspective by the benighted traveller whilst crossing some cheerless desert, apprising him that there is still one human being who, like himself, is keeping watch amidst the silence and obscurity of night. Noirtier's hair was long and white, and flowed over his shoulders; whilst in his eyes, shaded by thick, black lashes, was concentrated, as it often happens with any organ which is used to the exclusion of the others, all the activity, address, force, and intelligence, which were formerly diffused over his whole body; certainly, the movement of the arm, the sound of the voice, and the agility of the body, were wanting, but the speaking eye sufficed for all. He commanded with it; it was the medium through which his thanks were conveyed. In short, his whole appearance produced on the mind the impression of a corpse with living eyes, and nothing could be more startling than to observe the expression of anger or joy suddenly lighting up these organs, while the rest of the rigid and marble-like features were utterly deprived of the power of participation. Three persons only could understand this language of the poor paralytic; these were Villefort, Valentine, and the old servant, of whom we have already spoken. But as Villefort saw his father but seldom, and then only when absolutely obliged, and as he never took any pains to please or gratify him when he was there, all the old man's happiness was centred in his grand-daughter. Valentine, by means of her love, her patience, and her devotion, had learned to read in Noirtier's look all the varied feelings which were passing in his mind. To this dumb language, which was so unintelligible to others, she answered by throwing her whole soul into the expression of the countenance, and in this manner were the conversations sustained between the bloom-ing girl and the helpless invalid, whose body could scarcely be called a living one, but who, nevertheless, possessed a fund of knowledge and penetration, united with a will as powerful as ever, although clogged by a body rendered utterly incapable of obeying its impulses. Valentine had solved this strange problem, and was able easily to understand his thoughts, and to convey her own in return; and by her untiring and devoted assiduity, it was seldom that, in the ordinary transactions of everyday life, she failed to anticipate the wishes of the living, thinking mind, or the wants of the almost inanimate body. As to the servant, he had, as we have said, been with his master for five-and-twenty years, therefore he knew all his habits, and it was seldom that Noirtier found it necessary to ask for anything, so prompt was he in administering to all the necessities of the invalid. Villefort did not need the help of either Valentine or the domestic, in order to carry on with his father the strange conversation which he was about to begin. As we have said, he perfectly understood the old man's vocabulary; and if he did not use it more often, it was only indifference and *ennui* which prevented him from so doing. He, therefore, allowed Valentine to go into the garden, sent away Barrois, and after having taken a place on the right hand of his father, whilst Madame de Villefort seated herself on the left, he addressed him thus:—

"I trust you will not be displeased, sir, that Valentine has not come with us, or that I dismissed Barrois, for our conference will be one which could not with propriety be carried on in the presence of either; Madame de Villefort and I have a com-munication to make to you."

Noirtier's face remained perfectly passive during this long preamble; whilst, on the contrary, the eye of Villefort was endeavouring to penetrate into the inmost recesses of the old man's heart.

"This communication," continued the procureur du roi, in that cold and decisive tone which seemed ot once to preclude all discussion, "will, we are sure, meet with your approbation."

The eye of the invalid still retained that vacancy of expression which prevented his son from obtaining any knowledge of the feelings which were passing in his mind; he listened, nothing more.

"Sir," resumed Villefort, "we are thinking of marrying Valentine."

Had the old man's face been moulded in wax, it could not have shown less emotion at this news than was now to be traced there.

"The marriage will take place in less than three months," said Villefort.

Noirtier's eye still retained its inanimate expression.

Madame de Villefort now took her part in the conversation, and added:

"We thought this news would possess an interest for you, sir, who have always entertained a great affection for Valentine; it therefore only now remains for us to tell you the name of the young man for whom she is destined. It is one of the most desirable connections which could possibly be formed; he possesses fortune, a high rank in society, and every personal qualification like to render Valentine supremely happy; his name, however, cannot be wholly unknown to you. The person to whom we allude is M. Franz de Quesnel, Baron d'Epinay."

During the time that his wife was speaking, Villefort had narrowly watched the countenance of the old man. When Madame de Villefort pronounced the name of Franz, the pupil of M. Noirtier's eye began to dilate, and his eyelids trembled with the same movement as may be perceived on the lips of an individual about to speak, and he darted a lightning glance at Madame de Villefort and his son. The procureur du roi, who knew the political hatred which had formerly existed between M. Noirtier and the elder d'Epinay, well understood the agitation and anger which the announcement had produced; but, feigning not to perceive either, he immediately resumed the conversation commenced by his wife.

"Sir," said he, "you are aware that Valentine is about to enter her nineteenth year, which renders it important that she should lose no time in forming a suitable connection. Nevertheless, you have not been forgotten in our plans, and we have fully ascertained beforehand, that Valentine's future husband will consent, not to live in this house, for that might not be pleasant for the young people, but that you should live with them; so that you and Valentine, who are so attached to each other, would not be separated, and you would be able to pursue exactly the same course of life which you have hitherto done, and thus, instead of losing, you will be a gainer by the change, as it will secure to you two children instead of one, to watch over and comfort you."

Noirtier's look was furious: it was very evident that something desperate was passing in the old man's mind, for the cry of anger and grief rose to his throat, and not being able to find vent in utterance, appeared almost to choke him, for his face and lips turned quite purple with the struggle.

Villefort quietly opened a window, saying, " It is very warm and the heat affects M. Noirtier." He then returned to his place, but did not sit down.

" This marriage," added Madame de Villefort, " is quite agreeable to the wishes of M. d'Epinay and his family; besides, he had no relations nearer than an uncle and aunt, his mother having died at his birth, and his father having been assassinated in 1815, that is to say, when he was but two years old; it naturally followed that the child was permitted to choose his own pursuits, and he has, therefore, seldom acknowledged any other authority than that of his own will."

" That assassination was a mysterious affair," said Villefort, " and the perpetrators have hitherto escaped detection; although suspicion has fallen on the head of more than one person."

Noirtier made such an effort that his lips expanded into a smile.

" Now," continued Villefort, " those to whom the guilt really belongs, by whom the crime was committed, on whose heads the justice of man may probably descend here, and the certain judgment of God hereafter, would rejoice in the opportunity thus afforded of bestowing such a peace-offering as Valentine on the son of him whose life they so ruthlessly destroyed."

Noirtier had succeeded in mastering his emotion more than could have been deemed possible with such an enfeebled and shattered frame. " Yes, I understand! " was the reply contained in his look; and this look expressed a feeling of strong indignation mixed with profound contempt.

Villefort fully understood his father's meaning, and answered by a slight shrug of the shoulders. He then motioned to his wife to take leave.

"Now, sir," said Madame de Villefort, "I must bid you farewell. Would you like me to send Edward to you for a short time?"

It had been agreed that the old man should express his approbation by closing his eyes, his refusal by winking them several times, and if he had some desire or feeling to express, he raised them to heaven. If he wanted Valentine, he closed the right eye only; and if Barrois, the left.

At Madame de Villefort's proposition he instantly winked his eyes. Provoked by a complete refusal, she bit her lip, and said, "Then shall I send Valentine to you?"

The old man closed his eyes eagerly, thereby intimating that such was his wish.

M. and Madame de Villefort bowed and left the room, giving orders that Valentine should be summoned to her grandfather's presence, and feeling sure that she would have much to do to restore calmness to the perturbed spirit of the invalid.

Valentine, with a colour still heightened by emotion, entered the room just after her parents had quitted it. One look was sufficient to tell her that her grandfather was suffering, and that there was much on his mind which he was wishing to communicate to her.

"Dear grandpapa," cried she, "what has happened? They have vexed you, and you are angry?"

The paralytic closed his eyes in token of assent.

"Who has displeased you? Is it my father?"

"No."

"Madame de Villefort?"

"No."

"Me?"

The former sign was repeated.

"Are you displeased with me?" cried Valentine, in astonishment.

M. Noirtier again closed his eyes.

"And what have I done, dear grandpapa, that you should be angry with me?" cried Valentine.

There was no answer; and she continued: "I have not seen you all day. Has anyone been speaking to you against me?"

"Yes," said the old man's look, with eagerness.

"Let me think a moment. I do assure you, grandpapa—— Ah!—M. and Madame de Villefort have just left this room, have they not?"

"Yes."

"And it was they who told you something which made you

angry? What was it then? May I go and ask them, that I may have the opportunity of making my peace with you? "

" No, no! " said Noirtier's look.

" Ah! you frighten me. What can they have said? " and she again tried to think what it could be.

" Ah, I know," said she, lowering her voice, and going close to the old man, " they have been speaking of my marriage,— have they not? "

" Yes," replied the angry look.

" I understand; you are displeased at the silence I have preserved on the subject. The reason of it was, that they had insisted on my keeping the matter a secret, and begged me not to tell you anything of it; they did not even acquaint me with their intentions, and I only discovered them by chance; that is why I have been so reserved with you, dear grandpapa. Pray forgive me! "

But there was no look calculated to reassure her; all it seemed to say was, " It is not only your reserve which afflicts me."

" What is it, then? " asked the young girl. " Perhaps you think I shall abandon you, dear grandpapa, and that I shall forget you when I am married? "

" No."

" They told you then that M. d'Epinay consented to our all living together? "

" Yes."

" Then why are you still vexed and grieved? "

The old man's eyes beamed with an expression of gentle affection.

" Yes, I understand," said Valentine, " it is because you love me."

The old man assented.

" And you are afraid I shall be unhappy? "

" Yes."

" You do not like M. Franz? "

The eyes repeated several times, " No, no, no."

" Then you are vexed at the engagement? "

" Yes."

" Well, listen," said Valentine, throwing herself on her knees, and putting her arm round her grandfather's neck, " I am vexed too, for I do not love M. Franz d'Epinay."

An expression of intense joy illumed the old man's eyes.

" When I wished to retire into a convent, you remember how angry you were with me? "

A tear trembled in the eye of the invalid.

" Well," continued Valentine, " the reason of my proposing

it was that I might escape this hateful marriage, which drives me to despair."

Noirtier's breathing became thick and short.

" Then the idea of this marriage really grieves you too! Ah! if you could but help me; if we could both together defeat their plan! But you are unable to oppose them. You, whose mind is so quick, and whose will is so firm are, nevertheless, as weak and unequal to the contest as I am myself. Alas! you who would have been such a powerful protector to me in the days of your health and strength, can now only sympathise in my joys and sorrows, without being able to take any active part in them. However, this is much, and calls for gratitude; and Heaven has not taken away all my blessings when it leaves me your sympathy and kindness."

At these words there appeared in Noirtier's eyes an expression of such deep meaning, that the young girl thought she could read these words there, " You are mistaken; I can still do much for you."

" Do you think you can help me, dear grandpapa? " said Valentine.

" Yes." Noirtier raised his eyes; it was the sign agreed on between him and Valentine when he wanted anything.

" What is it you want, dear grandpapa? " said Valentine, and she endeavoured to recall to mind all the things which he would be likely to need; and as the ideas presented themselves to her mind, she repeated them aloud; but finding that all her efforts elicited nothing but a constant " No,"—" Come," said she, " since this plan does not answer, I will have recourse to another." She then recited all the letters of the alphabet from A down to N. When she arrived at that letter, the paralytic made her understand that was the initial letter of the thing which he wanted.

" Ah," said Valentine, " the thing you desire begins with the letter N; it is with N that we have to do, then. Well, let me see, what can you want that begins with N? Na ..., Ne ..., Ni ..., No ..."

" Yes, yes, yes," said the old man's eye.

" Ah, it is No, then? "

" Yes."

Valentine fetched a dictionary, which she placed on a desk before Noirtier; she opened it, and seeing that the old man's eye was thoroughly fixed on its pages, she ran her finger quickly up and down the columns. During the six years which had passed since Noirtier first fell into this sad state, Valentine's powers of invention had been too often put to the test not to render her expert in devising expedients for gaining a knowledge of his wishes, and the constant practice had so perfected her in the art, that she guessed the old man's meaning as quickly as if he himself had been able to seek for what he wanted. At the word *Notary*, Noirtier made a sign to her to stop.

"Notary," said she, "do you want a notary, dear grand-papa?"

The old man again signified that it was a notary he desired.

"You would wish a notary to be sent for, then?" said Valentine.

"Yes."

"Shall my father be informed of your wish?"

"Yes."

"Do you wish the notary should be sent for immediately?"

"Yes."

"Then they shall go for him directly, dear grandpapa. Is that all you want?"

"Yes."

Valentine rang the bell, and ordered the servant to tell Monsieur or Madame de Villefort that they were requested to come to M. Noirtier's room.

"Are you satisfied now?" inquired Valentine.

"Yes."

"I am sure you are; it is not very difficult to discover that;" and the young girl smiled on her grandfather, as if he had been a child.

M. de Villefort entered, followed by Barrois.

"What do you want me for, sir?" demanded he of the paralytic.

"Sir," said Valentine, "my grandfather wishes for a notary."

At this strange and unexpected demand, M. de Villefort and his father exchanged looks.

"Yes," motioned the latter, with a firmness which seemed to declare, that with the help of Valentine and his old servant, who both knew what his wishes were, he was quite prepared to maintain the contest.

"Do you wish for a notary?" asked Villefort.

"Yes."

"What to do?"

Noirtier made no answer.

"What do you want with a notary?" again repeated Villefort.

The invalid's eye remained fixed, by which expression he intended to intimate that his resolution was unalterable.

"Is it to do us some ill turn; do you think it is worth while?" said Villefort.

" Still," said Barrois, with the freedom and fidelity of an old servant, " if M. Noirtier asks for a notary, I suppose he really wishes for a notary, therefore I shall go at once and fetch one." Barrois acknowledged no master but Noirtier, and never allowed his desires in any way to be contradicted.

" Yes, I do want a notary," motioned the old man, shutting his eyes with a look of defiance, which seemed to say, " and I should like to see the person who dares to refuse my request."

" You shall have a notary, as you absolutely wish for one, sir," said Villefort; " but I shall explain to him your state of health, and make excuses for you, for the scene cannot fail of being a most ridiculous one."

" Never mind that," said Barrois, " I shall go and fetch a notary nevertheless "; and the old servant departed triumphantly on his mission.

60

The Will

As soon as Barrois had left the room, Noirtier looked at Valentine with that peculiar expression which conveyed so much deep meaning. The young girl perfectly understood the look, and so did Villefort, for his countenance became clouded, and he knitted his eyebrows angrily. He took a seat and quietly awaited the arrival of the notary.

Noirtier saw him seat himself with an appearance of perfect indifference, at the same time giving a side look at Valentine, which made her understand that she also was to remain in the room. Three-quarters of an hour after Barrois returned, bringing the notary with him.

" Sir," said Villefort, after the first salutations were over, " you were sent for by M. Noirtier, whom you see here. All his limbs have become completely paralysed; he has lost his voice also, and we ourselves find much trouble in endeavouring to catch some fragments of his meaning."

Noirtier cast an appealing look on Valentine, which look was at once so earnest and imperative, that she answered immediately:

" Sir," said she, " I perfectly understand my grandfather's meaning at all times."

" That is quite true," said Barrois; " and that is what I told the gentleman as we walked along."

" Permit me," said the notary, turning first to Villefort and then to Valentine, " permit me to state that the case in question is just one of those in which a public officer like myself cannot proceed to act without thereby incurring a dangerous responsibility. The first thing necessary to render an act valid is, that the notary should be thoroughly convinced that he has faithfully interpreted the will and wishes of the person dictating the act. Now, I cannot be sure of the approbation or disapprobation of a client who cannot speak; and as the object of his desire or his repugnance cannot be clearly proved to me, on account of his want of speech, my services here would be quite useless, and cannot be legally exercised."

The notary then prepared to retire. An imperceptible smile of triumph was expressed on the lips of the procureur du roi.

Noirtier looked at Valentine with an expression so full of grief, that she arrested the departure of the notary.

" Sir," said she, " the language which I speak with my grandfather may be easily learnt; and I can teach you, in a few minutes, to understand it almost as well as I can myself. Will you tell me what you require, in order to set your conscience quite at ease on the subject? "

" In order to render an act valid, I must be certain of the approbation or disapprobation of my client. Illness of the body would not affect the validity of the deed; but sanity of mind is absolutely requisite."

" Well, sir, by the help of two signs, with which I will acquaint you presently, you may ascertain with perfect certainty that my grandfather is still in the full possession of all his mental faculties. M. Noirtier, being deprived of voice and motion, is accustomed to convey his meaning by closing his eyes when he wishes to signify ' yes,' and to wink when he means ' no.' You now know quite enough to enable you to converse with M. Noirtier; try."

Noirtier gave Valentine such a look of tenderness and gratitude, that it was comprehended even by the notary himself.

" You have heard and understood what your granddaughter has been saying, sir, have you? " asked the notary.

Noirtier closed his eyes.

" And you approve of what she said; that is to say, you declare that the signs which she mentioned are really those by means of which you are accustomed to convey your thoughts? "

" Yes."

" It was you who sent for me? "

" Yes."

" To make your will? "

" Yes."

" And you do not wish me to go away without fulfilling your original intentions? "

The old man winked violently.

" Well, sir," said the young girl, " do you understand now, and is your conscience perfectly at rest on the subject? "

But before the notary could answer, Villefort had drawn him aside.

" Sir," said he, " do you suppose for a moment that a man can sustain a physical shock, such as M. Noirtier has received, without any detriment to his mental faculties? "

" It is not exactly that, sir," said the notary, " which makes me uneasy, but the difficulty will be in arriving at his thoughts and intentions, so as to be able to provoke his answers."

" You must see that to be an utter impossibility," said Villefort.

Valentine and the old man heard this conversation; and Noirtier fixed his eye so earnestly on Valentine, that she felt bound to answer to the look.

" Sir," said she, " that need not make you uneasy, however difficult it may at first sight appear to be. I can discover and explain to you my grandfather's thoughts, so as to put an end to all your doubts and fears on the subject. I have now been six years with M. Noirtier, and let him tell you if ever once, during that time, he has entertained a thought which he was unable to make me understand."

" No," signed the old man.

" Let us try what we can do, then," said the notary. " You accept this young lady as your interpreter, M. Noirtier? "

" Yes."

" Well, sir, what do you require of me, and what document is it that you wish to be drawn up? "

Valentine named all the letters of the alphabet till she came to W. At this letter the eloquent eye of Noirtier gave her notice that she was to stop.

" It is very evident that it is the letter W which M. Noirtier wants," said the notary.

" Wait," said Valentine; and, turning to her grandfather, she repeated, " Wa—We—Wi—"

The old man stopped her at the last syllable.

Valentine then took the dictionary, and the notary watched her whilst she turned over the pages. She passed her finger slowly down the columns, and when she came to the word " Will," M. Noirtier's eye bade her stop.

" Will! " cried the notary; " it is very evident that M. Noirtier is desirous of making his will."

"Yes, yes, yes!" motioned the invalid.

"Really, sir, you must allow that this is most extraordinary," said the astonished notary, turning to M. de Villefort.

"Yes," said the procureur; "and I think the Will promises to be yet more extraordinary; for I cannot see how it is to be drawn up without the intervention of Valentine, and she may, perhaps, be considered as too much interested in its contents to allow of her being a suitable interpreter of the obscure and ill-defined wishes of her grandfather."

"No, no, no!" replied the eye of the paralytic.

"What!" said Villefort, "do you mean to say that Valentine is not interested in your will?"

"No."

"Sir," said the notary, whose interest had been greatly excited, and who had resolved on publishing far and wide the account of this extraordinary and picturesque scene, "what appeared so impossible to me an hour ago, has now become quite easy and practicable; and this may be a perfectly valid will, provided it be read in the presence of seven witnesses, approved by the testator and sealed by the notary in the presence of the witnesses. As to the time, it will certainly occupy rather more than the generality of wills. There are certain forms necessary to be gone through, and which are always the same. As to the details; the greater part will be furnished afterwards, by the state in which we find the affairs of the testator, and by yourself, who, having had the management of them, can, doubtless, give full information on the subject. But, besides all this, in order that the instrument may not be contested, I am anxious to give it the greatest possible authenticity: therefore, one of my colleagues will help me, and, contrary to custom, will assist in the dictation of the testament. Are you satisfied, sir?" continued the notary, addressing the old man.

"Yes," looked the invalid, his eye beaming with delight at his meaning being so well understood.

"What is he going to do?" thought Villefort, whose position demanded so much reserve, but who was longing to know what were the intentions of his father. He left the room to give orders for another notary to be sent, but Barrois, who had heard all that passed, had guessed his master's wishes, and had already gone to fetch one. The procureur du roi then told his wife to come up.

In the course of a quarter of an hour everyone had assembled in the chamber of the paralytic; the second notary had also arrived. A few words sufficed for a mutual understanding between the two officers of the law. They read to Noirtier the formal copy of a will, in order to give him an idea of the terms in which such documents are generally couched; then, in order to test the capacity of the testator, the first notary said, turning towards him:

" When an individual makes his will, it is generally in favour or in prejudice of some person? "

" Yes."

" Have you an exact idea of the amount of your fortune? "

" Yes."

" I will name to you several sums, which will increase by graduation; you will stop me when I reach the one representing the amount of your own possessions? "

" Yes."

There was a kind of solemnity in this interrogation. Never had the struggle between mind and matter been more apparent than now; and if it was not a sublime, it was, at least, a curious spectacle. They had formed a circle round the invalid; the second notary was sitting at a table, prepared for writing, and his colleague was standing before the testator in the act of interrogating him on the subject to which we have alluded.

" Your fortune exceeds 300,000 francs, does it not? " asked he.

Noirtier made a sign that it did.

" Do you possess 400,000 francs? " inquired the notary.

Noirtier's eyes remained immovable.

" 500,000? "

The same expression continued.

" 600,000,—700,00,—800,000,—900,000? "

Noirtier stopped him at the last-named sum.

" You are then in possession of 900,000 francs? " asked the notary.

" Yes."

" In landed property? "

" No."

" In stock? "

" Yes."

" The stock is in your own hands? "

The look which M. Noirtier cast on Barrois showed that there was something wanted which he knew where to find; the old servant left the room, and presently returned, bringing with him a small casket.

" Do you permit us to open this casket? " asked the notary.

Noirtier gave his assent.

They opened it, and found 900,000 francs in bank scrip.

The first notary handed over each note, as he examined it, to his colleague. The total amount was found to be as M. Noirtier had stated.

" It is all as he has said; it is very evident that the mind still retains its full force and vigour." Then, turning towards the paralytic, he said, " You possess, then, 900,000 francs of capital, which, according to the manner in which you have invested it, ought to bring in an income of about 40,000 livres? "

" Yes."

" To whom do you desire to leave this fortune? "

" Oh! " said Madame de Villefort, " there is not much doubt on that subject. M. Noirtier tenderly loves his granddaughter, Mademoiselle de Villefort; it is she who has nursed and tended him for six years, and has, by her devoted attention, fully secured the affection, I had almost said the gratitude, of her grandfather; and it is but just that she should reap the fruit of her devotion."

The eye of Noirtier clearly showed by its expression that he was not deceived by the false assent given by Madame de Villefort's words and manner to the motives which she supposed him to entertain.

" Is it, then, to Madamoiselle Valentine de Villefort that you leave these 900,000 francs? " demanded the notary, thinking he had only to insert this clause, but waiting first for the assent of Noirtier, which it was necessary should be given before all the witnesses of this singular scene.

Valentine, when her name was made the subject of discussion, had stepped back to escape unpleasant observation; her eyes were cast down, and she was crying. The old man looked at her for an instant with an expression of the deepest tenderness; then, turning towards the notary, he significantly winked his eyes in token of dissent.

" What! " said the notary, " do you not intend making Mademoiselle Valentine de Villefort your residuary legatee? "

" No."

" You are not making any mistake, are you? " said the notary; " you really mean to declare that such is not your intention? "

" No, no."

Valentine raised her head; she was struck dumb with astonishment. It was not so much the conviction that she was disinherited which caused her grief, but her total inability to account for the feelings which had provoked her grandfather to such an act. But Noirtier looked at her with so much affectionate tenderness that she exclaimed:

" Oh, grandpa! I see now that it is only your fortune of which you deprive me; you still leave me the love which I have always enjoyed."

"Ah, yes, most assuredly!" said the eyes of the paralytic; for he closed them with an expression which Valentine could not mistake.

"Thank you! thank you!" murmured she.

The old man's declaration that Valentine was not the destined inheritor of his fortune had excited the hopes of Madame de Villefort; she gradually approached the invalid, and said:

"Then, doubtless, dear M. Noirtier, you intend leaving your fortune to your grandson, Edward de Villefort?"

The winking of the eyes which answered this speech was most decided and terrible, and expressed a feeling almost amounting to hatred.

"No!" said the notary; "then, perhaps, it is to your son, M. de Villefort?"

"No."

The two notaries looked at each other in mute astonishment and inquiry as to what were the real intentions of the testator. Villefort and his wife both blushed and changed colour, one from shame, the other from anger.

"What have we all done, then, dear grandpapa?" said Valentine; "you no longer seem to love any of us?"

The old man's eyes passed rapidly from Villefort and his wife, and rested on Valentine with a look of unutterable fondness.

"Well!" said she, "if you love me, grandpapa, try and bring that love to bear upon your actions at this present moment. You know me well enough to be quite sure that I have never thought of your fortune; besides, they say I am already rich in right of my mother, too rich even. Explain yourself, then."

Noirtier fixed his intelligent eyes on Valentine's hand.

"My hand?" said she.

"Yes."

"Her hand!" exclaimed everyone.

"Oh, gentlemen! you see it is all useless, and that my father's mind is really impaired," said Villefort.

"Ah!" cried Valentine suddenly, "I understand. It is my marriage you mean, is it not, dear grandpapa?"

"Yes, yes, yes," signed the paralytic, casting on Valentine a look of joyful gratitude for having guessed his meaning.

"You are angry with us all on account of this marriage, are you not?"

"Yes."

"Really this is too absurd," said Villefort.

"Excuse me, sir," replied the notary; "on the contrary, M. Noirtier's meaning is quite evident to me, and I can quite easily connect the train of ideas passing in his mind."

"You do not wish me to marry M. Franz d'Epinay?" observed Valentine.

"I do not wish it," said the eye of her grandfather.

"And you disinherit your granddaughter," continued the notary, "because she has contracted an engagement contrary to your wishes."

"Yes."

"So that, but for this marriage, she would have been your heir?"

"Yes."

There was a profound silence. The two notaries were holding a consultation as to the best means of proceeding with the affair; Valentine was looking at her grandfather with a smile of intense gratitude, and Villefort was biting his lips with vexation, whilst Madame de Villefort could not succeed in repressing an inward feeling of joy, which, in spite of herself, appeared in her whole countenance.

"But," said Villefort, who was the first to break the silence, "I consider that I am the best judge of the propriety of the marriage in question. I am the only person possessing the right to dispose of my daughter's hand. It is my wish that she should marry M. Franz d'Epinay—and she shall marry him!"

Valentine sank weeping into a chair.

"Sir," said the notary, "how do you intend disposing of your fortune in case Mademoiselle de Villefort still determines on marrying M. Franz?"

The old man gave no answer.

"You will, of course, dispose of it in some way or other?"

"Yes."

"In favour of some member of your family?"

"No."

"Do you intend devoting it to charitable purposes, then?" pursued the notary.

"Yes."

"But," said the notary, "you are aware that the law does not allow a son to be entirely deprived of his patrimony?"

"Yes."

"You only intend, then, to dispose of that part of your fortune which the law allows you to subtract from the inheritance of your son?"

Noirtier made no answer.

"Do you still wish to dispose of all?"

"Yes."

"But they will contest the Will after your death?"

"No."

"My father knows me," replied Villefort; "he is quite sure that his wishes will be held sacred by me; besides, he understands that in my position I cannot plead against the poor."

The eye of Noirtier beamed with triumph.

"What do you decide on, sir?" asked the notary of Villefort.

"Nothing, sir; it is a resolution which my father has taken, and I know he never alters his mind. I am quite resigned. These 900,000 francs will go out of the family in order to enrich some hospital; but it is ridiculous thus to yield to the caprices of an old man, and I shall, therefore, act according to my conscience."

Having said this, Villefort quitted the room with his wife, leaving his father at liberty to do as he pleased. The same day the Will was made, the witnesses were brought, it was approved by the old man, sealed in the presence of all, and given in charge to M. Des Champs, the family notary.

61

The Telegraph

M. AND MADAME DE VILLEFORT found on their return that the Count of Monte Cristo, who had come to visit them in their absence, had been ushered into the drawing-room, and was still awaiting them there. Madame de Villefort, who had not yet sufficiently recovered from her late emotion to allow of her entertaining visitors so immediately, retired to her bedroom, whilst the procureur du roi, who could better depend upon himself, proceeded at once to the drawing-room. Although M. de Villefort flattered himself that, to all outward view, he had completely masked the feelings which were passing in his mind, he did not know that the cloud was still lowering on his brow, so much that the count immediately remarked his sombre and thoughtful air.

"*Ma foi!*" said Monte Cristo, after the first compliments were over, "what is the matter with you, M. de Villefort? Have I arrived at the moment that you were drawing up some case of capital indictment?"

Villefort tried to smile.

"No, M. le Comte," replied M. de Villefort, "I am the only victim in this case. It is I who lose my cause; and it is ill-luck, obstinacy, and folly which have caused it to be decided against me."

"To what do you allude?" said Monte Cristo, with well-feigned interest. "Have you really met with some great misfortune?"

"Oh, M. le Comte," said Villefort, with a bitter smile, "it is only a loss of money which I have sustained,—nothing worth mentioning, I assure you."

"True," said Monte Cristo, "the loss of a sum of money becomes almost immaterial with a fortune such as you possess, and a mind raised, as yours is, above the common events of life."

"It is not so much the loss of the money which vexes me," said Villefort, "though, after all, 900,000 francs are worth regretting; but I am the more annoyed with this fate, chance, or whatever you please to call the power which has destroyed my hopes and my fortune, and may blast the prospects of my child also, as it is all occasioned by an old man relapsed into second childhood."

"What do you say?" said the count; "900,000 francs! It is indeed a sum which might be regretted even by a philosopher. And who is the cause of all this annoyance?"

"My father, as I told you."

"M. Noirtier! But I thought you told me he had become entirely paralysed, and that all his faculties were completely destroyed?"

"Yes, his bodily faculties, for he can neither move nor speak, nevertheless he thinks, acts, and wills in the manner I have described. I left him about five minutes ago, and he is now occupied in dictating his will to two notaries."

"But to do this he must have spoken?"

"He has done better than that—he has made himself understood."

"How was such a thing possible?"

"By the help of his eyes, which are still full of life, and, as you perceive, possess the power of inflicting mortal injury."

"My dear," said Madame de Villefort, who had just entered the room, "perhaps you exaggerate the evil."

"Good morning, madame!" said the count, bowing.

Madame de Villefort acknowledged the salutation with one of her most gracious smiles.

"What is this that M. de Villefort has been telling me?" demanded Monte Cristo, "and what incomprehensible misfortune——"

"Incomprehensible is not the word!" interrupted the procureur du roi, shrugging his shoulders. "It is an old man's caprice."

"And is there no means of making him revoke the decision?"

" Yes," said Madame de Villefort; " and it is still entirely in the power of my husband to cause the will, which is now in prejudice of Valentine, to be altered in her favour."

The count, who perceived that M. and Madame de Villefort were beginning to speak in parables, appeared to pay no attention to the conversation, and feigned to be busily engaged in watching Edward, who was mischievously pouring some ink into the bird's water-glass.

" My dear," said Villefort, in answer to his wife, " you know I have never been accustomed to play the patriarch in my family, nor have I ever considered that the fate of a universe was to be decided by my nod. Nevertheless, it is necessary that my will should be respected in my family, and that the folly of an old man and the caprice of a child should not be allowed to overturn a project which I have entertained for so many years. The Baron d'Epinay was my friend, as you know, and an alliance with his son is the most suitable thing that could possibly be arranged."

" Do you think," said Madame de Villefort, " that Valentine is in league with him? She has always been opposed to this marriage, and I should not be at all surprised if what we have just seen and heard is nothing but the execution of a plan concerted between them."

" Madame," said Villefort, " believe me, a fortune of 900,000 francs is not so easily renounced."

" She could, nevertheless, make up her mind to renounce the world, sir, since it is only about a year ago that she herself proposed entering a convent."

" Never mind," replied Villefort; " I say that this marriage *shall* be consummated! "

" Notwithstanding your father's wishes to the contrary? " said Madame de Villefort, selecting a new point of attack. " That is a serious thing! "

Monte Cristo, who pretended not to be listening, heard, however, every word that was said.

" Madame," replied Villefort, " I can truly say that I have always entertained a high respect for my father, because, to the natural feeling of relationship, was added the consciousness of his moral superiority. The name of father is sacred in two senses; he should be reverenced as the author of our being, and as a master whom we ought to obey. But, under the present circumstances, I am justified in doubting the wisdom of an old man who, because he hated the father, vents his anger on the son. It would be ridiculous in me to regulate my conduct by such caprices. I shall still continue to preserve the same respect towards M. Noirtier; I will suffer, without complaint, the pecuniary deprivation to which he has subjected me; but I will remain firm in my determination, and the world shall see which party has reason on his side. Consequently I shall marry my daughter to the Baron Franz d'Epinay, because I consider it would be a proper and eligible match for her to make, and, in short, because I choose to bestow my daughter's hand on whomsoever I please."

"What!" said the count, the approbation of whose eye Villefort had frequently solicited during this speech, "what! do you say that M. Noirtier disinherits Mademoiselle de Villefort because she is going to marry M. le Baron Franz d'Epinay?"

"Yes, sir, that is the reason," said Villefort, shrugging his shoulders.

"The apparent reason at least," said Madame de Villefort.

"The *real* reason, madame, I can assure you; I know my father."

"But I want to know in what way M. d'Epinay can have displeased your father more than any other person?"

"I believe I know M. Franz d'Epinay," said the count; "is he not the son of General de Quesnel, who was created Baron d'Epinay by Charles X?"

"The same," said Villefort.

"Well! but he is a charming young man, according to my ideas."

"He is, which makes me believe that it is only an excuse of M. Noirtier's to prevent his granddaughter marrying; old men are always so selfish in their affection," said Madame de Villefort.

"But," said Monte Cristo, "do you not know any cause for this hatred?"

"Ah, *ma foi*! who is to know?"

"Perhaps it is some political difference?"

"My father and the Baron d'Epinay lived in those stormy times of which I have only seen the few last days," said De Villefort.

"Was not your father a Bonapartist?" asked Monte Cristo; "I think I remember that you told me something of that kind."

"My father has been a Jacobin more than anything else," said Villefort, carried by his emotion beyond the bounds of prudence; "and the senator's robe, which Napoleon cast on his shoulders, only served to disguise the old man without any degree changing him. When my father conspired, it was not for the emperor, it was against the Bourbons; for M. Noirtier possessed this peculiarity, he never projected any Utopian schemes which could never be realised, but strove for possibilities, and he applied to the realisation of these possibilities the terrible theories of Montagne,* who never shrank from any means which he deemed necessary to their accomplishment."

"Well," said Monte Cristo, "it is just as I thought; it was politics which brought Noirtier and M. d'Epinay into personal contact. Although General d'Epinay served under Napoleon, did he not still retain Royalist sentiments? And was he not the person who was assassinated one evening on leaving a Bona-partist meeting to which he had been invited on the supposition of his favouring the cause of the emperor?"

Villefort looked at the count almost with terror.

"Am I mistaken, then?" said Monte Cristo.

"No, sir, the facts were precisely what you have stated," said Madame de Villefort; "and it was to prevent the renewal of old feuds that M. de Villefort formed the idea of uniting in the bonds of affection the two children of these inveterate enemies."

"It was a sublime and charitable thought," said Monte Cristo, "and the whole world should applaud it. It would be noble to see Mademoiselle Noirtier de Villefort assuming the title of Madame Franz d'Epinay."

Villefort shuddered, and looked at Monte Cristo as if he wished to read in his countenance the real feelings which had dictated the words he had just pronounced. But the count completely baffled the penetration of the procureur du roi, and pre-vented him from discovering anything beneath the never-varying smile he was so constantly in the habit of assuming.

"Although," said Villefort, "it will be a serious thing for Valentine to lose the fortune of her grandfather, I do not think the marriage will be prevented on that account, nor do I believe that M. d'Epinay will be frightened at this pecuniary loss. He will, perhaps, hold me in greater esteem than the money itself, seeing that I sacrifice everything in order to keep my word with him; besides, he knows that Valentine is rich in right of her mother, and that she will, in all probability, inherit the fortune of M. and Madame de Saint-Méran, her mother's parents, who both love her tenderly."

"And who are fully as well worth loving and tending as M. de Noirtier," said Madame de Villefort; "besides, they are to come to Paris in about a month, and Valentine, after the affront she has received, need not consider it necessary to continue to bury herself alive by being shut up with M. Noirtier."

The count listened with satisfaction to this tale of wounded self-love and defeated ambition.

"But it seems to me," said Monte Cristo, "and I must begin by asking your pardon for what I am about to say, that if M.

Noirtier disinherits Madamoiselle de Villefort on account of her marrying a man whose father he detested, he cannot have the same cause of complaint against this dear Edward."

"True," said Madame de Villefort, with an intonation of voice which it is impossible to describe; "is it not unjust,—shamefully unjust? Poor Edward is as much M. Noirtier's grandchild as Valentine, and yet, if she had not been going to marry M. Franz, M. Noirtier would have left her all his money; and supposing Valentine to be disinherited by her grandfather, she will still be three times richer than he."

The count listened and said no more.

"M. le Comte," said Villefort, "we will not entertain you any longer with our family misfortunes. It is true that my patrimony will go to endow charitable institutions, and my father will have deprived me of my lawful inheritance without any reason for doing so; but I shall have the satisfaction of knowing that I have acted like a man of sense and feeling. M. d'Epinay, to whom I had promised the interest of this sum, shall receive it, even if I endure the most cruel privations."

"However," said Madame de Villefort, returning to the one idea which incessantly occupied her mind, "perhaps it would be better to represent this unlucky affair to M. d'Epinay, in order to give him the opportunity of himself renouncing his claim to the hand of Mademoiselle de Villefort."

"Ah, that would be a great pity," said Villefort.

"A great pity!" said Monte Cristo.

"Undoubtedly," said Villefort, moderating the tones of his voice, "a marriage, once concerted and then broken off, throws a sort of discredit on a young lady; then, again, the old reports, which I was so anxious to put an end to, will instantly gain ground;—no, it will all go well; M. d'Epinay, if he is an honourable man, will consider himself more than ever pledged to Mademoiselle de Villefort; unless he were actuated by a decided feeling of avarice; but that is impossible."

"I agree with M. de Villefort," said Monte Cristo, fixing his eyes on Madame de Villefort; "and if I were sufficiently intimate with him to allow of giving my advice, I would persuade him, since I have been told M. d'Epinay is coming back, to settle this affair at once beyond all possibility of revocation. I will answer for the success of a project which will reflect so much honour on M. de Villefort."

The procureur du roi rose, delighted with the proposition, but his wife slightly changed colour.

"Well that is all that I wanted, and I will be guided by a counsellor such as you are," said he, extending his hand to

Monte Cristo. "Therefore let everyone here look upon what has passed to-day as if it had not happened, and as though we had never thought of such a thing as a change in our original plans."

"Sir," said the count, "the world, unjust as it is, will be pleased with your resolution; your friends will be proud of you, and M. d'Epinay, even if he took Mademoiselle de Villefort without any dowry, which he will not do, would be delighted with the idea of entering a family which could make such sacrifices in order to keep a promise and fulfil a duty."

At the conclusion of these words, the count rose to depart.

"Are you going to leave us, M. le Comte?" said Madame de Villefort.

"I am sorry to say I must do so, madame; I only came to remind you of your promise for Saturday."

"Did you fear that we should forget it?"

"You are very good, madame; but M. de Villefort has so many important and urgent occupations."

"My husband has given his word, sir," said Madame de Villefort; "you have just seen him resolve to keep it when he has all to lose, and surely there is more reason for his doing so where he has all to gain!"

"And," said Villefort, "is it at your house in the Champs-Elysées that you receive your visitors?"

"No," said Monte Cristo, "which is precisely the reason which renders your kindness more meritorious,—it is in the country."

"In the country?"

"Yes."

"Where is it, then? Near Paris, is it not?"

"Very near; only half a league from the Barriers,—it is at Auteuil."

"At Auteuil?" said Villefort; "true, Madame de Villefort told me you lived at Auteuil, since it was to your house that she was taken. And in what part of Auteuil do you reside?"

"Rue de la Fontaine."

"Rue de la Fontaine!" exclaimed Villefort, in an agitated tone; "at what number?"

"No. 28."

"Then," cried Villefort, "was it you who bought M. de Saint-Méran's house?"

"Did it belong to M. de Saint-Méran?" demanded Monte Cristo.

"Yes," replied Madame de Villefort; "and, would you believe, it, M. le Comte——"

" Believe what? "

" You think this house pretty, do you not? "

" I think it charming."

" Well! my husband would never live in it."

" Indeed! " returned Monte Cristo; " that is a prejudice on your part, M. de Villefort, for which I am quite at a loss to account."

" I do not like Auteuil, sir," said the procureur du roi, making an evident effort to appear calm.

" But I hope you will not carry your antipathy so far as to deprive me of the pleasure of your company, sir," said Monte Cristo.

" No, M. le Comte,—I hope—I assure you I will do all I can," stammered Villefort.

" Oh," said Monte Cristo, " I allow of no excuse. On Saturday, at six o'clock, I shall be expecting you, and if you fail to come I shall think—for how do I know to the contrary?—that this house, which has remained uninhabited for twenty years, must have some gloomy tradition or dreadful legend connected with it."

" I will come, M. le Comte,—I will be sure to come," said Villefort eagerly.

" Thank you," said Monte Cristo; " now you must permit me to take my leave of you."

" You said before you were obliged to leave us, M. le Comte," said Madame de Villefort, " and you were about to tell us the nature of the engagement which was to deprive us of the pleasure of your society, when your attention was called to some other subject."

" Indeed, madame! " said Monte Cristo; " I scarcely know if I dare tell you where I am going."

" Bah! "

" Well, then, it is to see a thing on which I have sometimes mused for hours together."

" What is it? "

" A telegraph. So now I have told my secret."

" What telegraph do you intend visiting? that of the home department, or of the observatory? "*

" Oh, no; I should find there people who would force me to understand things of which I would prefer to remain ignorant, and who would try to explain to me, in spite of myself, a mystery which even they do not understand. I shall, therefore, not visit either of these telegraphs, but one in the open country, where I shall find a good-natured simpleton, who knows no more than the machine he is employed to work."

" You are a singular man," said Villefort.

" What line would you advise me to study? "

" That which is most in use just at this time."

" The Spanish one, you mean, I suppose! Which is the nearest way? Bayonne? "

" Yes; the road to Bayonne."

" And afterwards the road to Chatillon? "

" Yes."

" By the tower of Montlhéry, you mean? "

" Yes."

" Thank you. Good-bye. On Saturday I will tell you my impressions concerning the telegraph."

At the door the count was met by the two notaries, who had just completed the act which was to disinherit Valentine, and who were leaving under the conviction of having done a thing which could not fail of redounding considerably to their credit.

62

The Bribe

NOT on the same night he had intended, but the next morning, the Count of Monte Cristo went out by the Barrier d'Enfer, taking the road to Orleans. Leaving the village of Linas, without stopping at the telegraph, which, at the moment the count passed, threw out its long bony arms, he reached the tower of Montlhéry, situated, as everyone knows, upon the highest point of the plain of that name. At the foot of the hill the count dismounted, and began to ascend the mountain by a little winding-path, about eighteen inches wide. When he reached the summit he found himself stopped by a hedge, upon which green fruit had succeeded to red and white flowers.

Monte Cristo looked for the door of the enclosure, and was not long in finding it. It was a little wooden gate, working on willow hinges, and fastened with a nail and string. The count soon understood its mechanism, and the door opened. He then found himself in a little garden, about twenty feet long by twelve wide, bounded on one side by part of the hedge, in which was formed the ingenious machine we have named a door; and on the other, by the old tower, covered with ivy and studded with wild flowers. No one would have thought to have seen it thus wrinkled and yet adorned, like an old lady whose grandchildren come to greet her on her birthday, that it could have related some terrible scenes, if it could have added a voice to the menacing ears which an old proverb awards to walls. The garden was crossed by a path of red gravel, edged by a border of thick box of many years' growth, and of a tone and colour that would have delighted the heart of Delacroix, our modern Rubens. This path was formed in the shape of the figure 8, thus, in its windings, making a walk of sixty feet in a garden of only twenty. Never had Flora, the fresh and smiling goddess of gardeners, been honoured with a purer or more minute worship than that which was paid to her in this little enclosure. In fact, of the twenty rose-trees which formed the *parterre*, not one bore the mark of the fly, nor were there to be seen any of those clusters of green insects which destroy plants growing in a damp soil. And yet it was not because the damp had been excluded from the garden; the earth, black as soot, the thick foliage of the trees, told it was there; besides, had natural humidity been wanting, it could have been immediately supplied by artificial means, thanks to a tank of water, sunk in one of the corners of the garden, and upon which were stationed a frog and a toad, who, from antipathy, no doubt, always remained on the two opposite sides of the basin. There was not a blade of grass to be seen in the paths, nor a weed in the flower-beds; no fine lady ever trained and watered her geraniums, her cactus, and rhododendrons, with more pains than this hitherto unseen gardener bestowed upon his little enclosure. Monte Cristo stopped after having closed the door and fastened the string to the nail and cast a look around.

"The man at the telegraph," said he, " must either engage a gardener or devote himself passionately to agriculture."

Suddenly he struck himself against something crouching behind a wheel-barrow filled with leaves; the something rose, uttering an exclamation of astonishment, and Monte Cristo found himself facing a man about fifty years old, who was plucking strawberries, which he was placing upon vine-leaves. He had twelve leaves and about as many strawberries, which, on rising suddenly, he let fall from his hand.

"You are gathering your crop, sir?" said Monte Cristo, smiling.

"Excuse me, sir," replied the man, raising his hand to his cap; "I am not up there, I know, but I have only just come down."

"Do not let me interfere with you in anything, my friend," said the count; "gather your strawberries, if, indeed, there are any left."

" I have ten left," said the man, " for here are eleven, and I had twenty-one, five more than last year. But I am not surprised; the spring has been warm this year, and strawberries require heat, sir. This is the reason that, instead of the sixteen I had last year, I have this year, you see, eleven, already plucked —twelve, thirteen, fourteen, fifteen, sixteen, seventeen, eighteen. Ah, I miss three! they were here last night, sir—I am sure they were here—I counted them. It must be the son of Mère Simon who has stolen them; I saw him strolling about here this morning. Ah, the young rascal! stealing in a garden—he does not know where that may lead him to."

" Certainly, it is wrong," said Monte Cristo; " but you should take into consideration the youth and greediness of the delinquent."

" Of course," said the gardener; " but that does not make it the less unpleasant. But, sir, once more I beg pardon; perhaps you are an officer that I am detaining here? " And he glanced timidly at the count's blue coat.

" Calm yourself, my friend," said the count, with that smile which at his will became so terrible or benevolent, and which this time beamed only with the latter expression; " I am not an inspector, but a traveller, conducted here by a curiosity he half repents of, since he causes you to lose your time."

" Ah! my time is not valuable," replied the man, with a melancholy smile. " Still, it belongs to government, and I ought not to waste it; but having received the signal that I might rest for an hour " (here he glanced at the sun-dial, for there was everything in the enclosure of Montlhéry, even a sun-dial), " and having ten minutes before me, and my strawberries being ripe, when a day longer—by the bye, sir, do you think dormice eat them? "

" Indeed, I should think not," replied Monte Cristo; " dormice are bad neighbours for us who do not eat them preserved, as the Romans did."

" What! did the Romans eat them? " said the gardener— " eat dormice? "

" I have read so in Petronius,'"said the count.

" Really! They can't be nice, though they do say, ' as fat as a dormouse.' It is not a wonder they are fat, sleeping all day, and only waking to eat all night. Listen; last year I had four apricots, they stole one. I had one nectarine, only one; well, sir, they ate half of it on the wall,—a splendid nectarine; I never ate a better."

" You ate it? "

" That is to say, the half that was left,—you understand; it was exquisite, sir. Ah, those gentlemen never choose the worst morsels; like Mère Simon's son, who has not chosen the worst strawberries. But this year," continued the horticulturist, " I'll take care it shall not happen, even if I should be forced to sit up the whole night to watch when the strawberries are ripe."

Monte Cristo had seen enough. Every man has a devouring passion in his heart, as every fruit has its worm; that of the man at the telegraph was horticulture. He began gathering the vine-leaves which screened the sun from the grapes, and won the heart of the gardener.

" Did you come here, sir, to see the telegraph? " he said.

" Yes; if it be not contrary to the rules."

" Oh, no! " said the gardener; " there are no orders against doing so, provided there is nothing dangerous, and that no one knows what we are saying."

" I have been told," said the count, " that you do not always yourselves understand the signals you repeat."

" Certainly, sir; and that is what I like best," said the man, smiling.

" Why do you like that best? "

" Because then I have no responsibility; I am a machine then, and nothing else; and so long as I work, nothing more is required of me."

" Is it possible," said Monte Cristo to himself, " that I can have met with a man that has no ambition? That would spoil my plans."

" Sir," said the gardener, glancing at the sun-dial, " the ten minutes are nearly expired; I must return to my post. Will you go up with me? "

" I follow you."

Monte Cristo entered the tower, which was divided into three stages; the lowest contained gardening implements, such as spades, rakes, watering-pots, hung against the wall; this was all the furniture. The second was the usual dwelling, or rather sleeping-place, of the man; it contained a few poor articles of household furniture—a bed, a table, two chairs, a stone pitcher and some dry herbs, hung up to the ceiling, which the count recognised as sweet peas, and of which the good man was pre-serving the seeds, having labelled them with as much care as if he had been master botanist in the Jardin des Plantes.

" Does it require much study to learn the art of telegraphing, sir? " asked Monte Cristo.

" The study does not take long; it was acting as a super-numerary that was so tedious."

" And what is the pay? "

" A thousand francs, sir."

" It is nothing."

" No; but then we are lodged, as you perceive."

Monte Cristo looked at the room.

They passed on to the third stage; it was the room of the telegraph. Monte Cristo looked in turns at the two iron handles by which the machine was worked.

" It is very interesting," he said; " but it must be very tedious for a lifetime."

" Yes. At first my neck was cramped with looking at it, but at the end of a year I became used to it; and then we have our hours of recreation and our holidays."

" Holidays? "

" Yes."

" When? "

" When we have a fog."

" Ah, to be sure."

" Those are, indeed, holidays to me; I go into the garden, I plant, I prune, I trim, I kill the insects all day long."

" How long have you been here? "

" Ten years, and five as a supernumerary make fifteen."

" You are——"

" Fifty-five years old."

" How long must you have served to claim the pension? "

" Oh, sir! twenty-five years."

" And how much is the pension? "

" A hundred crowns."

" Poor humanity! " murmured Monte Cristo.

" What did you say, sir? " asked the man.

" I was saying it was very interesting."

" What was? "

" All you were showing me. And you really understand none of these signals? "

" None at all."

" And have you never tried to understand them? "

" Never. Why should I? "

" But still there are some signals only addressed to you."

" Certainly."

" And do you understand them? "

" They are always the same."

" And then mean——"

" *Nothing new; You have an hour;* or, *To-morrow.*"

" This is simple enough," said the count; " but look, is not your correspondent putting itself in motion? "

" Ah, yes; thank you, sir! "

" And what is it saying—anything you understand? "

" Yes; it asks if I am ready."

" And you reply? "

" By the same sign, which, at the same time, tells my right-hand correspondent that I am ready, while it gives notice to my left-hand correspondent to prepare in his turn."

" It is very ingenious," said the count.

" You will see," said the man proudly, " in five minutes he will speak."

" I have, then, five minutes," said Monte Cristo to himself; " it is more time than I require. My dear sir, will you allow me to ask you a question? "

" What is it, sir? "

" You are fond of gardening? "

" Passionately."

" And you would be pleased to have, instead of this terrace of twenty feet, an enclosure of two acres? "

" Sir, I should make a terrestrial paradise of it."

" You live badly on your thousand francs? "

" Badly enough; but yet I do live."

" Yes; but you have only a wretched garden."

" True, the garden is not large."

" And, then, such as it is, it is filled with dormice, who eat everything."

" Ah! they are my scourges."

" Tell me, should you have the misfortune to turn your head while your right-hand correspondent was telegraphing—— "

" I should not see him."

" Then what would happen? "

" I could not repeat the signals."

" And then? "

" Not having repeated them, through negligence, I should be fined."

" How much? "

" A hundred francs."

" The tenth of your income—that would be fine work."

" Ah! " said the man.

" Has it ever happened to you? " said Monte-Cristo.

" Once, sir, when I was grafting a rose-tree."

" Well, suppose you were to alter a signal, and substitute another? "

" Ah, that is another case, I should be turned off and lose my pension."

" Three hundred francs? "

"A hundred crowns, yes, sir; so you see that I am not likely to do any of these things."

"Not even for fifteen years' wages? Come, it is worth thinking about?"

"For fifteen thousand francs!"

"Yes."

"Sir, you alarm me."

"Nonsense!"

"Sir, you are tempting me!"

"Just so; fifteen thousand francs, do you understand?"

"Sir, let me see my right-hand correspondent!"

"On the contrary, do not look at him, but on this."

"What is it?"

"What! do you not know these little papers?"

"Bank-notes!"

"Exactly; there are fifteen of them."

"And whose are they?"

"Yours, if you like."

"Mine!" exclaimed the man, half-suffocated.

"Yes; yours—your own property."

"Sir, my right-hand correspondent is signalling."

"Let him."

"Sir, you have distracted me; I shall be fined."

"That will cost you a hundred francs; you see it is your interest to take my bank-notes."

"Sir, my right-hand correspondent redoubles his signals; he is impatient."

"Never mind—take these;" and the count placed the packet in the hands of the man.

"Now this is not all," he said; "you cannot live upon your fifteen thousand francs."

"I shall still have my place."

"No, you will lose it, for you are going to alter the sign of your correspondent."

"Oh, sir, what are you proposing?"

"A jest."

"Sir, unless you force me——"

"I think I can effectually force you;" and Monte Cristo drew another packet from his pocket. "Here are ten thousand more francs," he said, "with the fifteen thousand already in your pocket, they will make twenty-five thousand. With five thousand you can buy a pretty little house with two acres of land; the remaining twenty thousand will bring you in a thousand francs a year."

"A garden with two acres of land!"

"And a thousand francs a year."

"Oh, heavens!"

"Come, take them!" and Monte Cristo forced the bank-notes into his hand.

"What am I to do?"

"Nothing very difficult."

"But what is it?"

"To repeat these signs;" Monte Cristo took a paper from his pocket, upon which were drawn three signs, with numbers to indicate the order in which they were to be worked.

"There, you see, it will not take long."

"Yes; but——"

"Do this, and you will have nectarines and all the rest."

The mark was hit; red with fever, while the large drops fell from his brow, the man executed, one after the other, the three signs, given by the count, notwithstanding the frightful contortions of the right-hand correspondent, who, not understanding the change, began to think the gardener had become mad. As to the left-hand one, he conscientiously repeated the same signals, which were definitely carried to the Minister of the Interior.

"Now you are rich," said Monte Cristo.

"Yes," replied the man, "but at what a price!"

"Listen, friend," said Monte Cristo. "I do not wish to cause you any remorse; believe me, then, when I swear to you that you have wronged no man, but on the contrary have benefited mankind."

The man looked at the bank-notes, felt them, counted them; he turned pale, then red; then rushed into his room to drink a glass of water, but he had not time to reach the water-jug, and fainted in the midst of his dried herbs.

Five minutes after, the new telegraph reached the minister; Debray had the horses put to his carriage, and drove to Danglars.

"Has your husband any Spanish bonds?" he asked of the baroness.

"I think so, indeed! He has six millions' worth."

"He must sell them at whatever price."

"Why?"

"Because Don Carlos has fled from Bourges, and has returned to Spain."

"How do you know?"

Debray shrugged his shoulders. "The idea of asking how I hear the news!" he said.

The baroness did not wait for a repetition; she ran to her husband, who immediately hastened to his agent, and ordered him to sell at any price.

When it was seen that Danglars sold, the Spanish funds fell directly. Danglars lost five hundred thousand francs; but he rid himself of all his Spanish shares.

The same evening the following was read in *Le Messager:*—

"Telegraphic despatch. The king, Don Carlos, has escaped the vigilance exercised over him at Bourges, and has returned to Spain by the Catalonian frontier. Barcelona has risen in his favour."

All that evening nothing was spoken of but the foresight of Danglars who had sold his shares, and of the luck of the stock-jobber, who only lost five hundred thousand francs by such a blow. Those who had kept their shares, or bought those of Danglars, looked upon themselves as ruined, and passed a very bad night.

The next morning *Le Moniteur* contained the following:—

"It was without any foundation that *Le Messager* yesterday announced the flight of Don Carlos and the revolt of Barcelona. The king (Don Carlos) has not left Bourges, and the Peninsula is in the enjoyment of profound peace. A telegraphic signal, improperly intercepted, owing to the fog, was the cause of this error."

The funds rose one per cent. higher than before they had fallen. This, reckoning his loss, and what he had missed gaining, made the difference of a million to Danglars.

"Good!" said Monte Cristo to Morrel, who was at his house when the news arrived of the strange reverse of fortune, of which Danglars had been the victim, "I have just made a discovery for twenty-five thousand francs. for which I would have paid a hundred thousand."

"What have you discovered?" asked Morrel.

"I have just discovered the method of ridding a gardener of the dormice that eat his peaches."

63

Shadows

At first sight the exterior of the house at Auteuil presented nothing splendid, nothing one would expect from the destined residence of the magnificent Count of Monte Cristo; but this simplicity was but according to the will of its master, who positively ordered nothing to be altered outside; this was seen by examining the interior. Indeed, scarcely could the door be opened before the scene changed. M. Bertuccio had outdone himself in the taste displayed in furnishing, and in the rapidity with which it was executed. As formerly the Duc d'Antin* had in a single night caused a whole avenue of trees to be cut down that annoyed Louis XIV, so in three days had M. Bertuccio planted an entirely bare court with poplars, large spreading sycamores shading the different parts of the house, before which, instead of the usual paving-stones, half hidden by the grass, there extended a turf-lawn but that morning laid down, and upon which the water was yet glistening. For the rest the orders had been issued by the count; he himself had given a plan to Bertuccio, marking the spot where each tree was to be planted, and the shape and extent of the lawn which was to succeed the paving-stones. Thus the house had become unrecognisable, and Bertuccio himself declared he scarcely knew it, encircled as it was by a framework of trees. The overseer would not have objected, while he was about it, to have made some improvements in the garden, but the count had positively forbidden it to be touched. Bertuccio made amends, however, by loading the ante-chambers, staircases, and chimneys with flowers. That which, above all, manifested the shrewdness of the steward, and the profound science of the master, the one in carrying out the ideas of the other, was that this house, which appeared only the night before so sad and gloomy, impregnated with that sickly smell one can almost fancy to be the smell of time, had, in one day, acquired the aspect of life, was scented with its master's favourite perfumes, and had the very light regulated according to his wish. When the count arrived, he had under his touch his books and arms, his eyes rested upon his favourite pictures; his dogs, whose caresses he loved, welcomed him in the ante-chamber; the birds, whose songs delighted him, cheered him with their music; and the house, awakened from its long sleep, like the Sleeping Beauty in the wood, lived, sang, and bloomed like the houses we have cherished, and in which, when we are forced to leave them, we leave a part of our souls. The servants passed gaily along the fine courtyard; some, belonging to the kitchens, gliding down the stairs, restored but the previous day, as if they had always inhabited the house; others filling the coach-houses, where the equipages, encased and numbered, appeared to have been installed for the last fifty years; and in the stables the horses replied by neighing to the grooms, who spoke to them with much more respect than many servants pay their masters.

The library was divided into two parts on either side of the wall, and contained upwards of two thousand volumes; one division was entirely devoted to novels, and even the one which had been published but the day before was to be seen in its place in all the dignity of its red and gold binding. On the other side of the house, to match with the library, was the conservatory, ornamented with rare flowers, blossoming in China jars; and in the midst of the greenhouse, marvellous alike to sight and smell, was a billiard-table, apparently abandoned during the last hour by the players, who had left the balls on the cloth.

One chamber alone had been respected by the magnificent Bertuccio. Before this room, to which you could ascend by the grand, and go out by the back staircase, the servants passed with curiosity, and Bertuccio with terror.

At five o'clock precisely, the count arrived before the house at Auteuil, followed by Ali. Bertuccio was awaiting this arrival with impatience, mingled with uneasiness; he hoped for some compliments, while, at the same time, he feared to have frowns. Monte Cristo descended in the courtyard, walked all over the house, without giving any sign of approbation or displeasure, until he entered his bedroom, situated on the opposite side of the closed room; then he approached a little piece of furniture, made of rosewood, which we remember to have noticed on a previous occasion.

" That will at least serve to put my gloves in," he said.

" Will your excellency deign to open it? " said the delighted Bertuccio, " and you will find gloves in it."

In all the rest of the furniture the count found everything he required, smelling-bottles, cigars, *bijouterie*.

" Good! " he said; and M. Bertuccio left enraptured: so great, so powerful, and real was the influence exercised by this man over all who surrounded him.

At precisely six o'clock the clatter of horses' hoofs was heard at the entrance door; it was our captain of Spahis, who had arrived on Medea.

"I am sure I am the first," cried Morrel; "I did it on purpose to have you a minute to myself before everyone came. Julie and Emanuel have a thousand things to tell you. Ah, really this is magnificent! But tell me, count, will your people take care of my horse?"

"Do not alarm yourself, my dear Maximilian; they understand."

"I mean, because he wants petting. If you had seen at what a pace he came—like the wind!"

"I should think so—a horse that cost 5000 francs!" said Monte Cristo, in the tone which a father would use towards a son.

"Do you regret them?" asked Morrel, with his open laugh.

"I? Certainly not!" replied the count. "No; I should only regret if the horse had not proved good."

"It is so good that I have distanced M. de Château-Renaud, one of the best riders in France, and M. Debray, who both mount the minister's Arabians; and close at their heels are the horses of Madame Danglars, who always go at six leagues an hour."

"Then they follow you?" asked Monte Cristo.

"See, they are here!"

And at the same minute a carriage with smoking horses, accompanied by two mounted gentlemen, arrived at the gate, which opened before them. The carriage drove round and stopped at the steps, followed by the horsemen. The instant Debray had touched the ground, he was at the carriage-door. He offered his hand to the baroness, who, descending, took it with a peculiarity of manner imperceptible to everyone but Monte Cristo. But nothing escaped the count's notice, and he observed a little note slipped with an indescribable ease, bespeaking the frequent practice of this manœuvre, from the hand of Madame Danglars to that of the minister's secretary.

After his wife, the banker descended, pale as though he had issued from the tomb instead of his carriage. Madame Danglars threw a rapid and inquiring glance around, which could only be interpreted by Monte Cristo, embracing the courtyard, the peristyle, and the front of the house; then, repressing a slight emotion, which must have been seen on her countenance if she had permitted her face to become pale, she ascended the steps, saying to Morrel:

"Sir, if you were a friend of mine, I should ask you if you would sell your horse?"

Morrel smiled with an expression very like a grimace, and then turned round to Monte Cristo as if to ask him to extricate him from his embarrassments. The count understood him.

" Ah, madame! " he said, " why did you not make that request of me? "

" With you, sir," replied the baroness, " one can wish for nothing, one is so sure to obtain it. If it were so with M. Morrel——"

" Unfortunately," replied the count, " I am witness that M. Morrel cannot give up his horse, his honour being engaged in keeping it."

" How so? "

" He laid a wager he would tame Medea in the space of six months. You understand now that if he were to get rid of it before the time named, he would not only lose his bet, but people would say he was afraid of it; and a brave captain of Spahis cannot risk this even to gratify a pretty woman, which is, in my opinion, one of the most sacred obligations in the world."

" You see my position, madame," said Morrel, bestowing a grateful smile on Monte Cristo.

" It seems to me," said Danglars, in his coarse tone, ill concealed by a forced smile, " that you have already got horses enough."

Madame Danglars seldom allowed remarks of this kind to pass unnoticed; but, to the surprise of the young people, she pretended not to hear it, and said nothing.

Monte Cristo smiled at her unusual humility, and showed her two immense porcelain jars, covered with marine plants of a size and delicacy that could alone emanate from nature. The baroness was astonished.

" Why," said she, " you could plant one of the chestnut-trees in the Tuileries inside! How can such enormous jars have been manufactured? "

" Ah, madame," replied Monte Cristo, " you must not ask of us, the manufacturers of glass-muslin, such a question; it is the work of another age, constructed by the genii of earth and water."

" How so? at what period can that have been? "

" I do not know; I have only heard that an emperor of China had an oven built expressly, and that in this oven twelve jars like this were successively baked. Two broke from the heat of the fire; the other ten were sunk three hundred fathoms deep into the sea. The sea, knowing what was required of her, threw over them her weeds, encircled them with coral, and encrusted them with shells; the whole was cemented by two hundred years beneath these almost impervious depths, for a revolution carried away the emperor who wished to make the trial, and only left the documents proving the manufacture of the jars and their descent into the sea. At the end of two hundred years the documents were found, and they thought of bringing up the jars. Divers descended in machines, made expressly on the discovery, into the bay where they were thrown; but of ten, three only remained, the rest having been broken by the waves. I am fond of these jars, upon which, perhaps, misshapen, frightful monsters have fixed their cold, dull eyes, and in which myriads of small fish have slept, seeking a refuge from the pursuit of their enemies."

Meanwhile Danglars, who had cared little for curiosities, was mechanically tearing off the blossoms of a splendid orange-tree, one after another. When he had finished with the orange-tree, he began at the cactus, but this not being so easily plucked as the orange-tree, pricked him dreadfully. He shuddered, and rubbed his eyes as though awaking from a dream.

" Sir," said Monte Cristo to him, " I do not recommend my pictures to you who possess such splendid paintings;* but, nevertheless, here are two by Hobbima, a Paul Potter, a Mieris, two Gerard Douw, a Raphael, a Vandyke, a Zurbaran, and two or three by Murillo, worth looking at."

" Stay! " said Debray; " I recognise this Hobbima."

" Ah, indeed! "

" Yes; it was proposed for the Museum."

" Which, I believe, does not contain one? " said Monte Cristo.

" No; and yet they refused to buy it."

" Why? " said Château-Renaud.

" You pretend not to know,—because government was not rich enough."

" Ah, pardon me! " said Château-Renaud; " I have heard of these things every day during the last eight years, and I cannot understand them yet."

" You will, by and by," said Debray.

" I think not," replied Château-Renaud.

" Major Bartolomeo Cavalcanti and Count Andrea Cavalcanti! " announced Baptistin.

A black satin stock, fresh from the maker's hands, gray moustaches, a bold eye, a major's uniform, ornamented with three medals and five crosses—in fact, the thorough bearing of an old soldier,—such was the appearance of Major Bartolomeo Cavalcanti, that tender father, with whom we are already acquainted. Close to him, dressed in entirely new clothes, advanced, smilingly, Count Andrea Cavalcanti, the dutiful son, whom we also know.

The three young people were talking together. On the entrance of the new-comers, their eyes glanced from father to son, and then, naturally enough, rested on the latter, whom they began criticising.

" Cavalcanti! " said Debray.

" A fine name," said Morrel.

" Yes," said Château-Renaud, " these Italians are well-named and badly dressed."

" You are fastidious, Château-Renaud," replied Debray; " those clothes are well cut and quite new."

" That is just what I find fault with. That gentleman appears to be well dressed for the first time in his life."

" Who are those gentlemen? " asked Danglars of Monte Cristo.

" You heard,—Cavalcanti."

" That tells me their name, and nothing else."

" Ah, true. You do not know the Italian nobility; the Cavalcanti are all descended from princes."

" Have they any fortune? "

" An enormous one."

" What do they do? "

" Try to spend it all. They have some business with you, I think, from what they told me the day before yesterday. I, indeed, invited them here to-day on your account. I will introduce you to them."

" But they appear to speak French with a very pure accent," said Danglars.

" The son has been educated in a college in the south; I believe near Marseilles. You will find him quite enthusiastic."

" Upon what subject? " asked Madame Danglars.

" The French ladies, madame. He has made up his mind to take a wife from Paris."

" A fine idea that of his! " said Danglars, shrugging his shoulders.

Madame Danglars looked at her husband with an expression which, at any other time, would have indicated a storm, but for the second time she controlled herself.

" The baron appears thoughtful to-day," said Monte Cristo to her; " are they going to put him in the ministry? "

" Not yet, I think. More likely he has been speculating on the Bourse, and has lost money."

" M. and Madame de Villefort! " cried Baptistin.

They entered. M. de Villefort, notwithstanding his self-control, was visibly affected; and when Monte Cristo touched his hand, he felt it tremble.

"Certainly women alone know how to dissimulate," said Monte Cristo to himself, glancing at Madame Danglars, who was smiling on the procureur du roi and embracing his wife. After a short time the count saw Bertuccio, who, until then, had been occupied on the other side of the house, glide into an adjoining room. He went to him.

"What do you want, M. Bertuccio?" said he.

"Your excellency has not stated the number of guests."

"Ah, true!"

"How many covers?"

"Count for yourself."

"Is everyone here, your excellency?"

"Yes."

Bertuccio glanced through the door, which was ajar. The count watched him.

"Good heavens!" he exclaimed.

"What is the matter?" said the count.

"That woman!—that woman!"

"Which?"

"The one with a white dress and so many diamonds—the fair one."

"Madame Danglars?"

"I do not know her name,—but it is she!—Sir, it is she!"

"Whom do you mean?"

"The woman of the garden!—she that was *enceinte*—she who was walking while she waited for——"

Bertuccio stood at the open door with his eyes starting and his hair on end.

"Waiting for whom?"

Bertuccio, without answering, pointed to Villefort with something of the gesture Macbeth uses to point out Banquo.

"Oh, oh!" he at length muttered; "do you see?"

"What?—Who?"

"Him!"

"Him?—M. de Villefort, the procureur du roi. Certainly, I see him."

"Then I did not kill him!"

"Really I think you are going mad, good Bertuccio," said the count.

"Then he is not dead?"

"No; you see plainly he is not dead; instead of striking between the sixth and seventh left rib, as your countrymen do, you must have struck higher or lower; and life is very tenacious in these lawyers; or, rather, there is no truth in anything you have told me; it was a flight of the imagination—a dream of your fancy. You went to sleep full of thoughts of vengeance; they weighed heavily upon your stomach; you had the nightmare—that's all. Come, calm yourself, and reckon: M. and Madame de Villefort, two; M. and Madame Danglars, four; M. de Château-Renaud, M. Debray, M. Morrel, seven; Major Bartolomeo Cavalcanti, eight."

" Eight! " repeated Bertuccio.

" Stop! You are in a shocking hurry to be off,—you forget one of my guests. Lean a little to the left. Stay! look at M. Andrea Cavalcanti—that young man, in a black coat, looking at Murillo's Madonna; now he is turning."

This time Bertuccio would have uttered an exclamation had not a look from Monte Cristo silenced him.

" Benedetto! " he muttered; " fatality! "

" Half-past six o'clock has just struck, M. Bertuccio," said the count severely; " I ordered dinner at that hour, and I do not like to wait; " and he returned to his guests; while Bertuccio, leaning against the wall, succeeded in reaching the dining-room. Five minutes afterwards, the doors of the drawing-room were thrown open, and Bertuccio appearing, said, with a violent effort:

" The dinner waits."

The Count of Monte Cristo offered his arm to Madame de Villefort.

" M. de Villefort," he said, " will you conduct the Baroness Danglars? "

Villefort complied, and they passed on to the dining-room.

64

The Dinner

IT was evident that one sentiment pervaded the whole of the guests on entering the dining-room. Each one asked himself what strange influence had conducted them to this house; and yet, astonished, even uneasy though they were, they still felt they would not like to be absent. The recent events, the solitary and eccentric position of the count; his enormous, nay, almost incredible fortune, should have made men cautious, and have altogether prevented ladies visiting a house where there was no one of their own sex to receive them; and yet both had passed the bounds of prudence and decorum. Stimulated by an invincible curiosity, there were none present, even including Cavalcanti and his son, notwithstanding the stiffness of the one and the carelessness of the other, who were not thoughtful, on finding themselves assembled at the house of this incomprehensible man.

Madame Danglars had started when Villefort, on the count's invitation, offered his arm; and Villefort felt that his glance was uneasy, beneath his gold spectacles, when he felt the arm of the baroness press upon his own. None of this had escaped the count, and even by this mere contact of individuals the scene had already acquired considerable interest for an observer.

M. de Villefort had on the right hand Madame Danglars, on his left Morrel. The count was seated between Madame de Villefort and Danglars; the other seats were filled by Debray, who was placed between the two Cavalcanti, and by Château-Renaud, seated between Madame de Villefort and Morrel.

The repast was magnificent; Monte Cristo had endeavoured completely to overturn the Parisian ideas, and to feed the curiosity as much as the appetite of his guests. It was an Oriental feast that he offered to them, but of such a kind as the Arabian fairies might be supposed to prepare. Every delicious fruit that the four quarters of the globe could provide was heaped in vases from China and jars from Japan. Rare birds, retaining their most brilliant plumage, enormous fish, spread upon massive silver dishes; together with every wine produced in the Archipelago, Asia Minor, or the Cape, sparkling in bottles, whose grotesque shape seemed to give an additional flavour to the wine;

all these, like one of those displays with which Apicius of old* gratified his guests, passed in review before the eyes of the astonished Parisians, who understood that it was possible to expend £1000 upon a dinner for ten persons, but only on the condition of eating pearls, like Cleopatra, or drinking beaten gold, like Lorenzo di Medici. Monte Cristo noticed the general astonishment, and began laughing and joking about it.

"Gentlemen," he said, "you will admit that, when arrived at a certain degree of fortune, the superfluities of life are all that can be desired; and the ladies will allow, that, after having risen to a certain eminence of position, the ideal alone can be more exalted. Now, to follow out this reasoning: what is the marvellous?—that which we do not understand. What is it that we really desire?—that which we cannot obtain. Now, to see things which I cannot understand, to procure impossibilities, these are the study of my life. I gratify my wishes by two means —my will and my money. I take as much interest in the pursuit of some whim as you do, M. Danglars, in forming a new railway line; you, M. de Villefort, in condemning a culprit to death; you, M. Debray, in pacifying a kingdom; you, M. de Château-Renaud, in pleasing a woman; and you Morrel, in breaking a horse that no one can ride. For example, you see these two fish; one brought fifty leagues beyond St. Petersburg, the other, five leagues from Naples. Is it not amusing to see them both on the same table?"

"What are the two fish?" asked Danglars.

"M. Château-Renaud, who has lived in Russia, will tell you the name of one, and Major Cavalcanti, who is an Italian, will tell you the name of the other."

"This one is, I think, a sterlet," said Château-Renaud.

"And that one, if I mistake not, a lamprey."

"Just so. Now, M. Danglars, ask these gentlemen where they are caught."

"Sterlets," said Château-Renaud, "are only found in the Volga."

"And," said Cavalcanti, "I know that Lake Fusaro alone supplies lampreys of that size."

"Exactly; one comes from the Volga, and the other from Lake Fusaro."

"Impossible!" cried all the guests simultaneously.

"Well, this is just what amuses me," said Monte Cristo. "I am like Nero—*cupitor impossibilium;** and that it is which is amusing you at this moment. This fish, which seems so exquisite to you, is, very likely, no better than perch or salmon; but it seemed impossible to procure it, and here it is."

" But how could you have these fish brought to France? "

" Oh, nothing more easy. Each fish was brought over in a cask, one filled with river herbs and weeds, the other with rushes and lake plants; they were placed in a wagon built on purpose; and thus the sterlet lived twelve days, the lamprey eight; and both were alive when my cook seized them, killing one with milk and the other with wine. You do not believe me, M. Danglars! "

" I cannot help doubting," answered Danglars, with his stupid smile.

" Baptistin," said the count, " have the other fish brought in— the sterlet and the lamprey which came in the other casks, and which are yet alive."

Danglars opened his bewildered eyes; the company clapped their hands. Four servants carried in two casks covered with aquatic plants, and in each of which was breathing a fish similar to those on the table.

" But why have two of each sort? " asked Danglars.

" Merely because one might have died," carelessly answered Monte Cristo.

" You are certainly an extraordinary man," said Danglars; " and philosophers may well say it is a fine thing to be rich."

" And to have ideas," added Madame Danglars.

" Oh, do not give me credit for this, madame; it was done by the Romans, who much esteemed them; and Pliny relates that they sent slaves from Ostia to Rome, who carried on their heads fish which he calls the *mulus*, and which, from the description, must probably be the goldfish. It was also considered a luxury to have them alive, it being an amusing sight to see them die; for, when dying, they change colour three or four times, and, like the rainbow when it disappears, pass through all the prismatic shades: after which they were sent to the kitchen. Their agony formed part of their merit; if they were not seen alive, they were despised when dead."

" Yes," said Debray; " but then Ostia is only a few leagues from Rome."

" True," said Monte Cristo; " but what would be the use of living 1800 years after Lucullus, if we can do no better than he could? "

The two Cavalcanti opened their enormous eyes, but had the good sense not to say anything.

" All this is very extraordinary," said Château-Renaud; " still, what I admire the most, I confess, is the marvellous promptitude with which your orders are executed. Is it not true that you only bought this house five or six days ago? "

"Certainly not longer."

"Well! I am sure it is quite transformed since last week. If I remember rightly, it had another entrance, and the courtyard was paved and empty; while, to-day, we have a splendid lawn, bordered by trees which appear to be a hundred years old."

"Why not? I am fond of grass and shade," said Monte Cristo.

"Yes," said Madame de Villefort, "the door was towards the road before; and on the day of my miraculous escape you brought me into the house from the road, I remember."

"Yes, madame," said Monte Cristo; "but I preferred having an entrance which would allow me to see the Bois de Boulogne over my gate."

"In four days!" said Morrel; "it is extraordinary!"

"Indeed," said Château-Renaud, "it seems quite miraculous to make a new house out of an old one; for it was very old and dull too. I recollect coming for my mother to look at it when M. de Saint-Méran advertised it for sale two or three years ago."

"M. de Saint-Méran!" said Madame de Villefort; "then this house belonged to M. de Saint-Méran before you bought it?"

"It appears so," replied Monte Cristo.

"How? do you not know of whom you purchased it?"

"No, indeed; my steward transacts all this business for me."

"It is certainly ten years since the house had been occupied," said Château-Renaud; "and it was quite melancholy to look at it, with the blinds closed, the doors locked, and the weeds in the court. Really, if the house had not belonged to the father-in-law of the procureur du roi, one might have thought it some accursed place where a horrible crime had been committed."

Villefort, who had hitherto not tasted the three or four glasses of rare wine which were placed before him, here took one, and drank it off. Monte Cristo allowed a short time to elapse, and then said:

"It is singular, baron, but the same idea came across me the first time I entered it; it looked so gloomy, I should never have bought it if my steward had not acted for me. Perhaps the fellow had been bribed by the notary."

"It is probable," stammered out De Villefort; "but, believe me, I have nothing to do with this corruption. This house is part of the marriage-portion of Valentine, and M. de Saint-Méran wished to sell it, for, if it had remained another year or two uninhabited, it would have fallen to ruin."

It was Morrel's turn to become pale.

"There was, above all, one room," continued Monte Cristo, "very plain in appearance, hung with red damask, which, I know not why, appeared to me quite dramatic."

" Why so? " said Danglars. " Why dramatic? "

" Can we account for instinct? " said Monte Cristo. " Are there not some places where we seem to breathe sadness—why, we cannot tell? It is a chain of recollections; an idea which carries you back to other times—to other places—which, very likely, have no connection with the present time and place. And there is something in this room which reminds me forcibly of the chamber of the Marchioness de Gange* or Desdemona. —Stay, since we have finished dinner, I will show it to you; and then we will take coffee in the garden. After dinner the play."

Monte Cristo looked inquiringly at his guests; Madame de Villefort rose, Monte Cristo did the same, and the rest followed their example. Villefort and Madame Danglars remained for a moment as if rooted to their seats; they interrogated each other with cold glazed eyes.

" Did you hear? " said Madame Danglars.

" We must go," replied Villefort, offering his arm.

Everyone else was already scattered in different parts of the house, urged by curiosity, for they thought the visit would not be limited to the one room, and that, at the same time, they would obtain a view of the rest of the building, of which Monte Cristo had created a palace. Each one went out by the open doors. Monte Cristo waited for the two who remained; then, when they had passed, he closed the march with a smile, which, if they could have understood it, would have alarmed them much more than a visit to the room they were about to enter.

They, therefore, began by walking through the apartments, many of which were fitted up in the Eastern style, with cushions and divans instead of beds, and pipes instead of furniture. The drawing-rooms were decorated with the rarest pictures, by the old masters; the boudoirs hung with draperies from China, of fanciful colours, fantastic design, and wonderful texture. At length they arrived at the famous room. There was nothing particular about it, excepting that, although daylight had disappeared, it was not lighted, and everything in it remained antique, while the rest of the rooms had been redecorated. These two causes were enough to give it a gloomy tinge.

" Oh," cried Madame de Villefort, " it is really frightful."

Madame Danglars tried to utter a few words, but was not heard. Many observations were made, the result of which was the unanimous opinion that there was a sinister appearance in the room.

" Is it not so? " asked Monte Cristo. " Look at that large clumsy bed, hung with such gloomy, blood-coloured drapery!

And those two crayon portraits, that have faded from the damp, do they not seem to say, with their pale lips and staring eyes, ' We have seen '? "

Villefort became livid; Madame Danglars fell into a long seat placed near the chimney.

" Oh," said Madame de Villefort, smiling, " are you courageous enough to sit down upon the very seat perhaps upon which the crime was committed? "

Madame Danglars rose suddenly.

" And then," said Monte Cristo, " this is not all."

" What is there more? " said Debray, who had not failed to notice the agitation of Madame Danglars.

" Ah! what else is there? " said Danglars, " for, at present, I cannot say that I have seen anything extraordinary. What do you say, M. Cavalcanti? "

" Ah," said he, " we have at Pisa the tower of Ugolino; at Ferrara, the prison of Tasso; at Rimini, the room of Francesca and Paolo."

" Yes, but you have not this little staircase," said Monte Cristo, opening a door concealed by the drapery. " Look at it, and tell me what you think of it."

" What a wicked-looking, crooked staircase," said Château-Renaud, smiling.

" I do not know whether the wine of Chios produces melancholy, but certainly everything appears to me black in this house," said Debray.

Ever since Valentine's dowry had been mentioned, Morrel had been silent and sad.

" Can you not imagine," said Monte Cristo, " some Othello or Abbé de Ganges, one stormy, dark night, descending these stairs step by step, carrying a heavy load, which he wishes to hide from the sight of man, if not from God? "

Madame Danglars half fainted on the arm of Villefort, who was obliged to support himself against the wall.

" Ah, madame," cried Debray, " what is the matter with you? how pale you look! "

" This is what is the matter with her," said Madame de Villefort; " it is very simple: M. de Monte Cristo is relating horrible stories to us, doubtless intending to frighten us to death."

" Yes," said Villefort, " really, count, you frighten the ladies."

" What is the matter? " asked Debray, in a whisper, of Madame Danglars.

" Nothing," she replied, with a violent effort. " I want air, that is all."

" Will you come into the garden? " said Debray, advancing towards the back staircase.

" No, no! " she answered, " I would rather remain here."

" Are you really frightened, madame? " said Monte Cristo.

" Oh, no, sir," said Madame Danglars; " but you suppose scenes in a manner which gives them the appearance of reality."

" Ah, yes! " said Monte Cristo, smiling; " it is all a matter of the imagination. Why should we not imagine this the apartment of an honest family woman? And this bed with red hangings, a bed visited by the goddess Lucina? And that mysterious staircase, the passage through which, not to disturb their sleep, the doctor and nurse pass, or even the father carrying the sleeping child? "

Here Madame Danglars, instead of being calmed by this soft picture, uttered a groan and fainted.

" Madame Danglars is ill," said Villefort; " it would be better to take her to her carriage."

" Oh, and I have forgotten my smelling-bottle! " said Monte Cristo.

" I have mine," said Madame de Villefort; and she passed over to Monte Cristo a bottle full of the same kind of red liquid whose good properties the count had tested on Edward.

" Ah! " said Monte Cristo, taking it from her hand.

" Yes," she said, " at your advice I have tried."

" And have you succeeded? "

" I think so."

Madame Danglars was carried into the adjoining room; Monte Cristo dropped a very small portion of the red liquid upon her lips; she returned to consciousness.

" Ah," she cried, " what a frightful dream! "

Villefort pressed her hand to let her know it was not a dream.

M. Danglars was sought, but little interested in poetical ideas, he had gone into the garden, and was talking with Major Cavalcanti on the projected railway from Leghorn to Florence.

Monte Cristo seemed in despair. He took the arm of Madame Danglars and conducted her into the garden, where they found Danglars taking coffee between the Cavalcanti.

" Really, madame," he said, " did I alarm you much? "

" Oh, no, sir," she answered; " but you know, things impress us differently according to the mood of our minds."

Villefort forced a laugh.

" And then, you know," he said, " an idea, a supposition, is sufficient."

" Well," said Monte Cristo, " you may believe me, if you

like, but it is my belief that a crime has been committed in this house."

"Take care!" said Madame de Villefort, "the procureur du roi is here."

"Ah," replied Monte Cristo, "since that is the case, I will take advantage of his presence to make my declaration."

"Your declaration!" said Villefort.

"Yes, before witnesses."

"Oh, this is very interesting," said Debray; "if there really has been a crime, we will investigate it."

"There has been a crime," said Monte Cristo. "Come this way, gentlemen; come, M. Villefort, for a declaration, to be available, should be made before the competent authorities."

He then took Villefort's arm, and, at the same time, holding that of Madame Danglars under his own, he dragged the procureur to the plantain-tree, where the shade was thickest. All the other guests followed.

"Stay," said Monte Cristo, "here in this very spot" (and he stamped upon the ground), "I had the earth dug up and fresh mould put in, to refresh these old trees; well, my man, digging, found a box, or rather the ironwork of a box, in the midst of which was the skeleton of a newly-born infant."

Monte Cristo felt the arm of Madame Danglars stiffen, while that of Villefort trembled.

"A newly-born infant!" repeated Debray; "this affair becomes serious!"

"Well," said Château-Renaud, "I was not wrong just now, then, when I said that houses had souls and faces like men, and that their exteriors carried the impress of their characters. This house was gloomy because it was remorseful; it was remorseful because it concealed a crime."

"Who said it was a crime?" asked Villefort, with a last effort.

"How? is it not a crime to bury a living child in a garden?" cried Monte Cristo. "And pray what do you call such an action?"

"But who said it was buried alive?"

"Why bury it there if it were dead? This garden has never been a cemetery."

"What is done to infanticides in this country?" asked Major Cavalcanti innocently.

"Oh, their heads are soon cut off," said Danglars.

"Ah, indeed!" said Cavalcanti.

"I think so: am I not right, M. de Villefort?" asked Monte Cristo.

"Yes, count," replied De Villefort, in a voice now scarcely human.

Monte Cristo saw that the two persons for whom he had prepared this scene could scarcely bear it, so, not wishing to carry it too far, he said:

"Come, gentlemen, some coffee, we seem to have forgotten it;" and he conducted the guests back to the table on the lawn.

"Indeed, count," said Madame Danglars, "I am ashamed to own it, but all your frightful stories have so upset me, that I must beg you to let me sit down;" and she fell into a chair. Monte Cristo bowed, and went to Madame de Villefort.

"I think, Madame Danglars again requires your bottle," he said.

But before Madame de Villefort could reach her friend, the procureur had found time to whisper to Madame Danglars:

"I must speak to you."

"When?"

"To-morrow."

"Where?"

"In my office, or in the court, if you like, that is the surest place."

"I will go."

At this moment Madame de Villefort approached.

"Thanks, my dear friend," said Madame Danglars, trying to smile; "it is over now, and I am much better."

THE evening passed on; Madame de Villefort expressed a desire to return to Paris, which Madame Danglars had not dared to do, notwithstanding the uneasiness she experienced. On his wife's request, M. de Villefort was the first to give the signal of departure. He offered a seat in his landau to Madame Danglars, that she might be under the care of his wife. As for M. Danglars, absorbed in an interesting conversation with M. Cavalcanti, he paid no attention to anything that was passing. While Monte Cristo had begged the smelling-bottle of Madame de Villefort, he had remarked the approach of Villefort to Madame Danglars, and he soon guessed all that had passed between them, though the words had been uttered in so low a voice as hardly to be heard by Madame Danglars. Without opposing their arrangements, he allowed Morrel, Château-Renaud, and Debray to leave on horseback, and the ladies in M. de Villefort's carriage. Danglars, more and more delighted with Major Cavalcanti, had offered him a seat in his carriage. Andrea Cavalcanti found his tilbury waiting at the door; the groom, in every respect a caricature of the English fashion, was standing on tiptoes to hold a large iron-gray horse. Andrea had spoken very little during dinner; he was an intelligent lad, and he feared to utter some absurdity before so many grand people, amongst whom he saw, with dilating eyes, the procureur du roi. Then he had been seized upon by Danglars, who, taking a rapid glance at the stiff-necked old major and his modest son, and taking into consideration the hospitality of the count, made up his mind that he was in the society of some nabob come to Paris to finish the worldly education of his only son. He contemplated with unspeakable delight the large diamond which shone on the major's little finger; for the major, like a prudent man, in case of any accident happening to his bank-notes, had immediately converted them into articles of value. Then after dinner, on the pretext of business, he questioned the father and son upon their mode of living; and the father and son, previously informed that it was through Danglars the one was to receive his 48,000 francs, and the other 50,000 livres annually, they were so full of affability, that they would have shaken hands even with the banker's servants, so much did their gratitude need an object to expend itself upon. One thing above all the rest heightened the respect, nay almost the veneration of Danglars for Cavalcanti. The latter, faithful to the principle of Horace, *nil admirari*, had contented himself in proving his knowledge by saying in what lake the best lampreys were caught. Then he had eaten some without saying a word; Danglars, therefore, concluded that these kind of luxuries were common at the table of the illustrious descendant of the Cavalcanti, who most likely in Lucca fed upon trout brought from Switzerland, and lobsters sent from England, by the same means used by the count to bring the lampreys from the Lake Fusaro, and the sterlet from the Volga. Thus it was with much politeness of manner that he heard Cavalcanti pronounce these words:

" To-morrow, sir, I shall have the honour of waiting upon you on business."

" And I, sir," said Danglars, " shall be most happy to receive you." Upon which he offered to take Cavalcanti in his carriage to the Hôtel de Princes, if it would not be depriving him of the company of his son. To this Cavalcanti replied, by saying, that for some time past his son had lived independently of him; that he had his own horses and carriages, and that not having come together, it would not be difficult for them to leave separately. The major seated himself, therefore, by the side of Danglars, who was more and more charmed with the ideas of order and economy which ruled this man, and yet who, being able to allow his son 50,000 francs a year, might be supposed to possess a fortune of 500,000 or 600,000 livres.

As for Andrea, he began, by way of showing off, to scold his groom; who, instead of bringing the tilbury to the steps of the house, had taken it to the outer door, thus giving him the trouble of walking thirty steps to reach it. The groom heard him with humility, took the bit of the impatient animal with his left hand, and with the right held out the reins to Andrea, who, taking them from him, rested his polished boot lightly on the step. At that moment a hand touched his shoulder. The young man turned round, thinking that Danglars or Monte Cristo had forgotten something they wished to tell him, and had returned just as they were starting. But, instead of either of these, he saw nothing but a strange face, sunburnt, and encircled by a beard, with eyes, brilliant as carbuncles, and a smile upon the mouth which displayed a perfect set of white teeth, pointed and sharp as the wolf's or jackal's. A red handkerchief encircled his gray head; torn and filthy garments covered his large bony limbs, which seemed as though, like those of a skeleton, they would rattle as he walked; and the hand with which he leant upon the young man's shoulder, and which was the first thing Andrea saw, seemed of a gigantic size.

Did the young man recognise that face by the light of the lantern in his tilbury, or was he merely struck with the horrible appearance of his interrogator? We cannot say; but only relate the fact that he shuddered and stepped back suddenly.

" What do you want of me? " he asked.

" Pardon me, my friend, if I disturb you," said the man with the red handkerchief, " but I want to speak to you."

" You have no right to beg at night," said the groom, endeavouring to rid his master of the troublesome intruder.

" I am not begging, my fine fellow," said the unknown to the servant, with so ironical an expression of eye, and so frightful a smile, that he withdrew; " I only wish to say two or three words to your master, who gave me a commission to execute about a fortnight ago."

" Come," said Andrea, with sufficient nerve for his servant not to perceive his agitation, " what do you want? Speak quickly, friend."

The man said in a low voice:

" I wish—I wish you to spare me the walk back to Paris. I am very tired, and not having eaten so good a dinner as you have, I can scarcely support myself."

The young man shuddered at this strange familiarity.

" Tell me," he said,—" tell me what you want? "

" Well, then, I want you to take me up in your fine carriage, and carry me back."

Andrea turned pale, but said nothing.

" Yes," said the man, thrusting his hands into his pockets, and looking impudently at the youth; " I have taken the whim into my head: do you understand, Master Benedetto? "

At this name the young man, no doubt, reflected a little, for he went towards his groom, saying:

" This man is right; I did indeed charge him with a commission, the result of which he must tell me; walk to the barrier, there take a cab, that you may not be too late."

The surprised groom retired.

" Let me, at least, reach a shady spot," said Andrea.

" Oh, as for that, I'll conduct you to a splendid spot," said the man with the handkerchief; and, taking the horse's bit, he led the tilbury to a place where it was certainly impossible for any one to witness the honour that Andrea conferred upon him.

" Don't think I want the honour of riding in your fine carriage," said he; " oh, no, it's only because I am tired, and also because I have a little business to talk over with you."

" Come, step in," said the young man.

It was a pity this scene had not occurred in daylight, for it was curious to see this rascal throwing himself heavily down on the cushion beside the young and elegant driver of the tilbury.

Andrea drove past the last house in the village, without saying a word to his companion, who smiled complacently, as though well pleased to find himself travelling in so comfortable a vehicle. Once out of Auteuil, Andrea looked around, in order to assure him el? that he could neither be seen nor heard; and then, stopping the horse and crossing his arms before the man, he asked:

" Now, tell me why you come to disturb my tranquillity? "

" Let me ask you why you deceived me? "

" How have I deceived you? "

" How! do you ask? When we parted at the Pont du Far, you told me you were going to travel through Piedmont and Tuscany; but instead of that, you come to Paris."

" How does that annoy you? "

" It does not; on the contrary, I think it will answer my purpose."

" So," said Andrea, " you are speculating upon me? "

" What fine words he uses! "

" I warn you, Master Caderousse, that you are mistaken."

" Well, well, don't be angry, my boy; you know well enough what it is to be unfortunate; and misfortunes make us jealous. I thought you were earning a living in Tuscany or Piedmont by acting as *facchino* or *cicerone*; and I pitied you sincerely, as I would a child of my own. You know I always did call you my child? "

" Come, come, what then? "

" Patience! patience! "

" I am patient, but go on."

" All at once I see you pass through the barrier with a groom, a tilbury, and fine new clothes. You must have discovered a mine, or else become a stockbroker."

" So that, as you acknowledge, you are jealous? "

" No, I am pleased; so pleased that I wished to congratulate you; but as I am not quite properly dressed, I chose my opportunity, that I might not compromise you."

" Yes, and a fine opportunity you have chosen! " exclaimed Andrea; " you speak to me before my servant."

" How can I help that, my boy? I speak to you when I can catch you. You have a quick horse, a light tilbury, you are naturally as slippery as an eel; if I had missed you to-night, I might not have had another chance."

"You see I do not conceal myself."

"You are lucky; I wish I could say as much: I do conceal myself; and then I was afraid you would not recognise me, but you did," added Caderousse, with his unpleasant smile; "it was very polite of you."

"Come," said Andrea, "what do you want?"

"You do not speak affectionately to me, Benedetto, my old friend; that is not right; take care, or I may become troublesome."

This menace smothered the young man's passion. He trotted his horse on.

"You should not speak so to an old friend like me, Caderousse, as you said just now; you are a native of Marseilles, I am——"

"Do you know then now what you are?"

"No; but I was brought up in Corsica; you are old and obstinate, I am young and wilful. Between folks like us threats are out of place, everything should be amicably arranged. Is it my fault, if Fortune, which has frowned on you, has been kind to me?"

"Fortune has been kind to you, then? Your tilbury, your groom, your clothes, are not then hired? Good, so much the better," said Caderousse, his eyes sparkling with avarice.

"Oh, you knew that well enough before speaking to me," said Andrea, becoming more and more excited. "If I had been wearing a handkerchief like yours on my head, rags on my back, and worn-out shoes on my feet you would not have known me."

"You wrong me, my boy; now I have found you, nothing prevents my being as well dressed as anyone, knowing as I do the goodness of your heart. If you have two coats you will give me one of them. I used to divide my soup and beans with you when you were hungry."

"True," said Andrea.

"What an appetite you used to have! Is it as good now?"

"Oh, yes," replied Andrea, laughing.

"How did you come to be dining with that prince whose house you have just left?"

"He is not a prince; simply a count."

"A count, and a rich one too, eh?"

"Yes; but you had better not have anything to say to him, for he is not a very good-tempered gentleman."

"Oh, be satisfied! I have no design upon your count, and you shall have him all to yourself. But," said Caderousse, again smiling with the disagreeable expression he had before assumed, " you must pay for it—you understand? "

" Well, what do you want? "

" I think that with a hundred francs per month——"

" Well? "

" I could live——"

" Upon a hundred francs! "

" Come—you understand me; but that with——"

" With? "

" With a hundred and fifty francs I should be quite happy."

" Here are two hundred," said Andrea; and he placed ten louis d'or in the hand of Caderousse.

" Good! " said Caderousse.

" Apply to the steward on the first day of every month, and you will receive the same sum."

" There now, again, you degrade me."

" How so? "

" By making me apply to the servants, when I want to transact business with you alone."

" Well, be it so then. Take it from me then, and so long at least as I receive my income, you shall be paid yours."

" Come, come; I always said you were a fine fellow, and it is a blessing when good fortune happens to such as you. But tell me all about it? "

" Why do you wish to know? " asked Cavalcanti.

" What! do you again defy me? "

" No; the fact is, I have found my father."

" What! a real father? "

" Yes, so long as he pays me——"

" You'll honour and believe him,—that's right. What is his name? "

" Major Cavalcanti."

" Is he pleased with you? "

" So far I have appeared to answer his purpose."

" And who found this father for you? "

" The Count of Monte Cristo."

" The man whose house you have just left? "

" Yes."

" I wish you would try and find me a situation with him as grandfather, since he holds the money-chest."

" Well, I will mention you to him. Meanwhile, what are you going to do? "

" I? "

" Yes, you."

" It is very kind of you to trouble yourself about me."

"Since you interest yourself in my affairs, I think it is now my turn to ask you some questions."

"Ah, true! Well, I shall rent a room in some respectable house, wear a decent coat, shave every day, and go and read the papers in a café. Then, in the evening, I will go to the theatre; I shall look like some retired baker. This is my wish."

"Come, if you will only put this scheme into execution, and be steady, nothing could be better."

"Do you think so, M. Bossuet? And you—what will you become? A peer of France?"

"Ah," said Andrea, "who knows?"

"Major Cavalcanti is already one, perhaps; but, then, hereditary rank is abolished."

"No politics, Caderousse!—And now that you have all you want, and that we understand each other, jump down from the tilbury, and disappear."

"Not at all, my good friend."

"How! not at all?"

"Why, just think for a moment; with this red handkerchief on my head, with scarcely any shoes, no papers, and ten gold napoleons in my pocket, without reckoning what was there before—making in all about two hundred francs,—why, I should certainly be arrested at the barrier! Then, to justify myself, I should say that you gave me the money; this would cause inquiries; it would be found that I left Toulon without giving due notice, and I should then be reconducted to the shores of the Mediterranean. Then I should become simply No. 106, and good-bye to my dream of resembling the retired baker! No, no, my boy; I prefer remaining honourably in the capital."

Andrea scowled. Certainly, as he had himself owned, the reputed son of Major Cavalcanti was a wilful fellow. He drew up for a minute, threw a rapid glance around him; and, after doing so, his hand fell instantly into his pocket, where it began playing with a pistol. But, meanwhile, Caderousse, who had never taken his eyes off his companion, passed his hand behind his back, and unclasped a long Spanish knife, which he always carried with him, to be ready in case of need. The two friends, as we see, were worthy of and understood one another. Andrea's hand left his pocket inoffensively, and was carried up to the red moustachio, which it played with for some time.

"Good Caderousse," he said, "how happy you will be!"

"I will do my best," said the innkeeper of the Pont du Gard, reclasping his knife.

"Well, then, we will go into Paris. But how will you pass

through the barrier without exciting suspicion? It seems to me that you are in more danger riding than on foot."

" Wait," said Caderousse, " you shall see." He then took the greatcoat with the large collar, which the groom had left behind in the tilbury, and put it on his back; then he took off Cavalcanti's hat, which he placed upon his own head; and finally assumed the careless attitude of a servant whose master drives himself.

" But, tell me," said Andrea, " am I to remain bareheaded? "

" Pooh! " said Caderousse; " it is so windy that your hat can easily appear to have blown off."

" Come, come; enough of this," said Cavalcanti.

" What are you waiting for? " said Caderousse. " I hope I am not the cause? "

" *Chut !* " exclaimed Andrea.

They passed the barrier without accident. At the first cross street Andrea stopped his horse, and Caderousse leaped out.

" Well! " said Andrea, " my servant's coat and my hat? "

" Ah," said Caderousse, " you would not like me to risk taking cold? "

" But what am I to do? "

" You! oh, you are young, whilst I am beginning to get old. *Au revoir*, Benedetto "; and, running into a court, he disappeared.

" Alas," said Andrea, sighing, " one cannot be completely happy in this world! "

66

A Conjugal Scene

AT the Place Louis XV the three young people separated,—
that is to say, Morrel went to the Boulevards, Château-
Renaud to the Pont de la Revolution, and Debray to the Quai.
Most probably Morrel and Château-Renaud returned to their
" domestic hearths," as they say in the gallery of the Chamber
in well-turned speeches, and in the theatre of the Rue Richelieu
in well-written pieces; but it was not the case with Debray.
When he reached the wicket of the Louvre, he turned to the left,
galloped across the Carrousel, passed through the Rue Saint-
Roch, and, issuing from the Rue de la Michodière, he arrived
at M. Danglars' door just at the same time that Villefort's landau,
after having deposited him and his wife at the Faubourg Saint
Honoré, stopped to leave the baroness at her own house. Debray,
with the air of a man familiar with the house, entered first into
the court, threw his bridle into the hands of a footman, and
returned to the door to receive Madame Danglars, to whom he
offered his arm, to conduct her to her apartments. The gate
once closed, and Debray and the baroness alone in the court,
he asked:

" What was the matter with you, Hermine? and why were
you so affected at that story, or rather fable, which the count
related? "

" Because I have been in such shocking spirits all the evening,
my friend," said the baroness.

" No, Hermine," replied Debray; " you cannot make me
believe that; on the contrary, you were in excellent spirits when
you arrived at the count's. M. Danglars was disagreeable,
certainly; but I know how much you care for his ill-humour.
Someone has vexed you; I will allow no one to annoy you."

" You are deceived, Lucien, I assure you," replied Madame
Danglars; " and what I have told you is really the case, added
to the ill-humour you remarked, but which I did not think it
worth while to allude to."

It was evident that Madame Danglars was suffering from that
nervous irritability which women frequently cannot account for
even to themselves; or that, as Debray had guessed, she had
experienced some secret agitation that she would not acknowledge

to anyone. Being a man who knew that the former of these symptoms was one of the elements of female life, he did not then press his inquiries, but waited for a more appropriate opportunity when he should again interrogate her, or receive an avowal *proprio motu*.

At the door of her apartment the baroness met Mademoiselle Cornélie, her confidential lady's-maid.

" What is my daughter doing? " asked Madame Danglars.

" She practised all evening, and then went to bed," replied Mademoiselle Cornélie.

" Yet I think I heard her piano."

" It is Mademoiselle Louise d'Arnilly, who is playing while Mademoiselle Danglars is in bed."

" Well," said Madame Danglars, " come and undress me."

They entered the bedroom. Debray stretched himself upon a large couch, and Madame Danglars passed into her dressing-room with Mademoiselle Cornélie.

" My dear M. Lucien," said Madame Danglars, through the door, " you are always complaining that Eugénie will not address a word to you."

" Madame," said Lucien, playing with a little dog, who, recognising him as a friend of the house, expected to be caressed, " I am not the only one who makes similar complaints; I think I heard Morcerf say that he could not extract a word from his *fiancée*."

" True," said Madame Danglars; " but yet I think this will all pass off, and that you will one day see her enter your study."

" My study? "

" At least that of the minister."

" Why so? "

" To ask for an engagement at the Opera. Really, I never saw such an infatuation for music; it is quite ridiculous for a young lady of fashion."

Debray smiled.

" Well," said he, " let her come, with your consent and that of the baron, and we will try and give her an engagement, though we are very poor to pay such talent as hers."

" Go, Cornélie," said Madame Danglars, " I do not require you any longer."

Cornélie obeyed, and the next minute Madame Danglars left her room in a charming loose dress, and came and sat down close to Debray. Then, thoughtful, she began to caress the little spaniel. Lucien looked at her for a moment in silence.

" Come, Hermine," he said, after a short time, " answer candidly,—something vexes you—is it not so? "

"Nothing," answered the baroness.

And yet, as she could scarcely breathe, she rose and went towards a looking-glass.

"I am frightful to-night," she said.

Debray rose, smiling, and was about to contradict the baroness upon this latter point, when the door opened suddenly. M. Danglars appeared; Debray reseated himself. At the noise of the door Madame Danglars turned round, and looked upon her husband with an astonishment she took no trouble to conceal.

"Good evening, madame!" said the banker; "good evening, M. Debray!"

Probably the baroness thought this unexpected visit signified a desire to repair the sharp words he had uttered during the day. Assuming a dignified air, she turned round to Debray, without answering her husband, "Read me something, M. Debray," she said.

Debray, who was slightly disturbed at this visit, recovered himself when he saw the calmness of the baroness, and took up a book marked by a mother-of-pearl knife inlaid with gold.

"Excuse me," said the banker, "but you will tire yourself, baroness, by such late hours, and M. Debray lives some distance from here."

Debray was petrified, not only to hear Danglars speak so calmly and politely, but that it was apparent that beneath this forced appearance there really lurked a determined spirit of opposition to do anything his wife wished that evening. The baroness was also surprised, and showed her astonishment by a look which would doubtless have had some effect upon her husband if he had not been intently occupied with the paper, where he was seeking the closing price of the funds. The result was, that the proud look entirely failed.

"M. Lucien," said the baroness, "I assure you I have no desire to sleep, and that I have a thousand things to tell you this evening, which you must listen to, even though you slept while hearing me."

"I am at your service, madame," replied Lucien coldly.

"My dear M. Debray," said the banker, "do not kill yourself to-night listening to the follies of Madame Danglars, for you can hear them as well to-morrow; but I claim to-night, and will dedicate it, if you will allow me, to talk over some serious matters with my wife."

This time the blow was so well aimed, and hit so directly, that Lucien and the baroness were staggered; and they interrogated each other with their eyes as if to seek help against this aggression, but the irresistible will of the master of the house prevailed, and the husband was victorious.

"Do not think I wish to turn you out, my dear Debray," continued Danglars; "oh, no, not at all! An unexpected occurrence forces me to ask my wife to have a little conversation with me; it is so rarely I make such a request, I am sure you cannot grudge it to me."

Debray muttered something, bowed, and went out, knocking himself against the edge of the door, like Nathan in *Athalie*.

"It is extraordinary," he said, when the door was closed behind him, "how easily these husbands, whom we ridicule, gain an advantage over us."

Lucien having left, Danglars took his place on the sofa, closed the open book, and placing himself in a dreadfully dictatorial attitude, he began playing with the dog; but the animal, not liking him so well as Debray, and attempting to bite him, Danglars seized him by the skin of his neck, and threw him to the other side of the room upon a couch. The animal uttered a cry during his transit, but, arrived at its destination, it crouched behind the cushions, and, stupefied at such unusual treatment, remained silent and motionless.

"Do you know, sir," asked the baroness, "that you are improving? Generally you are only rude, but to-night you are brutal."

"It is because I am in a worse humour than usual," replied Danglars.

Hermine looked at the banker with supreme disdain. These glances frequently exasperated the pride of Danglars, but this evening he took no notice of them.

"And what have I to do with your ill-humour?" said the baroness, irritated at the impassibility of her husband; "do these things concern me? Keep your ill-humour at home in your chests, or, since you have clerks whom you pay, vent it upon them."

"Not so," replied Danglars; "your advice is wrong, so I shall not follow it. My chests are my Pactolus, as, I think, M. Demoustier says, and I will not retard its course, or disturb its calm. My clerks are honest men, who earn my fortune, whom I pay much below their deserts, if I may value them according to what they bring in; therefore I shall not get into a passion with them; those with whom I will be in a passion are those who eat my dinners, mount my horses, and exhaust my fortune."

"And pray who are the persons who exhaust your fortune? Explain yourself more clearly, I beg, sir."

"Oh, make yourself easy!—I am not speaking riddles, and

you will soon know what I mean. The people who exhaust my fortune are those who draw out 700,000 francs in the course of an hour."

" I do not understand you, sir," said the baroness, trying to disguise the agitation of her voice and the flush of her face.

" You understand me perfectly, on the contrary," said Danglars; " but if you will persist, I will tell you that I have just lost 700,000 francs upon the Spanish loan."

" And pray," asked the baroness, " am I responsible for this loss? "

" Why not? "

" Is it my fault you have lost 700,000 francs? "

" Certainly it is not mine."

" Once for all, sir," replied the baroness sharply, " I tell you I will not hear cash named; it is a style of language I never heard in the house of my parents or in that of my first husband."

" Oh! I can well believe that, for neither of them was worth a penny."

" The better reason for my not being conversant with the slang of the bank, which is here dinning in my ears from morning to night; that noise of crowns jingling, which are constantly being counted and recounted, is odious to me. I only know one thing I dislike more, which is the sound of your voice."

" Really! " said Danglars. " Well, this surprises me, for I thought you took the liveliest interest in my affairs! "

" I! What could put such an idea into your head? "

" Yourself! "

" Ah!—what next? "

" Most assuredly."

" I should like to know upon what occasion? "

" Ah, that is very easily done! Last February you were the first who told me of the Haytian funds. You had dreamt that a ship had entered the harbour at Havre, that this ship brought news that a payment we had looked upon as lost was going to be made. I know how clear-sighted your dreams are; I therefore purchased immediately as many shares as I could of the Haytian debt, and I gained 400,000 francs by it, of which 100,000 have been honestly paid to you. You spent it as you pleased, that was your business. In March there was a question about a grant to a railway. Three companies presented themselves, each offering equal securities. You told me that your instinct,—and although you pretend to know nothing about speculations, I think, on the contrary, that your comprehension is very clear upon certain affairs,—well, you told me that your instinct led you to believe the grant would be given to the company called the Southern. I bought two-thirds of the shares of that company; as you had foreseen, the shares became of triple value, and I picked up a million ($40,000), from which 250,000 francs were paid to you for pin-money. How have you spent this 250,000 francs?—It is no business of mine."

"When are you coming to the point?" cried the baroness, shivering with anger and impatience.

"Patience, madame, I am coming to it."

"That's fortunate!"

"In April you went to dine at the minister's. You heard a private conversation respecting the affairs of Spain—on the expulsion of Don Carlos. I bought some Spanish shares. The expulsion took place, and I pocketed 600,000 francs the day Charles V repassed the Bidassoa. Of these 600,000 francs you took 50,000 crowns. They were yours, you disposed of them according to your fancy, and I asked no questions; but it is not the less true that you have this year received 500,000 livres."

"Well, sir, and what then?"

"Ah, yes, it was just after this that you spoiled everything!"

"Really your manner of speaking——"

"It expresses my meaning, and that is all I want. Well, three days after that you talked politics with M. Debray, and you fancied from his words that Don Carlos had returned to Spain. Well, I sold my shares, the news was spread, and I no longer sold but gave them; next day I find the news was false, and by this false report I have lost 700,000 francs."

"Well?"

"Well, since I give you a fourth of my gains, I think you owe me a fourth of my losses: the fourth of 700,000 francs is 175,000 francs."

"What you say is absurd, and I cannot see why M. Debray's name is mixed up in this affair."

"Because if you do not possess the 175,000 francs I reclaim, you must have lent them to your friends, and M. Debray is one of your friends."

"For shame!" exclaimed the baroness.

"Oh! let us have no gestures, no screams, no modern drama, or you will oblige me to tell you that I see Debray leave here, pocketing nearly the whole of the 500,000 livres you have handed over to him this year; while he smiles to himself, saying that he has found that which the most skilful players have never discovered; that is, a roulette, where he wins without paying, and is no loser when he loses."

The baroness became enraged.

"Wretch!" she cried, "will you dare to tell me you did not know that with which you now reproach me?"

"I do not say that I did know it, and I do not say that I did not know it. I merely tell you to look into my conduct during the last four years that we have ceased to be husband and wife, and see whether it has not always been consistent. Some time after our rupture, you wished to study music under the celebrated baritone who made such a successful *début* at the Théâtre Italien; at the same time I felt inclined to learn dancing of the *danseuse* who acquired such a reputation in London. This cost me, on your account and mine, about 100,000 francs. I said nothing, for we must have peace in the house; and 100,000 francs for a lady and gentleman to be properly instructed in music and dancing are not too much. Well, you soon became tired of singing, and you take a fancy to study diplomacy with the minister's secretary. You understand: it signifies nothing to me so long as you pay for your lessons out of your own cash-box. But to-day I find you are drawing on mine, and that your apprenticeship may cost me 700,000 francs per month. Stop there, madame, for this cannot last. Either the diplomatist must give his lessons gratis, and I will tolerate him, or he must never set his foot again in my house;—do you understand, madame?"

"Oh, this is too much," cried Hermine, choking: "you are worse than despicable."

"But," continued Danglars, "I find you did not even pause there——"

"Insults!"

"You are right: let us leave these facts alone, and reason coolly. I have never interfered in your affairs, excepting for your good; treat me in the same way. You say you have nothing to do with my cash-box. Be it so. Do as you like with your own, but do not fill or empty mine. Besides, how do I know that this was not a political trick; that the minister, enraged at seeing me in the opposition, and jealous of the popular sympathy I excite, has not concerted with M. Debray to ruin me?"

"A probable thing!"

"Why not? Whoever heard of such an occurrence as this?— A false telegraphic despatch—it is almost impossible for signals to have been made different to those of the two last telegraphs. It was done on purpose for me, I am sure of it."

"Sir," said the baroness humbly, "are you not aware that the man employed there was dismissed, that they talked of going to law with him, that orders were issued to arrest him, and that this order would have been put into execution if he had not escaped their researches by a flight, which proves either his madness or his culpability? It was a mistake."

"Yes, which made fools laugh, which caused the minister to have a sleepless night, which has caused the minister's secretaries to blacken several sheets of paper, but which has cost me 700,000 francs."

"But, sir," said Hermine suddenly, "if all this is, as you say, caused by M. Debray, why, instead of going direct to him, do you come and tell me of it? Why, to accuse the man, do you address the woman?"

"Do I know M. Debray?—do I wish to know him?—do I wish to know that he gives advice?—do I wish to follow it?—do I speculate? No; you do all this, not I."

"Still it seems to me, that as you profit by it——"

Danglars shrugged his shoulders.

"Foolish creature!" he exclaimed; "women fancy they have talent because they have managed two or three intrigues without being the talk of Paris! But know that if you had even hidden your irregularities from your husband, which is but the commencement of the art—for generally husbands *will* not see—you would then have been a faint imitation of most of your friends among the women of the world. But it has not been so with me,—I see, and always have seen, during the last sixteen years; you may, perhaps, have hidden a thought, but not a step, not an action, not a fault, has escaped me, while you flattered yourself upon your address, and firmly believed you had deceived me. What has been the result?—that, thanks to my pretended ignorance, there are none of your friends, from M. de Villefort to M. Debray, who have not trembled before me. There is not one who has not treated me as the master of the house, the only title I desire with respect to you; there is not one, in fact, who would have dared to speak of me as I have spoken of them this day. I will allow you to make me hateful, but I will prevent your rendering me ridiculous, and, above all, I forbid you to ruin me."

The baroness had been tolerably composed until the name of Villefort had been pronounced; but then she became pale, and, rising, as if touched by a spring, she stretched out her hands as though conjuring an apparition: she then took two or three steps towards her husband, as though to tear the secret from him, of which he was ignorant, or which he withheld from some odious calculation, as all his calculations were.

"M. de Villefort!—What do you mean?"

"I mean that M. de Nargonne, your first husband, being neither a philosopher nor a banker, or, perhaps, being both, and seeing there was nothing to be got out of a procureur du roi, died of grief or anger at finding, after an absence of nine months, that you had been *enceinte* six. I am brutal, I not only allow it, but boast of it; it is one of the reasons of my success in commercial business. Why did he kill himself instead of you? Because he had no cash to save. My life belongs to my cash. M. Debray has made me lose 700,000 francs; let him bear his share of the loss, and we will go on as before; if not, let him become bankrupt for the 250,000 livres, and do as all bankrupts do—disappear. He is a charming fellow, I allow, when his news is correct; but when it is not, there are fifty others in the world who would do better than he."

Madame Danglars was rooted to the spot; she made a violent effort to reply to this last attack, but she fell upon a chair, thinking of Villefort, of the dinner scene, of the strange series of misfortunes which had taken place in her house during the last few days, and changed the usual calm of her establishment to a scene of scandalous debate. Danglars did not even look at her, though she tried all she could to faint. He shut the bedroom door after him, without adding another word, and returned to his apartments; and when Madame Danglars recovered from her half-fainting condition, she could almost believe she had had a disagreeable dream.

67

Matrimonial Plans

THE day following this scene, at the hour the banker usually chose to pay a visit to Madame Danglars on his way to his office, his *coupé* did not appear in the court. At this time, that is, about half-past twelve, Madame Danglars ordered her carriage, and went out. Danglars, placed behind a curtain, watched the departure he had been waiting for. He gave orders that he should be informed directly Madame Danglars appeared, but at two o'clock she had not returned. He then called for his horses, drove to the Chamber, and inscribed his name to speak against the budget. From twelve to two o'clock Danglars had remained in his study, unsealing his despatches, and becoming more and more sad every minute, heaping figure upon figure, and receiving, among other visits, one from Major Cavalcanti, who, as stiff and as exact as ever, presented himself precisely at the hour named the night before, to terminate his business with the banker. On leaving the Chamber, Danglars, who had shown violent marks of agitation during the sitting, and been more bitter than ever against the ministry, re-entered his carriage, and told the coachman to drive to the Avenue des Champs-Elysées, No. 30.

Monte Cristo was at home; only he was engaged with someone, and begged Danglars to wait for a moment in the drawing-room. While the banker was waiting, the door opened, and a man dressed as an abbé entered, who, doubtless, more familiar with the house than he was, instead of waiting, merely bowed, and, passing on to the further apartments, disappeared. A minute after the door by which the priest had entered reopened, and Monte Cristo appeared.

" Pardon me," said he, " my dear baron, but one of my friends, the Abbé Busoni, whom you, perhaps, saw pass by, has just arrived in Paris; not having seen him for a long time, I could not make up my mind to leave him sooner, so I hope this will be sufficient reason for my having made you wait."

" Nay," said Danglars, " it is my fault; I have chosen my visit at a wrong time, and will retire."

" Not at all; on the contrary be seated: but what is the matter with you? You look careworn; really, you alarm me;

for a capitalist to be sad, like the appearance of a comet, presages some misfortune to the world."

"I have been in ill-luck for several days," said Danglars, "and I have heard nothing but bad news."

"Ah, indeed!" said Monte Cristo. "Have you had another fall at the Bourse?"

"No; I am safe for a few days at least. I am only annoyed about a bankrupt of Trieste."

"Really? Does it happen to be Jacopo Manfredi?"

"Exactly so: imagine a man who has transacted business with me for I do not know how long, to the amount of eight or nine hundred thousand francs during the year. Never a mistake or delay,—a fellow who paid like a prince. Well, I was a million in advance with him, and now my fine Jacopo Manfredi suspends payment!"

"Really?"

"It is an unheard-of fatality. I draw upon him for 600,000 francs, my bills are returned unpaid, and, more than that, I hold bills of exchange signed by him to the value of 400,000 francs, payable at his correspondent's in Paris at the end of this month. To-day is the 30th. I present them; but my correspondent has disappeared. This, with my Spanish affairs, made a pretty end to the month."

"Then you really lost by that affair in Spain?"

"Yes; only 700,000 francs out of my cash-box—nothing more!"

"Why, how could you make such a mistake—such an old stager?"

"Oh, it is all my wife's fault. She dreamed Don Carlos had returned to Spain; she believes in dreams. It is magnetism, she says; and when she dreams a thing it is sure to happen, she assures me. On this conviction, I allow her to speculate; she has her bank and her stockbroker; she speculated and lost. It is true she speculates with her own money, not mine; nevertheless, you can understand that when 700,000 francs leave the wife's pocket, the husband always finds it out. But do you mean to say you have not heard of this? Why, the thing has made a tremendous noise."

"Yes, I heard it spoken of, but I did not know the details; and then no one can be more ignorant than I am of the affairs in the Bourse."

"Then you do not speculate?"

"I?—How could I speculate when I already have so much trouble in regulating my income. I should be obliged, besides my steward, to keep a clerk and a boy. But touching these

Spanish affairs, I think the baroness did not dream the whole of this entrance of Don Carlos. The papers said something about it, did they not? "

" Well, this is what puzzles me," replied Danglars; " the news of the return of Don Carlos was brought by telegraph."

" So that," said Monte Cristo, " you have lost nearly 1,700,000 francs this month."

" Not nearly, indeed; that is exactly my loss."

" *Diable!* " said Monte Cristo compassionately, " it is a hard blow for a third-rate fortune! "

" Third-rate," said Danglars, rather humbled, " what do you mean by that? "

" Certainly," continued Monte Cristo, " I make three assortments in fortunes—first-rate, second-rate, and third-rate fortunes. I call those first-rate which are composed of treasures one possesses under one's hand, such as mines, lands, and funded property, in such states as France, Austria, and England, provided these treasures and property form a total of about a hundred millions; I call those second-rate fortunes, gained by manufacturing enterprises, joint-stock companies, viceroyalties, and principalities, not drawing more than 1,500,000 francs, the whole forming a capital of about fifty millions; finally, I call those third-rate fortunes, composed of a fluctuating capital, dependent upon the will of others, or upon chances which a bankruptcy involves or a false telegraph shakes, such as banks, speculations of the day— in fact, all operations under the influence of greater or less mischances, the whole bringing in a real or fictitious capital of about fifteen millions. I think this is about your position, is it not? "

" Confound it, yes! " replied Danglars.

" The result, then, of six more such months as this would be to reduce the third-rate house to despair."

" Oh," said Danglars, becoming very pale, " how you are running on! "

" Let us imagine seven such months," continued Monte Cristo, in the same tone. " Tell me have you ever thought that seven times 1,700,000 francs make nearly twelve millions? No, you have not;—well, you are right, for if you indulged in such reflections, you would never risk your principal, which is to the speculator what the skin is to civilised man. We have our clothes, some more splendid than others,—this is our credit; but when a man dies he has only his skin; in the same way, on retiring from business, you have nothing but your real principal of about five or six millions, at the most; for third-rate fortunes are never more than the fourth of what they appear to be, like the locomotive on a railway, the size of which is magnified by the smoke and steam surrounding it. Well, out of the five or six millions, which form your real capital, you have just lost nearly two millions, which must, of course, in the same degree diminish your credit and fictitious fortune; to follow out my simile, your skin has been opened by bleeding, which, repeated three or four times, will cause death—so pay attention to it, M. Danglars. Do you want money? Do you wish me to lend you some? "

" What a bad calculator you are! " exclaimed Danglars, calling to his assistance all his philosophy and dissimulation. " I have made money at the same time by speculations which have succeeded. I have made up for the loss of blood by nutrition. I lost a battle in Spain, I have been defeated in Trieste, but my naval army in India will have taken some galleons, and my Mexican pioneers will have discovered some mine."

" Very good, very good! But the wound remains, and will reopen at the first loss."

" No, for I am only embarked in certainties," replied Danglars, with the air of a mountebank, sounding out his own praises; " to involve me, three governments must crumble to dust."

" So much the better, my dear M. Danglars," said Monte Cristo; " I see I was deceived, and that you belong to the class of second-rate fortunes."

" I think I may aspire to that honour," said Danglars, with a sickly smile. " But, while we are speaking of business," he added, pleased to find an opportunity of changing the subject, " tell me what I am to do for M. Cavalcanti."

" Give him money, if he is recommended to you, and the recommendation seems good."

" Excellent; he presented himself this morning with a bond of 40,000 francs, payable at sight, on you, signed by Busoni, and returned by you to me, with your endorsement—of course, I immediately counted him over the forty bank-notes."

Monte Cristo nodded his head in token of assent.

" But that is not all," continued Danglars; " he has opened an account with my house for his son."

" May I ask, how much he allows the young man? "

" Five thousand francs per month."

" Sixty thousand francs per year. I thought I was right in believing that Cavalcanti to be a stingy fellow. How can a young man live upon 5000 francs a month? "

" But you understand that if the young man should want a few thousands more——"

" Do not advance it; the father will never repay it; you do not know these ultramontane millionaires; they are regular misers. And by whom were they recommended to you? "

" Oh, by the house of Fenzi, one of the best in Florence."

" I do not mean to say you will lose, but, nevertheless, mind you hold to the terms of the agreement."

" Would you not trust the Cavalcanti? "

" I? oh, I would advance six millions on his signature. I was only speaking in reference to the second-rate fortunes we were mentioning just now."

" And with all this, how plain he is! I should never have taken him for anything more than a mere major."

" And you would have flattered him, for certainly, as you say, he has no manner. The first time I saw him he appeared to me like an old lieutenant who had grown mouldy beneath his epaulette. But all the Italians are the same; they are like old Jews when they are not glittering in Oriental splendour."

" The young man is better," said Danglars.

" Yes; a little nervous, perhaps, but, upon the whole, he appeared tolerable. I was uneasy about him."

" Why? "

" Because you met him at my house, just after his introduction into the world, as they told me. He has been travelling with a very severe tutor, and had never been to Paris before."

" Ah, I believe noblemen marry amongst themselves, do they not? " asked Danglars carelessly; " they like to unite their fortunes."

" It is usual, certainly; but Cavalcanti is an original who does nothing like other people. I cannot help thinking he has brought his son to France to choose a wife."

" Do you think so? "

" I am sure of it."

" And you have heard his fortune mentioned? "

" Nothing else was talked of; only some said he was worth millions, and others that he did not possess a farthing."

" And what is your opinion? "

" I ought not to influence you, because it is only my own personal impression."

" Well, and it is that——"

" My opinion is, that all these old *podestas*, these ancient *condottieri*, for the Cavalcanti have commanded armies and governed provinces,—my opinion, I say, is, that they have buried their millions in corners, the secret of which they have only transmitted to their eldest sons, who have done the same from generation to generation, and the proof of this is seen in their yellow and dry appearance, like the florins of the republic, which, from being constantly gazed upon have become reflected in them. Oh, as I told you before, I think the good man very close!"

"Come, you do not flatter him."

"I scarcely know him; I think I have seen him three times in my life; all I know relating to him is through Busoni and himself. He was telling me this morning that, tired of letting his property lie dormant in Italy, which is a dead nation, he wished to find a method, either in France or England, of multiplying his millions; but remember, that though I place great confidence in Busoni, I am not responsible for this."

"Never mind; accept my thanks for the client you have sent me; it is a fine name to inscribe on my lists, and my cashier was quite proud of it when I explained to him who the Cavalcanti were. By the way, this is merely a simple question, when these kind of people marry their sons, do they give them any fortune?"

"Oh, that depends upon circumstances. I know an Italian prince, rich as a gold-mine, one of the noblest families in Tuscany, who, when his sons married according to his wish, gave them millions, and when they married against his consent, merely allowed them thirty crowns a month. Should Andrea marry according to his father's views, he will, perhaps, give him one, two, or three millions. For example, supposing it were the daughter of a banker, he might take an interest in the house of the father-in-law of his son; then again, if he disliked his choice, the major takes the key, double-locks his coffer, and Master Andrea would be obliged to live like the son of a Parisian family, by shuffling cards or rattling the dice."

"Ah! that boy will find out some Bavarian or Peruvian princess; he will want a crown and an immense fortune."

"No; these grand lords on the other side of the Alps frequently marry into plain families; like Jupiter, they like to cross the race. But do you wish to marry Andrea, my dear M. Danglars, that you are asking so many questions?"

"Ma foi!" said Danglars, "it would not be a bad speculation I fancy, and you know I am a speculator."

"You are not thinking of Madamoiselle Danglars, I hope; you would not like poor Andrea to have his throat cut by Albert?"

"Albert!" repeated Danglars, shrugging his shoulders; "ah, yes! he would care very little about it, I think."

"But he is betrothed to your daughter, I believe?"

"Certainly, M. de Morcerf and I have talked about this marriage, but Madame de Morcerf and Albert——"

" You do not mean to say that it would not be a good match? "

" Indeed, I imagine that Mademoiselle Danglars is as good as M. de Morcerf."

" Mademoiselle Danglars' fortune will be great, no doubt, especially if the telegraph should not make any more mistakes."

" Oh, I do not mean her fortune only; but tell me——"

" What? "

" Why did you not invite M. and Madame de Morcerf to your dinner? "

" I did so, but he excused himself on account of Madame de Morcerf being obliged to go to Dieppe for the benefit of sea air."

" Yes, yes," said Danglars, laughing, " it would do her a great deal of good."

" Why so? "

" Because it is the air she always breathed in her youth."

Monte Cristo took no notice of this ill-natured remark.

" But still if Albert be not so rich as Mademoiselle Danglars," said the count, " you must allow that he has a fine name? "

" So he has; but I like mine as well."

" Certainly, your name is popular, and does honour to the title they intended to adorn you with; but you are too intelligent not to know that according to a prejudice, too firmly rooted to be exterminated, a nobility which dates back five centuries is worth more than one that can only reckon twenty years."

" And for this very reason," said Danglars, with a smile, which he tried to make sardonic, " I prefer M. Andrea Cavalcanti to M. Albert de Morcerf."

" Still, I should not think the Morcerfs would yield to the Cavalcanti? "

" The Morcerfs!—Stay, my dear count," said Danglars, " you are a clever man, are you not? "

" I think so."

" And you understand heraldry? "

" A little."

" Well, look at my coat-of-arms; it is worth more than Morcerf's."

" Why so? "

" Because, though I am not a baron by birth, my real name is, at least, Danglars."

" Well, what then? "

" While his name is not Morcerf."

" How!—not Morcerf? "

" Not the least in the world."

" Go on."

" I have been made a baron, so that I actually am one; he made himself a count, so that he is not one at all."

" Impossible! "

" Listen, my dear count; M. de Morcerf has been my friend, or rather my acquaintance, during the last thirty years. You know I have made the most of my arms, though I never forgot my origin."

" A proof of great humility or great pride," said Monte Cristo.

" Well, when I was a clerk, Morcerf was a mere fisherman."

" And then he was called——"

" Fernand."

" Only Fernand? "

" Fernand Mondego."

" You are sure? "

" *Pardieu!* I have bought enough fish of him to know his name."

" Then, why did you think of giving your daughter to him? "

" Because Fernand and Danglars, being both *parvenus*, both having become noble, both rich, are about equal in worth, excepting that there have been certain things mentioned of him that were never said of me."

" What? "

" Oh, nothing! "

" Ah, yes; what you tell me recalls to mind something about the name of Fernand Mondego. I have heard that name in Greece."

" In conjunction with the affairs of Ali Pacha? "

" Exactly so."

" This is the mystery," said Danglars; " I acknowledge I would have given anything to find it out."

" It would be very easy if you much wished it."

" How so? "

" Probably, you have some correspondent in Greece? "

" I should think so."

" At Janina? "

" Everywhere."

" Well, write to your correspondent in Janina, and ask him what part was played by a Frenchman named Fernand Mondego in the catastrophe of Ali Tebelen."

" You are right," exclaimed Danglars, rising quickly: " I will write to-day."

Danglars rushed out of the room, and made but one leap into his *coupé*.

68

The Office of the Procureur du Roi

LET us leave the banker driving his horses at their fullest speed, and follow Madame Danglars in her morning excursion. We have said that, at half-past twelve o'clock, Madame Danglars had ordered her horses, and had left home in the carriage. She directed her course towards the Faubourg Saint-Germain, went down the Rue de Seine, and stopped at the Passage du Pont-Neuf. She descended and crossed the passage. She was very plainly dressed, as would be the case with a woman of taste walking in the morning. At the Rue Guénégaud she called a *fiacre*, and directed the driver to drive to the Rue de Harlay.

As soon as she was seated in the coach, she drew from her pocket a very thick black veil, which she tied on to her straw bonnet; she then replaced the bonnet, and saw with pleasure, in a little pocket mirror, that her white complexion and brilliant eyes were alone visible. The *fiacre* crossed the Pont-Neuf and entered the Rue de Harlay by the Place Dauphine; the driver was paid as the door opened, and, stepping lightly up the stairs, Madame Danglars soon reached the Salle des Pas-Perdus. There was a great press of people in M. de Villefort's antechamber, but Madame Danglars had no occasion even to pronounce her name; the instant she appeared, the door-keeper rose, came to her and asked whether she was not the person with whom M. le Procureur du Roi had made an appointment, and, on her affirmative answer being given, he conducted her by a private passage to M. de Villefort's office. The magistrate was seated in an arm-chair, writing, with his back towards the door; he heard it open and the door-keeper pronounce the words, " Walk in, madame! " and then reclose it, without moving; but no sooner had the man's footsteps ceased, than he started up, drew the bolts, closed the curtains, and examined every corner of the room. Then, when he had assured himself that he could neither be seen nor heard, and was, consequently, relieved of doubts, he said:

" Thanks, madame,—thanks for your punctuality "; and he offered a chair to Madame Danglars, which she accepted, for her heart beat so violently that she felt nearly suffocated.

" It is a long time, madame," said the procureur du roi,

describing a half-circle with his chair, so as to place himself directly opposite to Madame Danglars,—"it is a long time since I had the pleasure of speaking alone with you, and I regret that we have only now met to enter upon a painful conversation."

"Nevertheless, sir, you see I have answered your first appeal; although, certainly, the conversation must be much more painful for me than for you. When I look at this room, whence so many guilty creatures have departed trembling and ashamed,—when I look at that chair, before which I now sit trembling and ashamed, —oh, it requires all my reason to convince me that I am not a very guilty woman and you a menacing judge."

Villefort dropped his head and sighed.

"And I," he said, "I feel that my place is not in the judge's seat, but on the prisoner's stool."

"You?" said Madame Danglars.

"Yes, I."

"I think, sir, you exaggerate your situation," said Madame Danglars, whose beautiful eyes sparkled for a moment. "The paths of which you were just speaking have been traced by all young men of ardent imaginations. Besides the pleasure, there is always remorse, from the indulgence of our passions; and, after all, what have you men to fear from all this; the world excuses, and notoriety ennobles you?"

"Madame," replied Villefort, "you know that I am no hypocrite, or, at least, that I never deceive without a reason. If my brow be severe, it is because many misfortunes have clouded it; if my heart be petrified, it is that it might sustain the blows it has received. I was not so in my youth; I was not so on the night of the betrothal, when we were all seated round a table in the Rue de Cours at Marseilles. But since then everything has changed in and about me; I am accustomed to brave difficulties, and, in the conflict, to crush those who, by their own free will or by chance, voluntarily or involuntarily, interfere with me in my career. It is generally the case, that what we most ardently desire is as ardently withheld from us by those who wish to obtain it, or from whom we attempt to snatch it. Thus, the greater number of a man's errors come before him disguised under the specious form of necessity; then, after error has been committed in a moment of excitement, of delirium, or of fear, we see that we might have avoided and escaped it. The means we might have used, which we in our blindness could not see, then seem simple and easy, and we say, 'Why did I not do this instead of that?' Women, on the contrary, are rarely tormented with remorse; for the decision does not come from you,—your misfortunes are generally imposed upon you, and your faults the result of others' crimes."

"In any case, sir, you will allow," replied Madame Danglars, "that, even if the fault were alone mine, I last night received a severe punishment for it."

"Poor thing," said Villefort, pressing her hand, "it was too severe for your strength, for you were twice overwhelmed, and yet——"

"Well?"

"Well, I must tell you. Collect all your courage, for you have not yet heard all."

"Ah!" exclaimed Madame Danglars, alarmed, "what is there more to hear?"

"You only look back to the past; and it is, indeed, bad enough. Well, picture to yourself a future more gloomy still,—certainly frightful,—perhaps sanguinary."

The baroness knew how calm Villefort naturally was, and his present excitement frightened her so much, that she opened her mouth to scream, but the sound died in her throat.

"How has this terrible past been recalled?" cried Villefort: "how is it that it has escaped from the depths of the tomb and the recesses of our hearts, where it was buried, to visit us now, like a phantom?"

"Alas!" said Hermine, "doubtless it is chance."

"Chance!" replied Villefort; "no, no, madame, there is no such thing as chance."

"Oh, yes; has not a fatal chance revealed all this? Was it not by chance the Count of Monte Cristo bought this house? Was it not by chance he caused the earth to be dug? Is it not by chance that the unfortunate child was disinterred under the trees?—that poor innocent offspring of mine, which I never even kissed, but for whom I wept many, many tears. Ah! my heart clung to the count when he mentioned the dear spoil found beneath the flowers."

"Well, no, madame; this is the terrible news I have to tell you," said Villefort, in a hollow voice. "No, nothing was found beneath the flowers; there was no child disinterred,—no. You must not weep; no, you must not groan—you must tremble!"

"What can you mean?" asked Madame Danglars, shuddering.

"I mean that M. de Monte Cristo, digging underneath these trees, found neither skeleton nor chest, because neither of them was there."

"Neither of them there!" repeated Madame Danglars, fixing upon him her eyes, which, by their fearful dilation, indicated how much she was alarmed.

" No," said Villefort, burying his face in his hands,—" no, a hundred times—no! "

" Then you did not bury the poor child there, sir? Why did you deceive me? Where did you place it? tell me—where? "

" There! But listen to me—listen—and you will pity one who has for twenty years alone borne the heavy burden of the grief I am about to reveal, without casting the least portion upon you."

" Oh, you frighten me! But speak, I will listen."

" You recollect that sad night, when you were half expiring on that bed in the red damask room, while I, scarcely less agitated than you, awaited your delivery. The child was born—was given to me—without movement, without breath, without voice; we thought it dead."

Madame Danglars moved rapidly, as though she would spring from her chair; but Villefort stopped, and clasped his hands as if to implore her attention.

" We thought it dead," he repeated; " I placed it in the chest, which was to take the place of a coffin; I descended to the garden: I dug a hole, and then flung it down in haste. Scarcely had I covered it with mould, when the arm of the Corsican was stretched towards me; I saw a shadow rise, and, at the same time, a flash of light. I felt pain; I wished to cry out, but an icy shiver ran through my veins and stifled my voice. I fell lifeless, and fancied myself killed. Never shall I forget your sublime courage, when, having returned to consciousness, I dragged myself to the foot of the stairs, where, expiring yourself, you came to meet me. We were obliged to keep silent upon the dreadful catastrophe. You had the fortitude to regain the house, assisted by your nurse. A duel was the pretext for my wound. Though we scarcely expected it, our secret remained in our own keeping alone. I was taken to Versailles; for three months I struggled with death; at last, as I seemed to cling to life, I was ordered to the south. My recovery lasted six months; I never heard you mentioned, and I did not dare inquire for you. When I returned to Paris, I learned that, widow of M. de Nargonne, you had married M. Danglars.

" What had been the subject of my thoughts ever since consciousness had returned to me? Always the same,—always the child's corpse, which, every night in my dreams, rising from the earth, fixed itself above the grave with a menacing look and gesture. I inquired immediately on my return to Paris; the house had not been inhabited since we left it, but it had just been let for nine years. I found the tenant. I pretended that I disliked the idea of a house belonging to my wife's father and mother passing into the hands of strangers. I offered to pay them for yielding up the lease; they demanded 6000 francs. I would have given 10,000,—I would have given 20,000. I had the money with me; I made the tenant sign the cancelling deed; and when I had obtained what I so much wanted, I galloped to Auteuil. No one had entered the house since I had left it. It was five o'clock in the afternoon; I ascended into the red room, and waited for night. There all the thoughts which had disturbed me during my year of constant agony occurred with double force. The Corsican, who had declared the *vendetta* against me, who had followed me from Nîmes to Paris, who had hid himself in the garden, who had struck me, had seen me dig the grave, had seen me inter the child, he might become acquainted with your person; nay, he might even then have known it. Would he not one day make you pay for keeping this terrible secret? Would it not be a sweet revenge for him when he found I had not died from the blow of his dagger? It was therefore necessary, before everything else, and at all risks, that I should cause all traces of the past to disappear,—that I should destroy every material vestige; too much reality would always remain in my recollection. It was for this I had annulled the lease,—it was for this I had come,—it was for this I was waiting. Night arrived; I allowed it to become quite dark.

"Listen, Hermine! I consider myself as brave as most men; but when I drew from my breast the little key of the staircase which I had found in my coat,—that little key we both used to cherish so much, which you wished to have fastened to a golden ring,—when I opened the door, and saw the pale moon shedding a long stream of white light on the spiral staircase like a spectre, I leaned against the wall, and nearly shrieked. I seemed to be going mad. At last I mastered my agitation. I descended the staircase step by step; the only thing I could not conquer was a strange trembling in my knees. I grasped the railings; if I had relaxed my hold for a moment, I should have fallen. I reached the lower door. Outside this door a spade was placed against the wall; I took it and advanced towards the thicket. I had provided myself with a dark lantern. In the middle of the lawn I stopped to light it, then I continued my path. It was the end of November; all the freshness of the garden had disappeared, the trees were nothing more than skeletons with their long bony arms, and the dead leaves sounded on the gravel under my feet. My terror overcame me to such a degree as I approached the thicket, that I took a pistol from my pocket and armed myself. I fancied continually that I saw the figure of the Corsican between the branches. I examined the thicket with my dark lantern; it was empty. I cast my eyes all round; I was indeed alone; no noise disturbed the silence of the night but the owl, whose piercing cry seemed as if calling up the phantoms of the night. I tied my lantern to a forked branch I had remarked a year before at the precise spot where I stopped to dig the hole. The grass had grown very thickly there during the summer, and when autumn arrived, no one had been there to mow it. Still one place less covered attracted my attention; it evidently was there I had turned up the ground. I returned to work. The hour, then, for which I had been waiting during the last year had at length arrived. How I worked; how I hoped; how I sounded every piece of turf, thinking to find some resistance to my spade, but no,—I found nothing, though I had made a hole twice as large as the first. I thought I had been deceived, had mistaken the spot; I turned round; I looked at the trees; I tried to recall the details which had struck me at the time. I recollected that I was stabbed just as I was trampling the ground to fill up the hole; while doing so, I had leaned against a false ebony-tree; behind me was an artificial rock, intended to serve as a resting-place for persons walking in the garden; in falling, my hand relaxing its hold of the tree, felt the coldness of this stone. On my right I saw the tree, behind me the rock. I stood in the same attitude, and threw myself down; I rose, and again began digging and enlarging the hole; still I found nothing—nothing,—the chest was no longer there."

" The chest no longer there ! " murmured Madame Danglars, choking with fear.

" Think not I contented myself with this one effort," continued Villefort. " No, I searched the whole thicket. I thought the assassin, having discovered the chest, and supposing it to be a treasure, had intended carrying it off; but, perceiving his error, had dug another hole, and deposited it; but there was nothing. Then the idea struck me that he had not taken these precautions, and had simply thrown it in a corner. In the last case I must wait for daylight to resume my search. I regained the room and waited."

" Oh, Heaven! "

" When daylight dawned, I went down again. My first visit was to the thicket. I hoped to find some traces which had escaped me in the dark. I had turned up the earth over a surface of more than twenty feet square, and a depth of two feet. A labourer would not have done in a day what occupied me an hour. But I could find nothing—absolutely nothing. Then I renewed the search; supposing it had been thrown aside, it would probably be on the path which led to the little gate; but this examination was as useless as the first; and, with a bursting heart, I returned to the thicket, which now contained no hope for me."

"Oh," cried Madame Danglars, "it was enough to drive you mad."

"I hoped for a moment that it might," said Villefort; "but that happiness was denied me. However, recovering my strength and my ideas, 'Why,' said I, 'should that man have carried away the corpse?'"

"But you said," replied Madame Danglars, "he would require it as a proof."

"Ah, no, madame, that could not be, dead bodies are not kept a year; they are shown to a magistrate, and the evidence is taken; now nothing of the kind has happened."

"What then?" asked Hermine, trembling violently.

"Something more terrible, more fatal, more alarming for us; the child was, perhaps, alive, and the assassin may have saved it."

Madame Danglars uttered a piercing cry, and, seizing Villefort's hands, exclaimed:

"My child was alive!" said she; "you buried my child alive, sir! You were not certain my child was dead, and you buried it! Ah——"

Madame Danglars had risen, and stood before the procureur, whose hands she wrung in her feeble grasp.

"I know not; I merely suppose so, as I might suppose anything else," replied Villefort, with a look so fixed, it indicated that his powerful mind was on the verge of despair and madness.

"Ah, my child! my poor child!" cried the baroness, falling on her chair, and stifling her sobs in her handkerchief.

"You understand, then, that if it were so," said Villefort, rising in his turn, and approaching the baroness, to speak to her in a lower tone, "we are lost; this child lives, and someone knows it lives; someone is in possession of our secret; and since Monte Cristo speaks before us of a child disinterred, when the child could not be found, it is he who is in possession of our secret."

"Just God! avenging God!" murmured Madame Danglars. Villefort's only answer was a species of groan.

"But the child—the child, sir?" repeated the agitated mother.

"How have I searched for him!" replied Villefort, wringing his hands; "how have I called him in my long sleepless nights! How have I longed for royal wealth to purchase a million of secrets from a million of men, and to find mine among them. At last, one day when, for the hundredth time, I took up my spade, I asked myself again and again what the Corsican could have done with the child. A child encumbers a fugitive; perhaps, on perceiving it was still alive, he had thrown it into the river."

" Impossible! " cried Madame Danglars; " a man may murder another out of revenge, but he would not deliberately drown a child."

" Perhaps," continued Villefort, " he had put it in the foundling hospital? "

" Oh, yes, yes! " cried the baroness; " my child is there! "

" I ran to the hospital, and learned that the same night—the night of the 20th September—a child had been brought there, wrapped in part of a fine linen napkin, purposely torn in half. This portion of the napkin was marked with half a baron's crown and the letter H."

" Truly, truly," said Madame Danglars, " all my linen is marked thus; Monsieur de Nargonne was a baronet, and my name is Hermine. Thank God, my child was not then dead! Oh, where is it? "

Villefort shrugged his shoulders.

" Do I know? " said he; " and do you believe that if I knew I would relate to you all its trials and all its adventures as would a dramatist or a novel-writer? Alas! no, I know not. A woman, about six months after, came to claim it with the other half of the napkin. This woman gave all the requisite particulars, and it was intrusted to her."

" But you should have inquired for the woman; you should have traced her."

" And what do you think I did? I feigned a criminal process, and employed all the most acute bloodhounds and skilful agents in search of her. They traced her to Châlons; and there they lost her."

" They lost her? "

" Yes, for ever."

Madame Danglars had listened to this recital with a sigh, a tear, or a shriek, for every circumstance.

" And that is all? " said she; " and you stopped there? "

" Oh, no! " said Villefort; " I never ceased to search and to inquire. However, the last two or three years I had allowed myself some respite. But now I will begin with more perseverance and fury than ever, since fear urges me, not my conscience."

" But," replied Madame Danglars, " the Count of Monte Cristo can know nothing, or he would not seek our society as he does."

" Oh, the wickedness of man is very great," said Villefort, " since it surpasses the goodness of God. Did you observe that man's eyes while he was speaking to us? "

" No."

" But have you ever watched him carefully? "

" Doubtless he is capricious, but that is all; one thing alone struck me; of all the exquisite things he placed before us, he touched nothing; I might have suspected he was poisoning us."

" And you see you would have been deceived; believe me, that man has other projects. For that reason I wished to see you, to speak to you, to warn you against everyone, but especially against him. Tell me," cried Villefort, fixing his eyes more steadfastly on her than he had ever done before, " did you ever reveal to any one our connection? "

" Never, to any one! "

" You understand me? " replied Villefort affectionately; " when I say any one—pardon my urgency—to any one living, I mean."

" Yes, yes, I understand very well," ejaculated the baroness; " never, I swear to you."

" Were you ever in the habit of writing in the evening what had transpired in the morning? Do you keep a journal? "

" No; my life has been passed in frivolity; I wish to forget it myself."

" Do you talk in your sleep? "

" I sleep soundly, like a child; do you not remember? " The colour mounted to the baroness's face, and Villefort turned awfully pale.

" It is true," said he, in so low a tone that he could hardly be heard.

" Well? " said the baroness.

" Well, I understand what I now have to do," replied Villefort. " In less than one week from this time I will ascertain who this M. de Monte Cristo is, whence he comes, where he goes, and why he speaks in our presence of children which have been disinterred in a garden."

Villefort pronounced these words with an accent which would have made the count shudder had he heard him. Then he pressed the hand the baroness reluctantly gave him, and led her respectfully back to the door.

Madame Danglars returned in another hackney-coach to the passage, on the other side of which she found her carriage, and her coachman sleeping peacefully on his box while waiting for her.

69

A Summer Ball

THE same day, during the interview of Madame Danglars with the procureur, a travelling carriage entered the Rue du Helder, passed through the gateway of No. 27, and stopped in the yard. In a moment the door was opened, and Madame de Morcerf alighted, leaning on her son's arm. Albert soon left her, ordered his horses, and having arranged his toilet, drove to the Champs Elysées, to the house of Monte Cristo. The count received him with his habitual smile. It was a strange thing that no one ever appeared to advance a step in that man's favour. Those who would, as it were, force a passage to his heart, found an impassable barrier. Morcerf, who ran towards him with open arms, was chilled as he drew near, in spite of the friendly smile, and simply held out his hand.

Monte Cristo shook it coldly, according to his invariable practice.

" Here I am, dear count."

" Welcome home again."

" I arrived an hour since."

" From Dieppe? "

" No, from Tréport."

" Indeed! "

" And I am directly come to see you."

" That is extremely kind of you," said Monte Cristo, with a tone of perfect indifference.

" And what is the news? "

" You should not ask a stranger, a foreigner, for news."

" I know it; but in asking for news, I mean, have you done anything for me? "

" Had you commissioned me? " said Monte Cristo, feigning uneasiness.

" Come, come! " said Albert, " do not assume so much indifference. It is said, sympathy travels rapidly; and when at Tréport, I felt the electric shock; you have either been working for me or thinking of me."

" Possibly," said Monte Cristo, " I have indeed thought of you; but the magnetic wire I was guiding acted, indeed, without my knowledge."

" Indeed! Pray tell me how it happened? "

" Willingly. M. Danglars dined with me."

" I know it; to avoid meeting him, my mother and I left town."

" But he met here M. Andrea Cavalcanti."

" Your Italian prince? "

" Not so fast; M. Andrea only calls himself count."

" Calls himself, do you say? "

" Yes, calls himself."

" Is he not a count? "

" What can I know of him? He calls himself so. I, of course, give him the same title, and everyone else does the same."

" What a strange man you are! What next? You said M. Danglars dined here? "

" Yes, with Count Cavalcanti, the marquis his father, Madame Danglars, M. and Madame de Villefort,—charming people,— M. Debray, Maximilian Morrel, and M. de Château-Renaud."

" Did they speak of me? "

" Not a word."

" So much the worse."

" Why so? I thought you wished them to forget you? "

" If they did not speak of me, I am sure they thought about me, and I am in despair."

" How will that affect you, since Mademoiselle Danglars was not among the number here who thought of you? Truly she might have thought of you at home."

" I have no fear of that; or if she did, it was only in the same way in which I think of her."

" Touching sympathy! So you hate each other? " said the count.

" Listen," said Morcerf; " if Mademoiselle Danglars were disposed to take pity on my supposed martyrdom on her account, and would dispense with all matrimonial formalities between our two families, I am ready to agree to the arrangement. In a word, Mademoiselle Danglars would make a charming mistress, but a wife, *diable!* "

" And this," said Monte Cristo, " is your opinion of your intended spouse? "

" Yes; it is rather unkind, I acknowledge, but it is true. But as this dream cannot be realised, since Mademoiselle Danglars must become my lawful wife, live perpetually with me, sing to me, compose verses and music within ten paces of me, and that for my whole life, it frightens me. One may forsake a mistress, but a wife, good heavens! there she must always be; and to marry Mademoiselle Danglars would be awful."

" You are difficult to please, viscount."

" Yes, for I often wish for what is impossible."

" What is that? "

" To find such a wife as my father found."

Monte Cristo turned pale, and looked at Albert, while playing with some magnificent pistols.

" Your father was fortunate, then? " said he.

" You know my opinion of my mother, count; look at her, still beautiful, witty, better than ever. For any other son to have accompanied his mother four days at Tréport, it would have been a complaisance, an unprofitable toil; while I return, more contented, more peaceful,—shall I say more poetic?—than if I had taken Queen Mab or Titania as my companion."

" That is an overwhelming perfection, and you would make everyone vow to live a single life."

" Such are my reasons for not liking to marry Mademoiselle Danglars. Thus I shall rejoice when Mademoiselle Eugénie perceives I am but a pitiful atom, with scarcely as many hundred thousand francs as she has millions."

Monte Cristo smiled.

" One plan occurred to me," continued Albert. " Franz likes all that is eccentric. I tried to make him fall in love with Mademoiselle Danglars; but in spite of four letters, written in the most alluring style, he invariably answered, ' My eccentricity may be great, but it will not make me break my promise.' "

" That is what I call devoted friendship, to recommend to another one whom you would not marry yourself."

Albert smiled.

" *Apropos*," continued he, " Franz is coming soon, but it will not interest you; you dislike him, I think? "

" I? " said Monte Cristo; " my dear viscount, how have you discovered that I did not like M. Franz? I like everyone."

" And you include me in the expression everyone—many thanks! "

" Let us not mistake," said Monte Cristo; " I love everyone as God commands us to love our neighbour, as Christians, but I thoroughly hate but a few. Let us return to M. Franz d'Epinay. Did you say he was coming? "

" Yes; summoned by M. de Villefort, who is apparently as anxious to get Mademoiselle Valentine married as M. Danglars is to see Mademoiselle Eugénie settled. It must be a very, irksome office to be the father of a grown-up daughter; it seems to make them feverish, and to raise their pulse to ninety degrees until they get rid of them."

" But M. d'Epinay, unlike you, bears his misfortune patiently."

" Still more, he talks seriously about the matter, puts on a white cravat, and speaks of his family. He entertains a very high opinion of M. and Madame de Villefort."

" Which they deserve, do they not? "

" I believe they do. M. de Villefort has always passed for a severe, but a just man."

" There is, then, one," said Monte Cristo, " whom you do not condemn like poor Danglars? "

" Because I am not compelled to marry his daughter, perhaps," replied Albert, laughing.

" Indeed, my dear sir," said Monte Cristo, " you are revoltingly foppish."

" I foppish! how do you mean? "

" Yes; pray take a cigar, and cease to defend yourself, and to struggle to escape marrying Mademoiselle Danglars. Let things take their course; perhaps you may not have to retract."

" Bah! " said Albert, staring.

" Doubtless, M. le Vicomte, you will not be taken by force; and seriously, do you wish to break off your engagement? "

" I would give a hundred thousand francs to be able to do so."

" Then make yourself quite happy. M. Danglars would give double that sum to attain the same end."

" Am I, indeed, so happy? " said Albert, who still could not prevent an almost imperceptible cloud passing across his brow. " But, my dear count, has M. Danglars any reason? "

" Ah! there is your proud and selfish nature. You would expose the self-love of another with a hatchet, but you shrink if your own is attacked with a needle."

" But yet, M. Danglars appeared——"

" Delighted with you, was he not? Well, he is a man of bad taste, and is still more enchanted with another. I know not whom: study and judge for yourself."

" Thank you, I understand. But my mother—no, not my mother, I mistake—my father intends giving a ball."

" A ball at this season? "

" Summer balls are fashionable."

" If they were not, the countess has only to wish it, and they would become so."

" You are right; you know they are unmixed balls; those who remain in Paris in July must be true Parisians. Will you take charge of our invitation to Messieurs Cavalcanti? "

" When will it take place? "

" On Saturday."

" M. Cavalcanti's father will be gone."

" But the son will be here; will you invite young M. Cavalcanti? "

" I do not know him, viscount."

" You do not know him? "

" No, I had never seen him until a few days since, and am not responsible for him."

" But you receive him at your house? "

" That is another thing; he was recommended to me by a good abbé, who may be deceived. Give him a direct invitation, but do not ask me to present him. If he were afterwards to marry Mademoiselle Danglars, you would accuse me of intrigue, and would be challenging me; besides, I may not be there myself."

" Where? "

" At your ball."

" Why should you not be there? "

" Because you have not yet invited me."

" But I come expressly for that purpose."

" You are very kind, but I may be prevented."

" If I tell you one thing, you will be so amiable as to set aside all impediments."

" Tell me what it is."

" My mother begs you to come."

" The Countess de Morcerf? " said Monte Cristo, starting.

" Ah, count," said Albert, " I assure you Madame de Morcerf speaks freely to me, and if you have not felt those sympathetic fibres of which I spoke just now thrill within you, you must be entirely devoid of them, for during the last four days we have spoken of no one else."

" You have talked of me? "

" Yes; that is your privilege, being a living problem! "

" Then I am, also, a problem to your mother? I should have thought her too reasonable to be led by imagination."

" A problem, my dear count, for everyone—for my mother as well as others; much studied, but not solved, you still remain an enigma, do not fear. My mother is only astonished that you remain so long unsolved. I believe, while the Countess G——takes you for Lord Ruthven, my mother imagines you to be Cagliostro or Count Saint-Germain.* The first opportunity you have, confirm her in her opinion; it will be easy for you, as you have the philosophy of the one and the wit of the other."

" I thank you for the warning," said the count; " I shall endeavour to be prepared for all suppositions."

" You will, then, come on Saturday? "

" Yes, since Madame de Morcerf invites me."

" You are very kind."

" Will M. Danglars be there? "

" He has already been invited by my father. We shall try to persuade the great d'Aguesseau,* M. de Villefort, to come, but have not much hope of seeing him."

" ' Never despair,' says the proverb."

" Do you dance, count? "

" I dance? "

" Yes, you; it would not be astonishing.

" That is very well before one is above forty. No, I do not dance, but I like to see others. Does Madame de Morcerf dance? "

" Never; you can talk to her, she so delights in your conversation."

" Indeed! "

" Yes, truly; and I assure you, you are the only man of whom I have heard her speak with interest."

Albert rose, and took his hat; the count conducted him to the door.

" I have one thing to reproach myself with," said he, stopping Albert on the steps.

" What is it? "

" I have spoken to you indiscreetly about Danglars."

" On the contrary, speak to me always in the same strain about him."

" That is enough. *Apropos*, when do you expect M. d'Epinay? "

" Five or six days hence at the latest."

" And when is he to be married? "

" Immediately on the arrival of M. and Madame de Saint-Méran."

" Bring him to see me. Although you say I do not like him, I assure you I shall be happy to see him."

" I will obey your orders, my lord."

" Good-bye."

" Until Saturday, when I may expect you, may I not? "

" Yes, I promised you."

The count watched Albert waving his hand to him. When he had mounted his phaeton, Monte Cristo turned, and seeing Bertuccio, " What news? " said he.

" She went to the Palais," replied the steward.

" Did she stay long there? "

" An hour and a half."

" Did she return home? "

" Directly."

" Well, my dear Bertuccio," said the count, " I now advise you to go in quest of the little estate I spoke to you of in Normandy."

Bertuccio bowed, and as his wishes were in perfect harmony with the order he had received, he started the same evening.

70

The Inquiry

M. DE VILLEFORT kept the promise he had made to Madame Danglars to endeavour to find out how the Count of Monte Cristo had discovered the history of the house at Auteuil. He wrote the same day to M. de Boville, who, from having been an inspector of prisons, was promoted to a high office in the police, for the information he acquired; and the latter begged two days to ascertain exactly who would be most likely to give him full particulars.

At the end of the second day M. de Villefort received the following note:—

" The person called M. le Comte de Monte Cristo is an intimate acquaintance of Lord Wilmore, a rich foreigner, who is sometimes seen in Paris, and who is there at this moment: he is also known to the Abbé Busoni, a Sicilian priest, of high repute in the East, where he has done much good."

M. de Villefort replied by ordering the strictest inquiries to be made respecting these two persons; his orders were executed, and the following evening he received these details:—

" The abbé, who was in Paris for a month, inhabited a small house behind Saint-Sulpice, composed of one single storey over the ground-floor. Two rooms were on each floor, and he was the only tenant. The two lower rooms consisted of a dining-room, with a table, chairs, and sideboard of walnut-tree, and a wainscoted parlour, without ornaments, carpet, or timepiece. It was evident the abbé limited himself to objects of strict necessity.

" It was true the abbé preferred the sitting-room upstairs, which, being furnished with theological books and parchments, in which he delighted to bury himself during whole months, was more a library than a parlour. His valet looked at the visitors through a sort of wicket, and if their countenance was unknown to him or displeased him, he replied that M. l'Abbé was not in Paris,—an answer which satisfied most persons, because the abbé was known to be a great traveller. Besides, whether at home or not, whether in Paris or Cairo, the abbé always left something to give away, which the valet distributed through this wicket in his master's name.

" The other room near the library was a bedroom. A bed without curtains, four arm-chairs, and a couch, covered with yellow Utrecht velvet, composed, with a *prie-Dieu*, all its furniture.

" Lord Wilmore resided in Rue Fontaine-Saint-George. He was one of those English tourists who consume a large fortune in travelling. He hired the apartment in which he lived furnished, passed only a few hours in the day there, and rarely slept there. One of his peculiarities was never to speak a word of French, which he however wrote with great purity."

The day after these important particulars had been furnished to M. le Procureur, a man alighted from a carriage at the corner of the Rue Férou, and, rapping at an olive-green door, asked if the Abbé Busoni were within.

" No, he went out early this morning," replied the valet.

" I might not always be contented with that answer," replied the visitor, " for I come from one to whom everyone must be at home. But have the kindness to give the Abbé Busoni——"

" I told you he was not at home," repeated the valet.

" Then, on his return, give him that card and this sealed paper. Will he be at home at eight o'clock this evening? "

" Doubtless, unless he is at work, which is the same as if he were out."

" I will come again at that time," replied the visitor, who then retired.

At the appointed hour the same man returned in the same carriage, which, instead of stopping this time at the end of the Rue Férou, drove up to the green door. He knocked, and it was opened immediately to admit him.

From the signs of respect the valet paid him, he saw his note had produced a good effect.

" Is the abbé at home? " asked he.

" Yes; he is at work in his library, but he expects you, sir," replied the valet.

The stranger ascended a rough staircase, and before a table, whose surface was illumined by a lamp, whose light was concentrated by a large shade, whilst the rest of the apartment was in partial darkness, he perceived the abbé in a monk's dress, with a cowl on his head such as was used by learned men of the Middle Ages.

"Have I the honour of addressing the Abbé Busoni?" asked the visitor.

"Yes, sir," replied the abbé; "and are you the person whom M. de Boville, formerly an inspector of prisons, sends to me from the prefect of police?"

"Exactly, sir."

"One of the agents appointed to secure the safety of Paris?"

"Yes, sir," replied the stranger, with a slight hesitation, and blushing.

The abbé replaced the large spectacles, which covered, not only his eyes, but his temples, and sitting down, motioned to his visitor to do the same.

"I am at your service, sir," said the abbé, with a marked Italian accent.

"The mission with which I am charged, sir," replied the visitor, speaking with hesitation, "is a confidential one on the part of him who fulfils it, and him by whom he is employed."

The abbé bowed.

"Your probity," replied the stranger, "is so well known to the prefect, that he wishes, as a magistrate, to ascertain from you some particulars connected with the public safety; to ascertain which I am deputed to see you. It is hoped that no ties of friendship or humane consideration will induce you to conceal the truth."

"Provided, sir, the particulars you wish for do not interfere with my scruples or my conscience. I am a priest, sir, and the secrets of confession, for instance, must remain between me and God, and not between me and human justice."

"Do not alarm yourself, M. l'Abbé, we will duly respect your conscience."

At this moment the abbé pressed down his side of the shade, which raised it on the other, and threw a bright light on the face of the stranger, while his own remained obscured.

"Excuse me, abbé," said the envoy of the prefect of police, "but the light tries my eyes very much."

The abbé lowered the shade.

"Now, sir, I am listening—speak!"

"I will come at once to the point. Do you know the Count of Monte Cristo?"

"You mean M. Zaccone, I presume?"

"Zaccone!—is not his name Monte Cristo?"

" Monte Cristo is the name of an estate, or, rather, of a rock, and not a family name."

" Well, be it so—let us not dispute about words; and since M. de Monte Cristo and M. Zaccone are the same——"

" Absolutely the same."

" Let us speak of M. Zaccone."

" Agreed."

" I asked you if you knew him? "

" Extremely well."

" Who is he? "

" The son of a rich shipbuilder in Malta."

" I know that is the report, but, as you are aware, the police does not content itself with vague reports."

" However," replied the abbé, with an affable smile, " when that report is in accordance with the truth, everybody must believe it, the police as well as all the rest."

" Are you sure of what you assert? "

" What do you mean by that question? "

" Understand, sir, I do not in the least suspect your veracity; I ask you, are you certain of it? "

" I knew his father, M. Zaccone."

" Ah!—ah! "

" And when a child I often played with the son in the timber-yards."

" But whence does he derive the title of count? "

" You are aware that may be bought."

" In Italy? "

" Everywhere."

" And his immense riches, whence does he procure them? "

" They may not, perhaps, be so very great."

" How much do you suppose he possesses? "

" From one hundred and fifty to two hundred thousand livres per annum."

" That is reasonable," said the visitor; " I have heard he had three or four millions."

" Two hundred thousand per annum would make four millions of capital."

" But I was told he had four millions per annum? "

" That is not probable."

" Do you know his island of Monte Cristo? "

" Certainly; everyone who has returned from Palermo, from Naples, or from Rome to France, by sea, must know it, since he has passed close to it, and must have seen it."

" l am told it is a delightful place? "

" It is a rock."

" And why has the count bought a rock? "

" For the sake of being a count. In Italy one must have a county to be a count."

" You have, doubtless, heard the adventures of M. Zaccone's youth? "

" The father's? "

" No, the son's."

" I know nothing certain; at that period of his life, I lost sight of my young comrade."

" Did he go to war? "

" I think he entered the service."

" In what force? "

" In the navy."

" Are you not his confessor? "

" No, sir; I believe he is a Lutheran."

" A Lutheran? "

" I say, I believe such is the case, I do not affirm it; besides, liberty of conscience is established in France."

" Doubtless, and we are not now inquiring into his creed, but his actions; in the name of the prefect of police, I demand, what do you know of him? "

" He passes for a very charitable man. Our holy father, the Pope, has made him a knight of Jesus Christ for the services he rendered to the Christians in the East; he has five or six rings as testimonials from Eastern monarchs of his services."

" Does he wear them? "

" No, but he is proud of them; he is better pleased with rewards given to the benefactors of man than to his destroyers."

" He is a Quaker, then? "

" Exactly, he is a Quaker, with the exception of the peculiar dress."

" Has he any friends? "

" Yes, everyone who knows him is his friend."

" But has he any enemies? "

" One only."

" What is his name? "

" Lord Wilmore."

" Where is he? "

" He is in Paris just now."

" Can he give me any particulars? "

" Important ones; he was in India with Zaccone."

" Do you know his abode? "

" It is somewhere in la Chaussée d'Antin, but I know neither the street nor the number."

" Are you at variance with the Englishman? "

"I love Zaccone, and he hates him; we are consequently not friends."

"Do you think the Count of Monte Cristo had ever been in France before he made this visit to Paris?"

"To that question I can answer positively; no, sir, he had never been, because he applied to me six months since for the particulars he required, and as I knew not when I might again come to Paris, I recommended M. Cavalcanti to him."

"Andrea?"

"No, Bartolomeo, his father."

"Now, sir, I have but one more question to ask, and I charge you, in the name of honour, of humanity, and of religion, to answer me candidly."

"What is it, sir?"

"Do you know with what design M. de Monte Cristo purchased a house at Auteuil?"

"Certainly, for he told me."

"What was it, sir?"

"To make a lunatic asylum of it similar to that founded by the Count of Pisani at Palermo."

"Do you know that edifice?"

"I have heard of it."

"It is a magnificent institution."

Having said this, the abbé bowed to imply he wished to pursue his studies.

The visitor either understood the abbé's meaning, or had no more questions to ask; he rose, and the abbé accompanied him to the door.

"You are a great almsgiver," said the visitor, "and although you are said to be rich, I will venture to offer you something for your poor people; will you accept my offering?"

"I thank you, sir; I am only jealous of one thing, namely, that the relief I give should be entirely from my own resources."

"However——"

"My resolution, sir, is unchangeable: however, you have only to search for yourself, and you will find, alas! but too many objects upon whom to exercise your benevolence."

The abbé once more bowed as he opened the door, the stranger bowed and took his leave, and the carriage conducted him straight to the house of M. de Villefort.

An hour afterwards the carriage was again ordered, and this time it went to the Rue Fontaine-Saint-George, and stopped at No. 5, where Lord Wilmore lived.

The stranger had written to Lord Wilmore, requesting an interview, which the latter had fixed for ten o'clock. As the envoy of the prefect of police arrived ten minutes before ten, he was told that Lord Wilmore, who was precision and punctuality personified, was not yet come in, but that he would be sure to return as the clock struck. The visitor was introduced into the drawing-room, which was like all other furnished drawing-rooms. A mantelpiece, with two modern Sèvres vases, a timepiece representing Cupid with his bent bow, a looking-glass, with an engraving on each side, one representing Homer carrying his guide, the other Belisarius begging; a grayish paper, red and black tapestry —such was the appearance of Lord Wilmore's drawing-room. It was illuminated by lamps with ground-glass shades, which gave only a feeble light, as if out of consideration for the envoy's weak sight. After ten minutes' expectation the clock struck ten; at the fifth stroke the door opened, and Lord Wilmore appeared.

He was rather above the middle height, with thin, reddish whiskers, light complexion, and light hair, turning rather gray. He was dressed with all the English peculiarity, namely, in a blue coat with gilt buttons and high collar, in the fashion of 1811, a white kerseymere waistcoat, and nankeen pantaloons, three inches too short, but which were prevented by straps from slipping up to the knee. His first remark on entering was:

" You know, sir, I do not speak French? "

" I know you do not like to converse in our language," replied the envoy.

" But you may use it," replied Lord Wilmore; " I understand it."

" And I," replied the visitor, changing his idiom, " know enough of English to keep up the conversation. Do not put yourself to the slightest inconvenience."

" Heighho! " said Lord Wilmore, with that tone which is only known to natives of Great Britain.

The envoy presented his letter of introduction, which the latter read with English coolness; and having finished,—

" I understand," said he, " perfectly."

Then began the questions, which were similar to those which had been addressed to the Abbé Busoni. But as Lord Wilmore, in the character of the count's enemy, was less restrained in his answers, they were more numerous; he described the youth of Monte Cristo, who, he said, at ten years of age, entered the service of one of those petty sovereigns of India who make war on the English; it was there Wilmore had first met him and fought against him; in that war Zaccone had been taken prisoner, sent to England, put on the pontoon, whence he had escaped by swimming. Then began his travels, his duels, his passions, then came the insurrection in Greece, and he had served in the

Grecian ranks. While in that service he had discovered a silver mine in the mountains of Thessaly, but he had been careful to conceal it from everyone. After the battle of Navarino, when the Greek government was consolidated, he asked of King Otho a mining grant for that district, which was given him. Hence that immense fortune, which might, in Lord Wilmore's opinion, amount to one or two millions per annum, a precarious fortune, which might be momentarily lost by the failure of the mine.

"But," asked the visitor, "do you know why he came to France?"

"He is speculating in railways," said Lord Wilmore; "and being a clever theorist, he has discovered a new telegraph, which he is seeking to bring to perfection."

"How much does he spend yearly?" asked the prefect.

"Not more than five or six hundred francs," said Lord Wilmore; "he is a miser."

Hatred evidently inspired the Englishman, who, knowing no other reproach to bring on the count, accused him of avarice.

"Do you know his house at Auteuil?"

"Certainly."

"What do you know respecting it?"

"Do you wish to know why he bought it?"

"Yes."

"The count is a speculator, who will certainly ruin himself in experiments. He supposes there is in the neighbourhood of the house he has bought a mineral spring, equal to those at Baguères, Luchon, and Cauterets. He is going to turn his house into a *bad-haus*, as the Germans term it. He has already dug up all the garden two or three times, to find the famous spring, and, being unsuccessful, he will soon purchase all the contiguous houses. Now, as I dislike him, and hope his railway, his electric telegraph, or his search for baths, will ruin him, I am watching for his discomfiture, which must soon take place."

"What was the cause of your quarrel?"

"When in England he seduced the wife of one of my friends."

"Why do you not seek revenge?"

"I have already fought three duels with him," said the Englishman; "the first with the pistol, the second with the sword, and the third with the two-handed sword."

"And what was the result of those duels?"

"The first time he broke my arm, the second, he wounded me in the breast, and the third time made this large wound."

The Englishman turned down his shirt-collar, and showed a scar, whose redness proved it to be a recent one.

"So that, you see, there is a deadly feud between us."

This was all the visitor wished to ascertain, or, rather, all the Englishman appeared to know. The agent rose, and having bowed to Lord Wilmore, who returned his salutation with the stiff politeness of the English, he retired. Lord Wilmore having heard the door close after him, returned to his bedroom, where with one hand he pulled off his light hair, his red whiskers, his false jaw, and his wound, to resume his own black hair, the dark complexion, and the pearly teeth of the Count of Monte Cristo. It was M. de Villefort, and not the prefect, who returned to the house of M. de Villefort. The procureur du roi felt more at ease, although he had learned nothing really satisfactory, and, for the first time since the dinner-party at Auteuil, he slept soundly.

71

The Ball

IT was in the warmest days of July, when, in due course of time, the Saturday arrived upon which the ball of M. de Morcerf was to take place. It was ten o'clock at night; the large trees in the garden of the count's hotel threw up their branches towards the azure canopy of heaven, studded with golden stars, but where the last mists of a storm, which had threatened all day, yet glided. From the apartments on the ground-floor might be heard the sound of music, with the whirl of the waltz and galop, while brilliant streams of light shone through the openings of the Venetian blinds. At this moment the garden was only occupied by about ten servants, who had just received orders from their mistress to prepare the supper, the serenity of the weather continuing to increase. Until now it had been undecided whether the supper should take place in the dining-room, or under a long tent erected on the lawn; but the beautiful blue sky, covered with stars, had determined the case in favour of the lawn. The gardens were illuminated with coloured lanterns, according to the Italian custom, and, as usual in those countries where the luxuries of the table are well understood, the supper-table was loaded with wax lights and flowers. At the time the Countess de Morcerf returned to the rooms, after giving her orders, many guests were arriving, more attracted by the charming hospitality of the countess than by the distinguished position of the count; for, owing to the good taste of Mercédès, one was sure of finding some arrangements at her fête worthy of relating, or even copying in case of need.

Madame Danglars, in whom the events we have related had caused deep anxiety, had hesitated in going to Madame de Morcerf, when during the morning her carriage happened to cross that of De Villefort. The latter made a sign, and the carriages having drawn close together, he said:

" You are going to Madame de Morcerf's, are you not? "

" No," replied Madame Danglars, " I am too ill."

" You are wrong," replied Villefort significantly; " it is important that you should be seen there."

" In that case, I will go."

And the two carriages passed on towards their different destinations. Madame Danglars, therefore, came, not only beautiful in person, but radiant with splendour; she entered by one door at the same time that Mercédès appeared at the other. The countess took Albert to meet Madame Danglars; he approached, paid her some well-merited compliments on her toilet, and offered his arm to conduct her to a seat. Albert looked around him.

" You are looking for my daughter? " said the baroness, smiling.

" I confess it," replied Albert; " could you have been so cruel as not to bring her? "

" Calm yourself; she has met Mademoiselle de Villefort, and has taken her arm; see, they are following us, both in white dresses, one with a bouquet of camellias, the other with one of myosotis. But tell me——"

" Well, what do you wish to know? "

" Will not the Count of Monte Cristo be here to-night? "

" Seventeen! " replied Albert.

" What do you mean? "

" I only mean that the count seems the rage," replied the viscount, smiling, " and that you are the seventeenth person that has asked me the same question. The count is in fashion; I congratulate him upon it."

" And have you replied to everyone as you have to me? "

" Ah, to be sure, I have not answered you; be satisfied, we shall have this ' lion '; we are among the privileged ones."

" Were you at the Opera yesterday? "

" No."

" He was there."

" Ah, indeed! And did the eccentric person commit any new originality? "

" Can he be seen without doing so? Elssler was dancing in

*le Diable Boiteux;** the Greek princess was in ecstasies. After the cachucha he placed a magnificent ring on the stem of a bouquet, and threw it to the charming *danseuse*, who, in the third act, to do honour to the gift, reappeared with it on her finger.—And the Greek princess, will she be here? "

" No, you will be deprived of that pleasure; her position in the count's establishment is not sufficiently understood."

" Wait, leave me here, and go and speak to Madame de Villefort, who is longing to engage your attention."

Albert bowed to Madame Danglars, and advanced towards Madame de Villefort, whose lips opened as he approached.

" I wager anything," said Albert, interrupting her, " that I know what you were about to say."

" Well, what is it? "

" You were going to ask me if the Count of Monte Cristo were arrived, or expected."

" Not at all. It is not of him that I am now thinking. I was going to ask you if you had received any news of M. Franz? "

" Yes, yesterday."

" What did he tell you? "

" That he was leaving at the same time as his letter."

" Well—now then, the count? "

" The count will come; be satisfied."

" You know that he has another name besides Monte Cristo? "

" No, I did not know it."

" Monte Cristo is the name of an island, and he has a family name."

" I never heard it."

" Well, then, I am better informed than you; his name is Zaccone."

" It is possible."

" He is a Maltese."

" That is also possible."

" The son of a shipowner."

" Really, you should relate all this aloud; you would have the greatest success."

" He served in India, discovered a mine in Thessaly, and comes to Paris to form an establishment of mineral waters at Auteuil."

" Well, I'm sure! " said Morcerf; " this is indeed news! Am I allowed to repeat it? "

" Yes, but cautiously; tell one thing at a time, and do not say I told you."

" Why so? "

" Because it is a secret just discovered."

" By whom? "

" The police."

" Then the news originated——"

" At the prefect's last night. Paris, you can understand, is astonished at the sight of such unusual splendour, and the police have made inquiries."

" Good! Nothing more is wanting than to arrest the count as a vagabond, on the pretext of his being too rich."

" Indeed, this would doubtless have happened if his credentials had not been so favourable."

" Poor count! and is he aware of the danger he has been in? "

" I think not."

" Then it will be but charitable to inform him. When he arrives, I will not fail to do so."

Just then, a handsome young man with bright eyes, black hair, and glossy moustache, respectfully bowed to Madame de Villefort. Albert extended him his hand.

" Madame," said Albert, " allow me to present to you M. Maximilian Morrel, captain of Spahis, one of our best, and, above all, of our bravest officers."

" I have already had the pleasure of meeting this gentleman at Auteuil, at the house of the Count of Monte Cristo," replied Madame de Villefort, turning away with marked coldness of manner.

This answer, and, above all, the tone in which it was uttered, chilled the heart of poor Morrel. But a recompense was in store for him; turning round, he saw near the door a beautiful fair face, whose large blue eyes were without any marked expression fixed upon him, while the bouquet of myosotis was gently raised to the lips.

The salutation was so well understood, that Morrel, with the same expression in his eyes, placed his handkerchief to his mouth; and these two living statues, whose hearts beat so violently under their marble aspect, separated from each other by the whole length of the room, forgot themselves for a moment, or rather forgot the world in their mutual contemplation.

They might have remained much longer lost in one another, without anyone noticing their abstraction. The Count of Monte Cristo had just entered. He advanced through the crowd of curious glances and exchange of salutations towards Madame de Morcerf, who, standing before a mantelpiece, ornamented with flowers, had seen his entrance in a looking-glass placed opposite the door, and was prepared to receive him. She turned towards him with a serene smile just at the moment he was bowing to her.

No doubt she fancied the count would speak to her, while on his side the count thought she was about to address him; but both remained silent; and after a mere bow, Monte Cristo directed his steps to Albert, who received him cordially.

"Have you seen my mother?" asked Albert.

"I have just had the pleasure," replied the count, "but I have not seen your father."

"See, he is down there, talking politics with that little group of great geniuses."

Just then the count felt his arm pressed. He turned round; it was Danglars.

"Ah! is it you, baron?" said he.

"Why do you call me baron?" said Danglars; "you know that I care nothing for my title. I am not like you, viscount; you like your title, do you not?"

"Certainly," replied Albert, "seeing that without my title I should be nothing, while you, sacrificing the baron, would still remain the millionaire."

"Which seems to me the finest title under the royalty of July," replied Danglars.

"Unfortunately," said Monte Cristo, "one's title to a millionaire does not last for life, like that of baron, peer of France, or Academician; for example, the millionaires, Frank and Poulmann, of Frankfort, who have just become bankrupts."

"Indeed," said Danglars, becoming pale.

"Yes, I received the news this evening by a courier; I had about a million in their hands, but, warned in time, I withdrew it a month ago."

"Ah," exclaimed Danglars, "they have drawn on me for 200,000 francs."

"Well, you can guard against it; their signature is worth five per cent."

"Yes; but it is too late," said Danglars; "I have honoured their bills."

"Good!" said Monte Cristo, "here are 200,000 francs gone after——"

"Hush! Do not mention these things," said Danglars; then approaching Monte Cristo, he added, "especially before young M. Cavalcanti;" after which he smiled and turned towards the young man in question.

Albert had left the count to speak to his mother, Danglars to converse with young Cavalcanti,—Monte Cristo was for an instant alone. Meanwhile the heat became excessive. The footmen were hastening through the rooms with waiters loaded with ices. Monte Cristo wiped the perspiration from his forehead, but drew back when the waiter was presented to him; he took no refreshment. Madame de Morcerf did not lose sight of Monte Cristo. She saw that he took nothing, and even noticed the movement with which he withdrew from it.

"Albert," she asked, "did you notice that?"

"What, mother?"

"That the count will never accept an invitation to dine with us."

"Yes; but then he breakfasted with me,—indeed, he made his first appearance in the world on that occasion."

"But your house is not M. de Morcerf's," murmured Mercédès, "and since he has been here I have watched him."

"Well?"

"Well, he has taken nothing yet."

"The count is very temperate."

Mercédès smiled sadly.

"Approach him," said she, "and the next waiter that passes insist upon his taking something."

"But why, mother?"

"Oblige me, Albert," said Mercédès.

Albert kissed his mother's hand, and drew near to the count. Another salver passed, loaded as the preceding ones; she saw Albert attempt to persuade the count, but he obstinately refused. Albert rejoined his mother; she was very pale.

"Well," said she, "you see he refuses?"

"Yes; but why need this annoy you?"

"You know, Albert, women are singular creatures. I should like to have seen the count take something in my house, if only a morsel of pomegranate. Perhaps he cannot reconcile himself to the French style of living, and might prefer something else."

"Oh, no; I have seen him eat of everything in Italy; no doubt he does not feel inclined this evening."

"And besides," said the countess, "accustomed as he is to burning climates, possibly he does not feel the heat as we do."

"I do not think that, for he has complained of feeling almost suffocated, and asked why the Venetian blinds were not opened as well as the windows."

"In a word," said Mercédès, "it was a way of assuring me that his abstinence was intended."

And she left the room. A minute afterwards the blinds were thrown open, and through the jessamine and clematis that overhung the window, might be seen the garden ornamented with lanterns, and the supper laid under the tent. Dancers, players, talkers, all uttered an exclamation of joy; everyone inhaled with delight the breeze that floated in. At the same time, Mercédès reappeared, paler than before, but with an immovable expression of countenance which she sometimes wore. She went straight to the group of which her husband formed the centre.

" Do not detain these gentlemen here, count," she said; " they would prefer, I should think, to breathe in the garden, rather than suffocate here, since they are not playing."

" Ah," said a gallant old general, who, in 1809, had sung *Partant pour la Syrie!** " we will not go alone to the garden."

" Then," said Mercédès, " I will lead the way." Turning towards Monte Cristo, she added, " Count, will you oblige me with your arm? "

The count almost staggered at these simple words; then he fixed his eyes on Mercédès. It was but the glance of a moment, but it seemed to the countess to have lasted for a century, so much was expressed in that one look. He offered his arm to the countess; she leaned upon it, or, rather just touched it with her little hand, and they, together, descended the steps, lined with rhododendrons and camellias. Behind them, by another outlet, a group of about twenty persons rushed into the garden with loud exclamations of delight.

72

Bread and Salt

MADAME DE MORCERF entered an archway of trees with her companion; it was a grove of lindens, conducting to a conservatory.

" It was too warm in the room, was it not, count? " she asked.

" Yes, madame; and it was an excellent idea of yours to open the doors and the blinds."

As he ceased speaking, the count felt the hand of Mercédès tremble.

" But you," he said, " with that light dress, and without anything to cover you but that gauze scarf,—perhaps you feel cold? "

" Do you know where I am leading you? " said the countess, without replying to the question of Monte Cristo.

" No, madame," replied Monte Cristo; " but you see I make no resistance."

" We are going to the greenhouse that you see at the end of this grove."

The count looked at Mercédès as if to interrogate her, but she continued walking in silence; on his side, Monte Cristo also said nothing. They reached the building, ornamented with magnificent fruits, which ripen even in July, in the artificial temperature, which takes the place of the sun so frequently absent in our climate. The countess left the arm of Monte Cristo, and gathered a bunch of Muscatel grapes.

" See, count," she said, with a smile, so sad in its expression that one could almost see the tears on her eyelids—" see, our French grapes are not to be compared, I know, with yours of Sicily and Cyprus, but you will make allowance for our northern sun."

The count bowed, and stepped back.

" Do you refuse? " said Mercédès, in a tremulous voice.

" Pray, excuse me, madame," replied Monte Cristo, " but I never eat Muscatel grapes."

Mercédès let them fall, and sighed. A magnificent peach was hanging against an adjoining wall, ripened by the same artificial heat. Mercédès drew near, and plucked the fruit.

" Take this peach, then," she said.

The count again refused.

" What, again! " she exclaimed, in so plaintive an accent that it seemed but to stifle a sob; " really, you pain me."

A long silence succeeded this scene; the peach, like the grapes, was rolling on the ground.

" Count," added Mercédès, with a supplicating glance, " there is a beautiful Arabian custom, which makes eternal friends of those who have together eaten bread and salt beneath the same roof."

" I know it, madame," replied the count; " but we are in France, and not in Arabia; and in France eternal friendships are as rare as the custom of dividing bread and salt with one another."

" But," said the countess breathlessly, with her eyes fixed on Monte Cristo, whose arm she convulsively pressed with both hands, " we are friends, are we not? "

The count became pale as death, the blood rushed to his heart, and then again rising, dyed his cheeks with crimson; his eyes swam like those of a man suddenly dazzled.

" Certainly, we are friends," he replied; " why should we not be such? "

The answer was so little like the one Mercédès desired, that she turned away to give vent to a sigh, which sounded more like a groan.

" Thank you," she said.

And they recommenced walking. They went the whole length of the garden without uttering a word.

" Sir," suddenly exclaimed the countess, after their walk had continued ten minutes in silence, " is it true that you have seen so much, travelled so far, and suffered so deeply? "

" I have suffered deeply, madame," answered Monte Cristo.

" But now you are happy? "

" Doubtless," replied the count, " since no one hears me complain."

" And your present happiness, has it softened your heart? "

" My present happiness equals my past misery," said the count.

" Are you not married? " asked the countess.

" I, married! " exclaimed Monte Cristo, shuddering, " who could have told you so? "

" No one told me you were, but you have frequently been seen at the Opera with a young and lovely person."

" She is a slave whom I bought at Constantinople, madame, the daughter of a prince. I have adopted her as my daughter, having no one else to love in the world."

" You live alone, then? "

" I do."

" You have no sister—no son—no father? "

" I have no one."

"How can you exist thus, without any one to attach you to life?"

" It is not my fault, madame. At Malta, I loved a young girl, was on the point of marrying her, when war came and carried me away. I thought she loved me well enough to wait for me, and even to remain faithful to my grave. When I returned she was married. This is the history of most men who have passed twenty years of age. Perhaps my heart was weaker than those of the generality, and I suffered more than they would have done in my place; you know all."

The countess stopped for a moment, as if gasping for breath.

" Yes," she said, " and you have still preserved this love in your heart—one can only love once—and did you ever see her again? "

" Never! "

" Never? "

" I never returned to the country where she lived."

" At Malta? "

" Yes; at Malta."

" She is, then, now at Malta? "

" I think so."

" And have you forgiven her for all she has made you suffer? "

" Yes, I have pardoned *her*."

" But only her; do you, then, still hate those who separated you? "

" I hate them? not at all,—why should I? "

The countess placed herself before Monte Cristo, still holding in her hand a portion of the perfumed grapes.

" Take some," she said.

" Madame, I never eat Muscatel grapes," replied Monte Cristo, as if the subject had not been mentioned before.

The countess dashed the grapes into the nearest thicket, with a gesture of despair.

" Inflexible man! " she murmured.

Monte Cristo remained as unmoved as if the reproach had not been addressed to him. Albert at this moment ran in.

" Oh, mother," he exclaimed, " such a misfortune has happened! "

" What?—what has happened? " asked the countess, as though awaking from a sleep to the realities of life; " did you say a misfortune? Indeed I should expect misfortunes! "

" M. de Villefort is here."

" Well? "

" He comes to fetch his wife and daughter."

" Why so? "

" Because Madame de Saint-Méran is just arrived in Paris, bringing the news of M. de Saint-Méran's death, which took place on the first stage after he left Marseilles. Madame de Villefort, who was in very good spirits, would neither believe nor think of the misfortune; but Mademoiselle Valentine, at the first words, guessed the whole truth, notwithstanding all the precautions of her father; the blow struck her like a thunderbolt, and she fell senseless."

" And how was M. de Saint-Méran related to Mademoiselle de Villefort? " said the count.

" He was her grandfather on the mother's side. He was coming here to hasten her marriage with Franz."

" Ah, indeed! "

" Franz is delayed then. Why is not M. de Saint-Méran also grandfather to Mademoiselle Danglars? "

" Albert! Albert! " said Madame de Morcerf, in a tone of mild reproof, " what are you saying? Ah! count, he esteems you so highly, tell him that he has spoken amiss."

And she took two or three steps forward. Monte Cristo watched her with an air so thoughtful, and so full of affectionate admiration, that she returned, taking his hand; at the same time she grasped that of her son, and joined them together.

" We are friends; are we not? " she asked.

" Oh, madame, I do not presume to call myself your friend, but at all times I am your most respectful servant."

The countess left with an indescribable pang in her heart, and before she had taken ten steps the count saw her raise her handherchief to her eyes.

" Do not my mother and you agree? " asked Albert, astonished.

" On the contrary," replied the count, " did you not hear her declare that we were friends? "

They re-entered the drawing-room, which Valentine and Madame de Villefort had just quitted. Monte Cristo departed almost at the same time.

73

Madame de Saint-Méran

A GLOOMY scene had indeed just passed at the house of De Villefort. After the ladies had departed for the ball, whither all the entreaties of Madame de Villefort had failed in persuading him to accompany them, the procureur du roi had, as usual, shut himself up in his study, with a heap of papers, calculated to alarm anyone else, but which generally scarcely satisfied his inordinate desires. But this time the papers were a mere matter of form. Villefort had secluded himself, not to study, but to reflect; and, with the door locked, and orders given that he should not be disturbed, excepting for important business, he sat down in his arm-chair, and began to ponder over those events, the remembrance of which had, during the last eight days. filled his mind with so many gloomy thoughts and bitter recollections.

Then, instead of plunging into the mass of papers, piled before him, he opened the drawer of his desk, touched a spring, and drew out a parcel of notes, precious documents, amongst which he had carefully arranged, in characters only known to himself, the names of all those who, either in his political career, in money matters, at the bar, or in his mysterious love-affairs, had become his enemies. Their number was formidable, now that he had begun to fear, and yet these names, powerful though they were, had often caused him to smile with the same kind of satisfaction experienced by a traveller who, from the summit of a mountain, beholds at his feet the craggy eminences, the almost impassable paths, and the fearful chasms, through which he has so perilously climbed. When he had run over all these names in his memory, again read and studied them, commenting meanwhile upon his lists, he shook his head.

"No," he murmured, "none of my enemies would have waited so patiently and laboriously for so long a space of time, that they might now come and crush me with this secret. The story has been told by the Corsican to some priest, who, in his turn, has also repeated it. M. de Monte Cristo may have heard it, and to enlighten himself—but why should he wish to enlighten himself upon the subject?" asked Villefort, after a moment's reflection, "what interest can he take in discovering a gloomy, mysterious, and useless fact like this? However, amidst all the incoherent details given to me by the Abbé Busoni and by Lord Wilmore, by that friend and that enemy, one thing appears certain and clear in my opinion—that in no period, in no case, in no circumstance, could there have been any contact between him and me."

But Villefort uttered words which even he himself did not believe. He dreaded not the revelation so much, for he could reply to or deny its truth; but what he was really anxious for was to discover whose hand had traced them. While he was endeavouring to calm his fears,—and instead of dwelling upon the political future that had so often been the subject of his ambitious dreams, he was imagining a future limited to the enjoyments of home, fearing to awaken the enemy that had so long slept,—the noise of a carriage sounded in the yard, then he heard the steps of an aged person ascending the stairs, followed by tears and lamentations, such as servants always assume when they wish to appear interested in their master's grief. He drew back the bolt of his door, and almost directly an old lady entered, unannounced, carrying her shawl on her arm and her bonnet in her hand. The white hair was thrown back from her yellow forehead; and her eyes, already sunken by the furrows of age, now almost disappeared beneath the eyelids so swollen with grief.

" Oh, sir," she said; " oh, sir, what a misfortune! I shall die of it; oh, yes, I shall certainly die of it! "

And then, falling upon the chair nearest the door, she burst into a paroxysm of sobs. The servants, standing in the doorway, not daring to approach nearer, were looking at Noirtier's old servant, who, having heard a noise in his master's room, had run there also, and remained behind the others. Villefort rose, and ran towards his mother-in-law, for it was she.

" Why, what can have happened? " he exclaimed, " what has thus disturbed you? Is M. de Saint-Méran with you? "

" M. de Saint-Méran is dead! " answered the old marchioness, without preface and without expression; she appeared to be stupefied.

Villefort drew back, and, clasping his hands together, exclaimed:

" Dead! so suddenly? "

" A week ago," continued Madame de Saint-Méran, " we went out together in the carriage after dinner. M. de Saint-Méran had been unwell for some days; still, the idea of seeing our dear Valentine again inspired him with courage; and, notwithstanding his illness, he would leave. When, at six leagues from Marseilles, after having eaten some of the pastilles he is accustomed to take, he fell into such a deep sleep, that it appeared to me to be unnatural; still I hesitated to wake him, when I fancied his face became red, and that the veins in his temples throbbed more violently than usual. However, as it became dark, and I could no longer see, I fell asleep. I was soon awoke by a piercing shriek, as from a person suffering in his dreams, and he suddenly threw his head back. I stopped the postilion, I called M. de Saint-Méran, I applied my smelling-salts; but all was over, and I arrived at Aix by the side of a corpse."

Villefort stood with his mouth half open, quite stupefied.

"Of course, you sent for a doctor?"

"Immediately; but, as I have told you, it was too late."

"Yes; but then he could tell of what complaint the poor marquis had died."

"Oh, yes, sir, he told me; it appears to have been an apoplectic stroke."

"And what did you do then?"

"M. de Saint-Méran had always expressed a desire, in case of his death happening during his absence from Paris, that his body might be brought to the family vault. I had him put into a leaden coffin, and I am preceding him by a few days."

"Oh, my poor mother," said De Villefort, "to have such duties to perform at your age after such a blow!"

"God has supported me through all! And then, my dear marquis, he would certainly have done everything for me that I performed for him. It is true that since I left him, I seem to have lost my senses. I cannot cry; at my age they say that we have no more tears. Still, I think that when one is in trouble we should have the power of weeping. Where is Valentine, sir? It is on her account I am here; I wish to see Valentine."

Villefort thought it would be terrible to reply that Valentine was at a ball; so he only said that she had gone out with her stepmother, and that she should be fetched.

"This instant, sir—this instant, I beseech you" said the old lady.

Villefort placed the arm of Madame de Saint-Méran within his own, and conducted her to his apartment.

"Rest yourself, mother," he said.

The marchioness raised her head at this word, and beholding the man who so forcibly reminded her of her deeply-regretted child who still lived for her in Valentine, she felt touched at the name of mother, and bursting into tears, she fell on her knees before an arm-chair, where she buried her venerable head. Villefort left her to the care of the women, while old Barrois ran, half-scared, to his master; for nothing frightens old men so much as when death relaxes its vigilance over them for a moment in order to strike some other old man. Then, while Madame de Saint-Méran, still on her knees, remained praying fervently, Villefort sent for a hackney-coach, and went himself to fetch his wife and daughter from Madame de Morcerf's. He was so pale when he appeared at the door of the ballroom, that Valentine ran to him, saying:

" Oh, father, some misfortune has happened! "

" Your grandmamma has just arrived, Valentine," said M. de Villefort.

" And grandpapa? " inquired the young girl, trembling with apprehension.

M. de Villefort only replied by offering his arm to his daughter. It was just in time, for Valentine's head swam, and she staggered; Madame de Villefort instantly hastened to her assistance and aided her husband in dragging her to the carriage, saying:

" What a singular event! Who could have thought it? Ah, yes, it is indeed strange! "

And the wretched family departed, leaving a cloud of sadness hanging over the rest of the evening. At the foot of the stairs, Valentine found Barrois awaiting her.

" M. Noirtier wishes to see you to-night," he said, in an undertone.

" Tell him I will come when I leave my dear grandmamma," she replied, feeling, with true delicacy, that the person to whom she could be of the most service just then was Madame de Saint-Méran.

Valentine found her grandmother in bed; silent caresses, heartwrung sobs, broken sighs, burning tears, were all that passed in this sad interview, while Madame de Villefort, leaning on her husband's arm, maintained all outward forms of respect, at least towards the poor widow. She soon whispered to her husband:

" I think it would be better for me to retire, with your permission, for the sight of me appears still to afflict your mother-in-law."

Madame de Saint-Méran heard her.

" Yes, yes," she said softly to Valentine, " let her leave; but do you stay."

Madame de Villefort left, and Valentine remained alone beside the bed, for the procureur du roi, overcome with astonishment at the unexpected death, had followed his wife.

Meanwhile, Barrois had returned for the first time to old Noirtier, who having heard the noise in the house, had, as we have said, sent his old servant to inquire the cause; on his return, his quick and intelligent eye interrogated the messenger.

"Alas, sir," exclaimed Barrois, "a great misfortune has happened. Madame de Saint-Méran has arrived, and her husband is dead!"

M. de Saint-Méran and Noirtier had never been on strict terms of friendship; still, the death of one old man always considerably affects another. Noirtier let his head fall upon his chest, apparently overwhelmed and thoughtful; then he closed one eye, in token of inquiry.

"Mademoiselle Valentine?"

Noirtier nodded his head.

"She is at the ball, as you know, since she came to say good-bye to you in full dress."

Noirtier again closed the left eye.

"Do you wish to see her?"

Noirtier again made an affirmative sign.

"Well, they have gone to fetch her, no doubt, from Madame de Morcerf's; I will await her return, and beg her to come up here. Is that what you wish for?"

"Yes," replied the invalid.

Barrois, therefore, as we have seen, watched for Valentine, and informed her of her grandfather's wish. Consequently, Valentine came up to Noirtier, on leaving Madame de Saint-Méran, who in the midst of her grief had at last yielded to fatigue, and fallen into a feverish sleep. Within reach of her hand they placed a small table, upon which stood a bottle of orangeade, her usual beverage, and a glass. Then, as we have said, the young girl left the bedside to see M. Noirtier. Valentine kissed the old man, who looked at her with such tenderness that her eyes again filled with tears, whose sources he thought must be exhausted. The old gentleman continued to dwell upon her with the same expression.

"Yes, yes," said Valentine, "you mean that I have yet a kind grandfather left, do you not?"

The old man intimated that such was his meaning.

"Alas! happily I have," replied Valentine. "Without that, what would become of me?"

It was one o'clock in the morning. Barrois, who wished to go to bed himself, observed that after such sad events everyone stood in need of rest. Noirtier would not say that the only rest he needed was to see his child, but wished her good night, for grief and fatigue had made her appear quite ill.

The next morning she found her grandmother in bed; the

fever had not abated—on the contrary, her eyes glistened, and she appeared to be suffering from violent nervous irritability.

"Oh, dear grandmamma, are you worse?" exclaimed Valentine, perceiving all these signs of agitation.

"No, my child, no," said Madame de Saint-Méran; "but I was impatiently waiting your arrival that I might send for your father."

"My father?" inquired Valentine uneasily.

"Yes, I wish to speak to him."

Valentine durst not oppose her grandmother's wish, the cause of which she knew not; and an instant afterwards Villefort entered.

"Sir," said Madame de Saint-Méran, without using any circumlocution, and as if fearing she had no time to lose, "you wrote to me concerning the marriage of this child?"

"Yes, madame," replied Villefort; "it is not only projected, but arranged."

"Your intended son-in-law is named M. Franz d'Epinay?"

"Yes, madame."

"Is he not the son of General d'Epinay, who was on our side, and who was assassinated some days before the usurper returned from the Isle of Elba?"

"The same."

"Does he not dislike the idea of marrying the granddaughter of a Jacobin?"

"Our civil dissensions are now happily extinguished, mother," said Villefort; "M. d'Epinay was quite a child when his father died, he knows very little of M. Noirtier, and will meet him, if not with pleasure, at least with indifference."

"Is it a suitable match?"

"He is one of the most distinguished young men I know."

During the whole of this conversation Valentine had remained silent.

"Well, sir," said Madame de Saint-Méran, after a few minutes' reflection, "I must hasten the marriage, for I have but a short time to live."

"You, madame?" "You, dear mamma?" exclaimed M. de Villefort and Valentine at the same time.

"I know what I am saying," continued the marchioness; "I must hurry you, so that, having no mother, she may at least have a grandmother to bless her marriage. I am all that is left to her belonging to my poor Renée, whom you have so soon forgotten, sir."

"Ah, madame," said Villefort, "you forget that I was obliged to give a mother to my child."

"A stepmother is never a mother, sir. But this is not to the purpose—our business concerns Valentine; let us leave the dead in peace."

All this was said with such exceeding rapidity, that there was something in the conversation that seemed like the commencement of delirium.

"It shall be as you wish, madame," said Villefort; "more especially since your wishes coincide with mine; and as soon as M. d'Epinay arrives in Paris——"

"My dear grandmother," interrupted Valentine, "consider decorum—the recent death. You would not have me marry under such sad auspices?"

"My child," exclaimed the old lady sharply, "let us hear none of those conventional objections that deter weak minds from forming their fortunes. I also was married at the death-bed of my mother, and certainly I have not been less happy on that account."

"Still that idea of death, madame," said Villefort.

"Still?—Always! I tell you I am going to die—do you understand? Well, before dying I wish to see my son-in-law. I wish to tell him to make my child happy; I wish to read in his eyes whether he intends to obey me;—in fact, I will know him,—I will!" continued the old lady, with a fearful expression, "that I may rise from the depths of my grave to find him, if he should not fulfil his duty."

"Madame," said Villefort, "you must lay aside these exalted ideas, which almost assume the appearance of madness. The dead, once buried in their graves, rise no more."

"And I tell you, sir, that you are mistaken. This night I have had a fearful sleep. It seemed as though my soul were already hovering over my body; my eyes, which I tried to open, closed against my will; and what will appear impossible above all to you, sir, I saw with my eyes shut, in the spot where you are now standing, issuing from that corner where there is a door leading into Madame de Villefort's dressing-room—I saw, I tell you, silently enter, a white figure."

Valentine screamed.

"It was the fever that disturbed you, madame," said Villefort.

"Doubt, if you please, but I am sure of what I say. I saw a white figure, and as if to prevent my discrediting the testimony of only one of my senses, I heard my glass removed—the same which is there now on the table."

"Oh, dear mother, it was a dream."

"So little was it a dream, that I stretched my hand towards

the bell; but when I did so, the shade disappeared; my maid then entered with a light."

"But she saw no one?"

"Phantoms are visible to those only who ought to see them. It was the soul of my husband!—Well, if my husband's soul can come to me, why should not my soul reappear to guard my granddaughter? The tie is even more direct, it seems to me."

"Oh, madame," said Villefort, deeply affected, in spite of himself, "do not yield to those gloomy thoughts; you will long live with us, happy, loved, and honoured, and we will make you forget——"

"Never, never, never," said the marchioness. "When does M. d'Epinay return?"

"We expect him every moment."

"It is well. As soon as he arrives inform me. We must be expeditious. And then I also wish to see a notary, that I may be assured that all our property returns to Valentine."

"Ah, grandmamma!" murmured Valentine, pressing her lips on the burning brow of her grandmother, "do you wish to kill me? Oh, how feverish you are; we must not send for a notary, but for a doctor."

"A doctor!" said she, shrugging her shoulders, "I am not ill; I am thirsty—that is all."

"What are you drinking, dear grandmamma?"

"The same as usual, my dear, my glass is there on the table —give it me, Valentine."

Valentine poured the orangeade into a glass, and gave it to her grandmother with a certain degree of dread, for it was the same glass, she fancied, that had been touched by the spectre. The marchioness drained the glass at a single draught, and then turned on her pillow, repeating:

"The notary! the notary!"

M. de Villefort left the room, and Valentine seated herself at the bedside of her grandmother. The poor child appeared herself to require the doctor she had recommended to her aged relative. She was thinking of the despair of Maximilian, when informed that Madame de Saint-Méran, instead of being an ally, was unconsciously acting as his enemy. More than once she thought of revealing all to her grandmother, and she would not have hesitated a single moment, if Maximilian Morrel had been named Albert de Morcerf or Raoul de Château-Renaud; but Morrel was of plebeian extraction, and Valentine knew how the haughty Marquise de Saint-Méran despised all who were not noble. Her secret had each time been repressed when she was about to reveal it, by the sad conviction that it would be useless to do so, for, were it once discovered by her father and mother, all would be lost. Two hours passed thus; Madame de Saint-Méran was in a feverish sleep, and the notary had arrived. Though announced in a very low tone, Madame de Saint-Méran arose from her pillow.

"The notary!" she exclaimed; "let him come in."

The notary, who was at the door, immediately entered.

"Go, Valentine," said Madame de Saint-Méran, "and leave me with this gentleman."

The young girl kissed her grandmother, and left with her handkerchief to her eyes; at the door she found the valet-de-chambre, who told her the doctor was waiting in the dining-room. Valentine instantly ran down. The doctor was a friend of the family, and at the same time one of the cleverest men of the day, and very fond of Valentine, whose birth he had witnessed. He had himself a daughter about her age, but whose life was one continued source of anxiety and fear to him from her mother having been consumptive.

"Oh," said Valentine, "we have been waiting for you with such impatience, dear M. d'Avrigny." But, first of all, how are Madeleine and Antoinette?" Madeleine was the daughter of M. d'Avrigny, and Antoinette his niece.

M. d'Avrigny smiled sadly.

"Antoinette is very well," he said, "and Madeleine tolerably so. But you sent for me, my dear child. It is not your father or Madame de Villefort who is ill. As for you, although we doctors cannot divest our patients of nerves, I fancy you have no further need of me than to recommend you not to allow your imagination to take too wide a field."

Valentine coloured. M. d'Avrigny carried the science of divination almost to a miracle, for he was one of those doctors who always work upon the body through the mind.

"No," she replied, "it is for my poor grandmother. You know the calamity that has happened to us, do you not?"

"I know nothing," said M. d'Avrigny.

"Alas!" said Valentine, restraining her tears, "my grandfather is dead."

"M. de Saint-Méran?"

"Yes."

"Suddenly?"

"From an apoplectic stroke."

"An apoplectic stroke?" repeated the doctor.

"Yes, and my poor grandmother fancies that her husband, whom she never left, has called her, and that she must go and join him.   Oh, M. d'Avrigny, I beseech you, do something for her!"

"Where is she?"

"In her room with the notary."

"And M. Noirtier?"

"Just as he was, his mind perfectly clear, but the same incapability of moving or speaking."

"And the same love for you—eh, my dear child?"

"Yes," said Valentine; "he is very fond of me."

"Who does not love you?"

Valentine smiled sadly.

"What are your grandmother's symptoms?"

"An extreme nervous excitement and a strangely agitated sleep; she fancied this morning in her sleep that her soul was hovering above her body, which she at the same time watched. It must have been delirium; she fancies, too, that she saw a phantom enter her chamber, and even heard the noise it made on touching her glass."

"It is singular," said the doctor; "I was not aware that Madame de Saint-Méran was subject to such hallucinations."

"It is the first time I ever saw her thus," said Valentine; "and this morning she frightened me so, that I thought her mad; and my father, who you know is a strong-minded man, himself appeared deeply impressed."

"We will go and see," said the doctor; "what you tell me seems very strange."

The notary here descended, and Valentine was informed her grandmother was alone.

"Go upstairs," she said to the doctor.

"And you?"

"Oh, I dare not—she forbade my sending for you; and, as you say, I am myself agitated, feverish, and unwell. I will go and take a turn in the garden to recover myself."

The doctor pressed Valentine's hand, and while he visited her grandmother, she descended the steps. We need not say which portion of the garden was her favourite walk. She turned towards the avenue. As she advanced she fancied she heard a voice pronounce her name. She stopped astonished, then the voice reached her ear more distinctly, and she recognised it to be that of Maximilian.

74

The Promise

IT was, indeed, Maximilian Morrel, who had passed a wretched existence since the previous day. With that instinct peculiar to lovers he had anticipated, after the return of Madame de Saint-Méran and the death of the marquis, that something would occur at M. de Villefort's in connection with his attachment for Valentine. His presentiments were realised, as we shall see, and it was his uneasy forebodings which led him, pale and trembling, to the gate under the chestnut-trees. Valentine was ignorant of the cause of his sorrow and anxiety, and as it was not his accustomed hour for visiting her, pure chance, or rather a happy sympathy, led her at the moment to that spot.

Morrel called her, and she ran to the gate.

" You here, at this hour? " said she.

" Yes, my poor girl," replied Morrel; " I come to bring and to hear bad tidings."

" This is, indeed, a house of mourning," said Valentine; " speak, Maximilian; although the cup of sorrow seems already full."

" Dear Valentine," said Morrel, endeavouring to conceal his own emotion, " listen, I entreat you; what I am about to say is solemn. When are you to be married? "

" I will tell you all," said Valentine; " from you I have nothing to conceal. This morning the subject was introduced, and my dear grandmother, on whom I depended as my only support, not only declared herself favourable to it, but is so anxious for it, that they only await the arrival of M. d'Epinay, and the following day the contract will be signed."

A deep sigh escaped the young man, who gazed long and mournfully at her he loved.

" Alas! " replied he, " it is dreadful thus to hear my condemnation from your own lips. The sentence is passed, and, in a few hours, will be executed. It must be so, and I will not endeavour to prevent it. But, since you say nothing remains but for M. d'Epinay to arrive that the contract may be signed, and the following day you will be his, *to-morrow* you will be engaged to M. d'Epinay, for he came this morning to Paris."

Valentine uttered a cry.

"I was at the house of Monte Cristo an hour since," said Morrel; "we were speaking, he of the sorrow your family had experienced, and I of your grief, when a carriage rolled into the courtyard. Never, till then, had I placed any confidence in presentiments, but now I cannot help believing them, Valentine. At the sound of that carriage I shuddered; soon I heard steps on the staircase, which terrified me as much as the footsteps of the commander did Don Juan. The door at last opened; Albert de Morcerf entered first, and I began to hope my fears were vain, when, after him, another young man advanced, and the count exclaimed:

" 'Ah! M. le Baron Franz d'Epinay! '

"I summoned all my strength and courage to my support. Perhaps I turned pale and trembled, but certainly I smiled; and, five minutes after, I left, without having heard one word that had passed."

"Poor Maximilian!" murmured Valentine.

"Valentine, the time has arrived when you must answer me. And, remember, my life depends on your answer. What do you intend doing? "

Valentine held down her head; she was overwhelmed.

"Listen," said Morrel; "it is not the first time you have contemplated our present position, which is a serious and urgent one. Do you intend to struggle against our ill-fortune? Tell me, Valentine, for it is that I came to know."

Valentine trembled, and looked at him with amazement. The idea of resisting her father, her grandmother, and all the family, had never occurred to her.

"What do you say, Maximilian?" asked Valentine. "What do you term a struggle? Oh! it would be sacrilege. What! I resist my father's order, and my dying grandmother's wish? Impossible! "

Morrel started.

"You are too noble not to understand me, and you understand me so well that you already yield, dear Maximilian. No, no; I shall need all my strength to struggle with myself and support my grief in secret, as you say. But to grieve my father—to disturb my grandmother's last moments—never! "

"You are right," said Morrel calmly.

"In what a tone you speak! " cried Valentine.

"I speak as one who admires you, Mademoiselle."

"Mademoiselle! " cried Valentine; "mademoiselle! Oh, selfish man!—he sees me in despair, and pretends he cannot understand me! "

"You mistake—I understand you perfectly. You will not

oppose M. Villefort, you will not displease the marchioness, and to-morrow you will sign the contract which will bind you to your husband."

" But, tell me, how can I do otherwise? "

" Do not appeal to me, mademoiselle, I shall be a bad judge in such a case; my selfishness will blind me," replied Morrel, whose low voice and clenched hands announced his growing desperation.

" What would you have proposed, Morrel, had you found me willing to accede? "

" It is not for me to say."

" You are wrong; you must advise me what to do."

" Do you seriously ask my advice, Valentine? "

" Certainly, dear Maximilian, for if it is good, I will follow it; you know my devotion to you."

" Valentine," said Morrel, pushing aside a plank that was split, " give me your hand, in token of forgiveness for my anger; my senses are confused, and during the last hour the most extravagant thoughts have passed through my brain. Oh, if you refuse my advice——"

" What do you advise? " said Valentine, raising her eyes to heaven, and sighing.

" I am free," replied Maximilian, " and rich enough to support you. I swear to make you my lawful wife before my lips even shall have approached your forehead."

" You make me tremble! " said the young girl.

" Follow me," said Morrel; " I will take you to my sister, who is worthy also to be yours. We will embark for Algiers, for England, for America, or, if you prefer it, retire to the country, and only return to Paris when our friends have reconciled your family."

Valentine shook her head.

" I feared it, Maximilian," said she; " it is the counsel of a madman, and I should be more mad than you, did I not stop you at once with the word ' Impossible, Morrel, impossible! ' "

" You will then submit to what fate decrees for you without even attempting to contend with it? " said Morrel sorrowfully.

" Yes,—if I die."

" Well, Valentine," resumed Maximilian, " I again repeat you are right. Truly, it is I who am mad; and you prove to me that passion blinds the most correct minds. I appreciate your calm reasoning. It is then understood, to-morrow you will be irrevocably promised to M. Franz d'Epinay, not only by that theatrical formality invented to heighten the effect of a comedy called the signature of the contract, but your own will? "

" Again you drive me to despair, Maximilian," said Valentine,
" again you plunge the dagger in the wound! What would you
do, tell me, if your sister listened to such a proposition? "

" Mademoiselle," replied Morrel, with a bitter smile, " I am
selfish—you have already said so—and as a selfish man, I think
not of what others would do in my situation, but of what I intend
doing myself. I think only that I have known you now a whole
year. From the day I first saw you, all my hopes of happiness
have been in securing your affection. One day you acknowledged
that you loved me; and since that day my hope of future happiness has rested on obtaining you; for to gain you would be life
to me. Now, I think no more; I say only that fortune has turned
against me—I had thought to gain heaven, and now I have lost
it. It is an everyday occurrence for a gambler to lose not only
what he possesses, but also what he has not."

Morrel pronounced these words with perfect calmness;
Valentine looked at him a moment with her large, scrutinising
eyes, endeavouring not to let Morrel discover the grief which
struggled in her heart.

" But, in a word, what are you going to do? " asked she.

" I am going to have the honour of taking my leave of you,
mademoiselle, solemnly assuring you that I wish your life may be
so calm, so happy, and so fully occupied, that there may be no
place for me even in your memory."

" Oh! " murmured Valentine.

" Adieu, Valentine, adieu! " said Morrel, bowing.

" Where are you going? " cried the young girl, extending her
hand through the opening, and seizing Maximilian by his coat,
for she understood from her own agitated feelings that her lover's
calmness could not be real; " where are you going? "

" I am going that I may not bring fresh trouble into your
family; and to set an example which every honest and devoted
man, situated as I am, may follow."

" Before you leave me, tell me what you are going to do,
Maximilian."

The young man smiled sorrowfully.

" Speak, speak! " said Valentine; " I entreat you."

" Has your resolution changed, Valentine? "

" It cannot change, unhappy man; you know it must not! "
cried the young girl.

" Then adieu, Valentine! "

Valentine shook the gate with a strength of which she could
not have been supposed to be possessed, as Morrel was going
away, and passing both her hands through the opening, she
clasped and wrung them.

" I must know what you mean to do," said she. " Where are you going? "

" Oh, fear not," said Maximilian, stopping at a short distance, " I do not intend to render another man responsible for the rigorous fate reserved for me. Another might threaten to seek M. Franz, to provoke him, and to fight with him; all that would be folly. What has M. Franz to do with it? He saw me this morning for the first time, and has already forgotten he has seen me. He did not even know I existed when it was arranged by your two families that you should be united. I have no enmity against M. Franz, and promise you the punishment shall not fall on him."

" Oh whom, then?—on me? "

" On you, Valentine! Oh, Heaven forbid! Woman is sacred; the woman one loves is holy."

" On yourself, then, unhappy man; on yourself? "

" I am the only guilty person, am I not? " said Maximilian.

" Maximilian! " said Valentine, " Maximilian, return, I entreat you! "

He drew near, with his sweet smile, and, but for his paleness, one might have thought him in his usual happy frame.

" Listen, my dear, my adored Valentine," said he, in his melodious and grave tone, " those who, like us, have never had a thought for which we need blush before the world, such may read each other's heart. I never was romantic, and am no melancholy hero. I imitate neither Manfred nor Anthony; but without words, without protestations, and without vows, my life has entwined itself with yours; you leave me, and you are right in doing so,—I repeat it, you are right; but in losing you, I lose my life. The moment you leave me, Valentine, I am alone in the world. My sister is happily married; her husband is only my brother-in-law, that is, a man whom the ties of social life alone attach to me; no one then longer needs my useless life. This is what I shall do; I will wait until the very moment you are married, for I will not lose the shadow of one of those unexpected chances which are sometimes reserved for us, for, after all, M. Franz may die before that time; a thunderbolt may fall even on the altar as you approach it; nothing appears impossible to one condemned to die, and miracles appear quite reasonable when his escape from death is concerned. I will, then, wait until the last moment, and when my misery is certain, irremediable, hopeless, I will write a confidential letter to my brother-in-law, another to the prefect of police, to acquaint them with my intention, and at the corner of some wood, on the brink of some abyss, on the bank of some river, I will put an end to my existence, as certainly as I am the son of the most honest man who ever lived in France."

Valentine trembled convulsively; she loosed her hold of the gate, her arms fell by her side, and two large tears rolled down her cheeks. The young man stood before her, sorrowful and resolute.

" Oh, for pity's sake," said she, " you will live, will you not? "

" No, on my honour," said Maximilian; " but that will not affect you. You have done your duty, and your conscience will be at rest."

Valentine fell on her knees, and pressed her almost bursting heart.

" Maximilian," said she, " Maximilian, my friend, my brother on earth, my true husband in heaven, I entreat you, do as I do, live in suffering; perhaps we may one day be united."

" Adieu, Valentine," repeated Morrel.

" My God," said Valentine, raising both her hands to heaven with a sublime expression, " I have done my utmost to remain a submissive daughter; I have begged, entreated, implored; he has regarded neither my prayers, my entreaties, nor my tears. It is done," cried she, wiping away her tears, and resuming her firmness, " I am resolved not to die of remorse, but rather of shame. Live, Maximilian, and I will be yours. Say when shall it be? Speak, command, I will obey."

Morrel, who had already gone some few steps away, again returned, and, pale with joy, extended both hands towards Valentine through the opening.

" Valentine," said he, " dear Valentine, you must not speak thus—rather let me die. Why should I obtain you by violence, if our love is mutual? Is it from mere humanity you bid me live? I would then rather die."

" Truly," murmured Valentine, " who on this earth cares for me, if he does not? Who has consoled me in my sorrow but he? On whom do my hopes rest? On whom does my bleeding heart repose? On him, on him, always on him! Yes, you are right; Maximilian, I will follow you, I will leave the paternal home, I will give up all. Oh, ungrateful girl that I am," cried Valentine, sobbing, " I will give up all, even my dear old grandfather, whom I had nearly forgotten."

" No," said Maximilian, " you shall not leave him. M. Noirtier has evinced, you say, a kind feeling towards me. Well, before you leave, tell him all; his consent would be your justification in God's sight. As soon as we are married, he shall come and live with us; instead of one child, he shall have two. You have told me how you talk to him, and how he answers you; I shall very soon learn that language by signs, Valentine; and I promise you solemnly, that instead of despair, it is happiness that awaits us."

" Oh, see, Maximilian, see the power you have over me, you almost make me believe you; and yet, what you tell me is madness, for my father will curse me—he is inflexible—he will never pardon me. Now listen to me, Maximilian; if by artifice, by entreaty, by accident—in short, if by any means I can delay this marriage, will you wait? "

" Yes, I promise you, as faithfully as you have promised me, that this horrible marriage shall not take place, and that if you are dragged before a magistrate or a priest, you will refuse."

" I promise you by all that is most sacred to me in the world, namely, by my mother."

" We will wait, then," said Morrel.

" Yes, we will wait," replied Valentine, who revived at these words; " there are so many things which may save unhappy beings such as we are."

" I rely on you, Valentine," said Morrel; " all you do will be well done; only if they disregard your prayers, if your father and Madame de Saint-Méran insist that M. de Epinay should be called to-morrow to sign the contract——"

" Then you have my promise, Morrel."

" Instead of signing——"

" I will rejoin you, and we will fly; but from this moment until then, let us not tempt Providence, Morrel; let us not see each other. It is a miracle, it is a providence that we have not been discovered. If we were surprised, if it were known that we met thus, we should have no further resource."

" You are right, Valentine; but how shall I ascertain? "

" From the notary, M. Deschamps."

" I know him."

" And for myself—I will write to you, depend on me. I dread this marriage, Maximilian, as much as you."

" Thank you, my adored Valentine, thank you; that is enough. When once I know the hour, I will hasten to this spot, you can easily get over this fence with my assistance, a carriage will await us at the gate, in which you will accompany me to my sister's; there living, retired or mingling in society, as you wish, we shall be enabled to use our power to resist oppression, and not suffer ourselves to be put to death like sheep, which only defend themselves by sighs."

" Yes," said Valentine, " I will now acknowledge you are right, Maximilian; and now are you satisfied with your betrothal? " said the young girl sorrowfully.

" My adored Valentine, words cannot express one-half of my satisfaction."

Valentine had approached, or rather, had placed her lips so near the fence, that they nearly touched those of Morrel, which were pressed against the other side of the cold and inexorable barrier.

" Adieu, then, till we meet again," said Valentine, tearing herself away.

" I shall hear from you? "

" Yes."

" Thanks, thanks, dear love, adieu! "

The sound of a kiss was heard, and Valentine fled through the avenue. Morrel listened to catch the last sound of her dress brushing the branches, and of her footstep on the path, then raised his eyes with an ineffable smile of thankfulness to heaven for being permitted to be thus loved, and then also disappeared. The young man returned home and waited all the evening and all the next day without hearing anything. It was only on the following day at about ten o'clock in the morning, as he was starting to call on M. Deschamps, the notary, that he received from the postman a small billet, which he knew to be from Valentine, although he had not before seen her writing. It was to this effect:

" Tears, entreaties, prayers, have availed me nothing. Yesterday, for two hours, I was at the church of Saint-Philippe du Roule, and for two hours I prayed most fervently. Heaven is as inflexible as man, and the signature of the contract is fixed for this evening at nine o'clock. I have but one promise and but one heart to give; that promise is pledged to you, that heart is also yours. This evening, then, at a quarter to nine, at the gate.

".Your betrothed,

" VALENTINE DE VILLEFORT.

" PS.—My poor grandmother gets worse and worse; yesterday her fever amounted to delirium; to-day her delirium is almost madness. You will be very kind to me, will you not, Morrel, to make me forget my sorrow in leaving her thus? I think it is kept a secret from grandpapa Noirtier, that the contract is to be signed this evening."

Morrel went also to the notary, who confirmed his account of the proposed signature. Then he went to call on Monte Cristo, and heard still more. Franz had been to announce the solemnity, and Madame de Villefort had also written to beg the count to excuse her not inviting him; the death of M. de Saint-Méran, and the dangerous illness of his widow, would cast a gloom over the meeting which she would regret the count should share, whom she wished might enjoy every happiness. The day before Franz had been presented to Madame de Saint-Méran, who had left her bed to receive him, but had been obliged to return to it immediately after. It is easy to suppose that Morrel's agitation would not escape the count's penetrating eye. Monte Cristo was more affectionate than ever,—indeed, his manner was so kind, that several times Morrel was on the point of telling him all. But he recalled the promise he had made to Valentine, and kept his secret. The young man read Valentine's letter twenty times in the course of the day. It was her first, and on what an occasion! Each time he read it he renewed his vow to make her happy. Morrel longed intensely for the moment when he should hear Valentine say, "Here I am, Maximilian; come and help me." He had arranged everything for her escape; two ladders were hidden in the clover-field; a cabriolet was ordered for Maximilian alone, without a servant, without lights; at the turning of the first street they would light the lamps, as it would be foolish to attract the notice of the police by too many precautions. Occasionally he shuddered; he thought of the moment when, from the top of that wall, he should protect the descent of his dear Valentine, pressing in his arms for the first time her of whom he had yet only kissed the delicate hand.

At length the hour drew near. Never did a man, deeply in love, allow the clocks to go on peacefully. Morrel tormented his so effectually that they struck eight at half-past six. He then said, "It is time to start; the signature was indeed fixed to take place at nine o'clock; but, perhaps, Valentine would not wait for that." Consequently, Morrel having left the Rue Meslay at half-past eight by his timepiece, entered the clover-field while the clock of Saint-Philippe du Roule was striking eight. The horse and cabriolet were concealed behind a small ruin, where Morrel had often waited. The night gradually drew on, and the foliage in the garden assumed a deeper hue. Then Morrel came out from his hiding-place with a beating heart, and looked through the small opening in the paling; there was yet no one to be seen. The clock struck half-past eight, and still another half-hour was passed in waiting, while Morrel looked to and fro, and gazed more and more frequently through the opening. The garden became darker still, but in the darkness he looked in vain for the white dress, and in the silence he vainly listened for the sound of footsteps. The house, which was discernible through the trees, remained in darkness, and gave no indication that so important an event as the signature of a marriage-contract was going on. Morrel looked at his watch, which wanted a quarter to ten; but soon the same clock he had already heard strike two or three times rectified the error by striking half-past nine. This was already half an hour past the time Valentine had fixed. It was a terrible moment for the young man. The slightest rustling of the foliage, the least whistling of the wind, attracted his attention, and drew the perspiration on his brow; then he tremblingly fixed his ladder, and not to lose a moment, placed his foot on the first step. Amidst all these alternations of hope and fear, the clock struck ten.

" It is impossible," said Maximilian, " that the signing of a contract should occupy so long a time without unexpected interruptions. I have weighed all the chances, calculated the time required for all the forms; something must have happened." And then he walked rapidly to and fro, and pressed his burning forehead against the fence. Had Valentine fainted? or had she been discovered and stopped in her flight? These were the only obstacles which appeared possible to the young man.

The idea that her strength had failed her in attempting to escape, and that she had fainted in one of the paths, was the obstacle most impressed upon his mind. " In that case," said he, " I should lose her, and by my own fault." He dwelt on this thought one moment, then it appeared reality. He even thought he could perceive something on the ground at a distance; he ventured to call, and it seemed to him that the wind wafted back an almost inarticulate sigh. At last the half-hour struck. It was impossible to wait longer, his temples throbbed violently, his eyes were growing dim; he passed one leg over the wall, and in a moment leaped down on the other side. He was on Villefort's premises, had arrived there by scaling the wall. What might be the consequences? He followed a short distance close under the wall, then crossed a path, and entered a clump of trees. In a moment he had passed through them, and could see the house distinctly. Then Morrel was convinced of one thing, instead of lights at every window, as is customary on days of ceremony, he saw only a gray mass, which was veiled also by a cloud, which at that moment obscured the moon's feeble light. A light moved rapidly from time to time past three windows of the first floor. These three windows were in Madame de Saint-Méran's room. Another remained motionless behind some red curtains which were in Madame de Villefort's bedroom. Morrel guessed all this. So many times, in order to follow Valentine in thought at every hour in the day, had he made her describe the whole house, that without having seen it he knew it all. This darkness and silence alarmed Morrel still more than Valentine's absence had done. Almost mad with grief, and determined to venture everything in order to see Valentine once more, and be certain of the misfortune he feared, Morrel gained the edge of the clump of trees, and was going to pass as quickly as possible through the flower-garden, when the sound of a voice, still at some distance, but which was borne upon the wind, reached him. At this sound, as he was already partially exposed to view, he stepped back and concealed himself completely, remaining perfectly motionless. He had formed his resolution; if it was Valentine alone, he would speak as she passed; if she was accompanied, and he could not speak, still he should see her, and know that she was safe; if they were strangers, he would listen to their conversation, and might understand something of this hitherto incomprehensible mystery. The moon had just then escaped from behind the cloud which had concealed it, and Morrel saw Villefort come out upon the steps, followed by a gentleman in black; they descended and advanced towards the clump of trees, and Morrel soon recognised the other gentleman as Doctor d'Avrigny.

The young man seeing them approach, drew back mechanically, until he found himself stopped by a sycamore-tree in the centre of the clump; there he was compelled to remain. Soon the two gentlemen stopped also.

" Ah, my dear doctor," said the procureur, " Heaven declares itself against my house! What a dreadful death!—what a blow! Seek not to console me. Alas, nothing can alleviate so great a sorrow—the wound is too deep and too fresh! She is dead!—she is dead! "

A cold dampness covered the young man's brow, and his teeth chattered. Who could be dead in that house which Villefort himself had called accursed?

" My dear M. de Villefort," replied the doctor, with a tone which redoubled the terror of the young man, " I have not led you here to console you; on the contrary——"

" What can you mean? " asked the procureur, alarmed.

" I mean that behind the misfortune which has just happened to you, there is another, perhaps still greater."

" Can it be possible? " murmured Villefort, clasping his hands. " What are you going to tell me? "

" Are we quite alone, my friend? "

" Yes, quite. But why all these precautions? "

" Because I have a terrible secret to communicate to you," said the doctor. " Let us sit down."

Villefort fell rather than seated himself. The doctor stood before him with one hand placed on his shoulder.

"Speak, doctor, I am listening," said Villefort; "strike, I am prepared for everything!"

"Madame de Saint-Méran was, doubtless, advancing in years, but she enjoyed excellent health."

Morrel began again to breathe freely, which he had not done during the last ten minutes.

"Grief has consumed her," said Villefort,—"yes, grief, doctor! After living forty years with the marquis——"

"It is not grief, my dear Villefort," said the doctor; "grief may kill, although it rarely does, and never in a day, never in an hour, never in ten minutes."

Villefort answered nothing; he simply raised his head, which had been cast down before, and looked at the doctor with amazement.

"Were you present during the last struggle?" asked M. d'Avrigny.

"I was," replied the procureur; "you begged me not to leave."

"Did you notice the symptoms of the disease to which Madame de Saint-Méran has fallen a victim?"

"I did. Madame de Saint-Méran had three successive attacks, at intervals of some minutes, each one more serious than the former. When you arrived, Madame de Saint-Méran had already been panting for breath some minutes; she then had a fit, which I took to be simply a nervous attack, and it was only when I saw her raise herself in the bed, and her limbs and neck appear stiffened, that I became really alarmed. Then I understood from your countenance there was more to fear than I had thought. This crisis past, I endeavoured to catch your eye, but could not. You held her hand, you were feeling her pulse, and the second fit came on before you had turned towards me. This was more terrible than the first; the same nervous movements were repeated, and the mouth contracted and turned purple."

"And at the third she expired."

"At the end of the first attack I discovered symptoms of tetanus; you confirmed my opinion."

"Yes, before others," replied the doctor; "but now we are alone——"

"What are you going to say? Oh, spare me!"

"That the symptoms of tetanus and poisoning by vegetable substances are the same."

M. de Villefort started from his seat, then in a moment fell down again, silent and motionless.

"Listen," said the doctor; "I know the full importance of

the statement I have just made, and the disposition of the man to whom I have made it."

" Do you speak to me as a magistrate or as a friend? " asked Villefort.

" As a friend, and only as a friend, at this moment. The similarity in the symptoms of tetanus and poisoning by vegetable substances is so great, that were I obliged to affirm by oath what I have now stated, I should hesitate; I therefore repeat to you, I speak not to a magistrate, but to a friend. And to that friend I say, ' During the three-quarters of an hour that the struggle continued, I watched the convulsions and the death of Madame de Saint-Méran, and am thoroughly convinced that not only did her death proceed from poison, but I could also specify the poison.' "

" Indeed, sir!—indeed! "

" The symptoms are marked, do you see;—sleep disturbed by nervous fits, excitement of the brain, torpor of the system. Madame de Saint-Méran has sunk under a violent dose of brucine or of strychnine which by some mistake, perhaps, has been given to her."

Villefort seized the doctor's hand.

" Have pity on me, doctor! So many dreadful things have happened to me lately that I am on the verge of madness."

" Has any one beside me seen Madame de Saint-Méran? "
" No."

" Has anything been sent for from a chemist's that I have not examined? "

" Nothing."

" Had Madame de Saint-Méran any enemies? "

" Not to my knowledge."

" Would her death affect any one's interests? "

" It could not, indeed; my daughter is her only heiress— Valentine alone. Oh, if such a thought could present itself, I would stab myself to punish my heart for having for one instant harboured it."

" Indeed, my dear friend," said M. d'Avrigny, " I would not accuse anyone; I speak only of an accident, you understand,— of a mistake,—but whether accident or mistake, the fact is there; it speaks to my conscience, and compels me to speak aloud to you. Make inquiry."

" Of whom?—how?—of what? "

" May not Barrois, the old servant, have made a mistake, and have given Madame de Saint-Méran a dose prepared for his master? "

" But how could a dose prepared for M. Noirtier poison Madame de Saint-Méran? "

" Nothing is more simple. You know poisons become remedies in certain diseases, of which paralysis is one. For instance, having tried every other remedy to restore movement and speech to M. Noirtier, I resolved to try one last means, and for three months I have been giving him brucine; so that in the last dose I ordered for him there were six grains. This quantity, which it is perfectly safe to administer to the paralysed frame of M. Noirtier, which has become gradually accustomed to it, would be sufficient to kill another person."

" My dear doctor, there is no communication between M. Noirtier's apartment and that of Madame de Saint-Méran, and Barrois never entered my mother-in-law's room. In short, doctor, although I know you to be the most conscientious man in the world, and although I place the utmost reliance in you, I want, notwithstanding my conviction, to believe this axiom, *errare humanum est.*"

" Is there one of my brethren in whom you have equal confidence with myself? "

" Why do you ask me that?—what do you wish? "

" Send for him; I will tell him what I have seen, and we will consult together, and examine the body."

" And you will find traces of poison? "

" No, I did not say of poison, but we can prove what was the state of the body; we shall discover the cause of her sudden death, and we shall say, ' Dear Villefort, if this thing has been caused by negligence, watch over your servants; if from hatred, watch your enemies.' "

" What do you propose to me, D'Avrigny? " said Villefort, in despair; " so soon as another is admitted to our secret, an inquest will become necessary; and an inquest in my house, impossible! Still," continued the procureur, looking at the doctor with uneasiness, " if you wish it—if you demand it, it shall be done. But, doctor, you see me already so grieved—how can I introduce into my house so much scandal after so much sorrow? My wife and my daughter would die of it! And I, doctor—you know a man does not arrive at the post I occupy—one has not been procureur du roi twenty-five years without having amassed a tolerable number of enemies; mine are numerous. Let this affair be talked of, it will be a triumph for them which will make them rejoice, and cover me with shame. Pardon me, doctor, these worldly ideas; were you a priest I should not dare tell you that, but you are a man, and you know mankind. Doctor, pray recall your words; you have said nothing, have you? "

"My dear M. de Villefort," replied the doctor, "my first duty is humanity. I would have saved Madame de Saint-Méran if science could have done it; but she is dead, my duty regards the living. Let us bury this terrible secret in the deepest recesses of our hearts; I am willing, if anyone should suspect this, that my silence on this subject should be imputed to my ignorance. Meanwhile, sir, watch always—watch carefully, for, perhaps, the evil may not stop here. And when you have found the culprit, if you find him, I will say to you, 'You are a magistrate, do as you will!'"

"I thank you, doctor," said Villefort, with indescribable joy; "I never had a better friend than you." And as if he feared Doctor d'Avrigny would recall his promise, he hurried him towards the house.

When they were gone, Morrel ventured out from under the trees, and the moon shone upon his face, which was so pale it might have been taken for a phantom.

"I am manifestly protected in a most wonderful, but most terrible manner," said he; "but Valentine, poor girl! how will she bear so much sorrow?"

As he thought thus, he looked alternately at the window with red curtains and the three windows with white curtains. The light had almost disappeared from the former; doubtless Madame de Villefort had just put out her lamp, and the night-lamp alone reflected its dull light on the window.

At the extremity of the building, on the contrary, he saw one of the three windows open. A wax-light placed on the mantel-piece threw some of its pale rays without, and a shadow was seen for one moment on the balcony.

Morrel shuddered; he thought he heard a sob.

It cannot be wondered at that his mind, generally so courageous, but now disturbed by the two strongest human passions, love and fear, was weakened even to the indulgence of superstitious thoughts. Although it was impossible Valentine could see him, hidden as he was, he thought he heard the shadow at the window call him; his disturbed mind told him so. This double error became an irresistible reality, and by one of those incomprehensible transports of youth, he bounded from his hiding-place, and with two strides, at the risk of being seen, at the risk of alarming Valentine, at the risk of being discovered by some exclamation which might escape the young girl, he crossed the flower-garden, which, by the light of the moon, resembled a large white lake, and, having passed the rows of orange-trees which extended in front of the house, he reached the step, ran quickly up, and pushed the door, which opened without offering any resistance. Valentine had not seen him; her eyes, raised towards heaven, were watching a silvery cloud gliding over the azure; its form was that of a shadow mounting towards heaven; her poetic and excited mind pictured it as the soul of her grandmother. Meanwhile, Morrel had traversed the ante-room and found the staircase, which, being carpeted, prevented his approach being heard; and he had regained that degree of confidence that the presence of M. de Villefort even would not have alarmed him. Had he encountered him, his resolution was formed; he would have approached him and acknowledged all, begging him to excuse and sanction the love which united him to his daughter, and his daughter to him. Morrel was mad. Happily he did not meet anyone. Now, especially, did he find the description Valentine had given of the interior of the house useful to him; he arrived safely at the top of the staircase, and while feeling his way, a sob indicated the direction he was to take; he turned back: a door partly opened enabled him to see his road and to hear the sorrowing voice. He pushed it open and entered. At the other end of the room, under a white sheet which covered it, lay the corpse, still more alarming to Morrel since the account he had so unexpectedly overheard. By the side, on her knees, and her head buried in the cushion of an easy-chair, was Valentine, trembling and sobbing, her hands extended above her head, clasped and stiff. She had turned from the window which remained open, and was praying in accents that would have affected the most unfeeling; her words were rapid, incoherent unintelligible; for the burning weight of grief almost stopped her utterance. The moon shining through the open blinds made the lamp appear to burn paler, and cast a sepulchral hue over the whole scene. Morrel could not resist this; he was not exemplary for piety, he was not easily impressed, but Valentine suffering, weeping, wringing her hands before him, was more than he could bear in silence. He sighed, and whispered a name, and the head bathed in tears and pressed on the velvet cushion of the chair—a head resembling a Magdalen by Correggio—was raised and turned towards him. Valentine perceived him without betraying the least surprise. A heart overwhelmed with one great grief is insensible to minor emotions. Morrel held out his hand to her. Valentine, as her only apology for not having met him, pointed to the corpse under the sheet and began to sob again. Neither dared for some time to speak in that room. They hesitated to break the silence which death seemed to impose; at length Valentine ventured.

" My friend," said she, " how came you here? Alas, I would

say you are welcome, had not death opened the way for you into this house."

" Valentine," said Morrel, with a trembling voice, " I had waited since half-past eight, and did not see you come; I became uneasy, leaped the wall, found my way through the garden, when voices conversing about the fatal event——"

" What voices? " asked Valentine.

Morrel shuddered as he thought of the conversation of the doctor and M. de Villefort, and he thought he could see through the sheet the extended hands, the stiff neck, and purple lips.

" Your servants," said he, " who were repeating the whole of the sorrowful story; from them I learned it all."

" But it was risking the failure of our plan to come up here, love."

" Forgive me," replied Morrel; " I will go away."

" No," said Valentine, " you might meet someone; stay."

" But if anyone should come here——"

The young girl shook her head.

" No one will come," said she; " do not fear, there is our safeguard "; pointing to the bed.

" But what has become of M. D'Epinay? " replied Morrel.

" M. Franz arrived to sign the contract just as my dear grandmother was dying."

" Alas! " said Morrel, with a feeling of selfish joy; for he thought this death would cause the wedding to be postponed indefinitely.

" But what redoubles my sorrow," continued the young girl, as if this feeling was to receive its immediate punishment, " is that the poor old lady, on her death-bed, requested the marriage might take place as soon as possible; she also, thinking to protect me, was acting against me."

" Hark! " said Morrel.

They both listened; steps were distinctly heard in the corridor and on the stairs.

" It is my father, who has just left his cabinet."

" To accompany the doctor to the door," added Morrel.

" How do you know it is the doctor? " asked Valentine, astonished.

" I imagine it must be," said Morrel.

Valentine looked at the young man; they heard the street-door close; then M. de Villefort locked the garden-door, and returned upstairs. He stopped a moment in the ante-room, as if hesitating whether to turn to his own apartment or into Madame de Saint-Méran's; Morrel concealed himself behind a door; Valentine remained motionless, grief seemed to deprive her of all fear. M. de Villefort passed on to his own room.

"Now," said Valentine, "you can neither go out by the front door nor by the garden."

Morrel looked at her with astonishment.

"There is but one way left you that is safe," said she; "it is through my grandfather's room." She rose; "Come," she added.

"Where?" asked Maximilian.

"To my grandfather's room."

"I in M. Noirtier's apartment?"

"Yes."

"Can you mean it, Valentine?"

"I have long wished it; he is my only remaining friend, and we both need his help,—come."

"Be careful, Valentine," said Morrel, hesitating to comply with the young girl's wishes; "I now see my error—I acted as a madman in coming in here. Are you sure you are more reasonable?"

"Yes," said Valentine; "and I have but one scruple, namely, that of leaving my dear grandmother's remains, which I had undertaken to watch."

"Valentine," said Morrel, "death is in itself sacred."

"Yes," said Valentine; "besides, it will not be for long."

She then crossed the corridor, and led the way down a narrow staircase to M. Noirtier's room; Morrel followed her on tiptoe; at the door they found the old servant.

"Barrois," said Valentine, "shut the door, and let no one come in."

She passed first. Noirtier, seated in his chair, and listening to every sound, was watching the door; he saw Valentine, and his eye brightened. There was something grave and solemn in the approach of the young girl which struck the old man; and immediately his bright eye began to interrogate.

"Dear grandfather," said she hurriedly, "you know poor grandmamma died an hour since, and now I have no friend in the world but you."

His expressive eyes evinced the greatest tenderness.

"To you alone, then, may I confide my sorrows and my hopes?"

The paralytic motioned, "Yes."

Valentine took Maximilian's hand.

"Look attentively, then, at this gentleman."

The old man fixed his scrutinising gaze with slight astonishment on Morrel.

" It is M. Maximilian Morrel," said she; " the son of that good merchant of Marseilles whom you doubtless recollect."

" Yes," said the old man.

" He brings an irreproachable name, which Maximilian is likely to render glorious, since at thirty years of age he is a captain, an officer of the Legion of Honour."

The old man signified that he recollected him.

" Well, grandpapa," said Valentine, kneeling before him, and pointing to Maximilian, " I love him, and will be only his; were I compelled to marry another, I would destroy myself."

The eyes of the paralytic expressed a multitude of tumultuous laughs.

" You like M. Maximilian Morrel, do you not, grandpapa? " asked Valentine.

" Yes."

" And you will protect us, who are your children, against the will of my father? "

Noirtier cast an intelligent glance at Morrel, as if to say " Perhaps I may."

Maximilian understood him.

" Mademoiselle," said he, " you have a sacred duty to fulfil in your deceased grandmother's room, will you allow me the honour of a few minutes' conversation with M. Noirtier? "

" That is it," said the old man's eye. Then he looked anxiously at Valentine.

" Do you fear he will not understand you? "

" Yes."

" Oh, we have so often spoken of you that he knows exactly how I talk to you."

Then turning to Maximilian, with an adorable smile, although shaded by sorrow,—

" He knows everything I know," said she.

Valentine rose, placed a chair for Morrel, requested Barrois not to admit anyone, and having tenderly embraced her grand-papa, and sorrowfully taken leave of Morrel, she went away.

To prove to Noirtier that he was in Valentine's confidence and knew all their secrets, Morrel took the dictionary, a pen and some paper, and placed them all on a table where there was a light.

" But first," said Morrel, " allow me, sir, to tell you who I am, how much I love Mademoiselle Valentine, and what are my designs respecting her."

Noirtier made a sign that he would listen.

It was an imposing sight to witness this old man, apparently a mere useless burden, becoming the sole protector, support, and adviser of the lovers, who were both young, beautiful, and strong. His remarkably noble and austere expression struck Morrel, who began his recital with trembling. He related the manner in which he had become acquainted with Valentine, and how he had loved her; and that Valentine, in her solitude and her misfortune, had accepted the offer of his devotion. He told him his birth, his position, his fortune; and more than once, when he consulted the look of the paralytic, that look answered, "That is good, proceed."

"And now," said Morrel, when he had finished the first part of his recital, "now I have told you of my love and my hopes, may I inform you of my intentions?"

"Yes," signified the old man.

"This was our resolution: a cabriolet was in waiting at the gate, in which I intended to carry off Valentine to my sister's house, to marry her, and to wait respectfully M. de Villefort's pardon."

"No," said Noirtier.

"We must not do so?"

"No."

"You do not sanction our project?"

"No."

"There is another way," said Morrel.

The old man's interrogating eye said, "Which?"

"I will go," continued Maximilian, "I will seek M. Franz d'Epinay—I am happy to be able to mention this in Mademoiselle de Villefort's absence—and will conduct myself towards him so as to compel him to challenge me."

Noirtier's look continued to interrogate.

"You wish to know what I will do?"

"Yes."

"I will find him as I told you; I will tell him the ties which bind me to Mademoiselle Valentine. If he be a sensible man, he will prove it by renouncing of his own accord the hand of his betrothed, and will secure my friendship and love until death; if he refuse, either through interest or ridiculous pride, after I have proved to him that he would be forcing my wife from me, that Valentine loves me, and will love no other, I will fight with him, give him every advantage, and I shall kill him, or he will kill me; if I am victorious, he will not marry Valentine, and if I die, I am very sure Valentine will not marry him."

Noirtier watched, with indescribable pleasure, this noble and sincere countenance, on which every sentiment his tongue uttered was depicted, adding by the expression of his fine features all that colouring adds to a sound and faithful drawing. Still, when

Morrel had finished, he shut his eyes several times, which was his manner of saying " No."

" No? " said Morrel; " you disapprove of this second project, as you did of the first? "

" I do," signified the old man.

" But what must then be done? " asked Morrel. " Madame de Saint-Méran's last request was, that the marriage might not be delayed; must I let things take their course? "

Noirtier did not move.

" I understand," said Morrel; " I am to wait."

" Yes."

" But delay may ruin our plan, sir," replied the young man. " Alone, Valentine has no power; she will be compelled to submit. I am here almost miraculously, and can scarcely hope for so good an opportunity to occur again. Believe me, there are only the two plans I have proposed to you; forgive my vanity, and tell me which you prefer. Do you authorise Mademoiselle Valentine to intrust herself to my honour? "

" No."

" Do you prefer I should seek M. d'Epinay? "

" No."

" Whence then will come the help we need—from chance? " resumed Morrel.

" No."

" From you? "

" Yes."

" You thoroughly understand me, sir? Pardon my eagerness, for my life depends on your answer. Will our help come from you? "

" Yes."

" You are sure of it? "

" Yes."

There was so much firmness in the look which gave this answer, no one could, at any rate, doubt his will, if they did his power.

" Oh, thank you a thousand times! But how, unless a miracle should restore your speech, your gesture, your movement, how can you, chained to that arm-chair, dumb and motionless, oppose this marriage? "

A smile lit up the old man's face, a strange smile of the eyes on a paralysed face!

" Then I must wait? " asked the young man.

" Yes."

" But the contract? "

The same smile returned.

" Will you assure me it shall not be signed? "

" Yes," said Noirtier.

" The contract shall not be signed! " cried Morrel. " Oh! pardon me, sir; I can scarcely realise so great a happiness. Will they not sign it? "

" No," said the paralytic.

Notwithstanding that assurance, Morrel still hesitated. Whether Noirtier understood the young man's indecision, or whether he had not full confidence in his docility, he looked steadily at him.

" What do you wish, sir? " asked Morrel; " that I should renew my promise of remaining tranquil? "

Noirtier's eye remained fixed and firm, as if to imply that a promise did not suffice; then it passed from his face to his hands.

" Shall I swear to you, sir? " asked Maximilian.

" Yes," said the paralytic, with the same solemnity.

Morrel understood that the old man attached great importance to an oath.

He extended his hand.

" I swear to you, on my honour," said he, " to await your decision respecting the course I am to pursue with M. d'Epinay."

" That is right," said the old man.

" Now," said Morrel, " do you wish me to retire? "

" Yes."

" Without seeing Mademoiselle Valentine? "

" Yes."

Morrel made a sign that he was ready to obey.

" But," said he, " first allow me to embrace you as your granddaughter did just now."

Noirtier's expression could not be understood.

The young man pressed his lips on the same spot, on the old man's forehead, where Valentine's had been.

Then he bowed a second time and retired. He found the old servant outside the door, to whom Valentine had given directions; he conducted Morrel along a dark passage, which led to a little door opening on the garden.

Morrel soon found the spot where he had entered; with the assistance of the shrubs he gained the top of the wall, and by his ladder was, in an instant, in the clover-field, where his cabriolet was still waiting for him. He got in it, and, thoroughly wearied by so many emotions, he arrived about midnight in the Rue Meslay, threw himself on his bed, and slept soundly.

75

The Villefort Family Vault

Two days after, a considerable crowd was assembled, towards ten o'clock in the morning, round the door of M. de Villefort's house, and a long file of mourning-coaches and private carriages extended along the Faubourg Saint-Honoré and the Rue de la Pépinière. Among them was one of a very singular form, which appeared to have come from a distance. It was a kind of covered wagon, painted black, and was one of the first at the rendezvous. Inquiry was made, and it was ascertained that, by a strange coincidence, this carriage contained the corpse of the Marquis of Saint-Méran, and that those who had come, thinking to attend one funeral, would follow two.

Their number was great. The Marquis de Saint-Méran, one of the most zealous and faithful dignitaries of Louis XVIII and King Charles X,* had preserved a great number of friends, and these, added to the persons whom the usages of society gave Villefort a claim on, formed a considerable body.

Due information was given to the authorities, and permission obtained that the two funerals should take place at the same time. A second hearse, decked with the same funeral pomp, was brought to M. de Villefort's door, and the coffin removed into it from the post-wagon. The two bodies were to be interred in the cemetery of Père-la-Chaise,* where M. de Villefort had long since had a tomb prepared for the reception of his family. The remains of poor Renée were already deposited there, whom, after ten years of separation, her father and mother were now going to rejoin. The Parisians, always curious, always affected by funereal display, looked on, with religious silence, while the splendid procession accompanied to their last abode two of the number of the old aristocracy—the greatest protectors of commerce and sincere devotees to their principles.

In one of the mourning-coaches, Beauchamp, Debray, and Château-Renaud, were talking of the very sudden death of the marchioness.

" I saw Madame de Saint-Méran only last year at Marseilles, and should have supposed she might have lived to be a hundred years old, from her apparent sound health and great activity of mind and body. How old was she? "

" Franz assured me," replied Albert, " that she was seventy years old. But she has not died of old age, but of grief; it appears, since the death of the marquis, which affected her very deeply, she has not completely recovered her reason."

" But of what disease did she, then, die? " asked Debray.

" It is said to have been a congestion of the brain, or apoplexy, which is the same thing, is it not? "

" Nearly."

" It is difficult to believe it was apoplexy," said Beauchamp. " Madame de Saint-Méran, whom I once saw, was short, of slender form, and of a much more nervous than sanguine temperament;* grief could hardly produce apoplexy in such a constitution as that of Madame de Saint-Méran."

" At any rate," said Albert, " whatever disease or doctor may have killed her, M. de Villefort, or rather Mademoiselle Valentine, or, still rather, our friend Franz, inherits a magnificent fortune, amounting, I believe, to 80,000 livres per annum."

" And this fortune will be doubled at the death of the old Jacobin, Noirtier."

" That is a tenacious old grandfather," said Beauchamp. " *Tenacem propositi virum.** One thing only puzzles me, namely, how Franz d'Epinay will like a grandfather who cannot be separated from his wife. But where is Franz? "

" In the first carriage, with M. de Villefort, who considers him already as one of the family."

Such was the conversation in almost all the carriages; these two sudden deaths, so quickly following each other, astonished everyone; but no one suspected the terrible secret which M. d'Avrigny had communicated in his nocturnal walk to M. de Villefort.

They arrived in about an hour at the cemetery; the weather was mild, but dull, and in harmony with the funeral ceremony. Among the groups which flocked towards the family vault, Château-Renaud recognised Morrel, who had come alone in a cabriolet, and walked silently along the path bordered with yew-trees.

" You here! " said Château-Renaud, passing his arm through the young captain's; " are you a friend of Villefort's? How is it I have never met you at his house? "

" I am no acquaintance of M. de Villefort's," answered Morrel, " but I was of Madame de Saint-Méran."

Albert came up to them at this moment with Franz.

" The time and place are but ill suited for an introduction," said Albert; " but we are not superstitious. M. Morrel, allow me to present to you M. Franz d'Epinay, a delightful travelling companion, with whom I made the tour of Italy. My dear Franz, M. Maximilian Morrel, an excellent friend I have acquired in your absence, and whose name you will hear me mention every time I make any allusion to affection, wit, or amiability."

Morrel hesitated for a moment; he feared it would be hypocritical to accost in a friendly manner the man whom he was tacitly opposing, but his oath and the gravity of the circumstances recurred to his memory; he struggled to conceal his emotion, and bowed to Franz.

" Mademoiselle de Villefort is in deep sorrow, is she not? " said Debray to Franz.

" Extremely," replied he; " she looked so pale this morning, I scarcely knew her."

These apparently simple words pierced Morrel to the heart. This man had then seen Valentine, and spoken to her! The young and high-spirited officer required all his strength of mind to resist breaking his oath. He took the arm of Château-Renaud, and turned towards the vault, where the attendants had already placed the two coffins.

The Villefort vault formed a square of white stones, about twenty feet high; an interior partition separated the two families, and each compartment had its entrance-door. Here were not, as in other tombs, those ignoble drawers one above another, where economy encloses its dead with an inscription resembling a ticket; all that was visible within the bronze gates was a gloomy-looking room, separated by a wall from the vault itself. The two doors before mentioned were in the middle of this wall, and enclosed the Villefort and Saint-Méran coffins.

The two coffins were placed on trestles previously prepared for their reception in the right-hand division belonging to the Saint-Méran family. Villefort, Franz, and a few near relatives alone entered the sanctuary.

As the religious ceremonies had all been performed at the door, and there was no address given, the party all separated; Château-Renaud, Albert, and Morrel went one way, and Debray and Beauchamp the other. Franz remained with M. de Villefort: at the gate of the cemetery Morrel made an excuse to wait; he saw Franz and M. de Villefort get into the same mourning-coach, and thought this *tête-à-tête* foreboded evil. He then returned to Paris, and although in the same carriage with Château-Renaud and Albert, he did not hear one word of their conversation. As Franz was about to take leave of M. Villefort, " When shall I see you again? " said the latter.

" I am at your command, sir; shall we return together? "

" If not unpleasant to you."

" On the contrary, I shall feel much pleasure."

Thus, the future father and son-in-law stepped into the same carriage, and Morrel, seeing them pass, became uneasy.

Villefort and Franz returned to the Faubourg Saint-Honoré. The procureur, without going to see either his wife or his daughter, passed rapidly to his cabinet, and, offering the young man a chair,—

" M. d'Epinay," said he, " allow me to remind you at this moment,—which is, perhaps, not so ill chosen as at first sight may appear, for obedience to the wishes of the departed is the first offering which should be made at their tomb,—allow me, then, to remind you of the wish expressed by Madame de Saint-Méran on her death-bed, that Valentine's wedding might not be deferred. You know the affairs of the deceased are in perfect order, and her will bequeaths to Valentine the entire property of the Saint-Méran family; the notary showed me the documents yesterday, which will enable us to draw up the contract immediately. You may call on the notary, M. Deschamps, Place Beauvau, Faubourg Saint-Honoré, and you have my authority to inspect those deeds."

" Sir," replied M. d'Epinay, " it is not, perhaps, the moment for Mademoiselle Valentine, who is in deep distress, to think of a husband; indeed, I fear——"

" Valentine will have no greater pleasure than that of fulfilling her grandmamma's last injunctions; there will be no obstacle from that quarter, I assure you."

" In that case," replied Franz, " as I shall raise none, you may make arrangements when you please; I have pledged my word, and shall feel pleasure and happiness in adhering to it."

" Then," said Villefort, " nothing further is required; the contract was to have been signed three days since; we shall find it all ready, and can sign it to-day."

" But the mourning? " said Franz, hesitating.

" Fear not," replied Villefort; " no ceremony will be neglected in my house. Mademoiselle de Villefort may retire during the prescribed three months to her estate of Saint-Méran; I say hers, for she inherits it to-day. There, after a few days, if you like, the civil marriage shall be celebrated without pomp or ceremony. Madame de Saint-Méran wished her granddaughter should be married there. When that is over, you, sir, can return to Paris, while your wife passes the time of her mourning with her mother-in-law."

" As you please, sir," said Franz.

" Then," replied M. de Villefort, " have the kindness to wait half an hour. Valentine shall come down into the drawing-room.

I will send for M. Deschamps; we will read and sign the contract before we separate, and this evening Madame de Villefort shall accompany Valentine to her estate, where we will rejoin them in a week."

" Sir," said Franz, " I have one request to make."

" What is it? "

" I wish Albert de Morcerf and Raoul de Château-Renaud to be present at this signature; you know they are my witnesses."

" Half an hour will suffice to apprise them; will you go for them yourself, or will you send? "

" I prefer going, sir."

" I shall expect you, then, in half an hour, baron; and Valentine will be ready."

Franz bowed and left the room. Scarcely had the door closed, when M. de Villefort sent to tell Valentine to be ready in the drawing-room in half an hour, as he expected the notary and M. d'Epinay and his witnesses.

The news caused a great sensation throughout the house; Madame de Villefort would not believe it, and Valentine was thunderstruck. She looked round for help, and would have gone down to her grandfather's room, but meeting M. de Villefort on the stairs, he took her arm, and led her into the drawing-room.

In the ante-room, Valentine met Barrois, and looked despairingly at the old servant. One moment after, Madame de Villefort entered the drawing-room with her little Edward. It was evident that she had shared the grief of the family, for she was pale and looked fatigued. She sat down, took Edward on her knees, and, from time to time, pressed, almost convulsively, to her bosom, this child on whom her affections appeared centred. Two carriages were soon heard to enter the courtyard. One was the notary's; the other, that of Franz and his friends. In a moment the whole party was assembled. Valentine was so pale, one might trace the blue veins from her temples, round her eyes and down her cheeks. Franz was deeply affected. Château-Renaud and Albert looked at each other with amazement; the ceremony which was just concluded had not appeared more sorrowful than did that which was commencing. Madame de Villefort had placed herself in the shade behind a velvet curtain; and as she constantly bent over her child, it was difficult to read the expression of her face. M. de Villefort was, as usual, unmoved.

The notary, after having, according to the customary method, arranged the papers on the table, taken his place in an armchair, and raised his spectacles, turned towards Franz:

" Are you M. Franz de Quesnel, Baron d'Epinay? " asked he, although he knew it perfectly.

" Yes, sir," replied Franz.

The notary bowed.

" I have, then, to inform you, sir, at the request of M. de Villefort, that your projected marriage with Mademoiselle de Villefort has changed the feeling of M. Noirtier towards his grandchild; and that he disinherits her entirely of the fortune he would have left her. Let me hasten to add," continued he, " that the testator, having only the right to alienate a part of his fortune, and having alienated it all, the will will not bear scrunity, and is declared null and void."

" Yes," said Villefort; " but I warn M. d'Epinay, that during my lifetime, my father's will shall never be scrutinised, my position forbidding any doubt to be entertained."

" Sir," said Franz, " I regret much such a question has been raised in the presence of Mademoiselle Valentine; I have never inquired the amount of her fortune, which, however limited it may be, exceeds mine. My family has sought consideration in this alliance with M. de Villefort; all I seek is happiness."

Valentine imperceptibly thanked him, while two silent tears rolled down her cheeks.

" Besides, sir," said Villefort, addressing himself to his future son-in-law, " excepting the loss of a portion of your hopes, this unexpected will need not personally wound you; M. Noirtier's weakness of mind sufficiently explains it. It is not because Mademoiselle Valentine is going to marry you that he is angry, but because she will marry; a union with any other would have caused him the same sorrow. Old age is selfish, sir, and Mademoiselle de Villefort has been a faithful companion to M. Noirtier, which she cannot be when Madame la Baronne d'Epinay. My father's melancholy state prevents our speaking to him on many subjects, which the weakness of his mind would incapacitate him from understanding, and I am perfectly convinced that at the present time, although he knows his granddaughter is going to be married, M. Noirtier has even forgotten the name of his intended grandson."

M. de Villefort had scarcely said this, when the door opened, and Barrois appeared.

" Gentlemen," said he, in a tone strangely firm for a servant speaking to his masters under such solemn circumstances— " gentlemen, M. Noirtier de Villefort wishes to speak immediately to M. Franz de Quesnel, Baron d'Epinay ": he, as well as the notary, that there might be no mistake in the person, gave all his titles to the bridegroom-elect.

Villefort started, Madame de Villefort let her son slip from her knees, Valentine rose, pale and dumb as a statue. Albert and Château-Renaud exchanged a second look, more full of amazement than the first. The notary looked at Villefort.

"It is impossible," said the procureur du roi; " M. d'Epinay cannot leave the drawing-room at present."

"It is at this moment," replied Barrois, with the same firmness, " that M. Noirtier, my master, wishes to speak on important subjects to M. Franz d'Epinay."

"Grandpapa Noirtier can speak now, then," said Edward, with his usual quickness. However, his remark did not make Madame de Villefort even smile, so much was every mind engaged, and so solemn was the situation.

Astonishment was at its height. A kind of smile was perceptible on Madame de Villefort's countenance. Valentine instinctively raised her eyes, as if to thank Heaven.

"Pray go, Valentine," said M. de Villefort, " and see what this new fancy of your grandfather's is."

Valentine rose quickly, and was hastening joyfully towards the door, when M. de Villefort altered his intention.

"Stop!" said he; " I will go with you."

"Excuse me, sir," said Franz, " since M. Noirtier sent for me, I am ready to attend to his wish; besides, I shall be happy to pay my respects to him, not having yet had the honour of doing so."

"Pray, sir," said Villefort, with marked uneasiness, " do not disturb yourself."

"Forgive me, sir," said Franz, in a resolute tone. " I would not lose this opportunity of proving to M. Noirtier how wrong it would be of him to encourage feelings of dislike to me, which I am determined to conquer, whatever they may be, by my devotedness." And without listening to Villefort he rose, and followed Valentine, who was running downstairs with the joy of a shipwrecked mariner who finds a rock to cling to.

M. de Villefort followed them. Château-Renaud and Morcerf exchanged a third look of still increasing wonder.

76

A Signed Statement

NOIRTIER was prepared to receive them, dressed in black, and installed in his arm-chair. When the three persons he expected had entered, he looked at the door, which his valet immediately closed.

"Listen," whispered Villefort to Valentine, who could not conceal her joy; "if M. Noirtier wishes to communicate anything which would delay your marriage I forbid you to understand him."

Valentine blushed, but did not answer. Villefort, approaching Noirtier,—

"Here is M. Franz d'Epinay," said he; "you requested to see him. We have all wished for this interview. and I trust it will convince you how ill-formed are your objections to Valentine's marriage."

Noirtier answered only by a look which made Villefort's blood run cold. He motioned to Valentine to approach. In a moment, thanks to her habit of conversing with her grandfather, she understood he asked for a key. Then his eye was fixed on the drawer of a small chest between the windows. She opened the drawer and found a key; and, understanding that was what he wanted, again watched his eyes, which turned towards an old secretaire, long since forgotten, and supposed to contain none but useless documents.

"Shall I open the secretaire?" asked Valentine.

"Yes," said the old man.

"And the drawers?"

"Yes."

"Those at the side?"

"No."

"The middle one?"

"Yes."

Valentine opened it and drew out a bundle of papers.

"Is that what you wish for?" asked she.

"No."

She took successively all the other papers out till the drawer was empty.

"But there are no more," said she.

Noirtier's eye was fixed on the dictionary.

" Yes, I understand, grandfather," said the young girl.

She pointed to each letter of the alphabet. At the letter S the old man stopped her. She opened and found the word " secret."

" Ah, is there a secret spring? " said Valentine.

" Yes," said Noirtier.

" And who knows it? "

Noirtier looked at the door where the servant had gone out.

" Barrois? " said she.

" Yes."

Valentine went to the door, and called Barrois. Villefort's impatience during this scene made the perspiration roll from his forehead, and Franz was stupefied. The old servant came.

" Barrois," said Valentine, " my grandfather has told me to open that drawer in the secretaire, but there is a secret spring in it, which you know—will you open it? "

Barrois looked at the old man. " Obey," said Noirtier's intelligent eye. Barrois touched a spring, the false bottom came out, and they saw a bundle of papers tied with a black string.

" Is that what you wish for? " said Barrois.

" Yes."

" Shall I give these papers to M. de Villefort? "

" No."

" To Mademoiselle Valentine? "

" No."

" To M. Franz d'Epinay? "

" Yes."

Franz, astonished, advanced a step.

" To me, sir? " said he.

" Yes."

Franz took them from Barrois, and, casting his eye on the cover, read:—

" To be given, after my death, to General Durand, who shall bequeath the packet to his son, with an injunction to preserve it as containing an important document."

" Well, sir," asked Franz, " what do you wish me to do with this paper? "

" To preserve it, sealed up as it is, doubtless," said the procureur du roi.

" No, no," replied Noirtier eagerly.

" Do you wish him to read it? " said Valentine.

" Yes," replied the old man.

" You understand, baron, my grandfather wishes you to read this paper," said Valentine.

" Then let us sit down," said Villefort impatiently, " for it will take some time."

" Sit down," said the old man.

Villefort took a chair, but Valentine remained standing by her father's side, and Franz before him, holding the mysterious paper in his hand.

" Read," said the old man.

Franz untied it, and in the midst of the most profound silence, read:—

" *Extract of the Procès-verbal of a meeting of the Bonapartist Club in the Rue Saint-Jacques, held February 5th, 1815.*"

Franz stopped.

" February 5th, 1815!" said he; " it is the day my father was murdered."

Valentine and Villefort were dumb; the eye of the old man alone seemed to say clearly, " Go on."

" But it was on leaving this club," said he, " my father disappeared."

Noirtier's eye continued to say, " Read."

He resumed:—

" The undersigned Louis Jacques Beaurepaire, lieutenant-colonel of artillery, Etienne Duchampy, general of brigade, and Claude Lecharpal, keeper of woods and forests,

" Declare, that on the 4th of February, a letter arrived from the Isle of Elba, recommending to the kindness and the confidence of the Bonapartist Club General Flavien de Quesnel, who, having served the emperor from 1804 to 1814, was supposed to be devoted to the interests of the Napoleon dynasty, notwithstanding the title of baron, which Louis XVIII had just granted to him with his estate of Epinay.

" A note was, in consequence, addressed to General de Quesnel, begging him to be present at the meeting next day, the 5th. The note indicated neither the street nor the number of the house, the meeting was to be held; it bore no signature, but it announced to the general that someone would call for him if he would be ready at nine o'clock.

" The meetings were always held from that time till midnight.

" At nine o'clock, the president of the club presented himself; the general was ready; the president informed him one of the conditions of his introduction was, that he should be eternally ignorant of the place of meeting, and that he would allow his eyes to be bandaged, swearing that he would not endeavour to take off the bandage.

"The General de Quesnel accepted the condition, and promised, on his honour, not to seek to discover the road they took. The general's carriage was ready, but the president told him it was impossible he could use it, for it was useless to blindfold the master if the coachman knew through what streets he went.

"'What must, then, be done?' asked the general.

"'I have my carriage here,' said the president.

"'Have you, then, so much confidence in your servant that you can intrust him with a secret you will not allow me to know?'

"'Our coachman is a member of the club,' said the president; 'we shall be driven by a State-Councillor.'

"'Then we run another risk,' said the general, laughing, 'that of being upset.'

"We insert this joke to prove that the general was not in the least compelled to attend this meeting, but that he came willingly.

"When they were seated in the carriage the president reminded the general of his promise to allow his eyes to be bandaged, to which he made no opposition. On the road the president thought he saw the general make an attempt to remove the handkerchief, and reminded him of his oath.

"'True,' said the general.

"The carriage stopped at a passage leading to the Rue Saint-Jacques. The general alighted, leaning on the arm of the president, of whose dignity he was not aware, considering him simply as a member of the club; they crossed the passage, mounted to the first storey, and entered the meeting-room.

"The deliberations had already commenced. The members, apprised of the sort of presentation which was to be made that evening, were all in attendance. When in the middle of the room the general was invited to remove his bandage. He did so immediately, and was surprised to see so many well-known faces in a society of whose existence he had till then been ignorant. They questioned him as to his sentiments but he contented himself with answering that the letters from the Isle of Elba ought to have informed them——"

Franz interrupted himself by saying:

"My father was a royalist; they need not have asked his sentiments, which were well known."

"And hence," said Villefort, "arose my affection for your father, my dear M. Franz. A similarity of opinion soon binds."

"Read," again said the old man.

Franz continued:—

"The president then sought to make him speak more explicitly; but M. de Quesnel replied, that he wished first to know what they wanted with him.

"He was then informed of the contents of the letter from the Isle of Elba, in which he was recommended to the club as a man who would be likely to advance the interests of their party.

"One paragraph alluded to the return of Bonaparte, and promised another letter, and further details on the arrival of the *Pharaon*, belonging to the shipbuilder Morrel, of Marseilles, whose captain was entirely devoted to the emperor.

"During all this time, the general, on whom they thought to have relied as on a brother, manifested evidently signs of discontent and repugnance.

"When the reading was finished, he remained silent, with knit brow.

"'Well,' asked the president, 'what do you say to this letter, general?'

"'I say that it is too soon after declaring myself for Louis XVIII to break my vow in behalf of the ex-emperor.'

"This answer was too clear to be mistaken as to his sentiments.

"'General,' said the president, 'we acknowledge no King Louis XVIII, nor an ex-emperor, but his majesty the emperor and king, driven from France, which is his kingdom, by violence and treason.'

"'Excuse me, gentlemen,' said the general, 'you may not acknowledge Louis XVIII, but I do, as he has made me a baron and a field-marshal, and I shall never forget that for these two titles I am indebted to his happy return to France.'

"'Sir,' said the president, rising with gravity, 'be careful what you say; your words clearly show us that they are deceived concerning you in the Isle of Elba, and have deceived us! The communication has been made to you in consequence of the confidence placed in you, and which does you honour. Now we discover our error: a title and promotion attach you to the government we wish to overturn. We will not constrain you to help us; we enrol no one against his conscience, but we will compel you to act generously, even if you are not disposed to do so.'

"'You would call acting generously, knowing your conspiracy

and not informing against you; that is what I should call becoming your accomplice. You see I am more candid than you.' "

" Ah, my father! " said Franz, interrupting himself, " I understand now why they murdered him."

Valentine could not help casting one glance towards the young man, whose filial enthusiasm it was delightful to behold. Villefort walked to and fro behind them. Noirtier watched the expression of each one, and preserved his dignified and commanding attitude. Franz returned to the manuscript, and continued:—

" ' Sir,' said the president, ' you have been invited to join this assembly—you were not forced here; it was proposed to you to come blindfolded—you accepted. When you complied with this twofold request you well knew we did not wish to secure the throne to Louis XVIII, or we should not take so much care to avoid the vigilance of the police. It would be conceding too much to allow you to put on a mask to aid you in the discovery of our secret, and then to remove it that you may ruin those who have confided in you. No, no, you must first say, if you declare yourself for the king of a day who now reigns, or for his majesty the emperor.'

" ' I am a royalist,' replied the general; ' I have taken the oath of allegiance to Louis XVIII, and I will adhere to it! '

" These words were followed by a general murmur; and it was evident several of the members were discussing the propriety of making the general repent of his rashness.

" The president again rose, and having imposed silence, said:

" ' Sir, you are too serious and too sensible a man not to understand the consequences of our present situation, and your candour has already dictated to us the conditions which remain for us to offer you.'

" The general, putting his hand on his sword, exclaimed:

" ' If you talk of honour, do not begin by disavowing its laws; and impose nothing by violence.'

" ' And you, sir,' continued the president, with a calmness still more terrible than the general's anger, ' do not touch your sword, I advise you.'

" The general looked around him with slight uneasiness; however, he did not yield, but recalling all his strength,—

" ' I will not swear,' said he.

" ' Then you must die,' replied the president calmly.

" M. d'Epinay became very pale; he looked round him a second time, several members of the club were whispering, and getting their arms from under their cloaks.

"'General,' said the president, 'do not alarm yourself, you are among men of honour, who will use every means to convince you before resorting to the last extremity; but as you have said you are among conspirators, you are in possession of our secret, and you must restore it to us.'

"A significant silence followed these words, and as the general did not reply,—

"'Close the doors,' said the president to the doorkeepers.

"The same deadly silence succeeded these words. Then the general advanced, and making a violent effort to control his feelings,—

"'I have a son,' said he, 'and I ought to think of him, finding myself among assassins.'

"'General,' said the chief of the assembly, 'one man may insult fifty—it is the privilege of weakness. But he does wrong to use his privilege. Follow my advice, swear, and do not insult.'

"The general, again daunted by the superiority of the chief, hesitated a moment; then advancing to the president's desk,—

"'What is the form?' said he.

"'It is this:—"I swear by my honour not to reveal to any one what I have seen and heard on the 5th of February, 1815, between nine and ten o'clock in the evening; and I plead guilty of death should I ever violate this oath."'

"The general appeared to be affected by a nervous shudder, which prevented his answering for some moments, then, overcoming his manifest repugnance, he pronounced the required oath, but in so low a tone as to be scarcely audible to the majority of the members, who insisted on his repeating it clearly and distinctly, which he did.

"'Now am I at liberty to retire?' said the general.

"The president rose, appointed three members to accompany him, and got into the carriage with the general after bandaging his eyes.

"One of those three members was the coachman who had driven them there. The other members silently dispersed.

"'Where do you wish to be taken?' asked the president.

"'Anywhere out of your presence,' replied M. d'Epinay.

"'Beware, sir,' replied the president; 'you are no longer in the assembly, and have only to do with individuals; do not insult them unless you wish to be held responsible.'

"But instead of listening, M. d'Epinay went on:

"'You are still as brave in your carriage as in your assembly, because you are still four against one.'

"The president stopped the coach.

" They were at that part of the Quai des Ormes where the steps lead down to the river.

" ' Why do you stop here? ' asked D'Epinay.

" ' Because, sir,' said the president, ' you have insulted a man, and that man will not go one step farther without demanding honourable reparation.'

" ' Another method of assassination? ' said the general, shrugging his shoulders.

" ' Make no noise, sir, unless you wish me to consider you as one of those men whom you designated just now as cowards, who take their weakness for a shield. You are alone, one alone shall answer you; you have a sword by your side, I have one in my cane; you have no witness, one of these gentlemen will serve you. Now, if you please, remove your bandage.'

" The general tore the handkerchief from his eyes.

" ' At last,' said he, ' I shall know with whom I have to do.'

" They opened the door, and the four men alighted."

Franz again interrupted himself, and wiped the cold drops from his brow; there was something awful in hearing the son, trembling and pale, read aloud these details of his father's death, which had hitherto remained unknown.

Valentine clasped her hands as if in prayer. Noirtier looked at Villefort with an almost sublime expression of contempt and pride.

Franz continued:—

" It was, as we said, the 5th of February. For three days there had been five or six degrees of frost; the steps were covered with ice. The general was stout and tall; the president offered him the side of the railing to assist him in getting down. The two witnesses followed.

" It was a dark night. The ground from the steps to the river was covered with snow and hoarfrost, the water of the river looked black and deep. One of the seconds went for a lantern in a coal-barge near, and by its light they examined the arms.

" The president's sword, which was simply, as he had said, one he carried in his cane, was five inches shorter than the general's, and had no guard. The general proposed to cast lots for the swords, but the president said it was he who had given the provocation, and when he had given it he had supposed each would use his own arms. The witnesses endeavoured to insist, but the president bade them be silent.

" The lantern was placed on the ground, the two adversaries arranged themselves, and the duel commenced.

" The light made the two swords appear like flashes of lightning; as for the men, they were scarce perceptible, the darkness was so great.

" M. le Général d'Epinay passed for one of the best swordsmen in the army, but he was pressed so closely in the onset that he missed his aim and fell. The witnesses thought he was dead, but his adversary, who knew he had not struck him, offered him the assistance of his hand to rise. This circumstance irritated instead of calming the general, and he rushed on his adversary. But his opponent did not miss one stroke. Receiving him on his sword, three times the general drew back, and finding himself foiled, returned to the charge. At the third he fell again. They thought he slipped as at first, and the witnesses, seeing he did not move, approached and endeavoured to raise him, but the one who passed his arm round the body found it was moistened with blood. The general, who had almost fainted, revived.

" ' Ah,' said he, ' they have sent some fencing-master to fight with me.'

" The president, without answering, approached the witness who held the lantern, and raising his sleeve, showed him two wounds he had received in his arm; then opening his coat, and unbuttoning his waistcoat, displayed his side, pierced with a third wound. Still he had not even uttered a sigh.

" The General d'Epinay died five minutes after."

Franz read these last words in a voice so choked that they were hardly audible, and then stopped, passing his hand over his eyes as if to dispel a cloud. But after a moment's silence, he continued:

" The president went up the steps, after pushing his sword into his cane; a track of blood on the snow marked his course. He had scarcely arrived at the top when he heard a heavy splash in the water—it was the general's body, which the witnesses had just thrown into the river after ascertaining he was dead. The general fell, then, in a loyal duel, and not in ambush, as it might have been reported.

" In proof of this we have signed this paper to establish the truth of the facts, lest the moment should arrive when either of the actors in this terrible scene should be accused of premeditated murder or of infringement of the laws of honour.

" Signed,

" BEAUREPAIRE, DUCHAMPY, and LECHARPAL."

When Franz had finished reading this account, so dreadful for a son—when Valentine, pale with emotion, had wiped away a tear—when Villefort, trembling and crouched in a corner, had endeavoured to lessen the storm by supplicating glances at the implacable old man,—

" Sir," said d'Epinay to Noirtier, " since you are well acquainted with all these details, which are attested by honourable signatures, —since you appear to take some interest in me, although you have only manifested it hitherto by causing me sorrow, refuse me not one final satisfaction—tell me the name of the president of the club, that I may at least know who killed my father."

Villefort mechanically felt for the handle of the door; Valentine, who understood sooner than any one her grandfather's answer, and who had often seen two scars upon his right arm, drew back a few steps.

" Mademoiselle," said Franz, turning towards Valentine, " unite your efforts with mine to find out the name of the man who made me an orphan at two years of age."

Valentine remained dumb and motionless.

" Hold, sir! " said Villefort, " do not prolong this dreadful scene. The names have been purposely concealed; my father himself does not know who this president was, and if he knows, he cannot tell you: proper names are not in the dictionary."

" Oh, misery! " cried Franz; " the only hope which sustained me and enabled me to read to the end was that of knowing, at least, the name of him who killed my father! Sir!—sir! " cried he, turning to Noirtier, " do what you can!—make me understand in some way! "

" Yes," replied Noirtier.

" Oh, mademoiselle!—mademoiselle! " cried Franz, " your grandfather says he can indicate the person. Help me!—lend me your assistance! "

Noirtier looked at the dictionary. Franz took it, with a nervous trembling, and repeated the letters of the alphabet successively, until he came to M.

At that letter the old man signified " Yes."

" M? " repeated Franz.

The young man's finger glided over the words, but at each one Noirtier answered by a negative sign.

Valentine hid her head between her hands.

At length, Franz arrived at the word MYSELF.

" Yes! "

" You! " cried Franz, whose hair stood on end; " you, M. Noirtier!—you killed my father? "

" Yes! " replied Noirtier, fixing a majestic look on the young man.

Franz fell powerless on a chair; Villefort opened the door and escaped, for the idea had entered his mind to stifle the little remaining life in the old man's heart.

77

Progress of M. Cavalcanti the Younger

MEANWHILE M. Cavalcanti the elder had returned to his service, not in the army of his majesty the Emperor of Austria, but at the gaming-table of the baths of Lucca, of which he was one of the most assiduous courtiers. He had spent every farthing that had been allowed for his journey as a reward for the majestic and solemn manner in which he had maintained his assumed character of father. M. Andrea at his departure inherited all the papers, which proved that he had indeed the honour of being the son of the Marquis Bartolomeo and the Marchioness Oliva Corsinari.

He was now fairly launched in that Parisian society which gives such ready access to foreigners, and treats them, not as what they really are, but as what they wish to be considered.

Besides, what is required of a young man in Paris? To speak its language tolerably, to make a good appearance, to be a good gamester, and to pay in cash. They are certainly less particular with a foreigner than with a Frenchman.

Andrea had, then, in a fortnight, attained a very fair position. He was entitled M. le Comte, he was said to possess 50,000 livres per annum; and his father's immense riches, buried in the quarries of Saravezza, were a constant theme.

Such was the state of society in Paris at the period we bring before our readers, when Monte Cristo went one evening to pay M. Danglars a visit. M. Danglars was out, but the count was asked to go and see the baroness, and he accepted the invitation. When Monte Cristo entered the boudoir, to which we have already once introduced our readers, and where the baroness was examining some drawings, which her daughter passed to her after having looked at them with M. Cavalcanti, his presence soon produced its usual effect; and it was with smiles that the baroness received the count, although she had been a little disconcerted at the announcement of his name.

The latter took in the whole scene at a glance.

The baroness was partially reclining on a *causeuse*, Eugénie sat near her, and Cavalcanti was standing. Cavalcanti, dressed in black, like one of Goethe's heroes, with japanned shoes and open white silk stockings, passed a white and tolerably nice-looking hand through his light hair, in the midst of which sparkled a diamond, which, in spite of Monte Cristo's advice, the vain young man had been unable to resist putting on his little finger. This movement was accompanied by killing glances at Mademoiselle Danglars, and sighs addressed to the same party.

Mademoiselle Danglars was still the same—cold, beautiful, and satirical. Not one of these glances, nor one sigh, was lost on her; they might have been said to fall on the shield of Minerva, which some philosophers assert protected sometimes the breast of Sappho. Eugénie bowed coldly to the count, and availed herself of the first moment when the conversation became earnest to escape to her study, whence very soon two cheerful and noisy voices being heard, in connection with some notes of the piano, assured Monte Cristo that Mademoiselle Danglars preferred to his society and to that of M. Cavalcanti the company of Mademoiselle Louise d'Armilly, her singing governess.

It was then, especially while conversing with Madame Danglars, and apparently absorbed by the charm of the conversation, the count remarked M. Andrea Cavalcanti's solicitude, his manner of listening to the music at the door he dared not pass, and of manifesting his admiration.

The banker soon returned. His first look was certainly directed towards Monte Cristo, but the second was for Andrea. As for his wife, he bowed to her, as some husbands do to their wives, but in a way which bachelors will never comprehend, until a very extensive code is published on conjugal life.

" Have not the ladies invited you to join them at the piano? " said Danglars to Andrea.

" Alas! no, sir," replied Andrea, with a sigh, still more remarkable than the former ones.

Danglars immediately advanced towards the door and opened it.

The two young ladies were seen seated on the same chair, at the piano, accompanying themselves, each with one hand, a fancy to which they had accustomed themselves, and performed admirably. Mademoiselle d'Armilly, whom they then perceived through the open doorway, formed with Eugénie one of those living pictures of which the Germans are so fond. She was somewhat beautiful, and exquisitely genteel—a little fairy-like figure, with large curls falling on her neck, which was rather too long, as Perugino sometimes makes his Virgins, and her eyes dull from fatigue. She was said to have a weak chest, and like Antonia of the " Violon de Crémone,"* she would die one day while singing.

Monte Cristo cast one rapid and curious glance round this sanctum; it was the first time he had ever seen Mademoiselle d'Armilly, of whom he had heard much.

" Well," said the banker to his daughter, " are we then all to be excluded? "

He then led the young man into the study, and, either by chance or manœuvre, the door was partially closed after Andrea, so that from the place where they sat neither the count nor the baroness could see anything; but as the banker had accompanied Andrea, Madame Danglars appeared to take no notice of it.

The count soon heard Andrea's voice, singing a Corsican song, accompanied by the piano. While the count smiled at hearing this song, which made him lose sight of Andrea in the recollection of Benedetto, Madame Danglars was boasting to Monte Cristo of her husband's strength of mind, who that very morning had lost three or four hundred thousand francs by a failure at Milan.

The praise was well deserved, for had not the count heard it from the baroness, or by one of those means by which he knew everything, the baron's countenance would not have led him to suspect it.

" Hem! " thought Monte Cristo, " he begins to conceal his losses; a month since he boasted of them." Then, aloud,—

" Oh, madame, M. Danglars is so skilful, he will soon regain at the Bourse what he loses elsewhere."

" I see you are maintaining an erroneous idea, as well as many more," said Madame Danglars.

" What is it? " said Monte Cristo.

" That M. Danglars gambles, whereas he never plays."

" Truly, madame, I recollect M. Debray told me—à propos, what has become of him? I have seen nothing of him the last three or four days."

" Nor I," said Madame Danglars; " but you began a sentence, sir, and did not finish."

" Which? "

" M. Debray had told you——"

" Truly, he told me it was you who sacrificed to the demon of the card-table."

" I was once very fond of it, but I do not play now."

" Then you are wrong, madame. Fortune is precarious, and

if I were a woman, and fate had made me a banker's wife, whatever might be my confidence in my husband's good fortune, still in speculation, you know, there is great risk. Well, I would secure for myself a fortune independent of him, even if I acquired it by placing my interest in hands unknown to him."

Madame Danglars blushed, in spite of all her efforts.

"Stay," said Monte Cristo, as though he had not observed her confusion, "I have heard of a lucky hit that was made yesterday on the Neapolitan bonds."

"I have none—nor have I ever possessed any; but really we have talked long enough of money, count, we are like two stockbrokers; have you heard how fate is persecuting the poor Villeforts?"

"What has happened?" said the count, apparently ignorant of all.

"You know the Marquis of Saint-Méran died a few days after he had set out on his journey to Paris, and the marchioness a few days after her arrival?"

"Yes," said Monte Cristo, "I have heard that."

"But that is not all."

"Not all?"

"No; they were going to marry their daughter——"

"To M. Franz d'Epinay. Is it broken off?"

"Yesterday morning, it appears, Franz declined the honour."

"Indeed! And is the reason known?"

"No."

"How extraordinary! And how does M. de Villefort bear it?"

"As usual. Like a philosopher."

Danglars returned at this moment alone.

"Well," said the countess, "do you leave M. Cavalcanti with your daughter?"

"And Mademoiselle d'Armilly," said the banker; "do you consider her no one?"

Then, turning to Monte Cristo, he said, "Prince Cavalcanti is a charming young man, is he not? but is he really a prince?"

"I will not answer for it," said Monte Cristo. "His father was introduced to me as a marquis, so he ought to be a count; but I do not think he has much claim to that title."

"Why?" said the banker. "If he is a prince, he is wrong not to maintain his rank; I do not like anyone to deny his origin."

"Oh, you are a pure democrat," said Monte Cristo, smiling.

"But do you see to what you are exposing yourself? If, perchance, M. de Morcerf came, he would find M. Cavalcanti in that room, where he, the betrothed of Eugénie, has never been admitted."

"You may well say, perchance," replied the banker; "for he comes so seldom, it would seem only chance that brings him."

"But should he come and find that young man with your daughter, he might be displeased."

"He! you are mistaken; M. Albert would not do us the honour to be jealous, he does not like Eugénie sufficiently. Besides, I care not for his displeasure."

The valet announced M. le Vicomte Albert de Morcerf.

The countess rose hastily, and was going into the study, when Danglars stopped her.

"Stay!" said he.

She looked at him in amazement.

Monte Cristo appeared to be unconscious of what passed. Albert entered, looking very handsome, and in high spirits. He bowed politely to the countess, familiarly to Danglars, and affectionately to Monte Cristo. Then turning to the countess,—

"May I ask how Mademoiselle Danglars is?" said he.

"She is quite well," replied Danglars quickly; "she is at the piano with M. Cavalcanti."

Albert preserved his calm and indifferent manner; he might feel perhaps annoyed, but he knew Monte Cristo's eye was on him.

"M. Cavalcanti has a fine tenor voice," said he, "and Mademoiselle Eugénie a splendid soprano; and then she plays on the piano like Thalberg.* The concert must be a delightful one."

"They suit each other remarkably well," said Danglars.

Albert appeared not to notice this remark, which was, however, so rude that Madame Danglars blushed.

"I, too," said the young man, "am a musician—at least, my masters used to tell me so; but it is strange that my voice never would suit any other, and a soprano less than any."

Danglars smiled, and seemed to say, It is of no consequence. Then hoping, doubtless, to effect his purpose, he said:

"The prince and my daughter were universally admired yesterday. You were not of the party, M. de Morcerf?"

"What prince?" asked Albert.

"Prince Cavalcanti," said Danglars, who persisted in giving the young man that title.

"Pardon me," said Albert, "I was not aware he was a prince. And Prince Cavalcanti sang with Mademoiselle Eugénie yesterday? It must have been charming, indeed. I regret not having heard them. But I was unable to accept your invitation, having promised to accompany my mother to a German concert given by the Countess of Château-Renaud."

This was followed by rather an awkward silence.

" May I also be allowed," said Morcerf, " to pay my respects to Mademoiselle Danglars? "

" Wait a moment," said the banker, stopping the young man; " do you hear that delightful cavatina? Ta, ta, ta, ti, ta, ti, ta; it is charming; let them finish—one moment. Bravo! bravi! brava! " The banker was enthusiastic in his applause.

" Indeed," said Albert, " it is exquisite; it is impossible to understand the music of his country better than Prince Cavalcanti does. You said prince, did you not? But he can easily become one, if he is not already; it is no uncommon thing in Italy. But to return to the charming musicians—you should give us a treat, Danglars, without telling them there is a stranger. Ask them to sing one more song; it is so delightful to hear music in the distance, when the musicians are unrestrained by observation."

Danglars was quite annoyed by the young man's indifference. He took Monte Cristo aside.

" What do you think of our lover? " said he.

" He appears cool. But, then, your word is given."

" Yes, doubtless, I have promised to give my daughter to a man who loves her, but not to one who does not. Even if Albert had Cavalcanti's fortune, he is so proud, I would not care to see him marry her."

" Oh," said Monte Cristo, " my fondness may blind me, but, I assure you, I consider Morcerf far preferable; and his father's position is good."

" Hem! " said Danglars.

" Why do you doubt? "

" The past—that obscurity on the past."

" But that does not affect the son. A month since you thought well of him; and I know nothing of young Cavalcanti, although you met him at my house."

" But I do."

" Have you made inquiry? "

" Yes; and I know him to be rich."

" What do you suppose him worth? "

" Fifty thousand per annum; and he is well educated."

" Hem! " said Monte Cristo, in his turn.

" He is a musician."

" So are all Italians."

" Come, count, you do not do that young man justice."

"Well, I acknowledge it annoys me, knowing your connection with the Morcerf family, to see him throw himself in the way."

Danglars burst out laughing.

"What a Puritan you are!" said he; "that happens every day."

"But you cannot break it off thus; the Morcerfs are depending on this union."

"Indeed?"

"Positively."

"Then let them explain themselves. You should give the father a hint, you who are so intimate with the family."

"I?—where the devil did you find out that?"

"At their ball; it was apparent enough. Why, did not the countess, the proud Mercédès, the disdainful Catalane, who will scarcely open her lips to her oldest acquaintances, take your arm, lead you into the garden, into the private walks, and remain there for half an hour?—But will you undertake to speak to the father?"

"Willingly, if you wish it."

"But let it be done explicitly and positively. If he demands my daughter, let him fix the day—declare his conditions; in short, let us either understand each other, or quarrel. You understand—no more delay."

"Yes, sir, I will give my attention to the subject."

"I do not say I expect him with pleasure, but I do expect him. A banker must, you know, be a slave to his promise."

And Danglars sighed as M. Cavalcanti had done half an hour before.

"Bravo!" cried Morcerf, as the scene closed.

Danglars began to look suspiciously at Morcerf, when someone came and whispered a few words to him.

"I shall soon return," said the banker to Monte Cristo; "wait for me. I shall, perhaps, have something to say to you."

The baroness took advantage of her husband's absence to push open the door of her daughter's study, and M. Andrea, who was sitting before the piano with Mademoiselle Eugénie, started up like a spring.

Albert bowed to Mademoiselle Danglars with a smile, who, not appearing in the least disturbed, returned his bow with her usual coolness.

Cavalcanti was evidently embarrassed; he bowed to Morcerf, who replied with the most impertinent look possible.

Then Albert launched out in praise of Mademoiselle Danglars' voice, and on his regret, after what he had just heard, he had been unable to be present the previous evening.

Cavalcanti being left alone, turned to Monte Cristo.

" Come," said Madame Danglars, " leave music and compliments, and let us go and take tea."

" Come, Louisa," said Mademoiselle Danglars to her friend.

They passed into the next drawing-room, where tea was prepared. Just as they were beginning, in the English fashion, to leave the spoon in their cups, the door again opened, and Danglars entered, visibly agitated. Monte Cristo observed it particularly, and, by a look, asked the banker for an explanation.

" I have just received my courier from Greece," said Danglars.

" Ah, ah! " said the count; " that was the reason of your running away from us."

" Yes."

" How is King Otho? " asked Albert, in the most sprightly tone.

Danglars cast another suspicious look towards him without answering, and Monte Cristo turned away to conceal the expression of pity which passed over his features, but which was gone in a moment.

" We shall go together, shall we not? " said Albert to the count.

" If you like," replied the latter.

Albert could not understand the banker's look, and turning to Monte Cristo, who understood it perfectly,—

" Did you see," said he, " how he looked at me? "

" Yes," said the count; " but did you think there was anything particular in his look? "

" Indeed I did; and what does he mean by his news from Greece? "

" How can I tell you? "

" Because I imagine you have correspondents in that country."

Monte Cristo smiled significantly.

" Stop," said Albert, " here he comes. I shall compliment Mademoiselle Danglars on her cameo, while the father talks to you."

Albert advanced towards Eugénie, smiling, while Danglars, stooping to Monte Cristo's ear, " Your advice was excellent," said he; " there is a whole history connected with the names Fernand and Yanina."*

" Indeed! " said Monte Cristo.

" Yes, I will tell you all; but take away the young man; I cannot endure his presence."

" He is going with me. Shall I send the father to you? "

" Immediately."

" Very well."

The count made a sign to Albert; they bowed to the ladies and took their leave; Albert perfectly indifferent to Mademoiselle Danglars' contempt; Monte Cristo reiterating his advice to Madame Danglars on the prudence a banker's wife should exercise in providing for the future.

M. Cavalcanti remained master of the field.

78

Haydée

SCARCELY had the count's horses cleared the angle of the boulevard, than Albert, turning towards the count, burst into a loud fit of laughter—much too loud, in fact, not to give the idea of its being rather forced and unnatural.

" Well," said he, " how have I played my little part? "

" To what do you allude? " asked Monte Cristo.

" To the installation of my rival at M. Danglars'."

" What rival? "

" Ma foi! what rival? why, your protégé, M. Andrea Cavalcanti! "

" Ah, no joking, viscount, if you please; I do not patronise M. Andrea—at least, not as concerns M. Danglars."

" And you would be to blame for not assisting him, if the young man really needed your help in that quarter; but, happily for me, he can dispense with it."

" What! do you think he is paying his addresses? "

" I am certain of it; his languishing looks and modulated tones when addressing Mademoiselle Danglars fully proclaim his intentions. He aspires to the hand of the proud Eugénie."

" What does that signify, so long as they favour your suit? "

" But it is not the case, my dear count; on the contrary, I am repulsed on all sides."

" What! "

" It is so, indeed; Mademoiselle Eugénie scarcely answers me, and Mademoiselle d'Armilly, her confidante, does not speak to me at all."

" But the father has the greatest regard possible for you," said Monte Cristo.

" He? oh, no! he has plunged a thousand daggers into my

heart; tragedy-weapons, I own, which, instead of wounding, sheathe their points in their own handles, but daggers which he nevertheless believed to be real and deadly."

" Jealousy indicates affection."

" True; but I am not jealous."

" He is."

" Of whom?—of Debray? "

" No, of you."

" Of me? I will engage to say that before a week is past the door will be closed against me."

" You are mistaken, my dear viscount."

" Prove it to me."

" Do you wish me to do so? "

" Yes."

" Well, I am charged with the commission of endeavouring to induce M. le Comte de Morcerf to make some definite arrangement with the baron."

" By whom are you charged? "

" By the baron himself."

" Oh," said Albert, with all the cajolery of which he was capable. " You surely will not do that, my dear count? "

" Certainly I shall, Albert, as I have promised to do it."

" Well," said Albert, with a sigh, " it seems you are determined to marry me."

" I am determined to try and be on good terms with every-body, at all events," said Monte Cristo. " But à propos of Debray, how is it that I have not seen him lately at the baron's house? "

" There has been a misunderstanding."

" What, with the baroness? "

" No, with the baron."

" Has he perceived anything? "

" Ah, that is a good joke! "

" Do you think he suspects? " said Monte Cristo, with a charming naïveté.

" Where have you come from, my dear count," said Albert.

" From Congo, if you will."

" It must be farther off than even that."

" But what do I know of your Parisian husbands? "

" Oh, my dear count, husbands are pretty much the same everywhere; an individual husband of any country is a pretty fair specimen of the whole race."

" But, then, what can have led to the quarrel between Danglars and Debray? they seemed to understand each other so well! " said Monte Cristo, with renewed energy.

" Ah! now you are trying to penetrate into the mysteries of

Isis, in which I am not initiated. When M. Andrea Cavalcanti has become one of the family, you can ask him that question."

The carriage stopped.

" Here we are," said Monte Cristo; " it is only half-past ten o'clock, come in."

" Certainly I will."

" My carriage shall take you back."

" No, thank you; I gave orders for my *coupé* to follow me."

" There it is, then," said Monte Cristo, as he stepped out of the carriage.

They both went into the house; the drawing-room was lighted up—they entered it.

" You will make tea for us, Baptistin," said the count.

Baptistin left the room without waiting to answer, and in two seconds reappeared, bringing on a waiter all that his master had ordered, ready prepared, and appearing to have sprung from the ground, like the repasts which we read of in fairy-tales.

" Really, my dear count," said Morcerf, " what I admire in you is, not so much your riches, for perhaps there are people even wealthier than yourself, nor is it only your wit, for Beaumarchais*might have possessed as much,—but it is your manner of being served, without any questions, in a moment, in a second; it is as if they guessed what you wanted by your manner of ringing, and made a point of keeping everything you can possibly desire in constant readiness. Ah! but what do I hear?" and Morcerf inclined his head towards the door, through which sounds seemed to issue resembling those of a guitar.

" *Ma foi!* my dear viscount, you are fated to hear music this evening; you have only escaped from the piano of Mademoiselle Danglars to be attacked by the guzla of Haydée."

" Haydée! what an adorable name! Are there, then, really women who bear the name of Haydée*anywhere but in Byron's poems? "

" Certainly there are. Haydée is a very uncommon name in France, but it is common enough in Albania and Epirus; it is as if you said, for example, Chastity, Modesty, Innocence,—it is a kind of baptismal name, as you Parisians call it."

" Oh, that is charming! " said Albert; " how I should like to hear my countrywomen called Mademoiselle Goodness, Mademoiselle Silence, Mademoiselle Christian Charity! Only think, then, if Mademoiselle Danglars, instead of being called Claire-Marie-Eugénie, had been named Mademoiselle Chastity-Modesty-Innocence Danglars, what a fine effect that would have produced on the announcement of her marriage! "

" Silence! " said the count, " do not joke in so loud a tone; Haydée may hear you, perhaps."

" And you think she would be angry? "

" No, certainly not," said the count, with a haughty expression.

" She is very amiable, then, is she not? " said Albert.

" It is not to be called amiability, it is her duty; a slave does not dictate to a master."

" Come! you are joking yourself now. Are there any more slaves to be had who bear this beautiful name? "

" Undoubtedly."

" Really, count, you do nothing, and have nothing, like other people. The slave of M. le Comte de Monte Cristo! why, it is a rank of itself in France, and from the way in which you lavish money, it is a place that must be worth a hundred thousand francs a year."

" A hundred thousand francs! The poor girl originally possessed much more than that; she was born to treasures, in comparison with which those recorded in the *Thousand and One Nights* would seem but poverty."

" She must be a princess, then? "

" You are right; and she is one of the greatest in her country, too! "

" I thought so. But how did it happen that such a great princess became a slave? "

" How was it that Dionysius the Tyrant became a schoolmaster? The fortune of war, my dear viscount,—the caprice of fortune; that is the way in which these things are to be accounted for."

" And is her name a secret? "

" As regards the generality of mankind it is; but not for you, my dear viscount, who are one of my most intimate friends, and on whose silence I feel I may rely, if I consider it necessary to enjoin it: may I not do so? "

" Certainly! on my word of honour."

" You know the history of pacha of Yanina, do you not? "

" Of Ali Tebelen? Oh, yes; it was in his service that my father made his fortune."

" True, I had forgotten that."

" Well, what is Haydée to Ali Tebelen? "

" Merely his daughter."

" What! the daughter of Ali Pacha? "

" Of Ali Pacha and the beautiful Vasiliki."

" And your slave? "

" *Ma foi!* yes."

" But how did she become so? "

" Why, simply from the circumstance of my having bought her one day, as I was passing through the market at Constantinople."

" Wonderful! Really, my dear count, you seem to throw a sort of magic influence over all in which you are concerned; when listening to you, existence no longer seems reality, but a waking dream. Now, I am perhaps going to make an imprudent and thoughtless request, but——"

" Say on."

" But, since you go out with Haydée, and sometimes even take her to the Opera——"

" Well? "

" I think I may venture to ask you this favour."

" You may venture to ask me anything."

" Well, then, my dear count, present me to your princess."

" I will do so; but on two conditions."

" I accept them at once."

" The first is, that you will never tell anyone that I have granted the interview."

" Very well," said Albert, extending his hand; " I swear I will not."

" The second is, that you will not tell her that your father ever served hers."

" I give you my oath that I will not."

" Enough, viscount; you will remember these two vows, will you not? But I know you to be a man of honour."

The count again struck the gong. Ali reappeared.

" Tell Haydée," said he, " that I will take coffee with her, and give her to understand that I desire permission to present one of my friends to her."

Ali bowed and left the room.

" Now, understand me," said the count, " no direct questions, my dear Morcerf; if you wish to know anything tell me, and I will ask her."

" Agreed."

Ali reappeared for the third time, and drew back the tapestried hanging which concealed the door, to signify to his master and Albert that they were at liberty to pass on.

" Let us go in," said Monte Cristo.

Albert passed his hand through his hair and curled his moustache, then, having satisfied himself as to his personal appearance, followed the count into the room, the latter having previously resumed his hat and gloves. Ali was stationed as a kind of advanced guard, and the door was kept by the three French femmes-de-chambre, commanded by Myrtho. Haydée was awaiting her visitors in the first room of her suite of apartments, which was the drawing-room. Her large eyes were dilated with surprise and expectation, for it was the first time that any man, except Monte Cristo, had been accorded an entrance into her presence. She was sitting on a sofa placed in an angle of the room, with her legs crossed under her in the Eastern fashion, and seemed to have made for herself, as it were, a kind of nest in the rich Indian silks which enveloped her. Near her was the instrument on which she had just been playing; it was elegantly fashioned, and worthy of its mistress. On perceiving Monte Cristo, she rose and welcomed him with a kind of smile peculiar to herself, expressive at once of the most implicit obedience and also of the deepest love. Monte Cristo advanced towards her and extended his hand, which she, as usual, raised to her lips.

Albert had proceeded no farther than the door, where he remained rooted to the spot, being completely fascinated by the sight of such surpassing beauty, beheld, as it was, for the first time, and of which an inhabitant of more northern climates could form no adequate idea.

" Whom do you bring? " asked the young girl, in Romaic, of Monte Cristo; " is it a friend, a brother, a simple acquaintance, or an enemy? "

" A friend," said Monte Cristo, in the same language.

" What is his name? "

" Count Albert; it is the same man whom I rescued from the hands of the banditti at Rome."

" In what language would you like me to converse with him? "

Monte Cristo turned to Albert.

" Do you know modern Greek," asked he.

" Alas, no," said Albert; " nor even ancient Greek, my dear count; never had Homer or Plato a more unworthy scholar than myself."

" Then," said Haydée, proving by her remark that she had quite understood Monte Cristo's question and Albert's answer,— " then I will speak either in French or Italian, if my lord so wills it."

Monte Cristo reflected one instant.

" You will speak in Italian," said he. Then, turning towards Albert,—

" It is a pity you do not understand either ancient or modern Greek, both of which Haydée speaks so fluently; the poor child will be obliged to talk to you in Italian, which will give you but a very false idea of her powers of conversation."

The count made a sign to Haydée to address his visitor.

"Sir," said she to Morcerf, "you are most welcome as the friend of my lord and master."

This was said in excellent Tuscan, and with that soft Roman accent which makes the language of Dante as sonorous as that of Homer. Then, turning to Ali, she directed him to bring coffee and pipes; and when he had left the room to execute the orders of his young mistress, she beckoned Albert to approach nearer to her. Monte Cristo and Morcerf drew their seats towards a small table, on which were arranged music, drawings, and vases of flowers. Ali then entered, bringing coffee and chibouques; as to M. Baptistin, this portion of the building was interdicted to him. Albert refused the pipe which the Nubian offered him.

"Oh, take it—take it," said the count; "Haydée is almost as civilised as a Parisian; the smell of an Havana is disagreeable to her, but the tobacco of the East is a most delicious perfume, you know."

Ali left the room. The cups of coffee were all prepared, with the addition of a sugar-glass, which had been brought for Albert. Monte Cristo and Haydée took the liquor in the original Arabian manner, that is to say, without sugar. Haydée took the porcelain cup in her little slender fingers, and conveyed it to her mouth with all the innocent *naïveté* of a child when eating or drinking something which it likes. At this moment two women entered, bringing salvers filled with ices and sherbet, which they placed on two small tables appropriated to that purpose.

"My dear host, and you, signora," said Albert, in Italian, "excuse my apparent stupidity. I am quite bewildered, and it is natural that it should be so. Here I am in the heart of Paris; but a moment ago I heard the rumbling of the omnibuses and the tinkling of the bells of the lemonade-sellers, and now I feel as if I were suddenly transported to the East; not such as I have seen it, but such as my dreams have painted it. Oh, signora, if I could but speak Greek, your conversation, added to the fairy-scene which surrounds me, would furnish an evening of such delight as it would be impossible for me ever to forget."

"I speak sufficient Italian to enable me to converse with you, sir," said Haydée quietly; "and if you like what is Eastern, I will do my best to secure the gratification of your tastes while you are here."

"On what subject shall I converse with her?" said Albert, in a low tone to Monte Cristo.

"Just what you please; you may speak of her country and of her youthful reminiscences, or, if you like it better, you can talk of Rome, Naples, or Florence."

"Oh," said Albert, "it is of no use to be in the company of a Greek if one converses just in the same style as with a Parisian; let me speak to her of the East."

"Do so, then, for of all themes which you could choose that will be the most agreeable to her taste."

Albert turned towards Haydée.

"At what age did you leave Greece, signora?" asked he.

"I left it when I was but five years old," replied Haydée.

"And have you any recollection of your country?"

"When I shut my eyes and think, I seem to see it all again. The mind has its organ of vision as well as the body, with this additional perfection, that the objects presented to its view are indelibly impressed."

"And how far back into the past do your recollections extend?"

"I could scarcely walk when my mother, who was called Vasiliki, which means royal," said the young girl, tossing her head proudly, "took me by the hand, and after putting in our purse all the money we possessed, we went out, both covered with veils, to solicit alms for the prisoners, saying, 'He who giveth to the poor lendeth to the Lord.' Then when our purse was full, we returned to the palace, and without saying a word to my father we sent it to the convent, where it was divided amongst the prisoners."

"And how old were you at that time?"

"I was three years old," said Haydée.

"Then you remember all which was passing around you when you were but three years old?" said Albert.

"All."

"Count," said Albert, in a low tone to Monte Cristo, "do allow the signora to tell me something of her history. You prohibited my mentioning my father's name to her, but, perhaps, she will allude to him of her own accord in the course of the recital, and you have no idea how delighted I should be to hear our name pronounced by such beautiful lips."

Monte Cristo turned to Haydée, and with an expression of countenance which commanded her to pay the most implicit attention to his words, he said in Greek:

"Tell us the fate of your father; but neither the name of the traitor nor the treason."

Haydée sighed deeply, and a shade of sadness clouded her beautiful brow.

"What are you saying to her?" said Morcerf, in an undertone.

"I again reminded her that you were a friend, and that she need not conceal anything from you."

"Then," said Albert, "this pious pilgrimage in behalf of the prisoners was your first remembrance; what is the next?"

"Oh! then I remember as if it were but yesterday, sitting under the shade of some sycamore-trees, on the borders of a lake, in the waters of which the trembling foliage was reflected as in a mirror. Under the oldest and thickest of these trees, reclining on cushions, sat my father; my mother was at his feet, and I, child-like, amused myself by playing with his long white beard, which descended to his waist, or with the diamond-hilt of the scimitar attached to his girdle. Then from time to time there came to him an Albanian, who said something, to which I paid no attention, but which he always answered in the same tone of voice, either, 'Kill or pardon.'"

"It is very strange," said Albert, "to hear such words proceed from the mouth of anyone but an actress on the stage; and one needs constantly to be saying to oneself, 'This is no fiction, it is all reality,' in order to believe it. And how does France appear in your eyes, accustomed as they have been to gaze on such enchanted scenes?"

"I think it is a fine country," said Haydée; "but I see France as it really is, because I look on it with the eyes of a woman, whereas my own country, which I can only judge of from the impression produced on my childish mind, always seems enveloped in a doubtful atmosphere, which is luminous or otherwise, according as my remembrances of it are sad or joyous."

"So young," said Albert, forgetting at the moment the count's command that he should ask no questions of the slave herself, "is it possible that you can have known what suffering is except by name?"

Haydée turned her eyes towards Monte Cristo, who, making at the same time some imperceptible sign, murmured:

"Go on."

"Nothing is ever so firmly impressed on the mind as the memory of our early childhood, and with the exception of the two scenes I have just described to you, all my earliest reminiscences are fraught with deepest sadness."

"Speak, speak, signora," said Albert, "I am listening with the most intense delight and interest to all you say."

Haydée answered his remark with a melancholy smile.

"You wish me, then, to relate the history of my past sorrows?" said she.

"I beg of you to do so," replied Albert.

"Well, I was but four years old, when one night I was suddenly awoke by my mother. We were in the palace of Yanina; she snatched me from the cushions on which I was sleeping, and on opening my eyes I saw hers were filled with tears. She took me away without speaking. When I saw her weeping I began to cry too. 'Silence, child!' said she. At other times, in spite of maternal endearments or threats, I had, with a child's caprice, been accustomed to indulge my feelings of sorrow or anger by crying as much as I felt inclined; but on this occasion there was an intonation of such extreme terror in my mother's voice when she enjoined me to silence, that I ceased crying as soon as her command was given. She bore me rapidly away. I saw then that we were descending a large staircase; around us were all my mother's servants carrying trunks, bags, ornaments, jewels, purses of gold, with which they were hurrying away in the greatest distraction. Behind the women came a guard of twenty men armed with long guns and pistols, and dressed in the costume which the Greeks have assumed since they have again become a nation. You may imagine there was something startling and ominous," said Haydée, shaking her head, and turning pale at the mere remembrance of the scene, " in this long file of slaves and women, only half aroused from sleep, or at least so they appeared to me, who was myself scarcely awake. Here and there, on the walls of the staircase, were reflected gigantic shadows, which trembled in the flickering light of the pine-torches, till they seemed to reach to the vaulted roof above.

" 'Quick !' said a voice at the end of the gallery. This voice made everyone bow before it, resembling in its effect the wind passing over a field of corn, by its superior strength forcing every ear to yield obeisance. As for me, it made me tremble. This voice was that of my father. He marched the last, clothed in his splendid robes, and holding in his hand the carbine with which your emperor presented him. He was leaning on the shoulder of his favourite Selim, and he drove us all before him, as a shepherd would his straggling flock. My father," said Haydée, raising her head, " was that illustrious man known in Europe under the name of Ali Tebelen, pacha of Yanina, and before whom Turkey trembled."

Albert, without knowing why, started on hearing these words pronounced with such a haughty and dignified accent; it appeared to him as if there was something supernaturally gloomy and terrible in the expression which gleamed from the brilliant eyes of Haydée at this moment; she appeared like a Pythoness evoking a spectre, as she recalled to his mind the remembrance of the fearful death of this man, to the news of which all Europe had listened with horror.

" Soon," said Haydée, " we halted on our march, and found ourselves on the borders of a lake. My mother pressed me to her throbbing heart, and, at the distance of a few paces, I saw my father, who was glancing anxiously around. Four marble steps led down to the water's edge, and below them was a boat floating on the tide. From where we stood I could see, in the middle of the lake, a large black mass; it was the kiosk, to which we were going. This kiosk appeared to me to be at a considerable distance, perhaps on account of the darkness of the night, which prevented any object from being more than partially discerned.

" We stepped into the boat. I remember well that the oars made no noise whatever in striking the water, and when I leaned over to ascertain the cause, I saw they were muffled with the sashes of our Palicares.* Besides the rowers, the boat contained only the women, my father, mother, Selim, and myself. The Palicares had remained on the shore of the lake, ready to cover our retreat; they were kneeling on the lowest of the marble steps, and in that manner intended making a rampart of the three others in case of pursuit.

" Our bark flew before the wind.

" ' Why does the boat go so fast? ' asked I of my mother.

" ' Silence, child! Hush! we are flying.'

" I did not understand. Why should my father fly?—he, the all-powerful—he, before whom others were accustomed to fly,—he, who had taken for his device—

' THEY HATE ME, THEN THEY FEAR ME! '*

" It was indeed a flight which my father was trying to effect. I have been told since, that the garrison of the castle of Yanina, fatigued with long service——"

Here Haydée cast a significant glance at Monte Cristo, whose eyes had been riveted on her countenance during the whole course of her narrative. The young girl then continued, speaking slowly, like a person who is either inventing or suppressing some feature of the history which he is relating.

" You were saying, signora," said Albert, who was paying the most implicit attention to the recital, " that the garrison of Yanina, fatigued with long service——"

" Had treated with the Seraskier Kourchid,* who had been sent by the sultan to gain possession of the person of my father; it was then that Ali Tebelen took the resolution of retiring, after having sent to the sultan a French officer in whom he reposed great confidence, to the asylum which he had long before prepared for himself, and which he called *kataphygion,* or the refuge."

" And this officer," asked Albert, " do you remember his name, signora? "

Monte Cristo exchanged a rapid glance with the young girl, which was quite unperceived by Albert.

"No," said she, "I do not remember it just at this moment; but if it should occur to me presently, I will tell it you."

Albert was on the point of pronouncing his father's name, when Monte Cristo gently held up his finger in token of reproach; the young man recollected his vow, and was silent.

"It was towards this kiosk that we were rowing.

"A ground-floor, ornamented with arabesques, bathing its terraces in the water, and another floor, looking on the lake, was all which was visible to the eye. But beneath the ground-floor, stretching out into the island, was a large subterranean cavern, to which my mother, myself, and the women, were conducted. In this place were together 60,000 purses and 200 barrels; the purses contained 25,000,000 of money in gold, and the barrels were filled with 30,000 pounds of gunpowder.

"Near these barrels stood Selim, my father's favourite, whom I mentioned to you just now. It was his duty to watch day and night a lance, at the end of which was a lighted match, and he had orders to blow up all—kiosk, guards, women, gold, and Ali Tebelen himself, at the first signal given by my father. I remember well that the slaves, convinced of the precarious tenure on which they held their lives, passed whole days and nights in praying, crying, and groaning. As for me, I can never forget the pale complexion and black eye of the young soldier; and whenever the Angel of Death summons me to another world, I am quite sure I shall recognise Selim. I cannot tell you how long we remained in this state; at that period I did not even know what time meant. Sometimes, but very rarely, my father summoned me and my mother to the terrace of the palace; these were my hours of recreation; I who never saw anything in the dismal cavern but the gloomy countenances of the slaves and the fiery lance of Selim. My father was endeavouring to pierce with his eager looks the remotest verge of the horizon, examining attentively every black speck which appeared on the lake, whilst my mother, reclining by his side, rested her head on his shoulder, and I played at his feet, admiring everything I saw with that unsophisticated innocence of childhood which throws a charm round objects insignificant in themselves, but which in its eyes are invested with the greatest importance. The heights of Pindus towered above us; the castle of Yanina rose white and angular from the blue waters of the lake, and the immense masses of black vegetation which, viewed in the distance, gave the idea of lichens clinging to the rocks, were, in reality, gigantic fir-trees and myrtles.

" One morning my father sent for us; my mother had been crying all the night, and was very wretched; we found the pacha calm, but paler than usual.

" ' Take courage, Vasiliki,' said he; ' to-day arrives the firman of the master, and my fate will be decided. If my pardon be complete, we shall return triumphant to Yanina; if the news be inauspicious, we must fly this night.'

" ' But supposing our enemy should not allow us to do so? ' said my mother.

" ' Oh, make yourself easy on that head,' said Ali, smiling; ' Selim and his flaming lance will settle that matter. They would be glad to see me dead, but they would not like themselves to die with me.'

" My mother only answered by sighs to these consolations, which she knew did not come from my father's heart. She prepared the iced water which he was in the habit of constantly drinking, for, since his sojourn at the kiosk, he had been parched by the most violent fever, after which she anointed his white beard with perfumed oil, and lighted his chibouque, which he sometimes smoked for hours together, quietly watching the wreaths of vapour, which, ascending in spiral clouds, gradually mixed itself with the surrounding atmosphere. Presently he made such a sudden movement that I was paralysed with fear. Then, without taking his eyes from the object which had first attracted his attention, he asked for his telescope. My mother gave it him; and as she did so, looked whiter than the marble against which she leaned.

" I saw my father's hand tremble.

" ' A boat!—two!—three! ' murmured my father; ' four! '

" He then rose, seizing his arms and priming his pistols.

" ' Vasiliki,' said he to my mother, trembling perceptibly, ' the instant approaches which will decide everything. In the space of half an hour we shall know the emperor's answer. Go into the cavern with Haydée.'

" ' I will not quit you,' said Vasiliki; ' if you die, my lord, I will die with you.'

" ' Go to Selim! ' cried my father.

" ' Adieu, my lord,' murmured my mother, determining quietly to await the approach of death.

" ' Take away Vasiliki! ' said my father to his Palicares.

" As for me, I had been forgotten in the general confusion; I ran towards Ali Tebelen; he saw me hold out my arms to him, and he stooped down and pressed my forehead with his lips. Oh, how distinctly I remember that kiss! it was the last he ever gave me, and I feel as if it were still warm on my forehead. On descending we distinguished through the lattice-work several boats which were gradually becoming more distinct to our view. At first they appeared like black specks, and now they looked like birds skimming the surface of the waves.

" During this time, in the kiosk, at the feet of my father, were seated twenty Palicares, concealed from view by an angle of the wall, and watching with eager eyes the arrival of the boats. They were armed with their long guns inlaid with mother-of-pearl and silver, and cartouches, in great numbers, were lying scattered on the floor. My father looked at his watch, and paced up and down with a countenance expressive of the greatest anguish. This was the scene which presented itself to my view when I quitted my father after that last kiss. My mother and I traversed the gloomy passage leading to the cavern. Selim was still at his post, and smiled sadly on us as we entered. We fetched our cushions from the other end of the cavern, and sat down by Selim. In great dangers the devoted ones cling to each other; and young as I was, I quite understood that some imminent danger was hanging over our heads."

Albert had often heard, not from his father, for he never spoke on the subject, but from strangers, the description of the last moments of the vizier of Yanina; he had read different accounts of his death, but this history seemed to borrow new life from the voice and expression of the young girl: the living accent and the melancholy expression of countenance at once charmed and horrified him.

As to Haydée, these terrible reminiscences seemed to have overpowered her for the moment, for she ceased speaking, her head leaning on her hand like a beautiful flower bowing beneath the violence of the storm, and her eyes, gazing on vacancy, indicated that she was mentally contemplating the green summit of the Pindus and the blue waters of the lake of Yanina, which, like a magic mirror, seemed to reflect the sombre picture which she sketched. Monte Cristo looked at her with an indescribable expression of interest and pity.

" Go on," said the count, in the Romaic language.

Haydée looked up abruptly, as if the sonorous tones of Monte Cristo's voice had awakened her from a dream, and she resumed her narrative.

" It was about four o'clock in the afternoon, and although the day was brilliant out of doors, we were enveloped in the gloomy darkness of the cavern. One single solitary light was burning there, and it appeared like a star set in a heaven of blackness; it was Selim's flaming lance. My mother was a Christian, and she prayed.

"Selim repeated from time to time these sacred words:

" 'God is great!'

"However, my mother had still some hope. As she was coming down, she thought she recognised the French officer who had been sent to Constantinople, and in whom my father placed so much confidence, for he knew that all the soldiers of the French emperor were naturally noble and generous. She advanced some steps towards the staircase and listened.

" 'They are approaching,' said she; 'perhaps they bring us peace and liberty!'

" 'What do you fear, Vasiliki?' said Selim, in a voice at once so gentle and yet so proud; 'if they do not bring us peace we will give them war; if they do not bring life we will give them death.'

"And he renewed the flame of his lance with an alacrity which reminded one of the Dionysian festivals among the ancient Cretans. But I, who was only a little child, was terrified by this undaunted courage, which appeared to me both ferocious and senseless, and I recoiled with horror from the idea of the frightful death amidst fire and flame which probably awaited us.

"My mother experienced the same sensations, for I felt her tremble.

" 'Mamma, mamma,' said I, 'are we really to be killed?'

"And at the sound of my voice the slaves redoubled their cries, and prayers, and lamentations.

" 'My child,' said Vasiliki, 'may God preserve you from ever wishing for that death which to-day you so much dread!'

"Then, whispering to Selim, she asked what were his master's orders.

" 'If he send me his poniard, it will signify that the emperor's intentions are not favourable, and I am to set fire to the powder; if, on the contrary, he send me his ring, it will be a sign that the emperor pardons him, and I extinguish the match and leave the magazine untouched.'

" 'My friend,' said my mother, 'when your master's order arrives, if it is the poniard which he sends, instead of despatching us by that horrible death which we both so much dread, you will mercifully kill us with this same poniard, will you not?'

" 'Yes, Vasiliki,' replied Selim tranquilly.

"Suddenly we heard loud cries; we listened: they were cries of joy. The name of the French officer, who had been sent to Constantinople, resounded on all sides amongst our Palicares; it was evident that he brought the answer of the emperor, and that it was favourable."

"And do you not remember the Frenchman's name?" said Morcerf, quite ready to aid the memory of the narrator.

Monte Cristo made a sign to him to be silent.

"I do not recollect it," said Haydée.

"The noise increased, steps were heard approaching nearer and nearer; they were descending the steps leading to the cavern.

"Selim made ready his lance.

"Soon a figure appeared in the gray twilight at the entrance of the cave, formed by the reflection of the few rays of daylight which had found their way into this gloomy retreat.

"'Who are you?' cried Selim. 'But whoever you may be I charge you not to advance another step.'

"'Long live the emperor!' said the figure. 'He grants a full pardon to the Vizier Ali, and not only gives him his life, but restores to him his fortune and his possessions.'

"My mother uttered a cry of joy, and clasped me to her bosom.

"'Stop!' said Selim, seeing that she was about to go out, 'you see I have not yet received the ring.'

"'True,' said my mother. And she fell on her knees, at the same time holding me up towards heaven, as if she desired, whilst praying to God in my behalf, to raise me actually to his presence.'"

And for the second time Haydée stopped, overcome by such violent emotion that the perspiration stood upon her pale brow, and her stifled voice seemed hardly able to find utterance, so parched and dry were her throat and lips. Monte Cristo poured a little iced water into a glass and presented it to her, saying, with a mildness in which was also a shade of command:

"Courage."

Haydée dried her eyes and continued:

"By this time our eyes, habituated to the darkness, had recognised the messenger of the pacha,—it was a friend. Selim had also recognised him; but the brave young man only acknowledged one duty, which was to obey.

"'In whose name do you come?' said he to him.

"'I come in the name of our master, Ali Tebelen.'

"'If you come from Ali himself,' said Selim, 'you know what you were charged to remit to me?'

"'Yes,' said the messenger, 'and I bring you his ring.'

"At these words he raised his hand above his head to show the token; but it was too far off, and there was not light enough to enable Selim, where he was standing, to distinguish and recognise the object presented to his view.

" ' I do not see what you have in your hand,' said Selim.

" ' Approach, then,' said the messenger, ' or I will come nearer to you, if you prefer it.'

" ' I will agree to neither one nor the other,' replied the young soldier; ' place the object which I desire to see in the ray of light which shines there, and retire whilst I examine it.'

" ' Be it so,' said the envoy; and he retired after having first deposited the token agreed on in the place pointed out to him by Selim.

" Oh, how our hearts palpitated; for it did, indeed, seem to be a ring which was placed there. But was it my father's ring? that was the question.

" Selim, still holding in his hand the lighted match, walked towards the opening in the cavern, and aided by the faint light which streamed in through the mouth of the cave, picked up the token.

" ' It is well! ' said he kissing it; ' it is my master's ring! ' And throwing the match on the ground, he trampled on it and extinguished it.

" The messenger uttered a cry of joy, and clapped his hands. At this signal four soldiers of the Seraskier Kourchid suddenly appeared, and Selim fell pierced by five blows. Each man had stabbed him separately; and, intoxicated by their crime, though still pale with fear, they sought all over the cavern to discover if there was any fear of fire, after which they amused themselves by rolling on the bags of gold.

" At this moment my mother seized me in her arms, and bounding lightly along numerous turnings and windings, known only to ourselves, she arrived at a private staircase of the kiosk, where was a scene of frightful tumult and confusion. The lower rooms were entirely filled with the Tchodoars of Kourchid, that is to say, with our enemies. Just as my mother was on the point of pushing open a small door, we heard the voice of the pacha sounding in a loud and threatening tone. My mother applied her eye to the crack between the boards; I luckily found a small opening which afforded me a view of the apartment and what was passing within.

" ' What do you want? ' said my father to some people who were holding a paper inscribed with characters of gold.

" ' What we want,' replied one of them, ' is to communicate to you the will of his highness. Do you see this firman? '*

" ' I do,' said my father.

" ' Well, read it; he demands your head.'

" My father answered with a loud laugh, which was more frightful than even threats would have been, and he had not ceased when two reports of a pistol were heard: he had fired them himself, and had killed two men.

" The Palicares, who were prostrated at my father's feet, now sprang up and fired, and the room was filled with fire and smoke. At the same instant the firing began on the other side, and the balls penetrated the boards all round us.

" Oh, how noble did the grand vizier, my father, look at that moment, in the midst of the balls, his scimitar in his hand, and his face blackened with the powder of his enemies! and how he terrified them even then, and made them fly before him!

" ' Selim, Selim! ' cried he, ' guardian of the fire, do your duty! '

" ' Selim is dead! ' replied a voice, which seemed to come from the depths of the earth, ' and you are lost, Ali! ' At the same moment an explosion was heard, and the flooring of the room in which my father was sitting was suddenly torn up and shivered to atoms; the Tchodoars were firing underneath. Three or four Palicares fell with their bodies literally ploughed with wounds.

" My father howled aloud. He plunged his fingers into the holes which the balls had made, and tore up one of the planks entire. But immediately through this opening twenty more shots were fired, and the flame rushing up like fire from the crater of a volcano, soon gained the tapestry, which it quickly devoured. In the midst of all this frightful tumult and these terrific cries, two reports, fearfully distinct, followed by two shrieks more heart-rending than all, froze me with terror. These two shots had mortally wounded my father, and it was he who had given utterance to these frightful cries. However, he remained standing, clinging to a window. My mother tried to force the door that she might go and die with him, but it was fastened on the inside. All around him were lying the Palicares, writhing in convulsive agonies; whilst two or three, who were only slightly wounded, were trying to escape by springing from the windows. At this crisis the whole flooring suddenly gave way; my father fell on one knee, and at the same moment twenty hands were thrust forth armed with sabres, pistols, and poniards—twenty blows were instantaneously directed against one man, and my father disappeared in a whirlwind of fire and smoke kindled by these demons, and which seemed like hell itself opening beneath his feet. I felt myself fall to the ground; it was my mother who had fainted."

Haydée's arms fell by her side, and she uttered a deep groan, at the same time looking towards the count as if to ask if he were satisfied with her obedience to his commands. Monte Cristo rose and approached her; he took her hand, and said to her in Romaic:

"Calm yourself, my dear child, and take courage in remembering that there is a God who will punish traitors."

"It is a frightful story, count," said Albert, terrified at the paleness of Haydée's countenance, "and I reproach myself now for having been so cruel and thoughtless in my request."

"Oh, it is nothing!" said Monte Cristo.

Then patting the young girl on the head, he continued:

"Haydée is very courageous; and she sometimes even finds consolation in the recital of her misfortunes."

"Because, my lord," said Haydée eagerly, "my miseries recall to me the remembrance of your goodness."

Albert looked at her with curiosity, for she had not yet related what he most desired to know, namely, how she had become the slave of the count. Haydée saw at a glance the same expression pervading the countenances of her two auditors; she exclaimed:

"When my mother recovered her senses we were before the seraskier.

"'Kill me,' said she, 'but spare the honour of the widow of Ali.'

"'It is not me to whom you must address yourself,' said Kourchid.

"'To whom then?'

"'To your new master.'

"'Who and where is he?'

"'He is here.'

"And Kourchid pointed out one who had more than any contributed to the death of my father," said Haydée, in a tone of chastened anger.

"Then," said Albert, "you became the property of this man?"

"No," replied Haydée, "he did not dare to keep us, so we were sold to some slave-merchants who were going to Constantinople. We traversed Greece, and arrived half dead at the imperial gates. They were surrounded by a crowd of people, who opened a way for us to pass, when, suddenly, my mother having directed her eye to the object which was attracting their attention, uttered a piercing cry and fell to the ground, pointing as she did so to a head which was placed over the gates, and beneath which were inscribed these words:

'THIS IS THE HEAD OF ALI TEBELEN, PACHA OF YANINA.'

"I cried bitterly, and tried to raise my mother from the earth, but she was dead! I was taken to the slave-market, and was purchased by a rich Armenian. He caused me to be instructed, gave me masters, and when I was thirteen years of age he sold me to the Sultan Mahmoud."

" Of whom I bought her," said Monte Cristo, " as I told you, Albert, with the emerald which formed a match to the one I had made into a box for the purpose of holding my pastilles of hatchis."

" Oh, you are good, you are great, my lord! " said Haydée, kissing the count's hand, " and I am very fortunate in belonging to such a master."

Albert remained quite bewildered with all he had seen and heard.

" Come! finish your cup of coffee," said Monte Cristo; " the history is ended."

79

Yanina

IF Valentine could have seen the trembling step and agitated countenance of Franz when he quitted the chamber of M. Noirtier, even she would have been constrained to pity him. Villefort had only just given utterance to a few incoherent sentences, and then retired to his study, where he received about two hours afterwards the following letter:—

" After all the disclosures which were made this morning, M. Noirtier de Villefort must see the utter impossibility of any alliance being formed between his family and that of M. Franz d'Epinay. M. d'Epinay must say that he is shocked and astonished that M. de Villefort, who appeared to be aware of all the circumstances detailed this morning, should not have anticipated him in this announcement."

No one who had seen the magistrate at this moment so thoroughly unnerved by the recent inauspicious combination of circumstances would have supposed for an instant that he had anticipated the annoyance; although it certainly never had occurred to him that his father would carry candour, or rather rudeness, so far as to relate such a history. And in justice to Ville-fort, it must be understood that M. Noirtier, who never cared for the opinion of his son on any subject, had always omitted to explain the affair to Villefort, so that he had all his life entertained the belief that the General de Quesnel, or the Baron d'Epinay, as he was alternately styled, according as the speaker wished to identify him by his own family name or by the title which had been conferred on him, fell the victim of assassination, and not that he was killed fairly in a duel. This harsh letter, coming as it did from a man generally so polite and respectful, struck a mortal blow at the pride of Villefort. Hardly had he read the letter when his wife entered. The sudden departure of Franz after being summoned by M. Noirtier had so much astonished everyone that the position of Madame de Villefort, left alone with the notary and the witnesses, became every moment more embarrassing. Determined to bear it no longer, she rose and left the room, saying she would go and make some inquiries into the cause of his sudden disappearance.

M. de Villefort's communications on the subject were very limited and concise. He told her, in fact, that an explanation had taken place between M. Noirtier, M. d'Epinay, and himself, and that the marriage of Valentine and Franz would consequently be broken off. This was an awkward and unpleasant thing to have to report to those who were awaiting her return in the chamber of her father-in-law. She, therefore, contented herself with saying that M. Noirtier having, at the commencement of the discussion, been attacked by a sort of apoplectic fit, the affair would necessarily be deferred for some days longer. This news, false as it was, followed so singularly in the train of the two similar misfortunes which had so recently occurred, evidently astonished the auditors, and they retired without a remark. During this time, Valentine at once terrified and happy, after having embraced and thanked the feeble old man for thus breaking, with a single blow, the chain which she had been accustomed to consider as indissoluble, asked leave to retire to her own room in order to recover her composure, and Noirtier looked the permission which she solicited. But instead of going to her own room, Valentine having once gained her liberty, entered the gallery, and opening a small door at the end of it, found herself at once in the garden. It was high time for her to make her appearance at the gate, for Maximilian had long awaited her coming. He had half guessed what was going on when he saw Franz quit the cemetery with M. de Villefort. He followed M. d'Epinay, saw him enter, afterwards go out, and then re-enter with Albert and Château-Renaud. He had no longer any doubts as to the nature of the conference; he therefore quickly resumed his original position, prepared to hear the result of the proceedings, and very certain that Valentine would hasten to him the first moment she should be set at liberty. He was not mistaken; his eye, which was peering through the crevices of the wooden partition, soon discovered the young girl, who, throwing aside all her usual precautions, walked at once to the gate. The first glance which Maximilian directed towards her entirely reassured him, and the first words she pronounced made his heart bound with delight.

" We are saved! " said Valentine.

" Saved! " repeated Morrel, not being able to conceive such intense happiness; " by whom? "

" By my grandfather. Oh, Morrel, pray love him for all his goodness to us! "

Morrel swore to love him with all his soul; and at that moment he could safely promise to do so, for he felt as though it were not enough to love him merely as a friend or even as a father.

" But tell me, Valentine, how has it all been effected? What strange means has he used to compass this blessed end? "

Valentine was on the point of relating all that had passed, but she suddenly remembered that in doing so she must reveal a terrible secret which concerned others as well as her grandfather, and she said:

" At some future time I will tell you all about it."

" But when will that be? "

" When I am your wife."

The conversation had now turned upon a topic so pleasing to Morrel, that he was ready to accede to anything that Valentine thought fit to propose; and he likewise felt that a piece of intelligence such as he had just heard, ought to be more than sufficient to content him for one day. However, he would not leave without the promise of seeing Valentine again the next night.

During the time occupied by the interview we have just detailed, Madame de Villefort had gone to visit M. Noirtier. The old man looked at her with that stern and forbidding expression with which he was accustomed to receive her.

" Sir," said she, " it is superfluous for me to tell you that Valentine's marriage is broken off, since it was here that the affair was concluded."

Noirtier's countenance remained immovable.

" But one thing I can tell you, of which I do not think you are aware; that is, that I have always been opposed to this marriage, and that the contract was entered into entirely without my consent or approbation."

Noirtier regarded his daughter-in-law with a look of a man desiring an explanation.

" Now that this marriage, which I know you so much disliked

is done away with, I come to you on an errand which neither M. de Villefort nor Valentine could consistently undertake."

Noirtier's eyes demanded the nature of her mission.

" I come to entreat you, sir," continued Madame de Villefort, " as the only one who has the right of doing so inasmuch as I am the only one who will receive no personal benefit from the transaction,—I come to entreat you to restore, not your love, for that she has always possessed, but to restore your fortune to your granddaughter."

There was a doubtful expression in Noirtier's eyes; he was evidently trying to discover the motive of this proceeding, and he could not succeed in doing so.

" May I hope, sir," said Madame de Villefort, " that your intentions accord with my request? "

Noirtier made a sign that they did.

" In that case, sir," rejoined Madame de Villefort, " I will leave you overwhelmed with gratitude and happiness at your prompt acquiescence to my wishes."

She then bowed to M. Noirtier and retired.

The next day M. Noirtier sent for the notary. The first will was torn up and a second made, in which he left the whole of his fortune to Valentine, on condition that she should never be separated from him. It was then generally reported that Mademoiselle de Villefort, the heiress of the Marquis and Marchioness of Saint-Méran, had regained the good graces of her grandfather, and that she would ultimately be in possession of an income of 300,000 livres.

Whilst all the proceedings relative to the dissolution of the marriage-contract were being carried on at the house of M. de Villefort, Monte Cristo had paid his visit to the Comte de Morcerf, who, in order to lose no time in responding to M. Danglars' wishes, and at the same time to pay all due deference to his position in society, donned his uniform of lieutenant-general, which he ornamented with all his crosses, and, thus attired, ordered his finest horses and drove to the Rue de la Chaussée d'Antin. Danglars was balancing his monthly accounts, and it was, perhaps, not the most favourable moment for finding him in his best humour. At the first sight of his old friend, Danglars assumed his majestic air and settled himself in his easy-chair.

Morcerf, usually so stiff and formal, accosted the banker in an affable and smiling manner, and feeling sure that the overture he was about to make would be well received, he did not consider it necessary to adopt any manoeuvres in order to gain his end, but went at once straight to the point.

" Well, baron," said he, " here I am at last; some time has

elapsed since our plans were formed, and they are not yet executed."

Morcerf paused at these words, quietly waiting till the cloud should have dispersed which had gathered on the brow of Danglars, and which he attributed to his silence; but, on the contrary, to his great surprise, it grew darker and darker.

"To what do you allude, M. le Comte?" said Danglars; as if he was trying in vain to guess at the possible meaning of the general's words.

"Ah," said Morcerf, "I see you are a stickler for forms, my dear sir, and you would remind me that the ceremonial rites should not be omitted. *Ma foi!* I beg your pardon, but as I have but one son, and it is the first time I have ever thought of marrying him, I am still serving my apprenticeship, you know; come, I will reform." And Morcerf, with a forced smile, rose, and, making a low bow to M. Danglars, said:

"M. le Baron, I have the honour of asking of you the hand of Mademoiselle Eugénie Danglars for my son, Vicomte Albert de Morcerf."

But Danglars, instead of receiving this address in the favourable manner which Morcerf had expected, knit his brow, and without inviting the count, who was still standing, to take a seat, he said:

"M. le Comte, it will be necessary to reflect before I give you an answer."

"To reflect!" said M. Morcerf, more and more astonished; "have you not had enough time for reflection during the eight years which have elapsed since this marriage was first discussed between us?"

"M. le Comte," said the banker, "things are constantly occurring in the world to induce us to lay aside our most established opinions, or, at all events, to cause us to remodel them according to the change of circumstances which may have placed affairs in a totally different light to that in which we at first viewed them."

"I do not understand you, M. le Baron," said Morcerf.

"What I mean to say is this, sir; that during the last fortnight unforeseen circumstances have occurred——"

"Excuse me," said Morcerf; "but is it a play we are acting?"

"A play?"

"Yes, for it is like one; pray let us come more to the point, and endeavour thoroughly to understand each other."

"That is quite my desire."

"You have seen M. de Monte Cristo, have you not?"

"I see him very often," said Danglars, drawing himself up; "he is a particular friend of mine."

" Well, in one of your late conversations with him, you said that I appeared to be forgetful and irresolute concerning this marriage: did you not? "

" I did say so."

" Well, here I am, proving at once that I am really neither the one nor the other, by entreating you to keep your promise on that score."

Danglars did not answer.

" Have you so soon changed your mind," added Morcerf, " or have you only provoked my request that you may have the pleasure of seeing me humbled? "

Danglars seeing, that if he continued the conversation in the same tone in which he had begun it, the whole thing might turn out to his own disadvantage, turned to Morcerf, and said:

" M. le Comte, you must doubtless be surprised at my reserve, and I assure you it costs me much to act in such a manner towards you; but, believe me when I say, that imperative necessity has imposed the painful task upon me."

" These are all so many empty words, my dear sir," said Morcerf; " they might satisfy a new acquaintance, but the Comte de Morcerf does not rank in that list; and when a man like him comes to another, recalls to him his plighted word, and this man fails to redeem the pledge, he has, at least, a right to exact from him a good reason for so doing."

Danglars was a coward, but did not wish to appear so; he was piqued at the tone which Morcerf had just assumed.

" I am not without a good reason for my conduct," replied the banker.

" What do you mean to say? "

" I mean to say, that I have a good reason, but that it is difficult to explain."

" You must be aware, at all events, that it is impossible for me to understand motives before they are explained to me; but one thing at least is clear, which is, that you decline allying yourself with my family."

" No, sir," said Danglars; " I merely suspend my decision, that is all."

" And do you really flatter yourself that I shall yield to all your caprices, and quietly and humbly await the time of again being received into your good graces? "

" Then, M. le Comte, if you will not wait, we must look upon these projects as if they had never been entertained."

The count bit his lips till the blood almost started, to prevent the ebullition of anger which his proud and irritable temper scarcely allowed him to restrain. Understanding, however, that in the present state of things the laugh would decidedly be against him, he turned from the door, towards which he had been directing his steps, and again confronted the banker. A cloud settled on his brow, evincing decided anxiety and uneasiness, instead of the expression of offended pride which had lately reigned there.

"My dear Danglars," said Morcerf, "we have been acquainted for many years, and consequently we ought to make some allowances for each other's failings. You owe me an explanation, and really it is but fair that I should know what circumstance has occurred to deprive my son of your favour."

"It is from no personal ill-feeling towards the viscount, that is all I can say, sir," replied Danglars, who resumed his insolent manner as soon as he perceived that Morcerf was a little softened and calmed down.

"And towards whom do you bear this personal ill-feeling, then?" said Morcerf, turning pale with anger.

The expression of the count's face had not remained unperceived by the banker; he fixed on him a look of greater assurance than before, and said:

"You may, perhaps, be better satisfied that I should not go further into particulars."

A trembling, caused by repressed rage, shook the whole frame of the count, and making a violent effort over himself, he said:

"I have a right to insist on your giving me an explanation. Is it Madame de Morcerf who has displeased you? is it my fortune which you find insufficient? is it because my opinions differ from yours?"

"Nothing of the kind, sir," replied Danglars; "if such had been the case, I only should have been to blame, inasmuch as I was aware of all these things when I made the engagement. No, do not seek any longer to discover the reason. I really am quite ashamed to have been the cause of your undergoing such severe self-examination; let us drop the subject, and adopt the middle course, namely, delay, which implies neither a rupture nor an engagement. *Ma foi!* there is no hurry. My daughter is only seventeen years old, and your son twenty-one. Whilst we wait time will be progressing, events will succeed each other; things which in the evening look dark and obscure appear but too clearly in the light of morning, and sometimes the utterance of one word, or the lapse of a single day, will reveal the most cruel calumnies."

"Calumnies, did you say, sir?" cried Morcerf, turning livid with rage. "Does anyone dare to slander me?"

" M. le Comte, I told you that I considered it best to avoid all explanation."

" Then, sir, I am patiently to submit to your refusal? "

" Yes, sir, although I assure you the refusal is as painful for me to give, as it is for you to receive, for I had reckoned on the honour of your alliance, and the breaking off of a marriage-contract always injures the lady more than the gentleman."

" Enough, sir," said Morcerf; " we will speak no more on the subject." And clenching his gloves with passion, he left the apartment.

Danglars remarked that during the whole conversation Morcerf had never once dared to ask if it was on his own account that Danglars recalled his word. That evening there was a long conference between several friends, and M. Cavalcanti, who had remained in the drawing-room with the ladies, was the last to leave the house of the banker.

The next morning, directly he awoke, Danglars asked for the newspapers; they were brought to him; he laid aside three or four, and at last fixed on *l'Impartial:* it was the paper of which Beauchamp was the chief editor. He hastily tore off the cover, opened the journal with nervous precipitation, passed contemptuously over *le premier Paris*, and arriving at the miscellaneous intelligence, stopped, with a malicious smile, at a paragraph headed " YANINA."

" Very good! " observed Danglars, after having read the paragraph; " here is a little article on Colonel Fernand, which, if I am not mistaken, would render the explanation which the Comte de Morcerf required of me perfectly unnecessary."

At the same moment, that is, at nine o'clock in the morning, Albert de Morcerf, dressed in a black coat buttoned up to his chin, might have been seen walking with a quick and agitated step in the direction of Monte Cristo's house in the Champs Elysées. When he presented himself at the gate the porter informed him that the count had gone out about half an hour previously.

" Did he take Baptistin with him? "

" No, M. le Vicomte."

" Call him, then; I wish to speak to him."

The *concierge* went to seek the valet-de-chambre, and returned with him in an instant.

" My good friend," said Albert, " I beg pardon for my intrusion; but I was anxious to know from your own mouth if your master was really out or not."

" He is really out, sir," replied Baptistin.

" Out, even to me? "

" I know how happy my master always is to receive M. le

Vicomte," said Baptistin; "and I should therefore never think
of including him in any general order."

"You are right; and now I wish to see him on an affair of
great importance. Do you think it will be long before he
comes in?"

"No, I think not, for he ordered his breakfast at ten o'clock."

"Well, I will go and take a turn in the Champs Elysées, and
at ten o'clock I will return here; meanwhile, if M. le Comte
should come in, will you beg him not to go out again without
seeing me?"

"You may depend on my doing so, sir," said Baptistin.

Albert left the *fiacre* in which he had come standing at the door
of the count, intending to take a turn on foot. As he was passing
the Allée des Veuves, he thought he saw the count's horses
standing at Gossett's shooting-gallery;* he approached, and soon
recognised the coachman.

"Is M. le Comte shooting in the gallery?" said Morcerf.

"Yes, sir," replied the coachman.

Whilst he was speaking, Albert had heard the report of two
or three pistol-shots. He entered, and on his way met the
waiter.

"Excuse me, M. le Vicomte," said the lad; "but will you
have the kindness to wait a moment?"

"What for, Philip?" asked Albert, who, being a constant
visitor there, did not understand this opposition to his entrance.

"Because the person who is now in the gallery prefers being
alone, and never practises in the presence of anyone."

"Not even before you, Philip? Then who loads his pistols?"

"His servant."

"A Nubian?"

"A Negro."

"It is he, then."

"Do you know this gentleman?"

"Yes, and I am come to look for him; he is a friend of mine."

"Oh, that is quite another thing, then. I will go immediately
and inform him of your arrival."

And Philip, urged by his own curiosity, entered the gallery;
a second afterwards, Monte Cristo appeared on the threshold.

"I ask your pardon, my dear count," said Albert, "for
following you here; and I must first tell you that it was not the
fault of your servants that I did so. I alone am to blame for the
indiscretion. I went to your house, and they told me you were
out, but that they expected you home at ten o'clock to breakfast.
I was walking about in order to pass away the time till ten
o'clock, when I caught sight of your carriage and horses."

" What you have just said induces me to hope that you intend breakfasting with me."

" No, thank you, I am thinking of other things besides breakfast, just now; perhaps we may take that meal at a later hour and in worse company."

" What on earth are you talking of? "

" I am to fight to-day."

" What for? "

" I am going to fight——"

" Yes, I understand that, but what is the quarrel? People fight for all sorts of reasons, you know."

" I fight in the cause of honour."

" Ah, that is something serious."

" So serious, that I come to beg you to render me a service."

" What is it? "

" To be my second."

" That is a serious matter, and we will not discuss it here; let us speak of nothing till we get home. Ali, bring me some water."

The count turned up his sleeves, and passed into the little vestibule where the gentlemen were accustomed to wash their hands after shooting.

" Come in, M. le Vicomte," said Philip, in a low tone, " and I will show you something droll."

Morcerf entered, and instead of the usual mark, he perceived some playing-cards fixed against the wall. At a distance Albert thought it was a complete suit, for he counted from the ace to the ten.

" Ah! ah! " said Albert, " I see you were preparing for a game of cards."

" No," said the count, " I was making a suit of cards."

" How? " said Albert.

" Those are really aces and twos which you see, but my balls have turned them into threes, fives, sevens, eights, nines, and tens."

Albert approached.

In fact the balls had actually pierced the cards in the exact places which the painted signs would otherwise have occupied, the lines and distances being as regularly kept as if they had been ruled with a pencil.

" *Diable!* " said Morcerf.

" What would you have, my dear viscount? " said Monte Cristo, wiping his hands on the towel which Ali had brought him; " I must occupy my leisure moments in some way or other. But come, I am waiting for you."

Both then entered Monte Cristo's chariot, which in the course of a few minutes deposited them safely at No. 30. Monte Cristo took Albert into his study, and pointing to a seat, placed another for himself.

" Now let us talk the matter over quietly," said the count.

" You see I am perfectly composed," said Albert.

" With whom are you going to fight? "

" With Beauchamp."

" Is he one of your friends? "

" Of course; it is always with friends that one fights."

" I suppose you have some cause of quarrel? "

" I have."

" What has he done to you? "

" There appeared in his journal last night—— But wait, read for yourself."

And Albert handed over the paper to the count, who read as follows:—

" A correspondent at Yanina informs us of a fact of which until now we had remained in ignorance. The castle which formed the protection of the town was given up to the Turks by a French officer named Fernand, in whom the Grand Vizier, Ali Tebelen, had reposed the greatest confidence."

" Well," said Monte Cristo, " what do you see in that to annoy you? "

" What do I see in it? "

" Yes; what does it signify to you if the castle of Yanina was given up by a French officer? "

" It signifies to my father, the Count of Morcerf, whose Christian name is Fernand."

" Did your father serve Ali Pacha? "

" Yes; that is to say, he fought for the independence of the Greeks, and hence arises the calumny."

" Oh, my dear viscount, do talk reason! "

" I do not desire to do otherwise."

" Now just tell me, who the devil should know in France that the officer Fernand and the Comte de Morcerf are one and the same person? and who cares now about Yanina, which was taken as long ago as the year 1822 or 1823? "

" That just proves the blackness of the perfidy: they have allowed all this time to elapse, and then, all of a sudden, rake up events which have been forgotten, to furnish materials for scandal, in order to tarnish the lustre of our high position. I inherit my father's name, and I do not choose that the shadow of disgrace should darken it. I am going to Beauchamp, in whose journal this paragraph appears, and I shall insist on his retracting the assertion before two witnesses."

"Beauchamp will never retract."

"Then he must fight."

"No, he will not, for he will tell you, what is very true, that perhaps there were fifty officers in the Greek army bearing the same name."

"We will fight, nevertheless. I will efface that blot on my father's character. My father, who was such a brave soldier, whose career was so brilliant——"

"Oh, well, he will add, 'We are warranted in believing that this Fernand is not the illustrious Comte de Morcerf, who also bears the same Christian name.'"

"I am determined not to be content with anything short of an entire retractation."

"And you intend to make him do it in the presence of two witnesses, do you?"

"Yes."

"You do wrong."

"Which means, I suppose, that you refuse the service which I asked of you?"

"You know my theory regarding duels; I told you my opinion on that subject, if you remember, when we were at Rome."

"Nevertheless, my dear count, I found you this morning engaged in an occupation but little consistent with the notions you profess to entertain."

"Because, my dear fellow, you understand one must never be eccentric. If one's lot is cast amongst fools, it is necessary to study folly. I shall, perhaps, find myself one day called out by some hare-brained scamp, who has no more real cause of quarrel with me than you have with Beauchamp; he may take me to task for some foolish trifle or other, he will bring his witnesses, or will insult me in some public place, and I suppose I am expected to kill him for all that."

"You admit that you would fight, then? Well, if so, why do you object to my doing so?"

"I do not say that you ought not to fight, I only say that a duel is a serious thing, and ought not to be undertaken without due reflection."

"Did he reflect before he insulted my father?"

"If he spoke hastily, and owns that he did so, you ought to be satisfied."

"Ah, my dear count, you are far too indulgent."

" And you far too exacting. Supposing, for instance, and do not be angry at what I am going to say——"

" Well! "

" Supposing the assertion to be really true? "

" A son ought not to submit to such a stain on his father's honour."

" *Ma foi!* we live in times when there is much to which we must submit."

" That is precisely the fault of the age."

" And do you undertake to reform it? "

" Yes, as far as I am personally concerned."

" *Ma foi!* you are indeed rigid, my dear fellow! "

" Well, I own it."

" Are you quite impervious to good advice? "

" Not when it comes from a friend."

" And do you accord me that title? "

" Certainly I do."

" Well, then, before going to Beauchamp with your witnesses, seek further information on the subject."

" From whom? "

" From Haydée."

" Why, what can be the use of mixing a woman up in the affair?—what can she do in it? "

" She can declare to you, for example, that your father had no hand whatever in the defeat and death of the vizier, or if by chance he had indeed the misfortune to——"

" I have already told you, my dear count, that I would not for one moment admit of such a supposition."

" You reject this means of information, then? "

" I do—most decidedly."

" Then let me offer one more word of advice."

" Do so, then, but let it be the last."

" You do not wish to hear it, perhaps? "

" On the contrary, I request it."

" Do not take any witnesses with you when you go to Beauchamp—visit him alone."

" That would be contrary to all custom."

" Your case is not an ordinary one."

" And what is your reason for advising me to go alone? "

" Because then the affair will rest between you and Beauchamp."

" Explain yourself."

" I will do so. If Beauchamp be disposed to retract, you ought at least to give him the opportunity of doing it of his own free will; the satisfaction to you will be the same. If, on the contrary, he refuses to do so, it will then be quite time enough to admit two strangers into your secret."

" They will not be strangers, they will be friends."

" Ah, but the friends of to-day are the enemies of to-morrow; Beauchamp, for instance."

" So you recommend——"

" I recommend you to be prudent."

" Then you advise me to go alone to Beauchamp? "

" I do, and I will tell you why. When you wish to obtain some concession from a man's self-love, you must avoid even the appearance of wishing to wound it."

" I believe you are right."

" I am glad of it."

" Then I will go alone."

" Go; but you would do better still by not going at all."

" That is impossible."

" Do so, then; it will be a wiser plan than the first which you proposed."

" But if, in spite of all my precautions, I am at last obliged to fight, will you not be my second? "

" My dear viscount," said Monte Cristo gravely, " you must have seen before to-day that at all times and in all places I have been at your disposal, but the service which you have just demanded of me is one which it is out of my power to render you."

" Why? "

" Perhaps you may know at some future period; and, in the meantime, I request you to excuse my declining to put you in possession of my reasons."

" Well, I will have Franz and Château-Renaud; they will be the very men for it."

" Do so, then."

" But if I do fight, you will surely not object to giving me a lesson or two in shooting and fencing? "

" That, too, is impossible."

" What a singular being you are!—you will not interfere in anything."

" You are right—that is the principle on which I wish to act."

" We will say no more about it, then. Good-bye, count."

Morcerf took his hat, and left the room. He found his chariot at the door, and doing his utmost to restrain his anger, he drove at once to Beauchamp's house.

Beauchamp was in his office. It was one of those gloomy, dusty-looking apartments, such as journalists' offices have always been from time immemorial.

The servant announced M. Albert de Morcerf. Beauchamp repeated the name to himself, as though he could scarcely believe that he had heard right, and then gave orders for him to be admitted. Albert entered.

Beauchamp uttered an exclamation of surprise on seeing his friend leap over and trample under foot all the newspapers which were strewed about the room.

" Here, here, my dear Albert! " said he, holding out his hand to the young man. " Are you out of your senses, or do you come peaceably to take breakfast with me? Try and find a seat— there is one by that geranium, which is the only thing in the room to remind me that there are other leaves in the world besides leaves of paper."

" Beauchamp," said Albert, " it is of your journal that I come to speak."

" Indeed! what do you wish to say about it? "

" I desire that a statement contained in it should be rectified."

" To what do you allude? But pray sit down."

" Thank you," said Albert, with a cold and formal bow.

" Will you now have the kindness to explain the nature of the statement which has displeased you? "

" An announcement has been made which implicates the honour of a member of my family."

" What is it? " said Beauchamp, much surprised; " surely you must be mistaken."

" It is an article headed Yanina."

" Yanina? "

" Yes; really you appear to be totally ignorant of the cause which brings me here."

" Such is really the case, I assure you, upon my honour! Baptiste, give me yesterday's paper," cried Beauchamp.

" Here, I have brought mine with me," replied Albert.

Beauchamp took the paper, and read the article to which Albert pointed in an undertone.

" You see it is a serious annoyance," said Morcerf, when Beauchamp had finished the perusal of the paragraph.

" Is the officer alluded to a relation of yours, then? " demanded the journalist.

" Yes," said Albert, blushing.

" Well, what do you wish me to do for you? " said Beauchamp mildly.

" My dear Beauchamp, I wish you to contradict this statement."

Beauchamp looked at Albert with a benevolent expression.

" Come," said he, " this matter will want a good deal of

talking over; a retractation is always a serious thing, you know. Sit down, and I will read it again."

Albert resumed his seat, and Beauchamp read, with more attention than at first, the lines denounced by his friend.

"Well," said Albert, in a determined tone, "you see that your paper has insulted a member of my family, and I insist on a retractation being made."

"You insist?"

"Yes, I insist."

"Permit me to remind you that you are not in the Chamber, my dear viscount."

"Nor do I wish to be there," replied the young man, rising. "I repeat that I am determined to have the announcement of yesterday contradicted. You have known me long enough," continued Albert, biting his lips convulsively, for he saw that Beauchamp's anger was beginning to rise,—"you have been my friend, and therefore sufficiently intimate with me to be aware that I am likely to maintain my resolution on this point."

"If I have been your friend, Morcerf, your present manner of speaking would almost lead me to forget that I ever bore that title. But wait a moment, do not let us get angry, or, at least, not yet. You are irritated and vexed—tell me how this Fernand is related to you?"

"He is merely my father," said Albert; "M. Fernand Mondego, Comte de Morcerf, an old soldier, who has fought in twenty battles, and whose honourable scars they would denounce as badges of disgrace."

"Is it your father?" said Beauchamp; "that is quite another thing. Then I can well understand your indignation, my dear Albert. I will re-peruse;" and he read the paragraph for the third time, laying a stress on each word as he proceeded. "But the paper nowhere identifies this Fernand with your father."

"No; but the connection will be seen by others, and therefore I will have the article contradicted."

At the words *I will*, Beauchamp steadily raised his eye to Albert's countenance, and then as gradually lowering them, he remained thoughtful for a few moments.

"You will retract this assertion, will you not, Beauchamp?" said Albert, with increased though stifled anger.

"Yes," replied Beauchamp.

"Immediately?" said Albert.

"When I am convinced that the statement is false."

"What?"

"The thing is worth looking into, and I will take pains to investigate the matter thoroughly."

" But what is there to investigate, sir? " said Albert, enraged beyond measure at Beauchamp's last remark. " If you do not believe that it is my father, say so immediately; and if, on the contrary, you believe it to be him, state your reasons for doing so."

Beauchamp looked at Albert with the smile which was so peculiar to him, and which, in its numerous modifications, served to express every varied feeling of his mind.

" Sir," replied he, " if you came to me with the idea of demanding satisfaction, you should have gone at once to the point, and not have entertained me with the idle conversation to which I have been patiently listening for the last half-hour. Am I to put this construction on your visit? "

" Yes, if you will not consent to retract that infamous calumny."

" Wait a moment—no threats, if you please, M. Fernand Mondego, Vicomte de Morcerf; I never allow them from my enemies, and, therefore, shall not put up with them from my friends. You insist on my contradicting the article relating to General Fernand, an article in which, I assure you, on my word of honour, I have not taken the slightest share? "

" Yes, I insist on it! " said Albert, whose mind was beginning to get bewildered with the excitement of his feelings.

" And if I refuse to retract, you wish to fight, do you? " said Beauchamp, in a calm tone.

" Yes," replied Albert, raising his voice.

" Well," said Beauchamp, " here is my answer, my dear sir. The article was not inserted by me—I was not even aware of it; but you have by the step you have taken called my attention to the paragraph in question, and it will remain until it shall be either contradicted or confirmed by someone who has a right to do so."

" Sir," said Albert, rising, " I will do myself the honour of sending my seconds to you, and you will be kind enough to arrange with them the place of meeting and the arms which we are to use; do you understand me? "

" Certainly, my dear sir."

" And this evening, if you please, or to-morrow at the latest, we will meet."

" No, no! I will be on the ground at the proper time; but, in my opinion (and I have a right to dictate the preliminaries, as it is I who have received the provocation)—in my opinion, the time ought not to be yet. I know you to be well skilled in the management of the sword, whilst I am only moderately so; I know, too, that you are a good marksman—there we are about equal. I know that a duel between us two would be a serious affair, because you are brave, and I am brave also. I do not therefore wish either to kill you, or to be killed myself, without a cause. Now I am going to put a question to you, and one very much to the purpose, too. Do you insist on this retractation so far as to kill me if I do not make it, although I have repeated more than once, and affirmed, on my honour, that I was ignorant of the thing with which you charge me, and although I still declare that it is impossible for anyone but you to recognise the Comte de Morcerf under the name of Fernand? "

" I maintain my original resolution."

" Very well, my dear sir, then I consent to cut throats with you. But I require three weeks' preparation; at the end of that time I shall come and say to you, ' The assertion is false, and I retract it,' or, ' The assertion is true,' when I shall immediately draw the sword from its sheath, or the pistols from the case, whichever you please."

" Three weeks! " cried Albert; " they will pass as slowly as three centuries, when I am all the time suffering dishonour."

" Had you continued to remain on amicable terms with me, I should have said, ' Patience, my friend '; but you have constituted yourself my enemy, therefore I say, ' What does that signify to me, sir? ' "

" Well, let it be three weeks, then," said Morcerf; " but remember, at the expiration of that time, no delay or subterfuge will justify you in——"

" M. Albert de Morcerf," said Beauchamp, rising in his turn. " I cannot throw you out of window for three weeks, that is to say, for twenty-four days to come, nor have you any right to split my skull open till that time has elapsed. To-day is the 29th of August, the 21st of September will, therefore, be the conclusion of the term agreed on, and till that time arrives we will refrain from growling and barking like two dogs chained within sight of each other."

When he had concluded this speech, Beauchamp bowed coldly to Albert, turned his back upon him, and retired to his printing-office. As Albert in his chariot was crossing the barrier, he perceived Morrel, who was walking with a quick step and a bright eye. He was passing the Chinese Baths, and appeared to have come from the direction of the Porte Saint-Martin, and to be going towards the Magdalen.

" Ah," said Morcerf, " there goes a happy man! "

And Albert was not mistaken in his opinion.

80

The Lemonade

MORREL was, in fact, very happy. M. Noirtier had just sent for him, and he was in such haste to know the reason of his doing so, that he had not stopped to take a *fiacre*, placing infinitely more dependence on his own two legs than on the four legs of a cab-horse. He had, therefore, set off at a furious rate from the Rue Meslay, and was hastening with rapid strides in the direction of the Faubourg Saint-Honoré. Morrel advanced with a firm, manly tread, and poor Barrois followed him, as he best might. Morrel was only thirty-one, Barrois was sixty years of age; Morrel was deeply in love, and Barrois was dying with heat and exertion. These two men, thus opposed in age and interests, resembled two parts of a triangle, presenting the extremes of separation, yet, nevertheless, possessing their point of union. This point of union was Noirtier, and it was he who had just sent for Morrel with the request that he would lose no time in coming to him,—a command which Morrel obeyed to the letter, to the great discomfiture of Barrois.

On arriving at the house, Morrel was not even out of breath, for love lends wings to our desires; but Barrois, who had long forgotten what it was to love, was sorely fatigued by the expedition he had been constrained to use.

The old servant introduced Morrel by a private entrance, closed the door of the study, and soon the rustling of a dress announced the arrival of Valentine. She looked marvellously beautiful in her deep mourning dress, and Morrel experienced such intense delight in gazing upon her, that he felt as if he could almost have dispensed with the conversation of her grandfather. But the easy-chair of the old man was heard rolling along the floor, and he soon made his appearance in the room. Noirtier acknowledged by a look of extreme kindness and benevolence the thanks which Morrel lavished on him for his timely intervention on behalf of Valentine and himself,—an intervention which had saved them from despair. Morrel then cast on the invalid an interrogative look as to the new favour which he designed to bestow on him. Valentine was sitting at a little distance from them, timidly awaiting the moment when she should be obliged to speak. Noirtier fixed his eyes on her.

" Am I to say what you told me? " asked Valentine.

Noirtier made a sign that she was to do so.

" M. Morrel," said Valentine to the young man, who was regarding her with the most intense interest, " my grandfather, M. Noirtier, had a thousand things to say, which he told me three days ago; and now he has sent for you, that I may report them to you. I will repeat them, then; and since he has chosen me as his interpreter, I will be faithful to the trust, and will not alter a word of his intentions."

" Oh, I am listening with the greatest impatience," replied the young man; " speak, I beg of you."

Valentine cast down her eyes; this was a good omen for Morrel, for he knew that nothing but happiness could have the power of thus overcoming Valentine.

" My grandfather intends leaving this house," said she, " and Barrois is looking out suitable apartments for him in another."

" But you, Mademoiselle de Villefort, you, who are necessary to M. Noirtier's happiness——"

" Me? " interrupted Valentine, " I shall not leave my grandfather, that is an understood thing between us. My apartment will be close to his. Now M. de Villefort must either give his consent to this plan or his refusal; in the first case, I shall leave directly, and in the second, I shall await my majority, which will be completed in about ten months. Then I shall be free, I shall have an independent fortune, and——"

" And what? " demanded Morrel.

" And with my grandfather's consent I shall fulfil the promise which I have made you."

Valentine pronounced these few last words in such a low tone, that nothing but Morrel's intense interest in what she was saying could have enabled him to hear them.

" Have I not explained your wishes, grandpapa? " said Valentine, addressing Noirtier.

" Yes," looked the old man.

" Once under my grandfather's roof, M. Morrel can visit me in the presence of my good and worthy protector, if we still feel that the union we contemplated will be likely to insure our future comfort and happiness; in that case I shall expect M. Morrel to come and claim me. But alas! I have heard it said, that hearts inflamed by obstacles to their desire grow cold in time of security; I trust we shall never find it so in our experience."

" Oh," cried Morrel, almost tempted to throw himself on his knees before Noirtier and Valentine, and to adore them as two superior beings, " what have I ever done in my life to merit such unbounded happiness? "

" Until that time," continued the young girl, in a calm and self-possessed tone of voice, " we will conform to circumstances, and be guided by the wishes of our friends, so long as those wishes do not tend finally to separate us; in one word, and I repeat it, because it expresses all I wish to convey,—we will wait."

" And I swear to make all the sacrifices which this word imposes, sir," said Morrel, " not only with resignation, but with cheerfulness."

" Therefore," continued Valentine, looking playfully at Maximilian, " no more inconsiderate actions, no more rash projects; for you surely would not wish to compromise the feelings of her who from this day regards herself as destined, honourably and happily, to bear your name? "

Morrel looked obedience to her commands. Noirtier regarded the lovers with a look of ineffable tenderness, whilst Barrois, who had remained in the room in the character of a man privileged to know everything that passed, smiled on the youthful couple as he wiped the perspiration from his bald forehead.

" How hot you look, my good Barrois! " said Valentine.

" Ah! I have been running very fast, mademoiselle, but I must do M. Morrel the justice to say that he ran still faster."

Noirtier directed their attention to a waiter, on which was placed a decanter containing lemonade and a glass. The decanter was nearly full, with the exception of a little, which had been already drunk by M. Noirtier.

" Come, Barrois," said the young girl, " take some of this lemonade; I see you are coveting a good draught of it."

" The fact is, mademoiselle," said Barrois, " I am dying with thirst, and since you are so kind as to offer it me, I cannot say I should at all object to drinking your health in a glass of it."

" Take some, then, and come back immediately."

Barrois took away the waiter, and hardly was he outside the door which, in his haste, he forgot to shut, than they saw him throw back his head and empty to the very dregs the glass which Valentine had filled. Valentine and Morrel were exchanging their adieux in the presence of Noirtier when a ring was heard at the door-bell. It was the signal of a visit. Valentine looked at her watch.

" It is past noon," said she, " and to-day is Saturday; I dare say it is the doctor, grandpapa."

Noirtier looked his conviction that she was right in her supposition.

" He will come in here, and M. Morrel had better go: do you not think so, grandpapa? "

" Yes," signed the old man.

" Barrois! " called Valentine; " Barrois! "

" I am coming, mademoiselle," replied he.

" Barrois will open the door for you," said Valentine, addressing Morrel. " And now remember one thing, Mr. Officer, that my grandfather commands you not to take any rash or ill-advised step which would be likely to compromise our happiness."

" I promised him to wait," replied Morrel; " and I will wait."

At this moment Barrois entered.

" Who rang? " asked Valentine.

" Doctor d'Avrigny," said Barrois, staggering as if he would fall.

" What is the matter, Barrois? " said Valentine.

The old man did not answer, but looked at his master with wild staring eyes, whilst with his cramped hand he grasped a piece of furniture to enable him to stand upright.

" He is going to fall! " cried Morrel.

The trembling which had attacked Barrois gradually increased, the features of the face became quite altered, and the convulsive movement of the muscles appeared to indicate the approach of a most serious nervous disorder. Noirtier, seeing Barrois in this pitiable condition, showed by his looks all the various emotions of sorrow and sympathy which can animate the heart of man. Barrois made some steps towards his master.

" Ah, sir," said he, " tell me what is the matter with me? I am suffering—I cannot see. A thousand fiery darts are piercing my brain. Ah, don't touch me, pray don't."

By this time, his haggard eyes had the appearance of being ready to start from their sockets; his head fell back, and the lower extremities of the body began to stiffen.

Valentine uttered a cry of horror; Morrel took her in his arms, as if to defend her from some unknown danger.

" M. d'Avrigny, M. d'Avrigny! " cried she, in a stifled voice. " Help! help! "

Barrois turned round, and, with a great effort, stumbled a few steps, then fell at the feet of Noirtier, and resting his hand on the knee of the invalid, exclaimed, " My master, my good master! "

At this moment M. de Villefort, attracted by the noise, appeared on the threshold. Morrel relaxed his hold on Valentine, and retreating to a distant corner of the room, he remained half-hidden behind a curtain. Pale as if he had been gazing on a serpent, he fixed his terrified eye on the agonised sufferer.

Noirtier, burning with impatience and terror, was in despair at his utter inability to help his old domestic, whom he regarded more in the light of a friend than a servant. One might trace the terrible conflict which was going on between the living, energetic mind and the inanimate and helpless body, by the fearful swelling of the veins of his forehead and the contraction of the muscles round the eye. Barrois, his features convulsed, his eyes suffused with blood, and his head thrown back, was lying at full length, beating the floor with his hands, whilst his legs had become so stiff that they looked as if they would break rather than bend. A slight appearance of foam was visible round the mouth, and he breathed painfully and with extreme difficulty.

Villefort seemed stupefied with astonishment, and remained gazing intently on the scene before him, without uttering a word. He had not seen Morrel. After a moment of dumb contemplation, during which his face became pale, and his hair seemed to stand on end, he sprang towards the door, crying out:

" Doctor, doctor! come instantly, pray come."

" Madame, madame! " cried Valentine, calling her step-mother, and running upstairs to meet her; " come quick, quick! and bring your bottle of smelling-salts with you."

" What is the matter? " said Madame de Villefort, in a harsh and constrained tone.

" Oh, come, come! "

" But where is the doctor? " exclaimed Villefort; " where is he? "

Madame de Villefort now deliberately descended the staircase. In one hand she held her handkerchief, with which she appeared to be wiping her face, and in the other a bottle of English smelling-salts. Her first look on entering the room was at Noirtier, whose face, independent of the emotion which such a scene could not fail of producing, proclaimed him to be in possession of his usual health; her second glance was at the dying man. She turned pale, and her eye passed quickly from the servant and rested on the master.

" In the name of Heaven, madame," said Villefort, " where is the doctor?—he was with you just now. You see this is a fit of apoplexy, and he might be saved if he could but be bled! "

" Has he eaten anything lately? " asked Madame de Villefort, eluding her husband's question.

" Madame," replied Valentine, " he has not even breakfasted. He has been running very fast on an errand with which my grandfather charged him, and when he returned he took nothing but a glass of lemonade."

" Ah! " said Madame de Villefort; " why did he not take wine? lemonade was a very bad thing for him."

" Grandpapa's bottle of lemonade was standing just by his side; poor Barrois was very thirsty, and was thankful to drink anything he could find."

Madame de Villefort started. Noirtier looked at her with a glance of the most profound scrutiny.

" He has such a short neck," said she.

" Madame," said De Villefort, " I ask where is M. d'Avrigny? In God's name answer me! "

" He is with Edward, who is not quite well," replied Madame de Villefort, no longer being able to avoid answering.

Villefort rushed upstairs to fetch him himself.

" Take this," said Madame de Villefort, giving her smelling-bottle to Valentine. " They will, no doubt, bleed him; therefore I will retire, for I cannot endure the sight of blood "; and she followed her husband upstairs.

Morrel now emerged from his hiding-place, where he had remained quite unperceived, so great had been the general confusion.

" Go away as quick as you can, Maximilian," said Valentine, " and stay till I send for you. Go."

Morrel looked towards Noirtier for permission to retire. The old man, who had preserved all his usual *sang froid*, made a sign to him to do so. The young man pressed Valentine's hand to his lips, and then left the house by a back staircase. At the same moment that he quitted the room, Villefort and the doctor entered by an opposite entrance. Barrois was now showing signs of returning consciousness, the crisis seemed past, a low moaning was heard, and he raised himself on one knee. D'Avrigny and Villefort laid him on a couch.

" What do you prescribe, doctor? " demanded Villefort.

" Give me some water and ether; you have some in the house, have you not? "

" Yes."

" Send for some oil of turpentine and tartar emetic."

Villefort immediately despatched a messenger.

" And now let everyone retire."

" Must I go, too? " asked Valentine timidly.

" Yes, mademoiselle, you especially," replied the doctor abruptly.

Valentine looked at M. d'Avrigny with astonishment, kissed her grandfather on the forehead, and left the room. The doctor closed the door after her with a gloomy air.

" Look, look, doctor," said Villefort; " he is quite coming

round again; I really do not think, after all, it is anything of consequence."

M. d'Avrigny answered by a melancholy smile.

" How do you feel yourself, Barrois? " asked he.

" A little better, sir."

" Will you drink some of this ether and water? "

" I will try; but don't touch me."

" Why not? "

" Because I feel that if you were only to touch me with the tip of your finger, the fit would return."

" Drink."

Barrois took the glass, and raising it to his purple lips, took about half of the liquid offered him.

" Where do you suffer? " asked the doctor.

" Everywhere; I feel cramp over my whole body."

" Do you find any dazzling sensation before the eyes? "

" Yes."

" Any noise in the ears? "

" Frightful."

" When did you first feel that ? "

" Just now."

" Suddenly? "

" Yes, like a clap of thunder."

" Did you feel nothing of it yesterday or the day before? "

" Nothing."

" No drowsiness? "

" None."

" What have you eaten to-day? "

" I have eaten nothing; I only drank a glass of my master's lemonade—that's all; " and Barrois turned towards Noirtier, who, immovably fixed in his arm-chair, was contemplating this terrible scene without allowing a word or a movement to escape him.

" Where is this lemonade? " asked the doctor eagerly.

" Downstairs, in the decanter."

" Whereabouts downstairs? "

" In the kitchen."

" Shall I go and fetch it, doctor? " inquired Villefort.

" No, stay here, and try to make Barrois drink the rest of this glass of ether and water. I will go myself and fetch the lemonade."

D'Avrigny bounded towards the door, flew down the back staircase, and almost knocked down Madame de Villefort in his haste, who was herself going down to the kitchen. D'Avrigny paid no attention to her; possessed with but one idea, he cleared the last four steps with a bound, and rushed into the kitchen, where he saw the decanter about three parts empty still standing on the waiter, where it had been left. He darted upon it as an eagle would seize upon its prey. Panting with loss of breath, he returned to the room he had just left. Madame de Villefort was slowly ascending the steps which led to her room.

" Is this the decanter you spoke of? " asked D'Avrigny.

" Yes, doctor."

" Is this the same lemonade of which you partook? "

" I believe so."

" What did it taste like? "

" It had a bitter taste."

The doctor poured some drops of the lemonade into the palm of his hand, put his lips to it, and after having rinsed his mouth as a man does when he is tasting wine, he spat the liquor into the fireplace.

" It is no doubt the same," said he. " Did you drink some too, M. Noirtier? "

" Yes."

" And did you also discover a bitter taste? "

" Yes."

" Oh, doctor," cried Barrois, " the fit is coming on again. Oh, have pity on me."

The doctor flew to his patient.

" That emetic, Villefort; see if it is coming."

Villefort sprang into the passage, exclaiming:

" The emetic! the emetic!—is it come yet? "

No one answered. The most profound terror reigned throughout the house.

" If I had anything by means of which I could inflate the lungs," said D'Avrigny, looking around him, " perhaps I might prevent suffocation. But there is nothing which would do!—nothing! "

" Oh, sir," cried Barrois, " are you going to let me die without help? Oh, I am dying! Oh, save me! "

" A pen! a pen! " said the doctor.

There was one lying in the table; he endeavoured to introduce it into the mouth of the patient, who, in the midst of his convulsions, was making vain attempts to vomit; but the jaws were so clenched, that the pen could not pass them. This second attack was much more violent than the first, and he had slipped from the couch to the ground, where he was writhing in agony.

The doctor left him in this paroxysm, knowing that he could do nothing to alleviate it, and going up to Noirtier, said abruptly: " How do you find yourself?—well? "

" Yes."

" Have you any weight on the chest; or does your stomach feel light and comfortable?—eh? "

" Yes."

" Then you feel pretty much as you generally do after you have had the dose which I am accustomed to give you every Sunday? "

" Yes."

" Did Barrois make your lemonade? "

" Yes."

" Was it you who asked him to drink some of it? "

" No."

" Was it M. de Villefort? "

" No."

" Madame? "

" No."

" It was your granddaughter, then, was it not? "

" Yes."

A groan from Barrois, accompanied by a yawn which seemed to crack the very jawbones, attracted the attention of M. d'Avrigny; he left M. Noirtier and returned to the sick man.

" Barrois," said the doctor, " can you speak? "

Barrois muttered a few unintelligible words.

" Try and make an effort to do so, my good man," said D'Avrigny.

Barrois reopened his blood-shot eyes.

" Who made the lemonade? "

" I did."

" Did you bring it to your master directly it was made? "

" No."

" You left it somewhere, then, in the meantime? "

" Yes, I left it in the pantry, because I was called away."

" Who brought it into this room, then? "

" Mademoiselle Valentine."

D'Avrigny struck his forehead with his hand.

" Gracious Heaven! " exclaimed he.

" Doctor, doctor! " cried Barrois, who felt another fit coming on.

" Will they never bring that emetic? " asked the doctor.

" Here is a glass with one all ready prepared," said Villefort, entering the room.

" Who prepared it? "

" The chemist who came here with me."

" Drink it," said the doctor to Barrois.

" Impossible, doctor, it is too late; my throat is closing up.

I am choking! Oh, my heart!—Oh, my head!—Oh!—what agony!—Shall I suffer like this long? "

" No, no, friend," replied the doctor, " you will soon cease to suffer."

" Ah, I understand you," said the unhappy man. " My God, have mercy upon me! " and, uttering a fearful cry, Barrois fell back as if he had been struck by lightning.

D'Avrigny put his hand to his heart, and placed a glass before his lips.

" Well? " said Villefort.

" Go to the kitchen, and get me some syrup of violets."

Villefort went immediately.

" Do not be alarmed, M. Noirtier," said D'Avrigny; " I am going to take my patient into the next room to bleed him; this sort of attack is very frightful to witness."

And taking Barrois under the arms, he dragged him into an adjoining room; but, almost immediately, he returned to fetch the remainder of the lemonade.

Noirtier closed his right eye.

" You want Valentine, do you not? I will tell them to send her to you."

Villefort returned, and D'Avrigny met him in the passage.

" Well, how is he now? " asked he.

" Come in here," said D'Avrigny; and he took him into the chamber where the sick man lay.

" Is he still in a fit? " said the procureur du roi.

" He is dead."

Villefort drew back a few steps, and, clasping his hands, exclaimed, with real amazement and sympathy:

" Dead! and so soon too! "

" Yes, it is very soon," said the doctor, looking at the corpse before him; " but that ought not to astonish you; Monsieur and Madame de Saint-Méran died as soon. People die very suddenly in your house, M. de Villefort."

" What! " cried the magistrate, with an accent of horror and consternation, " are you still harping on that terrible idea? "

" Still, sir; and I shall always do so," replied D'Avrigny, " for it has never for one instant ceased to retain possession of my mind; and that you may be quite sure I am not mistaken this time, listen well to what I am going to say, M. de Villefort."

The magistrate trembled convulsively.

" There is a poison which destroys life almost without leaving any perceptible traces. I know it well; I have studied it in all its qualities and in the effect which it produces. I recognised the presence of this poison in the case of poor Barrois as well as in that of Madame de Saint-Méran. There is a way of detecting its presence. It restores the blue colour of litmus-paper reddened by an acid, and it turns syrup of violets green. We have no litmus-paper, but, hark! here they come with the syrup of violets."

The doctor was right; steps were heard in the passage. M. d'Avrigny opened the door, and took from the hands of the femme-de-chambre a cup which contained two or three spoonfuls of the syrup; he then carefully closed the door.

" Look," said he to the procureur du roi, whose heart beat so loudly that it might almost be heard; " here is in this cup some syrup of violets, and this decanter contains the remainder of the lemonade of which M. Noirtier and Barrois partook. If the lemonade be pure and inoffensive, the syrup will colour; if, on the contrary, the lemonade be drugged with poison, the syrup will become green. Look well at it! "

The doctor then slowly poured some drops of the lemonade from the decanter into the cup, and, in an instant, a kind of light cloudy sediment began to form at the bottom of the cup; this sediment first took a blue shade, then from the colour of sapphire it passed to that of opal, and from opal to emerald. Arrived at this last hue, it changed no more. The result of the experiment left no doubt whatever on the mind.

" The unfortunate Barrois has been poisoned," said D'Avrigny, " and I will maintain this assertion before God and man! "

Villefort said nothing, but he clasped his hands, opened his haggard eyes, and, overcome with his emotion, sank into a chair.

81

The Accusation

M. D'AVRIGNY soon restored the magistrate to consciousness, who had looked like a second corpse in that chamber of death.

" Oh, death is in my house! " cried Villefort.

" Say, rather, crime! " replied the doctor.

" M. d'Avrigny," cried Villefort, " I cannot tell you all I feel at this moment,—terror, grief, madness."

" Yes," said M. d'Avrigny, with an imposing calmness, " but I think it is now time to act. I think it is time to stop this torrent of mortality. I can no longer bear to be in possession of these secrets without the hope of seeing the victims and society generally revenged."

Villefort cast a gloomy look around him.

" In my house! " murmured he; " in my house! "

" Come, magistrate," said M. d'Avrigny, " show yourself a man; as an interpreter of the law, do honour to your profession by sacrificing your selfish interests to it."

" You make me shudder, doctor! Do you talk of a sacrifice? "

" I do."

" Do you then suspect anyone? "

" I suspect no one; death raps at your door—it enters—it goes, not blindfolded, but circumspectly, from room to room. Well, I follow its course, I track its passage; I adopt the wisdom of the ancients, and feel my way, for my friendship for your family and my respect for you are as a twofold bandage over my eyes; well——"

" Oh, speak, speak, doctor; I shall have courage."

" Well, sir, you have in your establishment, or in your family, perhaps, one of those frightful phenomena of which each century produces only one. Locusta and Agrippina, living at the same time, were an exception, and proved the determination of Providence to effect the entire ruin of the Roman Empire, sullied by so many crimes. Brunehault and Frédégonde* were the results of the painful struggle of civilisation in its infancy, when man was learning to control mind, were it even by an emissary from the realms of darkness. All these women have been, or were, beautiful. The same flower of innocence had flourished, or was still flourishing, on their brow, that is seen on the brow of the culprit in your house."

Villefort shrieked, clasped his hands, and looked at the doctor with a supplicating air. But the latter pursued without pity.

" ' Seek whom the crime would profit,' says an axiom of jurisprudence."

" Doctor," cried Villefort, " alas, doctor, how often has man's justice been deceived by those fatal words! I know not why, but I feel that this crime——"

" You acknowledge, then, the existence of the crime? "

" Yes, I see too plainly that it does exist. But it seems that it is intended to affect me personally. I fear an attack myself, after all these disasters."

" Oh, man," murmured D'Avrigny, " the most selfish of all animals, the most personal of all creatures, who believes the earth turns, the sun shines, and death strikes for him alone,—an ant cursing God from the top of a blade of grass! And have those who have lost their lives lost nothing?—M. de Saint-Méran, Madame de Saint-Méran, M. Noirtier——"

" How! M. Noirtier? "

" Yes; think you it was the poor servant's life was coveted? No, no; like Shakespeare's Polonius, he died for another. It was Noirtier the lemonade was intended for—it is Noirtier, logically speaking, who drank it; the other drank it only by accident; and although Barrois is dead, it was Noirtier whose death was wished for."

" But why did it not kill my father? "

" I told you one evening, in the garden, after Madame de Saint-Méran's death, because his system is accustomed to that very poison; and the dose was trifling for him, which would be fatal for another: because no one knows, not even the assassin, that, for the last twelve months, I have given M. Noirtier brucine for his paralytic affection; while the assassin is not ignorant, for he has proved it, that brucine is a violent poison."

" Pity, pity! " murmured Villefort, wringing his hands.

" Follow the culprit's steps; he first kills M. de Saint-Méran——."

" Oh, doctor! "

" I would swear to it; what I heard of his symptoms agrees too well with what I have seen in the other cases."

Villefort ceased to contend; he only groaned.

" He first kills M. de Saint-Méran," repeated the doctor, " then Madame de Saint-Méran,—a double fortune to inherit."

Villefort wiped the perspiration from his forehead.

" Listen attentively."

" Alas," stammered Villefort, " I do not lose a single word."

" M. Noirtier," resumed M. d'Avrigny, in the same pitiless tone,—" M. Noirtier had once made his will against you—against your family,—in favour of the poor, in fact; M. Noirtier is spared, because nothing is expected from him. But he has no sooner destroyed his first will and made a second than, for fear he should make a third, he is struck down. The will was made the day before yesterday, I believe; you see there has been no time lost."

" Oh, mercy, M. d'Avrigny! "

" No mercy, sir! The physician has a sacred mission on earth; and to fulfil it he begins at the source of life, and goes down to the mysterious darkness of the tomb. When crime has been committed, and God, doubtless in anger, turns away his face, it is for the physician to bring the culprit to justice."

" Have mercy on my child, sir! " murmured Villefort.

" You see it is yourself who have first named her—you, her father! "

" Have pity on Valentine! Listen! it is impossible. I would as willingly accuse myself! Valentine, whose heart is pure as a diamond or a lily."

" No pity, M. le procureur du roi; the crime is flagrant. Mademoiselle herself packed all the medicines which were sent to M. de Saint-Méran; and M. de Saint-Méran is dead. Mademoiselle de Villefort prepared all the cooling draughts which Madame de Saint-Méran took, and Madame de Saint-Méran is dead. Mademoiselle de Villefort took from the hands of Barrois, who was sent out, the lemonade which M. Noirtier has every morning, and he has escaped only by a miracle. Mademoiselle de Villefort is the culprit!—She is the poisoner! M. le procureur du roi, I denounce Mademoiselle de Villefort; do your duty."

" Doctor, I resist no longer; I can no longer defend myself: I believe you; but, for pity's sake, spare my life, my honour! "

" M. de Villefort," replied the doctor, with increased vehemence, " there are occasions when I dispense with all foolish human circumspection. If your daughter had committed only one crime, and I saw her meditating another, I would say, ' Warn her, punish her, let her pass the remainder of her life in a convent, weeping and praying.' If she had committed two crimes, I would say, ' Here, M. de Villefort, is a poison that the poisoner is not acquainted with, one that has no known antidote, quick as thought, rapid as lightning, mortal as the thunderbolt; give her that poison, recommending her soul to God, and save your honour and your life, for it is yours she aims at; and I can picture her approaching your pillow with her hypocritical smiles and her sweet exhortations. Woe to you, M. de Villefort, if you do not strike first! ' This is what I would say had she only killed two persons; but she has seen three deaths,—has contemplated three murdered persons,—has knelt by three corpses! To the scaffold with the poisoner!—to the scaffold! Do you talk of your honour? Do what I tell you, and immortality awaits you! "

Villefort fell on his knees.

" Listen! " said he; " I have not the strength of mind you have, or rather that which you would not have, if instead of my daughter Valentine your daughter Madeleine were concerned."

The doctor turned pale.

" Doctor, every son of woman is born to suffer and to die; I am content to suffer and to await death."

" Beware," said M. d'Avrigny; " it may come slowly; you will see it approach after having struck your father, your wife, perhaps your son."

Villefort, suffocating, pressed the doctor's arm.

" Listen! " cried he; " pity me,—help me! No, my daughter is not guilty. If you drag us both before a tribunal I will still say, ' No, my daughter is not guilty;—there is no crime in my house. I will not acknowledge a crime in my house; for when crime enters a dwelling, it is like death: it does not come alone.' Listen!—What does it signify to you if I am murdered?—Are you my friend?—Are you a man?—Have you a heart? No, you are a physician!—Well, I tell you I will not drag my daughter before a tribunal, and give her up to the executioner! The bare idea would kill me,—would drive me like a madman to dig my heart out with my finger-nails! And if you were mistaken, doctor! —if it were not my daughter!—If I should come one day, pale as a spectre, and say to you, ' Assassin, you have killed my child! ' Hold! if that should happen, although I am a Christian, M. d'Avrigny, I should kill myself."

" Well," said the doctor, after a moment's silence, " I will wait."

Villefort looked at him as if he had doubted his words.

" Only," continued M. d'Avrigny, with a slow and solemn tone, " if anyone falls ill in your house, if you feel yourself attacked, do not send for me, for I will come no more. I will consent to share this dreadful secret with you; but I will not allow shame and remorse to grow and increase in my conscience, as crime and misery will in your house."

" Then you abandon me, doctor? "

" Yes, for I can follow you no farther; and I only stop at the foot of the scaffold. Some further discovery will be made, which will bring this dreadful tragedy to a close. Adieu."

" I entreat you, doctor! "

" All the horrors that disturb my thoughts make your house odious and fatal. Adieu, sir."

" One word,—one single word more, doctor! You go leaving me in all the horror of my situation, after increasing it by what you have revealed to me. But what will be reported of the sudden death of this poor old servant? "

" True," said M. d'Avrigny; " we will return."

The doctor went out first, followed by M. de Villefort. The terrified servants were on the stairs and in the passage where the doctor would pass.

" Sir," said d'Avrigny to Villefort, so loud that all might hear, " poor Barrois has led too sedentary a life of late; accustomed formerly to ride on horseback, or in the carriage, to the four corners of Europe, the monotonous walk round that arm-chair had killed him ; his blood has thickened. He was stout, had a short, thick neck; he was attacked with apoplexy, and I was called in too late. *À propos*," added he, in a low tone, " take care to throw away that cup of syrup of violets in the ashes."

The doctor, without shaking hands with Villefort, without adding a word to what he had said, went out amid the tears and lamentations of the whole household.

The same evening all Villefort's servants, who had assembled in the kitchen, and had a long consultation, came to tell Madame Villefort they wished to leave. No entreaty, no proposition of increased wages, could induce them to remain; to every argument they replied, " We must go, for death is in this house." They all left in spite of prayers and entreaties, testifying their regret at leaving so good a master and mistress, and especially Mademoiselle Valentine, so good, so kind, and so gentle.

Villefort looked at Valentine as they said this. She was in tears; and, strange as it was, in spite of the emotions he felt at the sight of these tears, he looked also at Madame de Villefort, and it appeared to him as if a slight gloomy smile had passed over her thin lips like those meteors which are seen passing inauspiciously between two clouds in a stormy sky.

82

The Room of the Retired Baker

THE evening of the day on which the Comte de Morcerf had left Danglars' house with feelings of shame and anger, caused by the banker's declining the projected alliance between their two families, M. Andrea Cavalcanti, with curled hair, moustaches in perfect order, and white gloves which fitted admirably, had entered the courtyard of the banker's house in La Chaussée d'Antin. He had not been more than ten minutes in the drawing-room before he drew Danglars aside into the recess of a bow-window, and, after an ingenious preamble, related to him all his anxieties and cares since his noble father's departure. He acknowledged the extreme kindness which had been shown him by the banker's family, in which he had been received as a son, and where, besides, his warmest affections had found an object on which to centre in Mademoiselle Danglars.

Danglars listened with the most profound attention; he had expected this declaration the last two or three days, and when at last it came, his eyes glistened as much as they had lowered on listening to Morcerf. He would not, however, yield immediately to the young man's request, but made a few conscientious scruples.

" Are you not rather young, M. Andrea, to think of marrying? "

" I think not, sir," replied M. Cavalcanti; " in Italy the nobility generally marry young; life is so uncertain, we ought to secure happiness while it is within our reach."

" Well, sir," said Danglars, " in case your proposals, which do me honour, are accepted by my wife and daughter, by whom shall the preliminary arrangements be settled? So important a negotiation should, I think, be conducted by the respective fathers of the young people."

" Sir, my father is a man of great foresight and prudence. Imagining I might wish to settle in France, he left me at his departure, together with the papers constituting my identity, a letter promising, if he approved of my choice, 150,000 livres per annum from the day I was married. So far as I can judge, I suppose this to be a quarter of my father's revenue."

" I," said Danglars, " have always intended giving my daughter 500,000 francs as her dowry; she is, besides, my sole heiress."

"All would then be easily arranged if the baroness and her daughter are willing. We should command an annuity of 175,000 livres. Supposing, also, I should persuade the marquis to give me my capital, which is not likely, but still is possible, we would place these two or three millions in your hands, whose talent might make it realise ten per cent."

"I never give more than four per cent, and generally only three and a half; but to my son-in-law I would give five, and we would share the profit."

"Very good, father-in-law," said Cavalcanti, yielding to his low-born nature, which would escape sometimes through the aristocratic gloss with which he sought to conceal it.

Correcting himself immediately, he said, "Excuse me, sir; hope alone makes me almost mad—what will not reality do?"

"But," said Danglars, who, on his part, did not perceive how soon the conversation, which was at first disinterested, was turning to a business transaction, "there is, doubtless, a part of your fortune your father could not refuse you?"

"Which?" asked the young man.

"That you inherit from your mother."

"Truly, from my mother, Leonora Corsinari."

"How much may it amount to?"

"Indeed, sir," said Andrea, "I assure you I have never given the subject a thought; but, I suppose, it must have been at least two millions."

Danglars felt as much overcome with joy as the miser who finds a lost treasure, or as the shipwrecked mariner who feels himself on the solid ground instead of in the abyss which he expected would swallow him up.

"Well, sir," said Andrea, bowing to the banker respectfully, "may I hope?"

"You may not only hope," said Danglars, "but consider it a settled thing, if no obstacle arises on your part."

"I am, indeed, rejoiced," said Andrea.

"But," said Danglars thoughtfully, "how is it that your patron, M. de Monte Cristo, did not make this proposal for you?"

Andrea blushed imperceptibly.

"I have just left the count, sir," said he, "he is, doubtless, a delightful man, but inconceivably singular in his ideas. He esteems me highly. He even told me he had not the slightest doubt that my father would give me the capital instead of the interest of my property. He has promised to use his influence to obtain it for me; but he also declared that he never had taken on himself the responsibility of making proposals for another, and he never would. I must, however, do him the justice to add, that he assured me if ever he had regretted the repugnance he felt to such a step, it was on this occasion, because he thought the projected union would be a happy and suitable one. Besides, if he will do nothing officially, he will answer any questions you propose to him. And now," continued he, with one of his most charming smiles, " having finished talking to the father-in-law, I must address myself to the banker."

" And what may you have to say to him? " said Danglars, laughing in his turn.

" That the day after to-morrow I shall have to draw upon you for about four thousand francs; but the count, expecting my bachelor's revenue could not suffice for the coming month's outlay, has offered me a draft for twenty thousand francs. It bears his signature, as you see, which is all-sufficient."

" Bring me a million such as that," said Danglars, " I shall be well pleased," putting the draft in his pocket. " Fix your own hour for to-morrow, and my cashier shall call on you with a check for eighty thousand francs."

" At ten o'clock then, if you please; I should like it early, as I am going into the country to-morrow."

" Very well, at ten o'clock; you are still at the Hôtel des Princes? "

" Yes"

The following morning, with the banker's usual punctuality, the eighty thousand francs were placed in the young man's hands, as he was on the point of starting, having left two hundred francs for Caderousse. He went out chiefly to avoid this dangerous enemy, and returned as late as possible in the evening. But scarcely had he stepped out of his carriage, when the porter met him cap in hand.

" Sir," said he, " the man has been."

" What man? " said Andrea carelessly, apparently forgetting him whom he but too well recollected.

" Him to whom your excellency pays that little annuity."

" Oh," said Andrea, " my father's old servant. Well, you gave him the two hundred francs I had left for him? "

" Yes, your excellency."

Andrea had expressed a wish to be thus addressed.

" But," continued the porter, " he would not take them."

Andrea turned pale; but as it was dark, no one noticed his paleness.

" What! he would not take them? " said he, with slight emotion.

" No, he wished to speak to your excellency; I told him

you were gone out, which, after some dispute, he believed, and gave me this letter, which he had brought with him already sealed."

"Give it me," said Andrea, and he read by the light of his carriage-lamp:

" You know where I live; I expect you to-morrow morning at nine o'clock."

Andrea examined it carefully, to ascertain if the letter had been opened, or if any indiscreet eyes had seen its contents; but it was so carefully folded, no one could have read it, and the seal was perfect.

" Very well," said he. " Poor man! he is a worthy creature."

He left the porter to ponder on these words, not knowing which most to admire, the master or the servant.

" Take out the horses quickly, and come up to me," said Andrea to his groom.

In two seconds the young man had reached his room and burnt Caderousse's letter. The servant entered just as he had finished.

" You are about my height, Peter," said he.

" I have that honour, your excellency."

" You had a new livery yesterday? "

" Yes, sir."

" I have an engagement with a pretty little girl for this evening, and do not wish to be known; lend me your livery till to-morrow. I may sleep, perhaps, at an inn."

Peter obeyed. Five minutes after, Andrea left the hotel, completely disguised, took a cabriolet, and ordered the driver to take him to the Cheval Rouge, at Picpus. The next morning he left that inn, as he had left the Hôtel des Princes, without being noticed, walked down the Faubourg St. Antoine, along the Boulevard to Rue Ménilmontant, and stopping at the door of the third house on the left, looked for someone of whom to make inquiry in the porter's absence.

" Who are you looking for, my fine fellow? " asked the fruiteress on the opposite side.

" M. Pailletin, if you please, my good woman," replied Andrea.

" A retired baker? " asked the fruiteress.

" Exactly."

" He lives at the end of the yard, on the left, on the third storey."

Andrea went as she directed him, and on the third floor he found a hare's paw, which, by the hasty ringing of the bell, it was evident he pulled with considerable ill-temper. A moment after, Caderousse's face appeared at the grating in the door.

"Ah, you are punctual," said he, as he unbolted the door.

"Confound you and your punctuality!" said Andrea, throwing himself into a chair in a manner which implied that he would rather have flung it at the head of his host.

"Come, come, my little fellow, don't be angry. See, I have thought about you—look at the good breakfast we are going to have; nothing but what you are fond of."

Andrea, indeed, inhaled the scent of something cooking which was not unwelcome to him, hungry as he was; it was that mixture of fat and garlic peculiar to provincial kitchens of an inferior order, added to that of dried fish, and above all, the pungent smell of musk and cloves. These odours escaped from two deep dishes, which were covered, and placed on a stove, and from a copper pan placed in an old iron pot.

In an adjoining room, Andrea saw also a tolerably clean table prepared for two, two bottles of wine sealed, the one with green, the other with yellow, a considerable portion of brandy in a decanter, and a measure of fruit in a cabbage-leaf, cleverly arranged on an earthenware plate.

"What do you think of it, my little fellow?" said Caderousse; "ay, that smells good! You know I used to be a good cook; do you recollect how you used to lick your fingers? You were among the first who tasted any of my dishes, and I think you relished them tolerably."

While speaking, Caderousse went on peeling a fresh supply of onions.

"But," said Andrea ill-temperedly, "*pardieu!* if it was only to breakfast with you, you disturbed me, I wish the devil had taken you!"

"My boy," said Caderousse sententiously, "one can talk while eating. And then, you ungrateful being, are you not pleased to see an old friend? I am weeping with joy."

"Hold your tongue, hypocrite!" said Andrea; "you love me!"

"Yes, I do, or may the devil take me. I know it is a weakness," said Caderousse, "but it overpowers me."

"And yet it has not prevented your sending for me to play me some trick."

"Come!" said Caderousse, wiping his large knife on his apron, "if I did not like you, do you think I should endure the wretched life you lead me? Think for a moment. You have your servant's clothes on—you therefore keep a servant; I have none, and am obliged to prepare my own meals. You abuse my cookery because you dine at the table d'hôte of the Hôtel des Princes, or the Café de Paris. Well, I, too, could keep a servant; I, too, could have a tilbury; I, too, could dine where I like; but why do I not? Because I would not annoy my little Benedetto. Come! just acknowledge that I could, eh?"

This address was accompanied by a look which it was by no means difficult to understand.

"Well," said Andrea, "admitting your love, why do you want me to breakfast with you?"

"That I may have the pleasure of seeing you, my little fellow."

"What is the use of seeing me after we have made all our arrangements?"

"Eh, dear friend," said Caderousse, "are wills ever made without codicils? But you first came to breakfast, did you not? Well, sit down, and let us begin with these pilchards, and this fresh butter, which I have put on some vine-leaves to please you, wicked one. Ah, yes; you look at my room, my four straw chairs, my images, three francs each. But what do you expect? this is not the Hôtel des Princes."

"Come! you are growing discontented, you are no longer happy; you who only wished to appear a retired baker."

Caderousse sighed.

"Well, what have you to say? you have seen your dream realised."

"I can still say, it is a dream; a retired baker, my poor Benedetto, is rich—he has an annuity."

"Well, you have an annuity."

"I have?"

"Yes, since I bring you your two hundred francs."

Caderousse shrugged up his shoulders.

"It is humiliating," said he, "thus to receive money given grudgingly; an uncertain supply which may soon fail. You see I am obliged to economise, in case your prosperity should cease. Well, my friend, fortune is inconstant, as said the chaplain of —— regiment. I know your prosperity is great, rascal; you are to marry the daughter of Danglars."

"What! of Danglars?"

"Yes, to be sure; must I say Baron Danglars? I might as well say Count Benedetto. He was an old friend of mine, and if he had not so bad a memory, he ought to invite me to your wedding, seeing he came to mine. Yes, yes, to mine; forsooth! he was not so proud then; he was an under-clerk to the good M. Morrel. I have dined many times with him and the Comte de Morcerf; so you see I have some high connections, and were

I to cultivate them a little, we might meet in the same drawing-rooms."

"Come, your jealousy represents everything to you in the wrong light."

"That is all very fine, my Benedetto, but I know what I am saying. Perhaps I may one day put on my best coat, and presenting myself at the great gate, introduce myself. Meanwhile, let us sit down and eat."

Caderousse set the example, and attacked the breakfast with good appetite, praising each dish he set before his visitor. The latter seemed to have resigned himself; he drew the corks, and partook largely of the fish with the garlic and fat.

"Ah, compeer," said Caderousse, "you are getting on better terms with your old landlord!"

"Faith, yes," replied Andrea, whose hunger prevailed over every other feeling.

"So you like it, you rogue?"

"So much that I wonder how a man who can cook thus can complain of hard living."

"Do you see," said Caderousse, "all my happiness is marred by one thought!"

"What is that?"

"That I am dependent on another; I who have always gained my own livelihood honestly."

"Do not let that disturb you; I have enough for two."

"No, truly; you may believe me if you will; at the end of every month I am tormented by remorse."

"Good Caderousse!"

"So much so, that yesterday I would not take the two hundred francs."

"Yes, you wished to speak to me; but was it indeed remorse, tell me?"

"True remorse; and, besides, an idea had struck me."

Andrea shuddered; he always did so at Caderousse's ideas.

"It is miserable—do you see?—always to wait till the end of the month."

"Oh," said Andrea philosophically, determined to watch his companion narrowly, "does not life pass in waiting? Do I, for instance, fare better? Well, I wait patiently, do I not?"

"Yes, because instead of expecting two hundred wretched francs, you expect five or six thousand, perhaps ten, perhaps even twelve; for you take care not to let anyone know the utmost. Down there, you always had little presents and Christmas boxes which you tried to hide from your poor friend Caderousse. Fortunately he is a cunning fellow, that Caderousse."

" There you are beginning again to ramble, to talk again and again of the past! But what is the use of teasing me with so much repetition? "

" Ah, you are only one-and-twenty, and can forget the past; I am fifty, and am obliged to recollect it. But let us return to business."

" Yes."

" I was going to say, if I were in your place——"

" Well? "

" I would realise——"

" How would you realise? "

" I would ask for six months' in advance, under pretence of being able to purchase a farm, then with my six months' I would decamp."

" Well, well," said Andrea, " that is no bad thought! "

" My dear friend," said Caderousse, " eat of my bread, and take my advice, you will be none the worse off, physically or morally."

" But," said Andrea, " why do you not act on the advice you give me? Why do you not realise a six months', a year's advance even, and retire to Brussels? Instead of living the retired baker, you might live as a bankrupt, using his privileges; that would be very good."

" But how the devil would you have me retire on twelve hundred francs? "

" Ah, Caderousse," said Andrea, " how covetous you are! Two months since you were dying with hunger."

" In eating the appetite grows," said Caderousse, grinning, and showing his teeth, like a monkey laughing or a tiger growling. " And," added he, biting off, with those large white teeth, an enormous mouthful of bread, " I have formed a plan."

Caderousse's plans alarmed Andrea still more than his ideas; ideas were but the germ, the plan was reality.

" Let me see your plan; I dare say it is a pretty one."

" Why not? Who formed the plan by which we left the establishment of M——! eh? was it not I! and it was no bad one I believe, since here we are! "

" I do not say," replied Andrea, " that you never make a good one; but let us see your plan."

" Well," pursued Caderousse, " can you, without expending one sou, put me in the way of getting fifteen thousand francs? No, fifteen thousand are not enough, I cannot again become an honest man with less than thirty thousand francs."

" No," replied Andrea dryly, " no, I cannot."

"I do not think you understand me," replied Caderousse calmly; "I said without your laying out a sou."

"Do you want me to commit a robbery to spoil all my good fortune—and yours with mine—and both of us to be dragged down there again?"

"It would make very little difference to me," said Caderousse, "if I were retaken; I am a poor creature to live alone, and sometimes pine for my old comrades; not like you, heartless creature, who would be glad never to see them again!"

Andrea did more than tremble this time, he turned pale.

"Come, Caderousse, no nonsense!" said he.

"Don't alarm yourself my little Benedetto, but just point out to me some means of gaining those thirty thousand francs without your assistance, and I will contrive it."

"Well, I will see! I will recollect you!" said Andrea.

"Meanwhile you will raise my month to five hundred francs, my little fellow? I have a fancy, and mean to get a housekeeper."

"Well! you shall have your five hundred francs," said Andrea; "but it is very hard for me, my poor Caderousse—you take advantage——"

"Bah," said Caderousse, "when you have access to countless stores."

One would have said Andrea anticipated his companion's words, so did his eye flash like lightning, but it was but for a moment.

"True," he replied, "and my protector is very kind."

"That dear protector," said Caderousse; "and how much does he give you monthly?"

"Five thousand francs."

"As many thousands as you give me hundreds! truly, it is only bastards who are thus fortunate. Five thousand francs per month! what the devil can you do with all that?"

"Oh, it is no trouble to spend that; and I am like you, I want a capital."

"A capital!—yes—I understand—everyone would like a capital."

"Well! and I shall get one."

"Who will give it you—your prince?"

"Yes, my prince! But unfortunately I must wait."

"You must wait for what?" said Caderousse.

"For his death."

"The death of your prince?"

"Yes."

"How so?"

"Because he has made his will in my favour."

" Indeed? "

" On my honour."

" For how much? "

" For five hundred thousand."

" Only that? It's little enough! "

" But so it is."

" No, it cannot be! "

" Are you my friend, Caderousse? "

" Yes, in life or death."

" Well! I will tell you a secret."

" What is it? "

" But remember——"

" Ah, *pardieu!* mute as a carp."

" Well! I think——"

Andrea stopped and looked round him.

" You think? Do not fear, *pardieu!* we are alone."

" I think I have discovered my father."

" Your true father? "

" Yes."

" Not old Cavalcanti? "

" No, for he is gone again; the true one, as you say."

" And that father is——"

" Well! Caderousse, it is Monte Cristo."

" Bah! "

" Yes, you understand, that explains all. He cannot acknowledge me openly, it appears, but he does it through M. Cavalcanti, and gives him fifty thousand francs for it."

" Fifty thousand francs for being your father! I would have done it for half that, for twenty thousand, for fifteen thousand; why did you not think of me, ungrateful man? "

" Did I know anything about it, when it was all done when I was down there? "

" Ah, truly! And you say that by his will——"

" He leaves me five hundred thousand livres."

" Are you sure of it? "

" He showed it me; but that is not all; there is a codicil, as I said just now."

" Probably."

" And in that codicil he acknowledges me."

" Oh, the good father, the brave father, the very honest father! " said Caderousse, twirling a plate in the air between his two hands.

" Now, say if I conceal anything from you! "

" No, and your confidence makes you honourable in my opinion; and your princely father, is he rich, very rich? "

"Yes, in truth; he does not himself know the amount of his fortune."

"Is it possible?"

"It is evident enough to me who am always at his house. The other day, a banker's clerk brought him fifty thousand francs in a portfolio about the size of your plate; yesterday, his banker brought him a hundred thousand francs in gold."

Caderousse was filled with wonder; the young man's words sounded to him like metal, and he thought he could hear the rushing of cascades of louis.

"And you go into that house?" cried he briskly.

"When I like."

Caderousse was thoughtful for a moment. It was easy to perceive he was revolving some important idea in his mind. Then suddenly,—

"How I should like to see all that," cried he; "how beautiful it must be!"

"It is, in fact, magnificent," said Andrea.

"And does he not live in the Champs-Elysées?"

"Yes, No. 30."

"Ah," said Caderousse, "No. 30."

"Yes, a fine house standing alone, between a courtyard and a garden, you must know it."

"Possibly; but it is not the exterior I care for, it is the interior. What beautiful furniture there must be in it!"

"Have you ever seen the Tuileries?"

"No."

"Well, it surpasses that."

"It must be worth one's while to stoop, Andrea, when that good M. Monte Cristo lets fall his purse."

"It is not worth while to wait for that," said Andrea; "money is as plentiful in that house as fruit in an orchard."

"But you should take me there one day with you."

"How can I? On what plea?"

"You are right; but you have made my mouth water. I must absolutely see it; I shall find a way."

"No nonsense, Caderousse!"

"I will offer myself as a frotteur."

"The rooms are all carpeted."

"Well, then, I must be contented to imagine it."

"That is the best plan, believe me."

"Try, at least, to give me an idea of what it is."

"How can I?"

"Nothing is easier. Is it large?"

"Middling."

" How is it arranged? "

" Faith, I should require pen, ink, and paper, to make a plan."

" They are all here," said Caderousse briskly.

He fetched from an old secretaire a sheet of white paper, and pen and ink.

" Here," said Caderousse, " trace me all that on paper, my boy."

Andrea took the pen with an imperceptible smile, and began,—

" The house, as I said, is between the court and the garden; in this way, do you see? "

Andrea traced the garden, the court, and the house.

" High walls? "

" Not more than eight or ten feet."

" That is not prudent," said Caderousse.

" In the court are orange-trees in pots, turf, and clumps of flowers."

" And no steel-traps? "

" No."

" The stables? "

" Are on either side of the gate, which you see there."

And Andrea continued his plan.

" Let us see the ground-floor," said Caderousse.

" On the ground-floor, dining-room, two drawing-rooms, billard-room, staircase in the hall, and little back staircase."

" Windows? "

" Magnificent windows, so beautiful, so large, that I believe a man of your size could pass through each frame."

" Why the devil have they any stairs with such windows? "

" Luxury has everything."

" But shutters? "

" Yes, but they are never used. That Count of Monte Cristo is an original, who loves to look at the sky, even at night."

" And where do the servants sleep? "

" Oh, they have a house to themselves. Picture to yourself a pretty coach-house at the right-hand side where the ladders are kept. Well! over that coach-house are the servants' rooms, with bells corresponding with the different apartments."

" Ah, *diable!* bells did you say? "

" What do you mean? "

" Oh, nothing! I only say they cost a load of money to hang; and what is the use of them I should like to know? "

" There used to be a dog let loose in the yard at night; but it has been taken to the house at Auteuil, to that you went to, you know."

" Yes."

" I was saying to him only yesterday, ' You are imprudent, M. le Comte; for when you go to Auteuil, and take your servants, the house is left unprotected.'

" ' Well,' he said, ' what next? '

" ' Well, next, some day you will be robbed.' "

" What did he answer? "

" He quietly said, ' What do I care if I am? ' "

" Andrea, he has some secretaire with a spring? "

" How do you know? "

" Yes, which catches the thief in a trap and plays a tune. I was told there was such at the last exhibition."

" He has simply a mahogany secretaire, in which the key is always kept."

" And he is not robbed? "

" No; his servants are all devoted to him."

" There ought to be some money in that secretaire? "

" There may be. No one knows what there is."

" And where is it? "

" On the first floor."

" Sketch me the plan of that floor, as you have done of the ground-floor, my boy."

" That is very simple." Andrea took the pen. " On the first storey, do you see, there is the ante-room and drawing-room; to the right of the drawing-room, a library and a study; to the left, a bedroom and a dressing-room. The famous secretaire is in the dressing-room."

" Is there a window in the dressing-room? "

" Two, one here and one there."

Andrea sketched two windows in the room, which formed an angle on the plan, and appeared a smaller square added to the long square of the bedroom. Caderousse became thoughtful.

" Does he often go to Auteuil? " added he.

" Two or three times a week. To-morrow, for instance, he is going to spend the day and night there."

" Are you sure of it? "

" He has invited me to dine there."

" There is a life, for instance," said Caderousse; " a town-house and a country-house."

" That is what it is to be rich."

" And shall you dine there? "

" Probably."

" When you dine there, do you sleep there? "

" If I like; I am at home there."

Caderousse looked at the young man as if to get at the truth from the bottom of his heart. But Andrea drew a cigar-case from his pocket, took a Havana, quietly lit it, and began smoking.

"When do you want your five hundred francs?" said he to Caderousse.

"Now, if you have them."

Andrea took five-and-twenty louis from his pocket.

"Yellow boys?" said Caderousse; "no, I thank you."

"Oh, you despise them."

"On the contrary, I esteem them, but will not have them."

"You can change them, idiot; gold is worth five sous."

"Exactly; and he who changes them will follow friend Caderousse, lay hands on him, and demand what farmers pay him their rent in gold. No nonsense, my good fellow; silver simply, round coins with the head of some monarch or other on them. Anybody may possess a five-franc piece."

"But do you suppose I carry five hundred francs about with me? I should want a porter."

"Well, leave them with your porter; he is to be trusted. I will call for them."

"To-day?"

"No, to-morrow; I shall not have time to-day."

"Well, to-morrow I will leave them when I go to Auteuil."

"May I depend on it?"

"Certainly."

"Because I shall secure my housekeeper on the strength of it."

"Stop, will that be all? Eh! And will you not torment me any more?"

"Never."

Caderousse had become so gloomy that Andrea feared he should be obliged to notice the change. He redoubled his gaiety and carelessness.

"How sprightly you are," said Caderousse; "one would say you were already in possession of your property."

"No, unfortunately; but when I do obtain it——"

"Well?"

"I shall remember old friends, I only tell you that."

"Yes, since you have such a good memory."

"What do you want? I believe you wish to impose upon me."

"I? What an idea! I, who am going to give you another piece of good advice."

"What is it?"

"To leave behind you the diamond you have on your finger. We shall both get in trouble. You will ruin both yourself and me by your folly."

"How so?" said Andrea.

"How! You put on livery; you disguise yourself as a servant, and yet keep a diamond on your finger worth four or five thousand francs."

"You guess well."

"I know something of diamonds; I have had some."

"You do well to boast of it," said Andrea, who, without becoming angry, as Caderousse feared, at this new extortion, quietly resigned the ring. Caderousse looked so closely at it, that Andrea well knew that he was examining if all the edges were perfect.

"It is a false diamond," said Caderousse.

"You are joking now," replied Andrea.

"Do not be angry; we can try it."

Caderousse went to the window, touched the glass with it, and found it would cut.

"*Confiteor!*" said Caderousse, putting the diamond on his little finger; "I was mistaken; but those thieves of jewellers imitate so well that it is no longer worth while to rob a jeweller's shop—it is another branch of industry paralysed."

"Have you finished now?" said Andrea,—"do you want anything more?—will you have my waistcoat or my certificate? Make free now you have begun."

"No; you are, after all, a good companion; I will not detain you, and will try to cure myself of my ambition."

"But take care the same thing does not happen to you in selling the diamond you feared with the gold."

"I shall not sell it—do not fear it."

"Not at least till the day after to-morrow," thought the young man.

"Happy rogue," said Caderousse; "you are going to find your servants, your horses, your carriage, and your betrothed!"

"Yes," said Andrea.

"Well, I hope you will make me a handsome wedding-present the day you marry Mademoiselle Danglars."

"I have already told you it is a fancy you have taken in your head."

"What fortune has she?"

"But I tell you——"

"A million?"

Andrea shrugged up his shoulders.

"Let it be a million," said Caderousse; "you can never have so much as I wish you."

"Thank you," said the young man.

" Oh, I wish it you with all my heart," added Caderousse, with his hoarse laugh. " Stop, let me show you the way."

" It is not worth while."

" Yes, it is."

" Why? "

" Because there is a little secret, a precaution I thought it desirable to take, one of Huret and Fitchet's* locks, revised and improved by Gaspard Caderousse; I will manufacture you a similar one when you are a capitalist."

" Thank you," said Andrea; " I will let you know a week beforehand."

They parted. Caderousse remained on the landing until he had not only seen Andrea go down the three storeys, but also cross the court. Then he returned hastily, shut his door carefully, and began to study, like a clever architect, the plan Andrea had left him.

" Dear Benedetto," said he, " I think he will not be sorry to inherit his fortune, and he who hastens the day when he can touch his five hundred thousand will not be his worst friend."

83

The Burglary

THE day following that on which the conversation we have related took place, the Count of Monte Cristo set out for Auteuil, accompanied by Ali and several attendants, and also taking with him some horses whose qualities he was desirous of ascertaining. He was induced to undertake this journey, of which the day before he had not even thought, and which had not either occurred to Andrea, by the arrival of Bertuccio from Normandy, with intelligence respecting the house and sloop. The house was ready, and the sloop, which had arrived a week before, lay at anchor in a small creek, with her crew of six men, who, after having observed all the requisite formalities, were ready again to put to sea.

The count praised Bertuccio's zeal, and ordered him to prepare for a speedy departure, as his stay in France would not be prolonged more than a month.

" Now," said he, " I may require to go in one night from Paris to Tréport; let eight fresh horses be in readiness on the road, which will enable me to go fifty leagues in ten hours."

"Your highness had already expressed that wish," said Bertuccio, "and the horses are ready. I have bought them, and stationed them myself at the most desirable posts, namely, in villages, where no one generally stops."

"That's well," said Monte Cristo; "I remain here a day or two, arrange accordingly."

As Bertuccio was leaving the room to give the requisite orders, Baptistin opened the door: he held a letter on a silver waiter.

"What do you do here?" asked the count, seeing him covered with dust; "I did not send for you, I think?"

Baptistin, without answering, approached the count, and presented the letter.

"Important and urgent," said he.

The count opened the letter, and read:—

"M. de Monte Cristo is apprised that this night a man will enter his house in the Champs-Elysées with intention of carrying off some papers supposed to be in the secretaire in the dressing-room. The count's well-known courage will render unnecessary the aid of the police, whose interference might seriously affect him who sends this advice. The count, by any opening from the bedroom, or by concealing himself in the dressing-room, would be able to defend his property himself. Many attendants or apparent precautions would prevent the villain from the attempt, and M. de Monte Cristo would lose the opportunity of discovering an enemy whom chance has revealed to him who now sends this warning to the count,—a warning he might not be able to send another time, if this first attempt should fail and another be made."

The count's first idea was that this was an artifice—a gross deception, to draw his attention from a minor danger in order to expose him to a greater. He was on the point of sending the letter to the commissary of police, notwithstanding the advice of his anonymous friend, or, perhaps, *because* of that advice, when suddenly the idea occurred to him that it might be some personal enemy, whom he alone should recognise, and over whom, if such were the case, he alone could gain any advantage.

"They do not want my papers," said Monte Cristo, "they want to kill me; they are no robbers but assassins. I will not allow the police to interfere with my private affairs."

The count recalled Baptistin, who had left the room after delivering the letter.

"Return to Paris," said he, "assemble the servants who remain there. I want all my household at Auteuil."

" But will no one remain in the house, my lord? " asked Baptistin.

" Yes, the porter."

" My lord will remember that the lodge is at a distance from the house."

" Well? "

" The house might be stripped without his hearing the least noise."

" By whom? "

" By thieves."

" You are a fool, M. Baptistin; thieves might strip the house—it would annoy me less than to be disobeyed."

Baptistin bowed.

" You understand me? " said the count; " bring your comrades here, one and all; but let everything remain as usual, only close the shutters of the ground-floor."

" And those of the first floor? "

" You know they are never closed. Go! "

The count signified his intention of dining alone, and that no one but Ali should attend him. Having dined with his usual tranquillity and moderation, the Count making a signal to Ali to follow him, went out by the side gate, and on reaching the Bois de Boulogne, turned, apparently without design, towards Paris, and at twilight found himself opposite his house in the Champs-Elysées. All was dark; one solitary, feeble light was burning in the porter's lodge, about forty paces distant from the house, as Baptistin had said.

Monte Cristo leant against a tree, and, with that eye which was so rarely deceived, searched the double avenue, examined the passers-by, and carefully looked down the neighbouring streets, to see that no one was concealed. Ten minutes passed thus, and he was convinced no one was watching him. He hastened to the side-door with Ali, entered precipitately, and, by the servants' staircase, of which he had the key, gained his bed-room without opening or disarranging a single curtain, without even the porter having the slightest suspicion that the house which he supposed empty contained its chief occupant. Arrived in his bedroom the count motioned to Ali to stop; then he passed into the dressing-room, which he examined: all was as usual—the precious secrétaire in its place, and the key in the secrétaire. He doubly locked it, took the key, returned to the bedroom door, removed the double staple of the bolt, and went in.

Meanwhile Ali had procured the arms the count required, namely, a short carbine and a pair of double-barrelled pistols, with which as sure an aim might be taken as with a single-barrelled one. It was about half-past nine; the count and Ali ate in haste a crust of bread and drank a glass of Spanish wine, then Monte Cristo slipped aside one of the movable panels, which enabled him to see into the adjoining room. He had within his reach his pistols and his carbine, and Ali, standing near him, held one of those small Arabian hatchets, whose form has not varied since the crusades. Through one of the windows of the bedroom, on a line with that in the dressing-room, the count could see into the street. Two hours passed thus. It was intensely dark; still Ali, thanks to his wild nature, and the count, thanks, doubtless, to his long confinement, could distinguish in the darkness the slightest movement of the trees. The little light in the lodge had been long extinct. It might be expected that the attack, if indeed an attack was projected, would be made from the staircase of the ground-floor, and not from a window; in Monte Cristo's idea the villains sought his life, not his money. It would be his bedroom they would attack, and they must reach it by the back staircase or by the window in the dressing-room.

The clock of the Invalides struck a quarter to twelve; the west wind bore on its moistened gusts the doleful vibration of the three strokes. As the last stroke died away, the count thought he heard a slight noise in the dressing-room; this first sound, or, rather, this first grinding, was followed by a second, then a third; at the fourth the count knew what to expect. A firm and well-practised hand was engaged in cutting the four sides of a pane of glass with a diamond. The count felt his heart beat more rapidly. He made a sign to apprise Ali, who, understanding that danger was approaching from the other side, drew nearer to his master. Monte Cristo was eager to ascertain the strength and number of his enemies. The window whence the noise proceeded was opposite the opening by which the count could see into the dressing-room. He fixed his eyes on that window, he distinguished a shadow in the darkness; then one of the panes became quite opaque, as if a sheet of paper were stuck on the outside, then the square cracked without falling. Through the opening an arm was passed to find the fastening. A second after, the window turned on its hinges, and a man entered. He was alone.

" That's a daring rascal," whispered the count.

At that moment Ali touched him slightly on the shoulder; he turned. Ali pointed to the window of the room in which they were, facing the street.

" Good," said he, " there are two of them; one acts while the other watches."

He made a sign to Ali not to lose sight of the man in the street, and returned to the one in the dressing-room. The glass-cutter had entered, and was feeling his way, his arms stretched out before him. At last he appeared to have made himself familiar with all parts. There were two doors; he bolted them both. When he drew near to that of the bedroom Monte Cristo expected he was coming in, and raised one of his pistols; but he simply heard the sound of the bolts sliding in their copper rings. It was only a precaution. The nocturnal visitor, ignorant of the count's having removed the staples, might now think himself at home, and pursue his purpose with full security. Alone and uncontrolled, the man then drew from his pocket something which the count could not discern, placed it on a stand, then went straight to the secretaire, felt the lock, and contrary to his expectation, found that the key was missing. But the glass-cutter was a prudent man, who had provided for all emergencies. The count soon heard the rattling of a bunch of shapeless keys, such as the locksmith brings when called to force a lock, and which thieves call nightingales, doubtless from the music of their nightly song when they turn the precious lock.

" Ah, ah! " whispered Monte Cristo, with a smile of disappointment, " he is only a thief! "

But the man in the dark could not find the right key. He reached the instrument he had placed on the stand, touched a spring, and immediately a pale light, just bright enough to render objects distinct, was reflected on the hands and countenance of the man.

" Hold," exclaimed Monte Cristo, starting back, " it is——"

Ali raised his hatchet.

" Don't stir," whispered Monte Cristo, " and put down your hatchet; we shall require no arms."

Then he added some words in a low tone, for the exclamation which surprise had drawn from the count, weak as it had been, had startled the man, who remained in the attitude of an old knife-grinder.

It was an order the count had just given, for immediately Ali went noiselessly, and returned, bearing a black dress and a three-cornered hat. Meanwhile Monte Cristo had rapidly taken off his greatcoat, waistcoat, and shirt, and one might distinguish by the glimmering through the opening panel that he wore a pliant tunic of steel mail. This tunic soon disappeared under a long cassock, as did his hair under a priest's wig; the three-cornered hat over this effectually transformed the count into an abbé.

The man, hearing nothing more, had again raised himself,

and while Monte Cristo was completing his disguise, had advanced straight to the secretaire, whose lock was beginning to crack under his nightingale.

" Well done," whispered the count, who depended on the secret spring, which was unknown to the picklock, clever as he might be,—" well done!—you have a few minutes' work there." And he advanced to the window.

The man whom he had seen seated on a fence had got down, and was still pacing the street; but, strange as it appeared, he cared not for those who might pass from the avenue of the Champs-Elysées or by the Faubourg St. Honoré; his attention was engrossed with what was passing at the count's, and his only aim appeared to be to discern every movement in the dressing-room.

Monte Cristo suddenly struck his finger on his forehead, and a smile passed over his lips. Then drawing near to Ali, he whispered:

" Remain here, concealed in the dark, and whatever noise you hear, whatever passes, only come in, or show yourself if I call you."

Ali bowed in token of strict obedience. Monte Cristo then drew a lighted taper from a closet, and when the thief was deeply engaged with his lock, silently opened the door, taking care that the light should shine directly on his face. The door opened so quietly that the thief heard no sound; but, to his astonishment, the room was in a moment light. He turned.

" Good-evening, dear M. Caderousse," said Monte-Cristo; " what are you doing here at such an hour? "

" The Abbé Busoni! " exclaimed Caderousse; and, not knowing how this strange apparition could have entered when he had bolted the doors, he let fall his bunch of keys, and remained motionless and stupefied.

The count placed himself between Caderousse and the window, thus cutting off from the thief his only chance of retreat.

" The Abbé Busoni," repeated Caderousse, fixing his haggard gaze on the count.

" Yes, doubtless!—the Abbé Busoni himself," replied Monte Cristo, " and I am very glad you recognise me, dear M. Caderousse; it proves you have a good memory, for it must be about ten years since we last met."

This calmness of Busoni, combined with his irony and boldness, staggered Caderousse.

" L'abbé, l'abbé! " murmured he, clenching his fists, and his teeth chattering.

" So you would rob the Count of Monte Cristo? " continued the false abbé.

" M. l'Abbé," murmured Caderousse, seeking to regain the window, which the count pitilessly intercepted,—" M. l'Abbé, I don't know—believe me—I take my oath——"

" A pane of glass out," continued the count, " a dark lantern, a bunch of false keys, a secretaire half forced; it is tolerably evident——"

Caderousse was choking; he looked round for some corner to hide in—some way of escape.

" Come, come," continued the count, " I see you are still the same—an assassin."

" M. l'Abbé, since you know everything, you know it was not I, it was La Carconte; that was proved at the trial, since I was only condemned to the galleys."

" Is your time then expired, since I find you in a fair way to return there? "

" No, M. l'Abbé, I have been liberated by someone."

" That someone has done society a great kindness."

" Ah," said Caderousse, " I had promised——"

" And you are breaking your promise," interrupted Monte Cristo.

" Alas, yes! " said Caderousse, very uneasily.

" A bad relapse! That will lead you, if I mistake not, to the Place de Grève. So much the worse—so much the worse, *diavolo!* as they say in my country."

" M. l'Abbé, I am impelled——"

" Every criminal says the same thing."

" Poverty——"

" Pshaw! " said Busoni disdainfully; " poverty may make a man beg, steal a loaf of bread at a baker's door, but not cause him to open a secretaire in a house supposed to be inhabited. And when the jeweller Joannes had just paid you 45,000 francs for the diamond I had given you, and you killed him to get the diamond and the money both, was that also poverty? "

" Pardon, M. l'Abbé! " said Caderousse, " you have saved my life once, save me again! "

" That is but poor encouragement."

" Are you alone, M. l'Abbé, or have you there soldiers ready to seize me? "

" I am alone," said the abbé, " and I will again have pity on you and will let you escape, at the risk of the fresh miseries my weakness may lead to, if you tell me the truth."

" Ah, M. l'Abbé," cried Caderousse, clasping his hands, and

drawing nearer to Monte Cristo, " I may indeed say you are my deliverer."

" You mean to say you have been freed from confinement."

" Yes, in truth, M. l'Abbé."

" Who was your liberator? "

" An Englishman."

" What was his name? "

" Lord Wilmore."

" I know him; I shall know if you lie."

" M. l'Abbé, I tell you the simple truth."

" Was this Englishman protecting you? "

" No, not me, but a young Corsican, my companion."

" What was this young Corsican's name? "

" Benedetto."

" Is that his Christian name? "

" He had no other; he was a foundling."

" Then this young man escaped with you? "

" He did."

" In what way? "

" We were working at St. Mandrier, near Toulon. Do you know St. Mandrier? "

" I do."

" In the hour of rest, between noon and one o'clock——"

" Galley-slaves having a nap after dinner! We may well pity the poor fellows," said the abbé.

" Nay," said Caderousse, " one can't always work—one is not a dog! "

" So much the better for the dogs," said Monte Cristo.

" While the rest slept, then, we went away a short distance; we severed our fetters with a file the Englishman had given us, and swam away."

" And what is become of this Benedetto? "

" I don't know."

" You ought to know."

" No, in truth; we parted at Hyères."

And to give more weight to his protestation, Caderousse advanced another step towards the abbé, who remained motionless in his place, as calm as ever, and pursuing his interrogation.

" You lie," said the Abbé Busoni, with a tone of irresistible authority.

" M. l'Abbé! "

" You lie! This man is still your friend, and you, perhaps, make use of him as your accomplice."

" Oh, Monsieur l'Abbé! "

" Since you left Toulon what have you lived on? Answer me! "

" On what I could get."

" You lie," repeated the abbé, a third time, with a still more imperative tone.

Caderousse, terrified, looked at the count.

" You have lived on the money he has given you."

" True," said Caderousse; " Benedetto has become the son of a great lord."

" How can he be the son of a great lord? "

" A natural son."

" And what is that great lord's name? "

" The Count of Monte Cristo, the very same in whose house we are."

" Benedetto the count's son! " replied Monte Cristo, astonished in his turn.

" Forsooth! I suppose so, since the count has found him a false father—since the count gives him four thousand francs a month, and leaves him 500,000 francs in his will."

" Ah, ah! " said the false abbé, who began to understand; " and what name does the young man bear meanwhile? "

" Andrea Cavalcanti."

" Is it, then, that young man whom my friend the Count of Monte Cristo has received into his house, and who is going to marry Mademoiselle Danglars? "

" Exactly."

" And you suffer that, you wretch!—you who know his life and his crime? "

" Why should I stand in a comrade's way? " said Caderousse.

" You are right; it is not you who should apprise M. Danglars, it is I."

" Do not do so, M. l'Abbé."

" Why not? "

" Because you would bring us to ruin."

" And you think that to save such villains as you I will become an abettor of their plot—an accomplice in their crimes? "

" M. l'Abbé," said Caderousse, drawing still nearer.

" I will expose all to M. Danglars."

" By Heaven! " cried Caderousse, drawing from his waistcoat an open knife, and striking the count in the breast, " you shall disclose nothing, l'Abbé."

To Caderousse's great astonishment, the knife, instead of piercing the count's breast, flew back blunted. At the same moment the count seized with his left hand the assassin's wrist, and wrung it with such strength that the knife fell from his stiffened fingers, and Caderousse uttered a cry of pain. But the count, disregarding his cry, continued to wring the bandit's wrist until, his arm being dislocated, he fell first on his knees, then flat on the floor. The count then placed his foot on his head, saying:

"I know not what restrains me from crushing thy skull, rascal!"

"Ah, mercy—mercy!" cried Caderousse.

The count withdrew his foot.

"Rise!" said he.

Caderousse rose.

"What a wrist you have, M. l'Abbé!" said Caderousse, stroking his arm, all bruised by the fleshy pincers which had held it,—"what a wrist!"

"Silence! God gives me strength to overcome a wild beast like you; in the name of that God I act—remember that, wretch! —and to spare thee at this moment is still serving him."

"Oh!" said Caderousse, groaning with pain.

"Take this pen and paper, and write what I dictate."

"I don't know how to write, M. l'Abbé."

"You lie! Take this pen, and write!"

Caderousse, awed by the superior power of the abbé, sat down and wrote:—

"Sir,—The man whom you are receiving at your house, and to whom you intend to marry your daughter, is a felon who escaped with me from confinement at Toulon. He was No. 59, and I No. 58. He was called Benedetto; but he is ignorant of his real name, having never known his parents."

"Sign it!" continued the count.

"But would you ruin me?"

"If I sought your ruin, fool, I should drag you to the first guard-house; besides, when that note is delivered, in all probability you will have no more to fear. Sign it, then!"

Caderousse signed it.

"The address: À Monsieur le Baron Danglars, banker, Rue de la Chaussée d'Antin."

Caderousse wrote the address. The abbé took the note.

"Now," said he, "that suffices—begone!"

"Which way?"

"The way you came."

"You wish me to get out at that window?"

"You got in very well."

"Oh! you have some design against me, M. l'Abbé."

"Idiot! what design can I have?"

"Why, then, not let me out by the door?"

"What would be the advantage of waking the porter?"

" M. l'Abbé, tell me, do you not wish me dead? "

" I wish what God wills."

" But swear that you will not strike me as I go down."

" Cowardly fool! "

" What do you intend doing with me? "

" I ask you what can I do? I have tried to make you a happy man, and you have turned out a murderer."

" M. l'Abbé," said Caderousse, " make one more attempt— try me once more! "

" I will," said the count. " Listen!—you know if I may be relied on."

" Yes," said Caderousse.

" If you arrive safely at home——"

" What have I to fear, except from you? "

" If you reach your home safely, leave Paris, leave France; and wherever you may be, so long as you conduct yourself well, I will send you a small annuity; for if you return home safely, then——"

" Then? " asked Caderousse, shuddering.

" Then I shall believe God has forgiven you, and I will forgive you too."

" As true as I am a Christian," stammered Caderousse, " you will make me die of fright! "

" Now, begone," said the count, pointing to the window.

Caderousse, scarcely yet relying on this promise, put his legs out of the window and stood on the ladder.

" Now go down," said the abbé, folding his arms. Under-standing he had nothing more to fear from him, Caderousse began to go down.

Then the count brought the taper to the window, that it might be seen in the Champs-Elysées that a man was getting out of the window while another held a light.

" What are you doing, M. l'Abbé? Suppose a watchman should pass? "

And he blew out the light. He then descended, but it was only when he felt his foot touch the ground that he was satisfied he was safe. Monte Cristo returned to his bedroom, and glancing rapidly from the garden to the street, he saw first Caderousse, who, after walking to the end of the garden, fixed his ladder against the wall at a different part from where he came in. The count then looking over into the street, saw the man who appeared to be waiting run in the same direction, and place himself against the angle of the wall where Caderousse would come over. Caderousse climbed the ladder slowly, and looked over the coping to see if the street was quiet. No one could be seen or heard. The clock of the Invalides struck one. Then Caderousse sat astride the coping, and drawing up his ladder, passed it over the wall; then began to descend, or rather to slide down by the two stanchions, which he did with an ease which proved how accustomed he was to the exercise.

But, once started, he could not stop. In vain did he see a man start from the shade when he was half-way down—in vain did he see an arm raised as he touched the ground. Before he could defend himself that arm struck him so violently in the back, that he let go the ladder, crying, " Help! " A second blow struck him almost immediately in the side, and he fell, calling, " Help, murder! " Then, as he rolled on the ground, his adversary seized him by the hair, and struck him a third blow in the chest. This time Caderousse endeavoured to call again, but he could only utter a groan, and he shuddered as the blood flowed from his three wounds. The assassin, finding he no longer cried, lifted his head up by the hair; his eyes were closed, and mouth distorted. The murderer, supposing him dead, let fall his head and disappeared. Then Caderousse, feeling that he was leaving him, raised himself on his elbow, and with a dying voice cried with great effort:

" Murder! I am dying! Help, M. l'Abbé—help! "

This mournful appeal pierced the darkness. The door of the back staircase opened, then the side-gate of the garden, and Ali and his master were on the spot with lights.

84

The Hand of God

CADEROUSSE continued to call piteously:
"M. l'Abbé, help! help!"

"What is the matter?" asked Monte Cristo.

"Help," cried Caderousse; "I am murdered!"

"We are here;—take courage!"

"Ah, it's all over! You are come too late;—you are come to see me die. What blows, what blood!"

He fainted. Ali and his master conveyed the wounded man into a room. Monte Cristo motioned to Ali to undress him, and he then examined his dreadful wounds.

"My God!" he exclaimed, "thy vengeance is sometimes delayed, but only that it may fall the more effectually."

Ali looked at his master for further instructions.

"Conduct here immediately the procureur du roi, M. de Villefort, who lives in the Faubourg St. Honoré. As you pass the lodge, wake the porter, and send him for a surgeon."

Ali obeyed, leaving the abbé alone with Caderousse, who had not yet revived. When the wretched man again opened his eyes, the count looked at him with a mournful expression of pity, and his lips moved as if in prayer.

"A surgeon, M. l'Abbé—a surgeon!" said Caderousse.

"I have sent for one," replied the abbé.

"I know he cannot save my life, but he may strengthen me to give my evidence."

"Against whom?"

"Against my murderer."

"Did you recognise him?"

"Yes—it was Benedetto."

"The young Corsican?"

"Yes. After giving me the plan of this house, doubtless hoping I should kill the count and he thus become his heir, or that the count would kill me and I should be out of his way, he waylaid me, and has murdered me."

"I have also sent for the procureur du roi."

"He will not come in time;—I feel my life fast ebbing."

"Stop!" said Monte Cristo.

He left the room, and returned in five minutes with a phial.

The dying man's eyes were all the time riveted on the door, through which he hoped succour would arrive.

" Hasten, M. l'Abbé!—hasten! I shall faint again! "

Monte Cristo approached, and dropped on his purple lips three or four drops of the contents of the phial. Caderousse drew a deep breath.

" Oh," said he, " that is life to me;—more, more! "

" Two drops more would kill you," replied the abbé.

" Oh, send for someone to whom I can denounce the wretch! "

" Shall I write your deposition? You can sign it."

" Yes, yes," said Caderousse; and his eyes glistened at the thought of this posthumous revenge.

Monte Cristo wrote:—

" I die murdered by the Corsican Benedetto, my comrade in the galleys at Toulouse, No. 59."

" Quick, quick! " said Caderousse, " or I shall be unable to sign it."

Monte Cristo gave the pen to Caderousse, who collected all his strength, signed it, and fell back on the bed, saying:

" You will relate all the rest, M. l'Abbé; you will say he calls himself Andrea Cavalcanti. He lodges at the Hôtel des Princes. Oh, I am dying! "

He again fainted. The abbé made him smell the contents of the phial, and he again opened his eyes. His desire for revenge had not forsaken him.

" Ah, you will tell all I have said; will you not, M. l'Abbé? "

" Yes, and much more."

" What more will you say? "

" I will say he had doubtless given you the plan of this house, in the hope the count would kill you. I will say, likewise, he had apprised the count, by a note, of your intention; and the count being absent, I read the note, and sat up to await you. I will say that he followed and watched you the whole time, and, when he saw you leave the house, ran to the angle of the wall to conceal himself."

" Did you see all that? "

" Remember my words: ' If you return home safely, I shall believe God has forgiven you, and I will forgive you also.' "

" And you did not warn me," cried Caderousse, raising himself on his elbows. " You knew I should be killed on leaving this house, and did not warn me! "

" No, for I saw God's justice placed in the hands of Benedetto, and should have thought it sacrilege to oppose the designs of Providence."

" God's justice! Speak not of it, M. l'Abbé. If God were just, you know many would be punished who now escape."

" Listen," said the abbé, extending his hand over the wounded man, as if to command him to believe; " this is what the God in whom, on your death-bed, you refuse to believe, has done for you: he gave you health, strength, regular employment, even friends—a life, in fact, which a man might enjoy with a calm conscience. Instead of improving these gifts, rarely granted so abundantly, this has been your course: you have given yourself up to sloth and drunkenness, and in a fit of intoxication have ruined your best friend."

" Help! " cried Caderousse, " I require a surgeon, not a priest; perhaps I am not mortally wounded—I may not die; perhaps they can yet save my life."

" Your wounds are so far mortal, that without the three drops I gave you, you would now be dead. Listen, then." ·

" Ah," murmured Caderousse, " what a strange priest you are; you drive the dying to despair instead of consoling them."

" Listen," continued the abbé; " when you had betrayed your friend, God began not to strike, but to warn you; poverty overtook you; you had already passed half your life in coveting that which you might have honourably acquired, and already you contemplated crime under the excuse of want, when God worked a miracle in your behalf, sending you, by my hands, a fortune—brilliant, indeed, for you, who had never possessed any. But this unexpected, unhoped-for, unheard-of fortune sufficed you no longer when once you possessed it; you wished to double it; and how? by a murder! You succeeded, and then God snatched it from you, and brought you to justice."

" It was not I who wished to kill the Jew," said Caderousse; " it was La Carconte."

" Yes," said Monte Cristo, " and God, I cannot say in justice, for his justice would have slain you—but God, in his mercy, spared your life."

" Pardieu! to transport me for life; how merciful! "

" You thought it a mercy then, miserable wretch! The coward, who feared death, rejoiced at perpetual disgrace, for, like all galley-slaves, you said, ' I may escape from prison, I cannot from the grave.' And you said truly; the way was opened for you unexpectedly. An Englishman visited Toulouse, who had vowed to rescue two men from infamy, and his choice fell on you and your companion; you received a second fortune, money and tranquillity were restored to you, and you who had been condemned to a felon's life, might live as other men. Then, wretched creature! then you tempted God a third time. ' I have not enough,' you said, when you had more than you before possessed, and you committed a third crime, without reason, without excuse. God is wearied; he has punished you."

Caderousse was fast sinking.

" Give me drink," said he; " I thirst—I burn! "

Monte Cristo gave him a glass of water.

" And yet that villain, Benedetto, will escape! "

" No one, I tell you, will escape; Benedetto will be punished."

" Then you, too, will be punished, for you did not do your duty as a priest—you should have prevented Benedetto from killing me."

" I! " said the count, with a smile which petrified the dying man, " when you had just broken your knife against the coat of mail which protected my breast! Yet, perhaps, if I had found you humble and penitent, I might have prevented Benedetto from killing you; but I found you proud and bloodthirsty, and I left you in the hands of God."

" I do not believe there is a God! " howled Caderousse; " you do not believe it: you lie—you lie! "

" Silence! " said the abbé; " you will force the last drop of blood from your veins. What! you do not believe in God when he is striking you dead?—you will not believe in him, who requires but a prayer, a word, a tear, and he will forgive?—God, who might have directed the assassin's dagger so as to end your career in a moment, has given you this quarter of an hour for repentance. Reflect, then, wretched man, and repent."

" No," said Caderousse, " no; I will not repent. There is no God, there is no Providence—all comes by chance."

" There is a Providence, there is a God," said Monte Cristo, " of which you are a striking proof, as you lie in utter despair, denying him; while I stand before you, rich, happy, safe, and entreating that God in whom you endeavour not to believe, while in your heart you still believe in him."

" But who are you, then? " asked Caderousse, fixing his dying eyes on the count.

" Look well at me," said Monte Cristo, putting the light near his face.

" Well! the abbé—the Abbé Busoni."

Monte Cristo took off the wig which disfigured him, and let fall his black hair, which added so much to the beauty of his pallid features.

" Oh! " said Caderousse, thunderstruck, " but for that black hair, I should say you were the Englishman, Lord Wilmore."

" I am neither the Abbé Busoni nor Lord Wilmore," said Monte Cristo; " think again, do you not recollect me? "

There was a magic effect in the count's words which once more revived the exhausted powers of the miserable man.

" Yes, indeed," said he, " I think I have seen you and known you formerly."

" Yes, Caderousse, you have seen me, you knew me once."

" Who, then, are you? and why, if you knew me, do you let me die? "

" Because nothing can save you; your wounds are mortal. Had it been possible to save your life, I should have considered it another proof of God's mercy, and I would again have endeavoured to restore you, I swear by my father's tomb."

" By your father's tomb! " said Caderousse, supported by a supernatural power, and half raising himself to see more distinctly the man who had just taken this oath which all men hold sacred; " who, then, are you? "

The count had watched the approach of death. He knew this was the last struggle,—he approached the dying man, and leaning over him with a calm and melancholy look, he whispered:

" I am—I am——"

And his almost closed lips uttered a name so low that the count himself appeared afraid to hear it.

Caderousse, who had raised himself on his knees, and stretched out his arms, tried to draw back, then clasping his hands, and raising them with a desperate effort,—

" Oh, my God, my God! " said he, " pardon me for having denied thee; thou dost exist; thou art, indeed, man's father in heaven, and his judge on earth. My God, my Lord, I have long despised thee! Pardon me, my God; receive me, O my Lord! "

Caderousse sighed deeply, and fell back with a groan. The blood no longer flowed from his wounds. He was dead.

" One! " said the count mysteriously, his eyes fixed on the corpse, disfigured by so awful a death.

Ten minutes afterwards the surgeon and the procureur du roi arrived; the one accompanied by the porter, the other by Ali, and were received by the Abbé Busoni, who was praying by the side of the corpse.

85

Beauchamp

THE daring attempt to rob the count was the topic of conversation throughout Paris for the next fortnight. The dying man had signed a deposition declaring Benedetto to be the assassin. The police had orders to make the strictest search for the murderer. Caderousse's knife, dark lantern, bunch of keys, and clothing, excepting the waistcoat, which could not be found, were deposited at the registry; the corpse was conveyed to La Morgue. The count told everyone this adventure had happened during his absence at Auteuil, and that he only knew what was related by the Abbé Busoni, who that evening, by mere chance, had requested to pass the night in his house to examine some valuable books in his library. Bertuccio alone turned pale whenever Benedetto's name was mentioned in his presence, but there was no reason why anyone should notice his doing so. Villefort, being called on to prove the crime, was preparing the breviate with the same ardour as he was accustomed to exercise when called on to speak in criminal cases.

But three weeks had already passed, and the most diligent search had been unsuccessful; the attempted robbery and the murder of the robber by his comrade were almost forgotten in anticipation of the approaching marriage of Mademoiselle Danglars to the Count Andrea Cavalcanti. It was expected this wedding would shortly take place, as the young man was received at the banker's as the betrothed. Letters had been despatched to M. Cavalcanti, the count's father, who highly approved of the union, regretted his inability to leave Parma at that time, and promised a wedding-gift of a hundred and fifty thousand livres. It was agreed that the three millions should be intrusted to Danglars to improve; some persons had warned the young man of the circumstances of his future father-in-law, who had of late sustained repeated losses, but with sublime disinterestedness and confidence the young man refused to listen, or to express a single doubt to the baron. The baron adored Count Andrea Cavalcanti; not so Mademoiselle Eugénie Danglars. With an instinctive hatred of matrimony, she suffered Andrea's attentions in order to get rid of Morcerf; but when Andrea urged his suit, she betrayed an utter dislike to him. The baron might possibly have perceived it, but attributing it to caprice, feigned ignorance.

The delay demanded by Beauchamp had nearly expired. Morcerf appreciated the advice of Monte Cristo to let things die away of their own accord; no one had taken up the remark about the general, and no one had recognised in the officer who betrayed the castle of Yanina the noble count in the House of Peers. Albert, however, felt no less insulted; the few lines which had irritated him were certainly intended as an insult. Besides, the manner in which Beauchamp had closed the conference left a bitter recollection in his heart. He cherished the thought of the duel, hoping to conceal its true cause even from his seconds. Beauchamp had not been seen since the day he visited Albert; and those of whom the latter inquired always told him he was out on a journey which would detain him some days. Where he was no one knew.

One morning Albert was awoke by his valet-de-chambre, who announced Beauchamp. Albert rubbed his eyes, ordered his servant to introduce him into the small smoking-room on the ground-floor, dressed himself quickly, and went down. He found Beauchamp pacing the room; on perceiving him Beauchamp stopped.

" Your arrival here, without waiting my visit at your house to-day, looks well, sir," said Albert. " Tell me, may I shake hands with you, saying, ' Beauchamp, acknowledge you have injured me, and retain my friendship,' or must I simply propose to you a choice of arms? "

" Albert," said Beauchamp, with a look of sorrow which stupefied the young man, " let us first sit down and talk."

" Rather, sir, before we sit down, I must demand your answer."

" Albert," said the journalist, " these are questions which it is difficult to answer."

" I will facilitate it by repeating the question, ' Will you, or will you not, retract? ' "

" Morcerf, it is not enough to answer Yes or No to questions which concern the honour, the social interest, and the life of such a man as Lieutenant-General the Count of Morcerf, peer of France."

" What must then be done? "

" What I have done, Albert. I reasoned thus: Money, time, and fatigue are nothing compared with the reputation and interests of a whole family; probabilities will not suffice, only facts will justify a deadly combat with a friend. If I strike with the sword, or discharge the contents of a pistol at a man with whom, for three years, I have been on terms of intimacy, I must, at least, know why I do so; I must meet him with a heart at ease, and that quiet conscience which a man needs when his own arm must save his life."

"Well," asked Morcerf impatiently, "what does all this mean?"

"It means that I have just returned from Yanina."

"From Yanina?"

"Yes, here is my passport; examine the *visa*,—Geneva, Milan, Venice, Trieste, Delvino, Yanina. Will you believe the government of a republic, a kingdom, and an empire?"

Albert cast his eyes on the passport, then raised them in astonishment to Beauchamp.

"You have been to Yanina?" said he.

"Albert, had you been a stranger, a foreigner, a simple lord, like that Englishman who came to demand satisfaction three or four months since, and whom I killed to get rid of, I should not have taken this trouble; but I thought this mark of consideration due to you. I took a week to go, another to return, four days of quarantine, and forty-eight hours to stay there; that makes three weeks. I returned last night; and here I am."

"What circumlocution!—How long you are before you tell me what I most wish to know!"

"Because, in truth, Albert——"

"You hesitate!"

"Yes,—I fear."

"You fear to acknowledge that your correspondent has deceived you? Oh, no self-love, Beauchamp. Acknowledge it, Beauchamp; your courage cannot be doubted."

"Not so," murmured the journalist; "on the contrary——"

Albert turned frightfully pale; he endeavoured to speak, but the words died on his lips.

"My friend," said Beauchamp, in the most affectionate tone, "I should gladly make an apology; but, alas!——"

"But what?"

"The paragraph was correct, my friend."

"What! that French officer——"

"Yes."

"Fernand?"

"Yes."

"The traitor who surrendered the castle of the man in whose service he was——"

"Pardon me, my friend, that man was your father!"

Albert advanced furiously towards Beauchamp; but the latter restrained him more by a mild look than by his extended hand.

"My friend," said he, "here is a proof of it."

Albert opened the paper; it was an attestation of four notable inhabitants of Yanina, proving that Colonel Fernand Mondego, in the service of Ali Tebelen, had surrendered the castle for two million crowns. The signatures were perfectly legal. Albert tottered and fell overpowered in a chair. It could no longer be doubted; the family name was fully given. After a moment's mournful silence, his heart overflowed, and he gave way to a flood of tears. Beauchamp, who had watched with sincere pity the young man's paroxysm of grief, approached him.

" Now, Albert," said he, " you understand me?—Do you not? I wished to see all, and to judge of everything for myself, hoping the explanation would be in your father's favour, and that I might do him justice. But, on the contrary, the particulars which are given prove that Fernand Mondego, raised by Ali Pacha to the rank of governor-general, is no other than Comte Fernand de Morcerf; then recollecting the honour you had done me, in admitting me to your friendship, I hastened to you."

Albert, still extended on the chair, covered his face with both hands, as if to prevent the light from reaching him.

" I hastened to you," continued Beauchamp, " to tell you, Albert, in this changing age, the faults of a father cannot revert upon his children. Few have passed through this revolutionary period, in the midst of which we were born, without some stain of infamy or blood to soil the uniform of the soldier, the gown, or statesman. Now I have these proofs, Albert, and I am in your confidence, no human power can force me to a duel which your own conscience would reproach you with as criminal, but I come to offer you what you can no longer demand of me. Do you wish these proofs, these attestations, which I alone possess, to be destroyed? Do you wish this frightful secret to remain with us? Confided to me, it shall never escape my lips; say, Albert, my friend, do you wish it? "

Albert threw himself on Beauchamp's neck.

" Ah, noble fellow! " cried he.

" Take these," said Beauchamp, presenting the papers to Albert.

Albert seized them with a convulsive hand, tore them in pieces, and, trembling lest the least vestige should escape, and one day appear to confront him, he approached the wax-light, always kept burning for cigars, and consumed every fragment.

" Dear, excellent friend! " murmured Albert, still burning the papers.

" Let all be forgotten as a sorrowful dream," said Beauchamp; " let it vanish as the last sparks from the blackened paper, and disappear as the smoke from those silent ashes."

"Yes, yes," said Albert, "and may there remain only the eternal friendship which I promised to my deliverer, which shall be transmitted to our children's children, and shall always remind me that I owe my life and the honour of my name to you; for had this been known, oh, Beauchamp, I should have destroyed myself; or,—no, my poor mother! I could not have killed her by the same blow,—I should have fled from my country."

"Dear Albert!" said Beauchamp.

But this sudden and factitious joy soon forsook the young man and was succeeded by still greater grief.

"Well," said Beauchamp, "what still oppresses you, my friend?"

"I am broken-hearted," said Albert. "Listen, Beauchamp! I cannot thus, in a moment, relinquish the respect, the confidence, and pride with which a father's untarnished name inspires a son. Oh, Beauchamp, Beauchamp! how shall I now approach mine! Shall I draw back my forehead from his embrace, or withhold my hand from his? I am the most wretched of men. Ah, my mother, my poor mother!" said Albert, gazing through his tears at his mother's portrait; "if you know this how much must you suffer?"

"Come," said Beauchamp, taking both his hands, "take courage, my friend."

"But how came that first note inserted in your journal? Some unknown enemy,—an invisible foe has done this."

"The more must you fortify yourself, Albert. Let no trace of emotion be visible on your countenance; bear your grief as the cloud bears within it ruin and death; a fatal secret, known only when the storm bursts. Go, my friend, reserve your strength for the moment when the crash shall come."

"You think, then, all is not over yet?" said Albert, horror-stricken.

"I think nothing, my friend; but all things are possible. À propos——"

"What?" said Albert, seeing Beauchamp hesitated.

"Are you going to marry Mademoiselle Danglars?"

"Why do you ask me now?"

"Because the rupture or fulfilment of this engagement is connected with the person of whom we were speaking."

"How?" said Albert, whose brow reddened; "you think, M. Danglars——"

"I ask you only how your engagement stands. Pray put no construction on my words I do not mean they should convey, and give them no undue weight."

"No," said Albert, "the engagement is broken off."

"Well!" said Beauchamp. Then, seeing the young man was about to relapse into melancholy, "Let us go out, Albert," said he; "a ride in the wood in the phaeton, or on horseback, will refresh you; we will then return to breakfast, and you shall attend to your affairs, and I to mine."

"Willingly," said Albert; "but let us walk; I think a little exertion would do me good."

The two friends walked out on the fortress. When arrived at La Madeleine,—

"Since we are out," said Beauchamp, "let us call on M. de Monte Cristo; he is admirably adapted to revive one's spirits, because he never interrogates; and, in my opinion, those who ask no questions are the best comforters."

"Gladly," said Albert; "I love him—let us call."

86

The Journey

MONTE CRISTO uttered a joyful exclamation on seeing the young people together.

"Ah, ah!" said he, "I hope all is over, explained and settled."

"Yes," said Beauchamp; "the absurd reports have died away, and should they be renewed, I would be the first to oppose them; so let us speak no more of it."

"Albert will tell you," replied the count, "that I gave him the same advice. Look," added he, "I am finishing the most execrable morning's work."

"What is it?" said Albert; "arranging your papers apparently."

"My papers, thank God, no! my papers are all in capital order, because I have none; but M. Cavalcanti's."

"M. Cavalcanti's?" asked Beauchamp.

"Yes; do you not know that this is a young man whom the count is introducing?" said Morcerf.

"Let us not misunderstand each other," replied Monte Cristo; "I introduce no one, and certainly not M. Cavalcanti."

"And who," said Albert with a forced smile, "is to marry Mademoiselle Danglars instead of me, which grieves me cruelly."

"What! Cavalcanti is going to marry Mademoiselle Danglars?" asked Beauchamp.

"Certainly! do you come from the end of the world?" said Monte Cristo; "you, a journalist, the husband of renown! it is the talk of all Paris."

"And you, count, have made this match?" asked Beauchamp.

"I? Silence, Monsieur le Nouveliste, do not spread that report. I make a match! No, you do not know me; I have done all in my power to oppose it."

"Ah, I understand," said Beauchamp, "on our friend Albert's account."

"On my account?" said the young man; "oh, no, indeed; the count will do me the justice to assert that I have, on the contrary, always entreated him to break off my engagement, and happily it is ended. The count pretends I have not him to thank; but I perfectly well know to whom I am indebted."

"Listen," said Monte Cristo; "I have had little to do with it, for I am at variance both with the father-in-law and the young man; there is only Mademoiselle Eugénie, who appears but little charmed with the thoughts of matrimony, and who, seeing how little I was disposed to persuade her to renounce her dear liberty, retains any affection for me."

"And do you say this wedding is at hand?"

"Oh, yes, in spite of all I could say. I do not know the young man; he is said to be of good family and rich, but I never trust to vague assertions. I have warned M. Danglars of it till I am tired, but he is fascinated with his Lucquois. I have even informed him of a circumstance I consider very serious; the young man was either changed by his nurse, stolen by gipsies, or lost by his tutor, I scarcely know which. But I do know his father lost sight of him for more than ten years; what he did during these ten years, God only knows. Well, all that was useless. They have commissioned me to write to the major to demand papers; and here they are. I send them, but will have nothing more to do with the matter."

"And what does Mademoiselle d'Armilly say to you for robbing her of her pupil?"

"Forsooth! I know not; but I understand she is going to Italy. Madame Danglars asked me for letters of recommendation for the impresari; I gave her a few lines for the director of the Valle Theatre, who is under some obligation to me. But what is the matter, Albert? you look dull; are you, after all, unconsciously in love with Mademoiselle Eugénie?"

"I am not aware of it," said Albert, smiling sorrowfully.

Beauchamp turned to look at some paintings.

"But," continued Monte Cristo, "you are not in your usual spirits?"

"I have a dreadful headache," said Albert.

"Well, my dear viscount," said Monte Cristo, "I have an infallible remedy to propose to you."

"What is that?" asked the young man.

"A change."

"Indeed!" said Albert.

"Yes; and as I am just now excessively annoyed, I shall go from home. Shall we go together?"

"You annoyed, count?" said Beauchamp; "and by what?"

"*Pardieu!* you think very lightly of it; I should like to see you with a breviate preparing in your house."

"What breviate?"

"The one M. de Villefort is preparing against my amiable assassin,—some brigand escaped from the galleys apparently."

"True," said Beauchamp; "I saw it in the paper. Who is this Caderousse?"

"Some provincial, it appears. M. de Villefort heard of him at Marseilles, and M. Danglars recollects having seen him. Consequently M. le Procureur is very active in the affair, and the prefect of police very much interested; and, thanks to that interest, for which I am very grateful, they send me all the robbers of Paris and the neighbourhood, under pretence of their being Caderousse's murderers; so that in three months, if this continue, every robber and assassin in France will have the plan of my house at his fingers' end. I am resolved to desert them and to go to some remote corner of the earth, and shall be happy if you will accompany me, viscount."

"Willingly; but where?"

"To sea, viscount; you know I am a sailor. I was rocked when an infant in the arms of old Ocean, and on the bosom of the beautiful Amphitrite; I have sported with the green mantle of the one and the azure robe of the other; I love the sea as a mistress, and pine if I do not often see her."

"Let us go, count."

"You accept, viscount; well, there will be in my courtyard this evening a good travelling britska, with four post-horses, in which one may rest as in a bed. M. Beauchamp, it holds four very well, will you accompany us?"

"Thank you, I have just returned from sea."

"What! you have been to sea?"

"Yes. I have just made a little excursion to the Borromées Islands."*

"What of that? come with us," said Albert.

"No, dear Morcerf, you know I only refuse when the thing is impossible. Besides, it is important," added he in a low tone, " that I should remain in Paris just now to watch the paper."

" Ah, you are a good and an excellent friend," said Albert; " yes, you are right; watch, watch, Beauchamp, and try to discover the enemy who made this disclosure."

Albert and Beauchamp parted; the last pressure of their hands expressed what their tongues could not before a stranger.

" Beauchamp is a worthy fellow," said Monte Cristo, when the journalist was gone; " is he not, Albert? "

" Yes, and a sincere friend; I love him devotedly. But now we are alone, although it is immaterial to me, where are we going? "

" Into Normandy, if you like."

" Delightful; shall we be quite retired? have no society, no neighbours? "

" Our companions will be riding-horses, dogs to hunt with, and a fishing-boat."

" Exactly what I wish for; I will apprise my mother of my intention, and return to you."

" But shall you be allowed to go into Normandy? "

" I may go where I please."

" Yes, I am aware you may go alone, since I once met you in Italy—but to accompany the mysterious Monte Cristo? "

" You forget, count, that I have often told you of the deep interest my mother takes in you; instead of opposing, she will encourage me."

" Adieu, then, until five o'clock; be punctual, and we shall arrive at twelve or one."

" At Tréport? "

" Yes; or in the neighbourhood."

" But can we travel forty-eight leagues in eight hours? "

" Easily," said Monte Cristo.

" You are certainly a prodigy; you will soon not only surpass the railway,* which would not be very difficult in France, but even the telegraph."

" Meanwhile, viscount, since we cannot perform the journey in less than seven or eight hours, do not keep me waiting."

" Do not fear, I have little to prepare."

Monte Cristo smiled as he nodded to Albert, then remained a moment absorbed in deep meditation. But passing his hand across his forehead as if to dispel his reverie, he rang the bell twice, and Bertuccio entered.

" Bertuccio," said he, " I intend going this evening to Normandy, instead of to-morrow or the next day; you will have sufficient time before five o'clock; despatch a messenger to apprise the grooms at the first station. M. de Morcerf will accompany me."

Bertuccio obeyed, despatched a courier to Pontoise to say the travelling-carriage would arrive at six o'clock. From Pontoise another express was sent to the next stage, and in six hours all the horses stationed on the road were ready. Before his departure, the count went to Haydée's apartments, told her his intention, and resigned everything to her care.

Albert was punctual. The journey soon became interesting from its rapidity, of which Morcerf had formed no previous idea.

"Truly," said Monte Cristo, "with your post-horses going at the rate of two leagues an hour, and that absurd law that one traveller shall not pass another without permission, so that an invalid or ill-tempered traveller may detain those who are well and active, it is impossible to move; I escape this annoyance by travelling with my own postilion and horses; do I not, Ali?"

The count put his head out of the window and whistled, and the horses appeared to fly. The carriage rolled with a thundering noise over the pavement, and everyone turned to notice the dazzling meteor. Ali, smiling, repeated the sound, grasped the reins with a firm hand, and spurred his horses, whose beautiful manes floated in the breeze.

"I never knew till now the delight of speed," said Morcerf, and the last cloud disappeared from his brow; "but where the devil do you get such horses? are they made to order?"

"Precisely," said the count; "six years since I bought a horse in Hungary remarkable for its swiftness. The thirty-two that we shall use to-night are its progeny; they are all entirely black, with the exception of a star upon the forehead."

"That is perfectly admirable; but what do you do, count, with all these horses?"

"You see, I travel with them."

"But you are not always travelling."

"When I no longer require them, Bertuccio will sell them, and he expects to realise thirty or forty thousand francs by the sale."

"My dear count, if you tell me many more marvellous things, I warn you I shall not believe them."

The whole journey was performed with the utmost rapidity; the thirty-two horses, dispersed at seven stages, arrived in eight hours. At midnight they arrived at the gate of a beautiful park. The porter was in attendance; he had been apprised by the groom of the last stage, of the count's approach. At half-past two in the morning Morcerf was conducted to his apartments.

where a bath and supper were prepared. The servant who had travelled at the back of the carriage waited on him; Baptistin, who rode in front, attended the count.

Albert bathed, took his supper, and went to bed. All night he was lulled by the melancholy noise of the swell of the sea. On rising, he went to his window which opened on a terrace, having the sea in front, and at the back a pretty park bounded by a small forest. In a creek lay a little sloop, with a narrow keel and high masts, bearing on its flag the Monte Cristo arms, which were a mountain, or, on a sea azure, with a cross gules on the shield. Around the schooner lay a number of small fishing-boats belonging to the fishermen of the neighbouring village, as humble subjects awaiting orders from their queen. There, as in every spot where Monte Cristo stopped, if but for two days, all was comfort: life became easy.

Albert found in his ante-room two guns, with all the accoutrements for hunting; a higher room, on the ground-floor, containing all the ingenious instruments the English have invented for fishing. The day passed in pursuing those exercises in which Monte Cristo excelled; they killed a dozen pheasants in the park, as many trout in the stream, dined in a turret overlooking the ocean, and took tea in the library. Towards the evening of the third day, Albert, completely tired with the exercise, which appeared sport to Monte Cristo, was sleeping in an arm-chair near the window, while the count was designing with his architect the plan of a conservatory in his house, when the sound of a horse at full speed on the high-road made Albert look up. He was disagreeably surprised to see his own valet-de-chambre, whom he had not brought, that he might not inconvenience Monte Cristo.

" Florentin here! " cried he, starting up; " is my mother ill? " And he hastened to the door.

Monte Cristo watched him, he saw him approach the valet, who drew a small sealed parcel from his pocket, containing a newspaper and a letter.

" From whom is this? " said he eagerly.

" From M. Beauchamp," replied Florentin.

" Did he send you? "

" Yes, sir; he sent for me to his house, gave me money for my journey, procured a horse, and made me promise not to stop till I had rejoined you: I have come in fifteen hours."

Albert opened the letter with fear, uttered a shriek on reading the first line, and seized the paper. His sight was dimmed, his legs sunk under him, and he would have fallen had not Florentin supported him.

" Poor young man! " said Monte Cristo, with a low voice; " it is then true that the sin of the father shall fall on the children to the third and fourth generation."*

Meanwhile Albert had revived, and continuing to read, he threw back his hair, saying:

" Florentin, is your horse fit to return immediately? "

" It is a poor lame post-horse."

" In what state was the house when you left? "

" All was quiet; but on returning from M. Beauchamp's I found madame in tears; she had sent for me to know when you would return. I told her my orders from M. Beauchamp; she first extended her arms to prevent me, but after a moment's reflection, ' Go,' said she, ' Florentin, and fetch him.' "

" Yes, my mother," said Albert, " I will return, and woe to the infamous wretch! But first I must go——"

He returned completely changed to the room where he had left Monte Cristo; he had gone out as usual, but returned with a trembling voice, a feverish look, a threatening eye, and a tottering step.

" Count," said he, " I thank you for your hospitality, which I would gladly have enjoyed longer; but I must return to Paris."

" What has happened? "

" A great misfortune, more important to me than life. Question me not, I pray you, but lend me a horse."

" My stables are at your command, viscount; but you will kill yourself by riding on horseback. Take a post-chaise or a carriage."

" No, it would delay me, and I require that fatigue you fear; it will do me good."

Albert reeled as if shot with a cannon-ball, and fell on a chair near the door. Monte Cristo saw not this second weakness; he was at the window, calling:

" Ali, a horse for M. Morcerf! quick, he is in a hurry; "

These words restored Albert; he darted from the room, followed by the count.

" Thank you! " cried he, throwing himself on his horse. " Return as soon as you can, Florentin. Must I use any password to procure a horse? "

" Only dismount; another will be immediately saddled."

Albert hesitated a moment.

" You may think my departure strange and foolish," said the young man; "' you know not how a paragraph in a newspaper may exasperate. Read that," said he, " when I am gone, that you may not be witness of my anger."

While the count picked up the paper he put spurs to his horse, and started with the rapidity of an arrow. The count watched him with a feeling of compassion, and when he had completely disappeared, read as follows:—

" The French officer in the service of Ali, pacha of Yanina, alluded to three weeks since in the *Impartial*, who not only surrendered the castle of Yanina, but sold his benefactor to the Turks, styled himself truly at that time Fernand, as our honourable brother states; but he has since added to his Christian name a title of nobility and a family name. He now calls himself the Count of Morcerf, and ranks among the peers."

Thus this terrible secret, which Beauchamp had so generously destroyed, appeared again as an armed phantom; and another paper, cruelly informed, had published, two days after Albert's departure for Normandy, the few lines which had almost distracted the unfortunate young man.

87

The Trial

AT eight o'clock in the morning Albert had arrived at Beauchamp's door. The valet-de-chambre had received orders to introduce him into his master's room, who was just then bathing.

" Here I am," said Albert.

" Well, my poor friend," replied Beauchamp, " I expected you."

" I need not say, I think you too faithful and too kind to have spoken of that painful circumstance. Your having sent for me is another proof of your affection. So, without losing time, tell me, have you the slightest idea whence this terrible blow proceeds? "

" I think I have some clue."

" But first tell me all the particulars of this shameful plot."

Beauchamp proceeded to relate to the young man, overwhelmed with shame and grief, the following facts:—Two days previously, the article had appeared in another paper besides the *Impartial*, and, what was more serious, one that was well known as a govern-

ment paper. Beauchamp was breakfasting when he read the
passage. He sent immediately for a cabriolet, and hastened to
the publisher's office. Although professing diametrically opposite
principles from those of the editor of the accusing paper, Beauchamp—as it sometimes, we may say often, happens—was his
intimate friend. Beauchamp declared himself interested in the
article referring to Morcerf.

" I think you are running a great risk of a prosecution for
defamation of character," he said.

" Not at all: we have received with the information all the
requisite proofs, and we are quite sure M. de Morcerf will not
raise his voice against us; besides, it is rendering a service to
one's country to denounce those wretched criminals who are
unworthy of the honour it bestows on them."

Beauchamp remained thunderstruck.

" Who, then, has so correctly informed you? " asked he; " for
my paper, which had announced the subject, has been obliged
to stop for want of proof; and yet we are more interested than
you in exposing M. de Morcerf, as he is a peer of France, and we
are of the opposition."

" Oh, that is very simple; we have not sought to scandalise;
this news was brought to us. A man arrived, yesterday, from
Yanina, bringing the formidable bundle; and as we hesitated to
publish the accusatory article, he told us it should be inserted in
some other paper."

Beauchamp understood that nothing remained but to submit,
and left the office to despatch a courier to Morcerf. But he had
been unable to send to Albert the following particulars, as the
events had transpired after the messenger's departure; namely,
that the same day, a great agitation was manifest in the House of
Peers among the usually calm groups of the noble assembly.
Everyone had arrived almost before the usual hour, and was
conversing on the melancholy event which was to attract the
attention of the public towards one of their most illustrious
members. Some were perusing the article, others making comments, and recalling circumstances which substantiated the
charges still more. The count was no favourite with his colleagues.
Like all upstarts, he had had recourse to a great deal of haughti-
ness to maintain his position. The true nobility laughed at him,
the talented repelled him, and the honourable instinctively
despised him. Such were the extremities to which the count was
driven: the finger of God once pointed at him, everyone was
prepared to raise the hue and cry after him. The Comte de
Morcerf alone was ignorant of the news. He did not take in the
paper containing the defamatory article, and had passed the

morning in writing letters and in trying a horse. He arrived at his usual hour, with a proud look and insolent demeanour; he alighted, passed through the corridors, and entered the house without observing the hesitation of the door-keepers or the coolness of his colleagues. Business had already commenced half an hour when he entered.

Everyone held the accusing paper; but, as usual, no one liked to take upon himself the responsibility of the attack. At length an honourable peer, Morcerf's acknowledged enemy, ascended the tribune with that solemnity which announced the expected moment had arrived. There was an imposing silence; Morcerf alone knew not why such profound attention was given to an orator who was not always listened to with so much complacency. The count did not notice the introduction, in which the speaker announced that his communication would be of that vital importance that it demanded the undivided attention of the House; but at the names Yanina and Colonel Fernand, he turned so awfully pale, that every member shuddered and fixed his eyes upon him. The article having been read during this painful silence, a universal shudder pervaded the assembly, and immediately the closest attention was restored when the orator resumed. He stated his scruples and the difficulties of the case: it was the honour of M. de Morcerf, and that of the whole house, he proposed to defend, by provoking a debate on those personal questions always so warmly agitated. He concluded by calling for an examination, which might confound the calumnious report before it had time to spread, and restore M. de Morcerf to the position he had long held in public opinion. Morcerf was so completely overwhelmed by this enormous and unexpected calamity that he could scarcely stammer a few words as he looked round on the assembly. This timidity, which might proceed from the astonishment of innocence as well as the shame of guilt, conciliated some in his favour; for men who are truly generous are always ready to compassionate when the misfortune of their enemy surpasses the limits of their hatred.

The president put it to the vote, and it was decided the examination should take place. The count was asked what time he required to prepare his defence. Morcerf's courage had revived when he found himself alive after this horrible blow.

" My lords," answered he, " it is not by time I could repel the attack made on me by enemies unknown to me, and, doubtless, hidden in obscurity; it is immediately, and by a thunderbolt, I must repel the flash of lightning which, for a moment, startled me. Oh! that I could, instead of taking up this defence, shed my last drop of blood to prove to my noble colleagues that I am their equal in worth."

These words made a favourable impression on behalf of the accused.

" I demand, then, that the examination should take place as soon as possible, and I will furnish the House with all necessary information."

" What day do you fix? " asked the president.

" To-day I am at your service," replied the count.

The president rang the bell.

" Does the House approve that the examination should take place to-day? "

" Yes! " was the unanimous answer.

A committee of twelve members was chosen to examine the proofs brought forward by Morcerf. The examination would commence at eight o'clock that evening in the committee-room, and if it were necessary to postpone it, it would be resumed each evening at the same hour. Morcerf asked leave to retire; he had to collect the documents he had long been preparing against this storm, which his sagacity had foreseen.

Albert listened, trembling now with hope, then with anger, and then again with shame; for, from Beauchamp's confidence, he knew his father was guilty; and he asked himself how, since he was guilty, he could prove his innocence.

Beauchamp hesitated to continue his narrative.

" What next? " asked Albert.

" What next? My friend, you impose a painful task on me. Must you know all? "

" Absolutely; and rather from your lips than another's."

" Prepare your courage, then; for never will you have required it more."

Albert passed his hand over his forehead, as if to try his strength, as a man who is preparing to defend his life proves his shield and bends his sword. He thought himself strong enough, for he mistook fever for energy.

" Proceed," said he.

" The evening arrived; all Paris was in expectation. I used all my influence with one of the committee, a young peer of my acquaintance, to get introduced into a sort of gallery. He called for me at seven o'clock, and, before anyone had arrived, asked one of the door-keepers to place me in a box. I was concealed by a column, and might witness the whole of the terrible scene which was about to take place.

" At eight o'clock all were in their places, and M. de Morcerf entered at the last stroke. He held some papers in his hand; his countenance was calm, and his step firm, his dress particularly nice, and, according to the ancient military costume, buttoned completely up to the chin. His presence produced a good effect. His committee was composed of Liberal men, several of whom came forward to shake hands with him."

Albert felt his heart bursting at these particulars, but gratitude mingled with his sorrow: he would gladly have embraced those who had given his father this proof of esteem at a moment when his honour was so powerfully attacked.

" At this moment one of the door-keepers brought in a letter for the president.

" ' You are at liberty to speak, M. de Morcerf,' said the president, as he unsealed the letter; and the count began his defence, I assure you, Albert, in a most eloquent and skilful manner. He produced documents proving that the vizier of Yanina had, to the last moment, honoured him with his entire confidence, since he had intrusted him with a negotiation of life and death with the emperor. He produced the ring, his mark of authority, with which Ali Pacha generally sealed his letters, and which the latter had given him that he might, on his return at any hour of the day or night, or even in his harem, gain access to him. Unfortunately, the negotiation failed, and when he returned to defend his benefactor, he was dead. ' But,' said the count, ' so great was Ali Pacha's confidence, that on his death-bed he resigned his favourite mistress and her daughter to my care.' "

Albert started on hearing these words; the history of Haydée recurred to him, and he remembered what she had said of that message and the ring, and of the manner in which she had been sold and made a slave.

" And what effect did this discourse produce? " anxiously inquired Albert.

" I acknowledge it affected me, and, indeed, all the committee also," said Beauchamp.

" Meanwhile, the president carelessly opened the letter which had been brought to him; but the first lines aroused his attention; he read them again and again, and fixing his eyes on M. de Morcerf,—

" ' M. le Comte,' said he, ' you have said the vizier of Yanina had confided his wife and daughter to your care? '

" ' Yes, sir,' replied Morcerf, ' but in that, like all the rest, misfortune pursued me; on my return, Vasiliki and her daughter Haydée had disappeared.'

" ' Did you know them? '

" ' My intimacy with the pacha and his unlimited confidence had gained me an introduction to them, and I had seen them above twenty times.'

" ' Have you any idea what became of them? '

" ' Yes, sir, I heard they had fallen victims to their sorrow, and, perhaps, to their poverty. I was not rich; my life was in constant danger; I could not seek them, to my great regret.'

" The president frowned imperceptibly.

" ' Gentlemen,' said he, ' you have heard M. le Comte de Morcerf's defence. Can you, M. le Comte, produce any witnesses to the truth of what you have asserted? '

" ' Alas! no, sir,' replied the count; ' all those who surrounded the vizier, or who knew me at his court, are either dead or scattered. Alone, I believe, of all my countrymen, I survived that dreadful war. I have only the letters of Ali Tebelen, which I have placed before you; the ring, a token of his goodwill, which is here; and, lastly, the most convincing proof I can offer, after an anonymous attack, namely, the absence of all witness against my veracity and the purity of my military life.'

" A murmur of approbation ran through the assembly; and at this moment, Albert, had nothing more transpired, your father's cause had been gained. It only remained to put it to the vote, when the president resumed:

" ' Gentlemen, and you, M. le Comte, you will not be displeased, I presume, to listen to one who calls himself a very important witness, and who has just presented himself. He is, doubtless, come to prove the perfect innocence of our colleague. Here is a letter I have just received on the subject; shall it be read, or shall it be passed over? and shall we not regard this incident? '

" M. de Morcerf turned pale, and clenched his hands on the papers he held.

" The committee decided to hear the letter; the count was thoughtful and silent. The president read:

" ' MR. PRESIDENT,—I can furnish the committee of inquiry into the conduct of the Lieutenant-General the Count of Morcerf in Epirus and in Macedonia with important particulars.'

" The president paused, and the count turned pale. The president looked at his auditors.

" ' Proceed,' was heard on all sides. The president resumed:

" ' I was on the spot at the death of Ali Pacha; I was present during his last moments; I know what is become of Vasiliki and Haydée. I am at the command of the committee, and even claim the honour of being heard. I shall be in the lobby when this note is delivered to you.'

" ' And who is this witness, or rather this enemy? ' asked the count, in a tone in which there was a visible alteration.

" ' We shall know, sir,' replied the president. ' Is the committee willing to hear this witness? '

" ' Yes, yes,' said they all at once.

" The door-keeper was called.

" ' Is there anyone in the lobby? ' said the president.

" ' Yes, sir.'

" ' Who is it? '

" ' A female, accompanied by a servant.'

" Everyone looked at his neighbour.

" ' Introduce the female,' said the president.

" Five minutes after the door-keeper again appeared; all eyes were fixed on the door, and I," said Beauchamp, " shared the general expectation and anxiety. Behind the door-keeper walked a female enveloped in a large veil, which completely concealed her. It was evident, from her figure and the perfumes she had about her, that this was a young and elegant woman, but that was all. The president requested her to throw aside her veil, and it was then seen she was dressed in the Grecian costume, and was remarkably beautiful."

" Ah," said Albert, " it was she."

" Who? "

" Haydée."

" Who told you that? "

" Alas, I guess it. But go on, Beauchamp. You see I am calm and strong. And yet we must be drawing near the disclosure."

" M. de Morcerf," continued Beauchamp, " looked at this female with surprise and terror. Her lips were about to pass his sentence of life or death. To all the committee the adventure was so extraordinary and curious, that the interest they had felt for the count's safety became now quite a secondary matter. The president himself advanced to place a seat for the young lady; but she declined availing herself of it. As for the count, he had fallen on his chair; it was evident his legs refused to support him.

" ' Madame,' said the president, ' you have engaged to furnish the committee with some important particulars respecting the affair at Yanina, and you have stated that you were an eyewitness of the events.'

" ' I was, indeed! ' said the stranger, with a tone of sweet melancholy, and with the sonorous voice peculiar to the East.

" ' But allow me to say, you must have been very young then.'

" ' I was four years old; but as those events deeply concerned me, not a single particular has escaped my memory.'

" ' In what manner could those events concern you? and who are you, that they should have made so deep an impression on you? '

" ' On them depended my father's life,' replied she. ' I am Haydée, the daughter of Ali Tebelen, pacha of Yanina, and of Vasiliki, his beloved wife.'

" The blush of mingled pride and modesty which suddenly suffused the cheeks of the young female, the brilliancy of her eye, and her highly important communication, produced an inexpressible effect on the assembly. As for the count, he could not have been more overwhelmed if a thunderbolt had fallen at his feet and opened before him an immense gulf.

" ' Madame,' replied the president, bowing with profound respect, ' allow me to ask one question, it shall be the last: Can you prove the authenticity of what you have now stated? '

" ' I can, sir,' said Haydée, drawing from under her veil a satin satchel highly perfumed; ' for here is the register of my birth, signed by my father and his principal officers, and that of my baptism, my father having consented to my being brought up in my mother's faith—this latter has been sealed by the grand primate of Macedonia and Epirus; and lastly (and perhaps the most important), the record of the sale of my person and that of my mother to the Armenian merchant, El-Kobbir, by the French officer, who, in his infamous bargain with the Porte, had reserved his part of the booty, the wife and daughter of his benefactor, whom he sold for the sum of four hundred thousand francs.'

" A greenish paleness spread over the count's cheeks, and his eyes became blood-shot, at these terrible imputations, which were listened to by the assembly with an ill-foreboding silence.

" Haydée, still calm, but whose calmness was more dreadful than the anger of another would have been, handed to the president the record of her sale, registered in Arabic. It had been supposed some of these papers might be registered in the Arabian, Romaic, or Turkish language, and the interpreter of the house was in attendance. One of the noble peers, who was familiar with the Arabian language, having studied it during the sublime Egyptian campaign, followed with his eye as the translator read aloud:

" ' I, El-Kobbir, a slave-merchant, and furnisher of the harem of his Highness, acknowledge having received for transmission to the sublime emperor, from the French lord, Count of Monte Cristo, an emerald valued at eight hundred thousand francs, as the ransom of a young Christian slave of eleven years of age, named Haydée, the acknowledged daughter of the late lord Ali Tebelen, pacha of Yanina, and of Vasiliki, his favourite; she having been sold to me seven years previously, with her mother, who had died on arriving at Constantinople, by a French colonel in the service of the Vizier Ali Tebelen, named Fernand Mondego. The above-mentioned purchase was made on his Highness's account, whose mandate I had, for the sum of four hundred thousand francs.

" ' Given at Constantinople by authority of his Highness, in the year 1247 of the Hegira.

" ' Signed   EL-KOBBIR.

" ' That this record should have all due authority, it shall bear the imperial seal, which the vender is bound to have affixed to it.'

" Near the merchant's signature there was, indeed, the seal of the Sublime Emperor.

" A dreadful silence succeeded the reading of this paper; the count could only look, and his gaze, fixed as if unconsciously on Haydée, seemed one of fire and blood.

" ' Madame,' said the president, ' may reference be made to the Count of Monte Cristo, who is now, I believe, in Paris? '

" ' Sir,' replied Haydée, ' the Count of Monte Cristo, my foster-father, has been in Normandy the last three days.'

" ' Who, then, has counselled you to take this step, one for which the court is deeply indebted to you, and which is perfectly natural, considering your birth and your misfortunes? '

" ' Sir,' replied Haydée, ' I have been led to take this step from a feeling of respect and grief. Although a Christian, may God forgive me! I have always sought to revenge my illustrious father. Since I set my foot in France, and knew the traitor lived in Paris, I have watched carefully. I live retired in the house of my noble protector, but I do it from choice; I love retirement and silence, because I can live with my thoughts and recollections of past days. But M. le Comte de Monte Cristo surrounds me with every paternal care, and I am ignorant of nothing which passes in the world. I learn all in the silence of my apartments. For instance, I see all the newspapers, every periodical, as well as every new melody; and by thus watching the course of the life of others, I learned what has transpired this morning in the House of Peers, and what was to take place this evening—then, I wrote.'

" 'Then,' remarked the president, ' the Count of Monte Cristo knows nothing of your present proceedings? '

" 'He is quite unaware of them, and I have but one fear, which is, that he should disapprove of what I have done; but it is a glorious day for me,' continued the young girl, raising her ardent gaze to heaven, ' that on which I find at last an opportunity of revenging my father.'

" The count had not uttered one word the whole of this time; his colleagues looked at him, and, doubtless, pitied his blighted prospects which sank under the perfumed breath of a woman; his misery was depicted by sinister lines on his countenance.

" 'M. de Morcerf,' said the president, ' do you recognise this lady as the daughter of Ali Tebelen, pacha of Yanina? '

" 'No,' said Morcerf, attempting to rise; ' it is a base plot, contrived by my enemies.'

" Haydée, whose eyes had been fixed upon the door, as if expecting someone, turned hastily, and seeing the count standing, shrieked.

" 'You do not know me? ' said she: ' well, I fortunately recognise you! You are Fernand Mondego, the French officer who led the troops of my noble father. It is you who surrendered the castle of Yanina! It is you who, sent by him to Constantinople, to treat with the emperor of the life or death of your benefactor, brought back a false mandate granting full pardon! It is you, who, with that mandate, obtained the pacha's ring, which gave you authority over Selim, the fire-keeper! It is you who stabbed Selim! It is you who sold us, my mother and me, to the merchant El-Kobbir! Assassin! assassin! assassin! you have still on your brow your master's blood! Look, gentlemen, all! ' "

" These words had been pronounced with such enthusiasm and evident truth, that every eye was fixed on the count's forehead, and he himself passed his hand across it, as if he felt Ali's blood still moist upon it.

" 'You positively recognise M. de Morcerf as the officer, Fernand Mondego? '

" 'Indeed I do! ' cried Haydée. ' Oh, my mother! it was you who told me, " You were free, you had a beloved father, you were destined to be almost a queen. Look well at that man;

it is he who raised your father's head on the point of a spear,—
it is he who sold us, it is he who forsook us! Look well at his
right hand, on which he has a large wound; if you forgot his
features, you would know him by that hand into which fell one
by one the golden pieces of the merchant El-Kobbir!" I know
him! Ah, let him say now if he does not recognise me!'

" Each word fell like a dagger on Morcerf, and deprived him
of a portion of his energy; as she uttered the last, he hid hastily
in his bosom his hand, which had indeed been mutilated by a
wound, and fell back on his chair, overwhelmed by wretchedness
and despair. This scene completely changed the opinion of the
assembly respecting the accused count.

"' M. le Comte de Morcerf,' said the president, ' do not
allow yourself to be depressed; answer: the justice of the court
is supreme and impartial as that of God; it will not suffer you
to be trampled on by your enemies without giving you an opportunity of defending yourself. Shall further inquiries be made?
Shall two members of the House be sent to Yanina? Speak!'

" Morcerf did not reply.

" Then all the members looked at each other with terror.
They knew the count's energetic and violent temper. It must
be, indeed, a dreadful blow which would deprive him of courage
to defend himself; they expected this silence, resembling a sleep,
would be followed by an awakening like a thunderbolt.

"' Well!' asked the president, ' what is your decision?'

"' I have no reply to make,' said the count, in a low tone.

"' Has the daughter of Ali Tebelen spoken the truth?' said
the president. ' Is she then the terrible witness to whose charge
you dare not plead " Not guilty?" Have you really committed
the crimes of which you are accused?'

" The count looked round him with an expression which
might have softened tigers, but which could not disarm his
judges. Then he raised his eyes towards the ceiling, but withdrew
them immediately, as if he feared the roof would open and reveal
to his distressed view that second tribunal called heaven, and
that other judge named God. Then, with a hasty movement, he
tore open his coat, which seemed to stifle him, and flew from the
room like a madman; his footstep was heard one moment in
the corridor, then the rattling of his carriage-wheels, as he was
driven rapidly away.

"' Gentlemen,' said the president, when silence was restored,
' is M. le Comte de Morcerf convicted of felony, treason, and
outrage?'

"' Yes,' replied all the members of the committee of inquiry
with a unanimous voice.

"Haydée had remained until the close of the meeting; she heard the count's sentence pronounced without betraying an expression of joy or pity; then drawing her veil over her face, she bowed majestically to the councillors, and left with that dignified step which Virgil attributes to his goddesses."

88

The Challenge

"THEN," continued Beauchamp, "I took advantage of the silence and the darkness to leave the house without being seen. The door-keeper who had introduced me was waiting for me at the door, and he conducted me through the corridors to a private entrance opening into La Rue de Vaugirard. I left with mingled feelings of sorrow and delight. Excuse me, Albert, sorrow on your account, and delighted with that noble girl, thus pursuing paternal vengeance. Yes, Albert, from whatever source the blow may have proceeded, it may be from an enemy; but that enemy is only the agent of Providence."

Albert held his head between his hands; he raised his face, red with shame, and bathed in tears, and seizing Beauchamp's arm,—

"My friend," said he, "my life is ended; I cannot calmly say with you, ' Providence has struck the blow,' but I must discover who pursues me with his hatred; and when I have found him I will kill him, or he will kill me. I rely on your friendship to assist me, Beauchamp, if contempt has not banished it from your heart."

"Contempt, my friend! how does this misfortune affect you! No, happily that unjust prejudice is forgotten which made the son responsible for the father's actions. Review your life, Albert; although it is only just beginning, did a lovely summer's day ever dawn with greater purity than has marked the commencement of your career? No, Albert, take my advice, you are young and rich; leave Paris, all is soon forgotten in the great Babylon of excited life and changing taste; you will return after three or four years with a Russian princess for a bride, and no one will think more of what occurred yesterday than if it had happened sixteen years ago."

"Thank you, my dear Beauchamp, thank you for the excellent feeling which prompts your advice; but it cannot be thus.

I have told you my wish; or, if it must be so, I will say, determination. You understand, that interested as I am in this affair, I cannot see it in the same light as you do. What appears to you to emanate from a celestial source, seems to me to proceed from one far less pure. Providence appears to me to have no share in this affair; and, happily so, for instead of the invisible, impalpable agent of celestial rewards and punishments, I shall find one both palpable and visible, on whom I shall revenge myself, I assure you, for all I have suffered during the last month. Now, I repeat, Beauchamp, I wish to return to human and material existence; and if you are still the friend you profess to be, help me to discover the hand that struck the blow."

" Be it so," said Beauchamp; " if you must have me descend to earth, I submit; and if you will seek your enemy, I will assist you; and I will engage to find him, my honour being almost as deeply interested as yours."

" Well, then, you understand, Beauchamp, that we begin our research immediately. Each moment's delay is an eternity for me. The calumniator is not yet punished, and he may hope he will not be; but on my honour, if he thinks so, he deceives himself."

" Well, listen, Morcerf."

" Ah, Beauchamp, I see you know something already; you will restore me to life."

" I do not say there is any truth in what I am going to tell you; but it is, at least, as a light in the dark night; by following it we may, perhaps, discover something more certain."

" Tell me; satisfy my impatience."

" Well, I will tell you what I did not like to mention on my return from Yanina."

" Say on."

" I went, of course, to the chief banker of the town to make inquiries. At the first word, before I had even mentioned your father's name——"

" ' Ah,' said he, ' I guess what brings you here.'

" ' How, and why! '

" ' Because a fortnight since I was questioned on the same subject.'

" ' By whom? '

" ' By a banker of Paris, my correspondent.'

" ' Whose name is——'

" ' Danglars.' "

" He! " cried Albert; " yes, it is indeed he who has so long pursued my father with jealous hatred. He, the man who would be popular, cannot forgive the Count of Morcerf for being created a peer; and this marriage, broken off without a reason being assigned,—yes, it is all from the same cause."

"Inquire, Albert, but do not be angry without reason,—inquire, and if it is true——"

"Oh, yes; if it is true," cried the young man, "he shall pay me all I have suffered."

"Beware, Morcerf, he is already an old man."

"I will respect his age as he has respected the honour of my family; if my father had offended him, why did he not attack him personally? Oh, no, he was afraid to encounter him face to face."

"I do not condemn you, Albert; I only restrain you. Act prudently."

"Oh, do not fear; besides, you will accompany me. Beauchamp, solemn transactions should be sanctioned by a witness. Before this day closes, if M. Danglars is guilty, he shall cease to live or I will die."

"When such resolutions are made, Albert, they should be promptly executed. Do you wish to go to M. Danglars? Let us go immediately."

They sent for a cabriolet. On entering the banker's mansion, they perceived the phaeton and servant of M. Andrea Cavalcanti.

"Ah, *parbleu*! that's good," said Albert, with a gloomy tone; "if M. Danglars will not fight with me, I will kill his son-in-law; Cavalcanti will certainly fight."

The servant announced the young man; but the banker, recollecting what had transpired the day before, did not wish him admitted. It was, however, too late; Albert had followed the footman, and hearing the order given, forced the door open, and, followed by Beauchamp, found himself in the banker's cabinet.

"Sir," cried the latter, "am I no longer at liberty to receive whom I choose in my house? You appear to forget yourself sadly."

"No, sir," said Albert coldly; "there are circumstances in which one cannot, except through cowardice—I offer you that refuge,—refuse to admit certain persons at least."

"What is your errand, then, with me, sir?"

"I mean," said Albert, approaching, without apparently noticing Cavalcanti, who stood with his back towards the fireplace, "I mean to propose a meeting in some retired corner where two men having met, one of them will remain on the ground."

Danglars turned pale; Cavalcanti moved a step forward, and Albert turned towards him.

"And you, too," said he, "come, if you like, M. le Comte;

you have a claim, being almost one of the family, and I will give as many rendezvous of that kind as I can find persons willing to accept them.".

Cavalcanti looked at Danglars with a stupefied air; and the latter, making an effort, rose and advanced between the two young people. Albert's attack on Andrea had placed him on a different footing, and he hoped this visit had another cause than that he had at first supposed.

" Indeed, sir," said he to Albert, " if you are come to quarrel with this gentleman, because I have preferred him to you, I shall resign the case to the procureur du roi."

" You mistake, sir," said Morcerf, with a gloomy smile; " I am not alluding in the least to matrimony, and I only addressed myself to M. Cavalcanti, because he appeared disposed to interfere between us. In one respect you are right, for I am ready to quarrel with everyone to-day; but you have the first claim, M. Danglars."

" Sir," replied Danglars, pale with anger and fear, " I warn you, when I have the misfortune to meet with a mad dog, I kill it; and far from thinking myself guilty of a crime, I believe I do society a kindness. Now, if you are mad, and try to bite me, I will kill you without pity. Is it my fault that your father has dishonoured himself? "

" Yes, miserable wretch! " cried Morcerf, " it is your fault."
Danglars retreated a few steps.

" Who wrote to Yanina? "

" To Yanina? "

" Yes. Who wrote for particulars concerning my father? "

" I imagine anyone may write to Yanina."

" But one person only wrote, and that was you! "

" I, doubtless, wrote. It appears to me that when about to marry your daughter to a young man, it is right to make some inquiries respecting his family; it is not only a right but a duty."

" You wrote, sir, knowing what answer you would receive."

" I, indeed! I assure you," cried Danglars, with a confidence and security proceeding less from fear than from the interest he really felt for the young man, " I solemnly declare to you that I should never have thought of writing to Yanina, did I know anything of Ali Pacha's misfortunes."

" Who then urged you to write? Tell me."

" Pardieu! it was the most simple thing in the world. I was speaking of your father's past history. I said the origin of his fortune remained obscure. The person to whom I addressed my scruples asked me where your father had acquired his property? I answered, ' In Greece.' ' Then,' said he, ' write to Yanina.' "

" And who thus advised you? "

" No other than your friend Monte Cristo."

" The Count of Monte Cristo told you to write to Yanina? "

" Yes; and I wrote, and will show you my correspondence, if you like."

Albert and Beauchamp looked at each other.

" Sir," said Beauchamp, who had not yet spoken, " you appear to accuse the count, who is absent from Paris at this moment, and cannot justify himself."

" I accuse no one, sir," said Danglars; " I relate, and I will repeat before the count what I have said to you."

" Does the count know what answer you received? "

" Yes, I showed it to him."

" Did he know my father's Christian name was Fernand, and his family name Mondego."

" Yes; I had told him that long since, and I did nothing more than any other would have done in my circumstances, and perhaps less. When, the day after the arrival of this answer, your father came, by the advice of Monte Cristo, to ask my daughter's hand for you, I decidedly refused him, but without any explanation or exposure. In short, why should I have any more to do with the affair? How did the honour or disgrace of M. de Morcerf affect me? It neither increased or decreased my income."

Albert felt the colour mounting to his brow; there was no doubt upon the subject. Danglars defended himself with the baseness, but at the same time with the assurance, of a man who speaks the truth at least in part, if not wholly,—not for conscience' sake, but through fear. Besides, what was Morcerf seeking? It was not whether Danglars or Monte Cristo was more or less guilty; it was a man who would answer for the offence, whether trifling or serious; it was a man who would fight, and it was evident Danglars would not fight.

And, in addition to this, everything forgotten or unperceived before presented itself now to his recollection. Monte Cristo knew everything, as he had bought the daughter of Ali Pacha; and, knowing everything, he had advised Danglars to write to Yanina. The answer known, he had yielded to Albert's wish to be introduced to Haydée, and allowed the conversation to turn on the death of Ali, and had not opposed Haydée's recital (but having, doubtless, warned the young girl, in the few Romaic words he spoke to her, not to discover Morcerf's father). Besides, had he not begged of Morcerf not to mention his father's name before Haydée? Lastly, he had taken Albert to Normandy when he knew the final blow approached. There could be no doubt that all had been calculated and previously arranged; Monte Cristo then was in league with his father's enemies. Albert took Beauchamp aside, and communicated these ideas to him.

"You are right," said the latter; "M. Danglars has only been a secondary agent in this sad affair, and it is of M. de Monte Cristo that you must demand an explanation."

Albert turned.

"Sir," said he to Danglars, "understand that I do not take a final leave of you; I must ascertain if your insinuations are just, and am going now to inquire of the Count of Monte Cristo." He bowed to the banker, and went out with Beauchamp without appearing to notice Cavalcanti. Danglars accompanied him to the door, where he again assured Albert no motive of personal hatred influenced him against the Count de Morcerf.

89

The Insult

AT the banker's door Beauchamp stopped Morcerf.
"Listen," said he; "just now I told you it was of M. de Monte Cristo you must demand an explanation."

"Yes, and we are going to his house."

"Reflect, Morcerf, one moment before you go."

"On what shall I reflect?"

"On the importance of the step you are taking."

"Is it more serious than going to M. Danglars?"

"Yes; M. Danglars is a money-lover, and those who love money, you know, think too much of what they risk to be easily induced to fight a duel. The other is, on the contrary, to all appearance a true nobleman; but do you not fear to find in him the bravo?"

"I only fear one thing, namely, to find a man who will not fight."

"Do not be alarmed," said Beauchamp, "he will meet you. My only fear is that he will be too strong for you."

"My friend," said Morcerf, with a sweet smile, "that is what I wish. The happiest thing that could occur to me, would be to die in my father's stead; that would save us all."

"Your mother would die of grief."

"My poor mother!" said Albert, passing his hand across his eyes, "I know she would; but better so than die of shame."

" Are you quite decided, Albert? "

" Yes; let us go."

They ordered the driver to take them to No. 30 Champs-Elysées. Beauchamp wished to go in alone; but Albert observed, as this was an unusual circumstance, he might be allowed to deviate from the etiquette of duels. The cause which the young man espoused was one so sacred that Beauchamp had only to comply with all his wishes: he yielded, and contented himself with following Morcerf. Albert bounded from the porter's lodge to the steps. He was received by Baptistin. The count had, indeed, just arrived, but he was bathing, and had forbidden that anyone should be admitted.

" But after his bath? " asked Morcerf.

" My master will go to dinner."

" And after dinner? "

" He will sleep an hour."

" Then? "

" He is going to the Opera."

" Are you sure of it? " asked Albert.

" Quite, sir; my master has ordered his horses at eight o'clock precisely."

" Very good," replied Albert; " that is all I wished to know." Then turning towards Beauchamp, " If you have anything to attend to, Beauchamp, do it directly; if you have any appointment for this evening, defer it till to-morrow. I depend on you to accompany me to the opera; and, if you can, bring Château-Renaud with you."

Beauchamp availed himself of Albert's permission, and left him, promising to call for him at a quarter before eight. On his return home, Albert expressed his wish to Franz, Debray, and Morrel, to see them at the opera that evening. Then he went to see his mother, who, since the events of the day before, had refused to see anyone, and had kept her room. He found her in bed, overwhelmed with grief at this public humiliation. The sight of Albert produced the effect which might naturally be expected on Mercédès; she pressed her son's hand, and sobbed aloud; but her tears relieved her. Albert stood one moment speechless by the side of his mother's bed. It was evident, from his pale face and knit brows, that his resolution to revenge himself was growing weaker.

" My dear mother," said he, " do you know if M. de Morcerf has any enemy? "

Mercédès started; she noticed that the young man did not say my father.

" My son," she said, " persons in the count's situation have many secret enemies. Those who are known are not the most dangerous."

"I know it, and appeal to your penetration. You are of a superior mind, nothing escapes you."

"Why do you say so?"

"Because, for instance, you noticed, on the evening of the ball we gave, M. de Monte Cristo would eat nothing in our house."

Mercédès raised herself on her feverish arm.

"M. de Monte Cristo!" she exclaimed; "and how is he connected with the question you asked me?"

"You know, my mother, M. de Monte Cristo is almost an Oriental, and it is customary with them to secure full liberty of revenge by not eating or drinking in the house of their enemies."

"Do you say M. de Monte Cristo is our enemy?" replied Mercédès, becoming paler than the sheet which covered her. "Who told you so? Why, you are mad, Albert! M. de Monte Cristo has only shown us kindness. M. de Monte Cristo saved your life; you yourself presented him to us. Oh, I entreat you, my son, if you had entertained such an idea, dispel it; and my counsel to you—even more, my prayer is, retain his friendship."

"My mother," replied the young man, "you have special reasons for telling me to conciliate that man."

"I!" said Mercédès, blushing as rapidly as she had turned pale, and again becoming paler than ever.

"Yes, doubtless; and is it not because he can never do us any harm?"

Mercédès shuddered, and fixing on her son a scrutinising gaze,—

"You speak strangely," said she to Albert, "and you appear to have some singular prejudices. What has the count done? Three days since you were with him in Normandy; only three days since we looked on him as our best friend."

An ironical smile passed over Albert's lips. Mercédès saw it, and, with her double instinct of a woman and a mother, she guessed all; but, prudent and strong-minded, she concealed both her sorrows and her fears.

Albert was silent; an instant after the countess resumed. "You came to inquire after my health; I will candidly acknowledge I am not well. You should install yourself here and cheer my solitude. I do not wish to be left alone."

"My mother," said the young man, "you know how gladly I would obey your wish; but an urgent and important affair obliges me to leave you the whole evening."

" Well," replied Mercédès, sighing; " go, Albert, I will not make you a slave to your filial piety."

Scarcely had he shut her door than Mercédès called a confidential servant, and ordered him to follow Albert wherever he should go that evening, and to come and tell her immediately what he observed. Then she rang for her lady's maid, and, weak as she was, she dressed, in order to be ready for whatever might happen. The footman's mission was an easy one. Albert went to his room, and dressed with unusual care. At ten minute to eight Beauchamp arrived; he had seen Château-Renaud, who had promised to be in the orchestra before the curtain was raised. Both got into Albert's coupé, who, having no reason to conceal where he was going, called aloud, " To the Opera." In his impatience, he had arrived before the commencement of the performance. Château-Renaud was at his post: apprised by Beauchamp of the circumstances, he required no explanation from Albert. The conduct of this son, seeking to avenge his father, was so natural, that Château-Renaud did not seek to dissuade him, and was content with renewing his assurances of devotedness to Albert. Debray was not yet come, but Albert knew he seldom lost a scene at the Opera. Albert wandered about the theatre until the curtain was drawn up. He hoped to meet with M. de Monte Cristo either in the lobby or on the stairs. The bell summoned him to his seat, and he entered the orchestra with Château-Renaud and Beauchamp. But his eyes scarcely quitted the box between the columns, which remained obstinately closed during the whole of the first act. At last, as Albert was looking at his watch, about the hundredth time, at the commencement of the second act the door opened, and Monte Cristo, dressed in black, entered, and, leaning over the front of the box, looked round the pit. Morrel followed him, and looked also for his sister and brother-in-law; he soon discovered them in another box, and kissed his hand to them.

The count, in his survey of the pit, encountered a pale face and threatening eyes, which evidently sought to gain his attention. He recognised Albert, but thought it better not to notice him, as he looked so angry and discomposed. Without communicating his thoughts to his companion, he sat down, drew out his operaglass, and looked another way. Although apparently not noticing Albert, he did not, however, lose sight of him; and when the curtain fell at the end of the second act, he saw him leave the orchestra with his two friends. Then his head was seen passing at the back of the boxes, and the count knew the approaching storm was intended to fall on him. He was at the moment conversing cheerfully with Morrel, but he was well-prepared for what might happen. The door opened, and Monte Cristo, turning round, saw Albert, pale and trembling, followed by Beauchamp and Château-Renaud.

"Well," cried he, with that benevolent politeness which distinguished his salutation from the common civilities of the world, "my cavalier has attained his object. Good-evening, M. de Morcerf."

The countenance of this man, who possessed such extraordinary control over his feelings, expressed the most perfect cordiality. Morrel only then recollected the letter he had received from the viscount, in which, without assigning any reason, he begged him to go to the Opera, but he understood that something terrible was brooding.

"We are not come here, sir, to exchange hypocritical expressions of politeness or false professions of friendship," said Albert; "but to demand an explanation, count."

The trembling voice of the young man was scarcely audible.

"An explanation at the Opera?" said the count, with that calm tone and penetrating eye which characterises the man who knows his cause is good. "Little acquainted as I am with the habits of Parisians, I should not have thought this the place for such a demand."

"Still, if people will shut themselves up," said Albert, "and cannot be seen because they are bathing, dining, or asleep, we must avail ourselves of the opportunity whenever they are to be seen."

"I am not difficult of access, sir; for yesterday, if my memory does not deceive me, you were at my house."

"Yesterday I was at your house, sir," said the young man; "because then I knew not who you were."

In pronouncing these words Albert had raised his voice so as to be heard by those in the adjoining boxes and in the lobby. Thus the attention of many was attracted by this altercation.

"Where are you come from, sir? You do not appear to be in the possession of your senses."

"Provided I understand your perfidy, sir, and succeed in making you understand that I will be revenged, I shall be reasonable enough," said Albert furiously.

"I do not understand you, sir," replied Monte Cristo; "and if I did, your tone is too high. I am at home here, and I alone have a right to raise my voice above another's. Leave the box, sir!" Monte Cristo pointed towards the door with the most commanding dignity.

"Ah, I shall know how to make you leave your home!"

replied Albert, clasping in his convulsed grasp the glove, which Monte Cristo did not lose sight of.

"Well, well!" said Monte Cristo quietly, "I see you wish to quarrel with me; but I would give you one counsel, and do not forget it: it is a bad habit to make a display of a challenge. Display is not becoming to everyone, M. de Morcerf."

At this name a murmur of astonishment passed round the group of spectators of this scene. They had talked of no one but Morcerf the whole day.

Albert understood the allusion in a moment, and was about to throw his glove at the count, when Morrel seized his hand, while Beauchamp and Château-Renaud, fearing the scene would surpass the limits of a challenge, held him back.

But Monte Cristo, without rising, and leaning forward in his chair, merely extended his hand, and, taking the damp, crushed glove from the clenched hand of the young man,—

"Sir," said he, in a solemn tone, "I consider your glove thrown, and will return it you round a bullet. Now leave me, or I will summon my servants to throw you out at the door."

Wild, almost unconscious, and with eyes inflamed, Albert stepped back, and Morrel closed the door. Monte Cristo took up his glass again as if nothing had happened; he certainly must have had a heart of brass and face of marble.

Morrel whispered, "What have you done to him?"

"I? nothing—at least personally," said Monte Cristo.

"But there must be some cause for this strange scene."

"The Comte de Morcerf's adventure exasperates the young man."

"Have you anything to do with it?"

"It was by Haydée the house was informed of his father's treason."

"Indeed!" said Morrel. "I had been told, but would not credit it, that the Grecian slave I have seen with you here in this very box was the daughter of Ali Pacha."

"It is, notwithstanding, true."

"Then," said Morrel, "I understand it all, and this scene was premeditated."

"How so?"

"Yes. Albert wrote to request me to come to the Opera, doubtless that I might be a witness of the insult he meant to offer you."

"Probably," said Monte Cristo, with his imperturbable tranquillity.

"But what will you do with him?"

"As certainly, Maximilian, as I now press your hand, I will kill him before ten o'clock to-morrow morning."

Morrel in his turn took Monte Cristo's hand in both of his, and he shuddered to feel how cold and steady it was.

"Ah, count," said he, " his father loves him so much! "

"Do not speak to me of that," said Monte Cristo, with the first movement of anger he had betrayed; "I will make him suffer."

Morrel, amazed, let fall Monte Cristo's hand.

"Count, count! " said he.

"Dear Maximilian," interrupted the count; "listen how adorably Duprez is singing that line. I was the first to discover Duprez at Naples, and the first to applaud him. 'Bravo, bravo! '"

Morrel saw it was useless to say more, and refrained.

The curtain, which had been drawn up during the scene with Albert, again fell, and a rap was heard at the door.

"Come in," said Monte Cristo, without his voice betraying the least emotion; and immediately Beauchamp appeared.

"Good-evening, M. Beauchamp," said Monte Cristo, as if this was the first time he had seen the journalist that evening; "take a seat."

Beauchamp bowed, and sitting down,—

"Sir," said he, " I just now accompanied M. de Morcerf, as you saw."

"And that means," replied Monte Cristo, laughing, "that you had probably just dined together. I am happy to see, M. Beauchamp, you are more sober than he was."

"Sir," said Beauchamp, "Albert was wrong, I acknowledge, to betray so much anger, and I come, on my own account, to apologise for him. And having done so, on my own account only you understand, M. le Comte, I would add that I believe you too gentlemanly to refuse giving him some explanation concerning your connection with Yanina. Then I will add two words about the young Greek girl."

Monte Cristo motioned to him to be silent.

"Come," said he, laughing, "there are all my hopes about to be destroyed."

"How so? " asked Beauchamp.

"Doubtless you wish to make me appear a very eccentric character. I am, in your opinion, a Lara, a Manfred, a Lord Ruthven; then, just as I am arriving at the climax, you defeat your own end, and seek to make a common man of me. You bring me down to your own level, and demand explanations! Indeed, M. Beauchamp, it is quite laughable."

" Yet," replied Beauchamp haughtily, " there are occasions when probity commands——"

" M. Beauchamp," interrupted this strange man, " the Count of Monte Cristo bows to none but the Count of Monte Cristo himself. Say no more, I entreat you. I do what I please, M. Beauchamp, and it is always well done."

" Sir," replied the young man, " honest men are not to be paid with such coin. I require honourable guarantees."

" I am, sir, a living guarantee," replied Monte Cristo, motionless, but with a threatening look; " we have both blood in our veins which we wish to shed—that is our mutual guarantee. Tell the viscount so, and·that to-morrow, before ten o'clock, I shall see what colour his is."

" Then I have only to make arrangements for the duel," said Beauchamp.

" It is quite immaterial to me," said Monte-Cristo, " and it was very unnecessary to disturb me at the Opera for such a trifle. In France people fight with the sword or pistol, in the colonies with the carbine, in Arabia with the dagger. Tell your client, that although I am the insulted party, in order to carry out my eccentricity, I leave him the choice of arms, and will accept, without discussion, without dispute, anything, even combat by drawing lots, which is always stupid, but with me different from other people, as I am sure to gain."

" Sure to gain! " repeated Beauchamp, looking with amazement at the count.

" Certainly," said Monte Cristo, slightly shrugging up his shoulders, " otherwise I would not fight with M. de Morcerf. I shall kill him—I cannot help it. Only by a single line this evening at my house let me know the arms and the hour; I do not like to be kept waiting."

" Pistols, then, at eight o'clock, in the Bois de Vincennes," said Beauchamp, quite disconcerted, not knowing if he was dealing with an arrogant braggadocio or a supernatural being.

" Very well, sir," said Monte Cristo. " Now all that is settled, do let me see the performance, and tell your friend Albert not to come any more this evening; he will hurt himself with all his ill-chosen barbarisms: let him go home and go to sleep."

Beauchamp left the box perfectly amazed.

" Now," said Monte Cristo, turning towards Morrel, " I may depend upon you, may I not? "

" Certainly," said Morrel, " I am at your service, count; still——"

" What? "

" It is desirable I should know the real cause."

" That is to say, you would rather not? "

" No."

" The young man himself is acting blindfolded, and knows not the true cause, which is known only to God and to me; but I give you my word, Morrel, that God, who does know it, will be on our side."

" Enough," said Morrel, " who is your second witness? "

" I know no one in Paris, Morrel, on whom I could confer that honour besides you and your brother Emmanuel. Do you think Emmanuel would oblige me? "

" I will answer for him, count."

" Well, that is all I require. To-morrow morning, at seven o'clock, you will be with me, will you not? "

" We will."

" Hush! the curtain is rising. Listen! I never lose a note of this opera if I can avoid it; the music of *William Tell* is so sweet! "

90

Mercédès

M DE MONTE CRISTO waited, according to his usual custom, until Duprez had sung his famous " Suivez moi "; then he rose, and went out. Morrel took leave of him at the door, renewing his promise to be with him the next morning at seven o'clock, and to bring Emmanuel with him. Then he stepped into his coupé, calm and smiling, and was at home in five minutes. No one who knew the count could mistake his expression, when, on entering, he said:

" Ali, bring me my pistols with an ivory cross."

Ali brought the box to his master, who examined his arms with a solicitude very natural to a man who is about to entrust his life to a little powder and shot.

These were particular pistols, which Monte Cristo had had made to shoot at a target in his room. A cap was sufficient to drive out the ball, and from the adjoining room no one would have suspected the count was, as sportsmen would say, keeping his hand in. He was just taking one in his hand, and looking for the point to aim at, on a little iron plate, which served him as a target, when his cabinet door opened, and Baptistin entered.

Before he had spoken a word the count perceived in the next

room a veiled female, who had followed closely after Baptistin, and now seeing the count with a pistol in his hand and swords on the table, rushed in.

Baptistin looked at his master, who made a sign to him, and he went out, closing the door after him.

" Who are you, madame? " said the count to the veiled female.

The stranger cast one look around her, to be certain they were quite alone, then bending, as if she would have knelt, and joining her hands, she said with an accent of despair:

" Edmond, you will not kill my son? "

The count retreated a step, uttered a slight exclamation, and let fall the pistol he held.

" What name did you pronounce then, Madame de Morcerf? " said he.

" Yours! " cried she, throwing back her veil,—" yours, which I alone, perhaps, have not forgotten. Edmond, it is not Madame de Morcerf who is come to you, it is Mercédès."

" Mercédès is dead, madame," said Monte Cristo; " I know no one now of that name."

" Mercédès lives, sir, and she remembers, for she alone recognised you when she saw you, and even before she saw you, by your voice, Edmond,—by the simple sound of your voice; and from that moment she has followed your steps, watched you, feared you, and she needs not to inquire what hand has dealt the blow which now strikes M. de Morcerf."

" Fernand do you mean? " replied Monte Cristo, with bitter irony; " since we are recalling names, let us remember them all."

Monte Cristo had pronounced the name of Fernand with such an expression of hatred, that Mercédès felt a thrill of terror run through every vein.

" You see, Edmond, I am not mistaken, and have cause to say, ' Spare my son! ' "

" And who told you, madame, I have any hostile intentions against your son? "

" No one, in truth; but a mother has a twofold sight. I guessed it all; I followed him this evening to the Opera, and have seen all."

" If you have seen all, madame, you know that the son of Fernand has publicly insulted me," said Monte Cristo, with awful calmness.

" Oh, for pity's sake! "

" You have seen that he would have thrown his glove in my face if Morrel, one of my friends, had not stopped him."

" Listen to me: my son has also guessed who you are; he attributes his father's misfortunes to you."

" Madame, you are mistaken, they are not misfortunes,—it is a punishment. It is not I who strike M. de Morcerf; it is Providence which punishes him."

" And why do you represent Providence? " cried Mercédès. " Why do you remember when it forgets? What are Yanina and its vizier to you, Edmond? What injury has Fernand Mondego done you in betraying Ali Tebelen? "

" And, madame," replied Monte Cristo, " all this is an affair between the French captain and the daughter of Vasiliki. It does not concern me, you are right; and if I have sworn to revenge myself, it is not on the French captain, nor on the Count de Morcerf, but on the fisherman Fernand, the husband of the Catalan Mercédès."

" Ah, sir," cried the countess, " how terrible a vengeance for a fault which fatality made me commit! for I am the only culprit, Edmond; and if you owe revenge to anyone, it is to me, who had not fortitude to bear your absence and my solitude."

" But," exclaimed Monte Cristo, " why was I absent? And why were you alone? "

" Because you had been arrested, Edmond, and were a prisoner."

" And why was I arrested? Why was I a prisoner? "

" I do not know," said Mercédès.

" You do not, madame; at least I hope not. But I will tell you. I was arrested and became a prisoner, because under the arbour of La Réserve, the day before I was to marry you, a man named Danglars wrote this letter which the fisherman Fernand himself posted."

Monte Cristo went to a secretaire, opened a drawer by a spring, from which he took a paper which had lost its original colour, and the ink of which had become a rusty hue: this he placed in the hands of Mercédès. It was Danglars' letter to the procureur du roi, which the Count of Monte Cristo, disguised as a clerk from the house of Thomson and French, had taken from the bundle of Edmond Dantès, on the day he had paid the two hundred thousand francs to M. de Boville. Mercédès read with terror the following lines:—

" The procureur du roi is informed by a friend to the throne and the religious institutions of his country, that an individual, named Edmond Dantès, second in command on board the *Pharaon*, this day arrived from Smyrna, after having touched at Naples and Porto-Ferrajo, has been the bearer of a letter from

Murat to the usurper, and again taken charge of another letter from the usurper to the Bonapartist club in Paris. Ample corroboration of this statement may be obtained by arresting the above-mentioned Edmond Dantès, who either carries the letter for Paris about with him, or has it at his father's abode. Should it not be found in possession of either father or son, then it will assuredly be discovered in the cabin belonging to the said Dantès on board the *Pharaon*."

"How dreadful!" said Mercédès, passing her hand across her brow, moist with perspiration; "and that letter——"

"I bought it for two hundred thousand francs, madame," said Monte Cristo; "but that is a trifle, since it enables me to justify myself to you."

"And the result of that letter——"

"You well know, madame, was my arrest; but you do not know how long that arrest lasted. You do not know that I remained for fourteen years within a quarter of a league of you, in a dungeon in the Château d'If. You do not know that each day of those fourteen years I renewed the vow of vengeance which I had made the first day; and yet I knew not you had married Fernand, my calumniator, and that my father had died of hunger!"

"Can it be?" cried Mercédès, shuddering.

"That is what I heard on leaving my prison, fourteen years after I had entered it, and that is why, on account of the living Mercédès and my deceased father, I have sworn to revenge myself on Fernand, and—I have revenged myself."

"And you are sure the unhappy Fernand did that?"

"I am satisfied, madame, he did what I have told you; besides, that is not much more odious than a Frenchman, by adoption, having passed over to the English; a Spaniard by birth, having fought against the Spaniards; a stipendiary of Ali, having betrayed and murdered Ali. Compared with such things, what is the letter you have just read? A lover's deception, which the woman who has married that man ought certainly to forgive; but not so the lover who was to have married her. Well! the French did not avenge themselves on the traitor; the Spaniards did not shoot the traitor; Ali, in his tomb, left the traitor unpunished; but I, betrayed, sacrificed, buried, have risen from my tomb, by the grace of God, to punish that man. He sends me for that purpose, and here I am."

The poor woman's head and arms fell; her legs bent under her, and she sank on her knees.

"Forgive, Edmond, forgive for my sake, who loves you still!"

The dignity of the wife stopped the enthusiasm of the lover and the mother. Her forehead almost touched the carpet, when the count sprang forward and raised her. Then, seated on a chair, she looked at the manly countenance of Monte Cristo, on which grief and hatred still impressed a threatening expression.

" Not crush that accursed race! " murmured he; " abandon my purpose at the moment of its accomplishment! Impossible, madame, impossible! "

" Edmond," said the poor mother, who tried every means, " when I call you Edmond, why do you not call me Mercédès? "

" Mercédès! " repeated Monte Cristo; " Mercédès! Well, yes, you are right; that name has still its charms, and this is the first time for a long period that I have pronounced it so distinctly. Oh, Mercédès! I have uttered your name with the sigh of melancholy, with the groan of sorrow, with the last effort of despair; I have uttered it when frozen with cold, crouched on the straw in my dungeon; I have uttered it, consumed with heat, rolling on the stone floor of my prison. Mercédès, I must revenge myself, for I suffered fourteen years,—fourteen years I wept, I cursed; now I tell you, Mercédès, I must revenge myself! "

The count, fearing to yield to the entreaties of her he had so ardently loved, recalled his sufferings to the assistance of his hatred.

" Revenge yourself, then, Edmond," cried the poor mother; " but let your vengeance fall on the culprits; on him, on me, but not on my son! "

Monte Cristo groaned, and seized his beautiful hair with both hands.

" Edmond," continued Mercédès, with her arms extended towards the count, " since I first knew you, I have adored your name, have respected your memory. Edmond, my friend, do not compel me to tarnish that noble and fine image reflected incessantly on the mirror of my heart. Edmond, if you knew all the prayers I have addressed to God for you while I thought you were living and since I have thought you must be dead! Yes, dead, alas! I thought your dead body was buried at the foot of some gloomy tower; I thought your corpse was precipitated to the bottom of one of those gulfs where gaolers roll their dead prisoners, and I wept! What could I do for you, Edmond, besides pray and weep? Listen; during ten years I dreamed each night the same dream. I had been told you had endeavoured to escape; that you had taken the place of another prisoner; that you had slipped into the winding-sheet of a dead body;

that you had been precipitated alive from the top of the Château d'If, and the cry you uttered as you dashed upon the rocks first revealed to your gaolers that they were your murderers. Well! Edmond, I swear to you by the head of that son for whom I entreat your pity,—Edmond, during ten years I have seen every night men balancing something shapeless and unknown at the top of a rock; during ten years I have heard each night a terrible cry which has awoke me, shuddering and cold. And I, too, Edmond—oh, believe me—guilty as I was—oh, yes, I too have suffered much! "

" Have you felt your father die in your absence? " cried Monte Cristo, again thrusting his hands in his hair: " have you seen the woman you loved giving her hand to your rival while you were perishing at the bottom of a dungeon? "

" No," interrupted Mercédès, " but I have seen him whom I loved on the point of murdering my son."

Mercédès pronounced these words with such deep anguish, with an accent of such intense despair, that Monte Cristo could not restrain a sob. The lion was daunted; the avenger was conquered.

" What do you ask of me? " said he,—" your son's life? Well, he shall live! "

Mercédès uttered a cry which made the tears start from Monte Cristo's eyes.

" Oh," said she, seizing the count's hand, and raising it to her lips; " oh, thank you, thank you, Edmond! now you are exactly what I dreamt you were, such as I always loved you. Oh, now I may say so."

" So much the better," replied Monte Cristo; " as that poor Edmond will not have long to be loved by you. Death is about to return to the tomb, the phantom to retire in darkness."

" What do you say, Edmond? "

" I say, since you command me, Mercédès, I must die."

" Die! and who told you so? who talks of dying? whence have you these ideas of death? "

" You do not suppose, that publicly outraged in the face of a whole theatre, in the presence of your friends and those of your son,—challenged by a boy, who will glory in my pardon as in a victory,—you do not suppose I can for one moment wish to live. What I most loved after you, Mercédès, was myself, my dignity, and that strength which rendered me superior to other men; that strength was my life. With one word you have crushed it, and I die."

" But the duel will not take place, Edmond, since you forgive? "

" It will take place," said Monte Cristo, in a most solemn

tone; "but instead of your son's blood which will stain the ground, mine will flow."

Mercédès shrieked, and sprang towards Monte Cristo, but suddenly stopping:—

"Edmond," said she; "there is a God above us, since you live, since I have seen you again; I trust to him from my heart. While waiting his assistance I trust to your word; you have said my son should live, have you not?"

"Yes, madame, he shall live," said Monte Cristo, surprised that, without more emotion, Mercédès had accepted the heroic sacrifice he made for her.

Mercédès extended her hand to the count.

"Edmond," said she, and her eyes were wet with tears while looking at him to whom she spoke, "how noble it is of you, how great the action you have just performed; how sublime to have taken pity on a poor woman who offered herself to you with every chance against her! Alas, I am grown old with grief more than with years, and cannot now remind my Edmond by a smile, or by a look, of that Mercédès whom he once spent so many hours in contemplating. Ah, believe me, Edmond, I told you, I too had suffered much; I repeat it, it is melancholy to pass one's life without having one joy to recall, without preserving a single hope; but that proves that all is not yet over. No, it is not finished, I feel it by what remains in my heart. Oh, I repeat it, Edmond; what you have just done is beautiful,—it is grand; it is sublime."

"Do you say so now, Mercédès, and what would you say if you knew the extent of the sacrifice I make to you? But, no, no, you cannot imagine what I lose in sacrificing my life at this moment."

Mercédès looked at the count with an air which depicted at the same time her astonishment, her admiration, and her gratitude. Monte Cristo pressed his forehead on his burning hands, as if his brain could no longer bear alone the weight of its thoughts.

"Edmond," said Mercédès, "I have but one word more to say to you."

The count smiled bitterly.

"Edmond," continued she, "you will see if my face is pale, if my eyes are dull, if my beauty is gone; if Mercédès, in short, no longer resembles her former self in her features, you will see her heart is still the same. Adieu, then, Edmond; I have nothing more to ask of heaven—I have seen you again—and have found you as noble and as great as formerly you were. Adieu, Edmond, adieu, and thank you."

But the count did not answer. Mercédès opened the door of the cabinet and had disappeared before he had recovered from the painful and profound reverie into which his thwarted vengeance had plunged him. The clock of the Invalides struck one when the carriage which conveyed Madame de Morcerf away rolled on the pavement of the Champs-Elysées, and made Monte Cristo raise his head.

91

The Meeting

AFTER Mercédès had left Monte Cristo, a gloomy shadow seemed to overspread everything. Around him and within him the flight of thought appeared stopped; his energetic mind slumbered as does the body after extreme fatigue.

" What! " said he to himself, while the lamp and the wax lights were nearly burnt out, and the servants were waiting impatiently in the ante-room; " what! this edifice which I have been so long preparing,—which I have reared with so much care and toil, is to be crumbled by a single touch, a word, even a slight breath! Yes, this self, of whom I thought so much, of whom I was so proud, who had appeared so worthless in the dungeons of the Château D'If, and whom I had succeeded in making so great, will be but a lump of clay to-morrow. Alas! it is not the death of the body I regret; for is not that destruction of the vital principle the rest to which everything is tending, to which every unhappy being aspires, the repose of matter after which I so long sighed, and which I was seeking to attain by the painful process of starvation when Faria appeared in my dungeon? What is death for me but one step more towards repose? No, it is not existence, then, that I regret, but the ruin of my projects, so slowly carried out, so laboriously framed. Providence is now opposed to them when I most thought it would be propitious. It is not God's will they should be accomplished. This burden, almost as heavy as a world, which I had raised, and had thought to bear to the end, was too great for my strength, and I was compelled to lay it down in the middle of my career. Oh, shall I then again become a fatalist, whom fourteen years of despair and ten of hope had rendered a believer in Providence? and all this, all this, because my heart, which I thought dead, was only sleeping—because it has awoke and has beaten again, because I have yielded to the pain of the emotion excited in my breast by a woman's voice. Yet," continued the count, becoming each moment more absorbed in the anticipation of the dreadful sacrifice for the morrow, which Mercédès had accepted, " yet, it is impossible that so noble-minded a woman should thus, through selfishness, consent to my death when in the prime of life and strength; it is impossible she can carry to such a point maternal love, or rather delirium. There are virtues which become crimes by exaggeration. No, she must have conceived some pathetic scene; she will come and throw herself between us, and what would be sublime here will appear there ridiculous."

The blush of pride mounted to the count's forehead as this thought passed through his mind.

" Folly, folly, folly! to carry generosity so far as to place myself as a mark for that young man to aim at. He will never believe my death was a suicide; and yet it is important for the honour of my memory (and this, surely, is not vanity, but a justifiable pride), it is important the world should know that I have consented, by my free will, to stop my arm, already raised to strike, and that with that arm, so powerful against others, I have struck myself. It must be—it shall be."

Seizing a pen, he drew a paper from a secret drawer in his bureau, and traced at the bottom of that paper, which was no other than his will, made since his arrival in Paris, a sort of codicil, clearly explaining the nature of his death.

" I do this, O my God! " said he, with his eyes raised to heaven, " as much for thy honour as for mine. I have during ten years considered myself the agent of thy vengeance; and other wretches, like Morcerf, a Danglars, a Villefort, even that Morcerf himself must not imagine that chance has freed them from their enemy. Let them know, on the contrary, that their punishment which had been decreed by Providence is only delayed by my present determination, that although they escape it in this world, it awaits them in another, and that they are only exchanging time for eternity."

While he was thus agitated by these gloomy uncertainties, these wretched waking dreams of grief, the first rays of twilight pierced his windows, and shone upon the pale blue paper on which he had just traced his justification of Providence. It was just five o'clock in the morning, when a slight noise reached his ear, which appeared like a stifled sigh. He turned his head, looked round him, and saw no one; but the sound was repeated distinctly enough to convince him of its reality. He arose, and quietly opening the door of the drawing-room, saw Haydée, who had fallen on a chair with her arms hanging down, and her beautiful head thrown back. She had been standing at the door to prevent his going out without seeing her, until sleep, which the young cannot resist, had overpowered her frame, wearied as she was with watching so long. The noise of the door did not awaken her, and Monte Cristo gazed at her with affectionate regret.

"She remembered she had a son," said he; "and I forgot I had a daughter." Then shaking his head sorrowfully, "Poor Haydée!" said he; "she wished to see me to speak to me; she has feared or guessed something. Oh, I cannot go without taking leave of her; I cannot die without confiding her to someone." He quietly regained his seat, and wrote under the other lines:—

"I bequeath to Maximilian Morrel, captain, and son of my former patron, Pierre Morrel, shipowner at Marseilles, the sum of twenty millions, a part of which may be offered to his sister Julia and brother-in-law Emmanuel, if he does not fear this increase of fortune may mar their happiness. These twenty millions are concealed in my grotto at Monte Cristo, of which Bertuccio knows the secret. If his heart is free, and he will marry Haydée, the daughter of Ali, pacha of Yanina, whom I have brought up with the love of a father, and who has shown the love and tenderness of a daughter for me, he will thus accomplish my last wish.

"This will has already constituted Haydée heiress of the rest of my fortune, consisting in lands, rents on England, Austria, and Holland, furniture in my different palaces and houses, and which, without the twenty millions, and the legacies to my servants, may still amount to sixty millions."

He was finishing the last line when a cry behind him made him start and the pen fell from his hand.

"Haydée," said he, "did you read it?"

"Oh, my lord," said she, "why are you writing thus at such an hour? why are you bequeathing all your fortune to me? Are you going to leave me?"

"I am going on a journey, dear child," said Monte Cristo, with an expression of infinite tenderness and melancholy; "and if any misfortune should happen to me——" The count stopped.

"Well," asked the young girl, with an authoritative tone the count had never observed before, and which startled him.

"Well! if any misfortune happen to me," replied Monte Cristo, "I wish my daughter to be happy."

Haydée smiled sorrowfully and shook her head.

" Do you think of dying, my lord? " said she.

" The wise man has said, It is good to think of death, my child."

" Well, if you die," said she, " bequeath your fortune to others; for, if you die, I shall require nothing; " and, taking the paper, she tore it in four pieces and threw it in the middle of the room. Then the effort having exhausted her strength, she fell, not asleep this time, but fainting on the floor. The count leant over her and raised her in his arms; and seeing that sweet face pale, those lovely eyes closed, that beautiful form motionless, and to all appearance lifeless, the idea occurred to him for the first time, that perhaps she loved him otherwise than a daughter loves a father.

" Alas," murmured he, with intense suffering; " I might then have been happy yet." Then he carried Haydée to her room, resigned her to the care of her attendants, and returning to his cabinet, which he shut quickly this time, he again copied the destroyed will. As he was finishing, the sound of a cabriolet entering the yard was heard. Monte Cristo approached the window, and saw Maximilian and Emmanuel alight.

" Good," said he; " it was time," and he sealed his will with three seals. One moment afterwards he heard a noise in the drawing-room, and went to open the door himself. Morrel was there; he had come twenty minutes before the time appointed.

" I am, perhaps, come too soon, count," said he, " but I frankly acknowledge, I have not closed my eyes all night, nor anyone in my house. I required to see you strong in your courageous assurance to recover myself."

Monte Cristo could not resist this proof of affection; he not only extended his hand to the young man, but flew to him with open arms.

" Morrel," said he; " it is a happy day for me, to feel I am beloved by such a man as you. Good-morning, Emmanuel; you will come with me then, Maximilian? "

" Did you doubt it? " said the young captain.

" But if I were wrong——"

" I watched you during the whole scene of that challenge yesterday; I have been thinking of your firmness all this night, and I said, Justice must be on your side, or man's countenance is no longer to be relied on."

" But, Morrel, Albert is your friend? "

" A simple acquaintance, sir."

" You met on the same day you first saw me? "

" Truly; but I should not have recollected it had you not reminded me."

" Thank you, Morrel."

Then, ringing the bell once; " Look," said he to Ali, who came immediately, " take that to my solicitor. It is my will, Morrel. When I am dead, you will go and examine it."

" What! " said Morrel, " you dead? "

" Yes; must I not be prepared for everything, dear friend? But what did you do yesterday after you left me? "

" I went to Tortoni,* where, as I expected, I found Beauchamp and Château-Renaud. I own I was seeking them."

" Why, when all was arranged? "

" Listen, count, the affair is serious and unavoidable."

" Did you doubt it? "

" No; the offence was public, and everyone is already talking of it."

" Well? "

" Well! I hoped to get an exchange of arms, to substitute the sword for the pistol. The pistol is blind."

" Have you succeeded? " asked Monte Cristo quickly, with an imperceptible gleam of hope.

" No; for your skill with the sword is so well known."

" Ah, who has betrayed me? "

" The skilful swordsman, whom you have conquered."

" And you failed? "

" They positively refused."

" Morrel," said the count, " have you ever seen me fire a pistol? "

" Never."

" Well, we have time: look."

Monte Cristo took the pistols he held in his hand when Mercédès entered, and fixing an ace of clubs against the iron plate, with four shots he successively shot off the four sides of the club.* At each shot Morrel turned pale. He examined the balls with which Monte Cristo performed this dexterous feat, and saw that they were no larger than deer-shot.

" It is astonishing," said he; " look, Emmanuel."

Then turning towards Monte Cristo: " Count," said he, " in the name of all that is dear to you, I entreat you not to kill Albert! the unhappy youth has a mother."

" You are right," said Monte Cristo; " and I have none."

These words were uttered in a tone which made Morrel shudder.

" You are the offended party, count."

" Doubtless; what does that imply? "

" That you will fire first."

" I fire first? "

" Oh, I obtained, or rather claimed that; we had conceded enough for them to yield us that."

" And at what distance? "

" Twenty paces."

A terrific smile passed over the count's lips.

" Morrel," said he, " do not forget what you have just seen."

" The only chance for Albert's safety, then, will arise from your emotion."

" I suffer from emotion? " said Monte Cristo.

" Or from your generosity, my friend; to so good a marksman as you are, I may say what would appear absurd to another."

" What is it? "

" Break his arm—wound him—but do not kill him."

" I will tell you, Morrel," said the count, " that I do not need entreating to spare the life of M. de Morcerf; he shall be so well spared, that he will return quietly with his two friends, while I——"

" And you? "

" That's another story; I shall be carried home."

" What do you mean? " cried Maximilian, almost beside himself.

" As I told you, my dear Morrel, M. de Morcerf will kill me."

Morrel looked at the count as though he could no longer grasp his meaning.

" But what has happened then, since last evening, count? "

" The same thing which happened to Brutus the night before the battle of Philippi; I have seen a phantom."

" And that phantom——"

" Told me, Morrel, I had lived long enough."

Maximilian and Emmanuel looked at each other.

Monte Cristo drew out his watch.

" Let us go," said he; " it is five minutes past seven, and the appointment was for eight o'clock."

A carriage was in readiness at the door. Monte Cristo stepped into it with his two friends. He had stopped a moment in the passage to listen at a door, and Maximilian and Emmanuel, who had considerately passed forward a few steps, thought they heard him answer by a sigh, a sob from within.

As the clock struck eight, they drove up to the place of meeting.

" We are the first," said Morrel, looking out of the window.

" Truly," said Emmanuel, " I perceive two young men down there, who are evidently waiting."

Monte Cristo drew Morrel, not aside, but a step or two behind his brother-in-law.

" Maximilian," said he, " are your affections disengaged? "

Morrel looked at Monte Cristo with astonishment.

" I do not seek your confidence, my dear friend. I only ask you a simple question; answer it,—that is all I require."

" I love a young girl, count."

" Do you love her much? "

" More than my life! "

" Another hope defeated! " said the count. Then, with a sigh, " Poor Haydée! " murmured he.

" In truth, count, if I knew less of you, I should think you were less brave than you are."

" Because I sigh when thinking of someone I am leaving? Come, Morrel, it is not like a soldier to be so bad a judge of courage. Do I regret life? What is it to me, who have passed twenty years between life and death? Moreover, do not alarm yourself, Morrel: this weakness, if it is such, is betrayed to you alone. I know the world is a drawing-room, from which we must retreat politely and honestly; that is, with a bow, and all debts of honour paid."

" That is to the purpose. Have you brought your arms? "

" I?—what for? I hope those gentlemen have theirs."

" I will inquire," said Morrel.

" Do, but make no treaty—you understand me? "

" You need not fear."

Morrel advanced towards Beauchamp and Château-Renaud, who, seeing his intention, came to meet him.

The three young people bowed to each other courteously, if not affably.

" Excuse me, gentlemen," said Morrel, " but I do not see M. de Morcerf."

" He sent us word this morning," replied Château-Renaud, " that he would meet us on the ground."

" Ah! " said Morrel.

Beauchamp pulled out his watch. " It is only five minutes past eight," said he to Morrel; " there is not much time lost yet."

" Oh, I made no allusion of that kind," replied Morrel.

" There is a carriage coming," said Château-Renaud.

It advanced rapidly along one of the avenues leading towards the open space where they were assembled.

" You are doubtless provided with pistols, gentlemen? M. de Monte Cristo yields his right of using his."

" We had anticipated this kindness on the part of the count," said Beauchamp, " and I have brought some arms which I bought eight or ten days since, thinking to want them on a similar occasion. They are quite new, and have not yet been used. Will you examine them? "

" Oh, M. Beauchamp, if you assure me M. de Morcerf does not know these arms, you may readily believe your word will be quite sufficient."

" Gentlemen," said Château-Renaud, " it is not Morcerf coming in that carriage;—faith, it is Franz and Debray! "

The two young men he announced were indeed approaching.

" What chance brings you here, gentlemen? " said Château-Renaud, shaking hands with each of them.

" Because," said Debray, " Albert sent this morning to request us to come."

Beauchamp and Château-Renaud exchanged looks of astonishment.

" I think I understand his reason," said Morrel.

" What is it? "

" Yesterday afternoon I received a letter from M. de Morcerf, begging me to attend the Opera."

" And I," said Debray.

" And I, also," said Franz.

" And we, too," added Beauchamp and Château-Renaud. " Having wished you all to witness the challenge, he now wishes you to be present at the combat."

" Exactly so," said the young men; " you have probably guessed right."

" But, after all these arrangements, he does not come himself," said Château-Renaud; " Albert is ten minutes after time."

" There he comes," said Beauchamp, " on horseback, at full gallop, followed by a servant."

" How imprudent," said Château-Renaud, " to come on horseback to fight with the pistol, after all the instructions I had given him."

" And besides," said Beauchamp, " with a collar above his cravat, an open coat and white waistcoat! Why has he not painted a spot upon his heart?—it would have been more simple."

Meanwhile Albert had arrived within ten paces of the group formed by the five young men. He jumped from his horse, threw the bridle on his servant's arm, and joined them. He was pale, and his eyes were red and swollen; it was evident he had not slept. A shade of melancholy gravity overspread his countenance, which was not natural to him.

" I thank you, gentlemen," said he, " for having complied with my request; I feel extremely grateful for this mark of friendship."

Morrel had stepped back as Morcerf approached, and remained at a short distance.

" And to you also, M. Morrel, my thanks are due. Come, there cannot be too many."

" Sir," said Maximilian, " you are not perhaps aware I am M. de Monte Cristo's friend? "

" I was not sure, but I expected it. So much the better; the more honourable men there are here the better I shall be satisfied."

" M. Morrel," said Château-Renaud, " will you apprise the Count of Monte Cristo that M. de Morcerf is arrived, and we are at his command? "

Morrel was preparing to fulfil his commission. Beauchamp had meanwhile drawn the box of pistols from the carriage.

" Stop, gentlemen! " said Albert; " I have two words to say to the Count of Monte Cristo."

" In private? " asked Morrel.

" No, sir; before all who are here."

Albert's witnesses looked at each other. Franz and Debray exchanged some words in a whisper, and Morrel, rejoiced at this unexpected incident, went to fetch the count, who was walking in a retired path with Emmanuel.

" What does he want with me? " said Monte Cristo.

" I do not know, but he wishes to speak to you."

" Ah," said Monte Cristo, " I trust he is not going to tempt me by some fresh insult! "

" I do not think such is his intention," said Morrel.

The count advanced, accompanied by Maximilian and Emmanuel; his calm and serene look formed a singular contrast to Albert's grief-stricken face, who approached also, followed by the four young people.

When at three paces distant, Albert and the count stopped.

" Approach, gentlemen," said Albert; " I wish you not to lose one word of what I am about to have the honour of saying to the Count of Monte Cristo; for it must be repeated by you to all who will listen to it, strange as it may appear to you."

" Proceed, sir," said the count.

" Sir," said Albert, at first with a tremulous voice, but which gradually became firmer; " I reproached you with exposing the conduct of M. de Morcerf in Epirus, for, guilty as I knew he was, I thought you had no right to punish him; but I have since learned you have that right. It is not Fernand Mondego's treachery towards Ali Pacha which induces me so readily to excuse you, but the treachery of the fisherman Fernand towards you, and the almost unheard-of miseries which were its consequences; and I say, and proclaim it publicly, that you were justified in revenging yourself on my father; and I, his son, thank you for not using greater severity."

Had a thunderbolt fallen in the midst of the spectators of this unexpected scene, it would not have surprised them more than did Albert's declaration.

As for Monte Cristo, his eyes slowly rose towards heaven with an expression of infinite gratitude. He could not understand how Albert's fiery nature, of which he had seen so much among the Roman bandits, had suddenly stooped to this humiliation. He recognised the influence of Mercédès, and saw why her noble heart had not opposed the sacrifice she knew beforehand would be useless.

"Now, sir," said Albert, "if you think my apology sufficient, pray give me your hand. Next to the merit of infallibility which you appear to possess, I rank that of candidly acknowledging a fault. But this confession concerns me only. I acted well as a man, but you have acted better than man. An angel alone could have saved one of us from death—that angel came from heaven, if not to make us friends (which, alas, fatality renders impossible), at least to make us esteem each other."

Monte Cristo, with moistened eye, heaving breast, and lips half open, extended to Albert a hand, which the latter pressed with a sentiment resembling respectful fear.

"Gentlemen," said he, "M. de Monte Cristo receives my apology; I had acted hastily towards him. Hasty actions are generally bad ones. Now my fault is repaired. I hope the world will not call me cowardly for acting as my conscience dictated. But if anyone should entertain a false opinion of me," added he, drawing himself up as if he would challenge both friends and enemies, "I shall endeavour to correct his mistake."

"What has, then, happened during the night?" asked Beauchamp to Château-Renaud; "we appear to make a very sorry figure here."

"In truth, what Albert has just done is either very despicable or very noble," replied the baron.

"What can it mean?" said Debray to Franz. "The Count of Monte Cristo acts dishonourably to M. de Morcerf, and is justified by his son! Had I ten Yaninas in my family, I should only consider myself the more bound to fight ten times."

As for Monte Cristo, his head was bent down, his arms were powerless. Bowing under the weight of twenty-four years' reminiscences, he thought not of Albert, of Beauchamp, of Château-Renaud, or of any of that group; but he thought of that courageous woman who had come to plead for her son's life, to whom he had offered his, and who had now saved it by the revelation of a dreadful family secret, capable of destroying for ever, in that young man's heart, every feeling of filial piety.

"Providence still," murmured he; "now only am I fully convinced of being the emissary of God!"

92

The Mother and Son

THE Count of Monte Cristo bowed to the five young people with a melancholy and dignified smile, and got into his carriage with Maximilian and Emmanuel. Albert, Beauchamp, and Château-Renaud, remained alone. The young man's look at his two friends, without being timid, appeared to ask their opinion of what he had just done.

"Indeed, my dear friend," said Beauchamp, first, who had either the most feeling or the least dissimulation, "allow me to congratulate you; this is a very unhoped-for conclusion of a very disagreeable affair."

Albert remained silent and wrapped in thought. Château-Renaud contented himself with tapping his boot with his flexible cane.

"Are we not going?" said he, after this embarrassing silence.

"When you please," replied Beauchamp; "allow me only time to compliment M. de Morcerf, who has given proof to-day of such chivalric generosity, so rare!"

"Oh, yes," said Château-Renaud.

"It is magnificent," continued Beauchamp, "to be able to exercise so much self-control!"

"Assuredly; as for me, I should have been incapable of it," said Château-Renaud, with most significant coolness.

"Gentlemen," interrupted Albert, "I think you did not understand that something very serious had passed between M. de Monte Cristo and myself."

"Possibly, possibly," said Beauchamp immediately; "but every simpleton would not be able to understand your heroism, and, sooner or later, you will find yourself compelled to explain it to them more energetically than would be convenient to your bodily health and the duration of your life. May I give you a friendly counsel? Set out for Naples, the Hague, or St. Petersburg —calm countries, where the point of honour is better understood than among our hot-headed Parisians. Seek quietude and oblivion, so that you may return peaceably to France after a few years. Am I not right, M. de Château-Renaud? "

" That is quite my opinion," said the gentleman; " nothing induces serious duels so much as a fruitless one."

" Thank you, gentlemen," replied Albert, with a smile of indifference; " I shall follow your advice, not because you gave it, but because I had before intended to quit France. I thank you equally for the service you have rendered me in being my seconds. It is deeply engraved on my heart, since after what you have just said. I remember that only."

Château-Renaud and Beauchamp looked at each other; the impression was the same on both of them, and the tone in which Morcerf had just expressed his thanks was so determined, that the position would have become embarrassing for all if the conversation had continued.

" Farewell, Albert," said Beauchamp suddenly, carelessly extending his hand to the young man, without the latter appearing to rouse from his lethargy; in fact he did not notice the offered hand.

" Farewell," said Château-Renaud in his turn, keeping the little cane in his left hand, and saluting with his right.

Albert's lips scarcely whispered " Farewell! " but his look was more explicit; it embraced a whole poem of restrained anger, proud disdain, and generous indignation. He preserved his melancholy and motionless position for some time after his two friends had regained their carriage; then, suddenly loosing his horse from the little tree to which his servant had fastened it, he sprang on it, and galloped off in the direction of Paris. In a quarter of an hour he was entering the hotel of the Rue du Helder. As he alighted, he thought he saw behind the curtain of the count's bedroom his father's pale face; Albert turned away his head with a sigh, and went to his own apartments. He cast one lingering look on all the luxuries which had rendered life so easy and so happy since his infancy; he looked at the pictures, whose faces seemed to smile, and the landscapes which appeared painted in brighter colours. Then he took away his mother's portrait, with its oaken frame, leaving the gilt frame, from which he took it, black and empty. Then he arranged all his beautiful Turkish arms, his fine English guns, his Japanese China, his cups mounted in silver, his artistic bronzes, signed Feuchères, or Barye;* examined the cupboards, and placed the key in each; threw into a drawer of his secretaire, which he left open, all the pocket-money he had about him; and with it the thousand fancy jewels from his vases and his jewel-boxes; made an exact inventory of all, and placed it in the most conspicuous part of the table, after putting aside the books and papers which encumbered it. At the commencement of this work, his servant, notwithstanding his prohibition, came to his room.

" What do you want? " asked he, with a more sorrowful than angry tone.

" Pardon me, sir," replied the valet; " you had forbidden me to disturb you, but the Count of Morcerf had called me."

" Well? " said Albert.

" I did not like to go to him without first seeing you."

" Why? "

" Because the count is doubtless aware that I accompanied you to the meeting this morning."

" It is probable," said Albert.

" And since he has sent for me, it is doubtless to question me on what happened there. What must I answer? "

" The truth."

" Then I shall say the duel did not take place? "

" You will say I apologised to the Count of Monte Cristo. Go."

The valet bowed and retired; and Albert returned to his inventory.

As he was finishing this work the sound of horses prancing in the yard, and the wheels of a carriage shaking his window, attracted his attention. He approached the window, and saw his father get into it, and it drove away. The door was scarcely closed when Albert bent his steps to his mother's room; and no one being there to announce him, he advanced to her bedroom, and, distressed by what he saw and guessed, stopped for one moment at the door. As if the same soul had animated these two beings, Mercédès was doing the same in her apartments as he had just done. Everything was in order; laces, dresses, jewels, linen, money, all were arranged in the drawers, and the countess was carefully collecting the keys.

Albert saw all these preparations; he understood them, and exclaiming:

" My mother! " he threw his arms round her neck.

The artist who could have depicted the expression of these two countenances would certainly have made of them a beautiful picture. All these proofs of an energetic resolution, which Albert did not fear on his own account, alarmed him for his mother.

" What are you doing? " asked he.

" What were you doing," replied she.

" Oh, my mother! " exclaimed Albert, so overcome he could scarcely speak; " it is not the same with you and me—you cannot have made the same resolution I have, for I am come to warn you that I bid adieu to your house, and—and to you."

" I also," replied Mercédès, " am going, and I acknowledge I had depended on your accompanying me; have I deceived myself? "

" My mother," said Albert, with firmness, " I cannot make you share the fate I have planned for myself. I must live henceforth without rank and fortune, and to begin this hard apprenticeship I must borrow from a friend the loaf I shall eat until I have earned one. So, my dear mother, I am going at once to ask Franz to lend me the small sum I shall require to supply my present wants."

" You, my poor child, suffer poverty and hunger! Oh, say not so, it will break my resolutions."

" But not mine, mother," replied Albert. " I am young and strong; I believe I am courageous, and since yesterday I have learned the power of will. Alas! my dear mother, some have suffered so much, and yet live, and have raised a new fortune on the ruin of all the promises of happiness which heaven had made them, on the fragments of all the hope which God had given them! I have seen that, my mother; I know that from the gulf in which their enemies have plunged them they have risen with so much vigour and glory, that in their turn they have ruled their former conquerors, and have punished them. No, my mother, from this moment I have done with the past, and accept nothing from it; not even a name, because you can understand your son cannot bear the name of a man who ought to blush before another."

" Albert, my child," said Mercédès, " if I had a stronger heart, that is the counsel I would have given you; your conscience has spoken when my voice became too weak; listen to its dictates. You had friends, Albert; break off their acquaintance, but do not despair. You have life before you, my dear Albert, for you are yet scarcely twenty-two years old; and as a pure heart like yours wants a spotless name, take my father's; it was Herrera. I am sure, my Albert, whatever may be your career, you will soon render that name illustrious. Then, my friend, return to the world still more brilliant from the reflection of your former sorrows; and if I am wrong, still let me cherish these hopes, for I have no future to look forward to: for me the grave opens when I pass the threshold of this house."

" I will fulfil all your wishes, my dear mother," said the young man. " Yes, I share your hopes; the anger of heaven will not pursue us—you so pure, and I so innocent. But since our resolution is formed, let us act promptly. M. de Morcerf went out about half an hour since; the opportunity is favourable to avoid an explanation."

" I am ready, my son," said Mercédès.

Albert ran to fetch a hackney-coach. He recollected there was a small furnished house to let in the Rue des Saints-Pères, where his mother would find a humble, but decent lodging, and thither he intended conducting the countess. As the hackney-coach stopped at the door, and Albert was alighting, a man approached, and gave him a letter. Albert recognised the bearer.

" From the count," said Bertuccio.

Albert took the letter, opened it, and read it; then looked round for Bertuccio, but he was gone. He returned to Mercédès, with tears in his eyes and heaving breast, and, without uttering a word, he gave her the letter. Mercédès read:—

" ALBERT,—While showing you that I have discovered your plans, I hope also to convince you of my delicacy. You are free, you leave the count's hotel, and you take your mother to your home; but reflect. Albert, you owe her more than your poor noble heart can pay her. Keep the struggle for yourself, bear all the suffering, but spare her the trial of poverty which must accompany your first efforts; for she deserves not even the shadow of the misfortune which has this day fallen on her, and Providence wills not the innocent should suffer for the guilty. I know you are going to leave the Rue du Helder without taking anything with you; do not seek to know how I discovered it—I know it, that is sufficient. Now, listen, Albert. Twenty-four years ago I returned, proud and joyful, to my country. I had a betrothed, Albert, a lovely girl, whom I adored, and I was bringing to my betrothed a hundred and fifty louis, painfully amassed by ceaseless toil. This money was for her. I destined it for her, and knowing the treachery of the sea, I buried our treasure in the little garden of the house my father lived in at Marseilles, on the Allées de Meillan. Your mother, Albert, knows that poor house well. A short time since I passed through Marseilles, and went to see the old house, which revived so many painful recollections, and in the evening I took a spade and dug in the corner of the garden where I had concealed my treasure. The iron box was there, no one had touched it; it was under a beautiful fig-tree my father had planted the day I was born, which overshadowed the spot. Well, Albert, this money, which was formerly designed to promote the comfort and tranquillity of the woman I adored, may now, from a strange and painful circumstance, be devoted to the same purpose. Oh, feel for me, who could offer millions to that poor woman, but who return her only the piece of black bread, forgotten under my poor roof since the day I was torn from her I loved. You are a generous man, Albert, but, perhaps, you may be blinded by pride or resentment: if you refuse me, if you ask another for what I have a right to offer you, I will say it is ungenerous of you to refuse the life of your mother at the hands of a man whose father was allowed to die in all the horrors of poverty and despair by your father."

Albert stood pale and motionless to hear what his mother would decide after she had finished reading this letter. Mercédès turned her eyes with an ineffable look towards heaven.

"I accept it," said she; "he has a right to pay the dowry, which I shall take with me to some convent."

Putting the letter in her bosom, she took her son's arm, and with a firmer step than she even herself expected, she went downstairs.

93

The Suicide

MEANWHILE Monte Cristo had also returned to town with Emmanuel and Maximilian. Their return was cheerful. Emmanuel did not conceal his joy at having seen peace succeed to war, and acknowledged aloud his philanthropic tastes. Morrel, in a corner of the carriage, allowed his brother-in-law's gaiety to expend itself in words, while he felt equal inward joy, which, however, betrayed itself only by his look. At the Barrière du Trône they met Bertuccio, who was waiting there, motionless as a sentinel at his post. Monte Cristo put his head out of the window, exchanged a few words with him in a low tone, and the steward disappeared.

"M. le Comte," said Emmanuel, when they were at the end of the Place Royale, "put me down at my door, that my wife may not have a single moment of needless anxiety on my account or yours."

"If it were not ridiculous to make a display of our triumph, I would invite the count to our house; besides that, he doubtless has some trembling heart to comfort. So we will take leave of our friend, and let him hasten him home."

"Stop a moment," said Monte Cristo; "do not let me lose both my companions. Return, Emmanuel, to your charming wife, and present my best compliments to her; and do you, Morrel, accompany me to the Champs-Elysées."

"Willingly," said Maximilian; "particularly as I have business in that quarter."

"Shall we wait breakfast for you?" asked Emmanuel.

"No," replied the young man.

The door was closed, and the carriage proceeded.

"See what good fortune I brought you!" said Morrel, when he was alone with the count. "Have you not thought so?"

"Yes," said Monte Cristo, "for that reason I wished to keep you near me."

"It is miraculous!" continued Morrel, answering his own thoughts.

"What?" said Monte Cristo.

"What has just happened."

"Yes," said the count, "you are right—it is miraculous."

"For Albert is brave," resumed Morrel.

"Very brave," said Monte Cristo; "I have seen him sleep with a sword suspended over his head."

"And I know he has fought two duels," said Morrel. "How can you reconcile that with his conduct this morning?"

"All owing to your influence," replied Monte Cristo, smiling.

"It is well for Albert he is not in the army," said Morrel.

"Why?"

"An apology on the ground!" said the young captain, shaking his head.

"Come," said the count mildly, "do not entertain the prejudices of ordinary men, Morrel! Acknowledge, if Albert is brave, he cannot be a coward; he must then have had some reason for acting as he did this morning, and confess that his conduct is more heroic than otherwise."

"Doubtless, doubtless," said Morrel; "but I shall say like the Spaniard, 'He has not been so brave to-day as he was yesterday.'"

"You will breakfast with me, will you not, Morrel?" said the count, to turn the conversation.

"No; I must leave you at ten o'clock."

"Your engagement was for breakfast, then?" said the count. Morrel smiled and shook his head.

"Still you must breakfast somewhere."

"But if I am not hungry?" said the young man.

"Oh," said the count, "I only know two things which destroy the appetite; grief (and as I am happy to see you very cheerful, it is not that) and love. Now, after what you told me this morning of your heart, I may believe——"

" Well, count," replied Morrel gaily, " I will not dispute it."

" But you will not make me your confidant, Maximilian? " said the count, in a tone which showed how gladly he would have been admitted to the secret.

" I showed you this morning I had a heart, did I not, count? "

Monte Cristo only answered by extending his hand to the young man.

" Well," continued the latter, " since that heart is no longer with you in the Bois de Vincennes, it is elsewhere, and I must go and find it."

" Go," said the count deliberately, " go, dear friend, but promise me, if you meet with any obstacle, to remember that I have some power in this world; that I am happy to use that power in the behalf of those I love, and that I love you, Morrel."

" I will remember it," said the young man, " as selfish children recollect their parents when they want their aid. When I need your assistance, and the moment may come, I will come to you, count."

" Well, I rely upon your promise. Farewell. Adieu, till we meet again."

They had arrived in the Champs Elysées. Monte Cristo opened the carriage-door, Morrel sprang out on the pavement, Bertuccio was waiting on the steps. Morrel disappeared through the avenue of Marigny, and Monte Cristo hastened to join Bertuccio.

" Well? " asked he.

" She is going to leave her house," said the steward.

" And her son? "

" Florentin, his valet, thinks he is going to do the same."

" Come this way."

Monte Cristo took Bertuccio into his cabinet, wrote the letter we have seen, and gave it to the steward.

" Go," said he quickly. " *À propos*, let Haydée be informed I have returned."

" Here I am," said the young girl, who, at the sound of the carriage, had run downstairs, and whose face was radiant with joy at seeing the count return safely.

Bertuccio left. Every transport of a daughter finding a father, all the delight of a mistress seeing an adored lover, were felt by Haydée during the first moments of this meeting, which she had so eagerly expected. Doubtless, although less evident, Monte Cristo's joy was not less intense. Joy to hearts which have suffered long is like the dew on the ground after a long drought; both the heart and the ground absorb that beneficent moisture falling on them, and nothing is outwardly apparent. Monte Cristo was beginning to think, what he had not for a long time dared to believe, that there were two Mercédès in the world, and he might yet be happy. His eye, elate with happiness, was reading eagerly the moistened gaze of Haydée, when suddenly the door opened. The count knit his brow.

" M. de Morcerf! " said Baptistin, as if that name sufficed for his excuse.

In fact, the count's face brightened.

" Which," asked he, " the viscount or the count? "

" The count."

" Oh," exclaimed Haydée, " is it not yet over? "

" I know not if it is finished, my beloved child," said Monte Cristo, taking the young girl's hands; " but I do know you have nothing more to fear."

" But it is the wretched——"

" That man cannot injure me, Haydée," said Monte Cristo; " it was his son alone there was cause to fear."

" And what I have suffered," said the young girl, " you shall never know, my lord."

Monte Cristo smiled.

" By my father's tomb! " said he, extending his hand over the head of the young girl, " I swear to you, Haydée, that if any misfortune happens, it will not be to me."

" I believe you, my lord, as implicitly as if God had spoken to me," said the young girl, presenting her forehead to him.

Monte Cristo pressed on that pure beautiful forehead a kiss, which made two hearts throb at once, the one violently, the other secretly.

" Oh," murmured the count, " shall I then be permitted to love again? Ask M. de Morcerf into the drawing-room," said he to Baptistin, while he led the beautiful Greek girl to a private staircase.

We must explain this visit, which, although Monte Cristo expected, is unexpected to our readers. While Mercédès, as we have said, was making a similar inventory of her property to Albert's, while she was arranging her jewels, shutting her drawers, collecting her keys, to leave everything in perfect order, she did not perceive a pale and sinister face at a glass door which threw light into the passage, from which everything could be both seen and heard. He who was thus looking, without being heard or seen, probably heard and saw all that passed in Madame de Morcerf's apartments. From that glass door the pale-faced man went to the count's bedroom, and raised the curtain of a window overlooking the courtyard. He remained there ten minutes, motionless and dumb, listening to the beating of his own heart. For him those ten minutes were very long.

It was then Albert, returned from his rendezvous, perceived his father watching for his arrival behind a curtain, and turned aside. The count's eye expanded; he knew Albert had insulted the count dreadfully, and that, in every country in the world, such an insult would lead to a deadly duel. Albert returned safely —then the count was revenged. An indescribable ray of joy illumined that wretched countenance, like the last ray of the sun before it disappears behind a mass of clouds which appear more like its tomb than its couch. But as we have said, he waited in vain for his son to come to his apartment with the account of his triumph. He easily understood why his son did not come to see him before he went to avenge his father's honour; but when that was done, why did not his son come and throw himself in his arms? "

Then it was that the count, being unable to see Albert, sent for his servant. It was known that he was authorised to conceal nothing from the count. Ten minutes afterwards, General Morcerf was seen on the steps in a black coat with a military collar, black pantaloons, and black gloves. He had apparently given previous orders; for, as he reached the bottom step, his carriage came from the coach-house ready for him. The valet threw into the carriage his military cloak, in which two swords were wrapped, and shutting the door, he took his seat by the side of the coachman. The coachman stooped down for his orders.

" To the Champs-Elysées," said the general; " the Count of Monte Cristo's. Hurry! "

The horses bounded beneath the whip, and, in five minutes, they stopped before the count's door. M. de Morcerf opened the door himself, and, as the carriage rolled away, he passed up the walk, rang, and entered the open door with his servant.

A moment afterwards, Baptistin announced the Comte de Morcerf to M. de Monte Cristo; and the latter, leading Haydée aside, ordered the Comte de Morcerf to be asked into the drawing-room. The general was pacing the room the third time, when, in turning, he perceived Monte Cristo at the door.

" Eh! it is M. de Morcerf," said Monte Cristo quietly; " I thought I had heard wrong."

" Yes, it is I," said the count, whom a frightful contraction of the lips prevented from articulating freely.

" May I know the cause which procures me the pleasure of seeing M. de Morcerf so early? "

" Had you not a meeting with my son this morning? " asked the general.

" I had," replied the count.

" And I know my son had good reasons to wish to fight with you, and to endeavour to kill you."

" Yes, sir, he had very good ones; but you see, in spite of them, he has not killed me, and did not even fight."

" Yet he considered you the cause of his father's dishonour, the cause of the fearful ruin which has fallen on my house."

" Truly, sir," said Monte Cristo, with his dreadful calmness, " a secondary cause, but not the principal."

" Doubtless you made, then, some apology or explanation? "

" I explained nothing, and it is he who apologised to me."

" But to what do you attribute this conduct? "

" To the conviction, probably, that there was one more guilty than me."

" And who was that? "

" His father."

" That may be," said the count, turning pale; " but, you know, the guilty do not like to find themselves convicted."

" I know it. And I expected this result."

" You expected my son would be a coward? " cried the count.

" M. Albert de Morcerf is no coward! " said Monte Cristo.

" A man who holds a sword in his hand, and sees a mortal enemy within reach of that sword, and does not fight, is a coward! Why is he not here, that I may tell him so? "

" Sir," replied Monte Cristo coldly, " I did not expect you had come here to relate to me your little family affairs. Go and tell M. Albert that, and he may know what to answer you."

" Oh, no, no! " said the general, smiling faintly, " I did not come for that purpose; you are right! I came to tell you that I also look upon you as my enemy! I came to tell you that I hate you instinctively! That it seems as if I had always known you, and always hated you; and, in short, since the young people of the present day will not fight, it remains for us to do it. Do you think so, sir? "

" Certainly. And when I told you I had foreseen the result, it is the honour of your visit I alluded to."

" So much the better. Are you prepared? "

" Yes, sir."

" You know that we shall fight till one of us is dead! " said the general, whose teeth were clenched with rage.

" Until one of us dies," repeated Monte Cristo, moving his head slightly up and down.

" Let us start, then; we need no witnesses."

"Truly," said Monte Cristo, "it is unnecessary, we know each other so well!"

"On the contrary," said the count, "we know so little of each other."

"Indeed!" said Monte Cristo, with the same indomitable coolness; "let us see. Are you not the soldier Fernand, who deserted on the eve of the battle of Waterloo? Are you not the Lieutenant Fernand who served as guide and spy to the French army in Spain? Are you not the Captain Fernand who betrayed, sold, and murdered his benefactor, Ali? And have not all these Fernands, united, made the Lieutenant-General, the Count of Morcerf, peer of France?"

"Oh!" cried the general, as if branded with a hot iron, "wretch! to reproach me with my shame, when about, perhaps, to kill me! No, I did not say I was a stranger to you; I know well, demon, that you have penetrated into the darkness of the past, and that you have read, by the light of what flambeau I know not, every page of my life; but, perhaps, I may be more honourable in my shame than you under your pompous coverings. No—no, I am aware you know me; but I know you not, adventurer, sewn up in gold and jewellery. You have called yourself, at Paris, the Count of Monte Cristo; in Italy, Sinbad the Sailor; in Malta, I forget what. But it is your real name I want to know, in the midst of your hundred names, that I may pronounce it when we meet to fight, at the moment when I plunge my sword through your heart."

The Count of Monte Cristo turned dreadfully pale; his eye seemed to burn with a devouring fire. He bounded towards a dressing-room, near his bedroom, and, in less than a moment, tearing off his cravat, his coat, and waistcoat, he put on a sailor's jacket and hat, from beneath which rolled his long black hair. He returned thus, formidable and implacable, advancing with his arms crossed on his breast, towards the general, who could not understand why he had disappeared; but who, on seeing him again, and feeling his teeth chatter and his legs sink under him, drew back, and only stopped when he found a table to support his clenched hand.

"Fernand," cried he, "of my hundred names I need only tell you one to overwhelm you! But you guess it now; do you not?—or, rather, you remember it? For, notwithstanding all my sorrows and my tortures, I show you to-day a face which the happiness of revenge makes young again—a face you must often have seen in your dreams since your marriage with Mercédès, my betrothed!"

The general, with his head thrown back, hands extended, gaze fixed, looked silently at this dreadful apparition; then seeking the wall to support him, he glided along close to it until he reached the door, through which he went out backwards, uttering this single mournful, lamentable, distressing cry:

" Edmond Dantès! "

Then, with sighs which were unlike any human sound, he dragged himself to the door, reeled across the courtyard, and falling into the arms of his valet, he said, in a voice scarcely intelligible:

" Home, home! "

The fresh air and the shame he felt at having exposed himself before his servants, partially recalled his senses; but the ride was short, and as he drew near his house all his wretchedness revived. He stopped at a short distance from the house and alighted. The door of the hotel was wide open, a hackney-coach was standing in the middle of the yard—a strange sight before so noble a mansion. The count looked at it with terror; but without daring to ask, he rushed towards his apartment. Two persons were coming down the stairs: he had only time to creep into a cabinet to avoid them. It was Mercédès leaning on her son's arm, and leaving the hotel. They passed close by the unhappy being, who, concealed behind the damask door, almost felt Mercédès' dress brush past him, and his son's warm breath pronouncing these words:

" Courage, my mother! Come, this is no longer our home! "

The words died away, the steps were lost in the distance. The general drew himself up, clinging to the door; he uttered the most dreadful sob which ever escaped from the bosom of a father abandoned at the same time by his wife and son. He soon heard the clatter of the iron step of the hackney-coach, then the coachman's voice, and then the rolling of the heavy vehicle shook the windows. He darted to his bedroom to see once more all he had loved in the world; but the hackney-coach drove on without the head of either Mercédès or her son appearing at the window to take a last look at the house or the deserted father or husband. And at the very moment when the wheels of that coach crossed the gateway a report was heard, and a thick smoke escaped through one of the panes of the window, which was broken by the explosion.

94

Valentine

WE may easily conceive where Morrel's appointment was. On leaving Monte Cristo, he walked slowly toward Villefort's; we say slowly, for Morrel had more than half an hour to spare to go five hundred steps, but he had hastened to take leave of Monte Cristo because he wished to be alone with his thoughts. He knew his time well—the hour when Valentine was giving Noirtier his breakfast, and was sure not to be disturbed in the performance of this pious duty. Noirtier and Valentine had given him leave to go twice a week, and he was now availing himself of that permission.

He arrived; Valentine was expecting him. Uneasy and almost wandering, she seized his hand and led him to her grandfather. This uneasiness, amounting almost to wildness, arose from the report Morcerf's adventure had made in the world; the affair of the Opera was generally known. No one at Villefort's doubted that a duel would ensue from it. Valentine, with her woman's instinct, guessed that Morrel would be Monte Cristo's witness, and from the young man's well-known courage and his great affection for the count, she feared he would not content himself with the passive part assigned to him.

We may easily understand how eagerly the particulars were asked for, given, and received; and Morrel could read an indescribable joy in the eyes of his beloved, when she knew that the termination of this affair was as happy as it was unexpected.

"Now," said Valentine, motioning to Morrel to sit down near her grandfather, while she took her seat on his footstool,—" now let us talk about our own affairs. You know, Maximilian, grandpapa once thought of leaving this house, and taking an apartment away from M. de Villefort's."

"Yes," said Maximilian, "I recollect this project, of which I highly approved."

"Well," said Valentine, "you may approve again, for grandpapa is again thinking of it."

"Bravo!" said Maximilian.

"And do you know," said Valentine, "what reason grandpapa gives for leaving this house?"

Noirtier looked at Valentine to impose silence, but she did not notice him; her looks, her eyes, her smile, were all for Morrel.

" Oh, whatever may be M. Noirtier's reason," answered Morrel, " I will readily believe it to be a good one."

" An excellent one," said Valentine. " He pretends the air of the Faubourg Saint-Honoré is not good for me."

" Indeed! " said Morrel; " in that M. Noirtier may be right; your health has not appeared good the last fortnight."

" Not very," said Valentine. " And grandpapa is become my physician, and I have the greatest confidence in him, because he knows everything."

" Do you then really suffer? " asked Morrel quickly.

" Oh, it must not be called suffering; I feel a general uneasiness, that is all. I have lost my appetite, and my stomach feels to be struggling to become accustomed to something."

Noirtier did not lose a word of what Valentine said.

" And what treatment do you adopt for this singular complaint? "

" A very simple one," said Valentine. " I swallow every morning a spoonful of the mixture prepared for my grandfather. When I say one spoonful, I began by one—now I take four. Grandpapa says it is a panacea."

Valentine smiled, but it was evident she suffered.

Maximilian, in his devotedness, gazed silently at her. She was very beautiful, but her usual paleness had increased; her eyes were more brilliant than ever, and her hands, which were generally white like mother-of-pearl, now more resembled wax, to which time was adding a yellowish hue. From Valentine the young man looked towards Noirtier. The latter watched with strange and deep interest the young girl, absorbed by her affection; and he also, like Morrel, following those traces of inward suffering which were so little perceptible to a common observer—they escaped the notice of everyone but the grandfather and the lover.

" But," said Morrel, " I thought this mixture, of which you now take four spoonfuls, was prepared for M. Noirtier? "

" I know it is very bitter," said Valentine; " so bitter, that all I drink afterwards appears to have the same taste."

Noirtier looked inquiringly at his granddaughter.

" Yes, grandpapa," said Valentine, " it is so. Just now, before I came down to you, I drank a glass of *eau sucrée;* I left half, because it seemed so bitter."

Noirtier turned pale, and made a sign that he wished to speak. Valentine rose to fetch the dictionary. Noirtier watched her with evident anguish. In fact the blood was rushing to the young girl's head already, her cheeks were becoming red.

" Oh," cried she, without losing any of her cheerfulness, " this is singular! A dimness! Did the sun shine in my eyes? " And she leaned against the window.

" The sun is not shining," said Morrel, more alarmed by Noirtier's expression than by Valentine's indisposition.

He ran towards her. The young girl smiled.

" Comfort yourself! " said she to Noirtier.   " Do not be alarmed, Maximilian; it is nothing, and has already passed away. But listen! Do I not hear a carriage in the courtyard? " She opened Noirtier's door, ran to a window in the passage, and returned hastily. " Yes," said she, " it is Madame Danglars and her daughter, who are come to call on us. Good-bye! I must run away, for they would send here for me; or rather, farewell till I see you again. Stay with grandpapa, Maximilian; I promise you not to persuade them to stay."

Morrel watched her as she left the room; he heard her ascend the little staircase which led both to Madame de Villefort's apartments and to hers. As soon as she was gone Noirtier made a sign to Morrel to take the dictionary. Morrel obeyed; guided by Valentine, he had learned how to understand the old man quickly. Accustomed, however, as he was, and having to repeat most of the letters of the alphabet, and to find every word in the dictionary, it was ten minutes before the thought of the old man was translated by these words, " Fetch the glass of water and the decanter from Valentine's room."

Morrel rang immediately for the servant who had taken Barrois' situation, and in Noirtier's name gave that order. The servant soon returned. The decanter and the glass were completely empty. Noirtier made a sign that he wished to speak.

" Why are the glass and decanter empty? " asked he. " Valentine said she only drank half the glassful."

The translation of this new question occupied another five minutes.

. " I do not know," said the servant. " But the housemaid is in Mademoiselle Valentine's room; perhaps she has emptied them! "

" Ask her," said Morrel, translating Noirtier's thought this time by his look.

The servant went out, but returned almost immediately.

" Mademoiselle Valentine passed through the room to go to Madame de Villefort's," said he; " and in passing, as she was thirsty, she drank what remained in the glass; as for the decanter, Master Edward had emptied that to make a pond for his ducks."

Noirtier raised his eyes to heaven as a gambler does who stakes his all on one stroke. From that moment the old man's eyes were fixed on the door and did not quit it.

It was indeed Madame Danglars and her daughter whom Valentine had seen; they had been ushered into Madame de Villefort's room, who had said she would receive them there. That is why Valentine passed through her room, which was on a level with Valentine's, and only separated from it by Edward's.

The two ladies entered the drawing-room with that sort of official stiffness which announced a communication. Between worldly people a shadow is soon caught. Madame de Villefort received them with equal solemnity. Valentine entered at this moment, and the formalities were resumed.

" My dear friend," said the countess, while the two young people were shaking hands, " I and Eugénie are come to be the first to announce to you the approaching marriage of my daughter with Prince Cavalcanti."

Danglars kept up the title of prince. The popular banker found it answered better than count.

" Allow me to present you my sincere congratulations," replied Madame de Villefort. " M. le Prince Cavalcanti appears a young man of rare qualities."

" Listen," said the countess, smiling; " speaking to you as a friend, I would say the prince does not yet appear all he will be. He has about him a little of that foreign manner by which French persons recognise at first sight the Italian or German nobleman. Besides, he gives evidence of great kindness of disposition, much keenness of wit, and, as to suitableness, M. Danglars assures me his fortune is majestic,—that is his term."

" And then," said Eugénie, while turning over the leaves of Madame de Villefort's album, " add that you have taken a great fancy to the young man."

" And," said Madame de Villefort, " I need not ask you, if you share that fancy."

" I! " replied Eugénie, with her usual candour. " Oh, not the least in the world, madame! My wish was not to confine myself to domestic cares or the caprices of any man, but to be an artist, and, consequently, free in heart, in person, and in thought."

Eugénie pronounced these words with so firm a tone that the colour mounted to Valentine's cheeks. The timid girl could not understand that vigorous nature which appeared to have none of the timidities of woman.

" At any rate," said she, " since I am to be married whether I will or not, I ought to be thankful to Providence for having released me from my engagement with M. Albert de Morcerf, or I should this day have been the wife of a dishonoured man."

" It is true," said the countess, with that strange simplicity sometimes met with among fashionable ladies, and of which plebeian intercourse can never entirely deprive them,—" it is very true that, had not the Morcerfs hesitated, my daughter would have married that M. Albert. The general depended much on it; he even came to force M. Danglars. We have had a narrow escape."

" But," said Valentine timidly, " does all the father's shame revert upon the son? M. Albert appears to me quite innocent of the treason charged against the general."

" Excuse me," said the implacable young girl; " M. Albert claims and well deserves his share. It appears that after having challenged M. de Monte Cristo at the Opera yesterday, he apologised on the ground to-day."

" Impossible! " said Madame de Villefort.

" Ah, my dear friend," said Madame Danglars, with the same simplicity we before noticed, " it is a fact! I heard it from M. Debray, who was present at the explanation."

Valentine also knew the truth, but she did not answer. Deeply engaged with a sort of inward contemplation, she had ceased for a moment to join in the conversation. She would, indeed, have found it impossible to repeat what had been said during the last few minutes, when suddenly Madame Danglars' hand, pressed on her arm, aroused her from her dream.

" What is it? " said she, starting at Madame Danglars' touch as she would have done from an electric shock.

" It is, my dear Valentine," said the baroness, " that you are, doubtless, suffering."

" I? " said the young girl, passing her hand across her burning forehead.

" Yes, look at yourself in that glass: you have turned pale and red successively, three or four times in one minute."

" Indeed," cried Eugénie, " you are very pale! "

" Oh, do not be alarmed! I have been so for some days."

Artless as she was, the young girl knew this was an opportunity to leave; besides, Madame de Villefort came to her assistance.

" Retire, Valentine," said she; " you are really suffering, and these ladies will excuse you; drink a glass of pure water, it will restore you."

Valentine kissed Eugénie, bowed to Madame Danglars, who had already risen to take her leave, and went out.

" That poor child," said Madame de Villefort, when Valentine was gone, " she makes me very uneasy, and I should not be astonished if she had some serious illness."

Meanwhile, Valentine, in a sort of excitement which she could not quite understand, had crossed Edward's room without noticing some naughtiness or other of the child, and through her own had reached the little staircase. She was at the bottom excepting three steps; she already heard Morrel's voice, when suddenly a cloud passed over her eyes, her stiffened foot missed the step, her hands had no power to hold the baluster, and, falling against the wall, she rolled down these three steps rather than walked. Morrel bounded to the door, opened it, and found Valentine extended on the floor. Rapid as lightning he raised her in his arms and placed her in a chair. Valentine opened her eyes.

" Oh, what a clumsy thing I am! " said she, with feverish volubility; " I no longer know my way. I forgot there were three more steps before the landing."

" You have hurt yourself, perhaps," said Morrel. " What can I do for you, Valentine? "

Valentine looked round her; she saw the deepest terror depicted in Noirtier's eyes.

" Comfort yourself, dear grandpapa," said she, endeavouring to smile; " it is nothing,—it is nothing; I was giddy, that is all."

" Another giddiness! " said Morrel, clasping his hands. " Oh, attend to it, Valentine, I entreat you! "

" But no," said Valentine,—" no, I tell you it is all past, and it was nothing. Now, let me tell you some news: Eugénie is to be married in a week, and in three days there is to be a grand feast, a sort of betrothing festival. We are all invited, my father, Madame de Villefort, and I—at least I understood it so."

" When will it, then, be our turn to think of these things? Oh, Valentine, you, who have so much influence over your grandpapa, try to make him answer—soon."

" And do you," said Valentine, " depend on me to stimulate the tardiness and arouse the memory of grandpapa? "

" Yes," cried Morrel, " be quick! So long as you are not mine, Valentine, I shall always think I may lose you."

" Oh! " replied Valentine, with a convulsive movement,— " Oh! indeed, Maximilian, you are too timid for an officer, for a soldier who, they say, never knows fear. Ah! ah! ah! "

She burst into a forced and melancholy laugh, her arms stiffened and twisted, her head fell back on her chair, and she remained motionless. The cry of terror which was stopped on Noirtier's lips, seemed to start from his eyes. Morrel understood it, he knew he must call assistance. The young man rang the bell violently, the housemaid who had been in Mademoiselle Valentine's room, and the servant who had replaced Barrois, ran in at the same moment. Valentine was so pale, so cold, so inanimate, that, without listening to what was said to them, they were seized with the fear which pervaded that house, and they flew into the passage crying for help. Madame Danglars and Eugénie were going out at that moment; they heard the cause of the disturbance.

" I told you so! " cried Madame de Villefort. " Poor child! "

95

The Confession

AT the same moment M. de Villefort's voice was heard calling from his cabinet, " What is the matter? " Morrel consulted Noirtier's look, who had recovered his self-command, and with a glance indicated the closet where once before, under somewhat similar circumstances, he had taken refuge. He had only time to get his hat, and throw himself breathless into the closet; the procureur's footstep was heard in the passage. Villefort sprang into the room, ran to Valentine, and took her in his arms.

" A physician! a physician! M. d'Avrigny! " cried Villefort; " or rather I will go for him myself."

He flew from the apartment, and Morrel, at the same moment, darted out at the other door. He had been struck to the heart by a frightful recollection,—the conversation he had heard between the doctor and Villefort the night of Madame de Saint-Méran's death recurred to him; these symptoms, to a less alarming extent, were the same which had preceded the death of Barrois. At the same time Monte Cristo's voice seemed to resound in his ear, who had said only two hours before, " Whatever you want, Morrel, come to me, I have great power." More rapidly than thought he darted down the Rue Matignon, and thence to the Avenue des Champs Elysées.

Meanwhile M. de Villefort arrived in a hired cabriolet at M. d'Avrigny's door. He rang so violently, that the porter came alarmed. Villefort ran upstairs without saying a word. The porter knew him, and let him pass, only calling to him:

" In his cabinet, M. le Procureur du roi,—in his cabinet! "

Villefort pushed, or rather forced, the door open.

" Ah! " said the doctor, " is it you? "

" Yes," said Villefort, closing the door after him, " it is I, who am come in my turn to ask you if we are quite alone. Doctor, my house is accursed! "

" What! " said the latter, with apparent coolness, but with deep emotion, " have you another invalid? "

" Yes, doctor," cried Villefort, seizing, with a convulsive grasp, a handful of hair, " yes! "

D'Avrigny's look implied, " I told you it would be so." Then he slowly uttered these words, " Who is now dying in your house? What new victim is going to accuse you of weakness before God? "

A mournful sob burst from Villefort's heart; he approached the doctor, and seizing his arm,—

" Valentine! " said he, " it is Valentine's turn! "

" Your daughter! " cried D'Avrigny, with grief and surprise.

" You see you were deceived," murmured the magistrate; " come and see her, and on her bed of agony entreat her pardon for having suspected her."

" Each time you have applied to me," said the doctor, " it has been too late: still I will go. But let us make haste, sir; with the enemies you have to do with there is no time to be lost."

" Oh! this time, doctor, you shall not have to reproach me with weakness. This time I will know the assassin, and will pursue him."

" Let us try first to save the victim before we think of revenging her," said D'Avrigny. " Come."

The same cabriolet which had brought Villefort took them back at full speed, at the same moment when Morrel rapped at Monte Cristo's door.

The count was in his cabinet, and was reading, with an angry look, something which Bertuccio had brought in haste. Hearing Morrel announced, who had left him only two hours before, the count raised his head. He, as well as the count, had evidently been much tried during these two hours, for he had left him smiling, and returned with a disturbed air. The count rose, and sprang to meet him.

" What is the matter, Maximilian? " asked he; " you are pale, and the perspiration rolls from your forehead."

Morrel fell, rather than sat, down on a chair.

" Yes," said he, " I came quickly; I wanted to speak to you."

" Is all your family well? " asked the count, with an affectionate benevolence, whose sincerity no one could for a moment doubt.

" Thank you, count,—thank you," said the young man, evidently embarrassed how to begin the conversation; " yes, everyone in my family is well."

" So much the better; yet you have something to tell me? " replied the count, with increased anxiety.

"Yes," said Morrel, "it is true; I have just left a house where death has just entered to run to you."

"Are you then come from M. de Morcerf's?" asked Monte Cristo.

"No," said Morrel; "is someone dead in his house?"

"The general has just blown his brains out," replied Monte Cristo, with great coolness.

"Oh! what a dreadful event!" cried Maximilian.

"Not for the countess, nor for Albert," said Monte Cristo; "a dead father or husband is better than a dishonoured one; blood washes out shame."

"Poor countess!" said Maximilian, "I pity her very much; she is so noble a woman!"

"Pity Albert also, Maximilian; for, believe me, he is the worthy son of the countess. But let us return to yourself: you have hastened to me; can I have the happiness of being useful to you?"

"Yes, I need your help; that is, I thought, like a madman, you could lend me your assistance in a case where God alone can succour me."

"Tell me what it is," replied Monte Cristo.

"Oh!" said Morrel, "I know not, indeed, if I may reveal this secret to mortal ears; but fatality impels me, necessity constrains me, count——"

Morrel hesitated.

"Do you think I love you?" said Monte Cristo, taking the young man's hand affectionately in his.

"Oh! you encourage me! and something tells me there" (placing his hand on his heart) "that I ought to have no secret from you."

"You are right, Morrel; God is speaking to your heart, and your heart speaks to you. Tell me what it says."

"Count, will you allow me to send Baptistin to inquire after someone you know?"

"I am at your service, and still more my servants."

"Oh; I cannot live if she is not better."

"Shall I ring for Baptistin?"

"No, I will go and speak to him myself."

Morrel went out, called Baptistin, and whispered a few words to him. The valet ran directly.

"Well, have you sent?" asked Monte Cristo, seeing Morrel return.

"Yes, and now I shall be more calm."

"You know I am waiting," said Monte Cristo, smiling.

" Yes, and I will tell you. One evening I was in a garden; a clump of trees concealed me; no one suspected I was there. Two persons passed near me,—allow me to conceal their names for the present; they were speaking in an undertone, and yet I was so interested in what they said that I did not lose a single word."

" This is a gloomy introduction, if I may judge from your paleness and shuddering, Morrel."

" Oh, yes, very gloomy, my friend! Someone had just died in the house to which that garden belonged. One of those persons whose conversation I overheard was the master of the house, the other, the physician. The former was confiding to the latter his grief and fear; for it was the second time within a month that death had entered suddenly and unexpectedly that house, apparently destined to destruction by some exterminating angel, as an object of God's anger."

" Ah, ah! " said Monte Cristo, looking earnestly at the young man, and, by an imperceptible movement, turning his chair, so that he remained in the shade while the light fell full on Maximilian's face.

" Yes," continued Morrel, " death had entered that house twice within one month."

" And what did the doctor answer? " asked Monte Cristo.

" He replied—he replied, that the death was not a natural one, and must be attributed——"

" To what? "

" To poison! "

" Indeed! " said Monte Cristo, with a slight cough, which, in moments of extreme emotion, helped him to disguise a blush or his paleness, or the intense interest with which he listened; " indeed, Maximilian, did you hear that? "

" Yes, my dear count, I heard it; and the doctor added, that if another death occurred in a similar way he must appeal to justice."

Monte Cristo listened, or appeared to do so, with the greatest calmness.

" Well! " said Maximilian, " death came a third time, and neither the master of the house nor the doctor said a word. Death is now, perhaps, striking a fourth blow. Count, what am I bound to do, being in possession of this secret? "

" My dear friend," said Monte Cristo, " you appear to be relating an adventure which we all know by heart. I know the house where you heard it, or one very similar to it; a house with a garden, a master, a physician, and where there have been three unexpected and sudden deaths. Well! I have not intercepted your confidence, and yet I know all that as well as you, and I have no conscientious scruples. No! it does not concern me. You say an exterminating angel appears to have devoted that house to God's anger,—well! who says your supposition is not reality? Do not notice things which those whose interest it is to see them pass over. If it is God's justice, instead of His anger, which is walking through that house, Maximilian, turn away your face, and let His justice accomplish its purpose."

Morrel shuddered. There was something mournful, solemn, and terrible in the count's manner.

"Besides," continued he, in so changed a tone, that no one would have supposed it was the same person speaking,—" besides, who says that it will begin again? "

"It has returned, count! " exclaimed Morrel; " that is why I hastened to you."

"Well! what do you wish me to do? Do you wish me, for instance, to give information to the procureur du roi? "

Monte Cristo uttered the last words with so much meaning, that Morrel, starting up, cried out:

"You know of whom I speak, count, do you not? "

"Perfectly well, my good friend, and I will prove it to you by putting the dots to the *i*, or, rather, by naming the persons. You were walking one evening in M. de Villefort's garden: from what you relate, I suppose it to have been the evening of Madame de Saint-Méran's death. You heard M. de Villefort talking to M. d'Avrigny about the death of M. de Saint-Méran, and that no less surprising of the countess. M. d'Avrigny said, he believed they both proceeded from poison; and you, honest man, have ever since been asking your heart, and sounding your conscience, to know if you ought to expose or conceal this secret. Why do you torment them? ' Conscience, what hast thou to do with me? ' as Sterne said. My dear fellow, let them sleep on, if they are asleep; let them grow pale in their drowsiness, if they are disposed to do so; and pray do you remain in peace, who have no remorse to disturb you."

Deep grief was depicted on Morrel's features; he seized Monte Cristo's hand.

"But it is beginning again, I say! "

"Well! " said the count, astonished at his perseverance, which he could not understand, and looking still more earnestly at Maximilian, " let it begin again: it is a family of Atrides; God has condemned them, and they must submit to their punishment. They will all disappear like the fabrics children build with cards, and which fall, one by one, under the breath of their builder, even if there are two hundred of them. Three months since, it was M. de Saint-Méran: Madame de Saint-Méran two months since: the other day it was Barrois: to-day the old Noirtier or young Valentine."

"You knew it?" cried Morrel, in such a paroxysm of terror that Monte Cristo started, he whom the falling heavens would have found unmoved; "you knew it, and said nothing?"

"And what is it to me?" replied Monte Cristo, shrugging his shoulders: "do I know those people? and must I lose the one to save the other? Faith, no, for between the culprit and the victim I have no choice."

"But I," cried Morrel, groaning with sorrow,—"I love her!"

"You love!—whom?" cried Monte Cristo, starting on his feet and seizing the two hands which Morrel was raising towards heaven.

"I love most fondly—I love madly—I love as a man who would give his life-blood to spare her a tear—I love Valentine de Villefort, who is being murdered at this moment! Do you understand me? I love her; and I ask God and you how I can save her!"

Monte Cristo uttered a cry, which those only can conceive who have heard the roar of a wounded lion.

"Unhappy man!" cried he, wringing his hands in his turn; "you love Valentine!—that daughter of an accursed race!"

Never had Morrel witnessed such an expression—never had so terrible an eye flashed before his face,—never had the genius of terror he had so often seen, either on the battlefield or in the murderous nights of Algeria, shaken around him more dreadful fires. He drew back terrified.

As for Monte Cristo, after this ebullition, he closed his eyes, as if dazzled by internal light. In a moment he restrained himself so powerfully that the tempestuous heaving of his breast subsided, as turbulent and foaming waves yield to the sun's genial influence when the cloud has passed. This silence, self-control, and struggle, lasted about twenty seconds, then the count raised his pallid face.

"See," said he, "my dear friend, how God punishes the most thoughtless and unfeeling men for their indifference, by presenting dreadful scenes to their view. I, who was looking on, an eager and curious spectator,—I, who was watching the working of this mournful tragedy,—I, who, like a wicked angel, was laughing at the evil men committed, protected by secrecy (a secret is easily kept by the rich and powerful), I am, in my turn, bitten by the serpent whose tortuous course I was watching, and bitten to the heart!"

Morrel groaned.

"Come, come," continued the count, "complaints are unavailing; be a man, be strong, be full of hope, for I am here, and will watch over you."

Morrel shook his head sorrowfully.

"I tell you to hope. Do you understand me?" cried Monte Cristo. "Remember that I never utter a falsehood, and am never deceived. It is twelve o'clock, Maximilian; thank heaven that you came at noon rather than in the evening or to-morrow morning. Listen, Morrel!—it is noon; if Valentine is not now dead, she will not die."

"How so?" cried Morrel, "when I left her dying?"

Monte Cristo pressed his hand to his forehead. What was passing in that brain, so loaded with dreadful secrets? What does the angel of light, or the angel of darkness, say to that mind at once implacable and generous?—God only knows!

Monte Cristo raised his head once more; and this time he was calm as a child awaking from its sleep.

"Maximilian," said he, "return home. I command you not to stir—attempt nothing; not to let your countenance betray a thought, and I will send you tidings. Go!"

"Oh, count, you overwhelm me with that coolness. Have you, then, power against death?—Are you superhuman?—Are you an angel?"

And the young man who had never shrunk from danger, shrank before Monte Cristo with indescribable terror. But Monte Cristo looked at him with so melancholy and sweet a smile that Maximilian felt the tears filling his eyes.

"I can do much for you, my friend," replied the count. "Go; I must be alone."

Morrel, subdued by the extraordinary ascendancy Monte Cristo exercised over everything around him, did not endeavour to resist it. He pressed the count's hand and left. He stopped one moment at the door for Baptistin, whom he saw in the Rue Matignon, and who was running.

Meanwhile, Villefort and D'Avrigny had made all possible haste. Valentine had not revived from her fainting fit on their arrival, and the doctor examined the invalid with all the care the circumstances demanded, and with an interest which the knowledge of the secret doubled.

Villefort, closely watching his countenance and his lips, waited the result of the examination. Noirtier, paler even than the young girl, more eager than even Villefort for the decision, was watching also intently and affectionately. At last D'Avrigny slowly uttered these words:

"She is still alive!"

" Still? " cried Villefort, " oh, doctor, what a dreadful word is that! "

" Yes," said the physician, " I repeat it; she is still alive, and I am astonished at it."

" But is she safe? " asked the father.

" Yes, since she lives."

At that moment D'Avrigny's glance met Noirtier's eye. It glistened with such extraordinary joy, so rich and full of thought, that the physician was struck. He placed the young girl again on the chair; her lips were scarcely discernible, they were so pale and white, as well as her whole face; and remained motionless, looking at Noirtier, who appeared to anticipate and commend all he did.

" Sir," said D'Avrigny to Villefort, " call Mademoiselle Valentine's maid, if you please."

Villefort went himself to find her, and D'Avrigny approached Noirtier.

" Have you something to tell me? " asked he.

The old man winked his eye expressively, which we may remember was his only way of expressing his approval.

" Privately? "

" Yes," said Noirtier.

" Well; I will remain with you."

At this moment Villefort returned, followed by the lady's maid; and after her came Madame de Villefort.

" What is the matter, then, with this dear child? she has just left me, and she complained of feeling unwell; but I did not think seriously of it."

The young woman, with tears in her eyes and every mark of affection of a true mother, approached Valentine and took her hand.

D'Avrigny continued to look at Noirtier; he saw the eyes of the old man dilate and become round, his cheeks turn pale and tremble; the perspiration stood in drops upon his forehead.

" Ah! " said he, involuntarily following Noirtier's eyes, which were fixed on Madame de Villefort, who repeated:

" This poor child would be better in bed. Come, Fanny, we will put her in."

M. d'Avrigny, who saw that would be a means of his remaining alone with Noirtier, expressed his opinion that it was the best thing that could be done; but he forbade anything being given to her besides what he ordered.

They carried Valentine away: she had revived, but could scarcely move or speak, so shaken was her frame by the attack. She had, however, just power to give her grandfather one parting look; who, in losing her, seemed to be resigning his very soul. D'Avrigny followed the invalid, wrote a prescription, ordered Villefort to take a cabriolet, go in person to a chemist's to get the prescribed medicine, bring it himself, and wait for him in his daughter's room. Then, having renewed his injunction not to give Valentine anything, he went down again to Noirtier, shut the doors carefully, and after convincing himself no one was listening,—

"Do you," said he, "know anything of this young lady's illness?"

"Yes," said the old man.

"We have no time to lose; I will question, and do you answer me."

Noirtier made a sign that he was ready to answer.

"Did you anticipate the accident which has happened to your granddaughter?"

"Yes."

D'Avrigny reflected a moment; then approaching Noirtier,—

"Pardon what I am going to say," added he, "but no indication should be neglected in this terrible situation. Did you see poor Barrois die?"

Noirtier raised his eyes to heaven.

"Do you know of what he died?" asked D'Avrigny, placing his hand on Noirtier's shoulder.

"Yes," replied the old man.

"Do you think he died a natural death?"

A sort of smile was discernible on the motionless lips of Noirtier.

"Then you have thought Barrois was poisoned?"

"Yes."

"Do you think the poison he fell a victim to was intended for him?"

"No."

"Do you think the same hand which unintentionally struck Barrois has now attacked Valentine?"

"Yes."

"Then will she die too?" asked D'Avrigny, fixing his penetrating gaze on Noirtier.

He watched the effect of this question on the old man.

"No!" replied he, with an air of triumph, which would have puzzled the most clever diviner.

"Then you hope?" said D'Avrigny, with surprise.

"Yes."

"What do you hope?"

The old man made him understand with his eyes that he could not answer.

" Ah, yes, it is true! " murmured D'Avrigny. Then returning to Noirtier,—

" Do you hope the assassin will be tried? "

" No."

" Then you hope the poison will take no effect on Valentine? "

" Yes."

" It is no news to you," added D'Avrigny, " to tell you an attempt has been made to poison her? "

The old man made a sign that he entertained no doubt upon the subject.

" Then how do you hope Valentine will escape? "

Noirtier kept his eyes steadily fixed on the same spot. D'Avrigny followed the direction, and saw they were fixed on a bottle containing the mixture which he took every morning.

" Ah! ah! " said D'Avrigny, struck with a sudden thought, " has it occurred to you——"

Noirtier did not let him finish.

" Yes," said he.

" To prepare her system to resist poison? "

" Yes."

" By accustoming her by degrees——"

" Yes, yes, yes," said Noirtier, delighted to be understood.

" Truly, I had told you there was brucine in the mixture I give you? "

" Yes."

" And by accustoming her to that poison, you have endeavoured to neutralise the effect of a similar poison? "

Noirtier's joy continued.

" And you have succeeded," exclaimed D'Avrigny. " Without that precaution Valentine would have died before assistance could have been procured. The dose has been excessive, but she has only been shaken by it; and this time, at any rate, Valentine will not die."

A superhuman joy expanded the old man's eyes, which were raised towards heaven with an expression of infinite gratitude. At this moment Villefort returned.

" Here, doctor," said he, " is what you sent me for."

" Was this prepared in your presence? "

" Yes," replied the procureur du roi.

" Have you not let it go out of your hands? "

" No."

D'Avrigny took the bottle, poured some drops of the mixture it contained in the hollow of his hand, and swallowed them.

" Well," said he, " let us go to Valentine; I will give instructions to everyone, and you, M. de Villefort, will yourself see that no one deviates from them."

At the moment when D'Avrigny was returning to Valentine's room, accompanied by Villefort, an Italian priest, of serious demeanour, and calm and firm tone, hired for his use the house adjoining the hotel of M. de Villefort. No one knew how the three former tenants of that house left it. About two hours afterwards its foundation was reported to be unsafe; but the report did not prevent the new occupant establishing himself there with his modest furniture the same day at five o'clock. The lease was drawn up for three, six, or nine years by the new tenant, who, according to the rule of the proprietor, paid six months in advance. This new tenant, who, as we have said, was an Italian, was called Il Signor Giacomo Busoni. Workmen were immediately called in, and the same night the passengers at the end of the faubourg saw with surprise carpenters and masons occupied in repairing the lower part of the tottering house.

96

The Father and Daughter

WE have seen in a preceding chapter Madame Danglars coming formally to announce to Madame de Villefort the approaching marriage of Eugénie Danglars and M. Andrea Cavalcanti. This announcement, which implied, or appeared to imply, a resolution taken by all the parties concerned in this great affair, had been preceded by a scene to which our readers must be admitted. We beg them to take one step backwards, and to transport themselves, the morning of that day of great catastrophes, into the beautifully gilded saloon we have before shown them, and which was the pride of its owner, the Baron Danglars. In this room, at about ten o'clock in the morning, the banker himself had been walking some minutes, thoughtful, and evidently uneasy, watching each door, and listening to every sound. When his patience was exhausted, he called his valet.

"Stephen," said he, "see why Mademoiselle Eugénie has asked me to meet her in the drawing-room, and why she makes me wait so long."

Having given this vent to his ill-humour, the baron became more calm. Mademoiselle Danglars had that morning requested an interview with her father, and had fixed on that drawing-room as the spot. The singularity of this step, and, above all, its formal character, had not a little surprised the banker, who had immediately obeyed his daughter by repairing the first to the drawing-room. Stephen soon returned from his errand.

"Mademoiselle's lady's maid says, sir, that mademoiselle is finishing her toilet, and will be here shortly."

Danglars nodded, to signify he was satisfied. To the world and to his servants Danglars assumed the good-natured man and the weak father. This was one of his characters in the popular comedy he was performing; it was a physiognomy he had adopted, and which appeared as suitable to him as it was to the right side of the profile masks of the fathers of the ancient theatres to have a turned-up and laughing lip, while, on the left side, it was drawn down and ill-tempered. Let us hasten to say, that in private, the turned-up and laughing lip descended to the level of the drawn-down and ill-tempered one; so that, generally, the indulgent man disappeared to give place to the brutal husband and domineering father.

"Why the devil does that foolish girl, who pretends to wish to speak to me, not come into my cabinet: and why, above all, can she want to speak to me at all?"

He was revolving this worrying thought in his brain for the twentieth time, when the door opened, and Eugénie appeared, attired in a figured black satin dress, her hair arranged, and gloves on, as if going to the Italian Opera.

"Well, Eugénie, what is it you want with me? and why in this solemn drawing-room when the cabinet is so comfortable?"

"You are right, sir, and have proposed two questions which include all the conversation we are going to have. I will answer them both, and, contrary to the usual method, the last first, as being the least complex. I have chosen the drawing-room, sir, as our place of rendezvous, in order to avoid the disagreeable impressions and influences of a banker's cabinet. Those cash-books, gilded as they may be, those drawers, locked like gates of fortresses, those heaps of bank-bills, come from I know not where, and the quantities of letters from England, Holland, Spain, India, China, and Peru, have generally a strange influence on a father's mind, and make him forget there is in the world an interest greater and more sacred than the good opinion of his correspondents. I have, therefore, chosen this drawing-room, where you see, smiling and happy in their magnificent frames, your portrait, mine, my mother's, and all sorts of rural landscapes and touching pastorals. I rely much on external impressions; perhaps, with regard to you, they are immaterial; but I should be no artist if I had not some fancies."

" Very well," replied M. Danglars, who had listened to all this preamble with imperturbable coolness, but without understanding a word, engaged as he was, like every man burdened with thoughts of the past, in seeking the thread of his own ideas in those of the speaker.

" There is, then, the second point cleared up, or nearly so," said Eugénie, without the least confusion and with that masculine pointedness which distinguished her gesture and her language; " and you appear satisfied with the explanation. Now, let us return to the first! You ask me why I have requested this interview; I will tell you in two words, sir; I will not marry M. le Comte Andrea Cavalcanti."

Danglars bounded from his chair, and with this motion raised his eyes and arms towards heaven.

" Yes, indeed, sir," continued Eugénie, still quite calm; " you are astonished, I see; for since this little affair commenced, I have not manifested the slightest opposition; sure, as I always am, when the opportunity arrives, to oppose to people who have not consulted me, and things which displease me, a determined and absolute will. However, this time, this tranquillity, this passiveness, as philosophers say, proceeded from another source; it proceeded from a wish, like a submissive and devoted daughter (a slight smile was observable on the purple lips of the young girl), to practise obedience."

" Well? " asked Danglars.

" Well, sir," replied Eugénie, " I have tried to the very last; and now the moment has come, in spite of all my efforts, I feel it is impossible."

" But," said Danglars, whose weak mind was at first quite overwhelmed with the weight of this pitiless logic, marking evident premeditation and force of will, " what is your reason for this refusal, Eugénie? what reason do you assign? "

" My reason? " replied the young girl. " Well! it is not that the man is more ugly, more foolish, or more disagreeable than any other; no; M. Andrea Cavalcanti may appear to those who look at men's faces and figures a very good model. It is not, either, that my heart is less touched by him than any other; that would be a school-girl's reason, which I consider quite beneath me. I actually love no one, sir; you know it, do you not? I do not, then, see why, without real necessity, I should encumber my life with a perpetual companion. Has not some sage said, ' Rien de trop' ; and another, ' Portez tout avec vous-même! ' I have been taught these two aphorisms in Latin and in Greek; one is, I believe, from Phædrus, and the other from Bias.* Well, my dear father, in the shipwreck of life, for life is an eternal shipwreck of our hopes, I cast into the sea my useless encumbrance, that is all, and I remain with my own will, disposed to live perfectly alone, and, consequently, perfectly free."

"Unhappy girl! unhappy girl!" murmured Danglars, turning pale, for he knew, from long experience, the solidity of the obstacle he so suddenly encountered.

"Unhappy girl!" replied Eugénie, "unhappy girl! do you say, sir? No, indeed, the exclamation appears quite theatrical and affected. Happy, on the contrary, for what am I in want of? The world calls me beautiful. It is something to be well received: I like a favourable reception; it expands the countenance, and those around me do not then appear so ugly. I possess a share of wit, and a certain relative sensibility, which enables me to draw from general life, for the support of mine, all I meet with that is good, like the monkey who cracks the nut to get at its contents. I am rich, for you have one of the first fortunes in France; I am your only daughter, and you are not so tenacious as the fathers of La Porte Saint-Martin and La Gaieté,* who disinherited their daughters because they will give them no grandchildren. Besides, the provident law has deprived you of the power to disinherit me, at least, entirely, as it has also of the power to compel me to marry a particular person. Thus, beautiful, witty, somewhat talented, as the comic operas say, and rich— and that is happiness, sir—why do you call me unhappy?"

Danglars, seeing his daughter smiling, and proud even to insolence, could not entirely repress his brutal feelings; but they betrayed themselves only by an exclamation. Under the inquiring gaze of his daughter, before that beautiful black eyebrow, contracted by interrogation, he prudently turned away, and calmed himself immediately, daunted by the iron hand of circumspection.

"Truly, my daughter," replied he, with a smile, "you are all you boast of being, excepting one thing; I will not too hastily tell you which, but would rather leave you to guess it."

Eugénie looked at Danglars, much surprised that one flower of her crown of pride with which she had so superbly decked herself should be disputed.

"My daughter," continued the banker, "you have perfectly explained to me the sentiments which influence a girl like you who is determined she will not marry; now it remains for me to tell you the motives of a father like me, who has decided his daughter shall marry."

Eugénie bowed, not as a submissive daughter, but as an adversary prepared for a discussion.

"My daughter," continued Danglars, "when a father asks his daughter to choose a husband, he has always some reason for wishing her to marry. Some are affected with the mania to which you alluded just now, that of living again in their grand-children. That is not my weakness, I tell you at once,—family joys have no charms for me. I may acknowledge this to a daughter whom I know to be philosophical enough to understand my indifference, and not to impute it to me as a crime."

"À la bonne heure," said Eugénie; "let us speak candidly, sir, I admire it."

"Oh!" said Danglars; "I can, when circumstances render it desirable, adopt your system, although it may not be my general practice. I will therefore proceed. I have proposed to you to marry, not for your sake, for, indeed, I did not think of you in the least at the moment (you admire candour, and will now be satisfied, I hope); but because it suited me to marry you as soon as possible, on account of certain commercial specula-tions I am desirous of entering into."

Eugénie became uneasy.

"It is just so, I assure you, and you must not be angry with me, for you have sought this disclosure. I do not willingly enter into all these arithmetical explanations with an artist like you, who fear to enter my cabinet lest you should imbibe disagreeable or anti-poetic impressions and sensations. But in that same banker's cabinet, where you very willingly presented yourself yesterday to ask for the thousand francs I give you monthly for pocket-money, you must know, my dear young lady, many things may be learned, useful even to a girl who will not marry. There one may learn, for instance, what, out of regard to your nervous susceptibility, I will inform you of in the drawing-room, namely, that the credit of a banker is his physical and moral life; that credit sustains him as breath animates the body; and M. de Monte Cristo once gave me a lecture on that subject, which I have never forgotten. There we may learn that as credit sinks, the body becomes a corpse; and this is what must happen very soon to the banker who is proud to own so good a logician as you for his daughter."

But Eugénie, instead of stooping, drew herself up under the blow.

"Ruined!" said she.

"Exactly, my daughter; that is precisely what I mean," said Danglars, almost digging his nails into his breast, while he pre-served on his harsh features the smile of the heartless, though clever man; "ruined! yes, that is it."

"Ah!" said Eugénie.

"Yes, ruined! now it is revealed, this secret so full of horror, as the tragic poet says. Now, my daughter, learn from my lips how you may alleviate this misfortune, so far as it will affect you."

" Oh! " cried Eugénie, " you are a bad physiognomist, if you imagine I deplore, on my own account, the catastrophe you announce to me. I ruined, and what will that signify to me? Have I not my talent left? Can I not like la Pasta, la Malibran, la Grisi, acquire for myself what you would never have given me, whatever might have been your fortune, a hundred or a hundred and fifty thousand livres per annum, for which I shall be indebted to no one but myself; and which, instead of being given as you gave me those poor twelve thousand francs with pouting looks and reproaches for my prodigality, will be accompanied with acclamations, with bravos, and with flowers? And if I do not possess that talent, which your smile proves to me you doubt, should I not still have that furious love of independence, which will be a substitute for all treasure, and which in my mind supersedes even the instinct of self-preservation? No, I grieve not on my own account, I shall always find a resource; my books, my pencils, my piano, all those things which cost but little, and which I shall be able to procure, will remain my own. Do you think I sorrow for Madame Danglars? undeceive yourself again; either I am greatly mistaken, or she has provided against the catastrophe which threatens you, and which will pass over without affecting her; she has taken care for herself, at least I hope so, for her attention has not been diverted from her projects by watching over me; she has fostered my independence by professedly indulging my love for liberty. Oh! no, sir; from my childhood I have seen too much, and understood too much, of what has passed around me, for misfortune to have an undue power over me; from my earliest recollections, I have been beloved by no one—so much the worse; that has naturally led me to love no one—so much the better: now you have my profession of faith."

" Then," said Danglars, pale with anger, which did not emanate from offended paternal love,—" then, mademoiselle, you persist in your determination to accelerate my ruin? "

" Your ruin? I accelerate your ruin! what do you mean? I do not understand you."

" So much the better, I have a ray of hope left: listen."

" I am all attention," said Eugénie, looking so earnestly at her father, that it was an effort to the latter to bear her powerful gaze.

" M. Cavalcanti," continued Danglars, " is about to marry you, and will place in my hands his fortune, amounting to three million livres."

" That is admirable! " said Eugénie, with sovereign contempt, smoothing her gloves out one upon the other.

" You think I shall deprive you of those three millions," said Danglars; " but do not fear it. They are destined to produce at least ten. I and a brother banker have obtained a grant of a railway, the only speculation which in the present day offers any prospect of immediate success, like the chimerical Mississippi, which Law formerly supplied for the good Parisians, those Cockneys in speculation. In my estimation, a million's worth in the railway is equal to an acre of uncultivated land on the banks of the Ohio. It is a deposit, belonging to a mortgage, which is an advance, as you see, since we gain at least ten, fifteen, twenty or a hundred livres' worth of iron in exchange for our money. Well, within a week, I am to deposit four millions for my share; these four millions, I promise you, will produce ten or twelve."

" But during my visit to you the day before yesterday, sir, which you appear to recollect so well," replied Eugénie, " I saw you lay up—is not that the term?—five millions and half; you even pointed them out to me in two drafts on the treasury, and you were astonished that so valuable a paper did not dazzle my eyes like lightning."

" Yes, but those five millions and a half are not mine, and are only a proof of the great confidence placed in me; my title of popular banker has gained me the confidence of the hospitals, and the five millions and a half belong to the hospitals; at any other time I should not have hesitated to make use of them, but the great losses I have recently sustained are well known, and as I told you my credit is rather shaken. That deposit may be at any moment withdrawn, and if I had employed it for another purpose, I should bring on me a disgraceful bankruptcy. I do not despise bankruptcies, believe me, those which enrich, but not those which ruin. Now if you marry M. Cavalcanti, and I touch the three millions, or even if it is thought I am going to touch them, my credit will be restored, and my fortune, which for the last month or two has been swallowed up in gulfs which have been opened in my path by an inconceivable fatality, will revive. Do you understand me? "

" Perfectly; you pledge me for three millions, do you not? "

" The greater the amount, the more flattering it is to you; it gives you an idea of your value."

" Thank you. One word more, sir; do you promise me to make what use you can of the report of the fortune M. Cavalcanti will bring, without touching the sum? This is no act of selfishness, but of delicacy. I am willing to help rebuild your fortune, but I will not be an accomplice in the ruin of others."

" But since I tell you," cried Danglars, " that with these three millions——"

" Do you expect to recover your position, sir, without touching those three millions? "

" I hope so, if the marriage should take place and confirm my credit."

" Shall you be able to pay M. Cavalcanti the five hundred thousand francs you promise for my dowry? "

" He shall receive them on returning from the town-hall."

" Well! "

" What next?' what more do you want? "

" I wish to know, if in demanding my signature, you leave me entirely free in my person? "

" Absolutely! "

" Then, well, as I said before, sir, I am ready to marry M. Cavalcanti."

" But what are your projects? "

" Ah! that is my secret. What advantage should I have over you, if knowing your secret, I were to tell you mine? "

Danglars bit his lips.

" Then," said he, " you are ready to pay the official visits, which are absolutely indispensable? "

" Yes," replied Eugénie.

" And to sign the contract in three days? "

" Yes."

" Then in my turn, I will say, well! "

Danglars pressed his daughter's hand in his. But it was extraordinary, neither did the father say " Thank you, my child," nor did the daughter smile at her father.

" Is the conference ended? " asked Eugénie, rising.

Danglars motioned that he had nothing more to say. Five minutes afterwards the piano resounded to the touch of Mademoiselle d'Armilly's fingers, and Mademoiselle Danglars was singing Brabantio's malediction on Desdemona.* At the end of the piece Stephen entered, and announced to Eugénie that the horses were in the carriage, and the baroness was waiting for her to pay her visits. We have seen them at Villefort's; they proceeded then on their course.

97

The Contract

THREE days after the scene we have just described, namely, towards five o'clock in the afternoon of the day fixed for the signature of the contract between Mademoiselle Eugénie Danglars and Andrea Cavalcanti,—whom the banker persisted in calling prince,—a fresh breeze agitated all the leaves in the little garden situated in front of the Count of Monte Cristo's house, and the latter was preparing to go out. While his horses were impatiently pawing the ground, held in by the coachman, who had been seated a quarter of an hour on his box, the elegant phaeton with which we are familiar rapidly turned the angle of the entrance-gate, and threw, rather than set down, in the steps of the door, M. Andrea Cavalcanti, as much decked and as gay as if he, on his side, was going to marry a princess.

He inquired after the count with his usual familiarity, and, bounding lightly to the first storey, met him on the top of the stairs. · The count stopped on seeing the young man. As for Andrea, he was launched, and when once launched nothing stopped him.

"Ah! good-morning, my dear count," said he, " were you going out or just returned? "

" I was going out, sir."

" Then, in order not to hinder you, I will get up with you, if you please, in your carriage; I have a thousand things to talk about."

" No," said the count, with an imperceptible smile of contempt, for he had no wish to be seen in the young man's society, —" no; I prefer listening to you here, my dear M. Andrea; we can chat better indoors, and there is no coachman to overhear our conversation."

The count returned to a small drawing-room on the first floor, sat down, and, crossing his legs, motioned to the young man to take a seat also.

Andrea assumed his gayest manner.

" You know, my dear count," said he, " the ceremony is to take place this evening. At nine o'clock the contract is to be signed at my father-in-law's."

" Well," said Monte Cristo, " you are fortunate, M. Cavalcanti! it is a most suitable alliance you are contracting, and Mademoiselle Danglars is a pretty girl."

" Yes, indeed she is," replied Cavalcanti, with a very modest tone.

" Above all, she is very rich,—at least I believe so," said Monte Cristo.

" Very rich, do you think? " replied the young man.

" Doubtless; it is said M. Danglars conceals at least half of his fortune."

" And he acknowledges fifteen or twenty millions," said Andrea, with a look sparkling with joy.

" Without reckoning," added Monte Cristo, " that he is on the eve of entering into a sort of speculation already in vogue in the United States and in England, but quite novel in France."

" Yes, yes, I know what you allude to—the railway, of which he has obtained the grant, is it not? "

" Precisely! it is generally believed he will gain ten millions by that affair."

" Ten millions! Do you think so? It is magnificent! " said Cavalcanti, who was quite confounded at the metallic sound of these golden words.

" Without reckoning," replied Monte Cristo, " that all his fortune will come to you, and justly too, since Mademoiselle Danglars is an only daughter. Besides, your own fortune, as your father assured me, is almost equal to that of your betrothed. But, enough of money matters. Do you know, M. Andrea, I think you have managed this affair rather skilfully? "

"'Not badly, by any means," said the young man; " I was born for a diplomatist."

" Well, you must become a diplomatist; it is a knowledge not to be acquired, you know; it is instinctive. Have you lost your heart? "

" Indeed, I fear it," replied Andrea, in the tone in which he had heard Dorante or Valère reply to Alceste* in the Théâtre Français.

" Is your love returned? "

" I suppose so," said Andrea, with a triumphant smile, " since I am accepted. But I must not forget one grand point."

" Which? "

" That I have been singularly assisted."

" By circumstances? "

" No; by you."

" By me? Not at all, prince," said Monte Cristo, laying a marked stress on the title; " what have I done for you? Are not your name, your social position, and your merit sufficient? "

" No," said Andrea,—" no; it is useless for you to say so, count. I maintain that the position of a man like you has done more than my name, my social position, and my merit."

" You are completely mistaken, sir," said Monte Cristo coldly, who felt the perfidious manœuvre of the young man, and understood the bearing of his words; " you only acquired my protection after the influence and fortune of your father had been ascertained; for, after all, who procured for me, who had never seen either you or your illustrious father, the pleasure of your acquaintance?—Two of my good friends, Lord Wilmore and the Abbé Busoni. Who encouraged me not to become your surety, but to patronise you?—It was your father's name, so well known in Italy and so highly honoured. Personally, I do not know you."

This calm tone and perfect ease made Andrea feel he was, for the moment, restrained by a more muscular hand than his own, and that the restraint could not be easily broken through.

" Oh! then, my father has really a very large fortune, count? "

" It appears so, sir," replied Monte Cristo.

" Do you know if my promised dowry is come? "

" I have been advised of it."

" But the three millions? "

" The three millions are probably on the road."

" Then, I shall really have them? "

" Forsooth! " said the count, " I do not think you have yet known the want of money."

Andrea was so surprised, he reflected for a moment. Then arousing from his reverie,—

" Now, sir, I have one request to make to you, which you will understand, even if it should be disagreeable to you."

" Proceed," said Monte Cristo.

" I have formed an acquaintance, thanks to my good fortune, with many noted persons, and have, at least for the moment, a crowd of friends. But marrying, as I am about to do, before all Paris, I ought to be supported by an illustrious name, and, in the absence of the paternal hand, some powerful one ought to lead me to the altar: now, my father is not coming to Paris, is he? He is old, covered with wounds, and suffers dreadfully, he says, in travelling."

" Indeed! "

" Well, I am come to ask a favour of you."

" Of me? "

" Yes, of you."

" And pray what may it be? "

" Well, to take his part."

" Ah, my dear sir! What! after the numerous relations I have had the happiness to sustain towards you, you know me so little as to ask such a thing! Ask me to lend you half a million, and, although such a loan is somewhat rare, on my honour you would annoy me less! Know, then, what I thought I had already told you, that, in its moral participation particularly with this world's affairs, the Count of Monte Cristo has never ceased to entertain the scruples and even the superstitions of the East. I who have a seraglio at Cairo, one at Smyrna, and one at Constantinople, preside at a wedding—never! "

" Then you refuse me? "

" Decidedly; and were you my son or my brother I would refuse you in the same way."

" But what must be done? " said Andrea, disappointed.

" You said, just now, you had a hundred friends."

" Agreed; but you introduced me at M. Danglars'."

" Not at all! let us recall the exact facts. You met him at a dinner-party at my house, and you introduced yourself at his house; that is a totally different affair."

" Yes, but my marriage, you have forwarded that."

" I! not in the least, I beg you to believe. Recollect what I told you when you asked me to propose you. ' Oh! I never make matches, my dear prince, it is my settled principle.' "

Andrea bit his lips.

" But, at least, you will be there? "

" Will all Paris be there? "

" Oh, certainly! "

" Well, like all Paris, I shall be there too," said the count.

" And will you sign the contract? "

" I see no objection to that; my scruples do not go thus far."

" Well, since you will grant me no more, I must be content with what you give me. But, one word more, count."

" What is it? "

" Advice."

" Be careful; advice is worse than a service."

" Oh! you can give me this without compromising yourself."

" Tell me what it is."

" Is my wife's fortune five hundred thousand livres? "

" That is the sum M. Danglars himself announced."

" Must I receive it, or leave it in the hands of the notary? "

" This is the way such affairs are generally arranged when it is wished to do them stylishly:—Your two solicitors appoint a meeting, when the contract is signed, for the next day or the following; then they exchange the two portions, for which they each give a receipt; then, when the marriage is celebrated, they place the amount at your disposal as chief of the community."

" Because," said Andrea, with a certain ill-concealed uneasiness, " I thought I heard my father-in-law say he intended embarking our property in that famous railway affair of which you spoke just now."

" Well," replied Monte Cristo, " it will be the way everybody says, of trebling your fortune in twelve months. The Baron Danglars is a good father, and knows how to calculate."

" Come, then," said Andrea, " all is well, excepting your refusal, which quite grieves me. This evening, then, at nine o'clock."

" Adieu till then."

The four or five remaining hours before nine o'clock arrived, Andrea employed in riding, paying visits destined to interest those of whom he had spoken, to appear at the banker's in their gayest equipages. In fact, at half-past eight in the evening, the grand salon, the gallery adjoining, and the three other drawing-rooms on the same floor, were filled with a perfumed crowd, who sympathised but little in the event, but who all participated in that love of being present wherever there is anything fresh to be seen.

No one could dispute that the rooms were splendidly illuminated; the light streamed forth on the gold mouldings and the silk hangings; and all the bad taste of this furniture, which had only its richness to boast of, shone in its splendour. Mademoiselle Eugénie was dressed with elegant simplicity in a figured white silk dress, and a white rose half concealed in her jet-black hair was her only ornament, unaccompanied by a single jewel. Her eyes, however, betrayed that perfect confidence which contradicted the girlish simplicity of this modest attire. Madame Danglars was chatting at a short distance with Debray, Beauchamp, and Château-Renaud. Debray was admitted to the house for this grand solemnity, but like everyone else, and without any particular privilege. M. Danglars, surrounded by deputies and men connected with the revenue, was explaining a new theory of taxation which he intended to adopt, when the course of events had compelled government to call him into the ministry. Andrea, on whose arm hung one of the most consummate dandies of the Opera, was explaining to him rather cleverly, since he was obliged to be bold to appear at ease, his future projects and the new luxuries he meant to introduce to Parisian fashions with his hundred and seventy-five thousand livres per annum. The crowd moved to and fro in those rooms like an ebb and flow of turquoises, rubies, emeralds, opals, and diamonds.

At each moment, in the midst of the crowd, the buzzing and the laughter, the door-keeper's voice was heard announcing some name well known in the financial department, respected in the army, or illustrious in the literary world, and which was acknowledged by a slight movement in the different groups. But for one whose privilege it was to agitate that ocean of human waves, how many were received with a look of indifference or a sneer of disdain! At the moment when the hand of the massive timepiece, representing Endymion asleep, pointed to nine on its golden face, and the hammer, the faithful type of mechanical thought, struck nine times, the name of Comte de Monte Cristo resounded in its turn, and, as if by an electric shock, all the assembly turned towards the door.

A circle was formed immediately round the door. The count perceived at one glance Madame Danglars at one end of the drawing-room, M. Danglars at the other, and Eugénie in front of him. He first advanced towards the baroness, who was chatting with Madame Villefort, who had come alone, Valentine being still an invalid; and without turning aside, so clear was the road left for him, he passed from the baroness to Eugénie, whom he complimented in such rapid and measured terms, that the proud artist was quite struck. Near her was Mademoiselle Louise d'Armilly, who thanked the count for the letters of introduction he had so kindly given her for Italy, which she intended immediately to make use of. On leaving these ladies he found himself with Danglars, who had advanced to meet him.

Having accomplished these three social duties, Monte Cristo stopped, looking round him with that expression peculiar to a certain class, which seems to say, " I have done my duty, now let others do theirs." Andrea, who was in an adjoining room, had shared in the sensation caused by the arrival of Monte Cristo, and now came forward to pay his respects to the count. He found him completely surrounded; all were eager to speak to him, as is always the case with those whose words are few and weighty. The solicitors arrived at this moment, and arranged their scrawled papers on the velvet cloth embroidered with gold which covered the table prepared for the signature; it was a gilt table supported on lions' claws. One of the notaries sat down, the other remained standing. They were about to proceed to the reading of the contract which half Paris assembled was to sign. All took their places, or rather the ladies formed a circle, while the gentlemen commented on the feverish agitation of Andrea, on M. Danglars' riveted attention, Eugénie's composure, and the light and sprightly manner in which the baroness treated this important affair.

The contract was read during a profound silence. But as soon as it was finished, the buzz was redoubled through all the drawing-rooms: the brilliant sums, the rolling millions which were to be at the command of the two young people, and which crowned the display which had been made in a room entirely appropriated for the purpose of the wedding presents and the young lady's diamonds, had resounded with all their delusion on the jealous assembly. Mademoiselle Danglars' charms were heightened in the opinion of the young men, and for the moment seemed to outvie the sun in splendour.

As for the ladies, it is needless to say that, while jealous of these millions, they thought they did not require them to render them beautiful. Andrea, surrounded by his friends, complimented, flattered, beginning to believe in the reality of his dream, was almost bewildered. The notary solemnly took the pen, flourished it above his head, and said:

" Gentlemen, the contract is to be signed."

The baron was to sign first, then the representative of M. Cavalcanti, senior, then the baroness, afterwards the future couple, as they are styled on the ceremonious stamped papers. The baron took the pen and signed, then the representative.

The baroness approached, leaning on Madame de Villefort's arm.

" My dear," said she, as she took the pen, " is it not vexatious? An unexpected incident, in the affair of murder and theft at the Count of Monte Cristo's, in which he nearly fell a victim, deprives us of the pleasure of seeing M. de Villefort."

" Indeed! " said M. Danglars, in the same tone in which he would have said, " Faith, I care very little about it! "

" Indeed," said Monte . Cristo, approaching, " I am much afraid I am the involuntary cause of that absence."

" What! you, count? " said Madame Danglars, signing; " if you, are, take care, for I shall never forgive you."

Andrea pricked up his ears.

" But it is not my fault, as I shall endeavour to prove."

Everyone listened eagerly: Monte Cristo, who so rarely opened his lips, was about to speak.

" You remember," said the count, during the most profound silence, " that the unhappy wretch who came to rob me, died at my house; it was supposed he was stabbed by his accomplice, on attempting to leave it. In order to examine his wounds, he was undressed, and his clothes were thrown into a corner, where officers of justice picked them up, with the exception of the waist-coat, which they overlooked."

Andrea turned pale, and drew towards the door; he saw a

cloud rising in the horizon, which appeared to forebode a coming storm.

"Well! this waistcoat was discovered to-day, covered with blood, and with a hole over the heart."

The ladies screamed, and two or three prepared to faint.

"It was brought to me. No one could guess what the dirty rag could be; I alone supposed it was the waistcoat of the victim. My valet, in examining this mournful relic, felt a paper in the pocket and drew it out; it was a letter addressed to you, baron."

"To me?" cried Danglars.

"Yes, indeed, to you; I succeeded in deciphering your name under the blood with which the letter was stained," replied Monte Cristo, amid the general burst of amazement.

"But," asked Madame Danglars, looking at her husband with uneasiness, "how could that prevent M. de Villefort——"

"In this simple way, madame," replied Monte Cristo; "the waistcoat and the letter were both, what is termed, convictive evidence: I therefore sent it all to M. le Procureur du Roi. You understand, my dear baron, legal proceedings are the safest in criminal cases; it was perhaps some plot against you."

Andrea looked steadily at Monte Cristo, and disappeared in the second drawing-room.

"Possibly," said Danglars; "was not this murdered man an old galley-slave?"

"Yes," replied the count; "a felon named Caderousse."

Danglars turned slightly pale; Andrea reached the ante-room beyond the little drawing-room.

"But go on signing," said Monte Cristo; "I perceive my story has caused a general emotion, and I beg to apologise to you, baroness, and to Mademoiselle Danglars."

The baroness, who had signed, returned the pen to the notary.

"Prince Cavalcanti!" said the latter; "Prince Cavalcanti, where are you?"

"Andrea! Andrea!" repeated several young people, who were already on sufficiently intimate terms with him to call him by his Christian name.

"Call the prince; inform him it is his turn to sign!" cried Danglars to one of the door-keepers.

But at the same instant the crowd of guests rushed, terrified, into the principal salon. There was, indeed, reason to retreat, to be alarmed, and to scream. An officer was placing two soldiers at the door of each drawing-room, and was advancing towards Danglars, preceded by a commissioner of police, girded with his scarf.

Madame Danglars uttered a scream and fainted. Danglars, who thought himself threatened (certain consciences are never calm),—Danglars appeared before his guests with a terrified countenance.

"What is the matter, sir?" asked Monte Cristo, advancing to meet the commissioner.

"Which of you, gentlemen," asked the magistrate, without replying to the count, "answers to the name of Andrea Cavalcanti?"

A cry of stupor was heard from all parts of the room.

They searched; they questioned.

"But who then is Andrea Cavalcanti?" asked Danglars, in amazement.

"A galley-slave, escaped from confinement at Toulouse."

"And what crime has he committed?"

"He is accused," said the commissary, with his inflexible voice, "of having assassinated the man named Caderousse, his former companion in prison, at the moment he was making his escape from the house of the Count of Monte Cristo."

Monte Cristo cast a rapid glance around him. Andrea was gone.

98

The Departure for Belgium

A FEW minutes after the scene of confusion produced in the salons of M. Danglars by the unexpected appearance of the brigade of soldiers, and by the disclosure which had followed, the large hotel was deserted with a rapidity which the announcement of a case of plague or of cholera morbus among the guests would have caused. There remained in the banker's hotel only Danglars, closeted in his cabinet, and making his statement to the officer of the detachment; Madame Danglars, terrified, in the boudoir with which we are acquainted; and Eugénie, who, with haughty air and disdainful lip, had retired to her room with her inseparable companion, Mademoiselle Louise d'Armilly. As for the numerous servants (more numerous that evening than usual, for their number was augmented by the cooks and butlers of the Café de Paris), venting on their employers their anger at what they termed the insult, they collected in groups in the hall, in the kitchens, or in their rooms, thinking very little of their duty, which was thus naturally interrupted.

Of all this household, only two individuals deserve our notice; these are Mademoiselle Eugénie Danglars and Mademoiselle Louise d'Armilly. The betrothed had retired, as we said, with haughty air, disdainful lip, and the demeanour of an outraged queen, followed by her companion, paler and more affected than herself, On reaching her room, Eugénie locked her door, while Louise fell on a chair.

" Ah, what a dreadful thing! " said the young musician; " who would have suspected it? M. Andrea Cavalcanti a murderer —a galley-slave escaped—a convict! "

An ironical smile curled the lip of Eugénie. " In truth I was fated," said she; " I escaped the Morcerf only to fall into the Cavalcanti."

" Oh, do not confound the two, Eugénie! "

" Hold your tongue! The men are all infamous; and I am happy to be able now to do more than detest them—I despise them! "

" What shall we do? " asked Louise.

" Why, the same we had intended doing three days since— set off."

"What! although you are not now going to be married, you intend still——"

"Listen, Louise! I hate this life of the fashionable world, always ordered, measured, ruled like our music-paper. What I have always wished for, desired, and coveted, is the life of an artist, free and independent, relying only on my own resources, and accountable only to myself. Remain here! what for?— that they may try, a month hence, to marry me again; and to whom?—to M. Debray, perhaps, as it was once proposed. No, Louise, no! This evening's adventure will serve for my excuse. I did not seek one, I did not ask for one. God sends me this, and I hail it joyfully!"

"How strong and courageous you are!" said the fair frail girl to her brunette companion.

"Did you not yet know me? Come, Louise, let us talk of our affairs. The post-chaise——"

"Was happily bought three days since."

"Have you had it sent where we are to go for it?"

"Yes."

"Our passport?"

"Here it is!"

And Eugénie, with her usual precision, opened a printed paper, and read:

"M. Léon d'Armilly, twenty years of age; profession, artist; hair black, eyes black; travelling with his sister."

"Capital! How did you get this passport?"

"When I went to ask M. de Monte Cristo for letters for the directors of the theatres at Rome and at Naples, I expressed my fears of travelling as a female. He perfectly understood them, and undertook to procure for me a man's passport; and two days after I received this, to which I have added with my own hand, ' travelling with his sister.'"

"Well," said Eugénie cheerfully, "we have then only to pack up our trunks; we shall start the evening of the signature, instead of the evening of the wedding—that is all."

"Reflect well, Eugénie!"

"Oh, I have finished all my reflections! I am tired of hearing only of reports, of the end of the month, of up and down, of Spanish funds, of Haïtian paper. Instead of that, Louise—do you understand?—air, liberty, melody of birds, plains of Lombardy, Venetian canals, Roman palaces, the bay of Naples. How much have we, Louise?"

The young girl to whom this question was addressed drew

from an inlaid secretaire a small portfolio with a lock, in which she counted twenty-three bank-notes.

" Twenty-three thousand francs," said she.

" And as much, at least, in pearls, diamonds, and jewels," said Eugénie. " We are rich. With forty-five thousand francs we have enough to live on as princesses during two years, and comfortably during four; but before six months—you with your music, and I with my voice—we shall double our capital. Come, you shall take charge of the money, I of the jewel-box; so that if one of us had the misfortune to lose her treasure, the other would still have hers left. Now, the portmanteau!—let us make haste—the portmanteau! "

And the two young girls began to heap into a trunk all the things they thought they should require.

" There, now! " said Eugénie, " while I change my costume do you lock the portmanteau."

Louise pressed with all the strength of her little hands on the top of the portmanteau.

" But I cannot," said she; " I am not strong enough; do you shut it."

" Ah, you are right! " said Eugénie, laughing; " I forgot I was Hercules, and you only the pale Amphale! " And the young girl, kneeling on the top, pressed the two parts of the portmanteau together, and Mademoiselle d'Armilly passed the bolt of the padlock through.

When this was done, Eugénie opened a drawer, of which she kept the key, and took from it a wadded violet silk travelling cloak.

" Here," said she, " you will see I have thought of everything; with this cloak you will not be cold."

" But you? "

" Oh, I am never cold, you know! Besides, with those men's clothes——"

" Will you dress here? "

" Certainly."

" Shall you have time? "

" Do not be uneasy, you little coward! All our servants are busy, discussing the grand affair. Besides, what is there astonishing, when you think of the grief I ought to be in, that I shut myself up?—tell me! "

" No, truly—you comfort me."

" Come and help me."

From the same drawer she took a complete man's costume, from the boots to the coat, and a provision of linen, where there was nothing superfluous, but every requisite.

Then, with a promptitude which indicated this was not the first time she had amused herself by adopting the garb of the opposite sex, Eugénie drew on the boots and pantaloons, tied her cravat, buttoned her waistcoat up to the throat, and put on a coat which admirably fitted her beautiful figure.

" Oh, that is very good!—indeed it is very good! " said Louise, looking at her with admiration; " but that beautiful black hair, those magnificent braids, which made all the ladies sigh with envy, will they go under a man's hat like the one I see down there? "

" You shall see," said Eugénie.

And seizing with her left hand the thick mass, which her long fingers could scarcely grasp, she seized with her right hand a pair of long scissors, and soon the steel met through the rich and splendid hair, which fell entire at the feet of the young girl, who leaned back to keep it from her coat. Then she passed to the front hair, which she also cut off, without expressing the least regret; on the contrary, her eyes sparkled with greater pleasure than usual under her eyebrows black as ebony.

" Oh, the magnificent hair! " said Louise, with regret.

" And am I not a hundred times better thus? " cried Eugénie, smoothing the scattered curls of her hair, which had now quite a masculine appearance; " and do you not think me handsomer so? "

" Oh, you are beautiful—always beautiful! " cried Louise. " Now, where are you going? "

" To Brussels if you like; it is the nearest frontier. We can go to Brussels, Liège, Aix-la-Chapelle; then up the Rhine to Strasburg. We will cross Switzerland, and go down into Italy by Mount St. Gothard. Will that do? "

" Yes."

" What are you looking at? "

" I am looking at you; indeed you are adorable like that! One would say you were carrying me off."

" And they would be right, *par Dieu!* "

" Oh! I think you swore, Eugénie."

And the two young girls, whom everyone might have thought plunged in grief, the one on her own account, the other from interest in her friend, burst out laughing, as they cleared away every visible trace of the disorder which had naturally accompanied the preparations for their escape. Then, having blown out their lights, with an inquiring eye, listening ear, and extended neck, the two fugitives opened the door of a dressing-room which led by a side staircase down to the yard, Eugénie going first, and holding with one arm the portmanteau, which by the opposite handle Mademoiselle d'Armilly scarcely raised with both hands.

The yard was empty; the clock was striking twelve. The porter was not yet gone to bed. Eugénie approached softly, and saw the old man sleeping soundly in an arm-chair in his lodge. She returned to Louise, took up the portmanteau, which she had placed for a moment on the ground, and they reached the archway under the shadow of the wall.

Eugénie concealed Louise in an angle of the gateway, so that if the porter chanced to awake he might see but one person. Then placing herself in the full light of the lamp which lit the yard,—

" Gate! " cried she, with her finest contralto voice, and rapping at the window.

The porter got up as Eugénie expected, and even advanced some steps to recognise the person who was going out, but seeing a young man striking his boot impatiently with his riding-whip, he opened it immediately. Louise slid through the half-open gate like a snake, and bounded lightly forward. Eugénie, apparently calm, although in all probability her heart beat somewhat faster than usual, went out in her turn. A porter was passing; they gave him the portmanteau; then the two young girls having told him to take it to No. 36 Rue de la Victoire, walked behind this man, whose presence comforted Louise. As for Eugénie, she was strong as a Judith or a Dalilah. They arrived at the appointed spot. Eugénie ordered the porter to put down the portmanteau, gave him some pieces of money, and, having rapped at the shutter, sent him away.

The shutter where Eugénie had rapped was that of a little laundress, who had been previously apprised, and was not yet gone to bed. She opened the door.

" Mademoiselle," said Eugénie, " let the porter get the post-chaise from the coach-house and fetch some post-horses from the hotel. Here are five francs for his trouble."

In a quarter of an hour the porter returned with a post-boy and horses, which were harnessed and put in the post-chaise in a minute, while the porter fastened the portmanteau on with the assistance of a cord and a strap.

" Here is the passport," said the postilion; " which way are we going, young gentleman? "

" To Fontainebleau," replied Eugénie, with an almost masculine voice.

" What do you say? " said Louise.

" I am giving the slip," said Eugénie; " this woman to whom we have given twenty louis may betray us for forty; we will soon alter our direction."

And the young girl jumped into the britska,* which was admirably arranged for sleeping in, without scarcely touching the step.

"You are always right," said the singing governess, seating herself by the side of her friend.

A quarter of an hour afterwards the postilion, having been put in the right road, passed, cracking his whip, through the gateway of Barrière Saint-Martin.

M. Danglars had lost his daughter.

99

The Hotel of the Bell and Bottle

AND now let us leave Mademoiselle Danglars and her friend pursuing their way to Brussels, and return to poor Andrea Cavalcanti, so uncomfortably interrupted in his career of fortune. Notwithstanding his youth, Master Andrea was a very skilful and intelligent boy. We have seen that, on the first rumour which reached the salon, he had gradually approached the door, and, crossing two or three rooms, at last disappeared. But we have forgotten to mention one circumstance, which, nevertheless, ought not to be omitted; it was, that in one of the rooms he crossed, the trousseau of the bride-elect was exposed to view; consisting of cases of diamonds, cashmere shawls, Valenciennes lace, English veils, and, in fact, all those tempting things, the bare mention of which makes the hearts of young girls bound with joy, and which is called the *corbeille*. Now, in passing through this room, Andrea proved himself not only to be clever and intelligent, but also provident, for he helped himself to the most valuable of the ornaments before him. Furnished with this plunder, Andrea leaped with a lighter heart from the window, intending to slip through the hands of the gendarmes. Tall and well-proportioned as an ancient gladiator, and muscular as a Spartan, he walked for a quarter of an hour without knowing where to direct his steps, actuated by the sole idea of removing himself from the spot where he knew he must be taken. Having passed through the Rue Mont Blanc, he found himself, with the instinct which thieves have in avoiding barriers, at the end of the Rue Lafayette. There he stopped, breathless and panting. He was quite alone: on one side was the vast wilderness of the Saint-Lazare, on the other, Paris in all its darkness.

" Am I lost? " he cried; " no, not if I can use more activity than my enemies. My safety is now a mere question of speed."

At this moment he perceived a cab at the top of the Faubourg Poissonnière. The dull driver, smoking his pipe, appeared to be seeking to regain the extremities of the Faubourg Saint Denis, where, no doubt, he ordinarily stood.

" Ho, friend! " said Benedetto.

" What do you want, sir? " asked the driver.

" Is your horse tired? "

" Tired? oh, yes, tired enough!—he has done nothing the whole of this blessed day! Four wretched fares, and twenty sous over, making in all seven francs, are all that I have earned, and I ought to take ten to the owner."

" Will you add these twenty francs to the seven you have? "

" With pleasure, sir; twenty francs are not to be despised. Tell me what I am to do for this."

" A very easy thing, if your horse be not tired."

" I tell you he will go like the wind; only tell me which way to drive."

" Towards the Louvres."

" Ah! I know it!—the land of ratafia."*

" Exactly so; I merely wish to overtake one of my friends, with whom I am going to hunt to-morrow at Chapelle-en-Serval. He should have waited for me here with a cabriolet till half-past eleven; it is twelve, and, tired of waiting, he must have gone on. Will you try and overtake him? "

" Nothing I should like better."

" If you do not overtake him before we reach Bourget you shall have twenty francs; if not before Louvres, thirty."

" And if we do overtake him? "

" Forty," said Andrea, after a moment's hesitation, at the end of which he remembered that he might safely promise.

" That will do! " said the man; " get in, and we're off! Prrrrrouuu! "

Andrea got into the cab, which passed rapidly through the Faubourg Saint-Denis, along the Faubourg Saint-Martin, crossed the barrier, and threaded its way through the interminable Villette. They never overtook the chimerical friend, yet Andrea frequently inquired of walking passers and at the inns which were not yet closed, for a green cabriolet and bay horse; and as there are a great many cabriolets to be seen on the road to the Pays-Bas, and nine-tenths of them are green, the inquiries increased at every step. Everyone had just seen it pass; it was only five hundred, two hundred, one hundred steps in advance; at length they reached it, but it was not the friend. Once the cab was also passed by a calèche, rapidly whirled along by two post-horses.

"Ah!" said Cavalcanti to himself, "if I only had that britska, those two good post-horses, and, above all, the passport that carries them on!" And he sighed deeply.

The calèche contained Mademoiselle Danglars and Mademoiselle d'Armilly.

"Onwards! onwards!" said Andrea, "we must overtake him soon." And the poor horse resumed the desperate gallop it had never slackened since leaving the barrier, and arrived smoking at Louvres.

"Certainly," said Andrea, "I shall not overtake my friend, but I shall kill your horse, therefore I had better stop. Here are thirty francs; I will sleep at the Cheval Rouge, and will secure a place in the first coach. Good-night, friend!" And Andrea, after placing six pieces of five francs each in the man's hand, leaped lightly on to the pathway.

The coachman joyfully pocketed the sum, and turned back on his road to Paris. Andrea pretended to go towards the hotel of the Cheval Rouge, but after leaning an instant against the door, and hearing the last sound of the cab, which was disappearing to view, he went on his road, and with a firm tread prepared for a walk of two leagues. Then he rested; he must be near Chapelle-en-Serval, where he pretended to be going. It was not fatigue that stayed Andrea here; it was that he might form some resolution, adopt some plan. It would be impossible to make use of a diligence, equally so to engage post-horses; to travel either way a passport was necessary. It would also be impossible to remain in the department of the Oise, one of the most open and strictly guarded in France. He sat down by the side of the moat, buried his face in his hands and reflected. Ten minutes after he raised his head; his resolution was made. He threw some dust over the paletot, which he had found time to unhook from the ante-chamber and button over his ball costume, and, going to Chapelle-en-Serval, he knocked loudly at the door of the only inn in the place. The host opened it.

"My friend," said Andrea, "I was coming from Mortefontaine to Senlis, when my horse, which is a troublesome creature, stumbled and threw me. I must reach Compiègne to-night, or I shall cause deep anxiety to my family. Could you let me hire a horse of you?"

An innkeeper has always a horse to let, whether it be good or bad. The host of La Chapelle-en-Serval called the stable-boy, and ordered him to saddle Le Blanc; then he awoke his son, a child of seven years, whom he ordered to ride before the gentleman and bring back the horse. Andrea gave the innkeeper twenty francs, and, in taking them from his pocket, dropped a visiting-card. This belonged to one of his friends at the Café de Paris, so that the innkeeper, picking it up after Andrea had left, was convinced that he had let his horse to M. le Comte de Mauléon, 25 Rue Saint-Dominique, that being the name and address on the card.

Le Blanc was not a fast animal, but it went equally and steadily; in three hours and a half Andrea had run over the nine leagues which lie between Compiègne, and four o'clock struck as he reached the place where the diligences stop. There is an excellent hotel at Compiègne,˙ well remembered by those who have ever been there. Andrea, who had often stayed there in his rides about Paris, recollected the hotel of the Bell and Bottle; he turned round, saw the sign by the light of a reflected lamp, and having dismissed the child, giving him all the small coin he had about him, he began knocking at the door, reflecting, with justice, that, having now three or four hours before him, he had best fortify himself against the fatigues of the morrow by a sound sleep and a good supper. A waiter opened the door.

" My friend," said Andrea, " I have been dining at Saint-Jean-au-Bois, and expected to catch the coach which passes by at midnight, but, like a fool, I have lost my way, and have been walking for the last four hours in the forest. Show me into one of those pretty little rooms which overlook the court, and bring me a cold fowl and a bottle of Bordeaux."

The waiter had no suspicions; Andrea spoke with perfect composure, he had a cigar in his mouth, and his hands in the pocket of his paletot; his clothes were elegant, his chin smooth, his boots irreproachable; he looked merely as if he had stayed out very late, that was all. While the waiter was preparing his room, the hostess rose. Andrea assumed his most charming smile, and asked if he could have No. 3, which he had occupied on his last stay at Compiègne. Unfortunately, No. 3 was engaged by a young man who was travelling with his sister. Andrea appeared in despair, but consoled himself when the hostess assured him that No. 7, prepared for him, was situated precisely the same as No. 3, and while warming his feet and chatting about the last races at Chantilly, he waited until they announced his room to be ready.

Andrea had not spoken without cause of the pretty rooms looking out upon the court of the Bell Hotel; which, with its triple stages of galleries, looking like a theatre, with the jessamine and clematis twining round the light columns, forms one of the prettiest entrances to an inn you can imagine. The fowl was fresh, the wine old, the fire clear and sparkling, and Andrea was surprised to find himself eating with as good an appetite as though nothing had happened. Then he went to bed, and almost immediately fell into that deep sleep which is sure to visit men of twenty years of age, even when they are torn with remorse. Now here we are obliged to own that Andrea ought to have felt remorse, but that he did not.

This was the plan which had appeared to him to afford the best chance of his security. Before daybreak he would awake, leave the hotel after rigorously discharging his bill, and reaching the forest, he would, under pretence of making studies in painting, test the hospitality of some peasants; procure himself the dress of a woodcutter and a hatchet, casting off the lion's skin to assume that of the woodman: then, with his hands covered with dirt, his hair darkened by means of a leaden comb, his complexion embrowned with a preparation for which one of his old comrades had given him the recipe, he intended, through different forests, to reach the nearest frontier, walking by night and sleeping in the day in the forests and quarries, and only entering inhabited districts to buy a loaf from time to time. Once past the frontier, Andrea proposed making money of his diamonds; and, by uniting the proceeds to ten bank-notes he always carried about with him in case of accident, he would then find himself possessor of about 50,000 livres, which he philosophically considered as no very deplorable condition after all. Moreover, he reckoned much on its being to the interest of the Danglars to hush up the rumour of their own misadventures. These were the reasons which, added to the fatigue, caused Andrea to sleep so soundly. In order that he might wake early, he did not close the shutters, but contented himself with bolting the door, and placing on the table an unclasped and long-pointed knife, whose temper he well knew, and which was never absent from him. About seven in the morning Andrea was awakened by a ray of sunlight, which, warm and brilliant, played upon his face. In all well-organised brains, the predominating idea—and there always is one—is sure to be the last thought before sleeping, and the first upon waking in the morning. Andrea had scarcely opened his eyes when his predominating idea presented itself, and whispered in his ear that he had slept too long. He jumped out of bed and ran to the window. A gendarme was crossing the court. A gendarme is one of the most striking objects in the world, even to a man void of uneasiness; but for one who has a timid conscience, and with good cause too, the yellow, blue, and white uniform is really very alarming.

"Why is that gendarme there?" asked Andrea of himself.

Then all at once he replied with that logic which the reader has, doubtless, remarked in him, " There is nothing astonishing in seeing a gendarme at an inn; instead of being astonished, let me dress myself! "

And the youth dressed himself with a rapidity his valet-de-chambre had failed to divest him of during the few months of fashionable life he had led in Paris.

" Good! " said Andrea, while dressing himself. " I'll wait till he leaves, and then I'll slip away."

And, saying this, Andrea, who had now put on his boots and cravat, stole gently to the window, and a second time lifted up the muslin curtain. Not only was the first gendarme still there, but the young man now perceived a second yellow, blue, and white uniform at the foot of the staircase, the only one by which he could descend, while a third on horseback, holding a musket in his fist, was posted as a sentinel at the great street door which alone afforded the means of egress. This appearance of the third gendarme was particularly decisive, for a crowd of curious loungers was extended before him, effectually blocking the entrance to the hotel.

" They seek me! " was the first thought of Andrea. " *Diable!* "

A pallor overspread the young man's forehead, and he looked around him with anxiety. His room, like all those on the same floor, had but one outlet to the gallery in the sight of everybody.

" I am lost! " was his second thought; and, indeed, for a man in Andrea's situation, an arrest comprehended the assizes, the trial, and death,—death without mercy or delay. For a moment he convulsively pressed his head within his hands, and during that brief period he became nearly mad with terror: but soon a ray of hope glanced through the crowd of thoughts which bewildered his mind, and a faint smile played upon his white lips and pallid cheeks. He looked round and saw the objects of his search upon the chimney-piece; they were a pen, ink, and paper. With forced composure he dipped the pen in the ink, and wrote the following lines upon a sheet of paper:—

" I have no money to pay my bill, but I am not a dishonest man; I leave behind me as a pledge this pin, worth ten times the amount. I shall be excused for escaping at daybreak, for I was ashamed."

He then drew the pin from his cravat and placed it on the paper. This done, instead of leaving the door fastened, he drew back the bolts, and even placed the door ajar, as though he had left the room, forgetting to close it, and, sliding up the chimney like a man accustomed to those sort of gymnastic exercises, having effaced the very marks of his feet upon the floor, he commenced climbing the hollow tunnel, which afforded him the only means of escape left. At this precise time, the first gendarme Andrea had noticed walked upstairs, preceded by the commissary of police, and supported by the second gendarme who guarded the staircase, and was himself reinforced by the one stationed at the door. Andrea was indebted for this visit to the following circumstances:—At day break, the telegraphs were set at work in all directions; and almost immediately the authorities in every district had exerted their utmost endeavours to arrest the murderer of Caderousse. Compiègne, that royal residence and fortified town, is well furnished with authorities, gendarmes, and commissaries of police: they, therefore, commenced operations as soon as the telegraphic despatch arrived; and the Bell and Bottle being the first hotel in the town, they had naturally directed their first inquiries there. Now, besides the reports of the sentinels guarding the Hôtel de Ville, which is next door to the Bell and Bottle, it had been stated that a number of travellers had arrived there during the night. The sentinel, who was relieved at six o'clock in the morning, remembered perfectly that, just as he was taking his post a few minutes past four, a young man arrived on horseback, with a little boy before him. The young man, having dismissed the boy and horse, knocked at the door of the hotel, which was opened, and again closed after his entrance. This late arrival had attracted much suspicion, and the young man being no other than Andrea, the commissary and gendarme, who was a brigadier, directed their steps towards his room. They found the door ajar.

" Oh, oh! " said the brigadier, who thoroughly understood the trick, " a bad sign to find the door open! I would rather find it triply bolted."

And indeed the little note and pin upon the table confirmed, or rather supported, the sad truth. Andrea had fled. We say supported, because the brigadier was too experienced to yield to a single proof. He glanced round, looked in the bed, shook the curtains, opened the closets, and finally stopped at the chimney. Andrea had taken the precaution to leave no traces of his feet in the ashes, but still it was an outlet, and in this light was not to be passed over without serious investigation. The brigadier sent for some sticks and straw, and having filled the chimney with them, set a light to it. The fire crackled, and the smoke ascended like the dull vapour from a volcano; but still no prisoner fell down as they expected. The fact was, that

Andrea, at war with society ever since his youth, was quite as deep as a gendarme, even though he were advanced to the rank of brigadier, and, quite prepared for the fire, he had reached the roof, and was crouching down against the chimney pots. At one time he thought he was saved, for he heard the brigadier exclaim, in a loud voice, to the two gendarmes, " He is not here! " But venturing to peep, he perceived that the latter, instead of retiring, as might have been reasonably expected upon this announcement, were watching with increased attention. It was now his turn to look about him. The Hôtel de Ville, a massive building of the sixteenth century, was on his right. Anyone could descend from the openings in the tower, and examine every corner of the roof below; and Andrea expected momentarily to see the head of a gendarme appear at one of these openings. If once discovered, he knew he would be lost, for the roof afforded no chance of escape. He therefore resolved to descend, not through the same chimney by which he arrived, but by a similar one conducting to another room. He looked round for a chimney from which no smoke issued, and having reached it, he disappeared through the orifice without being seen by anyone. At the same minute, one of the little windows of the Hôtel de Ville was thrown open, and the head of a gendarme appeared. For an instant it remained motionless as one of the stone decorations of the building, then after a long sigh of disappointment, the head disappeared. The brigadier, calm and dignified as the law he represented, passed through the crowd, without answering the thousand questions addressed to him, and re-entered the hotel.

" Well? " asked the two gendarmes.

" Well, my boys," said the brigadier, " the brigand must really have escaped early this morning; but we will send to the Villers-Coterets and Noyon roads, and search the forest, when we shall catch him, no doubt."

The honourable functionary had scarcely expressed himself thus, in that intonation which is peculiar to brigadiers of the gendarmerie, when a loud scream, accompanied by the violent ringing of a bell, resounded through the court of the hotel.

" Ah! what is that? " cried the brigadier.

" Some traveller seems impatient," said the host. " What number was it that rang? "

" No. 3."

" Run, waiter! "

At this moment the screams and ringing were redoubled.

" Aha! " said the brigadier, stopping the servant, " the person who is ringing appears to want something more than a waiter;

we will attend upon him with a gendarme. Who occupies No. 3?"

"The little fellow who arrived last night in a post-chaise with his sister, and who asked for a double-bedded room."

The bell here rang for a third time, with another shriek of anguish.

"Follow me, M. le Commissaire!" said the brigadier; "tread in my steps."

"Wait an instant," said the host; "No. 3 has two staircases, an interior and an exterior."

"Good!" said the brigadier. "I will take charge of the interior. Are the carbines loaded?"

"Yes, brigadier."

"Well, you guard the exterior, and if he attempts to fly, fire upon him; he must be a great criminal from what the telegraph says."

The brigadier, followed by the commissary, disappeared by the interior staircase, accompanied by the noise which his assertions respecting Andrea had excited in the crowd. This is what had happened: Andrea had very cleverly managed to descend two-thirds of the chimney, but then his foot slipped, and notwithstanding his endeavours, he came into the room with more speed and noise than he intended. It would have signified little had the room been empty, but unfortunately, it was occupied. Two ladies, sleeping in one bed, were awakened by the noise, and fixing their eyes upon the spot whence the sound proceeded, they saw a man. One of these ladies, the fair one, uttered those terrible shrieks which resounded through the house; while the other, rushing to the bell-rope, rang with all her strength. Andrea, as we can see, was surrounded by misfortune.

"For pity's sake!" he cried, pale and bewildered, without seeing whom he was addressing,—"for pity's sake do not call assistance! Save me! I will not harm you."

"Andrea the murderer!" cried one of the ladies.

"Eugénie! Mademoiselle Danglars!" exclaimed Andrea, stupefied.

"Help, help!" cried Mademoiselle d'Armilly, taking the bell from her companion's hand, and ringing it yet more violently.

"Save me, I am pursued!" said Andrea, clasping his hands. "For pity, for mercy's sake, do not deliver me up!"

"It is too late; they are coming," said Eugénie.

"Well, conceal me somewhere; you can say you were needlessly alarmed; you can turn their suspicions, and save my life!"

The two ladies, pressing closely to one another, and drawing the bed-clothes tightly round them, remained silent to this supplicating voice; all their repugnance, all their fear, rose in their imaginations.

"Well! be it so," at length said Eugénie; "return by the same road you came, and we will say nothing about you, unhappy wretch."

"Here he is! here he is!" cried a voice in the landing-place; "here he is! I see him!"

The brigadier had put his eye to the keyhole, and had perceived Andrea standing and entreating. A violent blow from the butt-end of the musket burst open the lock, two more forced out the bolts, and the broken door fell in. Andrea ran to the other door, leading to the gallery, ready to rush out; but he was stopped short; and he stood with his body a little thrown back, pale, and with the useless knife in his clenched hand.

"Fly, then!" cried Mademoiselle d'Armilly, whose pity returned as her fears diminished; "fly!"

"Or kill yourself!" said Eugénie, in a tone which a Vestal in the circle would have used, while ordering the victorious gladiator to finish his vanquished adversary.

Andrea shuddered, and looked on the young girl with an expression which proved how little he understood such ferocious humour.

"Kill myself!" he cried, throwing down his knife; "why should I do so?"

"Why, you said," answered Mademoiselle Danglars, "that you would be condemned to die like the worst criminals."

"Bah!" said Cavalcanti, crossing his arms, "one has friends!"

The brigadier advanced to him, sword in hand.

"Come, come," said Andrea, "sheathe your sword, my fine fellow; there is no occasion to make such a fuss, since I yield myself;" and he held out his hands to be manacled.

The two girls looked with horror upon this horrid meta-morphosis, the man of the world shaking off his covering and appearing the galley-slave. Andrea turned towards them, and with an impertinent smile, asked:

"Have you any message for your father, Mademoiselle Danglars, for, in all probability, I shall return to Paris?"

Eugénie covered her face with her hands.

"Oh, oh!" said Andrea, "you need not be ashamed, even though you did post after me. Was I not nearly your husband?"

And with this raillery Andrea went out, leaving the two girls a prey to their own sufferings of shame and to the commentaries of the crowd. An hour after they stepped into their calèche, both dressed in female attire. The gate of the hotel had been closed to screen them from sight, but they were forced when the door was opened to pass through a throng of curious glances and whispering voices. Eugénie closed her eyes; but though she could not see she could hear, and the sneers of the crowd reached her in the carriage. The next day they stopped at the Hôtel de Flandre, at Brussels. The same evening Andrea was secured in the Conciergerie.

100

The Law

WE have seen how quietly Mademoiselle Danglars and Mademoiselle d'Armilly accomplished their transformation and flight; the fact being that everyone was too much occupied in his or her own affairs to think of theirs. We will leave the banker contemplating the enormous columns of his debt before the phantom of bankruptcy, and follow the baroness, who, after remaining for a moment as if crushed under the weight of the blow which had struck her, had gone to seek her usual adviser, Lucien Debray. The baroness had looked forward to this marriage as a means of ridding her of a guardianship which, over a girl of Eugénie's character, could not fail to be rather a troublesome undertaking; for in those tacit understandings which maintain the bond of family union, the mother is only really the mistress of her daughter upon the condition of continually representing herself to her as a model of wisdom and type of perfection. Now, Madame Danglars feared the penetration of Eugénie and the advice of Mademoiselle d'Armilly: she had frequently observed the contemptuous expression with which her daughter looked upon Debray,—an expression which seemed to imply that she understood all her mother's amorous and pecuniary relationships with the intimate secretary. Unfortunately in this world of ours, each person views things through a certain medium, which prevents his seeing them in the same light as others; and Madame Danglars, therefore, very much regretted that the marriage of Eugénie had not taken place, not only because the match was good, and likely to ensure the happiness of her child, but because it would also set her at liberty. She ran therefore to Debray's, who, after having, like the rest of Paris, witnessed the contract scene and the scandal attending it, had retired in haste to his club, where he was chatting with some friends upon the events, which served as a subject of conversation for three-fourths of that city, known as the capital of the world. At the precise time when Madame Danglars, dressed in black and concealed in a long veil, was ascending the stairs leading to the apartments of Debray, notwithstanding the assurances of the young man that his master was not at home, Debray was occupied in repelling the insinuations of a friend, who tried to persuade him that after the terrible scene which had just taken place he ought, as a friend of the family, to marry Mademoiselle Danglars and her two millions. Debray did not defend himself very warmly, for the idea had sometimes crossed his mind. Tea, play, and the conversation, which had become interesting during the discussion of such serious affairs, lasted till one o'clock in the morning.

Meanwhile Madame Danglars, veiled and fainting, awaited the return of Debray in the little green-room, seated between two baskets of flowers, which she had that morning sent, and which, it must be confessed, Debray had himself arranged and watered with so much care that his absence was half excused in the eyes of the poor woman. At forty minutes past eleven, Madame Danglars, tired of waiting, returned home. Women of a certain grade are like grisettes in one respect, they seldom return home after twelve o'clock. The baroness returned to the hotel with as much caution as Eugénie used in leaving it; she ran lightly upstairs, and with an aching heart entered her apartment, contiguous, as we know, to that of Eugénie. She was fearful of exciting any remark, and believed firmly in her daughter's innocence and fidelity to her paternal roof. She listened at Eugénie's door; then, hearing no sound, she tried to enter, but the bolts were drawn. Madame Danglars fancied that, fatigued with the terrible excitement of the evening, she had retired to her bed and slept. She called her lady's-maid and questioned her.

"Mademoiselle Eugénie," she said, " retired to her apartment with Mademoiselle d'Armilly; they then took tea together, after which they desired me to leave, saying they required me no longer." Since then the lady's-maid had been below, and, like everyone else, she thought the young ladies were in their own room; Madame Danglars, therefore, went to bed without a shadow of suspicion, and began to muse over the past events. In proportion as her ideas became clearer, so did occurrences at the scene of the contract increase in magnitude; it no longer appeared mere confusion; it was a tumult; it was no longer something distressing, but disgraceful. And then the baroness remembered that she had felt no pity for poor Mercédès, who had been afflicted with as severe a blow through her husband and son.

"Eugénie," she said to herself, "is lost, and so are we. The affair, as it will be reported, will cover us with shame; for in society, such as ours, satire inflicts a painful and incurable wound. How fortunate that Eugénie is possessed of that strange character which has so often made me tremble!" And her glance was turned towards heaven, where that mysterious Providence disposes all things; and out of a fault, nay, even a vice, sometimes produces a blessing. And then her thoughts, cleaving through space as a bird in the air, rested on Cavalcanti. This Andrea was a wretch, a robber, an assassin, and yet his manners indicated a sort of education, if not a complete one; he had been presented to the world with the appearance of an immense fortune, supported by an honourable name. How could she extricate herself from this labyrinth? To whom would she apply to help her out of this painful situation? Debray could but give her advice; she must apply to someone more powerful than he. The baroness then thought of M. de Villefort. It was M. de Villefort who had caused Cavalcanti to be arrested; it was M. de Villefort who had remorselessly brought misfortune into her family, as though they had been strangers. But, no; on reflection the procureur du roi was not a merciless man; and it was not the magistrate, slave to his duties, but the friend, the loyal friend, who, roughly but firmly, cut into the very core of the corruption; it was not the executioner, but the surgeon, who wished to withdraw the honour of Danglars from the ignominious association with the lost young man they had presented to the world as their son-in-law. From the moment that Villefort, the friend of Danglars, acted thus, no one could suppose that the banker had been previously acquainted with, or had lent himself to, any of the intrigues of Andrea. The conduct of Villefort, therefore, upon reflection, appeared to the baroness as if shaped for their mutual advantage. But the inflexibility of the procureur du roi should stop there: she would see him the next day, and if she could not make him fail in his duties as a magistrate, she would, at least, obtain all the indulgence he could allow. She would invoke the past, recall old recollections; M. de Villefort would stifle the affair. And after this reasoning she slept easily.

At nine o'clock next morning she rose, and without ringing for her maid, or giving the least sign of her existence, she dressed herself in the same simple style as on the previous night; then running downstairs, she left the hotel, walked to the Rue de Provence, called a *fiacre*, and drove to M. de Villefort's house. For the last month this wretched house had presented the gloomy appearance of a lazaretto infected with the plague. Some of the apartments were closed within and without; and the neighbours would say to each other in a low voice, " Shall we to-day see another bier leave the house of M. le Procureur du Roi? "

Madame Danglars involuntarily shuddered at the aspect of the desolate house; descending from the *fiacre*, she approached the door with trembling knees, and rang the bell. Three times did the bell ring with a dull, heavy sound, seeming to participate in the general sadness, before the concierge appeared and peeped through the door, which he opened just wide enough to allow his words to be heard. He saw a lady, a fashionable, elegantly dressed lady, and yet the door remained almost closed.

" Do you intend opening the door? " said the baroness.

" First, madame, who are you? "

" Who am I? You know me well enough."

" We no longer know anyone, madame."

" You must be mad, my friend," said the baroness.

" Where do you come from? "

" Oh, this is too much! "

" Madame, these are my orders; excuse me. Your name? "

" The Baroness Danglars; you have seen me twenty times."

" Possibly, madame. And now, what do you want? "

" Oh, how extraordinary! I shall complain to M. de Villefort of the impertinence of his servants."

" Madame, this is precaution, not impertinence; no one enters here without an order from M. d'Avrigny, or without speaking to M. le Procureur du Roi."

" Well, my business is with M. le Procureur du Roi."

" Is it pressing business? "

" You can imagine so, since I have not even brought my carriage out yet. But enough of this; here is my card; take it to your master."

" Madame will await my return? "

" Yes; go."

The concierge closed the door, leaving Madame Danglars in the street. She had not long to wait; directly afterwards the door was opened wide enough to admit her, and when she had passed through it was again shut. Without losing sight of her for an instant, the concierge took a whistle from his pocket as soon as they entered the court and sounded it. The valet-de-chambre appeared on the doorstep.

" You will excuse this poor fellow, madame," he said, as he preceded the baroness; " but his orders are precise, and M. de Villefort begged me to tell you he could not act otherwise than he had done."

The baroness ascended the steps; she felt herself strongly infected with the sadness which, as it were, seemed to enlarge the circle of her own, and still guided by the valet-de-chambre, who never lost sight of her for an instant, she was introduced to the study of the magistrate. Preoccupied as Madame Danglars had been with the object of her visit, the treatment she had received from these underlings appeared to her so insulting that she began by complaining of it. But Villefort, raising his head, bowed down by grief, looked up at her with so sad a smile that her complaints died upon her lips.

"Forgive my servants," he said, "for a terror I cannot blame them for; from being suspected they have become suspicious."

Madame Danglars had often heard of the terror to which the magistrate alluded, but without the evidence of her own eyesight she could never have believed the sentiment had been carried so far.

"You too, then, are unhappy?" she said.

"Yes, madame," replied the magistrate.

"Then you pity me?"

"Sincerely, madame."

"And you understand what brings me here?"

"You wish to speak to me about the circumstance which has just happened?"

"Yes, sir, a fearful misfortune."

"You mean a mischance."

"A mischance!" repeated the baroness.

"Alas, madame," said the procureur du roi, with his imperturbable calmness of manner, "I consider those alone misfortunes which are irreparable."

"And do you suppose this will be forgotten?"

"Everything will be forgotten, madame," said Villefort; "your daughter will be married to-morrow, if not to-day,—in a week, if not to-morrow. And I do not think you can regret the intended husband of your daughter."

Madame Danglars gazed on Villefort, stupefied to find him so almost insultingly calm.

"Am I come to a friend?" she asked, in a tone full of mournful dignity.

"You know that you are, madame," said Villefort, whose pale cheeks became slightly flushed as he gave her the assurance. And truly this assurance carried him back to different events to those now occupying the baroness and him.

"Well, then, be more affectionate, my dear Villefort," said the baroness. "Speak to me not as a magistrate, but as a friend;

and when I am in bitter anguish of spirit, do not tell me I ought to be gay."

Villefort bowed.

"When I hear misfortunes named, madame," he said, "I have within the last few months contracted the bad habit of thinking of my own, and then I cannot help drawing up an egotistical parallel in my mind. This is the reason that by the side of my misfortunes yours appear to me mere mischances; this is why my dreadful position makes yours appear enviable. But this annoys you; let us change the subject. You were saying, madame——"

"I came to ask you, my friend," said the baroness, "what will be done with this impostor."

"Impostor!" repeated Villefort; "certainly, madame, you appear to extenuate some cases and exaggerate others. Impostor, indeed!—M. Andrea Cavalcanti, or rather M. Benedetto, is nothing more nor less than an assassin."

"Sir, I do not deny the justice of your correction; but the more severely you arm yourself against that unfortunate, the more deeply will you strike our family. Come, forget him for a moment, and, instead of pursuing him, let him fly."

"You are too late, madame, the orders are issued."

"Well, should he be arrested—do you think they will arrest him?"

"I hope so."

"If they should arrest him (I know that sometimes prisons afford means of escape), will you leave him in prison?"

The procureur du roi shook his head.

"At least keep him there till my daughter be married."

"Impossible, madame: justice has its formalities."

"What! even for me?" said the baroness, half jesting, half in earnest.

"For all, even for myself among the rest," replied Villefort.

"Ah!" exclaimed the baroness, without expressing the ideas which the exclamation betrayed.

Villefort looked at her with that piercing glance which read the secrets of the heart.

"Yes, I know what you mean," he said; "you allude to those terrible rumours spread abroad in the world, that all those deaths which have kept me in mourning for the last three months, and from which Valentine has only escaped by a miracle, have not happened by natural means."

"I was not thinking of that," replied Madame Danglars quickly.

"Yes, you were thinking of it, and with justice. You could

not help thinking of it, and saying to yourself, ' You, who pursue crime so vindictively, answer now, Why are there unpunished crimes in your dwelling? ' "

The baroness became pale.

" You were saying this, were you not? "

" Well, I own it."

" I will answer you."

Villefort drew his arm-chair near to Madame Danglars; then, resting both hands upon his desk, he said, in a voice more hollow than usual:

" There are crimes which remain unpunished because the criminals are unknown, and we might strike the innocent instead of the guilty; but when the culprits are discovered " (Villefort here extended his hand towards a large crucifix placed opposite to his desk),—" when they are discovered, I swear to you, by all I hold most sacred, that whoever they may be, they shall die. Now, after the oath I have just taken, and which I will keep, madame, dare you ask for mercy for that wretch? "

" But, sir, are you sure he is as guilty as they say? "

" Listen, this is his description, ' Benedetto, condemned, at the age of sixteen, for five years to the galleys for forgery '; he promised well, as you see; first a runaway, then an assassin."

" And who is this wretch? "

" Who can tell?—a vagabond, a Corsican."

" Has no one owned him? "

" No one; his parents are unknown."

" But who was the man who brought him from Lucca? "

" Another rascal like himself, perhaps his accomplice."

The baroness clasped her hands.

" Villefort! " she exclaimed, in her softest and most captivating manner.

" For Heaven's sake, madame," said Villefort, with a firmness of expression not altogether free from harshness,—" for Heaven's sake, do not ask pardon of me for a guilty wretch. What am I? —the law. Has the law any eyes to witness your grief? Has the law ears to be melted by your sweet voice? Has the law a memory for all those soft recollections you endeavour to recall? No, madame, the law has commanded, and when it commands it strikes. You will tell me that I am a living being, and not a code; a man, and not a volume. Look at me, madame, look around me. Have mankind treated me as a brother? have they loved me? Have they spared me? Has anyone shown the mercy towards me that you now ask at my hands? No, madame, they struck me, always struck me! Woman! siren that you are, do you persist in fixing on me that fascinating eye, which reminds me that I ought to blush? Well, be it so, let me blush for the faults you know, and perhaps—perhaps for even more than those! But having sinned myself, it may be more deeply than others, I never rest till I have torn the disguises from my fellow-creatures, and found out their weaknesses. I have always found them; and more, I repeat with joy, with triumph, I have always found some proof of human perversity or error. Every criminal I condemn seems to me a living proof that I am not a hideous exception to the rest. Alas! alas! alas! all the world is wicked, let us therefore strike at wickedness!"

Villefort pronounced these last words with a feverish rage, which gave a ferocious eloquence to his words.

"But," said Madame Danglars, resolving to make a last effort, "this young man, though a murderer, is an orphan, abandoned by everybody."

"So much the worse, or rather so much the better; it has been so ordained that he may have none to weep his fate."

"But this is trampling on the weak, sir."

"The weakness of a murderer!"

"His dishonour reflects upon us."

"Is not death in my house?"

"Oh, sir," exclaimed the baroness, "you are without pity for others. Well, then, I tell you they will have no mercy on you!"

"Be it so!" said Villefort, raising his arms to heaven.

"At least delay the trial till the next assizes; we shall then have six months before us."

"No, madame," said Villefort; "instructions have been given; there are yet five days left; five days are more than I require. Do you not think that I also long for forgetfulness? While working night and day, I sometimes lose all recollection of the past, and then I experience the same sort of happiness I can imagine the dead to feel; still it is better than suffering."

"But, sir, he has fled; let him escape—inaction is a pardonable offence."

"I tell you it is too late; early this morning the telegraph was employed, and at this very minute——"

"Sir," said the valet-de-chambre, entering the room, "a dragoon has brought this despatch from the Minister of the Interior."

Villefort seized the letter, and hastily unsealed it. Madame Danglars trembled with fear; Villefort started with joy.

"Arrested!" he exclaimed; "he was taken at Compiègne, and all is over."

Madame Danglars rose from her seat pale and cold.

"Adieu, sir," she said.

"Adieu, madame," replied the procureur du roi, as in an almost joyful manner he conducted her to the door. Then, turning to his desk, he said, striking the letter with his right hand, "Come, I had a forgery, three robberies, and two incendiaries; I only wanted a murder, and here it is. It will be a splendid session!"

IOI

The Apparition

As the procureur du roi had told Madame Danglars, Valentine was not yet recovered. Bowed down with fatigue, she was indeed confined to her bed, and it was in her own room, and from the lips of Madame de Villefort, that she heard all the strange events we have related; we mean the flight of Eugénie and the arrest of Andrea Cavalcanti, or rather Benedetto, together with the accusation of murder pronounced against him. But Valentine was so weak that this recital scarcely produced the same effect it would have done had she been in her usual state of health. Indeed her brain was only the seat of vague ideas; and confused forms, mingled with strange fancies, alone presented themselves before her eyes. During the daytime Valentine's perceptions remained tolerably clear, owing to the constant presence of M. Noirtier, who caused himself to be carried to his granddaughter's room, and watched her with his paternal tenderness; Villefort also on his return from the Palais frequently passed an hour or two with his father and child. At six o'clock Villefort retired to his study, at eight M. d'Avrigny arrived himself, bringing the night draught prepared for the young girl, and then M. Noirtier was carried away. A nurse of the doctor's choice succeeded them, and never left till about ten or eleven o'clock, when Valentine was asleep. As she went downstairs she gave the keys of Valentine's room to M. de Villefort, so that no one could reach the sick-room excepting through that of Madame de Villefort and little Edward's. Every morning Morrel called on Noirtier to receive news of Valentine, and, extraordinary as it seemed, each day found him less uneasy. Certainly, though Valentine still laboured under dreadful nervous excitement, she was better, and moreover Monte Cristo had told him when, half distracted, he had rushed to his house, that if she was not dead in two hours she was saved. Now four days had elapsed, and Valentine still lived. The nervous excitement of which we speak pursued Valentine even in her sleep, or rather in that state of somnolence which succeeded her waking hours; it was then in the silence of night, in the dim light shed from the alabaster lamp on the chimney-piece, that she saw those shadows pass and repass, which hover over the bed of sickness, and fan the fever with their trembling wings. First she fancied she saw her stepmother threatening her, then Morrel stretched his arms towards her, sometimes mere strangers, like the Count of Monte Cristo, appeared to visit her; even the very furniture in these moments of delirium seemed to move; and this state lasted till about three o'clock in the morning, when a deep, heavy slumber overcame the young girl, from which she did not awake till morning. On the evening of the day on which Valentine had learnt of the flight of Eugénie and the arrest of Benedetto, Villefort having retired as well as Noirtier and D'Avrigny, her thoughts wandered in a confused maze, alternately reviewing her own situation, and the events she had just heard.

Eleven o'clock had struck. The nurse, having placed the beverage prepared by the doctor within reach of the patient, and locked the door, was listening with terror to the comments of the servants in the kitchen, and storing her memory with all the horrible stories which had for some months past amused the occupants of the ante-chambers in the house of the procureur du roi. Meanwhile an unexpected scene was passing in the room which had been so carefully locked.

Ten minutes had elapsed since the nurse had left; Valentine, who for the last hour had been suffering from the fever which returned nightly, incapable of controlling her ideas, was forced to yield to the excitement which exhausted itself in producing and reproducing a succession and recurrence of the same fancies and images. The night-lamp threw out countless rays, each resolving itself into some strange form to her disordered imagination, when suddenly, by its flickering light, Valentine thought she saw the door of her library, which was in the recess by the chimney-piece, open slowly, though she in vain listened for the sound of the hinges on which it turned. At any other time Valentine would have seized the silken bell-pull and summoned assistance, but nothing astonished her in her present situation. Her reason told her that all the visions she beheld were but the children of her imagination, and the conviction was strengthened by the fact that, in the morning, no traces remained of the nocturnal phantoms, who disappeared with the daylight. From behind the door a human figure appeared, but she was too familiar with such apparitions to be alarmed, and therefore, only stared, hoping to recognise Morrel. The figure advanced towards the bed, and appeared to listen with profound attention. At this moment a ray of light glanced across the face of the midnight visitor.

" It is not he! " she murmured, and waited, in the assurance of its being but a dream, for the man to disappear or assume some other form. Still she felt her pulse, and finding it throbbed violently, she remembered that the best method of dispelling such illusions was to drink, for a draught of the beverage prepared by the doctor to allay her fever seemed to cause a reaction of the brain, and, for a short time, she suffered less. Valentine therefore reached her hand towards the glass, but as soon as her trembling arm left the bed the apparition advanced more quickly towards her, and approached the young girl so closely, that she fancied she heard his breath, and felt the pressure of his hand. This time the illusion, or rather the reality, surpassed anything Valentine had before experienced; she began to believe herself really alive and awake, and the belief that her reason was this time not deceived made her shudder. The pressure she felt was evidently intended to arrest her arm, and she slowly withdrew it. Then the figure, from whom she could not detach her eyes, and who appeared more protecting than menacing, took the glass, and walking towards the night-light, held it up, as if to test its transparency. This did not seem sufficient; the man, or rather the phantom, for he trod so softly that no sound was heard, then poured out about a spoonful into the glass, and drank it. Valentine witnessed this scene with a sentiment of stupefaction. Every minute she had expected that it would vanish and give place to another vision; but the man, instead of dissolving like a shadow, again approached her, and said, in an agitated voice:

" Now you may drink."

Valentine shuddered. It was the first time one of these visions had ever addressed her in a living voice, and she was about to utter an exclamation.

The man placed his finger on her lips.

" The Count of Monte Cristo! " she murmured.

It was easy to see that no doubt now remained in the young girl's mind as to the reality of the scene; her eyes started with terror, her hands trembled, and she rapidly drew her bed-clothes closer to her. Still the presence of Monte Cristo at such an hour, his mysterious, fanciful, and extraordinary entrance into her room, through the wall, might well seem impossibilities to her shattered reason.

" Do not call anyone—do not be alarmed," said the count,—

" do not let a shade of suspicion or uneasiness remain in your breast; the man standing before you, Valentine (for this time it is no phantom), is nothing more than the tenderest father and the most respectful friend you could dream of."

Valentine could not reply; the voice which indicated the real presence of a being in the room alarmed her so much that she feared to utter a syllable; still the expression of her eyes seemed to inquire, " If your intentions are pure, why are you here? "

The count's marvellous sagacity understood all that was passing in the young girl's mind.

" Listen to me," he said, " or, rather, look upon me; look at my face, paler even than usual, and my eyes, red with weariness— for four days I have not closed them, for I have been constantly watching you, to protect and preserve you for Maximilian."

The blood mounted rapidly to the cheeks of Valentine, for the name just pronounced by the count dispelled all the fear with which his presence had inspired her.

" Maximilian! " she exclaimed, and so sweet did the sound appear to her, that she repeated it,—" Maximilian! has he then owned all to you? "

" Everything. He told me your life was his, and I have promised him you shall live."

" You have promised him that I shall live? '

" Yes."

" But, sir, you spoke of vigilance and protection. Are you a doctor? "

" Yes, the best you could have at the present time, believe me."

" But you say you have watched," said Valentine uneasily; " where have you been?—I have not seen you."

The count extended his hand towards the library. " I was hidden behind that door," he said, " which leads into the next house, which I have rented."

Valentine turned her eyes away, and, with an indignant expression of pride and modest fear, exclaimed:

" Sir, I think you have been guilty of an unparalleled intrusion, and that which you call protection is more resembling an insult."

" Valentine," he answered, " during my long watch over you, all I have observed has been what people visited you, what nourishment was prepared, and what beverage was served; then when the latter appeared dangerous to me, I entered, as I have now done, and substituted, in the place of the poison, a healthy draught; which, instead of producing the death intended, caused life to circulate in your veins."

" Poison! Death! " exclaimed Valentine, half believing herself under the influence of some feverish hallucination; " what are you saying, sir? "

" Hush, my child," said Monte Cristo, again placing his finger upon her lips; " I did say poison and death. But drink some of this "; and the count took a bottle from his pocket containing a red liquid, of which he poured a few drops into the glass.

" Drink this, and then take nothing more to-night."

Valentine stretched out her hand; but scarcely had she touched the glass than she drew back in fear. Monte Cristo took the glass, and drank half its contents, and then presented it to Valentine, who smiled, and swallowed the rest.

" Oh, yes," she exclaimed, " I recognise the flavour of my nocturnal beverage, which refreshed me so much, and seemed to ease my aching brain. Thank you, sir, thank you! "

" This is how you have lived during the last four nights, Valentine," said the count. " But, oh, how I passed that time! Oh, the wretched hours I have endured! the torture to which I have submitted when I saw the deadly poison poured into your glass, and how I trembled lest you would drink it before I could find time to throw it away! "

" Sir," said Valentine at the height of her terror, " you say you endured tortures when you saw the deadly poison poured into my glass; but if you saw this, you must also have seen the person who poured it? "

" Yes."

Valentine raised herself in bed, and drew over her chest, which appeared whiter than snow, the embroidered cambric, still moist with the cold dews of delirium, to which were now added those of terror.

" You saw the person? " repeated the young girl.

" Yes," repeated the count.

" That which you tell me is horrible, sir. You wish to make me believe something too dreadful. What! attempt to murder me in my father's house—in my room—on my bed of sickness? Oh, leave me, sir; you are tempting me; you make me doubt the goodness of Providence; it is impossible, it cannot be! "

" Are you the first that this hand has stricken? Have you not seen M. de Saint-Méran, Madame de Saint-Méran, Barrois, all fall? Would not M. Noirtier also have fallen a victim, had not the treatment he has been pursuing for the last three years neutralised the effects of the poison? "

" Oh heaven! " said Valentine; " is this the reason why grandpapa has made me share all his beverages during the last month? "

" And have they all tasted of a slightly bitter flavour, like that of dried orange-peel? "

" Oh, yes! oh, yes! "

" Then that explains all," said Monte Cristo. " Your grandfather knows, then, that a poisoner lives here; perhaps he even suspects the person. He has been fortifying you, his beloved child, against the fatal effects of the poison, which would have failed from the constant habit of imbibing it. But even this would have availed little against a more deadly medium of death employed four days ago, which is generally but too fatal."

" But who, then, is this assassin—this murderer? "

" Let me also ask you a question. Have you never seen anyone enter your room at night? "

" Oh, yes; I have frequently seen shadows pass close to me, approach, and disappear; but I took them for visions raised by my feverish imagination, and indeed, when you entered, I thought I was under the influence of delirium."

" Then you do not know who it is that attempts your life? "

" No," said Valentine; " who could desire my death? "

" You shall know it now, then," said Monte Cristo, listening.

" How do you mean? " said Valentine, looking terrified around.

" Because you are not feverish or delirious to-night, but thoroughly awake; midnight is striking, which is the hour murderers choose."

" Oh heavens! " exclaimed Valentine, wiping off the drops which ran down her forehead. Midnight struck slowly and sadly; every hour seemed to strike with leaden weight upon the heart of the poor girl.

" Valentine," said the count, " summon up all your courage; still the beatings of your heart; do not let a sound escape you, and feign to be asleep; then you will see."

Valentine seized the count's hand. " I think I hear a noise," she said; " leave me."

" Good-bye for the present," replied the count, walking upon tiptoe towards the library door, and smiling with an expression so sad and paternal, that the young girl's heart was filled with gratitude. Before closing the door he turned round once more, and said, " Not a movement,—not a word; let them think you asleep; or, perhaps, you may be killed before I have the power of helping you." And with this fearful injunction the count disappeared through the door, which noiselessly closed after him.

102

The Serpent

VALENTINE was alone; two other clocks, slower than that of Saint-Philippe du Roule, struck the hour of midnight from different situations; and, excepting the rumbling of a few carriages, all was silent. Then Valentine's attention was engrossed by the clock in her room, which marked the seconds. She began counting them, remarking that they were much slower than the beatings of her heart; and still she doubted,—the inoffensive Valentine could not imagine anyone desiring her death. Why should they? To what end? What had she done to excite the malice of an enemy? There was no fear of her falling asleep. One terrible idea pressed upon her mind, that someone existed in the world who had attempted to assassinate her, and who was about to endeavour to do so again. Supposing this person, wearied at the inefficiency of the poison, should, as Monte Cristo said, have recourse to steel!—What if the count should have no time to run to her rescue!—What if her last moments were approaching, and she would never again see Morrel! When this terrible chain of ideas presented itself, Valentine was nearly persuaded to ring the bell, and call for help. But through the door she fancied she saw the luminous eye of the count,—that eye which lived in her memory, and the recollection overwhelmed her with so much shame, that she asked herself whether any amount of gratitude could ever repay his dangerous and devoted friendship. Twenty minutes,—twenty tedious minutes, passed thus, then ten more, and at last the clock struck the half-hour. Just then the sound of finger-nails slightly grating against the door of the library informed Valentine that the count was still watching, and recommended her to do the same; at the same time, on the opposite side, that is towards Edward's room, Valentine fancied she heard the creaking of the floor; she listened attentively, holding her breath till she was nearly suffocated; the lock turned, and the door slowly opened. Valentine had raised herself upon her elbow, and had scarcely time to throw herself down on the bed and shade her eyes with her arm; then, trembling, agitated, and her heart beating with indescribable terror, she awaited the event. Someone approached the bed and drew back the curtains. Valentine summoned every effort, and breathed with that regular respiration which announces tranquil sleep.

"Valentine!" said a low voice.

Still silent: Valentine had promised not to wake. Then everything remained still, excepting that Valentine heard the almost noiseless sound of some liquid being poured into the glass she had just emptied. Then she ventured to open her eyelids, and glance over her extended arm. She saw a female in a white dressing-gown pouring a liquor from a phial into her glass. During this short time Valentine must have held her breath, or moved in some slight degree, for the woman, disturbed, stopped and leaned over the bed, in order the better to ascertain whether Valentine slept: it was Madame de Villefort.

On recognising her stepmother, Valentine could not repress a shudder, which caused a vibration in the bed. Madame de Villefort instantly stepped back close to the wall, and there, shaded by the bed-curtains, she silently and attentively watched the slightest movement of Valentine. The latter recollected the terrible caution of Monte Cristo; she fancied that the hand not holding the phial clasped a long sharp knife. Then collecting all her remaining strength, she forced herself to close her eyes; but this simple operation upon the most delicate organs of our frame, generally so easy to accomplish, became almost impossible at this moment, so much did curiosity struggle to retain the eyelid open and learn the truth.

Madame de Villefort, however, reassured by the silence, which was alone disturbed by the regular breathing of Valentine, again extended her hand, and, half hidden by the curtains, succeeded in emptying the contents of the phial into the glass. Then she retired so gently that Valentine did not know she had left the room. She only witnessed the withdrawal of the arm—that fair round arm of a woman, but twenty-five years old, and who yet spread death around her.

It is impossible to describe the sensations experienced by Valentine during the minute and a half Madame de Villefort remained in the room. The grating against the library door roused the young girl from the state of stupor in which she was plunged, and which almost amounted to insensibility. She raised her head with an effort. The noiseless door again turned on its hinges, and the Count of Monte Cristo reappeared.

"Well," said he, "do you still doubt?"

"Oh!" murmured the young girl.

"Have you seen?"

"Alas!"

"Did you recognise?"

Valentine groaned. " Oh, yes," she said, " I saw, but I cannot believe! "

" Would you rather die, then, and cause Maximilian's death? "

" Oh," repeated the young girl, almost bewildered, " can I not leave the house?—can I not escape? "

" Valentine, the hand which now threatens you will pursue you everywhere; your servants will be seduced with gold, and death will be offered to you disguised in every shape. You will find it in the water you drink from the spring, in the fruit you pluck from the tree."

" But did you not say that my kind grandfather's precaution had neutralised the poison? "

" Yes, but not against a strong dose; the poison will be changed and the quantity increased."

He took the glass and raised it to his lips.

" It is already done," he said; " brucine is no longer employed, but a simple narcotic! I can recognise the flavour of the alcohol in which it has been dissolved. If you had taken that which Madame de Villefort has poured into your glass, Valentine, Valentine, you would have been lost! "

" But," exclaimed the young girl, " why am I thus pursued? "

" How! are you so kind—so good—so unsuspicious of ill, that you cannot understand, Valentine? "

" No, I have never injured her."

" But you are rich, Valentine; you have 200,000 livres a year, and you prevent her son from enjoying these 200,000 livres."

" How so? The fortune is not her gift, but is inherited from my relations! "

" Certainly; and this is why M. and Madame de Saint-Méran have died; this is why M. Noirtier was sentenced the day he made you his heir; this is why you, in turn, are to die: it is because your father would inherit your property, and your brother, his only son, succeed to his."

" Edward? Poor child! are all these crimes committed on his account? "

" Ah! then you at length understand? "

" Heaven grant that this may not be visited upon him! "

" Valentine, you are an angel! "

" But why is my grandfather allowed to live? "

" It was considered, that you dead, the fortune would naturally revert to your brother, unless he were disinherited; and besides, the crime appearing useless, it would be folly to commit it."

" And is it possible that this frightful combination of crimes has been invented by a woman? "

"Do you recollect in the harbour of the Hôtel des Postes, at Perusa, seeing a man in a brown cloak, whom your stepmother was questioning upon *aqua tofana*? Well, ever since then, the infernal project has been ripening in her brain."

"Ah, then, indeed, sir," said the sweet girl, bathed in tears, "I see that I am condemned to die!"

"No, Valentine, for I have foreseen all their plots; no, your enemy is conquered since we know her, and you will live, Valentine—live to be happy yourself, and to confer happiness upon a noble heart; but to insure this you must rely on me."

"Command me, sir,—what am I to do?"

"You must blindly take what I give you."

"Alas, were it only for my own sake, I should prefer to die!"

"You must not confide in anyone—not even in your father."

"My father is not engaged in this fearful plot, is he, sir?" asked Valentine, clasping her hands.

"No; and yet your father, a man accustomed to judicial accusations, ought to have known that all these deaths have not happened naturally; it is he who should have watched over you —he should have occupied my place—he should have emptied that glass—he should have risen against the assassin! Spectre against spectre!" he murmured in a low voice, as he concluded his sentence.

"Sir," said Valentine, "I will do all I can to live, for there are two beings whose existence depends upon mine—my grandfather and Maximilian."

"I will watch over them as I have over you."

"Well, sir, do as you will with me;" and then she added, in a low voice, "Oh heavens! what will befall me?"

"Whatever may happen, Valentine, do not be alarmed; though you suffer; though you lose sight, hearing, consciousness, fear nothing; though you should awake and be ignorant where you are, still do not fear; even though you should find yourself in a sepulchral vault or coffin. Reassure yourself, then, and reflect: 'At this moment a friend, a father, who lives for my happiness and that of Maximilian, watches over me!'"

"Alas! alas! what a fearful extremity!"

"Valentine, would you rather denounce your stepmother?"

"I would rather die a hundred times!—oh, yes, die!"

"No, you will not die; but will you promise me, whatever happens, that you will not complain, but hope?"

"I will think of Maximilian!"

"My child, believe in my devotion to you as you believe in the goodness of Providence and the love of Maximilian."

Then he drew from his waistcoat-pocket the little emerald box, raised the golden lid, and took from it a pastille, about the size of a pea, which he placed in her hand. She took it, and looked attentively on the count; there was an expression on the face of her intrepid protector which commanded her veneration. She evidently interrogated him by her look.

" Yes," said he.

Valentine carried the pastille to her mouth, and swallowed it.

" And now, my dear child, adieu for the present. I will try and gain a little sleep, for you are saved."

" Go," said Valentine; " whatever happens I promise you not to fear."

Monte Cristo for some time kept his eyes fixed on the young girl, who gradually fell asleep, yielding to the effects of the narcotic the count had given her. Then he took the glass, emptied three parts of the contents in the fireplace, that it might be supposed Valentine had taken it, and replaced it on the table; then he disappeared, after throwing a farewell glance on Valentine, who slept with the confidence and innocence of an angel.

103

Valentine

THE night-light continued to burn on the chimney-piece, exhausting the last drops of oil which floated on the surface of the water; a dull and dismal light was shed over the bed-clothes and curtains surrounding the young girl. All noise in the streets had ceased, and the silence was frightful. It was then that the door of Edward's room opened, and a head we have before noticed appeared in the glass opposite; it was Madame de Villefort, who came to witness the effects of the draught. She stopped in the doorway, listened for a moment to the flickering of the lamp, the only sound in that deserted room, and then advanced to the table, to see if Valentine's glass were empty. It was still about a quarter full, as we before stated. Madame de Villefort emptied the contents into the ashes, which she disturbed, that they might the more readily absorb the liquid; then she carefully rinsed the glass, and wiping it with her handkerchief, replaced it on the table. If anyone could have looked into the room just then, he would have noticed the hesitation with which Madame de Villefort approached the bed and looked fixedly on Valentine. The dim light, the profound silence, and the gloomy thoughts inspired by the hour, and still more by her own conscience, all combined to produce a sensation of fear; the poisoner was terrified to contemplate her own work. At length she rallied, drew aside the curtain, and leaning over the pillow, gazed intently on Valentine. The young girl no longer breathed, no breath issued through the half-closed teeth; the white lips no longer quivered; the eyes appeared floating in a bluish vapour, and the long black lashes rested on a cheek white as wax. Madame de Villefort gazed upon the face so expressive even in its stillness; then she ventured to raise the coverlet, and press her hand upon the young girl's heart. It was cold and motionless. She only felt the pulsation in her own fingers, and withdrew her hand with a shudder. One arm was hanging out of the bed, that beautiful arm which seemed moulded by a sculptor; but the other appeared slightly distorted by convulsion, and the hand, so delicately formed, was resting with stiff and outstretched fingers on the framework of the bed. The nails, too, were turning blue. Madame de Villefort had no longer any doubt; all was over; she had consummated the last terrible work she had to accomplish. There was no more to do in the room, so the poisoner retired stealthily, as though fearing to hear the sound of her own footsteps; but as she withdrew she still held aside the curtain, absorbed in the irresistible attraction always offered by the picture of death, so long as it remains merely mysterious without exciting disgust. Just then the lamp again flickered; the noise startled Madame de Villefort, who shuddered and dropped the curtain. Immediately afterwards the light expired and the room was plunged in terrible obscurity, while the clock at that minute struck half-past four. Overpowered with agitation the poisoner succeeded in groping her way to the door, and reached her room in an agony of fear. The darkness lasted two hours longer; then by degrees a cold light crept through the Venetian blinds, until at length it revealed the objects in the room. About this time the nurse's cough was heard on the stairs, and the woman entered the room with a cup in her hand. To the tender eye of a father or a lover, the first glance would have sufficed to convince them of Valentine's state; but to this hireling, Valentine only appeared to sleep.

"Good!" she exclaimed, approaching the table, "she has taken part of her draught; the glass is three-quarters empty."

Then she went to the fireplace and lit the fire, and although she had but just left the bed, she could not resist the temptation offered by Valentine's sleep, so she threw herself into an arm-chair to snatch a little more rest. The clock striking eight awoke her. Astonished at the prolonged sleep of the patient, and frightened to see that the arm was still hanging out of bed, she advanced towards Valentine, and for the first time noticed the white lips. She tried to replace the arm, but it moved with a frightful stiffness which could not deceive a sick-nurse. She screamed aloud: then running to the door exclaimed:

"Help, help!"

"What do you mean?" asked M. d'Avrigny, at the foot of the stairs, it being the hour he usually visited her.

"What do you mean?" asked Villefort, rushing from his room. "Doctor, do you hear them call for help?"

"Yes, yes; let us hasten up; it was in Valentine's room."

But before the doctor and the father could reach the room, the servants who were on the same floor had entered, and seeing Valentine pale and motionless on her bed, they lifted up their hands towards heaven and stood transfixed, as though struck by lightning.

"Call Madame de Villefort! wake Madame de Villefort!"

cried the procureur du roi from the door of his chamber, which it seemed he scarcely dared to leave.

But instead of obeying him, the servants stood watching M. d'Avrigny, who ran to Valentine, and raised her in his arms.

" What! this one, too! " he exclaimed. " Oh, when will this cease? "

Villefort rushed into the room.

" What are you saying, doctor? " he exclaimed, raising his hand to heaven.

" I say that Valentine is dead! " replied d'Avrigny, in a voice terrible in its solemn calmness.

M. de Villefort staggered and buried his head in the bed. On the exclamation of the doctor and the cry of the father, the servants all fled with muttered imprecations; they were heard running down the stairs and through the long passages, then there was a rush in the court, afterwards all was still; they had, one and all, deserted from the accursed house. Just then, Madame de Villefort, in the act of slipping on her dressing-gown, threw aside the drapery, and for a moment remained still, as though interrogating the occupants of the room, while she endeavoured to call up some rebellious tears. On a sudden she stepped, or rather bounded, with outstretched arms towards the table. She saw D'Avrigny curiously examining the glass, which she felt certain of having emptied during the night. It was now a third full, just as it was when she threw the contents into the ashes. The spectre of Valentine rising before the poisoner would have alarmed her less. It was, indeed, the same colour as the draught she had poured into the glass, and which Valentine had drunk; it was indeed the poison, which could not deceive M. d'Avrigny, which he now examined so closely; it was doubtless a miracle from heaven, that, notwithstanding her precautions, there should be some trace, some proof remaining to denounce the crime. While Madame de Villefort remained rooted to the spot like a statue of terror, and Villefort, with his head hidden in the bed-clothes, saw nothing around him, D'Avrigny approached the window, that he might the better examine the contents of the glass, and dipping the tip of his finger in, tasted it.

" Ah," he exclaimed, " it is no longer brucine that is used; let me see what it is! "

Then he ran to one of the cupboards in Valentine's room, which had been transformed into a medicine-closet, and taking from its silver case a small bottle of nitric acid, dropped a little of it into the liquor, which immediately changed to a blood-red colour.

" Ah! " exclaimed D'Avrigny, in a voice in which the horror of a judge unveiling the truth was mixed with the delight of a student discovering a problem. Madame de Villefort was overpowered; her eyes first flashed and then swam; she staggered towards the door and disappeared. Directly afterwards the distant sound of a heavy weight falling on the ground was heard, but no one paid any attention to it; the nurse was engaged in watching the chemical analysis, and Villefort was still absorbed in grief. M. d'Avrigny alone had followed Madame de Villefort with his eyes, and watched her precipitate retreat. He lifted up the drapery over the entrance to Edward's room, and his eye reaching as far as Madame de Villefort's apartment, he beheld her extended lifeless on the floor.

" Go to the assistance of Madame de Villefort," he said to the nurse. " Madame de Villefort is ill."

" But Mademoiselle de Villefort——" stammered the nurse.

" Mademoiselle de Villefort no longer requires help," said D'Avrigny, " since she is dead."

" Dead!—dead! " groaned forth Villefort, in a paroxysm of grief which was the more terrible from the novelty of the sensation in the iron heart of that man.

" Dead! " repeated a third voice. " Who said Valentine was dead? "

The two men turned round, and saw Morrel standing at the door, pale and terror-stricken.

This is what had happened. At the usual time, Morrel had presented himself at the little door leading to Noirtier's room. Contrary to custom, the door was open, and, having no occasion to ring, he entered. He waited for a moment in the hall, and called for a servant to conduct him to M. Noirtier; but no one answered, the servants having, as we know, deserted the house. Morrel had no particular reason for uneasiness; Monte Cristo had promised him that Valentine should live, and, until then, he had always fulfilled his word. Every night the count had given him news, which was the next morning confirmed by Noirtier. Still, this extraordinary silence appeared strange to him, and he called a second and a third time; still no answer. Then he determined to go up.

Noirtier's room was open, like all the rest. The first thing he saw was the old man sitting in his arm-chair in his usual place; but his eyes expressed an internal fright, which was confirmed by the pallor which overspread his features.

" How are you, sir? " asked Morrel, with a sickness of heart.

" Well," answered the old man, by closing his eyes; but his appearance manifested increasing uneasiness.

"You are thoughtful, sir," continued Morrel; "you want something; shall I call one of the servants?"

"Yes," replied Noirtier.

Morrel pulled the bell, but, though he nearly broke the cord, no one answered. He turned towards Noirtier; the pallor and anguish expressed on his countenance momentarily increased.

"Oh," exclaimed Morrel, "why do they not come? Is anyone ill in the house?"

The eyes of Noirtier seemed as though they would start from their sockets.

"What is the matter? You alarm me. Valentine? Valentine?"

"Yes, yes," sighed Noirtier.

Maximilian tried to speak, but he could articulate nothing; he staggered, and supported himself against the wainscot. Then he pointed to the door.

"Yes, yes, yes," continued the old man.

Maximilian rushed up the little staircase, while Noirtier's eyes seemed to say:

"Quicker, quicker!"

In a minute the young man darted through several rooms, till, at length, he reached Valentine's. There was no occasion to push the door, it was wide open. A sob was the only sound he heard. He saw, as though in a mist, a black figure kneeling, and buried in a confused mass of white drapery. A terrible fear transfixed him. It was then he heard a voice exclaim, "Valentine is dead!" and another voice which, like an echo, repeated:

"Dead!—dead!"

104

Maximilian

Villefort rose, half ashamed of being surprised in such a paroxysm of grief. The terrible office he had held for twenty-five years had succeeded in making him more or less than man. His glance, at first wandering, fixed itself upon Morrel.

" Who are you, sir," he asked, " that forget that this is not the manner to enter a house stricken with death? Go, sir, go! "

But Morrel remained motionless; he could not detach his eyes from that disordered bed, and the pale corpse of the young girl who was lying on it.

" Go!—do you hear? " said Villefort, while D'Avrigny advanced to lead Morrel out. Maximilian stared for a moment at the corpse, gazed all round the room, then upon the two men; he opened his mouth to speak, but finding it impossible to give utterance to the innumerable ideas that occupied his brain, he went out, thrusting his hands through his hair in such a manner, that Villefort and D'Avrigny, for a moment diverted from the engrossing topic, exchanged glances, which seemed to convey:

" He is mad! "

But, in less than five minutes, the staircase groaned beneath an extraordinary weight. Morrel was seen carrying, with super-human strength, the arm-chair containing Noirtier, upstairs. When he reached the landing, he placed the arm-chair on the floor and rapidly rolled it into Valentine's room. This could only have been accomplished by means of unnatural strength supplied by powerful excitement. But the most fearful spectacle was Noirtier being pushed towards the bed, his face expressing all his meaning, and his eyes supplying the want of every other faculty.

That pale face and flaming glance appeared to Villefort like a frightful apparition. Each time he had been brought into contact with his father, something terrible had happened.

" See what they have done! " cried Morrel, with one hand leaning on the back of the chair, and the other extended towards Valentine. " See, my father, see! "

Villefort drew back and looked with astonishment on the young man, who, almost a stranger to him, called Noirtier his father. At this moment the whole soul of the old man seemed centred in his eyes, which became bloodshot; the veins of the throat swelled; his cheeks and temples became purple, as though he were struck with epilepsy; nothing was wanting to complete this but the utterance of a cry. And the cry issued from his pores, if we may thus speak—a cry, frightful in its silence. D'Avrigny rushed towards the old man and made him inhale a powerful restorative.

"Sir," cried Morrel, seizing the moist hand of the paralytic, "they ask me who I am, and what right I have to be here. Oh, you know it; tell them, tell them!"

And the young man's voice was choked by sobs.

As for the old man, his chest heaved with his panting respiration. One could have thought he was undergoing the agonies preceding death. At length, happier than the young man, who sobbed without weeping, tears glistened in the eyes of Noirtier.

"Tell them," said Morrel, in a hoarse voice,—"tell them I am her betrothed. Tell them she was my beloved, my noble girl, my only blessing in the world. Tell them—oh, tell them, that corpse belongs to me!"

The young man, who presented the dreadful spectacle of a strong frame crushed, fell heavily on his knees before the bed, which his fingers grasped with convulsive energy. D'Avrigny, unable to bear the sight of this touching emotion, turned away; and Villefort, without seeking any further explanation, and attracted towards him by the irresistible magnetism which draws us towards those who have loved the people for whom we mourn, extended his hand towards the young man. But Morrel saw nothing; he had grasped the hand of Valentine, and, unable to weep, vented his agony in gnawing the sheets. For some time nothing was heard in that chamber but sobs, exclamations, and prayers. At length Villefort, the most composed of all, spoke.

"Sir," said he to Maximilian, "you say you loved Valentine, that you were betrothed to her. I knew nothing of this engagement, of this love, yet I, her father, forgive you, for I see your grief is real and deep; and besides, my own sorrow is too great for anger to find a place in my heart. But you see the angel whom you hoped for has left this earth—she has nothing more to do with the adoration of men. Take a last farewell, sir, of her sad remains; take the hand you expected to possess once more within your own, and then separate yourself from her for ever. Valentine now alone requires the priest who will bless her."

"You are mistaken, sir," exclaimed Morrel, raising himself on one knee, his heart pierced by a more acute pang than any he had yet felt; "you are mistaken; Valentine, dying as she has, not only requires a priest, but an avenger. *You*, M. de Villefort, send for the priest, *I* will be the avenger."

" What do you mean, sir? " asked Villefort, trembling at the new idea inspired by the delirium of Morrel.

" I tell you, sir, that two persons exist in you; the father has mourned sufficiently, now let the procureur du roi fulfil his office."

The eyes of Noirtier glistened, and D'Avrigny approached.

" Gentlemen," said Morrel, reading all that passed· through the minds of the witnesses to the scene, " I know what I am saying, and you know as well as I do what I am about to say— Valentine has been assassinated! "

Villefort hung his head; D'Avrigny approached nearer; and Noirtier expressed " Yes " with his eyes.

" Now, sir," continued Morrel, " in these days no one can disappear by violent means without some inquiries being made as to the cause of her disappearance, even were she not a young beautiful, and adorable creature like Valentine. M. le Procureur du Roi," said Morrel, with increasing vehemence, " no mercy is allowed; I denounce the crime; it is your place to seek the assassin."

The young man's implacable eyes interrogated Villefort, who, on his side, glanced from Noirtier to D'Avrigny. But instead of finding sympathy in the eyes of the doctor and his father, he only saw an expression as inflexible as that of Maximilian.

" Yes," indicated the old man.

" Assuredly," said D'Avrigny.

" Sir," said Villefort, striving to struggle against this triple force and his own emotion,—" sir, you are deceived; no one commits crimes here. I am stricken by fate. It is horrible, indeed, but no one assassinates."

The eyes of Noirtier lighted up. with rage, and D'Avrigny prepared to speak. Morrel, however, extended his arm, and commanded silence.

" And I say that murders *are* committed here," said Morrel, whose voice, though lower in tone, lost none of its terrible distinctness; " I tell you that this is the fourth victim within the last four months. I tell you, Valentine's life was attempted by poison four days ago, though she escaped owing to the precautions of M. Noirtier! I tell you that the dose has been doubled, the poison changed, and that this time it has succeeded. I tell you that you know these things as well as I do, since this gentleman has forewarned you, both as a doctor and a friend."

" Oh, you rave, sir! " exclaimed Villefort, in vain endeavouring to escape the net in which he was taken.

" I rave? " said Morrel; " well, then, I appeal to M. d'Avrigny himself. Ask him, sir, if he recollects some words he uttered in the garden of this hotel on the night of Madame de Saint-Méran's death. You thought yourselves alone, and talked about that tragical death, and the fatality you mentioned then is the same as that which has caused the murder of Valentine."

Villefort and D'Avrigny exchanged looks.

" Yes, yes," continued Morrel, " recall the scene, for the words you thought were only given to silence and solitude fell into my ears. Certainly, after witnessing the culpable indolence manifested by M. de Villefort towards his own relations, I ought to have denounced him to the authorities; then I should not have been an accomplice to thy death, as I now am, sweet, beloved Valentine: but the accomplice shall become the avenger. This fourth murder is apparent to all, and if thy father abandon thee, Valentine, it is I, and I swear it, that shall pursue the assassin."

And this time, as though nature had at last taken compassion on the vigorous frame, nearly bursting with its own strength, the words of Morrel were stifled in his throat; his breast heaved; the tears, so long rebellious, gushed from his eyes; and he threw himself, weeping, on his knees, by the side of the bed.

Then D'Avrigny spoke.

" And I too," he exclaimed, in a low voice. " I unite with M. Morrel in demanding justice for crime; my blood boils at the idea of having encouraged a murderer by my cowardly concession! "

" Oh, merciful heavens! " murmured Villefort.

Morrel raised his head, and reading the eyes of the old man, which gleamed with unnatural lustre,—

" Stay," he said, " M. Noirtier wishes to speak."

" Yes," indicated Noirtier, with an expression the more terrible, from all his faculties being centred in his glance.

" Do you know the assassin? " asked Morrel.

" Yes," replied Noirtier.

" And will you direct us? " exclaimed the young man. " Listen, M. d'Avrigny, listen! "

Noirtier looked upon Morrel with one of those melancholy smiles which had so often made Valentine happy, and thus fixed his attention. Then having riveted the eyes of his interlocutor on his own, he glanced towards the door.

" Do you wish me to leave? " said Morrel sadly.

" Yes," replied Noirtier.

" Alas, alas! sir, have pity on me! "

The old man's eyes remained fixed on the door.

" May I at least, return? " asked Morrel.

"Yes."

"Must I leave alone?"

"No."

"Who am I to take with me?—M. le Procureur du Roi?"

"No."

"The doctor?"

"Yes."

"You wish to remain alone with M. de Villefort?"

"Yes."

"But can he understand you?"

"Yes."

"Oh," said Villefort, inexpressibly delighted to think the inquiries were to be made *tête-à-tête*, "oh, be satisfied, I can understand my father."

D'Avrigny took the young man's arm, and led him out of the room. A more than death-like silence then reigned in the house. At the end of a quarter of an hour a faltering footstep was heard, and Villefort appeared at the door of the apartment where D'Avrigny and Morrel had been staying, one absorbed in meditation, the other in grief.

"You can come!" he said, and led them back to Noirtier.

Morrel looked attentively on Villefort. His face was livid, large drops rolled down his face; and in his fingers he held the fragments of a pen which he had torn to atoms.

"Gentlemen," he said in a hoarse voice, "give me your word of honour that this horrible secret shall for ever remain buried amongst ourselves!"

The two men drew back.

"I entreat you——" continued Villefort.

"But," said Morrel, "the culprit—the murderer—the assassin."

"Do not alarm yourself, sir, justice will be done," said Villefort. "My father has revealed the culprit's name; my father thirsts for revenge as much as you do, yet even he conjures you as I do to keep this secret. Do you not, father?"

"Yes," resolutely replied Noirtier.

Morrel suffered an exclamation of horror and surprise to escape him.

"Oh, sir," said Villefort, arresting Maximilian by the arm, "if my father, the inflexible man, makes this request, it is because he knows, be assured, that Valentine will be terribly avenged. Is it not so, father?"

The old man made a sign in the affirmative. Villefort continued:

" He knows me, and I have pledged my word to him. Rest assured, gentlemen, that within three days, in a less time than justice would demand, the revenge I shall have taken for the murder of my child will be such as to make the boldest heart tremble; " and as he spoke these words he ground his teeth, and grasped the old man's senseless hand.

" Will this promise be fulfilled, M. Noirtier? " asked Morrel, while D'Avrigny looked inquiringly.

" Yes," replied Noirtier, with an expression of sinister joy.

" Swear then," said Villefort, joining the hands of Morrel and D'Avrigny, " swear that you will spare the honour of my house, and leave me to avenge my child."

D'Avrigny turned round and uttered a very feeble " Yes "; but Morrel, disengaging his hand, rushed to the bed, and after having pressed the cold lips of Valentine with his own, hurriedly left, uttering a long deep groan of despair and anguish.

We have before stated that all the servants had fled. M. de Villefort was, therefore, obliged to request M. d'Avrigny to superintend all those arrangements consequent upon a death in a large city, more especially a death under such suspicious circumstances. It was something terrible to witness the silent agony, the mute despair of Noirtier, whose tears silently rolled down his cheeks. Villefort retired to his study, and D'Avrigny left to summon the doctor of the mayoralty, whose office it is to examine bodies after decease, and who is expressively named " the doctor of the dead." M. Noirtier could not be persuaded to quit his grandchild. At the end of a quarter of an hour M. d'Avrigny returned with his associate. The district doctor approached the corpse with the indifference of a man accustomed to spend half his time amongst the dead; he then lifted the sheet which was placed over the face, and just unclosed the lips.

" Alas! " said D'Avrigny, " she is indeed dead, poor child! You can leave."

" Yes," answered the doctor laconically, dropping the sheet he had raised.

Noirtier uttered a kind of hoarse, rattling sound; the old man's eye sparkled, and the good doctor understood that he wished to behold his child. He therefore approached the bed, and while his companion was dipping the fingers with which he had touched the lips of the corpse in chloride of lime, he uncovered that calm and pale face which looked like that of a sleeping angel. A tear, which appeared in the old man's eye, expressed his thanks to the doctor. The doctor of the dead then laid his *procès-verbal* on the corner of the table, and having executed his office, was conducted out by D'Avrigny. Villefort met them at the door of his study; having in a few words thanked the district doctor, he returned to D'Avrigny and said:

" And now the priest! "

" Is there any particular priest you wish to pray with Valentine? " asked D'Avrigny.

" No," said Villefort; " fetch the nearest."

" The nearest," said the district doctor, " is a good Italian abbé, who lives next door to you. Shall I call on him as I pass? "

" D'Avrigny," said Villefort, " be so kind, I beseech you, as to accompany this gentleman. Here is the key of the door, so that you can go in and out as you please; you will bring the priest with you, and will oblige me by introducing him into my child's room."

" Do you wish to see him? "

" I only wish to be alone. You will excuse me, will you not? A priest can understand a father's grief." And M. de Villefort, giving the key to D'Avrigny, again bade farewell to the strange doctor, and retired to his study, where he began to work. For some temperaments work is a remedy for all afflictions.

As the doctors entered the street, they saw a man in a cassock standing on the threshold of the next door.

" This is the abbé of whom I spoke," said the doctor to D'Avrigny.

D'Avrigny accosted the priest.

" Sir," he said, " are you disposed to confer a great obligation on an unhappy father who has just lost his daughter? I mean M. de Villefort, the procureur du roi."

" The servants who fled from the house informed me of the death of the young girl. I also know that her name is Valentine, and I have already prayed for her."

" Thank you, sir," said D'Avrigny; " since you have commenced your sacred office, deign to continue it. Come and watch by the dead, and all the wretched family will be grateful to you."

" I am going, sir, and I do not hesitate to say that no prayers will be more fervent than mine."

D'Avrigny took the priest's hand, and without meeting Villefort, who was engaged in his study, they reached Valentine's room, which on the following night was to be occupied by the undertakers. On entering the room, Noirtier's eyes met those of the abbé, and no doubt he read some particular expression in them, for he remained in the room. D'Avrigny recommended the attention of the priest to the living as well as to the dead, and the abbé promised to devote his prayers to Valentine and his attentions to Noirtier. In order, doubtless, that he might not be disturbed while fulfilling his sacred mission, the priest, as soon as D'Avrigny departed, rose, and not only bolted the door through which the doctor had just left, but also that leading to Madame de Villefort's room.

105

Danglars' Signature

THE next morning rose dull and cloudy. During the night the undertakers had executed their melancholy office and folded the corpse in the winding-sheet, which, whatever may be said about the equality of death, is at least a last proof of the luxury so pleasing in life. During the evening two men, engaged for the purpose, had carried Noirtier from Valentine's room into his own, and, contrary to all expectation, there was no difficulty in withdrawing him from his child. The Abbé Busoni had watched till daylight, and then left without calling any one. D'Avrigny returned about eight o'clock in the morning; he met Villefort on his way to Noirtier's room and accompanied him to see how the old man had slept. They found him in the large arm-chair, which served him for a bed, enjoying a calm, nay, almost a smiling sleep. They both stood in amazement at the door.

" See," said D'Avrigny to Villefort, " nature knows how to alleviate the deepest sorrow. No one can say M. Noirtier did not love his child, and yet he sleeps."

" Yes, you are right," replied Villefort, surprised; " he sleeps indeed! And this is the more strange, since the least contradiction keeps him awake all night."

" Grief has stunned him," replied D'Avrigny, and they both returned thoughtfully to the study of the procureur du roi.

" See, I have not slept," said Villefort, showing his undisturbed bed; " grief does not stun me. I have not been in bed for two nights; but then look at my desk; see what I have written during these two days and nights, I have filled those papers and have made out the accusation against the assassin Benedetto. Oh, work! work! my passion, my joy, my delight! it is for thee to alleviate my sorrows! " and he convulsively grasped the hand of D'Avrigny.

" Do you require my services now? " asked D'Avrigny.

"No," said Villefort, " only return again at eleven o'clock; at twelve the—the, oh, heavens! my poor, poor child! " And the procureur du roi, again becoming a man, lifted up his eyes and groaned.

" Shall you be present in the reception-room? "

" No; I have a cousin who has undertaken this sad office. I shall work, doctor—when I work I forget everything." And, indeed, no sooner had the doctor left the room, than he was again absorbed in study. On the doorstep D'Avrigny met the cousin whom Villefort had mentioned. He was punctual, dressed in black, with crape around his hat, and presented himself at his cousin's with a face made up for the occasion, and which he could alter as might be required.

At twelve o'clock the mourning-coaches rolled into the paved court, and the Rue du Faubourg Saint-Honoré was filled with a crowd of idlers, equally pleased to witness the festivities of the mourning of the rich, and who rush with the same avidity to a funeral procession as to the marriage of a duchess.

Gradually the reception-room filled, and some of our old friends made their appearance,—we mean Debray, Château-Renaud and Beauchamp, accompanied by all the leading men of the day at the bar, in literature, or the army, for M. de Villefort moved in the first Parisian circles, less owing to his social position than to his personal merit. Those who were acquainted soon formed into little groups. One of these was composed of Debray, Château-Renaud, and Beauchamp.

" Poor girl! " said Debray, like the rest, paying an involuntary tribute to the sad event,—" poor girl! so young! so rich! so beautiful! Could you have imagined this scene, Château-Renaud, when we saw her, at the most three weeks ago, about to sign that contract? "

" Indeed, no! " said Château-Renaud.

" Did you know her? "

" I spoke to her once or twice at Madame de Morcerf's, amongst the rest; she appeared to me charming, though rather melancholy. Where is her stepmother? Do you know? "

" She is spending the day with the wife of the worthy gentleman who is receiving us."

" Doctor d'Avrigny, who attends my mother," said Château-Renaud, " declares that the procureur du roi is in despair. But whom are you seeking, Debray? "

" I am seeking the Count of Monte Cristo," said the young man.

" I met him on the Boulevard, on my road here," said Beauchamp. " I think he is about to leave Paris; he was going to his banker."

" His banker? Danglars is his banker, is he not? " asked Château-Renaud of Debray.

" I believe so," replied the secretary, with slight uneasiness. " But Monte Cristo is not the only one I miss here; I do not see Morrel."

" Morrel! Do they know him? " asked Château-Renaud. " I think he has only been introduced to Madame de Villefort."

" Still he ought to have been here," said Debray. " I wonder what will be talked about to-night; this funeral is the news of the day. But hush! here comes our minister of justice; he will feel obliged to make some little speech to the cousin." And the three young men drew near to listen.

Beauchamp told the truth when he said that on his road to the funeral he had met Monte Cristo, who was directing his steps towards the Rue de la Chaussée d'Antin to M. Danglars. The banker saw the carriage of the count enter the courtyard, and advanced to meet him with a sad though affable smile.

" Well," said he, extending his hand to Monte Cristo, " I suppose you have come to sympathise with me, for indeed misfortune has taken possession of my house. When I perceived you, I was just saying that a number of my acquaintances have been very unfortunate this year. For example, look at the puritanical procureur du roi, who has just lost his daughter. And in fact nearly all his family in so singular a manner; Morcerf dishonoured and dead; and then myself, covered with ridicule through the villainy of Benedetto; besides——"

" Besides what? " asked the count.

" Alas! do you not know? "

" What new calamity? "

" My daughter Eugénie has left us! "

" Good heavens! what are you telling me? "

" The truth, my dear count. Oh, how happy you must be in not having either wife or children! "

" Do you think so? And so Mademoiselle Danglars——"

" She could not endure the insult offered to us by that wretch, so she asked permission to travel."

" And is she gone? "

" The other night she left."

" With Madame Danglars? "

" No, with a relation. But still, we have quite lost our dear Eugénie; for I doubt whether her pride will ever allow her to return to France."

" Still, baron," said Monte Cristo, " family griefs, or indeed any other affliction which would crush a man whose child was his only treasure, are endurable to a millionaire. Philosophers may well say, and practical men will always support the opinion, that money mitigates many trials; and if you admit the efficacy of this sovereign balm, you ought to be very easily consoled; you, the king of finance, who form the intersecting point of all the powers in Europe, nay, the world! "

Danglars smiled at the good-natured pleasantry of the count.

" That reminds me," he said, " that when you entered, I was on the point of signing five little bonds; I have already signed two, will you allow me to do the same to the others? "

" Pray do so."

There was a moment's silence, during which the noise of the banker's pen was alone heard, while Monte Cristo examined the gilt mouldings of the ceiling.

" Are they Spanish, Haytian, or Neapolitan bonds? " said Monte Cristo.

" Neither," said Danglars, smiling; " they are bonds on the Bank of France, payable to the bearer. Stay," he added, " count, you who may be called the emperor, if I claim the title of king of finance, have you many pieces of paper of this size, each worth a million? "

The count took the papers which Danglars had so proudly presented to him, into his hands, and read:

" To the Governor of the Bank. Please to pay to my order, from the fund deposited by me, the sum of a million.

" BARON DANGLARS."

" One, two, three, four, five," said Monte Cristo; " five millions! why, what a Crœsus you are! "

" This is how I transact business! " said Danglars.

" It is really wonderful," said the count; " above all, if, as I suppose, it is payable at sight."

" It is, indeed," said Danglars.

" It is a fine thing to have such credit; really, it is only in France these things are done. Five millions on five little scraps of paper!—it must be seen to be believed."

" Well, you shall be convinced: take my clerk to the bank, and you will see him leave it with an order on the Treasury for the same sum."

" No," said Monte Cristo, folding the five notes, " most decidedly not; the thing is so curious, I will make the experiment myself. I am credited on you for six millions. I have drawn nine hundred thousand francs, you therefore still owe me five millions and a hundred thousand francs. I will take the five scraps of paper that I now hold as bonds, with your signature alone, and here is a receipt in full for the six millions between us. I had prepared it beforehand, for I am much in want of money to-day."

And Monte Cristo placed the bonds in his pocket with one hand, while with the other he held out the receipt to Danglars.

If a thunderbolt had fallen at the banker's feet, he could not have experienced greater terror.

"What!" he stammered, "do you mean to take that money? Excuse me, excuse me, but I owe this money to the hospital,—a deposit which I promised to pay this morning."

"Oh! well, then," said Monte-Cristo, "I am not particular about these five notes, pay me in a different form; I wished, from curiosity, to take these, that I might be able to say, that without any advice or preparation the house of Danglars had paid me five millions without a minute's delay: it would have been so remarkable. But here are your bonds; pay me differently;" and he held the bonds towards Danglars, who seized them like a vulture extending its claws to withhold the food attempted to be wrested from it. Suddenly he rallied, made a violent effort to restrain himself, and then a smile gradually widened the features of his disturbed countenance.

"Certainly," he said, "your receipt is money."

"Oh dear, yes; and if you were at Rome, the house of Thomson and French would make no more difficulty about paying the money on my receipt than you have just done."

"Pardon me, count, pardon me."

"Then I may keep this money?"

"Yes," said Danglars, while the perspiration started from the roots of his hair. "Yes, keep it—keep it."

Monte Cristo replaced the notes in his pocket with that indescribable expression which seemed to say, "Come, reflect; if you repent there is still time."

"No," said Danglars, "no, decidedly no; keep my signatures. But you know none are so formal as bankers in transacting business; I intended this money for the hospitals, and I seemed to be robbing them if I did not pay them with these precise bonds. How absurd! as if one crown were not as good as another. Excuse me"; and he began to laugh loudly, but nervously.

"Certainly, I excuse you," said Monte Cristo graciously, "and pocket them." And he placed the bonds in his pocket-book.

"But," said Danglars, "there is still a sum of one hundred thousand francs?"

"Oh, a mere nothing," said Monte Cristo. "The balance would come to about that sum; but keep it, and we shall be quits."

"Count," said Danglars, "are you speaking seriously?"

"I never joke with bankers," said Monte Cristo, in a freezing manner, which repelled impertinence; and he turned towards the door, just as the valet-de-chambre announced:

"M. de Boville, receiver-general of the hospitals."

"*Ma foi!*" said Monte Cristo; "I think I arrived just in time to obtain your signatures, or they would have been disputed with me."

Danglars again became pale, and hastened to conduct the count out. Monte Cristo exchanged a ceremonious bow with M. de Boville, who was standing in the waiting-room, and who was introduced into Danglars' room as soon as the count had left. The count's sad face was illumined by a faint smile, as he noticed the portfolio which the receiver-general held in his hand. At the door he found his carriage, and was immediately driven to the bank. Meanwhile Danglars, repressing all emotion, advanced to meet the receiver-general.

"Good-morning, creditor!" said he; "for I wager anything it is the creditor who visits me."

"You are right, baron," answered M. de Boville; "the hospitals present themselves to you through me: the widows and orphans depute me to receive alms to the amount of five millions from you."

"And yet they say orphans are to be pitied," said Danglars, wishing to prolong the jest. "Poor things?"

"Here I am in their name," said M. de Boville; "but did you receive my letter yesterday?"

"Yes."

"I have brought my receipt."

"My dear M. de Boville, your widows and orphans must oblige me by waiting twenty-four hours, since M. de Monte Cristo, whom you just saw leaving here—you did see him, I think?"

"Yes; well?"

"Well, M. de Monte Cristo has just carried off their five millions."

"How so?"

"The count had unlimited credit upon me; a credit opened by Thomson and French of Rome: he came to demand five millions at once, which I paid him with cheques on the bank; my funds are deposited there; and you can understand that if I draw out ten millions on the same day, it will appear rather strange to the governor. Two days will be a different thing," said Danglars, smiling.

" Come," said Boville, with a tone of entire incredulity; " five millions to that gentleman who just left, and who bowed to me as though he knew me! "

" Perhaps he knows you, though you do not know him; M. de Monte Cristo knows everybody."

" Five millions! "

" Here is his receipt. Believe your own eyes."

M. de Boville took the paper Danglars presented him, and read:

" Received of Baron Danglars the sum of five millions one hundred thousand francs, which will be repaid whenever he pleases by the house of Thomson and French, of Rome."

" It is really true," said De Boville.

" Do you know the house of Thomson and French? "

" Yes, I once had business to transact with it to the amount of 200,000 francs; but, since then, I have not heard it mentioned."

" It is one of the best houses in Europe," said Danglars, carelessly throwing down the receipt on his desk.

" And he had five millions in your hands alone! Why this Count of Monte Cristo must be a nabob? "

" Indeed I do not know what he is: he has three unlimited credits; one on me, one on Rothschild, one on Lafitte; and, you see," he added carelessly, " he has given me the preference, by leaving a balance of 100,000 francs."

M. de Boville manifested signs of extraordinary admiration.

" I must visit him," he said, " and obtain some pious grant from him."

" Oh, you may make sure of him; his charities alone amount to 20,000 francs per month."

" It is magnificent! I will set before him the example of Madame de Morcerf and her son."

" What example? "

" They gave all their fortune to the hospitals."

" For what reason? "

" Because they would not spend money so guiltily acquired."

" And what are they to live upon? "

" The mother retires into the country, and the son enters the army."

" And how much did they possess? "

" Oh, not much! from twelve to thirteen hundred thousand francs. But to return to our millions."

"Certainly," said Danglars, in the most natural tone in the world. "Are you, then, pressed for this money?"

"Yes; for the examination of our cash takes place to-morrow."

"To-morrow!—Why did you not tell me so before? Why, it is as good as a century! At what hour does the examination take place?"

"At two o'clock."

"Send at twelve," said Danglars, smiling.

M. de Boville said nothing, but nodded his head, and took up the portfolio.

"Now I think of it, you can do better," said Danglars.

"How do you mean?"

"The receipt of M. de Monte Cristo is as good as money; take it to Rothschild's or Lafitte's, and they will take it of you directly."

"What, though payable at Rome?"

"Certainly; it will only cost you a discount of five or six thousand francs."

The receiver started back.

"*Ma foi!*" he said, "I prefer waiting till to-morrow. What a proposition!"

"I thought, perhaps," said Danglars, with supreme impertipence, "that you had a deficiency to make up?"

"Indeed!" said the receiver.

"And if that were the case, it would be worth while to make some sacrifice."

"Thank you; no, sir."

"Then it will be to-morrow?"

"Yes; I shall come myself."

"Be it so; it will afford me the pleasure of seeing you again."

They shook hands.

"By the way," said M. de Boville, "are you not going to the funeral of poor Mademoiselle de Villefort, which I met on my road here?"

"No," said the banker; "I have appeared rather ridiculous since that affair of Benedetto, so I remain in the background."

"Everybody pities you, sir; and, above all, Mademoiselle Danglars!"

"Poor Eugénie!" said Danglars; "do you know she is going to embrace a religious life?"

"No."

"Alas, it is unhappily but too true. The day after the event, she decided on leaving Paris with a nun of her acquaintance; they are gone to seek a very strict convent in Italy or Spain."

"Oh, it is terrible!" and M. de Boville retired with this

exclamation, after expressing acute sympathy with the father. But he had scarcely left before Danglars, with an energy of action those can alone understand who have seen Robert Macaire represented by Frédéric,* exclaimed:

" Fool!!! "

Then, enclosing Monte Cristo's receipt in a little pocket-book, he added:

" Yes, come at twelve o'clock; I shall then be far away."

Then he double-locked his door, emptied all his drawers, collected about fifty thousand francs in bank-notes, burned several papers, left others exposed to view, and then commenced writing a letter which he addressed:—

" To Madame la Baronne Danglars."

" I will place it on her table myself to-night," he murmured.

Then taking a passport from his drawer, he said:

" Good! it is available for two months longer."

106

The Cemetery of Père-la-Chaise

M. DE BOVILLE had indeed met the funeral procession which conducted Valentine to her last home on earth. The weather was dull and stormy, a cold wind shook the few remaining yellow leaves from the boughs of the trees, and scattered them amongst the crowd which filled the Boulevards. M. de Villefort, a true Parisian, considered the cemetery of Père-la-Chaise alone worthy of receiving the mortal remains of a Parisian family. He had therefore purchased a vault, which was quickly occupied by members of his family. On the front of the monument was inscribed: " The families of Saint-Méran and Villefort," for such had been the last wish expressed by poor Renée, Valentine's mother. The pompous procession therefore wended its way towards Père-la-Chaise from the Faubourg Saint-Honoré. More than fifty private carriages followed the twenty mourning-coaches, and behind them more than five hundred persons joined the procession on foot.

These last consisted of all the young people, whom Valentine's death had struck like a thunderbolt; and who, notwithstanding the raw chilliness of the season, could not refrain from paying a last tribute to the memory of the beautiful, chaste, and adorable girl, thus cut off in the flower of her youth. As they left Paris, an equipage with four horses, at full speed, was seen to draw up suddenly; it contained Monte Cristo. The count left the carriage and mingled in the crowd who followed on foot. Château-Renaud perceived him, and immediately alighting from his coupé, joined him. The count looked attentively through every opening in the crowd; he was evidently watching for someone, but his search ended in disappointment.

" Where is Morrel? " he asked; " do either of these gentlemen know where he is? "

" We have already asked that question," said Château-Renaud, " for none of us have seen him."

The count was silent, but continued to gaze around him.

At length they arrived at the cemetery. The piercing eye of Monte Cristo glanced through clusters of bushes and trees, and was soon relieved from all anxiety, for he saw a shadow glide between the yew-trees, and Monte Cristo recognised him whom he sought. This shadow passed rapidly behind the tomb of Abelard and Héloïse,* and placed itself close to the horses' heads belonging to the hearse, and, following the undertaker's men, arrived with them at the spot appointed for the burial. Each person's attention was occupied. Monte Cristo saw nothing but the shadow, which no one else observed. Twice the count left the ranks to see whether the object of his interest had any concealed weapon beneath his clothes. When the procession stopped, this shadow was recognised as Morrel, who, with his coat buttoned up to his throat, his face livid, and convulsively crushing his hat between his fingers, leaned against a tree, situated on an elevation commanding the mausoleum, so that none of the funeral details could escape his observation. Everything was conducted in the usual manner. Monte Cristo heard and saw nothing, or rather he only saw Morrel, whose calmness had a frightful effect on those who knew what was passing in his heart.

" See," said Beauchamp, pointing out Morrel to Debray. " What is he doing up there? " And they called Château-Renaud's attention to him.

" How pale he is! " said Château-Renaud, shuddering.

" He is cold! " said Debray.

" Not at all," said Château-Renaud slowly; " I think he is violently agitated. He is very susceptible."

" Bah! " said Debray; " he scarcely knew Mademoiselle de Villefort; you said so yourself."

" True. Still I remember he danced three times with her at Madame de Morcerf's. Do you recollect that ball, count, where you produced such an effect? "

" No, I do not," replied Monte Cristo, without even knowing

of what or to whom he was speaking; so much was he occupied in watching Morrel, who was holding his breath with emotion. "The discourse is over; farewell, gentlemen," said the count.

And he disappeared without anyone seeing whither he went. The funeral being over, the guests returned to Paris. Château-Renaud looked for a moment for Morrel; but while watching the departure of the count, Morrel had quitted his post, and Château-Renaud failing in his search, joined Debray and Beauchamp. Monte Cristo concealed himself behind a large tomb, and waited the arrival of Morrel, who, by degrees, approached the tomb now abandoned by spectators and workmen. Morrel threw a glance around, but before it reached the spot occupied by Monte Cristo, the latter had advanced yet nearer, still unperceived. The young man knelt down. The count, with outstretched neck, and glaring eyes, stood in an attitude ready to pounce upon Morrel upon the first occasion. Morrel bent his head till it touched the stone, then clutching the grating with both hands, he murmured:

" Oh, Valentine! "

The count's heart was pierced by the utterance of these two words; he stepped forward, and touching the young man's shoulder, said:

" I was looking for you, my friend."

Monte Cristo expected a burst of passion, but he was deceived, for Morrel, turning round, said with calmness:

" You see, I was praying."

The scrutinising glance of the count searched the young man from head to foot. He then seemed more easy.

" Shall I drive you back to Paris? " he asked.

" No, thank you."

" Do you wish anything? "

" Leave me to pray."

The count withdrew without opposition, but it was only to place himself in a situation where he could watch every movement of Morrel, who at length rose, brushed the dust from his knees, and turned towards Paris, without once looking back. He walked slowly down the Rue de la Roguette. The count, dismissing his carriage, followed him about a hundred paces behind. Maximilian crossed the canal, and entered the Rue Meslay by the Boulevards. Five minutes after the door had been closed on Morrel's entrance, it was again opened for the count. Julie was at the entrance of the garden, where she was attentively watching Penelon, who, entering with zeal into his profession of a gardener, was very busy grafting some Bengal roses.

"Ah, count!" she exclaimed, with the delight manifested by every member of the family whenever he visited the Rue Meslay.

"Maximilian has just returned, has he not, madame?" asked the count.

"Yes, I think I saw him pass; but pray, call Emmanuel."

"Excuse me, madame, but I must go up to Maximilian's room this instant," replied Monte Cristo. "I have something of the greatest importance to tell him."

"Go, then," she said, with a charming smile which accompanied him until he had disappeared.

Monte Cristo soon ran up the staircase conducting from the ground-floor to Maximilian's room; when he reached the landing he listened attentively, but all was still. Like many old houses occupied by a single family, the room door was panelled with glass. But it was locked, Maximilian was shut in, and it was impossible to see what was passing in the room, owing to a red curtain being drawn before the glass. The count's anxiety was manifested by a bright colour, which seldom appeared on the face of that impassible man.

"What shall I do?" he uttered, and reflected for a moment, "shall I ring? No, the sound of a bell, announcing a visitor, will but accelerate the resolution of one in Maximilian's situation, and then the bell would be followed by a louder noise."

Monte Cristo trembled from head to foot, and as if his determination had been taken with the rapidity of lightning, he struck one of the panes of glass with his elbow; the glass was shivered to atoms, then withdrawing the curtain, he saw Morrel, who had been writing at his desk, bound from his seat at the noise of the broken window.

"I beg a thousand pardons!" said the count; "there is nothing the matter, but I slipped down and broke one of your panes of glass with my elbow. Since it is open, I will take advantage of it to enter your room; do not disturb yourself—do not disturb yourself!"

And passing his hand through the broken glass, the count opened the door. Morrel, evidently discomposed, came to meet Monte Cristo, less with the intention of receiving him than to exclude his entry.

"Ma foi!" said Monte Cristo, rubbing his elbow, "it's all your servant's fault; your stairs are so polished, it is like walking on glass."

"Are you hurt, sir?" coldly asked Morrel.

"I believe not. But what are you about there? You were writing."

" I? "

" Your fingers are stained with ink."

" Ah, true, I was writing. I do sometimes, soldier though I am."

Monte Cristo advanced into the room; Maximilian was obliged to let him pass, but he followed him.

" You were writing? " said Monte Cristo, with a searching look.

" I have already had the honour of telling you I was," said Morrel.

The count looked around him.

" Your pistols are beside your desk," said Monte Cristo, pointing with his finger to the pistols on the table.

" I am on the point of starting on a journey," replied Morrel disdainfully.

" My friend! " exclaimed Monte Cristo, in a tone of exquisite sweetness.

" Sir? "

" My friend, my dear Maximilian, do not make a hasty resolution, I entreat you."

" I make a hasty resolution? " said Morrel, shrugging his shoulders; " is there anything extraordinary in a journey? "

" Maximilian," said the count, " let us both lay aside the mask we have assumed. You no more deceive me with that false calmness than I impose upon you with my frivolous solicitude. You can understand, can you not, that to have acted as I have done, to have broken those windows, to have intruded on the solicitude of a friend—you can understand, that to have done all this I must have been actuated by real uneasiness, or rather by a terrible conviction. Morrel, you are going to destroy yourself! "

" Indeed, count," said Morrel, shuddering; " what has put this into your head? "

" I tell you that you are about to destroy yourself," continued the count, " and here is the proof of what I say; " and approaching the desk he removed the sheet of paper which Morrel had placed over the letter he had begun, and took the latter in his hands.

Morrel rushed forward to tear it from him. But Monte Cristo, perceiving his intention, seized his wrist with his iron grasp.

" You wish to destroy yourself," said the count; " you have written it."

" Well," said Morrel, changing his expression of calmness for one of violence; " well, and if I do intend to turn this pistol against myself, who shall prevent me? who will dare prevent me? All my hopes are blighted, my heart is broken, my life a burden, everything around me is sad and mournful; earth has become distasteful to me, and human voices distract me. It is a mercy to let me die, for if I live I shall lose my reason and become mad. When, sir, I tell you all this with tears of heartfelt anguish, can you reply that I am wrong, can you prevent my putting an end to my miserable existence? Tell me, sir, could you have the courage to do so? "

" Yes, Morrel," said Monte Cristo, with a calmness which contrasted strangely with the young man's excitement; " yes, I would do so."

" You! " exclaimed Morrel, with increasing anger and reproach; " you, who have deceived me with false hopes, who have cheered and soothed me with vain promises, when I might, if not have saved her, at least have seen her die in my arms! you, who pretend to understand everything, even the hidden sources of knowledge! you, who enact the part of guardian angel upon earth, and could not even find an antidote to a poison administered to a young girl! Ah, sir, indeed you would inspire me with pity, were you not hateful in my eyes."

" Morrel——"

" Yes; you tell me to lay aside the mask, and I will do so! Be satisfied! When you spoke to me at the cemetery, I answered you, my heart was softened; when you arrived here, I allowed you to enter. But since you abuse my confidence, since you have devised a new torture after I thought I had exhausted them all, then, Count of Monte Cristo, my pretended benefactor,—then, Count of Monte Cristo, the universal guardian, be satisfied, you shall witness the death of your friend; " and Morrel, with a maniacal laugh, again rushed towards the pistols."

" And I again repeat, you shall not commit suicide."

" Prevent me, then! " replied Morrel, with another struggle, which, like the first, failed in releasing him from the count's iron grasp.

" I will prevent you."

" And who are you, then, that arrogate to yourself this tyrannical right over free and rational beings? "

" Who am I? " repeated Monte Cristo. " Listen; I am the only man in the world having the right to say to you,— ' Morrel, your father's son shall not die to-day '; " and Monte Cristo, with an expression of majesty and sublimity, advanced with his arms folded towards the young man, who, involuntarily overcome by the command of this man, recoiled a step.

" Why do you mention my father? " stammered he; " why do you mingle a recollection of him with the affairs of to-day? "

" Because I am he who saved your father's life when he wished to destroy himself, as you do to-day,—because I am the man who sent the purse to your young sister, and the *Pharaon* to old Morrel, —because I am the Edmond Dantès who nursed you, a child, on my knees."

Morrel made another step back, staggering, breathless, crushed; then all his strength gave way, and he fell prostrate at the feet of Monte Cristo. Then his admirable nature underwent a complete and sudden revulsion; he rose, bounded out of the room, and rushed to the stairs, exclaiming energetically:

" Julie! Julie! Emmanuel! Emmanuel! "

Monte Cristo endeavoured also to leave, but Maximilian would have died rather than relax his hold of the handle of the door, which he closed upon the count. Julie, Emmanuel, and some of the servants, ran up in alarm on hearing the cries of Maximilian. Morrel seized their hands, and opening the door, exclaimed in a voice choked with sobs:

" On your knees! on your knees! he is our benefactor! the saviour of our father! He is——"

He would have added " Edmond Dantès," but the count seized his arm and prevented him. Julie threw herself into the arms of the count; Emmanuel embraced him as a guardian angel; Morrel again fell on his knees, and struck the ground with his forehead. Then the iron-hearted man felt his heart swell in his breast; a flame seemed to rush from his throat to his eyes, he bent his head and wept. For a while, nothing was heard in the room but a succession of sobs, while the incense from their grateful hearts mounted to heaven. Julie had scarcely recovered from her deep emotion when she rushed out of the room, descended to the next floor, ran into the drawing-room with childlike joy, and raised the crystal globe which covered the purse given by the unknown of the Allées de Meillan. Meanwhile, Emmanuel, in a broken voice, said to the count:

" Oh, count, how could you, hearing us so often speak of our unknown benefactor, seeing us pay such homage of gratitude and adoration to his memory, how could you continue so long without discovering yourself to us? Oh, it was cruel to us, and —dare I say it?—to you also."

" Listen, my friend," said the count—" I may call you so, since we have really been friends for the last eleven years; the discovery of this secret has been occasioned by a great event which you must never know. I wished to bury it during my whole life in my own bosom, but your brother, Maximilian, wrested it from me by a violence he repents of now, I am sure." Then turning round, and seeing that Morrel, still on his knees, had thrown himself into an arm-chair, he added in a low voice, pressing Emmanuel's hand significantly:

" Watch over him."

" Why so? " asked the young man, surprised.

" I cannot explain myself; but watch over him."

Emmanuel looked round the room and caught sight of the pistols. His eyes rested on the arms, and he pointed to them. Monte Cristo bent his head. Emmanuel went towards the pistols.

" Leave them," said Monte Cristo. Then walking towards Morrel, he took his hand; the tumultuous agitation of the young man was succeeded by a profound stupor. Julie returned, holding in her hands the silken purse, while tears of joy rolled down her cheeks, like dew-drops on the rose.

" Here is the relic," she said; " do not think it will be less dear to us now we are acquainted with our benefactor! "

" My child," said Monte Cristo, colouring, " allow me to take back that purse? Since you now know my face, I wish to be remembered alone through the affection I hope you will grant me."

" Oh! " said Julie, pressing the purse to her heart; " no, no, I beseech you do not take it; for some unhappy day you will leave us: will you not? "

" You have guessed rightly, madame," replied Monte Cristo, smiling; " in a week I shall have left this country, where so many persons who merit the vengeance of Heaven lived happily, while my father perished of hunger and grief."

While announcing his departure, the count fixed his eyes on Morrel, and remarked that the words, " I shall have left this country," had failed to rouse him from his lethargy. He then saw that he must make another struggle against the grief of his friend, and taking the hands of Emmanuel and Julie, which he pressed within his own, he said, with the mild authority of a father:

" My kind friends, leave me alone with Maximilian."

Julie saw the means offered of carrying off her precious relic, which Monte Cristo had forgotten. She drew her husband to the door.

" Let us leave them," she said.

The count was alone with Morrel, who remained motionless as a statue.

" Come," said Monte Cristo, touching his shoulder with his finger, " are you a man again, Maximilian? "

" Yes; for I begin to suffer again."

The count frowned, apparently in gloomy hesitation.

" Maximilian, Maximilian," he said, " the ideas you yield to are unworthy of a Christian."

" Oh, do not fear, my friend," said Morrel, raising his head, and smiling with a sweet expression on the count. " I shall no longer attempt my life."

" Then we are to have no more pistols, no more arms? "

" No, I have found a better remedy for my grief than either a bullet or knife."

" Poor fellow!—what is it? "

" My grief will kill me of itself."

" My friend," said Monte Cristo, with an expression of melancholy equal to his own, " listen to me; one day, in a moment of despair like yours, since it led to a similar resolution, I, like you, wished to kill myself: one day, your father, equally desperate, wished to kill himself too. If anyone had said to your father at the moment he raised the pistol to his head—if anyone had told me, when in my prison I pushed back the food I had not tasted for three days—if anyone had said to either of us then, ' Live! the day will come when you will be happy, and will bless life; no matter whose \ ice had spoken, we should have heard him with the smile of doubt, or the anguish of incredulity; and yet how many times has your father blessed life while embracing you! how often have I myself——"

" Ah! " exclaimed Morrel, interrupting the count, " you had only lost your liberty, my father had only lost his fortune, but I have lost Valentine."

" Look at me," said Monte Cristo, with that expression which sometimes made him so eloquent and persuasive,—" look at me, there are no tears in my eyes, nor is there fever in my veins, yet I see you suffer—you, Maximilian, whom I love as my own son. Well, does not this tell you that in grief, as in life, there is always something to look forward to beyond? Now, if I entreat, if I order you to live, Morrel, it is in the conviction that one day you will thank me for having preserved your life."

" Oh heavens! " said the young man; " oh, heavens! what are you saying, count? Take care. But, perhaps, you have never loved! "

" Child! " replied the count.

" I mean, as I love. You see I have been a soldier ever since I attained manhood; I reached the age of twenty-nine without loving, for none of the feelings I before then experienced merit the appellation of love; well, at twenty-nine I saw Valentine; during two years I have loved her, during two years I have seen written in her heart as in a book all the virtues of a daughter and wife. Count, to possess Valentine, would have been a happiness too infinite, too ecstatic, too complete, too divine for this world, since it has been denied me; but without Valentine the earth is desolate."

" I have told you to hope," said the count.

" Then have a care, I repeat, for you seek to persuade me, and if you succeed, I should lose my reason, for I should hope, that I could again behold Valentine."

The count smiled.

" My friend, my father," said Morrel, with excitement, " have a care, I again repeat, for the power you wield over me alarms me. Weigh your words before you speak, for my eyes have already become brighter, and my heart rebounds; be cautious, or you will make me believe in supernatural agencies. I must obey you; so in mercy be cautious."

" Hope, my friend," repeated the count.

" Ah," said Morrel, falling from the height of excitement to the abyss of despair, " ah, you are playing with me, like those good or rather selfish mothers who soothe their children with honied words, because their screams annoy them. No, my friend, I was wrong to caution you; do not fear, I will bury my grief so deep in my heart, I will disguise it so, that you shall not even care to sympathise with me. Adieu, my friend, adieu."

" On the contrary," said the count, " after this time you must live with me—you must not leave me; and in a week we shall have left France behind us."

" And you still bid me hope."

" I tell you to hope, because I have a method of curing you."

" Count, you render me sadder than before, if it be possible. You think the result of this blow has been to produce an ordinary grief, and you would cure it by an ordinary remedy, change of scene." And Morrel dropped his head with disdainful incredulity.

" What can I say more? " asked Monte Cristo. " I have confidence in the remedy I propose, and only ask you to permit me to assure you of its efficacy."

" Count, you prolong my agony."

" Then," said the count, " your feeble spirit will not even grant me the trial I request? Come! do you know of what the Count of Monte Cristo is capable? do you know that he holds terrestrial beings under his control? nay, that he can almost work a miracle! Well! wait for the miracle I hope to accomplish, or——"

" Or? " repeated Morrel.

" Or, take care, Morrel, lest I call you ungrateful."

" Have pity on me, count! "

" I feel so much pity towards you, Maximilian, that—listen to me attentively—if I do not cure you in a month, to the day, to the very hour, mark my words, Morrel, I will place loaded pistols before you, and a cup full of the deadliest Italian poison —a poison, more sure and prompt than that which has killed Valentine."

" Will you promise me? "

" Yes; for I am a man, and have suffered like yourself, and also contemplated suicide; indeed, often since misfortune has left me, I have longed for the delights of an eternal sleep."

" But you are sure you will promise me this? " said Morrel, intoxicated.

" I not only promise, but swear it," said Monte Cristo, extending his hand.

" In a month then, on your honour, if I am not consoled, you will let me take my life into my own hands, and whatever may happen, you will not call me ungrateful? "

" In a month, to the day; the very hour and the date is a sacred one, Maximilian. I do not know whether you remember that this is the 5th of September;* it is ten years to-day since I saved your father's life, who wished to die."

Morrel seized the count's hand and kissed it; the count allowed him to pay the homage he felt due to him.

" In a month you will find on the table, at which we shall be then sitting, good pistols and a delicious draught; but on the other hand, you must promise me not to attempt your life before that time."

" Oh, I also swear it."

Monte Cristo drew the young man towards him, and pressed him for some time to his heart.

" And now," he said, " after to-day, you will come and live with me; you can occupy Haydée's apartment, and my daughter will at least be replaced by my son."

" Haydée? " said Morrel, " what has become of her? "

" She departed last night."

" To leave you? "

" To wait for me. Hold yourself ready then to join me at the Champs Elysées, and lead me out of this house without anyone seeing my departure."

Maximilian hung his head, and obeyed with childlike reverence.

107

The Division

THE first floor of the house in the Rue Saint-Germain-des-Prés, chosen by Albert and Madame de Morcerf for their residence, consisting of one room, was let to a very mysterious person. This was a man, whose face the concierge himself had never seen; for in the winter his chin was buried in one of those large red handkerchiefs worn by gentlemen's coachmen on a cold night, and in the summer he made a point of always blowing his nose just as he approached the door. Contrary to custom, this gentleman had not been watched, for as the report ran that he was a person of high rank, and one who would allow no impertinent interference, his incognito was strictly respected. His visits were tolerably regular, though occasionally he appeared a little before or after his time, but generally, both in summer and winter, he took possession of his apartment about four o'clock, though he never spent the night there. At half-past three in the winter the fire was lighted by the discreet servant, who had the superintendence of the little apartment, and in the summer ices were placed on the table at the same hour. At four o'clock, as we have already stated, the mysterious personage arrived. Twenty minutes afterwards a carriage stopped at the house, a lady alighted in a black or dark blue dress, and always thickly veiled; she passed like a shadow through the lodge, and ran upstairs without a sound escaping under the touch of her light foot. No one ever asked her where she was going. Her face, therefore, like that of the gentleman, was perfectly unknown to the two concierges, who were, perhaps, unequalled throughout the capital for discretion. We need not say she stopped at the first floor. Then she tapped at a door in a peculiar manner, which, after being opened to admit her, was again fastened, and all was done. The same precautions were used in leaving as on entering the house. The lady always left first, and stepping into her carriage it drove away, sometimes towards the right hand, sometimes the left; then, about twenty minutes afterwards, the gentleman would also leave, buried in his cravat or concealed by his handkerchief.

The day after Monte Cristo had called upon Danglars, the

mysterious lodger entered at ten o'clock in the morning instead of four in the afternoon. Almost directly afterwards, without the usual interval of time, a hackney-coach arrived, and the veiled lady ran hastily upstairs. The door opened, but before it could be closed, the lady exclaimed:

" Oh, Lucien! oh, my friend! "

The concierge, therefore, heard for the first time that the lodger's name was Lucien; still, as he was the very perfection of a doorkeeper, he made up his mind not to tell his wife.

" Well, what is the matter, my dear? " asked the gentleman, whose name the lady's agitation revealed; " tell me what is the matter."

" Oh, Lucien, can I confide in you? "

" Of course, you know you can do so. But what can be the matter? Your note of this morning has completely bewildered me. This precipitation—this disordered meeting. Come, ease me of my anxiety, or else frighten me at once."

" Lucien, a great event has happened! " said the lady, glancing inquiringly at Lucien,—" M. Danglars left last night! "

" Left!—M. Danglars left! Where is he gone to? "

" I do not know."

" What do you mean? Is he gone intending not to return? "

" Undoubtedly; at ten o'clock at night his horses took him to the barrier of Charenton; there a post-chaise was waiting for him—he entered it with his valet-de-chambre, saying that he was going to Fontainebleau."

" Then what did you mean—— "

" Stay!—he left a letter for me."

" A letter? "

" Yes; read it."

And the baroness took from her pocket a letter which she gave to Debray.

Debray paused a moment before reading, as if trying to guess its contents, or, perhaps, while making up his mind how to act, whatever it might contain. No doubt his ideas were arranged in a few minutes, for he began reading the letter which caused so much uneasiness in the heart of the baroness, and which ran as follows:

" Madame and most faithful wife."

Debray mechanically stopped and looked at the baroness, whose face became covered with blushes.

" Read," she said.

Debray continued:—

"When you receive this, you will no longer have a husband!
Oh, you need not be alarmed, you will only have lost him as you
have lost your daughter; I mean that I shall be travelling on
one of the thirty or forty roads leading out of France. I owe you
some explanations for my conduct, and as you are a woman that
can perfectly understand me, I will give them. Listen then: I
this morning received five millions, which I paid away; almost
directly afterwards another demand for the same sum was presented to me; I postponed this creditor till to-morrow, and I
intend leaving to-day to escape that to-morrow, which would be
rather too unpleasant for me to endure. You understand this,
do you not, my most precious wife? I say you understand this,
because you are as conversant with my affairs as I am; indeed,
I think you understand them better, since I am ignorant of
what has become of a considerable portion of my fortune, once
very tolerable, while I am sure, madame, that you are perfectly
acquainted with it. For women have infallible instincts; they
can even explain the marvellous by an algebraic calculation they
have invented; but I, who only understand my own figures,
know nothing more than that one day these figures deceived me.
Have you admired the rapidity of my fall? Have you been
slightly dazzled at the sudden fusion of my ingots? I confess
I have seen nothing but the fire; let us hope you have found
some gold amongst the ashes. With this consoling idea, I leave
you, madame, and most prudent wife, without any conscientious
reproach for abandoning you; you have friends left, and the
ashes I have already mentioned, and, above all, the liberty I
hasten to restore to you. And here, madame, I must add another
word of explanation. So long as I hoped you were working for
the good of our house and for the fortune of our daughter, I
philosophically closed my eyes; but as you have transformed
that house into a vast ruin, I will not be the foundation of another
man's fortune. You were rich when I married you, but little
respected. Excuse me for speaking so very candidly, but as this
is intended only for ourselves, I do not see why I should weigh
my words. I have augmented our fortune, and it has continued
to increase during the last fifteen years, till extraordinary and
unexpected catastrophes have suddenly overturned it, without
any fault of mine, I can honestly declare. You, madame, have
only sought to increase your own, and I am convinced you have
succeeded. I leave you, therefore, as I took you, rich, but little
respected. Adieu! I also intend from this time to work on my

own account. Accept my acknowledgments for the example you have set me, and which I intend following.

"Your very devoted husband,

"BARON DANGLARS."

The baroness had watched Debray while reading this long and painful letter, and saw him, notwithstanding his self-control, change colour once or twice. When he had ended the perusal, he folded the letter, and resumed his pensive attitude.

"Well?" asked Madame Danglars, with an anxiety easy to be understood.

"Well, madame?" unhesitatingly repeated Debray.

"With what ideas does that letter inspire you?"

"Oh, it is simple enough, madame; it inspires me with the idea that M. Danglars has left suspiciously."

"Certainly; but is this all you have to say to me?"

"I do not understand you," said Debray, with freezing coldness.

"He is gone! Gone, never to return!"

"Oh, madame, do not think that!"

"I tell you he will never return; I know his character, he is inflexible in any resolutions formed for his own interests. If he could have made any use of me, he would have taken me with him; he leaves me in Paris, as our separation will conduce to his benefit; therefore he has gone, and I am free for ever," added Madame Danglars, in the same supplicating tone.

Debray, instead of answering, allowed her to remain in an attitude of nervous inquiry.

"Well!" she said at length, "do you not answer me?"

"I have but one question to ask you,—what do you intend to do?"

"I was going to ask you," replied the baroness, with a beating heart.

"Ah, then, you wish to ask advice of me?"

"Yes; I do wish to ask your advice," said Madame Danglars, with anxious expectation.

"Then if you wish to take my advice," said the young man coldly, "I would recommend you to travel."

"To travel!" she murmured.

"Certainly; as M. Danglars says, you are rich and perfectly free. In my opinion, a withdrawal from Paris is absolutely necessary after the double catastrophe of Mademoiselle Danglars' broken contract and M. Danglars' disappearance. The world will think you abandoned and poor, for the wife of a bankrupt would never be forgiven were she to keep up the appearance of opulence. You have only to remain in Paris for about a fortnight, telling the world you are abandoned, and relating the details of this desertion to your best friends, who will soon spread the report. Then you can quit your house, leaving your jewels, and giving up your jointure, and everyone's mouth will be filled with praises of your disinterestedness. They will know you are deserted, and think you also poor; for I alone know your real financial position, and am quite ready to give up my accounts as an honest partner."

The dread with which the baroness, pale and motionless, listened to this, was equalled by the calm indifference with which Debray had spoken.

"Deserted!" she repeated; "ah, yes, I am, indeed, deserted! You are right, sir, and no one can doubt my position."

These were the only words uttered by the proud and violent woman.

"But then you are rich,—very rich, indeed," continued Debray, taking out some papers from his pocket-book, which he spread upon the table.

Madame Danglars saw them not; she was fully engaged in stilling the beatings of her heart, and restraining the tears which were ready to gush forth. At length a sense of dignity prevailed, and if she did not entirely master her agitation, she at least succeeded in preventing the fall of a single tear.

"Madame," said Debray, "it is nearly six months since we have been associated. You furnished a principal of 100,000 francs. Our partnership began in the month of April. In May we commenced operations, and in the course of the month gained 450,000 francs. In June the profit amounted to 900,000. In July we added 1,700,000 francs,—it was, you know, the month of the Spanish bonds. In August we lost 300,000 francs at the beginning of the month, but on the 13th we made up for it, and we now find that our accounts, reckoning from the first day of partnership up to yesterday, when I closed them, showed a capital of 2,400,000 francs, that is, 1,200,000 for each of us. Now, madame," said Debray, delivering up his accounts in the methodical manner of a stockbroker, "there are still 80,000 francs, the interest of this money in my hands."

"But," said the baroness, "I thought you never put the money out to interest?"

"Excuse me, madame," said Debray coldly, "I had your permission to do so, and I have made use of it. There are then 40,000 francs for your share, besides the 100,000 you furnished me to begin with, making, in all, 1,340,000 francs for your portion. Now, madame, I took the precaution of drawing out your money the day before yesterday; it is not long ago you see, and I might be suspected of continually expecting to be called on to deliver up my accounts. There is your money, half in bank-notes, the other half in cheques payable to the bearer. I say *there*, for as I did not consider my house safe enough, nor lawyers sufficiently discreet, and as landed property carries evidence with it, and, moreover, since you have no right to possess anything independent of your husband,* I have kept this sum, now your whole fortune, in a chest concealed under that closet, and, for greater security, I myself fastened it in. Now, madame," continued Debray, first opening the closet, then the chest,—" now, madame, here are 800 notes of 1000 francs each, resembling, as you see, a large book bound in iron; to this I add a dividend of 25,000 francs; then, for the odd cash, making, I think, about 110,000 francs, here is a cheque upon my banker, who, not being M. Danglars, will pay you the amount, you may rest assured."

Madame Danglars mechanically took the cheque, the dividend, and the heap of bank-notes. This enormous fortune made no great appearance on the table. Madame Danglars, with tearless eyes, but with her breast heaving with concealed emotion, placed the bank-notes in her bag, put the dividend and cheque into her pocket-book, and then, standing pale and mute, awaited one kind word of consolation. But she waited in vain.

" Now, madame," said Debray, " you have a splendid fortune, an income of about 60,000 livres a year, which is enormous for a woman who cannot keep an establishment here for a year at least. You will be able to indulge all your fancies; besides, should you find your income insufficient, you can, for the sake of the past, madame, make use of mine; and I am ready to offer you all I possess on loan."

" Thank you, sir,—thank you," replied the baroness; " you forget that what you have just paid me is much more than a poor woman requires, who intends for some time, at least, to retire from the world."

Debray was, for a moment, surprised, but immediately recovering himself, he bowed with an air which seemed to convey:

" As you please, madame."

Madame Danglars had, until then, perhaps hoped for something; but when she saw the careless bow of Debray and the glance by which it was accompanied, together with his significant silence, she raised her head, and, without passion, or violence, or even hesitation, ran downstairs, disdaining to address a last farewell to one who could thus part from her.

" Bah! " said Debray, when she had left, " these are fine

projects! she will remain at home, read novels, and speculate at cards, since she can no longer do so on the Bourse."

Then taking up his account-book, he cancelled, with the greatest care, all the amounts he had just paid away.

" I have 1,060,000 francs remaining," he said. " What a pity Mademoiselle de Villefort is dead! She suited me in every respect, and I would have married her."

And he calmly waited till the twenty minutes had elapsed after Madame Danglars' departure before he left the house. During this time he occupied himself in making figures, with his watch by his side.

Asmodeus*—that diabolical personage, who would have been created by every fertile imagination, if Le Sage had not acquired the priority in his *chef d'œuvre*—would have enjoyed a singular spectacle, if he had lifted up the roof of the little house in the Rue Saint-Germain-des-Prés, while Debray was casting up his figures.

Above the room in which Debray had been dividing two millions and a half with Madame Danglars was another, inhabited by persons who have played too prominent a part in the incidents we have related for their appearance not to create some interest. Mercédès and Albert were in that room. Mercédès was much changed within the last few days; her eye no longer sparkled, her lips no longer smiled, and there was now a hesitation in uttering the words which formerly fell so fluently from her ready wit. It was not poverty which had broken her spirit; it was not a want of courage which rendered her poverty burdensome. Mercédès appeared like a queen, fallen from her palace to a hovel, and who, reduced to strict necessity, could neither become reconciled to the earthen vessels she was herself forced to place upon the table, nor to the humble pallet which succeeded her bed.

The beautiful Catalane and noble countess had lost both her proud glance and charming smile, because she saw nothing but misery around her: the walls were hung with one of those gray papers which economical landlords choose as not likely to show the dirt; the floor was uncarpeted; the furniture attracted the attention to the poor attempt at luxury; indeed, everything offended the eyes accustomed to refinement and elegance. Madame Morcerf had lived there since leaving her house. The continual silence of the spot oppressed her. Still, seeing that Albert continually watched her countenance, to judge the state of her feelings, she constrained herself to assume a monotonous smile of the lips alone, which contrasted sadly with the sweet and beaming expression that usually shone from her eyes.

Albert, too, was ill at ease; the remains of former luxury

prevented him from getting accustomed to his actual position. If he wished to go out without gloves, his hands appeared too white; if he wished to walk through the town, his boots seemed too highly polished. Yet these two noble and intelligent creatures, united by the indissoluble ties of maternal and filial love, had succeeded in tacitly understanding one another, and economising their stores, and Albert had been able to tell his mother without extorting a change of countenance,—

" Mother, we have no more money."

Mercédès had never known misery. She had often, in her youth, spoken of poverty, but between want and necessity, though synonymous words, there is a wide difference. Amongst the Catalans, Mercédès wished for a thousand things, but still she never really wanted any. So long as the nets were good, they caught fish; and so long as they sold their fish, they were able to buy thread for new nets. And then, shut out from friendship, having but one affection, which could not be mixed up with her ordinary pursuits, she thought of herself—of no one but herself. Upon the little she earned she lived as well as she could; now there were two to be supported, and nothing to live upon.

Winter approached. Mercédès had no fire in that cold and naked room—she, who was accustomed to stoves which heated the house from the hall to the boudoir; she had not even one little flower—she, whose apartment had been a conservatory of costly exotics. But she had her son. Hitherto the excitement of fulfilling a duty had sustained them. Excitement, like enthusiasm, sometimes renders us unconscious to the things of earth. But the excitement had calmed down, and they felt themselves obliged to descend from dreams to reality; after having exhausted the ideal, they found they must talk of the actual.

" Mother," exclaimed Albert, just as Madame Danglars was descending the stairs, " let us reckon our riches, if you please; I want a capital to build my plans upon."

" Capital—nothing! " replied Mercédès, with a mournful smile.

" No, mother,—capital, 3000 francs. And I have an idea of our leading a delightful life upon this 3000 francs."

" Child! " sighed Mercédès.

" Alas, dear mother," said the young man, " I have unhappily spent too much of your money not to know the value of it. These 3000 francs are enormous, and I intend building upon this foundation a miraculous certainty for the future."

" You say this, my dear boy, but do you think we ought to accept these 3000 francs? " said Mercédès, colouring.

"I think so," answered Albert, in a firm tone. "We will accept them the more readily, since we have them not here; you know they are buried in the garden of the little house in the Allées de Meillan, at Marseilles. With 200 francs we can reach Marseilles."

"With 200 francs?—think well, Albert."

"Oh, as for that, I have made inquiries respecting the diligences and steamboats, and my calculations are made. You will take your place in the coupé to Chalons. You see, mother, I treat you handsomely for thirty-five francs."

Albert then took a pen and wrote:—

	Frs.
"Coupé, thirty-five francs	35
From Chalons to Lyons you will go on by the steamboat—six francs	6
From Lyons to Avignon (still by steamboat), sixteen francs	16
From Avignon to Marseilles, seven francs	7
Expenses on the road, about fifty francs ..	50
Total ..	114 frs."

"Let us put down 120," added Albert, smiling. "You see I am generous; am I not, mother?"

"But you, my poor child?"

"I? do you not see I reserve eighty francs for myself? A young man does not require luxuries; besides, I know what travelling is."

"With a post-chaise and valet-de-chambre?"

"Any way, mother."

"Well, be it so. But these 200 francs?"

"Here they are, and 200 more besides. See, I have sold my watch for 100 francs, and the guard and seals for 300. How fortunate the ornaments were worth more than the watch. Still the same story of superfluities! Now I think we are rich, since, instead of the 114 francs we require for the journey, we find ourselves in possession of 250."

"But we owe something in this house?"

"Thirty francs; but I pay that out of my 150 francs; that is understood; and, as I require only eighty francs for my journey, you see I am overwhelmed with luxury. But that is not all. What do you say to this, mother?"

And Albert took out of a little pocket-book with golden clasps, a remnant of his old fancies, or perhaps a tender *souvenir* from one of those mysterious and veiled ladies who used to knock at his little door,—Albert took out of this pocket-book a note of 1000 francs.

"What is this?" asked Mercédès.

"A thousand francs."

"But whence have you obtained them?"

"Listen to me, mother, and do not yield too much to agitation."

And Albert, rising, kissed his mother on both cheeks, then stood looking at her.

"Dear child!" said Mercédès, endeavouring in vain to restrain a tear which glistened in the corner of her eye. "Indeed, you only wanted misfortune to change my love for you to admiration. I am not unhappy while I possess my son!"

"Ah, just so," said Albert; "here begins the trial. Do you know the decision we have come to, mother?"

"Have we come to any?"

"Yes; it is decided that you are to live at Marseilles, and that I am to leave for Africa, where I will earn for myself the right to use the name I now bear instead of the one I have thrown aside."

Mercédès sighed.

"Well, mother, I yesterday engaged myself in the Spahis," added the young man, lowering his eyes with a certain feeling of shame, for even he was unconscious of the sublimity of his self-abasement. "I thought my body was my own, and that I might sell it. I yesterday took the place of another. I sold myself for more than I thought I was worth," he added, attempting to smile; "I fetched 2000 francs."

"Then these 1000 francs——" said Mercédès, shuddering.

"Are the half of the sum, mother; the other will be paid in a year."

Mercédès raised her eyes to heaven with an expression it would be impossible to describe, and tears, which had hitherto been restrained, now yielded to her emotion and ran down her cheeks.

"The price of his blood!" she murmured.

"Yes, if I am killed," said Albert, laughing. "But I assure you, mother, I have a strong intention of defending my person, and I never felt half so strong an inclination to live as at present."

"Merciful heavens!"

"Besides, mother, why should you make up your mind that I am to be killed? Has Lamoricière, that Ney of the South, been killed? Has Changarnier been killed? Has Bedeau been killed? Has Morrel, whom we know, been killed? Think of your joy, mother, when you see me return with an embroidered uniform! I declare, I expect to look magnificent in it, and chose that regiment only from vanity."

Mercédès sighed while endeavouring to smile: the devoted mother felt she ought not to allow the whole weight of the sacrifice to fall upon her son.

"Well, now you understand, mother!" continued Albert; "here are more than 4000 francs settled on you; upon these you can live at least two years."

"Do you think so?" said Mercédès.

These words were uttered in so mournful a tone that their real meaning did not escape Albert; he felt his heart beat, and, taking his mother's hand within his own, he said tenderly:

"Yes, you will live!"

"I shall live!—then you will not leave me, Albert?"

"Mother, I must go," said Albert, in a firm, calm voice; "you love me too well to wish me to remain useless and idle with you; besides, I have signed."

"You will obey your own wish and the will of Heaven!"

"Not my own wish, mother, but reason—necessity. Are we not two despairing creatures? What is life to you?—Nothing. What is life to me?—Very little without you, mother; for, believe me, but for you, I should have ceased to live on the day I doubted my father and renounced his name. Well, I will live, if you promise me still to hope; and if you grant me the care for your future prospects, you will redouble my strength. Then I will go to the governor of Algeria; he has a royal heart, and is essentially a soldier; I will tell him my gloomy story. I will beg him turn his eyes now and then towards me; and if he keep his word, and interest himself for me, in six months I shall be an officer or dead. If I am an officer, your fortune is certain, for I shall have money enough for both, and, moreover, a name we shall both be proud of, since it will be our own. If I am killed—well, then, mother, you can also die, and there will be an end of our misfortunes."

"It is well," replied Mercédès, with her eloquent glance; "you are right, my love; let us prove to those who are watching our actions that we are worthy of compassion."

"But let us not yield to gloomy apprehensions," said the young man; "I assure you we are, or rather we shall be, very happy. You are a woman, at once full of spirit and resignation; I have become simple in my tastes, and am without passion, I hope. Once in service, I shall be rich—once in M. Dantès' house, you will be at rest. Let us strive, I beseech you,—let us strive to be cheerful."

" Yes, let us strive, for you ought to live, and to be happy, Albert."

" And so our division is made, mother," said the young man, affecting ease of mind. " We can now part; come, I shall engage your passage."

" And you, my dear boy? "

" I shall stay here for a few days longer; we must accustom ourselves to parting. I want recommendations, and some information relative to Africa. I will join you again at Marseilles."

" Well, be it so; let us part," said Mercédès, folding round her shoulders the only shawl she had taken away, and which, accidentally, happened to be a valuable black cashmere.

Albert gathered up his papers hastily, rang the bell to pay the thirty francs he owed to the landlord, and, offering his arm to his mother, they descended the stairs. Someone was walking down before them, and this person, hearing the rustling of a silk dress, turned round.

" Debray! " muttered Albert.

" You, Morcerf! " replied the secretary, resting on the stairs. Curiosity had vanquished the desire of preserving his incognito, and he was recognised. It was indeed, strange, in this unknown spot, to find the young man whose misfortunes had made so much noise in Paris.

" Morcerf! " repeated Debray.

Then, noticing, in the dim light, the still youthful and veiled figure of Madame de Morcerf,—

" Pardon me," he added, with a smile, " I leave you, Albert." Albert understood his thoughts.

" Mother," he said, turning towards Mercédès, " this is M. Debray, secretary of the minister for the interior, once a friend of mine."

" How once? " stammered Debray; " what do you mean? "

" I say so, M. Debray, because I have no friends now, and I ought not to have any. I thank you for having recognised me, sir."

Debray stepped forward and cordially pressed the hand of his interlocutor.

" Believe me, dear Albert," he said, with all the emotion he was capable of feeling, " believe me, I feel deeply for your misfortunes, and if, in any way, I can serve you, I am yours."

" Thank you, sir," said Albert, smiling. " In the midst of our misfortunes we are still rich enough not to require assistance from anyone. We are leaving Paris, and when our journey is paid, we shall have 5000 francs left."

The blood mounted to the temples of Debray, who held a

million in his pocket-book; and, unimaginative as he was, he could not help reflecting that the same house had contained two women,. one of whom, justly dishonoured, had left it poor with 1,500,000 francs under her cloak, while the other, unjustly stricken, but sublime in her misfortune, was yet rich with a few deniers. This parallel disturbed his usual politeness; the philosophy he witnessed appalled him; he muttered a few words of general civility, and ran downstairs.

The next day, about five o'clock in the afternoon, Madame de Morcerf, after having affectionately embraced her son, entered the coupé of the diligence, which closed upon her. A man was hidden in Lafitte's banking-house, behind one of the little arched windows which are placed above each desk; he saw Mercédès enter the diligence, and he also saw Albert withdraw. Then he passed his hand across his forehead, which was clouded with doubt.

" Alas," he exclaimed, " how can I restore the happiness I have taken away from these poor innocent creatures? God help me! "

108

The Lions' Den

ONE division of La Force,* in which the most dangerous and desperate prisoners are confined, is called the Court of Saint-Bernard. The prisoners, in their expressive language, have named it the Lions' Den, probably because the captives possess teeth which frequently gnaw the bars, and sometimes the keepers also. It is a prison within a prison; the walls are double the thickness of the rest. The courtyard of this quarter is enclosed by enormous walls, over which the sun glances obliquely, when it deigns to penetrate into this gulf of moral and physical deformity. On this paved yard are to be seen, pacing from morning till night, pale, careworn and haggard, like so many shadows, the men whom justice holds beneath the steel she is sharpening. There, crouched against the side of the wall, which attracts and retains the most heat, they may be seen sometimes talking to one another, but more frequently alone, watching the door, which sometimes opens to call forth one from the gloomy assemblage, or to throw in another outcast from society.

The Court of Saint-Bernard has its own particular parlour;

it is a long square, divided by two upright gratings, placed at a distance of three feet from one another, to prevent a visitor from shaking hands with or passing anything to the prisoners. It is a wretched, damp, nay, even horrible spot, more especially when we consider the fearful conferences which have taken place between those iron bars. And yet, frightful though this spot may be, it is considered as a kind of paradise to the men whose days are numbered; it is so rare for them to leave the Lions' Den for any other place than the barrier Saint-Jacques or the galleys!

In the court which we have attempted to describe, and from which a damp vapour was rising, a young man might be seen walking, with his hands in his pockets, who had excited much curiosity amongst the inhabitants of the " Den." The cut of his clothes would have made him pass for an elegant man, if those clothes had not been torn to ribands; still they were not worn, and the fine cloth soon recovered its gloss in the parts which were still perfect, beneath the careful hands of the prisoner, who tried to make it assume the appearance of a new coat. He bestowed the same attention upon the cambric front of a shirt, which had considerably changed in colour since his entrance into the prison, and he polished his varnished boots with the corner of a hand-kerchief embroidered with initials surmounted by a coronet. Some of the inmates of the " Lions' Den " were watching the operations of the prisoner's toilet with considerable interest.

" See, the prince is beautifying himself," said one of the thieves.

" He is naturally very handsome," said another; " and if he had only a comb and some pomatum, he would soon eclipse all the gentlemen in white kids."

" His coat looks nearly new, and his boots are brilliant. It is pleasant to have such well-dressed brethren; but didn't those gendarmes behave shamefully? What jealousy! to tear such clothes! "

" He appears to be someone of consequence," said another; " he dresses in first-rate style. And, then, to be here so young! —oh, it is splendid! "

Meanwhile the object of this hideous admiration approached the wicket, against which one of the keepers was leaning.

" Come, sir," he said, " lend me twenty francs; you will soon be paid; you run no risks with me. Remember, I have relations who possess more millions than you have deniers. Come, I beseech you, lend me twenty francs, so that I may buy a dressing-gown; it is intolerable always to be in a coat and boots! And what a coat, sir, for a prince of the Cavalcanti! "*

The keeper turned his back, and shrugged his shoulders; he

did not even laugh at what would have caused anyone else to do so; he had heard so many utter the same things,—indeed he heard nothing else..

" Come," said Andrea, " you are a man void of compassion! I will cause you to lose your place."

This made the keeper turn round, and he burst into a loud laugh. The prisoners then approached and formed a circle.

" I tell you that with that wretched sum," continued Andrea, " I could obtain a coat, and a room in which to receive the illustrious visitor I am daily expecting."

" He is right! he is right! " said the prisoners, " anyone can see he is a gentleman! "

" Well, then, lend him the twenty francs," said the keeper, leaning on the other shoulder; " surely you will not refuse a comrade! "

" I am no comrade of these people," said the young man proudly; " you have no right to insult me thus! "

" Do you hear him? " said the keeper, with a disagreeable smile; " he rates you handsomely. Come, lend him the twenty francs—eh? "

The thieves looked at one another with low murmurs, and a storm gathered over the head of the aristocratic prisoner, raised less by his own words than by the manner of the keeper. The latter, sure of quelling the tempest when the waves became too violent, allowed them to rise to a certain pitch, that he might be revenged on the importunate Andrea, and, besides, it would afford him some recreation during the long day.

The thieves had already approached Andrea, some screaming:

" *La savate!—La savate!* "—a cruel operation, which consists in flogging any comrade who may have fallen into disgrace, not with an old shoe, but with an iron-heeled one. Others proposed *l'anguille*, another kind of recreation, in which a handkerchief is filled with sand, pebbles, and halfpence when they have them, which the wretches discharge like a flail against the head and shoulders of the unhappy sufferer.

" Let us horsewhip the fine gentleman! " said others.

But Andrea, turning towards them, winked his eyes, rolled his tongue round his cheeks, and smacked his lips in a manner equivalent to a hundred words among the bandits when forced to be silent. It was a masonic sign Caderousse had taught him. He was immediately recognised as one of them; the handkerchief was thrown down, and the iron-heeled shoe replaced on the foot of the wretch to whom it belonged. Some voices were heard to say that the gentleman was right; that he intended to be civil in his way, and that they would set the example of liberty of conscience; and the mob retired. The keeper was so stupefied at this scene that he took Andrea by the hands, and began examining his person, attributing the sudden submission of the inmates of the Lions' Den to something more substantial than mere fascination. Andrea made no resistance, though he protested against it. Suddenly a voice was heard at the wicket.

" Benedetto! " exclaimed an inspector.

The keeper relaxed his hold.

" I am called," said Andrea.

" To the parlour! " said the same voice.

" You see someone pays me a visit. Ah, my dear sir, you will see whether a Cavalcànti is to be treated like a common person! "

And Andrea, gliding through the court like a black shadow, rushed out through the wicket, leaving his comrades and even the keeper lost in wonder.

Certainly a call to the parlour had scarcely astonished Andrea less than themselves; for the wily youth, instead of making use of his privilege of waiting to be claimed on his entry into La Force, had maintained a rigid silence.

" Everything," he said, " proves me to be under the protection of some powerful person; this sudden fortune, the facility with which I have overcome all obstacles; an unexpected family and an illustrious name awarded to me; gold showered down upon me; and the most splendid alliances about to be entered into. An unhappy lapse of fortune and the absence of my protector have reduced me, certainly, but not for ever. The hand which has retreated for a while will be again stretched forth to save me, at the very moment when I shall think myself sinking into the abyss! Why should I risk an imprudent step? It might alienate my protector. He has two means of extricating me from this dilemma: the one by a mysterious escape, managed through bribery; the other by buying off my judges with gold. I will say and do nothing until I am convinced that he has quite abandoned me; and then——"

Andrea had formed a plan which was tolerably clever. The unfortunate youth was intrepid in the attack, and rude in the defence. He had borne with the public prison, and with the privations of all sorts; still by degrees nature, or rather custom, had prevailed, and he suffered from being naked, dirty, and hungry. It was at this moment of *ennui* that the inspector's voice called him to the visiting-room.

Andrea felt his heart leap with joy. It was too soon for a visit from the *juge d'instruction*, and too late for one from the director of the prison or the doctor;—it must, then, be the visitor he hoped for. Behind the grating of the room into which Andrea had been led, he saw, while his eyes dilated with surprise, the dark and intelligent face of M. Bertuccio, who was also gazing with sad astonishment upon the iron bars, the bolted doors, and the shadow which moved behind the other grating.

" Ah! " said Andrea, deeply affected.

" Good-morning, Benedetto," said Bertuccio, with his deep, hollow voice.

" You—you! " said the young man, looking fearfully around him.

" Do you not recognise me, unhappy child? "

" Silence!—be silent! " said Andrea, who knew the delicate sense of hearing possessed by the walls; " for Heaven's sake do not speak so loud! "

" You wish to speak with me alone, do you not? " said Bertuccio.

" Oh, yes! "

" That is well! " And Bertuccio, feeling in his pocket, signed to a keeper whom he saw through the window of the wicket.

" Read," he said.

" What is that? " asked Andrea.

" An order to conduct you to a room, and to leave you there to talk with me."

" Oh! " cried Andrea, leaping with joy.

Then he mentally added:

" Still my unknown protector! I am not forgotten! They wish for secrecy, since we are to converse in a private room. I understand Bertuccio has been sent by my protector."

The keeper spoke for a moment with a superior, then opened the iron gates, and conducted Andrea to a room on the first floor.

The room was whitewashed, as is the custom in prisons; but it looked quite brilliant to a prisoner, though a stove, a bed, a chair, and a table formed the whole of its sumptuous furniture.

Bertuccio sat down upon the chair; Andrea threw himself upon the bed; the keeper retired.

" Now," said the steward, " what have you to tell me? "

" And you? " said Andrea.

" You speak first."

" Oh, no! You must have much to tell me, since you have come to seek me."

" Well, be it so! You have continued your course of villainy; you have robbed, you have assassinated."

" Good! If you had me taken to a private room only to tell me this, you might have spared yourself the trouble. I know all these things. But there are some with which, on the contrary,

I am not acquainted; let us talk of those, if you please. Who sent you?"

"Come, come, you are going on quickly, M. Benedetto!"

"Yes, and to the point. Let us dispense with useless words. Who sends you?"

"No one."

"How did you know I was in prison?"

"I recognised you, some time since, as the insolent dandy who so gracefully mounted his horse in the Champs Elysées."

"Oh, the Champs Elysées! Ah, ah! we burn, as they say at some game. The Champs Elysées! Come, let us talk a little about my father!"

"Who, then, am I?"

"You, sir?—you are my adopted father. But it was not you, I presume, who placed at my disposal 100,000 francs, which I spent in four or five months; it was not you who manufactured an Italian gentleman for my father; it was not you who introduced me into the world, and had me invited to a certain dinner at Auteuil, which I fancy I am eating at this moment, in company with the most distinguished people in Paris—amongst the rest, with a certain procureur du roi, whose acquaintance I did very wrong not to cultivate, for he would have been very useful to me just now;—it was not you, in fact, who bailed me for one or two millions when the fatal discovery of the *pot aux roses** took place. Come, speak, my worthy Corsican, speak!"

"What do you wish me to say?"

"I will help you. You were speaking of the Champs Elysées just now, worthy foster-father!"

"Well?"

"Well, in the Champs Elysées there resides a very rich gentleman."

"At whose house you robbed and murdered, did you not?"

"I believe I did."

"The Count of Monte Cristo?"

"You have named him. Well, am I to rush into his arms, and strain him to my heart, crying, as they do in the dramas, 'My father! my father!'"

"Do not let us jest," gravely replied Bertuccio, "and dare not to utter that name again as you have pronounced it."

"Bah!" said Andrea, a little overcome by the solemnity of Bertuccio's manner, "why not?"

"Because the person who bears it is too highly favoured by heaven to be the father of such a wretch as you!"

"Oh, these are fine words!"

"And there will be fine doings if you do not take care!"

"Menaces!—I do not fear them. I will say——"

"Do you think you are engaged with a pigmy like yourself?" said Bertuccio, in so calm a tone, and with so steadfast a look, that Andrea was moved to the very soul. "Do you think you have to do with galley-slaves, or novices in the world? Benedetto, you are fallen into terrible hands; they are ready to open for you—make use of them! Do not play with the thunderbolt they have laid aside for a moment, but which they can take up again instantly, if you attempt to intercept their movements."

"My father—I will know who my father is!" said the obstinate youth; "I will perish if I must, but I *will* know it. What does scandal signify to me? What possessions, what reputation have I? You great people always lose something by scandal, notwithstanding your millions. Come, who is my father?"

"I came to tell you."

"Ah," cried Benedetto, his eyes sparkling with joy.

Just then the door opened, and the gaoler, addressing himself to Bertuccio, said:

"Excuse me, sir, but the *juge d'instruction* is waiting for the prisoner."

"And so closes our interview," said Andrea to the worthy steward; "I wish the troublesome fellow were at the devil!"

"I will return to-morrow," said Bertuccio.

"Good! Gendarmes, I am at your service. Ah, sir, do leave a few crowns for me at the gate, that I may have some things I am in need of!"

"It shall be done," replied Bertuccio.

109

The Judge

WE remember that the Abbé Busoni remained alone with Noirtier in the chamber of death, and that the old man and the priest were the sole guardians of the young girl's body. Perhaps it was the Christian exhortations of the abbé, perhaps his kind charity, perhaps his persuasive words, which had restored the courage of Noirtier; for ever since he had conversed with the priest his volent despair had yielded to a calm resignation, which surprised all who knew his excessive affection for Valentine.

M. de Villefort had not seen his father since the morning of the death. The whole establishment had been changed; another valet-de-chambre was engaged for himself, a new servant for Noirtier; two women had entered Madame de Villefort's service; in fact everywhere, to the concierge and coachman, new faces were presented to the different masters of the house, thus widening the division which had always existed between the members of the same family. The assizes, also, were about to commence; and Villefort, shut up in his room, exerted himself with feverish anxiety in drawing up the case against the murderer of Caderousse. This affair, like all those in which the Count of Monte Cristo had interfered, caused a great sensation in Paris. The proofs were certainly not convincing, since they rested upon a few words written by an escaped galley-slave on his death-bed, and who might have been actuated by hatred or revenge in accusing his companion. But the mind of the procureur du roi was made up: he felt assured that Benedetto was guilty, and he hoped by his skill in conducting this aggravated case, to flatter his self-love, which was about the only vulnerable point left in his frozen heart.

Once only had Villefort seen his father; it was the day after that upon which Bertuccio had paid his second visit to Benedetto, when the latter was to learn his father's name. The magistrate, harassed and fatigued, had descended to the garden of his hotel, and in a gloomy mood paced the avenue. Accidentally he turned his eyes towards the house, where he heard the sound of his son, returned from school to spend the Sunday and Monday with his mother, playing noisily. While doing so, he observed M. Noirtier at one of the open windows, where the old man had been placed that he might enjoy the last rays of a sun which yet yielded some heat, and was now shining upon the dying flowers and red leaves of the creeper which twined round the balcony.

The eye of the old man was riveted upon a spot which Villefort could scarcely distinguish. His glance was so full of hate, of ferocity, and savage impatience, that Villefort turned out of the path he had been pursuing to see upon what person this dark look was directed. Then he saw beneath a thick clump of linden-trees, which were nearly divested of foliage, Madame de Villefort sitting with a book in her hand, the perusal of which she frequently interrupted to smile upon her son, or to throw back his elastic ball which he obstinately threw from the drawing-room into the garden. Villefort became pale; he understood the old man's meaning. Noirtier continued to look at the same object, but suddenly his glance was carried from the wife to the husband, and Villefort himself had to submit to the searching investigation of those eyes, which, while changing their object and even their language, had lost none of their menacing expression. Madame de Villefort, unconscious of all those passions that exhausted their fire over her head, at that moment held her son's ball, and was making signs to him to reclaim it with a kiss. Edward begged for a long while, the maternal kiss probably not offering sufficient recompense for the trouble he must take to obtain it; however, at length, he decided, leaped out of the window into a cluster of heliotropes and daisies, and ran to his mother, his forehead streaming with perspiration. Madame de Villefort wiped his forehead, pressed her lips upon it, and sent him back with the ball in one hand and some bonbons in the other.

Villefort, drawn by an irresistible attraction, like that of the bird to the serpent, walked towards the house. As he approached it, Noirtier's gaze followed him, and his eyes appeared of such a fiery brightness that Villefort felt them pierce to the depths of his heart. In that earnest look might be read a deep reproach as well as a terrible menace. Then Noirtier raised his eyes to heaven as though to remind his son of a forgotten oath.

" It is well, sir," replied Villefort from below,—" it is well; have patience but one day longer; what I have said I will do."

Noirtier appeared calmed by these words, and turned his eyes with indifference to the other side. Villefort violently unbuttoned his greatcoat, which seemed to strangle him, and passing his livid hand across his forehead, entered his study.

The next day, Monday, was the first sitting of the assizes. The morning rose bleak and gloomy, and Villefort saw the dim gray light shine upon the lines he had traced in red ink. The magistrate had slept for a short time while the lamp sent forth its final struggles; its flickerings awoke him, and he found his fingers as damp and purple as though they had been dipped in blood. He opened the window; a bright yellow streak crossed the sky, and seemed to divide in half the poplars, which stood out in black relief on the horizon. In the clover-fields beyond the chestnut-trees, a lark was mounting up to heaven while pouring out her clear morning song. The damps of the dew bathed the head of De Villefort and refreshed his memory.

"To-day," he said with an effort,—"to-day the man who holds the knife of justice must strike wherever there is guilt."

Involuntarily his eyes wandered towards the window of Noirtier's room, whence he had seen him the preceding night. The curtain was drawn, and yet the image of his father was so vivid to his mind, that he addressed the closed window as though it had been open, and as if through the opening he had beheld the menacing old man.

"Yes," he murmured,—"yes, be satisfied."

His head dropped upon his breast, and in this position he paced his room; then he threw himself, dressed as he was, upon a sofa, less to sleep than to rest his limbs, cramped with study and with the cold, which crept to the very marrow of his bones. By degrees everyone awoke. Villefort from his room heard the successive noises which constitute the life of a house; the opening and shutting of doors, the ringing of Madame de Villefort's bell, to summon the waiting-maid, mingled with the first shouts of the child who rose full of the enjoyment of his age. Villefort also rang; his new valet-de-chambre brought him the papers, and with them a cup of chocolate.

"What are you bringing me?" said he.

"A cup of chocolate."

"I did not ask for it. Who has paid me this attention?"

"My mistress, sir. She said you would have to speak a great deal on the case of the murder, and that you should take something to keep up your strength;" and the valet placed the cup on the table nearest to the sofa, which was, like all the rest, covered with papers. The valet then left the room.

Villefort looked for an instant with a gloomy expression, then, suddenly taking it up with a nervous motion, he swallowed its contents at one draught. It might have been thought that he hoped the beverage would be mortal, and that he sought for death to deliver him from a duty which he would rather die than fulfil.

He then rose and paced his room with a smile it would have been terrible to witness. The chocolate was inoffensive, but M.

de Villefort felt no effects. The breakfast-hour arrived, but M. de Villefort was not at table. The valet-de-chambre re-entered.

"Madame de Villefort wishes to remind you, sir," he said, "that eleven o'clock has just struck, and that the trial commences at twelve."

"Well," said Villefort, "what then?"

"Madame de Villefort is dressed; she is quite ready, and wishes to know if she is to accompany you, sir?"

"Where to?"

"To the Palais."

"What to do?"

"My mistress wishes much to be present at the trial."

"Ah!" said Villefort, with a startling accent; "does she wish that?"

The servant drew back and said:

"If you wish to go alone, sir, I will go and tell my mistress."

Villefort remained silent for a moment, and dented his pale cheeks with his nails.

"Tell your mistress," he at length answered, "that I wish to speak to her, and I beg she will wait for me in her own room."

"Yes, sir."

"Then come to dress and shave me."

"Directly, sir."

The valet-de-chambre reappeared almost instantly, and, having shaved his master, assisted him to dress entirely in black. When he had finished he said:

"My mistress said she should expect you, sir, as soon as you had finished dressing."

"I am going to her." And Villefort, with his papers under his arm and hat in hand, directed his steps towards the apartment of his wife. At the door he paused for a moment to wipe his damp, pale brow. He then entered the room.

Madame de Villefort was sitting on an ottoman, and impatiently turning over the leaves of some newspapers and pamphlets which young Edward, by way of amusing himself, was tearing in pieces before his mother could finish reading them. She was dressed to go out, her bonnet was placed beside her on a chair, and her gloves were on her hands.

"Ah, here you are, sir," she said, in her naturally calm voice; "but how pale you are! Have you been working all night? Why did you not come down to breakfast? Well, will you take me, or shall I take Edward?"

Madame de Villefort had multiplied her questions in order to gain one answer, but to all her inquiries M. de Villefort remained mute and cold as a statue.

"Edward," said Villefort, fixing an imperious glance on the child, "go and play in the drawing-room, my dear; I wish to speak to your mamma."

Madame de Villefort shuddered at the sight of that cold countenance, that resolute tone, and the awfully strange preliminaries. Edward raised his head, looked at his mother, and then, finding that she did not confirm the order, began cutting off the heads of his leaden soldiers.

"Edward," cried M. de Villefort, so harshly that the child started on the carpet, "do you hear me?—Go!"

The child, unaccustomed to such treatment, rose, pale and trembling; it would be difficult to say whether his emotion were caused by fear or passion. His father went up to him, took him in his arms, and kissed his forehead.

"Go," he said, "go, my child!"

Edward ran out. M. de Villefort went to the door, which he closed behind the child, and bolted.

"Oh heavens!" said the young woman, endeavouring to read her husband's inmost thoughts, while a smile passed over her countenance which froze the impassibility of Villefort. "What is the matter?"

"Madame, where do you keep the poison you generally use?" said the magistrate, without any introduction, placing himself between his wife and the door.

Madame de Villefort must have experienced somewhat of the sensation of a bird, which, looking up, sees the murderous trap closing over its head. A hoarse, broken tone, which was neither a cry nor a sigh, escaped from her, while she became deadly pale.

"Sir," she said, "I—I do not understand you." And, as in her first paroxysm of terror, she had raised herself from the sofa, in the next, stronger very likely than the other, she fell down again on the cushions.

"I asked you," continued Villefort, in a perfectly calm tone, "where you conceal the poison by the aid of which you have killed my father-in-law, M. de Saint-Méran, my mother-in-law, Madame de Saint-Méran, Barrois, and my daughter, Valentine."

"Ah, sir," exclaimed Madame de Villefort, clasping her hands, "what do you say?"

"It is not for you to interrogate, but to answer."

"Is it to the judge or to the husband?" stammered Madame de Villefort.

"To the judge,—to the judge, madame!"

It was terrible to behold the frightful pallor of that woman, the anguish of her look, the trembling of her whole frame.

"Ah, sir!" she muttered, "ah, sir!" and this was all.

"You do not answer, madame!" exclaimed the terrible interrogator. Then he added, with a smile yet more terrible than his anger, "It is true, then; you do not deny it!"

She moved forward.

"And you cannot deny it," added Villefort, extending his hand towards her, as though to seize her in the name of justice. "You have accomplished these different crimes with impudent address, but which could only deceive those whose affection for you blinded them. Since the death of Madame de Saint-Méran I have known that a poisoner lived in my house. M. d'Avrigny warned me of it. After the death of Barrois my suspicions were directed towards an angel,—those suspicions which, even when there is no crime, are always alive in my heart: but after the death of Valentine, there has been no doubt in my mind, madame, and not only in mine, but in those of others; thus your crime, known by two persons, suspected by many, will soon become public, and, as I told you just now, you no longer speak to the husband, but to the judge."

The young woman hid her face in her hands.

"Oh, sir," she stammered, "I beseech you, do not believe appearances."

"Are you, then, a coward?" cried Villefort, in a contemptuous voice. "But I have always remarked that poisoners were cowards. Can you be a coward, you who have had the courage to witness the death of two old men and a young girl murdered by you?"

"Sir! Sir!"

"Can you be a coward," continued Villefort, with increasing excitement, "you who could count, one by one, the minutes of four death-agonies? *You*, who have arranged your infernal plans, and removed the beverages with a talent and precision almost miraculous? Have you, then, who have calculated everything with such nicety, have you forgotten to calculate one thing, I mean where the revelation of your crimes will lead you to? Oh! it is impossible—you must have saved some surer, more subtle and deadly poison than any other, that you might escape the punishment you deserve. You have done this—I hope so, at least."

Madame de Villefort stretched out her hands, and fell on her knees.

"I understand," he said, "you confess; but a confession made to the judges, a confession made at the last moment, extorted when the crime cannot be denied, diminishes not the punishment inflicted on the guilty!"

"The punishment!" exclaimed Madame de Villefort, "the punishment, sir! Twice you have pronounced that word!"

"Certainly. Did you hope to escape it, because you were four times guilty? Did you think the punishment would be withheld because you are the wife of him who pronounces it?—No, madame, no, the scaffold awaits the poisoner, whoever she may be, unless, as I just said, the poisoner has taken the precaution of keeping for herself a few drops of her deadliest poison."

Madame de Villefort uttered a wild cry, and a hideous and uncontrollable terror spread over her distorted features.

"Oh, do not fear the scaffold, madame," said the magistrate, "I will not dishonour you, since that would be to dishonour myself: no, if you have heard me distinctly, you will understand that you are not to die on the scaffold."

"No, I did not understand; what do you mean?" stammered the unhappy woman, completely overwhelmed.

"I mean that the wife of the first magistrate in the capital shall not, by her infamy, soil an unblemished name; that she shall not, with one blow, dishonour her husband and her child."

"No, no—oh, no!"

"Well, madame, it will be a laudable action on your part, and I will thank you for it!"

"You will thank me—for what?"

"For what you have just said."

"What did I say? Oh, my brain whirls; I no longer understand anything, Oh heavens! oh heavens!" And she rose, with her hair dishevelled and her lips foaming.

"Have you answered the question I put to you on entering the room: Where do you keep the poison you generally use, madame?"

Madame de Villefort raised her arms to heaven, and convulsively struck one hand against the other.

"No, no!" she vociferated, "no, you cannot wish that?"

"What I do not wish, madame, is, that you should perish on the scaffold. Do you understand?" asked Villefort.

"Oh, mercy, mercy, sir!"

"What I require is, that justice be done. I am on the earth to punish, madame," he added, with a flaming glance; "any other woman, were it the queen herself, I would send to the executioner; but to you I shall be merciful. To you I will say, 'Have you not, madame, put aside some of the surest, deadliest, most speedy poison?'"

"Oh! pardon me, sir; let me live!"

"She is cowardly," said Villefort.

"Reflect that I am your wife!"

" You are a poisoner."

" In the name of heaven! "

" No! "

" In the name of the love you once bore me! "

" No, no! "

" In the name of our child! Ah, for the sake of our child, let me live! "

" No! no! no! I tell you; one day, if I allow you to live, you will, perhaps, kill him as you have the others! "

" I!—I kill my boy! " cried the distracted mother, rushing towards Villefort. " I kill my son! Ha! ha! ha! " and a frightful demoniac laugh finished the sentence, which was lost in a hoarse rattle.

Madame de Villefort fell at her husband's feet. He approached her.

" Think of it, madame," he said; " if, on my return, justice has not been satisfied, I will denounce you with my own mouth and arrest you with my own hands! "

She listened, panting, overwhelmed, crushed; her eye alone lived, and glared horribly.

" Do you understand me? " he said. " I am going down there to pronounce the sentence of death against a murderer. If I find you alive on my return, you shall sleep to-night in the Conciergerie."*

Madame de Villefort sighed; her nerves gave way, and she sunk on the carpet. The procureur du roi seemed to experience a sensation of pity, he looked upon her less severely, and bowing to her, said slowly:

" Farewell, madame, farewell! "

That farewell struck Madame de Villefort like the executioner's knife. She fainted. The procureur du roi went out, after having double-locked the door.

110

The Assizes

THE Benedetto affair, as it was called in the Palais, and by people in general, had produced a tremendous sensation. Frequenting the Café de Paris, the Boulevard de Gand, and the Bois de Boulogne, during his brief career of splendour, the false Cavalcanti had formed a host of acquaintances. The papers had related his various adventures, both as the man of fashion and the galley-slave; and as everyone who had been personally acquainted with the Prince Cavalcanti experienced a lively curiosity in his fate, they all determined to spare no trouble in endeavouring to witness the trial of M. Benedetto for the murder of his comrade. In the eyes of many Benedetto appeared, if not a victim to, at least an instance of, the fallibility of the law. M. Cavalcanti, his father, had been seen in Paris, and it was expected he would reappear to claim the illustrious outcast. Many, also, who were not aware of the circumstances attending his withdrawal from Paris, were struck with the worthy appearance, the gentlemanly bearing, and the knowledge of the world displayed by the old patrician, who certainly played the nobleman very well, so long as he said nothing, and made no arithmetical calculations. As for the accused himself, many remembered him as being so amiable, so handsome, and so liberal, that they chose to think him the victim of some conspiracy, since in this world large fortunes frequently excite the malevolence and jealousy of some unknown enemy.

Everyone, therefore, ran to the court; some to witness the sight, others to comment upon it. From seven o'clock in the morning a crowd was stationed at the iron gates, and an hour before the trial commenced the hall was full of the privileged. Beauchamp, one of the kings of the press, and therefore claiming the right of a throne everywhere, was looking round on every side. He perceived Château-Renaud and Debray, who had just gained the good graces of a sergent-de-ville, and who had persuaded the latter to let them stand before instead of behind him, as he ought to have done. The worthy agent had recognised the minister's secretary and the millionaire, and by way of paying extra attention to his noble neighbours, promised to keep their places while they paid a visit to Beauchamp.

" Well," said Beauchamp, " we shall see our friend! "

" Yes, indeed! " replied Debray.   " That worthy prince. Deuce take those Italian princes! "

" A man, too, who could boast of Dante for a genealogist, and could reckon as far back as the *Divina Commedia.*"*

" A nobility of the rope! " said Château-Renaud phlegmatically.

" He will be condemned, will he not? " asked Debray of Beauchamp.

" My dear fellow, I think we should ask you that question; you know such news much better than we do; did you see the president at the minister's last night? "

" Yes."

" What did he say? "

" Something which will surprise you."

" Oh! make haste and tell me then; it is a long time since that has happened."

" Well, he told me that Benedetto, who is considered a serpent of subtlety and a giant of cunning, is really but a very subordinate, silly rascal, and altogether unworthy of the experiments that will be made on his phrenological organs after his death."

" Bah! " said Beauchamp; " he played the prince very well."

" Yes, for you who detest those unhappy princes, Beauchamp, and are always delighted to find fault with them; but not for me who discover a gentleman by instinct, and who scent out an aristocratic family like a very bloodhound of heraldry."

" Then you never believed in the principality? "

" Yes; in the principality, but not in the prince."

" Not so bad," said Beauchamp; " still, I assure you he passed very well with many people; I saw him at the ministers' houses."

" Ah, yes! " said Château-Renaud. " The idea of thinking ministers understand anything about princes! "

" There is something in what you have just said," said Beauchamp, laughing.

" But," said Debray to Beauchamp, " if I spoke to the president, *you* must have been with the procureur du roi."

" It was an impossibility: for the last week M. de Villefort has secluded himself. It is natural enough; this strange chain of domestic afflictions followed by the no less strange death of his daughter——"

" Strange! What do you mean, Beauchamp? "

" Oh, yes! Do you pretend that all this has been unobserved at the minister's? " said Beauchamp, placing his eyeglass in his eye, where he tried to make it remain.

" My dear sir," said Château-Renaud, " allow me to tell you that you do not understand that manœuvre with the eyeglass half so well as Debray. Give him a lesson, Debray."

" Stay," said Beauchamp, " surely I am not deceived."

" What is it? "

" It is she! "

" Whom do you mean? "

" They said she had left."

" Mademoiselle Eugénie? " said Château-Renaud; " has she returned? "

" No; but her mother."

" Madame Danglars?—Nonsense! Impossible! " said Château-Renaud, " only ten days after the flight of her daughter, and three days from the bankruptcy of her husband? "

Debray coloured slightly, and followed with his eyes the direction of Beauchamp's glance.

" Come! " he said, " it is only a veiled lady, some foreign princess, perhaps the mother of Cavalcanti. But hush, gentlemen, here is the court; let us get back to our places."

A noise was heard in the hall; the sergent-de-ville called his two protégés with an energetic " Hem! " and the door-keeper appearing called out, with that shrill voice peculiar to his order, even in the days of Beaumarchais:*

" The court, gentlemen! "

The judges took their places in the midst of the most profound silence; the jury took their seats; M. de Villefort, the object of unusual attention, and we had almost said of general admiration, sat in the arm-chair, and cast a tranquil glance around him. Every person looked with astonishment on that grave and severe face, the calm expression of which personal griefs had been unable to disturb; and the aspect of a man who was a stranger to all human emotions excited a kind of terror.

" Gendarmes," said the president, " lead in the accused."

At these words the public attention became more intense, and all eyes were turned towards the door through which Benedetto was to enter. The door soon opened, and the accused appeared. His features bore no sign of that deep emotion which stops the beating of the heart and blanches the cheek. His hands gracefully placed, one upon his hat, the other in the opening of his white waistcoat, were not at all tremulous; his eye was calm, and even brilliant. Scarcely had he entered the hall when he glanced at the whole body of magistrates and assistants: his eye rested longer on the president, and still more so on the procureur du roi. By the side of Andrea was placed the lawyer who was to conduct his defence, and who had been chosen by the court.

The president called for the deed of accusation, corrected, as we know, by the clever and implacable pen of De Villefort.

During the reading of this, which was long, the public attention was continually drawn towards Andrea, who bore the burden with Spartan unconcern. Villefort had never been so concise and eloquent: the former life of the prisoner, his transformation, a review of his life from the earliest period, were set forth with all the talent that a knowledge of human life could furnish to a mind like that of the procureur du roi. Benedetto was thus for ever lost in public opinion before the sentence of the law could be pronounced. Andrea paid no attention to the successive charges which were brought against him. M. de Villefort, who examined him attentively, and who no doubt practised upon him all the psychological studies he was accustomed to use, in vain endeavoured to make him lower his eyes, notwithstanding the depth and profundity of his gaze. At length the deed was read.

" Accused," said the president, " your name and surname? "

Andrea rose.

" Excuse me, M. le Président," he said, in a clear voice, " but I see you are going to adopt a course of questions through which I cannot follow you. I have an idea, which I will explain by and by, of making an exception to the usual form of accusation. Allow me, then, if you please, to answer in different order, or I will not do so at all."

The astonished president looked at the jury, who themselves looked upon the procureur du roi. The whole assembly manifested great surprise. But Andrea appeared quite unmoved.

" Your age? " said the president; " will you answer that question? "

" I will answer that question as well as the rest, M. le Président, but in its turn."

" Your age? " repeated the president.

" I am twenty-one years old; or rather I shall be in a few days, as I was born the night of the 27th of September, 1817."

M. de Villefort, who was busy taking down some notes, raised his head at the mention of this date.

" Where were you born? " continued the president.

" At Auteuil, near Paris."

M. de Villefort a second time raised his head, looked at Benedetto as if he had been gazing at the head of Medusa, and became livid. As for Benedetto, he gracefully wiped his lips with a fine cambric pocket-handkerchief.

" Your profession? "

" First I was a forger," answered Andrea, as calmly as possible; " then I became a thief, and lately have become an assassin."

A murmur, or rather storm, of indignation burst from all parts of the assembly. The judges themselves appeared stupefied; and the jury manifested tokens of disgust for a stoicism so unexpected from a fashionable man. M. de Villefort pressed his hand upon his brow, which, at first pale, had become red and burning; then he suddenly rose, and looked around as though he had lost his senses—he wanted air.

" Are you looking for anything, M. le Procureur du Roi? " asked Benedetto, with his most pleasing smile.

M. de Villefort answered nothing, but sat, or rather threw himself down again, upon his chair.

" And now, prisoner, will you consent to tell your name? " said the president. " The brutal affectation with which you have enumerated and classified your crimes calls for a severe reprimand on the part of the court, both in the name of morality, and for the respect due to humanity. You appear to consider this a point of honour, and it may be for this reason you have delayed acknowledging your name. You wished it to be preceded by all these titles."

" It is quite wonderful, M. le Président, how entirely you have read my thoughts," said Benedetto, in his softest voice and most polite manner. " This is, indeed, the reason why I begged you to alter the order of the questions."

The public astonishment had reached its height. There was no longer any deceit or bravado in the manner of the accused. The audience seemed like some thunder-cloud about to burst over the gloomy scene.

" Well," said the president; " your name? "

" I cannot tell you my name, since I do not know it; but I know my father's, and will pronounce it."

" Repeat your father's name," said the President.

Not a whisper, not a breath was heard in that vast assembly; everyone waited anxiously.

" My father is the procureur du roi," replied Andrea calmly.

" The procureur du roi? " said the president, stupefied, and without noticing the agitation which spread over the face of M. de Villefort; " the procureur du roi? "

" Yes; and if you wish to know his name, I will tell it,—he is named Villefort."

The explosion, which had been so long restrained, from a feeling of respect to the court of justice, now burst forth like thunder from the breasts of all present; the court itself did not seek to restrain the movement of the multitude. The exclamations, the insults addressed to Benedetto, who remained perfectly unconcerned, the energetic gestures, the movement of the gendarmes, the sneers of the scum of the crowd, always sure to rise to the surface in case of any disturbance, all this lasted five minutes, before the door-keepers and magistrates were able to restore silence. Several persons hurried up to M. de Villefort, who was nearly buried in his chair, offering him consolation, encouragement, and protestations of zeal and sympathy. Order was re-established in the hall, with the exception of a few who still moved and whispered. A lady, it was said, had just fainted; they had supplied her with a smelling-bottle, and she had recovered. During the scene of tumult, Andrea had turned his smiling face towards the assembly; then leaning with one hand on the oaken rail of his bench in the most graceful attitude possible, he said:

"Gentlemen, I assure you, I had no idea of insulting the court, or of making a useless disturbance in the presence of this honourable assembly. They ask my age; I tell it. They ask where I was born; I answer. They ask my name; I cannot give it, since my parents abandoned me. But though I cannot give my own name, not possessing one, I can tell them my father's. Now I repeat, my father is named M. de Villefort, and I am ready to prove it."

There was an energy, a conviction, and a sincerity in the manner of the young man, which silenced the tumult. All eyes were turned for a moment towards the procureur du roi, who sat as motionless as though a thunderbolt had changed him into a corpse.

"Gentlemen," said Andrea, commanding silence by his voice and manner; " I owe you the proofs and explanations of what I have said."

"But," said the irritated president, "you called yourself Benedetto, declared yourself an orphan, and claimed Corsica as your country."

"I said anything I pleased, in order that the solemn declaration I have just made should not be withheld, which otherwise would certainly have been the case. I now repeat that I was born at Auteuil on the night of the 27th September, 1817, and that I am the son of the procureur du roi, M. de Villefort. Do you wish for any further details? I will give them. I was born in No. 28 Rue de la Fontaine, in a room hung with red damask: my father took me in his arms, telling my mother I was dead; wrapped me in a napkin marked with an H and an N; and carried me into a garden, where he buried me alive."

A shudder ran through the assembly when they saw that the confidence of the prisoner increased in proportion with the terror of M. de Villefort.

" But how have you become acquainted with all these details? " asked the president.

" I will tell you, M. le Président. A man who had sworn vengeance against my father, and had long watched his opportunity to kill him, had introduced himself that night into the garden in which my father buried me. He was concealed in a thicket; he saw my father bury something in the ground, and stabbed him in the midst of the operation; then, thinking the deposit might contain some treasure, he turned up the ground and found me still living. The man carried me to the hospital for *enfants trouvés*, where I was inscribed under the number 37. Three months afterwards, a woman travelled from Rogliano to Paris to fetch me, and having claimed me as her son, carried me away. Thus, you see, though born in Paris, I was brought up in Corsica."

There was a moment's silence, during which one could have fancied the hall empty, so profound was the stillness.

" Proceed! " said the president.

" Certainly, I might have lived happily amongst those good people, who adored me, but my perverse disposition prevailed over the virtues which my adopted mother endeavoured to instil into my heart. I increased in wickedness till I committed crime. One day, when I cursed Providence for making me so wicked and ordaining me to such a fate, my adopted father said to me, ' Do not blaspheme, unhappy child! the crime is your father's, not yours; your father's, who devoted you to death, or to a life of misery, in case by a miracle you should escape his doom.' Since then I cease to blaspheme, but I cursed my father. This is why I have uttered the words for which you blame me; this is why I have filled this whole assembly with horror. If I have committed an additional crime, punish me; but if you will allow that ever since the day of my birth my fate has been sad, bitter, and lamentable, then pity me."

" But your mother? " asked the president.

" My mother thought me dead; she is not guilty. I did not even wish to know her name, nor do I know it."

Just then a piercing cry, ending in a sob, burst from the centre of the crowd, who encircled the lady who had before fainted, and who now fell into a violent fit of hysterics. She was carried out of the hall, and in doing so, the thick veil which concealed her face dropped off, and Madame Danglars was recognised. Notwithstanding his shattered nerves, the stunning sensation in his ears, and the species of madness which turned his brain, Villefort rose as he perceived her.

"The proofs! the proofs!" said the president; "remember this tissue of horrors must be supported by the clearest proofs."

"The proofs?" said Benedetto, laughing,—"do you want proofs?"

"Yes."

"Well, then, look at M. de Villefort, and then ask me for proofs."

Everyone turned towards the procureur du roi, who, unable to bear the universal gaze now riveted on him alone, advanced staggering into the midst of the tribunal, with his hair dishevelled, and his face indented with the mark of his nails. The whole assembly uttered a long murmur of astonishment.

"Father," said Benedetto, "I am asked for proofs, do you wish me to give them?"

"No, no, it is useless!" stammered M. de Villefort, in a hoarse voice; "no, it is useless!"

"How! useless?" cried the president; "what do you mean?"

"I mean that I feel it impossible to struggle against this deadly weight which crushes me! Gentlemen, I know I am in the hands of an avenging God! We need no proofs; everything relating to this young man is true."

A dull, gloomy silence, like that which precedes some awful phenomenon of nature, pervaded the assembly, who shuddered in dismay.

"What! M. de Villefort," cried the president, "do you yield to a hallucination? What! are you no longer in possession of your senses? This strange, unexpected, terrible accusation has disordered your reason. Come, recover."

The procureur du roi dropped his head: his teeth chattered like those of a man under a violent attack of fever, and yet he was deadly pale.

"I am in possession of all my senses, sir," he said; "my body alone suffers, as you may suppose. I acknowledge myself guilty of all the young man has brought against me, and from this hour hold myself under the authority of the procureur du roi who will succeed me."

And as he spoke these words with a hoarse, choking voice, he staggered towards the door, which was mechanically opened by a door-keeper. The whole assembly were dumb with astonishment at the revelation and confession which had produced a catastrophe so different to that which had been expected during the last fortnight by the Parisian world.

"The sitting is adjourned, gentlemen," said the president;

" fresh inquiries will be made, and the case will be tried next session by another magistrate."

As for Andrea, who was as calm and more interesting than ever, he left the hall, escorted by gendarmes, who involuntarily paid him some attention.

" Well, what do you think of this, my fine fellow? " asked Debray of the sergent-de-ville, slipping a louis into his hand.

" There will be extenuating circumstances," he replied.

III

Expiation

NOTWITHSTANDING the density of the crowd, M. de Villefort saw it open before him. There is something so awe-inspiring in great afflictions, that even in the worst times the fiːst emotion of a crowd has generally been to sympathise with the sufferer in a great catastrophe. Many people have been assassinated in a tumult; but even criminals have rarely been insulted during their trial.

Thus Villefort passed through the mass of spectators and officers of the Palais and withdrew. Though he had acknowledged his guilt, he was protected by his grief. There are some situations which men understand by instinct, though their reason cannot explain them; in such cases the greatest orator is he who utters the loudest and most natural cry, which conveys a whole story to the mob. It would be difficult to describe the state of stupor in which Villefort left the Palais. Every pulse beat with feverish excitement, every nerve was strained, every vein swollen, and every part of the body seemed to suffer distinctly from the rest, thus multiplying his agony a thousandfold. Habit alone guided him through the passage; he threw aside his magisterial robe, he could not bear the weight on his shoulders. Having staggered as far as the Rue Dauphiné, he perceived his carriage, awoke his sleeping coachman by opening the door himself, threw himself on the cushions, and pointed towards the Faubourg Saint-Honoré: the carriage drove on. All the weight of his fallen fortune seemed suddenly to crush him; he could not foresee the consequences; he could not contemplate the future with the indifference of a cold murderer. One thought filled his mind; he saw the workings of a divine hand in all that had happened. The carriage rolled rapidly. Villefort, while turning restlessly on the cushions, felt something press against him. He put out his hand to remove the object; it was a fan which Madame de Villefort had left in the carriage; this fan awakened a recollection which darted through his mind like lightning. He thought of his wife.

His wife! he had just acted the inexorable judge with her, he had condemned her to death; and she, crushed by remorse, struck with terror, covered with the shame inspired by the eloquence of *his* irreproachable virtue, she might at that very moment, perhaps, be preparing to die! An hour had elapsed since her condemnation: at that moment, doubtless, she was recalling all her crimes to her memory; she was asking pardon for her sins; perhaps she was even writing a letter imploring forgiveness from her virtuous husband,—a forgiveness she was purchasing with her death. Villefort again groaned with anguish and despair.

" Ah! " he exclaimed, " that woman became criminal only from associating with me! I carried the infection of crime with me, and she has caught it as she would the typhus fever, the cholera, the plague! And yet I have punished her—I have dared to tell her—*I* have, ' Repent and die! ' But no! she must not die, she shall live and follow me. We will flee from Paris, and go as far as the earth reaches. I told her of the scaffold, and I forgot that it awaits me also! Yes, we will fly: I will confess all to her, I will tell her daily that I also have committed a crime!—Oh! what an alliance with the tiger and the serpent! worthy wife of such as I am! She *must* live that my infamy may diminish hers."

" Yes, yes! " repeated Villefort, as he approached his home— " yes, that woman must live, she must repent, and educate my son, the sole survivor, with the exception of the indestructible old man, of the wreck of my house. She loves him; it was for his sake she has committed these crimes. We ought never to despair of softening the heart of a mother who loves her child; she will repent; no one will know she has been guilty; the crimes which have taken place in my house, though they now occupy the public mind, will be forgotten in time; or if, indeed, a few enemies should persist in remembering them, why, then, I will add them to my guilty list. What will it signify if one, two, or three more are added? My wife and child shall escape from this gulf, carrying treasures with them; she will live and may yet be happy, since her child, in whom all her love is centred, will be with her. I shall have performed a good action, and my heart will be lighter." And the procureur du roi breathed more freely than he had done for some time.

The carriage stopped at the door of the hotel. Villefort leaped out of the carriage, and saw his servants surprised at his early return: he could read no other expression on their features. Neither of them spoke to him, they merely stood aside to let him pass by, as usual, nothing more. As he passed by M. Noirtier's room, he perceived, through the half-open door, two figures; but he experienced no curiosity to know who was visiting his father; anxiety carried him on farther.

" Come," he said, as he ascended the stairs leading to his wife's room, " nothing is changed here."

He then closed the door of the landing.

" No one must disturb us," he said; " I must speak freely to her, accuse myself, and say—" He approached the door, touched the crystal handle, which yielded to his hand. " Not locked! " he cried; " that is well." And he entered the little room in which Edward slept; for though the child went to school during the day, his mother could not allow him to be separated from her at night. With a single glance Villefort's eye ran through the room.

" Not here," he said; " doubtless she is in her bedroom."

He rushed towards the door; it was bolted; he stopped, shuddering. " Héloïse! " he cried. He fancied he heard the sound of a piece of furniture being removed. " Héloïse! " he repeated.

" Who is there? " answered the voice of her he sought.

He thought that voice more feeble than usual.

" Open the door! " cried Villefort; " open, it is I."

But notwithstanding this request, notwithstanding the tone of anguish in which it was uttered, the door remained closed. Villefort burst it open with a violent blow.

At the entrance of the room which led to her boudoir, Madame de Villefort was standing erect, pale, her features contracted, and her eyes glaring horribly.

" Héloïse! Héloïse! " he said, " what is the matter? Speak! "

The young woman extended her stiff white hand towards him.

" It is done, sir," she said, with a rattling which seemed to tear her throat. " What more do you want? " and she fell on the floor.

Villefort ran to her and seized her hand, which convulsively clasped a crystal bottle with a golden stopper. Madame de Villefort was dead.

Villefort, maddened with horror, stepped back to the threshold of the door, fixing his eyes on the corpse. " My son! " he exclaimed suddenly, " where is my son?—Edward, Edward! "

and he rushed out of the room, still crying, " Edward, Edward! "
The name was pronounced in such a tone of anguish that the
servants ran up.

" Where is my son? " asked Villefort; " let him be removed
from the house, that he may not see——"

" Master Edward is not downstairs, sir," replied the valet-de-
chambre.

" Then he must be playing in the garden; go and see."

" No, sir; Madame de Villefort sent for him half an hour
ago; he went into her room, and has not been downstairs
since."

A cold perspiration burst out in Villefort's brow; his legs
trembled, and his brain filled with a confused maze of ideas.

" In Madame de Villefort's room? " he murmured, and slowly
returned, with one hand wiping his forehead, and with the other
supporting himself against the wall. To enter the room, he
must again see the body of his unhappy wife. To call Edward,
he must reawaken the echo of that room which now appeared
like a sepulchre: to speak seemed like violating the silence of
the tomb. His tongue clave to the roof of his mouth.

" Edward! " he stammered, " Edward! " The child did not
answer. Where, then, could he be, if he had entered his mother's
room and not since returned? He stepped forward. The corpse
of Madame de Villefort was stretched across the doorway leading
to the room in which Edward must be; those glaring eyes seemed
to watch over the threshold, and the lips expressed a terrible and
mysterious irony. Through the open door a portion of the boudoir
was visible, containing an upright piano and a blue satin couch.
Villefort stepped forward two or three paces, and beheld his
child lying—no doubt asleep on the sofa. The unhappy man
uttered at exclamation of joy; a ray of light seemed to penetrate
the abyss of despair and darkness. He had only to step over the
corpse, enter the boudoir, take the child in his arms, and flee
far, far away.

He leaped over the corpse as though it had been a furnace.
He took the child in his arms, pressed him, shook him, called him,
but the child replied not. He pressed his burning lips to the
cheeks, but they were icy cold and pale; he felt his stiffened
limbs; he pressed his hand upon the heart, but it no longer
beat: the child was dead. A folded paper fell from Edward's
breast.

Villefort, thunderstruck, fell upon his knees; the child dropped
from his arms, and rolled on the floor by the side of its mother.
He picked up the paper, and recognising his wife's writing, ran
his eyes rapidly over its contents: they were as follows:

" You know that I was a good mother, since it was for my son's sake I became criminal. A good mother cannot depart without her son."

Villefort could not believe his eyes,—he could not believe his reason; he dragged himself towards the child's corpse, and examined it as a lioness contemplates its dead cub. Then a piercing cry escaped from his breast, and he cried, " Still the hand of God." The two victims alarmed him; he could not bear the solitude only shared by two corpses. He rose, his head bent beneath the weight of grief, and shaking his damp, dishevelled hair, he who had never felt compassion for anyone determined to seek his father, that he might have someone to whom he could relate his misfortunes—someone by whose side he might weep. He descended the little stairs with which we are acquainted, and entered Noirtier's room.

The old man appeared to be listening attentively and as affectionately as his infirmities would allow to the Abbé Busoni, who looked cold and calm, as usual.

Villefort, perceiving the abbé, passed his hand across his brow. He recollected the call he had made upon him after the dinner at Auteuil, and then the visit the abbé had himself paid to his house on the day of Valentine's death.

" You here, sir! " he exclaimed; " do you, then, never appear but to act as an escort to death? "

Busoni turned round, and perceiving the excitement depicted on the magistrate's face, the savage lustre of his eyes, he understood that the scene of the assizes had been accomplished; but beyond this he was ignorant. " I came to pray over the body of your daughter."

" And, now, why are you here? "

" I come to tell you that you have sufficiently repaid your debt, and that from this moment I will pray to God to forgive you as I do."

" Good heavens! " exclaimed Villefort, stepping back fearfully, " surely that is not the voice of the Abbé Busoni! "

" No! " The abbé threw off his false tonsure, shook his head, and his hair, no longer confined, fell in black masses around his manly face.

" It is the face of the Count of Monte Cristo! " exclaimed the procureur du roi, with a haggard expression.

" You are not exactly right, M. le Procureur du roi; you must go further back."

" That voice! that voice!—where did I first hear it? "

" You heard it for the first time at Marseilles, twenty-three years ago, the day of your marriage with Mademoiselle de Saint-Méran. Refer to your papers."

"You are not Busoni?—you are not Monte Cristo? Oh heavens! you are then some concealed, implacable, and mortal enemy! I must have wronged you in some way at Marseilles. Oh! woe to me!"

"Yes: you are, indeed, right," said the count, crossing his arms over his broad chest; "you condemned me to a horrible, tedious death,—you killed my father,—you deprived me of liberty, of love, and happiness."

"Who are you, then? Who are you?"

"I am the spectre of a wretch you buried in the dungeons of the Château d'If. The form of the Count of Monte Cristo was given to that spectre when he at length issued from his tomb, enriched with gold and diamonds to reconduct him to you!"

"Ah! I recognise you! I recognise you!" exclaimed the procureur du roi; "you are——"

"I am Edmond Dantès!"

"You are Edmond Dantès!" cried Villefort, seizing the count by the wrist, "then come here!" And he dragged Monte Cristo up the stairs; who, ignorant of what had happened, followed him in astonishment, presaging some new catastrophe. "Hold! Edmond Dantès!" he said, pointing to the bodies of his wife and child. "See! are you well revenged?"

Monte Cristo became pale at this horrible sight; he felt he had passed beyond the bounds of vengeance, and that he could no longer say, "God is for and with me." With an expression of indescribable anguish, he threw himself upon the body of the child, reopened its eyes, felt its pulse, and then rushed with him into Valentine's room, of which he double-locked the door.

"My child!" cried Villefort. "He carries away the body of my child! Oh! curses, woe, death to you!" and he tried to follow Monte Cristo; but, as though in a dream, he was transfixed to the spot; his eyes glared as though they were starting through the sockets; he gripped the flesh on his chest, until his nails were stained with blood; the veins of his temple swelled and boiled as though they would burst their narrow boundary, and deluge his brain with living fire. This lasted several minutes, until the frightful overturn of reason was accomplished; then, uttering a loud cry, followed by a burst of laughter, he rushed down the stairs.

A quarter of an hour afterwards, the door of Valentine's room opened, and Monte Cristo reappeared. Pale, with a dull eye and heavy heart, all the noble features of that face, usually so calm and serene, appeared overturned by grief. In his arms he held the child, whom no skill had been able to recall to life. Bending on one knee he placed it reverently by the side of its mother, with its head upon her breast. Then rising, he went out, and meeting a servant on the stairs, he asked:

" Where is M. de Villefort? "

The servant, instead of answering, pointed to the garden. Monte Cristo ran down the steps, and, advancing towards the spot designated, beheld Villefort, encircled by his servants, with a spade in his hand, and digging the earth with fury.

" It is not here! " he cried. " It is not here! " And then he moved farther on, and recommenced digging.

Monte Cristo approached him, and said, in a low voice, with an expression almost humble:

" Sir, you have indeed lost a son; but——"

Villefort interrupted him; he had neither listened nor heard.

" Oh, I *will* find it! " he cried; " you may pretend he is not here, but I *will* find him, though I dig for ever! "

Monte Cristo drew back in horror.

" Oh! " he said, " he is mad! " And as though he feared that the walls of the accursed house would crumble around him, he rushed into the street, for the first time doubting whether he had the right to do as he had done.

" Oh! enough of this,—enough of this," he cried, " let me save the last."

On entering his house he met Morrel, who wandered about like a ghost.

" Prepare yourself, Maximilian," he said, with a smile; " we leave Paris to-morrow."

" Have you nothing more to do there? " asked Morrel.

" No," replied Monte Cristo; " God grant I may not have done too much already."

The next day they indeed left, accompanied alone by Baptistin. Haydée had taken away Ali, and Bertuccio remained with Noirtier.

112

The Departure

THE recent events formed the theme of conversation throughout all Paris. Emmanuel and his wife conversed with natural astonishment in their little apartment in the Rue-Meslay upon the three successive sudden and most unexpected catastrophes of Morcerf, Danglars, and Villefort. Maximilian, who was paying them a visit, listened to their conversation, or rather was present at it, plunged in his accustomed state of apathy.

"Indeed," said Julie, "might we not almost fancy, Emmanuel, that those people, so rich, so happy but yesterday, had forgotten in their prosperity, that an evil genius hovered over them, who, like the wicked fairies in Perrault's stories, presenting themselves unbidden, at some wedding or baptism, has appeared all at once to revenge himself for their fatal neglect?"

"What a dire misfortune!" said Emmanuel, thinking of Morcerf and Danglars.

"What dreadful sufferings!" said Julie, remembering Valentine, but whom with a delicacy natural to woman, she did not name before her brother.

"If the Supreme Being has directed the fatal blow," said Emmanuel, "it must be that he in his great goodness has perceived nothing in the past lives of these people to merit mitigation of their awful punishment."

"Do you not form a very rash judgment, Emmanuel?" said Julie. "When my father, with a pistol in his hand, was once on the point of committing suicide, had anyone then said, 'This man deserves his misery,' would not that person have been deceived?"

"Yes, but your father was not allowed to fall; a being was commissioned to arrest the fatal hand of Death about to descend on him."

Emmanuel had scarcely uttered these words, when the sound of the bell was heard, the well-known signal given by the porter that a visitor had arrived. Nearly at the same instant, the door of the room was opened, and the Count of Monte Cristo appeared on the threshold. The young people uttered a cry of joy, while Maximilian raised his head, but let it fall again immediately.

"Maximilian," said the count, without appearing to notice

the different impressions which his presence produced on the little circle, " I come to seek you."

" To seek me? " repeated Morrel, as if awakening from a dream.

" Yes," said Monte Cristo, " has it not been agreed that I should take you with me, and did I not tell you yesterday to prepare for departure? "

" I am ready," said Maximilian, " I came expressly to wish them farewell."

" Whither are you going, count? " asked Julie.

" In the first instance to Marseilles, madame."

" To Marseilles! " exclaimed the young couple.

" Yes, and I take your brother with me."

" Oh! count," said Julie, " will you restore him to us cured of his melancholy? "

Morrel turned away to conceal the confusion of his countenance.

" You perceive, then, that he is not happy? " said the count.

" Yes," replied the young woman; " and I fear much that he finds our home but a dull one."

" I will undertake to divert him," replied the count.

" I am ready to accompany you, sir," said Maximilian. " Adieu, my kind friends! Emmanuel! Julie! Farewell! "

" How farewell? " exclaimed Julie; " do you leave us thus, so suddenly, without any preparations for your journey, without even a passport? "

" Needless delays but increase the grief of parting," said Monte Cristo, " and Maximilian has doubtless provided himself with everything requisite; at least I advised him to do so."

" I have a passport, and my clothes are ready packed," said Morrel, in his tranquil but mournful manner.

" Good! " said Monte Cristo, smiling; " in these prompt arrangements we recognise the order of a well-disciplined soldier."

" And you quit us thus? " said Julie, " at a moment's warning, you do not give us a day—no, not even an hour before your departure? "

" My carriage is at the door, madame; and I must be in Rome in five days."

" But does Maximilian go to Rome? " exclaimed Emmanuel.

" I am going wherever it may please the count to lead me," said Morrel, with a smile full of grief; " I am devoted to him for the next month."

" Oh! heavens! how strangely he expresses himself, count! " said Julie.

" Maximilian accompanies *me*," said the count, in his kindest and most persuasive manner, " therefore do not make yourself uneasy on your brother's account."

" Once more farewell, my dear sister; Emmanuel, adieu! " Morrel repeated.

" His carelessness and indifference touch me to the heart," said Julie. " Oh! Maximilian, Maximilian, you are certainly concealing something from us."

" Pshaw! " said Monte Cristo, " you will see him return to you gay, smiling, and joyful."

Maximilian cast a look of disdain, almost of anger, on the count.

" We must leave you," said Monte Cristo. " And on the eve of departure, I carry my egotism so far as to say, ' Do not forget me, my kind friends, for probably you will never see me again.' "

" Never see you again! " exclaimed Emmanuel, whilst two large tears rolled down Julie's cheeks; " never behold you again! It is not a man then, but some angel that leaves us, and this angel is on the point of returning to heaven after having appeared on earth to do good."

" Say not so," quickly returned Monte Cristo,—" say not so, my friends; angels never err, celestial beings remain where they wish to be: fate is not more powerful than they; it is they who, on the contrary, overcome fate. No! Emmanuel, I am but a man, and your admiration is as unmerited as your words are sacrilegious."

And pressing his lips on the hand of Julie, who rushed into his arms, he extended his other hand to Emmanuel; then tearing himself from this house, the abode of peace and happiness, he made a sign to Maximilian, who followed him passively with the indifference which was perceptible in him ever since the death of Valentine had so stunned him."

" Restore my brother to peace and happiness," whispered Julie to Monte Cristo.

And the count pressed her hand in reply, as he had done eleven years before on the staircase leading to Morrel's study.

" You still confide, then, in Sinbad the Sailor? " asked he, smiling.

" Oh, yes! " was the ready answer.

" Well, then, sleep in peace, and put your trust in the Lord."

As we have before said, the post-chaise was waiting; four powerful horses were already pawing the ground with impatience, whilst at the foot of the steps, Ali, his face bathed in perspiration, and apparently just arrived from a long walk, was standing.

" Well," asked the count in Arabic, " have you been to the old man's? "

Ali made a sign in the affirmative.

" And have you placed the letter before him, as I ordered you to do? "

The slave respectfully signalised that he had.

" And what did he say, or rather do? "

Ali placed himself in the light, so that his master might see him distinctly, and then imitating in his intelligent manner the countenance of the old man, he closed his eyes, as Noirtier was in the custom of doing when saying " yes."

" Good! he accepts," said Monte Cristo; " now let us go."

These words had scarcely escaped him, when the carriage was on its road; and the feet of the horses struck a shower of sparks from the pavement. Maximilian settled himself in his corner without uttering a word. Half an hour had fled, when the carriage stopped suddenly; the count had just pulled the silken check-string, which was fastened to Ali's finger. The Nubian immediately descended, and opened the carriage-door. It was a lovely starlight night—they had just reached the top of the hill of Villejuif, the platform from whence Paris, like some dark sea, is seen to agitate its millions of lights, resembling phosphoric waves,—waves indeed, more noisy, more passionate, more changeable, more furious, more greedy, than those of the tempestuous ocean,—waves which never lie calm, like those of the vast sea,—waves ever destructive, ever foaming, and ever restless.

The count remained alone, and on a sign from his hand, the carriage advanced some steps. He contemplated for some time, with his arms crossed, the vast city. When he had fixed his piercing look on this modern Babylon, which equally engages the contemplation of the religious enthusiast, the materialist, and the scoffer:

" Great city! " murmured he, inclining his head and joining his hands as if in prayer, " less than six months have elapsed since first I entered thy gates. I believe that the spirit of God led my steps to thee, and that he also enables me to quit thee in triumph; the secret cause of my presence within thy walls I have confided alone to him, who only has had the power to read my heart. God only knows that I retire from thee without pride or hatred, but not without many regrets; he only knows that the power confided to me has never been made subservient to my personal good or to any useless cause. Oh! great city! it is in thy palpitating bosom that I have found that which I sought; like a patient miner, I have dug deep into thy very entrails to root out evil thence; now my work is accomplished, my mission

is terminated, now thou canst neither afford me pain nor pleasure.
Adieu Paris! Adieu! "

His look wandered over the vast plain like that of some genius
of the night; he passed his hand over his brow, and, getting
into the carriage, the door was closed on him, and it quickly
disappeared on the other side of the hill in a cloud of dust and
noise.

113

The House in the Allées de Meillan

TEN leagues were passed without a single word being pronounced. Morrel was dreaming, and Monte Cristo was
looking at the dreamer.

" Morrel," said the count to him at length, " do you repent
having followed me? "

" No, count; but to leave Paris——"

" If I thought happiness might await you in Paris, Morrel,
I would have left you there."

" Valentine reposes within the walls of Paris, and to leave
Paris is like losing her a second time."

" Maximilian," said the count, " the friends that we have lost
do not repose in the bosom of the earth, but are buried deep in
our hearts; and it has been thus ordained, that we may always
be accompanied by them. I have two friends, who in this way
never depart from me; the one who gave me being, and the
other who conferred knowledge and intelligence on me. Their
spirits live in me. Listen to the voice of your heart, Morrel, and
ask it whether you ought to preserve this melancholy exterior
towards me."

" My friend," said Maximilian, " the voice of my heart is
very sorrowful, and points out the future in most unhappy
colours."

" It is ever thus that weakened minds see everything as through
a black veil; the soul forms its own horizons; your soul is
darkened, and consequently the sky of the future appears stormy
and unpromising."

" That may possibly be true," said Maximilian; and he again
subsided into his thoughtful mood.

The journey was performed with that marvellous rapidity
which the unlimited power of the count ever commanded. The

following morning they arrived at Châlons, where the count's steamboat waited for them; without an instant being lost, the carriage was placed on board, and the two travellers embarked without delay. The boat was built for speed; her two paddle-wheels resembled two wings with which she skimmed the water like a bird. Morrel was not insensible to that sensation of delight which is generally experienced in passing rapidly through the air, and the wind, which occasionally raised the hair from his forehead, seemed on the point of dispelling momentarily the clouds collected there. As the distance increased between the travellers and Paris, an almost superhuman serenity appeared to surround the count; he might have been taken for an exile about to revisit his native land.

Ere long Marseilles presented herself to view. With one accord they stopped on the Cannebière. A vessel was setting sail for Algiers, on board of which the bustle usually attending departure prevailed. The passengers and their relations crowded on the deck, friends taking a tender, but sorrowful, leave of each other, some weeping, others noisy in their grief, formed a spectacle, exciting even to those who witnessed similar ones daily, but which had not the power to disturb the current of thought that had taken possession of the mind of Maximilian from the moment he had set foot on the broad pavement of the quay.

"Here," said he, leaning heavily on the arm of Monte Cristo, "here is the spot where my father stopped, when the *Pharaon* entered the port; it was here that the good old man, whom you saved from death and dishonour, threw himself into my arms. I yet feel his warm tears on my face,—and his were not the only tears shed, for many who witnessed our meeting wept also."

Monte Cristo gently smiled and said:

"I was there;" at the same time pointing to the corner of a street. As he spoke, and in the very direction he indicated, a groan, expressive of bitter grief, was heard; and a woman was seen waving her hand to a passenger on board the vessel about to sail. Monte Cristo looked at her with an emotion that must have been remarked by Morrel had not his eyes been fixed on the vessel.

"Oh heavens!" exclaimed Morrel, "I do not deceive myself—that young man who is waving his hat, that youth in the uniform of a lieutenant, is Albert de Morcerf!"

"Yes," said Monte Cristo, "I recognised him."

"How so?—you were looking the other way."

The count smiled, as he was in the habit of doing when he did not wish to make any reply, and he again turned his looks towards the veiled female who soon disappeared at the corner of the street. Turning to his friend,—

" Dear Maximilian," said the count, " have you nothing to do in this land? "

" I have to weep over the grave of my father," replied Morrel, in a broken voice.

" Well, then, go—wait for me there, and I will soon join you. I have a pious visit to pay."

Morrel allowed his hand to fall into that which the count extended to him; then with an inexpressibly melancholy inclination of the head he quitted the count, and bent his steps to the east of the city. Monte Cristo remained on the same spot until Maximilian was out of sight; he then walked slowly towards the Allées de Meillan to seek out a small house with which our readers must have been familiar at the commencement of this story. It yet stood under the shade of the fine avenue of lime-trees, which forms one of the most frequented walks of the idlers of Marseilles; covered by an immense vine, which spread its aged and blackened branches over the stone front, burnt yellow by the ardent sun of the south. Two stone steps, worn away by the friction of the feet, led to the door, made of three planks, which, owing to their never having made acquaintance with paint or varnish, parted annually to reunite again when the damp season arrived. This house, with all its crumbling antiquity and apparent misery, was yet cheerful and picturesque, and was the same that old Dantès formerly inhabited—the only difference being that the old man occupied merely the garret, while the whole house was now placed at the command of Mercédès by the count.

The female whom the count had seen leave the ship with so much regret entered this house; she had scarcely closed the door after her when Monte Cristo appeared at the corner of a street, so that he found and lost her again almost at the same instant. The worn-out steps were old acquaintances of his; he knew better than anyone else how to open that weather-beaten door, with a large-headed nail, which served to raise the latch within. He entered without knocking, or giving any other intimation of his presence, as if he had been the friend or the master of the place. At the end of a passage, paved with bricks, was seen a little garden, bathed in sunshine, and rich in warmth and light— it was in this garden that Mercédès found, in the place indicated by the count, the sum of money which he, through a sense of delicacy, intimated had been placed there four-and-twenty years previously. The trees of the garden were easily seen from the steps of the street door. Monte Cristo, on stepping into the house, heard a sigh, almost resembling a deep sob; he looked in the direction whence it came, and there, under an arbour of Virginian jessamine, with its thick foliage, and beautiful long purple flowers, he perceived Mercédès seated, with her head bowed, and weeping bitterly. She had raised her veil, and with her face hidden by her hands, was giving free scope to those sighs and tears which had been so long restrained by the presence of her son. Monte Cristo advanced a few paces, which were heard on the gravel. Mercédès raised her head and uttered a cry of terror on beholding a man before her.

"Madame," said the count, "it is no longer in my power to restore you to happiness, but I offer you consolation; will you deign to accept it as coming from a friend?"

"I am, indeed, most wretched," replied Mercédès. "Alone in the world, I had but my son, and he has left me!"

"He possesses a noble heart, madame," replied the count, "and he has acted rightly. He feels that every man owes a tribute to his country. Had he remained with you, his life must have become a hateful burden, nor would he have participated in your griefs. He will increase in strength and honour by struggling with adversity, which he will convert into prosperity. Leave him to build up the future for you, and I venture to say, you will confide it to safe hands."

"Oh," replied the wretched woman, mournfully shaking her head, "the prosperity of which you speak, and which, from the bottom of my heart, I pray God in his mercy to grant him, I can never enjoy. The bitter cup of adversity has been drained by me to the very dregs, and I feel that the grave is not far distant. You have acted kindly, count, in bringing me back to the place where I have enjoyed so much bliss. I ought to meet death on the same spot where happiness was once all my own."

"Alas!" said Monte Cristo, "your words sear and embitter my heart, the more so as you have every reason to hate me; I have been the cause of all your misfortunes; but why do you pity, instead of blame me? You render me still more unhappy."

"Hate you,—blame you,—*you*, Edmond! Hate—reproach the man that has spared my son's life! For was it not your fatal and sanguinary intention to destroy that son of whom M. de Morcerf was so proud? Oh, look at me well, and discover, if you can, even the semblance of a reproach in me."

The count looked up, and fixed his eyes on Mercédès, who, partly rising from her seat, extended both her hands towards him.

"Oh, look at me," continued she, with a feeling of profound

melancholy; "my eyes no longer dazzle by their brilliancy, for the time has long fled since I used to smile on Edmond Dantès, who anxiously looked out for me from the window of yonder garret, then inhabited by his old father. Years of grief have created an abyss between those days and the present.—I neither reproach you nor hate you, my friend! Oh, no, Edmond, it is myself that I blame,—myself that I hate! Oh, miserable creature that I am!" cried she, clasping her hands, and raising her eyes to heaven. "I once possessed piety, innocence, and love,—the three ingredients of the happiness of angels,—and now what am I?"

Monte Cristo approached her, and silently took her hand.

"No," said she, withdrawing it gently, "no, my friend, touch me not. You have spared me, yet of all those who have fallen under your vengeance I was the most guilty. They were influenced by hatred, by avarice, and by self-love; but I was base, and, for want of courage, acted against my judgment. Nay, do not press my hand, Edmond! You are thinking of some kind expression, I am sure, to console me, but do not bestow it on me, for I am no longer worthy of kindness. See" (and she exposed her face completely to view), "see, misfortune has silvered my hair; my eyes have shed so many tears that they are encircled by a rim of purple; and my brow is wrinkled. You, Edmond, on the contrary,—you are still young, handsome, dignified; it is because you have never doubted the mercy of God, and he has supported and strengthened you in all your trials."

As Mercédès spoke, the tears chased each other down her wan cheeks; the unhappy woman's heart was breaking, as memory recalled the changeful events of her life. Monte Cristo, however, took her hand, and imprinted a kiss on it, but she herself felt that it was with no greater warmth than he would have respectfully bestowed on the hand of some marble statue of a saint.

"It often happens," continued she, "that a first fault destroys the prospects of a whole life. I believed you dead; why did I survive you? What good has it done me to mourn for you eternally in the secret recesses of my heart? Only to make a woman of nine-and-thirty look like one of fifty years of age. Why, having recognised you, and I the only one to do so, why was I able to save my son alone? Ought I not also to have rescued the man that I had accepted for a husband, guilty though he were? Yet I let him die; what do I say? Oh merciful heavens! was I not accessary to his death by my supine insensibility, by my contempt for him, not remembering, or not willing to remember, that it was for my sake he had become a traitor and a perjurer? In what am I benefited by accompanying my son so far, since I now abandon him, and allow him to depart alone to the baneful climate of Africa? Oh, I have been base, cowardly, I tell you; I have abjured my affections, and, like all renegades, I am of evil omen to those who surround me! "

" No, Mercédès," said Monte Cristo, " no; you judge yourself with too much severity. You are a noble-minded woman, and it was your grief that disarmed me. Still I was but an agent, led on by an invisible and offended Deity, who chose not to withhold the fatal blow that I was destined to hurl. I take that God to witness, at whose feet I have prostrated myself daily for the last ten years, that I would have sacrificed my life to you, and, with my life, the projects that were indissolubly linked with it. But— and I say it with some pride, Mercédès—God required me, and I lived. Examine the past and the present, and endeavour to pierce futurity, and then say whether I am not a Divine instrument. The most dreadful misfortunes, the most frightful sufferings, the abandonment of all those who loved me, the persecution of those who did not know me, formed the trials of my youth; when suddenly, from captivity, solitude, misery, I was restored to light and liberty, and became the possessor of a fortune so brilliant, so unbounded, so unheard-of, that I must have been blind not to be conscious that God had endowed me with it to work out his own great designs. From that time I viewed this fortune as confided to me for a particular purpose. Not a thought was given to a life which you once, Mercédès, had the power to render blissful,— not one hour of peaceful calm was mine, but I felt myself driven on like an exterminating angel. Like those adventurous captains about to embark on some enterprise full of danger, I laid in my provisions, I loaded my arms, I collected every means of attack and defence; I inured my body to the most violent exercises, my soul to the bitterest trials; I taught my arm to slay, my eyes to behold excruciating sufferings, and my mouth to smile at the most horrid spectacles. From good-natured, confiding, and for-giving, I became revengeful, cunning, and wicked, or rather immovable as fate. Then I launched out into the path that was opened to me; I overcame every obstacle and reached the goal. But woe to those who met me in my career."

" Enough," said Mercédès, " enough, Edmond! Believe me that she who alone recognised you has been the only one to comprehend you. And had she crossed your path, and you had crushed her like a frail glass, still, Edmond, still she must have admired you! Like the gulf between me and the past, there is an abyss between you, Edmond, and the rest of mankind; and I tell you freely, that the comparison I drew between you and other men will ever be one of my greatest tortures. No! there is nothing in the world to resemble you in worth and goodness! But we must say farewell, Edmond, and let us part."

" Before I leave you, Mercédès, have you no request to make?" said the count.

" I desire but one thing in this world, Edmond—the happiness of my son."

" Pray to the Almighty to spare his life, and I will take upon myself to promote his happiness."

" Thanks, thanks, Edmond! "

" But have you no request to make for yourself, Mercédès? "

" For myself I want nothing. I live, as it were, between two graves. The one, that of Edmond Dantès—lost to me long, long since. He had my love! That word ill becomes my faded lip now, but it is a memory dear to my heart, and one that I would not lose for all that the world contains. The other grave is that of the man who met his death from the hand of Edmond Dantès. I approve of the deed, but I must pray for the dead."

" Yes, your son shall be happy, Mercédès," repeated the count.

" Then I shall enjoy as much happiness as this world can possibly confer."

" But what are your intentions? "

" To say that I shall live here, like the Mercédès of other times, gaining my bread by labour, would not be true, nor would you believe me. I have no longer the strength to do anything but to spend my days in prayer. However, I shall have no occasion to work, for the little sum of money buried by you, and which I found in the place you mentioned, will be sufficient to maintain me. Rumour will probably be busy respecting me, my occupations, my manner of living—that will signify but little! "

" Mercédès," said the count, " I do not say it to blame you, but you made an unnecessary sacrifice in relinquishing the whole of the fortune amassed by M. de Morcerf; half of it, at least, by right belonged to you, in virtue of your vigilance and economy."

" I perceive what you are intending to propose to me; but I cannot accept it, Edmond—my son would not permit it."

" Nothing shall be done without the full approbation of Albert de Morcerf. I will make myself acquainted with his intentions, and will submit to them. But if he be willing to accept my offers, will you oppose them? "

" You know well, Edmond, that I am no longer a reasoning creature. I have no will, unless it be the will never to decide. I have been so overwhelmed by the many storms that have broken over my head, that I am become passive in the hands of the Almighty, like a sparrow in the talons of an eagle. I live, because it is not ordained for me to die. If succour be sent to me I will accept it."

"Ah, madame," said Monte Cristo, "you should not talk thus! It is not so we should evince our resignation to the will of Heaven; on the contrary, we are all free agents."

"Alas!" exclaimed Mercédès, "if it were so, if I possessed free-will, but without the power to render that will efficacious, it would drive me to despair."

Monte Cristo dropped his head and shrank from the vehemence of her grief.

"Will you not even say you will see me again?" he asked.

"On the contrary, we shall meet again," said Mercédès, pointing to heaven with solemnity. "I tell you so to prove to you that I still hope." And after pressing her own trembling hand upon that of the count, Mercédès rushed up the stairs and disappeared.

Monte Cristo slowly left the house and turned towards the quay. But Mercédès saw not his departure, though she was seated at the little window of the room which had been occupied by old Dantès. Her eyes were straining to see the ship which was carrying her son over the vast sea. But still her voice involuntarily murmured softly:

"Edmond! Edmond! Edmond!"*

The count departed with a sad heart from the house in which he had left Mercédès, probably never to behold her again.

He turned towards the cemetery, where he felt sure of finding Morrel. He, too, ten years ago, had piously sought out a tomb, and sought it vainly. He, who returned to France with millions, had been unable to find the grave of his father, who had perished from hunger. Morrel had, indeed, placed a cross over the spot, but it had fallen down, and the gravedigger had burnt it, as he did all the old wood in the churchyard.

The worthy merchant had been more fortunate. Dying in the arms of his children, he had been by them laid by the side of his wife, who had preceded him in eternity by two years. Two large slabs of marble, on which were inscribed their names, were placed on either side of a little enclosure, railed in, and shaded by four cypress-trees.

Morrel was leaning against one of these, mechanically fixing his eyes on the graves. His grief was so profound, he was nearly unconscious.

"Maximilian," said the count, "you should not look on the graves, but there;" and he pointed upwards.

"The dead are everywhere," said Morrel; "did you not yourself tell me so as we left Paris?"

" Maximilian," said the count, " you asked me during the journey to allow you to remain some days at Marseilles. Do you still wish to do so? "

" I have no wishes, count; only I fancy I could pass the time less painfully here than anywhere else."

" So much the better, for I must leave you; but I carry your word with me, do I not? "

" You have my promise," he said, after a minute's pause, extending his hand to Monte Cristo. " Only remember——"

" On the 5th of October, Morrel, I shall expect you at the island of Monte Cristo. On the 4th a yacht will wait for you in the port of Bastia, it will be called the *Eurus*. You will deliver your name to the captain, who will bring you to me. It is understood—is it not? "

" But, count, do you remember that the 5th of October——"

" Child! " replied the count, " not to know the value of a man's word! I have told you twenty times that if you wish to die on that day I will assist you. Morrel, farewell! "

" Do you leave me? "

" Yes; I have business in Italy. I leave you alone with your misfortunes and with hope, Maximilian."

" When do you leave? "

" Immediately; the steamer waits, and in an hour I shall be far from you. Will you accompany me to the harbour, Maximilian? "

" I am entirely yours, count."

Morrel accompanied the count to the harbour; the white steam was ascending like a plume of feathers from the black chimney. The steamer soon disappeared, and in an hour afterwards, as the count had said, was scarcely distinguishable in the horizon amidst the fogs of the night.

114

Peppino

AT the same time the steamer disappeared behind Cape Morgiou, a man, travelling post on the road from Florence to Rome, had just passed the little town of Aquapendente. He was travelling fast enough to make a great deal of ground without becoming altogether suspicious.

This man, dressed in a greatcoat, or rather a surtout, a little the worse for the journey, but which exhibited the riband of the Legion d'Honneur still fresh and brilliant, a decoration which also ornamented the under coat, might be recognised, not only by these signs, but also from the accent with which he spoke to the postilion, to be a Frenchman. Another proof that he was a native of the universal country was apparent in the fact of his knowing no other Italian words than the terms used in music.

" *Allegro!* " he called out to the postilions at every ascent. " *Moderato!* " he cried as they descended. And anyone who has ever travelled that road, knows there are hills enough between Rome and Florence by the way of Aquapendente!

These two words greatly amused the men to whom they were addressed. On reaching La Storta, the point from whence Rome is first visible, the traveller evinced none of the enthusiastic curiosity which usually leads strangers to stand up and endeavour to catch sight of the dome of St. Peter's, which may be seen long before any other object is distinguishable. No, he merely drew a pocket-book from his pocket, and took from it a paper folded in four, and, after having examined it in a manner almost reverential, he said:

" Good! I have it still."

The carriage entered by the Porte del Popolo, turned to the left, and stopped at the Hôtel d'Espagne. Maître Pastrini, our old acquaintance, received the traveller at the door hat in hand. The traveller alighted, ordered a good dinner, and inquired the address of the house of Thomson and French, which was immediately given to him, as it was one of the most celebrated in Rome. It was situated in the Via dei Banchi, near St. Peter's.

In Rome, as everywhere else, the arrival of a post-chaise is an event. Ten young descendants of Marius and the Gracchi, barefooted and out at elbows, with one hand resting on the hip, and the other arm gracefully curved above the head, stared at the traveller, the post-chaise, and the horses; to these were added about fifty little vagabonds from the states of his holiness, who made a collection for plunging into the Tiber at high water from the bridge of St. Angelo.

Now, as these *gamins* of Rome, more fortunate than those of Paris, understand every language, more especially the French, they heard the traveller order an apartment, a dinner, and finally inquire the way to the house of Thomson and French. The result was, that when the new-comer left the hotel with the cicerone, a man detached himself from the rest of the idlers, and, without having been seen by the traveller, and appearing to excite no attention from the guide, followed the stranger with as much skill as a Parisian agent of police would have used.

The Frenchman had been so impatient to reach the house of Thomson and French that he would not wait for the horses to be harnessed, but left word for the carriage to overtake him on the road, or to wait for him at the banker's door. He reached it before the carriage arrived.

The Frenchman entered, leaving his guide in the ante-room, who immediately entered into conversation with two or three of those industrious idlers, who are always to be found in Rome at the doors of banking-houses, churches, museums, or theatres. With the Frenchman, the man who had followed him entered too; the Frenchman knocked at the inner door, and entered the first room; his shadow did the same.

" Messrs. Thomson and French? " inquired the stranger.

A kind of footman rose at a sign from a confidential clerk belonging to the first desk.

" Whom shall I announce? " said the footman.

" The Baron Danglars."

" Follow me! " said the man. A door opened, through which the footman and the baron disappeared.

The man who had followed Danglars sat down on a bench. The clerk continued to write for the next five minutes; the man also preserved profound silence, and remained perfectly motionless. Then the pen of the clerk ceased to move over the paper; he raised his head, and appearing to be perfectly sure of a *tête-à-tête*,—

" Ah, ha! " he said, " here you are, Peppino! "

" Yes," was the laconic reply.

" You have found out that there is something worth having about this large gentleman? "

" There is no great merit due to me, for we were informed of it."

" You know his business here, then? "

" *Pardieu!* he has come to draw, but I don't know how much! "

" You will know presently, my friend."

" Very well, only do not give me false information, as you did the other day."

" What do you mean?—of whom do you speak? Was it the Englishman who carried off 3000 crowns from here the other day? "

" No; he really had 3000 crowns, and we found them. I mean the Russian prince, who you said had 30,000 livres, and we only found 22,000."

" You must have searched badly."

" Luigi Vampa himself searched."

" Indeed! But you must let me make my observations, or the Frenchman will transact his business without my knowing the sum."

Peppino nodded, and, taking a rosary from his pocket, began to mutter a few prayers, while the clerk disappeared through the same door by which Danglars and the footman had gone out. At the expiration of ten minutes the clerk returned, with a bright countenance.

" Well? " asked Peppino of his friend.

" Joy, joy!—the sum is large."

" Five or six millions, is it not? "

" Yes, you know the amount."

" On the receipt of the Count of Monte Cristo? "

" Why, how came you to be so well acquainted with all this? "

" I told you we were informed beforehand."

" Then why do you apply to me? "

" That I may be sure I have the right man."

" Yes, it is indeed he! Five millions—a pretty sum, eh, Peppino? "

" Hush!—here is our man! "

The clerk seized his pen, and Peppino his beads; one was writing, and the other praying, when the door opened.

Danglars looked radiant with joy; the banker accompanied him to the door.

Peppino followed Danglars.

According to the arrangements, the carriage was waiting at the door. The guide held the door open. Guides are useful people, who will turn their hands to anything. Danglars leaped into the carriage like a young man of twenty. The cicerone reclosed the door, and sprang up by the side of the coachman. Peppino mounted the seat behind.

" Will your excellency visit St. Peter's? " asked the cicerone.

" I did not come to Rome to see," said Danglars aloud; then he added softly, with an avaricious smile, " I came to touch! " and he tapped his pocket-book, in which he had just placed a letter.

" Then your excellency is going——"

" To the hotel."

" Casa Pastrini! " said the cicerone to the coachman, and the carriage drove rapidly on.

Ten minutes afterwards the baron entered his apartment, and Peppino stationed himself on the bench outside the door of the hotel, after having whispered something in the ear of one of the descendants of Marius and the Gracchi whom we noticed at the beginning of the chapter, who immediately ran down the road leading to the Capitol at his fullest speed.

Danglars was tired and sleepy; he therefore went to bed, placing his pocket-book under his pillow.

Peppino had a little spare time, so he had a game of *mora** with the facchina, lost three crowns, and then to console himself, drank a bottle of vin d'Orvieto.

The next morning Danglars awoke late, though he went to bed so early; he had not slept well for five or six nights, even if he had slept at all. He breakfasted heartily, and caring little, as he said, for the beauties of the Eternal City, ordered post-horses at noon. But Danglars had not reckoned upon the formalities of the police and the idleness of the posting-master. The horses only arrived at two o'clock, and the cicerone did not bring the passport till three. All these preparations had collected a number of idlers round the door of Maître Pastrini's; the descendants of Marius and the Gracchi were also not wanting. The baron walked triumphantly through the crowd, who, for the sake of gain, styled him " your excellency." As Danglars had hitherto contented himself with being called a baron, he felt rather flattered at the title of excellency, and distributed a dozen pauls* amongst the *canaille*, who were ready for twelve more to call him " your highness."

" Which road? " asked the postilion in Italian.

" The Ancona road," replied the baron.

Maître Pastrini interpreted the question and answer, and the horses galloped off.

Danglars intended travelling to Venice, where he would receive one part of his fortune, and then proceeding to Vienna, where he would find the rest, he meant to take up his residence in the latter town, which he had been told was a city of pleasure.

He had scarcely advanced three leagues out of Rome when daylight began to disappear. Danglars had not intended starting so late, or he would have remained; he put his head out and asked the postilion how long it would be before they reached the next town.

" *Non capisco,*" was the reply.

Danglars bent his head, which he meant to imply, " Very well."

The carriage again moved on.

" I will stop at the first posting-house," said Danglars to himself.

He still felt the same self-satisfaction which he had experienced the previous evening, and which had procured him so good a night's rest. He was luxuriously stretched in a good English calèche, with double springs; he was drawn by four good horses, at full gallop; he knew the relay to be at a distance of seven leagues. What subject of meditation could present itself to the banker, so fortunately become bankrupt?

Danglars thought for ten minutes upon his wife in Paris; another ten minutes upon his daughter travelling about with Mademoiselle d'Armilly; the same period was given to his creditors, and the manner in which he intended spending their money; and then, having no subject left for contemplation, he shut his eyes and fell asleep.

Now and then a jolt more violent than the rest caused him to open his eyes; then he felt that he was still carried with vast rapidity over the same country, so thickly strewn with broken aqueducts, which look like granite giants petrified in the midst of their course. But the night was cold, dull, and rainy; and it was much more pleasant for a traveller to remain in the warm carriage than to put his head out of the window to make inquiries of a postilion, whose only answer was, " *Non capisco.*"

Danglars therefore continued to sleep, saying to himself that he would be sure to awake at the posting-house.

The carriage stopped. Danglars fancied they had reached the long-desired point; he opened his eyes, looked through the window, expecting to find himself in the midst of some town, or at least village; but he saw nothing but a kind of ruin, whence three or four men went and came like shadows. Danglars waited for a moment, expecting the postilion to come and demand payment, having finished his stage. He intended taking advantage of the opportunity to make fresh inquiries of the new conductor; but the horses were unharnessed, and others put in their places, without anyone claiming money from the traveller. Danglars, astonished, opened the door; but a strong hand pushed him back, and the carriage rolled on.

The baron was completely roused.

" Eh! " he said to the postilion,—" eh, *mio caro*? "

This was another little piece of Italian the baron had learnt from hearing his daughter sing Italian duets with Cavalcanti.

But *mio caro* replied not. Danglars then opened the window.

" Come, my friend," he said, thrusting his hand through the opening, " where are we going? "

" *Dentro la testa!* " answered a solemn and imperious voice, accompanied by a menacing gesture.

Danglars thought *dentro la testa* meant " Put in your head! " He was making rapid progress in Italian.

He obeyed, not without some uneasiness, which, momentarily increasing, caused his mind, instead of being as unoccupied as it was when he began his journey, to fill with ideas which were very likely to keep a traveller awake, more especially one in such a situation as Danglars. His eyes acquired that quality which in the first moment of strong emotion enables them to see distinctly, and which afterwards fails from being too much taxed. Before we are alarmed, we see correctly; when we are alarmed, we see double; and when we have been alarmed, we see nothing but trouble.

Danglars observed a man in a cloak galloping at the right hand of the carriage.

" Some gendarme! " he exclaimed. " Can I have been signalled by the French telegraphs to the pontifical authorities? " He resolved to end his anxiety. " Where are you leading me? " he asked. " *Dentro la testa*," replied the same voice, with the same menacing accent.

Danglars turned to the left; another man on horseback was galloping on that side.

" Decidedly," said Danglars, with the perspiration on his forehead, " I must be taken." And he threw himself back in the calèche, not this time to sleep, but to think. Directly afterwards the moon rose. He then saw the great aqueducts, those stone phantoms which he had before remarked; only then they were on the right hand; now they were on the left. He understood that they had described a circle, and were bringing him back to Rome.

" Oh, unfortunate! " he cried, " they must have obtained my arrest."

The carriage continued to roll on with frightful speed. A terrible hour elapsed, for every spot they passed indicated they were on the road back. At length, he saw a dark mass, against which it seemed the carriage must dash; but it turned round, leaving behind it the mass, which was no other than one of the ramparts encircling Rome.

"Oh! oh!" cried Danglars, "we are not returning to Rome; then it is not justice which is pursuing me! Gracious heavens! another idea presents itself; what if they should be——"

His hair stood on end. He remembered those interesting stories so little believed in Paris respecting Roman bandits; he remembered the adventures that Albert de Morcerf had related when it was intended he should marry Mademoiselle Eugénie.

"They are robbers, perhaps!" he muttered.

Just then the carriage rolled on something harder than the gravelled road. Danglars hazarded a look on both sides of the road, and perceived monuments of a singular form; and his mind now recalled all the details Morcerf had related, and comparing them with his own situation, he felt sure he must be on the Appian Way. On the left, in a sort of valley, he perceived a circular excavation. It was Caracalla's circle.* On a word from the man who rode at the side of the carriage, it stopped.

At the same time the door was opened.

"*Scendi!*" exclaimed a commanding voice.

Danglars instantly descended; though he did not yet speak Italian, he understood it very well. More dead than alive, he looked around him. Four men surrounded him, besides the postilion.

"*Di quà*," said one of the men, descending a little path leading out of the Appian Way. Danglars followed his guide without opposition, and had no occasion to turn round to see whether the three others were following him. Still it appeared as though they stopped at equal distances from one another like sentinels. After walking for about ten minutes, during which Danglars did not exchange a single word with his guide, he found himself between a hillock and a clump of high weeds; three men, standing silent, formed a triangle, of which he was the centre. He wished to speak, but his tongue refused to move.

"*Avanti!*" said the same sharp and imperative voice.

This time Danglars had double reason to understand, for if the word and gesture had not explained the speaker's meaning, it was clearly expressed by the man walking behind him, who pushed him so rudely, that he struck against the guide. This guide was our friend Peppino, who dashed into the thicket of high weeds, through a path which none but lizards or polecats could have imagined to be an open road. Peppino stopped before a pit overhung by thick hedges; the pit, half open, afforded a passage to the young man, who disappeared like the evil spirits in the fairy tales. The voice and gesture of the man who followed Danglars ordered him to do the same. There was no longer any doubt; the bankrupt was in the hands of Roman banditti.

Danglars acquitted himself like a man placed between two dangerous positions, and who is rendered brave by fear. Notwithstanding his large stomach, certainly not intended to penetrate the fissures of an Italian road, he slid down like Peppino, and closing his eyes, fell upon his feet. As he touched the ground, he opened his eyes. The path was wide, but dark. Peppino, who cared little for being recognised now he was in his own territories, struck a light, and lit a torch. Two other men descended after Danglars, forming the rearguard, and pushing Danglars whenever he happened to stop, they arrived by a gentle declivity at the centre of a cross-road of sinister appearance. Indeed, the walls hollowed out in sepulchres, placed one above the other, seemed, in contrast with the white stones, to open their large dark eyes, like those which we see on the faces of the dead. A sentinel struck his carbine against his left hand.

" Who goes there? " he cried.

" Friends! friends! " said Peppino; " but where is the captain? "

" There! " said the sentinel, pointing over his shoulder to a sort of large hall, hollowed out of the rock, the lights from which shone into the passage through the large arched openings.

" Fine spoil! captain—fine spoil! " said Peppino in Italian, and taking Danglars by the collar of his coat, he dragged him to an opening resembling a door, through which they entered the hall of which the captain appeared to have made his dwelling-place.

" Is this the man? " asked the captain, who was attentively reading Plutarch's *Life of Alexander*.

" Himself, captain,—himself."

" Very well, show him to me."

At this rather impertinent order, Peppino raised his torch to Danglars' face, who hastily withdrew, that he might not have his eyelashes burnt. His agitated features presented the appearance of pale and hideous terror.

" The man is tired," said the captain, " conduct him to his bed."

" Oh," murmured Danglars, " that bed is probably one of the coffins hollowed in the wall, and the sleep I shall enjoy will be death from one of the poniards I see glistening in the shade."

From the depths of the hall were now seen to rise from their beds of dried leaves or calf's-skin the companions of the man who had been found by Albert de Morcerf reading *Cæsar's Commentaries*, and by Danglars studying the *Life of Alexander*. The banker uttered a groan and followed his guide; he neither supplicated nor exclaimed. He no longer possessed strength, will, power, or feeling; he followed where they led him. At length, he found himself at the foot of a staircase, and he mechanically lifted his foot five or six times. Then a low door was opened before him, and bending his head to avoid striking his forehead, he entered a small room cut out of the rock. The cell was clean, though naked, and dry, though situated at a great distance under the earth. Danglars, on beholding it, brightened, fancying it a type of safety.

" Oh, God be praised! " he said; " it is a real bed! "

" *Ecco!* " said the guide, and pushing Danglars into the cell, he closed the door upon him.

A bolt grated; Danglars was a prisoner; besides, had there been no bolt, it would have been impossible for him to pass through the midst of the garrison who held the catacombs of St. Sebastian, encamped round a master whom our readers must have recognised as the famous Luigi Vampa. Danglars, too, had recognised the bandit, whose existence he would not believe when Albert de Morcerf mentioned him in Paris; and not only did he recognise him, but also the cell in which Albert had been confined, and which was probably kept for the accommodation of strangers. These recollections were dwelt upon with some pleasure by Danglars, and restored him to some degree of tranquillity. Since the bandits had not despatched him at once, he felt that they would not kill him at all. They had arrested him for the purpose of robbery, and as he had only a few louis about him, he doubted not he would be ransomed. He remembered that Morcerf had been taxed at 4000 crowns, and as he considered himself of much greater importance than Morcerf, he fixed his own price at 8000 crowns: 8000 crowns amounted to 48,000 livres: he would then have about 5,050,000 francs. With this sum he could manage to keep out of difficulties.

Therefore, tolerably secure in being able to extricate himself from his position, provided he were not rated at the unreasonable sum of 5,050,000 francs, he stretched himself on his bed, and, after turning round two or three times, he fell asleep with the tranquillity of the hero whose life Luigi Vampa was studying.

115

Luigi Vampa's Bill of Fare

WE awake from every sleep except the one dreaded by
Danglars. He awoke. To a Parisian accustomed to silken
curtains, walls hung with velvet drapery, and the soft perfume of
burning wood, the white smoke of which diffuses itself in graceful
curves around the room, the appearance of the whitewashed cell
which greeted his eyes on awaking seemed like the continuation
of some disagreeable dream. But in such a situation a single
moment suffices to change the strongest doubt into certainty.

" Yes, yes," he murmured, " I am in the hands of the brigands
of whom Albert de Morcerf spoke."

His first idea was to breathe, that he might know whether he
was wounded. He borrowed this from *Don Quixote*, the only
book he had ever read, but which he still slightly remembered.

" No," he cried, " they have not wounded, but perhaps they
have robbed me! " and he thrust his hands into his pockets.
They were untouched; the hundred louis he had reserved for
his journey from Rome to Venice were in his trousers' pocket,
and in that of his greatcoat he found the little note-case containing
his letter of credit for 5,050,000 francs.

" Singular bandits! " he exclaimed; " they have left me my
purse and pocket-book. As I was saying last night, they intend
me to be ransomed. Holla! here is my watch! Let me see what
time it is."

Danglars' watch, one of Breguet's chef-d'œuvres, which he
had carefully wound up on the previous night, struck half-past
five. Without this Danglars would have been quite ignorant of
the time, for daylight did not reach his cell. Should he demand
an explanation from the bandits, or should he wait patiently for
them to propose it? The last alternative seemed the most prudent,
so he waited until twelve o'clock. During all this time a sentinel,
who had been relieved at eight o'clock, had been watching his
door.

Danglars suddenly felt a strong inclination to see the person
who kept watch over him. He had remarked that a few rays, not
of daylight, but from a lamp, penetrated through the ill-joined
planks of the door; he approached it just as a brigand was
refreshing himself with a mouthful of brandy, which, owing to

the leather bottle containing it, sent forth an odour which was extremely unpleasant to Danglars.

"Faugh!" he exclaimed, retreating to the extreme corner of his cell.

At twelve this man was replaced by another functionary, and Danglars, wishing to catch sight of his new guardian, approached the door again. He was an athletic, gigantic bandit, with large eyes, thick lips, and a flat nose; his red hair fell in dishevelled masses like snakes around his shoulders.

"Ah, ah," cried Danglars, "this fellow is more like an ogre than anything else; however, I am rather too old and tough to be very good eating!"

We see that Danglars was quite collected enough to jest; at the same time, as though to disprove the ogreish propensities, the man took some black bread, cheese, and onions from his wallet, which he began devouring voraciously.

"May I be hanged," said Danglars, glancing at the bandit's dinner through the crevices of the door,—"may I be hanged if I can understand how people can eat such filth!" and he withdrew to seat himself upon his goatskin, which recalled to him the smell of the brandy.

But the secrets of nature are incomprehensible, and there are certain invitations contained in even the coarsest food which appeal very irresistibly to a fasting stomach. Danglars felt his own not to be very well supplied just then; and gradually the man appeared less ugly, the bread less black, and the cheese more fresh, while those dreadful vulgar onions recalled to his mind certain sauces and side-dishes, which his cook prepared in a very superior manner whenever he said, "M. Deniseau, let me have a nice little fricassée to-day." He rose and knocked at the door; the bandit raised his head. Danglars knew that he was heard, so he redoubled his blows.

"*Che cosa?*" asked the bandit.

"Come, come," said Danglars, tapping his fingers against the door, "I think it is quite time to think of giving me something to eat!"

But whether he did not understand him, or whether he had received no orders respecting the nourishment of Danglars, the giant, without answering, recommenced his dinner.

Danglars felt his pride hurt, and not wishing to commit himself with the brute, threw himself down again on his goatskin and did not breathe another word.

Four hours passed by; the giant was replaced by another bandit. Danglars, who really began to experience sundry gnawings at the stomach, rose softly, and again applied his eye to the crack of the door, and recognised the intelligent countenance of his guide. It was, indeed, Peppino, who was preparing to mount guard as comfortably as possible by seating himself opposite to the door, and placing between his legs an earthen pan, containing chick-pease stewed with bacon. Near the pan he also placed a pretty little basket of grapes and a bottle of vin d'Orvieto. Peppino was decidedly an epicure.

While witnessing these preparations Danglars' mouth watered. "Come," he said to himself, "let me try if he will be more tractable than the other;" and he tapped gently at the door.

"Coming!" exclaimed Peppino, who, from frequenting the house of Maître Pastrini, understood French perfectly.

Danglars immediately recognised him as the man who had called out in such a furious manner, "Put in your head!" But this was not the time for recrimination, so he assumed his most agreeable manner and said with a gracious smile:

"Excuse me, sir, but are they not going to give me any dinner? "

"Does your excellency happen to be hungry? "

"Happen to be hungry! that's excellent, when I have not eaten for twenty-four hours!" muttered Danglars. Then he added aloud, "Yes, sir, I am hungry—very hungry!"

"What would your excellency like? " and Peppino placed his pan on the ground so that the steam rose directly under the nostrils of Danglars. "Give your orders! "

"Have you kitchens here? "

"Kitchens?—of course! complete ones."

"And cooks? "

"Excellent! "

"Well, a fowl, fish, game,—it signifies little, so that I eat."

"As your excellency pleases! You mentioned a fowl, I think."

"Yes, a fowl."

Peppino, turning round, shouted, "A fowl for his excellency! "

His voice yet echoed in the archway when a young man, handsome, graceful, and half naked, appeared, bearing a fowl in a silver dish on his head, without the assistance of his hands.

"I could almost believe myself at the Café de Paris," murmured Danglars.

"Here, your excellency," said Peppino, taking the fowl from the young bandit and placing it on the worm-eaten table, which, with a stool and the goatskin bed, formed the entire furniture of the cell.

Danglars asked for a knife and fork.

"Here, excellency," said Peppino, offering him a little blunt knife and a boxwood fork.

Danglars took the knife in one hand and the fork in the other, and was about to cut up the fowl.

"Pardon me, excellency," said Peppino, placing his hand on the banker's shoulder; "people pay here before they eat. They might not be satisfied and——"

"Ah, ah," thought Danglars, "this is no longer like Paris, without reckoning that I shall probably be fleeced! Never mind, I will carry it off well! I have always heard how cheap poultry is in Italy; I should think a fowl is worth about twelve sous at Rome."

"There," he said, throwing a louis down.

Peppino picked up the louis, and Danglars again prepared to carve the fowl.

"Stay a moment, your excellency," said Peppino, rising; "you still owe me something."

"I said they would fleece me," thought Danglars; but resolving to resist the extortion, he said, "Come, how much do I owe you for this fowl?"

"Your excellency has given me a louis on account."

"A louis on account for a fowl?"

"Certainly; and your excellency now owes me 4999 louis."

Danglars opened his enormous eyes on hearing this gigantic joke.

"Come, come, this is very droll—very amusing—I allow; but, as I am very hungry, pray allow me to eat. Stay, here is another louis for you."

"Then, that will make only 4998 louis," said Peppino, with the same indifference. "I shall get them all in time."

"Oh, as for that," said Danglars, exasperated at his perseverance in the jest,—"as for that, you will never succeed. Go to the devil! You do not know with whom you have to deal!"

Peppino made a sign, and the youth hastily removed the fowl. Danglars threw himself upon his goatskin, and Peppino, reclosing the door, again began eating his pease and bacon. Though Danglars could not see Peppino, the noise of his teeth allowed no doubt as to his occupation. He was certainly eating, and noisily too, like an ill-bred man.

"Brute!" said Danglars.

Peppino pretended not to hear him, and, without even turning his head, continued to eat slowly.

Danglars' stomach felt so empty, it seemed as though it would be impossible ever to fill it again; still he had patience for another half-hour, which appeared to him like a century. He again rose and went to the door.

"Come, sir, do not keep me starving here any longer, but tell me what they want."

"Nay, your excellency, it is you who should tell us what you want. Give your orders, and we will execute them."

"Then open the door directly."

Peppino obeyed.

"*Pardieu!* I want something to eat! To eat! Do you hear?"

"Are you hungry?"

"Come, you understand me."

"What would your excellency like to eat?"

"A piece of dry bread, since the fowls are beyond all price in this accursed place."

"Bread! Very well. Holloa, there! Some bread!" he exclaimed.

The youth brought a small loaf.

"How much?" asked Danglars.

"Four thousand nine hundred and ninety-eight louis," said Peppino. "You have paid two louis in advance."

"What! 100,000 francs for a loaf?"

"One hundred thousand francs!" repeated Peppino.

"But you asked only 100,000 francs for a fowl!"

"We have a fixed price for all our provisions. It signifies nothing whether you eat much or little—whether you have ten dishes or one,—it is always the same price."

"What! still keeping up this silly jest? My dear fellow, it is perfectly ridiculous—stupid! You had better tell me at once that you intend starving me to death."

"Oh, dear, no, your excellency, unless you intend to commit suicide. Pay and eat."

"And what am I to pay with, brute?" said Danglars, enraged. "Do you suppose I carry 100,000 francs in my pocket?"

"Your excellency has 5,050,000 francs in your pocket; that will be fifty fowls at 100,000 francs apiece, and half a fowl for the 50,000."

Danglars shuddered. The bandage fell from his eyes, and he understood the joke, which he did not think quite so stupid as he had done just before.

"Come," he said, "if I pay you the 100,000 francs, will you be satisfied, and allow me to eat at my ease?"

"Certainly," said Peppino.

"But how can I pay them?"

"Oh, nothing easier; you have an account opened with Messrs. Thomson and French, Via dei Banchi, Rome. Give me a bill for 4998 louis on these gentlemen, and our banker shall take it."

Danglars thought it as well to comply with a good grace; so he took the pen, ink, and paper Peppino offered him, wrote the bill, and signed it.

"Here," he said, "here is a bill at sight."

"And here is your fowl."

Danglars sighed while he carved the fowl; it appeared very thin for the price it had cost. As for Peppino, he read the paper attentively, put it in his pocket, and continued eating his peas.

116

The Pardon

THE next day Danglars was again hungry; certainly the air of that dungeon was very appetising. The prisoner expected that he would be at no expense that day, for, like an economical man, he had concealed half of his fowl and a piece of the bread in the corner of his cell. But he had no sooner eaten than he felt thirsty; he had forgotten that. He struggled against his thirst till his tongue clave to the roof of his mouth; then no longer able to resist, he called out. The sentinel opened the door; it was a new face. He thought it would be better to transact business with his old acquaintance; so he sent for Peppino.

"Here I am, your excellency," said Peppino, with an eagerness which Danglars thought favourable to him. "What do you want?"

"Something to drink."

"Your excellency knows that wine is beyond all price near Rome."

"Then give me water," cried Danglars, endeavouring to parry the blow.

"Oh, water is even more scarce than wine, your excellency, there has been such a drought!"

"Come," thought Danglars, "we are going to repeat the old story." And while he smiled as he attempted to regard the affair as a joke, he felt his temples moist with perspiration.

"Come, my friend," said Danglars, seeing he made no impression on Peppino, "you will not refuse me a glass of wine?"

"I have already told you that we do not sell retail."

"Well, then, let me have a bottle of the least expensive."

"They are all the same price."

"And what is that?"

"Twenty-five thousand francs per bottle."

"Tell me," cried Danglars, in a voice of extreme bitterness,—
"tell me that you wish to despoil me of all; it will be sooner
over than devouring me piecemeal."

"It is possible such may be the master's intention."

"The master!—who is he?"

"The person to whom you were conducted yesterday."

"Where is he?"

"Here."

"Let me see him."

"Certainly." And the next moment Luigi Vampa appeared
before Danglars.

"You sent for me," he said to the prisoner.

"Are you, sir, the chief of the people who brought me here?"

"Yes, your excellency. What then?"

"How much do you require for my ransom?"

"Merely the 5,000,000 you have about you."

Danglars felt a dreadful spasm dart through his heart.

"But this is all I have left in the world," he said, "out of an
immense fortune. If you deprive me of that, take away my life
also."

"We are forbidden to shed your blood."

"And by whom are you forbidden?"

"By him we obey."

"You do, then, obey someone?"

"Yes; a chief."

"I thought you said you were the chief?"

"So I am of these men; but there is another over me."

"And did your superior tell you to treat me thus?"

"Yes."

"But my purse will be exhausted."

"Probably."

"Come," said Danglars, "will you take a million?"

"No."

"Two millions?—Three?—Four? Come—four? I will give
them to you on condition that you let me go."

"Why do you offer me 4,000,000 for what is worth 5,000,000?
That is a kind of usury, banker, I do not understand."

"Take all, then! Take all, I tell you, and kill me!"

"Come, come, calm yourself. You will excite your blood, and
that would produce an appetite it would require a million a day
to satisfy. Be more economical!"

"But when I have no more money left to pay you?" asked
the infuriated Danglars.

"Then you must suffer hunger."

"Suffer hunger?" said Danglars, becoming pale.

" Most likely," replied Vampa coolly.

" But you say you do not wish to kill me? "

" No."

" And yet you will let me perish with hunger? "

" Ah, that is a different thing! "

" Well, then, wretches! " cried Danglars, " I will defy your infamous calculations; I would rather die at once; you may torture—torment—kill me,—but you shall not have my signature again."

" As your excellency pleases," said Vampa, as he left the cell.

Danglars, raving, threw himself on the goatskin.

Who could these men be? Who was the invisible chief? What could be his projects towards him? And why, when every one else was allowed to be ransomed, might he not also be? Oh, yes! certainly a speedy, sudden death would be a fine means of deceiving these remorseless enemies, who appeared to pursue him with such incomprehensible vengeance. But to die! For the first time in his life, Danglars contemplated death with a mixture of dread and desire; the time had come when the implacable spectre, which exists in the mind of every human creature, arrested his sight, and called out with every pulsation of his heart, " Thou shalt die! "

Danglars resembled a timid animal excited in the chase; first it flies, then despairs, and, at last, by the very force of desperation, succeeds in escaping. Danglars meditated an escape. But the walls were solid rock; a man was sitting reading at the only outlet to the cell, and behind that man figures armed with guns continually passed.

His resolution not to sign lasted two days, after which he offered a million for some food.

They sent him a magnificent supper and took his million.

From this time the prisoner resolved to suffer no longer, but to yield to all his exigencies. At the end of twelve days, after having made a splendid dinner, he reckoned his accounts, and found he had only 50,000 francs left. Then a strange reaction took place; he who had just abandoned 5,000,000 endeavoured to save the 50,000 francs he had left, and, sooner than give them up, he resolved to enter again upon his life of privation; he yielded to rays of hope resembling madness. He, who for so long a time had forgotten God, began to think that miracles were possible; that the accursed cave might be discovered by the officers of the Papal States, who would release him; that then he would have 50,000 francs remaining, which would be sufficient to save him from starvation; and, finally, he prayed that this sum might be preserved to him,—and, as he prayed, he wept.

Three days passed thus, during which his prayers were frequent, if not heartfelt. Sometimes he was delirious, and fancied he saw an old man stretched on a pallet. He, also, was dying of hunger.

On the fourth, he was no longer a man, but a living corpse. He had picked up every crumb that had been left from his former meals, and was beginning to eat the matting which covered the floor of his cell. Then he entreated Peppino, as he would a guardian angel, to give him food; he offered him 1000 francs for a mouthful of bread.

But Peppino did not answer.

On the fifth day he dragged himself to the door of the cell.

"Are you not a Christian?" he said, falling on his knees. "Do you wish to assassinate a man who, in the eyes of heaven, is a brother? Oh, my former friends, my former friends!" he murmured, and fell with his face to the ground. Then rising with a species of despair, he exclaimed, "The chief! the chief!"

"Here I am," said Vampa, instantly appearing, "what do you want?"

"Take my last gold," muttered Danglars, holding out his pocket-book, "and let me live here; I ask no more for liberty, I only ask to live."

"Then you suffer a great deal?"

"Oh, yes, yes! cruelly."

"Still there have been men who suffered more than you."

"I do not think so."

"Yes; those who have died of hunger."

Danglars thought of the old man whom, in his hours of delirium, he had seen groaning on his bed. He struck his forehead on the ground and groaned.

"Yes," he said, "there have been some who have suffered more than I have, but then they must have been martyrs, at least."

"Do you repent?" asked a deep, solemn voice, which caused Danglars' hair to stand on end. His feeble eyes endeavoured to distinguish objects, and behind the bandit he saw a man enveloped in a cloak, half lost in the shadow of a stone column.

"Of what must I repent?" stammered Danglars.

"Of the evil you have done," said the voice.

"Oh, yes! oh, yes! I do indeed repent." And he struck his breast with his emaciated fist.

"Then I forgive you," said the man, dropping his cloak, and advancing to the light.

"The Count of Monte Cristo!" said Danglars, more pale

from terror than he had been just before from hunger and misery.

" You are mistaken,—I am not the Count of Monte Cristo! "

" Then who are you? "

" I am he whom you sold and dishonoured,—I am he whose betrothed you prostituted,—I am he upon whom you trampled that you might raise yourself to fortune,—I am he whose father you condemned to die of hunger,—I am he whom you also condemned to starvation, and who yet forgives you, because he hopes to be forgiven,—I am Edmond Dantès! "

Danglars uttered a cry and fell prostrate.

" Rise," said the count, " your life is safe; the same good fortune has not happened to your accomplices: one is mad, the other dead. Keep the 50,000 francs you have left, I give them to you. The 5,000,000 you robbed from the hospitals has been restored to them by an unknown hand. And now eat and drink; I will entertain you to-night. Vampa, when this man is satisfied, let him be free."

Danglars remained prostrate while the count withdrew; when he raised his head he saw nothing more than a kind of shadow disappearing in the passage, before which the bandits bowed.

According to the count's directions, Danglars was waited on by Vampa, who brought him the best wine and fruits of Italy; then, having conducted him to the road, and pointed to his post-chaise, he left him leaning against a tree. He remained there all night, not knowing where he was. When daylight dawned, he saw that he was near a stream; he was thirsty, and dragged himself towards it. As he stooped down to drink, he perceived that his hair had become quite white.

117

The Fifth of October

IT was about six o'clock in the evening; an opal-coloured light, through which an autumnal sun shed its golden rays, descended on the blue sea. The heat of the day had gradually decreased, and a light breeze arose, seeming like the respiration of nature on awaking from the burning siesta of the south; a delicious zephyr played along the coasts of the Mediterranean, and wafted from shore to shore the sweet perfume of plants, mingled with the fresh smell of the sea.

A light yacht, chaste and elegant in its form, was gliding amidst the first dews of night over the immense lake, extending from Gibraltar to the Dardanelles, and from Tunis to Venice. The motion resembled that of a swan with its wings opened towards the wind, gliding on the water. It advanced, at the same time, swiftly and gracefully, leaving behind it a glittering track. By degrees the sun disappeared behind the western horizon; but, as though to prove the truth of the fanciful ideas in heathen mythology, its indiscreet rays reappeared on the summit of each wave, seeming to reveal that the god of fire had just enfolded himself in the bosom of Amphitrite,* who in vain endeavoured to hide her lover beneath her azure mantle. The yacht moved rapidly on, though there did not appear to be sufficient wind to ruffle the curls on the head of a young girl. Standing on the prow was a tall man, of a dark complexion, who saw with dilating eyes that they were approaching a dark mass of land in the shape of a cone, rising from the midst of the waves, like the hat of a Catalan.

" Is that Monte Cristo? " asked the traveller, to whose orders the yacht was for the time submitted, in a melancholy voice.

" Yes, your excellency," said the captain, " we have reached it."

" We have reached it! " repeated the traveller, in an accent of indescribable sadness. Then he added, in a low tone, " Yes; that is the haven." And then he again plunged into a train of thought, the character of which was better revealed by a sad smile than it would have been by tears. A few minutes afterwards, a flash of light, which was extinguished instantly, was seen on the land, and the sound of firearms reached the yacht.

" Your excellency," said the captain, " that was the land signal, will you answer it yourself? "

" What signal? "

The captain pointed towards the island, up the side of which ascended a volume of smoke, increasing as it rose.

" Ay, yes," he said, as if awaking from a dream. " Give it to me."

The captain gave him a loaded carbine; the traveller slowly raised it, and fired in the air. Ten minutes afterwards, the sails were brailed, and they cast anchor about one hundred paces from the little harbour. The canoe was already in the sea, manned with four rowers and the pilot. The traveller descended, and instead of sitting down at the stern of the boat, which had been decorated with a blue carpet for his accommodation, stood up with his arms crossed. The rowers waited, with oars half lifted out of the water, like birds drying their wings.

" Proceed! " said the traveller. The eight oars fell into the sea simultaneously without splashing a drop of water, and the boat, yielding to the impulsion, glided forward. In an instant they found themselves in a little harbour, formed in a natural creek; the boat touched the fine sand.

" Will your excellency be so good as to mount the shoulders of two of our men, they will carry you ashore? "

The young man answered this invitation with a gesture of indifference, and stepping out of the boat, the sea immediately rose to his waist.

" Ah, your excellency," murmured the pilot, " you should not have done so; our master will scold us for it."

The young man continued to advance, following the sailors, who chose a firm footing. After about thirty paces they landed; the young man stamped on the ground to shake off the wet, and looked round for someone to show him his road, for it was quite dark. Just as he turned, a hand rested on his shoulder, and a voice which made him shudder, exclaimed:

" Good-evening, Maximilian! you are punctual, thank you! "

" Ah, is it you, count? " said the young man, in an almost joyful accent, pressing Monte Cristo's hand with both his own.

" Yes; you see I am as exact as you are. But you are dripping, my dear fellow; you must change your clothes, as Calypso said to Telemachus.* Come, I have a habitation prepared for you, in which you will soon forget fatigue and cold."

Monte Cristo perceived that the young man had turned round; indeed Morrel saw with surprise, that the men who had brought him had left without being paid or uttering a word.

Already the sound of their oars might be heard as they returned to the yacht.

"Oh, yes," said the count, "you are looking for the sailors."

"Yes; I paid them nothing, and yet they are gone."

"Never mind that, Maximilian," said Monte Cristo, smiling. "I have made an agreement with the navy, that the access to my island shall be free of all charge. I have made a bargain."

Morrel looked at the count with surprise.

"Count," he said, "you are not the same here as in Paris."

"How so?"

"Here you laugh."

The count's brow became clouded.

"You are right to recall me to myself, Maximilian," he said; "I was delighted to see you again, and forgot for the moment that all happiness is fleeting."

"Oh, no, no, count," cried Maximilian, seizing the count's hands, "pray laugh; be happy, and prove to me, by your indifference, that life is endurable to sufferers. Oh, how charitable, kind, and good you are; you affect this gaiety to inspire me with courage."

"You are wrong, Morrel; I was really happy."

"Then you forget me; so much the better."

"How so?"

"Yes; for as the gladiator said to the emperor, when he entered the arena, 'He who is going to die salutes you.'"

"Then you are not consoled?" asked the count, surprised.

"Oh," exclaimed Morrel, with a glance full of bitter reproach. "do you think it possible I could be?"

"Listen," said the count. "Do you understand the meaning of my words? You cannot take me for a commonplace man, a mere rattle emitting a vague and senseless noise. When I ask you, if you are consoled, I speak to you as a man for whom the human heart has no secrets. Well, Morrel, let us both examine the depths of your heart. Do you still feel the same feverish impatience of grief which made you start like a wounded lion? Have you still that devouring thirst, which can only be appeased in the grave? Are you still actuated by the regret which drags the living to the pursuit of death, or are you only suffering from the prostration of fatigue and the weariness of 'hope deferred'? Has the loss of memory rendered it impossible for you to weep? Oh, my dear friend, if this be the case, if you can no longer weep, if your frozen heart be dead, if you put all your trust in God, then, Maximilian, you are consoled—do not complain."

"Count," said Morrel, in a firm, and at the same time soft, voice, "listen to me, as to a man whose thoughts are raised to heaven, though he remains on earth; I come to die in the arms of a friend. Certainly, there are people whom I love; I love my sister, Julie—I love her husband, Emmanuel; but I require a strong mind to smile on my last moments. My sister would be bathed in tears and fainting; I could not bear to see her suffer. Emmanuel would tear the weapon from my hand, and alarm the house with his cries. You, count, who are more than mortal, will, I am sure, lead me to death by a pleasant path, will you not? "

." My friend," said the count, " I have still one doubt—are you weak enough to pride yourself upon your sufferings? "

" No, indeed—I am calm," said Morrel, giving his hand to the count; " my pulse does not beat slower or faster than usual. No, I feel I have reached the goal, and I will go no farther. You told me to wait and hope; do you know what you did, unfortunate adviser? I waited a month, or rather I suffered for a month! I did hope (man is a poor wretched creature), I did hope. What, I cannot tell: something wonderful, an absurdity, a miracle—of what nature, he alone can tell who has mingled with our reason that folly we call hope. Yes; I did wait;—yes; I did hope, count, and during this quarter of an hour we have been talking together, you have unconsciously wounded, tortured my heart, for every word you have uttered proved that there was no hope for me. Oh, count, I shall sleep calmly, deliciously in the arms of death! " Morrel pronounced these words with an energy which made the count shudder. " My friend," continued Morrel, " you named the fifth of October as the term of the delay you asked—to-day is the fifth of October," he took out his watch; " it is now nine o'clock—I have yet three hours to live."

" Be it so! " said the count, " come."

Morrel mechanically followed the count, and they had entered the grotto before he perceived it. He felt a carpet under his feet, a door opened, perfumes surrounded him, and a brilliant light dazzled his eyes. Morrel hesitated to advance, he dreaded the enervating effect of all that he saw. Monte Cristo drew him in gently.

" Why should we not spend the last three hours remaining to us of life, like those ancient Romans, who when condemned by Nero, their emperor and heir, sat down at a table covered with flowers, and gently glided into death, through the perfume of heliotropes and roses? "

Morrel smiled. " As you please," he said, " death is always death, that is forgetfulness, repose, exclusion from life, and therefore from grief." He sat down, and Monte Cristo placed himself opposite to him. They were in the marvellous dining-room before described, where the statues had baskets on their heads always filled with fruits and flowers. Morrel had looked carelessly around, and had probably noticed nothing.

" Let us talk like men," he said, looking at the count.

" Proceed."

" Count," said Morrel, " you are the epitome of all human knowledge, and you seem to me a being descended from a wiser and a more advanced world than ours."

" There is something true in what you say," said the count, with that smile which made him so handsome, " I have descended from a planet, called grief."

" I believe all you tell me without questioning its sense; in proof, you told me to live, and I did live; you told me to hope, and I almost did so. I am almost inclined to ask you, as though you had experienced death, ' Is it painful to die? ' "

Monte Cristo looked upon Morrel with indescribable tenderness. " Yes," he said, " yes, doubtless it is painful, if you violently break the outer covering which obstinately begs for life. If you plunge a dagger into your flesh, if you insinuate a bullet into your brain, which the least shock disorders, certainly, then, you will suffer pain, and you will repent quitting a life for a repose you have bought at so dear a price."

" Yes; I understand there is a secret of luxury and pain in death, as well as in life; the only thing is to understand it."

" You have spoken truly, Maximilian, according to the care we bestow upon it, death is either a friend who rocks us gently as a nurse, or an enemy who violently drags the soul from the body. Some day, when the world is much older, and when mankind will be masters of all the destructive powers in nature, to serve for the general good of humanity; when mankind, as you were just saying, have discovered the secrets of death, then that death will become as sweet and voluptuous as a slumber in the arms of your beloved."

" And if you wished to die, you would choose this death, count? "

" Yes."

Morrel extended his hand. " Now I understand," he said, " why you had me brought here to this desolate spot, in the midst of the ocean, to this subterranean palace; it was because you loved me, was it not, count? It was because you loved me, well enough to give me one of those sweet means of death of which we were speaking, a death without agony, a death which allows me to fade away while pronouncing Valentine's name and pressing your hand."

" Yes; you have guessed rightly, Morrel," said the count,
" that is what I intended."

" Thanks! the idea, that to-morrow I shall no longer suffer,
is sweet to my heart."

" Do you then regret nothing? "

" No," replied Morrel.

" Not even me? " asked the count, with deep emotion.

Morrel's clear eye was for the moment, clouded, then it shone
with unusual lustre, and a large tear rolled down his cheek.

" What! " said the count, " do you still regret anything in the
world, and yet die? "

" Oh, I entreat you," exclaimed Morrel, in a low voice, " do
not speak another word, count, do not prolong my punishment."

The count fancied he was yielding, and this belief revived the
horrible doubt that had overwhelmed him at the Château d'If.
" I am endeavouring," he thought, " to make this man happy;
I look upon this restitution as a weight thrown into the scale to
balance the evil I have wrought. Now, supposing I am deceived,
if this man has not been unhappy enough to merit happiness.
Alas! what would become of me, who can only atone for evil
by doing good? " Then he said aloud, " Listen, Morrel, I see
your grief is great, but still you do not like to risk your soul."

Morrel smiled sadly. " Count," he said, " I swear to you, my
soul is no longer my own."

" Maximilian, you know I have no relation in the world.
I have accustomed myself to regard you as my son: well, then,
to save my son, I will sacrifice my life, nay, even my fortune."

" What do you mean? "

" I mean, that you wish to quit life because you do not understand all the enjoyments which are the fruits of a large fortune.
Morrel, I possess nearly a hundred millions; I give them to you;
with such a fortune you can attain every wish. Are you ambitious?
every career is open to you. Overturn the world, change its
character, yield to mad ideas, be even criminal—but live."

" Count, I have your word," said Morrel coldly; then taking
out his watch, he added, " It is half-past eleven."

" Morrel, can you intend it, in my house, beneath my eyes? "

" Then let me go," said Maximilian, " or I shall think you
did not love me for my own sake, but for yours; " and he rose.

" It is well," said Monte Cristo, whose countenance brightened
at these words; " you wish it; you are inflexible; yes, as you
said, you are indeed wretched, and a miracle alone can cure you;
sit down, Morrel, and wait."

Morrel obeyed; the count rose, and unlocking a closet with
a key suspended from his gold chain, took from it a little silver

casket, beautifully carved and chased, the corners of which represented four bending figures, similar to the Caryatides, the forms of women, symbols of the angels aspiring to heaven. He placed the casket on the table; then opening it, took out a little golden box, the top of which flew open when touched by a secret spring. This box contained an unctuous substance, partly solid, of which it was impossible to discover the colour, owing to the reflection of the polished gold, sapphires, rubies, emeralds, which ornamented the box. It was a mixed mass of blue, red, and gold. The count took out a small quantity of this with a gilt spoon, and offered it to Morrel, fixing a long steadfast glance upon him. It was then observable that the substance was greenish.

"This is what you asked for," he said, "and what I promised to give you."

"I thank you from the depths of my heart," said the young man, taking the spoon from the hands of Monte Cristo.

The count took another spoon, and again dipped it into the golden box.

"What are you going to do, my friend?" asked Morrel, arresting his hand.

"*Ma foi!* Morrel, I was thinking that I too am weary of life, and since an opportunity presents itself——"

"Stay," said the young man, "you, who love and are beloved; you, who have faith and hope, oh, do not follow my example; in your case it would be a crime. Adieu, my noble and generous friend, adieu; I will go and tell Valentine what you have done for me."

And slowly, though without any hesitation, only waiting to press the count's hand fervently, he swallowed the mysterious substance offered by Monte Cristo. Then they were both silent. Ali, mute and attentive, brought the pipes and coffee, and disappeared. By degrees the lamps gradually faded in the hands of the marble statues which held them, and the perfumes appeared less powerful to Morrel. Seated opposite to him, Monte Cristo watched him in the shadow, and Morrel saw nothing but the bright eyes of the count. An overpowering sadness took possession of the young man; his hands relaxed their hold; the objects in the room gradually lost their form and colour; and his disturbed vision seemed to perceive doors and curtains open in the wall.

"Friend," he cried, "I feel that I am dying; thanks!" He made a last effort to extend his hand, but it fell powerless beside him. Then it appeared to him that Monte Cristo smiled, not with that strange and fearful expression, which had sometimes revealed to him the secrets of his heart, but with the benevolent kindness of a father for an infant. At the same time the count appeared to increase in stature; his form, nearly double its usual height, stood out in relief against the red tapestry, his black hair was thrown back, and he stood in the attitude of a menacing angel.

Morrel, overpowered, turned round in the arm-chair; a delicious torpor was insinuated into every vein; a change of ideas presented themselves to his brain, like a new design on the kaleidoscope; enervated, prostrate, and breathless, he became unconscious of outward objects, he seemed to be entering that vague delirium preceding death. He wished once again to press the count's hand; but his own was immovable: he wished to articulate a last farewell, but his tongue lay motionless and heavy in his throat, like a stone at the mouth of a sepulchre. Involuntarily his languid eyes closed; and still through his eyelashes a well-known form seemed to move amid the obscurity with which he thought himself eneveloped.

The count had just opened a door. Immediately a brilliant light from the next room, or rather from the palace adjoining, shone upon the room in which he was gently gliding into his last sleep. Then he saw a woman of marvellous beauty appear on the threshold of the door separating the two rooms. Pale, and sweetly smiling, she looked like an angel of mercy conjuring the angel of vengeance.

" Is it heaven that opens before me? " thought the dying man, " that angel resembles the one I have lost."

Monte Cristo pointed Morrel to the young woman, who advanced towards him with clasped hands and a smile upon her lips.

" Valentine! Valentine! " he mentally ejaculated, but his lips uttered no sound; and as though all his strength were centred in that internal emotion, he sighed and closed his eyes.

Valentine rushed towards him; his lips again moved.

" He is calling you," said the count, " he to whom you have confided your destiny, he from whom death would have separated you, calls you to him. Happily I vanquished death. Henceforth, Valentine, you will never again be separated on earth, since he has rushed into death to find you. Without me you would both have died. May God accept my atonement of these two existences! "

Valentine seized the count's hands, and in her irresistible impulse of joy carried it to her lips.

" Oh, thank me again! " said the count, " tell me till you are weary that I have restored you to happiness; you do not know how much I require this assurance."

" Oh, yes, yes, I thank you with all my heart," said Valentine;

" and if you doubt the sincerity of my gratitude, oh, then, ask Haydée, ask my beloved sister Haydée, who ever since our departure from France, has caused me to wait patiently for this happy day, while talking to me of you."

" You then love Haydée? " asked Monte Cristo, with an emotion he in vain endeavoured to dissimulate.

" Oh, yes, with all my soul."

" Well, then, listen, Valentine," said the count, " I have a favour to ask of you."

" Of me? Oh, am I happy enough for that? "

" Yes; you have called Haydée your sister; let her become so indeed, Valentine: render to her all the gratitude you fancy you owe me; protect her, for " (the count's voice was thick with emotion) " henceforth she will be alone in the world."

" Alone in the world! " repeated a voice behind the count, " and why? "

Monte Cristo turned round; Haydée was standing pale, motionless, looking at the count with an expression of fearful amazement.

" Because to-morrow, Haydée, you will be free; you will then assume your proper position in society, for I will not allow my destiny to overshadow yours. Daughter of a prince! I restore to you the riches and name of your father."

Haydée became pale, and lifting her transparent hands to heaven, exclaimed in a voice hoarse with tears:

" Then you leave me, my lord? "

" Haydée, Haydée, you are young and beautiful, forget even my name, and be happy! "

" It is well," said Haydée, " your order shall be executed, my lord; I will forget even your name, and be happy." And she stepped back to retire.

" Oh heavens! " exclaimed Valentine, who was supporting the head of Morrel on her shoulder, " do you not see how pale she is? Do you not see how she suffers? "

Haydée answered with a heartrending expression.

" Why should he understand this, my sister? He is my master, and I am his slave; he has the right to notice nothing."

The count shuddered at the tones of a voice which penetrated the inmost recesses of his heart; his eyes met those of the young girl, and he could not bear their brilliancy.

" Oh heavens! " exclaimed Monte Cristo, " can my suspicions be correct? Haydée, would it please you not to leave me? "

" I am young," gently replied Haydée, " I love the life you have made so sweet to me, and should regret to die."

" You mean, then, that if I leave you, Haydée——"

" I should die; yes, my lord."

" Do you then love me? "

" Oh, Valentine, he asks if I love him! Valentine, tell him if you love Maximilian."

The count felt his heart dilate and throb; he opened his arms, and Haydée, uttering a cry, sprang into them.

" Oh, yes," she cried, " I do love you! I love you as one loves a father, brother, husband! I love you as my life, for you are the best, the noblest of created beings! "

" Let it be, then, as you wish, sweet angel; God has sustained me in my struggle with my enemies, and has given me this victory; he will not let me end my triumph with this penance; I wished to punish myself, but he has pardoned me! Love me then, Haydée! Who knows? perhaps your love will make me forget all I wish not to remember."

" What do you mean, my lord? "

" I mean that one word from you has enlightened me more than twenty years of slow experience; I have but you in the world, Haydée; through you I again connect myself with life, through you I shall suffer, through you rejoice."

" Do you hear him, Valentine? " exclaimed Haydée, " he says that through me he will suffer,—through *me*, who would yield my life for his."

The count withdrew for a moment.

" Have I discovered the truth? " he said; " but whether it be for recompense or punishment, I accept my fate. Come, Haydée, come! " and throwing his arm round the young girl's waist, he pressed the hand of Valentine and disappeared.

An hour had nearly passed, during which Valentine, breathless and motionless, watched steadfastly over Morrel. At length she felt his heart beat, a faint breath played upon his lips, a slight shudder, announcing the return of life, passed through the young man's frame. At length his eyes opened, but they were at first fixed and expressionless; then sight returned, and with it feeling and grief.

" Oh," he cried, in an accent of despair, " the count has deceived me; I am yet living," and extending his hand towards the table, he seized a knife.

" Dearest! " exclaimed Valentine, with her adorable smile, " awake, and look on my side."

Morrel uttered a loud exclamation, and frantic, doubtful, dazzled as though by a celestial vision, he fell upon his knees.

.   .   .   .   .   .

The next morning, at daybreak, Valentine and Morrel were

walking arm-in-arm on the seashore, Valentine relating how Monte Cristo had appeared in her room; how he had unveiled everything; how he had revealed the crime; and, finally, how he had saved her life by allowing her to seem dead. They had found the door of the grotto open, and went forth, the few remaining stars yet pressing through the morning light. Morrel soon perceived a man standing amidst the group of rocks, who was awaiting a sign from them to advance; he pointed him out to Valentine.

"Ah, it is Jacopo," she said, "the captain of the yacht;" and she beckoned him towards them.

"Do you wish to speak to us?" asked Morrel.

"I have a letter to give you from the count."

"From the count!" murmured the two young people.

"Yes; read it."

Morrel opened the letter and read:

"MY DEAR MAXIMILIAN,—

"There is a felucca for you at anchor. Jacopo will conduct you to Leghorn, where M. Noirtier waits his granddaughter, whom he wishes to bless before you lead her to the altar. All that is in this grotto, my friend, my house in the Champs Elysées, and my château at Tréport, are the marriage gifts bestowed by Edmond Dantès upon the son of his old master, Morrel. Mademoiselle de Villefort will share them with you; for I entreat her to give to the poor the immense fortune reverting to her from her father, now a madman, and her brother, who died last September with his mother. Tell the angel who will watch over your future destiny, Morrel, to pray sometimes for a man who, like Satan, thought himself, for an instant, equal to God; but who now acknowledges, with Christian humility, that God alone possesses supreme power and infinite wisdom. Perhaps those prayers may soften the remorse he feels in his heart. As for you, Morrel, this is the secret of my conduct towards you. There is neither happiness nor misery in the world; there is only the comparison of one state with another, nothing more. He who has felt the deepest grief is best able to experience supreme happiness. We must have felt what it is to die, Morrel, that we may appreciate the enjoyments of life.

"Live, then, and be happy, beloved children of my heart, and never forget, that until the day when God will deign to reveal the future to man, all human wisdom is contained in these two words,—'Wait and hope.'—Your friend,

"EDMOND DANTÈS,

"COUNT OF MONTE CRISTO."

During the perusal of this letter, which informed Valentine, for the first time, of the madness of her father and the death of her brother, she became pale, a heavy sigh escaped from her bosom, and tears, not the less painful because they were silent, ran down her cheeks; her happiness cost her very dear. Morrel looked round uneasily.

" But," he said, " the count's generosity is too overwhelming; Valentine will be satisfied with my humble fortune. Where is the count, friend? Lead me to him."

Jacopo pointed towards the horizon.

" What do you mean? " asked Valentine. " Where is the count?—where is Haydée? "

" Look! " said Jacopo.

The eyes of both were fixed upon the spot indicated by the sailor, and on the blue line separating the sky from the Mediterranean Sea, they perceived a large white sail.

" Gone! " said Morrel; " gone!—Adieu, my friend!—adieu, my father! "

" Gone! " murmured Valentine: " adieu, my friend!—adieu, my sister! "

" Who can say whether we shall ever see them again? " said Morrel, with tearful eyes.

" Darling," replied Valentine, " has not the count just told us that all human wisdom was contained in these two words,— *Wait and hope* '? "

EXPLANATORY NOTES

2 *M. Morrel*: in his travel books Dumas several times mentions a 'Monsieur Morel' (*sic*) whom he had met on his visits to the Midi. It is more than likely that the 'Morrel' of the novel bears some resemblance to the 'Morel' of reality.

2 *£1000*: all sums of money were converted by the translator in 1846 according to the exchange rate of 25 francs to the pound, which remained steady until the end of the nineteenth century but has since changed dramatically. If the sums involved seem absurdly small, the reader might like to bear in mind that a *curé*'s stipend, like the annual subscription to the Jockey-Club was 1,000 francs (£40), while the highest paid cabinet minister received 20,000 francs (£800) a year.

3 *supercargo*: in the merchant navy, the officer responsible for sales and all the commercial transactions of the ship.

4 *a packet for the Maréchal Bertrand*: Henri-Gratien, comte Bertrand (1773–1844) followed Napoleon into exile first to Elba, after the abdication of 6 April 1814, and later to Saint Helena, after the second abdication on 22 June 1815 following the Hundred Days and Waterloo. It was Bertrand who brought Napoleon's remains back to France in 1840.

8 *a second Marseilles*: the glamour with which *The Count of Monte Cristo* invested Marseilles—Phocea to the Ancients and the 'Gateway to Africa' famed for its handsome main street, La Canebière—so improved the city's image that Dumas subsequently found that Marseillais cab drivers and ferrymen refused to take his money on the ground they were in fact very much in *his* debt.

25 *par le déluge*: 'They drink only water that have evil in their blood, / A truth attested by the coming of the Flood'. Part of the third couplet of the *Chanson morale* by Louis-Philippe Ségur (1753–1830), soldier, ambassador to Saint Petersburg, and man of letters who was also Napoleon's Grand Master of Ceremonies.

28 *Murat*: husband of Napoleon's sister, Caroline Bonaparte, Maréchal de France, and King of Naples 1808–15, Joachim Murat (1767–1815) was shot after an unsuccessful attempt to retake Naples after the escape from Elba of Napoleon (the 'usurper' to Royalist supporters). Dumas fills in the background at the start of Chapter 6.

44 *religious strife*: the political divisions which divided the French in 1814 and 1815 were aggravated in the Protestant South by a tradition of religious persecution which went back to the sectarian wars of the sixteenth century.

44 *the Empress Josephine*: anti-bonapartists were free to criticise Napoleon only after his downfall in 1814. Not only were recent disasters like the retreat from Moscow (1812) and the defeat at Leipzig in 1813 openly discussed for the first time, but older scandals resurfaced, such as the divorce of the Empress Joséphine (1763–1814) in 1809.

45 *Hartwell*: Louis XVIII (1755–1824), who fled into exile in 1791, lived at Hartwell in Buckinghamshire from 1807 until he returned to France on 26 April 1814. Dumas the liberal here gives a surprisingly flattering portrait of Louis XVIII who in fact made every effort to reintroduce the illiberal *ancien régime*. His passion for Horace and Virgil is, however, well documented.

46 *9th Thermidor and 4th of April*: the execution of Robespierre on 9 Thermidor (28 July 1794) marked the end of the Revolutionary Terror. On 4 April 1814 Napoleon bowed to political pressures and abdicated two days later.

65 *Chateau d'If*: A fortified castle was built by François I in 1524 on If, one of a number of small islands situated in the bay of Marseilles, about three kilometres out to sea. It was subsequently used as a state prison for about twenty detainees. Recent inmates had included Mirabeau and Philippe Egalité, brother of Louis XVI. Dumas visited it in 1834 and inspected Mirabeau's cell.

74 *Gryphius*: Sebastian Gryphius (1493–1556) set up as a typesetter in Lyons in 1528 and is known as one of the finest Renaissance printers. His edition of Horace was published in 1540.

74 *Blacas?*: Le duc de Blacas d'Aulps (1771–1839), fled France in
    1790 and entered the service of the future Louis XVIII in
    1803. In 1815, he became a Minister of State and later served
    as ambassador to Naples and Rome. After the Revolution of
    1830, he went into exile and died in Austria.

74 "*Canimus surdis!*": 'We sing to those who have no ears'. The
    tag (which is misquoted: *non canimus surdis*) is taken from Vir-
    gil's tenth Eclogue.

74 *Pastor quàm traheret*: 'The shepherd who was leading ...'.
    Horace, *Odes*, i. 15.

75 "*Mala ducis avi domum,*": from the same Ode: 'You bring home
    dark portents'.

75 *M. Dandré*: Antoine-Balthazar-Joseph Dandré (1759–1825)
    entered the Revolution of 1789 as a constitutional monar-
    chist. As an elected deputy and member of numerous revolu-
    tionary committees, he was several times required to affirm
    his opposition to Royalism. In 1792, he emigrated to England
    and in 1796 to Germany. He returned to France in 1814
    when he was named Minister of Police. During the Hundred
    Days, he followed Louis XVIII into Belgium.

75 *bella, horrida bella!*: 'War, and all the horrors of war' (Virgil,
    Aeneid, vi. 86).

75 *prurigo?*: 'the itch'.

77 '*Molli fugies anhelitu*': 'You will run away panting for breath'
    (Horace, *Odes*, vii 15).

77 *a telegraph*: a telegraph system, consisting of observation posts
    each equipped with an apparatus using mechanical arms
    invented by abbé Claude Chappe (1763–1805) in 1792, was
    first used in 1794. The first relay system to be installed linked
    Paris with Nantes, and by 1845, when the first electric line
    was introduced, there were 5,000 kilometres of 'aerial tele-
    graph' in existence: it was reasonably efficient but was, of
    course, useless at night and in fog. The Paris–Lyons link was
    inaugurated in 1805 but was not extended to Toulon until
    1828 when it took four hours to transmit a message along its
    entire length. In 1815 traditional land dispatches were still
    used to connect Lyons with the far South. Although experi-

ments had begun in the eighteenth century, the electric telegraph was not perfected until 1837.

78 *Noirtier the Girondin? . . . the senator?*: the Girondins, one of the
two major parties in the Revolutionary Assembly, became
increasingly moderate after the September Massacres of 1792
and the death of Louis XVI in January 1793. In the Autumn
of 1793, the Jacobins under Robespierre waged a successful
political campaign for control against the Girondins and
many were guillotined. This clearly makes Noirtier a moderate, though later he is described as a Jacobin (see note to
p. 615). As a member of the rubber-stamping Senate of 1806,
a body which was not elected but directly appointed by
Napoleon, Noirtier the Senator clearly enjoyed the favour of
France's Emperor.

78 "*Justum et tenacem propositi virum*": 'The just and unwavering
man' (Horace, *Odes*, iii. 3).

78 *Brezé*: Henri Evrard, Marquis de Dreux-Brézé (1762–1829)
emigrated in 1792 and became Louis XVIII's Grand Master
of Ceremonies in 1815. He makes a brief appearance in *Ange
Pitou* (1851, chap. 24) as an obsequious courtier who fawns on
Marie-Antoinette.

81 *the 1st of March*: Dumas's dates here are slightly inaccurate.
Napoleon left Elba on 26 February 1815 and not the 28th.
The news of his landing on French soil arrived in Paris on 5
March and not 1 March.

83 *forgotten nothing!*: this judgement on the restored Bourbon
monarchy is generally attributed to Talleyrand.

85 *General Quesnel*: two generals of this name may have contributed something to the making of Dumas's 'Quesnel'. General
Quesnel, Baron du Torpt (1765–1819) served in Napoleon's
Army of the Alps in 1814: he was permanently retired in September 1815. Louis Quesnel (1770–1815), a former actor and
officer in Napoleon's Imperial Guard, was taken prisoner in
Russia in 1812 but returned to France in 1814; a Royalist
convert, he was assassinated by the Bonapartist faction in
1815. It is possible that Dumas amalgamated the two soldiers
though, given the son attributed to 'Quesnel' later in the

novel, it seems unlikely that they would have been very suitable models.

85 *Legion of Honour*: the Order of the *Légion d'honneur* was instituted on 19 May 1802 by Napoleon as First Consul in recognition of distinguished military and civil service.

91 *20th or 25th at Paris*: in fact, Napoleon reached Lyons on 10 March and entered the Tuileries in Paris on 20 March.

95 *The Hundred Days*: the period of Napoleon's return lasted from his entry into Paris on 20 March until his defeat at Waterloo (18 June) and his second abdication four days later.

98 *Fenestrelles, to Pignerol, or to the Iles Sainte-Marguerite*: Fenestrelle, 72 kilometres from Turin on the Franco–Italian border, was a prison-fortress designed by Louis XIV to curb the Huguenots: it was dismantled in 1836. Pignerol, 30 kilometres to the south-east, was built in the sixteenth century and among its prisoners were Fouquet, Lauzun, and the Man in the Iron Mask. The Ile Sainte-Marguerite is the largest of the Lerin Islands off Cannes and was also a fortified prison: the Man in the Iron Mask was held there too between 1687 and 1698.

104 "*L'Abbé Faria*": José-Custodio de Faria (1756–1819), born in Goa, was a part-Indian Portuguese cleric who arrived in Paris in 1788. In 1792 he was denounced for not taking the oath the Revolution required of all clergy, but survived a series of perils. In *Les Mémoires d'Outre-tombe* (Paris, 1948–9, ii. 59), Chateaubriand recalls meeting him in about 1802 at the house of Madame de Custines: Faria was obliged to leave the room after failing to hypnotize a canary to death as he had claimed he could. A man of considerable learning, both of orthodox and unorthodox matters, he taught philosophy in Marseilles and Nîmes but on his return to Paris in 1813, he set up as a teacher of 'magnetism'. His public demonstrations of hypnotism brought him considerable notoriety, but the clergy spoke out against him and his *séances* were disrupted. Thereafter he earned his living as a chaplain in a girls' convent and had finished the first volume of a treatise on 'wakeful trances' when he suddenly died in 1819. He is now regarded as a serious investigator of the phenomenon of

suggestion. In the Preface to *Les Compagnons de Jéhu* (*The Companions of Jehu*, 1857), Dumas claims that his Faria was entirely the product of his imagination. He was of course too young to have known the real abbé, but he certainly knew of the reputation of Faria whose swarthy features, foreign accent, and piercing eyes had created an aura of mystery. Because of this mysterious presence but perhaps too because of Faria's mixed blood, it was only a matter of time before the Portuguese wizard would find his way into a Dumas romance, albeit in a quite altered guise. For further details, see Santana Rodrigues, *O Abade Faria* (Lisboa, 1946).

105 *Archimedes when the soldier of Marcellus slew him*: When Syracuse fell to the Romans in 212 BC, Archimedes is said to have been sitting in a public square peering at geometric figures he had drawn in the dust. Instead of complying with his polite request not to tread on his circles and triangles, a centurion cut him down brutally.

105 *Cardinal Spada's secretary*: Italian history seems full of notable figures of this name. Goldoni stayed with a Spada in 1731 and Casanova encountered another in the 1750s. However, given the facts of Faria's life (see note to p. 104), it seems most likely that 'Cardinal Spada' (of whom further details are given on p. 154) is an invention.

108 *the government of Ham*: a prison, near Péronne in north-eastern France, which held Polignac and his ministers after the July Revolution of 1830.

109 *sighed for the galleys*: the galleys had been used as a punishment for criminals and especially for heretics since the Middle Ages. Between the Revocation of the Edict of Nantes in 1685 and 1715, 38,000 Protestants were sent to the galleys at Marseilles and Toulon, but there were also galleys at Brest and Dunkirk. The 'Corps des Galères' was abolished in 1748, though galleys continued to be manned by convicted criminals into the nineteenth century. Their use was never officially ended. Advances in boat-building simply made them redundant.

110 *Martin's pictures*: probably the English artist John Martin (1789–1854) whose enormous, dramatic paintings of biblical

and allegorical scenes attracted the attention of the litho-
graphers who made him extraordinarily popular throughout
Europe.

110 *in the Inferno of Dante*: Count Ugolino was betrayed and imprisoned in 1289 by Ruggieri degli Ubaldini, Archbishop of
Pisa. At the start of Canto XXXIII of the *Inferno*, he explains
the reasons for his 'fierce repast'.

119 *Isle de Daume or the Isle of Tiboulen*: these, along with Ratonneau, Pomègue, and Lemaire (or Maire) (see pp. 127 and
176), are all situated a few miles off the coast near Marseilles.
Only Ratonneau and Pomègue are of any size, the rest being
rocky outcrops.

124 *the very scheme Napoleon wished to realise in 1811*: by 1809, the
numerous states and principalities of Italy had formed into
three major zones: areas absorbed into the French Empire,
the Kingdom of Italy ruled by a French Vice-roy, and the
Kingdom of Naples under Murat. Under the French, important steps were taken for the regeneration of Italy which
acquired civil and religious freedom, equality before the law,
rationalized administrative and financial structures, and so
on. It is this 'civilizing' programme which Dumas here attributes to Napoleon. In 1814 the kings and princes of Italy
returned and Murat was unsuccessful in his attempt to raise
the flag of Italian liberation after Napoleon's final overthrow.
Dumas turns Faria into a forerunner of Garibaldi, later
Dumas's friend and the architect of Italian unity.

128 *cases of successful evasion*: the Duc de Beaufort (1616–69)
escaped from the prison at Vincennes in 1648: Dumas incor-
porates the episode into Chapter XVIII of *Twenty Years After*.
The Abbé Dubuquoi (1650–1740), who called himself the
Comte de Bucquoy, was a soldier and later a Trappist monk
who was jailed for speaking out against despotism in 1706: his
account of his escape from the Bastille was published in 1719.
Jean-Henri Masers de Latude (1725–1805) was incarcerated
in 1749 and spent the next 35 years in various prisons. His
memoirs (1791–3) made him a European celebrity.

129 *Lavoisier, . . . Cabanis*: Antoine-Laurent de Lavoisier (1743–94)
was one of the founders of modern chemistry. Georges

Cabanis (1757–1808) was highly regarded for his work on the relationship between man's physical and moral being which reduced the spiritual side of human nature to a function of physiology.

154 *History of the City of Rome*: the French text merely mentions 'a history' and refers to chapter XX. The text is an invention of Dumas.

162 *the Isle of Monte Cristo*: Monte Cristo is a barren island which rises out of the Mediterranean east of Corsica to a height of 645 metres. Dumas describes in his *Causeries* (1860, vol. i, chap. 10) how he saw the Island in 1842, but did not land there.

179 *a Genoese tartane*: a single-masted vessel, used mainly for commercial purposes in the Mediterranean. It was rigged with a mainsail and a foresail.

189 *the gabelle*: the *gabelle* was a feudal tax on salt which was abolished in France 1789 but persisted in areas such as Sardinia and Sicily which remained outside the imperial control of Napoleon.

189 *Voltaire's Doctor Pangloss*: in *Candide* (1759), Voltaire satirized the current of philosophical optimism in the person of the ridiculous Pangloss who believed that the world was in its optimum condition (hence 'optimism') and that progress was not merely impossible but unnecessary.

194 *Lucius Brutus*: in his history of Rome, Livy (*Ab urbe condita libri*, bk. I, chap. 66) relates how Lucius Junius Brutus and the sons of Tarquin were told by the Delphic oracle that the first of them to kiss his mother would acquire sovereign power: Brutus promptly kissed the earth, 'mother to all men'.

200 *vessel of the speronare class*: a light sailing vessel. Dumas had sailed on such a boat for three months in the company of Sicilian sailors, as he relates in his travel book *Le Speronare* (1842).

202 *those who buried Alaric*: Alaric I, conqueror of Rome, died at Cosenza in Calabria around AD 410 at the age of 34. One tradition tells that his body was laid to rest in the bed of the

Busento. To ensure that his remains did not fall into Roman hands, the slaves who carried out the work were put to death.

213   *a pedestrian excursion to the south of France*: in 1834 Dumas himself undertook such a tour of the south of France with a painter friend, visited the major cities including Beaucaire, and published his *Nouvelles impressions de voyage: Le Midi de la France* (*New Travel Impressions: The South of France*) in 1841.

235   *support the Greeks*: the Turkish mastery of Greece, established by Mohammed II in 1453, lasted until the revival of Greek national consciousness in 1821. Within a year Greek independence was regained, then lost in 1824 and, with help from Britain, France, and Russia, finally won in 1828. It was a cause that inspired the Romantic imagination: Byron, its most famous champion, died fighting for Greek freedom in 1824.

235   *Ali Pacha*: Ali Pasha (1741–1822), called 'the Lion', rose to power in Albania, Thessaly, and Epirus through murder, terror, and shifting loyalties. Within his dominions he maintained security, order, and justice, and encouraged industry, so that European visitors regarded him as an active and intelligent governor. The Turks finally moved against him in 1820 at Jannina, of which he was Pasha. He resisted for two years but finally surrendered to Khourchid Pasha on the security of an oath that his life and property would be spared. Nevertheless, he was put to death on 5 February 1822.

236   *"Frailty, thy name is woman"*: *Hamlet*, I. ii.

245   *Le Drapeau Blanc*: an ultra-Royalist daily which appeared between 1819 and 1827 and again from 1829 until July 1830 when it was suppressed. The white flag of the title was the flag of the Bourbons.

252   *Cape Blanc and Cape Bogador*: thirty years before the Suez canal was opened, the *Pharaon*, bound from Calcutta on a south-westerly course, must have foundered in the Indian Ocean on its way to the Cape of Good Hope. Both the Capes mentioned here appear to be inventions.

252   *the dust at Montredon*: Montredon-Labessonie in south-west

France was reputed for making scythes and knives and for its sawmills, and hence for its dusty atmosphere.

259 *the Ecole Polytechnique*: the École Polytechnique was created in 1795 to train civil and military engineers. Napoleon, who later regarded it as 'a goose that laid golden eggs', incorporated it into his system of *lycées* and higher education establishments through which he hoped to equip France with an effective class of technocrats and administrators.

259 *and read the Semaphore*: Le Sémaphore de Marseille (1828) was briefly a shipping trade paper before turning into a mouthpiece for the new liberalism. After the July Revolution of 1830, it continued to hold to its liberal views until the 1870s when it moved to the right.

270 *Maître Pastrini*: Dumas had patronized the establishment of Pastrini during a visit to Rome in 1835: see *Le Speronare*, chap. 1.

272 *capture of Algiers*: from the time of Haruk Barbarossa (who was executed in 1518), Algeria was a troublesome mixture of military despotism and piracy which the English, Dutch, French, Spaniards, and Americans from time to time made vain efforts to overturn. In 1830 Algiers capitulated to a French fleet, an event which marked the beginning of France's long-running efforts to conquer Algeria and acquire an African empire.

272 *the romances of Cooper and Captain Marryat*: the ripping yarns of the American James Fenimore Cooper (1789–1851) and Frederick Marryat (1792–1848) were enormously popular in France.

273 *like the giant Adamastor*: in Book V of *The Lusiads*, the Portuguese poet Camões (1525–80) relates that when Vasco da Gama attempted to sail round the Cape of Good Hope, Adamastor, the Giant of the Storm, rose out of the sea to oppose him. Adamastor does not figure in Greek mythology and was an invention of Camões.

275 *in a Corsican's nature to revenge himself*: romantic, savage Corsica and the vendetta were favourite subjects for nineteenth-century novelists and short-story writers from Balzac (*La*

vendetta (1830)) and Mérimée (*Mateo Falcone* (1829) and *Colomba* (1840)) to Maupassant (*Une vendetta* (1883)) and beyond.

277 *that Turkish phrase of Molière's*: in *Le Bourgeois Gentilhomme* (1670, IV. vii), Cléonte, disguised as a Turk, says 'Bel-men', meaning 'I don't know'. Clovielle, who is interpreting, tells M. Jourdain that this means that he must dress in ceremonial clothes, call on his daughter, and conclude her marriage. Taken aback, Monsieur Jourdain remarks: 'So many ideas in just two words!'

282 *the Huguenots*: *Les Huguenots*, with score by Meyerbeer and libretto by Scribe and Deschamps, was first performed at the Paris Opera on 29 February 1836.

283 *yataghan*: a Turkish sword with a lightly curved blade which had neither guard nor cross-piece but often boasted a decorated pommel.

284 *M. Appert, and the little man in the blue cloak*: Nicolas Appert (1750–1841) discovered a method of preserving food by boiling and vacuum-sealing, and thus qualifies as a social benefactor. 'The man in the blue cloak' was Edme Champion (1764–1852), a retired diamond merchant who, thus attired, devoted his fortune to the relief of the poor.

286 *Hassen-ben Sabah*: Hassan ibn el-Sabbah (d. 1124), 'the Old Man of the Mountain', was founder of the Muslim sect of the Assassins, from which the word 'hashish' is derived.

286 *hatchis!*: i.e. hashish. Hallucinants (hashish and opium in the main) were an important part of the Romantic quest for new experience and 'the multiplication of the personality' both in England (Crabbe, Coleridge, de Quincey, Keats, etc.) and in France from the painter Meissonier and Théophile Gautier (*Le Club des Haschichins* (1846)) to Baudelaire's *Paradis artificiels* (1860) and thence to Villiers de l'Isle-Adam and Rimbaud.

288 *Lorelay, . . . Amphion*: Heine had written of the Lorelei on the banks of the Rhine as had Nerval with whom Dumas had travelled and collaborated in 1838. When Amphion, son of Zeus and Antiope, strummed his lyre, stones stirred and built themselves into walls.

296 *shepherds of the Landes*: until the 1930s, shepherds in the Landes in south-west France used stilts to cover the vast distances which often separated the areas where they grazed their sheep.

298 *the Decesaris and the Gasparones*: banditry was rife and these gangs were named after their leaders: see p. 304. Mastrilla (see p. 299) was also a model for Cucumetto.

300 '*Let him die*': in Corneille's *Horace* (1640), the hero does not stand his ground and confront the three Curiace brothers but runs away. Subsequently we learn that his 'dishonourable' action was part of a strategy: by separating his opponents, he succeeds in killing all three. Ignorant of the final outcome, his stern father does not accept that he had any choice but to fight and when asked what he should have done, replies: 'he should have died'. The '*qu'il mourût*' of *Le Vieil Horace* (III. vi) had long been a byword for a rigid code of honour.

300 *Jean Sbogar or Lara*: in *Jean Sbogar* (1818) by Charles Nodier (1780–1844), a romantic and rather soulful bandit chief melodramatically rejects the laws of convention. Byron's 'tale', *Lara* (1814), featured a proud, gloomy, doomed hero of the kind which so appealed to overheated Romantic imaginations.

300 *Bréguet*: Abraham-Louis Bréguet (1747–1823) was one of France's finest watchmakers. His son, Louis-Antoine (1776–1858) continued the family tradition.

304 *Manfred*: the hero of Byron's dramatic poem, *Manfred* (1817).

317 *the times of Florian*: Jean-Pierre Claris de Florian (1755–94) wrote novels, plays, and fables, but was especially remembered for his idyllic but excessively sentimental romances.

318 *Leopold Robert or Schnetz*: the Swiss artist Léopold Robert (1794–1835) was particularly known for the harvest scenes which he painted in Italy: Dumas refers to one of these on p. 337. Jean-Victor Schnetz (1787–1870), a pupil of David, was a historical and genre painter.

324 *mazzolato*: the *mazzolata* (from *mazzuola*, a mallet), was the execution of criminals by clubbing. See also Chapter 36.

327 *Parisina*: The opera *Parisina* by Donizetti (1797–1848) was first performed in Florence in 1833 and his *Lucia di Lammer-moor*, based on the novel by Walter Scott, at Naples in 1835. On *Parisina*, see p. 332.

328 *Opera buffa … Italian Opera*: Albert compares Italian theatres with theatres he knows in Paris—the Opéra comique and the Opéra. The French *opéra bouffe*, less farcical than the Italian *opera buffa*, was already well established before the opening of the Théâtre des Bouffes-parisien in 1855 which became the home of Offenbach and parodic comic opera.

329 "*Countess G——*": the part of the manuscript preserved at Villers-Cotterêt reads 'la comtesse Giuci——'; later the count-ess adds 'mon titre de confrère de Lord Biron me servira d'introduction'. On p. 334 she speaks of Byron's views on vampires. These indications make it certain that Dumas had in mind the contessa Teresa Giucciolo who was Byron's mis-tress during his stay in Venice between 1817 and 1819. She reappears in Chapter 54.

331 *Medora*: in Byron's *Corsair* (1814), Medora is the ideal of 'Oriental' womanhood whose very life is the love she bears her lord and master.

331 *Henri*: when the Opéra-Comique left the Salle Ventadour, it was replaced by the 'Théâtre nautique', so called because it boasted a water tank which enabled spectacular aquatic effects to be obtained. The Théâtre nautique opened in June 1834 and closed early in 1835. Henri was its Ballet Master. He subsequently resumed his career in Italy.

334 *Lord Ruthven*: Charles Nodier's novel *Lord Ruthven, ou les Vam-pires* (1820) was based on a tale improvised by Byron to frighten a circle of ladies he had met at Geneva: we learn sub-sequently that Countess G—— 'had known Lord Ruthven' (p. 401). The same year, Nodier, in collaboration with Car-mouche and Jouffroy, staged a melodrama starring Marie Dorval entitled *Le Vampire*. Dumas, newly arrived in Paris, attended a revival of the play in 1823 at which he sat next to Nodier: see *Mes Mémoires*, ii, chaps. 73 and 78. The Roman-tics' interest in vampires lingered on (Dumas wrote a play called *Le Vampire* in 1850) and eventually led to Bram

Stoker's *Dracula* (1899) which is the immediate source of our century's fascination with the legend.

336 *Blin or Humann*: the Blin family was well known in the textile industry as progressive and philanthropic employers. Humann was a fashionable tailor who had opened premises in the rue Neuve-des-Petits-Champs in 1822.

339 *the ring of Gyges*: Plato tells how Gygès acquired a magic ring which he used to make himself invisible, murder the king of Lydia, and usurp the throne.

342 *the sound of a guzla*: a violin-shaped instrument, popular in the Balkans. Played with a bow, it has one or sometimes two strings and is used to accompany the human voice in unison.

345 *Comte de Chalais*: Henri de Talleyrand, Comte de Chalais (1599–1626) was clumsily executed at Nantes by the orders of Richelieu against whom he was accused of plotting. On the *mandaïa*, see p. 351.

347 *broken on the wheel*: the guillotine was first called the *louisette* after its inventor Dr Louis, who based his decapitation machine on Italian models, but it was subsequently associated with the professor of anatomy at the Paris Faculty of Médecine Dr Guillotin, who recommended its use to the Constituent Assembly. Its introduction in 1792 was widely regarded as one of the humanitarian acts of the Revolution. Previously, serious crimes were punished by the wheel: convicted criminals were bound to a horizontally hung cartwheel and their limbs were broken by an executioner wielding an iron bar. In cases where mercy was recommended, the victim was first strangled before being broken. For attempting to kill Louis XV in 1757, Damiens was broken on the wheel while still conscious. His limbs were then attached to four horses which were whipped hard until he was torn apart.

348 *Castaing*: Dr Edme-Samuel Castaing (1797–1823) used his knowledge of poisons to carry out a number of murders designed to remove all obstacles between himself and the fortune of the Ballet family. The case was a sensation in 1823 and it is likely that Dumas incorporated details concerning the administration of poisons which emerged during the trial

in Chapter 53 ('Toxicology'). Dumas devoted a chapter of his *Mémoires* (ii, chap. 41) to the Castaing affair.

354 *costume of paillasse*: i.e. *Pagliacci*, a clown or buffoon.

356 *Callot's Temptation of St. Anthony*: the painter and engraver Jacques Callot (1592–1635) was admired by Romantic writers and artists for the grotesque realism with which he showed suffering and poverty. His *Tentation de Saint-Antoine* dealt with a subject which was to have a particular fascination for Flaubert.

356 *The Bear and the Pacha*: Odry (1779–1853) played the lead in *L'Ours et le Pacha*, a one-act vaudeville by Scribe, which was first performed at the Théâtre des Variétés in 1820.

358 *l'Italienne à Alger!*: it was with *The Italian Girl in Algiers*, first performed in Venice in 1813, that Rossini established his name.

361 *bajocco*: a *bajocca* or *baiocco* was a low denomination coin current in the Papal States.

361 *worthy of Didier or Anthony*: Didier is the hero of Hugo's verse drama, *Marion Delorme* (1831), and Anthony is the main character in Dumas's own *Antony* which was also first performed in 1831. Both are prime examples of the sultry, doomed romantic hero.

363 *Gregory XVI*: Gregory XVI (1765–1846) was elected Pope in 1831.

364 *moccoletto*: a candle: see p. 367.

366 *barberi*: i.e. Barbary horses, about to begin the race.

383 *M. Aguado and M. Rothschild*: the financier Alexander Aguado (1784–1842), a Spaniard who had become a French citizen in 1828, had opened a bank in Paris in 1815. All five sons of Meyer Amschel Rothschild became international bankers: Dumas had met Baron Charles de Rothschild (1788–1855) in Naples.

387 *the bandits of Colomba*: Mérimée's *Colomba* appeared in 1840, about a year after the events described here.

390 *Grisier, Cook, and Charles Lecour*: François Grisier (1791–1865) was a celebrated fencing master and author of *Les Armes et le duel* (1847) for which Dumas wrote a preface. Cook ran a

gymnasium while Charles Leboucher (who is always called Lecour in English translations) taught French boxing (which rather unsportingly allows the use of the feet).

390 *Bernard de Palissy*: Bernard Palissy (1510–90) was a Huguenot potter and naturalist. His high-relief ware was particularly valued by Catherine de Medici. A new edition of his writings had just been published in 1844.

391 *Roller and Blanchet*: in 1826 Pierre Blanchet had gone into partnership with Roller, the inventor of the upright piano. In 1827 they exhibited at the Louvre their 'bridge' piano which provided a hollow in the form of an arch to make room for the feet of the performer.

391 *Weber, ... Grétry, and Porpora*: Carl-Maria von Weber (1786–1826), the pioneer of German Romantic opera; André-Erneste-Modeste Grétry (1741–1813), popular composer of comic operas: Nicolo Antonio Porpora (1686–1766), a prolific composer of operas and oratorios, now rarely performed.

392 *get them at Borel's*: that is the celebrated Borrel who had opened his first restaurant, the *Rocher de Cancale*, in the rue Montorgueil in 1816. In 1842 he moved to 112, rue de Richelieu, to premises formerly occupied by the *Frascati* pleasure gardens which closed after the July Revolution of 1830.

392 *the affairs of the Peninsula*: in 1833, on the death of his brother, Don Carlos de Bourbon (1788–1855) laid claim to the Spanish throne. The coronation of Isabella II led to a civil war (1834–40) which ended with the defeat of the Carlist absolutists. Both France and England were interested in Spanish affairs and in September 1843 arrangements were made for the succession. Don Carlos renounced his claims to the Spanish throne in 1844 in favour of his son and withdrew to Austria.

397 *the raising of the siege*: after an abortive mission against the Bey of Constantine in November 1836, a second French expedition succeeded in taking the city on 13 October 1837.

398 *from Klugmann* [*sic*] *or Marochetti*: Jean-Baptiste Klagmann (1810–67) was a sculptor who worked on the decoration of the *Théâtre historique* founded by Dumas in 1847. Charles

Marochetti (1805–62), one of the most noted sculptors of his day, was an Italian who had taken French nationality.

401 *Mehemet Ali*: the rebellion of Mehemet Ali (1769–1849), Vice-Roy of Egypt, against the Turkish Sultan during the 1830s was backed by France which hoped thereby to further its interests in the Middle East. Britain opposed French support for Mehemet Ali whose revolt eventually collapsed.

401 *the famous sea serpent of the Constitutionnel*: Le Constitutionnel, founded in 1815 as a liberal, anti-clerical newspaper, was in the 1830s a popular opposition paper which also spoke out against the Romantic movement. After 1844, when it was bought by Dr Louis Désiré Véron, its fortunes were revived by its serializations of George Sand, Eugène Sue, and Dumas. It regularly advocated the adoption of a parliamentary regime based on the English model: this was its King Charles's Head or 'violon d'Ingres' or obsession—which is all 'un serpent de mer' means in French.

404 *karrick in India*: read 'curry'.

409 *the Charivari*: Le Charivari was a kind of French *Punch*, founded in 1832 by Charles Philippon, which was famous for satirical cartoons (by Daumier, Gavarni, Cham, etc.) lampooning the July Monarchy, Louis-Philippe, and the *bourgeoisie*. It survived into the twentieth century.

409 "*Faubourg Saint-Germain*": this was the part of Paris which was home to the aristocracy, politicians, and diplomats. The Faubourg Saint Honoré, where Villefort lives (p. 487), was already popular with the new financial bourgeois who were also moving into the Chaussée d'Antin (Danglars has his house there (p. 468) and the Boulevard de l'Opéra which were the fashionable and artistic centres. The Champs-Elysées, where Monte-Cristo rents a town house, was built only along half its length and was regarded as leading to 'the country'.

409 *chibouque*: a long-stemmed Turkish pipe.

413 *modern art*: Dumas parades his knowledge of modern artists, and includes the names of a number of his friends. Jules Dupré (1811–89) was a landscape painter of the Barbizon group,

and Eugène Delacroix (1798–1863) the leader of the Romantic School. Louis Boulanger (1806–67) was a painter and a close friend of Victor Hugo many of whose books he illustrated. Narcisse Diaz de la Pena (1807–76) painted flowers and woodland scenes. Alexandre-Gabriel Decamps (1803–60) was the most celebrated of French Romantic Orientalist painters. Salvator Rosa (1615–73) was poet and musician as well as a painter known for the energy of his compositions and his liking for strong colour. Eugène Giraud (1806–81) was a friend and travelling companion of Dumas whose portrait he drew for the first illustrated edition of *The Count of Monte Cristo* (1846). There were several artists named Müller, but Adrien Dauzats (1804–68) provided material and drawings for Dumas who used them as the basis of his text for their *Quinze jours au Sinaï* (*Two weeks in the Sinai Desert*) (1839).

414 *portrait by Gros*: Jean-Antoine Gros (1771–1835), a pupil of David, was known especially for his scenes from French history and for his heroic paintings of Napoleon's battles.

416 *Hozier and Jaucourt*: Pierre de la Garde d'Hozier (1592–1660), one of France's most noted genealogists, was the author of *Généalogie des principales familles de France* in 150 volumes. His work was continued by his son René (1640–1732). Louis de Jaucourt (1704–79) was one of Diderot's chief collaborators in *L'Encyclopédie* (1751–72) and was remembered for his 'encyclopaedic' knowledge.

416 *the wars of Greece and Spain*: see notes to pp. 235 and 392.

417 *Marshall Bourmont*: Le comte Louis de Bourmont (1773–1846), one of Napoleon's generals, went over to Louis XVIII in 1815, was a loyal servant of the Restoration and commanded the army which captured Algiers in 1830.

421 *Byron's heroes*: these 'heroes', all rebels doomed to fail, gave their names to Byron's influential poems: *Manfred* (1814), *Lara* (1817), and *Werner* (1822).

427 "*I have been almost obliged to wait*": Louis XIV's comment to an unpunctual courtier ('I was almost on the point of waiting for you') is still quoted as an example of the devastating put-down.

440 *Rue d'Enfer*: the 'Hospice des Enfants Assistés' was opened in
1814 in the rue d'Enfer (now the rue Denfert-Rochereau).
Though gruesome by modern standards, it was an improvement on the old Paris foundling hospital which, in the 1770s,
was an efficient infanticide agency: then, only hundreds survived of the 7,000 abandoned children admitted each year to
the 'Enfants trouvés'.

470 *Albano and Fattore*: Francesco Albani (called Albano) (1488–
1528) and Giovan Francesco Penni (known as *il Fattore*)
(1578–1660) are two more Italian painters with whom
Dumas hoped to impress his reader.

470 *Montmorency and Lafayette?*: Mathieu-Félicité, Duke de Montmorency (1767–1826) fought with Lafayette in America,
went over to the Third Estate in 1789, and signed the decree
which abolished the nobility on 17 June 1790. His extreme
royalist sympathies after 1815 rather spoil Monte-Cristo's
argument. The liberalism, however, of Marie-Joseph, Marquis de Lafayette (1757–1834), was beyond reproach. A hero
of the struggle for American Independence, he never lost faith
with the progressive ideals of the French Revolution. During
the 1820s he was a prominent opposition spokesman and
Dumas had known him during the July Revolution.

473 *Rothschild, ... Lafitte*: on the first, see note to p. 383. The banker
Jacques Lafitte (1767–1844) played a considerable role in the
political affairs of France from the time of Napoleon until the
Bourgeois monarchy of Louis-Philippe whose Minister of
Finance he was for a brief period. Lafitte rescued Dumas in
1828, before he was famous, by giving him an interest-free
loan of 3,000 francs.

478 *the Théâtre Français, ... is nowhere*: not for the first time in its history, the leading French theatre was divided by wranglings
which had led Marie Dorval to leave the company in 1837.
Dumas, a man of the theatre, remembered the squabbling
clearly. In 1838, however, with the arrival of Rachel, the
greatest tragic actress of her day, the classical repertoire
became fashionable again when the excesses of Romantic
drama began to lose favour.

478 *races held in the Champ de Mars and Satory*: the Champ-de-Mars, between the École Militaire and the Eiffel Tower (built in 1889), was the scene of the first Fête de la Fédération (1790), the Fête de l'Etre suprême (1794), and of Napoleon's first distribution of Legion of Honour awards in 1804 (see note to p. 85). After the Restoration, it was used for horse-racing: Frédérick Moreau takes Rosannette to the Hippodrome there in Flaubert's *Education sentimentale* (Part II, chap. 4). Satory, south west of Versailles, was mainly used for Army manœuvres but also boasted a race-track.

489 *a Harlay or a Molé*: Achille de Harlay (1536–1619), president of the Paris *parlement*, is remembered for his opposition to the Duke de Guise and his loyalty to the throne. Mathieu Molé (1584–1656) also enjoyed a high reputation as a distinguished president of the Paris *parlement*.

492 *pede claudo*: the dictum, *pede poena clauda* (Horace, *Odes*, III. 2, 32), means literally 'punishment (comes) with limping foot'. It warns that though punishment may not follow the crime at once, it will nevertheless come sooner or later.

497 *non bis in idem*: the legal principle that a man shall not be tried twice for the same offence.

504 *la Presse and les Débats*: La Presse (1836) was one of the new cheap daily newspapers which relied for their revenue on advertisements. *Le Journal des débats* (1789) was one of the four political newspapers which survived Napoleon's reform of 1811. It turned ultra-royalist after 1815 but soon rallied to the cause of constitutional monarchy and press freedom. After 1830 it moderated its liberalism somewhat but was known for the quality of its writers: Berlioz contributed polemical articles on music between 1835 and 1863. *Monte Cristo* first appeared in its pages in serial form. It survived until 1944.

519 *aristocracy of the lance ... nobility of the cannon*: for a variety of reasons—the Revolution of 1789, the Imperial pretensions of the Napoleonic court and the nascent industrial revolution— the French upper classes continued the process of renewal through intermarriage, though 'true' aristocratic values continued to dominate polite society.

521 *Algiers*: see note to p. 272.

526 *on different subjects*: Perugino (1445–1523) was among the masters of Raphael (1483–1520), though the Umbrian city of Perugina (i.e. 'Perusa') was associated with this poison only at a later date. *Aqua Tofana* (or *Aqua di Perugia*) was discovered in Naples at the end of the seventeenth century by a Sicilian woman named Toffania who sold it as 'Manna of St Nicolas of Bari'. It was, like most of the 'mysterious' poisons of the time, arsenic-based and it produced its effects imperceptibly by weakening the appetite and respiratory organs. After causing directly or indirectly the deaths of 600 persons, Toffania was tried and strangled in 1719.

527 "*Mithridates, rex Ponticus*": Mithridates VII Eupator, 'the Great', King of Pontus (123–63 BC), in addition to speaking twenty-two languages and perpetually fighting the Romans, was said to have studied from youth all forms of vegetable poisons.

528 *Cornelius Nepos*: a Roman historian (b. 99 BC), known especially for his biographies of famous men (*De Viris Illustribus*).

529 *Brucœa ferruginea*: in action, the alkaloid brucine resembles strychnine, but has only a twelfth of its strength. When mixed with nitric acid, it turns blood-red. It is this test that Dr D'Avrigny will carry out in Chapter 80.

530 *Flamel, a Fontana, or a Cabanis*: Nicolas Flamel (1330–1418) amassed a fortune in so mysterious a manner (probably by usury) that it was widely believed that he had dabbled in alchemy and discovered the philosopher's stone. Félix Fontana (1730–1805), an Italian doctor and anatomist, was known for his study of the action of poisons on the human body. On Cabanis, see note to p. 129. A more immediate source for Dumas's knowledge of poison was the well-publicized trial of Castaing in 1823: see note to p. 348.

530 *Galland*: Antoine Galland (1646–1715), an Orientalist at the Collège de France, was the translator of *The Arabian Nights* (1704–17). Though defective, Galland's version acted powerfully on the imagination of French readers and writers for generations.

531 *Desrues*: the trial and execution of Antoine Desrues (1734–77), a multiple poisoner, stirred the popular imagination and was still remembered two generations later. His wife was branded and jailed for life in 1779 for her part in his crimes. Dumas told their story in volume VII of his *Causes célèbres* (1839–41).

532 *Asmodeus*: Asmodeus appears in the Apocryphal Book of Tobit as the demon of matrimonial unhappiness; in the Talmud he is said to have driven Solomon from his kingdom. In *Le Diable boîteux* (*The Devil on Two Sticks*) (1707), Lesage tells how Asmodée is released from a bottle where he has been imprisoned. To reward his benefactor, he lifts the roofs of houses and exposes what goes on inside, thus enabling Lesage to provide a satirical picture of life in Paris, thinly disguised as 'Madrid'.

532 *Adelmonte of Taormine*: Adelmonte appears to be an invention of Dumas: see p. 533 for his manner of proceeding.

532 *Monthyon* [*sic*] *prizes*: Jean-Baptiste-Antoine Auget, baron de Montyon (1733–1820) was a philanthropist who used his immense fortune to establish a number of prizes, distributed annually by the *Institut*, which rewarded the poor for public-spirited works and acts.

532 *Borgias, ... Trenck*: Romantic dramatists were fascinated by the home life of the Borgias and Medicis and regularly showed them feeding poison to persons they did not care for. Cosimo Ruggieri (who appears in Dumas's *Henri III et sa cour* (*Henry III and His Court*) (1829)) and René le Florentin were respectively parfumier and astrologer to Catherine de Medici. Friedrich von der Trenck (1726–94) was a German adventurer who spent many years in prison. The publication of his autobiography in 1787 made him a European celebrity and episodes from his romantic life were turned into numerous plays. He returned to Paris in 1791, was accused of being an Austrian agent, and was executed.

533 *M. Magendie or M. Flourens*: François Magendie (1783–1855) and Marie-Jean-Pierre Flourens (1794–1867) were both noted physiologists.

534 *by raising the tip of the finger*: what would most people do if, without fear of discovery, they could make themselves rich by

killing a Mandarin in far-off China, simply by an effort of will, 'just by lifting a finger'? The question was raised in this form by Chateaubriand (*Le Génie du christianisme*, 1. vi. 2). Though it occurs nowhere in Rousseau's writings, the 'paradox' was, however, regularly associated with Rousseau who warned that conscience is the greatest casuist of all. It is likely that Dumas found the idea in Balzac's *Le Père Goriot* (1949, ed. Conard, vi. 361) where it forms what some critics regard as the crucial moral choice which Rastignac, Balzac's ambitious but naïve hero, is required to make. Subsequently, the expression 'tuer le mandarin' ('to kill the mandarin') was applied to anyone who got rich quickly by suspect means. 'Rousseau's mandarin' figures elsewhere in various guises, as a fisherman or, in Balzac's *Argow le pirate* (chap. 12), as a New Zealander. On the origin and history of 'Rousseau's paradox', see L. W. Keates's 'Mysterious Miraculous Mandarin', *Revue de littérature comparée*, 40 (1966, 497–525).

536 *M. Planchét*; [*sic*] ... *Hoffmann's drops*: the father of the dramatic critic Gustave Planche (1808–57) was a well-known chemist with premises in the Chaussée d'Antin. Hoffmann's drops, the invention of Friedrich Hoffmann (1660–1742), a doctor who advanced the 'organicist' view that soul and matter are made of a single substance, were a preparation of alcohol and ether and were recommended as a treatment for convulsions.

538 *Robert le Diable*: it was with *Robert le Diable* (1831), with libretto by Scribe and Delavigne, that Jacques Meyerbeer began his career as one of the most popular and influential composers of his age.

538 *Levasseur*: Nicolas-Prosper Levasseur (1791–1871) was a bass who made his début at the Paris Opera in 1813. After a number of seasons in Italy, he became known especially for his roles in Rossini and (as here) Meyerbeer.

545 *coronation of the Queen of England ... Mademoiselle Mars' diamonds*: the reference to the coronation of Queen Victoria (28 June 1837) reveals the occasional faultiness of Dumas's chronology, since Monte Cristo does not resurface in Italy until 'the commencement of the year 1838' (p. 270). Mademoiselle Mars was the stage name of Anne-Françoise-Hippolyte

Boutet (1779–1847). A star of the *Théâtre Français*, she was much admired for her roles in the great romantic dramas and for her playing of Molière and Marivaux.

547 *Cagliostro*: Joseph Balsamo (1743–95), known as Alexandre, comte de Cagliostro, acquired a European reputation as physician, necromancer, philosopher, alchemist, and freemason. Disgraced for his part in the Affair of the Diamond Necklace (which Dumas recounts in *Le Collier de la Reine* (*The Queen's Necklace*) (1849–50)), he was sent to the Bastille but succeeded in clearing his name. In 1789, in Rome, the Inquisition condemned him to life-imprisonment for Freemasonry. He died, perhaps strangled by his jailors, in 1795. Dumas's *Mémoires d'un médecin: Joseph Balsamo* (*The Memoirs of a Physician*) (1846–8) tells his story with relish, for Dumas clearly had a certain sympathy for the man and his ideas. Thus the liberal Dr Gilbert (*Ange Pitou* (1851), chap. 20) informs a startled Mme de Stael: 'To that "mountebank" I owe my knowledge, and perhaps the world will be indebted to him for its liberty'.

547 *Potemkin*: Prince Gregory Potemkin (1736–91), the most powerful of Catherine II's favourites, was an energetic and intelligent but coarse and unscrupulous man who, in spite of his ostentatious extravagance, amassed a large personal fortune.

547 *little Thumb*: in *Le Petit Poucet*, one of the collection of fairy tales published in 1697 by Charles Perrault (1628–1703), we learn how resourceful Tom Thumb, like Hansel, lays a trail of white pebbles to guide his steps back from the dark forest where his woodcutter father wishes to abandon him and his brothers and sisters.

552 *Mesdemoiselles Noblet, Julie, and Leroux*: of these dancers who performed the 'Ballet des Nonnes' in *Robert le Diable*, the most celebrated was Marie-Elisabeth Noblet (1803–52) who made her début at the Opera in 1817 and began taking leading roles in 1823. In 1832, she played Jenny in Dumas's *Richard Darlington*.

553 *the court of Ali Tebelen*: Ali Pasha (see note to p. 235) was governor of Jannina, on the shores of lake Jannina in Northern

Greece, when he was killed in 1822. He was born in Tebelen in Albania. Haydée's version of events will be found in Chapters 78 and 87.

556 *Bayard . . . Duguesclin*: Pierre du Terrail (1473–1524), seigneur de Bayard, is one of the folk heroes of French military history. His loyalty and courage earned him the title of 'Chevalier sans peur et sans reproche' ('A parfit, gentil knight'). Bertrand de la Motte-Broons (*c.*1320–80), Chevalier Du Guesclin, is another French byword for disinterested courage.

558 *della metà*: literally 'Money and saintliness (*santità*), / half of the half', a proverb meaning that tales about both are usually exaggerated.

558 *écarté*: écarté is usually a two-handed game which uses thirty-two cards only. Before the game begins, both players may discard (*écarter*) any of their cards and have them replaced with fresh ones. For *La Bouillotte*, players are dealt three cards only: Maximilian Morrel wins a considerable sum at *la bouillotte* on p. 593. Boston is a kind of solo-whist, invented by French soldiers during the War of American Independence, in which one of the four players bids to take a certain number of tricks, or none, or lose all but one, etc.

561 *Grand Référendaire*: a senior Senator who was responsible for the conduct of business in the House and for applying the seal of the Assembly to all measures approved by the Senate.

562 *in the tenth canto of L'Inferno*: Cavalcante Cavalcanti, father of Guido, one of Dante's earliest friends, begins to speak at line 45.

564 "*Lucullus dines with Lucullus*": Lucullus (*c.*109–57 BC), a Roman General enriched by his campaigns, is said, when dining alone, to have spoken these words in admonishment to his servant who had served him an unacceptably simple meal.

615 *theories of Montagne*: 'Montagne' was not a person, as the translator suggests, but the name given to the group of members of the Convention (21 September 1792–26 October 1795) who occupied the highest tiers of seats in the Assembly and normally voted for the extremest measures. Their opponents, mainly Girondin parliamentary moderates, sat on the right

while the lower seats were occupied by uncommitted *deputés* collectively known as 'the Plain'. By making Villefort say that his father had been 'a Jacobin more than anything else', Dumas seems to forget that Noirtier was first introduced as a Girondin: see p. 78. Overall, however, his political stance is clear: he was an unwavering opponent of the Bourbons and the *ancien régime* which they lost in 1789 and restored in 1815.

618 *of the home department, or of the observatory?*: i.e. the Ministry of the Interior and the Observatoire.

621 *I have read so in Petronius*: mice were on the menu at the dinner given by Trimalcio in section 31 of the *Satyricon* of Petronius (d. AD 65) where they were served with honey and poppy seeds.

627 *Le Moniteur ... Le Messager*: founded in 1789, *La Gazette nationale, ou le Moniteur universel*, began as a liberal daily. As the Revolution proceeded, it printed official documents and provided full reports of parliamentary proceedings, By 1800 it had acquired a semi-official status which it retained until 1868 when it was replaced by the *Journal officiel*. After 1830 it increased its literary coverage and serialized the work of Gautier, Musset, Mérimée, Dumas, etc. *Le Messager des chambres* first appeared February 1828 as an opposition paper but thereafter passed through many hands before being bought by the government whose point of view it expressed from about 1840 until it closed in 1846.

628 *the Duc d'Antin*: Louis-Antoine, duc d'Antin (1665–1736) was steward of the royal fabric.

632 *such splendid paintings*: again Dumas airs his artistic knowledge. Meindert Hobbema (1638–1709) was a Dutch landscape painter: Paul Potter (1625–54), also a Dutch master, was known for his paintings of landscapes and animals; Franz Van Mieris (1635–81) of Leyden, portraitist and genre painter, was a pupil of Gerard Dow (1613–75). For good measure, Dumas adds an Italian, Raphael (1483–1520), the Flemish artist Van Dyck (1599–1641), and two Spaniards. Francisco de Zurburan (1598–1664), painter of religious portraits and scenes, and Bartolomeo Esteban (1617–82).

637 *Apicius of old*: Parcus Gabius Apicius, a first-century Roman gastronomer, was known as a lavish host.

637 *cupitor impossibilium*: the Emperor Nero (AD 37–68) was 'he who desired the impossible'.

638 *Lucullus*: see note to p. 564.

640 *Marchioness de Gange* [*sic*]: the Marquise de Ganges died of poison in 1667, after being subjected to a number of grisly attempts on her life by the brothers of her husband, the Chevalier and the abbé de Ganges. The story is included in Dumas's *Causes célèbres* (1839–41).

642 *projected railway from Leghorn to Florence*: the age of railways was just beginning throughout Europe: the first Italian line was opened in October 1839. François Zola, father of the novelist Emile Zola, was one of the first Italian railway engineers. Later, we shall see Danglars speculating in railways.

656 *My chests are my Pactolus, as, ... M. Demoustier says*: according to legend, King Midas was allowed to bathe in the river Pactolus to which his regrettable ability to turn everything to gold was thereupon transferred. According to the French text, Danglars's *offices* are his goldmine. Charles Demoustier (or Desmoutiers) (1760–1801), a descendant of Racine, was known as a writer of overblown prose. Dumas remembered him particularly because he was born only a short distance from the house at Villers-Cotterêts where Demoustiers died.

683 *the Count Saint-Germain*: on Ruthven and Cagliostro, see notes to pp. 334 and 547. The Comte de Saint-Germain (d. 1784) was an adventurer who imposed himself on the court of Louis XV by claiming occult powers. He was much admired by Cagliostro.

684 *the great d'Aguesseau*: Henri-François Daguesseau (1668–1751) was a learned and highly respected magistrate of moderate views. Though unsympathetic to the ideas of the *philosophes*, it was the Chancelier Daguesseau who authorized the publication of Diderot's *Encyclopédie*.

691 *kerseymere waistcoat, and nankeen pantaloons*: kerseymere was a coarse woollen cloth, usually ribbed, used mainly for the manufacture of men's trousers; etymologically, a corruption

of 'cassimere', a twilled fabric. Nankeen was a cotton cloth, usually yellow, originally from Nanking in China, but widely imitated and also used principally for making trousers.

692 *the battle of Navarino*: in 1827 the Turkish and Egyptian navies were destroyed off the Pelopponesian port of Navarino by the combined French, British, and Russian fleets under Codrington. Otto of Bavaria (1815–67) was chosen King of Greece in 1832. He was deposed in 1862.

692 *Baguères*: read Bagnères-de-Bigorre which, with Bagnères-de-Luchon and Cauterets, were already the most popular Pyrenean spa towns.

695 *Elssler was dancing in Le Diable Boiteux*: the Austrian dancer, Fanny Elssler (1810–84) danced *Le Diable boïteux* (*The Devil on Two Sticks*) with score by Casimir Gide, in 1836. 'La cachucha' was a kind of bolero: it was with a well-publicized performance of 'la cachucha' that Lola Montès made her name in Paris at the age of twenty.

699 *Partant pour la Syrie!*: a rousing song which, already the Bonapartist anthem during the Restoration, was officially adopted during the Second Empire. The tune was by Philippe Droult and the words were attributed variously to Queen Hortense or to the archaeologist Alexandre de Laborde.

712 *M. d'Avrigny*: it has been suggested that Dr D'Avrigny (who also appears in *Amaury* (1844)) was modelled on a medical friend of Dumas named Thibaut. In *Mes Mémoires* (ii. 279), Dumas mentions that the experiments which they carried out together in Thibaut's rooms were his introduction 'to the poisons used by Mme de Villefort in *Monte Cristo*, my studies being pursued and later completed with Ruolz' (the chemist Henri-Catherine Ruolz-Montchal (1808–87)).

736 *Charles X*: Charles X succeeded Louis XVIII in 1824 and ruled with increasing conservatism until forced to abdicate on 2 August 1830 in the aftermath of the July Revolution.

736 *Père-la-Chaise*: François de La Chaise (1624–1709) was a Jesuit priest who developed a site in the Eastern part of Paris into a place of rest used by his Order. It became a municipal

cemetery in 1803 and looms large in nineteenth-century literature: Balzac's Old Goriot was buried there.

737 *sanguine temperament*: though the universal theory of the 'humours' was being challenged (by Cabanis, who argued that mental states are dependent upon physiology, or by the successors of Mesmer who experimented with hypnotism), it remained widely current until it was overtaken by Freudian psychoanalysis.

737 "*Tenacem propositi virum*": see note to p. 78.

755 "*Violon de Crémone*": in the mysterious tale of this title by E. T. A. Hoffmann, Krespel falls into a kind of dream in which he sees and hears his daughter Antonia singing: when he wakes, she is dead.

757 *Thalberg*: Sigismond Thalberg (1812–71) was one of the rivals of Chopin and Liszt in an age of piano virtuosi. He made his Paris début in 1835.

760 *Yanina*: see note to p. 553.

763 *Beaumarchais*: Pierre Caron de Beaumarchais (1732–99) was the son of a watchmaker whose ready wit made his name and his fortune. Dumas, who was also a self-taught and self-made man, had a special affection for the creator of Figaro.

763 *the name of Haydée*: see Byron's *Don Juan* (Canto II, cxxviii ff.). Haidee, 'the greatest heiress of the Eastern Isles', lives on one of the smaller Cyclades.

771 *Palicares*: the name given to soldiers of the Greek militia who fought in the War of Independence.

771 '*They hate me, then they fear me!*': a version of a line from a lost play by Quintius Ennius quoted by Cicero (*De Officiis*, I. xxviii) meaning 'If I am hated, I am feared'.

771 *Kourchid*: Seraskier was the Turkish rank of commander-in-chief. On Kourchid, see note to p. 235.

777 *firman?*: an edict or order issued by any Oriental sovereign (here, the Sultan of Turkey) for a variety of special purposes: to sanction an enterprise, to grant safe passage to travellers, to authorize the movement of goods, etc.

787 *l'Impartial*: a short-lived literary paper of this name appeared

in 1822 while another, funded by political and business interests, ran from 1833 to 1836. Beauchamp's paper is an invention of Dumas.

788 *Gossett's shooting-gallery*: Gosset's shooting gallery (which Dumas frequented in 1835, according to *Mes Mémoires*, iii. 85), was situated on the Champs-Elysées. The Allée des Veuves is now part of the Avenue Montaigne.

809 *Locusta and Agrippina, ... Brunehault and Frédégonde*: with the aid of Locusta, a woman skilled in poisons, Agrippina (AD 15–59) murdered her third husband, the emperor Claudius, and succeeded making her son Nero caesar. Brunhilda (*c*.534–613) divided the government of the Frankish world with her rival, the unscrupulous Frédégonde who killed anyone who came between her young son and the throne. After the death of Frédégonde in 598, Brunhilda became sole ruler of the Merovingian dominions until she was overthrown in 613: she was dragged to death at the heels of a wild horse.

829 *Huret and Fitchet's*: Calixte-Léopold Huret (1786–1857) was a cabinet-maker who also made safes and combination locks from his premises in the rue de Castiglione. Alexandre Fichet (1799–1862) was a provincial locksmith who opened a shop in the rue Rameau in 1825 and subsequently moved to 77, rue Richelieu.

846 *La Morgue*: the Paris Morgue was housed in the Grand Châtelet from the seventeenth century until 1863 when it was relocated in premises situated behind Notre Dame. In 1923 its function was taken over by the Institut médico-légal.

846 *preparing the breviate*: i.e. the statement containing his findings.

852 *his Lucquois*: Major Cavalcanti claimed to be a native of Lucca, and so his 'son' must therefore also be a 'Lucquois'.

852 *Valle Theatre*: one of Rome's numerous opera houses, rebuilt in 1823. It had staged operas by Rossini and from 1832 all of Bellini was performed there. A second heyday began in 1841 with the appointment of the impresario Jacovacci.

853 *Borromées Islands*: the four Borromean Islands sit picturesquely at the western end of Lake Maggiore. They are named after

the Borromeo family who transformed them with terraces and gardens in the seventeenth century.

854 *surpass the railway*: see note to p. 642. Dumas, who here speaks so disparagingly of the railways, was later to see a number of his own books published in Hachette's popular 'Bibliothèque du chemin de fer' and, in England, in Routledge's 'Railway Library' series.

857 *third and fourth generation*: Exodus 20. 5.5. This strikes a very Old Testament note, which is perfectly consistent with the themes of vengeance and retribution.

880 *Duprez*: Gilbert-Louis Duprez (1806–96) made his début in Paris in 1825 but sang for some years in Italy (where he scored a triumph in *Parisina* (see note to p. 327)) before returning to Paris in 1837 where he was acclaimed for his role in a revival of Rossini's *William Tell*.

893 *Tortoni*: Tortoni's, on the corner of the rue Taitbout and the Boulevard des Italiens, was one of the most fashionable of Parisian cafés. It was then at the height of its vogue.

893 *the four sides of the club*: in spite of Dumas's odd phrasing here, the sign of clubs was then, as now, a trefoiled clover with a stalk.

900 *signed Feuchères* [*sic*], *or Barye*: Jean-Jacques Feuchère (1807–52) began his career as a goldsmith before turning into one of the most archetypal Romantic sculptors. Antoine-Louis Barye (1796–1875) specialized in portraying animals.

930 *Phædrus, . . . Bias*: 'rien de trop' ('Nothing to excess') comes in fact from Plato's *Philebus*. Bias, who flourished around the middle of the sixth century BC, was one of the Seven Wise Men of Greece. Among his apothegms were: 'Know and then act' and 'He is unfortunate who cannot bear misfortune'. It is said that when his fellow citizens were busy bearing away their possessions in anticipation of an attack by a pillaging enemy, Bias was seen to be empty-handed. When asked why this was so, he replied in words which in Latin became a proverb: 'Omnia meum mecum porto' ('I carry all my possessions with me').

931 *La Porte Saint-Martin and La Gaieté*: here Dumas seems to mock

the melodramatic traditions of these two popular theatres—
even though a number of his own plays had been performed
at the Porte Saint-Martin.

933 *la Pasta, la Malibran, la Grisi*: there were two sisters named
Grisi, Guiditta (1805–40) and Giulia (1811–69), who were
both famous sopranos: their cousin Ernesta, who also sang
professionally, married Théophile Gautier. Maria Felicia
Garcia (1808–36), who sang under the name of Malibran,
was of Spanish origin: she was in the audience for the first
night of Dumas's *Henri III et sa cour* (*Henry III and His Court*) in
1829. Giuditta Pasta (1798–1865) had a vocal range wide
enough to allow her to sing both soprano and contralto parts:
she was best known for her performances in Bellini's *Norma*
and *La Sonnambula*, both performed in 1831.

934 *the chimerical Mississipi*: John Law (1671–1729), a Scot born in
Edinburgh and advocate of the notion of credit, became
France's General Controller of Finances during the Regency.
He set up the French India Company which sought to col-
onize Louisiana. The venture was over-subscribed and when
the 'Louisiana Bubble' burst in 1719, there were widespread
bankruptcies. It was said that the only person to emerge with
a profit was the hunchback who rented out his hump as a
mobile desk on which deals were signed. Dumas invents a
similar Panamanian scheme as the final confidence trick of
the hero of *Le capitaine Pamphile* (1840).

935 *Brabantio's malediction on Desdemona*: in Rossini's *Otello* (1816),
Brabantio curses his daughter for marrying a Moor. It seems
an odd choice of song in the circumstances.

937 *reply to Alceste*: neither Dorante nor Valère figure in Molière's
Le Misanthrope (1666), though Andrea catches something of
the pompous tone of the obsequious Oronte. Like Danglars
(see p. 929), he acts a role.

950 *the britska*: a light, partly covered, four-wheeled carriage of
Polish origin.

951 *the Louvres ... the land of ratafia*: not *the* Louvre but Louvres in
the Val d'Oise, near the present-day airport at Roissy, where
ratafia, an aromatic liqueur, had been manufactured since

the seventeenth century: Aramis and Athos drink a glass of ratafia at Louvres in Chapter 83 of *Twenty Years After*.

999 *Robert Macaire represented by Frédéric*: Robert Macaire is the hero-villain of what is probably the most famous of all French melodramas, *L'Auberge des Adrets* (1823) by Antier, Saint-Amant, and Paulyanthe. There was a sequel in 1834 entitled *Robert Macaire*. Macaire was played with extraordinary panache by Frederic Lemaître (1800–76), the quintessentially Romantic actor who created a number of roles for Dumas, notably in *Kean* (1837). According to *The Times* (19 January 1835). 'He is by no means a good actor, regarded either according to the French or the English estimate of good acting; but he is clever, and although coarse is striking. The subject of *Robert Macaire* is of that violent and vulgar class which our neighbours on the other side of the Channel have of late so strangely encouraged.' For a view of Lemaître at work, see Marcel Carné's film *Les Enfants du Paradis* (1944–5) in which he is played to the hilt by Pierre Brasseur.

1000 *Abelard and Héloïse*: innumerable eighteenth-century versions of the story of Héloïse (1101–64) and Pierre Abélard (1079–1142), philosopher and scholar, ensured that they were known as lovers every whit as pure and tragic as Romeo and Juliet.

1009 *this is the 5th of September*: alert readers will note that the time appointed for the duel between Albert de Morcerf and Beauchamp (three weeks from 29 August, according to p. 797) has already come and gone. Dumas's chronology, dislocated here by the temptation of a sentimental anniversary, is rather hurried in the closing stages. The whole 'Paris' section of the novel, which begins on 21 May and ends on 5 October, occupies a period of just over four months.

1015 *no right to posssess anything independent of your husband*: the *Code civil* (1804), drawn up with the active participation of Napoleon, allowed women as many legal rights as were permitted to children and mad persons. In particular, a woman's right to own property outside the marriage settlement was severely curtailed. In spite of the vociferous pro-feminist trend of the 1830s, Mme Danglars's legal position is delicate, and Debray makes the most of it.

1016 *Asmodeus*: see note to p. 532.

1019 *Lamoricière, ... Changarnier ... Bedau*: Louis-Christophe-Léon Juchault de Lamoricière (1806–65) and Nicolas Changarnier (1793–1877, who later became governor of Algeria) both distinguished themselves at the siege of Constantine in 1837. Marie-Alphonse Bedau (1804–63) also fought in North Africa.

1022 *La Force*: La Force, in the Marais, was one of the Revolutionary prisons where the Septembre Massacres took place in 1792. It was decommissioned in 1850.

1023 *price of the Cavalcanti*: for 'price' read 'Prince'.

1027 *pot aux roses*: the expression simply means 'a secret'.

1036 *the Conciergerie*: the most famous Paris prison after the Bastille and perhaps the oldest in Europe. It formed part of the Palais de Justice and among recent prisoners held there were Marie-Antoinette, Danton, and Robespierre.

1037 *Boulevard de Gand*: the Boulevard de Gand was, during the Restoration, the name given to the Boulevard des Italiens in which the capital's most fashionable cafés were located: the Café de Paris was at no. 24.

1038 *the Divina Commedia*: See note to p. 562.

1039 *the days of Beaumarchais*: a reference to the court-room scene of *Le Mariage de Figaro* (III. xiv) where the Usher bellows not 'La cour, messieurs!' of Dumas's text but 'L'Audience!'

1052 *Perrault's stories*: see note to p. 547.

1063 *Edmond!*: at this point, the standard French text includes a significant episode absent from our text. On leaving Mercédès, Edmond takes a boat out to If and visits the cell where he had suffered for so long. The old hatred and thirst for vengeance return but are silenced when the jailor shows him a manuscript in the hand of the abbé Faria. This reminder of the wisdom of his mentor brings him peace and, back in Marseilles, thoughts of Haydée complete his conversion: his vengeance was just but it is now finished.

1068 *a game of mora*: an old game, still common in Italy, in which one player raises his right hand and then lowers it rapidly with one or more fingers extended. The other players have to guess how many.

1068 *a dozen pauls*: a *paul* was a coin of small denomination current in the Papal States.

1071 *Caracalla's circle*: among the ruins of buildings put up by Caracalla (188–217), one of the more disagreeable later Roman Emperors, are the Thermae Caracallae and the circus which Danglars recognizes here.

1074 *Breguet's*: see note to p. 300.

1084 *Amphitrite*: goddess of the sea, daughter of Oceanus, and wife of Neptune.

1085 *as Calypso said to Telemachus*: in Homer's *Odyssey*, Odysseus/Telemachus is wrecked on the island of Ogygia where he is rescued by Calypso who treats him kindly and promises him immortality if he would marry her.

The Oxford World's Classics Website

www.worldsclassics.co.uk

- Information about new titles
- Explore the full range of Oxford World's Classics
- Links to other literary sites and the main OUP webpage
- Imaginative competitions, with bookish prizes
- Peruse the Oxford World's Classics Magazine
- Articles by editors
- Extracts from Introductions
- A forum for discussion and feedback on the series
- Special information for teachers and lecturers

www.worldsclassics.co.uk

American Literature

British and Irish Literature

Children's Literature

Classics and Ancient Literature

Colonial Literature

Eastern Literature

European Literature

History

Medieval Literature

Oxford English Drama

Poetry

Philosophy

Politics

Religion

The Oxford Shakespeare

A complete list of Oxford Paperbacks, including Oxford World's Classics, Oxford Shakespeare, Oxford Drama, and Oxford Paperback Reference, is available in the UK from the Academic Division Publicity Department, Oxford University Press, Great Clarendon Street, Oxford OX2 6DP.

In the USA, complete lists are available from the Paperbacks Marketing Manager, Oxford University Press, 198 Madison Avenue, New York, NY 10016.

Oxford Paperbacks are available from all good bookshops. In case of difficulty, customers in the UK can order direct from Oxford University Press Bookshop, Freepost, 116 High Street, Oxford OX1 4BR, enclosing full payment. Please add 10 per cent of published price for postage and packing.